PRAISE FOR WILBUR SMITH

'Wilbur Smith rarely misses a trick'
Sunday Times

'The world's leading adventure writer'
Daily Express

'Action is the name of Wilbur Smith's game
and he is a master'
Washington Post

'The pace would do credit to a Porsche, and the invention
is as bright and explosive as a fireworks display'
Sunday Telegraph

'A bonanza of excitement'
New York Times

'. . . a natural storyteller who moves confidently and
often splendidly in his period and sustains a flow of
convicing incident'
Scotsman

'Raw experience, grim realism, history and romance welded
with mystery and the bewilderment of life itself'
Library Journal

'A thundering good read'
Irish Times

Wilbur Smith was born in Central Africa in 1933. He was educated at Michaelhouse and Rhodes University. He became a full-time writer in 1964 after the successful publication of *When the Lion Feeds*, and has since written thirty novels, all meticulously researched on his numerous expeditions world-wide. His books are now translated into twenty-six different languages.

Also by Wilbur Smith

THE COURTNEYS
When the Lion Feeds
The Sound of Thunder
A Sparrow Falls
Birds of Prey
Monsoon
The Triumph of the Sun

THE COURTNEYS OF AFRICA
The Burning Shore
Power of the Sword
Rage
A Time to Die
Golden Fox

THE BALLANTYNE NOVELS
A Falcon Flies
Men of Men
The Angels Weep
The Leopard Hunts in Darkness

Also
The Dark of the Sun
Shout at the Devil
Gold Mine
The Diamond Hunters
The Sunbird
Eagle in the Sky
The Eye of the Tiger
Cry Wolf
Wild Justice
Elephant Song
River God
The Seventh Scroll
Warlock

WILBUR SMITH

BLUE HORIZON
&
HUNGRY AS THE SEA

PAN BOOKS

Blue Horizon first published 2003 by Macmillan.
First published in paperback 2004 by Pan Books.
Hungry as the Sea first published 1978 by William Heinemann.
First published in paperback 1979 by Pan Books.

This omnibus first published 2007 by Pan Books
an imprint of Pan Macmillan Ltd
Pan Macmillan, 20 New Wharf Road, London N1 9RR
Basingstoke and Oxford
Associated companies throughout the world
www.panmacmillan.com

ISBN 978-0-330-45233-5

1 3 5 7 9 8 6 4 2

A CIP catalogue record for this book is available from
the British Library.

Typeset by SetSystems Ltd, Saffron Walden, Essex
Printed and bound in Great Britain by
Mackays of Chatham plc, Chatham, Kent

BLUE HORIZON

This book is for my wife, Mokhiniso.

Our first three years together have been enchantment.
I look forward eagerly to the next thirty.

The three stood at the very edge of the sea and watched the moon laying a pathway of shimmering iridescence across the dark waters.

'Full of the moon in two days,' Jim Courtney said confidently. 'The big reds will be hungry as lions.' A wave came sliding up the beach and foamed around his ankles.

'Let's get her launched, instead of standing here jabbering,' his cousin, Mansur Courtney, suggested. His hair shone like newly minted copper in the moonlight, his smile sparkling as brightly. Lightly he elbowed the black youth who stood beside him, wearing only a white loincloth. 'Come on, Zama.' They bent to it together. The small craft slid forward reluctantly, and they heaved again, but this time it stuck fast in the wet sand.

'Wait for the next big one,' Jim ordered, and they gathered themselves. 'Here it comes!' The swell humped up far out, then raced towards them, gathering height. It burst white on the break-line, then creamed in, throwing the bows of the skiff high and making them stagger with its power – they had to cling to the gunwale with the water swirling waist high around them.

'Together now!' Jim yelled, and they threw their combined weight on the boat. 'Run with her!' She came unstuck and rode free, and they used the backwash of the wave to take her out until they were shoulder deep. 'Get on the oars!' Jim spluttered as the next wave broke over his head. They reached up, grabbed the side of the skiff and hauled themselves on board, the seawater running off them. Laughing with excitement, they seized the long oars that were lying ready and thrust them between the thole pins.

'Heave away!' The oars bit, swung and came clear, dripping with silver in the moonlight, leaving tiny luminous whirlpools on the surface. The skiff danced clear of the turbulent break-line, and they fell into the easy rhythm of long practice.

1

'Which way?' Mansur asked. Both he and Zama looked naturally to Jim for the decision: Jim was always the leader.

'The Cauldron!' Jim said, with finality.

'I thought so.' Mansur laughed. 'You still got a grudge against Big Julie.' Zama spat over the side without missing the stroke.

'Have a care, Somoya. Big Julie still has a grudge against you.' Zama spoke in Lozi, his native tongue. 'Somoya' meant 'wild wind'. It was the name that Jim had been given in childhood for his temper.

Jim scowled at the memory. None of them had ever laid eyes on the fish they had named Big Julie, but they knew it was a hen not a cock because only the female grew to such size and power. They had felt her power transferred from the depths through the straining cod line. The seawater squirted out of the weave, and smoked as it sped out over the gunwale, cutting a deep furrow in the hardwood as blood dripped from their torn hands.

'In 1715 my father was on the old *Maid of Oman* when she went aground at Danger Point,' Mansur said, in Arabic, his mother's language. 'The mate tried to swim ashore to carry a line through the surf and a big red steenbras came up under him when he was half-way across. The water was so clear they could see it coming up from three fathoms down. It bit off the mate's left leg above the knee and swallowed it in a gulp, like a dog with a chicken wing. The mate was screaming and beating the water, all frothed up with his own blood, trying to scare the fish off, but it circled under him and took the other leg. Then it pulled him under and took him deep. They never saw him again.'

'You tell that story every time I want to go to the Cauldron,' Jim grunted darkly.

'And every time it scares seven different colours of dung out of you,' said Zama, in English. The three had spent so much time together that they were fluent in each other's language – English, Arabic and Lozi. They switched between them effortlessly.

Jim laughed, more to relieve his feelings than from amuse-

2

ment, 'Where, pray, did you learn that disgusting expression, you heathen?'

Zama grinned. 'From your exalted father,' he retorted, and for once Jim had no answer.

Instead he looked to the lightening horizon. 'Sunrise in two hours. I want to be over the Cauldron before then. That's the best time for another tilt at Julie.'

They pulled out into the heart of the bay, riding the long Cape swells that came marching in unfettered ranks from their long journey across the southern Atlantic. With the wind full into the bows they could not hoist the single sail. Behind them rose the moonlit massif of Table Mountain, flat-topped and majestic. There was a dark agglomeration of shipping lying close in below the mountain, riding at anchor, most of the great ships with their yards down. This anchorage was the caravanserai of the southern seas. The trading vessels and warships of the Dutch East India Company, the VOC, and those of half a dozen other nations used the Cape of Good Hope to victual and refit after their long ocean passages.

At this early hour few lights showed on the shore, only dim lanterns on the walls of the castle and in the windows of the beachfront taverns where the crews from the ships in the bay were still revelling. Jim's eyes went naturally to a single prick of light separated by over a sea mile of darkness from the others. That was the godown and office of the Courtney Brothers Trading Company and he knew the light shone from the window of his father's office on the second floor of the sprawling warehouse.

'Papa is counting the shekels again.' He laughed to himself. Tom Courtney, Jim's father, was one of the most successful traders at Good Hope.

'There's the island coming up,' Mansur said, and Jim's attention came back to the work ahead. He adjusted the tiller rope, which was wrapped around the big toe of his bare right foot. They altered course slightly to port, heading for the north point of Robben Island. 'Robben' was the Dutch word for the seals that swarmed over the rocky outcrop. Already they could smell the animals on the night air: the stench of their fish-

3

laden dung was chokingly powerful. Closer in, Jim stood up on the thwart to get his bearing from the shore, checking the landmarks that would enable him to place the skiff accurately over the deep hole they had named the Cauldron.

Suddenly he shouted with alarm and dropped back on to the thwart. 'Look at this great oaf! He's going to run us down. Pull, damn you, pull!' A tall ship flying a great mass of canvas, had come silently and swiftly around the north point of the island. Driven on the north-wester it was bearing down on them with terrifying speed.

'Bloody cheese-headed Dutchman!' Jim swore, as he heaved on the long oar. 'Murderous landlubbing son of a tavern whore! He's not even showing a light.'

'And where, pray, did *you* learn such language?' Mansur panted, between desperate strokes.

'You're as big a clown as this stupid Dutchman,' Jim told him grimly. The ship loomed over them, her bow wave shining silver in the moonlight.

'Hail her!' There was a sudden edge to Mansur's voice as the danger became even more apparent.

'Don't waste your breath,' Zama retorted. 'They're fast asleep. They won't hear you. Pull!' The three strained on the oars and the little vessel seemed to fly through the water, but the big ship came on even faster.

'We will have to jump?' There was a question in Mansur's strained tone.

'Good!' Jim grunted. 'We're right over the Cauldron. Test your father's story. Which of your legs will Big Julie bite off first?'

They rowed in a silent frenzy, sweat bursting out and shining on their contorted faces in the cool night. They were heading for the safety of the rocks where the big ship could not touch them, but they were still a full cable's length out and now the high sails towered over them, blotting out the stars. They could hear the wind drumming in the canvas, the creaking of her timbers, and the musical burble of her bow wave. Not one of the boys spoke, but as they strained on the oars they stared up at her in dread.

4

'Sweet Jesus, spare us!' Jim whispered.

'In Allah's Name!' Mansur said softly.

'All the fathers of my tribe!'

Each called out to his own god or gods. Zama never missed the stroke but his eyes glared white in his dark face as he watched death bear down on them. The pressure wave ahead of the bows lifted them, and suddenly they were surfing on it, flung backwards, racing stern-first down the side of the wave. The transom went under and icy water poured in, flooding her. All three boys were hurled over the side, just as the massive hull hit them. As he went under Jim realized that it had been a glancing blow. The skiff was hurled aside, but there was no crack of rending timbers.

Jim was driven deep, but he tried to swim deeper still. He knew that contact with the bottom of the ship would be fatal. She would be heavily encrusted with barnacles after her ocean passage, and the razor-sharp shells would strip the flesh from his bones. He tensed every muscle in his body in anticipation of the agony, but it did not come. His lungs were burning and his chest was pumping with the compelling urge to breathe. He fought it until he was sure that the ship was clear, then turned for the surface and drove upwards with arms and legs. He saw the golden outline of the moon through limpid water, wavering and insubstantial, and swam towards it with all his strength and will. Suddenly he burst out into the air and filled his lungs with it. He rolled on to his back, gasped, choked and sucked in the life-giving sweetness. 'Mansur! Zama!' he croaked, through the pain of his aching lungs. 'Where are you? Pipe up, damn you. Let me hear you!'

'Here!' It was Mansur's voice, and Jim looked for him. His cousin was clinging to the swamped skiff, his long red curls slicked down over his face like a seal's pelt. Just then another head popped through the surface between them.

'Zama.' With two overarm strokes he reached him, and lifted his face out of the water. Zama coughed and brought up an explosive jet of seawater and vomit. He tried to throw both arms around Jim's neck, but Jim ducked him until he released his grip, then dragged him to the side of the wallowing skiff.

5

'Here! Take hold of this.' He guided his hand to the gunwale. The three hung there, struggling for breath.

Jim was the first to recover sufficiently to find his anger again. 'Bitch-born bastard!' he gasped, as he stared after the departing ship. She was sailing on sedately. 'Doesn't even know he almost killed us.'

'She stinks worse than the seal colony.' Mansur's voice was still rough, and the effort of speech brought on a coughing fit.

Jim sniffed the air and caught the odour that fouled it. 'Slaver. Bloody slaver,' he spat. 'No mistaking that smell.'

'Or a convict ship,' Mansur said hoarsely. 'Probably transporting prisoners from Amsterdam to Batavia.' They watched the ship alter course, her sails changing shape in the moonlight as she rounded up to enter the bay and join the other shipping anchored there.

'I'd like to find her captain in one of the gin hells at the docks,' Jim said darkly.

'Forget it!' Mansur advised him. 'He'd stick a knife between your ribs, or in some other painful place. Let's get the skiff bailed out.' There was only a few fingers of free board so Jim had to slide in over the transom. He groped under the thwart and found the wooden bucket still lashed under the seat. They had tied down all the gear and equipment securely for the hazardous launch through the surf. He began bailing out the hull, sending a steady stream of water over the side. By the time it was half cleared, Zama had recovered sufficiently to climb aboard and take a spell with the bucket. Jim hauled in the oars, which were still floating alongside, then checked the other equipment. 'All the fishing tackle's still here.' He opened the mouth of a sack and peered inside. 'Even the bait.'

'Are we going on?' Mansur asked.

'Of course we are! Why not, in the name of the Devil?'

'Well . . .' Mansur looked dubious. 'We were nearly drowned.'

'But we weren't,' Jim pointed out briskly. 'Zama has got her dry, and the Cauldron is less than a cable's length away. Big Julie is waiting for her breakfast. Let's go and feed it to her.' Once again they took their positions on the thwarts, and plied

6

the long oars. 'Bastard cheesehead cost us an hour's fishing time,' Jim complained bitterly.

'Could have cost you a lot more, Somoya,' Zama laughed, 'if I hadn't been there to pull you out—' Jim picked up a dead fish from the bait bag and threw it at his head. They were swiftly recovering their high spirits and camaraderie.

'Hold the stroke, we're coming up on the marks now,' Jim warned, and they began the delicate business of manoeuvring the skiff into position over the rocky hole in the green depths below them. They had to drop the anchor on to the ledge to the south of the Cauldron, then let the current drift them back over the deep subterranean canyon. The swirling current that gave the place its name complicated their work, and twice they missed the marks. With much sweat and swearing they had to retrieve the fifty-pound boulder that was their anchor and try again. The dawn was sneaking in from the east, stealthily as a thief, before Jim plumbed the depth with an unbaited cod line to make certain they were in the perfect position. He measured the line between the span of his open arms as it streamed over the side.

'Thirty-three fathoms!' he exclaimed, as he felt the lead sinker bump the bottom. 'Nearly two hundred feet. We're right over Big Julie's dining room.' He brought up the sinker swiftly with a swinging double-handed action. 'Bait up, boys!' There was a scramble for the bait bag. Jim reached in and, from under Mansur's fingers, he snatched the choicest bait of all, a grey mullet as long as his forearm. He had netted it the previous day in the lagoon below the company godown. 'That's too good for you,' he explained reasonably. 'Needs a real fisherman to handle Julie.' He threaded the point of the steel shark hook through the mullet's eye sockets. The bight of the hook was two handspans across. Jim shook out the leader. It was ten feet of steel chain, light but strong. Alf, his father's blacksmith, had hand-forged it especially for him. Jim was certain it would resist the efforts of even a great king steenbras to sheer it against the reef. He swung the bait round his head, letting the heavy cod line pay out with each swing, until at last he released it and sent it with the chain leader to streak

7

far out across the green surface. As the bait sank into the depths he let the line stream after it. 'Right down Big Julie's throat,' he gloated. 'This time she isn't going to get away. This time she's mine.' When he felt the lead sinker hit the bottom, he laid out a coil of the line on the deck and stood firmly on it with his bare right foot. He needed both hands on the oar to counter the current and keep the skiff on station above the Cauldron with the heavy line running straight up and down.

Zama and Mansur were fishing with lighter hooks and lines, using small chunks of mackerel as bait. Almost immediately they were hauling in fish – rosy red stumpnose, wriggling silvery bream, spotted tigers that grunted like piglets as the boys twisted out the hook and threw them into the bilges.

'Baby fish for little boys!' Jim mocked them. Diligently he tended his own heavy line, rowing quietly to hold the skiff steady across the current. The sun rose clear of the horizon and took the chill out of the air. The three stripped off their outer clothing until they were clad only in breech clouts.

Close at hand the seals swarmed over the rocks of the island, dived and roiled close around the anchored skiff. Suddenly a big dog seal dived under the boat and seized the fish Mansur was bringing up, tore it from the hook and surfaced yards away with it in its jaws.

'Abomination, cursed of God!' Mansur shouted in outrage as the seal held the plundered fish on its chest and tore off hunks of flesh with gleaming fangs. Jim dropped the oar and reached into his tackle bag. He brought out his slingshot, and fitted a water-worn pebble into the pouch. He had selected his ammunition from the bed of the stream at the north end of the estate, and each stone was round, smooth and perfectly weighted. Jim had practised with the slingshot until he could bring down a high-flying goose with four throws out of five. He wound up for the throw, swinging the slingshot overhead until it hummed with power. Then he released it and the pebble blurred from the pouch. It caught the dog seal in the centre of its rounded black skull and they heard the fragile bone shatter. The animal died instantly, and its carcass drifted away on the current, twitching convulsively.

8

'He won't be stealing any more fish.' Jim stuffed the slingshot back in the bag. 'And the others will have learned a lesson in manners.' The rest of the seal pack sheered away from the skiff. Jim took up the oar again, and they resumed their interrupted conversation.

Only the previous week Mansur had returned on one of the Courtney ships from a trading voyage up the east coast of Africa as far as the Horn of Hormuz. He was describing to them the wonders he had seen and the marvellous adventures he had shared with his father, who had captained the *Gift of Allah*.

Mansur's father, Dorian Courtney, was the other partner in the company. In his extreme youth he had been captured by Arabian pirates and sold to a prince of Oman, who had adopted him and converted him to Islam. His half-brother Tom Courtney was Christian, while Dorian was Muslim. When Tom had found and rescued his younger brother they had made a happy partnership. Between them they had entry to both religious worlds, and their enterprise had flourished. Over the last twenty years they had traded in India, Arabia and Africa, and sold their exotic goods in Europe.

As Mansur spoke Jim watched his cousin's face, and once again he envied his beauty and his charm. Mansur had inherited it from his father, along with the red-gold hair that hung thickly down his back. Like Dorian he was lithe and quick, while Jim took after his own father, broad and strong. Zama's father, Aboli, had compared them to the bull and the gazelle.

'Come on, coz!' Mansur broke off his tale to tease Jim. 'Zama and I will have the boat filled to the gunwales before you have even woken up. Catch us a fish!'

'I have always prized quality above mere quantity,' Jim retorted, in a pitying tone.

'Well, you have nothing better to do, so you can tell us about your journey to the land of the Hottentots.' Mansur swung another gleaming flapping fish over the side of the skiff.

Jim's plain, honest face lit up with pleasure at the memory of his own adventure. Instinctively he looked northwards

9

across the bay at the rugged mountains, which the morning sun was painting with brightest gold. 'We travelled for thirty-eight days,' he boasted, 'north across the mountains and the great desert, far beyond the frontiers of this colony, which the Governor and the Council of the VOC in Amsterdam have forbidden any man to cross. We trekked into lands where no white man has been before us.' He did not have the fluency or the poetic descriptive powers of his cousin, but his enthusiasm was contagious. Mansur and Zama laughed with him, as he described the barbaric tribes they had encountered and the endless herds of wild game spread across the plains. At intervals he appealed to Zama, 'It's true what I say, isn't it, Zama? You were with me. Tell Mansur it's true.'

Zama nodded solemnly. 'It is true. I swear it on the grave of my own father. Every word is true.'

'One day I will go back.' Jim made the promise to himself, rather than to the others. 'I will go back and cross the blue horizon, to the very limit of this land.'

'And I will go with you, Somoya!' Zama looked at him with complete trust and affection.

Zama remembered what his own father had said of Jim when at last he lay dying on his sleeping kaross, burnt out with age, a ruined giant whose strength had seemed once to hold the very sky suspended. 'Jim Courtney is the true son of his father,' Aboli had whispered. 'Cleave to him as I have to Tom. You will never regret it, my son.'

'I will go with you,' Zama repeated, and Jim winked at him.

'Of course you will, you rogue. Nobody else would have you.' He clapped Zama on the back so hard he almost knocked him off the thwart.

He would have said more but at that moment the coil of cod line jerked under his foot and he let out a triumphant shout. 'Julie knocks at the door. Come in, Big Julie!' He dropped the oar and snatched up the line. He held it strung between both his hands with a slack bight ready to feed out over the side. Without being ordered to do so the other two retrieved their own rigs, stripping the line in over the gunwale, hand over hand, working with feverish speed. They knew how

10

vital it was to give Jim open water in which to work with a truly big fish.

'Come, my prettyling!' Jim whispered to the fish, as he held the line delicately between thumb and finger. He could feel nothing, just the soft press of the current. 'Come, my darling! Papa loves you,' he pleaded.

Then he felt a new pressure on the line, a gentle almost furtive movement. Every nerve in his body jerked bowstring taut. 'She's there. She's still there.'

The line went slack again, 'Don't leave me, sweetest heart. Please don't leave me.' Jim leaned out over the side of the skiff, holding the line high so that it ran straight from his fingers into the green swirl of the waters. The others watched without daring to draw breath. Then, suddenly, they saw his raised right hand drawn down irresistibly by some massive weight. They watched the muscles in his arms and back coil and bunch, like an adder preparing to strike, and neither spoke or moved as the hand holding the line almost touched the surface of the sea.

'Yes!' said Jim quietly. 'Now!' He reared back with the weight of his body behind the strike. 'Yes! And yes and yes!' Each time he said it he heaved back on the line, swinging with alternate arms, right, left and right again. There was no give even to Jim's strength.

'That can't be a fish,' said Mansur. 'No fish is that strong. You must have hooked the bottom.' Jim did not answer him. Now he was leaning back with all his weight, his knees jammed against the wooden gunwale to give himself full purchase. His teeth were gritted, his face turned puce and his eyes seemed to bulge from their sockets.

'Tail on to the line!' he gasped, and the other two scrambled down the deck to help him, but before they reached the stern Jim was jerked off his feet, and sprawled against the side of the boat. The line raced through his fingers, and they could smell the skin, burning like mutton ribs grilling on the coals, as it tore from his palm.

Jim yelled with pain but held on grimly. With a mighty effort he managed to get the line across the edge of the

11

gunwale and tried to jam it there. But he lost more skin as his knuckles slammed into the wood. With one hand he snatched off his cap to use as a glove while he held the line against the wood. All three were yelling like demons in hellfire.

'Give me a hand! Grab the end!'

'Let him run. You'll straighten the hook.'

'Get the bucket. Throw water on it! The line will burst into flames!'

Zama managed to get both hands on the line, but even with their combined strength they could not stop the run of the great fish. The line hissed with the strain as it raced over the side, and they could feel the sweep of the great tail pulsing through it.

'Water, for the love of Christ, wet it down!' Jim howled, and Mansur scooped a bucketful from alongside and dashed it over their hands and the sizzling line. There was a puff of steam as the water boiled off.

'By God! We've almost lost all of this coil,' Jim shouted, as he saw the end of the line in the bottom of the wooden tub that held it. 'Quick as you can, Mansur! Tie on another coil.' Mansur worked quickly, with the dexterity for which he was renowned, but he was only just in time; as he tightened the knot the rope was jerked from his grasp and pulled through the fingers of the other two, ripping off more skin, before it went over the side and down into the green depths.

'Stop!' Jim pleaded with the fish. 'Are you trying to kill us, Julie? Will you not stop, my beauty?'

'That's half the second coil gone already,' Mansur warned them. 'Let me take over from you, Jim. There's blood all over the deck.'

'No, no.' Jim shook his head vehemently. 'She's slowing down. Heart's almost broken.'

'Yours or hers?' Mansur asked.

'Go on the stage, coz,' Jim advised him grimly. 'Your wit is wasted here.'

The running line began to slow as it passed through their torn fingers. Then it stopped. 'Leave the water bucket,' Jim ordered. 'Get a grip on the line.' Mansur hung on behind

Zama and, with the extra weight, Jim could let go with one hand and suck his fingers. 'Do we do this for fun?' he asked, wonderingly. Then his voice became businesslike. 'Now it's our turn, Julie.'

Keeping pressure on the line while they moved, they rearranged themselves down the length of the deck, standing nose to tail, bent double with the line passed back between their legs.

'One, two and a tiger!' Jim gave them the timing, and they heaved the line in, swinging their weight on it together. The knotted joint came back in over the side, and Mansur, as third man, coiled the line back into the tub. Four times more the great fish gathered its strength and streaked away and they were forced to let it take out line, but each time the run was shorter. Then they turned its head and brought it back, struggling and jolting, its strength slowly waning.

Suddenly Jim at the head of the line gave a shout of joy. 'There she is! I can see her down there.' The fish turned in a wide circle deep below the hull. As she came round her bronze-red side caught the sunlight and flashed like a mirror.

'Sweet Jesus, she's beautiful!' Jim could see the fish's huge golden eye staring up at him through the emerald-coloured water. The steenbras's mouth opened and closed spasmodically, the gill plates flaring as they pumped water through, starving for oxygen. Those jaws were cavernous enough to take in a grown man's head and shoulders, and they were lined with serried ranks of fangs as long and thick as his forefinger.

'Now I believe Uncle Dorry's tale.' Jim gasped with the exertion. 'Those teeth could easily bite off a man's leg.'

At last, almost two hours after Jim had first set the hook in the hinge of the fish's jaw, they had it alongside the skiff. Between them they lifted the gigantic head clear of the water. As soon as they did so the fish went into its last frenzy. Its body was half as long again as a tall man, and as thick around the middle as a Shetland pony. It pulsed and flexed until its nose touched the wide flukes of its tail, first on the one side, then on the other. It threw up sheets of seawater that came aboard in solid gouts, drenching the three lads as though they

13

stood under a waterfall. They held on grimly, until the violent paroxysms weakened. Then Jim called out, 'Hang on to her! She's ready for the priest.'

He snatched up the billy from its sling under the transom. The end of the club was weighted with lead, balanced and heavy in his big right hand. He lifted the fish's head high and swung his weight behind the blow. It caught the fish across the bony ridge above those glaring yellow eyes. The massive body stiffened in death and violent tremors ran down its shimmering sun-red flanks. Then the life went out of it and, white belly uppermost, it floated alongside the skiff with its gill plates open wide as a lady's parasol.

Drenched with sweat and seawater, panting wildly, nursing their torn hands, they leaned on the transom and gazed in awe upon the marvellous creature they had killed. There were no words to express adequately the overpowering emotions of triumph and remorse, of jubilation and melancholy that gripped them now that the ultimate passion of the hunter had come to its climax.

'In the Name of the Prophet, this is Leviathan indeed,' Mansur said softly. 'He makes me feel so small.'

'The sharks will be here any minute.' Jim broke the spell. 'Help me get her on board.' They threaded the rope through the fish's gills, then all three hauled on it, the skiff listing dangerously close to the point of capsizing as they brought it over the side. The boat was barely large enough to contain its bulk and there was no room for them to sit on the thwarts so they perched on the gunwale. A scale had been torn off as the fish slid over the side: it was the size of a gold doubloon and as bright.

Mansur picked it up, and turned it to catch the sunlight, staring at it with fascination. 'We must take this fish home to High Weald,' he said.

'Why?' Jim asked brusquely.

'To show the family, my father and yours.'

'By nightfall she'll have lost her colour, her scales will be dry and dull, and her flesh will start to rot and stink.' Jim shook his head. 'I want to remember her like this, in all her glory.'

'What are we going to do with her then?'

'Sell her to the purser of the VOC ship.'

'Such a wonderful creature. Sell her like a sack of potatoes? That seems like sacrilege,' Mansur protested.

'"I give you of the beasts of the earth and the fish of the sea." Kill! Eat!' Jim quoted. 'Genesis. God's very words. How could it be sacrilege?'

'Your God, not mine,' Mansur contradicted him.

'He's the same God, yours and mine. We just call him different names.'

'He is my God also.' Zama was not to be left out. 'Kulu Kulu, the Greatest of the Great Ones.'

Jim wrapped a strip of cloth round his injured hand. 'In the name of Kulu Kulu then. This steenbras is the means to get aboard the Dutch ship. I am going to use it as a letter of introduction to the purser. It's not just one fish I'm going to sell him, it's all the produce from High Weald.'

With the north-westerly breeze blowing ten knots behind them they could hoist the single sail, which carried them swiftly into the bay. There were eight ships lying at anchor under the guns of the castle. Most had been there for weeks and were already well provisioned.

Jim pointed out the latest arrival. 'They will not have set foot on land for months. They will be famished for fresh food. They are probably riddled with scurvy already.' Jim put the tiller over and wove through the anchored shipping. 'After what they almost did to us, they owe us a nice bit of profit.' All the Courtneys were traders to the core of their being and for even the youngest of them the word 'profit' held almost religious significance. Jim headed for the Dutch ship. It was a tall three-decker, twenty guns a side, square-rigged, three masts, big and beamy, obviously an armed trader. She flew the VOC pennant and the flag of the Dutch Republic. As they closed with her Jim could see the storm damage to hull and rigging. Clearly she had endured a rough passage. Closer still, Jim could make out the ship's name on her stern in faded gilt lettering: *Het Gelukkige Meeuw*, the *Lucky Seagull*. He grinned at how inappropriately the shabby old lady had

15

been named. Then his green eyes narrowed with surprise and interest.

'Women, by God!' He pointed ahead. 'Hundreds of them.' Both Mansur and Zama scrambled to their feet, clung to the mast and peered ahead, shading their eyes against the sun.

'You're right!' Mansur exclaimed. Apart from the wives of the burghers, their stolid, heavily chaperoned daughters and the trollops of the waterfront taverns, women were rare at the Cape of Good Hope.

'Look at them,' Jim breathed with awe. 'Just look at those beauties.' Forward of the mainmast the deck was crowded with female shapes.

'How do you know they're beautiful?' Mansur demanded. 'We're too far away to tell. They're probably ugly old crones.'

'No, God could not be so cruel to us.' Jim laughed excitedly. 'Every one of them is an angel from heaven. I just know it!'

There was a small group of officers on the quarter-deck, and knots of seamen were already at work repairing the damaged rigging and painting the hull. But the three youths in the skiff had eyes only for the female shapes on the foredeck. Once again they caught a whiff of the stench that hung over the ship, and Jim exclaimed with horror: 'They're in leg irons.' He had the sharpest eyesight of the three and had seen that the ranks of women were shuffling along the deck in single file, with the hampered gait of the chained captive.

'Convicts!' Mansur agreed. 'Your angels from heaven are female convicts. Uglier than sin.'

They were close enough now to make out the features of some of the bedraggled creatures, the grey, greasy hair, the toothless mouths, the wrinkled pallor of ancient skin, the sunken eyes and, on most of the miserable faces, the ugly blotches and bruises of scurvy. They stared down on the approaching boat with dull, hopeless eyes, showing no interest, no emotion of any kind.

Even Jim's lascivious instincts were cooled. These were no longer human beings, but beaten, abused animals. Their coarse

16

canvas shifts were ragged and soiled. Obviously they had worn them ever since leaving Amsterdam, without water to wash their bodies, let alone their clothing. There were guards armed with muskets stationed in the mainmast bitts and the fore-castle overlooking the deck. As the skiff came within hail a petty officer in a blue pea-jacket hurried to the ship's side and raised a speaking trumpet to his lips. 'Stand clear,' he shouted in Dutch. 'This is a prison ship. Stand off or we will fire into you.'

'He means it, Jim,' Mansur said. 'Let's get away from her.'

Jim ignored the suggestion and held up one of the fish. '*Vars vis*! Fresh fish,' he yelled back. 'Straight out of the sea. Caught an hour ago.' The man at the rail hesitated, and Jim sensed his opportunity. 'Look at this one.' He pointed at the huge carcass that filled most of the skiff. 'Steenbras! Finest eating fish in the sea! There's enough here to feed every man on board for a week.'

'Wait!' the man yelled back, and hurried across the deck to the group of officers. There was a brief discussion, then he came back to the rail. 'Good, then. Come! But keep clear of our bows. Hook on to the stern chains.'

Mansur dropped the tiny sail and they rowed under the side of the ship. Three seamen stood at the rail, aiming their muskets down into the skiff.

'Don't try anything clever,' the petty officer warned them, 'unless you want a ball in your belly.'

Jim grinned up at him ingratiatingly and showed his empty hands. 'We mean no harm, Mijnheer. We are honest fisher-men.' He was still fascinated by the lines of chained women, and stared up at them with revulsion and pity as they shuffled in a sorry line along the near rail. Then he switched his attention to bringing the skiff alongside. He did this with a seamanlike flourish, and Zama tossed the painter up to a sea-man who was waiting in the chains above them.

The ship's purser, a plump bald man, stuck his head over the side and peered down into the skiff to inspect the wares on offer. He looked impressed by the size of the giant steenbras carcass. 'I'm not going to shout. Come up here where we can

17

talk,' the purser invited Jim, and ordered a seaman to drop a rope-ladder over the side. This was the invitation Jim had been angling for. He shinned up and over the high tumble-home of the ship's side like an acrobat, and landed on the deck beside the purser with a slap of his bare feet.

'How much for the big one?' The purser's question was ambiguous, and he ran a pederast's calculating glance over Jim's body. A fine bit of beef, he thought, as he studied the muscled chest and arms, and the long, shapely legs, smooth and tanned by the sun.

'Fifteen silver guilders for the entire load of our fish.' Jim placed emphasis on the last word. The purser's interest in him was obvious.

'Are you an escaped lunatic?' the purser retorted. 'You, your fish and your dirty little boat together are not worth half that much.'

'The boat and I are not for sale,' Jim assured him, with relish. When he was bargaining he was in his element. His father had trained him well. He had no compunction in taking advantage of the purser's sexual predilections to push him for the best price. They settled on eight guilders for the full load.

'I want to keep the smallest fish for my family's dinner.' Jim said, and the purser chuckled. 'You drive a hard bargain, *kerel*.' He spat on his right hand and proffered it. Jim spat on his own and they shook hands to seal the bargain.

The purser held on to Jim's hand for a little longer than was necessary. 'What else have you got for sale, young stallion?' He winked at Jim and ran his tongue round his fat, sun-cracked lips.

Jim did not answer him at once, but went to the rail to watch the crew of *Het Gelukkige Meeuw* lower a cargo net into the skiff. With difficulty Mansur and Zama slid the huge fish into it. Then it was hoisted up and swung on to the deck. Jim turned back to the purser. 'I can sell you a load of fresh vegetables – potatoes, onions, pumpkins, fruit, anything you want at half the price they will charge you if you buy from the Company gardens,' Jim told him.

18

'You know full well that the VOC has the monopoly,' the purser demurred. 'I am forbidden to buy from private traders.'

'I can fix that with a few guilders in the right pocket.' Jim touched the side of his nose. Everyone knew how simple it was to placate the Company officials at Good Hope. Corruption was a way of life in the colonies.

'Very well, then. Bring me out a load of the best you have,' the purser agreed, and laid an avuncular hand on Jim's arm. 'But don't get caught at it. We don't want a pretty boy like you all cut up with the lash.' Jim evaded his touch without making it obvious. Never upset a customer. There was a sudden commotion on the foredeck and, grateful for the respite from these plump and sweaty attentions, Jim glanced over his shoulder.

The first group of women prisoners was being herded down below decks, and another line was coming up into the open air for their exercise. Jim stared at the girl at the head of this new file of prisoners. His breath came short and his pulse pounded in his ears. She was tall, but starved thin and pale. She wore a shift of threadbare canvas, with a hem so tattered that her knees showed through the holes. Her legs were thin and bony, the flesh melted off by starvation, and her arms were the same. Under the shapeless canvas her body seemed boyish, lacking the swells and round contours of a woman. But Jim was not looking at her body: he was gazing at her face.

Her head was small but gracefully poised on her long neck, like an unopened tulip on its stem. Her skin was pale and flawless, so fine in texture that he imagined he could see her cheekbones through it. Even in her terrible circumstances she had clearly made an effort to prevent herself sinking into the slough of despair. Her hair was pulled back from her face, plaited into a thick rope that hung forward over one shoulder, and she had contrived somehow to keep it clean and combed. It reached down almost to her waist, fine as spun Chinese silk and blonde, dazzling as a golden guinea in the sunlight. But it was her eyes that stopped Jim's breath altogether for a long minute. They were blue, the colour of the high African sky in midsummer. When she looked upon him for the first time they opened wide. Then her lips parted and her teeth were white and even, with no gaps between them. She stopped abruptly, and the woman behind stumbled into her. Both lost their balance and almost fell. Their leg irons clanked, and the other woman thrust her forward roughly, cursing her in the accents of the Antwerp docklands. 'Come on, princess, move your pretty pussy.'

The girl did not seem to notice.

One of the gaolers stepped up behind her. 'Keep moving, you stupid cow.' With the length of knotted rope he hit her across the top of her thin bare arm, raising a vivid red welt. Jim fought to stop himself rushing to protect her, and the nearest guard sensed the movement. He swung the muzzle of his musket towards Jim, who stepped back. He knew that at that range the buckshot would have disembowelled him. But the girl had seen his gesture too, recognized something in him. She stumbled forward, her eyes filled with tears of pain from the lash, massaging the crimson welt with her other hand. She kept those haunting eyes on his face as she passed where Jim stood rooted to the deck. He knew it was dangerous and futile to speak to her, but the words were out before he could bite down on them and there was pity in his tone. 'They've starved you.'

A pale travesty of a smile flickered across her lips, but she gave no other sign of having heard him. Then the harridan in the line behind her shoved her forward: 'No young cock for you today, your highness. You'll have to use your finger. Keep moving.' The girl went on down the deck away from him.

'Let me give you some advice, *kerel*,' said the purser at his shoulder. 'Don't try anything with any of those bitches. That's the shortest way to hell.'

Jim mustered a grin. 'I'm a brave man, but not a stupid one.' He held out his hand and the purser counted eight silver coins into his palm. He swung a leg over the rail. 'I'll bring out a load of vegetables for you tomorrow. Then perhaps we can go ashore together and have a grog in one of the taverns.' As he dropped down into the skiff, he muttered, 'Or I could break your neck and both your fat legs.' He took his place at the tiller.

'Cast off, hoist the sail,' he called to Zama, and brought the skiff on to the wind. They skimmed down the side of the *Meeuw*. The port-lids on the gunports were open to let light and air into the gundecks. Jim looked into the nearest as he came level. The crowded, fetid gundeck was a vision from hell, and the stench was like a pig-sty or cesspit. Hundreds of human beings had been crowded into that low, narrow space for months without relief.

Jim tore away his gaze, and glanced up at the ship's rail, high above his head. He was still looking for the girl, but he expected to be disappointed. Then his pulse leaped as those unbelievably blue eyes stared down at him. In the line of women prisoners the girl was shuffling along the rail near the bows.

'Your name? What's your name?' he called urgently. At that moment to know it was the most important thing in the world.

Her reply was faint on the wind, but he read it on her lips: 'Louisa.'

'I'll come back, Louisa. Be of good cheer,' he shouted recklessly, and she stared at him expressionlessly. Then he did something even more reckless. He knew it was madness, but she was starved. He snatched up the red stumpnose he had kept back from the sale. It weighed almost ten pounds but he tossed it up lightly. Louisa reached out and caught it in both hands, with a hungry, desperate expression on her face. The grotesque troll in the line behind her jumped forward and tried to wrest it out of her grasp. Immediately three or four other women joined the struggle, fighting over the fish like a pack of she-wolves. Then the gaolers rushed in to break up the mêlée, flogging and lashing the shrieking women with the knotted ropes. Jim turned away, sick to the guts, his heart torn with pity and with some other emotion he did not recognize for he had never experienced it before.

The three sailed on in grim silence, but every few minutes Jim turned to look back at the prison ship.

21

'There is nothing you can do for her,' Mansur said at last. 'Forget her, coz. She's out of your reach.'

Jim's face darkened with anger and frustration. 'Is she? You think you know everything, Mansur Courtney. We shall see. We shall see!'

On the beach ahead one of the grooms was holding a string of harnessed mules, ready to help them beach the skiff. 'Don't just sit there like a pair of cormorants drying your wings on a rock. Get the sail down,' Jim snarled at the other two with the formless, undirected anger still dark upon him.

They waited on the first line of the surf, hanging on the oars, waiting for the right wave. When Jim saw it coming he shouted, 'Here we go. Give way together. Pull!'

It swept under the stern and then suddenly, exhilaratingly, they were surfing on the brow of the curling green wave, racing on to the beach. The wave carried them high, then pulled back to leave them stranded. They jumped out and when the groom galloped in with the team of mules, they hitched on to the trek chain. They ran beside the team, whooping to drive them on, dragging the skiff well above the high-water mark, then unhitched it.

'I'll need the team again first thing tomorrow morning,' Jim told the groom. 'Have them ready.'

'So, we're going out to that hell ship again, are we?' Mansur asked flatly.

'To take them a load of vegetables.' Jim feigned innocence.

'What do you want to trade in return?' Mansur asked, with equal insouciance. Jim punched his arm lightly and they jumped on to the bare backs of the mules. Jim took one last, brooding look across the bay to where the prison ship was anchored, then they rode round the shore of the lagoon, up the hill towards the whitewashed buildings of the estate, the homestead and the godown that Tom Courtney had named High Weald after the great mansion in Devon where he and Dorian had been born, and which neither of them had laid eyes on for so many years.

The name was the only thing that the two houses had in common. This one was built in the Cape style. The roof was

22

thatched thickly with reeds. The graceful gabled ends and the archway leading into the central courtyard had been designed by the celebrated Dutch architect, Anreith. The name of the estate and the family emblem were incorporated into the ornate fresco of cherubs and saints above the archway. The emblem depicted a long-barrelled cannon on its wheeled carriage with a ribbon below it, and the letters 'CBTC' for Courtney Brothers Trading Company. In a separate panel was the legend: 'High Weald, 1711'. The house had been built in the same year that Jim and Mansur were born.

As they clattered through the archway and into the cobbled courtyard, Tom Courtney came stamping out of the main doors of the warehouse. He was a big man, over six foot tall, heavy in the shoulders. His dense black beard was shot through with silver and his pate was innocent of a single strand of hair, but thick curls surrounded the shiny bald scalp and bushed down the back of his neck. His belly, once flat and hard, had taken on a magisterial girth. His craggy features were laced with webs of laughter lines, while his eyes gleamed with humour and the contentment of a supremely confident, prosperous man.

'James Courtney! You've been gone so long I'd forgotten what you looked like. It's good of you to drop in. I hate to trouble you, but do any of you intend doing any work this day?'

Jim hunched his shoulders guiltily. 'We were almost run down by a Dutch ship, damned nigh sunk us. Then we caught a red steenbras the size of a carthorse. It took two hours to bring it in. We had to take it out to sell to one of the ships in the bay.'

'By Jesus, boy, you've had a busy morning. Don't tell me the rest of your tribulations, let me guess. You were attacked by a French ship-of-the-line, and charged by a wounded hippo.' Tom roared with delight at his own wit. 'Anyway, how much did you get for a carthorse-sized steenbras?' he demanded.

'Eight silver guilders.'

Tom whistled. 'It must have been a monster.' Then his

expression became serious. 'Ain't no excuse, lad. I didn't give you the week off. You should have been back hours ago.'

'I haggled with the purser of the Dutch ship,' Jim told him. 'He will take all the provender we can send him – and at good prices, Papa.'

A shrewd expression replaced the laughter in Tom's eyes. 'Seems you ain't wasted your time. Well done, lad.'

At that moment a fine-looking woman, almost as tall as Tom, stepped out of the kitchens at the opposite end of the courtyard. Her hair was scraped up into a heavy bun on top of her head, and the sleeves of her blouse were rolled up around her plump sun-browned arms. 'Tom Courtney, don't you realize the poor child left this morning without breakfast. Let him eat a meal before you bully him any more.'

'Sarah Courtney,' Tom shouted back, 'this poor child of yours isn't five years old any longer.'

'It's your lunchtime too.' Sarah changed tack. 'Yasmini, the girls and I have been slaving over the stove all morning. Come along now, all of you.'

Tom threw up his hands in capitulation. 'Sarah, you're a tyrant, but I could eat a buffalo bull with the horns on,' he said. He came down off the veranda and put one arm around Jim's shoulders, the other round Mansur's and led them towards the kitchen door, where Sarah waited for them with her arms powdered to the elbows with flour.

Zama took the team of mules and led them out of the courtyard towards the stables. 'Zama, tell my brother that the ladies are waiting lunch for him,' Tom called after him,

'I will tell him, *oubaas*!' Zama used the most respectful term of address for the master of High Weald.

'As soon as you have finished eating, you get back here with all the men,' Jim warned him. 'We have to pick and load a cargo of vegetables to take out to the *Lucky Seagull* tomorrow.'

The kitchen was bustling with women, most of them freed house slaves, graceful, golden-skinned Javanese women from Batavia. Jim went to embrace his mother.

Sarah pretended to be put out, 'Don't be a great booby,

24

James,' but she flushed with pleasure as he lifted her and bussed her on both cheeks. 'Put me down at once and let me get on.'

'If you don't love me then at least Aunt Yassie does.' He went to the delicate, lovely woman who was wrapped in the arms of her own son. 'Come now, Mansur! It's my turn now.' He lifted Yasmini out of Mansur's embrace. She wore a long *ghāgrā* skirt and a *colī* blouse of vivid silk. She was as slim and light as a girl, her skin a glowing amber, her slanting eyes dark as onyx. The snowy blaze through the front of her dense dark hair was not a sign of age: she had been born with it, as had her mother and grandmother before her.

With the women fussing over them, the men seated themselves at the top of the long yellow-wood table, which was piled with bowls and platters. There were dishes of bobootie curry in the Malayan style, redolent with mutton and spices, rich with eggs and yoghurt, an enormous venison pie, made with potatoes and the meat of the springbuck Jim and Mansur had shot out in the open veld, loaves of bread still hot from the oven, pottery crocks of yellow butter, jugs of thick sour milk and small beer.

'Where is Dorian?' Tom demanded, from the head of the table. 'Late again!'

'Did someone call my name?' Dorian sauntered into the kitchen, still lean and athletic, handsome and debonair, his head a mass of copper curls to match his son's. He wore high riding boots that were dusty to the knees, and a wide-brimmed straw hat. He spun the hat across the room, and the women greeted him with a chorus of delight.

'Quiet! All of you! You sound like a flock of hens when a jackal gets into the coop,' Tom bellowed. The noise subsided almost imperceptibly. 'Come on, sit down, Dorry, before you drive these women wild. We are to hear the tale of the giant steenbras the boys caught, and the deal they have done with the VOC ship lying out in the bay.'

Dorian took the chair beside his brother, and sank the blade of his knife through the crust of the venison pie. There was a sigh of approval from all of the company as a fragrant cloud of steam rose to the high stinkwood beams of the ceiling. As Sarah spooned the food on to the blue willow-pattern plates the room was filled with banter from the men, giggles and spontaneous demonstrations of affection from the women.

'What's wrong with Jim Boy?' Sarah looked across the table, and raised her voice above the pandemonium.

'Nothing,' said Tom, with the next spoonful half-way to his mouth. He looked sharply at his only son. 'Is there?'

Slowly silence settled over the table and everyone stared at Jim. 'Why aren't you eating?' Sarah demanded with alarm. Jim's vast appetite was a family legend. 'What you need is a dose of sulphur and molasses.'

'I'm fine, just not hungry.' Jim glanced down at the pie he had barely touched, then at the circle of faces. 'Don't look at me like that. I'm not going to die.'

Sarah was still watching him. 'What happened today?'

Jim knew she could see through him as though he was made of glass. He jumped to his feet. 'Please excuse me,' he said, pushed back his stool and stalked out of the kitchen into the yard.

Tom lumbered to his feet to follow him, but Sarah shook her head. 'Leave him be, husband,' she said. Only one person could give Tom Courtney orders, and he subsided obediently on to his stool. In contrast to the mood of only moments before, the room was plunged into a heavy, fraught silence.

Sarah looked across the table. 'What happened out there today, Mansur?'

'Jim went aboard the convict ship in the bay. He saw things that upset him.'

'What things?' she asked.

'The ship is filled with women prisoners. They had been chained, starved and beaten. The ship sinks like a pig-sty,' Mansur said, repugnance and pity in his voice. Silence descended again as they visualized the scene Mansur had described.

Then Sarah said softly, 'And one of the women on board was young and pretty.'

26

'How did you know that?' Mansur stared at her with astonishment.

Jim strode out through the archway and down the hill towards the paddock at the edge of the lagoon. As the track emerged from the trees he put two fingers into his mouth and whistled. The stallion was a little separated from the rest of the herd, grazing on the green grass at the edge of the water. He threw up his head at the sound, and the blaze on his forehead shone like a diadem in the sunlight. He arched his neck, flared his wide Arabian nostrils and stared across at Jim with luminous eyes. Jim whistled again. 'Come, Drumfire,' he called. 'Come to me.'

Drumfire glided from a standstill into a full gallop in a few strides. For such a large animal he moved with the grace of an antelope. Just watching him Jim felt his black mood begin to evaporate. The animal's coat gleamed like oiled mahogany and his mane streamed out over his back like a war banner. His steel-shod hoofs tore chunks out of the green turf with the thunder of rapid fire from a massed battery of cannon, the sound for which Jim had named him.

Riding against the burghers of the colony and the officers of the cavalry regiment, Jim and Drumfire had won the Governor's Gold Plate last Christmas Day. In doing so Drumfire had proved he was the fastest horse in Africa, and Jim had spurned an offer of two thousand guilders for him from Colonel Stephanus Keyser, the commander of the garrison. Horse and rider had won honour but no friends that day.

Drumfire swept down the track, running straight at Jim. He loved to try to make his master flinch. Jim stood his ground and, at the very last instant, Drumfire swerved so close that the wind of his passing ruffled Jim's hair. Then he came to a dead stop on braced front legs, nodding and neighing wildly.

'You great showman,' Jim told him. 'Behave yourself.' Suddenly docile as a kitten Drumfire came back and nuzzled his chest, snuffling at the pockets of his coat until he smelt the slice of plum cake. 'Cupboard love,' Jim told him firmly.

Drumfire pushed him with his forehead, gently at first but then so demandingly that Jim was lifted off his feet. 'You don't deserve it, but . . .' Jim relented and held out the cake. Drumfire drooled into his open palm as he picked up every last crumb with velvet lips. Jim wiped his hand on the shining neck, then laid one hand on the horse's withers and leaped lightly on to his back. At the touch of his heels, Drumfire glided again into that miraculous stride, and the wind whipped tears from the corners of Jim's eyes. They raced along the edge of the lagoon, but when Jim touched him behind the shoulder with his toe the stallion did not hesitate. He turned and plunged into the shallows, startling a shoal of mullet into brief flight like a handful of spinning silver guilders across the green surface. Abruptly Drumfire was into the deep and Jim slipped into the water beside him as he swam. He grasped a handful of the long mane, and let the stallion tow him along. Swimming was another of Drumfire's great joys and the horse gave loud grunts of pleasure. As soon as he felt the bottom of the far shore under the horse's hoofs Jim slid on to his back again, and they burst out on to the beach at full stride.

Jim turned him down towards the seashore, and they crossed the high dunes, leaving deep hoofprints in the white sand, and went down the other side to where the surf crashed on to the beach. Without check Drumfire galloped along the edge of the water, running first on the hard wet sand, then belly deep through salt water as the waves came ashore. At last Jim slowed him to a walk. The stallion had galloped away his black mood, his anger and guilt left on the wind. He jumped up and stretched to his full height on Drumfire's back, and the horse adjusted his gait smoothly to help him balance. This was just one of the tricks they had taught each other.

Standing high Jim gazed out over the bay. The *Meeuw* had swung on her anchor so that she lay broadside to the beach. From this distance she looked as honest and respectable as a burgher's goodwife, giving no outward sign of the horrors hidden within her drab hull.

'Wind's changed,' Jim told his horse, who cocked an ear back to listen to his voice. 'It'll blow up a hell-storm in the next few days.' He imagined the conditions below the decks of the convict ship if she were still anchored in the bay, which was open to the west, when it came. His black mood was returning. He dropped back astride Drumfire and rode on at a more sedate pace towards the castle. By the time they arrived below the massive stone walls his clothing had dried, although his *velskoen* boots made of kudu skin were still damp.

Captain Hugo van Hoogen, the quartermaster of the garrison, was in his office beside the main powder magazine. He gave Jim a friendly welcome, then offered him a pipe of Turkish tobacco and a cup of Arabian coffee. Jim refused the pipe but drank the dark, bitter brew with relish – his aunt Yasmini had introduced them all to it. Jim and the quartermaster were old accomplices. It was accepted between them that Jim was the unofficial go-between of the Courtney family. If Hugo signed a licence stating that the Company was unable to supply provisions or stores to any ship in the bay, then the private chandler designated in the document was allowed to make good the shortfall. Hugo was also an avid fisherman, and Jim related the saga of the steenbras, to a chorus from Hugo of '*Ag nee*, man!' and '*Dis nee war nee*! It's not true!'

When Jim shook hands with him and took his leave, he had in his pocket a blank licence to trade in the name of Courtney Brothers Trading Company. 'I will come and drink coffee with you again on Saturday.' Jim winked.

Hugo nodded genially. 'You will be more than welcome, my young friend.' From long experience he knew that he could trust Jim to bring his commission in a little purse of gold and silver coin.

Back in the stables on High Weald Jim rubbed Drumfire down, rather than letting one of the grooms do the job, then left him with a manger of crushed corn, over which he had dribbled molasses. Drumfire had a sweet tooth.

The fields and orchards behind the stables were filled with freed slaves gathering in the fresh produce destined for the *Meeuw*. Most of the bushel baskets were already filled with

29

potatoes and apples, pumpkins and turnips. His father and Mansur were supervising the harvest. Jim left them to it, and went down to the slaughterhouse. In the cavernous cool room, with its thick, windowless walls, dozens of freshly slaughtered sheep carcasses hung from hooks in the ceiling. Jim drew the knife from the sheath on his belt and whipped the blade, with practised strokes, across the whetstone as he went to join his uncle Dorian. To prepare all the produce they needed to supply to the ship, everyone on the estate had to help with the work. Freed slaves dragged in fat-tailed Persian sheep from the holding pen, held them down and pulled back their heads to expose the throats to the stroke of the knife. Other willing hands lifted the dead animals on to the hooks and stripped off the bloody fleeces.

Weeks ago, Carl Otto, the estate butcher, had filled his smokeroom with hams and sausages for just such an opportunity. In the kitchens all the women from eldest to youngest were helping Sarah and Yasmini to bottle fruit and pickle vegetables.

Despite their best efforts it was late in the afternoon before the convoy of mule carts was fully loaded and had set off down to the beach. The transfer of the provisions from the carts to the beached bumboats took most of the rest of the night, and it was almost dawn before they were loaded.

Despite Jim's misgivings the wind had not increased in strength and the sea and surf were manageable as the mule teams dragged the heavily laden boats down the sand. The first glimmer of dawn was in the eastern sky by the time the little convoy was on its way. Jim was at the tiller in the leading boat and Mansur was on the stroke oar.

'What have you got in the bag, Jim?' he asked, between strokes.

'Ask no questions and you'll hear no lies.' Jim glanced down at the waterproof canvas bag that lay between his feet. He kept his voice low so that his father did not overhear. Luckily Tom Courtney, who stood in the bows, had fired so many heavy muskets in his long career as a hunter that his hearing was dull.

'Is it a gift for a sweetheart?' Mansur grinned slyly in the darkness, but Jim ignored him. That arrow was too near the bullseye for comfort. Jim had carefully packed into the bag a bundle of salted, sun-dried venison, the ubiquitous *biltong* of the Cape Boers, ten pounds of hard ship's biscuit wrapped in a cloth, a folding knife and a triangular-bladed file that he had pilfered from the estate workshop, a tortoiseshell comb, which belonged to his mother, and a letter written on a single sheet of paper in Dutch.

They came up to the *Meeuw*, and Tom Courtney hailed her in a bull bellow: 'Longboat with supplies. Permission to hook on?'

There was an answering shout from the ship and they rowed in, bumping lightly against the tall hull.

With her long legs folded under her, Louisa Leuven sat on the hard deck in the noisome semi-darkness that was lit only by the feeble light of the fighting-lanterns. Her shoulders were covered with a single thin cotton blanket of the poorest quality. The gunports were closed and bolted. The guards were taking no chances: with the shore so close, some of the women might take the risk in the cold green currents, undeterred by the possibility of drowning or being devoured by the monstrous sharks that were attracted to these waters by the swarming seal colony on Robben Island. While the women had been on deck that afternoon the cook had thrown overboard a bucket of guts from the red steenbras. The head gaoler had pointed out to his prisoners the triangular fins of the sharks as they sped in to snatch these bloody morsels.

'Don't any of you filthy slatterns get ideas of escape,' he cautioned them.

At the beginning of the voyage Louisa had claimed for herself this berth under one of the huge bronze cannons. She was stronger than most of the other wizened undernourished convicts and, of necessity, she had learned how to protect herself. Life on board was like being in a pack of wild animals:

the women around her were every bit as dangerous and merciless as wolves, but shrewder and more cunning. At the beginning Louisa knew she had to procure a weapon so she had managed to prise loose a strip of the bronze beading from under the carriage of the cannon. She had spent long hours of the night stropping this against the cannon barrel until it had a sharp double stiletto edge. She tore a strip of canvas from the hem of her shift and wrapped it round the hilt to make a handle. She carried the dagger, day and night, in the pouch she wore strapped around her waist under the canvas shift. So far she had been forced to cut only one of the other women.

Nedda was a Frieslander, with heavy thighs and bottom, fat arms and a pudding face covered with freckles. She had once been a notorious whore-mistress for the nobility. She had specialized in procuring young children for her rich clients, until she became too greedy and tried to blackmail one. On a hot, tropical night as the ship lay becalmed a few degrees south of the equator, Big Nedda had crept up on Louisa in the night, and pinned her down under her suffocating weight. None of the gaolers or any of the women had come to Louisa's rescue as she screamed and struggled. Instead they had giggled and egged Nedda on.

'Give it to the high and mighty bitch.'

'Listen to her squealing for it. She loves it.'

'Go on, Big Nedda. Shove your fist up that prim royal *poesje*.'

When Louisa felt the woman prise her legs apart with a fat knee, she reached down, slipped the blade out of its pouch and slashed Nedda's chubby red cheek. Nedda howled and rolled off her, clutching the deep, spurting wound. Then she crept away, sobbing and moaning, into the darkness. During the next few weeks the wound had festered, and Nedda had crouched like a bear in the darkest recess of the gundeck, her face swollen to double its size, pus leaking out through the dirty bandage, dripping yellow and thick as cream from her chin. Since then Nedda had kept well clear of Louisa, and the other women had learned from her example. They left her well alone.

For Louisa this dreadful voyage seemed to have lasted all her life. Even during this respite from the open sea, while the *Meeuw* lay at anchor in Table Bay, the magnitude of the ordeal she had undergone still haunted her. She cowered further into her refuge under the cannon and shuddered as each of the separate memories pricked her like thorns. The throng of humanity was pressed close about her. They were packed so tightly into every inch of the deck that it was almost impossible to escape the touch of other filthy bodies crawling with lice. In rough weather the latrine buckets slopped over, and the sewage ran down the crowded deck. It soaked the women's clothing and their thin cotton blankets where they lay. During the occasional spells of calm weather the crew pumped seawater down the hatches and the women went down on their knees to scrub the planks with the coarse holystones. It was in vain, for during the next storm the filth splashed over them again. In the dawn when the hatches were taken off the companionways, they took turns to carry the reeking wooden buckets up the ladders to the deck and empty them over the side while the crew and the guards jeered at them.

Every Sunday, in any kind of weather, the prisoners were mustered on deck while the guards stood over them with loaded muskets. The women, in their leg irons and ragged canvas shifts, shivered and hugged themselves with their thin arms, their skin blue and pimpled with the cold, while the Dutch Reform dominie harangued them for their sins. When this ordeal was over the crew set up canvas screens on the foredeck, and in groups the prisoners were forced behind them while streams of seawater were sprayed over them from the ship's pumps. Louisa and some of the more fastidious women stripped off their shifts and tried as best they could to wash off the filth. The screens fluttered in the wind and afforded them almost no privacy, and the seamen on the pumps or in the rigging overhead whistled and called ribald comments.

'Look at the dugs on that cow!'

'You could sail a ship-of-the-line up that great hairy harbour.'

Louisa learned to use her wet shift to cover herself, as she crouched low, screening herself behind the other women. The few hours of cleanliness were worth the humiliation, but as soon as her shift dried and the warmth of her body hatched the next batch of nits she began to scratch again. With her bronze blade she whittled a splinter of wood into a fine-tooth comb and spent hours each day under the gun carriage combing the nits out of her long, golden hair, and from the tufts of her body hair. Her pathetic attempts at bodily hygiene seemed to highlight the slovenliness of the other women, which infuriated them.

'Look at her royal bloody highness, at it again. Combing her *poesje* hairs.'

'She's better than the rest of us. Going to marry the Governor of Batavia when we get there, didn't you know?'

'You going to invite us to the wedding, Princess?'

'Nedda here will be your bridesmaid, won't you, Nedda *lieveling*?' The livid scar down Nedda's fat cheek twisted into a grotesque grin, but her eyes were filled with hatred in the dim lantern-light.

Louisa had learned to ignore them. She heated the point of her blade in the smoky flame of the lantern in the gimbal above her head, ran the blade down the seams of the shift in her lap, and the nits popped and frizzled. She held the blade back in the flame and, while she waited for it to heat again, she ducked her head to peer through the narrow slit in the joint of the port-lid.

She had used the point of her blade to enlarge this aperture until she had an unobstructed view. There was a padlock on the port-lid, but she had worked for weeks to loosen the shackles. Then she had used soot from the lantern to darken the raw wood, rubbing it in with her finger to conceal it from the weekly inspection of the ship's officers, carried out on Sunday while the convicts were on the open deck for the prayer meeting and ablutions. Louisa always returned to her berth terrified that her work had been discovered. When she found that it had not, her relief was so intense that often she broke down and wept.

34

Despair was always so near at hand, lurking like a wild beast, ready to pounce at any moment and devour her. More than once over the past months she had sharpened her little blade until the edge could shave the fine blonde hairs of her forearm. Then she had hidden away under the gun carriage and felt for the pulse in her wrist where the blue artery beat so close to the surface. Once she had laid the sharp edge against the skin and steeled herself to make the deep incision, then she had looked up at the thin chink of light coming through the joint of the port-lid. It seemed to be a promise.

'No,' she whispered to herself. 'I am going to escape. I am going to endure.'

To bolster her determination she spent hours during those terrible endless days when the ship crashed through the high, turbulent storms of the southern Atlantic daydreaming of the bright, happy days of her childhood, which now seemed to have been in another hazy existence. She trained herself to retreat into her imagination, and to shut out the reality in which she was trapped.

She dwelt on the memory of her father, Hendrick Leuven, a tall, thin man with his black suit buttoned high. She saw again his crisp white lace stock, the stockings that covered his scrawny shanks lovingly darned by her mother, and the pinch-beck buckles on his square-toed shoes, polished until they shone like pure silver. Under the wide brim of his tall black hat the lugubriousness of his features was given the lie by mischievous blue eyes. She had inherited hers from him. She remembered all of his funny, fascinating and poignant stories. Every night when she was young he had carried her up the stairs to her cot. He had tucked her in, and sat beside her reciting them to her while she tried desperately to fight off sleep. When she was older she had walked with him in the garden, her hand in his, through the tulip fields of the estate, going over the day's lessons with him. She smiled secretly now as she recalled his endless patience with her questions, and his sad, proud smile when she arrived at the right answer to a mathematical problem with only a little prompting.

Hendrick Leuven had been tutor to the van Ritters family,

35

one of the pre-eminent merchant families of Amsterdam. Mijnheer Koen van Ritters was one of Het Zeventien, the board of directors of the VOC. His warehouses ran for a quarter of a mile along both banks of the inner canal and he traded around the world with his fleet of fifty-three fine ships. His country mansion was one of the most magnificent in Holland.

During the winter his numerous household lived in Huis Brabant, the huge mansion overlooking the canal. Louisa's family had three rooms at the top of the house to themselves and from the window of her tiny bedroom she could look down on the heavily laden barges, and the fishing-boats coming in from the sea.

However, the spring was the time she loved the most. That was when the family moved out into the country, to Mooi Uitsig, their country estate. In those magical days Hendrick and his family lived in a cottage across the lake from the big house. Louisa remembered the long skeins of geese coming up from the south as the weather warmed. They landed with a great splash on the lake and their honking woke her in the dawn. She cuddled under her eiderdown and listened to her father's snores from the next room. She had never again felt so warm and safe as she did then.

Louisa's mother, Anne, was English. Her father had brought her to Holland when she was a child. He had been a corporal in the bodyguard of William of Orange, after he had become King of England. When Anne was sixteen she had been engaged as a junior cook in the van Ritters household, and had married Hendrick within a year of taking up her post.

Louisa's mother had been plump and jolly, always surrounded by an aura of the delicious aromas of the kitchen: spices and vanilla, saffron and baking bread. She had insisted that Louisa learn English, and they always spoke it when they were alone. Louisa had an ear for language. In addition Anne taught her cooking and baking, embroidery, sewing and all the feminine skills.

Louisa had been allowed, as a special concession by Mijnheer van Ritters, to take her lessons with his own children, although she was expected to sit at the back of the classroom and keep quiet. Only when she was alone with her father could she ask the questions that had burned all day on the tip of her tongue. Very early she had learned deferential manners.

Only twice in all the years had Louisa laid eyes on Mevrou van Ritters. On both occasions she had spied on her from the classroom window as she stepped into the huge black-curtained carriage, assisted by half a dozen servants. She was a mysterious figure, clad in layers of black brocaded silks and a dark veil that hid her face. Louisa had overheard her mother discussing the chatelaine with the other servants. She suffered from some skin disease which made her features as monstrous as a vision of hell. Even her own husband and children were never allowed to see her unveiled.

On the other hand Mijnheer van Ritters sometimes visited the classroom to check on his offspring's progress. He often smiled at the pretty, demure little girl who sat at the back of the room. Once he even paused beside Louisa's desk to watch her writing on her slate in a neat and well-formed script. He smiled and touched her head. 'What lovely hair you have, little one,' he murmured. His own daughters tended towards plump and plain.

Louisa blushed. She thought how kind he was, and yet as remote and powerful as God. He even looked rather like the image of God in the huge oil painting in the banquet hall. It had been painted by the famous artist, Rembrandt Harmenszoon van Rijn, a protégé of the van Ritters family. It was said that Mijnheer's grandfather had posed for the artist. The painting depicted the Day of Resurrection, with the merciful Lord lifting the saved souls into Paradise, while in the background the condemned were herded into the burning pit by demons. The painting had fascinated Louisa and she spent hours in front of it.

Now, in the reeking gundeck of the *Meeuw*, combing the nits from her hair, Louisa felt like one of the unfortunates destined for Hades. She felt tears near the surface, and tried to put the sad thoughts from her mind, but they kept crowding

37

back. She had been just ten when the black plague had struck Amsterdam again, beginning as before in the rat-infested docks, then sweeping through the city.

Mijnheer van Ritters had fled with all his household from Huis Brabant, and they had taken refuge at Mooi Uitsig. He ordered that all the gates to the estate were to be locked and armed sentries placed at each to deny access to strangers. However, when the servants unpacked one of the leather trunks they had brought from Amsterdam a huge rat leaped out and scuttled down the staircase. Even so, for weeks they believed themselves safe, until one of the housemaids collapsed in a dead faint while she was waiting on the family at dinner.

Two footmen carried the girl into the kitchen and laid her on the long table. When Louisa's mother opened the top of her blouse, she gasped as she recognized the necklace of red blotches around the girl's throat, the stigmata of the plague, the ring of roses. She was so distressed that she took little notice of the black flea that sprang from the girl's clothing on to her own skirts. Before sunset the following day the girl was dead.

The next morning two of the van Ritters children were missing when Louisa's father called the classroom to order. One of the nurserymaids came into the room and whispered in his ear. He nodded, then said, 'Kobus and Tinus will not be joining us today. Now, little ones, please open your spelling books at page five. No, Petronella, that is page ten.'

Petronella was the same age as Louisa and she was the only one of the van Ritters children who had been friendly to her. They shared a double desk at the back of the room. She often brought small gifts for Louisa, and sometimes invited her to play with her dolls in the nursery. On Louisa's last birthday she had given her one of her favourites. Of course, her nurse had made Louisa give it back. When they walked along the edge of the lake Petronella held Louisa's hand. 'Tinus was so sick last night,' she whispered. 'He vomited! It smelt awful.'

Half-way through the morning Petronella stood up suddenly and, without asking permission, started towards the door.

'Where are you going, Petronella?' Hendrick Leuven demanded sharply. She turned and stared at him with a bloodless face. Then, without a word, she collapsed on to the floor. That evening Louisa's father told her, 'Mijnheer van Ritters has ordered me to close the classroom. None of us is allowed up to the Big House again until the sickness has passed. We are to stay here in the cottage.'

'What will we eat, Papa?' Louisa, like her mother, was always practical.

'Your mother is bringing down food for us from the pantries: cheese, ham, sausage, apples and potatoes. I have my little vegetable garden, and the rabbit hutch and the chickens. You will help me work in the garden. We will continue your lessons. You will make swifter progress without the duller children to hold you back. It will be like a holiday. We will enjoy ourselves. But you are not allowed to leave the garden, do you understand?' he asked her seriously, as he scratched the red flea-bite on his bony wrist.

For three days they had enjoyed themselves. Then, the next morning, as Louisa was helping her mother prepare breakfast, Anne fainted over the kitchen stove and spilled boiling water down her leg. Louisa helped her father carry her up the stairs and lay her on the big bed. They wrapped her scalded leg in bandages soaked in honey. Then Hendrick unbuttoned the front of her dress and stared in terror at the red ring of roses around her throat.

The fever descended upon her with the speed of a summer storm. Within an hour her skin was blotched with red and seemed almost too hot to touch. Louisa and Hendrick sponged her down with cold water from the lake. 'Be strong, my *lieveling*,' Hendrick whispered to her, as she tossed and groaned, and soaked the mattress with her sweat. 'God will protect you.'

They took turns to sit with her during the night, but in the dawn Louisa screamed for her father. When he came scrambling up the stairs Louisa pointed at her mother's naked lower body. On both sides of her groin, at the juncture of her thighs with her belly, monstrous carbuncles had swelled to the size of Louisa's clenched fist. They were hard as stones and a furious purple, like ripe plums.

'The buboes!' Hendrick touched one. Anne screamed wildly in agony at his light touch, and her bowels let loose an explosion of gas and yellow diarrhoea that soaked the sheets.

Hendrick and Louisa lifted her out of the stinking bed and laid her on a clean mattress on the floor. By evening her pain was so intense and unrelenting that Hendrick could bear his wife's shrieks no longer. His blue eyes were bloodshot and haunted. 'Fetch my shaving razor!' he ordered Louisa. She scurried across to the wash-basin in the corner of the bedroom, and brought it to him. It had a beautiful mother-of-pearl handle. Louisa had always enjoyed watching her father in the early mornings lathering his cheeks, then stripping off the white soapsuds with the straight, gleaming blade.

'What are you going to do, Papa?' she asked, as she watched him sharpening the edge on the leather strop.

'We must let out the poison. It is killing your mother. Hold her still!'

Gently Louisa took hold of her mother's wrists. 'It's going to be all right, Mama. Papa is going to make it better.'

Hendrick took off his black coat and, in his white shirt, came back to the bed. He straddled his wife's legs to hold her down. Sweat was pouring down his cheeks, and his hand shook wildly as he laid the razor edge across the huge purple swelling in her groin.

'Forgive me, O merciful God,' he whispered, then pressed down and drew the blade across the carbuncle, cutting deeply and cleanly. For a moment nothing happened, then a tide of black blood and custard yellow pus erupted out of the deep wound. It splattered across the front of Hendrick's white shirt and up to the low ceiling of the bedroom above his head.

Anne's back arched like a longbow and Louisa was hurled against the wall. Hendrick cringed into a corner, stunned by the violence of his wife's contortions. Anne writhed and rolled and screamed, her face in a rictus so horrible that Louisa was terrified. She clasped both hands over her own mouth to prevent herself screaming as she watched the blood spurt in powerful, regular jets from the wound. Gradually the pulsing scarlet fountain shrivelled, and Anne's agony eased. Her screams died away, until at last she lay still and deadly pale in a spreading pool of blood.

Louisa crept back to her side and touched her arm. 'Mama, it's all right now. Papa has let all the poison out. You are going to be well again soon.' Then she looked across at her father. She had never seen him like this: he was weeping, and his lips were slack and blubbery. Saliva dripped from his chin.

'Don't cry, Papa,' she whispered. 'She will wake up soon.'

But Anne never woke again.

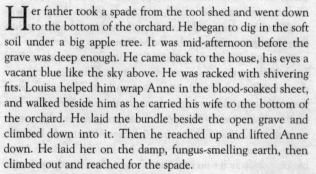

Her father took a spade from the tool shed and went down to the bottom of the orchard. He began to dig in the soft soil under a big apple tree. It was mid-afternoon before the grave was deep enough. He came back to the house, his eyes a vacant blue like the sky above. He was racked with shivering fits. Louisa helped him wrap Anne in the blood-soaked sheet, and walked beside him as he carried his wife to the bottom of the orchard. He laid the bundle beside the open grave and climbed down into it. Then he reached up and lifted Anne down. He laid her on the damp, fungus-smelling earth, then climbed out and reached for the spade.

Louisa sobbed as she watched him fill in the grave and tamp down the earth. Then she went out into the field beyond the hedge and picked an armful of flowers. When she came back her father was no longer in the orchard. Louisa arranged the tulips over where her mother's head must be. It seemed that the well of her tears had dried up. Her sobs were painful and dry.

When she went back to the cottage she found her father sitting at the table, his shirt filthy with his wife's blood and the grave soil. His head was cupped in his hands, his shoulders racked by shivering. When he lifted his head and looked at her, his face was pale and blotched, and his teeth chattered.

'Papa, are you sick too?' She started towards him, then shrank back as he opened his mouth and a solid stream of bile-brown vomit burst through his lips and splashed across the scrubbed wooden tabletop. Then he slumped out of his chair on to the stone-flagged floor. He was too heavy for her to lift, or even to drag up the stairs, so she tended him where he lay, cleaning away the vomit and liquid excrement, sponging him with icy lake water to bring down the fever. But she could not bring herself to take the razor to him. Two days later he died on the kitchen floor.

'I have to be brave now. I am not a baby, I'm ten years old,' she told herself. 'There is nobody to help me. I have to take care of Papa myself.'

She went down into the orchard. The spade was lying beside her mother's grave, where her father had dropped it. She began to dig. It was hard, slow work. When the grave was deep, and her thin, childish arms did not have the strength to throw up the wet earth, she fetched an apple basket from the kitchen, filled it with earth and pulled up each basketload from the bottom of the grave with a rope. When darkness fell she worked on in the grave by lantern-light. When it was as deep as she was tall, she went back to where her father lay and tried to drag him to the door. She was exhausted, her hands were raw and blistered from the handle of the spade, and she could not move him. She spread a blanket over him to cover his pale, blotched skin and staring eyes, then lay down beside him and slept until morning.

When she woke, sunlight was streaming through the window into her eyes. She got up and cut a slice from the ham hanging in the pantry and a wedge of cheese. She ate them with a hunk of dry bread. Then she went up to the stables at the rear of the big house. She remembered that she had been forbidden to go there, so she crept down behind the hedge. The stables were deserted and she realized that the grooms must have fled with the other servants. She ducked through the secret hole in the hedge that she and Petronella had discovered. The horses were still in their stalls, unfed and unwatered. She opened the doors and shooed them out into the paddock. Immediately they galloped straight down to the lake shore and lined up along the edge to drink.

She fetched a halter from the tack room, and went to Petronella's pony while it was still drinking. Petronella had allowed her to ride the pony whenever she wanted to, so the animal recognized and trusted her. As soon as it lifted its head, water dripping from its muzzle, Louisa slipped the halter over its ears, and led it back to the cottage. The back door was wide enough for the pony to pass through.

For a long while Louisa hesitated while she tried to think of some more respectful manner in which to take her father to his grave, but in the end she found a rope, hitched it to his heels and the pony dragged him into the orchard, with his head bouncing over the uneven ground. As he slipped over the lip of the shallow grave Louisa wept for him for the last time. She took the halter off the pony and turned the animal loose in the paddock. Then she climbed down beside her father and tried to arrange his limbs neatly, but they were rigid. She left him as he lay, went out into the field, gathered another armful of flowers and strewed them over his body. She knelt beside the open grave and, in a high, sweet voice, sang the first verse of 'The Lord Is My Shepherd' in English, as her mother had taught her. Then she began to shovel the earth on top of him. By the time she had filled in the last spadeful night had fallen and she crept back to the cottage, emotionally and physically numbed with exhaustion.

She had neither the strength nor the desire to eat, nor even to climb the stairs to her bed. She lay down next to the hearth and, almost immediately, fell into a deathlike sleep. She woke before morning, consumed by thirst and with a headache that felt as though her skull was about to burst open. When she tried to rise she staggered and fell against the wall. She was nauseous and giddy, her bladder swollen and painful. She tried to make her way out into the garden to relieve herself, but a wave of nausea swept over her. She doubled over slowly and vomited in the middle of the kitchen floor, then with horror stared down at the steaming puddle between her feet. She staggered to the row of her mother's copper pots, which hung on hooks along the far wall, and looked at her reflection in the polished bottom of one. Slowly and reluctantly she touched her throat and stared at the rosy necklace that adorned her milky skin.

Her legs gave way and she subsided on to the stone flags. Dark clouds of despair gathered in her mind and her vision faded. Then, suddenly, she discovered a spark still burning in the darkness, a tiny spark of strength and determination. She clung to it, shielding it like a lamp flame fluttering in a high wind. It helped her to drive back the darkness.

'I have to think,' she whispered to herself. 'I have to stand up. I know what will happen, just the way it did to Mama and Papa. I have to get ready.' Using the wall she pulled herself to her feet, and stood swaying. 'I must hurry. I can feel it coming quickly.' She remembered the terrible thirst that had consumed her dying parents. 'Water!' she whispered. She staggered with the empty water bucket to the pump in the yard. Each stroke of the long handle was a trial of her strength and courage. 'Not everyone dies,' she whispered to herself, as she worked. 'I heard the grown-ups talking. They say that some of the young, strong ones live. They don't die.' Water flowed into the bucket. 'I won't die. I won't! I won't!'

When the bucket was full she staggered to the rabbit hutch, then to the chicken run, and released all the animals and fowls to fend for themselves. 'I am not going to be able to take care of you,' she explained to them.

Carrying the water bucket, she staggered unsteadily back to the kitchen, water slopping down her legs. She placed the bucket beside the hearth with a copper dipper hooked over the side. 'Food!' she murmured, through the giddy mirages in her head. She fetched the remains of the cheese and ham and a basket of apples from the pantry and placed them where she could reach them.

'Cold. It will be cold at night.' She dragged herself to the linen chest where her mother had kept what remained of her dowry, took out a bundle of woollen blankets and a sheepskin rug and laid them out beside the hearth. Then she fetched an

44

armful of firewood from the stack in the corner and, as the shivering fits began, she built up the fire.

'The door! Lock the door!' She had heard that in the city starving pigs and dogs had broken into the houses where people lay too sick to defend themselves. The animals had eaten them alive. She closed the door and placed the locking bar in the brackets. She found her father's axe and a carving knife, and laid them beside her mattress.

There were rats in the thatch and the walls of the cottage. She had heard them scurrying about in the night, and her mother had complained of their nocturnal depredations in her pantry. Petronella had described to Louisa how a huge rat had got into the nursery of the big house while the new nursemaid was drunk on gin. Her father had found the horrid beast in her little sister's cot and had ordered the grooms to thrash the drunken nurse. The wretched woman's screams had penetrated the classroom, and the children had exchanged glances of delicious horror as they listened. Now Louisa's skin crawled at the thought of lying helpless under a rat's razor fangs.

With the last of her strength she brought down the largest of her mother's copper pots from its hook on the wall, and placed it in the corner with the lid in place. She was a fastidious child, and the thought of fouling herself as her parents had done was abhorrent to her.

'That's all I can do,' she whispered, and collapsed on to the sheepskin. Dark clouds swirled in her head and her blood seemed to boil in her veins with the heat of fever. 'Our Father, which art in heaven . . .' She recited the prayer in English, as her mother had taught her, but the sweltering darkness overwhelmed her.

Perhaps an eternity passed before she rose slowly to the surface of her mind, like a swimmer coming up from great depth. The darkness gave way to a blinding white light. Like sunlight on a snowfield, it dazzled and blinded her. The cold came out of the light, chilling her blood and frosting her bones, so she shivered wildly.

Moving painfully she drew the sheepskin over herself, and

rolled herself into a ball, hugging her knees to her chest. Then, fearfully, she reached behind: the flesh had wasted from her buttocks leaving the bones poking through. She explored herself with a finger, dreading the feel of wet, slimy faeces, but her skin was dry. She sniffed her finger tentatively. It was clean.

She remembered overhearing her father talking to her mother, 'Diarrhoea is the worst sign. Those who survive do not scour their bowels.'

'It's a sign from Jesus,' Louisa whispered to herself, through chattering teeth. 'I did not dirty myself. I am not going to die.' Then the scalding heat came back to burn away the cold and the white light. She tossed on the mattress in delirium, crying to her father and her mother, and to Jesus. Thirst woke her: it was a fire in her throat and her tongue filled her parched mouth like a sun-heated stone. She fought to raise herself on one elbow and reach for the water dipper. On the first attempt she spilled most of it over her chest, then choked and gasped on what remained in the copper dipper. The few mouthfuls that she was able to swallow renewed her strength miraculously. On her next attempt she forced down the entire contents of the dipper. She rested again, then drank another dipperful. She was satiated at last and the fires in her blood for the moment seemed quenched. She curled under the sheepskin, her belly bulging with the water she had drunk. This time the sleep that overcame her was deep but natural.

Pain roused her. She did not know where she was, or what had caused it. Then she heard a harsh ripping sound close at hand. She opened her eyes and looked down. One of her feet protruded from under the sheepskin. Hunched over her bare foot was something as big as a tomcat, grey and hairy. For a moment she did not know what it was, but then the tearing sound came again and the pain. She wanted to kick out at it, or scream, but she was frozen with terror. This was her worst nightmare come true.

The creature lifted its head and peered at her with bright, beadlike eyes. It wiggled the whiskers on its long, pointed nose, and the sharp curved fangs that overlapped its lower lip were rosy pink with her blood. It had been gnawing at her ankle. The little girl and the rat stared at each other, but Louisa was still paralysed with horror. The rat lowered its head and bit into her flesh again. Slowly Louisa reached out for the carving knife beside her head. With the speed of a cat she slashed out at the foul creature. The rat was almost as quick: it leaped high in the air, but the point of the knife split open its belly. It squealed, and flopped over.

Louisa dropped the knife and watched, wide-eyed, as the rat dragged itself across the stone floor, the slimy purple tangle of its entrails slithering after it. She was panting and it took a long time for her heart to slow and her breathing to settle. Then she found that the shock had made her feel stronger. She sat up and examined her injured foot. The bites were deep. She tore a strip off her petticoat and wrapped it round her ankle. Then she realized she was hungry. She crawled to the table and pulled herself up. The rat had been at the ham, but she hacked away the chewed area, and cut a thick slice, and placed it on a slab of bread. Green mould was already growing on the cheese, evidence of how long she had lain unconscious on the hearth. Mould and all, it was delicious. She drank the last dipperful of water. She wished she could replenish the bucket, but she knew she was not strong enough, and she was afraid to open the door.

She dragged herself to the big copper pot in the corner and squatted over it. While she piddled, she lifted her skirt high and examined her lower belly. It was smooth and unblemished, her innocent little cleft naked of hair. But she stared at the swollen buboes in her groin. They were hard as acorns and painful when she touched them, but not the same terrifying colour or size of those that had killed her mother. She thought about the razor, but knew she did not have the courage to do that to herself.

'I am not going to die!' For the first time she truly believed it. She smoothed down her skirt and crawled back to her mattress. With the carving knife clutched in her hand she slept again. After that, the days and nights mingled into a dream-like succession of sleeping and brief intervals of wakefulness.

Gradually these periods became longer. Each time she woke she felt stronger, more able to care for herself. When she used the pot in the corner she discovered that the buboes had subsided and had changed from red to pink. They were not nearly so painful when she touched them, but she knew she had to drink.

She summoned every last shred of her courage and strength, tottered out into the yard and refilled the water bucket. Then she locked herself into the kitchen again. When the ham was just a bare bone and the apple basket was empty, she found that she was strong enough to make her way into the garden, where she pulled up a basketful of turnips and potatoes. She rekindled the fire with her father's flint, and cooked a stew of vegetables flavoured with the ham bone. The food was delicious, and the strength flowed back into her. Each morning after that she set herself a task for the day.

On the first she emptied the copper vessel she had been using as a chamber-pot into her father's compost pit, then washed it out with lye and hot water, and hung it back on its hook. She knew her mother would have wanted that. The effort exhausted her and she crept back to the sheepskin.

The next morning she felt strong enough to fill the bucket from the pump, strip off her filthy clothing and wash herself from head to toe with a ladleful of the precious soap her mother made by boiling sheep's fat and wood ash together. She was delighted to find that the buboes in her groin had almost disappeared. With her fingertips she could press them quite hard and the pain was bearable. When her skin was pink and glowing, she scrubbed her teeth with a finger dipped in salt and dressed the rat bite on her leg from her mother's medicine chest. Then she chose fresh clothes from the linen chest.

The next day she was hungry again. She caught one of the rabbits that were hopping trustingly around the garden, held it up by the ears, steeled herself, and broke its neck with the stick her father had kept for that purpose. She gutted and skinned the carcass as her mother had taught her, then

48

quartered it and placed it in the pot with onions and potatoes. When she had eaten it, she sucked the bones white.

The following morning she went down to the bottom of the orchard and spent the morning tidying and tending her parents' graves. Until now she had not left the security of the cottage garden, but she gathered her courage, climbed through the hole in the hedge and crept up to the greenhouse. She made certain that no one was anywhere to be seen. The estate seemed deserted still. She picked out some of the choicest blooms from the vast array on the shelves, placed them in a handcart, trundled them back to the cottage and planted them in the newly smoothed earth of the graves. She chatted away to her parents as she worked, telling them every detail of her ordeal, about the rat, and the rabbit, and how she had cooked the stew in the black three-legged pot.

'I am so sorry I used your best copper pot, Mama,' she hung her head in shame, 'but I have washed it and hung it back on the wall.'

When the graves had been decorated to her satisfaction curiosity rose in her again. Once more she slipped through the hedge and took a circuitous route through the plantation of fir trees until she could approach the big house from the south side. It was silent and bleak: all the windows were shuttered. When she sidled up cautiously to the front door she found that it was locked and barred. She stared at the cross that someone had sketched crudely on the door in red. The paint had run like tears of blood down the panel. It was the plague warning.

Suddenly she felt lonely and bereft. She sat down on the steps that led up to the doorway. 'I think I'm the only person left alive in the world. All the others are dead.'

At last she stood up and, made bold by desperation, ran round to the back door, which led to the kitchen and the servants' quarters. She tried it. To her astonishment it swung open. 'Hello!' she called. 'Is anyone there? Stals! Hans! Where are you?'

The kitchen was deserted. She went through to the scullery

and stuck her head through the door. 'Hello!' There was no answer. She went through the entire house, searching every room, but they were all deserted. Everywhere there was evidence of the family's hasty departure. She left everything untouched and closed the kitchen door carefully when she left.

On the way back to the cottage a thought occurred to her. She turned off the path and went down to the chapel at the end of the rose garden. Some of the headstones in the cemetery were two hundred years old and covered with green moss, but near the door there was a line of new graves. The headstones had not yet been set in place. The posies of flowers on them had faded and withered. Names and final messages were printed on black-edged cards on each pile of fresh earth. The ink had run in the rain, but Louisa could still read the names. She found one that read 'Petronella Katrina Susanna van Ritters'. Her friend lay between two of her younger brothers.

Louisa ran back to the cottage, and that night she sobbed herself to sleep. When she woke she felt sick and weak again, and her sorrow and loneliness had returned in full measure. She dragged herself out into the yard and washed her face and hands under the pump. Then, abruptly, she lifted her face, water running into her eyes and dripping off her chin. She cocked her head and, slowly, an expression of delight lit her face. Her eyes sparkled with blue lights. 'People!' she said aloud. 'Voices.' They were faint, and came from the direction of the big house. 'They have come back. I am not alone any more.'

Her face still wet, she raced to the hole in the hedge, jumped through and set off towards the big house. The sound of voices grew louder as she approached. At the potting shed she paused to catch her breath. She was about to run out on to the lawns, when some instinct warned her to be cautious. She hesitated, then put her head slowly round the corner of the red-brick wall. A chill of horror ran up her spine.

She had expected to see coaches with the van Ritters' coat-

50

of-arms drawn up on the gravel driveway, and the family disembarking, with the coachmen, grooms and footmen hovering around them. Instead a horde of strangers was running in and out of the front doors, carrying armfuls of silver, clothing and paintings. The doors had been smashed open, and the shattered panels hung drunkenly on their hinges.

The looters were piling the treasures on to a row of handcarts, shouting and laughing with excitement. Louisa could see that they were the dregs of the city, of its docks and slums, army deserters, from prisons and barracks that had thrown open their gates when all the trappings of civilized government had been swept away by the plague. They were dressed in the rags of the back-streets and gutters, in odd pieces of military uniform and the ill-fitting finery of the rich they had plundered. One rascal, wearing a high plumed hat, brandished a square-faced bottle of gin as he staggered down the main staircase with a solid gold salver under his other arm. His face, flushed and marked with drink and dissipation, turned towards Louisa. Stunned by the scene, she was too slow to duck back behind the wall and he spotted her. 'A woman. By Satan and all the devils of hell, a veritable woman! Young and juicy as a ripe red apple.' He dropped the bottle and drew his sword. 'Come here, you sweet little filly. Let's take a look at what you're hiding under those pretty skirts.' He bounded down the steps.

A wild cry went up from all his companions: 'A woman! After her, lads! The one who catches her gets the cherry.'

They came in a screaming pack across the lawn towards her. Louisa swirled about and ran. At first she headed instinctively for the safety of the cottage, then realized that they were close behind her and would trap her there like a rabbit in its warren pursued by a troop of ferrets. She veered away across the paddock towards the woods. The ground was soft and muddy and her legs had not yet recovered their full strength after her sickness. They were gaining on her, their shouts loud and jubilant. She reached the treeline only just ahead of the leaders, but she knew these woods intimately for they were her playground. She twisted and turned along paths that were barely discernible, and ducked through thickets of blackberry and gorse.

Every few minutes she stopped to listen, and each time the sounds of pursuit were fainter. At last they dwindled into silence. Her terror receded, but she knew it was still dangerous to leave the shelter of the forest. She found the densest stretch of thorns and crept into it, crawling on her belly until she was hidden. Then she burrowed into the dead leaves until only her mouth and eyes were showing, so she could watch the clearing she had just left. She lay there, panting and trembling. Gradually she calmed down, and lay without moving until the shadows of the trees stretched long upon the earth. Eventually, when there were still no more sounds of her hunters, she began to crawl back towards the clearing.

She was just about to stand up when her nose wrinkled and she sniffed the air. She caught a whiff of tobacco smoke and sank down again, pressing herself to the earth. Her terror returned at full strength. After many silent, tense minutes she lifted her head slowly. At the far side of the clearing, a man sat with his back to the trunk of the tallest beech tree. He was smoking a long-stemmed clay pipe, but his eyes roved from side to side. She recognized him instantly. It was the man in the plumed hat who had first spotted her and who had led the chase. He was so close that she could hear every puff he took on his pipe. She buried her face in the leaf mould and tried to still her trembling. She did not know what he would do to her if he discovered her, but she sensed that it would be beyond her worst nightmares.

She lay and listened to the suck and gurgle of his spittle in the bowl of the pipe, and her terror mounted. Suddenly he hawked and spat a glob of thick mucus. She heard it splatter close to her head, and her nerve almost broke. It was only by exerting all her courage and self-discipline that she stopped herself jumping to her feet and running again.

Time seemed to stand still, but at last she felt the air turn cold on her bare arms. Still she did not lift her head. Then she heard rustling in the leaves, and heavy footsteps coming directly towards her across the clearing. They stopped close by her head, and a great bull voice bellowed, so close to her that her heart seemed to clench and freeze, 'There you are! I can see you! I'm coming! Run! You'd better run!' Her frozen heart came to life, and hammered against her ribs, but she forced herself not to move. There was another long silence, then the footsteps walked away from where she lay. As he went she could hear him muttering to himself, 'Dirty little whore, she's probably riddled with the pox, anyway.'

She lay without moving until the darkness was complete, and she heard an owl hoot in the top of the beech tree. Then she stood up and crept through the woods, starting and trembling at every rustle and scurry of the small night creatures.

She did not leave the cottage again for some days. During the day she immersed herself in her father's books. There was one in particular that fascinated her and she read it from the first page to the last, then started again at the beginning. The title was In Darkest Africa. The tales of strange animals and savage tribes enchanted her, and wiled away the long days. She read of great hairy men who lived in the tops of the trees, of a tribe that ate the flesh of other men, and of tiny pygmies with a single eye in the centre of their foreheads. Reading became the opiate for her fears. One evening she fell asleep at the kitchen table, her golden head on the open book, the flame fluttering in the lamp.

The glimmer of the light showed through the uncurtained window, and from there through a chink in the hedge. Two dark figures, who were passing on the road, stopped and exchanged a few hoarse words. Then they crept through the gate in the hedge. One went to the front door of the cottage while the other circled round to the back.

'Who are you?'

The harsh bellow brought Louisa awake and on her feet in the same instant. 'We know you're in there! Come out now!'

She darted to the back door and struggled with the locking bar, then threw open the door and dashed out into the night. At that moment a heavy masculine hand fell on the back of her neck, and she was lifted by the scruff with her feet dangling and kicking as if she were a newborn kitten.

The man who held her opened the shutter of the bullseye lantern he carried and shone the beam into her face. 'Who are you?' he demanded.

In the lamplight she recognized his red face and bushy whiskers. 'Jan!' she squeaked. 'It's me! Louisa! Louisa Leuven.'

Jan was the van Ritters' footman. The belligerence in his expression faded, slowly replaced by amazement. 'Little Louisa! Is it really you? We all thought you must be dead with the rest of them.'

A few days later Jan travelled with Louisa to Amsterdam in a cart containing some of the salvaged possessions of the van Ritters family. When he led her into the kitchens of the Huis Brabant the servants who had survived crowded round to welcome her. Her prettiness, her sweet manner and sunny nature had always made her a favourite in the servants' quarters, so they grieved with her when they heard that Anne and Hendrick were dead. They could hardly believe that little Louisa, at just ten, had survived without her parents or friends, and had done so on her own resources and resolve. Elise the cook, who had been a dear friend of her mother, immediately took her under her protection.

Louisa had to tell her tale again and again as news of her survival spread, and the other servants, the workers and seamen from the van Ritters' ships and warehouses came to hear it.

Every week Stals, the butler and major-domo of the household, wrote a report to Mijnheer van Ritters in London, where he had taken refuge from the plague with the remainder of his family. At the end of one report he mentioned that Louisa, the schoolmaster's daughter, had been rescued. Mijnheer was gracious enough to reply, 'See that the child is taken in and set to work in the household. You may pay her as a scullerymaid. When I return to Amsterdam I shall decide what is to be done with her.'

In early December when the cold weather cleansed the city of the last traces of the plague, Mijnheer van Ritters brought home his family. His wife had been carried away by the plague, but her absence would make no difference to their lives. Out of the twelve children only five had survived the pestilence. One morning, when Mijnheer van Ritters had been over a month in Amsterdam, and had attended to all the more pressing matters that awaited his attention, he ordered Stals to bring Louisa to him.

She hesitated in the doorway to Mijnheer van Ritters' library. He looked up from the thick leatherbound ledger in which he was writing. 'Come in, child,' he ordered. 'Come here where I can see you.'

Stals led her to stand in front of the great man's desk. She curtsied to him, and he nodded approval. 'Your father was a good man, and he taught you manners.' He got up and went to stand in front of the tall bay windows. For a minute he looked out through the diamond panes at one of his ships, unloading bales of cotton from the Indies into the warehouse. Then he turned back to study Louisa. She had grown since last he had seen her, and her face and limbs had filled out. He knew that she had had the plague, but she had recovered well. There were no traces on her face of the ravages of the disease. She was a pretty girl, very pretty indeed, he decided. And it was not an insipid beauty: her expression was alert and intelligent. Her eyes were alive, and sparkled with the blue of precious sapphires. Her skin was creamy and unblemished, but her hair was her most attractive attribute: she wore it in two long plaits that hung forward over her shoulders. He asked her a few questions.

She tried to hide her fear and awe of him, and to answer in a sensible manner.

'Are you attending to your lessons, child?'

'I have all my father's books, Mijnheer. I read every night before I sleep.'

55

'What work are you doing?'

'I wash and peel the vegetables, and I knead the bread, and help Pieter wash and dry the pots and pans, Mijnheer.'

'Are you happy?'

'Oh, yes, Mijnheer. Elise, the cook, is so kind to me, like my own mother.'

'I think we can find something more useful for you to do.' Van Ritters stroked his beard thoughtfully.

Elise and Stals had lectured Louisa on how to behave when she was with him. 'Remember always that he is one of the greatest men in all the land. Always call him "Your Excellency" or "Mijnheer". Curtsy when you greet him and when you leave.'

'Do exactly what he tells you. If he asks a question, answer him directly, but never answer back.'

'Stand straight and don't slump. Keep your hands clasped in front of you, and do not fidget or pick your nose.'

There had been so many instructions that they had confused her. But now, as she stood in front of him, her courage returned. He was dressed in cloth of the finest quality, and his collar was of snowy lace. The buckles on his shoes were pure silver, and the hilt of the dagger on his belt was gold set with glowing rubies. He was tall and his legs in black silk hose were as shapely and as well turned as a man half his age. Although his hair was touched with silver, it was dense and perfectly curled and set. His beard was almost entirely silver, but neatly barbered and shaped in the Vandyke style. There were light laughter lines around his eyes, but the back of his hand as he stroked his pointed beard was smooth and unmarred by the blotches of age. He wore an enormous ruby on his forefinger. Despite his grandeur and dignity his gaze was kind. Somehow she knew she could trust him, just as she could always trust Gentle Jesus to look after her.

'Gertruda needs someone to look after her.' Van Ritters reached a decision. Gertruda was his youngest surviving daughter. She was seven years old, a plain, simple-witted, petulant girl. 'You will be her companion and help her with her lessons. I know you are a bright girl.'

Louisa's spirits fell. She had grown so close to Elise, the motherly woman who had replaced Anne as head cook in the kitchen. She did not want to forsake the aura of warmth and security that cosseted her in the servants' quarters, and have to go upstairs to care for the whining Gertruda. She wanted to protest, but Elise had warned her not to answer back. She hung her head and curtsied.

'Stals, see she is properly dressed. She will be paid as junior nursemaid, and have a room to herself near the nursery.' Van Ritters dismissed them and went back to his desk.

Louisa knew she would have to make the best of her circumstances. There was no alternative. Mijnheer was the lord of her universe. She knew that if she tried to pit herself against his dictates her suffering would be endless. She set herself to win over Gertruda. It was not easy, for the younger girl was demanding and unreasonable. Not content with having Louisa as a slave during the day, she would scream for her in the night when she woke from a nightmare, or even when she wanted to use the chamber-pot. Always uncomplaining and cheerful, Louisa gradually won her over. She taught her simple games, sheltered her from the bullying of her brothers and sisters, sang to her at bedtime, or read her stories. When she was haunted by nightmares, Louisa crawled into her bed, took her in her arms and rocked her back to sleep. Gradually Gertruda abandoned the role of Louisa's tormentor. Her own mother had been a remote, veiled figure whose face she could not remember. Gertruda had found a substitute and she followed Louisa about with puppylike trust. Soon Louisa was able to control her wild tantrums, when she rolled howling on the floor, hurled her food against the wall or tried to throw herself out of the windows into the canal. Nobody had been able to do this before, but with a quiet word Louisa would calm her, then take her by the hand and lead her back to her room. Within minutes she was laughing and clapping her hands, and reciting the chorus of a children's rhyme with

Louisa. At first Louisa felt only a sense of duty and obligation towards Gertruda, but slowly this turned to affection and then to a type of motherly love.

Mijnheer van Ritters became aware of the change in his daughter. On his occasional visits to nursery and classroom he often singled out Louisa for a kind word. At the Christmas party for the children he watched Louisa dancing with her charge. She was as supple and graceful as Gertruda was dumpy and ungainly. Van Ritters smiled when Gertruda gave Louisa a pair of tiny pearl earrings as her Christmas present, and Louisa kissed and hugged her.

A few months later van Ritters called Louisa to his library. For a while he discussed the progress that she was making with Gertruda, and told her how pleased he was with her. When she was leaving he touched her hair. 'You are growing into such a lovely young woman. I must be careful that some oaf does not try to take you from us. Gertruda and I need you here.' Louisa was almost overcome by his condescension.

On Louisa's thirteenth birthday Gertruda asked her father to give her a special birthday treat. Van Ritters was taking one of his elder sons to England, where he was to enter the great university at Cambridge, and Gertruda asked if she and Louisa might go with the party. Indulgently van Ritters agreed.

They sailed on one of the van Ritters ships, and spent most of that summer visiting the great cities of England. Louisa was enchanted by her mother's homeland, and took every opportunity to practise the language.

The van Ritters party stayed for a week in Cambridge as Mijnheer wanted to see his favourite son settled in. He hired all the rooms at the Red Boar, the finest tavern in the university town. As usual Louisa slept on a bed in the corner of Gertruda's room. She was dressing one morning and Gertruda was sitting on her bed chattering to her. Suddenly she reached out and pinched Louisa's bosom. 'Look, Louisa, you are growing titties.'

Gently Louisa removed her hand. In the last few months she had developed the stony lumps under her nipples that heralded the onset of puberty. Her breast buds were swollen, tender and sensitive. Gertruda's touch had been rough.

'You must not do that, Gertie, my *schat*. It hurts me, and that is an ugly word you used.'

'I am sorry, Louisa.' Tears formed in the child's eyes. 'I didn't mean to hurt you.'

'It's all right.' Louisa kissed her. 'Now what do you want for breakfast?'

'Cakes.' The tears were immediately forgotten. 'Lots of cakes with cream and strawberry jam.'

'Then afterwards we can go to the Punch and Judy show,' Louisa suggested.

'Oh, can we, Louisa? Can we really?'

When Louisa went to ask Mijnheer van Ritters' permission for the outing, he decided on an impulse to accompany them. In the carriage Gertruda, in her unpredictable fashion, returned to the morning's topic. She announced in a penetrating tone, 'Louisa has got pink titties. The tips stick out.'

Louisa lowered her eyes and whispered, 'I told you, Gertie, that's a rude word. You promised not to use it again.'

'I am sorry, Louisa. I forgot.' Gertruda looked stricken.

Louisa squeezed her hand. 'I am not cross, *schat*. I just want you to behave like a lady.'

Van Ritters seemed not to have overheard the exchange. He did not look up from the book that was open on his knee. However, during the puppet show, when the hook-nosed Punch was beating his shrieking wife about the head with a club, Louisa glanced sideways and saw that Mijnheer was studying the tender swellings beneath her blouse. She felt the blood rush to her cheeks, and drew her shawl more closely around her shoulders.

It was autumn when they sailed on the return journey to Amsterdam. On the first night at sea Gertruda was prostrate with seasickness. Louisa nursed her, and held the basin for her as she retched. At last she fell into a deep sleep and Louisa escaped from the fetid cabin. Longing for a breath of fresh sea air she hurried up the companionway to the deck. She stopped in the hatchway as she spotted the tall, elegant figure of van Ritters standing alone on the quarter-deck. The officers and crew had left the windward rail to him: as the ship's owner this was his prerogative. She would have gone below again immediately but he saw her, and called her to him. 'How is my Gertie?'

'She is sleeping, Mijnheer. I am sure she will feel much better in the morning.'

At that moment a larger wave lifted the ship's hull and she rolled sharply. Taken off balance Louisa was thrown against him. He put an arm round her shoulders. 'I am so sorry, Mijnheer.' Her voice was husky. 'I slipped.' She tried to draw back, but his arm held her firmly. She was confused, unsure what she should do next. She dared not pull away again. He made no move to release her, and then – she could hardly credit her senses – she felt his other hand close on her right breast. She gasped and shivered as she felt him roll her tender swollen nipple between his fingers. He was gentle, unlike his daughter had been. He did not hurt her at all. With a terrible burning shame she realized she was enjoying his touch. 'I am cold,' she whispered.

'Yes,' he said. 'You must go below before you catch a chill.' He released her and turned back to lean on the rail. Sparks streamed from the tip of his cheroot, and blew away on the wind.

When they returned to Huis Brabant, she did not see him again for several weeks. She heard Stals telling Elise that Mijnheer had gone to Paris on business. However, the brief incident on shipboard was never far from her mind. Sometimes she woke in the night and lay awake, burning with shame and remorse as she relived it. She felt that what had happened was her fault. A great man like Mijnheer van Ritters surely could not be to blame. When she thought about it her nipples burned and itched strangely. She felt a great evil in her, and climbed out of her bed to kneel and pray, shivering on the bare wooden floor. Gertruda called out in the dark, 'Louisa, I need the chamber-pot.'

With a sense of relief Louisa went to her before she could wet the bed. Over the following weeks the guilt faded, but never quite left her.

Then, one afternoon, Stals came to find her in the nursery. 'Mijnheer van Ritters wants to see you. You must go at once. I hope you have not done anything wrong, girl?' As Louisa brushed her hair hurriedly she told Gertruda where she was going.

'Can I come with you?'

'You must finish painting the picture of the boat for me. Try to stay inside the lines, my *schat*. I will be back soon.'

She knocked on the door of the library, her heart racing wildly. She knew he was going to punish her for what had happened on the ship. He might have her beaten by the grooms, like they had done to the drunken nursemaid. Worse still, he might dismiss her, have her thrown out into the street.

'Come in!' His voice was stern.

She curtsied in the doorway. 'You sent for me, Mijnheer.'

'Yes, come in, Louisa.' She stopped in front of his desk, but he gestured for her to come round and stand beside him. 'I want to talk to you about my daughter.'

Instead of his usual black coat and lace collar he wore a dressing-robe of heavy Chinese silk that buttoned up the front. From this informal attire and his calm, friendly expression she realized he was not angry with her. She felt a rush of relief. He was not going to punish her. His next words confirmed this. 'I was thinking that it might be time for Gertruda to begin riding lessons. You are a good horsewoman. I have seen you helping the grooms to exercise the horses. I want to hear your opinion.'

'Oh, yes, Mijnheer. I am sure Gertie would love it. Old Bumble is a gentle gelding . . .' Happily she started to help him develop the plan. She was standing close to his shoulder. A thick book with a green leather cover was lying on the desk in front of him. Casually he opened it. She could not avoid seeing the exposed page and her voice trailed away. She lifted both hands to her mouth as she looked at the illustration that filled the whole of one folio-sized page. It was obviously the work of a skilled artist. The man in the painting was young and handsome, he lolled back in a leather armchair. A pretty young girl stood in front of him, laughing, and Louisa saw that she might have been her own twin. The girl's large wide-set eyes were cerulean blue, and she was holding her skirts up to her waist so that the man could see the golden nest between her thighs. The artist had emphasized the pair of swollen lips that pouted at him through the curls.

That was enough to stop her breath, but there was worse – far worse. The front flap of the man's breeches was undone, and through the opening thrust a pale shaft with a pink head. The man was holding it lightly between his fingers and seemed to be aiming it at the girl's rosy opening.

Louisa had never seen a man naked. Even though she had listened to the other girls in the servants' quarters discussing it with gusto, she had not expected anything remotely like this. She stared at it in dreadful fascination, unable to tear her eyes away. She felt hot waves of blood rising up her throat and flooding her cheeks. She was consumed with shame and horror.

'I thought the girl looked like you, although not as pretty,' said van Ritters quietly. 'Don't you agree, my dear?'

'I – I don't know,' she whispered. Her legs almost folded under her as she felt Mijnheer van Ritters' hand settle lightly on her bottom. The touch seemed to burn her flesh through the petticoats. He cupped her small round buttock, and she knew she should ask him to stop, or run from the room. But she could not. Stals and Elise had warned her repeatedly that she must obey Mijnheer always. She stood paralysed. She belonged to him, like any of his horses or dogs. She was one of his chattels. She must submit to him without protest, even though she was not sure what he was doing, what he wanted from her.

'Of course, Rembrant has taken some artistic licence when it comes to dimensions.' She could not believe that the artist who had painted the figure of God had also painted this picture, yet it was possible: even a famous artist must do what the great man required of him.

'Forgive me, Gentle Jesus,' she prayed and shut her eyes tightly so that she did not have to look at that wicked picture. She heard the rustle of stiff silk brocade, and he said, 'There, Louisa, this is what it really looks like.'

Her eyelids were clenched tightly, and he ran his hand over her buttock, gently but insistently. 'You are a big girl now, Louisa. It is time you knew these things. Open your eyes, my dear.'

Obediently she opened them a crack. She saw that he had undone the front of his robe, and that he wore nothing under it. She stared at the thing that stood proud through the folds of silk. The painting was a bland and romanticized representation of it. It rose massively from a nest of coarse dark hair, and seemed as thick as her wrist. The head was not an insipid pink as in the painting, but the colour of a ripe plum. The slit in the end of it glared at her like a cyclopean eye. She shut her eyes again tightly.

'Gertruda!' she whispered. 'I promised to take her for a walk.'

'You are very good to her, Louisa.' His voice had a strange husky edge to it that she had never heard before. 'But now you must be good to me also.' He reached down and under her skirts, then ran his fingers up her naked legs. He lingered at the soft dimples at the back of her knees, and she trembled more violently. His touch was caressing, and strangely reassuring, but she knew it was wrong. She was confused by these contrary emotions, and she felt as though she were suffocating. His fingers left the soft back of her knees and moved up her thigh. The touch was neither furtive nor hesitant, but authoritative, not something she could deny or oppose.

'You must be good to me,' he had said, and she knew that he had every right to ask that of her. She owed him everything. If this was being good to him, then she had no choice, yet she knew it was wicked and that Jesus would punish her. Perhaps He would cease to love her for what they were doing. She heard the rustle of the page as he turned it with his free hand, and then he said, 'Look!' She tried to resist him in this at least, and shut her eyes again. His touch became more demanding and his hand moved up to the crease where her buttock joined the back of her thigh.

She opened her eyes, just a fraction, and looked through her lashes at the fresh page of the book. Then her eyes flew wide open. The girl who looked so like her was kneeling in front of her swain. Her skirts had hiked up behind her, and her exposed bottom was round and buttery. Both she and the boy were gazing down into his lap. The girl's expression was fond, as though she were looking down at a beloved pet, a kitten perhaps. She held it clasped in both her small hands, but her dainty fingers were not able to encompass its girth.

'Is it not a beautiful picture?' he asked, and despite the wickedness of the subject, she felt a strange empathy towards the young couple. They were smiling, and it seemed as though they loved each other and were enjoying what they were doing. She forgot to close her eyes again.

'You see, Louisa, that God has made men and women differently. On their own they are incomplete, but together they make a whole.' She was not sure exactly what he meant, but sometimes she had not understood what her father had told her, or the sermon preached by the dominie. 'That is why the couple in the painting are so happy and why you can see that they feel full of love for each other.'

With gentle authority his fingers moved between her legs, right up to the juncture of her thighs. Then he did something else to her there. She was not sure what it was, but she moved her feet apart so he could do it more easily. The sensation that overtook her was beyond anything she had experienced before. She could feel the happiness and love he had spoken about spreading out and suffusing her entire body. She stared down again into the opening of his robe, and her feelings of shock and fear faded. She saw that, like the picture in the book, it was really quite pleasing. No wonder the other girl looked at it like that.

He moved her gently, and she was pliant and unresisting. Still sitting in the chair, he turned towards her, and at the same time, drew her closer and placed one hand on her shoulder. She understood instinctively that he wanted her to do what the girl in the picture was doing. Under the pressure of the hand on her shoulder she sank down to her knees and that strangely ugly, beautiful thing was only inches from her face. Like the other girl she reached out and took it in her hands. He made a small grunting sound and she felt how hot and hard it was. It fascinated her. She squeezed gently, and felt a leap of life as though this thing had a separate existence. It belonged to her, and she felt a strange sense of power, as though she held the core of his being in her hands.

He reached down and placed his own hands over hers. He began to move them back and forth. At first she was not sure what he was doing, then understood that he was showing her what he wanted. She felt a strong desire to please him, and she learned quickly. While she moved her fingers as rapidly as a weaver working at the loom he lay back in the chair and groaned. She thought she had hurt him and she tried to stand up, but he stopped her with the hand on her shoulder again and, a desperate tone in his voice, said, 'No, Louisa, just like that. Don't stop what you're doing. You're such a good, clever girl.'

Suddenly he let out a deep, shuddering sigh and whipped a scarlet silk kerchief out of the pocket of his robe, covering his lap and both her hands with it. She did not want to let go of him, even when she felt a hot, viscous fluid pouring over her hands and soaking the silk cloth. When she tried to keep on with what she was doing, he grasped her wrists and held her hands still. 'That's enough, my dear. You have made me very happy.'

After a long time he roused himself. He took her little hands one at a time and wiped them clean with the silk cloth. She felt no sense of revulsion. He was smiling at her kindly, and he told her, 'I am very pleased with you, but you must not tell anyone what we did today. Do you understand, Louisa?' She nodded vehemently. The guilt had evaporated, and she felt instead gratitude and reverence.

'Now you can go back to Gertruda. We will begin her

riding lessons tomorrow. Of course, you will take her to the academy.'

Over the next few weeks Louisa saw him only once and at a distance. She was half-way up the staircase, on her way to Gertruda's room, when a footman opened the doors to the banquet room, and Mijnheer van Ritters led out a procession of his guests. They were all beautifully dressed, prosperous-looking ladies and gentlemen. Louisa knew at least four of the men were members of Het Zeventien, the directors of the VOC. They had obviously dined well and were jovial and noisy. She hid behind the curtains as they passed below her, but she watched Mijnheer van Ritters with a strange feeling of longing. He was wearing a long, curled wig, and the sash and the star of the Order of the Golden Fleece. He was magnificent. Louisa felt a rare flash of hatred for the smiling, elegant woman on his arm. After they had passed her hiding-place she ran to the room she shared with Gertruda, threw herself on the bed and wept.

'Why does he not want to see me again? Did I displease him?'

She thought about the incident in the library every day, especially after the lantern was out and she was in her bed across the room from Gertruda.

Then one day Mijnheer van Ritters arrived unexpectedly at the riding academy. Louisa had taught Gertruda how to curtsy. She was awkward and clumsy and Louisa had to help her back on to her feet when she lost her balance, but van Ritters smiled a little at this accomplishment, and returned the courtesy with a playful bow. 'Your devoted servant,' he said, and Gertruda giggled. He did not speak directly to Louisa, and she knew better than to address him uninvited. He watched Gertruda make a circuit of the ring, on the lead rein. Louisa had to walk beside the pony, and Gertruda's pudding face was screwed up with terror. Then van Ritters left as abruptly as he had appeared.

Another week passed and Louisa was torn with opposing emotions. At times the magnitude of her sin returned to plague her. She had allowed him to touch and play with her, and she had taken pleasure in handling that monstrous thing of his. She had even begun to have the most vivid dreams about it, and she woke in confusion, her newly fledged breasts and her private parts burning and itching. As though in punishment for her sins her breasts had swelled until they strained the buttons of her blouse. She tried to hide them, keeping her arms crossed over her chest, but she had seen the stable boys and the footmen looking at them.

She wanted to talk to Elise about what had happened to her and ask her advice, but Mijnheer van Ritters had warned her against this. So she kept silent.

Then, unexpectedly, Stals told her, 'You are to move to your own room. It is the Mijnheer's order.'

Louisa stared at him in astonishment. 'But what about Gertruda? She can't sleep alone.'

'The master thinks it is time she learned to do so. She, too, will have a new room and you will have the one beside her. She will have a bell to call you if she needs you in the night.'

The girls' new apartments were on the floor below the library and Mijnheer's bedroom suite. Louisa made a game of the move, and stilled Gertruda's misgivings. They took all her dolls up and held a party for them to introduce them to their new quarters. Louisa had learned to speak in a different voice for each toy, a trick that never failed to reduce Gertruda to shrieks of laughter. When each of her dolls in turn had told Gertruda how happy they were with their new home, she was convinced.

Louisa's own room was light and spacious. The furnishings were quite splendid, with velvet curtains and gilt chairs and bedstead. There was a feather mattress on the bed, and thick blankets. There was even a fireplace with a marble surround, although Stals cautioned her that she would be rationed to a single bucket of coal a week. But, wonder of wonders, there was a tiny cubicle that contained a commode with a lid that lifted to reveal a carved seat and the porcelain chamber-pot under it. Louisa was in a haze of delight as she crept into bed that first night. It seemed that she had never been warm in her life until this evening.

She came out of a deep, dreamless sleep and lay awake trying to place what had woken her. It must have been well past midnight for it was dark and the house was silent. Then the sound came again, and her heart raced. It was footsteps, but they came from the panelled wall at the far side of the room. She was gripped by superstitious dread, and could neither move nor scream. Then she heard the creak of a door opening, and a ghostly light glowed out of nowhere. Slowly a panel in the far wall swung wide open and a spectral figure stepped into the room. It was a tall, bearded man dressed in breeches and a white shirt with leg-o'-mutton sleeves and a high stock.

'Louisa!' His voice was hollow and echoed strangely. It was just the voice that she would have expected from a ghost. She pulled the covers over her head and lay without breathing. She heard footsteps crossing to her bedside, and she could see the wavering light through a slit in the bedclothes. The footsteps stopped beside her and suddenly her coverings were flung back. This time she screamed, but she knew it was futile: next door Gertruda would be sleeping in a mindless stupor from which nothing short of an earthquake could waken her, and there were only the two of them on this floor of Huis Brabant. She stared at the face above her, so far gone in terror that she did not recognize him even in the lantern-light.

'Don't be afraid, child. I will not hurt you.'

'Oh, Mijnheer!' She flung herself against his chest and clung to him with all the strength of her relief. 'I thought you were a ghost.'

'There, child.' He stroked her hair. 'It's all over. There is nothing to be afraid of.' It took her a long time to become calm again. Then he said, 'I won't leave you here alone. Come with me.'

He took her hand, and she followed him trustingly in her cotton nightdress on bare feet. He led her through the door in the panel. A spiral staircase was concealed behind it. They went up it, then through another secret doorway. Suddenly they were in a magnificent chamber, so spacious that even with fifty candles burning in their chandeliers the far reaches of the room and the ceilings were in shadow. He led her to the fireplace in which tall yellow flames leaped and twisted.

He embraced her and stroked her hair. 'Did you think I had forgotten you?'

She nodded. 'I thought I had made you angry, and that you did not like me any more.'

He chuckled and lifted her face to the light. 'What a beautiful little thing you are. This is how angry I am and how much I dislike you.' He kissed her mouth and she tasted the cheroot on his lips, a strong aromatic flavour that made her feel safe and secure. At last he broke the embrace and seated her on the sofa in front of the fire. He went to a table on which stood crystal glasses and a decanter of ruby red liquor. He poured a glass and brought it to her. 'Drink this. It will chase away the bad thoughts.'

She choked and coughed at the sting of the liquor, but then a marvellous glow spread through her, to her toes and fingertips. He sat beside her, stroked her hair and spoke to her softly, telling her how pretty she was, what a good girl, and how he had missed her. Lulled by the warmth in her belly and his mesmeric voice she leaned her head on his chest. He lifted the hem of her nightdress over her head and she wriggled out of it. Then she was naked. In the candlelight her child-like body was pale and smooth as cream in a jug. She felt no shame as he fondled her, and kissed her face. She turned this way and that at the gentle urging of his hands.

Suddenly he stood up and she watched him as he pulled off his shirt and breeches. When he came back to the sofa and stood in front of her he did not have to guide her hands and she reached for him naturally. She gazed at his sex as she slid back the loose skin to reveal the shiny plum-coloured head, as he had taught her. Then he reached down, removed her hands and sank to the floor in front of her. He pushed apart her knees and laid her back on the velvet-covered sofa. He lowered his face and she felt his moustaches tickling the inside of her thighs, then moving higher.

'What are you doing?' she cried, with alarm. He had not done this before, and she tried to sit up. He held her down and suddenly she cried out and sank her fingernails into his shoulders. His mouth had settled on her most secret parts. The sensation was so intense that she feared for a moment she might faint.

It was not every night that he came down the spiral staircase to fetch her. On many nights there was the rumble of carriage wheels on the cobbled streets below Louisa's window. She blew out her candle and peeped through the curtains to watch Mijnheer van Ritters' guests arriving for another banquet or fashionable soirée. Long after they had left she lay awake, hoping to hear his footstep on the staircase, but she was usually disappointed.

For weeks or even months at a time he was gone, sailing on one of his fine ships to places with strange and evocative names. While he was gone she was restless and bored. She found that she was even impatient with Gertruda, and unhappy with herself.

When he came back his presence filled the great house, and even the other servants were enlivened and excited by it. Suddenly all the waiting and pining were as if they had never happened as she heard him descending the staircase and leaped from her bed to meet him as he stepped through the secret door in the panelling. After that he devised a signal to summon her to his chamber so that he no longer had to come down to fetch her. At dinner time he would send a footman to deliver a red rose to Gertruda. None of the servants who delivered the bloom thought it odd: they all knew that Mijnheer had an inexplicable affection for his ugly slow-witted daughter. But on those nights the door at the top of the spiral staircase was unlocked, and when Louisa stepped through he was waiting for her.

These meetings were never the same. Every time he invented some new game for them to act out. He made her dress in fantastic costumes, play the role of milkmaid, stable-boy or princess. Sometimes he made her wear masks, the heads of demons and wild animals.

On other evenings they would study the pictures in the green book, and then enact the scenes they depicted. The first time he showed her the picture of the girl lying under the boy and his shaft buried in her to the hilt, she did not believe it was possible. But he was gentle, patient and considerate, so that when it happened there was little pain and only a few drops of her virgin blood on the sheets of the wide bed. Afterwards she felt a great sense of accomplishment and when she was alone she studied her lower body with awe. It amazed her that the parts she had been taught were unclean and sinful could be the seat of such delights. She was convinced now that there was nothing more that he could teach her. She believed that she had been able to pleasure him, and herself, in every conceivable way. But she was wrong.

He went away on one of his seemingly interminable voyages, this time to a place called St Petersburg in Russia to visit the court of Pyotr Alekseyevich, whom other men called Peter the Great, and to expand his interests in the trade in precious furs. When he returned Louisa was in a fever of excitement, and this time she did not have long to wait for his summons. That evening a footman delivered a single red rose to Gertruda while Louisa was cutting up her roasted chicken.

'Why are you so happy, Louisa?' Gertruda demanded, as she danced around the bedroom.

'Because I love you, Gertie, and I love everybody in the world,' Louisa sang.

Gertruda clapped her hands. 'And I love you too, Louisa.'

'Now it's time for your bed, and here is a cup of hot milk to make you sleep tight.'

That evening when Louisa stepped through the secret

71

doorway into Mijnheer van Ritters' bedchamber, she stopped dead in astonishment. This was a new game and she was at once confused and frightened. This was too real, too terrifying.

Mijnheer van Ritters' head was concealed with a tight-fitting black leather hood with round cutout eyeholes and a crude gash for a mouth. He wore a black leather apron and shiny black boots that reached to the top of his thighs. His arms were folded across his chest, and his hands were covered with black gloves. She could barely tear her gaze away from him to look at the sinister structure that stood in the centre of the floor. It was identical to the flogging tripod on which miscreants received public punishment in the square outside the law courts. However, in place of the usual chains, silk ropes dangled from the top of the tripod.

She smiled at him with trembling lips, but he stared back at her impassively through the eyeholes in the black hood. She wanted to run, but he seemed to anticipate her intentions. He strode to the door and locked it. Then he placed the key in the front pocket of his apron. Her legs gave way under her, and she sank to the floor. 'I am sorry,' she whispered. 'Please don't hurt me.'

'You have been sentenced for the sin of harlotry to twenty strokes of the whip.' His voice was stern and harsh.

'Please let me go. I don't want to play this game.'

'This is no game.' He came to her, and though she pleaded with him for mercy he lifted her and led her to the tripod. He tied her hands high above her head with the silken ropes, and she peered back at him over her shoulder with her long yellow hair hanging over her face. 'What are you going to do to me?'

He went to the table against the far wall and, with his back turned to her, picked up something. Then, with theatrical slowness, he turned back with the whip in his hand. She whimpered and tried to free herself from the silken bonds that pinioned her wrists, twisting and turning as she hung on the tripod. He came to her and placed one finger into the opening of her nightdress, and ripped it down to the hem. He stripped away the tatters and she was naked. He came to stand in front of her, and she saw a huge bulge under his leather apron, evidence of his arousal.

'Twenty strokes,' he repeated, in the cold, hard voice of a stranger, 'and you will count each one as it falls. Do you understand, you wanton little whore?' She winced at the word. Nobody had ever called her that before.

'I did not know I was doing wrong. I thought I was pleasing you.'

He cut the whip through the air, and the lash hissed close to her face. Then he went behind her, and she closed her eyes and tensed every muscle in her back, but still the pain of the stroke defied her belief and she shrieked aloud.

'Count!' he ordered, and through white, quivering lips she obeyed.

'One!' she screamed.

It went on and on without pity or respite, until she fainted. He held a small green bottle under her nose and the pungent fumes revived her. Then it started again.

'Count!' he ordered.

At last she was able to whisper, 'Twenty,' and he laid the whip back on the table. He was loosening the strings of his leather apron as he came back to her. She hung on the silk ropes, unable to lift her head or support herself. Her back, her buttocks and the tops of her legs felt as though they were on fire.

He came up behind her, and she felt his hands on her lower body, drawing her red, throbbing buttocks apart. Then there was a pain more dreadful than any that had gone before it. She was being impaled in the most unnatural way, ripped apart. Agony tore through her bowels, and she found fresh strength to scream and scream again.

At last he cut her down from the tripod, wrapped her in a blanket and carried her down the staircase. Without another word he left her sobbing on the bed. In the morning when she tottered to the cubicle and sat on the commode she found that she was still bleeding. Seven days later she had still not healed completely, and another red rose was delivered to

Gertruda. Trembling and weeping quietly, she climbed the staircase to answer his summons. When she entered his chamber the tripod stood in the middle of the floor and, once again, he wore the hood and apron of the executioner.

It took months for her to gather her courage, but at last she went to Elise and told her how Mijnheer was treating her. She lifted her dress and turned to show the welts and stripes across her back. Then she bent over and showed her the torn, festering opening.

'Cover yourself, you shameless strumpet,' Elise shouted, and slapped her cheek. 'How dare you make up filthy lies about such a great and good man? I shall have to report you to Mijnheer for this, but in the meantime I will tell Stals to lock you in the wine cellar.'

For two days Louisa crouched on the stone floor in a dark corner of the cellar. The agony in her lower belly was a fire that threatened to consume her very soul. On the third day a sergeant and three men of the city watch came to fetch her. As they led her up the stairs to the kitchen yard she looked for Gertruda, Elise or Stals but there was no sign of them or any of the other servants.

'Thank you for coming to rescue me,' she told the sergeant. 'I could not have borne it another day.' He gave her an odd enigmatic glance.

'We searched your room and found the jewellery you had stolen,' he said. 'What terrible ingratitude to a gentleman who treated you so kindly. We shall see what the magistrate has to say to you.'

The magistrate was suffering from the effects of the previous evening's overindulgence. He had been one of fifty dinner guests at Huis Brabant whose cellars and table were famous throughout the Low Countries. Koen van Ritters was an old friend, and the magistrate glowered at the young female prisoner arraigned before him. Koen had spoken to him about this hussy after last night's dinner, while they puffed on their cheroots and finished off a bottle of fine old cognac. He listened impatiently as the sergeant of the watch gave evidence

74

against her, and laid before the magistrate the package of stolen jewellery that they had found in her room.

'Prisoner is to be transported to the penal colony in Batavia for life,' the magistrate ordered.

Het Gelukkige Meeuw was lying in the harbour, almost ready to sail. They marched Louisa from the court room directly to the docks. At the top of the gangplank she was met by the head gaoler. He entered her name in the register, then two of his men locked leg irons on her ankles and shoved her down the hatchway to the gundeck.

Now almost a year later the *Meeuw* lay at anchor in Table Bay. Even through the thick oaken planking Louisa heard the hail, 'Longboat with supplies. Permission to hook on?'

She roused herself from her long reverie, and peeped through the chink in the joint of the port-lid. She saw the longboat being rowed towards the ship by a mixed crew of a dozen black and white men. There was a big, broad-shouldered ruffian standing in the bows, and she started as she recognized the man at the tiller. It was the young one who had asked her name and thrown the fish to her. She had fought for possession of that precious gift, then divided it with her little blade and shared it with three other women. They were not her friends, for there were no friends aboard this ship, but early in the voyage the four had forged a pact of mutual protection for survival. They had gobbled down the fish raw, watchful of the other starving women who crowded round them, waiting for an opportunity to snatch a scrap.

She remembered, with longing, the sweet taste of the raw fish now as she watched the heavily laden longboat moor against the side of the ship. There was a hubbub of banging and shouting, the squeal of sheave blocks and more shouted orders. Through the chink she watched the baskets and boxes of fresh produce being swung on board. She could smell the

75

fruit and the newly picked tomatoes. Saliva flooded her mouth, but she knew that most of this bounty would go to the officers' mess, and what remained to the gunroom and the common seamen's kitchen. None of it would find its way down to the prison decks. The convicts would subsist on the weevily hard biscuit and the rotten salt pork, crawling with maggots.

Suddenly she heard someone banging on one of the other gunports further down the deck, and a masculine voice from outside called softly but urgently, 'Louisa! Is Louisa there?'

Before she could answer, some of the other women howled and shouted back, '*Ja*, my *dottie*. I am Louisa. Do you want a taste of my honey-pot?' Then there were shrieks of laughter. Louisa recognized the man's voice. She tried to shout to him above the chorus of filth and invective, but her enemies swamped her with malicious glee and she knew he would not hear her. With rising despair she peered through her peephole, but the view was restricted.

'I am here,' she shouted in Dutch. 'I am Louisa.'

Abruptly his face rose into her view. He must have been standing on one of the thwarts of the longboat that was moored below her gunport.

'Louisa?' He put his eye to the other side of the chink and they stared at each other from a range of a few inches, 'Yes.' He laughed unexpectedly. 'Blue eyes! Bright blue eyes.'

'Who are you? What is your name?' On impulse she spoke in English, and he gaped at her.

'You speak English?'

'No, you weak-wit, it was Chinese,' she snapped back at him, and he laughed again. By the sound of him he was overbearing and cocky, but his was the only friendly voice she had heard in over a year.

'It's a saucy one you are! I have something else for you. Can you get this port-lid open?' he asked.

'Are any of the guards watching from the deck?' she asked. 'They will have me flogged if they see us talking.'

'No, we are hidden by the tumble-home of the ship's side.'

'Wait!' she said, and drew the blade from her pouch. Quickly she prised out the single shackle that still held the lock in place. Then she leaned back, placed both bare feet against the port-lid and pushed with all her might. The hinges creaked, then gave a few inches. She saw his fingers at the edge and he helped to pull it open a little wider.

Then he thrust a small canvas bag through the opening. 'There is a letter for you,' he whispered, his face close to hers. 'Read it.' And then he was gone.

'Wait!' she pleaded, and his face appeared in the opening again. 'You did not tell me. What's your name?'

'Jim. Jim Courtney.'

'Thank you, Jim Courtney,' she said, and let the port-lid thump shut.

The three women crowded round her in a tight circle of protection as she opened the bag. Quickly they divided up the dried meat and the packets of hard biscuit, and gnawed at the unappetizing fare with desperate hunger. When she found the comb tears came to Louisa's eyes. It was carved from dappled honey-coloured tortoiseshell. She stroked it through her hair, and it glided smoothly, not pulling painfully like the ugly hand-whittled thing she had been reduced to. Then she found the file and the knife wrapped together in a scrap of canvas. The knife was horn-handled, and the blade, when she tested it on her thumb, was keen, a fine weapon. The sturdy little file had three cutting edges. She felt a lift of hope, the first in all those long months. She looked down at the irons on her ankles. The skin beneath the cruel bonds was calloused.

Knife and file were invaluable gifts, but it was the comb that touched her deepest. It was an affirmation that he had seen her as a woman, not as gaol dregs from the slums and the gutter. She rummaged in the bottom of the bag for the letter he had promised. It was a single sheet of cheap paper, folded cunningly to form its own envelope. It was addressed to 'Louisa' in a bold but fair hand. She unfolded it, careful not to tear it. It was in poorly spelt Dutch, but she was able to make out the gist of it.

Use the file on your chains. I will have a boat under the
stern tomorrow night. When you hear the ship's bell strike

77

two bells in the middle watch, jump. I will hear the splash. Have courage.

Her pulse raced. At once she knew that the chances of success were negligible. A hundred things could go wrong, not least a musket ball or a shark. What mattered was that she had found a friend and with it new hope of salvation, no matter how remote. She tore the note into shreds and dropped them into the reeking latrine bucket. None of the guards would try to retrieve it from there. Then she crept back under the cannon, into the darkness that was her only privacy, and sat with her legs folded under her so she could easily reach the links of her leg irons. With the first stroke of the little file she cut a shallow but bright notch and a few grains of iron filtered down to the deck. The shackles had been forged from untempered steel of poor quality but it would take time and heartbreaking perseverance to cut through a single link.

'I have a day and a night. Until two bells in the middle watch tomorrow night,' she encouraged herself, and laid the file into the notch she had already cut. At the next stroke more iron filings dusted the deck.

The longboat had been relieved of the heavy load of produce and now she rode lightly. Mansur was at the tiller, and Jim gazed back over the stern as he rowed. Every now and again he grinned as he went over in his mind the brief meeting with Louisa. She spoke English, good English, with only a touch of a Dutch accent, and she was spirited and quick-witted. She had responded swiftly to the circumstances. This was no dull-witted lump of gaol-bait. He had seen her bare legs through the chink in the port-lid as she helped him prise it open. They were starved painfully thin, and galled by her chains, but they were long and straight, not twisted and deformed by rickets. 'Good breeding there!' as his father would say of a blood filly. The hand that had taken the canvas bag from his was grubby, and the nails were cracked and broken, but it was beautifully shaped, with gracefully tapered fingers. The hands of a lady, not a slave or scullerymaid. 'She does not smell like a posy of lavender. But she's been locked up in that filthy tub for Lord alone knows how long. What do you expect?' He made excuses for her. Then he thought about her eyes, those wondrous blue eyes, and his expression was soft and dreamy. 'In all my life, I have never laid eyes on a girl like that. And she speaks English.'

'Hey, coz!' Mansur shouted. 'Keep the stroke. You will have us on Robben Island if you're not more careful.' Jim started out of his day-dream just in time to meet the next swell that lifted the stern high.

'Sea's getting up,' his father grunted. 'Like as not it will be blowing a gale by tomorrow. We'll have to try to take out the last load before it gets too rough.'

Jim took his eyes off the receding shape of the ship, and looked beyond her. His spirits sank. The stormclouds were piling up high and heavy as mountains upon the horizon.

I have to think up an excuse to stay ashore when they take out the next load to the *Meeuw*, he decided. There is not going to be another chance to make ready.

As the mules dragged the longboat up the beach, Jim told his father, 'I have to take Captain Hugo his cut. He might scotch us if he doesn't have some coin in his fat fist.'

'Let him wait for it, the old sheep thief. I need you to help with the next shipment.'

'I promised Hugo and, anyway, you have a full crew for the next trip out to the ship.'

Tom Courtney studied his son with a searching gaze. He knew him well. He was up to something. It was not like Jim to shirk. On the contrary, he was a rock on which Tom could depend. It was he who had established good terms with the purser on the convict ship, he had obtained the licence to trade from Hugo, and he had supervised the loading of the first shipment. He could be trusted.

'Well, I don't know . . .' Tom stroked his chin dubiously.

Mansur stepped in quickly. 'Let Jim go, Uncle Tom. I can take over from him for the time being.'

'Very well, Jim. Go and visit your friend Hugo,' Tom acquiesced, 'but be back on the beach to help with the boats when we return.'

Later, from the top of the dunes, Jim watched the longboats rowing back towards the *Meeuw* with the final load of produce. It seemed to him that the swells were higher than they had been that morning, and the wind was starting to claw off the tops in a parade of leaping white horses.

'God spare us!' he said aloud. 'If the storm comes up I will not be able to get the girl off until it passes.' Then he remembered his instructions to her. He had told her to jump overboard at precisely two bells in the middle watch. He could not get another message to her to stop her doing that. Would she have the good sense to stay on board if there was a full gale blowing, realizing that he had not been able to keep the rendezvous, or would she throw herself overboard regardless and perish in the darkness? The thought of her drowning in the dark waters struck him like a fist in his belly, and he felt nauseous. He turned Drumfire's head towards the castle and pressed his heels into the horse's sides.

Captain Hugo was surprised but pleased to have his commission paid so promptly. Jim left him without ceremony, refusing even a mug of coffee, and galloped back along the beach. He was thinking furiously as he rode.

There had been so little time to lay his plans. It was only in the last few hours that he had been sure the girl had the spirit to chance such a hazardous escape. The first consideration, if he succeeded in getting her ashore, would be to find a safe hiding-place for her. As soon as her escape was discovered the entire castle garrison would be sent out to find her, a hundred infantry and a squadron of cavalry. The Company troops in the castle had little enough employment, and a manhunt or, better still, a woman-hunt would be one of the most exciting events in years. Colonel Keyser, the garrison commander, would be hot for the honour of capturing an escaped convict.

For the first time he allowed himself to consider the consequences if this hare-brained scheme fell to pieces. He worried that he might be making trouble for his family. The strict law laid down by the directors of the VOC, the almighty Zeventien in Amsterdam, was that no foreigner was permitted to reside or carry on a business in the colony. However, like so many other strict laws of the directors in Amsterdam, there were special circumstances by which they could be circumvented. Those special circumstances always involved a monetary token of esteem to His Excellency Governor van de Witten. It had cost the Courtney brothers twenty thousand guilders to obtain a licence to reside and trade in the Colony of Good Hope. Van de Witten was unlikely to revoke that licence. He and Tom Courtney were on friendly terms, and Tom contributed generously to van de Witten's unofficial pension fund.

Jim hoped that if he and the girl simply disappeared from the colony, there would be nothing to implicate the rest of his family. There might be suspicions, and at the worst it might cost his father another gift to van de Witten, but in the end it would blow over, just as long as he never returned.

There were only two avenues of escape from the colony. The natural and best was the sea. But that meant a boat. The Courtney brothers owned two armed traders, handy and fleet schooners with which they traded as far as Arabia and Bombay. However, at the present time both these vessels were at sea and were not expected back until the monsoon changed, which would not be for several months yet.

Jim had saved up a little money, perhaps enough to pay for a passage for the girl and himself on one of the ships lying in Table Bay at the moment. But the first thing Colonel Keyser would do as soon as the girl was reported missing was to send search parties aboard every ship. He could try to steal a small boat, a pinnace perhaps, something seaworthy enough in which he and the girl could reach the Portuguese ports on the Mozambique coast, but every captain was alert for piracy. The most likely reward for his efforts would be a musket ball in the belly.

Even in his most optimistic expectations he had to face the fact that the sea route was closed to them. There was only one other still open, and he turned and looked northwards at the far mountains on which the last of the winter snows had not yet thawed. He pulled up Drumfire and thought about what lay out there. Jim had not travelled more than fifty leagues beyond those peaks, but he had heard of others who had gone further into the hinterland and returned with a great store of ivory. There was even a rumour of the old hunter who had picked a shiny pebble out of a sandbank of a nameless river far to the north, and had sold the diamond in Amsterdam for a hundred thousand guilders. He felt his skin prickle with excitement. On countless nights he had dreamed of what lay beyond that blue horizon. He had discussed it with Mansur and Zama, and they had promised each other that one day they would make the journey. Had the gods of adventure overheard his boasts, and were they conspiring now to drive him out there into the wilderness? Would he have a girl with golden hair and blue eyes riding at his side? He laughed at the thought, and urged Drumfire on.

With his father, his uncle Dorian and almost all the servants and freed slaves out of the way for the next few hours, he had to work quickly. He knew where his father kept the keys to both the strongroom and the armoury. He selected six strong mules out of the herd in the kraal, pack-saddled them and took them on a lead rein up to the rear doors of the godown. He had to choose carefully as he selected goods from the warehouse to make up the loads. A dozen best Tower muskets and canvas ball-pouches, kegs of black powder, and lead bars and moulds to cast more ball; axes, knives and blankets; beads and cloth to trade with the wild tribes they might meet; basic medicines, pots and water bottles; needles and thread, and all the other necessities of existence in the wilderness, but no luxuries. Coffee was not a luxury, he consoled himself, as he added a sack of beans.

When they were loaded he led the string of mules away to a quiet place beside a stream in the forest almost two miles from High Weald. He relieved the animals of their packs so they could rest, and left them with knee-halters to allow them to graze on the lush grass on the stream bank.

By the time he returned to High Weald the longboats were on their way back from the *Meeuw*. He went down to meet his father, Mansur and the returning crews as they came back over the dunes. He rode along with them, and listened to their desultory conversation. They were all drenched with seawater and almost exhausted, for it had been a long haul back from the Dutch ship in the heavy seas.

Mansur described it to him succinctly: 'You were lucky to get out of it. The waves were breaking over us like a waterfall.'

'Did you see the girl?' Jim whispered, so his father would not overhear.

'What girl?' Mansur gave him a knowing glance.

'You know what girl.' Jim punched his arm.

Mansur's expression turned serious. 'They had all the convicts locked up and battened down. One of the officers told Uncle Tom that the captain is anxious to sail as soon as he can finish reprovisioning and filling his water butts. By tomorrow at the very latest. He does not want to be pinned down by the storm on this lee shore.' He saw Jim's despairing expression, and went on sympathetically, 'Sorry, coz, but like as not the ship will be gone by noon tomorrow. She would have been no good for you anyway, a convict woman. You know nothing about her, you don't know what crimes she has committed. Murder, perhaps. Let her go, Jim. Forget about her. There is more than one bird in the blue sky, more than a single blade of grass on the plains of Camdeboo.'

Jim felt anger flare and bitter words rose to his lips, but he held them back. He left the others and turned Drumfire towards the top of the dunes. From the height he looked out across the bay. The storm was mounting even as he watched,

83

bringing on the darkness prematurely. The wind moaned and ruffled his hair, and whipped Drumfire's mane into a tangle. He had to shield his eyes against the sting of flying sand and spume. The surface of the sea was a welter of breaking white spray, and tall, heaving swells that rose up and crashed down on the beach. It was a wonder that his father had been able to bring the boats in through that turmoil of wind and water, but Tom Courtney was a master mariner.

Almost two miles out the *Meeuw* was an indistinct grey shape that rolled and pitched with swinging bare masts, and disappeared as each fresh squall swept across the bay. Jim watched until the darkness hid her completely. Then he galloped down the back of the dune towards High Weald. He found Zama still working in the stables, bedding down the horses. 'Come with me,' he ordered, and obediently Zama followed him out into the orchard. When they were out of sight of the house they squatted down side by side. They were silent for a while, then Jim spoke in Lozi, the language of the forests, so that Zama would know there were deadly serious matters to discuss.

'I'm going,' he said.

Zama stared into his face, but his eyes were hidden by the darkness. 'Where, Somoya?' he asked. Jim pointed with his chin towards the north. 'When will you return?'

'I do not know, perhaps never,' said Jim.

'Then I must take leave of my father.'

'You're coming with me?' Jim asked.

Zama glanced at him pityingly. No answer was needed to such a fatuous question.

'Aboli was a father to me also.' Jim stood up and placed an arm around his shoulder. 'Let us go to his grave.'

They climbed the hill in the intermittent lightning flashes, but they both had the night-vision of youth so they went swiftly. The grave was on the eastern slope, sited deliberately to face each morning's sunrise. Jim remembered every detail of the funeral. Tom Courtney had slaughtered a black bull and Aboli's wives had stitched the old man's corpse into the wet hide. Then, Tom had carried Aboli's once great body, shrunken now with age, like a sleeping child, down into the deep shaft. He had sat him upright, then laid out all his weapons and his most treasured possessions around him. Lastly the entrance to the shaft was sealed with a round boulder. It had taken two full spans of oxen to drag it into position.

Now, in the darkness, Jim and Zama knelt before it and prayed to the tribal gods of the Lozi, and to Aboli, who in death had joined that dark pantheon. The rolling thunder counterpointed their prayers. Zama asked his father for his blessing on the journey that lay ahead of them, then Jim thanked him for teaching him the way of the musket and the sword, and reminded Aboli of when he had taken him to hunt his first lion. 'Protect us your sons as you shielded us that day,' he asked, 'for we go upon a journey we know not where.'

Then the two sat with their backs against the gravestone, and Jim explained to Zama what he must do. 'I have loaded a string of mules. They are tethered by the stream. Take them up into the mountains, to Majuba, the Place of Doves, and wait for me there.'

Majuba was the rude hut, hidden in the foothills, that was used by the shepherds who took the Courtney flocks up to the high pastures in the summer, and by the men of the Courtney family when they went out to hunt the quagga, the eland and the bluebuck. It was deserted at this season of the year. They said their last farewells to the old warrior who sat eternally in the darkness behind the boulder, and went down to the clearing beside the stream in the forest. Jim took a lantern from one of the packs and, by its light, helped Zama load the mules with the heavy packs. Then he set him on the path that led northwards into the mountains.

'I will come in two days, whatever happens. Wait for me!' Jim shouted as they parted, and Zama rode on alone.

By the time Jim arrived back at High Weald the household was asleep. But Sarah, his mother, had kept his dinner warm for him on the back of the stove. When she heard him clattering the pots, she came down in her nightgown and sat to watch him eat. She said little but her eyes were sad, and there was a droop at the corners of her mouth. 'God bless you, my son, my only son,' she whispered, as she kissed him goodnight. Earlier that day she had seen him lead away the mule train into the forest and, with a mother's instinct, she had known he was leaving. She picked up the candle and climbed the stairs to the bedroom where Tom snored peacefully.

Jim slept little that night, while the wind buffeted the house and rattled the window-frames. He was up long before the rest of the household. In the kitchen he poured a mug of bitter black coffee from the enamel kettle that always stood on the back of the stove. It was still dark as he went down to the stables, and led out Drumfire. He rode down to the seashore, and as he and the horse topped the dunes the full force of the wind came at them out of the darkness like a ravening monster. He took Drumfire back behind the shelter of the dune and tethered him to a low saltbush, then climbed again on foot to the crest. He wrapped his cloak closer round his shoulders and pulled his wide-brimmed hat low over his eyes as he squatted and waited for the first show of dawn. He thought about the girl. She had shown herself to be quick-witted but was she sensible enough to realize that no small boat could come out to the anchorage in the bay until this storm abated? Would she understand that he was not deserting her?

The low, scudding clouds delayed the dawn, and even when it broke it could hardly illuminate the wild scene before him. He stood up, and had to lean into the wind as though he were crossing a fast-flowing river. He held onto his hat with both hands and searched for a glimpse of the Dutch ship. Then, far out, he saw a flash of something not as evanescent as the leaping foam and spray that strove to extinguish it. He watched it avidly, and it persisted, constant in this raging seascape.

'A sail!' he cried, and the wind tore the words from his lips. However, it was not where he had expected to find the

Meeuw. This was a ship under sail, not lying at anchor. He must know if this was the *Meeuw*, trying to fight her way out of the bay, or if it was one of the other ships that had been anchored there. His small hunting telescope was in his saddle-bag. He turned and ran back through the soft sand to where he had left Drumfire out of the wind.

When he reached the crest again he searched for the ship. It took him minutes to find her, but then her sails flashed at him again. He sat flat in the sand and, using his knees and elbows like a tripod to steady himself against the buffeting of the wind, he trained the lens on the distant ship. He picked up her sails, but the swells obscured the hull until suddenly a freak combination of wave and wind lifted her high.

'It's her!' There was no doubt left. '*Het Gelukkige Meeuw.*' He was swamped by an enervating sense of doom. Before his eyes Louisa was being carried away to some foul prison at the far ends of the earth and there was nothing he could do to prevent it happening.

'Please, God, don't take her from me so soon,' he prayed, in despair, but the distant ship battled on through the storm, close-hauled, her captain trying to get clear of the deadly lee shore. Through the lens Jim watched her with a seaman's eye. Tom had taught him well, and he understood all the forces and counter-forces of wind, keel and sail. He saw how close to disaster she was hovering.

The light strengthened and, even with the naked eye, he could make out the detail of this dreadful contest of ship against storm. After another hour she was still locked in the bay and Jim trained the telescope from the ship on to the black, sharklike shape of Robben Island that guarded the exit. Every minute that passed made it more apparent that the *Meeuw* could not break out into the open sea on this tack. The captain would have to come about. He had no alternative: the bottom under him was already too deep for him to drop anchor again, and the storm was pushing him down inexorably on to the rocks of the island. If he went aground there, the hull would be smashed to splinters.

'Go about!' Jim jumped to his feet. 'Tack now! You're going

to murder them, you idiot!' He meant both the ship and the girl. He knew that Louisa would still be battened down below, and even if by some miracle she escaped from the gundeck the chains around her ankles would drag her under as soon as she went over the side.

Doggedly the ship held her course. The manoeuvre of bringing such an ungainly ship about in the weather would entail terrible risk, but soon the captain must realize that no other course lay open to him.

'It's too late!' Jim agonized. 'It's already too late.' Then he saw it begin to happen, the sails slanting and their silhouette altering as she turned her head to the storm. He watched her through the lens, his hand shaking as her turn slowed. At last she hung there, caught in stays, with all her sails flogging and hammering, unable to complete the turn on to the other tack. Then Jim saw the next squall bearing down on her. The sea boiled at the foot of the racing curtain of rain and wind, which caught her and laid the ship over until her bottom planking showed, thick and filthy with weed and barnacles. Then the squall smothered her. She was gone as though she had never existed. In anguish Jim watched for her to reappear. She might have turned turtle to float keel uppermost, or she might even have been trodden right under – there was no way for him to know. His eye burned and his vision blurred with the intensity of his stare through the lens of the telescope. It seemed to take an age for the squall to pass. Then, abruptly, the ship appeared again, but it seemed that it could not be the same vessel, so drastically had her silhouette altered.

'Dismasted!' Jim groaned. Though tears brought on by strain and wind ran down his cheeks, he could not take his eye from the lens. 'Main and fore! She's lost both masts.' Only the mizzen poked up from the rolling hull and the tangle of sails and masts hanging over her side barely slowed her as she paid off before the wind. It swept her back into the bay, clear of the rocks of Robben Island but straight towards the thundering surf on the beach below where Jim stood.

Swiftly Jim calculated the distance, angles and speed. 'She will be on the beach in less than an hour,' he whispered to himself. 'God help all those on board when she strikes.' He lowered the telescope and, with the back of his arm, wiped the wind-tears from his cheek. 'And, most of all, God help Louisa.' He tried to imagine the conditions on the gundeck of the *Meeuw* at that moment, but his imagination baulked.

Louisa had not slept all that night. For hour after hour, while the *Meeuw* rolled and surged and snubbed against her anchor cable, and the storm howled relentlessly through the rigging, she had crouched under the gun carriage, working away with the file. She had padded the chain links with the canvas bag to deaden the scraping sound of metal against metal. But the file handle had raised a blister in her palm. When it burst she had to use the bag to cushion the raw flesh. The first pale light of dawn showed through the chink in the port-lid, and there was only a thin sliver of metal holding the chain link when she lifted her head and heard the unmistakable sounds of the anchor cable being hauled in, the stamp of the bare feet of the sailors working at the windlass on the deck above her. Then, faintly, she heard the shouted orders of the officers on the main deck, and the rush of feet to the masts as men went aloft in the storm.

'We're sailing!' The word was passed along the gundeck and women cursed their misfortune, or shouted abuse at the captain and his crew on the deck above or at God as their mood dictated. The respite was over. All the tribulations of making passage in this hell-ship were about to begin again. They felt the altered motion of the hull as the anchor flukes broke out of the mud bottom, and the ship came alive to begin her struggle with the raging elements.

A dark, bitter anger swept over Louisa. Salvation had seemed so close. She crept to the chink in the port-lid. The light was too poor and the spray and rain were too thick to allow her more than a dim glimpse of the distant land. 'It is still close,' she told herself. 'By God's grace, I might reach it.' But in her heart she knew that across those miles of storm-driven sea the shore was far beyond her reach. Even if she managed to shed her leg irons, climb out through the gunport and leap overboard, there was no chance of her surviving more than a few minutes before she was driven under. She knew that Jim Courtney could not be there to rescue her.

'Better to go quickly by drowning,' she told herself, 'than to rot away in this lice-infested hell.' Frenziedly she sawed at the last sliver of steel that held the chain link closed. Around her the other prisoners were screaming and howling as they were thrown about mercilessly. Close-hauled against the gale the ship pitched and rolled wildly. Louisa forced herself not to look up from her work. Just a few strokes more of the file, the link parted and her chains fell to the deck. Louisa wasted only a minute to massage her swollen, galled ankles. Then she crawled back under the cannon and took out the horn-handled knife from where she had hidden it. 'Nobody must try to stop me,' she whispered grimly. She crawled back to the gunport, and prised loose the shackle of the lock. Then she tucked the knife into the pouch under her skirt. She wedged her back against the gun carriage and tried to force open the port-lid. The ship was on the starboard tack, and the heel of the deck was against her. With all her strength behind it she could push the heavy port-lid open only a few inches, and when she achieved this a solid jet of salt water spurted through the crack. She had to let it slam closed again.

'Help me! Help me get the port-lid open,' she called desperately to her three allies among the prisoners. They stared back at her with dull, bovine expressions. They would rouse themselves to help her only if their own survival depended on it. Between waves Louisa stole another quick glance through the chink of the port-lid, and saw the dark shape of the island not far ahead.

We will be forced to tack now, she thought, or we will be driven aground. Over the months aboard she had picked up a working knowledge and understanding of the ship's navigation and handling. On the other tack, I will have the heel of the hull to help me get it open. She crouched ready, and at last felt the bows coming up into the wind, the motion of the hull changing under her. Even above the keening of the wind she heard, from the deck above, the faint bellowing of orders and the running of frantic feet. She braced herself for the heel of the deck on to the opposite tack. But it did not happen, and the ship rolled with a heavy, slack motion, dead in the water.

One of the other prisoners, whose putative husband had been a boatswain on a VOC Indiaman shouted, with rising panic, 'Stupid pig of a captain has missed stays. Sweet Jesus, we're in irons!' Louisa knew what that meant. Head to the wind, the ship had lost her way through the water and now she could not pay off on the other tack. She was pinned down helplessly before the storm.

'Listen!' the woman screamed. Then, above the din of the storm, they all heard it coming. 'Squall! She's going to lay us over!' They crouched helplessly in their chains, and listened to it grow louder. The shriek of the approaching squall deafened them, and when it seemed that it could not rise higher, it struck the ship. She reeled and staggered and went over like a bull elephant shot through the heart. They were stunned by the crackling uproar of breaking rigging, then the cannon shot of the mainstay parting under the strain. The hull went on over, until the gundeck was vertical, and tackle, gear and human beings slid down the slope until they piled up against the hull. Loose iron cannon-balls slammed into the piles of struggling prisoners. Women were shrieking with pain and terror. One of the iron balls came rolling down the slanting deck towards where Louisa clung to her gun carriage. At the last moment she threw herself aside, and the cannon-ball hit the woman who crouched beside her. Louisa heard the bones in both her legs shatter. The woman sat and stared at the tangle of her own limbs with an expression of astonishment.

One of the great guns, nine tons of cast bronze, broke out of its tackle and came hurtling down the deck. It crushed the struggling women who lay in its path as though they were rabbits under the wheels of a chariot. Then it struck the hull. Even the massive oaken planking could not check its charge. It burst through and was gone. The sea poured through the splintered opening, and swamped the gundeck under an icy green wave. Louisa held her breath and clung to the gun carriage as she was engulfed. Then she felt the hull begin to right itself as the squall raced past and relinquished its grip on the ship. The water poured out through the gaping hole in the side of the hull, and sucked out a struggling, screaming knot of women. As they dropped into the sea their chains dragged them under instantly.

Still clinging to her gun carriage Louisa could look out of the gaping wound in the ship's side as though it were an open doorway. She saw the broken mast, the tangled ropes and canvas hanging down into the churning water from the deck above. She saw the bobbing heads of the seamen who had been swept over the side with the wreckage. Then, beyond it, she saw the shore of Africa, and the high surf bursting upon its beaches like volleys of cannonfire. The crippled ship was drifting down upon it, driven on by the gale. She watched the inexorable progress, terror mingled with burgeoning hope. With every second that passed the shore was drawing closer, and the runaway cannon had smashed open an escape hatch for her. Even through the driving rain and spray she could make out features on the shore, trees bending and dancing in the wind, a scattering of whitewashed buildings set back from the beach.

Closer and closer the stricken ship drifted in, and now she could make out tiny human figures. They were coming from the town, scurrying along the edge of the beach, some waving their arms, but if they were shouting their voices could not carry against that terrible wind. Now the ship was close enough for Louisa to tell the difference between man, woman and child in the gathering throng of spectators.

It took an immense effort for her to force herself to leave her place of safety behind the gun carriage, but she began to crawl along the heaving deck, over the shattered human bodies and sodden equipment. Cannon-balls still rolled aimlessly back and forth, heavy enough to crush her bones and she dodged those that trundled towards her. She reached the hole in the hull. It was wide enough for a horse to gallop through. She clung to the splintered planks, and peered through the spray and the breaking surf at the beach. Her father had taught her to tread water and to swim in a dog-paddle in the lake at Mooi Uitsig. With his encouragement, as he swam beside her, she had once succeeded in crossing from one side of the lake to the other. This was different. She knew she could keep afloat only for a few seconds in this maelstrom of crazed surf.

The shore was so close now that she could make out the expressions of the spectators who waited for the ship to strike. Some were laughing with excitement, two or three children were dancing and waving their arms above their heads. None showed any compassion or pity for the death struggle of a great ship and the mortal predicament of those aboard her. For them this was a Roman circus, with the prospect of profit from salvaging the wreckage as it washed ashore.

From the direction of the castle she saw a file of soldiers come down the beach at a dog-trot. A mounted officer in a fine uniform was leading them – she could see his insignia glinting on his green and yellow jacket even in this dull light. She knew that, even if she succeeded in reaching the shore, the soldiers would be waiting for her.

There was a fresh chorus of screams and heart-stopping cries from the women around her as they felt the vessel touch the bottom. The ship tore herself free and drifted on, only to touch again, the impact shivering the timbers of the hull. This time she stuck fast, pinned down on the sands, and the waves charged at her like rank after rank of a monstrous cavalry. The ship could not yield to their assault, and each wave struck with a malicious boom and a high white fountain of foam. Slowly the hull rolled over, and her starboard side came uppermost. Louisa scrambled out through the jagged opening. She stood upright on the high side of the heavily canted hull. The wind flung out her long yellow hair in a tangle, and flattened the threadbare canvas shift against her thin body. The wet cloth emphasized the thrust of her breasts, which were full and round.

She gazed towards the beach, saw the heads of the sailors

who had abandoned the ship bobbing in the wild waters. One reached the shallows and stood up only to be knocked flat by the next wave. Through the hole in the hull three other convicts followed her out, but as they clung to the planking their leg irons slowed their movements. Another wave swept the hull and Louisa grabbed one of the shrouds from the mainmast, which dangled close by. The waters swirled round her waist but she clung on. When the wave receded all three of the other women were gone, drawn instantly under the green water by their chains.

Using the shroud Louisa pulled herself to her feet again. The spectators were galvanized by the sight of her, seemingly rising like Aphrodite from the waves. She was so young and lovely, and in such mortal danger. This was better than any flogging or execution on the parade-ground of the castle. They danced and waved and shouted. Their voices were faint but in the lull in the wind she could make out their cries.

'Jump, Meisje.'

'Swim, let's see you swim!'

'Better than a gaol cell, Poesje?'

She could see the sadistic excitement on their faces, and hear the cruelty in their voices. She knew that there was no promise of help to be had from them. She raised her face to the sky and, at that moment, a movement caught her eye.

A horse and rider had appeared on the crest of the dune overlooking the stricken ship. The horse was a magnificent bay stallion. The rider sat astride the bare back. He had stripped off all his clothing except a breech clout knotted round his waist. His torso was pale as porcelain, but his strong young arms were tanned by the sun to the colour of fine leather and his dense dark curls danced in the wind. He gazed back at her across the beach and the booming surf, and suddenly he raised his arm above his head and waved at her. Then she recognized him.

Wildly she waved back, and screamed his name. 'Jim! Jim Courtney!'

94

With mounting horror Jim had watched the final moment of *Het Gelukkige Meeuw*'s agony. A few of the crew still huddled on the capsized hull, then some of the female convicts were creeping out of the open gunports and shattered hatches. The crowds on the beach taunted them as they clustered on the wave-swept hull. When a woman was washed overboard, and her chains pulled her under, there was an ironic chorus of laughter and cheers from the spectators. Then the ship's keel struck the sand and the impact hurled most of the convicts over the side.

As the ship was rolled and pummelled on to the beach by the waves, the crew leaped from the heavily listing deck into the sea. The water overpowered most of them. One or two drowned bodies were washed up on the beach and the spectators dragged them up above the high-water mark. As soon as it was evident there was no life in them they threw them into an untidy pile, and ran back to join the sport. The first of the survivors waded out through the surf and fell to his knees in prayerful gratitude for his escape. Three convict women were thrown ashore, clinging to a spar from the shattered rigging; it had supported them despite the weight of their chains. The soldiers from the castle rushed waist deep into the creaming surf to drag them out on to the beach and arrest them. Jim saw that one was an obese creature with flaxen hair. White breasts the size of a pair of Zeelander cheeses bulged out of her torn shift. Struggling with her captors she screamed an obscenity at Colonel Keyser as he rode up. Keyser leaned out of the saddle, lifted his sheathed sword and struck her a blow with the scabbard that knocked her to her knees. But she was still shrieking as she looked up at him. There was a livid purple scar down her fat cheek.

The next blow with the steel scabbard dropped her face down into the sand, and the soldiers dragged her away.

Desperately Jim searched the open deck for a glimpse of Louisa, but he could not find her. The hull dragged itself free of the sand and began once more to drift closer. Then she struck again solidly, and began to roll over. The surviving women slid down the listing deck, and one after another dropped over the side and splashed into the green water. The ship now lay on her side. There were no living souls clinging to the wreck. For the first time Jim saw the gaping hole through which the loose cannon had burst out. This opening was pointed to the sky, and suddenly a slim feminine form crawled out of it, and came to her feet shakily on the rounded hull. Her long yellow hair was streaming with seawater, and flapped heavily in the gale. Her tattered shift barely covered her coltish limbs. She might have been a boy, were it not for the full bosom under the rags. She gazed imploringly towards the crowds on the beach, who jeered and mocked her.

'Jump, gallows-bait,' they hooted.

'Swim. Swim for us, little fish.'

Jim focused the telescope on her face, and it did not need the sapphire flash of blue from the eyes in her gaunt and pale face for him to recognize her. He sprang to his feet and ran down the back slope of the dune to where Drumfire stood patiently. He lifted his head and whinnied when he saw Jim coming. As he ran Jim stripped off his clothing and left it strewn behind him. Hopping first on one leg and then the other he pulled off his boots, until he wore only his cotton breech clout. He reached the stallion's side, undid the girth and let the saddle drop into the sand. Then he swung himself on to Drumfire's bare back, urged him up the slope and halted him on the crest.

He looked out with dread that he might find that the girl had been washed off the wallowing hull. His spirits surged when he saw that Louisa was still perched there, as he had last seen her, but the ship was breaking up under the brutal hammer blows of the surf. He lifted his right arm high and waved at her. Her head jerked as she looked towards him, and he saw the moment that she recognized him. She waved back at him wildly, and although the wind smothered the sound she mouthed his name: 'Jim! Jim Courtney!'

'Ha! Ha!' he called to Drumfire, and the stallion leaped

forward down the slope of loose white sand, going back on his haunches to balance as they slid down the dune. They hit the beach at a gallop, and the crowd of onlookers scattered in front of Drumfire's flying hoofs. Keyser spurred his horse forward as if to intercept them. His plump, clean-shaven face was stern and the ostrich feathers in his hat were blowing like the white surf. Jim touched Drumfire's flank with his toe and the stallion swerved past the other horse and they raced down towards the sea.

A broken wave came tumbling to meet them, but its main force was spent. Without hesitation Drumfire gathered his forefeet under his chest and leapt over the leading edge of white water as though he were jumping a fence. When he splashed in on the other side, it was already too deep for his hoofs to find the bottom. He began to swim, and Jim slid off his back and wove his fingers into the horse's mane. With his free hand on the stallion's neck he guided him towards the wallowing wreck.

Drumfire swam like an otter, his legs pumping in a mighty rhythm beneath the surface. He had gone twenty yards before the next tall wave struck, and burst over them, submerging them.

The girl on the wreck stared in horrified fascination, and even the watchers on the beach were silenced as they searched for a sign of them in the swirling aftermath of the wave's passage. Then a shout went up as their heads appeared through the foam. They had been washed back half the distance gained, but the stallion was swimming strongly – and the girl could hear him snorting the seawater from his nostrils with each breath. Jim's long black hair was sleeked down his face and shoulders. She could hear his cries faint in the thunder of waters: 'Come, Drumfire. Ha! Ha!'

They swam on through the icy green seas, swiftly making up the distance lost. Another wave came in but they swam up and over the crest, and now they were almost half-way across the gap between shore and ship. The girl stood up and balanced precariously on the heaving hull, gathering herself for the leap over the side.

'No!' Jim yelled up at her. 'Not yet! Wait!' He had seen the next wave humping up against the horizon. This one dwarfed all those that had come before it. Its cliff-like face seemed to be carved from solid green malachite, laced with white spume. As it came on in ponderous majesty it blocked out half of the sky.

'Hold hard, Louisa!' Jim shouted, as the mighty wave crashed into the ship, and smothered her. It left her submerged in its wake. Then it gathered itself again like a predator pouncing on its prey. For long seconds horse and rider swam up its curling front. They were a pair of insects trapped on a wall of green glass. Then the face of the wave toppled forward, curling over them and falling in a solid avalanche as it crashed down on itself with such weight and power that the men on the beach felt the earth jump beneath their feet. Horse and rider were gone, driven so deeply under that surely they could never surface again.

The watchers who, only seconds before, had clamoured to see the storm prevail and its victims perish, now stood smitten with dread, waiting for the impossible to happen, for the heads of that gallant horse and his rider to reappear through the wild surf. Then the water subsided around the ship and as it poured away they saw the girl still lying on the hull, the loose ropes of the rigging holding her from being sucked over the side. She lifted her head and, with the water streaming from her long hair, searched desperately for any sign of horse and man. The seconds drew on and became minutes. Another wave crashed in, then another, but they were not as high and powerful as the one that had buried horse and rider.

Louisa felt despair settle on her. It was not for herself that she feared. She knew she was about to die, but her own life did not seem to matter any more. Instead she grieved for the young stranger who had given his own trying to save her. 'Jim!' she pleaded. 'Please don't die.'

As if in response to her call, the two heads burst out

through the surface. The undertow of the great wave that had pinned them under had also sucked them back almost to where they had disappeared.

'Jim!' she screamed, and leaped to her feet. He was so close that she could see the agony that contorted his face in the effort to draw breath, but he looked up at her, and tried to say something. Perhaps it was a farewell, but then she knew in her heart that this was not a man who would ever surrender, not even to death. He was trying to shout a command, but his breath only whistled and gurgled in his throat. The horse was swimming again, but when it tried to turn its head back towards the beach she saw Jim's hand in its mane guide it back towards her. Jim was still choking and could not use his voice, but he made a gesture with his free hand, and now he was close enough for her to see the determination in his eyes.

'Jump?' she shouted, against the wind. 'Shall I jump?'

He nodded his sodden curls emphatically, and she could just make out the hoarse croak of his voice: 'Come!'

She glanced over her shoulder and saw that, even in his distress, he had picked the slack between the waves to call her on. She threw aside the piece of rope that had saved her, took three running strides across the shattered deck and leaped over the side with her shift ballooning round her waist and her arms windmilling. She hit the water and went under, to reappear almost immediately. She struck out the way her father had taught her and swam to meet them.

Jim reached out and seized her wrist. His grip was so powerful that she thought it might crush her bones. And after what she had suffered at Huis Brabant she had thought that she would never allow a man to touch her again. But there was no time to think of that now. The next wave broke over her head, but his grip never slackened. They came up again and she was spluttering and gasping for breath, yet she seemed to feel strength flowing into her through his fingers. He guided her hand to the horse's mane, and now he had recovered some of his voice.

'Don't hamper him.' She understood what he meant for she knew horses, and she tried not to put her weight on the stallion's back but to swim beside him. Now they were heading towards the beach and each wave that came up behind them carried them forward. Louisa heard voices, faint at first but growing louder every second. The spectators on the beach were caught up in the excitement of the rescue and, fickle as any mob, they were cheering them on. They all knew this horse – most of them had seen him win on Christmas Day. Jim Courtney was a well-known figure in the town: some envied him as the son of a rich man, some thought him too brash, but they all were forced to pay him respect. This was a famous battle he was waging against the sea, and most of them were sailors. Their hearts went out to him.

'Courage, Jim!'

'Power to you, lad.'

'Good on you! Swim, Jim boy, swim.'

Drumfire had felt the shore shelving under his hoofs, and lunged forward powerfully. By now Jim had recovered his breath and coughed most of the water out of his lungs. He threw one leg over the stallion's back. As soon as he was astride he reached down and pulled Louisa up behind him. She wrapped both arms round his waist and hung on with all her strength. Drumfire burst out of the shallows, water exploding before his charge, and then they were out on the beach.

Jim saw Colonel Keyser galloping to intercept them, and urged Drumfire into full stride, swinging his head away until Keyser was trailng twenty strides behind.

'*Wag, jou donder*! Wait! She's an escaped prisoner. Hand the cow over to the law.'

'I will deliver her to the castle myself,' Jim yelled, without looking back.

'No, you don't! She's mine. Bring the bitch back!' Keyser's voice was thick with fury. As Jim urged Drumfire on down the beach he was determined on one thing only. He had already chanced too much ever to turn this girl over to anyone in the garrison, and in particular to Keyser. He had watched too many of the floggings and executions on the parade-ground outside the castle walls over which Keyser had presided. Jim's own great-grandfather had been tortured and executed on that very ground after being falsely convicted of piracy on the high seas.

'They aren't going to get this one,' he swore grimly. Her thin arms were clasped round his waist and he could feel the length of her body pressed against his naked back. Although she was half starved, wet and shivering with the cold of the green waters and the wind of Drumfire's speed, he could sense the courage and determination in her, which matched his own.

She's a fighter, this one. I can never let her down, he thought, and called back to her, 'Hold tight, Louisa. We're going to run the fat colonel into the dirt.' Though she did not answer and he could hear her teeth chattering, she tightened her grip round him and crouched low. He could feel by her balance and the way she adjusted to Drumfire's motion that she was a horsewoman.

He glanced back under his arm, and saw that they had opened the gap on Keyser. Jim had raced against Trouwhart before and he knew the mare's best points and her weaknesses. She was quick and game as her name, Trueheart, suggested, but Keyser overburdened her light frame. On firm, smooth going she was in her element and she probably had the legs of Drumfire out in the open, but on this soft beach sand or over rock and other heavy going, Drumfire's great strength gave him the advantage. Although the stallion was carrying a double load, Louisa was light as a sparrow and Jim was not as heavily built as the colonel. Yet Jim knew better than to underestimate the mare. He knew she had the heart of a lioness and had almost run Drumfire down over the last half-mile of the Christmas racing.

I must pick the course to our advantage, he decided. He had ridden every inch of the ground between here and the foothills, and knew every hill and marsh, salt pan and patch of forest where Trueheart would be at a disadvantage.

'Stop, *jongen*, or I will shoot.' There was another shout

behind and when Jim looked back, Keyser had drawn the pistol from the holster on the front of his saddle and was leaning out to avoid hitting his own horse. In that swift glance Jim saw that it was a single-barrelled weapon, and there was not a second in the holster. Jim swerved Drumfire to the left without a break in his stride, cutting sharply across the mare's nose. In an instant he had changed Keyser's target from a steady going-away shot to one with a sharp angle of deflection. Even an experienced soldier like the colonel, shooting from a galloping horse, would have difficulty judging the forward allowance.

Jim reached back, seized Louisa round the waist and swung her round on his off-side, tucking her under his armpit and shielding her with his own body. The pistol shot boomed out, and he felt the strike of the heavy ball. It was high in his back across his shoulders, but after the numbing shock his arms were still strong and his senses alert. He knew he was not badly wounded.

Only pricked me, he thought, and then he spoke: 'That's his one and only shot.' He said it to encourage Louisa, and swung her back into her place behind him.

'Mercy! You're hit,' she exclaimed fearfully. Blood was streaming down his back.

'We'll worry about that later,' he sang out. 'Now Drumfire and I are going to show you a few of our tricks.' He was enjoying himself. He had just been half drowned and shot, but he was still cocky. Louisa had found herself an indomitable champion, and her spirits soared.

But they had lost ground with that evasive turn, and close behind they heard Trueheart's hoofs slapping into the sand, and the scraping of steel in the scabbard as Keyser drew his sabre. Louisa glanced back and saw him rise up over her, standing in the stirrups with his blade held high, but the change of his balance wrong-footed the mare and she stumbled. Keyser swayed and grabbed at the pommel of his saddle to regain balance and Drumfire pulled ahead. Jim put him at the slope of the high dune, and here the stallion's great strength came into play. He went up in a series of violent lunges with the sand spurting out from under his hoofs. Trueheart dropped back sharply as she carried the colonel's weight up the slope.

They went over the top and slid down the far side. From the foot of the dune there was open ground and firm going to the edge of the lagoon. Louisa looked back. 'They're gaining again,' she warned Jim. Trueheart was striding out gracefully. Even though she was carrying the weight of the colonel, and all his weapons and accoutrements, she seemed to flirt with the earth.

'He's reloading his pistol.' There was an edge of alarm in her voice. Keyser was ramming a ball into the muzzle.

'Let's see if we can wet his powder for him,' Jim said, and they reached the edge of the lagoon and plunged in without a check.

'Swim again,' Jim ordered, and Louisa slipped into the water on Drumfire's other flank. They both looked back as Trueheart reached the edge of the lagoon and Keyser pulled her up. He jumped down and primed the pan of his pistol. Then he cocked the hammer, and aimed at them across the open water. There was a puff of white gunsmoke. A fountain of water jumped from the surface an arm's length behind them and, with a hum, the heavy ball ricocheted over their heads.

'Now throw your boots at us.' Jim laughed, and Keyser stamped with rage. Jim hoped that he would give up now. Surely, even in his anger, he must consider the fact that Trueheart was so heavily burdened, while they were almost naked and Drumfire's back was bare. Keyser made the decision, and swung up on to the mare's back. He pushed her into the water, just as Drumfire emerged on to the muddy bank on the far side. Immediately Jim turned him parallel to the shore and, keeping to the soft ground, led him along the shore at a trot.

'We must give Drumfire a chance to breathe,' he told Louisa as she ran behind him. 'That swim out to the ship would have drowned any other horse.' He was watching their pursuers. Trueheart was only half-way across the lagoon. 'Keyser wasted time with his pistol practice. One thing is certain, there will be no more of that. His powder is well and truly soaked by now.'

'The water washed the blood from your wound,' she told him, reaching out to touch his back lightly. 'I can see now it's a graze, not deep, thank the good Lord.'

'It's you we have to worry about,' he said. 'You're skin and bones, not a pound of meat on you. How long can you run on those skinny legs?'

'As long as you can,' she flared at him, and angry red spots appeared on her pale cheeks.

He grinned at her unrepentantly. 'You may have to prove that boast before this day is done. Keyser is across.'

Far behind them Trueheart came out on to the bank and, streaming water from his tunic, breeches and boots, Keyser mounted her and set out along the bank after them. He urged the mare into a gallop, but heavy clods of mud flew from her hoofs and it was immediately obvious that she was making heavy work of it. Jim had kept to the mud flats for just that reason, to test Trueheart's strength.

'Up you get.' Jim seized Louisa, threw her up on to the stallion's back and broke into a run. He kept a firm grip on Drumfire's mane so he was pulled along, keeping pace with horse's easy canter while saving the animal's strength. He kept glancing back to judge their relative speeds. He could afford to let Keyser gain a little ground now. Carrying only Louisa's weight Drumfire was going easily, while the mare was burning up her strength in this reckless pursuit.

Within half a mile Keyser's weight began to tell, and Trueheart slowed to a walk. She was still trailing by a half pistol-shot. Jim slowed to her speed to keep the gap constant.

'Come down, if you please, your ladyship,' he told Louisa. 'Give Drumfire another breather.'

She jumped down lightly, but flashed at him, 'Don't call me that.' It was a bitter reminder of the taunts she had endured from her fellow convicts.

'Perhaps we should rather call you Hedgehog?' he asked. 'The Lord knows, you have prickles enough to warrant it.'

Keyser must be almost exhausted by now, Jim thought, for he stayed in the saddle, not taking his weight off his mount. 'They are almost done in,' he told Louisa. He knew that not far ahead and still on the Courtney estate lay a salt pan that they called Groot Wit – Big White. That was where he was leading Keyser.

'He's coming on again,' Louisa warned him, and he saw that Keyser was pushing the mare into a canter. She was a game little filly, and she was responding to the whip.

'Mount!' he ordered.

'I can run as far as you can.' She shook the salt-crusted tangle of her long hair at him defiantly.

'In Jesus's name, woman, must you always argue?'

'Must you always blaspheme?' she riposted, but she allowed him to hoist her on to the stallion's back. They ran on. Within the mile Trueheart had slowed to a walk, and they could do the same.

'There is the beginning of the salt.' Jim pointed ahead and even under the low stormclouds and in the gathering dusk, it shone like a vast mirror.

'It looks flat and hard.' She shaded her eyes against the glare.

'It looks that way, but under the crust it's porridge. With that great fat Dutchman and all his equipment upon her back the mare will break through every few paces. It's almost three miles across the pan. They will be completely finished before they reach the other side and . . .' he looked at the sky '. . . by then it will be dark.'

Although it was hidden by the lowering blanket of cloud the sun must have been close to the horizon and the darkness was coming on apace as Jim led Drumfire, the girl staggering beside him, off the treacherous white plain. He paused at the edge of the forest, and they both looked back.

Like a long string of black pearls Drumfire's hoofprints were deeply scored into the smooth white surface. Even for him the crossing had been a terrible ordeal. Far behind they could just make out the small dark shape of the mare. Two hours earlier, with Keyser on her back, Trueheart had broken through the salt crust and into the quicksand beneath. Jim had stopped and watched Keyser struggle to free her. He had been tempted to turn back and help them. She was such a game, beautiful animal that he could not bear to watch her bogged down and exhausted. Then he remembered that he was unarmed and almost naked, while Keyser had his sabre and was a swordsman to be reckoned with. Jim had watched him leading his cavalry troop through their evolutions on the parade-ground outside the castle. While he hesitated Keyser had managed, by force, to drag the mare free of the mud and continue plodding in pursuit.

Now he was still following and Jim frowned. 'If there were ever a time to meet Keyser it would be when he comes off the salt. He will be exhausted and in the dark I would have the benefit of surprise. But he has his sabre and I have nothing,' he murmured. Louisa looked at him for a moment, then turned her back to him modestly, and reached under the skirt of her shift. She found the horn-handled clasp knife in the pouch she wore strapped round her waist and handed it to him without a word. He stared at it in astonishment, then burst out laughing as he recognized it.

'I withdraw everything I said about you. You look like a Viking maid and, by Jesus, you act like one too.'

'Watch your blaspheming tongue, Jim Courtney,' she said, but there was no fire in the rebuke. She was too tired to argue further, and the compliment had been a pretty one. As she turned away her head there was a weary half smile on her lips. Jim led Drumfire into the trees, and she followed them. After a few hundred paces, in a spot where the forest was thickest, he tethered the stallion and told Louisa, 'Now you can rest a while.'

This time she did not protest but sank down on the thick leaf mould on the forest floor, curled up, closed her eyes. In her weakened state she felt that she might never have the strength to stand up again. Hardly had the thought flashed through her mind than she was asleep.

Jim wasted a few moments admiring her suddenly serene

features. Until then he had not realized how young she was. Now she looked like a sleeping child. While he watched her he opened the blade of the knife and tested the point on the ball of his thumb. At last he tore himself away, and ran back to the edge of the forest. Keeping well hidden he peered out across the darkening salt pan. Keyser was still coming on doggedly, leading the mare.

Will he never give up? Jim wondered, and felt a twinge of admiration for him. Then he looked around for the best place to hide beside the tracks that Drumfire had left. He picked a patch of dense bush, crept into it and squatted there with the knife in his hand.

Keyser reached the edge of the pan, and staggered out on to the firm footing. By this time it was so dark that, although Jim could hear him panting for breath, he was just a dark shape. He came on slowly, leading the mare, and Jim let him pass his hiding-place. Then he slipped out of the bush and crept up behind him. Any sound he might have made was covered by the hoof-falls of the mare. From behind he locked his left arm around Keyser's throat and, at the same time, pressed the point of the knife into the soft skin under his ear. 'I will kill you if you force me to it,' he snarled, making his tone ferocious.

Keyser froze with shock. Then he regained his own voice. 'You can't hope to get away with this, Courtney. There is no place for you to run. Give me the woman, and I will settle things with your father and Governor van de Witten.'

Jim reached down and drew the sabre from the scabbard on the colonel's belt. Then he released his lock around the man's throat and stepped back, but he held the point of the sabre to Keyser's chest. 'Take off your clothes,' he ordered.

'You are young and stupid, Courtney,' Keyser replied coldly. 'I will try to make allowances for that.'

'Tunic first,' Jim ordered. 'Then breeches and boots.'

Keyser did not move. Jim pricked his chest, and at last, reluctantly, the colonel reached up and began to unbutton his tunic.

'What do you hope to achieve?' he asked, as he shrugged out of it. 'Is this some boyish notion of chivalry? The woman is a convicted felon. She is probably a whore and a murderess.'

'Say that again, Colonel, and I will spit you like a sucking pig.' This time Jim drew blood with the point. Keyser sat down to pull off his boots and his breeches. Jim stuffed them into Trueheart's saddlebags. Then, with the point of the sabre at the man's back, he escorted Keyser, barefoot and wearing only his undershirt, to the edge of the salt pan.

'Follow your own tracks, Colonel,' he told him, 'and you should be back at the castle in time for breakfast.'

'Listen to me, *jongen*,' Keyser said, in a thin tight voice. 'I will come after you. I will see you hanged on the parade, and I promise you it will be slow – very slow.'

'If you stand here talking, Colonel, you're going to miss your breakfast.' Jim smiled at him. 'You had far better start walking.'

He watched Keyser trudge away across the salt pan. Suddenly the heavy clouds were stripped away by the wind and the full moon burst through to light the pale surface as though it were day. It was bright enough to throw a shadow at Keyser's feet. Jim watched him until he was only a dark blob in the distance, and knew that he was not coming back. Not tonight, at least. But it's not the last we've seen of the gallant colonel, he thought, we can be sure of that. Then he ran back to Trueheart, and led her into the forest. He shook Louisa awake. 'Wake up, Hedgehog. We have a long journey ahead of us,' he told her. 'And by this time tomorrow we are going to have Keyser and a squadron of cavalry in full cry after us.'

When she sat up groggily he went to Trueheart. A rolled woollen cavalry cloak was strapped on top of Keyser's saddlebags.

'It will be cold when we get into the mountains,' he warned her. She was still half asleep and did not protest as he wrapped the cloak round her shoulders. Then he found the colonel's food bag. It held a loaf of bread, a wedge of cheese, a few apples and a flask of wine. 'The colonel dearly loves his food.' He tossed her an apple and she wolfed it down core and all.

'Sweeter than honey,' she said, through a mouthful. 'I never tasted anything like it before.'

'Greedy little Hedgehog,' he teased her and this time she gave him an urchin smile. Most people found it hard to be angry with Jim for long. He squatted on his haunches in front of her and, with the clasp knife, cut a hunk of bread and slapped a thick slice of cheese on top of it. She ate with ferocious intensity. He watched her pale face in the moonlight. She looked like a pixie.

'And you?' she asked. 'Aren't you eating?' He shook his head. He had decided that there would not be enough for both of them: this girl was starving.

'How did you learn to speak such good English?'

'My mother came from Devon.'

'My oath! That's where we're from. My great-great-grand-father was a duke, or something of that ilk.'

'So, shall I call you Duke?'

'That will do until I think of something better, Hedgehog.' She took another bite of bread and cheese so she could not reply. While she ate he sorted through the rest of Keyser's possessions. He tried on the gold-frogged tunic, and held the lapels together.

'Space for two of us in here, but it's warm.' The front flaps of the colonel's breeches went half-way again round Jim's middle but he belted them with one of the straps from the saddlebags. Then he tried the boots. 'At least these are a good fit.'

'In London I saw a play called *The Tin Soldier*,' she said. 'That's who you look like now.'

'You were in London?' Despite himself he was impressed. London was the centre of the world. 'You must tell me about it as soon as we have an opportunity.'

Then he led the horses to the well on the edge of the pan where the cattle were watered. He and Mansur had dug it themselves two years ago. The water in it was sweet, and the horses drank thirstily. When he led them back he found Louisa had fallen asleep again under the cloak. He squatted beside her and studied her face in the moonlight, and there was a strange hollow feeling under his ribs. He left her to sleep a little longer and went to feed the horses from the colonel's grain bag.

Then he selected what he needed from Keyser's equipment. The pistol was a lovely weapon, and tucked into the leather holster was a small canvas roll that contained the ramrod and all the accessories. The sabre was of the finest steel. In the tunic he found a gold watch and a purse filled with silver guilders and a few gold ducats. In the back pocket there was a small brass box that contained a flint and steel, and cotton kindling.

'If I steal his horse I might as well take the money too,' he told himself. However, he drew the line at filching Keyser's more personal possessions, so he placed the gold watch and the medals in one of the saddlebags, and left it lying conspicuously in the centre of the clearing. He knew that Keyser would return here tomorrow with his Bushman trackers, and would find his personal treasures. 'I wonder how grateful he will be for my generosity?' He smiled bleakly. He was carried along by a sense of reckless inevitability. He knew that there was no turning back. He was committed. He went to resaddle Trueheart, then squatted beside Louisa. She was curled into a ball under the cloak. He stroked her hair to wake her gently.

She opened her eyes and looked up at him. 'Don't touch me like that,' she whispered. 'Don't ever touch me like that again.'

Her voice was filled with such bitter loathing that he recoiled. Years ago Jim had captured a wild-cat kitten. Despite all his loving patience he had never been able to tame the creature. It snarled and bit and scratched. In the end he had taken it out into the veld and set it free. Perhaps this girl was like that. 'I had to wake you,' he said. 'We must go on.' She stood up immediately.

'Take the mare,' he said. 'She has a soft mouth and a gentle nature, yet she is fast as the wind. Her name is Trueheart.' He boosted her into the saddle, and she took the reins and wrapped the cloak tightly around her shoulders. He handed her the last of the bread and cheese. 'You can eat as we go.'

110

She ate as though she were still famished, and he wondered what terrible privations she had been forced to endure that had turned her into this starved, abused wild creature. He felt a fleeting doubt at his own ability to help or redeem her. He thrust it aside and smiled at her in what he imagined was a placatory way, but which to her seemed merely supercilious. 'When we get to Majuba, Zama will have the hunter's pot going. I hope he has filled it to the brim. I would place money on you in an eating contest with the good colonel.' He sprang up on Drumfire's back. 'First, though, we have something else to do here.'

He set off at a trot in the direction of High Weald, but he circled well clear of the homestead. By now it was after midnight, but still he did not want to chance running into his father or Uncle Dorian. The news of his escapade would have reached their ears almost as soon as he had plucked the girl out of the sea. He had seen many of the family freed slaves and servants among the spectators on the beach. He could not face his father now. We will get no sympathy there, he thought. He will try to force me to turn Louisa over to the colonel. He rode instead to a cluster of huts at the east side of the paddock. He dismounted in a stand of trees and handed Drumfire's reins to Louisa. 'Stay here. I won't be long.'

He approached the largest mud-walled hut in the village carefully and whistled. There was a long pause, then a lantern flared behind the uncured sheepskin that covered the single window in place of a curtain. The reeking fleece was drawn aside, and a dark head poked out suspiciously. 'Who's there?'

'Bakkat, it's me.'

'Somoya!' He came out into the moonlight with a greasy blanket tucked around his waist. He was as tiny as a child, his skin amber in the moonlight. His features were flattened and his eyes had a curious Asiatic slant. He was a Bushman, and he could track a lost beast for fifty leagues over desert and mountain, through blizzard and storm. He smiled up at Jim, and his eyes were almost hidden in a web of wrinkles. 'May the Kulu Kulu smile upon you, Somoya.'

'And on you also, old friend. Call out all the other

shepherds. Gather up the herds and drive them over every road. Especially all the paths heading towards the east and north. I want them to chop up the ground until it looks like a ploughed field. Nobody must be able to follow my tracks when I leave here, not even you. Do you understand?'

Bakkat cackled with laughter. 'Oh, *ja*, Somoya! I understand very well. We all saw the fat soldier chasing you when you ran off with that pretty little girl. Don't worry! By morning there won't be a single one of your tracks left for him to follow.'

'Good fellow!' Jim clapped him on the back. 'I am off.'

'I know where you are going. You are taking the Robbers' Road?' The Robbers' Road was the legendary escape route out of the colony, travelled only by fugitives and outlaws. 'Nobody knows where it leads, because nobody ever comes back. The spirits of my ancestors whisper to me in the night, and my soul pines for the wild places. Do you have a place for me at your side?'

Jim laughed. 'Follow and be welcome, Bakkat. I know that you'll be able to find me wherever I go. You could follow the tracks of a ghost over the burning rocks of hell. But, first, do what you must do here. Tell my father I am well. Tell my mother I love her,' he said, and ran back to where Louisa and the horses were still waiting.

They went on. The storm had blown itself out, the wind had dropped, and the moon was low in the west before they reached the foothills. He stopped beside a stream that ran down from the hills. 'We will rest and water the horses,' he told her. He did not offer to help her dismount, but she dropped to the ground as lithely as a cat, and took Trueheart to drink at the pool. She and the mare seemed already to have established an accord. Then she went into the bushes on her own. He wanted to call after her and warn her not to go far, but he held back the words.

The colonel's wine flask was half-empty. Jim smiled as he shook it. Keyser must have been nipping at it since breakfast time yesterday, he thought and went to the pool to dilute what remained with the sweet mountain water. He heard the girl come back through the bushes and, still hidden from him by a pile of tall rocks, go down to the water. There was a splash.

'Damn me if the mad woman is not taking a bath.' He shook his head, and shivered at the thought. There was still snow on the mountains, and the night air was chill. When Louisa returned she sat on one of the rocks at the edge of the pool, not too close to him nor again too far away. Her hair was wet and she combed it out. He recognized the tortoiseshell comb. He went over to her and passed her the wine flask. She paused long enough to drink from it.

'That's good.' She said it like a peace-offering, then went on combing the pale hair that reached almost to her waist. He watched her quietly but she did not look in his direction again.

A fishing owl darted down on the pool on silent wings like a gigantic moth. Hunting only by the last rays of the moon it snatched a small yellowfish from the waters and flew with it to a branch of the dead tree on the far bank. The fish flapped in its talons as the owl tore chunks of meat out of its back.

Louisa looked away. When she spoke again her voice was soft and the faint accent appealing. 'Don't think I'm not grateful for what you have done for me. I know you have risked your life and maybe more than that to help me.'

'Well, you must understand that I keep a menagerie of pets.' He spoke lightly. 'I needed only one more to add to it. A small hedgehog.'

'Perhaps you have the right to call me that,' she said, and sipped from the flask again. 'You know nothing about me. Things have happened to me. Things that you could never understand.'

'I know a little about you. I have seen your courage and your determination. I saw what it was like and how it smelt on board the *Meeuw*. Perhaps I might understand,' he replied. 'At least, I would try.'

He turned to her, then felt his heart break as he saw the

113

tears running down her cheeks, silver in the moonlight. He wanted to rush to her and hold her tightly, but he remembered what she had said: 'Never touch me like that again.'

Instead he said, 'Whether you like it or not, I'm your friend. I want to understand.'

She wiped her cheeks with the palm of one small dainty hand, and sat huddled, thin, pale and disconsolate in the cloak.

'There is just one thing I must know,' Jim said. 'I have a cousin called Mansur. He is closer to me than a brother could be. He said that perhaps you are a murderess. That burns my soul. I must know. Are you? Is that why you were on the *Meeuw*?'

She turned slowly towards him and, with both hands, parted the curtain of her damp hair so that he could see her face. 'My father and mother died of the plague. I dug their graves with my own hands. I swear to you, Jim Courtney, on my love for them and on the graves in which they lie, that I am no murderess.'

He heaved a great sigh of relief. 'I believe you. You don't have to tell me anything else.'

She drank again from the flask, then handed it back to him. 'Don't let me have more. It softens my heart when I need to be strong,' she said. They sat on in silence. He was just about to tell her that they must go on deeper into the mountains when she whispered, so quietly that he was not sure that she had spoken, 'There was a man. A rich and powerful man whom I trusted as once I trusted my dead father. He did things to me that he did not want other people to know about.'

'No, Louisa.' He held up his hand to stop her. 'Don't tell me this.'

'I owe you my life and my freedom. You have a right to know.'

'Please stop.' He wanted to jump to his feet and run into the bushes to escape her words. But he could not move. He was held mesmerized by them, as a mouse by the swaying dance of the cobra.

114

She went on in the same sweet, childlike tones. 'I will not tell you what he did to me. I will never tell anyone that. But I cannot let any man touch me again. When I tried to escape from him, he had his servants hide a packet of jewellery in my room. Then they called the watch to find it. They took me before the magistrate in Amsterdam. My accuser was not even in the court room when I was condemned to be transported for life.' They were both silent for a long time. Then she spoke again. 'Now you know about me, Jim Courtney. Now you know that I am a soiled and discarded plaything. What do you want to do now?'

'I want to kill him,' said Jim at last. 'If ever I meet this man I will kill him.'

'I have spoken honestly to you. Now you must speak honestly to me. Be sure of what you want. I have told you that I will let no man touch me again. I have told you what I am. Do you want to take me back to Good Hope and hand me over to Colonel Keyser? If you do, I am ready to go back with you.'

He did not want her to see his face. Not since he was a child had anyone seen him weep. He jumped to his feet and went to saddle Trueheart. 'Come, Hedgehog. It's a long ride to Majuba. We have no more time to waste in idle chatter.' She came to him obediently and mounted the horse. He led her into the deep defile in the mountains and up the steep gorge. It grew colder as they climbed, and in the dawn, the sun lit the mountain tops with a weird pink light. Patches of old unmelted snow gleamed among the rocks.

It was late in the morning before they paused on the crest at the limit of the treeline and looked down into a hidden valley. There was a tumbledown building among the rocks of the scree slope. She might not have noticed it, were it not for the thin column of smoke rising from the hole in the tattered thatch roof, and the small herd of mules in the stone-walled kraal.

'Majuba,' he told her, as he reined in, 'the Place of the Doves, and that is Zama.' A tall young man dressed in a loincloth had come out into the sunlight and was staring up at them. 'We have been together all our lives. I think you will like him.'

Zama waved and bounded up the slope to meet them. Jim slipped down from Drumfire's back to greet him. 'Have you got the coffee-pot on?' he asked.

Zama looked up at the girl on the horse. They studied each other for a moment. He was tall and well formed, with a broad, strong face, and very white teeth. 'I see you, Miss Louisa,' he said at last.

'I see you also, Zama, but how did you know my name?'

'Somoya told me. How did you know mine?'

'He told me also. He is a great chatterbox, is he not?' she said, and they laughed together. 'But why do you call him Somoya?' she asked.

'It is the name my father gave him. It means the Wild Wind,' Zama replied. 'He blows as he pleases, like the wind.'

'Which way will he blow now?' she asked, but she was looking at Jim with a small, quizzical smile.

'We shall see.' Zama laughed. 'But it will be the way we least expect.'

Colonel Keyser led ten mounted troopers clattering into the courtyard of High Weald. His Bushman tracker ran at his horse's head. Keyser stood in the stirrups and shouted towards the main doors of the godown: 'Mijnheer Tom Courtney! Come out at once!'

From every window and doorway white and black heads appeared, children and freed slaves gawked at him in round-eyed amazement.

'I am on dire Company business,' Keyser shouted again. 'Do not trifle with me, Tom Courtney.'

Tom came out through the tall doors of the warehouse. 'Stephanus Keyser, my dear friend!' he called, in jovial tones, as he pushed his steel-rimmed spectacles on to the top of his head. 'You are welcome indeed.'

The two had spent many evenings together in the Mermaid tavern. Over the years they had done each other many favours. Only last month Tom had found a string of pearls for Keyser's mistress at a favourable price, and Keyser had seen to it that the charges of public drunkenness and brawling laid against one of Tom's servants were quashed.

'Come in! Come in!' Tom spread his arms in invitation. 'My wife will bring us a pot of coffee, or do you prefer the fruit of the vine?' He called across the courtyard to the kitchens, 'Sarah Courtney! We have an honoured guest.'

She came out on to the terrace. 'Why, Colonel! This is a delightful surprise.'

'A surprise maybe,' he said sternly, 'but delightful, I doubt it, Mevrouw. Your son James is in serious trouble with the law.'

Sarah untied her apron and went to stand beside her husband. He put one thick arm around her waist. At that moment Dorian Courtney, slim and elegant, his dark red hair bound up in a green turban, stepped out of the shadows of the godown and stood at Tom's other hand. Together, the three presented a united and formidable front.

'Come inside, Stephanus,' Tom repeated. 'We cannot talk here.'

Keyser shook his head firmly. 'You must tell me where your son, James Courtney, is hiding.'

'I thought *you* might be able to tell *me* that. Yesterday evening all the world and his brothers saw you racing Jim over the dunes. Did he beat you again, Stephanus?'

Keyser flushed and fidgeted on his borrowed saddle. His spare tunic was too tight under the armpits. Only hours ago he had recovered his medals and the star of St Nicholas from the abandoned saddlebags his Bushman tracker had found on the edge of the salt pan. He had pinned these decorations on awry. He touched his pockets to reassure himself that his gold watch was still in place. His breeches were fit to burst their seams. His feet were raw and blistered from the long walk home in the darkness; his new boots pinched the sore spots.

117

He usually took pride in his appearance, and his present disarray and discomfort compounded the humiliation he had suffered at the hands of Jim Courtney.

'Your son has absconded with an escaped convict. He has stolen a horse and other valuable items. All these are hanging matters, I warn you. I have reason to believe that the fugitive is hiding here at High Weald. We have followed his tracks here from the salt pan. I am going to search every building.'

'Good!' Tom nodded. 'And when you are finished my wife will have refreshments ready for you and your men.' As Keyser's troopers dismounted and drew their sabres, Tom went on, 'But, Stephanus, you warn those ruffians of yours to leave my serving girls alone, otherwise it will really be a hanging matter.'

The three Courtneys withdrew into the cool shade of the godown, and crossed the wide, cluttered floor to the counting-house on the far side. Tom slumped into the leather-covered armchair beside the cold fireplace. Dorian sat cross-legged on a leather cushion on the far side of the room. With his green turban and embroidered waistcoat he looked like the Oriental potentate he had once been. Sarah closed the door but remained standing beside it to keep watch for any possible eavesdroppers. She studied the pair while she waited for Tom to speak. Brothers could scarcely have been more different: Dorian slim, elegant, marvellously handsome and Tom so big, solid and bluff. The strength of her feelings for him, even after all these years, still surprised her.

'I could happily wring the young puppy's neck.' Tom's genial smile had given way to a furious scowl. 'We can't be sure what he has got us all into.'

'You were young once, Tom Courtney, and you were always in hot water up to your neck.' Sarah gave him the smile of a loving wife. 'Why do you think I fell in love with you? It could never have been your looks.'

Tom tried not to let his smile reappear. 'That was different,' he declared. 'I never asked for trouble.'

'You never asked,' she agreed. 'You simply grabbed it with both hands.'

Tom winked at her and turned to Dorian. 'It must be wonderful to have a dutiful, respectful wife like Yasmini.' Then he was serious again.

'Has Bakkat returned yet?' The herder had sent one of his sons to Tom to tell him of Jim's nocturnal visit. Tom had felt a sneaking admiration for Jim's ruse in covering his tracks. 'It's the sort of thing I would have done. He may be wild as the wind but he's no fool,' he had told Sarah.

'No,' Dorian answered. 'Bakkat and the other herders are still moving all of the cattle and sheep over every path and road this side of the mountains. Even Keyser's Bushman will not be able to work out Jim's tracks. I think we can be sure that Jim has got clean away. But where did he go?' Both of them looked at Sarah for the answer.

'He planned it carefully,' she answered. 'I saw him with the mules a day or so ago. The shipwreck might have been a stroke of luck as far as he was concerned, but he was planning to get the girl off the ship one way or the other.'

'That damned woman! Why is it always a woman?' Tom lamented.

'You, of all people, should not have to ask that,' Sarah told him. 'You stole me away from my family with musket balls whizzing around our heads. Don't try to play the Pope with me, Tom Courtney!'

'Sweet heavens, yes! I'd almost forgotten about that. It was fun, though, wasn't it, my beauty?' He leaned across and pinched her bottom. She slapped his hand, and he went on unperturbed, 'But this woman Jim is with. What is she? A prison drab. A poisoner? A cutpurse? A whore mistress? Who knows what the idiot has picked for himself.'

Dorian had been watching this exchange with a fond expression while he got his hookah pipe to draw properly. It was a habit he had brought back from Arabia. Now he took out the ivory mouthpiece and remarked drily, 'I have spoken to at least a dozen of our people who were on the beach and saw it all. She may be all the other things you suggest, but she is no drab.' He blew a long feather of fragrant smoke. 'Reports of her vary. Kateng says she is an angel of beauty, Litila says

119

she is a golden princess. Bakkat says she is as lovely as the spirit of the rain goddess.'

Tom snorted with derision. 'A rain goddess out of a stinking convict ship? A sunbird hatching from a turkey buzzard's egg is more likely. But where has Jim taken her?'

'Zama has been missing since the day before yesterday. I didn't see him go, but my guess is that Jim sent him off with the mules to wait for him somewhere,' Sarah suggested. 'Zama will do whatever Jim asks.'

'And Jim spoke to Bakkat about the Robbers' Road,' Dorian added, 'and told him to sweep his tracks from the road to the east and the north of here.'

'The Robbers' Road is a myth,' said Tom firmly. 'There are no roads into the wilderness.'

'But Jim believes in it. I heard him and Mansur discussing it,' Sarah said.

Tom looked worried. 'It's madness. A babe and a prison drab going off empty-handed into the wilderness? They won't last a week.'

'They have Zama, and they are hardly empty-handed. Jim took six mule-loads of goods,' said Dorian. 'I've been checking what is missing from the stores, and he chose well. They are well set-up and provisioned for a long journey.'

'He didn't even say goodbye.' Tom shook his head. 'He's my son, my only son, and he didn't even say goodbye.'

'He was in somewhat of a hurry, brother,' Dorian pointed out.

Sarah rallied to her son's defence: 'He sent us a message through Bakkat. He didn't forget us.'

'It's not the same,' said Tom heavily. 'You know he might never come back. He has closed this door behind him. Keyser will catch him and hang him if he ever sets foot in the colony again. No, damn my eyes, I must see him again. Just once more. He is so headstrong and wild. I have to give him my counsel.'

'You have been giving him your counsel for the last nineteen years,' Dorian said wryly. 'Look where it has got us now.'

'Where was his rendezvous with Zama?' Sarah asked. 'That is where they will be.'

Tom thought about it for a moment, then grinned. 'Only one place it could be,' he said firmly.

Dorian nodded. 'I know what you're thinking,' he told Tom. 'Majuba is the obvious place for them to hide out. But we dare not follow them there. Keyser will be watching us like a leopard at the water-hole. If one of us leaves High Weald he will put that little yellow bloodhound of his on to us, and we will lead him straight to Majuba, and Jim.'

'If we're going to find him it must be soon, otherwise Jim will be gone from Majuba. They are well mounted. They have Drumfire and Keyser's mare. Jim will be half-way to Timbuktu before we can catch up with him.'

At that moment the tramp of boots and loud masculine voices echoed through the main storeroom of the godown.

'Keyser's men have searched the house.' Sarah glanced out of the door. 'Now they're starting on the warehouse and the outbuildings.'

'We'd better go out to keep an eye on those rogues,' Dorian stood up, 'before they start helping themselves.'

'We'll decide what to do about Jim once we've seen Keyser off,' Tom said, as they went through on to the main floor of the godown.

Four of the troopers were poking about aimlessly among the clutter. They were obviously tiring of their fruitless hunt. The long storeroom was piled to the high yellow-wood rafters. If they were to search it thoroughly they would need to clear the tons of goods with which the warehouse was congested. There were bales of silk from China, and cottons from the Indies; sacks of coffee beans and gum arabic from Zanzibar and other ports beyond the Horn of Hormuz; balks of sawn teak, sandalwood and ebony; mounds of pure gleaming copper cast into huge wheels so that armies of slaves could trundle them down the mountain tracks from the far interior of Ethiopia to the coast. There were bundles of the dried skins of exotic animals, tigers and zebras, and the furs of monkeys and seals, and the long curved horns of the rhinoceros, famous through China and the Orient for its aphrodisiac powers.

The Cape of Good Hope sat across the trade routes between Europe and the Orient. In former times the ships from the north had made the long voyage down the Atlantic. Even when they anchored in Table Bay they still faced another seemingly endless passage to the Indies and China, then even further north again to far Japan. A ship might be at sea for three or four years before it could return to Amsterdam, or the Pool of London.

Tom and Dorian had gradually evolved another network of trade. They had convinced a syndicate of ship-owners in Europe to send their ships only as far as the Cape. From the Courtney Brothers' warehouse they could fill their holds with choice goods, turn round in Table Bay and, with favourable winds, be back in their home ports in under a year. The profit the Courtneys exacted more than compensated for the additional years that the ships would be forced to spend at sea if they went further afield. In the same way ships coming from the east could discharge in Table Bay into the godown of the Courtney Brothers and be back in Batavia, Rangoon or Bombay in less than half the time it would have taken to make the journey across two great oceans.

This innovation was the foundation on which they had built their fortune. Added to this, they had their own trading schooners, which plied the African coast and were captained by Dorian's trusted Arab followers. As Muslims they could travel into waters forbidden to Christian captains, and venture as far as Muscat and Medina, the Luminous City of the Prophet of God. Although these vessels lacked the large holds in which to carry bulky cargoes, they dealt in the goods of higher value: copper and gum arabic, pearls and mother-of-pearl shells from the Red Sea, ivory from the markets of Zanzibar, sapphires from the mines of Kandy, yellow diamonds from the alluvial field along the great rivers of the empire of the Moguls, and cakes of black opium from the mountains of the Pathans.

There was only one commodity in which the Courtney

122

brothers refused to trade: human slaves. They had intimate knowledge of the barbaric practice. Dorian had spent most of his boyhood in slavery, until his owner, Sultan Abd Muhammad al-Malik, the ruler of Muscat, had adopted him as a son. In his younger days Tom had waged a bitter war against the Arab slave-traders of the East African coast, and had been a witness at first hand of the heartless cruelty of the trade. Many of the Courtney servants and sailors were former slaves who had come into their possession and whom they had manumitted at once. The means by which some of these unfortunates had been brought under the wing of the family varied – sometimes by force of arms, for Tom dearly loved a good fight, or by shipwreck, or in payment of debts, or even by outright purchase. Sarah could seldom bring herself to walk past a weeping orphan on the auction block without importuning her husband to buy the child and give it into her care. She had reared half of her house servants from infancy.

Sarah went out to the kitchens and came back almost immediately with her sister-in-law Yasmini, and a chattering, giggling train of housemaids all bearing jugs of freshly squeezed lime juice, trays of Cornish pasties, pork pies and samosas filled with spicy lamb curry. The bored, hungry troopers sheathed their blades and fell upon the fare with a will. Between bites they ogled and flirted with the maids. The soldiers who were supposed to be searching the coach-house and the stables saw the women carrying the provender out of the kitchens and found an excuse to follow them.

Colonel Keyser interrupted the feast and ordered his men back to work, but Tom and Dorian placated him and inveigled him into the counting house.

'I hope that now you will accept my word of honour, Colonel, that my son Jim is not anywhere on High Weald.' Tom poured him a glass of *jonge jenever* from a stone bottle; Sarah cut him a thick wedge of steaming Cornish pasty.

'*Ja*, very well, I accept that he is not here now, Tom. He has had enough time to get clean away – for the moment, that is. But I think you know where he is hiding.' He glared at Tom as he accepted the long-stemmed glass.

123

Tom assumed the expression of a choirboy about to receive the sacrament. 'You can trust me, Stephanus.'

'That I doubt.' Keyser washed down a mouthful of the pasty with a swallow of gin. 'But I warn you, I am not going to let that bumptious puppy of yours get away with what he has done. Do not try to soften my resolve.'

'Of course not! You have your duty to perform,' Tom agreed. 'I offer you only common hospitality and I am not attempting to influence you. The minute that Jim returns to High Weald I myself will frogmarch him up to the castle to account to you and His Excellency. You have my word on it as a gentleman.'

Only slightly mollified, Keyser allowed them to usher him out to where a groom was holding his horse. Tom slipped two more bottles of the young Hollands gin into his saddlebags and waved to him as he led his squadron out through the gates.

As they watched them go, Tom said quietly to his brother, 'I have to get a message to Jim. He must stay at Majuba until I can reach him. Keyser will be watching for me to ride into the mountains and show him the way, but I'll send Bakkat. He leaves no tracks.'

Dorian threw the tail of his turban over his shoulder. 'Listen to me well, Tom. Don't take Keyser too lightly. He is not the clown he pretends to be. If he gets his hands on Jim it will be a tragic day for this family. Never forget that our own grandfather died on the gallows of the castle parade.'

The rutted road from High Weald back to the town led through a forest of tall yellow-wood trees with trunks as thick as cathedral columns. Keyser halted his troop as soon as they were hidden from the homestead. He looked down at the little Bushman at his stirrup, who gazed back at him with the eager expression of a hunting dog.

'Xhia!' He pronounced the name with the explosive sound of a sneeze. 'Soon they will send someone with a message to wherever the young rogue is hiding. Watch for the messenger. Follow him. Do not let yourself be seen. When you have found the hiding-place, return to me swiftly. Do you understand?'

'I understand, Gwenyama.' He used the term of utmost respect, which meant He Who Devours His Enemies. He knew that Keyser enjoyed the title. 'I know who they will send. Bakkat is an old rival and enemy of mine. It will give me pleasure to bring him down.'

'Go, then. Keep watch.'

Xhia slipped away into the yellow-wood forest, silent as a shadow, and Keyser led the troop of horsemen back towards the castle.

The lodge at Majuba was a single long room. The low roof was thatched with reeds from the banks of the stream that flowed close by the door. The windows were slits in the stonework, curtained by the dried skins of eland and bluebuck. There was an open fireplace in the centre of the earthen floor, with a hole in the roof above to let the smoke escape. The far corner of the hut was screened off by a hanging curtain of rawhide.

'We put my father behind that curtain when we came hunting up here. We thought it might deaden the sound of his snores,' Jim told Louisa. 'Of course it didn't work. Nothing could deaden his snores.' He laughed. 'But now we will put you there.'

'I don't snore,' she protested.

'Even if you do, it won't be for long. We're going to move on as soon as I have rested the horses, repacked the loads and put some decent clothes on you.'

'How long will that be?'

'We will go on before they can send soldiers after us from the castle.'

'To where?'

'I don't know.' He smiled at her. 'But I will tell you when

125

we get there.' He gave her an appraising glance. Her tattered shift left her almost naked and she drew the cloak around herself. 'You are hardly dressed for dinner with the governor at the castle.' He went to one of the mule packs, which Zama had stacked against the wall. He rummaged in it and pulled out a roll of trade cloth, and a canvas housewife roll, which contained scissors, needles and thread. 'I hope you can sew?' he asked, as brought them to her.

'My mother taught me to make my own clothes.'

'Good,' he said. 'But we will sup first. I haven't eaten since breakfast two days ago.'

Zama ladled out venison stew from the three-legged hunter's pot standing on the coals. On top of it he placed a chunk of stiff maize cake. Jim took a spoonful. With his mouth full he asked Louisa, 'Did your mother teach you to cook also?'

Louisa nodded. 'She was a famous cook. She cooked for the Stadholder of Amsterdam, and the Prince of the House of Orange.'

'Then you have much employment here. You shall take over the cooking,' he said. 'Zama once poisoned a chief of the Hottentots, without even exerting himself. You may not think this a great accomplishment, but let me tell you that a Hottentot will grow fat on what kills the hyenas.'

She glanced at Zama uncertainly, her spoon half-way to her mouth. 'Is that true?'

'The Hottentots are the greatest liars in all Africa,' Zama answered, 'but none can match Somoya.'

'So it is a joke?' she asked.

'Yes, it is a joke,' Zama agreed. 'A bad English joke. It takes many years to learn to understand English jokes. Some people never succeed.'

When they had eaten, Louisa spread out the roll of cloth and began to measure and cut. Jim and Zama unpacked the mule loads that Jim had thrown together in such haste, and they noted and rearranged the contents. With relief Jim donned his own familiar boots and clothing, and gave Keyser's tunic and breeches to Zama. 'If we ever get into a battle with the wild tribes of the north, you can impress them with the uniform of a Company colonel,' he told him.

They cleaned and oiled the muskets, then replaced the flints in the locks. They placed the lead pot on the fire and melted lead to cast additional balls for the pistol Jim had captured from Colonel Keyser. The shot bags for the muskets were still full.

'You should have brought at least another five kegs of powder,' Zama told Jim, as he filled the powder flasks. 'If we meet hostile tribes when we start hunting, this will not last long.'

'I would have brought another fifty kegs, if I had found another twenty mules to carry them,' Jim said acidly. Then he called across the hut to where Louisa was kneeling over the bolt of material she had spread on the floor. She was using a stick of charcoal from the fireplace to mark her pattern before cutting it. 'Can you load and fire a musket?'

She looked abashed, and shook her head.

'Then I shall have to teach you.' He pointed to the material she was working on. 'What is that you are making?'

'A skirt.'

'A stout pair of trousers would be more useful, and would take less cloth.'

Her cheeks turned an intriguing shade of pink. 'Women don't wear trousers.'

'If they are going to ride astride, walk and run, as you are, then they should.' He nodded at her bare feet. 'Zama will make you a fine pair of *velskoen* boots from eland skin to go with your new trousers.'

Louisa cut the legs of her trousers very full, which made her appear even more boyish. She trimmed the tattered hem of her convict shift into a long shirt that she wore over the top and it hung half-way down her thighs. She gathered this in at the waist with a rawhide belt that Zama made for her. She learned that he was an expert sailmaker and leather-worker. The boots he made fitted her well. They reached half-way up her calves, and he turned the fur on the outside, which

127

gave them a dashing appearance and enhanced the length of her legs. Lastly, she made herself a canvas bonnet to cover her hair and keep off the sun.

Early the next morning Jim whistled for Drumfire. He charged up from the bank of the stream where he had been cropping the young spring grass. In his usual display of affection, he pretended he was going to run his master down. Jim bestowed on him a few affectionate insults while he slipped the bridle over his head.

Louisa appeared in the door of the hut. 'Where are you going?'

'To sweep the back trail,' he told her.

'What does that mean?'

'I must go back the way we came to make certain we are not being followed,' he explained.

'I would like to come with you, for the ride.' She looked out at Trueheart. 'Both the horses are well rested.'

'Saddle up!' Jim invited her.

Louisa had hidden a large chunk of maize bread in the pouch on her belt, but Trueheart smelt it as soon as she stepped out of the door of the hut. The mare came to her at once, and while she ate the bread Louisa settled the saddle on her back. Jim watched her buckle the girth and mount. She moved easily in her new breeches.

'She must be the luckiest horse in Africa,' Jim commented, 'to have exchanged the colonel for you. An elephant for a hedgehog.'

Jim had saddled Drumfire: he slid a long musket into the sheath, slung a powder horn over his shoulder then sprang on to Drumfire's back. 'Lead the way,' he told her.

'Back the way we came?' she asked, and without waiting for his reply she started up the slope. Louisa had a light hand on the reins, and a natural seat. The mare seemed not to notice her weight, and flew up the steep mountainside.

From behind Jim appraised her style. If she was accustomed

to the side-saddle, she had adapted readily to riding astride. He remembered how she had endured during the long night ride, and was amazed at how quickly she had recovered. He knew that she would be able to keep up, no matter how gruelling the pace he set.

When they reached the crest, he moved into the lead. Unerringly he found his way back through the labyrinth of valleys and defiles. To Louisa each sheer cliff and hillside seemed the same as the one before it, but he twisted and turned through the maze without hesitation.

Whenever a new stretch of ground opened before them he dismounted and climbed to a vantage-point to scan the terrain ahead through the lens of his telescope. These halts gave her respite to enjoy the grand scenery that surrounded them. After the flat country of her native land, these mountain tops seemed to reach to the heavens. The cliff walls were umber, red and purple. The scree slopes were densely clad with shrubs: some of their flowers looked like huge pincushions, and the colours were daffodil yellow and brilliant orange. Flocks of long-tailed birds swarmed over them, probing their curved beaks deeply into the flowers.

'*Suiker-bekkies* – sugar-beaks,' Jim told her, when she pointed them out. 'They are drinking the nectar from the protea bushes.'

It was the first time since the shipwreck that she had been able to look around her, and she felt drawn by the beauty of this strange new land. The horrors of the *Meeuw*'s gundeck were already fading, seemed now to belong to an old nightmare. The path they were following climbed another steep slope, and Jim stopped below the skyline and handed her Drumfire's reins to hold, while he climbed to the crest to observe the far side of the mountain.

She watched him idly. Suddenly his manner changed abruptly. He ducked down, doubled over, and scrambled back to where she waited. She was alarmed, and her voice shook: 'Are we being followed? Is it the colonel's men?'

'No, it's much better than that. It's meat.'

'I don't understand.'

'Eland. Herd of twenty or more. Coming straight up the far side towards us.'

'Eland?' she asked.

'The largest antelope in Africa. As big as an ox,' he explained, as he checked the priming in the pan of the musket. 'The flesh is rich with fat and closer to the taste of beef than any other antelope's. Salted and dried or smoked the flesh of a single eland will last us many weeks.'

'Are you going to kill one? What if the colonel is following us? Won't he hear the shot?'

'In these mountains the echoes will break up the sound and confuse the direction. In any event, I cannot miss this opportunity. We are already short of meat. I must take the chance if we are not to starve.'

He took hold of the bridles of both horses and led them off the path, then stopped behind an outcrop of raw red rock.

'Dismount. Hold the horses' heads, but try to stay out of sight. Don't move until I call you,' he ordered Louisa, and then, carrying the musket, he ran back up the slope. Just before he reached the crest he dropped into the grass. He glanced back and saw that she had followed his instructions. She was squatting down so that only her head was visible.

'The horses will not alarm the eland,' he told himself. The eland would take them for other wild game.

With his hat he wiped the sweat out of his eyes, and wriggled down more comfortably behind a small rock. He was sitting, not lying flat. Fired from the prone position the recoil of the heavy musket might break his collar-bone. He used his hat as a cushion and laid the stock of the musket on it, aiming up the slope.

The profound silence of the mountains settled over the valley; the soft hum of insects in the protea blossoms and the lonely, plaintive whistle of a red-winged mountain starling sounded abnormally loud.

The minutes passed as slowly as honey dripping, then Jim lifted his head. He had heard another sound that made his heartbeat trip. It was a faint clicking, like dry sticks being tapped together. Jim recognized it instantly. The eland antelope has a peculiar characteristic, unique in the African wild: the mighty sinews in its legs make a strange click with each step it takes.

Bakkat, the little yellow Bushman, had explained to Jim when he was a child how this had come about. One day in that far-off time when the sun had risen on the first day and the world was new with the dew still fresh upon it, Xtog who was the father of all the Khoisan, the Bushmen, caught in his cunning snare Impisi, the hyena. As all the world knows, Impisi was and still is a powerful magician. As Xtog was sharpening his flint knife to cut his throat, Impisi said to him, 'Xtog, if you set me free, I will make a magic for you. Instead of my flesh, which stinks of the carrion I eat, you will have hills of white fat and mountains of the sweet meat of the eland roasting on your fire every night of your life.'

'How can this be, O Hyena?' Xtog had wondered, although he was beginning to drown in his own saliva at the thought of the eland meat. But the eland was a cunning animal and difficult to find.

'I will place a spell on the eland so that wherever he roams over desert and mountain he will make a sound that will guide you to him.'

Thus Xtog had set Impisi free, and from that day onwards the eland has clicked as he walks to warn the hunter of his approach.

Jim grinned as he remembered Bakkat's story. Gently he drew back the heavy hammer of the musket to full cock, and settled the brassbound butt into his shoulder. The clicking sounds grew louder, stopping as the animals that made them paused, then coming on again. Jim watched the skyline just ahead of where he lay and suddenly a massive pair of horns rose against the blue. They were as long and thick as a strongman's arm, spiralled like the horn of the narwhal, polished black so the sun glinted upon them.

The clicking sound ceased and the horns turned slowly from side to side, as if the animal that carried them was listening. Jim heard his breath whistling in his ears, and his nerves tightened like the string of a crossbow. Then the

131

clicking sound began again and the horns rose higher, until two trumpet-shaped ears and a pair of huge eyes appeared beneath them. The eyes were dark and gentle, seeming to swim with tears. Long curling lashes veiled them. They stared directly into Jim's soul, and his breath stopped. The beast was so close that he could see it blink, and he dared not move.

Then the eland looked away, swinging its great head to stare down the slope up which it had come. Then it started forward towards Jim, and the rest of its body came into view. He could not have circled that thick neck with his arms: a heavy dewlap hung beneath it, swinging ponderously with each pace. Its back and shoulders were blue with age, and it stood as tall as Jim himself.

Only a dozen paces from where he sat it stopped and lowered its head to pull the new spring leaves from a cripple-wood bush. Over the ridge behind the bull, the rest of the herd came into view. The cows were a soft creamy brown, and although they carried the long spiral horns, their heads were more graceful and feminine. The calves were a ruddy chestnut, the younger ones hornless. One dropped its head and butted its twin playfully, then they bucked and chased each other in a circle. The mother watched with mild disinterest.

The hunter's instinct drew Jim's eyes back to the great bull. It was still chewing the cripplewood. It was an effort for Jim to reject this old animal. Despite the mighty trophy it carried, its flesh would be tough and gamy, its fat sparse.

Bakkat's philosophy came back to him: 'Leave the old bull to breed, and the cow to suckle her young.' Slowly Jim turned his head to examine the rest of the herd. At that moment the perfect quarry came up over the ridge.

This was a much younger bull, not more than four years old, his hindquarters so plump they seemed to be bursting from his glossy golden-brown hide. He turned aside, attracted by the shiny green leaves of a gwarrie tree. The branches were laden with ripe purple berries, and the young bull moved round until he was facing Jim. Then he stretched up to nibble at the berries, exposing the creamy curve of his throat.

Jim traversed the barrel of the musket towards him. His

movements were as slow as the advance of a chameleon on a fly. The frolicking calves kicked up dust and distracted the usually watchful gaze of the cows. Carefully Jim laid the bead of the foresight on the base of the bull's throat, on the crease of skin that encircled it like a necklace. He knew that even at such close range either of the beast's massive shoulder-blades would flatten and stop the musket ball. He had to find the gap in the animal's brisket through which he could drive the ball deep into the vitals to tear through the heart, lungs and pulsing arteries.

He took up the slack in the trigger and felt the resistance of the sear. Steadily he increased the pressure, staring hard at his aiming point on the throat, resisting any impulse to jerk the trigger that final hair-breadth. The hammer fell with a loud snap, and the flint struck a shower of sparks off the frizzen, the powder in the pan ignited in a puff of white smoke, and with a bass roar the butt slammed back into his shoulder. Before he could be unsighted by the heavy recoil and the gush of powder smoke, Jim saw the eland hump its back in a mighty spasm. He knew from this that the ball had sliced through its heart. He sprang to his feet to see over the bank of smoke. The young bull was still frozen in agony, its mouth gaping. Jim could see the bullet wound, a dark, bloodless hole in the smooth hide of the throat.

All around him the rest of the herd burst into flight, scattering away down the rocky hillside in a mad gallop, loose stones and dust flying from under their hoofs. The stricken bull backed away, racked in a gigantic contortion. Its legs shook and quivered, and it sank back on its haunches. It lifted its head to the sky and the bright lung blood sprayed from its gaping jaws. Then it twisted over and fell on its back, all four legs kicking spasmodically in the air. Jim stood and watched the beast's last throes.

His jubilation was gradually replaced by the melancholy of the true hunter, caught up in the beauty and tragedy of the kill. As the eland subsided and was still, he laid aside the musket and drew the knife from its sheath on his belt. Using the horns as a lever he pulled back the beast's head and, with

133

two expert incisions, he laid open the arteries on each side of the throat and watched the bright blood flow out. Then he lifted one of the massive back legs and cut away the scrotum.

Louisa rode up as he straightened with the furry white pouch in his hand. He felt bound to explain: 'It would taint the flesh if we left it.'

She looked away. 'What a magnificent animal. So big.' She seemed subdued by the enormity of what he had done. Then she sat up straighter in the saddle. 'What must I do to help you?'

'Tether the horses first,' he told her and she swung down from Trueheart's back and led the horses to the gwarrie tree. She hitched them to the trunk, then came back.

'Hold one of the back legs,' he said. 'If we leave the guts inside, the meat will sour and spoil in a few hours.'

It was heavy work, but she did not flinch from it. When he made the paunching stroke from the crotch to the ribs the bowels and entrails came ballooning out of the opening.

'This is when you get your hands messy,' he warned her, but before he could go on, another voice spoke near at hand, a piping, childlike voice.

'I taught you well, Somoya.'

Jim spun round, the knife held instinctively in the under-hand defensive grip, and stared at the little yellow man who sat on a rock watching them.

'Bakkat, you little *shaitan*,' Jim shouted, more in fright than anger. 'Don't ever do that again. Where in the name of the Kulu Kulu did you come from?'

'Did I startle you, Somoya?' Bakkat looked uncomfortable, and Jim remembered his manners. He had come close to giving offence to his friend.

'No, of course not. I saw you from afar.' You must never tell a Bushman that you had overlooked him: he will take it as an insulting reference to his tiny stature. 'You stand taller than the trees.'

Bakkat's face lit up at the compliment. 'I watched you from the beginning of the hunt. It was a fair stalk and a clean kill,

134

Somoya. But I think you need more than a young girl to help you dress the meat.' He hopped down from the rock. He paused in front of Louisa and crouched down, clapping his hands in greeting.

'What is he saying?' she asked Jim.

'He says that he sees you, and that your hair is like sunlight,' he told her. 'I think you have just been given your African name, Welanga, Girl of Sunlight.'

'Please tell him that I see him also, and that he does me great honour.' She smiled down at him and Bakkat cackled with delighted laughter.

Bakkat carried a native axe hooked over one shoulder, and his hunting bow over the other. He laid aside the bow and quiver, and hefted the axe as he came to help Jim with the huge carcass.

Louisa was amazed at how quickly the two of them worked. Each knew his job and did it without hesitation or argument. Bloody to the elbows they drew out the entrails and the bulging sac of the stomach. With barely a check in the work Bakkat cut a strip of the raw tripes. He slapped it against a rock to knock off the half-digested vegetation, then stuffed it into his mouth and chewed with unfeigned relish. When they pulled out the steaming liver, even Jim joined in the feast.

Louisa stared in horror. 'It's raw!' she protested.

'In Holland you eat raw herring,' he said, and offered her a sliver of the purple liver. She was about to refuse, then saw from his expression that this was a challenge. She hesitated still until she realized that Bakkat also was watching her with a sly smile, his eyes slitted between leathery wrinkles.

She took the slice of liver, gathered her courage and placed it in her mouth. She felt her gorge rise but forced herself to chew. After the first shock of the strong taste, it was not unpleasant. She ate slowly, and swallowed it. To her deep satisfaction Jim looked crestfallen. She took another slice from his bloody hand and began to chew at it.

Bakkat let out a squeal of laughter, and dug his elbow into Jim's ribs. He shook his head with delight, mocking Jim, and

135

miming the way she had won the silent contest, staggering around in a circle as he crammed imaginary lumps of liver into his mouth with both hands, weak with mirth.

'If you were half as funny as you think you are,' Jim told him sourly, 'you would be the wit of all the fifty tribes of the Khoisan. Now let's get back to work.'

They divided up the meat into loads for both the horses, and Bakkat made a sack of the wet skin into which he stuffed all the titbits of kidneys, tripes and liver. It weighed almost as much as he did, but he shouldered it and set off at a trot. Jim carried a shoulder of the eland, which almost buckled his knees, and Louisa led the horses. They covered the last mile down the gorge to Majuba in darkness.

Xhia trotted with the rapid bow-legged gait that the Bushmen call 'drinking the wind'. He could keep it up from first light in the morning until nightfall. As he went he talked to himself as if to a companion, replying to his own questions, chuckling at his jokes. Still on the run, he drank from his horn bottle and ate from the leather food bag slung over his shoulder.

He was reminding himself of how cunning and brave he was. 'I am Xhia the mighty hunter,' he said, and gave a little jump in the air. 'I have killed the great bull elephant with the poison that tips my arrow.' He remembered how he had followed it along the banks of the great river. Doggedly, he had kept up the hunt during the time that it had taken the new moon to wax to the full, then wane again. 'Not once did I lose the spoor. Could any other man do that?' He shook his head. 'No! Could Bakkat perform such a feat? Never! Could Bakkat have fired the arrow into the vein behind the ear so that the poison was taken straight to the heart of the bull? He could not have done it!' The frail reed arrow could barely pierce the thick pachyderm hide – it would never penetrate to heart or lung: he had had to find one of the great blood vessels close to the surface to carry the poison. It had taken the poison five days to bring the bull down. 'But I followed him all that time and I danced and sang the hunter's song when, at last, he fell like a mountain and raised the dust as high as the treetops. Could Bakkat have performed such a feat?' he asked the high peaks around him. 'Never!' he replied. 'Never!'

Xhia and Bakkat were members of the same tribe, but they were not brothers. 'We are not brothers!' Xhia shouted aloud, and he became angry.

Once there had been a girl, with skin as bright as the plumage of a weaver bird and a face shaped like a heart. Her lips were as full as the fruit of the ripe marula, her buttocks were like ostrich eggs and her breasts as round as two yellow Tsama melons warming in the Kalahari sun. 'She was born to be my woman,' Xhia cried. 'The Kulu Kulu took a piece of my heart while I slept and moulded it into that woman.' He could not bring himself to say her name. He had shot her with the tiny love arrow tipped with the feathers of the mourning dove to demonstrate to her how much he wanted her.

'But she went away. She would not come to lie on the sleeping mat of Xhia the hunter. She went instead with the despicable Bakkat and bore him three sons. But I am cunning. The woman died from the bite of the mamba.' Xhia had captured the snake himself. He had found its hiding-place under a flat rock. He had tethered a live dove as bait beside it and when the snake slid out from under the rock, he had pinned it behind the head. It was not a large mamba, only as long as one of his arms, but its venom was virulent enough to kill a bull buffalo. He placed it in the girl's harvesting bag while she and Bakkat slept. The next morning when she opened the mouth of the bag to place a tuber inside, the snake had bitten her three times, once on the finger and twice on the wrist. Her death, though swift, was terrible to behold. Bakkat wept as he held her in his arms. Concealed among the rocks, Xhia had watched it all. Now the memory of her death and Bakkat's grief was so sweet that Xhia jumped with both feet together like a grasshopper.

'There is no animal who can elude me. There is no man who can prevail against my guile. For I am Xhia!' he shouted, and the echo came back from the cliffs above. 'Xhia, Xhia, Xhia.'

After Colonel Keyser left him, he had waited two days and a night on the hills and in the forests of High Weald, watching for Bakkat. On the first morning he saw him come out of his hut in the dawn, yawn, scratch himself and laugh at the squeal of gas from between his buttocks. For the Bushmen a flourish of flatus was always a propitious sign of good health. He watched him let the herd out of the kraal and drive them down to the water. Lying like a partridge concealed in the grass Xhia saw the big white man with the black beard that they called Klebe, the hawk, ride down from the homestead. He was Bakkat's master and the two squatted in the middle of the open field with their heads close together and they spoke in whispers for a long time so that no one could overhear them. Even Xhia was not able to creep close enough to pick up their words.

Xhia grinned to watch their secret counsel. 'I know what you are saying, Klebe. I know you are sending Bakkat to find your son. I know you are telling him to take care that he is not followed but, like the spirit of the wind I, Xhia, will be watching when they meet.'

He watched Bakkat close the door of his hut at nightfall, and saw the glow of his cooking fire, but Bakkat did not come out again until the dawn.

'You try to lull me, Bakkat, but will it be tonight or tomorrow?' he asked, as he watched from the hilltop. 'Is your patience greater than mine? We shall see.' He watched Bakkat circle around his hut in the early light, searching the earth for the sign of an enemy, for someone who had come to spy upon him.

Xhia embraced himself with glee, and rubbed his back with both hands. 'Do you think I am such a fool as to come in close, Bakkat?' This was the reason he had sat all night upon the hilltop. 'I am Xhia and I leave no sign. Not even the high-flying vulture can discover my hiding-place.'

All that day he had watched Bakkat go about his business, tending his master's herds. At nightfall Bakkat went into his hut again. Xhia worked a charm in the darkness. He took a pinch of powder from one of the stoppered duiker-horn flasks on his beaded belt and placed it on his tongue. It was the ash of a leopard's whiskers, mixed with the dry, powdered dung of a lion and other secret ingredients. Xhia mumbled an incantation as it dissolved in his own saliva. It was the spell for outwitting prey. Then he spat three times in the direction of the hut in which Bakkat lived.

'This is a charm of great power, Bakkat,' he warned his enemy. 'No animal or man can resist its spell.' This was not always true, but whenever it failed there was always good reason for it. Sometimes it was because the wind had changed direction, or because a black crow flew overhead, or because the sore-eye lily was in bloom. Apart from these and similar circumstances it was an infallible charm.

Having cast the spell he settled down to wait. He had not eaten since the day before, so now he swallowed a few fragments of smoked meat from his food bag. Neither hunger nor the cold wind off the snows of the mountain deterred him. Like all his tribe he was inured to pain and hardship. The night was still, proof that his spell was efficacious. Even a small breeze would have covered the sounds for which he was listening.

It was soon after the moon had set that he heard a nightbird utter its alarm call in the forest behind Bakkat's home. He nodded to himself. 'Something moves there.'

A few minutes later he heard the nightjar's mate whirl up from the forest floor, and by correlating the two clues he guessed the direction in which his quarry was moving. He went down the hill, silent as shadow, testing each footfall with his bare toe for twigs or dry leaves that might crackle and disclose his presence. He stopped to listen at every second step, and heard, down by the stream, the dry rustle of a porcupine erecting its quills as a warning to a predator who had ventured too close. The porcupine might have seen a leopard, but Xhia knew it had not. The leopard would have lingered to harass its natural prey, but a man moved on immediately. Not even an adept of the San, such as Bakkat or even Xhia himself, could have avoided encountering the nightjar or the prowling porcupine in the darkness of the forest. Those little signs had been all that Xhia needed to work out how Bakkat was moving, and the direction he was taking.

Another hunter might have made the mistake of closing in too swiftly, but Xhia hung back. He knew that Bakkat would backtrack and circle to make certain he was not followed.

'He is almost as cunning in the lore of the wild as I am. But I am Xhia and there is no other like me.' Telling himself this made him feel strong and brave. He found where Bakkat had crossed the stream and, in the last rays of the waning moon he picked out a single wet footprint gleaming on the top of one of the river boulders. It was the size of a child's, but broader, and there was no arch.

'Bakkat!' He gave a little hop. 'I will remember the shape of your foot all the days of my life. Have I not seen it a hundred times running beside the track of the woman who should have been my wife?' He remembered how he had followed their tracks into the bush so that he could creep up on them and watch them as they coupled, writhing together in the grass. The memory made him hate Bakkat with a fresh, corroding passion. 'But you will never savour those melon breasts again. Xhia and the snake have seen to that.'

Now that he had clearly established the direction and run of the spoor, he could hang back to avoid, in the dark, the traps that Bakkat would surely set for him. 'Because he moves in darkness he will not be able to cover his sign as completely as he would in daylight. I will wait for the coming of the sun to read more clearly the sign he has left for me.'

In the first flush of the dawn he picked up the spoor again. The wet footprint had dried leaving no trace, but within a hundred paces he found a dislodged pebble. Another hundred paces and there was a broken blade of grass, dangling and beginning to wither. Xhia did not stop to pore over these clues. A quick darting glance confirmed his instinct and enabled him to make minute adjustments to his direction. He smiled and shook his head when he found where Bakkat had lain in wait beside his spoor. Because he had squatted unmoving for so long, his bare heels had left indentations in the earth. Then, much further on, he found where Bakkat had made a wide circle to wait again beside his own spoor, the same way as a wounded buffalo circles back to wait for the hunter who pursues him.

Xhia was so pleased with himself that he took a little snuff, sneezed softly and said, 'Know, Bakkat, that it is Xhia who follows, that Xhia is your master in all things!' He tried not to think of the honey-yellow girl, the one thing in which Bakkat had prevailed.

Once the spoor led into the mountains it became even more elusive. Up one long narrow valley he found where Bakkat had hopped from rock to rock, never touching soft earth or disturbing a blade of grass or other growing thing, except for the grey lichen that grew sparsely on the rocks. This plant was so dry and tough, and Bakkat so light, his sole so small and pliant, that he passed over it almost as softly as the mountain breeze. Xhia squinted to pick out the slightly different shade of lichen grey where his foot had touched. Xhia kept carefully to the side of the tracks furthest from the rising sun, to highlight the faint spoor and not to disturb it in case he was forced to come back to rework it.

Then even Xhia was confounded. The tracks climbed a scree slope, again moving from rock to rock. Then abruptly, half-way up the scree, the tracks ended. It was as though Bakkat had been plucked into the sky in the talons of an eagle. Xhia went on in the established line of the spoor until he reached the head of the valley, but he found nothing more. He went back to where the sign ended, squatted down and turned his head one way then the other to contemplate the faint smears on the lichen coating of the rocks.

As a last resort he took another pinch of the magical powder from the duiker horn and let it dissolve in his saliva. He closed his eyes to rest them, and swallowed the mixture. He half opened his eyes and, through the veil of his own lashes, he had a fleeting glimpse of movement, faint shadows like the flicker of bat's wings in the gloaming. When he looked

141

directly at them they disappeared as though they had never existed. The saliva dried in his mouth and the skin on his arms prickled. He knew that one of the spirits of the wilderness had touched him, and what he had seen was the memory of Bakkat's feet running across the rocks. They were running not upwards but back down the scree.

In that moment of heightened awareness, he realized, from the colour of the lichen, that Bakkat's feet had touched it twice, going up and coming back. He laughed out loud. 'Bakkat, you would have deceived any other man, but not Xhia.' He moved back down the scree and saw how he had done it. How he had run up the slope, bouncing from rock to rock and then, in mid-stride, he had reversed direction and run backwards, his tiny feet falling exactly in the same spoor. The only tell-tale sign was the slight colour difference of the double tracks.

Near the bottom of the slope the spoor passed under the low branch of a Boer bean tree. Lying on the earth beside the tracks was a fragment of dried bark no bigger than a thumb-nail. It had recently fallen or been dislodged from the branch above. At this point the double tracks on the lichen-coated rocks suddenly became single tracks again. Xhia laughed out loud.

'Bakkat has taken to the trees like the baboon that was his mother.' Xhia went to stand under the outspread branch, jumped, caught a hold and drew himself up until he stood upright, balancing on the narrow branch. He saw the marks Bakkat's feet had made on the bark. He ran along them to the main trunk of the tree, slid down to the earth, picked up the spoor again and ran along it.

Twice more Bakkat had set him puzzles to solve. The first of these was at the base of a red cliff and cost him more time. But after the Boer bean tree he had learned to look upwards and found the place where Bakkat had reached up high and traversed hand over hand along a ledge so that his feet had not touched the earth.

The sun had started down the sky by the time he reached the place where Bakkat had laid the second puzzle. This one

142

seemed to defy even his powers of solution. After a while he felt a superstitious tingle of his nerves that Bakkat had worked some counter-charm and grown wings like a bird. He swallowed another dose of the hunter's powder, but the spirits did not touch him again. Instead his head began to ache.

'I am Xhia. No man can deceive me,' he told himself, but even though he said it loudly he could not dispel the sense of failure that slowly overwhelmed him.

Then he heard a sound, dulled by distance but unmistakable. The echoes from the cliffs confirmed it, but at the same time muddled the direction so that Xhia turned his head from side to side to try to pinpoint it. 'Musket shot,' he whispered. 'My spirits have not deserted me. They lead me on.'

He left the spoor and climbed the nearest peak, squatted there and watched the sky. It was not long before he picked out a tiny black speck high against the blue. 'Where there is gunfire, there is Death. And Death has his faithful minions.'

Another speck appeared, then many more. They coalesced into a slow-turning wheel in the sky. Xhia sprang to his feet and trotted in that direction. As he approached, the specks resolved themselves into carrion birds, soaring on fixed wings, turning their repulsive naked heads to peer down at one spot among the mountains below them.

Xhia knew well all the five varieties of vulture, from the common tawny bird of the Cape to the huge bearded vulture with its patterned throat and triangular fan of tail feathers.

'Thank you, old friends,' Xhia called up to them. Since time beyond memory these birds had led him and his tribe to the feast. As he came closer to the centre of the spinning circle, he became more furtive, creeping from rock to rock, peering all around with those sharp bright eyes. Then he heard human voices coming from the far side of the ridge ahead of him and, like a puff of smoke, Xhia seemed simply to dissolve in the air.

From his place of concealment he watched the trio loading the butchered meat on to the horses. Somoya, he knew well. His was a familiar face in the colony. Xhia had watched him win the Christmas Day races from his own master. However, the woman was a stranger. 'This must be the one that Gwenyama seeks. The woman who escaped from the sinking ship.'

He chuckled when he recognized Trueheart tethered beside Drumfire. 'Soon you will return to our master,' he promised the mare. Then he concentrated all his attention on the dainty figure of Bakkat and his eyes slitted with hatred.

He watched the little band finish loading the horses, and move off out of sight along the game trail that meandered down the valley. As soon as they had gone Xhia ran down to dispute what remained of the eland carcass with the vultures. There was a puddle of blood lying where Jim had cut the eland's throat. It had coagulated to a black jelly, and Xhia scooped it up in his cupped hands, and dribbled it into his open mouth. Over the past two days he had eaten only sparingly from his food bag, and he was famished. He licked every last sticky clot from his fingers. He could not afford to spend much time on the carcass, for if Bakkat looked back he would notice that the vultures had not settled immediately, and know that something or someone was keeping them in the air. The hunters had not left much for him. There was the long rubbery tube of the small intestines, which they had not been able to carry away. He drew it through his fingers to squeeze out the liquid dung. The coating of excrement that remained gave it a pungent relish, which he savoured as he chewed. He was tempted to use a rock to crack open the massive leg bones and suck out the rich yellow marrow, but he knew that Bakkat would return to the kill, and he would not overlook such an obvious clue. Instead he used his knife to scrape off the shreds and strips of flesh that still adhered to the bones and ribcage. He stuffed these fragments into his food bag, then used a switch of dried grass to brush away his footprints. The birds would soon obliterate any small traces of his presence that he had overlooked. When Bakkat returned to sweep his back trail there would be nothing to alert him.

Chewing happily on strips of the reeking intestines, he left the carcass and went on after Bakkat and the white couple. He did not follow directly in their tracks but kept well out on

144

the slope above the valley. At three places he anticipated the twists and turns of the valleys ahead, cut across the high ground where the horses could not go and intercepted them on the far side. From a distance he picked out the smoke from the camp at Majuba and hurried ahead. He was watching from the peak when they arrived with the horses. He knew that he should go back at once to report to his master his success in discovering the hiding-place of the fugitives, but the temptation to linger and gloat over his old enemy, Bakkat, was too great to resist.

The three men, white, black and yellow, cut the raw eland meat into thick strips, and the woman sprinkled coarse sea salt from a leather bag on to them then rubbed it in with her palms and spread out the strips on the rocks to cure. In the meantime the men threw the lumps of white fat they trimmed from the meat into a three-legged pot on the fire to render it down for cooking or making soap.

Whenever Bakkat stood up or moved apart from the others, Xhia's eyes followed him with the malevolent gaze of a cobra. He fingered one of the arrows in his little bark quiver and dreamed of the day when he would sink the poisoned tip deep into Bakkat's flesh.

When the butcher's work was done, and the men were tending the horses and the mules, the white woman laid out the last strips of meat to dry. Then she left the camp and picked her way along the bank of the stream until she reached a green pool screened by the bend from the camp. She took off her bonnet and shook out her hair in a glowing cloud. Xhia was taken aback. He had never seen hair that colour and length. It was unnatural and repellent. The scalps of the women of his tribe were covered by crisp, furry peppercorns, pleasant to touch and look upon. Only a witch or some other disgusting creature would have hair like this one. He spat to ward away any evil influence she might emit.

The woman looked about her carefully, but no human eye could discover Xhia when he wished to remain concealed. Then she undressed, stepping out of the baggy clothes that covered her lower body, and stood naked at the edge of the pool. Again Xhia was repelled by her appearance. This was no female but some hermaphroditic thing. Her body was mis-shapen: her legs were elongated, her hips narrow, her belly concave and she had the buttocks of a starving boy. The San women gloried in their steatopygia. There was another puff of hair at the juncture of her thighs. It was the colour of the Kalahari desert sands and so fine that it did not completely screen her genitals. Her slit was like a tightly pursed mouth. There was no sign of the inner lips. The mothers of Xhia's tribe pierced their daughters' labia in infancy and hung stones upon them to stretch them and make them protrude attract-ively. In Xhia's estimation monumental buttocks and dangling labia were signs of true feminine beauty. Only her breasts proclaimed this woman's sex, yet they, too, were strangely shaped. They thrust out pointedly and the pale nipples pricked upwards like the ears of a startled dik-dik. Xhia covered his mouth and giggled at his own simile. 'What man could want a creature like that?' he asked himself.

The woman waded out into the pool until the water reached her chin. Xhia had seen enough and the sun was sinking. He slipped back over the skyline and set off at a trot towards the flat-topped mountain, blue and ethereal in the distance, that showed above the southern horizon. He would travel on through the night to bring the news to his master.

They sat close to the small fire in the centre of the hut, for the nights were still chill. They feasted on thick steaks cut from the long back strips of the eland, and kebabs of kidney, liver and fat grilled over the coals. The rich juices greased Bakkat's chin. When Jim sat back with a sigh of contentment, Louisa poured a mug of coffee for him. He nodded his thanks. 'Won't you take some?' he invited, but she shook her head.

'I do not like it.' This was untrue. She had developed a taste for it while she lived in Huis Brabant, but she knew how rare and expensive it was. She had seen how he treasured the small bag of beans, which would not last much longer. Her gratitude towards him, as her saviour and protector, was so strong that she did not want to deprive him of something that gave him so much pleasure. 'It's harsh and bitter,' she explained.

She went back to her place on the opposite side of the fire and watched the men's faces in the firelight as they talked. She did not understand what they were saying for the language was strange, but the sound was melodious and lulling. She was drowsy and well fed, and had not felt as safe and contented since she had left Amsterdam.

'I gave your message to Klebe, your father,' Bakkat told Jim. This was the first time they had mentioned the subject uppermost in both their minds. It was callow and ill-mannered to speak of important matters until the right moment for serious discussion.

'What was his reply?' Jim demanded anxiously.

'He told me to greet you in his name and in the name of your mother. He said that although you would leave a hole in their hearts that would never be filled, you must not return to High Weald. He said that the fat soldier from the castle would wait for your return with the patience of a crocodile buried in the mud of the water-hole.'

Jim nodded sadly. He had known what the consequences must be from the moment he had decided he must rescue the girl. Yet now that he heard his father confirm it, the enormity of his exile from the colony weighed like a stone. He was truly an outcast.

In the firelight Louisa saw his expression and instinctively she knew she was the cause of his grief. She looked down into the wavering flames, and her guilt was a knife under her ribs.

'What else did he say?' Jim asked softly.

'He said that the pain of parting from his only son would be too great to bear, unless he could hold you in his eye once more before you go.' Jim opened his mouth to speak, then closed it again. Bakkat went on, 'He knows that you intend to follow the Robbers' Road northwards into the wilderness. He said that you will not be able to survive with such meagre

147

stores as you were able to take with you. He intends to bring you more. He said that would be your inheritance.'

'How is that possible? I cannot go to him and he cannot come to me. The risk is too great.'

'He has already sent Bomvu, your uncle Dorian, and Mansur with two wagons laden with sacks of sand and chests filled with stones along the west coast road. This will draw Keyser away so that your father can come to meet you at an arranged place. He will have with him other wagons carrying his parting gifts to you.'

'Where is the place of meeting?' Jim asked. He felt a deep sense of relief and excitement that he might see his father. He had thought they were parted for ever. 'He cannot come here to Majuba. The road through the mountains is too steep and treacherous for wagons to pass.'

'No, he will not come here.'

'Where then?' Jim asked.

'Do you remember two years ago when we travelled together to the frontiers of the colony?' Jim nodded. 'We went through the mountains by the secret pass of the Gariep river.'

'I remember.' That journey had been the adventure of Jim's life.

'Klebe will take the wagons out through that pass and meet you on the edge of the unknown lands, by the *kopje* shaped like the head of a baboon.'

'Yes, that was where we hunted and killed the old gemsbuck bull. It was the last camp before we returned to the colony.' The disappointment he had felt when they turned back came to him vividly. 'I wanted to go on to the next horizon, and the next, until I reached the last.'

Bakkat laughed. 'You were always an impatient boy, and you still are. But your father will meet you at the Hill of the Baboon's Head. Can you find it without me to lead you, Somoya?' He mocked Jim lightly, but for once he could not draw him. 'Your father will only leave High Weald when he is sure that Keyser is following Bomvu and Mansur, and when I have returned with your reply.'

'Tell my father I will meet him there.'

Bakkat stood up and reached for his quiver and bow.

'You cannot leave yet,' Jim told him. 'It is still dark, and you have not rested since you left High Weald.'

'I have the stars to guide me,' Bakkat went to the door of the hut, 'and Klebe told me to return at once. We will meet again at the Hill of the Baboon's Head.' He crossed to the door of the hut, and smiled back at Jim. 'Until that day go in peace, Somoya. Keep Welanga beside you always, for it seems to me that, although she is young, she will grow to be a fine woman, like your own mother.' Then he was gone into the night.

Bakkat moved as swiftly through the darkness as any of the other night creatures, but it had been late when he left Majuba, and the dawn light was already strengthening when he reached the remains of the eland carcass. He squatted beside it and searched for clues as to who and what had visited it since the previous day. The vultures were roosting, hump-backed, on the surrounding cliffs and kranzes. The ground around the carcass was littered with their feathers where they had squabbled over the scraps, and white streaks of their liquid dung painted the rocks around the kill. Their talons had raked the earth, but he was able to pick out the tracks of a number of jackal and other small wild cats and scavengers in the softened earth. There were no signs of hyena, but that was not surprising: the mountains were too high and cold for them at this season of the year. Although picked bare, the skeleton of the eland was intact. Hyena would have chewed the bones to splinters.

If there had been a human visitor, any sign of him had been obliterated. However, Bakkat was confident that he had not been followed. Few men could have untangled the trail he had laid. Then his eyes fell on the ribcage of the eland. The bones were smooth and white. Suddenly he gave a soft whistle of alarm, and his confidence wavered. He touched the bare ribs, running his finger down them one after another. The marks on them were so light that they might have been natural or the toothmarks of one of the scavengers. But Bakkat felt a sick spasm of doubt tighten his stomach muscles. The marks were too smooth and regular, not those of teeth but of a tool. Someone had scraped the flesh off the bone with a blade.

If it were a man, he would have left the mark of boot or sandal, he thought, and made a quick cast around the carcass, wide enough to avoid the chaos created by the scavengers. Nothing! He returned to the skeleton and studied it again. Perhaps he was barefoot? he wondered. But the Hottentot wear sandals, and what would one of them be doing in the mountains in this season? They will be with their herds down in the plains. Perhaps, after all, I was followed? But only an adept could have read my sign. An adept who goes unshod? A San? One of my own kind? As he pondered it he became more anxious. Should I go on to High Weald, or should I go back to warn Somoya? He hesitated, then made his decision. I cannot go in both directions at the same time. I must go on. That is my duty. I must take my news to Klebe.

Now in the morning light he could move faster. As he ran, his dark eyes were never still and no sound or smell, however faint, eluded him. As he skirted a stand of cripplewood, whose stems were hung with beards of grey moss, his nostrils flared as he caught a whiff of faecal odour. He turned off the path to trace the source, and found it within a few paces. A single glance told him that these were the droppings of a carnivore, who had gorged recently on blood and meat: they were black, loose and foetid.

Jackal? he thought, then immediately knew that it was not. It must be human, for close by were the stained leaves with which he had cleaned himself. Only the San used the leaves of the wash-hand bush for that purpose: they were succulent and soft, and when rubbed between the palms of the hand they burst open and ran with herbal-scented juice. He knew then that the same man who had eaten at the eland carcass had defecated here, close to the path that led from Majuba down the mountains, and that the man was of the

San. Apart from himself how many adepts of the San lived within the borders of the colony? His people were of the deserts and the wilderness. Then his instincts told him who it must be.

'Xhia!' he whispered. 'Xhia, who is my enemy has followed me and learned my secrets. Now he runs back to his master in the castle. Soon they will ride out to Majuba with many horsemen to run down Somoya and Welanga.' He was immediately stricken by the same dreadful uncertainty. 'Must I go back to warn Somoya, or go on to High Weald? How far is Xhia ahead of me?' Then he reached the same decision. 'Somoya will already have left Majuba. Keyser and his troopers will move slower than Somoya. If I drink the wind, I might be able to warn both Klebe and Somoya before Keyser catches up with them.'

He began to run as he had seldom run before, as though he were following a wounded gemsbuck, or being chased by a hungry lion.

It was late at night when Xhia reached the colony. The gates of the castle were closed and would not open again until reveille and the hoisting of the VOC flag at daybreak. But Xhia knew that, these days, Gwenyama, his master, seldom slept in his sumptuous quarters within the high stone walls. There was a fresh and irresistible attraction for him in the town.

It was the decree of the VOC council in Amsterdam that the burghers of the colony, and more especially the servants of the Company, should not have congress with the natives of the country. Like many of the other decrees of the Zeventien they were written only on paper, and Colonel Keyser kept a discreet little cottage on the far side of the Company gardens. It was situated down an unpaved lane and was screened by a tall, flowering lantana hedge. Xhia knew better than to waste time arguing with the sentries at the gates of the castle. He went directly to the colonel's love nest, and slipped through

151

the opening in the lantana hedge. A lamp was burning in the kitchen at the rear of the cottage, and he tapped on the window. A shadow passed between the lamp and the pane, and a female voice he recognized called, 'Who is there?' Her tone was sharp and nervous.

'Shala! It is Xhia,' he called back, in the Hottentot tongue, and heard her lift the locking bar on the door. She swung it open and peered out. She was only a little taller than Xhia and looked childlike, but she was not.

'Is Gwenyama here?' Xhia asked. She shook her head. He looked at her with pleasure: the Hottentot were cousins of the San and Shala was Xhia's ideal of a beautiful woman. Her skin glowed like amber in the lamplight, her dark eyes slanted up at the corners, her cheekbones were high and wide, and her chin was narrow so that her face was the shape of an inverted arrowhead. The dome of her head was perfectly rounded, and covered with a pelt of peppercorn curls.

'No! He has gone away,' she repeated, and held open the door in invitation.

Xhia hesitated. From their previous encounters he had a clear picture of her sex in his mind. It resembled one of the succulent desert cactus flowers, with fleshy petals of a pouting purple texture. Added to that, there was an intense pleasure to be had from stirring his master's porridge pot. Shala had once described the colonel's manly part to Xhia. 'It is like the beak of a sugar-bird. Thin and curved. It sips my nectar only lightly, then flits away.'

The men of the San were famous for their priapism, and for penile dimensions unrelated to their diminutive stature. Shala, who had much first-hand experience in these matters, considered Xhia to be gifted beyond all his tribe.

'Where is he?' Xhia was torn between duty and temptation.

'He rode away yesterday with ten of his men.' She took Xhia's hand and drew him into the kitchen, closed the door behind him and replaced the locking bar.

'Where did they go?' he asked, as she stood before him and unwrapped her robe. Keyser delighted in dressing her in the gaudy silks of the Indies, and in pearls and other finery that he purchased at great expense from the godown of the Courtney brothers.

'He said they were following the wagons of Bomvu, the red-haired one,' she said, and let the robe slide down her body to the floor. He drew in his breath sharply. No matter how often he saw those breasts it was always with a shock of delight.

'Why is he following those wagons?' He reached out, took one of her breasts and squeezed it.

She smiled dreamily and swayed closer to him. 'He said they would lead him to the runaways, to Somoya, the son of the Courtneys, and the woman he stole from the shipwreck,' she answered, her voice husky. She lifted the front of his kilt and reached under it. Her eyes slanted lasciviously and she showed small white teeth as she smiled.

'I do not have much time,' he warned her.

'Then let us be quick,' she said, and sank to her knees in front of him.

'Which way did he go?'

'I watched them from the top of Signal Hill,' she replied. 'They went along the coastal road towards the west.'

She placed her elbows on the floor to brace herself and leaned forward until her extraordinary golden buttocks were raised towards the thatched ceiling. He went behind her, moved her knees apart, knelt between them and, both hands on her hips, pulled her back towards him. She gave a soft little squeal as he forced apart her fleshy petals and went in deeply.

At the end she squealed again, but this time as though in mortal agony and then she flopped forward on to her face and lay there in the centre of the kitchen floor writhing weakly.

Xhia stood up and adjusted his leather skirt. He picked up his quiver and bow and slung them over his shoulder.

'When will you come back?' She sat up shakily.

'When I can,' he promised, and went out into the night.

As Bakkat topped the hills above High Weald, he saw that the entire estate was bustling with unusual activity. Every one of the servants seemed frantically employed. The wagon drivers and the *voorlopers*, the lead boys, were bringing up the trek oxen from the kraals at the far end of the main paddock. They had inspanned four full teams of twelve bullocks each, which were trudging up the road to the homestead. Another group of herders had assembled small herds of fat-tailed sheep, milking cows with their unweaned calves, and spare trek bullocks, and were driving them slowly towards the north. They were already strung out over such a distance that the furthest of the small herds were specks almost obscured by their own dust.

'Already they are heading for the Gariep river pass to meet Somoya.' Bakkat nodded with satisfaction, and started down the hill towards the homestead.

As soon as he entered the courtyard he saw that the preparations for departure were well advanced. On the loading ramp of the warehouse Tom Courtney was in his shirt-sleeves giving orders to the men who were packing the last chests of goods into the wagon beds.

'What is in that chest?' he demanded of one. 'I don't recognize it.'

'The mistress told me to load it. I do not know what is in it.' The man shrugged. 'Woman's things, perhaps.'

'Put it into the second wagon.' Tom turned, and spotted Bakkat as he entered the yard. 'I saw you as soon as you came over the hill. You grow taller every day, Bakkat.'

Bakkat grinned with pleasure, squared his shoulders and puffed out his chest a little. 'I see your plan has worked, Klebe?' It was more a question than a statement.

'Within a few hours of Bomvu taking the wagons out along the west coast, Keyser and all his men were after them.' Tom laughed. 'But I don't know how soon he will realize that he is following the wrong game, and come rushing back. We have to get clear as soon as we can.'

'Klebe, I bring evil tidings.'

Tom saw the little man's expression and his own smile faded. 'Come! We will go where we can talk privately.' He led Bakkat into the warehouse, and listened seriously as the little man related all that had happened during his foray into the mountains. He exclaimed with relief when he heard that their guess had proved correct and Bakkat had found Jim at Majuba.

'So Somoya, Zama and the girl will already have left Majuba, and will be riding to the meeting place on the frontier at the Hill of the Baboon's Head,' Bakkat went on.

'This is good news,' Tom declared. 'So why do you wear such a gloomy countenance?'

'I was followed,' Bakkat admitted. 'Somebody followed me to Majuba.'

'Who was it?' Tom could not disguise his alarm.

'A San,' said Bakkat. 'An adept of my tribe, one who could unravel my spoor. One who was watching for me to leave High Weald.'

'Keyser's hunting dog!' Tom exclaimed furiously.

'Xhia,' Bakkat agreed. 'He tricked me and even now he must be hurrying back to his master. Within the next day he will lead Keyser to Majuba.'

'Does Somoya know he has been discovered by Xhia?'

'I only discovered Xhia's sign when I was half-way back from Majuba. I came on to warn you first,' Bakkat said. 'Now I can go back to find Somoya, warn him also, and lead him out of danger.'

'You must reach him before Keyser catches up with him.' Tom's bluff features were twisted with anxiety.

'Xhia must return to Majuba again before he can pick up Somoya's outgoing tracks. Keyser and his men will travel slowly for they are unaccustomed to the mountain paths,' Bakkat explained. 'He will be forced to make a wide loop to the south. On the other hand, I can cut through the mountains further north, get ahead of them and find Somoya before they do.'

'Go swiftly, old friend,' Tom told him. 'I place the life of my son in your hands.'

155

Bakkat bobbed his head in farewell. 'Somoya and I will be waiting for you at the Hill of the Baboon's Head.'

Bakkat turned to leave, but Tom called him back. 'The woman—' He broke off, unable to look at the little man's face. 'Is she still with him?' he asked gruffly, and Bakkat nodded.

'What is she—' Tom stopped, then tried to rephrase his question. 'Is she . . . ?'

Bakkat took pity on him. 'I have named her Welanga, for her hair is like sunlight.'

'That is not what I wanted to know.'

'I think that Welanga will walk beside him for a long, long time. Perhaps for the rest of his life. Is that what you wanted to know?'

'Yes, Bakkat, that is exactly what I wanted to know.'

From the loading ramp he watched Bakkat trot out of the gateway, and take the path back towards the mountains. He wondered when last the little man had rested or slept, but the question was irrelevant. Bakkat would keep on as long as his duty beckoned him.

'Tom!' He heard Sarah call his name, and turned to see her hurrying towards him from the kitchens. To his surprise he saw that she was wearing breeches, riding boots and a wide brimmed straw hat tied down with a red bandanna under her chin. 'What was Bakkat doing here?'

'He has found Jim.'

'And the girl?'

'Yes.' He nodded reluctantly. 'The girl also.'

'Then why aren't we ready to leave yet?' she demanded.

'We?' he asked. '*We* are going nowhere. But *I* will be ready to leave within the next hour.'

Sarah placed her clenched fists on her hips. He knew that that was the equivalent of the first rumbling of an active volcano about to erupt. 'Thomas Courtney,' she said coolly, but the light of battle shone in her eyes, 'James is my son. My only child. Do you think for one moment that I will sit here in my kitchen while you ride off to bid him farewell, possibly for ever?'

'I will give him your maternal love,' he offered, 'and when I return, I will describe the girl to you in minute detail.'

He argued a little longer, but when he rode out through the gates of High Weald Sarah rode at his side. Her chin was up, and she was trying not to smile triumphantly. She glanced sideways at him and said sweetly, 'Tom Courtney, you are still the most handsome man I have ever laid eyes upon, except when you are sulking.'

'I am not sulking. I never sulk,' he said sulkily.

'I will race you to the ford,' she said. 'Winner may claim a kiss.' She tickled the mare's rump with the switch she carried, and bounded forward. Tom tried to hold the stallion, but he danced in a circle, eager to be after them.

'Damn it! All right then.' Tom let him have his head. He had given the mare too much of a start, and Sarah was an expert horsewoman.

She was waiting for him at the ford, with flushed cheeks and sparkling eyes. 'Where is my kiss?' she asked. He leaned out of the saddle to take her in a bear-hug. 'That is just an instalment,' he promised, as he set her back in the saddle. 'You will get the main payment tonight.'

Jim had a well-developed sense of direction, but Bakkat knew it was not infallible. He remembered the time when Jim had slipped away from camp while everyone else was sleeping in the heat of noon. Jim had seen a small herd of gemsbuck on the horizon, and as they were short of meat he had ridden after them. Three days later, Bakkat had found him wandering in circles through the trackless hills, leading a lame horse, and half crazed with thirst.

Jim hated to be reminded of that episode, and before they parted at Majuba he had listened with full attention while Bakkat gave him detailed directions on how to find his way through the mountains, following the well-defined game trails used for centuries past by the elephant and eland herds. One of these would lead him to a ford on the Gariep river where it debouched on to the plains at the frontier where the wilderness began. From that point the Hill of the Baboon's Head stood out clearly on the horizon to the east. Bakkat could rely on Jim to follow those directions accurately, so he had a clear picture in his mind of where Jim might be now, and what route he must take to intercept him.

Bakkat cut through the foothills and was well out to the north before he turned back into the main range, and went up between tall umber-coloured cliffs into the high valleys. On the fifth day after leaving High Weald he cut their sign. With two steel-shod horses and six heavily laden mules they had left a well-trodden spoor. Before noon he had caught up with Jim's party. He did not announce himself, but instead circled out ahead of them to wait beside the path they must follow.

Bakkat watched Jim coming down the path at the head of the file. As Drumfire came level with his hiding-place, he popped up from behind his boulder like the *ajinni* from the lamp and shouted shrilly, 'I see you, Somoya!' Drumfire was so startled that he shied wildly. Jim, also taken by surprise, was thrown on to his neck, and Bakkat shrieked with laughter at the joke. Jim recovered his balance instantly and rode after him as Bakkat darted away down the game path, still hooting with laughter. Jim snatched off his hat, leaned out of the saddle and slapped him with it round the head and shoulders.

'You horrible little man! You are so small, so tiny, so minute that I did not even see you.' These insults sent Bakkat into such paroxysms of mirth that he fell and rolled on the earth.

When Bakkat had recovered sufficiently to stand up again, Jim looked him over carefully while they greeted each other with a little more formality. Now it was apparent how finely drawn Bakkat was. Even though his tribe were famous for their fortitude and endurance, over the past week Bakkat had run over a hundred leagues through mountainous terrain, without allowing himself time to eat or drink adequately, or to sleep for more than a few hours. Instead of being golden and glossy, his skin was as grey and dusty as the ashes of last night's campfire. His head looked like a skull, and his gaunt cheek-bones stood proud. His eyes had sunk deeply into their sockets. A Bushman's buttocks are like the camel's hump: when he is well-fed and rested they are majestic, and sway independently as he walks. Bakkat's backside had collapsed into folds of loose skin that dangled out of the back of his kilt. His legs and arms were as thin as the limbs of a praying mantis.

'Zama,' Jim called as he brought up the string of mules. 'Unload one of the *chagga* bags.'

When Bakkat started to make his report, Jim silenced him. 'Eat and drink first,' he ordered, 'and then sleep. We can talk later.'

Zama dragged up one of the leather bags filled with *chagga* made from the eland meat. The salted strips had been half dried in the sun, then packed so tightly into the bag that the air and the flies could not get to them. The first African travellers had probably taken the idea from the pemmican of the North American Indians. Treated like this the meat would not putrefy, but keep indefinitely. It retained much of its moisture, and though the taste was high and gamy, the salt disguised the tang of rot. It was a taste that, in circumstances of need, could be readily acquired.

Bakkat sat in the shade by the mountain stream and, with a heap of the black *chagga* sticks in front of him, began to eat. After Louisa had bathed in one of the pools further downstream she came to sit beside Jim and they watched Bakkat eat.

After a while she asked, 'How much more can he take in?'

'He is only now starting to get the taste for it,' Jim said.

Much later she said, 'Look at his stomach. It's beginning to swell.'

Bakkat stood up and went to kneel at the pool. 'He has finished!' Louisa said. 'I thought he would go on until he burst.'

'No.' Jim shook his head. 'He just needs to wash it down to make room for the next course.'

Bakkat returned from the pool, water dripping from his

chin, and fell on the pile of *chagga* with undiminished appetite. Louisa clapped her hands and laughed with amazement. 'He is so tiny, it does not seem possible! He is never going to stop.'

But at last he did. With an apparent effort he forced down one last mouthful. Then he sat cross-legged and glassy eyed and hiccuped loudly.

'He looks as though he is eight months along with child.' Jim pointed out his bulging stomach. Louisa blushed at such an intimate and improper reference, but she could not hold back her smile. It was an apt description. Bakkat smiled at her, then collapsed sideways, curled himself into a ball and began to snore.

In the morning his cheeks had filled out miraculously and his buttocks, although not yet restored to their former grandeur, showed a distinct bulge under his kilt. He set upon a breakfast of *chagga* with renewed gusto and, thus fortified, was ready to make his report to Jim.

Jim listened mostly in silence. When Bakkat told him of discovering the evidence that Xhia had followed them into the mountains, that he would certainly bring Keyser to Majuba, that they would follow their spoor from there, Jim looked worried. But then Bakkat gave him his father's message of love and support. The dark clouds around Jim seemed to lift, and his face lit with the familiar smile. When Bakkat had finished, they were both silent for a while. Then Jim stood up and went down to the pool. He sat on a rotten tree stump, and brooded heavily. He broke off a lump of rotten bark, picked out the white wood maggots he had exposed and flicked them into the water. A large yellow fish rose to the surface and, in a swirl of water, gobbled them down. At last he came back to where Bakkat waited patiently, and squatted, facing him. 'We cannot go on to the Gariep with Keyser following us. We will lead him straight to my father and the wagons.' Bakkat nodded. 'We must lead him away, and throw him off the spoor.'

'You have wisdom and understanding far beyond your tender years, Somoya.'

Jim picked up the sarcasm in his voice. He leaned across

160

and gave Bakkat an affectionate cuff. 'Tell me then, Prince of the Polecat Clan of the San, what must we do?'

Bakkat led them in a wide, meandering circle, away from the Gariep, back the way they had come, following game trails and crossing from one valley to the other until they arrived back above the Majuba camp. They did not approach within half a league of the stone and thatch hut, but camped instead behind the eastern watershed of the valley. They made no fire but ate their food cold and slept wrapped in jackal-skin karosses. During the day the men took turns to climb to the high ground with Jim's telescope and watch the camp at Majuba for Xhia, Keyser and his troopers to arrive.

'They cannot match my speed through these mountains,' Bakkat boasted. 'They will not arrive until the day after tomorrow. But until then we must keep well hidden for Xhia has the eyes of a vulture and the instincts of a hyena.'

Jim and Bakkat built a hide of dead cripplewood branches and grass below the crest. Bakkat examined it from all angles to make certain that it was invisible. When he was satisfied, he cautioned Jim and Zama not to use the telescope when the sun was at an angle to reflect from the lens. Jim set himself the first morning shift in the lookout hide.

He had settled down comfortably and sunk softly into a pleasant reverie. He thought about his father's promise of wagons and supplies. With this help, his dreams of a journey to the ends of this vast land might become reality. He thought about the adventures he and Louisa would experience, and the wonders they would find in that unexplored wilderness. He remembered the legends of riverbeds lined with gold nuggets, of the vast ivory herds, the deserts paved with glittering diamonds.

Suddenly he was startled to reality by the sound of a loose pebble rattling down the hillside behind him. He reached instinctively for the pistol on his belt. But he could not risk a shot. Bakkat had chided him none too gently about the musket shot that had brought down the eland and had led Xhia to them.

'Xhia would never have unravelled my spoor if you had not led him on, Somoya. That shot you fired confounded us.'

'Forgive me, Bakkat,' Jim had apologized ironically. 'And I know how you hate the taste of eland *chagga*. It would have been far better for us to starve.'

Now he dropped his hand from the pistol, and reached for the handle of his knife. The blade was long and sharp, and he held it poised for a defensive stroke, but at that moment Louisa whispered softly outside the back wall of the hide, 'Jim?'

The alarm he had felt at her approach was replaced with a lift of pleasure at the sound of her voice.

'Come in quickly, Hedgehog. Don't show yourself.' She crawled in through the low entrance. There was barely room inside the lookout for both of them. They sat side by side, only inches between them. The silence was heavy and awkward. He broke it at last. 'Is everything well with the others?'

'They are sleeping.' She did not look at him, but it was impossible for her not to be intensely aware of him. He was so close, and he smelt of sweat, leather and horses. He was so powerful and masculine that she felt confused and flustered. Dark memories mixed with new conflicting emotions, and she drew as far away from him as the space allowed. Immediately he did the same.

'Crowded in here,' he said. 'Bakkat built it to fit himself.'

'I didn't mean—' she started.

'I understand, Hedgehog,' he said. 'You explained to me once.' She shot him a glance from the corner of her eye, but saw with relief that his smile was unfeigned. She had learned over the past days that the name 'Hedgehog' was not a rebuke or an insult, but friendly teasing.

'You said you once wanted one as a pet.' She followed her thoughts.

'What?' He looked puzzled.

'A hedgehog. Why didn't you find yourself one?'

'Not easy. There aren't any in Africa.' He grinned. 'I've

162

seen them in books. You are the first in the flesh. You don't mind when I call you that?'

She thought about it, and realized that now he was not even teasing her, but using it as an endearment. 'I did at first, but now I am accustomed to it,' she said, and added softly, 'Let me tell you that hedgehogs are sweet little creatures. No, I don't mind too much.'

They were silent again, but it was no longer tense and awkward. After a while she made a peephole for herself in the grass of the front wall. He handed her the telescope and showed her how to focus it.

'You told me you are an orphan. Tell me about your parents,' he said. The question shocked her, and her temper flared. He had no right to ask that. She concentrated on her view through the telescope, but saw nothing. Then the anger subsided. She recognized a deep need to speak of her loss. She had never been able to before, not even to Elise while she still trusted the old woman.

'My father was a teacher, gentle and kind. He loved books and learning.' Her voice was almost inaudible but became stronger and surer as she remembered all the wonderful things about her mother and father, the love and kindness.

He sat beside her quietly, asking a question as her words faltered, leading her on. It was as though he had lanced an abscess in her soul, and let all the poison and the pain escape. She felt a growing trust in him, as though she could tell him everything and he would somehow understand. She seemed to lose track of time, until she was jerked into the present by a soft scratching sound at the back wall of the hide. Bakkat's voice whispered a question. Jim replied and Bakkat went again as silently as he had come.

'What did he say?' she asked.

'He came to take over the watch, but I sent him away.'

'I have been talking too much. What time is it?'

'Out here, time matters little. Go on with what you were saying. I like to listen to you.'

When she had told him everything she could remember of her parents, they went on to discuss other things, anything

163

that came into her head, or wherever his questions led her. It was such a joy for her to talk freely to someone again.

Now that she was at her ease, and her defences were lowered, Jim found, to his delight, that she had a dry, quirky sense of humour: she could be funny and self-deprecating, sometimes sharply observant or wickedly ironic. Her English was excellent, far surpassing the quality of his Dutch, but her accent made things sound fresh, and her occasional lapses and solecisms were enchanting.

The education she had received from her father had armed her with wide knowledge and understanding of a surprising range of subjects, and she had travelled to places that fascinated him. England was his ancestral and spiritual home, but he had never been there, and she described scenes and places he had heard of from his parents but seen only in books.

The hours sped away, and it was only when the long mountain shadows fell over the little hut that he saw the day was almost gone. Guiltily he realized that he had neglected his watch, had not so much as glanced out of his peephole for several hours.

He leaned forward and peered down the mountainside. Louisa jumped with surprise as his hand fell on her shoulder. 'They are here!' His voice was sharp and urgent, but for a moment she did not understand. 'Keyser and his men.'

Her pulse raced and the fine pale hair on her forearms rose. She peered out with trepidation, and saw movement in the valley far below. A column of horsemen was crossing the stream, but at this range it was not possible to identify the individual riders. Jim snatched the telescope out of her lap. He checked the angle of the sun with a glance, but the hut was already in shadow so there was no danger of a reflection from the lens. He refocused it swiftly.

'Xhia the Bushman is leading them. I know that little swine of old. He is as cunning as a baboon and as dangerous as a wounded leopard. He and Bakkat are mortal enemies. Bakkat swears he killed his wife with wizard craft. He says Xhia charmed a mamba to sting her.'

He traversed the telescope, and went on to describe what

164

he was seeing: 'Keyser is close behind Xhia. He is riding his grey. That's another good horse. Keyser is a wealthy man, from the bribes he has taken and with what he has stolen from the VOC. He has one of the finest stables in Africa. He is not as soft as his big belly would suggest. They have arrived a full day sooner than Bakkat expected them.'

Louisa shrank a little closer to him. She felt the cold reptiles of fear slither down her back. She knew what would happen to her if she fell into Keyser's hands.

Jim moved the glass on. 'That's Captain Herminius Koots following Keyser. Sweet Mother Mary, there's a naughty fellow for you! There are stories about Koots that would make you blush or faint. That's Sergeant Oudeman, behind him. He is Koots' boon companion, and they share the same tastes. What interests them mostly is gold and blood and what's under a skirt.'

'Jim Courtney, I'll thank you not to talk like that. Remember, I am a woman.'

'Then I'll not have to explain it to you, will I, Hedgehog?' He grinned, and she tried to look severe, but he ignored her disapproval and reeled off the names of the other troopers following Keyser.

'Corporals Richter and Le Riche are in the rear, bringing up the spare horses.' He counted ten in the little herd that followed the troop. 'No wonder they've made such good time. With all those spares, they'll be able to push us hard.'

Then he snapped the telescope shut. 'I'm going to explain what we have to do now. We have to lead Keyser away from the Gariep river where my father will be waiting for us with wagons and supplies. I'm sorry, but it's going to mean running away like this for days and even weeks more. It will mean much more hard living, no tents or time to build a shelter, short rations once the eland meat runs out – unless we can kill more, but at this season most of the game herds are down on the plains. With Keyser close behind us we won't be able to hunt. It's not going to be easy.'

She hid her fears behind a smile, and a cheerful tone: 'After the gundeck of the *Meeuw* it will seem like Paradise.'

She rubbed the chain galls on her ankles. These injuries were healing: the scabs were peeling away, leaving fresh pink skin underneath. Bakkat had concocted a balm of eland fat and wild herbs for her that was proving almost miraculously efficacious.

'I thought about sending you off to the Gariep with Zama to protect you and take you to the rendezvous with my father, while Bakkat and I led Keyser away, but when I discussed it with Bakkat we decided we could not take the risk. Keyser's Bushman tracker is a magician. You and Zama could never elude him, even with Bakkat playing all the tricks he knows. Xhia would pick up your spoor at the place where we parted and Keyser wants you almost as much as he wants me.' His face darkened as he thought of her left without protection to the mercy of Keyser and Koots and Oudeman. 'No, we will stay together.'

She was surprised at how relieved she felt that he would not leave her.

They watched as Keyser's men searched the deserted hut, then remounted and set off up the valley following the cold trail they had left. They disappeared into the mountains.

'They will return soon enough,' Jim predicted.

I t took Xhia three days to lead Keyser round the wide circuit of the spoor and return to the hills above Majuba. Jim had used this respite to graze and rest the horses and mules. While they waited Bakkat recovered his strength. His backside grew full and fat again while they watched the trail. At a little after noon on the third day, Keyser's column appeared again, doggedly following the old spoor. As soon as Bakkat had them in sight, Jim and his party began to retreat further and further into the mountain fastness. He adjusted their pace to that of the pursuit: they kept far enough ahead of Keyser to keep him under observation and be alert to any sudden dash he might make, or to any other stratagem he and Xhia might conceive to take them unawares.

Their order of march was to send Zama and Louisa ahead with the mules and the baggage. Zama set the best pace that the animals could sustain. They had to be allowed to graze and rest or they would soon weaken and break down. Fortunately the same restrictions on the rapidity of march applied to Keyser's animals, although he had spare horses. Even so, Zama and Louisa were able to keep well out in front.

Bakkat and Jim stayed under Keyser's nose, shadowing him, keeping loose contact, but trying to make certain of his exact whereabouts at all times. Whenever the trail led over a ridge or crossed a watershed they waited on the high ground until Keyser's troop came in sight. Before they moved on Jim counted horses and men through the telescope and made certain that none had detached.

When night fell Bakkat would creep back to watch Keyser's camp from the shadows in case he was planning mischief. He could not take Jim with him. Xhia was a constant danger and, skilled in bush lore as Jim might be, he was no match for Xhia in the darkness. With Louisa and Zama far ahead, Jim would eat alone at his own campfire, then leave it burning to mislead any watcher and slip away into the night, following the other two, guarding their back trail against a surprise attack.

Before it was light Bakkat would break off his vigil over the enemy camp and hurry back to Jim. Then, all that day, they would resume the same order of retreat.

Next morning Xhia was able to read all their movements when he studied the sign they had left. On the third night Keyser ordered a surprise attack. He set up camp at nightfall. His troopers secured the horses, ate their dinners and posted sentries, then the others rolled into their blankets and let the fires die down. They knew from Xhia's observations that Bakkat must be spying on them. As soon as it was dark, Xhia led Koots and Oudeman silently and secretly out of camp. They circled out to try to slip past Bakkat, and surprise Jim at his campfire. But the two white men, even though they

167

had removed their spurs and wrapped rags around their boots to deaden the sound, were no match for Bakkat. He heard every blundering step they took in the darkness. When Xhia and the two white men reached Jim's campfire it was long deserted and the flames had burned down to embers.

Two nights later Koots and Oudeman lay in wait for Bakkat well outside the perimeter of their camp. Bakkat had an animal instinct for survival. He smelt Koots from twenty paces: a white man's sweat and stale cigar smoke have a distinctive aroma. Bakkat rolled a small boulder down the hillside on top of him. Both Koots and Oudeman blazed away with their muskets at the sound. The camp erupted with shouting and gunfire, and neither Keyser nor any of his men got much sleep for the rest of the night.

The next day Jim and Bakkat were watching when the enemy mounted up and came after them again. 'When will Keyser give up, and turn back to the colony?' Jim wondered.

Running beside him, hanging on to a stirrup leather, Bakkat chuckled. 'You should not have stolen his horse, Somoya. I think you have angered him, and made it a matter of pride. We will either have to kill him or give him the slip. But he will not give up before that.'

'No killing, you bloodthirsty little devil. Abduction of a VOC convict and horse theft are bad enough. But even Governor van de Witten could not overlook the murder of his military commander. He would take it out on my family. My father—' Jim broke off. The consequences were too terrible to think about.

'Keyser is no dumbhead,' Bakkat went on. 'He knows by now that we are going to a meeting with your father. If he does not know where, all he has to do is follow us. If you are not going to kill him, you will need help from the Kulu Kulu himself to throw Xhia off our spoor. I could not be certain of doing it even if I were travelling alone. But now we are three men, a girl who has never been in the wilderness before, two horses and six loaded mules. What hope do we have against the eyes, nose and magic of Xhia?'

They reached another ridgeline where they stopped to rest Drumfire and let the pursuit come in sight once again.

'Where are we, Bakkat?' Jim rose in the stirrups and gazed around at the awe-inspiring chaos of mountain and valley that surrounded them.

'This place has no name for ordinary men do not come here, unless they are lost or mad.'

'Then which way are the sea and the colony?' He found it difficult to keep a sense of direction in the maze of the mountains.

Bakkat pointed without hesitation, and Jim squinted at the sun to check his bearings, but he did not question Bakkat's infallibility. 'How far?'

'Not far if you ride on an eagle's back.' Bakkat shrugged. 'Perhaps eight days if you know the road, and travel fast.'

'Keyser must be running out of supplies by now. Even we are down to the last bag of *chagga*, and twenty pounds of maize meal.'

'He will eat his spare horses before he gives up and lets you go to the meeting with your father,' Bakkat predicted.

Late that afternoon they watched, from a safe distance, as Sergeant Oudeman selected one of the horses from the remount herd and led it into a ravine near where Keyser's troop were camped. While Oudeman held its head, and Richter and Le Riche stropped their knives on a rock, Koots checked the flint and priming in his pistol. Then he walked up to the animal and placed the muzzle against the white blaze on its forehead. The shot was muted but the horse dropped instantly and kicked convulsively.

'Horse steaks for dinner,' Jim murmured. 'and Keyser has food for another week at the least.' He lowered his telescope. 'Bakkat, we cannot go on like this much longer. My father will not wait for ever at the Gariep.'

'How many horses do they have left?' Bakkat asked as he picked his nose thoughtfully, and examined what he had excavated.

Jim lifted the glass again and ran it over the distant herd.

'... sixteen, seventeen, eighteen,' he counted. 'Eighteen, including Keyser's grey.' He studied Bakkat's face, but it was innocent. 'The horses? Yes, of course!' he exclaimed. Bakkat's studied expression broke and his face creased into an impish grin. 'Yes. Their horses are the only way for us to attack them.'

The pursuit drove them on relentlessly into wild country where not even Bakkat had ventured before. Twice they saw game – once a herd of four eland crossing the skyline, then fifty beautiful bluebuck in a single herd together. But if they had turned aside to pursue the animals they would have lost ground and the gunfire would have brought Keyser and his troopers on at full tilt – he would be with them before they could butcher their kill. If they shot one of the mules, the same thing would happen. They rode on with the last of their provisions almost gone. Jim hoarded the last handful of coffee beans.

Gradually the pace Zama could maintain with Louisa and the mules fell off. The gap between the two parties dwindled until Jim and Bakkat caught up with them. Still Keyser's troopers came on apace, so that Jim's little band had more and more difficulty holding them off. Fresh horse steaks grilled over the fire seemed to have restored the strength and determination of Keyser's troopers. Louisa was flagging. She had been emaciated before the chase began, and now, with little food and rest, she was nearing the limit of her endurance.

To add to Jim's worries other hunters had joined the chase. Sleeping fitfully in the darkness, cold and hungry, unable to afford time during daylight even to collect firewood, expecting at any moment that Keyser's men might creep up on them, they were startled awake by a terrible sound. Louisa screamed before she could stop herself.

'What is that?'

Jim leaped out of his fur kaross and went to her. He put an arm round her shoulders. She was so terrified that she did not pull away. The sound came again: a series of deep grunts, each louder than the last, crescendoing into a thunder that echoed and rolled off the dark mountains.

'What is it?' Louisa's voice shook.

'Lions,' Jim told her. There was no point in trying to deceive her so, instead, he tried to distract her. 'Even the bravest of men is frightened by a lion three times – when first he sees its spoor, when first he hears its roar, when first he meets it face to face.'

'Once is enough for me,' she said, and although her voice quavered, she gave a small, uncertain laugh. Jim felt a lift of pride at her courage. Then he dropped his arm from her shoulders as he felt her shift uncomfortably in his embrace. She still could not bear a masculine touch. 'They are after the horses,' he told her. 'If fortune favours us, they might go after Keyser's animals instead of ours.' As if in answer to his wish, a few minutes later they heard a fusillade of musket fire further back down the valley where they had seen the enemy set up camp at nightfall.

'The lions must be on our side.' Louisa laughed again, a little more convincingly. At intervals during the rest of the night there came the clap of a distant musket shot.

'The lions are still harassing Keyser's camp,' Jim said. 'With luck they will lose some horses.'

At dawn as they began their flight again, Jim looked back through the telescope and saw that Keyser had lost none of his horses. 'They were able to drive off the lions, more's the pity,' he told Louisa.

'Let's hope they try again tonight,' she said.

It was the hardest day they had so far been forced to endure. During the afternoon a thunderstorm swept down from the north-west and drenched them with cold, driving rain. It blew over just as the sun was setting, and in the last light of the day they saw the enemy less than a league behind them, coming on steadily. Jim continued the retreat long after dark. It was a nightmare march over wet and treacherous ground, through rills that had swollen dangerously with rain. Jim knew in his heart that they could not carry on like this much longer.

171

When at last they halted Louisa almost fell from True-heart's back. Jim wrapped her in a sodden fur kaross and gave her a small stick of *chagga*, almost the last of their food.

'You have it. I am not hungry,' she protested.

'Eat it,' he commanded. 'No time for heroics now.'

She slumped and fell asleep before she had taken more than a few mouthfuls. Jim went to where Zama and Bakkat were sitting together. 'This is just about the end,' he said grimly. 'We have to do it tonight, or not at all. We have to get at their horses.' They had been planning all that day, but it would be a forlorn attempt. Although he kept a bold face, Jim knew it was almost certainly doomed.

Bakkat was the only one of them who had any chance at all of thwarting Xhia's vigilance and getting into the enemy camp undiscovered, and he could not untether all eighteen horses and bring them out on his own.

'One or two, yes,' he told Jim, 'but not eighteen.'

'We must take all of them.' He looked up at the sky. A sickle moon sailed through the streaming remnants of the rainclouds. 'Just enough light to do the job.'

'Bakkat could get into the horselines and cripple them, hamstring them,' Zama suggested.

Jim shifted uneasily: the idea of mutilating a horse was distasteful. 'The first animal would scream so loudly Bakkat would have the whole camp down on him. No, that won't work.'

At that moment Bakkat sprang to his feet and sniffed loudly. 'Hold the horses!' he cried. 'Quickly! The lions are here.'

Zama ran to Trueheart and seized her halter rope. Bakkat darted to the mules to control them. They would be more docile than the two thoroughbreds.

Jim was only just in time. He grabbed Drumfire's head as the stallion reared on his hind legs and whinnied shrilly with terror. Jim was lifted off his feet but he managed to throw an arm around Drumfire's neck, and hold him down. 'Steady, my darling. Whoa now! Easy! Easy!' he soothed him. But still the

172

horse stamped and reared and tried to break away. Jim shouted across at Bakkat, 'What is it? What's happening?'

'It's the lion,' Bakkat panted. 'Foul demon! He has circled upwind, and squirted his stinking piss for the horses to smell. The lioness will be waiting down wind to catch any that break away.'

'Sweet Christ!' Jim exclaimed. 'Even I can smell it!' It was a rank feline stench in the back of his throat, more repulsive than the spray of a tomcat. Drumfire reared again. The odour was driving him crazy. He was beyond control. This time Jim knew he could not hold him. He still had both arms around the stallion's neck but his feet barely touched the ground. Drumfire broke into a gallop dragging Jim along with him.

'The lioness!' Bakkat yelled. 'Beware! The lioness is waiting for you.'

Drumfire's hoofs thundered over the rocky ground, and Jim felt as though his arms were being wrenched out of their sockets.

'Let him go, Somoya. You cannot stop him!' Bakkat screamed after him. 'The lioness will get you too!'

Jim jackknifed his body forward and as his feet struck the earth he used the power of both legs to boost himself high and swing one leg over Drumfire's back. Balancing easily to the stallion's run, he snatch Keyser's pistol from his belt and cocked the hammer with a single movement.

'To your right, Somoya!' Bakkat's voice receded behind him, but he picked up the warning just in time. He saw the movement as the lioness broke from cover and streaked in from his right. She was ghostly pale in the faint moonlight, silent, huge and terrible.

He lifted the pistol and leaned forward. He tried to steer Drumfire with the pressure of his knees, but the horse was far beyond any restraint. He saw the lioness get ahead of them and crouch down, gathering herself to spring. Then she rose from the earth, launching herself straight at Jim. There was no time to aim. Instinctively he pointed the muzzle into her face. She was so close that he could see both her front paws,

173

reaching for him with great curved claws. Her open jaws were a black pit. Her teeth shone like porcelain in the moonlight, and the graveyard stench of her breath blew hot into his face as she roared.

He fired the pistol at the full reach of his right arm, and the muzzle flash blinded him. The weight of the lioness's body crashed into them. Even Drumfire reeled at the weight, but then he gathered himself and galloped on. Jim felt the lioness's claws rip into his boot, but they did not hold. The huge carcass dropped away, tumbled slackly across the hard ground, then lay in an inert pile.

It took seconds for Jim to realize that he had come through the attack unscathed. Then his next care was for Drumfire. He leaned forward and clasped him around the neck, calling to him soothingly, 'It's all over, my sweetheart. Whoa! There's a good boy.'

Drumfire's ears twitched back as he listened to Jim's voice. He slowed down to an easy trot, and at last to a walk. Jim steered him back up the slope. But as soon as he smelt the lioness's blood, he started mincing and dancing, throwing his head nervously.

'Lioness is dead,' Bakkat called out of the darkness. 'Shot through the mouth and out the back of her skull.'

'Where is the lion?' Jim shouted back.

As if in reply they heard the lion roar near the top of the mountain, a good mile off. 'Now she is of no further use to him, he has deserted his wife,' Bakkat sneered. 'Cowardly and thieving beast.'

It was with difficulty that Jim coaxed Drumfire back to where Bakkat stood beside the dead lioness. He was still skittish and nervous. 'I've never seen him so terrified,' Jim exclaimed.

'No animal can stay calm and brave with the smell of lion's piss or blood in his nostrils,' Bakkat told him. Then they exclaimed in the same voice: 'That's it! We have it!'

It was long after midnight by the time they reached the ridge overlooking the enemy camp. Keyser's watchfires had burned low, but they could see that the sentries were still awake.

'Just a small breeze from the east.' Jim held Drumfire's head to calm him. The stallion was still shivering and sweating with terror. Not even Jim's hand and voice could soothe him. Every time the carcass he was towing behind him slithered forward, he rolled his eyes until the whites glared in the moonlight.

'We must keep below the wind,' Bakkat murmured. 'The other horses must not catch the scent until we are ready.'

They had muffled Drumfire's hoofs with leather booties, and wrapped all the metal pieces of his tack. Bakkat went ahead to make sure that the way was clear as they circled out round the western perimeter of the enemy camp.

'Even Xhia has to sleep sometime,' Jim whispered to Bakkat, but he was unconvinced. They closed in slowly and were within half a pistol shot of the perimeter where they could see the enemy sentries outlined against the faint glow of their fire.

'Give me your knife, Somoya,' whispered Bakkat. 'It is sharper than mine.'

'If you lose it, I will have both your ears in exchange,' Jim muttered, as he handed it over.

'Wait for my signal.' Bakkat left him, in his disconcertingly abrupt fashion, seeming to vanish into the air. Jim stood at Drumfire's head, holding his nostrils closed to prevent him whickering at the smell of the other horses so close to him.

Like a wraith Bakkat drifted closer to the fires and his heart leaped as he saw Xhia. His enemy sat on the opposite side of the second fire, his kaross wrapped about his shoulders. Bakkat could see that his eyes were closed and his head nodded on the verge of sleep.

Somoya was right. Bakkat smiled to himself. He does sleep sometimes.

Nevertheless he kept well clear of Xhia, but he slipped almost contemptuously within touching distance past Corporal

Richter who was guarding the horselines. Keyser's grey was the first animal he came to. As Bakkat crept up to it, he began to hum in his throat, a lulling sound. The grey shifted slightly and pricked its ears, but made no other sound. Bakkat took only a moment to sever three strands of its halter rope. Then he moved on to the next horse in the line, still humming his lullaby, and drew the blade carefully across the rope that held it.

He was half-way down the line when behind him he heard Corporal Richter cough, hawk and spit. Bakkat sank to the earth and lay still. He heard Richter's booted footsteps coming down the line and watched him pause beside the grey's head to check the halter. In the darkness he overlooked the unravelling strands of the fraying rope. Then he came on and almost stepped on Bakkat. When he reached the end of the line he unfastened the fly of his breeches and urinated noisily on the earth. When he came back, Bakkat had crawled under the belly of one of the horses, and Richter passed without glancing in his direction. He went back to his place by the fire, and said something to Xhia who grunted a reply.

Bakkat gave them a few minutes to settle again, then crept on down the line of horses, and dealt with each of their halter ropes.

Jim heard the signal, the soft liquid call of a nightbird, so convincing that he hoped that it was indeed the little man and not a real bird that had uttered it.

'No going back now!' He swung up on to Drumfire's back. The stallion needed no urging, his nerves were raw, and as he felt Jim's heels he started forward. The carcass of the lioness, half disembowelled, her reeking guts hanging out of the cavity, slithered after him and Drumfire could stand it no longer. At full tilt he tore into the sleeping camp, and on his back Jim was howling, gibbering and waving his hat over his head.

Bakkat leaped out of the darkness on the far side grunting

and roaring at an incredible volume for such a small frame. It was a perfect imitation of the beast.

Corporal Richter, half asleep, staggered to his feet and fired his musket at Jim as he charged past. The ball missed Drumfire but hit one of the horses tethered in the lines, shattering its front leg. The animal screamed and plunged, snapping its weakened halter rope, then fell and rolled on its back kicking in the air. The other troopers woke and snatched up their muskets. The panic was contagious and they blazed away at imaginary lions and attackers, shouting challenges and orders.

'It's the Courtney bastard!' Keyser bellowed. 'There he is! Shoot him! Don't let him get away!'

The horses were bombarded with shouts and screams and roars, by blasts of gunfire and, finally, by the terrifying scent of lion blood and guts. On the previous night they had been attacked repeatedly by the lion pride, and that memory was still vivid. They could stand no more. They fought their head ropes, kicking, rearing and whinnying with terror. One after another the ropes snapped and the horses were free. They wheeled away and thundered out of the camp in a solid bunch, heading downwind. Close behind them rode Jim on Drumfire. Bakkat darted out of the shadows and seized one of his stirrup leathers. While Drumfire carried him along, Bakkat was still roaring like a ravening lion. In their dust ran Keyser and his troopers, bellowing with rage and firing as fast as they were able to reload.

'Stop them!' Keyser howled. 'They have got the horses! Stop them!' He tripped over a rock and fell to his knees, gasping for breath, his heart pounding as though it were about to burst. He stared after the vanishing herd, and the import of his predicament struck him with full force. He and his men were stranded in tractless, mountainous terrain, at least ten days' march from civilization. Their supplies were severely depleted even those they would not be able to carry with them.

'Swine!' he shouted. 'I will get you, Jim Courtney. I will

not rest until I see you swinging on the gibbet, until I see the maggots filling your skull and dribbling out of your eye-sockets. I swear by all that is holy, and may God be my witness.'

The runaway horses kept bunched together, and Jim herded them along. He cut the rope on which he was towing the lioness, and left her carcass behind. Glad to be rid of his odorous burden, Drumfire calmed down at once. Within a mile the running herd dropped from a gallop to a canter, but Jim kept them moving steadily. Within an hour he knew that none of the troopers, shod as they were and carrying their weapons and equipment, could overhaul them. He slowed down to a steady trot, a pace they could keep up for hours.

Before the attack on Keyser's camp, Jim had sent Zama and Louisa on ahead with Trueheart and the mules. They had had several hours' start, but Jim caught up with them an hour after sunrise. The meeting was emotional.

'We heard the gunfire in the night,' Louisa told Jim, 'and feared the worst, but I prayed for you. I didn't stop until a minute ago when I heard you shout behind us.'

'That's what did it, then, Hedgehog. You must be a champion prayer-maker.' Although he grinned, Jim felt an almost irresistible urge to lift her down from Trueheart's back and hold her close, to protect her and cherish her. She looked so thin, pale and exhausted. Instead he swung down from his own saddle. 'Make a fire, Zama,' he ordered. 'We can warm up and rest. Damn me, if we won't eat the last mouthful of the food, drink the last mug of coffee, then sleep until we wake up.' He laughed. 'Keyser is on his way back to the colony on Shanks's pony and we won't have any more trouble from him for a while.'

This time Jim would not allow Louisa to refuse a mug of coffee, and once she had tasted the bitter liquid she could no longer deny herself, and drank the rest thankfully. It revived her almost immediately. She stopped shivering and a little colour returned to her cheeks. She even raised a wan smile at a few of Jim's worst jokes. He refilled the canteen with boiling water every time it was emptied. Each brew of coffee became progressively weaker but it restored his spirits and he was cheerful and ebullient again. He described to Louisa how Keyser had reacted to the surprise raid, and imitated him staggering about barefoot, waving his sword over his head, bellowing threats and tripping over his own feet in the dark. Louisa laughed until tears ran down her cheeks.

Jim and Zama examined the horses they had captured. They were in good condition, considering the long, gruelling journey that had been forced on them. Keyser's grey gelding was the pick of the herd. Keyser had named him Zehn, but Jim translated that to the English, Frost.

Now that they had remounts they would be able to push on at speed towards the rendezvous on the Gariep. But first Jim rested and grazed the horses knowing that Keyser could not harass them. Louisa took full advantage of this respite. She curled under her kaross and slept. She lay so still that Jim was worried. Quietly he lifted a corner of the fur to make sure she was still breathing.

That morning, just before they had caught up with Zama and Louisa, Jim had spotted a small herd of four or five mountain rhebuck grazing among the rocks higher up the slope from the valley. Now he saddled Frost and Bakkat rode bareback on another of the captured horses. Jim left Louisa to sleep with Zama to guard her, and they rode back to where they had seen the rhebuck. They found that the herd had moved on and the slope was empty, but Jim knew they were unlikely to have gone far. They knee-haltered the horses and left them to graze on a patch of sweet grass with fluffy pink seedheads ripening in the spring sunshine. They climbed the slope.

Bakkat picked up the rhebuck spoor just below the crest, and worked it swiftly, trotting along over rocky ground with Jim striding after him. On the far side of the ridge they found the herd already bedded down in the lee of a cluster of large boulders that sheltered them from the cold wind. Bakkat led Jim in close, leopard-crawling with the musket cradled in the crook of his elbow. At seventy paces Jim knew they could not get closer without bolting the herd. He picked a fat dun-coloured ewe who was lying facing away from him, chewing the cud contentedly. He knew that the musket threw three inches to the right at a hundred paces, so he propped his elbows on his knees for a steady shot and laid off his aim a thumb's width. The ball struck at the base of the ewe's skull with a sound like a ripe melon dropped on a stone floor. She did not move again, except to drop her head flat against the earth. The rest of the herd bounded away, flashing their bushy white tails and whistling with alarm.

They skinned the ewe and gralloched her, feasting on raw liver as they worked. She was only a medium-sized antelope, but young and plump. They left the skin and head and entrails and between them carried the rest of the carcass back to the horses.

Once they had loaded it on to Frost's back, Bakkat stuffed his food bag with strips of fresh raw meat, and they parted. Armed with Jim's telescope, he rode back to spy on Keyser and his troopers. Jim wanted him to make certain that they had abandoned the chase, now that they had lost their horses, and that they were starting on the long, bitter march back through the mountains to the distant colony. Jim would not trust Keyser to do what was expected of him: he was learning to respect the colonel's tenacity, and the strength of his hatred.

By the time Jim reached the camp where he had left Louisa it was after noon, and she was still sleeping. The aroma of roasting rhebuck steaks roused her. Jim managed to brew one more watery canteen of coffee with the old beans, and Louisa ate with obvious relish.

In the late afternoon, just as the sun was settling on the peaks, painting them bloody and fiery, Bakkat rode back into camp. 'I found them about five miles from where we attacked them last night,' he told Jim. 'They have given up the chase. They have abandoned all of the supplies and equipment they could not carry on their backs – they did not even take the time to burn it. I brought back everything I thought we could use.'

While Zama helped him unload the booty, Jim asked, 'Which way are they heading?'

'As you hoped, Xhia is leading them back west again, straight towards the colony. But they are travelling slowly. Most of the white men are suffering. Their boots are better suited to riding than walking. The fat colonel is already limping, and using a stick. It does not seem as though he will be able to carry on much longer, not for the ten days' travel it will take them to reach the colony.' Bakkat looked at Jim. 'You said that you did not want to kill him. The mountains might kill him for you.'

Jim shook his head. 'Stephanus Keyser is no fool. He will send Xhia ahead to fetch fresh horses from the Cape. He might lose some of his belly, but he won't die,' he declared, with assurance he did not feel. He added silently, Or, at least, I hope not. He did not want Keyser's murder laid at the door of his family.

For the first time in weeks they did not have to run to keep ahead of their pursuers. Bakkat had found a small bag of flour and a bottle of wine in one of the saddlebags Keyser had abandoned. Louisa cooked flat unleavened breadcakes over the coals, and kebabs of rhebuck meat and liver, and they washed it down with Keyser's fine old claret. Alcohol is poison to the San, and Bakkat, giggling tipsily, almost fell into the fire when he tried to stand. The fur karosses had dried out after the soaking in the previous day's thunderstorm, and they collected armfuls of cedarwood to feed a fragrant campfire, so they enjoyed their first unbroken sleep for many a night.

Early the next morning they rode on, well fed, rested and mounted, towards the meeting place at the Hill of the Baboon's Head. Only Bakkat was still suffering the ill-effects of the three mouthfuls of wine he had drunk the night before. 'I am poisoned,' he muttered. 'I am going to die.'

'No, you won't,' Jim assured him. 'The ancestors will not take a rogue like you.'

For three days Colonel Stephanus Keyser limped along, leaning heavily on the staff that Captain Koots had cut for him, supported on the other side by Goffel, one of the Hottentot troopers. The trail was endless: steep descents followed by treacherous uphill stretches on which the loose round scree rubble rolled underfoot. An hour before noon on the third day of the march Keyser could go no further. He collapsed with a groan on a small boulder beside the game trail they were following.

'Goffel, you useless bastard, pull off my boots,' he shouted, and offered one of his feet. Goffel struggled with the large, scuffed, dusty boot, then staggered backwards as it came free in his hands. The others gathered around and stared in awe at the exposed foot. The stocking was in bloody ribbons. The blisters had burst and tatters of skin hung from the open wounds.

Captain Koots blinked his pale eyes. His eyelashes were colourless which gave him a perpetual bland stare. 'Colonel, sir, you cannot go on with your feet in that condition.'

'That's what I have been telling you for the last twenty miles, you gibbering idiot,' Keyser roared at him. 'Get your men to build me a carrying chair.'

The men exchanged glances. They were already heavily burdened with the equipment Keyser had insisted they carry back to the colony, including his English hunting saddle, his folding camp chair and bed, his canteen and bedroll. Now they were about to be accorded the honour of carrying the colonel himself.

'You heard the colonel.' Koots rounded on them. 'Richter! You and Le Riche find two cedarwood poles. Use your bayonets to trim them into shape. We will tie the colonel's saddle over them with strips of bark.' The troopers scattered to their tasks.

Keyser hobbled on bare, bleeding feet to the stream and sat on the bank. He soaked his feet in the cold clear water and sighed with relief. 'Koots!' he shouted, and the captain hurried to join him.

'Colonel, sir!' He stood to attention on the bank. He was a lean, hard man, with narrow hips and wide bony shoulders under the green baize tunic.

'How would you like to earn ten thousand guilders?' Keyser dropped his voice to a confidential tone. Koots thought about that sum of money. It represented almost five years' pay on his present level, and he had no illusions about climbing higher up the military ladder. 'It is a large sum of money, sir,' he said cautiously.

'I want that young bastard Courtney. I want him as much as anything I have ever wanted in my life.'

'I understand, Colonel.' Koots nodded. 'I would like to get my hands on him myself.' He smiled like a cobra at the thought, and clenched his fists instinctively at his sides.

'He is going to get away, Koots,' Keyser said heavily. 'Before we ever reach the castle he will be over the frontier of the colony and we will never see him again. He has made a jackass of me, and of the VOC.'

Koots showed no sign of distress at these trespasses. He could not prevent a bleak smile reaching his thin lips as he thought, That's no great feat. It doesn't take a genius to make a jackass of the colonel.

Keyser caught a glimmer of the smile. 'You, too, Koots. You will be the butt of every joke of every drunkard and whore in every tavern in the colony. You will be buying your own drinks for years to come.' Koots's face darkened into a murderous scowl. Keyser pressed the advantage. 'That is, Koots, unless you and I can see to it that he is captured and brought back to give a public performance of the rope dance on the parade outside the castle.'

'He is taking the Robbers' Road to the north,' Koots protested. 'The VOC cannot send troops after him. It's outside their suzerainty. Governor van de Witten would never allow it. He could not flout the orders in council of Het Zeventien.'

'I could arrange for you, my fine fellow, to take an indefinite leave of absence from the Company service. Paid leave, of course. I would also arrange a travel pass for you to cross the frontier on a hunting expedition. I would give you Xhia and two or three other good men – Richter and Le Riche, perhaps? I would provide all the supplies you needed.'

'And if I succeed? If I capture Courtney and bring him back to the castle?'

'I will see to it that Governor van de Witten and the VOC place a bounty on him of ten thousand guilders in gold. I would even settle for his head pickled in a vat of *brandewijn*.'

Koots's eyes widened as he thought about it. With ten thousand guilders he could leave this God-forsaken land for ever. Of course, he could never return to Holland. He was known by a name other than Koots in the old country, and he had unfinished business there that might end on the gallows. However, Batavia was Paradise compared to this backward colony on the tip of a barbaric continent. Koots allowed himself a fleeting erotic fantasy. The Javanese women were famous for their beauty. He had never developed a taste for the simian-featured Hottentots of the Cape. Moreover, there were opportunities in the east for a man who was good with a sword and gun, who did not flinch at the sight of blood, and even more so if he had a purse of gold guilders on his belt.

'What do you say to that, Koots?' Keyser interrupted his day-dreams.

'I say fifteen thousand.'

'You are a greedy fellow, Koots. Fifteen thousand is a fortune.'

'You are a wealthy man, Colonel,' Koots pointed out. 'I know that you paid two thousand each for Trueheart and Frost. I would bring back your two horses, along with Courtney's head.'

At the mention of his stolen horses Keyser's sense of outrage, which he had managed to hold under tenuous control, returned in full force. They were two of the finest animals outside Europe. He looked down at his ruined feet, the pain in them almost as bitter as the loss of his horses. Yet fifteen thousand guilders out of his own purse was indeed a fortune.

Koots saw him wavering. He needed only a gentle push. 'Then there is the stallion,' he said.

'What stallion?' Keyser looked up from his feet.

'The one who beat you at Christmas. Drumfire. Jim Courtney's stallion. I would throw him into the bargain.'

Keyser was weakening, but he set one last condition. 'The girl. The convict girl, I want her also.'

'I will have a little fun with her first.' Although his lean, hard features were impassive, Koots was enjoying the bargaining. 'I will bring her to you damaged but alive.'

'She is probably damaged already.' Keyser laughed. 'And will be more so when that young Courtney ram is finished with her. I want her only to make a good show on the gallows. The crowds always love to see a young girl on the rope. I don't mind what you do to her before that.'

'We have an agreement, then?' Koots asked.

'The man, the girl and the three horses.' Keyser nodded. 'Three thousand each, or fifteen thousand for all of them.'

There were ten men to share the labour of carrying the colonel. A team of four was changed every hour, timed with Keyser's gold watch. The saddle was in the English style, but the work of one of Holland's finest saddle-makers. They secured it in the centre of the carrying poles. Keyser sat at ease with his feet in the stirrups, while two men at each end lifted the poles on to their shoulders and walked away with them. It took them nine days to reach the colony, the last two without food. The shoulders of the men were sadly galled by the weight of the poles, but Keyser's feet had almost healed, and the enforced diet had slimmed down his belly and bulk; he looked ten years younger.

Keyser's first duty was to report to Governor Paulus Pieterzoon van de Witten. They were old comrades, and shared many secrets. Van de Witten was a tall dyspeptic-looking man of not yet forty. His father and grandfather before him had been members of Het Zeventien in Amsterdam, and his wealth and power were considerable. Very soon he would return to Holland and take his seat on the board of the VOC, as long as there were no blemishes on his career or reputation. The activities of this English bandit might conceivably leave such a stain on his reputation. Colonel Keyser described in detail the crimes against the property and dignity of the VOC perpetrated by the youngest Courtney. Slowly he stoked the flames of the governor's outrage, repeatedly hinting at van de Witten's own responsibility in the affair. Their discussion lasted several hours, helped along by the consumption of quantities of Hollands gin and French claret. Finally van de Witten capitulated and agreed that the VOC would offer a reward of fifteen thousand guilders for the capture of Louisa Leuven and James Archibald Courtney, or for positive proof of their execution.

The placing of rewards on the heads of criminals who had fled the colony was a long-established practice. Many of the hunters and traders who had licences to leave the colony supplemented their profits with bounty money for the VOC.

Keyser was well pleased with this result. It meant that he was not obliged to risk a single guilder of his own carefully accumulated fortune to contribute to the bounty he had agreed with Captain Koots.

That same night Koots visited him in the little cottage in the lane behind the Company gardens. Keyser advanced him four hundred guilders to cover the costs of provisioning the expeditionary force that was to pursue Jim Courtney. Five days later a small party of travellers assembled on the banks of the Eerste river, the first river after leaving the colony. They had come separately to the meeting place. There were four white men: Captain Koots, with his pale eyes and colourless hair, his skin reddened by the sun; Sergeant Oudeman, bald, but with heavy drooping moustaches, Koots's right-hand man and accomplice; Corporals Richter and Le Riche, who hunted together like a pair of wild dogs. Then there were five Hottentot troopers, including the notorious Goffel, who was the interpreter, and Xhia, the Bushman tracker. None of them wore VOC military uniform: they were dressed in the coarse homespun and leather of the Cape burghers. Xhia's loincloth was made of tanned springbuck skin decorated with beads of ostrich eggshell and Venetian trade beads. Over his shoulders he carried his bow and bark quiver of poisoned arrows, and round his waist a belt hung with an array of charms and buck horns filled with magical and medical potions, powders and unguents.

Koots swung up into the saddle and looked down at Xhia, the Bushman. 'Take the spoor, you little yellow devil, and drink the wind.' They followed Xhia in single file, each trooper leading a spare horse that carried a pack-saddle.

'Courtney's spoor will be many weeks old before we cut it again,' Koots watched Xhia's bare back and peppercorned head bobbing along ahead of his horse's nose, 'but this hunting dog is a *shaitan*. He could follow a snowball through the fires of hell.' Then he let himself savour the thought of the warrant in his saddlebag signed by Governor van de Witten, and the prospect of fifteen thousand guilders in gold. He smiled. It was not a pretty smile.

Bakkat knew that this was only a respite, and that Keyser would not allow them to escape so easily: sooner rather than later Xhia would be following their spoor again. He scouted well ahead and on the sixth day after the capture of Keyser's horses he found the place ideally suited to his purpose. Here, a stratum of black igneous rock cut diagonally across the floor of a wide valley, through the bed of a fast-flowing river, then climbed the steep far side of the valley. The stratum ran straight and stood out as clearly as a paved Roman road, for no grass or other vegetation grew upon it. Where it crossed the river it was so resistant to the erosion of the waters that it formed a natural weir. The river dropped over the far side, a thundering waterfall, into a whirlpool twenty feet below. The black rock was so hard that not even the steel-shod hoofs of the horses left a scratch upon the surface.

187

'Keyser will come back,' Bakkat told Jim, as they squatted on the shiny black floor. 'He is a stubborn man, and you have made it a matter of his pride and honour. He will not give up. Even if he does not come himself he will send others to follow you, and Xhia will guide them.'

'It will take even Xhia many days and weeks to reach the Cape and then return,' Jim demurred. 'By then we will be hundreds of leagues away.'

'Xhia can follow a spoor that is a year old, unless it has been carefully wiped clean.'

'How will you wipe our spoor, Bakkat?' Jim asked.

'We have many horses,' Bakkat pointed out, and Jim nodded. 'Perhaps too many,' Bakkat persisted.

Jim looked over the herd of mules and captured horses. There were over thirty. 'We do not need so many,' he agreed.

'How many do you need?' Bakkat asked.

Jim considered. 'Drumfire and Trueheart, Frost and Crow to ride, Stag and Lemon as spares and to carry the packs.'

'I will use the rest, horses and mules, to wipe our spoor and act as a decoy to lead Xhia away,' Bakkat declared.

'Show me!' Jim ordered, and Bakkat set about the preparations. While Zama watered the herd above the black rock weir, Louisa and Jim fashioned leather booties from the captured saddlebags and the skins of the eland and rhebuck. These would muffle the hoofs of the six horses they were taking with them. While they were busy with this task, Bakkat scouted downstream. He kept well up on the slope of the valley and never approached the river bank. When he returned they cut out the six chosen horses and strapped the booties over their hoofs. It would not take long for the steel shoes to bite through the leather, but it was only a few hundred yards to the river bank.

They secured the equipment to the backs of the six horses. Then, when all was in readiness, they assembled the entire herd of horses and mules into a tight bunch and walked them easily across the black rock. Half-way across they held the six loaded horses, and let the rest go on and start grazing on the far slope of the valley.

Jim, Louisa and Zama removed their own boots, strapped them on to the backs of their mounts, then led them barefoot along the black stone pathway. Bakkat came behind them, examining each inch of the ground they had covered. Even to his eye they left no sign. The leather booties had padded the hoofs, the bare human feet were soft and pliant, and they had walked slowly, not adding their weight to that of the horses. The hoofs had neither scored nor scratched the rock.

When they reached the river bank Jim told Zama, 'You go first. Once they hit the water the horses will want to swim straight to the bank. Your job will be to prevent them doing that.'

They watched anxiously as Zama waded out along the natural causeway, with the water reaching first to his knees, then to his waist. In the end he did not have to dive over the edge, the racing waters simply carried him away. He struck the surface of the pool twenty feet below and disappeared for what seemed to the watchers an age. Then his head broke out and he lifted one arm and waved up at them. Jim turned to Louisa.

'Are you ready?' he asked. She lifted her chin and nodded. She did not speak, but he saw the fear in her eyes. She walked firmly to the river's edge, but he could not let her go alone. He took her arm, and for once she made no move to pull away from him. They waded out side by side until the water reached over their knees. Then they stopped and teetered slightly, Jim bracing himself to hold her. 'I know you swim like a fish. I have seen you,' he said. She looked up and smiled at him, but her eyes were huge and dark blue with terror. He released his grip on her arm, and she did not hesitate but dived forward and instantly disappeared in the spray and thunder. Jim felt his heart go with her, and was frozen with dread as he peered down.

Then her head burst out of the creaming foam. She had tucked her hat under her belt, and her hair had come down. It streamed over her face like a sheet of shining silk. She looked up at him and, incredulously, he saw that she was laughing. The sound of the waterfall smothered her voice, but he could read her lips: 'Don't be afraid. I'll catch you.'

He guffawed with relief. 'Saucy wench!' he shouted back, and returned to the bank where Bakkat was holding the horses. He led them out one at a time, Trueheart first because she was the most tractable. The mare had watched Louisa take the leap and she went readily enough. She landed with a tall splash. As soon as she came up she tried to head for the bank, but Louisa swam to her head and turned her downstream. When they reached the tail of the pool the bottom shelved and they were able to stand. Louisa waved up at Jim again to signal that they were all right. She had replaced her hat on her head.

Jim brought out the other horses. Crow and Lemon, the two mares, went over without any ado. The geldings Stag and Frost were more difficult, but in the end Jim forced them to take the plunge. As soon as they hit the water Zama swam to them and steered them downstream to where Louisa waited to hold them, belly deep in the middle of the river.

Drumfire had watched the other horses jump, and when his turn came he decided he wanted no part of such madness. In the middle of the stone weir, with turbulent waters booming around them, he staged a battle of wills with Jim. He reared and plunged, losing his footing, then regaining it, backing away and throwing his head around. Jim hung on as he was tossed about, reciting a string of insults and threats in a tone that was meant to sound endearing and soothing. 'You demented creature, I'll use you as lion bait.' In the end he managed to wrestle Drumfire's head around into a position where he could make a flying mount. Once he was astride, he had the upper hand and he forced Drumfire to the edge, where the current did the rest. They went over together, and during the long drop Jim twisted free. If Drumfire had landed on top of him he would have been crushed, but he threw himself clear and as soon as Drumfire's head broke the surface he was ready to seize a handful of his mane, and swim him down to where Louisa and the rest of the horses stood.

Bakkat alone was still at the top of the waterfall. He gave Jim a brief hand signal to urge him on downstream, then went back along the black rock stratum, for a second time scrutinizing the surface for any sign he might have overlooked.

Satisfied at last, he reached the point where the rest of the herd had crossed the black rock. There he worked the masking spell for blinding the enemy. He lifted his leather skirt and urinated, intermittently pinching off the stream between thumb and forefinger as he turned in a circle.

'Xhia, you murderer of innocent women, with this spell I close your eyes so you cannot see the sun above you at noon.' He let fly a mighty squirt.

'Xhia, beloved of the darkest spirits, with this spell I seal your ears so that you might not hear the trumpeting of wild elephants.' He farted with the effort of expelling the next spurt, jumped in the air and laughed.

'Xhia, you stranger to the customs and traditions of your own tribe, with this spell I seal your nostrils so that you might not even smell your own dung.'

His bladder empty, he unstoppered one of the duiker horns on his belt, shook out the grey powder and let it blow away on the breeze. 'Xhia, you who are my enemy unto the death, I dull all your senses so that you will pass this place without divining the parting of the spoors.'

Then, at last, he lit a dried twig of the tong tree from his clay fire-pot and waved it over the spoor. 'Xhia, you nameless filth and excrement, with this smoke I mask my spoor that you may not follow.'

Satisfied at last, he looked down the valley and, in the distance, saw Jim and the others leading the horses away, keeping to the middle of the fast-flowing stream. They would not leave the water until they reached the place he had picked out for them almost a league downstream. Bakkat watched them disappear round the bend of the river.

The horses and mules they were leaving behind as decoys were already spread out down the valley, grazing quietly. Bakkat followed them, picked out a horse and mounted it. In an unhurried manner, not alarming the herd, he gathered it up and began to move it away from the river, crossing the divide into the next steep valley.

He went on for another five days, an aimless meandering through the mountainous terrain, making no effort to hide the

191

spoor. On the evening of the fifth day he strapped the hoofs of the dead rhebuck back-to-front on his own feet. Then he abandoned the herd of remaining horses and mules, and minced away imitating the gait and the length of stride of the living rhebuck. Once he was well clear he laid another magical spell to blind Xhia, in the unlikely event that his enemy had been able to unravel the spoor this far.

He was confident at last that Xhia would not find where the party had split on the rock, and that he would follow the more numerous, undisguised spoor of the herd. When he caught up with it, he would find a dead end.

Now, at last, he could circle back towards the riverine valley where he had parted from Jim and the others. When he reached it, he was not surprised to find that Jim had followed his instructions exactly. He had left the river on the rocky stretch of the bank that Bakkat had selected and doubled back towards the east. Bakkat followed, carefully wiping clean the light spoor the party had left. He used a broom made from a branch of the magical tong tree. When he was well clear of the river, he cast a third magical spell to confuse any pursuit, then followed at a faster pace. By this time he was almost ten days behind Jim, but he travelled so swiftly that even on foot he caught up with them four days later.

He smelt their campfire long before he reached it. He was pleased to find that, once they had eaten the evening meal, Jim had doused the fire under a heavy blanket of sand, then moved on in the dark to spend the night in another better-protected place.

Bakkat nodded his approval: only a fool sleeps beside his own campfire when he knows he may be followed. When he crept up to the camp he found Zama was the sentry. Bakkat bypassed him effortlessly, and when Jim woke in the first light of dawn he was sitting close beside him.

'Somoya, when you snore you shame the lions,' he greeted him.

When Jim recovered from the shock, he embraced him. 'I swear to the Kulu Kulu, Bakkat, that you have grown even

192

smaller since last I saw you. Soon I will be able to carry you in my pocket.'

Bakkat rode ahead on the gelding, Frost. He led them straight towards the cliff that blocked off the head of the valley like a mighty fortress. Jim pushed his hat to the back of his head and gazed up at the wall of rock.

'There is no way through.' He shook his head. High above them the vultures sailed across the rockface on wide wings, coming in to land on the ledges beside their bulky nests of sticks and twigs.

'Bakkat will find the way,' Louisa contradicted him. Already she had complete confidence and trust in the little Bushman. They shared not a single word of a common language, but in the evenings at the campfire the two often sat close together, communicating with hand signs and facial expressions, laughing at jokes that they both seemed to understand perfectly. Jim wondered how he could be jealous of Bakkat, but Louisa was not as at ease with him as she was with the Bushman.

They climbed on upwards, straight towards the solid wall of rock. Louisa had dropped back to ride with Zama, who was bringing up the two spare horses at the rear of the column. Zama had been her protector and constant companion during all the long, hard days of the flight from Keyser, while Jim had been occupied with guarding the back trail and keeping the pursuit at bay. They had developed a rapport too. Zama was teaching her the language of the forests, and as she had an ear for the language she was learning swiftly.

Jim had come to realize that Louisa possessed some quality that drew others to her. He tried to fathom what it was. He cast his mind back to their first encounter on the deck of the convict ship. For him the attraction had been immediate and compelling. He tried to put it into words. Is it that she emanates a feeling of compassion and goodness? He was not

193

sure. It seemed that she hid only from him behind the defensive armour he called her hedgehog prickles; to others she was open and friendly. It was confusing and at times he resented it. He wanted her to ride at his side, not with Zama.

She must have felt his gaze upon her for her head turned towards him. Even at that distance her eyes were an extraordinary blue. She smiled at him through the thin veil of dust kicked up by the hoofs of the horses.

Bakkat stopped half-way up the scree. 'Wait for me here, Somoya,' he said.

'Where are you going, old friend?' Jim asked.

'I go to speak to my fathers, and take them a gift.'

'What gift?'

'Something to eat, and something pretty.' Bakkat opened the pouch on his belt and brought out a stick of eland *chagga* half the length of his thumb that he had been hoarding, and the dried wing of a sunbird. The iridescent feathers gleamed like emeralds and rubies. He dismounted and handed Frost's reins to Jim. 'I have to ask permission to enter the sacred places,' he explained, and disappeared among the proteas and sugarbushes. Zama and Louisa came up and they unsaddled the horses and settled down to rest. Time passed and they were drowsing in the shade of the proteas when they heard the sound of a human voice, tiny with distance, but the echoes whispered along the cliff. Louisa scrambled to her feet and looked up the slope. 'I told you Bakkat knew the way,' she cried.

High above them he stood at the base of the cliff, and waved to them to follow. They saddled up quickly, and climbed up to meet him.

'Look! Oh, look!' Louisa pointed to the vertical gash that split the rockface from the base of the cliff to the crest. 'It is like a gateway, the entrance to a castle.'

Bakkat took Frost's reins from Jim and led the horse into the dark opening. They dismounted and, leading their own horses, they followed him. The passage was so narrow that they were forced to walk in single file with their stirrup irons almost scraping the rock walls on each side. On both sides of them the glassy smooth stone seemed to reach to the strip of blue high above them. The sky was so remote that it appeared thin as the blade of a rapier. Zama drove the spare horses into the opening behind them but their hoofbeats were muffled by the floor of soft white sand. Their voices echoed weirdly in the confined spaces as the passage twisted and turned through the depths of the rock.

'Oh, look! Look!' Louisa cried, with delight, and pointed to the paintings that covered the walls from the sandy floor to her eye-level. 'Who painted these? Surely they are not the work of men, but of fairies.'

The paintings depicted men and animals, herds of antelope that galloped wildly across the smooth stone, and dainty little men who pursued them with arrows nocked to their bows, ready to shoot. There were herds of giraffe, blotched with ochre and cream, long sinuous necks entwined like serpents. There were rhinoceros, dark and menacing, with nose horns longer than the little human hunters who surrounded them and fired arrows into them so that the red blood flowed and dribbled into pools beneath their hoofs. There were elephant, birds and snakes, all the profusion of creation.

'Who painted these, Bakkat?' Louisa asked again. Bakkat understood the sense of the question but not the language she spoke. He turned on Frost's back and answered her in a rush of clicking words that sounded like snapping twigs.

'What does he say?' Louisa turned to Jim.

'They were painted by his tribe, by his fathers and grandfathers. They are the hunting dreams of his people – praise-pictures to the courage and beauty of the quarry and the cunning of the hunters.'

'It's like a cathedral,' Louisa's voice was hushed with awe.

'It is a cathedral.' Jim agreed. 'It is one of the holy places of the San.'

The paintings covered the walls on both sides. Some must have been ancient, for the paint had faded and crumbled and other artists had painted over them, but the ghostly images of the ages blended together and formed a tapestry of infinity. They were silent at last, for the sound of their voices seemed sacrilegious in this place.

At last the rock opened ahead of them and they rode towards the narrow vertical blade of sunlight at the end of the passage. Then they emerged through the rock cleft and the sunlight dazzled them. They found themselves high above the world, with a vulture's view across a vastness that left them silent and astonished. Great plains stretched away, dun and limitless, laced with veins of green where the rivers flowed, and dotted with patches of darker forest. Beyond the plains, almost at the reach of the eye, rose an infinity of hills, rank upon rank, like the serrated fangs of a monstrous shark, fading with distance, purple and blue, until they merged with the blue of the tall African sky.

Louisa had never imagined a sky so high or a land so wide, and gazed upon it with a rapt expression, silent until Jim could bear it no longer. This was his land and he wanted her to share it with him and love it the way he loved it.

'Is it not grand?'

'If I had never believed in God before, I would now,' she whispered.

They reached the Gariep river the next morning, at the point where it debouched from the mountains. Over the aeons its waters had cut this deep pass through the rock. The river was running wide and apple green with the thawing of the high snows.

After the mountains, the air here was warm and caressing. The banks of the river were lined with dense stands of sweet thorn and wild willows, carpeted with spring flowers. The saffron-plumed weaver birds were shrieking and fluttering as they wove their basket nests on to the drooping wands of the willows. Five kudu bulls were drinking at the water's edge. They threw up their massive spiralled horns and stared with astonishment at the cavalcade of horses coming down the far bank to the ford. Then they fled into the sweet thorn with their horns laid back and water dripping from their muzzles.

Jim was the first across the river, and let out a hoot of triumph as he examined the deep tracks cut by steel-shod wheels into the soft earth of the opposite bank. 'The wagons!' he shouted. 'They passed through here less than a month ago!'

They rode on faster, Jim barely able to contain his eagerness. From a distance of many miles he picked out the single *kopje* that stood upon the plain ahead. A forest of camel-thorn trees surrounded the base of the hill, then the conical slopes rose steeply to a buttress of grey rock. This formed a plinth for the weird, wind-carved natural sculpture that surmounted it. It was the shape of a squatting bull baboon, with domed pate and low, beetling brows, his elongated muzzle pointed towards the north, staring out across the lion-coloured plain over which the springbuck herds drifted like puffs of cinnamon-coloured smoke.

Jim kicked his feet out of the stirrups and stood erect on Drumfire's back. Through the lens of the telescope he swept the base of the distant *kopje*. He laughed with joy as he picked out a flash of white in the sunlight, like the sail of a tall ship seen from afar.

'The wagons! They are there, waiting for us.' He dropped into the saddle and as his backside slapped against the leather Drumfire jumped forward and bore him away at full gallop.

Tom Courtney was butchering the venison he had killed that morning. Under the wagon tent one of the servants was turning the handle, another feeding the strips of fresh meat into the sausage-making machine. Sarah was working at the nozzle from which the paste oozed, filling the long tubes of pig's gut. Tom straightened up, glanced out across the veld and spotted the distant dustcloud raised by flying hoofs. He swept off his hat and used it to shade his eyes against the cruel white glare. 'Rider!' he called to Sarah. 'Coming fast.'

She looked up but kept the long coils of sausage running

between her fingers. 'Who is it?' she demanded. Of course, with a mother's instinct, she knew who it was, but she did not want to jinx it by saying the name until she could see his face.

'It's himself!' Tom cried. 'Or if it is not, I will shave my beard. The little devil must have succeeded in showing Keyser a clean pair of heels.'

For weeks they had waited, worried and tried to cheer each other, insisting that Jim was safe, while hope eroded with the passage of the long days. Now their relief and joy were unbounded.

Tom seized a bridle from the rack on the tailboard of the wagon and ran to one of the horses tethered in the shade. He slipped the bit between its jaws and tightened the cheek-strap. Scorning a saddle he went up on its bare back and galloped out to meet his son.

Jim saw him coming and rose in the stirrups, waving his hat over his head, hooting and bellowing like an escaped maniac. They raced towards each other and then as they came level, dismounted on the run, hurled by the momentum of their mounts into each other's arms. They hugged each other, beat each other on the back and danced in a circle trying to swing each other off their feet. Tom ruffled Jim's long hair and pulled and twisted his ears painfully.

'I should thrash you within an inch of your life, you little *skellum*,' he scolded. 'You have given your mother and me the worst days of our lives.' He held him at arm's length and glared at him lovingly. 'I don't know why we bothered. We should have let Keyser have you, and good riddance.' His voice choked, and he hugged Jim again. 'Come on, boy! Your mother is waiting for you. I hope she gives you a royal slice of her tongue.'

Jim's reunion with Sarah was less boisterous but if anything even more loving than it had been with his father. 'We were so worried about you,' she said. 'I thank God with all my heart for your deliverance.'

Then her first instinct was to feed him. Through mouthfuls of jam roly-poly and milk tart he gave his parents a colourful, if expurgated, account of his exploits since he had last seen them. He did not mention Louisa, and they were all aware of the omission.

At last Sarah could contain herself no longer. She stood over him and placed her fists on her hips. 'That's all very well and good, James Archibald Courtney, but what about the girl?' Jim choked on the tart, then looked shamefaced and at a loss for words.

'Out with it, boy!' Tom said, in support of his wife. 'What about the girl – or woman or whatever she may be?'

'You will meet her. She's coming now,' Jim said, in a subdued voice, and pointed to the horses and riders coming towards them across the plain in a cloud of their own dust. Tom and Sarah stood together and watched it drawing closer.

Tom spoke first. 'An't no girl there that I can see,' he said, with finality. 'Zama and Bakkat, yes, but no girl.'

Jim jumped up from the trestle table and came to join them. 'She must be . . .' His voice trailed off as he realized that his father was right. Louisa was not with them. He ran to meet Zama and Bakkat as they rode into camp. 'Where is Welanga? What have you done with her?'

Zama and Bakkat looked at each other, both waiting for the other to answer. At times such as these Bakkat could be conveniently mute. Zama shrugged and took the responsibility of replying. 'She will not come,' he said.

'Why not?' Jim shouted.

'She is afraid.'

'Afraid?' Jim was puzzled. 'What has she got to be afraid of?'

Zama did not reply but glanced significantly at Tom and Sarah.

'What a time for her to start jibbing!' Jim strode towards where Drumfire was enjoying a nosebag of oats. 'I will go and fetch her.'

'No, Jim!' Sarah called softly, but in a tone that stopped him in his tracks. He stared at his mother. 'Saddle Sugarbush for me,' she told him. 'I will go to her.'

From the saddle she looked down at Jim. 'What's her name?'

'Louisa,' he answered. 'Louisa Leuven. She speaks good English.'

Sarah nodded. 'I may be some time,' she said to her husband. 'Now, don't come looking for me, do you hear?' She had known Tom from girlhood, and loved him past the power of words to describe, but she knew that at times he had the tact of a wounded bull buffalo. She flicked the reins and Sugarbush cantered out of camp.

She saw the girl half a mile ahead, sitting under a camel-thorn tree on one of the fallen dead branches with Trueheart tethered beside her. Louisa scrambled to her feet when she saw Sarah riding towards her. On the vast plain she was a tiny forlorn figure. Sarah rode up to her and reined in Sugarbush. 'You are Louisa? Louisa Leuven?'

'Yes, Mistress Courtney.' Louisa took off her hat and her hair tumbled down. Sarah blinked at its golden profusion. Louisa bobbed a small curtsy and waited respectfully for her to speak again.

'How do you know who I am?' Sarah asked.

'He looks just like you, mistress,' Louisa explained, 'and he told me all about you and his father.' Her voice was low but sweet, and trembled on the verge of tears.

Sarah was taken aback. This was not at all what she had expected. But what *had* she expected of an escaped convict? Hard-boiled defiance? World-weariness? Corruption and depravity? She looked into those blue eyes and could find no vice in them.

'You're very young, Louisa?'

'Yes, mistress.' Her voice broke. 'I am so sorry. I didn't mean to get Jim into trouble. I didn't mean to take him away from you.' She was weeping slow, silent tears, which sparkled like jewels in the sunlight. 'We haven't done anything bad together, I promise you.'

Sarah stepped down from Sugarbush's back and went to her. She placed one arm round her shoulders and Louisa clung to her. Sarah knew that what she was doing was dangerous, but her maternal instincts were strong, and the girl was so young. The aura of innocence that surrounded her was almost palpable. Sarah found herself drawn irresistibly to her.

'Come, child.' Gently Sarah led her into the shade, and they sat side by side on the dead branch.

They talked while the sun climbed to its zenith, then began its slow slide down the sky. At first Sarah's questions were probing, and she fought her inclination to let down all her defences and allow this stranger into her inner keep, into the place of trust. From bitter experience she knew that the devil often conceals his true nature behind a beautiful exterior.

Louisa's replies were open, unstinted, almost disconcertingly honest. She never avoided Sarah's searching gaze. She seemed pathetically eager to please, and Sarah felt her reservations crumbling.

At last she took the girl's hand. 'Why do you tell me all this, Louisa?' she asked.

'Because Jim risked his life to save me, and you are Jim's mother. I owe you that at least.' Sarah felt her own tears rising to the surface. She was silent while she brought herself under control.

At last Louisa broke the quiet. 'I know what you are thinking, Mistress Courtney. You are wondering why I was on a convict ship. You wish to know what crime I am guilty of.' Sarah could not trust her voice to deny it. Of course, she wanted to know the answer. Her only son was in love with this girl, and she had to know.

'I will tell you,' Louisa said. 'I have told no one except Jim, but now I will tell you.'

And she did. When she had finished Sarah was weeping with her. 'It is late.' She glanced at the height of the sun, and stood up. 'Come, Louisa, we will go home now.'

Tom Courtney was astonished to see that his wife had been weeping. Her eyes were swollen and red. He could not remember the last time that had happened, for Sarah was not much given to tears. She did not dismount, or make any move to introduce him to the pale girl who rode beside her into the camp.

'We need to be alone for a while, before Louisa is ready to meet you,' she told him firmly, and the girl kept her head down and her eyes averted as they rode past and went to the last wagon in the line. The two women disappeared behind the afterclap, the canvas screen at the back of the wagon, and Sarah called for the servants to bring the copper hipbath and buckets of hot water from the cooking fire. The mysterious chest that she had ordered to be loaded on to the wagon, which they had carried with them from High Weald, contained everything that a girl might need.

The two men were sitting beside the fire on the *riempie* camp chairs, the backs and seats laced with the criss-crossed rawhide strips that gave the chairs the name. They were drinking coffee, and Tom had laced their mugs with a liberal dram of Hollands gin. They were still discussing everything that had overtaken the family since their last meeting, and were making plans on how to proceed. They both skirted tactfully around the subject of Louisa and how she fitted into these plans. The nearest Tom had come to it was to say, 'That is women's business. We will have to let your mother decide.'

Night had fallen and out on the plain the jackals were wailing. 'What is your mother doing?' Tom complained. 'It's long past my dinner time, and I'm hungry.' As if she had heard, Sarah came up from the last wagon carrying a lantern, and leading Louisa by the hand. As they stepped into the firelight, both men stared bemusedly at the girl. Jim was as amazed as his father.

Sarah had washed Louisa's hair with lavender-scented soap

from England, then rubbed it dry, brushed it, trimmed the ragged ends and caught it up with a satin ribbon. It hung down her back in a lustrous wave. Her blouse was buttoned demurely at the throat and the sleeves at the wrists. The full skirt just allowed her ankles to peep out from under the hem. White stockings hid the faint scars of the leg irons.

The firelight emphasized the smooth perfection of her skin, and the size of her eyes. Tom stared at her, and Sarah pre-empted any humorous remark he might come up with. 'This is Jim's friend, Louisa Leuven. She may be staying with us for a while.' It was an understatement. 'Louisa, this is my husband Mr Thomas Courtney.' Louisa made one of her graceful curtsies.

'You are welcome, Louisa.' Tom bowed.

Sarah smiled. She hadn't seen him do that for a while – her husband was not the courtly kind. So much for your prison drab, Tom Courtney, she thought complacently, I give you instead a golden Dutch daffodil.

She glanced at her only son, and saw his expression. No doubt about where Jim stands either. It seems that Louisa has been unanimously elected to the Courtney clan.

Later that night Sarah and Tom settled under the blankets in their nightclothes: even down here on the plains the nights were chilly. For twenty years they had slept like spoons, one body fitted into the curve of the other, changing places when one rolled over without waking or losing contact. That night they lay in poignant silence, neither wanting to be the first to speak.

Tom gave in first.

'She is rather pretty,' he ventured.

'You might say so,' Sarah agreed. 'You might even go so far as to say she's no prison drab.'

'I never said that.' Tom sat up indignantly, but she pulled him down again, and cuddled comfortably into the warm bulge of his belly. 'Well, if I did say it, I take it back now.'

She knew how much it cost him to admit that he was wrong, and her heart went out to him. 'I have spoken to her,' she said. 'She's a good girl.'

'Well, if you say so, that's all right, then.' He closed the subject. They began drifting towards sleep.

'I love you, Tom Courtney,' she murmured drowsily.

'I love you, Sarah Courtney,' he replied. 'Young Jim will be a lucky lad if she ever makes him half as happy as you make me.' Usually he scorned what he called mawkishness. This was a rare pronouncement.

'Why, Tom Courtney! Sometimes you can still surprise me,' she whispered.

They were all up before dawn. Louisa emerged from her wagon, which was parked close alongside Tom and Sarah's. Sarah had placed her there deliberately, and sequestered Jim in the furthest. If there had been any nocturnal shenanigans she would have heard every last whisper.

Poor child, Sarah thought with an inward smile. She had to listen to my Tom's snores all night long. In the event her precautions had proved unnecessary: Tom and the jackals had provided all the vocal entertainment and there had been not so much as a whisper from Louisa's wagon.

When Louisa saw Sarah already at the cooking fire she ran to help her with the breakfast, and soon the two were chatting like friends. While Louisa laid rows of sausages to splutter and hiss on the grill, Sarah poured batter on to the flat iron griddle and watched it brown into pancakes.

Tom and Jim were already inspecting the wagons Tom had brought up from the Cape. These were large, powerful vehicles, built in the colony to a design that was constantly being modified to suit the rough African conditions. They ran on four wheels, the front pair of which were used to steer. The pivoted front axle was connected to the *disselboom*, the long, sturdy main drag pole. The team of twelve oxen were inspanned in pairs by a simple system of yokes, yoke-pins and rawhide ropes. The main harness, or *trek-tow*, was connected to the front end of the *disselboom*. The rear wheels were much larger in diameter than the front pair.

The body of the vehicle was a capacious eighteen feet in length, with a breadth of four feet. At the bow the wooden sides were two feet high, rising to over three at the stern. Along both sides of the body, iron staples were riveted to hold the arched greenwood boughs over which was spread the tent. The interior was about five feet high, so a tall man had to stoop beneath it. The awning was double-layered. A strong canvas outer sail rendered it waterproof, or at least deterred the ingress of large quantities of rainwater. A mat of coarse coir fibre, woven from the husk of the coconut, insulated the interior from the worst heat of the sun. The long sail curtains at front and back were called the foreclap and afterclap. The driver's seat was a large chest that stretched the full breadth of the wagon, and there was a similar chest at the rear, the forechest and the afterchest. Along the outsides of the body and under the floorboards were rows of iron hooks from which were suspended pots and pans, tools, canvas bags, powder kegs and other heavy paraphernalia.

Within the wagon another row of hooks held the square-cut canvas side pockets into which were stuffed spare clothing, combs, brushes, soap and towels, tobacco and pipes, pistols, knives, and anything that might be needed urgently. There were also adjustable pegs to support the cardell, the comfortable and spacious bed upon which the traveller slept. By means of the pegs, this could be raised or lowered to make room for the bags, boxes, chests and kegs stored beneath it. Like the camp chairs, the bed was also strung with rawhide *riempies*, criss-crossed like the catgut strings of the racquets used in the royal game of tennis.

Tom had brought four of these enormous vehicles and the oxen to pull them. Each vehicle required a skilled driver, and a *voorloper*, a lad to lead the front oxen by a halter of kudu skin looped about the base of their horns.

All four wagons were heavily laden, and after breakfast Sarah and Louisa were summoned to help take an inventory of the contents. For this purpose the wagons had to be unloaded, and all the goods checked. Tom, as an old ship's captain, had made out an itemized bill-of-lading, and Jim had to know exactly where each item was stowed. It would be wasted and frustrating labour if somewhere out in the wilderness they had to unload and search all four wagons to find a lynch-pin, horse-shoes or a hank of sail twine.

Even Jim was amazed at what his father had provided for them. 'It's all your inheritance, my boy, and there's no more coming to you. Use it wisely.'

The huge yellow-wood chest that Sarah had packed for Louisa was placed in the bows of the wagon that would be Louisa's home over the months, perhaps years to come. It contained combs and brushes, needles and thread, a complete wardrobe of clothing and rolls of cloth to make more, gloves and bonnets to protect delicate skin from the sun, scissors and nail files, scented English soaps and medicines. Then there was a thick book of recipes and prescriptions written in Sarah's own hand, invaluable empirical knowledge gathered at first hand: instructions for cooking everything from an elephant's trunk to wild mushrooms, for making soap and tanning leather; lists of medicinal wild herbs and edible plants and tubers; cures for sunstroke, stomach upsets and a baby's teething problems. Then there was a small library of other books, including a medical lexicon published in London and an almanac beginning at the year 1731, the Holy Bible, ink, pens and writing paper, a box of watercolours and brushes, reams of fine-quality drawing paper, knitting needles and wool, a roll of soft tanned leather from which to make the uppers for footwear – the soles would be cut from buffalo rawhide. Then there was bed-linen, blankets, pillows stuffed with wild-goose down, shawls and knitted stockings, a beautiful kaross of jackal fur, a long coat of sheepskin, and a waterproof cape of tarpaulin with an attached hood. That was but the half of it.

Jim's chest was smaller and contained all his old and well-worn clothing, his razor and strop, his hunting and skinning knives, fishing line and hooks, the tinder box that held his flint and steel, a magnifying glass, a spare telescope, and other items that he would never have considered. They bespoke his mother's concern for his well-being: a long tarpaulin waterproof coat and a wide-brimmed hat of the same material, scarves and gloves, neckerchiefs and woollen socks, a dozen bottles of extract-of-lettuce cough mixture and another dozen of Dr Chamberlain's sovereign diarrhoea remedy.

When they came to the list of general stores and provisions, this seemed endless. At the head of it were eight quarter-chests of coffee beans, totalling six hundred pounds in weight, and three hundred pounds of sugar. Jim was overjoyed to see them. Then there were two hundred pounds of salt for preserving venison, ten pounds of pepper, a large box of strong curry powder, sacks of rice, flour and maize meal, bags of spices and bottles of flavouring essences for stews and cakes, bottles of jam and kegs of pickles from the kitchens of High Weald. Cheeses and hams hung from the hooks inside the wagons. There were pumpkins and sun-dried maize on the cob, and packets and boxes of vegetable seeds to be planted wherever they camped long enough to raise a crop.

For cooking and eating there were three-legged pots, baking, stewing and frying pans, saucepans, gridirons and kettles, water buckets, plates and mugs, forks, spoons and soup ladles. Each wagon was equipped with two fifty-gallon Fagies, or water casks. Then there were canteens and water bottles of military design to carry on horseback. There was fifty pounds of yellow soap, and when this was expended Jim could make more with hippopotamus fat and wood ash.

For the maintenance of the wagons there were two drums of tar to be mixed with animal fat to grease the wheel hubs, heavy coils of rawhide trek ropes, *riems* and straps, yokes and yoke-pins, lynch-pins for the wheel hubs, rolls of canvas and coir matting to repair the tents. One of the afterchests contained a selection of tools such as augers, brace and bits, wood planes and spoke shaves, chisels, a heavy vice, blacksmith's tongs and hammers, and a huge selection of other carpenter's and blacksmith's equipment stores, including two hundred horseshoes, bags of nails and drawing knives to trim hoofs.

'Now, these are important, Jim.' Tom showed him the iron pestle and mortar for crushing rock samples, and a nest of gold pans, each a broad flat dish with a groove around the circumference. The groove would capture the heavy flakes of gold when the ore or river-sands were washed.

'Old Humbert showed you how to use them.' Humbert had been Tom's gold-finder until his liver had succumbed to a steady diet of Hollands gin and cheap Cape brandy. 'There is also a tub of slow-match – two hundred yards of fuse for blasting open the reef when you find gold.'

As trade goods and gifts to African chieftains and potentates, Tom had selected stores that he knew were highly valued by all the wild tribes they might meet in the far interior: two hundred cheap knives, axe heads, bags of Venetian trade beads in fifty different patterns and colours, hand mirrors, tinder boxes, coils of thin copper and brass wire to be converted into bracelets, anklets and other ornaments by the indigenes who received them.

There were two fine English hunting-saddles and tack, common saddles for the servants, two pack-saddles for bringing in venison from the veld, a large bell tent for a kitchen and dining room, folding chairs and tables to furnish it.

For hunting and defence against attack by the more warlike tribes Tom had provided twenty naval cutlasses and thirty smooth-bore Brown Bess muskets, which most of the servants could load and fire with some proficiency, two heavy German elephant guns that threw four to the pound and could drive to the heart of an elephant or a rhinoceros, and a pair of iniquitously expensive London-made two-grooved double-barrelled rifles so accurate that Jim knew from experience that with the conical bullet he could bring down an oryx or kudu at four hundred paces. There was one other rifle, a lovely little lady's gun made in France. Its provenance was noble for the lock was gold inlaid with the coat of arms of the dukes of d'Ademas. Tom had given it to Sarah when Jim was born. It was light and accurate and there was a pink velvet cheek pad on the walnut stock. Although nowadays she seldom hunted, Jim had once seen his mother drop a running springbuck at two hundred paces with this weapon. Now she was giving it to Louisa. 'It may be useful.'

Sarah dismissed Louisa's thanks, but impulsively Louisa threw both arms round her and whispered, 'I shall treasure your gifts, and always remember your kindness to me.'

To serve this battery of guns there was an assortment of lead ladles, bullet moulds, loading ramrods, shot-belts and powder flasks. To manufacture ammunition there were five hundredweight of lead in bars, fifty pounds of pewter to harden the balls to be used against heavy game, twenty thousand prepared lead musket balls, twenty kegs of first-class sporting gunpowder for the rifles and a hundred kegs of coarse black powder for the Brown Bess muskets, two thousand gunflints, greased patches to ensure a tight fit of the conical bullets in the rifle bore, fine cotton cloth to be cut into more patches, and a large keg of rendered hippopotamus fat to grease them.

So great was this store of goods that by nightfall on the second day they had not finished reloading the wagons. 'That can wait until tomorrow,' Tom said expansively, 'but now the ladies are free to make supper for us.'

The last meal together was marred by melancholy silences when they were reminded of their imminent parting. These were followed by bursts of forced jollity. In the end Tom brought it to its conclusion with typical directness. 'Early start tomorrow.' He stood up and took Sarah's hand. As he led her to their quarters in the first wagon he whispered, 'Can we leave them alone? Should we not chaperone them?'

Sarah laughed gaily at him. 'Tom Courtney, what a time for you to turn prissy on me! They have already spent weeks alone in the wilderness together, and it seems they are about to spend several years more. What good could you do now?'

Tom grinned ruefully, picked her up in his arms and boosted her into the wagon. Later as they settled in the cardell bed Sarah murmured, 'Don't worry about Louisa. I have told you already that she is a good girl, and we have brought up Jim to behave like a gentleman. Nothing has happened between them yet, and nothing will until the time is ripe. Then herds of wild buffalo could not prevent it. If things have changed when next we all meet we can think of a wedding. As I recall, Tom Courtney, you showed less restraint when we first met, and there was some delay before we celebrated our own nuptials.'

'In these matters, at least, you are wiser than me,' Tom admitted and pulled her closer. 'Mind you, Mistress Courtney, there are no herds of wild buffalo present to prevent anything happening here tonight, between you and me.'

'Indeed, Mr Courtney, how perceptive of you,' she said, and giggled like a girl.

They had taken breakfast and completed the rest of the loading before the sun had fully dispersed the last of the night's chill. With a single stroke of his trek whip Smallboy, the huge head driver, gave the signal to begin inspanning the oxen. This formidable instrument was a bamboo pole twenty-two feet in length, with a whip thong even longer. Without leaving his seat on the wagon or removing his clay pipe from his mouth, Smallboy could kill a fly on the rump of the lead ox in his team with the tapered forelash of kudu hide and not disturb a hair on the beast's back.

Now as he cracked the long whip with a report like a double-shotted pistol that could be heard a mile away across the plain, the lead boys ran to yoke the oxen in pairs and bring them in from the veld where they had been grazing. They drove them in with shouted insults and well-aimed pebbles.

'Come, Scotland, you snake with twenty-two fathers and only one mother.'

'Hey! Squint Eye, look this way or you will fetch another stone.'

'Wake up, Lizard, you lazy *skellum*!'

'Move along, Blackheart, don't try any of your tricks today.'

Pair after pair the beasts were linked into the span. Then the leaders, the strongest and most tractable animals, were led to their places. Smallboy fired his great whip again and, without apparent strain, the oxen walked away and the heavily loaded wagon rolled smoothly after them. At intervals of a few hundred paces the other three wagons fell into caravan behind the leader. They maintained the wide spacing to avoid the dust raised by the hoofs of the leading oxen and the iron-rimmed wheels of the vehicles they pulled. Behind the wagons followed a loose herd of horses, spare oxen, milk cows and sheep and goats for slaughter. Although they spread out to graze, they were kept in a loose formation and brought along at a leisurely pace by four herd-boys. None of these lads was older than thirteen or younger than ten. They were some of the orphans Sarah had gathered over the years, and who had pleaded to be allowed to join in the great adventure with Somoya, whom they revered. At their heels ran a motley pack of mongrel hounds, who would earn their keep by hunting and finding wounded game or stray animals.

Soon only one small dog-cart remained in the encampment below the Baboon's Head *kopje*, but it was packed and the horses were grazing nearby, ready to take Tom and Sarah back to High Weald. The family were reluctant to part. They drew out the last hour together, drinking a final mug of coffee around the smouldering fire, remembering all the things they had forgotten to say over the last few days, and repeating all those that had been said many times already.

Tom had kept one of the most serious matters to the last. Now he fetched a mariner's tarpaulin chart case from the dog-cart and came back to sit beside Jim again. He opened the flat case, and drew out a chart. 'This is a copy of a chart I've been drawing up over the past fifteen years. I have kept the original, and this is the only copy. It's a valuable document,' he told Jim.

'I will keep it safe,' his son promised.

Tom spread the sheet of heavy parchment on the ground in front of them, and placed small stones on each corner to hold it down in the light morning breeze. Jim studied the finely drawn and coloured topography of the south continent. 'I had no idea, Father, that you were a talented artist.'

His father looked mildly uncomfortable and glanced at Sarah. 'Well,' he drawled, 'I had a little help.'

'You are too modest, Tom.' Sarah smiled. 'You did all the supervision.'

'Of course,' Tom chuckled, 'that was the difficult part.' Then he was serious again. 'The outline of the coast is accurate, more accurate than any other map I have seen. Your uncle Dorian and I made the observations as we sailed and traded along both the western and eastern coastlines over the last twenty years. You have been on one of these voyages with me, Jim, so you will remember these places.' He named them as he pointed them out. 'On the west coast the Bay of Whales and New Devon Harbour – I named it for the old country. On the east coast this is Frank's Lagoon, where your great-grandfather buried the treasure he captured from the Dutch galleon the *Standvastigheid*. It's a fine anchorage guarded from the open sea by an entrance protected by rocky headlands. Here much further north is another great bay, which the Portuguese call Nativity Bay, or Natal.'

'But you don't have godowns built at these ports, Father,' Jim interjected. 'I know that they are desolate, deserted places, all of them.'

'You're right, of course, Jim. But one of our schooners calls in at these places every six months or so, depending on the season and the winds. The natives know that we come regularly, and they wait for us there with hides, gum arabic, ivory and other goods to trade.'

Jim nodded.

Tom went on, 'Because you have already been there, you will recognize any of those places on the coast when you reach it. You know where the mail stones are.' These were large brightly painted flat stones set at prominent places on shore under which visiting sailors could leave letters in waterproof tarpaulin packets to be found by other ships and carried on to the person to whom they were addressed. 'If you leave a letter there you know that I or your uncle will find it in time. We also will leave them for you, on the off-chance.'

'Or I could wait there for the next visit of one of our ships.'

'Yes, Jim, you could do that. But make sure it's not a VOC

212

ship that you meet. By now Governor van de Witten will have a large bounty on your head and Louisa's too.'

They all looked serious as they considered the predicament in which the young couple now stood. Tom went on quickly to cover the pause: 'Before you reach the coast, however, you will have to cross hundreds, even thousands of leagues of virtually unexplored wilderness.' Tom spread his big scarred hand across the map. 'Just look what lies ahead of your wagons. It's an opportunity I've been hankering for all my life. This place where we are sitting now is as far into the interior as I have ever been able to travel.'

'You have nobody to blame for that but yourself, Thomas Courtney,' Sarah told him. 'I never stopped you, but you were always too busy making money.'

'And now it's too late. I'm getting old and fat.' Tom put on a lugubrious expression. 'But Jim here is going in my place.' He stared longingly at the map, then lifted his gaze across the plain to where the wagon train was rolling away in its own yellow dustcloud, and murmured, 'You lucky devil, you are going to see places never before looked upon by civilized eyes.'

Then he returned his attention to the map. 'Over the years I have sought out every man, black, white and yellow, who was ever reputed to have travelled beyond the borders of the Cape colony. I questioned them exhaustively. When Dorian and I went ashore on our trading expeditions we interrogated the natives we traded with. I have written everything that I ever learned from these sources on to this map. I have spelled the names as they sounded in my ear. Here, in the margins and on the reverse side, I have made notes of every story and legend I was told, the names of the different tribes, their villages, kings and chiefs. Then I have tried to mark in the rivers, lakes and water-holes, but there was no way of telling the distances between them and their compass bearings from each other. You, Bakkat, Zama and Smallboy between you speak a dozen or so native dialects. You will be able to hire guides and translators as you travel on and come in contact with new and unknown tribes.' Tom folded the map again and

213

placed it back with reverential care in the tarpaulin case. He handed it to Jim. 'Guard it well, my boy. It will guide you on your journey.'

Then he went back to the dog-cart and brought out a hard leather case. He opened it and showed Jim what it contained. 'I would have liked you to have one of those new-fangled chronometers that Harrison in London has so recently perfected, so that you could more accurately determine your latitude and longitude as you travel, but I have never even laid eyes on one, and they do say that even if you find one they cost five hundred pounds each. The same goes for one of John Hadley's reflecting quadrants. But here are my trusty old compass and octant. They belonged to your grandfather, but you know well how to use them, and with this copy of the Admiralty tables you will always be pretty sure at least of your latitude any time you can see the sun. You should be able to navigate to any of the places I have marked on the chart.'

Jim took the leather case from his father, opened it and lifted out the beautiful, complex instrument. It was of Italian manufacture. On top was the brass ring from which it could be suspended to establish its own level, then the rotating brass rings lovingly engraved with star charts, circles of latitude and a marginal circle of hours. The alidade, or diametral rule, which served as a sun sight, could pick up the sun's shadow, and throw it across the coinciding circles of time and latitude.

Jim fondled it, then looked up at his father. 'I shall never be able to repay you for all these wonderful gifts and for all you have done for me. I do not deserve such love and generosity.'

'Let your mother and me be the judge of that,' Tom said gruffly. 'And now we must start for home.' He called to the two servants who were returning to the colony with them. They ran to inspan the draught horses to the dog-cart, and to saddle Tom's big bay gelding.

Up on Drumfire and Trueheart, Jim and Louisa rode beside the dog-cart for almost a league, taking this last chance to repeat their farewells. When at last they knew they should go no further if they wanted to catch up with their own wagons before sunset, they lingered and watched the dog-cart dwindling across the dusty veld.

'He's coming back,' Louisa exclaimed, as she spotted Tom returning at a gallop. He reined in beside them again.

'Listen to me, Jim, my lad, don't you forget to keep a journal. I want you to record all your navigational notes. Don't forget the names of the native chiefs and their towns. Keep a lookout for any goods we might be able to trade with them in future.'

'Yes, Father. We have spoken about this already,' Jim reminded him.

'And the gold pans,' Tom went on.

'I will pan the sands of every riverbed we cross.' Jim laughed. 'I won't forget.'

'You remind him, Louisa. He is a scatterbrain, this son of mine. I don't know where he gets it from. Must be his mother.'

'I promise, Mr Courtney.' Louisa nodded seriously.

Tom turned back to Jim. 'James Archibald, you look after this young lady. She is obviously a sensible girl, and much too good for you.'

At last Tom left them and rode off after the dog-cart, turning in the saddle every few minutes to wave back at them. They saw him rejoin the distant cart, and then suddenly Jim exclaimed, 'Name of the devil, I forgot to send my respects and farewells to Mansur and Uncle Dorian. Come on!' They galloped in pursuit of the cart. When they caught up with it they all dismounted and embraced again.

'This time we really are leaving,' Jim said at last, but his father rode back with them a mile before he could bring himself to let them go, and he waved them out of sight.

The wagons had long ago disappeared into the distance, but the tracks of their iron-rimmed wheels were scored into the earth, and as easy to follow as a signposted road. As the two of them rode along it the herds of springbuck were driven ahead of them like flocks of sheep, the smaller herds mingling with those ahead, until the land seemed to seethe and the grass was hidden beneath this living sea.

Other larger wild animals became part of this tide of life.

Dark troops of gnu pranced and cavorted, shaking their shaggy manes, arching their necks like thoroughbreds and kicking their hind legs to the sky as they chased each other in circles. Squadrons of quagga galloped away in ranks, barking like packs of hounds. These wild horses of the Cape, striped like the zebra except for their plain brown legs, were so numerous that the Cape burghers killed them in thousands for their hides. They sewed them into grain bags and left the carcasses for the vultures and the hyenas.

Louisa looked upon this host with amazement. 'I have never seen such a marvellous sight,' she cried.

'In this land we are blessed with such multitudes that no man need stint himself or put up his gun until his arms are too exhausted to lift it,' Jim agreed. 'I know of one great hunter who lives in the colony. He destroyed three hundred head of big game in a single day, and rode four horses to a standstill to achieve it. What a feat that was.' Jim shook his head in admiration.

The campfires guided them to the laagered wagons in the last mile of darkness, where Zama had the black iron kettle boiling and coffee beans freshly ground in the mortar.

Relying on his father's chart and navigational instruments, Jim steered the wagons north by east. The days fell into a natural rhythm, and became weeks, which in their turn became months. Each morning Jim rode out with Bakkat to spy out the land that lay ahead, and to find the next water-hole or river. He took his breakfast with him in the canteen slung with his bedroll on the back of his saddle, and Bakkat led a pack-horse to bring in any game they bagged.

Often Louisa was busy around the wagons, mending and cleaning, directing the servants in running her movable home the way she wanted, but most days she was free to ride out with Jim on Trueheart. From the beginning she was enchanted by the animals and birds that teemed in every direction she cast her eye. Jim taught her the names of all of them and they

216

discussed their habits in detail. Bakkat joined in with an endless fund of facts and magical stories.

When they halted at midday to rest and graze the horses, Louisa brought out of her saddlebag one of the pads Sarah had given her and sketched the interesting things they had seen that day. Jim lounged nearby and advised on how she might improve each portrait, though secretly he was amazed at her artistic skills.

He insisted she always carry the little French rifle in the gun sheath under her right knee. 'When you need a gun you need it in a hurry,' he told her, 'and you had better be sure you know how to use it.' He rehearsed her in loading, priming and firing the weapon. With the report and recoil of her first shot she cried out with alarm and would have dropped the rifle, had not Jim been ready to snatch it out of her hands. After much reassurance and encouragement he convinced her that it had not been as fearful an experience as her reaction had indicated, and Louisa expressed herself ready for a second attempt. To encourage her, Jim placed his own hat on a low thornbush twenty paces away.

'I tell you now, Hedgehog, you'll not come within ten feet of it.' It was a calculated challenge. Louisa's eyes narrowed into blue diamond chips of determination. This time her hand was steady. When the gunsmoke cleared after the shot, Jim's hat was spinning high in the air. It was his favourite hat, and he raced after it. When he stuck his forefinger through the hole in the brim his expression was of such disbelief and dismay that Bakkat dissolved into hoots of mirth. He staggered in circles demonstrating with hand signals how the hat had sailed into the air. Then his legs gave way under him, and he collapsed in the dust and beat his belly with both hands, shrieking with laughter.

His mirth was infectious and Louisa broke into peals of laughter. Up to that time Jim had not heard her laugh so naturally and so wholeheartedly. He placed the riddled hat on his head, and joined in the merriment. Later he stuck an eagle feather in the hole and wore it proudly.

They sat in the shade of a sweet thorn tree and ate the

lunch of cold venison and pickles that Louisa had packed into his canteen. Every few minutes one of them would start laughing again and set off the other two.

'Let Welanga shoot your hat again,' Bakkat pleaded. 'It was the greatest joke of my life.'

Jim declined, and instead he blazed the trunk of the sweet thorn tree with his hunting knife. The bright white patch formed an idle target. He was learning that when Louisa set her mind on something she was determined and tenacious. She swiftly mastered the art of loading the rifle: measuring the powder charge from the flask, ramming the wad down upon it, selecting a symmetrical ball from the bag on her belt, wrapping it in the greased patch, and rodding it down the bore, tapping it home with the little wooden mallet until it seated on the wad, then priming the pan and closing the frizzen over it to prevent it spilling.

By the second day of instruction she could load and fire the weapon unaided, and soon she was able to hit the sap-oozing blaze on a tree with four balls out of five.

'This is becoming too easy for you now, Hedgehog. Time for your first real hunt.'

Early the next morning she loaded the rifle in the way he had trained her, and they rode out together. As they approached the first herds of grazing game Jim showed her how to use Trueheart as a stalking horse. They both dismounted and Jim led Drumfire, while she followed in his tracks leading the mare and staying close to her flank. Screened by the bodies of the horses they angled across the front of a small bachelor herd of springbuck rams. These animals had never seen human beings or horses before and they stood and stared with innocent amazement at the strange creatures passing by. Jim approached them on the diagonal, not heading directly towards the herd, which might have alarmed them and set them to flight.

At the point of closest approach, less than a hundred paces from the nearest animals in the herd, Jim halted Drumfire and whistled softly. Louisa dropped Trueheart's reins. The mare stopped and stood obediently, trembling in anticipation of the shot she knew was coming. Louisa sank down and, from a seated position, took careful aim at a ram who was standing broadside to her and slightly separated from the rest of the herd. Jim had drummed into her the point of aiming behind the shoulder, showing it to her on a drawing of the animal, and on carcasses that he had shot and brought into camp.

Nevertheless, she found this different from aiming at a blaze on a tree. Her heart was racing, her hands shook almost uncontrollably and her aim danced up and down and across.

Softly Jim called to her, 'Remember what I told you.'

In the excitement of the hunt she had forgotten his advice. 'Take a deep breath. Swing it up smoothly. Let half of your breath out. Don't hang on the trigger. Squeeze it off as your sights bear.'

She lowered the rifle, gathered herself and did it just the way he had taught her. The little rifle felt light as thistledown as it floated up, and fired of its own accord, so unexpectedly that she was startled by the crash of the shot and long spurt of gunsmoke.

There was a thud of the ball striking, the ram leaped high in the air, and came down in a graceful pirouette. Then its legs collapsed under it, it rolled like a ball across the sun-baked earth, and at last stretched out and lay still. Jim let out a whoop of triumph and raced out to where it lay. With the smoking rifle in her hand Louisa ran after him.

'Shot cleanly through the heart,' Jim cried. 'I could not have done it better myself.' He turned to meet her as she came running up. Her cheeks were flushed, her hair had escaped in glorious disarray from under her hat and her eyes sparkled. Despite her efforts to avoid the sun, her skin had taken on the colour of a ripe peach. Her excitement matched his own, and he thought he had never seen anything as beautiful as she was at that moment.

He reached out with both arms to take her into his embrace. She came up short, just out of his reach and backed away from him. With a mighty effort, he checked his impulse. They stared at each other, and he saw the horror replace the sparkle in her eyes, her revulsion at a masculine touch. It was

219

only a fleeting moment, but he knew how close he had come to disaster. All these months spent in building her trust, in showing her how he respected her, and cared for her well-being, how he wanted to protect and cherish her, all of that so nearly lost in a boisterously impulsive gesture.

He turned away quickly, giving her time to recover from her fright. 'It's a magnificent buck, fat as butter.'

As the animal relaxed in death, the long fold of skin that ran down the centre of its back opened, and it displayed the dorsal plume of snowy white hair. Jim stooped and ran one finger down the fold of skin, then raised the finger to his nose. 'It's the only animal that smells like a flower.' A pale yellow wax from the animal's sebaceous glands coated his finger. He did not look at her. 'Try it,' he suggested.

She averted her eyes from his as she combed her fingers through the animal's dorsal plume, then held them to her own nose. 'Perfumed!' she exclaimed, with surprise. He called Bakkat and between them they gralloched the springbuck and hoisted the carcass on to the pack-saddle. The wagons were tiny specks across the plain. They rode towards them, but the joyous mood of the morning was spoilt, and they were silent. Jim was consumed with despair. It seemed that he and Louisa had lost all the ground they had travelled together, and were back at the starting point of their relationship.

Fortunately, when they reached the wagons there was something to distract him. Smallboy had driven the lead wagon over the underground burrow of an antbear, and the earth had collapsed. The heavily laden vehicle had crashed into the excavation as far as its floorboards. A number of spokes in the offside front wheel were shattered, and the vehicle was firmly stuck. They had to unload it before it was light enough for a double span of oxen to heave it out. Darkness had fallen before they had freed the wagon. It was too late to start repairs to the broken front wheel. The shattered spokes would have to be replaced, and the work of shaving the new parts to fit was finicky and might take days.

Tired and sweat-drenched, Jim went to his own wagon. 'Bath! Hot water!' he shouted at Zama.

'Welanga has already ordered it,' Zama told him disapprovingly.

Well, at least, we know whose side you're on, Jim thought bitterly, but his mood lifted when he found the galvanized-iron bath filled with hot water waiting for him, a bar of soap and a clean towel laid out beside it. After he had bathed he went to the kitchen tent.

Louisa was working at the cooking fire. He was still feeling too affronted by her rejection to thank her or acknowledge her gesture of contrition in preparing his bath. When he entered the tent she glanced up then looked away again quickly.

'I thought you might like a dram of the Hollands that your father gave you.' The gin bottle stood on the camp table ready for him. This was the first time he had seen it since he had parted from his family. He did not know how to decline her offer gracefully, and tell her that he did not like to fuddle his senses with alcohol. He had been drunk only once in his life and regretted the experience. However, he did not wish to spoil this delicate mood, so he poured half a dram and drank it reluctantly.

Louisa had grilled fresh springbuck cutlets for dinner, and she served them with caramelized onions and herbs, a recipe Sarah had given her. This he fell on with great appetite, and his mood improved sufficiently to compliment her. 'Not only well shot, but perfectly cooked.' Yet after that their conversation was stilted and interspersed with awkward silences. They had come so close to being friends, he lamented silently, as he drank a mug of coffee.

'I am off to bed.' He stood up sooner than he usually did. 'How about you?'

'I want to write up my journal,' she answered. 'For me it has been a special day. My first hunt. And, what is more, I promised your father not to miss a day. I will come later.' He left her and made his way to his own wagon.

Each night the wagons were drawn up in a square, and the spaces between them filled with branches of thorn trees, to pen the domestic animals and keep out the predators. Louisa's wagon was always parked alongside Jim's, so that there was only the thickness of the two wagon tents between them. This ensured that Jim was always on hand if she needed him, and during the night, without leaving their separate beds, they were able to speak to each other.

That evening Jim lay awake, until he heard her footsteps coming from the kitchen tent, and saw the glow of her lantern pass along the wall of his tent. Later he heard her changing into her nightdress. The rustle of her clothing conjured up disturbing images of her, and he tried unsuccessfully to banish them. Then he heard her brushing her hair, every stroke of the brush a soft whisper like the wind in a field of ripe wheat. He could imagine the way it rippled and glowed in the lamplight. At last he heard the creak of the cardell bed as it took her weight. Then there was a long silence.

'Jim.' Her voice was low, almost a whisper. It shocked and thrilled him. 'Jim, are you awake?'

'Yes.' His voice sounded loud in his own ears.

'Thank you,' she said. 'I cannot remember when last I enjoyed a day so much.'

'I have enjoyed it also.' He almost added, 'Except—' but he bit back the word.

They were silent for so long that he thought she had fallen asleep, but she whispered again: 'Thank you also for your gentleness.'

He said nothing, for there was nothing to say. He lay long awake, and his hurt slowly gave way to anger. I do not deserve to be treated like this. I have given up everything for her, my home and my family. I have become an outlaw to save her, yet she treats me like some repulsive and poisonous reptile. Then she goes off to sleep as though nothing has happened. I hate her. I wish I had never laid eyes upon her.

222

Louisa lay rigid and wakeful on her bed. She knew he could hear any movement she made and she did not want him to know that she was unable to sleep. She was racked by guilt and remorse. She felt a deep sense of obligation to Jim. She knew only too well what he had sacrificed for her.

Added to this she liked him. It was impossible not to. He was so outgoing and cheerful, so strong, dependable and resourceful. She felt safe when he was near at hand. She liked the way he looked, big and strong, with an open, honest face. He could make her laugh. She smiled as she thought of the way he had reacted when she shot a hole through his hat. He had a quirky sense of humour that she was at last coming to understand. He could retell the day's events in a way that made her laugh with surprise, even though she had witnessed them. She felt that he was her friend when he called her Hedgehog, and teased her in that rude, almost incomprehensible English way.

Even now that he was sulking it was good to know that he was within call. Often in the night when she heard strange wild sounds, the gibbering of hyena or the roaring of a pride of lions, she was mortally afraid. Then he would speak to her quietly through the wall of the tent. His voice reassured her, calmed her fears, and she could sleep again.

Then there were the nightmares. Often she dreamed that she was at Huis Brabant again; she saw the tripod and the silk ropes and, in the candlelight, the dark figure dressed in the costume of the executioner, the black gloves and the leather mask with the eye slits. When the nightmares came upon her she was trapped in those dark fantasies, unable to escape, until his voice woke her, rescued her from the terror.

'Hedgehog! Wake up! It's all right. It's only a dream. I'm here. I won't let anything happen to you.' She always woke to a deep sense of gratitude.

She liked him a little more each day, and she trusted him. But she could not let him touch her. At even the most casual contact – if he adjusted her stirrup leather and touched her ankle, if he handed her some ordinary object like a spoon or a coffee mug and their fingers brushed – she felt afraid and repelled.

Strangely, from a distance she found him attractive. When he rode beside her and she smelt his warm man smell and listened to his voice and his laughter, it made her happy.

Once she had come upon Jim unexpectedly while he was washing in the river. He had still been wearing his breeches, but he had thrown his shirt and leather jacket on the bank; he was scooping handfuls of water and dashing them over his head. His back had been towards her so he had not seen her. For a long moment, before she turned away, she had stared at the smooth, unblemished skin of his bare back. It was in sharp contrast to his sun-browned arms. The muscles were strongly defined below the pale skin and changed shape as he lifted his arms.

She had felt again that wicked stirring of her senses, that shortness of breath, the melting heaviness of her loins, and the unfocused but lascivious longing that Koen van Ritters had awakened in her, before he plunged her into the horrors of his evil fantasy.

I don't want that ever again, she thought as she lay in darkness. I cannot let another man touch me. Not even Jim. I want him to be my friend, but I don't want *that*. I should go into the Church, a nunnery. That is the only escape for me.

But there was no nunnery in the wilderness, and at last she slept.

Xhia led Koots and his band of bounty-hunters back to the camp where Jim Courtney had stampeded their horses, the camp from which they had begun the long march back to the colony. Many weeks had passed since that night, and in the meantime there had been high winds and heavy rainfall in the mountains. To any other eye than Xhia's the elements had washed away every last vestige of the sign.

Xhia worked outwards from the old campsite, following the direction of the stampede, then instinctively divining the direction in which Jim would have driven the stolen herd once he had it under control again. A quarter of a league from the old camp he picked out the faintest trace of the spoor, the scrape of a steel horseshoe on shale that could not have been made by the hoof of an eland bull or any other wild game. He aged the sign, it was not too fresh, nor too old. This was the first peg upon which he began to build the picture of the chase.

He worked away from it searching in the sheltered places, between two rocks, in the lee of fallen trees, in the malleable clay of a donga bottom, in the stratas of shale soft enough to bear an imprint and hard enough to retain it.

Koots and his men followed at a distance, careful not to over-tread and spoil the ancient sign. Often when the spoor was so ethereal as to be obscured from even Xhia's sorcery, they unsaddled their horses and waited, smoking and bickering, playing dice, gambling for the reward money they would win with the capture of the fugitives. At last Xhia, with infinite patience, would unravel that part of the puzzle. He would call them, and they would mount up and follow him on through the mountains.

Gradually the sign became fresher as he narrowed the gap between them and their quarry, and Xhia moved along it with more confidence. None the less, it was three weeks after picking up that first faint hoofprint that Xhia caught up with the wandering herd of mules and horses that Jim and Bakkat had used to lure them on, then abandoned.

At first Koots could not understand how they had been gulled. Here were their horses but no human beings with them. Since the first day he had encountered great difficulty communicating with Xhia, for the Bushman's Dutch was rudimentary and hand signs were not adequate for explaining the complicated nature of the deceit that Bakkat had played upon them. Then it dawned upon Koots that the best horses were missing from this herd of strays: Frost, Crow, Lemon, Stag and, of course, Drumfire and Trueheart.

'They split off, and left this bunch of animals to lead us away.' Koots had understood at last and he blanched with fury. 'For all this time we have been wandering in circles, while those criminals got clear away in another direction.'

His anger needed a focus, and that was Xhia. 'Catch that yellow rat!' he shouted at Richter and Le Riche. 'I want some skin from this stinking little *swartze*.' They grabbed the Bushman before he realized their intention.

'Tie him to that tree.' Koots pointed out a large cripple-wood. They were enjoying this. Their anger with the Bushman was every bit as intense as Koots's: he was directly responsible for their hardship and discomfort over the past months, and retribution would be sweet. They bound him with leather thongs at ankles and wrists. Koots tore off Xhia's leather breech cloth and left him naked.

'Goffel!' Koots shouted at the Hottentot trooper. 'Cut me a bundle of thorn branches this thick.' He made a circle of thumb and forefinger. 'Leave the thorns on them.'

Koots shrugged off his leather coat, and windmilled his right arm, loosening the muscles. Goffel came up from the bank of the stream with an armful of thorn branches, and Koots took his time selecting one that had a pleasing whip and rigidity. Xhia watched him with huge eyes as he strained at his bonds. Koots chopped the thorns off the butt end of the stick of his choice so they would not prick his own fingers, but the rest of the limber wand bristled with the red-tipped spikes. He flourished the scourge as he advanced on Xhia. 'Now, you little reptile, you have led me a fine fandango, but it's your turn to dance now.'

He swung the first cut across Xhia's shoulder-blades. The cane raised a welt upon it, studded with an irregular rash of thorn punctures, from each of which oozed a drop of blood. Xhia howled with pain and outrage.

'Sing, you bastard mating of baboons,' Koots told him, with grim satisfaction. 'You must learn that you cannot take Herminius Koots for a fool.' He swung again. The green branch began to disintegrate with the force of the blows, and the thorns broke off and embedded themselves in Xhia's flesh.

226

Xhia twisted and fought against his bonds until his wrists were rubbed bloody and raw by the leather loops. In a voice too loud for his little frame he screamed his fury and his vows of revenge in a language that the white man could not understand.

'You will die for this, you white hyena! You eater of dung! You copulater with corpses! I shall kill you with the slowest of my poisons, you drinker of snake's piss and monkey sperm.'

Koots discarded the broken branch and selected another. He wiped the sweat off his face with the sleeve of his shirt and began again. He kept it up until both he and Xhia were exhausted. His shirt was sodden and his breathing hoarse. Xhia hung silently on the leather thongs and the blood ran in dark snakes down his back and buttocks to drip into the dust between his feet. Only then did Koots step back. 'Leave him hanging there tonight,' he ordered. 'He should be in a more willing mood by the morning. Nothing like a good thrashing to get these *zwartes* working properly.'

Slowly Xhia turned his head and looked into Koots's face. He spoke softly. 'I will give you the death of twenty days. You will plead with me to kill you at the end.'

Koots did not understand the words but when he saw the hatred in Xhia's beady black eyes he understood the sense, and stepped back involuntarily. 'Corporal Richter,' he said, 'we will have to keep him tied up until he gets over his sore back and his murderous temper.' He picked up Xhia's quiver of poisoned arrows and tossed it on to the fire. 'Don't let him have any weapon until he's learned his lesson. I don't want it between my shoulder-blades. They are treacherous bastards, these little apes.'

In the morning Goffel used the point of his bayonet to dig the thorns out of the punctures that covered Xhia's back, but some had been driven in too deeply. Over the following days they festered and suppurated, before they sloughed to the surface. With the fortitude of a wild thing Xhia recovered his strength and agility swiftly. His expression was inscrutable, and only when he looked at Koots did the hatred gleam out of those anthracite dark eyes.

'Drink the wind, Xhia,' Koots cuffed him casually as he would a recalcitrant dog, 'and don't look at me like that, or I'll waste another thorn tree on your stinking hide.' He pointed back along the trail that had led them to this place. 'Now go back and find where Jim Courtney split his spoor.'

They retraced their footsteps over the ground they had covered during the last ten days. They followed Xhia. Gradually his torn back clotted with festering scabs as his injuries started to heal. However, it seemed that the beating had indeed been beneficial for he worked hard. He seldom lifted his eyes from the ground, except to study the lie of the terrain ahead. They went swiftly for he had their own tracks to use as a marker. Sometimes he followed a spur for a short way until it proved false or illusory, then returned to the main trail.

At last they reached the stratum of black igneous rock beside the waterfall. On the way out they had passed this spot with only a brief pause. Even though this seemed an ideal location for Bakkat to stage a deception, Xhia's suspicions had been only mildly excited. Almost immediately he had picked up the strong clear spoor on the further side of the stratum, and followed it away.

Now he shook his head as he returned to the spot. 'I was a fool. Now I can smell Bakkat's treachery in the air.' He sniffed like a dog getting a whiff of the chase. He reached the place where Bakkat had cast the masking spell, and he picked up a fragment of black ash. He examined it carefully and saw it was the ash of the tong tree, the wizard's tree.

'Here he burned the tong and cast his spell to cheat me. I walked past this place with my eyes blinded.' He was angry at having been so easily deluded by a man he considered his inferior in cunning and wizard-craft. He went down on his hands and knees and snuffled the earth. 'This is where he would have pissed to cover his scent.' But the traces were months old and even his nose could distinguish no residual ammoniac odour of Bakkat's urine.

He stood up again and made a sign of separation to Koots, laying the palms of his hands together, then parting them with a swimming motion. 'This is the place,' he said in execrable

Dutch, pointing left and right. 'Horses go that way. Man go that way.'

'By the blood of the crucifixion, this time you had better be right or I will have your balls. Do you understand?'

'No understand.' Xhia shook his head.

Koots reached down and seized a handful of Xhia's genitalia, and with his other hand drew his dagger. He lifted Xhia on tiptoe by his scrotum, then made the gesture of drawing the blade across the stretched sac, almost touching the skin, but shaving past it by a hair's breadth.

'Cut your balls,' he repeated. '*Verstaan?*'

Xhia nodded soundlessly and Koots pushed him away. 'Get on with it, then.'

They camped on the bank above the waterfall, and Xhia worked both banks of the river for three miles upstream and down. First he covered the water's edge, but in the last ten days or so the river had come down in spate, then subsided again. At the high-water mark dry grass and debris were stranded in the branches of the trees that grew along the banks. Not even the heaviest trodden spoor could have survived the inundation.

Next Xhia moved out from the river bank, climbing up the slopes to the highest point that the flood waters had reached. He worked the ground painstakingly, scrutinizing every inch. All his experience and magic yielded nothing. The trail was gone, washed away. He had no way of knowing whether Bakkat had gone upstream or down. He had come up against an impenetrable wall.

Koots's nerves were already raw, and when he realized that Xhia had failed again he flew into a fit of fury more vicious than the last. He had Xhia bound again, but this time they hung him by his heels over a smouldering fire which Koots stoked carefully with green leaves. Xhia's peppercorn hair frizzled in the heat and he coughed, choked and retched in the smoke as he writhed and swung on the rope's end.

The rest of the band broke off their dice game to watch. They were all thoroughly bored and dispirited by this time, and the lure of the reward was waning as the trail grew colder each day. Richter and Le Riche had already started muttering threats of mutiny, of abandoning the pursuit, escaping from these harsh and merciless mountains and heading back to the colony.

'Kill the little monkey,' said Le Riche in a tone of disinterest. 'Have done with him, and let's go home.'

Instead Koots stood up and drew his knife, slashed the rope that held Xhia suspended, and the little man dropped headlong into the coals. He let out another shriek and rolled out of the fire, only slightly more singed than he had been already. Koots grabbed the end of the rope that was still round his ankles and dragged Xhia to the nearest tree. He tied him there, and left him while he went back to eat the midday meal.

Xhia crouched against the trunk of the tree, muttering to himself and examining his injuries. When Koots had finished eating he flicked the coffee grounds out of his mug, and shouted for Goffel. The Hottentot went with him to the tree and they both looked down at Xhia. 'I want you to tell this little bastard in his own language, that I am going to keep him tied up. He will receive no water or food and I will beat him every day until he does his job and finds the spoor again.'

Goffel translated this threat. Xhia hissed angrily and covered his face, to show how the sight of Koots offended him.

'Tell him I am in no hurry,' Koots instructed. 'Tell him I can wait until he shrivels up and dries in the sun like the baboon turd that he is.'

In the morning Xhia was still tied to the tree, but while Koots and his troopers were eating a breakfast of grilled corncakes and smoked Dutch sausage Xhia called out to Goffel in the language of the San. The Hottentot went to squat in front of him and they spoke together quietly for a long time. Then Goffel came back to Koots. 'Xhia says that he can find Somoya for you.'

'Well, he hasn't done a good job of it so far.' Koots spat a piece of sausage skin into the fire.

'He says that the only way to find the spoor now is to work a solemn magic.'

Le Riche and Richter guffawed scornfully, and Le Riche said, 'If we have come to witchcraft then I'm spending no more time here. I am going back to the Cape, and Keyser can stick his reward up his arsehole.'

'Shut your fat face,' Koots told him, and turned back to Goffel. 'What kind of solemn magic is this?'

'There is a sacred place in the mountains where the spirits of the San have their abode. There, their power is strongest. Xhia says that if we go to this place and sacrifice to the spirits Somoya's tracks will be revealed.'

Le Riche stood up. 'I have heard enough of this mumbo-jumbo. I have listened to it for almost three months and we are still no nearer having the gold guilders in hand.' He picked up his saddle and began to walk towards where his horse was grazing.

'Where are you going?' Koots asked.

'Are you deaf or just stupid?' Le Riche asked belligerently, and placed his right hand on the hilt of his sabre. 'I told you once, but I will tell you again. I am going back to the Cape.'

'It is called desertion and dereliction of duty, but I can understand why you want to go,' Koots said, in such a mild tone that Le Riche looked surprised. Koots went on, 'If anyone else wants to go with Le Riche, I will not stop them.'

Richter stood up slowly. 'I think I will,' he said.

'Good!' said Koots. 'But leave any VOC property when you go.'

'What do you mean, Koots?' Le Riche demanded.

'The saddle and bridle,' Koots said, 'the musket and your sabre are all Company issue. The horse and, of course, your boots and uniform, not to mention your water bottle and blanket.' Koots smiled. 'Just leave all that over there, and you can say goodbye.'

Richter had not yet committed himself, so he sat down again hurriedly. Le Riche stood uncertainly, looking from Koots to his grazing horse. Then, with a visible effort, he steeled himself. 'Koots,' he said, 'the first thing I will do when I get back to the Cape, even if it costs me five guilders, is fuck your wife.' Koots had recently married a beautiful young Hottentot girl. Her name was Nella, and she had been one of the most famous *filles de joie* in the colony. Koots had married her in an attempt to gain exclusive rights to her bountiful charms. That ruse had not been entirely successful, and he had already killed one man who had not understood the niceties of holy wedlock.

Koots glanced at Sergeant Oudeman, his old comrade in arms. Oudeman was bald as an ostrich egg, but he had a fine dark moustache. He understood Koots's unspoken orders, and he let one eyelid droop in acknowledgement. Koots stood up, and stretched like a leopard. He was tall and lean, and his pale eyes were dangerous beneath the colourless lashes. 'One other item I forgot to mention,' he said ominously. 'You can leave your testicles here also. I am coming to get them from you.' With a metallic scraping he drew his own sabre, and walked towards Le Riche. Le Riche dropped his saddle and spun to face him, his blade leaping from the scabbard in a flash of sunlight.

'A long time I have waited for a chance at you, Koots.'

'Now you have it,' Koots said, and lifted his point. He drifted in closer and Le Riche raised his own blade. Steel tapped lightly on steel as they measured each other. They knew one another well: they had trained and practised together over the years. They drew apart and circled.

'You are guilty of desertion,' said Koots. 'It is my duty to arrest you, or to kill you.' He smiled. 'I prefer the second option.'

Le Riche scowled and ducked his head aggressively. He was not as tall as Koots, but he had long simian arms and powerful shoulders. He attacked with a series of lunges, driving in hard and fast. Koots had been expecting this. Le Riche lacked finesse. Koots faded away before him, and when he reached the limit of his extension, Koots riposted with the strike of a puff adder. Le Riche jumped back only just in time but his sleeve was split and a few drops of blood dripped from the scratch on his forearm.

They engaged again, steel scraping and thrilling on steel, but they were neatly matched. They broke and circled, Koots trying to move him towards where Oudeman lounged against the trunk of a thorn tree. Over the years Koots and Oudeman had developed an understanding. Twice Koots almost had Le Riche in position for Oudeman to deal with him, but each time he moved out of the trap.

Oudeman left the thorn tree and moved out towards the cooking fire, as if to refill his coffee mug, but he kept his right hand behind his back. He usually went for the kidneys. A blade in the small of the back would paralyse the victim, and Koots would finish off Le Riche with a thrust through the throat.

Koots changed the direction and angle of his attack, squeezing Le Riche back towards where Oudeman waited. Le Riche jumped back and whirled suddenly, nimble as a ballerina. In the same instant, he slashed his blade across the knuckles of Oudeman's hand, which held the dagger. The knife flew out of his nerveless fingers, and Le Riche spun back to face Koots. He was still smiling. 'Why don't you teach your dog a new trick, Koots? I have seen that one too many times before, and it's becoming boring.'

Oudeman was swearing and clutching his injured hand, and Koots was clearly disconcerted by Le Riche's unexpected ploy. He glanced at his accomplice, and as his eyes left Le Riche's face, Le Riche attacked *en flèche*, the attack of the arrow: he went straight for Koots's throat. Koots stumbled back, and lost his footing. He went down on one knee, and Le Riche pressed home to end it. At the last moment he saw the flare of triumph in Koots's pale eyes and tried to turn aside, but his right foot was leading and Koots went in low, cutting under his guard. The razor steel sliced through the back of Le Riche's boot, and there was an audible pop as it severed his Achilles tendon. Koots was on his feet again in the same instant, and sprang back outside even Le Riche's long reach.

'There is a new trick for you, Corporal, and how do you like it?' he asked. 'Now, pray tell me, who has fucked whom?'

Blood was spurting from the gash in the back of Le Riche's boot, and he hopped back on his good leg, dragging his crippled foot behind him. His expression was desperate as Koots came in again fast, cutting and thrusting at his face. On one leg Le Riche could not hope to hold him off and he toppled over backwards. As he sprawled, Koots made the next cut with the precision of a surgeon. He slashed through the back of Le Riche's left boot and his other tendon parted cleanly. Koots ran his sabre back into its scabbard and walked away from him contemptuously. Le Riche sat up and, with shaking hands and pale sweating face, drew off his boots one at a time. He stared silently at the terrible crippling injuries. Then he tore the hem off his shirt and tried to bind up the wounds, but the blood soaked swiftly through the grubby cloth.

'Break camp, Sergeant,' Koots called to Oudeman. 'Everyone mounted and ready to leave in five minutes. The Bushman is taking us to this sacred place of his.'

The troop rode out of the camp in single file following Xhia. Oudeman was leading Le Riche's horse, and his musket, water bottle and all his other equipment were tied to the empty saddle.

Le Riche crawled after them. 'Wait! You can't leave me here.' He tried to stand, but he had no control of his feet, and he toppled over again. 'Please, Captain Koots, have mercy. In the name of Jesus, at least leave me my musket and water bottle.'

Koots turned his horse back and looked down at Le Riche from the saddle. 'Why should I waste valuable equipment? Soon you will have no further use for it.'

Le Riche crawled towards him on his hands and knees, his crippled feet flopping and dragging behind him like stranded fish. Koots backed his horse away, keeping just out of his reach.

'I can't walk, and you have taken my horse,' he pleaded.

'It's not your horse, Corporal. It belongs to the VOC,' Koots pointed out. 'But I have left you your boots and your testicles. That is enough generosity for one day.' He turned his horse's head and rode after the rest of his troop.

'Please!' Le Riche screamed after him. 'If you leave me here I will die.'

'Yes,' Koots agreed over his shoulder, 'but probably not until the vultures and the hyenas find you.' He rode away. The sound of the horses' hoofs faded, and the silence of the mountains pressed down upon Le Riche with such weight that he felt the last shreds of his courage and resolve crushed beneath it.

It did not take long before the first vulture planed overhead on widespread wings. It twisted its head on its long naked red neck and peered down at Le Riche. Then, satisfied that he was crippled and moribund, and unable to protect himself, it circled in for a landing on the rocky pinnacle above him. It flared its massive wings and stretched out its talons to find purchase on the rock. Then it settled, hump-backed, folded away the long wings, and watched him impassively. It was an enormous bird, black and lappet-faced.

Le Riche crawled to the nearest tree, and leaned against the trunk. He gathered every stone within reach, but they made a pathetically small pile. He hurled one at the crouching vulture, but the range was long, and from a sitting position his throw lacked power. The great bird blinked its eyes but made no other movement. A dead branch had fallen from the tree and lay just within Le Riche's reach. It was too heavy and too awkwardly shaped to wield effectively, nevertheless he placed it across his lap. It was his weapon of last resort, but when he studied the great bird, he knew just how puny it was.

They watched each other for the rest of that day. Once the vulture ruffled out its feathers, then preened them carefully and settled into immobility again. By nightfall Le Riche was thirsty, and the pain in his feet was almost unbearable. The brooding silhouette of the bird was satanic black against the background of stars. Le Riche thought about creeping up upon it as it slept and strangling it with his bare hands, but when he tried to move the pain in his feet held him as effectively as leg irons.

The midnight cold drained his vital force, and he sank into a delirious sleep. The faint warmth of the sun on his face and the dazzle of it in his eyes roused him. For many seconds he did not know where he was, but when he tried to move, the pain in his feet held him fast and brought back the horrors of his predicament in full force.

He groaned and turned his head, then screamed wildly with shock. The vulture had come down from its perch on the rocky pinnacle. It sat close by, just out of his reach. He had not realized the size of the creature. It seemed to tower over him as he sat. Close up it was even more hideous. Its naked head and neck were raw scaly red, and it reeked of carrion.

He snatched up a stone from the pile at his side and hurled it with all his strength. It glanced off the vulture's gleaming funereal plumage. The creature spread its huge wings, wider than he was tall, and hopped back a little, then folded them again.

'Leave me, you foul beast!' he sobbed with terror. At the sound of his voice, it raised its feathers, and ducked the monstrous head on its shoulders, but that was its only reaction. The day drew on and the heat of the sun rose until Le Riche felt that he was trapped in a bread oven, barely able to breathe, and his thirst became a terrible torment.

The vulture sat like a carved cathedral gargoyle and watched him. His senses reeled and the darkness drew in on him. The bird must have sensed it also, for suddenly it spread its wings like a black canopy. It uttered a guttural squawk and bounded towards him, hopping on spread talons. Its hooked beak gaped wide open. Le Riche howled with terror, snatched up the stick from his lap and struck out wildly. He fetched the vulture a blow along its naked neck, with just enough force to knock it off-balance. But it used its wings to recover and hopped back out of his reach again. It folded its wings and resumed its inscrutable vigil.

It was the vulture's indefatigable patience that drove him beyond the bounds of sanity. He raved at it through lips swollen with thirst and cracked by the baking sun until the blood dripped from his chin. The vulture never moved, except to blink its glittering eyes. In his madness he threw his precious stick at its head, his weapon of last resort. The vulture lifted its wings and croaked as the stick glanced off its armoured plumage. Then it settled down again to wait.

The sun reached its zenith, and Le Riche raved and shouted, challenging God and the devil, swearing at the patient bird. He scratched up handfuls of dust and sand to throw at it, until his fingernails were broken off to the quick. He sucked his bleeding fingers to find moisture to slake his thirst, but the dirt clogged his swollen tongue.

He thought about the stream they had crossed on their way here, but it was at least half a mile back down the valley. The picture of the cold tumbling waters excited his dementia. He left the illusionary shelter of the thorn tree, and started crawling slowly back along the rocky pathway towards the river. His feet flopped along behind him, and the crusted sabre cuts burst open and started bleeding again. The vulture smelt the blood, squawked hoarsely and hopped along behind him. Le Riche covered less than a hundred paces, and told himself, 'I will rest for a while.' He lowered his face on to his arm, and lapsed into unconsciousness. The pain woke him. It was as though a dozen spear-heads were being driven into his back.

The vulture was perched between his shoulder-blades, its curved talons locked deeply in his flesh. It was flapping its wings to maintain its balance as it lowered its head and, with a slash of its beak, tore away his shirt. Then it stuck in the hooked, pointed tip and ripped away a long strip of his flesh.

Le Riche screamed hysterically, and rolled over trying to crush the bird under his own body, but with a flap of its wings it rose and settled again close by.

Although his eyesight was blurring and wavering he watched it swallow his flesh, stretching its neck and gulping to force it down. Then it lifted its head and turned its eyes upon him again, holding his gaze unflinchingly.

He knew that it was waiting for him to slip once more into unconsciousness. He sat up and tried to remain alert, singing and shouting at it and clapping his hands, but slowly his voice became an incoherent mumble, his arms fell to his sides and his eyes closed.

This time when he came awake he could not believe the intensity of the pain that overwhelmed him. There was a battering whirlwind of wings around his head and it felt as though a steel hook had been driven through his eye-socket, that his brains were being drawn out of his skull.

He thrashed around weakly on his back, no longer with the strength to cry out, and tried to open his eyes, but he was blind and he could feel sheets of hot blood pouring down his face, filling his good eye, mouth and nostrils so that he was drowning in it.

He reached up with both hands, clutching at the bird's scaly neck, and realized that the bird had driven its beak deep into one of his eye-sockets. It was pulling out his eyeball on the long rubbery string that contained the optic nerve.

They always go for the eyes, he thought, with final resignation, past any further resistance. Blinded and now too weak to lift his hands he listened to the bird somewhere close at hand, gulping down his eyeball. He tried to peer at it through his remaining eye, but it was obscured by a streaming river of blood, too copious for him to blink away. Then the buffeting of heavy wing strokes burst around his head again. The last thing he felt was the point of the beak being driven deeply into his other eye.

Oudeman rode close behind Xhia, holding him on a long rope like a hunting dog on a leash. They all knew that if Xhia left them, perhaps slipping away into the night, none of them was likely to find his way out of this wilderness and back to the distant colony. After the treatment he had received from Koots, this eventuality was more than just a possibility, so they took turns to guard Xhia, keeping him on the rope night and day.

They crossed another small clear stream and turned a corner in the valley between two tall pinnacles of stone. An extraordinary vista opened before them. Their senses had become dulled by the wild grandeur of these mountains, but now they reined in their horses and stared in astonishment.

Xhia began to sing, a plaintive, repetitive chant, shuffling and dancing, as he looked up at the sacred cliffs that rose in front of them. Even Koots was awed. The riven walls of rock seemed to reach to the very sky, and the clouds rolled over the summit, like spilled milk.

Suddenly Xhia leaped high in the air and uttered a dreadful shriek, which startled Koots and raised the fine hair on his forearms. Xhia's cry was picked up in the great basin of stone, and flung back in a glissando of descending echoes.

'Hear the voices of my ancestors answer me!' Xhia cried, and jumped again. 'O holy ones, O wise ones, give me leave to enter.'

'Enter! Enter!' the echoes answered him and, still dancing and singing, Xhia led them up the scree to the foot of the cliffs. The walls of lichen-covered stone seemed to hang over them, and the clouds flying over the tops gave the illusion that the cliff was toppling down on them. The wind thrummed through the turrets and towers of stone like the voices of the long-dead, and the troopers were silent, their horses fidgeting nervously.

Half-way up the scree a massive boulder blocked their way. In ancient time it had fallen out of the cliff face and tumbled down to this resting place. It was the size of a cottage and so almost perfectly rectangular that it might have been shaped by human hand. Koots saw that in the near side of the block there was a small natural shrine. A strange collection of objects was laid in the niche: horns of bluebuck and rhebuck so old they were encrusted with the cocoons of the bacon beetle, the skull of a baboon and the wings of a heron, dry and brittle with age, a calabash half filled with pretty agate and quartz pebbles, water-worn and polished, a necklace of beads chipped from ostrich egg, flint arrow-heads and a quiver that was rotted and cracked.

'We must leave gifts here for the Old People,' Xhia said, and Goffel translated.

Koots looked uncomfortable. 'What gifts?' he asked.

'Something to eat or drink, and something pretty,' Xhia told him. 'Your little shiny bottle.'

'No!' Koots said, but without conviction. He had been saving the last few inches of Hollands gin in his silver flask, rationing himself to an occasional sip.

'The Old People will be angry,' Xhia warned. 'They will conceal the sign from us.'

Koots wavered, then reluctantly unfastened the flap of his saddlebag and brought out the silver flask. Xhia reached up for it, but Koots kept his grip. 'If you fail me again, I will have no further use for you, except to fatten the jackals.' He gave up the flask.

Chanting softly Xhia approached the shrine and poured a few drops of the gin down the face of the rock. Then he picked up a fist-sized stone and battered the metal flask. Koots winced, but kept silent. Xhia placed the flask with the other offerings in the niche, then backed away, still singing softly.

'Now what do we do?' Koots demanded. This place made him nervous. He wanted to be gone. 'What about the spoor?'

'If the Old People are pleased with your gift they will reveal it to us. We must go on into the sacred places,' Xhia told him. 'First you must take this rope from my neck, or the Old People will be angered that you treat one of their own tribe in this manner.'

Koots looked doubtful, but Xhia's plea made good sense. He reached a decision. He drew his musket from its sheath and cocked the hammer. 'Tell him that he must stay close. If he tries to run, I will ride him down and shoot him like a rabid dog. This gun is loaded with goose-shot and he has seen me shoot. He knows I don't miss,' he ordered Goffel, and waited while he translated for the little Bushman.

'Turn him loose.' He nodded to Oudeman. Xhia made no attempt to escape, and they followed him up to the base of the cliff. Abruptly Xhia vanished, as though by the magic of his forefathers.

With a shout of anger, Koots spurred his horse forward, his musket at the ready. Suddenly he reined in and stared with amazement into the narrow gateway in the rock that opened in front of him.

Xhia had disappeared into the dim depths of the passage. Koots hesitated to follow him in there. He could see that once he was inside it the passage was too narrow for him to turn his horse. The other troopers hung back behind him.

'Goffel!' Koots shouted. 'Go in there and pull the little bastard out.'

Goffel looked behind him, back down the slope, but Koots turned the cocked musket on him.

'If I can't have Xhia, then by God you will have to do.'

At that moment they heard Xhia's voice issue from the mouth of the passage, and he was singing.

'What is he saying?' Koots demanded, and Goffel looked mightily relieved.

'It is his song of victory. He is thanking his gods for their kindness in revealing the spoor to him.'

Koots's misgivings evaporated. He swung down from the saddle and strode into the passage. He found Xhia around the first bend, singing, clapping and giggling with triumph. 'What have you found?'

'Look under your feet, you white baboon,' Xhia told him, making sure he would not understand the insult, but pointing at the trampled white sand. Koots understood the gesture, but still he was uncertain. Any definition of the spoor was long ago obliterated: it was merely a dimpling of the surface.

'How can he be sure that this is our quarry?' Koots demanded of Goffel as he came up. 'It could be anything – a herd of quagga or eland.'

Xhia answered this objection with a rapid fire of denials, and Goffel spoke for him: 'Xhia says that this is a sacred place. No wild animal ever passes through here.'

'I don't believe that!' Koots scoffed. 'How would an animal know?'

'If you cannot feel the magic here, your eyes are blind and your ears are deaf indeed,' Xhia told him, but he went to the nearest wall of the passage and peered minutely at it. Then he began to pick things off the rock, the way a baboon picks nits

241

from a companion's scalp. He gathered whatever it was in the palm of his hand, then came back to Koots. Between forefinger and thumb he offered him something. Koots had to look closely to see that it was a hair.

'Behold, with your pale and disgusting eyes, O eater of dung!' he said, so Koots could not understand. 'This white hair came from the shoulder of the gelding, Frost. This brown and silky one from Trueheart when she touched the rock, and this yellow one from Lemon. This dark one is from Somoya's horse, Drumfire.' He hooted scornfully. 'And now do you believe that Xhia is the mightiest hunter of all the San, and that he has worked a great and solemn magic and revealed the spoor to you?'

'Tell the little yellow ape to stop chattering, and take us after them.' Koots tried, unsuccessfully, to disguise his elation.

'What river is that?' Koots asked. They stood on the peak and looked down from the mountains, over endless plains and vistas of rolling grassland, to another range of hills, pale against the milky blue of the tall African sky at noon day.

'It is called the river Gariep,' Goffel translated. 'Or, in the language of the San, Gariep Che Tabong, the River Where the Elephant Died.'

'Why is it called that?' Koots wanted to know.

'It was on the banks of this river when he was a young man that Xhia slew the great elephant he had followed for many days.'

Koots grunted. Since the Bushman had found the spoor again Koots was more kindly disposed towards him. He had treated his burns and other injuries from the field chest of medicines he carried on the pack-horse. Xhia healed quickly, the way a wild animal does.

'Tell him that if he can find where Somoya crossed this river, I will give him a fine cow as his own animal when we return to the colony. Then, if he can lead me to the capture or the killing of Somoya, I will give him five more fat cows.'

Koots was now regretting his previous harsh treatment of the Bushman. He knew that if he wanted to catch up with the fugitives, he must make amends and buy back Xhia's loyalty.

Xhia received this promise of wealth joyfully. Few men of the San owned a sheep, let alone a single head of kine. Childlike, his memory of abuse faded with the offer of reward. He started down the mountain slopes towards the plains and the river with such alacrity that even on horseback Koots was hard-pressed to keep him in sight. When they reached the river they found wild game concentrated on these waters in numbers that Koots had not imagined possible. The herds within the colony had been hunted extensively since the first Dutch colonists, under Governor van Riebeeck, had set foot ashore almost eighty years before. The burghers were all enthusiastic hunters, indulging in the pastime not only for the thrill of the chase but also for the meat, hides and ivory it yielded. Within the borders of the colony at any time of day one could hear the boom of their long *roers*, and in the season of the great animal migrations across the plains they had organized themselves into large mounted parties to hunt the wild horses, the quagga, for their hides, the springbuck and eland for their meat. After one of these great *jags* the vultures darkened the sky with their wings and the stench of death hung in the air for months thereafter. The bleached bones lay like banks of snowy arum lilies, gleaming in the sunlight.

As a consequence of these predations the game had been severely reduced in numbers, and even the quagga had become something of a rarity within the immediate environs of the town and castle. The last elephant herds had been driven far from the frontiers of the colony almost forty years before, and only a few hardy souls occasionally made the journey of months and even years into the remote wilderness to pursue them. In fact, not many white men had ventured even thus far from the safety and security of the colony, which was why this mighty gathering of wild beasts was a revelation to Koots.

Game had been scarce in the mountains, and they were hungry for fresh meat so Koots and Oudeman spurred ahead of the rest of the troop. Riding hard they caught up with a herd

243

of giraffe who had been grazing on the top branches of an isolated clump of acacia trees. These gigantic creatures ran with a ponderous, swaying motion, twisting their bushy tails up on to their haunches. They thrust their long, sinuous necks forward as though to counterbalance their massive bodies. Koots and Oudeman cut a young cow out of the herd of a dozen and, riding hard at her heels, with the stones and pebbles flung up by her hoofs whizzing past their ears they fired into her rump, trying to send a ball through the ridge of her spine, which showed clearly under her dappled brown and yellow skin. At last Koots pressed in so close to her that he almost touched her with the muzzle of his musket, and this time the ball flew true. It severed her spinal column and she collapsed in a cloud of dust and debris. Koots dismounted to reload and as soon as his weapon was recharged he ran close to her. She was thrashing about weakly, but he avoided the convulsive kicks of her long front legs, which could snap the spine of an attacking lion. Then he fired another ball into the back of her skull.

That night while the hyena squalled and squabbled with a pride of lions for possession of what remained of the colossal carcass, Koots and his men feasted around their campfire on marrow from the giraffe's thigh-bones. They cracked the roasted bones between two rocks, and out slid long cylindrical lumps of the rich yellow marrow, as thick as a man's arm and twice as long.

In the dawn when Koots awoke, he found Goffel, who was on sentry duty, fast asleep. Xhia was gone. Raging, Koots booted Goffel in the stomach and crotch, then laid into him with a bridle, swinging the bit end and the metal cheek buckles across his shoulders and close-cropped scalp. At last he stepped back and snarled, 'Now, take the spoor and catch that little yellow ape, or there'll be another helping of ginger for you.'

Xhia had made no attempt to cover his tracks so even Goffel could read them easily. Without breakfast they mounted up and rode after Xhia before he could make good his escape. On the open plain Koots hoped to spot him at a distance, and even a Bushman could not hope to outdistance a good horse.

Xhia's tracks led straight towards the dark green ribbon of riverine bush on the horizon that marked the course of the Gariep river. They were only half-way there when Koots saw the springbuck herds ahead pronking, leaping high in the air with all four feet together and noses almost touching their front hoofs, the snowy dorsal plumes flashing in full display.

'Something's alarming them,' Goffel said. 'Maybe it is the Bushman.' Koots spurred forward. Then, through the dust kicked up by the antics of the springbuck herds, he saw a tiny familiar figure trotting towards them.

'By the breath of Satan!' Koots swore. 'It's him. It's Xhia and he's coming back!'

As he came towards them Xhia broke into a dance and a litany of triumph and self-congratulation. 'I am Xhia, the greatest hunter of all my tribe. I am Xhia, the beloved of the ancestors. My eyes are like the moon for they see all, even in the night. My arrows are swift as swallows in flight, and no animal may run from them. My magic is so powerful that no man may avoid it.'

That same day Xhia led them to the Gariep river, and he showed Koots the wheel ruts of many wagons scored deeply into the soft alluvial earth along its banks.

'Four great wagons and one small one passed this way.' Through Goffel he explained the sign to Koots. 'With the wagons were many animals, horses and cattle and some sheep. See here! The small wagon has returned towards the colony, but the four great wagons have gone on into the wilderness.'

'Whose wagons are these?' Koots asked him.

'In all the colony there are few burghers rich enough to boast five wagons. One of those is Klebe, the father of Somoya.'

'I do not understand.' Koots shook his head.

Goffel explained: 'It seems that while Bakkat and Somoya led us on a chase through the mountains, Klebe came here to the Gariep with these wagons. When Somoya had stolen our horses and knew we could follow him no further, he came back here to meet his father.'

'What of the small wagon that went back towards the colony?' Koots wanted to know.

Xhia shrugged. 'Perhaps after he had given the great wagons to his son, Klebe returned to the Cape.' Xhia touched the wheel marks with his toe. 'See how deeply the wheels have bitten into the earth. They are heavily laden with goods.'

'How does Xhia know all this?' Koots demanded.

'Because I am Xhia, with eyes like the moon, that sees all.'

'That means the little bastard is guessing.' Koots lifted his hat and wiped the sweat from his balding pate.

'If we follow the wagons Xhia will give you proof,' Goffel suggested. 'Or if he does not, you will shoot him and save yourself the cattle you promised him.'

Koots replaced his hat. Despite his forbidding expression he felt more confident of eventual success than at any time since they had left the colony.

It is plain to see that they are carrying much cargo, Koots thought. It may be that those wagons are worth almost as much as the bounty money itself. He looked towards the heat-shimmering horizon where the tracks led. Out there, there is no civilized law. Head money or cargoes, one way or the other I smell a sweet profit in this.

He dismounted and inspected the wagon tracks more closely, giving himself time to think. 'How long since the wagons passed this way?'

Goffel referred the question to Xhia.

'Some months. It is not possible to say more than that. But wagons travel slowly, while horsemen travel fast.'

Koots nodded to Goffel. 'Good, very good! Tell him to follow, and find proof of who these wagons belong to.'

They found proof a hundred leagues further and twelve days later. They came to a place where one of the wagons had run into an antbear hole and been badly damaged. A number of the spokes in one of the front wheels had been shattered. The travellers had camped for some days at the site of the accident, making repairs to the wagon. They had whittled and shaved new spokes, and discarded the damaged ones.

Xhia retrieved one of the broken pieces from where it had been thrown into the grass. He cackled with triumph. 'Did not Xhia tell you this truth and that truth? Did you believe him? No! You did not believe him, you stupid white maggot.' He brandished the broken spar. 'Know now, once and for all time, white man, that Xhia sees all and knows all.' He brought the fragment of the spoke to Koots and showed him the design that had been burnt into the wood with a branding iron. 'Do you know this picture?' he demanded.

Koots grinned wolfishly and nodded with recognition.

It was the stylized picture of a cannon, a long nine-pounder on its carriage. In the ribbon below it were the letters CBTC. Koots had seen the same design on the flag that flew above the godown at High Weald, and on the pediment above the front wall of the main building. He knew that the initials stood for Courtney Brothers Trading Company.

He called his troopers and showed them the fragment of wood. They passed it from hand to hand. They all knew the design. The entire population of the colony was less than three thousand souls, and within its boundaries everyone knew everything about everyone else. After Governor van de Witten himself, the Courtney brothers were the richest, most influential men in the colony. Their coat-of-arms was almost as well known as that of the VOC. The brothers emblazoned it on all their possessions, their buildings, ships, wagons. It was the seal they used on their documents and the brand on their horses and livestock. There was no longer any doubt of the identity of the wagon train they were following.

Koots looked over his band, and picked out Richter. He tossed him the broken spoke. 'Corporal, do you know what that is you are holding?'

'Yes, Captain, sir. It's a wheel spoke.'

'No, Corporal!' Koots told him. 'That is thousands of guilders in gold coin in your hand.' He looked from the two white faces, Oudeman and Richter's, to the yellow and chocolate ones of Xhia and Goffel and the other Hottentots. 'Do any of you still want to go home? Unlike that miserable bastard Le Riche, this time I will let you take your horse when you leave. The reward money is not all that we will win. There are four wagons also, and a herd of domestic animals. Even Xhia will win more than the six head of cattle I promised him. The rest of you? Do any of you want to go home, yes or no?'

They grinned at each other, like a pack of wild hunting dogs with the smell of a wounded quarry in their nostrils, and shook their heads.

'Then there is the girl. Would any of you black bastards like to play with a white girl with golden hair?'

They burst into laughter at the suggestion, lewd and loud.

'I must apologize, but one of you will not have that pleasure.' He looked them over thoughtfully. There was one Hottentot trooper whom he would be pleased to see the back of. His name was Minna, and he had a squint. This gave him a sly, villainous expression, which Koots had realized reflected accurately his true nature. Minna had sulked and whined ever since leaving the colony, and he was the only one of the troop who was exhibiting no enthusiasm for following the tracks of Jim Courtney's wagons.

'Minna, you and I are brothers of the warrior blood,' Koots placed his arm around the man's shoulders, 'so it grieves me sorely that we must part. However, I need a good man and true to carry a message back to Colonel Keyser at the castle. I have to let him know of the success of our expedition. You, my dear and stalwart Minna, are the man for that job. I shall ask the colonel to reward you handsomely. Who knows? You may have some gold braid upon your sleeve, and gold in your pocket from this day's work.'

Koots hunched over his grubby notebook for almost an hour as he composed the message. He knew that Minna was illiterate. After extolling his own achievements in the conduct of the expedition the final paragraph of his report to Colonel Keyser read, 'The trooper who carries this message, Johannes Minna, lacks any soldierly virtues. It is my respectful recommendation that he be stripped of rank and privilege and discharged from the Company service without benefit of pension.'

And that, he thought, with satisfaction, when he folded the message, takes care of any obligation I might have to share the bounty with Minna when I bring Jim Courtney's head back to the colony. 'You have only to follow the wagon tracks, and they will lead you back to the Cape of Good Hope,' he told Minna. 'Xhia says it is less than ten days' ride.' He handed the message and the broken wagon spoke to Minna. 'Give these both to Colonel Keyser in person.'

Minna leered and went with alacrity to saddle his horse. He could hardly believe his good fortune in escaping this dreadful journey, and being offered a reward for doing so.

The days sped by much faster than the slow turning of the wagon wheels. It seemed that the hours were too short for them to enjoy in full measure all the wonders they saw, or to savour the adventures, great and small, that they encountered each day. Were it not for the journal that Louisa kept with such dedication they would soon have lost track of those golden days. She had to nag at Jim to keep his promise to his father. He made the solar observations of their position only when she insisted that he do so, and she recorded the results.

Jim was more reliable with the gold pans and he tested the sands of every river they crossed for the precious metal. On many occasions he found a bright yellow tail of metallic dust around the rim of the pan, but his excitement was short-lived when he tested it with hydrochloric acid from the gold-finder's chest, and the yellow metal bubbled and dissolved. 'Iron pyrites! Fool's gold!' he told Louisa bitterly. 'How old Humbert would laugh at me as a dupe.' But the disappointment and bitterness did not last long, and within hours Jim's enthusiasm would have fully regenerated. His boyish optimism was one of the things Louisa found endearing about him.

Jim looked for signs of other human presence, but there was little evidence of this. Once they found the tracks of wagon wheels preserved in the sterile crust of a salt pan, but Bakkat declared them to be very old indeed. Bakkat's concept of the passage of time was different from that of the European mind, so Jim pressed him further. 'How old is very old, Bakkat?'

'These tracks were made before you were born, Somoya,' he told Jim. 'The man whose wagon made them is probably dead of old age.'

There were other, fresher signs of human existence. These were of Bakkat's own people. Wherever they found a rock shelter or cave in the side of a hill or *kopje*, there were usually whimsical, vividly coloured paintings decorating the rock walls, and fairly recent hearths on which charcoal fragments showed how the little people had cooked their quarry, and discarded the bones on the midden piles nearby. Bakkat was able to recognize which clans of the tribe had passed this way by the symbols and styles of the paintings. Often when they were examining these artistic tributes to strange gods and quaint custom, Louisa sensed the deep longing and nostalgia that Bakkat felt for his people, who were living the free, careless existence that nature had decreed for them.

The land changed as they travelled across it, the plains giving way to forests and hills with rivers running through wide green valleys and straths. In places, the bush was so dense and thorny that they could not force a way through it. Even attempts to cut a roadway for the wagons failed. The tangled branches were iron hard and defied the sharpest axes. They were obliged to make detours of many days to pass around these jungles. In other places the veld was like English parkland, open and fertile, with great trees as tall as cathedral columns and widespread canopies of green leaf. Birds and monkeys shrieked and chattered in the treetops as they competed for fruit.

It seemed that there were animals and birds wherever they cast their eyes. The numbers and varieties never palled. They ranged in size from tiny sunbirds to ostriches taller than a mounted man with white plumes in their wings and tail tufts, from shrews not much bigger than Jim's thumb to hippopotamus as heavy as their largest oxen. These behemoths seemed to inhabit every pool and river, their huge bodies crowded so close together that they formed massive rafts on which the white egrets perched as though they were rocks.

Jim sent a hardened ball between the eyes of one old bull. Although he plunged below the surface in his death throes and disappeared from their sight, on the second day the gases in his belly brought him to the surface and he floated like a balloon with his stubby legs sticking into the air. With a span of oxen they dragged the carcass to the bank. The pure white fat that filled his body cavity filled a fifty-gallon water keg when rendered down. It was perfect for cooking and sausage-making, for the manufacture of soap, for lubricating the wheel hubs of the wagons, or for greasing the rifle patches.

There were so many kinds of antelope, each with flesh of different taste and texture: Louisa was able to order her favourites from Jim's rifle, like a housewife from her butcher. Herds of dun-coloured reedbuck lived on the grassland under the tall trees. Fantastically striped zebra galloped together in herds. They came across other horse-like antelope, with backs and limbs of ebony black, bellies of frosty white, and huge back-swept scimitar-shaped horns. In every thicket and thorn forest they found nervous kudu with spiral horns, and herds of bovine black buffalo, so numerous that they flattened the tangled bush when they stampeded.

Always Jim longed for his first sighting of elephant, and at night spoke of them with almost religious awe. He had never laid eyes on a living beast, but their tusks were piled high in the Company godown at High Weald. In his youth Jim's father had hunted the elephant in the eastern lands of Africa, a thousand miles and more from where Louisa and he now found themselves. Jim had been reared on tales of his father's chases after these legendary animals, and the thought of his first encounter with them became an obsession to him. 'We have travelled almost a thousand leagues since we left the Gariep,' he told Louisa. 'Surely no other man has travelled further from the colony. We must come up with the elephant herds very soon.'

Then his dreams had something to feed upon. They came upon a whole forest whose trunks had been thrown to earth as though by a hurricane of wind, and shattered to splinters. Those trees left standing had been stripped of their bark by the mighty pachyderms.

'See how they have chewed the juice out of the bark.' Bakkat showed Jim the huge balls of desiccated bark the animals had spat out. 'See how they have torn down this tree, which once stood higher than the mainmast of your father's ship – and they ate only the tender top leaves. Hau! They are truly wondrous beasts.'

'Follow them, Bakkat!' Jim pleaded. 'Show these beasts to me.'

'These signs were made a full season ago. See how the marks of the pads that they left in the mud of the last rains have dried hard as stone.'

'When will we find them?' Jim demanded. 'Will we ever find them?'

'We will find them,' Bakkat promised. 'And when we do, perchance you will wish we had not.' With a thrust of his chin he indicated one of the fallen trees: 'If they can do that to such a tree, what might they do to a man?'

Each day they rode out to explore the land ahead, to look for fresher elephant sign, and blaze a road for Smallboy and the wagons to follow. Always they had to make certain of sources of potable water and good fodder for the oxen and other domestic animals, and to refill the fagies against the times when their search for fresh water-holes might prove unsuccessful. Bakkat showed Jim how to watch the flight of flocks of sandgrouse and other birds, and the direction of travel of the thirsty game herds to the nearest water-holes. The horses were also good guides – they could smell it on the wind from many miles off.

Often they reached so far ahead of the wagon train that they were unable to return to its security and comfort before the setting of the sun, and they were forced to pitch a fly-camp wherever darkness and exhaustion overtook them. However, on those nights that they returned to the wagons it was always with a sense of joyous homecoming when they saw the campfires from a distance, or heard the lowing of the oxen. Then the dogs rushed out, barking with excitement, and Smallboy and the other drivers shouted greetings.

Louisa marked the calendar religiously, and she never missed the Sabbath. She insisted that she and Jim stay in camp for that day. They slept late on Sunday mornings, hearing each other wake as the sun shone through the chinks in the afterclap. Then they lay on their own cardell beds and chatted drowsily through the canvas of the wagon tents, until Louisa argued with Jim that it was time to be up and about. The smell of Zama brewing coffee at the campfire would convince him that she was right.

Louisa always cooked a special Sunday dinner, usually with some new recipe from the cookbook Sarah had given to her. In the meantime Jim saw to the small jobs around the camp that had been neglected during the week, from shoeing a horse to repairing a tear in the wagon tent or greasing the wheel hubs.

After lunch they often slung hammocks in the shade of the trees and read to each other from their small library of books. Then they discussed the events of the past week, and made plans for the week ahead. As a surprise for Jim on the first of his birthdays they spent together, Louisa secretly carved a set of chessmen and a board, using woods of different colours. Although he tried to look enthusiastic, Jim was not entirely enchanted by the gift for he had never played the game before. But she read him the rules from the back pages of the almanac, then set up the board under the spreading branches of a mighty camel-thorn tree.

'You can play white,' she told him magnanimously, 'which means you move first.'

'Is that good?' he demanded.

'It is of the utmost advantage,' she assured him. With a laugh he advanced a rook's pawn three squares. She made him correct this, then proceeded to give him a thorough and merciless drubbing. 'Checkmate!' she said and he looked startled.

253

Humiliated by the ease with which she had accomplished this feat, he examined the board minutely and argued the legitimacy of each move that had led to his defeat. When it became apparent that she had not cheated, he sat back and stared morosely at the board. Then, slowly, the light of battle dawned in his eyes, and he squared his shoulders. 'We will play again,' he announced ominously. But the result of their second game was no less humiliating. Perhaps for this reason Jim became captivated by it, and it soon became a major, binding force in their shared existence. With Louisa's tactful tuition he made such rapid progress that soon they were almost evenly matched. They fought many memorable, epic battles across the chequered board but, strangely, these encounters brought them closer together.

In one endeavour she could not match him, although she tried with all her determination and often came close to doing so. This was in shooting. On Sunday afternoons after dinner, Jim set up targets at fifty, a hundred and a hundred and fifty paces. Louisa shot with her little French rifle, while he used one of the pair of heavier London guns. The trophy was the bushy tail of a giraffe, and the winner of this weekly competition was entitled to hang the tail on the front of his or her wagon for the rest of the week. During the rare weeks that Louisa had that honour, Smallboy, the driver of her wagon, strutted, preened and fired his great whip more often, and with more force, than was necessary for the encouragement of the ox team.

Gradually Louisa developed such a sense of pride and fulfilment in the running of the camp and the ordering of their existence, and came to derive so much pleasure from Jim's companionship, that the dark memories of her old life began to recede. The nightmares became less frequent and terrifying. Slowly she regained the sense of fun and the enjoyment of life that more suited her age than defensiveness and suspicion.

Riding out together one afternoon they came upon a tsama vine in full fruit. The green and yellow striped melons were the size of a man's head. Jim filled his saddlebags with them, and when they returned to the wagons he cut one into thick wedges. 'One of the delicacies of the wilderness.' He handed her a piece, and she tasted it gingerly. It was running with juice, but the flavour was bland and only slightly sugary. To please him, Louisa pretended to enjoy it.

'My father says that one of these saved his life. He had been lost for days in the desert, and would have died of thirst had he not chanced upon a tsama vine like this one. Isn't it tasty?'

She looked at the pale yellow pith that filled the shell, then up at him. Unexpectedly she was filled with a girlish mischief she had not known since before the death of her parents.

'What are you grinning at?' Jim demanded.

'This!' she said, leaned across the camp table and mashed the soft wet fruit into his face. He gaped at her in astonishment as juice and the yellow flesh dripped off his nose and chin. 'Isn't it tasty?' she asked, and dissolved into peals of laughter. 'You look so silly!'

'We shall see who looks even more silly.' Jim recovered, and snatched up the remains of the melon. She squealed with alarm, leaped up from the table and ran. Jim pursued her through the camp brandishing the melon, with pips in his hair and juice down his shirt.

The servants were astounded as Louisa dodged and ducked around the wagons. But she was weak with laughter and at last Jim caught her, pinned her against the side of a wagon with one hand and took aim with the other.

'I am mortally sorry,' she gasped. 'Please forgive me. I am abject. It will not happen again.'

'No! It will never happen again,' he agreed. 'I'll show you what will happen if it does.' He gave her the same treatment, and by the time he had finished she had yellow melon in her hair and eyelashes, and in her ears.

'You are a beast, James Archibald!' She knew how he hated that name. 'I hate you.' She tried to glare at him, but burst into laughter again. She raised one hand to strike him, but he caught her wrist and she stumbled against him.

Suddenly neither of them was laughing. Their mouths were so close that their breath mingled and there was something in her eyes that he had not seen before. Then she began to tremble and her lips quivered. The emotion he had seen faded and was replaced with terror. He knew that all the servants were watching them.

With an effort he released her wrist and stepped back, but now his laughter was breathless. 'Beware, wench. Next time it will be a cold slimy lump of melon down the back of your neck.'

The moment hung precariously, for she was on the edge of tears. Bakkat saved them by breaking into a pantomime of their contest. He picked up the remains of the melon and hurled it at Zama. The drivers and *voorlopers* joined in, and melon rind flew in all directions. In the uproar Louisa slipped away to her wagon. When she emerged later she was demure in a fresh frock, her hair in long plaits. 'Would you like a game of chess?' she asked, not looking into his eyes.

He checkmated her in twenty moves, then doubted the merit of his victory. He wondered if she had purposely allowed him to win, or whether she had merely been distracted.

The next morning Jim and Louisa, with Bakkat, rode out before dawn, taking their breakfast with them tied in the canteens behind their saddles. Only an hour ahead of the wagons, they stopped to water the horses and eat their breakfast beside a small stream that meandered down from the line of lightly forested hills that lay across their path.

They sat opposite each other on fallen logs. They were shy and subdued, unable to meet each other's eyes. The memory of the moment from the previous day was still vivid in their minds, and their conversation was stilted and overly polite. After they had eaten Louisa took the canteens down to the stream to wash them while Jim resaddled the horses. When she came back he hesitated before helping her to step up into

Trueheart's saddle. She thanked him more profusely than the small act called for.

They rode up the hill, Bakkat leading the way on Frost. As he reached the crest he wheeled Frost back off the skyline, and raced towards them, his face contorted with some strong emotion, his voice reduced to an unintelligible squeak.

'What is it?' Jim shouted at him. 'What have you seen?' He seized Bakkat's arm and almost yanked him out of the saddle.

Bakkat found his voice at last. '*Dhlovu!*' he cried, as though in pain. 'Many, many.'

Jim threw his reins to Bakkat, jerked the small-bore rifle from its sheath and sprang out of the saddle. He knew better than to show himself on the skyline and stopped below the crest to gather himself. Excitement had clamped down on his chest and he could hardly breathe. His heart seemed on the point of leaping out of his mouth. Yet he still had the good sense to check the direction of the breeze: he picked a few blades of dry grass, shredded them between his fingers, and studied the drift of the tiny fragments. It was favourable.

Suddenly he felt Louisa's presence close beside him. 'What is it, Jim?' She had not understood the word Bakkat had used.

'Elephant!' Jim could barely enunciate the magical word.

She stared at him for only a moment, then her eyes flared like sunlight in blue sapphire. 'Oh, Jim! Show me!'

Even in the turmoil that had overwhelmed him, he was grateful she was there to share something he knew, deep in his heart, would stay with him all his days. 'Come!' he said, and, quite naturally, she took his hand. Despite all that had gone between them, this trusting gesture came as no surprise to him. Hand in hand they went to the crest of the hill and looked over.

Below them lay a vast bowl of land hemmed about with hills. It was carpeted with new growth, freshly sprung after the recent rains on ground that had been burned by grass-fires during the dry season. It was green as an English meadow, and scattered with clumps of tall mahoba-hoba trees, and copses of thornbush.

257

Spread out in the bottom of the bowl, alone or in small herds, were hundreds of elephant. For Jim, who had imagined this first encounter so many times and in so many ways, the reality far outweighed all his fantasy. 'Oh, sweet Mary!' he whispered. 'Oh, God, oh, beloved God!'

She felt his hand shaking in hers and tightened her grip. She recognized this as a seminal moment in his life and suddenly she was proud to be beside him, to share it with him. It seemed that this was her place: as though she had at last found where she belonged.

He could see at once from their relative size that most of the elephant herds consisted of females and their young. They formed grey agglomerations like reefs of granite, and the shapes of the herds changed only slowly, coming together, then flowing apart again. In all this mass of animals the great bulls stood apart and aloof, massive dark shapes, even at this remove dominating the herds that surrounded them, unmistakable in their majesty.

Close below where Jim and Louisa stood one particular animal made all the others seem insignificant. Perhaps it was merely the way the sunlight played upon him, but he was darker than any other. His ears were spread like the mainsail of a ship, and he fanned them with a lazy, flapping motion. With each movement the sun caught the curve of a huge tusk, and shot a ray towards them like the reflection of a mirror. Once the bull reached down with his trunk, and gathered up the dust at his feet and threw it back over his head and shoulders in a pale cloud.

'He is so big!' Louisa whispered. 'I never expected them to be that size.'

Her voice roused Jim from his trance of wonder, and he looked back to see Bakkat hovering close behind him.

'I have only this small-bore gun with me.' Jim had left the two big German four-to-the-pounders with the wagons. They were awkward weapons to carry and handle and, having been so often disappointed, he had not expected to run into elephant today, and certainly not in such numbers. He regretted the oversight now, but he knew it would be folly to use the little London rifle he had with him against a creature endowed with such bulk of muscle and sinew, such massive bone structure. Only with great luck could he hope to send such a light ball into its vitals.

'Ride back, Bakkat, as fast as Frost will carry you, and bring the two big guns to me with the powder flask and shotbelt.' No sooner had Jim finished speaking than Bakkat was up on Frost and going back down the hill at a mad gallop. They did not watch him go, but Jim and Louisa crept forward, using a small bush to break up their silhouette as they crossed the skyline. On the far slope they found a clump of thorny acacia that offered concealment, and settled among the fluffy branches and yellow blossom, sitting side by side while Jim focused his telescope on the great bull below them.

He gasped aloud, amazed at the animal's enhanced size when seen through the lens, and he stared in awe at the length and thickness of those shafts of ivory. Although he had not yet had his fill of such a magnificent sight he passed the glass to Louisa. By now she had learned to use it with expertise, and she trained it on the great animal. But after only a few minutes her attention was diverted to the playful antics of a group of calves further on: they were squealing and chasing each other through the forest.

When Jim saw the direction of the telescope wandering away from the patriarch he was strongly inclined to take it out of Louisa's hands and continue his study of the bull. Then he saw the tender smile on her face as she watched the calves at play, and he restrained himself. This in itself was a mark of his feelings for her: he was almost consumed by the hunter's passion and his heart beat hotly for the chase.

Then, to his delight, the bull left the shade of the mahoba-hoba tree and started ambling up the slope directly towards where they sat. He placed his hand on Louisa's shoulder to warn her. When she lowered the telescope he put a finger to his lips and pointed at the approaching bull.

Louisa's expression changed to awe as it drew closer, and loomed larger. Even in broad daylight there was something ghostly and unnerving about the utter silence of its walk: it

259

placed its feet with a precision and grace disproportionate to its size, and the huge spongy pads absorbed all sound. The trunk hung slackly, almost to the ground and only the tip unrolled and touched the earth, picking up a leaf or a seed pod with an extraordinary dexterity that matched human fingers, toying with it then tossing it aside.

Closer still, they could see clearly that its one visible eye was set in a web of deep grey wrinkles, like the concentric rings of a spider's web. A wet stain of tears ran from one corner down its weathered cheek, but the eye gleamed with a sheen of intelligence and sagacity. With every few slow strides the tip of one of those long tusks touched the ground and left a tiny furrow in the earth.

Closer it came until it seemed to fill the sky above them, and they held their breath, expecting to be trodden on or at least stabbed through by a thrust from one of those gleaming ivory shafts. Louisa stirred, ready to spring up and run, but Jim tightened his grip on her shoulder and restrained her.

The bull was making a deep rumble in his throat and belly, which sounded like distant thunder. Louisa trembled in sympathy, excitement mingling with dread. Slowly, so as not to alarm the animal, Jim raised the little rifle to his shoulder and looked over the sights at the great grey head. Beside him he felt Louisa stiffen in anticipation of the shot. Then he remembered all that his father had told him, where to aim for a shot to the brain.

'But only a fool and a braggart tries that shot,' Tom had told him. ''Tis such a tiny mark to hit in the huge bony castle of the skull. The true hunter makes certain of the kill. He uses a heavy bore that throws a weighty ball, and he shoots for the shoulder, for the heart and the lungs.'

Jim lowered the rifle, and beside him Louisa relaxed. The elephant passed their hiding-place with its stately stride, and fifty paces further on it reached a small gwarrie tree, began to strip its purple berries and lift them fastidiously to its mouth. When the withered, baggy rump was turned towards them, Jim rose cautiously and led Louisa back over the ridge. He picked out the feather of dust coming towards them from the direction of the wagons, and the pale shape of Frost at full gallop.

As Bakkat came up, Jim said, 'That was quick work, and well done.' He snatched one of the great guns from his hand before Bakkat had a chance to dismount. Quickly he examined the weapon. It was unloaded and thick with grease, but the flint was new and well shaped. Quickly he set about loading. He rammed the huge, glistening ball down the barrel. At four ounces, it was almost twice the size of a ripe grape. It had been rendered adamantine by the addition of pewter to the molten lead. When it was seated firmly on the wad and the heavy charge of black powder, he looked to the priming, then exchanged the weapon for the second of the pair Bakkat held out to him. When both were loaded, he said, 'There is a magnificent bull feeding close by, just over yonder ridge. I will attack him on foot but as soon as you hear my shot, bring up Drumfire and the second gun with all speed.'

'What must I do?' Louisa asked, and he hesitated. His instinct was to send her back to the wagons, but he knew that would be unfair. She should not be deprived of the excitement and adventure of this first chase after the mighty beasts. More importantly, she would probably refuse to obey him, and he did not have time now for an argument he would almost certainly lose. On the other hand he could not leave her here. He knew, from vivid accounts that his father had given him, that once the first shot was fired the bush would be swarming with panic-stricken beasts running in all directions. If one came upon her when she was unprotected she would be in mortal danger. 'Follow us, but not too closely. You must keep me or Bakkat in sight at all times, but you must also keep a watchful eye all around you. Elephant might come from any direction, even from behind. But you can rely on Trueheart to carry you out of danger.'

He drew back the hammer of the big gun to half-cock, ran to the crest of the ridge, and peered over. Nothing had changed in the time since he had last seen the bull. He was still feeding quietly on the gwarrie tree, facing away from Jim.

The herds below were resting, or feeding quietly, and the young calves were still frolicking around the legs of their dams.

Jim paused only to check the direction of the breeze once more. He felt its cool, light touch on his sweaty face, but he took a few moments to dribble a handful of dust through his fingers. The breeze was still steady and in his favour. He knew that there was little reason for concealment now. The eyesight of the elephant is poor, and they are unable to distinguish the form of a man at fifty paces, as long as he remains motionless. On the other hand, their sense of smell is phenomenal.

With the breeze in his favour, and stepping lightly, Jim crept up behind the feeding bull. His father's words came back to him: 'Close. Always get as close as you can. Every yard you close with the quarry makes the kill more certain. Thirty paces is too far. Twenty is not as good as ten. Five paces is perfect. From that range your ball will drive to the heart.'

As he drew in closer Jim's steps slowed. It was as though his legs were filling with molten lead. His breath became laboured, and he felt as though he was suffocating. The gun in his hands was becoming heavier. He had not expected to be afraid. I have never been scared before, he thought, and then, well, perhaps just a little, sometimes.

Closer and still closer. Then he remembered he had forgotten to fully cock the hammer of the big gun. He was so close that the bull would hear the click of the mechanism, and take fright. He hesitated, and the animal moved. With that ponderous, deliberate stride it began to circle the gwarrie tree. Jim's heart jumped against his ribs as its flank was exposed to him, and he could make out the outline of the massive shoulder-blade beneath the riven, creased hide. It was just as his father had drawn it for him. He knew exactly where to aim. He lifted the butt to his shoulder, but the bull kept moving round the tree, until its shoulder was covered by the twisted branches and thick, shiny green foliage. It stopped on the far side of the bush from him, and began to feed again. It was so close that Jim could see the individual bristles in its ear, and the thick, matted eyelashes surrounding the knowing little eye that seemed so incongruous in the ancient, mountainous head.

'Only a fool and a braggart shoots for the brain,' his father had warned him, but the shoulder was covered and he was so close. Surely he could not miss from this range. First he had to fully cock the rifle. He placed his hand over the action, trying to muffle it, and he inched back the engraved steel hammer. He felt the moment when the sear was about to engage and bit his tongue as he concentrated on easing it through that last fraction of the arc.

He was watching the bull, trying by the force of his will to lull it to the sound of metal on metal. The elephant was chewing with evident satisfaction, stuffing the ripe berries into its mouth; the inside of its lips was stained purple.

Click! To Jim the sound was deafening in the great silence of the wilderness. The elephant stopped chewing and froze in monumental stillness. It had heard that alien sound, and Jim knew that it was poised on the edge of flight.

Jim stared hard at the dark slit of the earhole, and slowly lifted the butt to his shoulder. The iron sights did not impinge upon his vision: he seemed to look through them. All his being was concentrated on that spot half a finger's length in front of the ear. He knew the pull and feel of the trigger intimately, but so intense was his concentration that the thunder of the shot surprised him.

The butt of the weapon pounded into his shoulder, driving him back two paces before he regained his balance. The long bluish plume of powder smoke gushed out from the muzzle and seemed to stroke the wrinkled grey skin of the bull's temple. Jim was unsighted by the recoil and by the cloud of smoke, so he did not see the strike of the ball, but he heard it crack against the skull like an axe blade against the trunk of an ironwood tree.

The bull threw back its great head and dropped with almost miraculous suddenness, hitting the earth with such force that he raised a cloud of dust. The ground under Jim's feet seemed to jump with the impact. Jim regained his balance and gaped with astonishment at what he had achieved. Then his heart soared and he whooped with triumph. 'He's down! With a single shot I have slain him.' He started forward to gloat over his kill, but there came the pounding of hoofs from behind.

When he glanced round Bakkat was galloping up on Frost, waving the second gun and leading Drumfire. 'Change guns, Somoya!' he shouted. 'Behold! There are *dhlovu* all about us. We may kill ten more if we ride hard.'

'I must see the bull I have killed,' Jim protested. 'I must cut off his tail.' This was the trophy his father had always taken from a downed beast, even in the heat of the chase.

'If he is dead he will stay dead.' Bakkat reined in, snatched the empty gun from his hand and thrust the loaded one towards him. 'The others will be gone before you have a chance to cut off the tail. Once they are gone you will never see them again.' Still Jim hesitated, looking longingly to where the fallen bull lay concealed behind the gwarrie tree. 'Come, Somoya! See the dust they raise as they run. Soon it will be too late.'

Jim looked down the slope and saw that his shot had startled the herds, and in the basin below them the elephant were scattering and fleeing in every direction. His father had told him of the peculiar instinctive horror that the elephant entertains towards man: even if they have never before encountered his cruel, warlike behaviour they will run a hundred leagues from their first contact with him. Still he hesitated, and Bakkat told him urgently, 'Somoya, the moment passes.' He pointed at two more great bulls charging past, less than a pistol shot from where they stood. Their ears were folded back against their shoulders and they were at full run. 'They will be gone before you can draw three more breaths. Follow! Follow with all speed!'

The bulls were already disappearing into the forest, but Jim knew he could catch up within a mile of hard riding. He hesitated no longer. With the loaded rifle in hand he leaped into Drumfire's saddle and booted him in the ribs. 'Ha! Ha! Drumfire! After them, my darling.' He turned the stallion's head down the slope and they tore off in pursuit. Drumfire caught the contagious excitement of his rider, and his eyes rolled wildly as he drove his head into each stride like a sledgehammer. They swung in behind the running bulls, closing swiftly. Jim slitted his eyes against the dust storm they were throwing up with the huge pads of their feet, and the thorn branches that whipped back into his face. He picked out the larger of the two great bulls. Even from his station dead astern he could see the wide curves of its tusks showing on each side of its heaving flanks.

'I will sup with the devil if he's not bigger than the first one I downed,' he exulted, and steered Drumfire out to one side, trying to come level with the bull, seeking to open his flank for a shot at the shoulder. He held the rifle across the pommel of his saddle and eased the hammer back into the half-cock position.

Then, from behind him, he heard the wild trumpeting of an enraged elephant, followed, almost immediately, by Louisa's scream.

The two dreadful sounds were almost drowned by distance and the thunder of Drumfire's hoofs. But there was a timbre to Louisa's cry that raked every nerve in his body and cut him to the heart. It was the wild ringing screech of abject terror. He swivelled in the saddle and looked back and saw her mortal predicament.

Obedient to Jim's instructions, Louisa had hung back, keeping Trueheart behind Frost as they crossed the ridge at a walk. She saw Jim two hundred paces ahead. His back was turned towards her, and he was moving forward deliberately, half crouched over the weapon he carried level with his waist.

For a moment she failed to see the bull. With its grey colour it seemed to blend like smoke into the bush around him. Then she gasped as her eyes picked out its form. It seemed mountainous, and Jim was so close to the beast that she was terrified for his safety. She stopped Trueheart and watched, with dreadful fascination, as Jim crept closer still.

She saw the bull change its position, move behind the gwarrie tree, and for a moment she thought it had eluded Jim's stalk. Then she saw Jim rise from his crouch and lift the long barrel of his rifle. When he aimed, the muzzle seemed to touch the bull's head, and then came the thunderous clap of the discharge, like the mainsail of the *Meeuw* filling with wind as she tacked into the storm.

The blue powder smoke boiled and churned in the breeze, and the bull went down as though struck by an avalanche. Then all was shouting and commotion as Bakkat spurred forward from beside her, and raced to where Jim stood, dragging Drumfire on the lead rein after him. Jim went up on Drumfire and, leaving the downed bull lying where it had fallen, he and Bakkat raced down the slope, chasing two more huge elephant that she had not noticed until that moment.

Louisa let them go. Without conscious volition, she found that Trueheart had responded to a slight pressure of her knees and was walking forward towards the gwarrie tree behind which the bull had fallen. She did not try to stop the mare and as they approached her curiosity increased. She raised herself in the stirrups to see over the tree, trying to catch a glimpse of the mighty creature she had seen fall there.

She was almost up to the tree when she saw a small flirt of movement, too insignificant to have been made by such a large beast. She rode closer, and this time she realized that what she had seen was a flick of the elephant's stubby tail. The clump of bristles at the end was worn and ragged as an old paintbrush.

She was about to dismount and lead Trueheart forward for a better view of the carcass and the curved, magnificent yellow tusks that intrigued her. Then, to her horrified disbelief, the bull stood up. It came to its feet in one swift motion, alert and agile as though waking from a light sleep. It stood for a moment, as though listening. A rivulet of bright scarlet blood poured from the wound in its temple, and down its grey, wrinkled cheek. Trueheart snorted with fright and shied away. In the act of dismounting, Louisa had only one foot in the stirrup and she was nearly thrown, but with an effort she regained her seat.

The bull had heard Trueheart snort, and turned towards them. Its huge ears flared out: it saw them as his tormentors. The horse and human scent filled its head, an alien odour it had never smelt before, but which reeked of danger.

The bull shook its head, the huge ears snapping and clattering with the strength of the movement, and it squealed its fury and affront. Blood splattered from the bullet wound, and the droplets pelted into Louisa's face, warm as monsoon rain, and she screamed with all her breath and all the strength of her lungs. 'Jim! Save me!'

The bull rolled its trunk up against its chest, and half cocked its ears back with the ends curled, the attitude of ultimate aggression. Then it charged straight at them. Trueheart wheeled away, laid her ears flat and burst into full gallop. She seemed to take flight, to skim lightly over the rough surface, but the bull stayed close at her tail, squealing again and again with fury, a pink feather of blood blowing back from its head wound.

With a burst of speed Trueheart opened the gap, pulling ahead, but suddenly there was a hedge of thorn bush in front of her and she was forced to check, and change direction to swerve round the obstacle. The bull did not hesitate, but burst through the thorn thicket as though it did not exist, regaining all the ground it had lost. It was now closer still.

With horror Louisa saw that there was rocky ground ahead and denser thickets of thorn bush blocking their path. The bull was driving them into a trap, in which even Trueheart's speed would be of little avail. Louisa remembered the small French rifle under her right leg. In her terror she had forgotten its existence, but now she knew it was all she had to stop the bull snatching her from the saddle. She glanced back and saw that the long ophidian trunk was already reaching out for her.

She drew the rifle from its leather sheath, swivelled round and cocked the weapon in the same movement. Again she screamed involuntarily as she saw the grasping trunk waving in her face, and threw up the rifle. The enormous head filled all her vision and she did not aim but fired blindly into the bull's face.

The light ball could never have penetrated the thick hide and the bony casket of the skull, but the bull was vulnerable in one place. By the wildest chance the ball found that mark. It entered the eye-socket at a raking angle, and burst the eyeball, blinding the bull instantly on the same side of its head as the wound Jim had inflicted.

The elephant reeled and staggered, losing ground on Trueheart, but it recovered almost immediately and started forward again. All of Louisa's attention was fastened on the task of reloading the rifle, but she had never done this on horseback at full gallop, and the gunpowder spewed from the flask and blew away in the wind. She glanced back and saw that the bull still had them in the focus of its right eye and was reaching for her again. She knew that this time it would have her.

So complete was her fascination with her fate that she did not see the thicket looming ahead. Trueheart swerved to avoid running full into it, and Louisa was thrown off balance teetering in the saddle. She dropped the rifle as she clutched at the pommel. The weapon clattered on the rocky ground.

Hanging half out of the saddle she was dragged down the length of the thicket. The hooked thorns were tipped with crimson and needle sharp. They bit into her clothing and into her flesh like myriad cats' claws. Their combined grip was irresistible and Louisa was jerked cleanly from Trueheart's back. The mare galloped on with an empty saddle, leaving Louisa dangling and struggling in the tenacious grip of the thorns.

The elephant had lost sight of her on his blind side, but it smelled her: the odour of the fresh blood from the tiny wounds inflicted by the thorns was strong. It let Trueheart run on unmolested and turned back. It began to search for Louisa with outstretched trunk, pushing its way into the thicket, its thick grey hide impervious to the hooked thorns, guided by the sound of Louisa's struggles and her scent. It closed in on her swiftly. She realized her danger and froze into stillness.

She lay quietly in the grip of the thorns and watched with resignation as the questing tip of the trunk groped towards her. It touched her boot, then locked round her ankle. With unimaginable strength she was torn out of the thicket, the clinging thorns breaking off in the folds of her clothing or in her skin.

She hung upside down, dangling by one leg from the trunk of the elephant. Its grip on her ankle tightened and she feared that at any moment the bone would crush to splinters. From all Jim had told her, she knew what would happen next. The bull would lift her high in the air and then, with all its monstrous power, would dash her head first against the rocky ground. It would beat her against the earth again and again, until almost every bone in her body was shattered and then it would kneel on her and crush her to pulp, driving the points of its tusks through and through.

Jim turned at the sound of her first scream and the shrill trumpeting of the huge bull. He broke off the chase after the two other elephants, and reined Drumfire hard down on his haunches. Then he stared back in horror and disbelief. 'I killed it!' he gasped. 'I left it dead.' But at the same time he remembered his father's warning. 'The brain is so small, and is not placed where you would expect it to be. If you miss it by even the breadth of your little finger, the animal will drop as though stone-dead, but it is stunned only. When it comes round, it will be unimpaired and many times more dangerous than before. I have seen good men killed that way. Never chance that shot, Jim, my boy, or you will live to regret it.'

'Bakkat!' Jim yelled. 'Stay close with the second gun!' He gave Drumfire the spurs, and sent him back at full gallop. Louisa and the bull were running directly away from him, and he overhauled them only gradually. He was seized by a feeling of debilitating impotence: he could see that Louisa would be killed before he could reach her, and it was his fault: he had left the enraged animal in a position where it could attack her.

'I'm coming!' he yelled. 'Hold hard!' He tried to give her courage but in the thunder of hoofs and the ringing trumpeting of the bull she showed no sign of having heard him. He watched her turn in the saddle and fire the little lady's rifle, but though the bull staggered slightly to the shot it did not leave her.

Then he watched in despair as Louisa ran into the bushes and was plucked from the saddle. The elephant turned back to hunt for her, as she was held powerless in the grip of the thorns. However, this check enabled Jim to push in so close that Drumfire baulked and shied at the gamy stench of the elephant, and at its threatening presence. Using his spurs without mercy, Jim drove him in closer still, watching for an opportunity to send in a telling shot. He knew that his ball must break bone or hit the vitals to distract the bull. However, all was confused movement, noise and flying dust. The elephant was wading through the thorn bush, and the waving branches protected his vulnerable parts and frustrated Jim's aim. Drumfire was skittering under him, throwing his head and trying to back away from the terrible menace of the elephant.

He saw Louisa tangled in the thorns. She showed no sign of life. He thought that her neck might have snapped in the fall or that her skull was crushed in. The idea of losing her was too agonizing to be borne, and he forced Drumfire forward with all his strength and will. Suddenly the bull found Louisa's limp body and hauled her out of the thicket. Jim dared not fire at its head for fear of hitting Louisa. He was forced to wait until the beast backed and turned broadside to him, at last exposing its flank. Jim leaned far out of the saddle, reaching up until the muzzle of the heavy gun almost touched the rough and baggy skin, and he fired.

The ball struck the point of the bull's shoulder, on the

heavy joint of humerus and scapula, shattering the bone. The elephant reeled back from the shot, and threw out its trunk to balance itself on three legs. It released its grip on Louisa's leg, and she fell back into the thicket where the branches cushioned her from the hard earth.

The elephant turned towards Jim, ears flaring, shrilling with pain and rage, then reached out with its trunk to pull him from the saddle. But it was pinned by its broken front leg, and Jim turned Drumfire away, swinging out of reach, and rode back to meet Bakkat who was coming up with the second gun. With expertise born of long practice they exchanged guns. 'Reload! As quick as you like!' Jim shouted, and with the second weapon in his hand he spurred back to confront the bull, which was dragging itself to meet him, hobbling on three legs, the crippled front leg twisted and useless.

Jim could see now that Louisa's shot had blinded one eye, for blood and eye jelly poured down its cheek. He changed direction, coming in from the bull's blind side, so close that the tip of one tusk grazed his shoulder, and as he went by he fired into its chest without checking Drumfire's gallop. The bull staggered. This time the heavy four-ounce ball had gone in deeply, cutting through the vital organs, the tangled arteries and veins deep in the chest cavity. It was a fatal wound but it would take time for the beast to fall.

He reckoned that Louisa was out of harm's way, as long as she stayed where she was, deeply hidden in the thicket. In the utmost haste Jim rode back to where Bakkat had dropped down from Frost's back, the better and swifter to reload the other gun. It took courage to dismount in the face of a wounded elephant.

Courage is one thing he lacks not! Jim thought, as he watched for him to finish the complicated business of reloading the heavy gun. Drumfire danced in nervous circles, and Jim glanced back to watch the bull. Then he shouted with alarm as he saw Louisa crawling out of the thorn bush on hands and knees, almost under the bull's trampling feet. Exposed as she now was, she was once again in terrible danger. He dropped the empty gun and, not waiting for Bakkat to finish reloading, galloped back. Again he swerved in from the bull's blind side so that he could risk a much closer pass.

Obviously half stunned, Louisa came to her feet, favouring her injured leg where the bull's trunk had seized her. She saw Jim riding towards her, hopped towards him and lifted her arms. She was a dreadful sight, her clothing torn by thorns and stained with blood. She was covered with scratches and dust, her long hair tumbling down over her face.

Drumfire brushed so closely along the bull's blind side that the blood that flowed down from the wound in its shoulder stained Jim's breeches at the knee, but when the elephant swung its trunk to swat him like a fly, Jim flattened himself along Drumfire's neck and ducked under the blow. They galloped up to Louisa and, without pausing, Jim leaned far out of the saddle, gripping only with his knees, flung one arm round Louisa and swung her up behind him. As soon as she was astride she locked both her arms around his waist and pressed her face into his sweaty shirt between his shoulder-blades. She was sobbing with pain and fright, unable to utter a word. He carried her to the crest of the hill, swung himself to the ground, and reached up to lift her down from Drumfire's back.

She was still unable to speak, but words were unnecessary and inadequate. Her eyes, close to his, expressed all her gratitude and gave him a glimpse of her other emotions, still too complex and confused for her to express.

Jim set her carefully on the ground. 'Where are you hurt?' he asked. His voice was choked with concern for her. The toll that their brush with death had exacted was clear to see on his face, and this rallied her. She clung to him still as he knelt over her.

'My ankle, but 'tis almost nothing,' she whispered.

'Let me see it,' he said, and she let her arms slip away from his neck. 'Which one?' he asked, and she showed him. He eased the boot from her foot and tested her leg gently. 'It's not broken,' he said.

'No.' She sat up. 'And 'tis only a little sore.' She brushed the golden hair off her dusty face and he saw that a thorn was stuck into her cheek. He plucked it out, and she winced but held his gaze. 'Jim!' she whispered.

'Yes, my little hedgehog?'

'No, 'tis nothing, except—' She broke off, unable to finish, then went on lamely, 'I like it well enough when you call me that.'

'I'm glad to have you back,' Jim said. 'For a moment I thought you had taken leave of us.'

'I must be a sight to give children nightmares.' She could look no longer into his eyes, and tried to wipe the dust from her face.

Only a woman could consider her appearance at such a time, Jim thought, but he did not say it. 'You are such a sight as I have dreamed on,' he said instead, and she blushed under the dirt.

Then Bakkat rode up on Frost with both the great guns loaded and primed. 'The bull will escape us yet, if you let him, Somoya.'

Jim roused himself to what was happening around them. He saw the old bull walking away slowly downhill, dragging one front leg and shaking its huge head as the agony of the burst eyeball raged through its skull.

'Oh, Jim,' Louisa whispered. 'The poor beast is in terrible extremes. You must not let him suffer so.'

'It will not take long,' he promised her. He stepped up into Drumfire's saddle and took the gun Bakkat handed up to him. Then he rode down the slope, circled out ahead of the maimed animal and stopped Drumfire squarely in its path. He cocked the hammer and waited.

The bull seemed not to notice them and came on slowly, painfully. At ten paces Jim fired into the front of its chest. As the ball socked heavily into the wrinkled hide, he spun Drumfire away like a dancer. The bull made no move to follow them. It stood still as a monument, and the heart blood pumped from the fresh bullet hole, bright as a fountain in the sunlight.

Jim changed guns with Bakkat, then brought Drumfire back

273

towards where the bull still stood. He came in on its blind side at a steady walk. The bull began to rock gently on its feet, once again making a soft rumbling sound deep in its chest. Jim felt all his warlike passions abating, to be replaced by a feeling of sadness and aching remorse. With this most noble of all quarry, he felt more intensely than ever the eternal tragedy of the kill. It was an effort to raise the gun and fire again. The bull shuddered when it received the ball, and began to back away, but its movements were slow and unsteady. Then, at last, it sighed, a laboured, gusty sound.

It fell the way a great tree goes down before the axe and cross-saw, slowly at first, then faster until it hit the earth with a crash that echoed from the hills across the valley.

Bakkat slipped off Frost's back, and went forward. The elephant's good eye was wide open, and Bakkat ran his finger lightly along the fringe of its lashes. It did not blink. 'It is over, Somoya. He belongs to you for ever.'

Despite her protests that her injuries were of no consequence, Jim would not let Louisa ride back to the wagons. He and Bakkat cut two long, supple poles and with a framework of lighter sticks fastened between them, the whole covered by the canvas ground sheets from their blanket rolls, they contrived a travois for Trueheart to drag behind her. Jim laid Louisa tenderly on it and picked the smoothest path to lead Trueheart back to the wagons.

Although Louisa laughed from this comfortable bed, and declared it the easiest journey she had ever made, by the time they reached the wagons her injuries had stiffened. When she rose from the travois she hobbled to her wagon like a very old lady.

Jim hovered around her anxiously, aware that any uninvited help he might offer would be rejected. He was surprised and delighted when she placed a hand on his shoulder as she climbed the wagon steps. He left her to take off her torn, soiled clothing while he supervised the heating of the water cauldron and the preparation of the copper hip-bath. Zama and the other servants removed the afterchest from her wagon and set up the bath in its place. Then they filled it with steaming water. When all was ready, Jim retired and listened through the canvas tent to her splashes, and winced in sympathy at her small cries and exclamations of pain as the water stung her abrasions and thorn pricks. When at last he judged that she had finished he asked permission to enter her wagon tent. 'Yes, you may come in, for I am as chastely attired as a nun.'

She was wearing the dressing-robe Sarah Courtney had given her. It reached from her chin to her ankles, and down to her wrists.

'Is there aught I can do to ease your discomfort?' he asked.

'I have rubbed your aunt Yasmini's sovereign balm and ointment upon my ankle and on most of my other afflictions.' She lifted the hem of the robe a few inches to show her ankle tightly wrapped in bandages. Dorian Courtney's wife was an adept of Arabian and Oriental medicine. Her famous ointment was the family cure-all. Sarah had packed a dozen large jars of it into the medical chest she had given them. There was an open jar beside Louisa's cardell bed, and the strong but pleasant herbal smell permeated the interior of the tent.

Jim was not sure where these remarks were leading, but he nodded wisely. Then she blushed again, and, without looking at him, murmured, 'However, I have thorns in places that I cannot reach. And bruises sufficient for two persons to share.'

It did not occur to him that she was asking for his help, and she had to make it more apparent. She reached over one shoulder and touched her back as far down as she could reach. 'It feels as though I have an entire forest of thorns embedded down there.' Still he stared at her, and she had to eschew all attempts at subtlety and modesty.

'In the chest you will find a pair of tweezers and a selection of needles you can use,' she said, turned her back to him and slipped the robe off her shoulder. 'There is one particular thorn here, just below my shoulderblade.' She touched the spot. 'It feels like a crucifixion nail.'

He gulped as he grasped her meaning, and reached for the tweezers. 'I shall try not to hurt you, but cry out if I do,' he said, but he was well practised in caring for sick and wounded animals, and his touch was firm but gentle.

She stretched out face down upon the sheepskin mattress, and gave herself over to his ministrations. Although her back was scratched and punctured in many places, and pale lymph and watery blood wept from the injuries, her skin was marble smooth and lustrously pale where it was undamaged. Although when he had first met her she had been a skinny waif, since then an abundance of good food and months of riding and walking had firmed and shaped her muscles. Even in her present straits, her body was the loveliest thing he had ever laid eyes on. He worked in silence, not trusting his voice, and except for the occasional gasp or small whimper Louisa said nothing.

When he folded back the hem of her robe to reach another hidden thorn, she moved slightly to make it easier for him. When he peeled back the silk a little further it revealed the beginning of the delicate cleft that separated her buttocks and down so fine and pale that it was invisible until the light fell upon it from a certain angle. Jim stood back and averted his eyes, although the effort required to do so was almost beyond him. 'I cannot go further,' he blurted.

'Pray, why not?' she asked, without lifting her face from the pillow. 'I can feel there are thorns that still demand your attention.'

'Modesty forbids it.'

'So you will not care if my injuries mortify, and I die of blood poisoning to save your precious modesty?'

'Do not jest so,' he exclaimed. The thought of her death struck deep into his soul. She had come so close to it this very morning.

'I jest not, James Archibald.' She raised her head from the pillow and regarded him frostily. 'I have no one else to whom I may turn. Think of yourself as a surgeon, and me as your patient.'

The lines of her naked bottom were pure and symmetrical beyond any geometrical or navigational diagram he had studied. Under his fingers her skin was warm and silken. When he had removed the thorns and anointed her various wounds with the balm, he measured a dose of laudanum to ease her discomfort. Then, at last, he was free to leave her wagon tent. But his legs seemed almost too weak to carry him.

J im ate dinner alone at the campfire. Zama had roasted a large slice of the elephant's trunk, considered by his father and other connoisseurs to be one of the great delicacies of the African bush. But Jim's jaw ached from the effort of chewing it and it had all the flavour of boiled woodchips. When the flames of the campfire died down, exhaustion overtook him. He had just sufficient energy to peep through the chink in the afterclap of Louisa's wagon tent. She was stretched out, face down under the kaross, and sleeping so soundly that he had to listen intently for the faint sound of her breathing. Then he left her and tottered to his own bed. He stripped off his clothing and dropped it on the floor, then collapsed on the sheepskin.

He woke in confusion not sure if what he was hearing was a dream or reality. It was Louisa's voice, shrill with terror: 'Jim, Jim! Help me!'

He sprang from his bed to go to her, then remembered he was naked. While he groped for his breeches she cried out again. He did not have time to don his breeches, but holding them before him, he went to her rescue. He skinned his knee on the tailboard of the wagon as he jumped down, then ran to hers and dived through the curtains of the afterclap. 'Louisa! Are you safe? What troubles you?'

'Ride! Oh, ride with all haste! Don't let it catch me!' she screamed. He realized that she was locked in a nightmare. This time it was difficult to wake her. He had to seize both of her shoulders and shake her.

'Jim, is it you?' At last she came back from the land of shadows. 'Oh, I had such a terrible dream. It was the elephant again.'

She clung to him, and he waited for her to calm. She was hot and flushed, but after a while he laid her back and pulled the fur kaross over her. 'Sleep now, little hedgehog,' he whispered. 'I will not be far away.'

'Don't leave me, Jim. Stay with me for a while.'

'Until you sleep,' he agreed.

But he fell asleep before she did. She felt him topple over slowly and lie full length beside her. Then his breathing became slow and even. He was not touching her, but his presence was reassuring and she let herself slip back into sleep. This time there were no dark fantasies to haunt her rest.

When she awoke in the dawn to the sounds of the camp stirring around her she reached out to touch him, but he was gone. She felt a sharp sense of loss.

She dressed and climbed painfully down from the wagon. Jim and Bakkat were busy at the horselines, washing the scratches and small injuries that Drumfire and Trueheart had received in yesterday's battle with the elephant, and feeding them a little of the precious oats and bran moistened with black molasses as a reward for their courage. When he looked up and saw Louisa struggling down from her wagon, Jim exclaimed with alarm and ran to her. 'You should keep to your bed. What are you doing here?'

'I am going to see to breakfast.'

'What madness is this? Zama can do without your instruction for a day. You must rest.'

'Do not treat me like a child,' she told him, but the reprimand lacked fire and she smiled at him as she limped to the cooking fire. He did not argue. It was a gorgeous morning, bright and cool, and this put them both in a sunny mood. They ate under the trees to the sound of birdsong from the branches above them, and the meal became a small celebration of the previous day's events. With animation they discussed every detail of the hunt and relived all the excitement and terror, but neither mentioned the events of the night, although they were uppermost in their minds.

'Now I must go back to the carcass to remove the tusks. It is not a task I can leave to others. A careless slip of the axe will damage the ivory irrevocably,' he told her, as he mopped his plate with a piece of unleavened pot bread. 'I will rest Drumfire today, he worked hard yesterday, and I will take Crow. Trueheart will stay in camp, for she is as lame as you are.'

'Then I shall ride Stag,' she said. 'It will not take me long to don my boots.' Stag was a strong but gentle gelding they had taken from Colonel Keyser.

'You should stay in camp to recuperate fully.'

'I must go with you to retrieve my rifle, which I dropped in the thorn thickets.'

'That is a feeble pretext. I can do that for you.'

'You do not truly believe that I shall not attend the removal of the tusks for which we risked our very lives?'

He opened his mouth to protest, but saw from her expression that it would be wasted effort. 'I shall tell Bakkat to saddle Stag.'

There were two traditional methods of withdrawing the tusks. The carcass could be left to decompose, and when the cartilage that held the tusks in their sockets had softened and disintegrated they could be pulled forcibly from the skull. This was a lengthy and malodorous business, and Jim was impatient to see his trophies revealed in all their magnificence. So was Louisa.

When they rode back they found a canopy of circling carrion birds darkening the sky above the body of the dead bull. In this vast assembly there was every species of vulture and eagle, as well as the undertaker storks with their monstrous beaks and bald pink heads, which seemed to have been parboiled. The branches of the trees around the dead bull groaned under the weight of this feathered horde. As Jim and Louisa rode up to the carcass, packs of hyena slunk away, and little red jackals peered at them from the cover of the thornbushes with pricked ears and bright eyes. These scavengers had picked out the eyes of the bull and burrowed in through his anus, but they had not been able to tear open the tough grey hide to reach the flesh. Where the vultures had perched upon the carcass their excrement had left white stains down its sides. Jim felt a sense of outrage at this desecration of such a noble beast. Angrily he drew his rifle from its sheath and fired at one of the black vultures on the top branches of the nearest tree. Struck squarely by the leaden ball, the hideous bird came tumbling down in a welter of feathers and flapping wings. The rest of the roosting flock rose and climbed to join their peers in the sky above.

When Louisa retrieved her rifle, she found that the woodwork was only lightly scratched. She came back and selected a vantage-point in the shade. Seated on a saddle blanket she sketched the proceedings, and made notes in the margins of the page.

Jim's first task was to sever the bull's immense head from the neck. This had to be done to make it easier to handle – it would have taken fifty men or more to roll the massive carcass from one side to the other. As it was, the decapitation took half the morning. Stripped to the waist the men were sweating in the noonday sun before it was accomplished.

Then came the painstaking work of removing the skin and chipping away the bone from around the roots of the tusks, with meticulous axe strokes. Jim, Bakkat and Zama took turns, not trusting the clumsy touch of the wagon drivers and servants on the precious ivory. First one and then the other tusk was lifted out of its bony canal and laid upon a mattress of cut grass. With quick strokes of her brush Louisa recorded the moment when Jim stooped over the tusks and, with the point of his knife, freed the long cone-shaped nerve from the hollow butt end of each one. They slithered out, white and glutinous as jelly.

They wrapped the tusks in cushions of cut grass, loaded them on to the backs of the pack-horses and bore them back to the wagons in triumph. Jim unpacked the scale his father had given him for this purpose and suspended it from the branch of a tree. Then, surrounded by everyone, he weighed the tusks one at a time. The right-hand shaft of ivory, the bull's working tusk, was more worn and weighed 143 pounds. The larger tusk weighed 150 pounds precisely. Both were stained brown by vegetable juices where they had been exposed, but the butts were a lovely cream colour, glossy as precious porcelain where they had been protected in the sheath of bone and cartilage. 'In all the hundreds of traded tusks I have seen pass through the godown at High Weald I have never seen one larger,' he told Louisa proudly.

They sat late beside the campfire that night for there seemed so much still to say. Bakkat, Zama and the other servants had all rolled themselves in their blankets and were sleeping beside their fires when Jim walked Louisa back to her wagon.

Afterwards he lay on his own bed, naked in the balmy night. As he drifted off he listened to the weird sobbing and laughter of the hyena patrolling the outskirts of the camp, attracted by the scent of the raw elephant meat curing on the smoking racks. His last thought was to wonder if Smallboy and the other drivers had placed the leather ropes and tackle of the wagon harness out of reach of those scavengers. With their formidable jaws the hyena could chew and swallow the toughest tanned leather as easily as he could devour a luscious oyster. But he knew that the safety and condition of the wagon harness was always Smallboy's first concern, and let himself drop into a sound sleep.

He woke suddenly, aware that the wagon had rocked lightly under him. His first thought was a continuation of the last: perhaps a hyena was raiding the camp. He sat up and reached for the loaded musket that always lay beside his bed, but before his hand could fall upon the stock he froze and stared towards the afterclap.

The moon still lacked two nights of full, and he could tell by its angle that it must be after midnight. Its light threw a soft glow through the canvas curtain of the afterclap. Louisa was silhouetted against it, an ethereal fairy figure. He could not see her face, for it was in shadow, but her hair came down in a pale cascade around her shoulders.

She took a hesitant pace towards his bed. Then she stopped again. He could see by the way in which she held her head that she was shy or afraid, maybe both. 'Louisa? What ails you?'

'I could not sleep,' she whispered.

'Is there anything I can do?'

She did not reply at once, but instead she came forward slowly and lay down at his side. 'Please, Jim, be kind to me. Be patient with me.'

They lay in silence, without touching, their bodies rigid. Neither knew what to do next.

Louisa broke the silence. 'Speak to me, Jim. Do you want me to go back to my own wagon?' It irked her that he who was usually so bold was timid now.

'No. Oh, please, no,' he blurted out.

'Then speak to me.'

'I'm not sure what you want me to say, but I will tell you all that is in my mind and heart,' he said. He thought for a while, and his voice sank to a whisper. 'When first I saw you on the deck of the ship, it seemed that I had been waiting all my life for that moment.'

She sighed softly, and he felt her relax beside him, like a cat spreading herself out in the warmth of the sun. Encouraged, he went on, 'I have often thought when I watch my father and mother together that for every man born God fashions a woman.'

'Adam's rib,' she murmured.

'I believe that you are my rib,' he said. 'I cannot find happiness and fulfilment without you.'

'Go on, Jim. Please don't stop.'

'I believe that all the terrible things that happened to you before we met, and all the hardships and dangers we have endured since then, have had but one purpose. That is to test and temper us, like steel in the furnace.'

'I had not thought of that,' she said, 'but now I see it is true.'

282

He reached out and touched her hand. It seemed to him that a spark passed between their fingertips like the crackling discharge of gunpowder in the pan. She jerked away her hand. He sensed that their moment, although close, had not yet arrived. He took back his own hand and she relaxed again.

His uncle Dorian had once given him a filly that no one else could break to the bit and saddle. It had been very much like this, weeks and months of slow progress, of advance and retreat, but in the end she had become his, as beautiful and wondrous a creature as it was possible to imagine. He had called her Windsong and had held her head as she died of the horse-sickness.

On an inspiration he told Louisa about Windsong, how he had loved her and how she had died. She lay beside him in the darkness and listened, captivated. When he came to the end of the story she wept like a child, but they were good tears, not the bitter hurting tears that had so often gone before.

Then she slept at last, still lying beside him, still not quite touching. He listened to her gentle breathing, and at last slept also.

They followed the elephant herds northwards for almost another month. It was as his father had warned him: when disturbed by man the great beasts moved hundreds of leagues to new country. They travelled at that long, striding walk that even a good horse could not match over a long distance. The entire southern continent was their domain, and the old matriarchs of the herds knew every mountain pass and every lake, river and water-hole along the way; they knew how to avoid the deserts and the desolate lands. They knew the forests that were rich in fruits and luxuriant growth, and they knew the fastness where they were safe from attack.

However, they left tracks that were clear to Bakkat's eye, and he followed them into wilderness where even he had never ventured. The tracks led them to good water, and to the easy passes through the mountains.

Thus, they came at last to a river set in a strath of grassy veld, and the waters were sweet and clear. Jim took his sights of the noon passage of the sun on five consecutive days until he was certain he had accurately fixed their position on his father's chart. Both he and Louisa were amazed at the great distance the leisurely turning wheels of the wagons had covered to bring them here.

They left the camp on the river bank each day and rode out to explore the country in all directions. On the sixth day they climbed to the top of a tall, rounded hill that overlooked the plains beyond the river.

'Since we left the frontier of the colony we have seen no sign of our fellow men,' Louisa remarked, 'just that one wagon track almost three months ago, and the paintings of Bakkat's tribe in the caves of the mountains.'

'It is an empty land,' Jim agreed, 'and I love it so, for it and everything in it belongs to me. It makes me feel like a god.'

She smiled as she watched his enthusiasm. To her he looked indeed like a young god. The sun had burned him brown, and his arms and legs were carved from granite muscle. Despite her frequent clipping with the sheep shears, his hair had grown down to his shoulders. Accustomed to staring at far horizons, his gaze was calm and steady. His bearing displayed his confidence and authority.

She could not much longer try to deceive herself, or deny how her feelings had changed towards him in these last months. He had proved his worth a hundred times. He now stood at the centre of her existence. However, she must first throw off the brake and burden of her past – even now when she closed her eyes she could see the sinister head in the black leather mask, and the cold eyes behind the slits. Van Ritters, the master of Huis Brabant, was with her still.

Jim turned back to face her, and she averted her eyes: surely her dark thoughts must be clear for him to see in them. 'Look!' she cried, and pointed across the river. 'There is a field of wild daisies growing there.'

He shaded his eyes and followed the direction of her out-thrust hand. 'I doubt that they are flowers.' He shook his head. 'They shine too bright. I think what you see is a bed of chalk stone or white quartz pebbles.'

'I am sure they are daisies, like those that grew beside the Gariep river.' Louisa pushed Trueheart forward. 'Come, let's cross to look at them. I wish to draw them.' She was already well down the hill, leaving him little choice but to follow her, although he had no great interest in flowers.

A well-trodden game path led them through a grove of wild willows to a shallow ford. They splashed through the green waters belly deep and rode up the steep cut of the far bank. They saw the mysterious white field not far ahead, glaring in the sunlight, and raced each other to it.

Louisa was a few lengths ahead, but suddenly she reined in and the laughter died on her lips. She stared down at the ground, speechless with horror. Jim stepped down from the stirrup and, leading Drumfire, walked forward slowly. The ground beneath his feet was thickly strewn with human bones. He stooped and picked up a skull from the macabre display. 'A child,' he said, and turned the tiny relic in his hands. 'Its head was staved in.'

'What has happened here, Jim?'

'There has been a massacre,' he answered, 'and not too long ago, for although the birds have picked the skeletons clean, the hyena have not yet devoured them.'

'How did it happen?' The tragic remains had moved her, and her eyes swam with tears.

He brought the child's skull to her, and held it up so she might examine it more closely. 'The imprint of a war club. A single blow to the back of the head. 'Tis how the Nguni despatch their enemies.'

'Children also?'

'It is said that they kill for the thrill and prestige.'

'How many have died here?' Louisa averted her gaze from the tiny skull, and looked instead to the piled skeletons, which lay in snowdrifts and windrows. 'How many?'

'We shall never know, but it seems that this was an entire

285

tribe.' Jim laid the little skull down on the spot where he had found it.

'No wonder we found no living man on all our long journey,' she whispered. 'These monsters have slain every one, and laid waste to the land.'

Jim fetched Bakkat from the wagons and he confirmed Jim's first estimate. He picked out from among the bones evidence to paint a broader picture of the slaughter. He found the broken head and the shaft of a war club, which he called a *kerrie*. It had been skilfully carved from a shoot of a knobthorn bush: the bulbous root section formed a natural head for the vicious club. The weapon must have snapped in the hand of the warrior who had wielded it. He also found a handful of glass trade beads scattered in the grass. They might once have been part of a necklace. They were cylindrical in shape, red and white.

Jim knew them well: identical beads were among the goods they carried in their own wagons. He showed them to Louisa. 'Beads like these have been common currency in Africa for a hundred years or more. Originally they were probably traded by the Portuguese to the northern tribes.'

Bakkat rubbed one between his fingers. 'They are highly prized by the Nguni. One of the warriors might have had a string of these torn from his neck, perhaps by the dying fingers of one of his victims.'

'Who were the victims?' Louisa asked, and spread her hands to indicate the bones that lay so thickly around them.

Bakkat shrugged. 'In this land men come from nowhere and depart again leaving no trace of their passing.' He tucked the beads into the pouch on his belt, which was made from the scrotum of a bull buffalo. 'Except my people. We leave our pictures on the rocks so that the spirits will remember us.'

'I would like to know who they were,' Louisa said. 'It is so tragic to think of the little ones who were snuffed out here, with no one to bury them or mourn their passing.'

She did not have to wait long to find out who the victims were.

The next day as the wagon train rolled northwards they saw, at a distance, the herds of wild antelope parting like the bow wave of an ocean-going vessel. Jim recognized that this was how animals reacted to the presence of human beings. He had no way of knowing what lay ahead, so he ordered Smallboy to form the wagons into a defensive square and issue a musket to each man. Then, taking Bakkat and Zama with them, he and Louisa rode out to scout the land ahead.

The grassy plain undulated like the swells of the ocean, and when they reached the next crest of higher ground and could see ahead, they reined in spontaneously and stared in silence at the strange sight that was revealed to them.

Tiny with distance a column of forlorn human figures toiled across the plain, moving so painfully slowly that they raised almost no dust. They had no domestic animals with them, and as they drew closer Jim could see through the telescope that they were carrying their meagre possessions on their heads: clay pots and calabashes, or bundles wrapped in animal skins. There was nothing hostile in their appearance, and Jim rode to meet them. As the distance narrowed more details became apparent.

The straggling file was made up almost entirely of women and their children. The infants were being carried in leather pouches slung on the backs or across the hips of their mothers. They were all wasted and thin, with legs like dried sticks. They walked with the slack, dragging gait of exhaustion. As Jim and Louisa watched, one of the skeletal women sagged to the ground. The bundle and the two small children she carried on her back were too great a burden. Her companions stopped to help her back to her feet. One held a water gourd to her mouth to allow her to drink.

It was a touching gesture. 'These people are dying on their feet,' Louisa said softly. As they rode closer she counted their heads: 'There are sixty-eight of them, but I may have missed some of the children.'

When they were within hail of the head of this sorry file, they stopped the horses and Jim rose in the stirrups. 'Who are you, and where do you come from?'

It seemed that they were so far gone they had not seen the party until then, for Jim's voice caused confusion and despair among them. Many of the women threw down their bundles and seized their children. They scattered back the way they had come, but their efforts at escape were pathetic, and one after another they staggered to a halt and collapsed in the grass, unable to run further. They tried to escape attention by lying flat and pulling their leather capes over their heads.

Only one had not run, an old man. He, too, was stick-thin and frail, but he straightened and stood with dignity. He let the shawl drop from his shoulders, let out a shrill, quavering war-cry and charged straight at Jim, brandishing a throwing spear. From fifty paces, out of range of his old arm, he hurled the spear, which pegged into the earth half-way between him and Jim. Then he sagged to his knees. Jim rode warily closer, alert for another warlike attack from the silver-headed ancient.

'Who are you, old father?' he repeated. He had to ask the same question in three different dialects before the man started with recognition, and answered: 'I know who you are, you who ride upon the back of wild animals and speak in tongues. I know you are one of the white crocodile wizards that come out of the great waters to devour men. How else would you know the language of my people? Yet I fear you not, foul demon, for I am old and ready to die. But I will die fighting against you who would devour my daughters and my grand-children.' He staggered to his feet and drew the axe from his belt. 'Come, and we will see if you have blood in your veins like other men.'

The dialect he spoke was of the northern Lozi, which old Aboli had taught Jim. 'You terrify me, bold warrior,' he told the old man gravely, 'but let us put aside our weapons and talk for a while before we do battle.'

'He looks confused and terrified,' Louisa said. 'The poor old man.'

'It may be that he is not accustomed to discourse with

288

wizards and demons,' Bakkat remarked drily, 'but one thing I know, if he is not fed soon the wind will blow him away.'

The old man was swaying on his bony legs. 'When did you last eat, great chieftain?' Jim asked.

'I do not parley with wizards or crocodile spirits,' announced the old man, with disdain.

'If you are not hungry, then tell me, chieftain, when did your daughters and your grandchildren last eat?'

The old man's defiance wavered. He looked back at his people, and his voice was low as he replied with simple dignity, 'They are starving.'

'I can see that,' Jim said grimly.

'Jim, we must fetch food for them from the wagons,' Louisa burst out.

'It will need more than our few fish and loaves to feed this multitude. Then, when they have eaten our pantry bare, we will starve with them,' Jim answered, and turned in the saddle to survey the herds of game that were scattered across the plains in every direction. 'They are starving in the midst of plenty. Their hunting skills and crude weapons will not bring down a single head of game from all this multitude,' he said, then looked back at the old man. 'I will use my witchcraft not to destroy your people but to feed them.'

They left him standing and rode out across the plain. Jim picked out a herd of cow-like wildebeest, strange-looking creatures with fringes of dark mane and lunate horns, their legs too thin for their robust bodies. These were the fools of the veld, and they gambolled ahead of Bakkat and Zama as they rode in a wide circle to surround them and drive them back towards Jim and Louisa. When the herd leaders were almost within gunshot, they sensed the danger and put down their ugly heads. Snorting and kicking up their heels they ran in earnest. Drumfire and Trueheart came up on them easily. Riding in close and shooting from the saddle Jim dropped a beast with a shot from each of his guns, and Louisa brought down another with the little French rifle. They roped the carcasses by the heels and dragged them behind the horses to where the old man was squatting in the grass.

He rose to his feet. When he realized what they had brought him, he cried out to his followers, in a quavering voice, 'Meat! The devils have brought us meat! Come quickly, and bring the children.'

Timidly one old woman crept forward, while the others hung back. The two old people started work on the carcasses, using the blade of the throwing spear as a butcher's knife. When the rest of the band saw that they were not being molested by the white devils they came swarming forward to the feast.

Louisa laughed aloud to see mothers hacking off lumps of raw meat, and chewing it to a pulp before spitting it into the mouths of their children, like mother birds feeding their chicks. When their first hunger was appeased, they built fires to roast and smoke the rest of the kill. Jim and Louisa hunted again, bringing in more prime game to provide enough smoked meat to feed even this number of mouths for some months.

Very soon the little tribe lost all fear and became so trusting that they no longer skittered away when Louisa walked among them. They even allowed her to pick up and dandle the little ones. Then the women clustered around her, touched her hair and stroked her pale skin with awe.

Jim and Bakkat sat with the old man and questioned him. 'What people are you?'

'We are of the Lozi, but our totem is the Bakwato.'

'How are you called, great chieftain of the Bakwato?' Jim asked.

'Tegwane, and in truth I am but a very small chief,' he replied. The tegwane was the little fish-eating brown stork with a feathered topknot that frequented every stream and river pool.

'Where do you come from?' The old man pointed to the north. 'Where are the young warriors of your tribe?'

'Slain by the Nguni,' Tegwane said, 'fighting to save their families. Now I am trying to find a place where the women and children will be safe, but I fear the killers are not far behind us.'

'Tell me about these Nguni,' Jim invited. 'I have heard the

name spoken with fear and awe, but I have never seen them, nor met any man who has.'

'They are killer devils,' Tegwane replied. 'They come swiftly as cloud shadows the plain, and they slaughter every living soul in their path.'

'Tell me all you know of them. What do they look like?'

'The warriors are big men built like ironwood trees. They wear black vulture feathers in their headdress. They have rattles on their wrists and ankles so their legions make the sound of the wind when they come.'

'What of their weapons?'

'They carry black shields of dried ox-hide, and they scorn the throwing spear. They like to come close with the short stabbing *assegai*. The wound from that blade is so wide and deep that it sucks the blood from the victim like a river as they pluck out the steel.'

'Where do they come from?'

'No man knows, but some say from a land far to the north. They travel with great herds of plundered cattle, and they send their cohorts ahead to slaughter all in their path.'

'Who is their king?'

'They have no king, but a queen. Her name is Manatasee. I have never seen her, but they say she is crueller and more warlike than any of her warriors.' He looked fearfully to the horizon. 'I must take my people on to escape her. Her warriors cannot be far behind us now. Perhaps if we cross the river they may not follow us.'

They left Tegwane and his women working over the fires to smoke the rest of the meat, and rode back to the wagons. That night, as they ate their dinner by the glow of the campfire under a canopy of glittering stars, they discussed the predicament of the little tribe of refugees. Louisa proposed to return next morning with their meagre chest of medicines, and bags of flour and salt.

'If you give them all we have, what will happen to us?' Jim asked reasonably.

'Just for the children?' she tried again, although she knew he was right and it was a forlorn hope that he might agree.

291

'Child or grown, we cannot take an entire tribe under our wing. We have provided them with food sufficient to see them to the river and beyond. This is a cruel land. Like us, they have to fend for themselves or perish.'

She did not come to his wagon that night, and he missed her. Although they were still as chaste as brother and sister, he had become accustomed to her presence in the night. When he woke she was already working at the campfire. During this hiatus on the river bank, their hens had been allowed out of their coop on the back of the wagon to forage. In gratitude they had produced half a dozen eggs. Louisa made an omelette for his breakfast, and served it without a smile, making her disapproval obvious.

'I had a dream last night,' she told him.

He suppressed a sigh. He was learning to make room in his life for her dreams. 'Tell me.'

'I dreamed that something terrible happened to our friends, the Bakwato.'

'You do not yield without a fight, do you?' he asked. She only smiled at him once they were riding back towards where they had left the small group of fugitives. During the ride he tried to think of other good reasons to dissuade her from taking on the role of benefactor and protector of the seventy starvelings, but he bided his time before he returned to the contest of wills.

The drifting smoke from the fires on which the meat was curing guided them the last league. As they crested the rise they reined in with surprise. Tegwane's encampment was not as they had last seen it. Dust mingled with the smoke of the fires to veil the scene, but many tiny figures were scurrying in and out of the low cloud. Jim pulled his telescope out of its case. After one glance through the lens he exclaimed, 'Sweet Jesus, the Nguni have found them already!'

'I knew it!' Louisa cried. 'I told you something terrible had happened, didn't I?'

She spurred forward and he had to ride hard to catch her. He grabbed Trueheart's rein and brought them to a halt.

'Wait! We must have a care. We don't know what we are riding into.'

'They are killing our friends!'

'The old man and his tribe are probably dead already and we do not want to join them.' Quickly he explained to Bakkat and Zama what he planned.

Fortunately the wagons were not far behind them. He gave orders to Zama to ride back and warn Smallboy and his men to stand on guard, and to bring all the oxen, spare horses and other animals into the centre of the laager.

'When they have secured the camp bring Smallboy and two of the other drivers back here, fast as you like! Bring two muskets for each man. Fill the bullet bags with goose-shot, and bring extra powder flasks.'

The smooth bores were quicker to reload than the rifles. A handful of goose-shot fired at close range would spread widely and might bring down more than one enemy with each discharge.

Although Louisa fretted and argued to go immediately to the rescue of the little band of refugees, he made her wait until Zama brought up the reinforcements of men and weapons. 'They will be here within the hour,' he assured her.

'By then the Bakwato will all be wiped out.'

She wanted to take the telescope from his hand, but he would not give it to her. 'It's better that you do not watch this.'

Through the lens he could see the sparkle of steel blades in the sunlight, waving war-shields and dancing feathered headdresses. Even his flesh crawled with horror as he saw a naked Bakwato woman run out of the dustclouds, clutching an infant to her breast. She was pursued by a tall plumed warrior. He came up behind her and stabbed her in the back. The point of the *assegai* came out between her breasts. Jim saw the steel flash pink with her blood, like the shine of a salmon's flank turning below the surface. She fell forward into the grass. The warrior stooped over her, then straightened up with her infant dangling from one hand. He threw the child high into the air,

293

and as it fell he caught it, neatly skewered on the point of the *assegai*. Then, brandishing the little corpse like a standard, he rushed back into the dust and smoke.

At last, but not too soon for Louisa, Zama galloped back with Smallboy, Klaas and Muntu, the other drivers. Swiftly Jim checked to see that their muskets were primed and loaded. They were all well versed in the use of the guns, but Jim had never seen their temper tested in a hard fight. He formed them into an extended line, and then, keeping the horses to a walk to save their strength, they rode towards the embattled encampment. Jim kept Louisa close to him. He would have preferred to send her back to the safety of the wagons, but he knew better than to suggest it.

As they closed in they could hear the outcry coming from the encampment, the screams and the wailing, the wild, triumphant ululations of the Nguni as they plied the *assegai* and the *kerrie*. Under the cloud of dust and smoke the grassland was littered with the broken bodies of the dead women and children, like flotsam thrown on a storm-swept beach.

They are all killed, Jim thought, and his anger became murderous. He glanced across at Louisa. Her face was blanched with horror as she looked upon the carnage. Then, incredibly, he saw that one, at least, of the Bakwato was still alive.

In the centre of the encampment there was a low outcrop of granite. It formed a natural strongpoint, a *zareeba* walled with rock. Here stood the gaunt figure of Tegwane, a club in one hand and a spear in the other. His body was painted with his own blood and that of his enemies. He was surrounded by Nguni warriors. They seemed to be toying with the old man, amused by his courage. Cats with a doomed mouse, they danced about him, mocking him and laughing at his warlike antics. Tegwane had regained a little of the strength and ferocity of his lost youth. His shrill war-cry and his shouts of defiance rang out, and Jim saw one of his attackers stagger back from a spear thrust into his face. He clutched the wound and blood spurted out between his fingers. This success sealed Tegwane's fate, and the Nguni moved in with purpose.

294

By now the thin line of horsemen was within a hundred paces of the periphery of the camp. So immersed were the Nguni in the joy of killing that none was aware as yet of their approach.

'How many of them are there?' Jim called to Louisa.

'I see not more than twenty or so,' she answered.

'A small scouting party,' Jim guessed. Then he shouted to his men, 'Have at them! Take them! Shoot them down like rabid jackals.'

They pushed the horses into a canter and charged down on the camp. Just ahead of the line a Nguni was prodding one of the younger women with his *assegai*, goading her into position for a thrust to her belly, but she was rolling and writhing on the ground like an eel, avoiding the bright steel point. He was so preoccupied with his cruel game that Louisa was almost on him before he looked up. Jim was not sure what she intended, but it took him by surprise when she raised the musket and fired. The charge of goose-shot slammed into the Nguni's sweat-glazed chest, and he was flung backwards by the force of it.

Louisa pulled the second musket from its sheath and kept her station at Jim's side, as they charged the knot of warriors that surrounded Tegwane. She fired again and another man dropped. Even in the exigency of the moment, Jim felt awed by her ruthlessness. This was not the girl he had thought he knew. She had just killed two men, coldly and efficiently, allowing none of the emotions that raged within her to show.

The warriors attacking Tegwane heard the gunfire behind them. The heavy reports were sounds alien to them, and when they turned to face the line of horsemen their astonishment and bewilderment showed clearly on their faces, which were speckled with the blood of their victims. Jim fired only seconds after Louisa. The heavy lead goose-shot tore into one naked belly, felling the man instantly, and shattered the arm of the warrior beside him. His *assegai* dropped from his grip and the arm hung uselessly at his side, half severed above the elbow.

The wounded man looked down at his dangling arm, then reached down and picked up his fallen *assegai* with his left hand and ran straight at Jim, who was astonished by his courage. Both his muskets were empty, and he was forced to draw the pistol from the holster on the front of his saddle. The ball hit the charging Nguni full in the throat. He made a gargling noise and blood sprayed from his severed windpipe, but his example was an inspiration to his comrades. They recovered from their surprise, left Tegwane and launched themselves at the horsemen, keening with eagerness, their faces alight with bloodlust, the rattles at their ankles buzzing with every stamp of their bare feet and thrust of their stabbing arms.

Zama and Bakkat fired together and each killed one. Two more were struck by the volley from Smallboy and the other drivers, but their aim was wild, and even the wounded Nguni came on strongly, almost closing within range of their short *assegais*.

'Back! Back to reload!' Jim shouted. The line of horsemen broke and wheeled away, galloping out of the encampment. The charge of the Nguni faltered and halted when they could not overtake the horses. Well out in the veld, Jim stopped his men and brought them under control again. 'Dismount and reload!' he ordered. 'Keep your mounts on the rein. You don't want to lose them now!'

They obeyed with alacrity. With the reins secured round their shoulders they poured powder and shot into the muzzles, and rodded a handful of goose-shot down on top.

'Smallboy and his lads may shoot like rabbits,' Jim muttered to Louisa, as he primed the pan of his second musket, 'but at least they are still under control.'

Louisa worked almost as quickly and neatly as he did and she finished loading both her weapons only a little after him. The Nguni were encouraged to see them halted. With savage shouts they broke into a run again, swiftly covering the open grassland towards the group of dismounted riders.

'At least we have drawn them away from their victims,' Louisa said, as she stepped into the saddle. Jim went up on Drumfire, but the rest of the men were still busy reloading. Jim saw that Louisa was right. All of the remaining enemy warriors had joined in the chase, and were streaming towards them across the grassland. At the granite outcrop old Tegwane stood alone, obviously badly hurt but still alive.

Bakkat finished priming the pan of his musket and, with the agility of a monkey, leaped into the saddle. He fell in beside Jim, but the others were still busy.

'Follow us when you're loaded,' Jim shouted, 'but hurry!' Then, to Louisa and Bakkat, 'Come on! We will give them a whiff of gunsmoke to blunt their appetite.' The three trotted out to meet the advancing band of warriors.

'They show no fear!' Louisa said, with reluctant admiration, as the Nguni bayed like a pack of hunting dogs and burst into a headlong charge, straight at them.

When only a hundred paces separated them, Jim halted. From the saddle they fired deliberately. Two of the attackers collapsed; a third fell to his knees and clutched his belly. They changed muskets and fired again. Both Jim and Bakkat brought down another man each, but the strain was telling on Louisa. The muskets were far too heavy for her, and she flinched instinctively at the painful recoil. Her second shot flew high. The other Nguni closed in howling savagely. Only a few were still on their feet, but their faces were lit with battle fever, and they held their black war-shields high.

'Back!' Jim ordered, and they turned away, almost under the shadow of the shields, and galloped towards where Zama, Smallboy and the rest of the company were at last reloaded and mounting. As they passed each other Jim shouted across at Smallboy, 'Don't let them get too close. Stand off and shoot them down. We'll reload and come after you.'

While Jim's party reloaded, he saw that Smallboy was obeying his orders. He and his men were keeping their horses just ahead of the charge of the Nguni, baiting them on, stopping to fire when they were in killing range, then spurring ahead again. They were doing better now: two more of the warriors were lying lifeless in the grass. When their muskets were empty Smallboy broke off his attack and led his men back.

By this time Jim's party had reloaded and were in the saddle again. The ranks of horsemen passed through each other as one retreated and the other went forward.

'Pretty shooting!' Jim encouraged Smallboy. 'Now it's our turn.'

The Nguni warriors saw them coming and stopped. For a moment, they stood in a small, uncertain group. By now, they had realized the futility of charging to meet these strangers mounted on the back of fleet, alien animals whose speed no man on foot could match. They had swiftly learned the menace of the weapons that boomed out smoke and struck men down from afar with the force of witchcraft. One broke away and fled. However, Jim noted that he did not discard his shield and *assegai*. It was clear he meant not to yield but to fight again. His companions seemed infected by his example. They turned and ran.

'Steady!' Jim cautioned his own men. 'Don't let them draw you in.' Tegwane had warned him that it was a favoured tactic of the Nguni to pretend flight, or even to feign death, to lure their enemy on.

One of them, the slowest runner, had fallen far behind the others. Jim went after him and caught him up swiftly. As he raised the musket the warrior turned at bay. Jim saw that he was no stripling: there were silver strands in his short, curling beard, and he wore a headdress of ostrich feathers and the cow tails of honour and courage around his spear arm. He displayed a sudden burst of speed and darted towards Jim. He might have driven his *assegai* blade into Drumfire's flank but Jim hit him full in the face with a load of goose-shot.

When he looked round he saw that Louisa had obeyed his order. She had not taken up the pursuit, and Bakkat and Zama had also turned back. Jim was pleased with this show of discipline and good sense: it might have been fatal to have his small force scattered across the veld. He rode back to where Louisa waited.

As he reached her side Jim saw from her face that her rage had vanished as swiftly as it had arisen. She was looking down at one of the dead Nguni with sadness and remorse in her eyes.

298

'We have driven them off, but they will return, I'm sure of that,' Jim told her, and she watched the distant figures of the surviving Nguni dwindle into the golden grassland, and disappear at last over the fold of the ground.

'It was enough,' she said. 'I'm glad you let them go.'

'Where did you learn to fight?' he asked.

'If you had spent a year on the gundeck of the *Meeuw*, you would understand.'

At that moment Smallboy and the other drivers rode up with their muskets recharged. 'We will follow them, Somoya,' he cried eagerly. It was clear that he was still gripped by the ecstasy of battle.

'No! Leave them!' Jim ordered sharply. 'Manatasee and all her army are probably waiting for you over the next hill. Your place is back at the wagons. Go there now, protect the cattle, and make ready to meet another attack.'

While Smallboy and the drivers rode off, Jim led the others back to the grisly encampment. Old Tegwane was sitting on a lump of granite, nursing his injuries and crooning a soft lament for his family and the other women and children of his tribe, whose corpses were scattered around him.

While Louisa gave him water from her flask, then washed his wounds and bound them up to staunch the bleeding, Jim went through the encampment. He approached the bodies of the fallen Nguni warily, loaded pistol at the ready. But all of them were dead: the goose-shot had inflicted terrible wounds. They were mostly big, handsome men, young and powerfully built. Their weapons were the work of skilled blacksmiths. Jim picked up one of the *assegais*. It had a marvellous balance in his hand and both edges were sharp enough to shave the hair from his forearm. The dead warriors all wore necklaces and bangles of carved ivory. Jim took one of these ornaments from the neck of the Nguni elder he had killed with his last shot. By the ostrich feathers in his headdress, and the white cow tails round his upper arms Jim judged that he must have been senior in the band. The ivory necklace was beautifully carved, tiny human figures threaded on to a leather thong.

'Each figure represents a man he has killed in battle,' Jim

299

guessed. It was obvious that the Nguni placed a high value on ivory. This intrigued Jim, and he slipped the necklace into his pocket.

As he went on through the camp he found that the Nguni had done their gruesome work thoroughly. The children had all been despatched with merciless efficiency. For most a single blow with a war club was all it had taken. Apart from Tegwane, they found only one other Bakwato still alive, the girl Louisa had saved with her first shot. She had a deep spear wound in her shoulder, but she was able to walk when Zama lifted her to her feet. Louisa saw that she was too young to have given birth to her first child, for her belly was flat and smooth, her breasts like unripe fruit. Tegwane let out a joyous cry when he saw she was still alive, and hobbled to embrace her.

'This is Intepe, the lily of my heart, my granddaughter,' he cried.

Louisa had noticed her at their first meeting with the tribe, for she was the prettiest of all the women. Intepe came to her trustingly and sat patiently as Louisa washed and dressed her wound. When Louisa had finished tending Tegwane and his granddaughter, she looked around at the dead who lay half hidden in the grass.

'What must we do with all these others?' she called to Jim.

'We have finished here,' Jim replied, then glanced up at the cloudless sky where, high above, the vultures were gathering. 'We will leave the rest of the work to them. Now we must hurry back to the wagons. We have much to do there before the Nguni return.'

Jim picked out the best defensive position along the river bank. Here a small tributary stream flowed down from the hills to join the main flow. It came in at an acute angle, forming a narrow wedge of ground bounded on one side by a pool of the main river. Jim plumbed the depth of the pool and found that it was deeper than a man was tall.

'The Nguni will never swim,' Tegwane assured him. 'Water is perhaps the only thing they fear. They will eat neither fish nor hippopotamus, for they have an abhorrence of anything that comes from water.'

'So the pool will protect our flank and rear.' Jim was relieved. Tegwane was proving a useful source of information. He boasted that he could speak the Nguni language fluently, and that he knew their customs. If this was true, he was well worth his keep.

Jim walked along the top of the steep bank of the tributary stream. The drop was over ten feet, a wall of greasy clay that would be difficult to scale without a ladder.

'This will protect the other flank. We have only to draw up the wagons across the neck between river and stream.'

They rolled them into position, and roped the wheels together with rawhide *riems*, to prevent the Nguni pushing them aside and forcing a breach. In the gaps between the wagon bodies, and under the wagon beds they packed thorn-branches, leaving no space for the warriors to crawl through. In the centre of the wagon line they left a narrow gate.

Jim ordered that the horses and the other domestic animals were to be herded and grazed close by, so that within minutes they could be driven into the protection of the laager and the gateway sealed off against attack with faggots of thornbush placed ready to hand.

'Do you truly believe that the Nguni will return?' Louisa tried to hide her fear as she asked the question. 'Don't you think they might have learned by hard experience and that they will pass us by?'

'Old Tegwane knows them well. He has no doubt that they will come if only because they dearly love a fight,' Jim replied.

'How many more of them are there?' she asked. 'Does Tegwane know?'

'The old man cannot count. He says only that they are many.'

Jim carefully measured and selected a spot well out in front of the wagons, where he made Smallboy and his drivers dig a shallow hole. In it he placed a fifty-pound keg of coarse black

301

gunpowder, set a fuse of slow-match in the bung-hole and ran it back between the wheels of the centre wagon. He covered the keg with sacks of pebbles from the river bed which he hoped would scatter like musket balls when the keg exploded.

He had the men cut firing loopholes into the wall of thorns through which they could lay down enfilading fire along the front of the defences. With the grindstone Smallboy sharpened the naval cutlasses and placed them ready to hand. Then the loaded muskets were stacked beside the cutlasses, with powder kegs and shot bags and spare ramrods close by. Louisa instructed and rehearsed the *voorlopers* and herd-boys in load-ing and priming the weapons. She had some difficulty in persuading them that if one handful of gunpowder resulted in such a satisfactory explosion, two would be no improvement; it might result in a burst gun barrel and even the decapitation of whoever pulled the trigger.

The water fagies were refilled from the river pool and made ready, either to slake the thirst of fighting men or to quench the flames if the Nguni latched on to the old trick of hurling lighted torches into the laager.

Two herd-boys were placed as lookouts on the crest of the low hill from which Louisa had first spied the charnel field. Jim gave them a clay fire-pot, and ordered them to light a fire of green leaves if they saw the main Nguni *impi*, or warrior band, approaching. The smoke would warn the camp and, when it was lit, they could race down the hill into the laager to spread the alarm. Jim made certain that the boys came down from the hilltop and were safely in the laager each evening before nightfall. It would have been heartless to leave them out there in the dark at the mercy of wild beasts and Nguni scouts.

'The Nguni never attack at night,' Tegwane told Jim. 'They say that the darkness is for cowards. A true warrior should die only in the sunlight.' Nevertheless Jim brought in his pickets and placed sentries around the periphery of the laager at nightfall, and inspected them regularly during the night to make certain that they stayed awake.

'They will come singing and beating their shields,' Tegwane

302

said. 'They wish to warn their enemy. They know that their fame precedes them, and that the sound of their voices and sight of their black headdresses fills the bellies of their enemy with fear.'

'Then we must prepare a fitting greeting for them,' Jim said.

They cleared the trees and underbrush for a hundred paces in front of the wagons, and the spans of trek oxen dragged away the felled trees. The ground was left open and bare. The attacking *impi* would have to cross this killing ground to reach the wagons. Then Jim paced out the distances in front of the defences, and laid a line of white river stones to mark the most effective range and spread patterns of the goose-shot. He impressed on his men that they must not open fire until the first rank of the attackers crossed this line.

When he had completed all his preparations, they settled down to wait. This was the worst time, and the slow drag of the hours was corrosive to their spirits. Jim took advantage of this delay by spending time with Tegwane, learning more about the enemy from him.

'Where do they keep their women and children?'

'They do not bring them to war. Perhaps they leave them in their homeland.'

'Do they have a great store of plunder and riches?'

'They have many cattle, and they love the ivory teeth of the elephant and the hippopotamus.'

'Tell me of their cattle.'

'They have huge herds. The Nguni love their cattle like their own children. They do not slaughter them to eat their meat. Instead they tap off their blood and mix it with the milk. This is their main food.'

A calculating look came into Jim's eyes as he listened. A prime ox fetched a hundred guilders in the colony.

'Tell me of their ivory.'

'They love ivory very much,' Tegwane replied. 'Perhaps they need it for trade with the Arabs of the north or with the Bulamatari.' The name meant Breakers of Rock, a reference to the Portuguese, whose prospectors chipped the reef for traces of gold. Jim was surprised that here, in the deep interior,

Tegwane had heard of these nations. He questioned him on this, and Tegwane smiled. 'My father's father knew of you crocodile wizards, and his father before him.'

Jim nodded. It was naïve of him. The Omani Arabs had been trading and slaving in Africa since the fifth century. It was a hundred and fifty years ago that Vasco da Gama landed at Mozambique island and the Portuguese had begun building their forts and trading stations on the mainland. Of course rumours of these events must have penetrated even to the most primitive tribes in the remotest corners of this vast land.

Jim showed the old man the tusks of the bull he had killed, and Tegwane was amazed. 'I have never seen teeth of this size before.'

'Where do the Nguni find the ivory? Do they hunt the elephant?'

Tegwane shook his head. 'The elephant is a mighty beast, and even the Nguni cannot kill him with their *assegais*.'

'Where, then, does the ivory come from?'

'I have heard that there are some tribes who dig pits to trap them, or hang a spear weighted with stones in a tree over the pathway they frequent. When the elephant touches the trip-rope the spear drops and pierces him to the heart.' Tegwane paused and glanced at Bakkat who was asleep under one of the wagons. 'I have also heard that those little yellow monkeys of the San sometimes kill them with their poisoned arrows. But they can kill few by these methods.'

'Then where do the Nguni get their ivory?' Jim persisted.

'Each season, especially in the time of the rains, some of the great beasts die of age or sickness or they flounder in mudholes or fall from the mountain passes. The ivory tusks lie there for any man to gather up. During my lifetime my own tribe has gathered up many.'

'What happened to the tusks of your tribe?' Jim leaned forward eagerly.

'When they slaughtered our young men, the Nguni stole them from us, as they steal them from every tribe they attack and massacre.'

'They must have a great store of ivory,' Jim said. 'Where do they keep it?'

'They carry it with them,' Tegwane replied. 'When they move they load the tusks onto the backs of their cattle. They have as much ivory as they have cattle to carry it. They have many cattle.'

Jim repeated the story to Louisa. 'I should like to find one of these herds, each beast with a fortune in ivory strapped to its back.'

'Would it belong to you?' she asked innocently.

'The spoils of war!' he said, with righteous indignation. 'Of course it would be mine.' He looked to the hills over which he expected the *impis* of the Nguni to appear. 'When will they come?' he wondered.

The longer they had to wait, the more it played on all their nerves. Jim and Louisa passed much of the time over the chessboard, but when that palled she painted his portrait again. While he posed for her, he read aloud *Robinson Crusoe*. It was his favourite book. Secretly he saw himself as the resourceful hero. Although he had read it many times, he still chuckled and exclaimed at Crusoe's adventures, and bewailed his misfortunes.

Two or three times during the day they rode out to inspect the lookouts on the hilltop and make sure the herd-boys were awake and alert, and had not wandered off in search of honey or some other childish distraction. Then they scouted the lie of the land around the laager to make certain the Nguni pickets were not creeping up on them through the gullies and the light forests that were interspersed in the grassy veld.

On the twelfth day after the massacre of the Bakwato, Jim and Louisa rode out alone. The herd-boys on the hilltop were bored and disgruntled, and Jim had to speak to them sternly to make them stay at their posts.

They came back down the hill and crossed the river at the ford. They rode out almost to the site of the massacre, but turned back before they reached it. Jim wanted to spare Louisa the harrowing memories associated with that place.

They returned to within sight of the laager, and Jim stopped to examine the defences through the lens of the telescope to see if he could pick out any weak spot he had overlooked. While he was preoccupied Louisa dismounted and looked around for some place where she could go about her private business. The ground was open here, and the grass had been grazed down by the game herds until it reached only half-way to her knees. However, she saw that close by ran a *donga*, a natural gully cut out by the rainwaters draining towards the river. She handed Trueheart's reins to Jim.

'I will not be gone long,' she said, and started towards the gully. Jim opened his mouth to caution her, then thought better of it and looked away to preserve her modesty.

As Louisa approached the lip of the gully she became aware of a strange sound, a whisper, a susurration, that seemed to tremble in the air. She kept on walking, but more slowly, puzzled but not alarmed. The sound grew louder, like running water or the hum of insects. She was not certain from which direction it came.

She glanced back at Jim, but he was gazing through the lens, not looking in her direction. It was clear that he had not heard the sound. She hesitated then stepped to the lip of the *donga* and looked down into it. As she did so, the sound rose to an angry buzz as though she had disturbed a nest of hornets.

The gully below her was closely packed with rank upon rank of Nguni warriors. They were sitting on their shields, but each man had his stabbing *assegai* in his right hand and they were pointing the blades at her, and at the same time shaking the weapons, a slight trembling movement that agitated the war rattles on each wrist. This gave off the buzzing sound that had troubled her. The small movement also set the glossy black feathers in their headdresses dancing. Their naked torsos were anointed with fat so that they shone like washed coal. The whites of their eyes staring up at her were the only contrast in this seething expanse of black. It seemed to Louisa that she was gazing down on an enormous dragon coiled in its lair, black scales glittering, angry and venomous, poised to strike.

306

She whirled and ran. 'Jim! Beware! They are here!'

Jim looked back, startled by her cry. He saw no sign of danger, only Louisa racing towards him with her face working with terror.

'What is it?' he called, and at that moment the ground seemed to open behind the running girl and from it erupted a mass of warriors. Their bare feet beat upon the hard earth and the war rattles on their ankles crashed in unison. They drummed on their black war-shields with the *assegais*, a deafening roar, and they shouted, '*Bulala! Bulala amathagati!* Kill! Kill the wizards!'

Louisa fled before this rolling tide. She ran like a whippet, nimble and quick, but one of her pursuers was quicker still. He was tall and lean, made taller by the headdress. The muscle started proud in his belly and shoulders, as he bounded after her. He threw aside his shield to unburden himself. Although Louisa had a lead of twenty paces or more, he was overhauling her swiftly. The haft of his *assegai* rested lightly on his shoulder, but the long blade was pointed forward, poised for the thrust between her shoulder-blades. Jim had a fleeting memory of the Bakwato girl run through in this way, the blade appearing magically out of the middle of her breast, smeared pink with her heart's blood.

He sent Drumfire into full gallop and, dragging Trueheart on the rein behind him, raced to meet Louisa. But he saw that the leading warrior was already too close. She would not have time to mount before he was on her, his blade transfixed through her body. He did not slow or check Drumfire's charge. They brushed past Louisa so closely that her hair fluttered in the wind of their passing. Jim tossed her Trueheart's reins.

'Get up and away!' he shouted as he went by. He had only one musket with him, for he had not expected a fight. He could not afford to waste that single shot. The light ball of the pistol might only wound and not kill cleanly. There was no latitude for error here. He had seen the warrior throw aside his shield. He jerked the naval cutlass from its scabbard. Under the eye of Aboli and his father he had practised with this weapon until he mastered the Manual of Arms. He did not brandish the blade to warn his man. He charged Drumfire straight at the Nguni, and saw him check and change his grip on the *assegai*. His dark eyes locked on Jim's face. Jim knew by his haughty expression that he would not deign to wound the horse under him, but would take him on man to man. He watched for the *assegai* thrust, leaning forward to meet it. The Nguni struck, and Jim dropped the cutlass into the classic counter, sweeping aside the point of the *assegai*, then reversed and, as he passed, he swung the cutlass back-handed. Smallboy had put a fine edge on the steel and it was sharp as a butcher's cleaver. Jim swept it across the back of the warrior's neck, and felt the hilt jar in his hand as it sheared cleanly through his vertebrae. The man dropped as though a gallow's trap had opened under him.

At the pressure of his knees Drumfire spun round like a weathercock in a fluke of wind. He saw that Louisa was having difficulty trying to mount Trueheart. The mare had smelt the Nguni and seen the ranks racing towards them. She was skittering sideways and throwing her head wildly. Holding on to the reins Louisa was being pulled off her feet.

Jim sheathed the bloody cutlass, and turned Drumfire in behind her. Leaning from the saddle he grabbed a handful of the baggy seat of her breeches and boosted her up into the saddle. Then he steadied her with a hand on her arm as they galloped back knee to knee. As soon as they were clear he drew his pistol and fired a shot into the air, to alert the sentries at the laager. As soon as he saw that they had heard it, he told Louisa, 'Ride back! Warn them to get the animals into the laager. Send Bakkat and Smallboy to help me delay them.'

To his relief she had the good sense not to argue, and raced away, pushing Trueheart to the top of her speed. He turned back to face the charging warriors, drew the musket from its sheath and walked Drumfire towards them. He picked out the *induna* in the front rank who was leading them. Tegwane had told him how to recognize the captains. 'They are always older men, and they wear ostrich plumes in their headdress and white cow tails on their arms.'

He touched Drumfire with his toes and broke into a trot,

heading directly for the *induna*. By now the Nguni must have understood the terrible menace of the firearms, but the man showed no fear: he increased the speed of his charge, and lifted his shield to clear his spear arm, his face twisted with the ferocity of his war-cry.

'*Bulala*! Kill! Kill!' Behind him his men surged forward. Jim let him come in close, then fired. Still at full run the *induna* went down, the *assegai* flew from his hand and he rolled in the grass. The spread of shot caught the two men directly behind him, and sent them tumbling too.

An angry roar went up from the black mass of the *impi* to see their captain and their comrades shot down, but Jim had wheeled away and was already galloping back to reload. The Nguni could not keep up the pace, and they slowed to a trot. But still they came on.

With the musket reloaded, Jim mounted again and rode to meet them. He wondered how many there were in that dark mass, but it was impossible to guess. He crossed their front at less than twenty paces and fired into them. He saw men stumble and fall, but their comrades swept over them so their bodies were hidden almost immediately. This time there was no angry shout to acknowledge the damage he had inflicted.

The *impi* slowed to a smooth, swinging trot, and began to sing. The deep African voices were beautiful, but the sound made the hair rise on the back of Jim's neck, and seemed to reverberate deep in his guts. They moved inexorably towards the fortified walls of the laager.

As Jim finished reloading again, he heard the sound of hoofs and looked up to see Bakkat and Louisa leading Zama and the other drivers out through the gateway between the wagons.

'Lord give me strength! I meant her to stay safely in the laager,' he muttered, but then he made the best of it. As she rode up and handed him his second musket, he said, 'The same drill as before, Hedgehog. You take command of the second section, Zama, Bakkat and Muntu with you. Smallboy and Klaas with me.'

He led his section in, right under the *assegais* of the front

309

rank of warriors, and they fired the first guns, then changed, came back and fired the second volley before breaking off and galloping back with empty guns.

'Pick out the *indunas*,' Jim called, 'kill their captains,' as Louisa led her section forward. Again and again the two sections changed places smoothly, and the steady volleys never faltered. Jim saw with grim satisfaction that most of the *indunas* at the front of the attack had fallen under the onslaught.

The Nguni wilted before this fearsome unrelenting attack. Their pace slowed, the singing sank away to an angry, frustrated hissing. At last they stopped only three hundred paces short of the laager. The horsemen kept up the steady attack.

Jim rode in once again at the head of his section, and saw the change. Some of the warriors in the front rank lowered their shields and glanced behind them. Jim and his men fired a volley with their first guns, then turned and rode back along the front with their second guns at the ready. The headdresses waved, the feathers fluttered like the wind in the grass. The next volley crashed into them, and the lead-shot clapped into living flesh. Men reeled and fell.

The echoes of the volley were still booming back from the hills when Louisa galloped forward with Zama, Bakkat and Muntu close behind her. The front rank of the Nguni saw them coming and broke. They turned back and shoved with their shields into the men behind them shouting, '*Emuva!* Back, go back!' but those behind shouted, '*Shikelela!* Forward! Push forward!'

The entire *impi* wavered, swaying back and forth, men struggling, their shields tangling and blocking each other's spear arms. Louisa and her men charged in close and they fired a rolling volley into the struggling mass. A groan of despair went up and the rear rank gave way. They turned and streamed back across the grassland, leaving their dead and wounded lying where they had fallen, their shields, spears and *kerries* strewn about them. Louisa's party galloped after them, firing their second guns into the ruck.

Jim saw the danger of them being drawn into a trap, and raced after them. Drumfire swiftly overhauled them. 'Stop!

310

Break off the chase!' Louisa obeyed at once and called off her men. All of them rode back. As soon as they were safely into the laager, a span of oxen dragged the faggots of thornbush into the gap in the defences to seal it off.

It seemed impossible that such a mass of humanity could disappear so swiftly, but by the time the gate was secured the *impi* were gone, and the only signs of the fighting were the dead and the trampled, bloodstained grass in front of the laager.

'We hurt them grievously. Will they come back?' Louisa asked anxiously.

'As surely as the sun will set and rise again tomorrow,' Jim said grimly, and nodded to where it was already sinking towards the horizon. 'That was probably only the scouting party, sent by Manatasee to test our mettle.'

He called for Tegwane, and the old man came at once, trying not to favour his wounds. 'The *impi* were lying up close to the laager. If Welanga had not come across them, they would have waited for nightfall to attack us. You were wrong, old man. They do fight at night.'

'Only the Kulu Kulu is never wrong,' Tegwane answered, with an unconvincing attempt at nonchalance.

'You can redeem yourself,' Jim told him sternly.

'I will do whatever you say.' Tegwane nodded.

'Some of the Nguni are not dead. As we rode back, I saw at least one still moving. Go out with Bakkat to guard you. Find one of the Nguni who still lives. I want to know the whereabouts of their queen. I also want to know where their baggage train is camped, the cattle and the ivory.'

Tegwane nodded, and loosened his skinning knife in its sheath. Jim was about to order him to leave his knife in the laager, but then he remembered the women and children of the old man's tribe, and the manner of their deaths.

'Go at once, great chief. Go before the coming of darkness and before the hyena find the wounded Nguni.' Then he turned to Bakkat. 'Have your musket ready. Never trust a Nguni, especially a dead one.'

Three times Jim looked up from inspecting the defences of

the laager at the sound of Bakkat's musket booming out across the battlefield. He knew that the little Bushman was finishing off the wounded enemy. Just as the light was fading, Bakkat and Tegwane returned to the laager. Both were carrying *assegais* and looted ivory ornaments. Tegwane had fresh blood on his hands.

'I spoke to a wounded *induna*, before he died. You were right. This was only a scouting party. However, Manatasee is very close, with the rest of her *impis* and the cattle. She will be here within two days.'

'What did you do with the man who told you this?'

'I recognized him,' Tegwane replied. 'He was the one who led the first attack on our village. Two of my sons died that day.' Tegwane was silent for a while, then smiled thinly. 'It would have been heartless to leave a fine warrior, such as he was, to the hyenas. I am a man of compassion.'

After dinner, the drivers and other servants drifted across from their fires and gathered at a respectful distance around Jim and Louisa. The drivers smoked their long-stemmed clay pipes. The smell of the strong Turkish tobacco was rank on the sweet night air. This was one of the informal councils, which they called *indaba*, that had become a tradition of camp life over the months. Although most of them listened more than they spoke, every man present – from Smallboy, the head driver, to Izeze, the youngest herd-boy – knew that he was entitled to state his views as strongly as he felt inclined.

They were all nervous. At even the most ordinary night sounds they started and peered out into the darkness beyond the walls of the laager. The yipping of a jackal might be the rallying call of the Nguni pickets. The whisper of the night wind in the thorn trees along the river bank might be the sound of their war rattles. The rumbling hoofs of a stampeding herd of wildebeest, frightened by a marauding pride of lions, might be the sound of *assegais* drumming on rawhide shields. Jim knew that his men had come to him to seek reassurance.

Though he was younger than any of the adults except Zama, he spoke to them like a father. He told them of the battles they had fought already, and singled them out one by one to praise their feats, their steadiness in the heat of the action, and the terrible losses they had inflicted on the enemy. He did not forget the part played by the herders and the *voorlopers*, and the boys grinned with pride. 'You have proved to me, and yourselves, that the Nguni cannot prevail against our horses and muskets – as long as we stand firm and hold hard.'

When they drifted away at last from the campfire to their own mattresses their mood had changed. They chatted cheerfully among themselves, and their laughter was unfeigned.

'They trust you,' Louisa said quietly. 'They will follow where you lead them.' She was silent a moment and then she said, so softly that he barely caught the words, 'And so will I.' She paused, then 'Come!' she said, took his hand and pulled him to his feet. Her voice was firm and decided. Before this she had always come to him surreptitiously once the rest of the camp was asleep. Now she went openly with him to his wagon. She could hear the murmur of other voices in the darkness and knew that the servants were watching them. It did not deter her.

'Hand me up,' she said when they reached the rear steps of the wagon. He stooped and lifted her in his arms. She placed both her arms round his neck and pressed her face into its curve. He made her feel as small and light as a child as he carried her up the ladder and brushed through the curtain of the afterclap. 'I am your woman,' she told him.

'Yes.' He laid her on the cardell bed. 'And I am your man.'

He stood over her and stripped off his clothing. His body was pale and strong in the lamplight. She saw that he was fully aroused, and felt no revulsion. She reached out unashamedly and took him in her hand, her thumb and fingers barely encompassing his girth. He was as hard as if he had been carved from a branch of ironwood. The tips of her breasts ached with wanting him. She sat up and unlaced the front of her tunic.

313

'I need you, Jim. Oh, how I need you,' she said, still staring at him. He was rough with haste, his need surpassing hers. He pulled off her boots, then stripped off her breeches. Then he stopped and stared in awe at the pale golden cluster of curls in the fork of her thighs.

'Touch me,' she said, her voice husky. For the first time he laid his hand upon the entry-port to her body and soul. She let her thighs fall apart, and he felt the heat almost scald his fingertips. Gently he parted the fleshy lips, and slippery beads of moisture anointed him.

'Hurry, Jim,' she whispered, and clasped him again. 'I can bear it no longer.' She tugged at him insistently, and he fell forward on top of her.

'Oh, God, my little hedgehog, how I love you.' His words were choked.

Clasping him in both her hands, she tried to guide him into herself, but there was a moment when she thought she was too small for him. 'Help me!' she cried again, and placed both hands upon his buttocks. She pulled him towards her desperately, and felt the hard round muscles convulse under her hands as he thrust forward with his hips. She cried out incoherently, for he was cleaving her apart. It was pleasure driven to the frontiers of agony. Then, suddenly, he forced his way past all resistance, and she felt the full slithering length of him. She screamed, but when he tried to pull back she locked both legs over his back to hold him. 'Don't leave me,' she cried. 'Don't ever leave. Stay with me for ever.'

When he woke, the first light of dawn was pearling the canvas curtain of the afterclap. She was awake and watching him, lying quietly with her head on his bare chest. When she saw his eyes open she traced with her forefinger the shape of his mouth. 'When you sleep you look like a little boy,' she whispered.

'I will prove to you that I am a big boy,' he whispered back.

'I want you to know, James Archibald, that I am always open to proof.' She smiled, then sat up and placed her hands on his shoulders to pin him down. In one lithe movement, as though she were mounting Trueheart, she straddled his lower body.

Their joy was so incandescent that it seemed to light the whole encampment, and changed the mood of all those around them. Even the herd-boys were aware that something monumental had taken place, and they giggled and nudged each other when they watched Jim and Louisa together. It gave them all something to gossip about, and even the threat of Manatasee and her *impis* seemed to recede in the face of this new fascination.

Jim sensed the lackadaisical mood that was spreading through the laager, and did all he could to keep them alert and vigilant. He exercised the mounted musketeers every morning, honing the tactics of the fighting withdrawal they had struck upon almost by chance.

Then he reviewed the defence of the laager. Each of the musketeers was allotted his station on the perimeter, and given two boys to load for him. Jim and Louisa together drilled the *voorlopers* and herd-boys at reloading the muskets. Jim nailed a gold guilder coin to the tailboard of his wagon. 'On Sunday, after Welanga reads to you from the Bible, we will hold a competition for the fastest gun team,' he promised, and hauled from his pocket the big chiming watch on its gold chain that Tom and Sarah had given him on his last birthday. 'I will time you with this, and the gold guilder goes to the champions.'

A gold coin was a fortune beyond the imagining of the boys, and the promise spurred them on until soon they were almost as quick as Louisa. Although some were so small that they had to stand on tiptoe to rod the charge down the long barrels, they learned to cant the weapon so they could reach the muzzle more readily. They weighed the powder charge by scooping a handful from the kegs, rather than fumbling with the flask, and stuffed the shot into their mouths to spit it into the muzzle. Within days they were able to keep a ripple of gunfire running up and down the barricade, handing the recharged muskets to the front almost as fast as the men could fire them. Jim felt that the expenditure of gunpowder and shot was worthwhile. The boys were inflamed with excitement as the day of the loading competition drew nearer, and the men gambled heavily on the outcome.

On Sunday Jim woke while it was still dark. He was immediately aware that something was amiss. He could not place it, but then he heard the horses moving restlessly in the lines, and the cattle milling about in the laager.

'Lions?' he wondered, and sat up. At that moment one of the dogs barked, and the others joined in. He jumped out of bed and reached for his breeches.

'What is it, Jim?' Louisa asked, and he could hear that she was still half asleep.

'The dogs. The horses. I'm not sure.' He pulled on his boots, sprang down from the wagon, and saw that most of the camp was already astir. Smallboy was throwing wood on to the fire and Bakkat and Zama were in the horselines trying to soothe the agitated animals with words and caresses. Jim strode to the barricade and spoke softly to the two boys who were crouched there, shivering in the dawn chill.

'Have you seen or heard anything out there?' They shook their heads and peered out into the darkness. It was still too dark to make out the tops of the thorn trees against the sky. He listened intently, but the only sound he heard was the dawn breeze in the grass. Nevertheless, he was as restless as the horses, and relieved that he had ordered all the livestock to be brought in from the veld at sunset the previous evening. The laager was sealed off and barricaded.

Louisa came to stand beside him. She was fully dressed with a shawl over her shoulders, and she had bound up her hair with a headcloth. They stood close together, waiting and listening. Trueheart whickered and the other horses stamped and jingled the chains of their halters. Every person in the laager was awake now, but their voices were strained and subdued.

Suddenly Louisa seized Jim's hand and squeezed it hard. She heard the singing before he did. The voices were faint, but bass and deep on the soft dawn breeze.

Tegwane came from the fire, still limping from his wounds. He stood by Jim's other side and they listened to the singing. 'It is the Death Song,' Tegwane said softly. 'The Nguni are asking the spirits of their fathers to prepare a feast to welcome them in the land of shades. They are singing that this day they will die in battle or bring great honour to the tribe.' They listened in silence for a while.

'They are singing now that tonight their women will weep or rejoice for them, and their sons will be proud.'

'When will they come?' Louisa asked softly.

'As soon as it is light,' Tegwane told her.

Louisa was still clinging to Jim's hand. Now she lifted her face to his. 'I have not said it before, but I must say it now. I love you, my man.'

'I have said it many times before, but I say it again,' he replied. 'I love you, my little hedgehog.'

'Kiss me,' she said, and their embrace was long and fierce. Then they drew apart.

'Go to your places now,' Jim called to the men. 'Manatasee has come.'

The herd-boys brought them their breakfast from the cooking fires, and they ate their salted porridge in darkness, standing by the guns. When daylight came, it came swiftly. First the tops of the trees showed against the brightening sky, then they could make out the vague shape of the hills beyond. Suddenly Jim drew breath sharply, and Louisa started next to him.

'The hills are dark,' she whispered. The light strengthened and the singing grew with it, rising in majestic chorus. Now they could make out the mass of the regiments that lay like a deep shadow upon the pale grassland. Jim studied them through the lens of the telescope.

'How many are there?' Louisa asked softly.

'As Tegwane has said, they are many. It is not possible to count their numbers.'

'And we are only eight.' Her voice faltered.

'You have not counted the boys.' He laughed. 'Don't forget the boys.'

Jim went back to where the boys waited beside the gun racks, and spoke to each of them. Their cheeks were stuffed with goose-shot, and they held the ramrods ready, but they grinned and bobbed their heads. Children make fine soldiers, he thought. They have no fear for they think it is a game, and they obey orders.

Then he walked along the line of men who stood behind the barricades. To Bakkat he said, 'The Nguni will have seen you from afar, for you stand tall as a granite hill in their path and strike terror into their hearts.'

'Have your long whips ready,' he told Smallboy and the drivers. 'After this little fight you will have a thousand head of cattle to drive down to the coast.'

He clasped Zama's shoulder. 'I am glad that you stand beside me as you have always done. You are my right hand, old friend.'

As he returned to Louisa's side the singing of the *impis* swelled to a crescendo, then ended with the stamp of hundreds of horny bare feet that rang out like a salvo of artillery. The silence after it was shocking.

'Now it begins,' Jim said and lifted the telescope.

The black ranks stood like a petrified forest. The only movement was the rising dawn wind ruffling the vulture feathers in their headdresses. Then Jim saw that the centre of the line was opening like the petals of a night orchid, and a column of men came through, winding like a serpent down the grassy hillside towards the laager. In stark contrast to the massed *impis* they wore kilts made of strips of white oxhide, and tall headdresses of snowy egret feathers. Twenty men led the column. On their hips were slung war drums made from hollowed-out logs. The rank behind them carried trumpets of kudu horn. In the centre of the column there was a massive litter whose interior was screened by leather curtains. Twenty men carried it on their shoulders, shuffling and swaying, dipping and turning.

One of the drummers began to tap out a tattoo, which throbbed like the pulse of all the world, and the *impis* swayed to the rhythm. One by one the other drummers joined in and the music swelled. Then the trumpeters lifted their kudu horns, and blew a warlike fanfare. The column opened into a single file with the great litter in the centre, and halted just out of range of the barricade of the laager. The trumpets sounded a second blast that rang against the hills, then another eerie silence fell.

By now the first rays of the rising sun played over the massed regiments. It struck sparks of light from the blades of the *assegais*.

'We should strike now,' Louisa said. 'We should sortie on horseback, and attack them first.'

'They are already too close. We would only get in two or three volleys before they drove us back into the laager,' Jim told her gently. 'Let them expend themselves on the barricades. I want to save the horses for what will come later.'

Again the trumpets sang out and the bearers lowered the litter to the ground. There was another trumpet blast, and from the litter emerged a single dark shape like a hornet from its nest.

'*Bayete!*' thundered the regiments. '*Bayete!*' The royal salute drowned the drums and trumpets. Hurriedly Jim snatched up the telescope and stared at the macabre figure.

The woman was slim and sinuous, taller than her bodyguards in their egret headdresses. She was stark naked, but her entire body was painted in fantastic patterns. There were glaring white circles around her eyes. A straight white line ran up her throat, over her chin and nose, between her eyes and over her shaven scalp, dividing her head into hemispheres. One half was painted blue as the sky, the other half blood red. She carried a small ceremonial *assegai* in her right hand, the haft covered with fine designs of beadwork and tassels of lion's mane hair.

Whorls and swirls of white paint highlighted her breasts and her mons Veneris. Diamond and arrowhead patterns enhanced the length of her slim arms and legs.

319

'Manatasee!' Tegwane said softly. 'The queen of death.'

Manatasee began to dance, a slow, mesmeric movement like that of an erect cobra. She came down the hillside towards the laager, graceful and deadly. None of the men in the laager moved or spoke and stared in dread fascination.

The *impis* moved forward behind her, as though she were the head of the dragon and they the monstrous body. Their weapons sparkled like reptilian scales in the low sun.

Manatasee stopped just short of the cut line that Jim had cleared in front of the wagons. She stood with her legs apart and her back arched, thrusting her hips towards them. Behind her the drums crashed out again and the kudu-horn trumpets shrilled.

'Now she will mark us for death.' Tegwane spoke loud enough for them all to hear, but Jim was not certain what he meant until from between her long painted legs Manatasee sent a powerful gush of urine arcing towards them.

'She pisses upon us,' Tegwane said.

Manatasee's stream dwindled and as the last yellow drops fell to earth she let out a wild scream and leaped high in the air. As she landed again she aimed the point of her *assegai* at the laager.

'*Bulala!*' she screeched. 'Kill them all!' A deafening roar went up from the *impis* and they surged forward.

Jim snatched up one of his London rifles, and tried to pick up the queen in the sights, but he had left it too late. As with all the others, Manatasee had held him enthralled. Before he could fire she was screened by the advancing wall of her warriors. A plumed *induna* had stepped in front of her, and in frustration Jim almost shot him down, but checked his trigger finger at the last instant. He knew that the sound of the shot would be echoed by his own men, and the first carefully aimed volley would be wasted before the enemy were in effective range. He lowered the rifle and strode down the barricades, calling to them: 'Steady now! Let them come in close. Don't be greedy. There will be enough for all of you.' Only Smallboy laughed at his joke. The sound was raucous and forced.

Jim moved back to his place beside Louisa, nonchalant and unhurried, setting an example to the musketeers and to the boys. The front rank of the *impi* was sweeping up to the line of white stones. They came dancing and singing, stamping their bare feet and shaking their war rattles, beating with the bright blades upon their shields. There were no gaps between the black shields.

I have let them come too close, Jim thought. To his fevered gaze, they seemed already within range with those deadly stabbing blades. Then he saw that they had not yet reached the stones. He steeled his nerve and shouted down the line, 'Wait! Hold your fire!'

He picked out the *induna* who was still in the front rank. He was horribly scarred. An axe cut ran from his scalp through his eye and down his cheek. The healed cicatrice was smooth and shiny, and over the top edge of his black shield the empty eye socket seemed to glare straight at Jim.

'Wait!' Jim called. 'Let them come.' Now he could see the separate drops of sweat sliding down the *induna*'s cheeks like grey seed pearls. The man's bare feet kicked over one of the cairns of white river stones.

'Now, fire!' Jim shouted, and the first volley was a single clap of thunder. The gunsmoke spurted out in a grey cloud-bank.

From such close quarters the rawhide shields were no protection at all. The goose-shot cut through, and the destruction was terrible. The front rank seemed to dissolve in the wash of smoke. The heavy lead pellets drove clean through flesh and bone, going on to rattle against the shields and bodies of those behind. The second rank stumbled over the dead and dying. Those warriors coming up behind were impatient to get within *assegai* range. They shoved forward with their shields, knocking off-balance the stunned survivors in the front rank.

The smoking gun was snatched from Jim's grip and a loaded musket thrust into his hands by one of the herd-boys. The second volley bellowed out with almost the same precision as the first, but then each successive volley became more ragged as some of the musketeers fired faster, served more quickly by their boys.

Mounds of dead and wounded piled up in front of the barricades, and the warriors coming up from the rear ranks had to clamber over them. The limp corpses were treacherous footing, and slowed them down, while the muskets were changed swiftly and a continuous rolling fire thundered down the line of wagons.

When the most determined Nguni reached the barricades they tried to tear away the thorn branches with their bare hands, but the musket fire never slackened. They climbed over their own dead and tried to scale the sides of the wagons. The relentless fire from the redoubts caught them in enfilade, and they tumbled back on to those below them.

The narrow wedge of land between the pool of the river and the high clay bank of the stream compressed the *impi* as they advanced in a solid mass. Like the sweep of a scythe, every blast of shot from the muskets cut swathes through them.

The wind was blowing from the direction of the river, into the faces of the attackers, and the gunsmoke rolled over them in a dense fog, half blinding them and confusing their attack. The same wind cleared the range for the defenders.

One of the warriors used the spokes of a wagon wheel as a ladder and succeeded in clambering over the tailboard of the central wagon. Jim was occupied with the Nguni storming the barricade directly in front of him when Louisa's scream alerted him. As he turned, the warrior stabbed at Louisa over the side of the wagon. She jumped back but the steel point slit the front of her tunic.

Jim dropped his empty musket and grabbed the cutlass he had pegged into the wood of the wagon, ready to hand. He sent a thrust deep into the man's chest, under his raised right arm. As he fell back, Jim jerked his blade clear and pegged the point back into the wagon, then reached back to take the loaded musket from the boy behind him.

322

'Good lad!' he grunted, and shot down the next attacker as he tried to pull himself up the side of the wagon. Jim glanced to his right and saw that Louisa had returned to her place by his side. The front of her tunic flapped open where the *assegai* had ripped it and a flash of her tender white skin showed in the tear.

'You're not hurt?' He smiled encouragement at her. Her face and arms were already blackened with the soot of gun-smoke, and her eyes were misty blue in contrast. She nodded without smiling, and took the next gun her loader handed her. She paused, let the oncoming warrior reach up to start scaling the barricade and then she fired. The recoil rocked her back on her feet, but the man cried out as the shot whipped into his face and throat and he slumped back onto the man beneath him.

Jim lost track of the passage of time. It all became a blur of smoke, sweat and gunfire. The smoke choked them, the sweat ran into their eyes, and the gunfire deafened and dazed them. Then, abruptly, the warriors who, a moment before, had been swarming like hiving bees upon the barricades were gone.

The defenders gazed about them in astonishment, seeking another target to fire at. The bank of gunsmoke drifted away, and it came as a shock to see the shattered *impis* running and staggering back up the hillside, dragging their wounded with them.

'To horse! We must mount and pursue them,' Louisa called to Jim.

He was amazed by her aggressive spirit, and that her grasp of tactics was so astute. 'Wait! They are not beaten yet.' He pointed beyond the retreating *impis*. 'Look! Manatasee still has half her forces in reserve.' Louisa shaded her eyes. Just below the crest of the high ground she saw the orderly ranks of warriors sitting on their shields, waiting for the order to attack.

The herd-boys ran up with the water bottles. They swallowed and gasped, and drank again, spluttering in their eagerness. Jim hurried down the line, anxiously questioning each of his men.

323

'Are you hurt? Are you all right?' It seemed impossible, but not one had been touched. Louisa had come closest, with the *assegai* thrust that had split open her tunic.

She scrambled through the afterclap of her own wagon and, within a short while, emerged again. Her face and arms were scrubbed pink. She wore a fresh tunic, and a starched, ironed headcloth bound about her hair. She hurried to help Zama relight the cooking fires and prepare a hasty meal for the defenders. She brought Jim a pewter plate piled with hunks of bread, and cuts of grilled venison and pickles.

'We have been fortunate,' she said, as she watched him wolf down the food. 'More than once I was certain they were going to overwhelm us.'

Jim shook his head and replied, with his mouth half full, 'Even the bravest men cannot prevail against firearms. Have no fear, Hedgehog, it's hard but in the end we will survive.'

She saw that he spoke to encourage her rather than out of conviction, and smiled. 'Whatever comes we will face it side by side.'

As she spoke the singing started again on the hillside. The defenders, who had been stretched out in the shade of the wagons, pulled themselves to their feet, and went back to their places at the barricade. The fresh *impis* were moving forward through the wounded and exhausted stragglers, who were scattered back from the battlefield. Manatasee danced ahead of the advancing cohorts, surrounded by her drummers.

Jim picked his best London rifle from the rack. He checked the priming. Louisa was watching him.

'If I can kill the she-wolf, her pack will lose heart,' he told her.

He stepped to the side of the wagon, and measured the shot. The range was long even for the rifle. The wind had risen and was swirling and gusting – it could blow even the heavy lead ball off its trajectory. Dust obscured the range, and Manatasee was dancing and twisting like a serpent. Jim handed the telescope to Louisa.

'Call the strike of my shot,' he told her, and braced himself, holding the rifle at high port, waiting for the moment. The wind gusted coolly against his sweaty cheek, then dropped. At the same time a gap opened in the curtain of dust, and Manatasee raised both arms above her head, and posed in this dramatic attitude. Jim swung up the rifle and picked up her tall shape in the notch of the rear sight. He did not try to hold the picture, but let the pip of the foresight ride smoothly up her painted body. At the same time his forefinger took up the slack of the trigger, and the shot crashed out as it came level with her eyes, aiming high to allow for the drop of the ball over the range.

For an instant Jim was unsighted by the recoil and the smoke, then he focused again. It took the heavy ball a heart-beat to cover the distance, and he saw Manatasee spin round and fall.

'You have struck her!' Louisa screamed with excitement. 'She is down.'

A growl went up from the *impis*, the voice of an angry beast.

'That will break their spirit,' Jim exulted. Then he grunted with surprise. 'Sweet Jesus, I do not believe my eyes!'

Manatasee had risen to her feet again. Even at this range Jim could see the tint of crimson on her painted skin, a rose petal of blood that ran down her flank.

'It has grazed across her ribs.' Louisa stared through the lens. 'She is only lightly wounded.'

Manatasee pirouetted before her *impis* showing herself to them, proving that she was still alive. They responded with a joyous shout and lifted their shields to salute her.

'*Bayete!*' they bellowed.

'*Zee!*' the queen screeched. '*Zee, Amadoda!*' and she began to ululate. The sound drove her *impis* into frenzy.

'*Zee!*' they exhorted themselves and those about them, and they came down to the wagons like lava pouring from the mouth of the volcano. Manatasee still pranced at the head of the charge.

Jim snatched up the second rifle of the pair, and fired again, trying to pick out her slender weaving figure from the flowing tide of blackness. The plumed *induna* at her side threw up his

325

arms and went down, struck squarely by the ball, but Manatasee danced on. Fortified by her rage, she seemed at every instant to grow stronger.

'Stand firm, and wait your chance,' Jim called to his men.

The first ranks of the attackers poured across the open ground, and clambered over the mounds of the dead and wounded.

'Now!' Jim yelled. 'Hit them! Hit them hard!'

The fusillade struck them as though they had run into a wall of stone, but those behind dragged the dead and wounded from the pile and scrambled up into the hellstorm of shot. The barrels of the muskets blistered the fingers of the musketeers when they touched them. The steel was so hot that it could have set off the gunpowder as it was poured into the muzzle. The gun barrels hissed and sizzled when the boys plunged them into the water kegs to quench them. Even in their haste they were careful not to immerse the locks and soak the flints.

The need to cool the guns slowed up the rate of reloading, the fire slackened as the defenders at the barricades shouted desperately for fresh muskets. Some of the smaller boys were almost exhausted by the gruelling work and were beginning to panic. Louisa left her place at the barricade and ran back to steady and encourage them. 'Remember your drill! Steady now, don't try to hurry!'

Through the haze of gunsmoke and over the heads of the attackers Jim glimpsed Manatasee again. She was close behind her *impi*, waving them forward to the attack. Her wild screams and ululation goaded them to mightier efforts. Many more of the warriors were swarming over the piles of corpses and reaching the barricade below where Jim stood. The smell of blood was in their nostrils and their expressions were wolfish. Their baying chilled the soul and weakened the arms of the defenders.

Unable to climb the barricades in the face of the steady volleys, the warriors began to rock the central wagon on its wheels. Fifty of them heaved together, and the wagon swayed dangerously back and forth. Jim realized that soon it would reach the critical point of balance and capsize. The warriors would swarm through the breach it left. The *assegais* would drink deeply of blood, and the fight would be over in minutes.

Manatasee had seen the opportunity, and sensed victory almost within her grasp. She pranced in close behind the rear rank of the attackers and climbed on to a mound of rocks to see over their heads.

'Zee!' she screamed. 'Zee!' Her warriors answered her and thrust with their shoulders against the wagon truck. It teetered at the limit of its balance, seemed at any moment to be going over, then fell back on to all four wheels.

'*Shikelela!*' shouted the *indunas*. 'Again!' The warriors gathered themselves, and bent to take their grip on the axles and the chassis of the wagon.

Jim looked back at Manatasee. The mound of rocks on which she stood was the one Jim had built to cover the keg of gunpowder. He glanced under the front wheels of the wagon. The end of the slow match was still lashed to one of the spokes, and the rest of the long fuse ran back under the chassis, under the heaps of the Nguni corpses to the mound on which Manatasee stood. He had buried the fuse under only a light layer of earth. He could see that in places it had been trampled and exposed by the feet of the attackers. Perhaps the other end of the fuse had been plucked from the bung-hole of the powder keg.

'Only one way to find out!' he told himself grimly. He snatched the next loaded musket that one of his gunboys handed him, and cocked the hammer, then ducked under the swaying body of the wagon.

If the wagon goes over now, I'll be crushed like a frog under the wheels, he thought, but he found the end of the fuse and laid it over the pan of the musket lock. He held it there with one hand and pulled the trigger. The falling flint struck a shower of sparks from the frizzen and the powder in the pan flared up in a puff of smoke. The musket jumped in his grip and the shot ploughed into the ground at his feet. The flash in the pan had ignited the fuse. It hissed and blackened, then the flame shot along its length, and disappeared into the earth, like a snake into its hole.

Jim sprang back on to the truck of the violently rocking wagon, and stared across at Manatasee. A fine slick of blood was running down her flank from the flesh wound his ball had inflicted. She saw him and pointed her *assegai* at his face. Her grotesquely painted features contorted with hatred, and spittle flew from her lips in a cloud and sparkled in the sunlight, as she screamed her death curses at him.

Then he saw the length of slow-match had been exposed across the last yard of trampled earth below the mound on which the queen stood. The swift flame shot along it, leaving the fuse blackened and twisted as it burned. Jim clenched his jaws and waited for the explosion. It hung fire for a terrible moment and in that pause the wagon finally toppled over, ripping a fatal gap in the barricade. Jim was thrown from his platform, and sprawled half under the wagon body. The attacking warriors shouted triumphantly and surged forward.

'*Bulala!*' they bellowed. 'Kill!'

Then the powder keg exploded beneath Manatasee's feet. A mighty tower of dust and stones shot higher than the treetops. The explosion tore the queen's body into three separate parts. One of her legs cartwheeled high into the air. The other, still attached to her torso, was thrown back into the ranks of her oncoming warriors, splattering them with her blood. Her head sailed like a cannon ball over the barricade and rolled across the open ground within the laager.

The blast swept over the Nguni who had overturned the wagon, and who were crowded into the gap they had opened. It cut them down, killing and maiming them and piling their corpses on to those of their comrades who had already fallen.

Jim was protected from the full force of the explosion by the body of the overturned wagon. Half dazed he came to his feet; his first concern for Louisa. She had been with the herd-boys, and the blast had knocked her to her knees, but she jumped up again and ran to him.

'Jim, you are hurt!' she cried, and he felt something warm

328

and wet running down from his nose into his mouth. It tasted metallic and salty. A flying splinter of rock had sliced across the bridge of his nose.

'A scratch!' he said, and hugged her to his chest. 'But thank God you are unhurt.' Still clinging together they gazed through the gap in the barricade at the carnage the explosion had wrought. The Nguni dead were lying waist deep, piled upon each other. Manatasee's *impis* were in full flight, back up the grassy hillside. Most had thrown aside their shields and weapons. Their terrified voices were filled with superstitious dread as they screamed to each other, 'The wizards are immortal.'

'Manatasee is dead.'

'She is slain by the lightning of the wizards.'

'The great black cow is devoured by witchcraft.'

'Flee! We cannot prevail against them.'

'They are ghosts, and the spirits of crocodiles.'

Jim looked along the wall of the laager. Smallboy was leaning on the ramparts, staring after the routed enemy, in a stupor of exhaustion. The other men had slumped down, some in attitudes of prayer, still holding their hot, smoking muskets. Only Bakkat was indefatigable. He had climbed on to the top of one of the wagons, and was shrieking insults at the routed *impis* as they fled.

'I defecate on your heads, I piss on your seed. May your sons be born with two heads. May your wives grow beards, and fire-ants eat your testicles.'

'What is the little devil telling them?' Louisa asked.

'He wishes them a fond farewell and lifelong happiness,' Jim said, and the sound of her laughter revived him.

'To horse!' he shouted at his men. 'Mount! Our hour has come.'

They stared at him dully, and he thought they might not have heard him, for his own ears still hummed with the memory of the guns.

'Come on!' he told Louisa. 'We must lead them out.' The two ran to the horselines. Bakkat jumped down from his perch and followed them. The horses were already saddled. They had been held ready for this moment. Jim and Louisa mounted, and the others came running.

Bakkat retrieved Manatasee's painted head, and spiked it on the point of a Nguni *assegai*. He carried it high as a Roman eagle standard. The queen's purple tongue lolled out of the corner of her mouth, and one eye was closed while the other glared white and malicious.

As the band of horsemen sallied forth through the gap the Nguni had torn in the laager wall, each carried two muskets, one in hand and the other in the gun sheath. They had shot-belts slung over each shoulder and powder flasks tied to the pommel. Behind them came the boys, riding bareback, each leading a spare horse loaded with powder kegs, shot-bags and water bottles.

'Keep together!' Jim exhorted them. 'Don't get cut off. Like cornered jackals the Nguni are still dangerous.'

They trampled the corpses and the fallen shields under their hoofs before they reached the open grassland and spurred forward, but Jim called again: 'Steady! Keep to a trot. There are still many hours of daylight ahead of us. Don't burn up the horses!'

In a wide line abreast they swept the veld, and the muskets began to boom out as they overtook the running warriors. Most of the Nguni had thrown away their weapons and lost their headdresses. When they heard the steady pounding of the hoofs coming up behind them, they ran until their legs gave way. Then they knelt in the grass and waited like dumb animals for the blast of goose-shot.

'I cannot do this,' Louisa called desperately to Jim.

'Then tomorrow they will return and do it to you,' he warned her.

Smallboy and his men revelled and rejoiced in the slaughter. The herd-boys had to replenish their powder flasks, and refill the shot-bags. Bakkat waved the head of Manatasee on high, and shrieked with excitement as he rode down on another isolated bunch of demoralized warriors.

'He's a bloodthirsty hobgoblin,' Louisa muttered, as they followed him. But when the Nguni saw the head of their queen they wailed with despair and threw themselves down in attitudes of surrender.

Ahead of the line of avenging riders rose another series of low, rolling hills, and it was towards these that the remnants of the broken *impis* were flying. Jim would not allow his men to increase their pace, and as they rode up towards the crest at a steady trot the musket fire had dwindled: the *impis* were scattering away to the horizon, and offered few targets.

Jim and Louisa reined in on the crest and looked down into a wide strath, a gently sloping valley through which another river meandered. Its banks were forested with magnificent trees, and open grass meadows lay beneath them. The air was blue with smoke from the fires of a vast encampment. Hundreds of small thatched huts were laid out on the grassland with military precision. They were deserted. What remained of the *impis* had fled: the tail end of the army disappearing over the far rise of the valley.

'Manatasee's camp!' Louisa exclaimed. 'This is where she mustered her *impis* before she attacked us.'

'And, by the love of all that is holy, there are her herds!' Jim pointed. Beneath the trees, along both banks of the river and spread out widely over the grassy saucer, were the dappled herds of cattle.

'They are Manatasee's treasury. The wealth of her nation. We have only to ride down and gather them up.' Jim's eyes sparkled as he surveyed them. Each herd was composed of animals of the same colour. The black cattle formed a dark stain on the golden veld, well separated from the red-brown herds and the dappled beasts.

'There are too many of them.' Louisa shook her head. 'We will not be able to manage such numbers.'

'My sweet hedgehog, there are some things of which a man can never have too much: love, money and cattle to name just a few.' He rose in his stirrups and ran the lens of his telescope over the multicoloured masses of animals, then over the last of the fleeing Nguni. He lowered the telescope. 'The *impis* are beaten and broken. We can call off the pursuit and count our winnings.'

Although the Nguni dead littered the grassland, not a single one of Jim's men had been wounded, apart from little Izeze who had caught his finger in the lock of a musket he was reloading and lost the first joint. Louisa had dressed it and Jim told him it was a wound of honour. Izeze held the finger aloft proudly and showed off the turban of white bandage to anyone who would look.

With the eye of a stockman born and raised, Jim appraised the booty as he rode among the captured herds. These were tough, hardy animals, with massive shoulder humps and a wide rack of horns. They were tame and trusting and showed no alarm as Jim rode within arm's length. All were in prime condition, glossy hides and rumps bulging with fat. At this first inspection Jim saw no evidence of the maggot-infested wounds of screw-worm, or the wall eyes of fly-borne ophthalmia. But he did notice with satisfaction the healed scars of sweat sickness on the glands of the throat, which proclaimed their immunity from further infection. For them to have survived in such fine condition he was sure they must also be salted against the disease of the tsetse fly.

'These are more valuable than any cattle brought from Europe,' he told Louisa. 'They have immunity to the diseases of Africa, and have been lovingly raised by the Nguni. As Tegwane told us, they love their cattle more than their own children.'

Zama had left the band of horsemen and disappeared into the encampment of thatched huts. Suddenly he rode back, his face working with agitation. He was speechless with excitement, and gesticulated for Jim to follow him.

He led Jim to a stockade of freshly hewn tree-trunks. They lifted the logs out of the gateway and Jim went through, then stopped to stare in wonder. Before him lay Manatasee's treasure house. The ivory was piled in stacks as high as a man could reach. The tusks had been graded by length and thickness. The immature ivory, some of which was no thicker than a human wrist, had been bound with strips of bark rope into fascicles, each making up a load that an ox could carry comfortably. The larger tusks were also bound with bark rope so that they could be secured to a pack-saddle for transportation. Some of the tusks were huge, but Jim saw none to match the pair he had taken from his own great bull.

While Smallboy and the other driver unsaddled the horses and took them down to the river to drink, Jim and Louisa wandered around the ivory storeroom. She watched his face as he gloated on this mass of treasure. He is like a little boy at Christmas time, she thought, as he came back to her and took her hand.

'Louisa Leuven,' he said, with solemn formality, 'I am at last a rich man.'

'Yes.' She tried to wipe the smile from her lips. 'I can see that you are. But, despite all your wealth, you are really quite a lovable lad.'

'I am pleased you have noticed that. That being agreed between us, will you marry me, and share my riches and my abundant charms?'

The laughter died on her lips. 'Oh, Jim!' she whispered, and then the strain of the battle and the pursuit of the *impis* caught up with her, and she began to weep. Her tears cut runnels through the gun-soot and dust that coated her cheeks. 'Oh, yes, Jim! I can think of nothing that would please me better than to become your wife.'

He caught her up and hugged her. 'Then this is the happiest day of my life.' He bussed her heartily. 'Now, dry your tears, Hedgehog. I'm sure we will find a priest somewhere, if not this year then next.'

With Louisa held in the crook of one arm, and his other hand laid possessively on one of the stacks of ivory, he looked over his newly acquired herds, which filled half of the valley with their abundance. Slowly his expression changed as he was struck by the age-old dilemma of the rich man.

How, in the name of Satan himself, do we keep our hands on what we have won, for every man and beast in Africa will be eager to take it from us? he wondered.

It was sunset before Jim could tear himself away from the captured encampment. Leaving Zama and half of his tiny force to guard the ivory and the herds, they set off back to the laager. The dazzling panoply of stars lit their way. As the group passed the corpses of the Nguni who had died that day, hyena and jackals scattered before the horses.

When they were almost within sight of the wagon laager they reined in their horses and stared at the night sky with awe. A mystic glow rose over the eastern horizon, and lit the world so clearly that they could see each other's startled faces turned upwards. It was as though the sun was rising from the wrong direction. They watched in awe as an enormous fireball climbed over the horizon and hurtled silently overhead. Some of the herd-boys whimpered and pulled their blankets over their heads.

''Tis nothing but a shooting star.' Jim reached across to take Louisa's hand and reassure her. 'They are common visitors in these African skies. This one is a little larger than most.'

'It is the spirit of Manatasee,' Smallboy cried. 'She begins her journey to the land of shades.'

'The death of kings,' Bakkat whimpered. 'The fall of tribes. War and death.'

'An omen of the worst kind.' Zama shook his head.

'I thought I had civilized you,' Jim laughed, 'but you are still a crew of superstitious savages at heart.'

The gigantic heavenly body swept down into the west, leaving its fiery trail clear across the sky behind it as it disappeared below the horizon. It lit the sky for the rest of that night, and the next, and for many nights thereafter.

By its ghostly light they reached the wagon laager. They found old Tegwane, spear in hand, his beautiful granddaughter at his side, guarding it like a pair of faithful watchdogs.

Although they were all nearly at the end of their tether, Jim roused the camp again before dawn. Using a span of oxen, and with much shouting and cracking of long whips, they heaved the overturned wagon back on to its wheels. The robust vehicle had suffered little damage, and within a few hours they had repacked its scattered load. Jim knew that they must leave the battlefield at once. In the heat of the sun the corpses would very soon putrefy, and, with the stench of their rotting, sickness and disease would come.

At his orders they inspanned every other wagon in the train. Then Smallboy and the other drivers fired the long whips and the oxen trundled the vehicles out of the gruesome laager and into the open grassland.

They set up camp that evening among the deserted thatched huts of the Nguni town, surrounded by the vast herds of humpbacked cattle, with the piles of ivory securely enclosed within the wagon laager.

The next morning, after breakfast, Jim summoned all his men to the *indaba*. He wanted to explain to them his future plans, and to tell them where he would lead them next. First he asked Tegwane to explain how the Nguni used their cattle to carry the ivory when they were on the march.

'Tell us how they place the loads, and secure them to the backs of the animals,' Jim ordered.

'That I do not know,' Tegwane admitted. 'I have only watched their advance from afar.'

'Smallboy will be able to work out the harness for himself,' Jim decided, 'but it would have been better to use a method to which the cattle are accustomed.' Then he turned to the small group of herd-boys and said, 'Can you men' – they liked to be called men and they had earned the right at the barricades – 'can you men take care of so many?'

They considered the vast herds of cattle that were scattered down the full length of the valley.

'They are not so very many,' said the eldest, who was the spokesman.

'We can herd many more than that,' said another.

'We have vanquished the Nguni in battle,' squeaked Izeze, smallest and cheekiest of the boys, his voice not yet broken. 'We can take care of their cattle, and their women also, when we capture them.'

335

'It may be, Izeze,' the name Jim had given him meant Little Flea, 'it may be that neither your whip nor your whistle are yet large enough for those tasks.'

Izeze's companions shrieked with laughter. 'Show it to us!' they cried, and tried to catch him, but like the insect that was his namesake he was quick and agile. 'Show us the weapon that will terrify the women of the Nguni.' Clinging to his loincloth to preserve his modesty and dignity Izeze fled, pursued by his peers.

'All of which brings us no closer to a solution of the problem,' Jim remarked as he and Louisa made the final inspection of the laager's defences before turning in for the night.

Although it seemed apparent that the Nguni *impis* had been shattered and would not return, Jim was taking no chances. He set his sentries at nightfall and the next morning they stood to their guns in the dawn.

'Sweet heavens!' Jim exclaimed, as the light strengthened. 'They have returned!' He seized Louisa's arm and pointed out to her the rows of shadowy figures squatting just out of musket shot beyond the barricades of the laager.

'Who are they?' she whispered, though in her heart she knew the answer well.

'Who else but the Nguni?' he told her grimly.

'I had thought it was over, the killing and the fighting. God grant that it was enough.'

'We shall soon find out,' he said, and called for Tegwane. 'Hail them!' he ordered the old man. 'Tell them that I will send our lightning down upon them as I did to Manatasee.'

Tegwane climbed shakily on to the side of the wagon, and called across the open grassland. A voice answered him from among the gathered Nguni, and a long shouted exchange followed.

'What do they want?' Jim demanded impatiently. 'Do they not know that their queen is dead and their *impis* shattered?'

'They know it well,' Tegwane said. 'They have seen her head carried upon the *assegai* as they fled the battlefield, and

336

her fiery spirit passing in the night sky as she travelled to meet her forefathers.'

'Then what is it they want?'

'They want to speak with the wizard who struck down their queen with his lightning.'

'A parley,' Jim explained to Louisa. 'It seems that these are some of the survivors of the battle.'

'Talk to them, Jim,' she urged. 'Perhaps you can prevent any more bloodshed. Anything is better than that.'

Jim turned back to Tegwane. 'Tell their *induna*, their leader, that he must come into the laager alone and unarmed. I will not harm him.'

He came dressed in a simple kilt of leather strips, without headdress or weapons. He was a fine-looking man in his middle years, with the body and limbs of a warrior and a handsome moon face the chocolate colour of freshly hewn mabanga wood. As soon as he entered the laager he recognized Jim. He must have seen him upon the battlefield. He went down on one knee, an attitude of respect, clapping his hands and chanting praises: 'Mightiest of warriors! Invincible wizard who comes out of the great waters! Devourer of *impis*! Slayer of Manatasee! Greater than all of her fathers!'

'Tell him that I see him, and that he may approach me,' Jim ordered. He realized the significance and importance of this delegation, and assumed a dignified manner and haughty expression. The *induna* went down on all fours and crawled towards him. He took Jim's right foot and placed it on his own bowed head. Jim was taken by surprise and almost lost his balance, but he recovered swiftly.

'Great white bull elephant,' the *induna* chanted, 'young in years but mighty in power and wisdom, grant me mercy.'

From his father and his uncle Jim had learned enough of African protocol to know how to conduct himself. 'Your worthless life is mine,' he said. 'Mine to take or spare. Why should I not send you on the same road through the sky as the one on which I sent Manatasee?'

'I am a child without a father or mother. I am an orphan. You have taken my children from me.'

337

'What is he talking about?' Jim demanded angrily of Tegwane. 'We killed no children.'

The *induna* heard his tone and realized he had given offence. He pressed his face into the dirt. When he answered Tegwane's questions his voice was hoarse with dust. Jim used the opportunity to remove his foot from the *induna*'s head: standing on one leg was uncomfortable and undignified.

At last Tegwane turned back to Jim. 'He was Manatasee's keeper of the royal herds. He calls the cattle his children. He begs you either to kill him, or to allow him the honour of becoming your keeper of the herds.'

Jim stared at the man in astonishment. 'He wants to work for me as my chief herdsman?'

'He says he has lived with the herds since he was a child. He knows each animal by name, which bull covered their dams. He knows each one's age and temper. He knows the remedy and the treatment for every disease to which the herds are prone. With his own *assegai* he has killed five lions who were attacking the animals. What is more . . .' Tegwane paused to draw breath.

'Enough.' Jim stopped him hastily. 'I believe what he says, but what of these others?' He pointed at the other files of squatting figures outside the laager. 'Who are they?'

'They are his herders. Like him they have been dedicated to the care of the royal cattle since childhood. Without the herds their lives are without purpose.'

'They, too, are offering themselves?' Jim was having difficulty grasping the extent of his good fortune.

'Every one of them wishes to become your man.'

'What do they expect from me?'

'They expect you to kill them if they err or fail in their duties,' Tegwane assured him. 'Manatasee would have done so.'

'That is not exactly what I meant,' Jim said in English, and Tegwane looked baffled. He went on quickly: 'What do they expect in return for their work?'

'The sunshine of your pleasure,' said Tegwane. 'As I do.'

Jim pulled his ear thoughtfully, and the *induna* rolled his head to watch his face, worried that their request would be denied and that the white wizard would strike him down as he had the queen. Jim was considering the expense of adding the *induna* and fifty or sixty of his comrades to the strength of his already numerous crew. However, there seemed to be no additional cost that he could fathom. From what Tegwane had told him he knew these herders would live on the blood and milk of the herds, and the venison that fell to his gun. He was sure he could expect a most extraordinary level of loyalty and dedication in return. These were skilled cattlemen and fearless spearmen. He would find himself at the head of his own tribe of warriors. With the Hottentot musketeers and the Nguni spearmen he need fear nothing in this wild and savage land. He would be a king. 'What is this man's name?' he asked Tegwane.

'He is called Inkunzi, for he is the bull of all the royal herds.'

'Tell Inkunzi that I look with favour on his request. He and his men are now my men. Their lives are in my hands.'

'*Bayete!*' Inkunzi shouted with joy when he heard this. 'You are my master and my sun.' Once again he placed Jim's right foot upon his head, and his men seeing this, knew they had been accepted.

They rose to their feet, drummed on their shields with their *assegais*, and shouted together, '*Bayete!* We are your men! You are our sun!'

'Tell them that the sun can warm a man, but it can also burn him to death,' Jim warned them solemnly. Then he turned to Louisa and explained to her what had just taken place.

Louisa looked upon this fearsome band of warriors, and remembered how, only days before, they had come singing to the laager. 'Can you trust them, Jim? Should you not disarm them?'

'I know the traditions of these people. Once they have sworn their allegiance I will trust them with my life.'

'And mine,' she pointed out softly.

The next day Jim made an observation of the noon passage of the sun, and plotted their position on his father's chart. 'According to my reckoning we are only a few degrees south of the latitude of the Courtney trading post at Nativity Bay. By my calculations, it should be less than a thousand leagues to the east, three months' travel. It is possible that we might encounter one of our ships there, or at least find a message from my family under the mail stones.'

'Is that where we are going next, Jim?' Louisa asked. He looked up from the parchment of the chart and raised an eyebrow. 'Unless you have a better suggestion?'

'No.' She shook her head. 'That will suit me as well as any other.'

The following morning they broke camp. Inkunzi and his herders brought in the captured royal herds, and Jim watched with interest as they loaded the ivory. The rawhide harness they used was simple, but had obviously been perfected by the Nguni to fit over the heavy hump and be secured behind the front legs. The loads of ivory were counterbalanced to hang comfortably but securely on each side of the beast's back, allowing it freedom of movement. Inkunzi and his men matched the weight of each load to the size and strength of the animal that would carry it. The cattle seemed unaware of their burden as they moved along at the leisurely pace set by the herders, grazing contentedly as they spread out like a river in flood across the veld. By the time the entire herd was on the move they covered several leagues.

Jim took a compass bearing along the line of march, and pointed out to Inkunzi a landmark on the horizon to head for. Inkunzi himself stalked along at the head of his herds, wrapped in his leather cloak with his *assegai* and his black war shield slung on his back. He played on a reed flute as he went, a sweet but monotonous tune, and the cattle followed him like faithful hounds. The wagon train brought up the rearguard.

Each morning Jim and Louisa rode out with Bakkat to

break trail and search ahead for any lurking danger or for fresh sign of the elephant herds. They scouted far ahead of the slowly moving caravan, picking out the passes through the hills, the fords and drifts across the rivers. The herds of wild game astonished them, but they found that the Nguni had swept the land bare of human presence. Villages had been burnt to the ground, only the smoke-blackened patterns of the foundation stones still standing, and the veld around was strewn with the white fields of human bones. There was no living soul.

'The *mefecane*,' Tegwane called this great slaughter. 'The pounding of the tribes, like corn between the grinding stones of the *impis*.'

Once Inkunzi had proved his worth and established his place high in the hierarchy of the band, he joined quite naturally in the *indabas* around the campfire. He was able from his own life to paint for them a picture of these terrible events. He told them how his people had their origins far to the north, along some mythical valley, a place he called the Beginning of All Things.

Generations before, his tribe had been overtaken by some cataclysmic event, another *mefecane*, and the famine that naturally followed. They and their herds had begun the long migration southwards plundering and killing all the other tribes that stood in their path. As pastoralists and nomads they always moved on, seeking grazing for their herds, more plunder and women. It was a tragic saga.

'We will never know how many human souls have perished on these lovely wild fields,' Louisa said softly.

Even Jim was subdued by the extent of the tragedy that had swept like the black plague across the continent. 'This is a savage land. To flourish it needs to be watered by the blood of man and beast,' he agreed with her.

When they scouted ahead of the wagons Jim was always on the lookout for signs of the rest of the Nguni, and drilled his small band in the defensive tactics they would adopt if they were attacked.

He was searching also for the elusive elephant herds, but as the weeks passed, and mile after mile of this grand and tractless land fell behind the turning wagon wheels, they discovered neither Nguni nor elephant.

Almost three months after they had turned east, they came abruptly upon a steep, broken escarpment where the land fell away before them into a sheer abyss.

'This seems to be the end of the world,' Louisa breathed. They stood together and stared in wonder. In the clear air and bright sunshine it seemed they could indeed see to the ends of the earth. Staring through the lens of his telescope Jim saw that as it blended with the distant horizon the sky shaded to an unearthly blue, bright and translucent as polished lapis-lazuli.

It took him some time to realize what he was looking at. Then the angle of the sunlight changed subtly and he exclaimed, 'In the name of all that is holy and beautiful, Hedgehog, 'tis the ocean at last.' He handed her the telescope. 'You shall now see what a famous navigator I am, for I shall lead you unerringly to the beach at Nativity Bay in the land of the elephants.'

Tom and Dorian Courtney rode up to the main gates of the castle. They were expected and the sergeant of the guard saluted and waved them through into the courtyard. Grooms came running to take their horses as they dismounted.

The Courtney brothers were accustomed to such respect. As two of the leading burghers of the colony and its most prosperous merchants, they were often guests of Governor van de Witten. The governor's secretary, himself an important VOC official, came scurrying out of his office to greet them and usher them through into the governor's private quarters.

They were not kept waiting in the anteroom, but taken immediately into the spacious council chamber. The long central table and all the twenty chairs around it were of stinkwood, one of the most beautifully grained timbers of Africa, lovingly carved by the skilled Malay slave cabinetmakers. The floors were of lustrous yellow-wood planks polished with beeswax until they shone like glass. The panes of the bay windows at the far end of the room were of jewel-like stained glass shipped down the length of the Atlantic from Holland. They looked out over the vista of Table Bay, with the monumental bulk of Lion's Head mountain beyond. The bay was cluttered with shipping, and whipped by the south-easter into a froth of prancing white horses.

The panelled walls were hung with the seventeen portraits of the council members of the VOC in Amsterdam: serious bulldog-faced men in black hats with lace collars, paper white on their high-buttoned black coats.

Two men rose from their seats at the council table to greet the brothers. Colonel Keyser was in the dress uniform he had designed for himself. It was of scarlet brocade, with sashes over both shoulders, one blue, the other gold. His ample girth was encircled by a sword belt embossed with gold medallions, and the hilt of his rapier was inlaid with semi-precious stones. There were three large enamelled diamanté stars pinned on his chest. The largest of these was the Order of St Nicholas. The tops of his glossy boots reached above his knees. His hat was wide-brimmed, crowned with a large bunch of ostrich feathers.

In contrast, Governor van de Witten wore the sombre dress that was almost the uniform of the most senior officials of the VOC: a black velvet skull-cap, a Flemish lace collar, and a black high-buttoned jacket. His thin legs were clad in black silk hose, and his square-toed shoes were buckled with solid silver.

'Mijnheeren, you do us honour by your presence,' he said, his face pale and lugubrious.

'The honour is ours alone. We came as soon as we received your invitation,' Tom said, and the brothers bowed together. Tom was dressed in dark broadcloth, but of first quality and London cut. Dorian wore a green silk jacket and voluminous breeches. His sandals were camel-skin, and his turban matched his jacket and was secured with an emerald pin. His short red beard was neatly trimmed and curled. It was in sharp contrast

343

to Tom's more luxuriant, silver-shot growth. Looking at them together nobody would have guessed they were brothers. Colonel Keyser came forward to greet them, and they bowed again.

'Your servant, Colonel, as ever,' Tom said.

'*Salaam aleikum*, Colonel,' Dorian murmured. Although when he was at High Weald and in the bosom of his own family he often forgot it, when he went abroad, and especially in these formal surroundings, he liked to remind the world that he was the adopted son of Sultan Abd Muhammad al-Malik, the Caliph of Muscat. 'Peace be unto you, Colonel.' Then he added in Arabic, making it sound like part of the greeting, 'I like not the fat one's expression. The tiger shark smiles in the same way.' This was entirely for Tom's benefit: he knew that the others in the room understood not a word of what he had said.

Governor van de Witten indicated the chairs facing his own across the glistening expanse of the table. 'Gentlemen, please be seated.' He clapped his hands, and immediately a small procession of Malay slaves appeared carrying silver salvers of choice morsels of food, and decanters of wine and spirits.

While they were being served the governor and his guests continued the customary exchange of compliments and small talk. Both Tom and Dorian refrained from more than a single glance at the mysterious object that lay in the centre of the stinkwood table between them. It was covered with a velvet cloth, beaded around the edges. Tom pressed his knee lightly against Dorian's. Dorian did not look at him, but touched the side of his nose, a signal that he had also noticed the object. Over the years they had grown so close that they could read each other's minds with accuracy.

The slaves at last backed out of the council chamber, and the governor turned to Tom. 'Mijnheer Courtney, you have already discussed with Colonel Keyser the distressing and reprehensible behaviour of your son, James Archibald Courtney.'

Tom stiffened. Although he had been expecting this, he

braced himself for what would follow. What new trick has Keyser come up with now? he wondered. As Dorian had pointed out, Keyser's expression was smug and gloating. Aloud he said, 'Indeed, Governor, I well recall our conversation.'

'You assured me that you disapproved of your son's behaviour, his interference with the course of justice, the abduction of a female prisoner, the theft of VOC property.'

'I remember it well,' Tom assured him hastily, anxious to cut short the list of Jim's transgressions.

However, van de Witten went on remorselessly: 'You gave me your assurance that you would keep me informed of your son's whereabouts as soon as you obtained knowledge of his movements. You promised that you would do all in your power to see to it that he and this female criminal, Louisa Leuven, were brought to the castle at the first opportunity to answer to me personally for their crimes. Did we not agree on this?'

'Yes, we did, Your Excellency. I also recall that, as an earnest of my good faith and intentions and to compensate the VOC for its losses, I made a payment to you of twenty thousand guilders in gold.'

Van de Witten ignored this solecism. He had never issued an official receipt for that payment, ten per cent of which had gone to Colonel Keyser and the balance into his own purse. As he went on speaking his expression became increasingly sorrowful: 'I have reason to believe, Mijnheer Courtney, that you have not kept your side of our bargain.'

Tom threw up his hands, and made theatrical sounds of amazement and denial, but did not go so far as to deny the charge outright.

'You would like me to substantiate what I have just said?' van de Witten asked, and Tom nodded warily. 'As Colonel Keyser is the officer responsible to me for the conduct of this case, I will ask him to explain what he has discovered.' He looked at the colonel. 'Would you please be kind enough to enlighten these gentlemen?'

'Certainly, Your Excellency, it will be my duty and privilege.' Keyser leaned across the table and touched the mysterious object under the beaded velvet cloth. All their eyes went to it. Teasingly, Keyser removed his hand and leaned back in his chair again.

'Let me first ask you, Mijnheer Courtney, if at any time during the last three months any of the wagons belonging to you and your brother,' he nodded at Dorian, 'left the colony.'

Tom pondered a moment, then turned to his brother. 'I don't remember that happening, do you, Dorry?'

'None of our vehicles received VOC permission to leave the colony.' Dorian begged the question neatly.

Once again Keyser leaned forward, but this time he whipped away the velvet cloth and they all stared at the broken stub of the wheel spoke. 'Is that your company cypher branded into the wood?'

'Where did you find it?' Tom asked ingenuously.

'An officer of the VOC found it lying beside the tracks of four wagons that left the colony near the headwaters of the Gariep river and headed north into the wilderness.'

Tom shook his head. 'I cannot explain it.' He tugged his beard. 'Can you, Dorian?'

'In March last year we sold one of the old lumber wagons to that Hottentot hunter, what was his name? Oompie? He said he was going to find ivory in the desert lands.'

'My sacred oath!' Tom exclaimed. 'I had forgotten that.'

'Did you get a receipt for the sale?' Keyser looked frustrated.

'Old Oompie cannot write,' Dorian murmured.

'So, then, let us get this clear. You never travelled with four heavily laden wagons to the borders of the colony, and you did not hand these wagons over to the fugitive from justice, James Courtney. And you never encouraged and abetted this runaway to flee the borders of the colony without VOC sanction. Is that what you are telling me?'

'That is correct.' Tom looked him steadily in the eyes across the table. Keyser grinned with triumph and glanced at Governor van de Witten for permission to continue. He nodded his agreement, and Keyser clapped his hands again. The double doors swung open and two uniformed VOC corporals entered, dragging between them a human figure.

For a moment neither Tom nor Dorian recognized him. He

wore only a pair of breeches that were filthy with dried blood and his own excrement. The nails had been plucked from his toes and fingers with blacksmith's tongs. His back had taken the lash until it was a bloody pulp. His face was swollen grotesquely. One eye was closed completely, and the other a mere slit in the bloated purple flesh.

'A pretty sight.' Keyser smiled. Governor van de Witten held a small sachet of dried herbs and flower petals to his nose. 'I beg your pardon, Your Excellency.' Keyser noticed the gesture. 'Animals must be treated as such.' He turned back to Tom. 'You know this man, of course. He is one of your wagon drivers.'

'Sonnie!' Tom started up, then thought better of it and sank back into his chair. Dorian looked distressed. Sonnie was one of their best men, when he was sober. He had been missing from High Weald for over a week, and they had presumed that he had gone off on one of his periodic binges, from which he always returned reeking of bhang, cheap brandy and even cheaper women, but chastened, apologetic and swearing on the grave of his father that it would not happen again.

'Ah, yes!' Keyser said. 'You do know him. He has been telling us interesting details of your movements, and those of your family. He says that last September two of your wagons led by Mijnheer Dorian Courtney's son, Mansur, set off along the coastal road to the north. This I can substantiate, because I led a full troop of my own men to follow those wagons. I now know that this was a diversion to draw my attention away from the other matters of more consequence.' Keyser looked at Dorian. 'I am sad that a fine lad like Mansur should have become embroiled in this sordid affair. He also must face the consequence of his actions.' It was said lightly, but the threat was undisguised.

Both Courtney brothers remained silent. Tom could not look at Sonnie, lest he lose his temper and self-control. Sonnie was a free spirit who, despite his multitudinous failings, stood high in his affections, and Tom felt paternally responsible for him.

347

Keyser turned his attention back to Tom. 'This man has also told us that soon after the two decoy wagons left High Weald, and when you were sure that my troops had followed them, you and Mevrouw Courtney slipped away with four other heavily loaded wagons, a large number of horses and other animals to the Gariep river. You waited there for some weeks, and eventually your son, James Courtney, and the escaped female prisoner came out of the mountains to join you. You handed over the wagons and the animals to them. They made good their escape into the wilderness, and you returned with assumed innocence to the colony.'

Keyser leaned back in his chair and clasped his hands over the buckle of his sword belt. The room was silent, until Sonnie blurted out, 'I am sorry, Klebe.' His voice was indistinct for his lips were cut and crusted with half-healed scabs, and there were black holes in the front of his mouth where two of his front teeth had been knocked out. 'I did not want to tell them, but they beat me. They said they would kill me, then do the same to my children.'

'It is not your fault, Sonnie. You only did what any man would do.'

Keyser smiled and inclined his head towards Tom. 'You are magnanimous, Mijnheer. If I were in your place I would not be so understanding.'

Governor van de Witten intervened: 'Can we be rid of this fellow now, Colonel?' he asked irritably. 'His stink is atrocious, and he is dripping blood and other less salubrious fluids on to my floor.'

'I beg your pardon, Your Excellency. He has served his purpose.' He nodded at the uniformed warders and waved them away. They dragged Sonnie out through the doors, and closed them as they left.

'If you set bail for him, I will pay it and take that poor wretch back to High Weald with me,' Tom said.

'That presupposes that the two of you are going back to High Weald,' Keyser pointed out. 'But, alas, even if you were, I could not allow you to take the witness with you. He must remain in the castle dungeons until your son James and the

348

escaped prisoner are brought to trial in front of the governor.' He unclasped his fingers and leaned forward. The smile faded and his expression became hard, his eyes cold and fierce. 'And until your own part in these matters has been made clear.'

'Are you arresting us?' Tom asked. 'On the unsubstantiated testimony of a Hottentot wagon driver?' Tom looked at Governor van de Witten. 'Your Excellency, under article 152 of the Criminal Procedure Act, laid down by the governors in Amsterdam, no slave or native may give evidence against a free burgher of the colony.'

'You have missed your vocation, Mijnheer. Your grasp of the law is impressive.' Van de Witten nodded. 'Thank you for bringing the Act to my attention.' He stood up and walked on those thin black-hosed legs to the stained-glass windows. He folded his arms over his pigeon chest and stared out at the bay. 'I see both your ships have returned to port.'

Neither brother answered this remark. It was superfluous. The two Courtney vessels were clearly visible from where he stood, lying at anchor off the foreshore. They had come into the bay in convoy two days previously, and had not yet offloaded. The *Maid of York* and the *Gift of Allah* were lovely schooners. They had been built in the yards at Trincomalee to Tom's own design. They were fast and handy, with shallow draught and well armed, perfect for inshore work, trading into estuaries and the shallows of a dangerous and hostile coast.

Sarah had been born in York and Tom had named one vessel for her. Dorian and Yasmini had chosen the name for the other ship.

'A lucrative voyage?' van de Witten asked. 'Or so I hear.'

Tom smiled thinly. 'We thank the Lord for what we have had, but for a little more we would be glad.'

Van de Witten acknowledged the witticism with an acidic smile, and returned to his chair. 'You ask if you are under arrest. The answer, Mijnheer Courtney, is no.' He shook his head. 'You are a pillar of our small society, a gentleman of the highest reputation, industrious and hard-working. You pay your taxes. Technically you are not a free Dutch burgher, but

349

a citizen of a foreign nation. However, you pay your residence-licence fees and, as such, you are entitled to the equivalent rights of a burgher. I would not even think of arresting you.' It was clear from Colonel Keyser's expression that in fact deep consideration had been given to the possibility.

'Thank you, Your Excellency.' Tom rose to his feet, and Dorian followed his example. 'Your good opinion means a great deal to us.'

'Please, Mijnheeren!' Van de Witten held up his hand to delay them. 'There are some other small matters that we should discuss before you go.' They sat down again.

'I would not want either of you, or any member of your family, to leave the colony without my express permission until this matter is fully resolved. That includes your son, Mansur Courtney, who was responsible for deliberately drawing out a troop of the VOC cavalry on a fruitless expedition to the northern borders of the colony.' He stared at Dorian. 'Do I make myself clear?' Dorian nodded.

'Is that all, Your Excellency?' Tom asked, with exaggerated politeness.

'No, Mijnheer. Not quite all. I have determined that you should place with me a nominal surety to ensure that you and your family abide by the conditions I have imposed.'

'Just how nominal?' Tom braced himself to hear the response.

'One hundred thousand guilders.' Van de Witten picked up the decanter of honey-golden Madeira wine. He came round the table to refill their spiral-stemmed glasses. A heavy silence hung over the room. 'I will make allowance for the fact you are foreigners and perhaps you did not understand me.' Van de Witten resumed his seat. 'I will repeat myself. I require a surety of one hundred thousand guilders from you.'

'That is a great deal of money,' Tom said at last.

'Yes, I would think it should be sufficient.' The governor nodded. 'But a relatively modest sum when we take into consideration the profits of your last trading voyage.'

'I will need some time to raise that amount in cash,' Tom

said. His face was almost impassive; a slight tic of one eyelid was all that betrayed his agitation.

'Yes, I understand that,' van de Witten agreed. 'However, while you are making provision for the surety, you should take into consideration that your residence-licence renewal fee is also due for payment within a few weeks. It would be just as well if you paid both amounts at the same time.'

'An additional fifty thousand guilders,' Tom said, trying to hide his dismay.

'No, Mijnheer. On account of these unforeseen circumstances I have had to reconsider the amount of the residence licence. It has been increased to one hundred thousand guilders.'

'That is piracy,' Tom snapped, losing his temper for the instant, then recovering it at once. 'I beg you pardon, Your Excellency. I withdraw that remark.'

'You should know about pirates, Mijnheer Courtney.' Van de Witten sighed mournfully. 'Your own grandfather was executed for that crime.' He pointed through the bay windows. 'Out there on the parade-ground within sight of this very room. We must pray that no other member of your family meets the same tragic end.' The threat was implicit, but it lay across the quiet room like the shadow of the gallows.

Dorian intervened for the first time: 'A fee of one hundred thousand on top of the surety deposit will beggar our company.'

Van de Witten turned to him. 'I think that you still misunderstand me,' he said sadly. 'The fee for your brother's family residence is one hundred thousand and for your family an additional one hundred thousand. Then you must add to that the surety for good behaviour.'

'Three hundred thousand!' Tom exclaimed. 'That is not possible.'

'I am sure it is!' van de Witten contradicted him. 'As a last resort you could always sell your ships and the contents of your warehouse. That will surely bring in the full amount.'

'Sell the ships?' Tom leaped to his feet. 'What madness is this? They are the blood and bones of our company.'

351

'I assure you it is not madness.' Van de Witten shook his head and smiled at Colonel Keyser. 'I think you should explain the position to these gentlemen.'

'Certainly, Your Excellency.' Keyser hoisted himself out of his chair and swaggered to the window. 'Ah, good! Just in time to illustrate the point.'

On the beach below the ramparts of the castle two platoons of VOC soldiers were drawn up. The bayonets were fixed on their muskets, and they carried full packs. Their green uniform jackets stood out sharply against the white sands. As Tom and Dorian watched they began to embark in two open lighters at the edge of the water, wading out knee-deep to reach them.

'I am taking the precaution of placing guards on board both your ships,' Keyser announced, 'merely to ensure your compliance with Governor van de Witten's edict.' Keyser settled back in his chair again. 'Until further notice, both of you will report every day before the noon gun to my headquarters to reassure me that you have not left the colony. Of course, as soon as you can produce a receipt from the treasury for the full amount you owe, and a passport from Governor van de Witten, you will be free to leave. I fear, however, that it might not be so easy to return next time.'

'Well, perhaps we have overstayed our welcome,' Tom said, and beamed round the room. The family was seated in the counting-house of the High Weald godown.

Sarah Courtney tried to show her disapproval in sternness, but an expression of resignation was not entirely hidden by her lowered lids. He will never cease to amaze me, this husband of mine, she thought. He revels in circumstances that would devastate other men.

'I think Tom is right.' Dorian joined in between puffs on his hookah. 'We Courtneys have always been voyagers on the oceans and wanderers on the continents. Twenty years in one spot on this earth is too long.'

'You are talking about my home,' Yasmini protested, 'the

place where I have spent half my life, and where my only son was born.'

'We will find both you and Sarah another home, and give you both more sons, if that is what will make you happy,' Dorian promised.

'You are as bad as your brother,' Sarah rounded on him. 'You don't understand a woman's heart.'

'Or her mind.' Tom chuckled. 'Come now, my sweeting, we cannot stay here to be beggared by van de Witten. You have been forced to up sticks and run before. Don't you remember how we had to clear out of Fort Providence at five minutes' notice when Zayn al-Din's men came calling?'

'I shall never forget it. You threw my harpsichord overboard to lighten the ship so we could clear the sandbars at the mouth of the river.'

'Ah, but I bought you another,' Tom said, and they all glanced across the room to the triangular instrument standing against the inner wall. Sarah stood up and crossed to it. She opened the lid of the keyboard, took her seat on the stool and played the opening bars of 'Spanish Ladies'. Tom hummed the chorus.

Abruptly Sarah closed the lid, and stood up. There were tears in her eyes. 'That was long ago, Tom Courtney, when I was a silly young girl.'

'Young? Yes. Silly? Never!' Tom went to her quickly and placed an arm round her shoulders.

'Tom, I am too old to start all over again,' she whispered.

'Nonsense, you are as young and strong as you ever were.'

'We will be destitute,' Sarah mourned. 'Beggars and homeless wanderers.'

'If you think that, you do not know me as well as you think you do.' Still holding her fondly he looked at his brother. 'Shall we show them, Dorry?'

'There will be no peace for us if we do not.' Dorian shrugged. 'They are scolds and martinets, these women of ours.'

Yasmini leaned over and tugged his curling red beard. 'I have always been a dutiful Muslim wife to you, al-Salil.' She

353

used his Arabic name, the Drawn Sword. 'How dare you accuse me of disrespect? Recant at once or you shall be deprived of all favours and privileges until next Ramadan comes round.'

'You are so lovely, full moon on my life. You grow sweeter and more docile with each day that passes.'

'I shall take that as a recantation.' She smiled and her great dark eyes glowed at him.

'Enough!' cried Tom. 'This dispute tears apart our family and our hearts.' They all laughed, even the women, and Tom seized the advantage. 'You know that Dorian and I were never such fools as to trust that gang of footpads and cutpurses who make up the board of governors of the VOC,' he said.

'We always knew that we were in this colony under sufferance,' Dorian went on. 'The Dutch looked upon us as milch cows. For the last twenty years they have been sucking our udders dry.'

'Well, not entirely dry,' Tom demurred, and went to the bookcase at the far end of the room, which reached from floor to ceiling. 'Lend a hand here, brother,' he said, and Dorian went to help him. The bookcase, filled with heavy leatherbound tomes, was set on steel rollers cunningly concealed beneath the dark wooden skirting-board. With both of them shoving at one end, it slid aside, with squealing protest from the rollers, to reveal a small door in the back wall, barred with iron crossbolts and locked with an enormous bronze padlock.

Tom lifted down a book, whose spine was embossed in gold leaf *Monsters of the Southern Oceans*. He opened the covers; in the hollowed-out interior lay a key.

'Bring the lantern,' he told Sarah, as he turned the key in the padlock, shot back the bolts and opened the door.

'How did you keep this from us over all these years?' Sarah demanded.

'With the greatest difficulty.' Tom took her hand, and led her into a tiny room, not much bigger than a cupboard. Dorian and Yasmini followed. There was barely enough space for them all and the stack of small wooden chests piled neatly against the far wall.

'The family fortune,' Tom explained. 'The profits of twenty years. We did not have the reckless courage or the lack of good sense to entrust it to the Bank of Batavia, which is owned by our old friends in Amsterdam, the VOC.' He opened the top chest, which was packed to the brim with small canvas bags. Tom handed one of the bags to each of the women.

'So heavy!' Yasmini exclaimed, and nearly dropped hers.

'An't nothing heavier,' Tom agreed.

When Sarah opened the mouth of the bag she held she gasped. 'Gold coins? All three chests filled with gold?'

'Naturally, my sweeting. We pay our expenses in silver, and keep the profits in gold.'

'Tom Courtney, you are a dark horse. Why did you never tell us of this hoard?'

'There was never a reason until now.' He laughed. 'The knowledge would have made you discontent, but now it has taken a weight off your heart.'

'How much have you and Dorry squirrelled away in here?' Yasmini asked, in wonder.

Tom knocked with his knuckles on each of the three chests in turn. 'Seems all three are still full. This is the most part of our savings. In addition we have an ample collection of sapphires from Ceylon and diamonds from the fabulous Kollur mine on the Krishna river in India. They are all large stones of the first water. If not quite a king's ransom, then at least a rajah's.' He chuckled richly. 'In truth, that is not quite all. Both our ships lying in the bay have their weighty cargoes still intact.'

'To say nothing of two platoons of VOC soldiers on board as well,' Sarah pointed out spicily, as she backed out of the concealed strongroom.

'That presents an interesting problem,' Tom admitted, as he locked the door and Dorian helped him push the bookcase back into position to cover it. 'But one that is not insoluble.' He went to take his seat again, and patted the chair next to

355

him. 'Come sit beside me, Sarah Courtney. I am going to need the benefit of your sharp wit and famous erudition now.'

'I think it is time that we invited Mansur to join the family deliberations,' Dorian suggested. 'He is old enough at last and, what is more, his life will be changed as profoundly as ours when we sail out of Table Bay. He will probably be distraught to be taken from his childhood home.'

'Quite right!' Tom agreed. 'But now speed is everything. Our exodus must take van de Witten and Keyser by surprise. They cannot be expecting us to abandon High Weald and all its contents. There is a great deal to be seen to, but we must set ourselves a limit.' He looked up at Dorian. 'Three days?'

'It will be a close-run thing.' Dorian frowned as he considered it. 'But, yes, we can be ready to sail in three days.'

Those three days were filled with frenzied activity, carefully concealed from the rest of the world. It was essential that even the most trusted of their servants had no inkling of their true intentions. Loyalty did not presuppose discretion: the serving girls were notorious chatterboxes, and the chambermaids even worse. Many had romantic attachments to men in the town and a few consorted with the soldiers and petty officers in the castle. To allay any suspicions, Sarah and Yasmini put it about that the sorting and packing of clothes and furniture was merely a seasonal reordering and cleaning of the rambling homestead. In the godown Tom and Dorian conducted their annual stock-taking three months earlier than was their usual custom.

An English East Indiaman was lying at anchor in the bay, and the captain was an old and trusted friend of Tom. They had dealt with each other over the last twenty years. Tom sent him an invitation to dinner and, during the meal, swore him to secrecy and informed him of their plans to leave Good Hope. Then he sold him the entire contents of the godown at High Weald for a fraction of its real value. In return Captain Welles promised not to take possession until after the two Courtney ships had sailed from the bay. He undertook to make payment for the goods directly into the CBTC account at Mr

Coutts's bank in Piccadilly immediately on his return to London.

The land and buildings of High Weald were held under perpetual quit-rent to the VOC. Mijnheer van de Velde, another prosperous burgher of the colony, had been importuning Tom and Dorian for years to sell the estate to him.

After midnight the brothers, dressed in black, their faces covered by the brims of their hats and the collars of their greatcoats, rode across to his homestead on the banks of the Black river, and knocked on the shutters of van de Velde's bedroom. After his initial alarm, angry shouts and threats, he came out in his nightshirt brandishing a bell-mouthed blunderbuss. He shone his lantern into their faces.

'Name of a dog, it is you!' he exclaimed, and led them into his counting-house. As the first light of dawn paled the sky and the doves cooed in the oaks outside the windows they shook hands on the bargain. Tom and Dorian signed the deed of transfer of High Weald and, grinning triumphantly, van de Velde handed over an irrevocable letter of credit drawn on the Bank of Batavia for an amount less than half of what he had been prepared to pay for it only a few months before.

On the planned evening of departure, as the sun set and the light faded, when they could not be observed from the beach or the castle walls, Mansur and a small crew rowed out to the anchored ships. Keyser had placed six Hottentot troopers under a corporal on board each. After five days at anchor, with the vessels pitching and rolling in the steep swells kicked up by the south-easter, those soldiers who were not prostrated with seasickness were bored and disenchanted with this duty. To add to their misery they could see the lights of the taverns along the beachfront and hear snatches of song and revelry drifting across the dark, wind-churned surface from the shore.

Mansur's arrival alongside was a pleasant distraction, and they crowded the rail to exchange jests and friendly insults with him and his rowers. Mansur was a favourite of the Hottentot community in the colony. The nickname they had bestowed upon him was Specht, Woodpecker, for his fiery topknot.

'You are not allowed on board, Specht,' the corporal told him sternly. 'Colonel Keyser's orders. No visitors allowed.'

'Do not fuss yourself. I am not coming on board. I would not want to be seen in the company of such rogues and ruffians,' Mansur shouted back.

'So you say, old Specht, but then what are you doing here? You should be giving the girls in the village sewing lessons.' The corporal shouted with laughter at his own wit. The word *naai* had a double meaning: not only to sew but also to fornicate. Mansur's red hair and startling good looks rendered him almost irresistible to the members of the fair sex.

'It's my birthday,' Mansur told them, 'and I have brought a present for you.' He kicked the keg of Cape *brandewijn* that lay in the bottom of the boat. 'Send down a cargo net.' They jumped to obey, and the keg swayed up on to the deck.

The Muslim captain of the *Gift of Allah* came up from his cabin to protest at this devil's brew, forbidden by the Prophet, coming on board.

'Peace be upon you, Batula,' Mansur called to him in Arabic. 'These men are my friends.' Batula had been Dorian's lance-bearer in the early days in the deserts, they had spent most of their lives together and the links between them were of iron. Batula had known Mansur from the day of his birth. He recognized Mansur's voice and his anger abated a little. He consoled himself that all his men were believers and they would not be tempted by Satan's liquor, unlike the *kaffir* soldiers.

The Hottentot corporal knocked the bung out of the brandy keg and filled a pewter mug. He took a mouthful of the neat spirits, gasped and exhaled the fumes noisily. '*Yis maar!*' he exclaimed. '*Dis lekker!* It's so good!'

Mugs in hand his men crowded round him for their turn at the keg, but the corporal relented his former strictures and called down to Mansur, 'Hey, Specht! Come on board and share a cup.'

Mansur waved an apology as they pulled away and headed for the other ship. 'Not now, perhaps later. I have another present for your men on the *Maid of York*.'

Sarah and Yasmini had been strictly charged by their husbands to restrict their luggage to two large travelling trunks each. Tom absolutely forbade Sarah to try to smuggle her harpsichord on to the ship. As soon as the men were occupied elsewhere, the two goodwives had the servants load their ten large chests on to the waiting cart, and the harpsichord sat four-square on top of this abundant cargo. The wheels of the cart were splayed under the weight.

'Sarah Courtney, you astound me. I know not what to say.' Tom glared at the offending instrument when he returned.

'Then say naught, Tom, you big booby. And I shall play you the sweetest rendition of "Spanish Ladies" you have ever heard when we reach the new home you shall build me.' That was his favourite song, and he stumped off in defeat to oversee the loading of the other wagons.

At this last hour it was not possible that word of their departure might reach Colonel Keyser's ear in time for him to intervene, so the servants were assembled and Tom and Dorian told them that the family was leaving High Weald for ever. There was not space on board the two ships for all of the servants and freed slaves that made up the High Weald household. Those who had been chosen to go with the family were given the right to refuse and stay in the colony. Not one took up that option. They were given an hour to pack. Those who were being left behind huddled in a forlorn group at the end of the wide veranda. The women were weeping softly. All the members of the Courtney family went down the line of familiar, well-beloved faces, talking to each in turn and embracing them. Tom and Dorian handed each a canvas purse, and a deed of manumission and release from service, with a glowing letter of character reference.

'Where is Susie?' Sarah asked, when she reached the end of the line, and looked around for one of her older housemaids. Susie was married to the wagon driver Sonnie, who was still a prisoner in the castle dungeons.

The other servants looked around with surprise. 'Susie was here,' one answered. 'I saw her at the end of the veranda.'

'She was probably overcome by the shock of hearing that we are leaving,' Yasmini suggested. 'When she has recovered I'm sure she will come back to take her leave.'

There was so much still to be done that Sarah was forced to put Susie's absence to the back of her mind. 'I'm sure she would never let us go without a word,' she said, and hurried down to make sure that the cart carrying her special treasures was ready to leave for the beach.

By the time the wagons were ready to leave the homestead the moon had risen, and by its light Susie was hurrying along the road to the castle. She had her shawl over her head, the tail of it wrapped round the lower half of her face. Her face was wet with tears, and she muttered to herself as she ran: 'They don't think about me and Sonnie. No, they leave my husband in the hands of the Boers, to be beaten and killed. They leave me here with three little ones to starve while they sail away.' The twenty years of kindness she had received from Sarah Courtney were swept from her mind and she burst into sobs as she thought about the cruelty of her employer.

She quickened her pace. 'Well, if they don't care for me and Sonnie and the little ones, why should I care for them?' Her voice hardened with her resolve. 'I will make a bargain with the Boers. If they let Sonnie go from the dungeon, I will tell them what Klebe and his wife are up to tonight.'

Susie did not waste time going to the castle to find Colonel Keyser. She went directly to the little cottage behind the Company gardens. The Hottentot community was close-knit and Shala, Colonel Keyser's paramour, was the youngest daughter of Susie's sister. Her liaison with the colonel gave Shala great prestige in the family.

Susie knocked on the shutters of the back room of the cottage. After some fumbling and grumbling in the darkened bedroom, lantern light flared behind the shutters and Shala's voice demanded sleepily, 'Who is it?'

'Shala, it's me. Tannie Susie.'

Shala opened the shutters. She stood naked in the light of her own lantern, and her fat honey-coloured breasts joggled together as she leaned over the window-sill. 'Auntie? How late is it? What do you want at this hour?'

'Is he here, child?' Susie's question was redundant. Keyser's snores rumbled from the darkened bedroom like distant thunder. 'Wake him up.'

'He will beat me if I do,' Shala protested. 'You also, he will thrash you.'

'I have important news for him,' Susie snapped. 'He will reward us both when he hears it. Your uncle Sonnie's life depends on it. Wake him at once.'

When the line of wagons set off from High Weald towards the seafront even those who were not sailing with the family walked alongside. When they reached the beach they helped load the cargo into the lighters that were already waiting at the edge of the surf. Before all the wagons had made their way down through the dunes both boats were fully loaded.

'In this surf we will risk a capsize if we burden them any more,' Tom decided. 'Dorian and I will take this load out to the ships and secure the guards.' He turned to Sarah and Yasmini. 'If they are not sufficiently lulled with Mansur's brandy, there may be a rumpus on board. I don't want you mixed up in that. You two must wait here and I will bring you out to the ships on the next trip.'

'The cart with our luggage has not arrived yet.' Sarah peered back worriedly into the darkness of the dunes.

'It will be here in short order,' Tom assured her. 'Now, please wait here and do not take Yassie and go wandering off to heaven knows where.' He embraced her and whispered in her ear, 'And I would be mightily obliged if you do as I ask just this once.'

'How can you think so poorly of your own wife?' she whispered back. 'Off you go. When you return I shall be here, as good as gold.'

'And twice as beautiful,' he added.

The men scrambled aboard the lighters and seized the oars. The pull out to the ships was rough and wet, for the laden vessels were low in the water. The spray came over the bows, soaking them to the skin. When at last they rowed into the calmer water in the lee of the *Gift of Allah* there was no challenge from the ship. Tom swarmed up the rope-ladder with Dorian and Mansur not far behind him. They drew their blades, ready to meet an attack from the VOC troops, but instead they found Captain Batula waiting at the entry-port.

'May the peace of God be upon you.' He greeted his ship's owners with the deepest respect. Dorian embraced Batula warmly. They had ridden thousands of leagues together and sailed even further. They had fought side by side in the battles that had won a kingdom. They had shared bread and salt. Their friendship was a rock.

'Where are the guards, Batula?' Tom cut short their greetings.

'The forecastle,' Batula told him. 'They are sodden with drink.'

Tom ran to the open companionway and jumped down. The cabin stank of brandy fumes and other less attractive odours. The VOC troopers and their corporal were lying comatose in puddles of their own vomit.

Tom sheathed his sword. 'These gentlemen are quite happy for a while. Tie them up and let them enjoy their rest until we are ready to leave. Let's get the gold chests and the rest of the cargo on board.'

Once the chests of gold coins were safely stowed in the main cabin, Tom left Dorian and Mansur to supervise the loading of the rest of the cargo. He took charge of the second lighter and they rowed across to the *Maid of York*. They found the VOC guards there in no better condition than their comrades on the *Gift of Allah*.

'Sunrise in eight hours, and we must be out of sight of land by then,' Tom told Kumrah, the Arab captain. 'Get this cargo on board as soon as you like.' The crew flew at the task and as the last bale of goods came on board, Tom looked across at the other ship and saw that Dorian had sent a single lantern to the masthead of the *Gift*, the signal that the first lighter was unloaded and returning to the beach to pick up the women and the remaining cargo.

As soon as the bales were lashed down, Tom had his crew carry the VOC soldiers up from the forecastle and dump them, trussed like chickens, into the lighter lying alongside. By then some were regaining consciousness, but on account of their gags and bonds they were unable to express their indignation except by grunting and rolling their eyes.

They pushed off from the ship's side and Tom took the tiller and steered back towards the shore following Dorian's lighter. As they came on to the sand Tom saw Dorian's boat was already on the beach, but nobody was at work loading it. Instead an agitated knot of servants and crew was gathered at the foot of the dunes. Tom jumped down into the shallow water and waded to the shore. He ran up the beach and saw Dorian arguing with the head driver.

'What has happened?' Then he saw that Sarah and Yasmini were missing. 'Where are the women?' Tom called.

'This idiot has let them go back.' Dorian's tone was edged with desperation.

'Go back?' Tom stopped dead and stared at him. 'What do you mean, go back?'

'The cart with their luggage broke down in the dunes. The axle snapped. Sarah and Yasmini have taken one of the empty wagons to fetch the load.'

'Those mad women!' Tom exploded, and then, with a great effort, brought his temper under control. 'Very well, we must make the best of it. Mansur, take the prisoners up above the high-water mark. Do not untie them. Leave them there for

363

Keyser to find in the morning. Then load these goods into the first lighter.' He pointed at the remaining boxes and crates piled on the beach. 'Send them out to the ships with the crew from the *Maid of York*. Thank the good Lord we have the gold chests on board already.'

'What shall I do after that?' asked Mansur.

'You have charge here at the landing. Wait with the second boat. Be ready to load up and launch as soon as we return with the women.' Mansur ran to obey, and Tom turned back to Dorian. 'Come, brother, you and I will go to fetch the sweet chickens that have flown the coop.'

They hurried to the horses. 'Loosen your blade in its scabbard, and make sure both your pistols are charged, Dorry. I like this turn in the road not at all,' Tom muttered, as they mounted. He took his own advice, loosened the blue sword in its scabbard, drew the pistols from the holsters on the front of his saddle, checked them, then thrust them back again.

'Come!' he said, and the two galloped back along the sandy track. Tom was expecting at any moment to come across the stranded cart, but when they rode down out of the dunes and started up through the paddocks towards the homestead they had still not found it.

'If the cart did not get very far,' Dorian muttered, 'you cannot place much blame on the driver. It collapsed under that great mountain of female baggage.'

'We should have packed it on the larger wagon.'

'The ladies would not have it so,' Dorian reminded him. 'They did not want their treasures contaminated by sharing the ride with common goods.'

'I see no call for levity in this, brother. Time runs us short.' Tom looked up at the eastern sky, but there was no sign of the dawn.

'There they are!' Ahead they saw the gleam of a lantern, and the dark shape of a wagon beside the lesser bulk of the capsized cart. They urged the horses to the top of their speed. As they came up Sarah stepped into the road, holding up the lantern, with Yasmini beside her.

'You are just in time to be too late, husband of mine.' Sarah laughed. 'Everything is safely repacked on board the wagon.'

At that moment Tom saw the driver behind her brandish his long whip, flicking out the lash to fire it over the backs of the oxen. 'Stay your hand, Henny, you damned fool. They will hear your whiplash down in the castle. You will bring the colonel and all his men upon us like a pride of lions!'

Guiltily Henny lowered the great whip, and instead he and his *voorloper* ran alongside the oxen slapping their rumps and urging them to pull away. The wagon began lumbering along towards the start of the dunes. The harpsichord swayed and rocked on top of the load. Tom spared it one bitter glance. 'May it fall and burst into a thousand pieces!' he grumbled.

'I choose to ignore that remark,' Sarah said primly, 'for I know you did not mean it.'

'Come up behind me, my sweeting.' Tom leaned out of the saddle to lift her up. 'I shall whisk you back to the beach and have you on board before you can blink an eye.'

'I thank you, no, my own true heart. I prefer to stay with the wagon, to see that no further mishaps befall my baggage.' In frustration Tom slapped the lead ox across its rump with the heavy sword scabbard.

They reached the first slope of the dunes and Tom looked back, and felt the first flare of alarm. There were lights showing around the homestead, which only minutes before had been in complete darkness.

'Look at that, brother,' he muttered to Dorian, keeping his voice low. 'What do you make of it?'

Dorian turned in the saddle. 'Mounted men carrying lighted torches,' Dorian exclaimed. 'They are coming up the hill from the direction of the colony. A large troop, riding in column. They must be cavalry.'

'Keyser!' Tom agreed. 'Stephanus Keyser! It can be no other. Somehow he has got wind of what we are about.'

'When he finds that we have left the homestead, he will come straight on to the landing on the shore.'

'He will catch us before we can load this baggage into the

boats,' Tom agreed. 'We must abandon the wagon, and run for the beach.'

He spurred back to where Sarah and Yasmini were walking alongside the span of oxen. They had cut sticks from the side of the road and were helping to drive the span onwards.

'Douse that lantern. Keyser has come,' Tom shouted at Sarah and pointed back. 'He will be after us in no time at all.'

'Leave the wagon. We must run.' Dorian was at Tom's side.

Sarah cupped her hand around the glass chimney of the lantern, blew out the flame. Then she turned on her husband. 'You cannot be sure it is Keyser,' she challenged him.

'Who else would be leading a troop of cavalry to High Weald at this time of the night?'

'He will not know that we are heading for the beach.'

'He may be fat, but that does not make him blind or stupid. Of course he will come after us.'

Sarah looked ahead. 'It's not far now. We can reach the shore before him.'

'A loaded ox-wagon against a troop of cavalry? Don't be daft, woman.'

'Then you must think of something,' she said, with simple faith. 'You always do.'

'Yes, I have already thought of something. Get up behind me, and we will run as though the devil is breathing fire down our necks.'

'Which he is!' said Dorian, and then to Yasmini, 'Come, my darling, let us go at once.'

'You may go, Yassie,' Sarah said, 'but I am staying.'

'I cannot leave you, Sarah, we have been together too long. I will stay with you,' said Yasmini, and moved closer to her side. They presented the men with an unassailable front. Tom hesitated just a moment longer. Then he turned back to Dorian.

'If I have learned nothing else in my life, this I know. They will not be moved.' He drew one of the pistols from its holster on the pommel of his saddle. 'Look to your priming, Dorry.' He turned back to Sarah and told her sternly, 'You will get us all killed. Perhaps then you will be satisfied. Make all haste.

366

When you reach the beach Mansur will be waiting with the lighter. Have it loaded and ready to shove off. When next you see us Dorry and I might be in somewhat of a hurry.' He was about to ride off when a sudden thought occurred to him. He leaned over and lifted the spare trek chain from its bracket at the back end of the wagon. Every wagon carried this piece of equipment: it was there for use when the teams had to be double spanned.

'What do you mean to do with that?' Dorian demanded. 'It will weigh down your mount.'

'Perhaps nothing.' Tom lashed the chain to the pommel of his saddle. 'But then again, perhaps a great deal.'

They left their two wives and the wagon after one last exhortation to make for the beach at their best speed, and galloped back up the hill. As they approached, the lights of the torches became brighter and the scene clearer. They reined in at the edge of the paddock, just below the homestead, and walked the horses into the deeper darkness below the out-spread branches of the trees. They saw at once that these visitors were uniformed troopers. Many were dismounted and running in and out of the buildings, their sabres drawn, searching the rooms. Tom and Dorian could clearly make out their faces and features.

'There is Keyser,' Dorian exclaimed, 'and, by the beard of the Prophet, that is Susie with him.'

'So, she is our Judas!' Tom's tone was grim. 'What possible reason would she have to betray us?'

'Sometimes there is no accounting for the treacherous spite of those we have loved and trusted most,' Dorian replied.

'Keyser won't waste much time searching for us in the homestead,' Tom grunted, as he untied the *riempie* that secured the heavy trek chain to the front of his saddle. 'Here is what you must do, Dorry.'

Quickly he outlined his plan. Almost as soon as he started talking Dorian had grasped it all.

'The gate above the main kraal,' Dorian agreed.

'When you have done, leave it open,' Tom warned him.

'You do have a hellish mind, brother Tom.' Dorian

367

chuckled. 'At times such as these, I am pleased that I am for you, not against.'

'Go quickly,' Tom said. 'Keyser has already discovered that the stable is empty and the birds have flown.' Tom mixed his metaphors cruelly.

Dorian left Tom under the trees and took the fork of the road that led down to the main cattle stockades above the lagoon. Tom noted that he had the good sense to keep to the verge so that the grass muffled his horse's hoofbeats. He watched until Dorian disappeared into the darkness, then switched his attention to what was happening around the buildings of High Weald.

The troopers had at last abandoned the search and were hurrying back to their horses. On the front *stoep* of the homestead Susie was cowering in front of Keyser, who was shouting at her. His angry tone carried to where Tom waited, but he was too distant to catch the words.

Perhaps Susie has been stricken by an attack of conscience, Tom thought, and watched Keyser lash the woman across the face with his riding crop. Susie fell to her knees. Keyser struck her again across her shoulders with a full overhead stroke of the whip. Susie screamed shrilly and pointed down the road to the dunes.

The cavalry troopers mounted hastily and fell in behind Keyser as he rode at the head of the column. By the light of the torches they carried, Tom watched them come down towards the paddock. The jingle of the harness and the clatter of the carbines and sabres in the scabbards grew louder. When they were so close that he could hear the breathing of their horses, Tom spurred his own horse out of the darkness into the middle of the road in front of them.

'Keyser, you treacherous bag of pig's lard! A curse on your black heart and a pox on your shrivelled genitals!' he shouted. Keyser was so taken aback that he reined in his horse. The troopers behind him bumped into each other. For a moment there was confusion in the column as the horses milled about.

'You will never take me, Keyser, you great round of cheese! Not on that donkey you call a horse.'

368

Tom lifted the double-barrelled pistol and aimed as close over the top of the ostrich plumes in Keyser's hat as he dared. Keyser ducked as the ball buzzed past his ear.

Tom spun his horse and sent him racing down the road towards the kraal. Behind him he heard the thud of answering pistol shots, and Keyser's furious bellows: 'Catch that man! After him! Alive if you can, but dead if you must. Either way, I want him!'

The troop of cavalry pounded after Tom. A blast of pellets from a cavalry carbine whirred around him like a covey of partridge rising from cover, and he lay flat on his horse's mane and lashed the loose end of the reins across its neck.

He looked back under his arm to judge the gap between himself and the pursuit, and when he saw that he was drawing ahead he slowed down a little into a firm gallop and let Keyser close in. The excited shouts and halloos of the troopers reassured Tom that they had him well in sight. Every few seconds there came the bang and thud of a pistol or carbine, and a few balls flew close enough for him to hear them pass. One struck his saddle only inches from his buttocks and went whining off into the night. If it had hit him, it would certainly have inflicted a wound that would have ended it all there and then.

Although he knew exactly where the gate was and he was looking ahead to find it, it still surprised him when it appeared suddenly out of the darkness ahead of him. He saw instantly that Dorian had done as he had asked and left it wide open. The hedge on each side of the opening was shoulder high, thick and dark with matted thorn. Tom had only a moment to steer away from the gateway, and aim at the hedge. As he gathered his mount for the jump with the pressure of his knees and his hands on the reins, from the corner of his eye he saw the glint of steel. Dorian had wrapped each end of the chain around the heavy wooden gate-posts and the links were stretched at waist height across the opening.

Tom let the horse under him judge the moment of take-off, moved his weight forward and helped him surge upwards. They brushed over the top of the hedge and landed well in hand on the far side. The instant Tom recovered his balance and steadied his mount he turned and looked back. One of the troopers had pulled well ahead of his comrades, and tried to follow Tom over the hedge. His horse shied and refused at the last moment, running out while his rider flew off his back and came sailing over the hedge, flying free. He struck the ground in a tangle of limbs and equipment and lay like a sack of beans.

Colonel Keyser saw his man unhorsed, waved his sword over his head and shouted, 'Follow me! Through the gate!'

His squadron bunched up close behind him and he charged into the gateway. With a metallic clash the chain sprang tight as the combined weight of animals and men crashed into it. In an instant the entire column was cut down, horses piling into each other as they fell. The bones of their legs snapped like dry firewood as they hit the chain. Their bodies filled the gateway in a struggling, kicking, screaming mass. Men were caught under the animals and their cries swelled the tumult.

Even Tom, who had engineered it, was appalled by the shambles. Instinctively he turned back his horse, tempted for a fleeting moment to try to render assistance to his victims. Dorian rode out from behind the wall of the kraal where he had been concealed and stopped beside Tom. The two stared in horror. Then Keyser struggled to his feet almost under the noses of their horses.

As the first into the trap, Keyser's mount had struck the chain cleanly, and as they went down Keyser was hurled from the saddle like a stone from a sling. He struck and rolled across the earth, but somehow retained his grip on his sabre. Now he stood up unsteadily and gazed back in disbelief at the pile of struggling men and horses. Then he let out a cry of rage and despair mingled. He raised his sword and rushed at Tom.

'For this I shall have your hide and heart!' he bellowed. With a flick of his sword Tom sent the sabre spinning from his grip to peg into the earth ten paces away. 'Don't be an idiot, man. There has been enough damage done for one day. See to your men.' Tom glanced at Dorian. 'Come, Dorry, let's go on.'

They turned their horses. Still half stunned Keyser staggered to retrieve his sword and as they rode away he shouted after them, 'This is not the end of the business, Tom Courtney. I shall come after you with all the might and authority of the VOC. You shall not escape my wrath.' Neither Tom nor Dorian looked back and he ran after them shouting threats, until they had pulled away and he had run out of breath. He stopped, panting, and hurled his sabre after them. 'I shall hunt you down and root you out, you and all your seed.'

Just as they were disappearing into the night, Keyser bellowed his last taunt: 'Koots has already captured your bitch-born bastard. He is bringing back Jim Courtney's head, and the head of his convict whore, pickled in a keg of brandy.'

Tom stopped and stared back at him.

'Yes, Koots has caught him,' Keyser shouted, with wild laughter.

'He is lying, brother. He says it to wound you.' Dorian laid a hand on Tom's arm. 'How could he know what has happened out there?'

'You are right, of course,' Tom whispered. 'Jim has got clean away.'

'We must get back to the women, and see them safely aboard,' Dorian insisted. They rode on and Keyser's shouts receded behind them.

Struggling for breath, Keyser tottered back to the tangle of men and horses. A few of his troopers were crawling to their feet, or sitting holding their heads or nursing other injuries.

'Find me a horse,' Keyser yelled.

His own horse, like most of the others, had broken its legs when it struck the chain, but a few animals, who had been in the rear rank of the charge, had been able to heave themselves upright and were standing, shivering and shaken. Keyser ran from one to another, checking their legs. He selected the one that seemed strongest, hoisted himself into the saddle and

371

shouted to his men who could still walk, 'Come on! Find yourselves a mount and follow me. We can still catch them on the beach.'

Tom and Dorian found the last wagon descending the final slope of the dunes. The women were walking beside it. Sarah had relit the lantern and held it high when she heard the horses galloping up.

'Will you not hurry, woman?' Tom was so agitated that he shouted at her from a distance.

'We *are* hurrying,' she replied, 'and your rough seaman's language will make us go no faster.'

'We have delayed Keyser for the moment, but he will be after us again soon enough.' Tom realized his mistake in adopting that brusque approach to his wife and, despite his agitation, tried to ameliorate his tone. 'We are in sight of the beach, and all your possessions are safe.' He pointed ahead. 'Will you now let me take you to the boat, my sweeting.'

She looked up at him and, even in the poor light of her lantern, could see the strain on his face. She relented. 'Lift me up, then, Tom.' She raised her arms to him like a small girl to her father. When he swung her up and placed her behind him she hugged him close, and whispered into the thick curls that bushed down the back of his neck, 'You are the finest husband God ever placed upon this earth, and I am the most fortunate of wives.'

Dorian gathered up Yasmini and they followed Tom down to where Mansur waited with the lighter at the water's edge. They placed the two women firmly on board. The wagon came trundling down, and as it reached the lighter it sank axle deep into the wet sand. But this made it easier to transfer the last of their possessions into the boat. Once the wagon was empty the oxen were able to haul it away.

While this was going on, Tom and Dorian kept glancing back into the darkness of the dunes, expecting the worst of Keyser's threats to materialize, but the harpsichord was at last lashed down and covered with a tarpaulin to protect it from the spray.

Mansur and the crewmen who were shoving out the boat were still waist deep, when there was an angry shout from the dunes and the flash and clap of a carbine shot. The ball slammed into the transom of the boat, and Mansur leaped in.

There was another shot and again the ball struck the hull. Tom pushed the women down until they were sitting on the deck, in an inch or more of bilge water, protected by the pile of hastily loaded cargo.

'I entreat you now to keep your heads well down. We can argue the merits of this suggestion later. However, I assure you those are real musket balls.'

He looked back and could just make out Keyser's distinctive outline against the pale sand, but his stentorian bellows carried clearly: 'You will not escape me, Tom Courtney. I shall see you hanged, drawn and quartered on the same scaffold as that bloody pirate, your grandfather. Every Dutch port in this world will be closed to you.'

'Take no notice of what he says,' Tom told Sarah, dreading that Keyser would repeat his gruesome description of Jim's fate and torment her beyond bearing. 'In his pique he utters only monstrous lies. Come, let us give him a farewell tune.'

To drown Keyser's threats, he launched into a hearty but off-key rendition of 'Spanish Ladies', and the others all joined in. Dorian's voice was as magnificent as ever and Mansur had inherited his ringing tenor. Yasmini's soprano lisped sweetly. Sarah leaned against Tom's reassuring bulk and sang with him.

'Farewell and adieu to you, fair Spanish ladies,
Farewell and adieu to you,' ladies of Spain
For we've received orders to sail for old England,
But we hope in a short time to see you again . . .

Then let every man here toss off a full bumper,
Then let every man here toss off his full bowl,
For we will be jolly and drown melancholy,
With a health to each jovial and true-hearted soul . . .'

Yasmini laughed and clapped her hands. 'That's the first naughty song Dorry ever taught me. Do you remember when first I sang it to you, Tom?'

'My oath on it, I will never forget it.' Tom chuckled as he steered for the *Maid of York*. ''Twas the day you brought Dorrie back to me after I had lost him for all those years.'

As Tom clambered aboard the *Maid of York* he gave orders to his captain: 'Captain Kumrah, in God's name, get this last load on board as quick as you like.' He went back to the rail and looked down at Dorian, who was still in the lighter. He called to him, 'As soon as you're on board the *Gift of Allah* douse all lights and hoist anchor, we must be clear of the land before first light. I don't want Keyser and the Dutch lookouts in the castle to spy out in which direction we are headed. Let them guess whether it be east or west, or even south to the Pole.'

The last of the baggage to come on board from the lighter was Sarah's harpsichord. As it dangled over the side, Tom called to the men on the fall of the tackle, 'A guinea for the man who lets that damn thing drop down to Davy Jones.'

Sarah prodded him sharply in the ribs, and the crewmen paused and looked at each other. They were never sure what to make of Tom's sense of humour. Tom put his arm around Sarah and went on, 'Of course, once you have your guinea, out of deference to the feeling of my wife, I shall be obliged to throw you in after it.'

They laughed uncertainly and swung the harpsichord on board. Tom strode back to the side. 'Be away with you then, brother,' he called to Dorian.

The crew of the lighter shoved off and Dorian hailed back, 'If we become separated in the dark, then the rendezvous will be off Cape Hangklip, as always?'

'As always, Dorry.'

The two ships sailed within minutes of each other, and for the first hour they were able to keep station. Then the wind increased to near gale force and the last sliver of moon went behind the clouds. In the darkness they lost contact with each other.

374

When dawn broke the *Maid* found herself alone, with the south-easter howling through her rigging. The land was a blue smear, low on the northern horizon, almost obscured by the breaking waves and the swirling sea fret.

'Fat chance that the Dutch will make us out in this weather,' Tom shouted at Kumrah, as the tails of his tarpaulin coat flapped around his legs, and the ship heeled over to the push of the storm. 'Make this your offing, and come about for Cape Hangklip.'

Close-hauled against the storm they raised the Cape the next morning, and found the *Gift* there before them, beating back and forth on the rendezvous. Once more in convoy they set out eastwards to round Cape Agulhas, the southernmost tip of Africa. The wind held steadily out of the east. They spent many weary days tacking back and forth, steering clear of the treacherous shoals that guarded Agulhas and clawing their way into their eastings. At last they were able to double the Cape and turn northwards along that rugged and inhospitable coast.

Three weeks after leaving High Weald they finally passed through the heads of grey rock that guarded the great Lagoon of the Elephants. They dropped anchor in the blessedly calm waters, clear as good Hollands gin and teaming with shoals of fish.

'This is where my grandfather Frankie Courtney fought his last battle with the Dutch. Here, they made him prisoner and took him down to Good Hope to perish on the gallows,' he told Sarah. 'My sacred oath, they were tough old devils those ancestors of mine,' he said with pride.

Sarah smiled at him. 'Are you suggesting that you are a milktoast and a caitiff when compared with them?' Then she shaded her eyes and peered up at the hillside that rose above the lagoon. 'Is that your famous post stone?'

Half-way up the hill a prominent lump of grey stone the size of a hayrick had been painted with a large, lop-sided letter P in scarlet paint, so that it was visible to any ship anchored in the lagoon.

'Oh, take me ashore immediately. I feel certain that there is a letter from Jim awaiting us.'

Tom was certain that her hopes were doomed to disappointment, but they rowed to the beach in the longboat. Sarah was first over the side with the water reaching to her thighs and soaking her skirts. Tom had difficulty keeping up with her as she lifted the sodden cloth to her knees and scrambled up the hillside. 'Look!' she cried. 'Someone has placed a cairn of stones on the summit. That surely is a sign that a letter is waiting for us.'

A hollow space had been burrowed out beneath the post stone, and the entrance to it was blocked with smaller ones. She pulled these apart and beyond them she found a bulky parcel. It was stitched up in a wrapper of heavy tarpaulin and sealed with tar.

'I knew it! Oh, yes, I knew it,' Sarah sang, as she dragged the parcel from its hiding-place. But when she read the inscription on it her face fell. Without another word she handed the packet to Tom and started back down the hill.

Tom read the inscription. It was in an ill-formed hand, misspelled and crude: 'Hail, you tru and worfy sole who doth this missif find. Tak it with you to London Town and gif it over to Nicolas Whatt Esquire at 51 Wacker Street close by the East Hindia Dok. He shall gif you a giny for it. Opun not this paket! Fayle me nefer! If you do so, then I do rot your balls and dam your eyes! May your mannikin never rise, you God forsaken boger!' The message was signed, 'Cpt Noah Calder abord the Brig *Larkspur* out bound for Bombay, 21 May in the yer of ow Lord Jassus 1731.'

'Words well chosen, and sentiments sweetly expressed.' Tom smiled as he replaced the packet in the recess and covered it with the stones. 'I am not headed for old London Town, so I will not risk the dire consequences of failure. It must wait for a bolder soul heading in the right direction.'

He went down the hill, and half-way to the beach he found Sarah sitting forlornly upon a rock. She turned away as he sat down beside her, and tried to stifle her sobs. He took her face between his big hands and turned it towards him. 'No, no, my love. You must not take on so. Our Jim is safe.'

'Oh, Tom, I was so sure it was his letter to us, and not that of some oaf of a sailor.'

'It was most unlikely that he would come here. Surely he will be heading further north. I do believe he had set upon Nativity. We shall find him there, and little Louisa with him. Mark my words. Nothing can befall our Jim. He is a Courtney, ten feet tall and made from billets of cast iron covered with elephant hide.'

She laughed through her tears. 'Tom, you silly man, you should be upon the stage.'

'Even Master Garrick could not afford my fee.' He laughed with her. 'Come along now, my own sweet girl. There is no profit in pining, and there is work to do if we purpose to sleep ashore this night.'

They went back down to the beach, and found that Dorian and his party from the *Gift* had already come ashore. Mansur was unloading the water casks into the longboat. He would refill them from the sweet-water stream that flowed into the top end of the lagoon. Dorian and his men were building shelters on the edge of the forest, weaving frameworks of saplings. They were thatching these with new reeds, fresh cut from the edge of the water. The smell of sweet sap perfumed the air.

After the trying weeks at sea in rough weather the women needed comfortable quarters on dry land in which to recuperate. It was over a year since the brothers had visited the lagoon on their last trading expedition along the coast. The huts they had built then they had burned to the ground when they sailed, for by now they would have been infested by scorpions, hornets and other unpleasant flying insects and crawling creatures.

There was a brief alarum when they heard a succession of musket shots banging out from the top end of the lagoon, but Dorian reassured them quickly: 'I told Mansur to bring us in fresh meat. He must have found game.'

When Mansur returned with the refilled water casks, he brought with him the carcass of a half-grown buffalo. Despite its tender age the beast was the size of an ox, enough to feed them all for weeks once it was salted and smoked. Then the other longboat returned from the edge of the channel where Tom had sent five of the crew to catch fish. The bins amidship were filled with sparkling silver mounds, still quivering and twitching.

Sarah and Yasmini set to work at once with their servants to prepare a suitable feast to celebrate their arrival. They ate under the stars, with sparks from the campfire rising into the dark sky in a torrent. After they had eaten their fill, Tom sent for Batula and Kumrah. They came ashore from the anchored ships and took their places, sitting cross-legged on their prayer mats in the circle around the fire.

'I ask your forgiveness for any disrespect,' Tom greeted the two captains. 'We should have heard the news you bring sooner than this. However, with the need to sail from Good Hope with such despatch, and the gale that assailed us since then, there has been no opportunity.'

'It is as you say, *effendi*,' Batula, the senior captain, replied. 'We are your men and there was never any disrespect.'

The servants brought coffee from the fire in brass kettles, and Dorian and the Arabs lit their hookahs. The water in the bowls bubbled with each breath of the perfumed Turkish tobacco smoke they drew.

First they discussed the trade and the goods that the captains had gathered during their last voyage along this coast. As Arabs they were able to travel where no Christian ship was allowed to pass. They had even sailed on past the Horn of Hormuz into the Red Sea as far as holy Medina, the luminous city of the Prophet.

On their return journey they had parted company, Kumrah in the *Maid* turning eastwards to call in at the ports of the empire of the Moguls, there to deal with the diamond merchants from the Kollur mines, and to buy bales of silken rugs from the souks of Bombay and Delhi. Meanwhile, Batula sailed along the Coromandel coast and loaded his ship with tea and spices. The two ships met again in the harbour of Trincomalee in Ceylon. There, they took on board cloves, saffron, coffee beans and choice packets of blue star sapphires. Then, in company, they had returned to Good Hope, to the anchorage off the beach of High Weald.

Batula was able to recite from memory the quantities of each commodity they had purchased, the prices they had paid, and the state of the various markets they had visited.

Tom and Dorian questioned them carefully and exhaustively, while Mansur wrote everything in the CBTC journal. This information was vital to their prosperity: any change in the state and condition of the markets and the supply of goods could spell great profit or, perhaps, even greater disaster to their enterprise.

'The largest profits still lie in the commerce of slaves,' Kumrah summed up delicately, and neither captain could meet Tom's eye as he said it. They knew his views on their trade, which he called 'an abomination in the face of God and man'.

Predictably Tom rounded on Kumrah. 'The only piece of human flesh I will ever sell is your hairy buttocks to the first man who will pay the five rupees I ask for them.'

'Effendi!' cried Kumrah, his expression a Thespian masterpiece: an unlikely mixture of contrition and pained sensibility. 'I would rather shave off my beard and feast on pig flesh than buy a single human soul from the slave block.'

Tom was about to remind him that slaving had been his chief enterprise before he entered the service of the Courtney brothers, when Dorian, playing the peace-maker, intervened smoothly: 'I hunger for news of my old home. Tell me what you have learned of Omani and Muscat, of Lamu and Zanzibar.'

'We knew that you would ask us this, so we have saved this news for the last. Those lands have been overtaken by momentous events, al-Salil.' They turned to Dorian eagerly, grateful to him for having diverted Tom's wrath.

'Good captains, tell us all you have learned,' Yasmini demanded. Until now she had sat behind her husband and held her peace as a dutiful Muslim wife should. Now, however, she could restrain herself no longer, for they were speaking of her homeland and her family. Although she and Dorian had fled the Zanzibar coast almost twenty years ago, her thoughts often returned there and her heart hankered for the lost years of her childhood.

It was true indeed that not all of her memories were happy ones. There had been times of loneliness in the isolation of the women's zenana, although she had been born a princess, daughter of Sultan Abd Muhammad al-Malik, the Caliph of Muscat. Her father had possessed more than fifty wives. He showed interest only in his sons, and could never bother himself to keep track of his daughters. She knew that he was barely aware of her existence, and could not remember any word he had spoken to her, or even a touch of his hand or a kindly glance. In all truth, she had laid eyes on him only on state occasions or when he visited his women in the zenana. Then it had been only at a distance, and she had trembled and covered her face in terror of his magnificence and his godlike presence. Even so she mourned and fasted the full forty days and nights stipulated by the Prophet when news of his death reached her in the African wilderness whence she had fled with Dorian.

Her mother had died in Yasmini's infancy, and she could not remember a single detail about her. As she grew older she learned that she had inherited from her the startling streak of silver hair that divided her own thick midnight black tresses. Yasmini had spent all her childhood in the zenana on Lamu island. The only maternal love she had known was given to her unstintingly by Tahi, the old slave woman who had nursed her and Dorian.

In the beginning Dorian, the adopted son of her own father, was with her in the zenana. This was before he reached his puberty and underwent the ordeal of the circumcision knife. As her adopted elder brother, he protected her, often with his fists and feet from the malice of her blood brothers. Her particular tormentor was Zayn al-Din. When Dorian defended her, he had made a mortal enemy of him; the rancour would persist througout their lives. To this day Yasmini remembered that dire confrontation between the two boys in every detail.

380

Dorian and Zayn had been only a few months short of puberty, and their departure from the zenana and entry into manhood and military service was looming large. That day Yasmini was playing alone on the terrace of the old saint's tomb, at the end of the zenana gardens. This was one of her secret places where she could escape from the bullying of their peers, and find solace in daydreams and childish games of fantasy. With Yasmini was her pet vervet monkey, Jinni. Zayn al-Din and Abubaker, both her half-brothers, had discovered her there.

Plump, sly and vicious, Zayn was bravest when he had one of his toadies with him. He wrested the little monkey from Yasmini and threw him into the open rainwater cistern. Though Yasmini screamed at the top of her lungs and jumped on his back, pummelling his head and trying to scratch lumps out of his skin, he ignored her and began systematically to drown Jinni, ducking the monkey's head each time he surfaced.

Summoned by Yasmini's screams Dorian came racing up the staircase from the garden. He took in the scene at a glance, then launched himself at the two bigger boys. Before his capture by the Arabs, his brother Tom had coached Dorian in the art of boxing, but Zayn and Abubaker had never before come into contact with bunched, flying fists. Abubaker fled from this terrible attack, but Zayn's nose burst in a spray of scarlet at the first punch, while the second sent him somersaulting down the steep staircase. When he struck the bottom, one of the bones in his right foot snapped. The bone set ill, and he would limp for the rest of his life.

In the years after he had left behind his childhood and the zenana, Dorian had become a prince in his own right and a famous warrior. Yasmini, however, was forced to remain behind, at the mercy of Kush, the head eunuch. Even after all these years, his monstrous cruelty lived vividly in her memory. Yasmini grew to lovely womanhood while Dorian fought his adopted father's enemies in the Arabian deserts far to the north. Covered in glory he had returned at last to Lamu, but he had almost forgotten his adopted sister and childhood sweetheart. Then Tahi, his ancient slave nurse, had come to him in the palace and reminded him that Yasmini was still languishing in the zenana.

With Tahi as a go-between they had arranged a dangerous tryst. When they became lovers they were committing a double sin from the consequences of which not even Dorian's exalted position could protect them. They were adopted brother and sister and, in the eyes of God, the Caliph and the council of mullahs, their union was both fornication and incest.

Kush had discovered their secret, and planned a punishment for Yasmini so unspeakably cruel that she still shuddered when she thought about it, but Dorian had intervened to save her. He killed Kush and buried him in the grave the eunuch had dug for Yasmini. Then Dorian disguised her as a boy and smuggled her out of the harem. Together they escaped from Lamu.

Many years later, after his father Abd Muhammad al-Malik had died of poisoning, Zayn – still limping from the injury Dorian had inflicted – ascended the Elephant Throne of Oman. One of his first acts as caliph was to send Abubaker to find and capture Dorian and Yasmini. When Abubaker caught up with the lovers there had been a terrible battle in which Dorian had killed him. Yasmini and Dorian had escaped once again from Zayn's vengeance and been reunited with Tom. However, Zayn al-Din sat on the mighty Elephant Throne to this day, and was still Caliph of Oman. They knew they were never entirely safe from his hatred.

Now, sitting by the campfire on this wild and savage shore, she reached out to touch Dorian. It was almost as though he had read her thoughts, for he took her hand and held it firmly. She felt strength and courage flowing from him into her like the balmy influence of the *kusi*, the trade wind of the Indian Ocean.

'Recount!' Dorian ordered his captains. 'Tell me these momentous tidings you bring from Muscat. Did you hear aught of the Caliph, Zayn al-Din?'

'Our tidings are all of Zayn al-Din. As Allah bears witness, he is Caliph in Muscat no longer.'

'What is this you say?' Dorian started up. 'Is Zayn dead at last?'

'Nay, my Prince. A *shaitan* is hard to kill. Zayn al-Din lives on.'

'Where is he, then? We must know all of this affair.'

'Forgive me, *effendi*.' Batula made a gesture of deep respect, touching his lips and his heart. 'There is one in our present company who knows all this far better than I do. He comes from the bosom of Zayn al-Din, and was once one of his trusted ministers and confidants.'

'Then he is no friend of mine. His master has tried on many occasions to kill me and my wife. It was Zayn who drove us into exile. He is my mortal enemy, and he has sworn a blood feud against us.'

'All this I know well, lord,' Batula replied, 'for I have been with you since that happy day when the man who then was Caliph, your sainted adoptive father al-Malik, made me your lance-bearer. Do you forget that I was at your side when you captured Zayn al-Din at the battle of Muscat and you roped him behind your camel and dragged him as a traitor to face the wrath and justice of al-Malik?'

'That I will never forget, as I will not forget your loyalty and service to me over all these years.' Dorian's expression became sad. 'Pity it is that my father's wrath was so short-lived, and his justice too heavily tempered with mercy. For he pardoned Zayn al-Din and clasped him once again to his bosom.'

'By God's Holy Name!' Batula's anger matched that of his master. 'Your father died from that show of mercy. It was Zayn's effeminate hand that held the poisoned cup to his lips.'

'And Zayn's fat buttocks that sat on the Elephant Throne when my father was gone.' Dorian's handsome features were marred by an expression of ferocity. 'Now you ask me to accept into my camp the minion and minister of this monster?'

'Not so, Highness. I said that this man was once all those

things to Zayn al-Din. But no longer. Like all who know him well, he became sickened to the heart by the monstrous cruelty of Zayn al-Din. He watched while Zayn tore the sinews and the heart of the nation to shreds. He watched helplessly while Zayn fed his pet sharks with the flesh of good and noble men, until they were almost too bloated to swim. He tried to protest when Zayn sold his birthright to the Sublime Porte, to the Turkish tyrants in Constantinople. In the end he was one of the chief conspirators in the plot against Zayn that overturned his throne and drove him out through the gates of Muscat.'

'Zayn is overthrown?' Dorian stared at Batula in astonishment. 'He was Caliph for twenty years. I thought he would stay in power until he died of old age.'

'Some men of great evil possess not only the savagery of the wolf but also that beast's instincts of survival. This man, Kadem al-Jurf, will tell you the rest of the story if you will allow it.'

Dorian glanced at Tom, who had been following every word with intense interest. 'What do you think, brother?'

'Let us hear the man's story,' Tom said.

Kadem al-Jurf must have been awaiting their summons for he came within minutes from the crew's encampment at the edge of the forest. They all realized that they had seen him often during the stormy voyage up from Good Hope. Although they had not known his name, they had understood that he was Batula's newly hired writer and purser.

'Kadem al-Jurf?' Dorian greeted him. 'You are a guest in my camp. You are under my protection.'

'Your beneficence lights my life like the sunrise, Prince al-Salil ibn al-Malik.' Kadem prostrated himself before Dorian. 'May the peace of God and the love of his last true Prophet follow you all the days of your long and illustrious life.'

'It is many years since any man has called me by that title.' Dorian nodded, gratified. 'Rise up, Kadem, and take a place in our council.' Kadem sat beside Batula, his sponsor. The servants brought him coffee in a silver cup and Batula passed him the ivory mouthpiece of his pipe. Both Dorian and Tom studied the new man carefully while he enjoyed these expressions of hospitality and favour.

Kadem al-Jurf was young, no more than a few years older than Mansur. He had a noble face. His features reminded Dorian of his own adoptive father. Of course, it was not impossible that he was a royal bastard. The Caliph had been a man indeed, and prolific with his seed. He had ploughed and sowed wherever the ground pleased him.

Dorian smiled faintly, then put aside the thought, and once more regarded Kadem with his full attention. His skin was the colour of fine polished teak. His brow was deep and wide, his eyes clear, dark and penetrating. He returned Dorian's scrutiny calmly and, despite his protestations of loyalty and respect, Dorian thought he recognized in his gaze the disconcerting gleam of the zealot. This is a man who lives by the Word of Allah alone, he thought. Here is one who places scant value in the law and opinions of men. He knew well how dangerous such men could be. While he composed his next question he looked at Kadem's hands. There were telltale calluses on his fingers and his right palm. He recognized these as the stigmata of the warrior, the gall of bowstring and sword hilt. He looked again at his shoulders and arms and saw the development of muscle and sinew that could only have been built up during long hours of practice with bow and blade. Dorian let none of these thoughts show in his own eyes as he asked gravely, 'You were in the service of Caliph Zayn al-Din?'

'Since childhood, Lord. I was an orphan and he took me under his protection.'

'You swore a blood oath of loyalty to him,' Dorian insisted. For the first time Kadem's steady gaze shifted slightly. He did not reply. 'Yet you have reneged on this oath,' Dorian persisted. 'Batula tells me you are no longer the Caliph's man. Is that true?'

'Your Highness, I swore that oath nearly twelve years ago, on the day of my circumcision. In those days I was a man in name only, but in reality I was a mere child and a stranger to the truth.'

'And now I can see that you have become a man.' Dorian went on appraising him. Kadem was supposedly a writer, a man of papers and ink, but he did not have that look. There was a latent fierceness about him, like a falcon at roost. Dorian was intrigued. He went on, 'But, Kadem al-Jurf, does this release you from a blood oath of fealty?'

'My lord, I believe that fealty is a dagger with two edges. He who accepts it has a responsibility towards he who offers it. If he neglects that duty and responsibility, then the debt is cancelled.'

'These are devious semantics, Kadem. I find them too convoluted to fathom. To me an oath is an oath.'

'My lord condemns me?' Kadem's voice was silky, but his eyes were cold as obsidian.

'Nay, Kadem al-Jurf. I leave judgement and condemnation to God.'

'*Bismallah!*' Kadem intoned, and Batula and Kumrah stirred.

'There is no God, but God,' said Batula.

'God's wisdom surpasses all understanding,' said Kumrah.

Kadem whispered, 'Yet I know that Zayn al-Din is your blood enemy. That is why I come to you, al-Salil.'

'Yes, Zayn is my adopted brother and my enemy. Many years ago he swore to kill me. Many times since then I have felt his baleful influence touch my life,' Dorian agreed.

'I have heard him relate to his courtiers how he owes his crippled foot to you,' Kadem went on.

'He owes me much else besides.' Dorian smiled. 'I had the great pleasure of placing a rope around his neck and dragging him before our father to face the Caliph's wrath.'

'Posterity and Zayn al-Din remember this deed of yours well.' Kadem nodded. 'This is part of the reason that we chose to come to you.'

'Before it was "I", but now it is "we"?'

'There are others who have repudiated their oaths of fealty to Zayn al-Din. We turn to you, for you are the last of the line of Abd Muhammad al-Malik.'

'How is that possible?' Dorian demanded, and suddenly he

was angry. 'My father had countless wives who bore him sons, and they in turn had sons and grandsons. My father's seed was fruitful.'

'Fruitful no longer. Zayn has harvested all his father's fruits. On the first day of Ramadan there was such a slaughter as to shame the Face of God and astound all Islam. Two hundred of your brothers and nephews were gathered up by Zayn al-Din's reapers. They died by poison, that coward's tool, and they died by steel and rope and water. Their blood soaked the desert sands and tinted the sea to rose. Every person who had a blood claim to the Elephant Throne in Muscat perished in that holy month. Murder was compounded ten thousand times by sacrilege.'

Dorian stared at him in horrified disbelief, and Yasmini choked back her sobs: her brothers and other kin must be among the dead. Dorian put aside his own shocked grief to comfort her. He stroked the silver blaze that shone like a diadem in her sable locks, and whispered softly to her before he turned back to Kadem. 'This is hard news and bitter,' he said. 'It takes great effort for the mind to encompass such evil.'

'My lord, neither were we able to treat with such monstrous evil. That is why we repudiated our vows and rose up against Zayn al-Din.'

'There has been a rising?' Although Batula had already warned him of this, Dorian wanted Kadem to confirm it: all this seemed too far beyond the frontiers of possibility.

'A battle raged within the walls of the city for many days. Zayn al Din and his adherents were driven into the keep of the fort. We believed that they would perish there but, alas, there was a secret tunnel under the walls that led down to the old harbour. Zayn escaped by this route, and his ships bore him away.'

'Whither did he flee?' Dorian demanded.

'He sailed back to his birthplace on Lamu island. With the help of the Portuguese and the collusion of the minions of the English East India Company at Zanzibar, he has seized the great fort and all the Omani settlements and possessions along the Fever Coast. Under the threat of the English guns his forces in those possessions have remained loyal to him, and have resisted our efforts to cast down the tyrant.'

'In God's name, you and your junta in Muscat must be preparing your fleet to exploit these successes and to attack Zayn in Zanzibar and Lamu, is that not so?' Dorian demanded.

'My lord prince, our ranks are riven by dissent. There is no successor of royal blood to head our junta. Thus we lack loyal support from the Omani nation. In particular the desert tribes are hesitating to declare against Zayn and join our standard.'

Dorian's expression became wooden and remote as he realized where Kadem's protestations were heading.

'Without a leader our cause grows weaker and more divided each day, while each day Zayn regains his stature and strength. He commands the Zanzibar coast. We have learned that he has sent envoys to the Great Mogul, the Supreme Emperor in Delhi, and to the Sublime Porte in Constantinople. His old allies are rallying to support him. Soon all of Islam and Christendom will unite against us. Our victory will drain away into the sands, like the ebb of the spring tide.'

'What do you want from me, Kadem al-Jurf?' Dorian asked softly.

'We need a leader with a rightful claim to the Elephant Throne,' Kadem replied. 'We need a tried warrior who has commanded the desert tribes in battle: the Saar, the Dahm and the Karab, the Bait Kathir and the Awamir, but most of all the Harasis who hold within their sway the plains of Muscat. Without these there can be no ultimate victory.'

Dorian sat quietly but his heart had beaten faster as Kadem recited those illustrious names. In his mind's eye he saw again the battle array, the glint of steel in the dustclouds and the banners unfurled. He heard the war-cries of the riders, '*Allah Akbar!* God is great!' and the roaring of the ranks of camels racing onwards across the sands of Oman.

Yasmini felt his arm tremble under her hand, and her heart quailed. I believed in my heart that the dark days were past for ever, she thought, that I might never again hear the beat of the war drums. I hoped that my husband would always stay beside me and never again ride away to war.

The company was silent, each of them thinking their own thoughts. Kadem was watching Dorian with that glittering, compulsive stare.

Dorian shook himself back to the present. 'Do you know these things are true?' he asked. 'Or are they merely the dreams born of desire?'

Kadem answered straight, without lowering his eyes: 'We have been in council with the desert sheikhs. They who are often divided all speak with a single voice. They say, "Let al-Salil take his place at the head of our armies, and we will follow wherever he leads."'

Dorian stood up abruptly and left the circle around the campfire. None of the others followed him, neither Tom nor Yasmini. He paced along the edge of the water, a romantic figure in his robes, tall and shining in the moonlight.

Tom and Sarah whispered together, but the others were silent.

'You must not let him go,' Sarah told Tom quietly, 'for Yasmini's sake and ours. You lost him once. You cannot let him go again.'

'And yet I cannot stop him. This is between Dorian and his God.'

Batula packed fresh tobacco in the bowl of the hookah, and it was almost consumed to ash before Dorian came back to the fire. He sat cross-legged with his elbows on his knees and his chin cupped in both hands, staring into the leaping flames.

'My lord,' Kadem whispered, 'give me your answer. With the trade winds standing fair, if you sail at once you can mount the Elephant Throne in Muscat at the beginning of the Feast of Lights. There can be no more propitious day than that to begin your reign as Caliph.'

Dorian was silent still, and Kadem went on – his tone was not wheedling, but strong and sure of his purpose: 'Your Highness, if you return to Muscat, the mullahs will declare *jihad*, a holy war, against the tyrant. God and all of Oman will be at your back. You cannot turn aside from your destiny.'

Dorian raised his head slowly. Yasmini drew a long slow breath and held it. Her nails sank into the hard muscles of his forearm.

'Kadem al-Jurf,' Dorian replied, 'this is a terrible decision. I cannot make it alone. I must pray for guidance.'

Kadem fell forward, prostrating himself on the sand before Dorian. His arms and legs were spread wide. 'God is great!' he said. 'There can be no victory without His benevolence. I shall wait for your answer.'

'I will give it to you tomorrow night at this same time and place.'

Yasmini let out her breath slowly. She knew that this was only a reprieve, and not a pardon.

Early the next day Tom and Sarah climbed to the top of the grey rocks that guarded the entrance to the lagoon, and found a sheltered nook out of the wind but full in the sun.

The Ocean of the Indies was spread beneath them, raked with creamy furrows. A sea bird used the wind to hang like a kite above the green waters. Suddenly it folded its wings and plunged from on high, hitting the surface with a tiny splash, rising again almost immediately with a silver fish wriggling in its beak. On the rocks above where they lay, the hyrax sat in the sun, rabbity brown balls of fluff watching them with huge, curious eyes.

'I want to have serious speech with you,' Sarah said.

Tom rolled on to his back and locked his fingers behind his head, grinning at her. 'Fool that I am, I thought you had brought me here to have your wicked way with me, to ravish my tender flesh.'

'Tom Courtney, will you never be serious?'

'Aye, lass, that I will, and I thank you for the invitation.' He reached for her, but she struck away his hand.

'I warn you, I shall scream.'

'I will cease and desist, for the moment at least. What is it that you wanted to discuss with me?'

''Tis Dorry and Yassie.'

'Why does this not come as any great surprise to me?'

'Yassie is sure that he will sail to Muscat to take up the offer of the throne.'

'I am sure she would not hate the thought of becoming a queen. What woman would?'

'It will destroy her life. She explained it all to me. You can have no conception of the intrigues and conspiracies that surround an Oriental court.'

'Can I not?' He raised an eyebrow. 'I have lived twenty years with you, my heart, which has given me good training.'

She went on as though he had not spoken: 'You are the elder brother. You must forbid him to leave. This offer of the Elephant Throne is a poisoned gift, which will destroy them and us also.'

'Sarah Courtney, you do not truly believe that I would forbid Dorian anything? It is a decision that only he can make.'

'You will lose him again, Tom. Do you not remember how it was when he was sold into slavery? How you thought he was dead, and part of you died with him?'

'I remember it well. But this is not slavery and death. It's a crown and power unbounded.'

'I think you begin to relish the thought of him going,' she accused him.

Tom sat up quickly. 'No, woman! He is blood of my blood. I want only what is best for him.'

'You think this may be best?'

'It was the life and the destiny for which he was trained. He has become a trader with me, but I have known all along that his heart is not truly in our enterprise. For me it is meat and wine, but Dorry hankers after more than we have here. Have you not heard him speak of his adoptive father and the days when he commanded the army of Oman? Do you not sometimes see the regret and longing in his eyes?'

'Tom, you look for signs that are not there,' Sarah protested.

'You know me well, my love.' He paused, then went on, 'It is my nature to dominate those around me. Even you.'

She laughed, a gay pretty sound. 'You do try, I grant you that.'

'I try with Dorry too, and with him I succeed better than I do with you. He is my dutiful younger brother, and over all these years I have treated him like that. Perhaps this summons to Muscat is what he has been waiting for.'

'You will lose him again,' she repeated.

'No, there will be only a little water between us, and I have a fast ship.' He lay back in the grass and pulled his hat down over his eyes to shield them from the sun. 'Besides, it will not be bad for business to have a brother able to issue licences for my ships to trade in all the forbidden ports of the Orient.'

'Tom Courtney, you mercenary monster. I do truly hate you.' She leaped on him and pummelled his chest with clenched fists. He rolled her easily on to her back in the grass and lifted her skirts away from her legs. They were still strong and shapely as those of a girl. She crossed them firmly.

'Sarah Courtney, show me how much you really hate me.' He held her down with one hand while he unbuckled his belt.

'Stop this at once, you lecherous knave. They're watching us.' She struggled but not too hard.

'Who?' he asked.

'Them!' She pointed at the ring of staring rock rabbits.

'Boo!' Tom shouted at them, and they shot down the entrances to their burrows. 'They aren't watching now!' said he.

Sarah uncrossed her legs.

The gathering at the campfire that night was solemn and fraught with uncertainty and anxiety. No one in the family knew what Dorian had decided. Yasmini, sitting beside

392

her husband, answered the silent question that Sarah flashed to her across the firelit circle with a resigned lift of her shoulders.

Tom alone was determinedly cheerful. While they ate grilled fish with chunks of new baked bread, he retold the story of their grandfather Francis Courtney, and the capture of the Dutch East India galleon off Cape Agulhas nearly sixty years before. He explained to them where Francis had hidden his booty, in a cave up at the head waters of the stream that ran into the lagoon, near where Mansur had shot the buffalo the previous day. Then he laughed as he pointed out the trenches and overgrown excavations all around their encampment that the Dutch had dug in their efforts to find and retrieve the plundered treasure. 'While they sweated and swore, our own father, Hal Courtney, had spirited away the booty long before,' he told them, but they had heard the story often enough not to be amazed by it. In the end even Tom was defeated by the silence, and instead of regaling them further he addressed himself to the bowl of spiced buffalo stew that the women had served after the fish.

Dorian ate little. Before the silver coffee-pot was brought from its cradle over the coals he told Tom, 'If you agree, brother, I will speak to Kadem now and give him my decision.'

'Aye, Dorry,' Tom agreed. ''Twould be best to have done with the whole business. The ladies have been sitting on a nest of ants since yesterday.' He shouted for Batula. 'Tell Kadem he might join our council, if he has a mind.'

Kadem came striding down the beach. He walked like a desert warrior, lithe and long-limbed, and prostrated himself before Dorian.

Mansur leaned forward eagerly. He and Dorian had left the camp earlier that day and passed many hours alone together in the forest. Only they knew what they had discussed. Yasmini looked at her son's shining face and her heart sank. He is so young and beautiful, she thought, so bright and strong. Of course he pines for such an adventure as he sees here. He knows only the ballad singers' romantic vision of

393

battle. He dreams of glory, power and a throne. For, depending on the choice Dorian makes this evening, the Elephant Throne of Oman might one day be his.

She drew the veil over her face to hide her fears. *My son does not understand what pain and suffering the crown will bring him all the days of his life. He knows nothing of the poison cup and the assassin's blade. He does not understand that the caliphate is a slavery more oppressive than the chains of the galley slave or those of the worker in the copper mines of Monomatapa.*

Her thoughts were interrupted when Kadem greeted Dorian. 'The Prophet's blessing upon you, Majesty, and the peace of God. May he bless our undertakings.'

'It is early to speak of Majesty, Kadem al-Jurf,' Dorian cautioned him. 'Wait rather until you have heard my decision.'

'Your decision has already been made for you by the prophet and saint Mullah al-Allama. He died in his ninety-ninth year, in the mosque on Lamu island, praising God with his last breath.'

'I did not know he was dead,' Dorian said sadly, 'though, in all truth, at that venerable age it could not have been otherwise. He was a holy man indeed. I knew him well. It was his hand that circumcized me. He was my wise councillor, and a second father to me.'

'In his last days he thought of you, and made a prophecy.'

Dorian inclined his head. 'You may recite the words of the holy mullah.'

Kadem had the gift of rhetoric, and his voice was strong but pleasing. 'The orphan from the sea, he who won the Elephant for his father, shall sit upon its back when the father has passed, and he shall wear a crown of red gold.' Kadem spread his arms. 'Majesty, the orphan of the prophecy can mean no other than you. For you are crowned now in red gold, and you were the victor of the battle that gave the Elephant Throne to your adoptive father, Caliph Abd Muhammad al-Malik.'

A long silence followed his ringing speech, and Kadem stood with arms outspread like the Prophet himself.

Dorian broke the silence at last. 'I have heard your pleas, and I will give you my decision that you must take back to the sheikhs of Oman. But first I must tell you how I have reached it.'

Dorian placed his hand upon Mansur's shoulder. 'This is my son, my only son. My decision touches him deeply. He and I have discussed it in every detail. His fierce young heart is hot for the enterprise, just as mine was at the same age. He has urged me to accept the invitation of the sheikhs.'

'Your son is wise far beyond his years,' said Kadem. 'If it please Allah, he shall rule in Muscat after you.'

'*Bismallah!*' cried Batula and Kumrah together.

'If God pleases!' cried Mansur in Arabic, his expression rapt with joy.

Dorian held up his right hand, and they fell silent again. 'There is another who is touched deeply by my decision.' He took Yasmini's hand. 'The Princess Yasmini has been my companion and my wife all these years, from childhood to this day. I swore an oath to her long ago, a blood oath.' He turned to her. 'Do you remember my marriage vows to you?'

'I remember, my lord husband,' she said softly, 'but I thought you might have forgotten.'

'I swore two vows to you. The first was that, even though the law and the prophets allow it, I would take no other wife than you. I have kept that vow.'

Yasmini was not able to speak, but she nodded. At the movement a tear that trembled on her long eyelashes detached itself and splashed upon the silk that covered her bosom, leaving a wet stain.

'The second oath I swore that day was that I would not cause you pain if it was in my power to prevent it.' Yasmini nodded again.

'Let all of you here present know that if I were to take up the invitation of the sheikhs to the Elephant Throne, it would cause the Princess Yasmini pain more poignant than the pain of death itself.'

The silence drew out, tingling, in the night, like the threat of summer thunder. Dorian stood up and spread his arms. 'This

395

is my reply. May God hear my words. May the holy prophets of Islam bear witness to my oath.'

Tom was amazed by the transformation that had overtaken his younger brother. Now he looked like a king indeed. But Dorian's next words shattered that illusion. 'Tell them that my love and admiration is with them still, as it was at the battle of Muscat and every day since then. Despite this, the burden they would place upon me is too heavy for my heart and my shoulders. They must find another for the Elephant Throne. I cannot take up the caliphate and keep true to my oath to the Princess Yasmini.'

Mansur gave a small involuntary cry of distress. He leaped to his feet and ran into the night. Tom jumped up and might have chased after him had not Dorian shaken his head. 'Let him go, brother. His disappointment is sharp, but it will pass.' He sat down again and turned to smile at Yasmini. An expression of adoration shone upon her lovely face. 'I have kept both my oaths to you,' Dorian said.

'My lord!' she whispered. 'My own heart.'

Kadem stood up again, his face expressionless. He bowed deeply to Dorian. 'As my prince commands,' he agreed softly. 'Would that I could call you "Majesty". It saddens me, but that is not to be. God's will be done.' He turned and strode away into the darkness, heading in the opposite direction to that taken by Mansur.

It was the time of the evening prayers and the man who called himself Kadem al-Jurf performed his ritual ablutions in the salt waters of the lagoon. Once he was cleansed, he climbed to a high place on the rocks above the ocean. He spread his prayer mat, recited the first prayer and made the first prostration.

For once neither the act of worship nor submission to the will of God could calm the anger that seethed within him. It required all his self-discipline and dedication to complete the prayers without letting his unruly emotions mar them. When he had finished, he built a small fire from the faggot of wood he had gathered on the way up the hill. When it was burning brightly Kadem sat cross-legged on the mat in front of it and gazed through the curtain of shimmering heat at the glowing wood.

Rocking slightly, as though he were riding a racing camel across the desert, he recited the twelve mystical *sura* of the Qur'an, and waited for the voices. They had been with him since childhood, since the day of his circumcision. Always they came to him clearly after praying or fasting. He knew they were the voices of God's angels and of his prophets. The first to speak was the one he dreaded most.

'You have failed in your task.' He recognized the voice of Gabriel, the avenging archangel, and quailed before the accusation.

'Highest of the high, it was not possible that al-Salil could spurn the bait that was so carefully prepared for him,' he murmured.

'Hear me, Kadem ibn Abubaker,' said the angel. 'It was your overweening pride that led you into failure. You were too certain of your own powers.'

The angel used his true name, for Kadem was the son of Pasha Abubaker, the general Dorian had slain in the battle on the banks of the river Lunga twenty years before.

Pasha Abubaker had been the half-brother and boon companion of Zayn al-Din, the Caliph of Oman. They had grown up together in the zenana on Lamu island, and it was there that their destinies had first become entangled with those of Dorian and Yasmini.

Much later, in the palace at Muscat, when their royal father was dead and Zayn al-Din was caliph, he had appointed Abubaker supreme military commander and a Pasha in the service of the caliphate. Then he had sent Abubaker with his army to Africa to hunt down and capture Dorian and Yasmini, the incestuous runaway couple.

At the head of his cavalry squadrons Abubaker had caught up with them as they were trying to escape down the river Lunga and reach the open sea in Tom's tiny ship, the *Swallow*.

Abubaker had attacked them while they were stranded on the sandbar at the mouth of the river. The battle was fierce and bloody, with Abubaker's cavalry squadrons charging through the shallows. But the ship had been armed with cannon and Dorian had touched off the blast of grape-shot that blew off Pasha Abubaker's head and drove off his troops in disarray.

Although Kadem had been an infant at the time of his father's death, Zayn al-Din had taken him under his protection and shown him the favour and preference he offered his own sons rather than treating him as a nephew. In doing so he made Kadem his liege man, his blood bondsman. He fettered him with chains of steel that could never be broken. Despite what Kadem had told Dorian at the campfire, the strength of his oath to Zayn al-Din was matched only by his awareness of his duty to take vengeance on the man who had slain his father. This was a holy duty, a blood feud imposed on him by God and his own conscience.

Zayn al-Din, who loved few men, loved Kadem, his nephew. He kept him close, and when he became a true warrior he made him the commander of the royal bodyguard. Only Kadem, of the possible heirs to the caliphate, was spared from the Ramadan massacre. During the uprising that followed, Kadem had fought like a lion to protect his caliph, and in the end it was Kadem who had led Zayn al-Din through the maze of underground passages, under the palace walls to the ship waiting in the harbour of Muscat. He had carried his master safely to the palace on Lamu island off the Fever Coast.

Kadem was the general who had overwhelmed the forts along the coast that attempted to rise in support of the revolutionary junta in Muscat. Kadem had negotiated the alliance with the English consul in Zanzibar, and Kadem had urged his master to send envoys to Constantinople and Delhi to garner support. During these campaigns along the Fever Coast, Kadem had captured most of the leaders of the factions who opposed Zayn. As a matter of course, the prisoners were handed over to his inquisitors so that they could extract from them all the information and intelligence they could.

In this way, by the intelligent and judicious application of the bastinado, the screw and the garotte, the inquisitors dredged up a precious gem: the whereabouts of al-Salil, the murderer of Pasha Abubaker and the sworn blood enemy of the Caliph.

Armed with this knowledge, Kadem pleaded with Zayn al-Din to allow him to be the instrument of retribution. Zayn consented, and Kadem would entrust his sacred duty to none of his underlings. He alone devised the stratagem of luring al-Salil into the Caliph's realm and power by impersonating an envoy of the rebel junta who still held the capital city of Muscat.

When Kadem revealed his plan to Zayn al-Din, the Caliph was delighted and gave the enterprise his blessing. He promised Kadem the title of pasha, like his father before him, and any other reward Kadem could ask for, if he succeeded in bringing al-Salil and his incestuous wife Yasmini back to Lamu island to face his wrath and retribution. Kadem asked only one reward; that when the time came for al-Salil to die, Kadem should be given the honour of strangling him with his own hands. He promised Zayn that the garotting would be slow and agonizing. Zayn smiled and granted this boon also.

Kadem had learned from the inquisitors that the trading ship, *Gift of Allah*, which called often at the ports of the Fever Coast, belonged to al-Salil. When next it arrived in the port of Zanzibar Kadem inveigled himself into the confidences of Batula, al-Salil's old lance-bearer. Kadem's plot had unfurled smoothly, until now, with the prize almost within his grasp, when he had been thwarted by al-Salil's unfathomable refusal to accept the lure. Now Kadem had to answer the accusation of God's angel.

'Highest of the high, I have indeed committed the sin of pride.' Kadem made the sign of penitence by wiping his face with open hands, as though washing away the sin.

'You believed that without divine intervention, you alone could bring the sinner to justice. This was vanity and foolishness.'

The accusations thundered in his head until it felt that his eardrums must burst. Kadem bore the pain stoically. 'Merciful

399

one, it did not seem possible that any mortal man could spurn the offer of a throne.' Kadem prostrated himself before the fire and the angel. 'Tell me what I should do to make amends for my arrogance and stupidity. Command me, O highest of the high.'

There was no reply. The only sounds were the crashing of the high surf on the rocks below and the mewing of the gulls as they circled overhead.

'Speak to me, holy Gabriel,' Kadem pleaded. 'Do not desert me now, not after all these years when I have done as you commanded.' He drew the curved dagger from his belt. It was a magnificent weapon. The blade was of Damascus steel and the hilt was rhinoceros horn covered with pure gold filigree. Kadem pressed the point of the blade into the ball of his own thumb, and blood flowed out.

'Allah! Allah!' he cried. 'With this blood I entreat you, give me guidance.'

Only then, through his pain, the other voice spoke, not the thunder of Gabriel but calm and measured, melodious. Kadem knew that this was the very voice of the Prophet, terrible in its quiet simplicity. He trembled and listened.

'You are fortunate, Kadem ibn Abubaker,' said the Prophet, 'for I have listened to your confession and been moved by your cries. I will allow you one last chance of redemption.'

Kadem threw himself down on his face, not daring to answer that voice. It spoke again. 'Kadem ibn Abubaker! You must wash your hands in the heart blood of the murderer of your father, the traitor and heretic, the sinner who wallows in incest, al-Salil.'

Kadem beat his head against the earth, weeping for joy at the mercy the Prophet had shown him. Then he sat back on his heels and held up his hand with fingers and thumb spread. The blood still dribbled from the self-inflicted wound. 'God is great,' he whispered. 'Show me a mark of your favour, I beseech you.' He stretched out his hand and held it in the leaping flames, which engulfed it. 'Allah!' he chanted. 'The One! The Only!'

In the flames the flow of bright blood shrivelled and dried.

400

Then miraculously the wound closed like the tentacled mouth of a sea anemone. His flesh healed before his eyes.

He lifted his hand out of the flames, still chanting God's praises, and held it aloft. There was no mark where the wound had been. There was no redness or blistering from the flames. His skin was smooth and flawless. It was the sign he had asked for.

'God is great!' he exulted. 'There is no God but God, and Muhammad is his last true Prophet!'

After they had eaten the evening meal with the rest of the family, Dorian and Yasmini took their leave. Yasmini embraced Sarah first, then her own son, Mansur. She kissed his eyes and stroked his hair, which gleamed in the firelight like molten copper poured from the melting pot.

Tom hugged Dorian so hard that his ribs creaked. 'Damn my eyes, Dorian Courtney, I thought we had got rid of you at last, and could pack you off to Oman.'

Dorian hugged him back. 'Are you not the unlucky one? I will be here to plague you for a while yet.'

Though Mansur embraced his father briefly, he did not speak or look into his eyes, and the line of his lips was hard with bitter disappointment. Dorian shook his head sadly. He knew that Mansur had set his heart on glory, and his own father had snatched it from him. The pain was still too intense to be assuaged by words. Dorian would console him later.

Dorian and Yasmini left the campfire, and started down the beach together. As soon as they were out of the ruddy light of the flames Dorian placed his arm round her. They did not speak, for they had said it all. The physical contact expressed their love more than words ever could. At the turning of the sandbar, where the deeper channel ran close in to the beach, Dorian stripped off his robes and unwound his turban. He handed his clothing to Yasmini and waded naked into the water. The tide was flowing strongly between the rocky heads and the water was chilled with the memory of the open ocean.

Dorian dived into the deep channel and surfaced again, gasping and snorting with the cold.

Yasmini sat on the sandbar and watched him. She did not share his love of cold water. She held his clothes in a bundle, then almost stealthily buried her face in them. She inhaled the masculine odour of her husband and delighted in it. Even after all these years she had never tired of it. The smell of him made her feel safe and secure. Dorian always smiled when she picked up the discarded robe he had worn all day and donned it in preference to her nightdress.

'I would wear your skin if it were possible,' she replied seriously to his gentle teasing. 'This way I can be close to you, part of your raiment, part of your body.'

At last Dorian waded ashore. The phosphorescence of the tiny plankton in the lagoon sparkled upon his body, and Yasmini exclaimed with delight. 'Even nature decks you in diamonds. God loves you, al-Salil, but not as much as I do.'

He stooped over her, kissed her with salty lips, took his turban from her and used it to dry himself. Then he wound it round his waist as a loincloth, and let his long wet hair hang down his back.

'This night breeze will finish the job before we reach our hut,' he told her, and they walked back along the sand to the encampment. The sentry greeted them and called a blessing as they passed the watchfire. Their own hut was well separated from that of Tom and Sarah. Mansur preferred to sleep with the ship's officers and the men.

Dorian lit the lanterns, and Yasmini carried one when she went behind the screen at the far end of the room. She had furnished the hut with Persian carpets, silk draperies, silk mattresses and cushions filled with wild-goose down. Dorian heard the purl of water from the jug into the basin, and Yasmini hummed and sang softly as she washed. Dorian felt his loins stir: this was Yasmini's prelude to lovemaking. He threw his robe and damp turban aside and stretched out on the mattress. He watched her silhouette, thrown by the lamp-light on to the design of birds and flowers that decorated the

Chinese screen. She had placed the lamp artfully and knew he was watching her. When she stood in the basin and bent over to wash her intimate parts, she turned so that he could watch the shadow show, and see how she was sweetening and preparing the way for him.

When at last she came out from behind the screen she hung her head demurely, allowing her hair to hang forward over her face like a dark silver-shot curtain. She covered her pudenda with both hands, then tilted her head and peeped at him with one eye through the veil. It was huge and luminous with the light of passion.

'You succulent, salacious little houri,' he said, and stiffened into full arousal. She saw what she had done to him, and tinkled with laughter. She let her hands fall to her sides, and her own sex was meticulously plucked free of hair. It was a plump and naked cleft below the ivory smooth curve of her belly. Her breasts were small and pert, so her body seemed that of a young girl.

'Come to me!' he commanded, and she obeyed with joy.

Much later in the night Yasmini felt him stir beside her and came fully awake immediately. She was always sensitive to his moods or needs. 'Are you well?' she whispered. 'Is there anything you need?'

'Sleep on, little one,' he whispered back. ''Tis only your friend and fervent admirer who demands to be taken in hand.' He stood up from the mattress.

'Please convey to the friend my respectful salaams and my wifely duty,' she whispered. He chuckled sleepily and kissed her lightly before he rose from their mattress. Dorian would only use the chamber-pot in the gravest emergency. Squatting was the woman's way. He slipped out through the back door, to the pit latrine which stood fifty yards from their hut, screened by the trees of the forest verge. The sand was cool under his bare feet, the night air soft and perfumed by forest flowers and the fret off the ocean. When Dorian had relieved himself, he started back. But he stopped before he reached the rear door of the hut. The night was so beautiful and the blaze

403

of the stars so dazzling that they mesmerized him. He stared up at them and, slowly, he found himself transported into a deep sense of peace.

Until this moment he had been storm-tossed by doubts. Had his decision to turn his back on the Elephant Throne been selfish, and unfair to Mansur? Had he failed in his duty to the peoples of Oman who were grinding under the cruel yoke of Zayn al-Din? He knew deep in his heart that Zayn had murdered their father. Did not the laws of man and God also place upon him the blood duty of retribution for the terrible crime of patricide?

All these doubts receded as he stood now under the stars. Even though the night was chilly and he was naked as a newborn, he was still warm from the arms of the only woman he had ever loved. He sighed with contentment. *Even if I have sinned, it was the sin of omission. My first duty is to the living, not the dead, and Yasmini needs me as much if not more than all the others.*

He started back towards the hut and at that moment he heard Yasmini scream. It was a shocking sound, terror and mortal agony blending.

As Dorian left the hut Yasmini sat up and shivered. The night had turned cold, much colder than it should have been. She wondered if it was a natural cold or the cold of evil. Perhaps some baleful spirit hovered over them. She believed implicitly in the other world, which overlapped their own so intimately, the realm in which the angels, the *djinni* and the *shaitans* existed. She shivered again, this time more in dread than with cold. She made the sign to avert the evil eye with thumb and forefinger. Then she stood up from the mattress and turned up the wick of the lantern, so that Dorian would have light when he returned. She went to where Dorian's robe hung over the screen and slipped it over her naked body. Sitting on the mattress, she wound his turban round her head.

It had dried but it still smelt of his hair. She lifted a fold of his robe to her nose, and smelt the odour of his sweat floating up from the cloth. She inhaled it with pleasure, and the comfort it imparted to her forced back the premonition of lurking evil. Just the faintest twinge of unease lingered.

'Where is Dorry?' she whispered. 'He should not take so long.' She was about to call out to him through the thatched wall when she heard a stealthy sound behind her. She turned and was confronted by a tall figure clad in black, a black headcloth swaddling its face. It seemed to be some evil manifestation, a *djinni* or a *shaitan*, rather than a human. It must have entered through the other door, and its ghastly influence seemed to fill the room with a choking, cloying emanation of pure evil. In its right hand a long curved blade glinted, reflecting the dim lantern light.

Yasmini screamed with all her strength and tried to rise, but the thing sprang towards her and she did not see the knife stroke for it was so swift as to cheat her eye. She felt the blade go in, so sharp that her tender flesh offered little resistance to its entry. There was only a stinging sensation deep in her bosom.

The assassin stood over her as she sagged down on legs that were suddenly without strength. He made no effort to pull out the long blade. Instead he cocked his wrist and held it rigid, so the blade was angled upwards. He allowed the razor edge to slice its own way out, enlarging the wound, cutting through muscle, vein and artery. When at last the blade came free, Yasmini fell back upon the mattress. The dark figure looked about, seeking the man who should have been present, but was not there. He had only realized that his victim was a woman when she screamed – but by then it was too late. He stooped and pulled the turban loose from Yasmini's face. He stared at her lovely features, now so pale and still in the lantern-light that they seemed carved from ivory.

'In God's Holy name, only half my work is done,' he whispered. 'I have killed the vixen but missed the fox.'

He whirled and ran for the door through which he had

entered the hut. At that moment Dorian burst naked into the room behind him. 'Guards!' Dorian shouted. 'Succour! On me! Here!'

Kadem ibn Abubaker recognized the voice and turned back on the instant. This was the victim he was seeking, this man and not his woman dressed in his robes. He leaped at Dorian who was slow to react, but threw up his right arm to deflect the blow. The blade raked him from shoulder to elbow. His blood sprang darkly in the lamplight and he yelled again, then dropped to his knees. His arms dangling at his sides, he looked up with a piteous expression at the man who was killing him.

Kadem knew that his victim was twice his age, and from his first reaction that the years had slowed him, that now he was helpless. This was his chance to end it swiftly and he sprang forward eagerly. But he should have been warned by the warlike reputation of al-Salil. As he stabbed down, going once more for the heart, two steely arms shot out, swiftly as striking adders. He found his knife arm trapped in a classic wrist block.

Dorian came to his feet, splattering blood from the long wound down his arm, and they whirled together. Kadem was intent on breaking the lock, so that he could stab again. Dorian was trying even more desperately to hold him, as he shouted for help. 'Tom!' he screamed. 'Tom! On me! On me!'

Kadem hooked his heel behind Dorian's foot and lunged against him to trip him and throw him over, but Dorian changed his weight smoothly to the other foot, and turned inside him, twisting the wrist of his knife hand back against the joint, straining the sinews and tendons. Kadem grunted with pain, and fell back a pace against the unbearable pressure. Dorian pressed forward. 'Tom!' he yelled. 'Tom, in God's Name.'

Kadem yielded to the pressure on his wrist. The release gave him just enough latitude to turn his hip into Dorian, and throw him across it. He broke Dorian's grip and sent him cartwheeling across the floor of the hut. Like a ferret on a rabbit, he went at him, and Dorian was only just able to catch his knife wrist again as he fell back. Once more they were chest to chest, but now Kadem was on top of him, and the difference in their ages and their state of martial fitness began to tell. Remorselessly Kadem forced the point of the curved blade down towards Dorian's chest. The assassin's face was still covered by the headcloth. Only his eyes glittered above the black folds, just inches from Dorian's.

'For my father's memory,' grated Kadem, his breath coming hard with the effort, 'I perform my duty.'

All Kadem's weight was behind his knife arm. Dorian could not hold it longer. His own arm buckled slowly. The knife point pricked the bare skin of his chest and slid on, deeper and still deeper, up to the hilt.

'Justice is mine!' Kadem cried in triumph.

Before the cry had died in Kadem's throat, Tom charged through the doorway behind him, furious and powerful as a black-maned lion. He took it all in at a glance, and swung the heavy pistol he carried in his right hand, not daring to fire it for fear of hitting his brother. The steel barrel crunched across the back of Kadem's skull. Without another sound he collapsed on top of Dorian.

As Tom stooped to drag the Arab off his brother's inert body, Mansur dashed into the hut. 'For the love of God, what's amiss?'

'This swine set upon Dorry.'

Mansur helped Tom to lift Dorian into a sitting position. 'Father, are you hurt?' Then they both saw the terrible knife wound in his bare chest. They stared at it in horror.

'Yassie!' Dorian wheezed. 'Look to her.'

Tom and Mansur turned towards the small figure curled on the mattress. Neither of them had noticed her until then.

'Yassie is all right, Dorry. She's sleeping,' Tom said.

'No, Tom, she is mortal hurt.' Dorian tried to shrug off their restraining hands. 'Help me. I must attend to her.'

'I will see to Mother.' Mansur jumped up and ran to the mattress. 'Mother!' he cried, and tried to lift her. Then he reeled back, staring at his hands, which were shining with Yasmini's blood.

Dorian crawled across the floor, dragged himself on to the

mattress and lifted Yasmini in his arms. Her head lolled lifelessly. 'Yassie, please don't leave me.' He wept tears of utter desolation. 'Don't go, my darling.'

His entreaties were in vain for Yasmini's elfin spirit was already well sped along the fatal way.

Sarah had been awakened by the uproar. She came swiftly to join Tom. A quick examination showed her that Yasmini's heartbeat had stilled, and she was past any help. She stifled her grief, and turned to Dorian for he was still alive, if only just.

At Tom's curt order, Batula and Kumrah dragged Kadem out of the hut. Using rawhide thongs, they tied his elbows and wrists behind his back. Then they pulled his ankles to his wrists and bound them together. His spine arched painfully as they riveted a steel slave collar round his neck and chained him to a tree in the centre of the encampment. As soon as the dreadful tidings of the assassination flashed through the camp, the women gathered around Kadem to curse and spit at him in anger and revulsion: they had all loved Yasmini.

'Keep him secure. Do not let them kill him, not yet, not until I order it,' Tom told Batula grimly. 'You sponsored this murderous swine. The duty is with you, on your own life.'

He went back into the hut to give what help he could. This was not much, for Sarah had taken charge. She was highly skilled in the medical arts. She had spent much of her life tending broken bodies and dying men. She only needed his strength to pull the compression bandages tightly enough to stem the bleeding. For the remainder of the time Tom hovered in the background, cursing his own stupidity for not anticipating the danger and taking precautions to forestall it.

'I am not an innocent child. I should have known.' His lamentations hampered rather than helped, and Sarah ordered him out of the hut.

When she had dressed Dorian's wound and he was lying more comfortably Sarah relented and allowed Tom to return.

She told him that although his brother was gravely injured, the blade had missed his heart – as far as she could divine. She thought it had pierced the left lung, for there was bloody froth on his lips.

'I have seen men less robust than Dorry recover from worse wounds. Now it is up to God and time.' That was the best reassurance she had for Tom. She gave Dorian a double spoonful of laudanum, and, once the drug had taken effect, left him with Tom and Mansur to tend him. Then she went to start the heartbreaking process of laying out Yasmini's body for burial.

The Malay servant girls, also Muslim, helped her. They carried Yasmini to Sarah's own hut at the far end of the encampment, laid her on the low table, and placed a screen round her. They took away the bloodied robe and burned it to ash on the watchfire. They closed the lids of those magnificent dark eyes, from which the luminosity had faded. They bathed Yasmini's childlike body and anointed her with perfumed oils. They bandaged the single dreadful wound that had stabbed through to her heart. They combed and brushed her hair, and the silver blaze shone as brightly as ever. They dressed her in a clean white robe and laid her on the funeral bier. She looked like a child asleep.

Mansur and Sarah, who after Dorian had loved her best, chose a burial site in the forest. With the crew of the *Gift*, Mansur stayed to help dig the grave, for the law of Islam decreed that Yasmini should be buried before sunset on the day of her death.

When they lifted Yasmini's bier and carried her from the hut, the lamentations of the women roused Dorian from the sleep of the poppy and he called weakly for Tom, who came at the run. 'You must bring Yassie to me,' Dorian whispered.

'No, brother, you must not move. Any movement could do you terrible ill.'

'If you will not bring her, then I will go to her.' Dorian tried to sit up, but Tom held him down gently, and shouted for Mansur to bring the funeral bier to Dorian's bedside.

At his insistence, Tom and Mansur supported Dorian so he

could kiss his wife's lips for the last time. Then Dorian worked free from his own finger the gold ring over which he had spoken his wedding vows. It came off with difficulty for he had never before removed it. Mansur guided his father's hand as he placed it on Yasmini's slim tapered finger. It was far too large for her, but Dorian folded her fingers around it so that it would not slip off.

'Go in peace, my love. And may Allah take you to His bosom.'

As Tom had warned, the effort and sorrow exhausted Dorian and he sank back on to the mattress. Bright new blood soaked into the bandages about his chest.

They carried Yassie out to the grave, and lowered her into it gently. Sarah placed a silk shawl over her face, and stood to one side. Tom and Mansur would let no one else undertake the harrowing task of covering her with earth. Sarah watched until they had finished. Then she took Tom's hand on one side and Mansur's on the other and led them back to the camp.

Tom and Mansur went directly to the tree where Kadem was chained. Tom was scowling darkly as he stood over the captive, arms akimbo. There was a large swelling on the back of Kadem's head from the blow with the pistol barrel. His scalp was split and the blood was already congealing into a black scab over the laceration. However, Kadem had recovered consciousness and he was once more alert. He stared up at Tom with a steely, fanatical gaze.

Batula came and prostrated himself before Tom. 'Lord Klebe, I deserve all your wrath. Your accusation is just. It was I who sponsored this creature and brought him into your camp.'

'Yes, Batula. The blame is indeed yours. It will take you the rest of your life to redeem yourself. In the end it may even cost you your own life.'

410

'As my lord says. I am ready to repay the debt I owe,' Batula said humbly. 'Shall I kill this eater of pig flesh now?'

'No, Batula. First he must tell us who he truly is and who was the master who sent him to carry out this vile deed. It may be difficult to make him tell us. I see by his eyes that this man lives not on an earthly plane, as other men.'

'He is ruled by demons,' Batula agreed.

'Make him speak, but make certain he does not die before he has done so,' Tom reiterated.

'As you say, lord.'

'Take him to some place where his cries will not affright the women.'

'I will go with Batula,' said Mansur.

'No, lad. It will be grisly work. You will not want to watch it.'

'The Princess Yasmini was my mother,' Mansur said. 'Not only will I watch but I shall delight in every scream he utters, and glory in every drop of his blood that flows.'

Tom stared at him in astonishment. This was not the winsome child he had known from birth. This was a hard man grown to full maturity in a single hour. 'Go with Batula and Kumrah then,' he agreed at last, 'and note well the replies of Kadem al-Jurf.'

They took Kadem in the longboat to the head-waters of the stream over a mile from the camp and found another tree to which to chain him. They tied a leather strap round his forehead, then back around the bole of the tree, twisting it tightly so that it cut into his flesh and he could not move his head. Mansur asked him his real name, and Kadem spat at him. Mansur looked at Batula and Kumrah.

'The work we must do now is just. In God's Name, let us begin,' said Mansur.

'*Bismallah!*' said Batula.

While Mansur guarded the prisoner, Batula and Kumrah went into the forest. They knew where to search, and within the hour they had found a nest of the fierce soldier ants. These insects were bright red in colour, and not much bigger than a

411

rice grain. The glistening head was armed with a pair of poisonous pincers. Careful not to injure them and even more careful to avoid their stings, Batula picked the ants out of the nest with a pair of bamboo tweezers.

When they returned Kumrah cut a hollow reed from the stream verge, and carefully worked one end of the tube as far as it would go into the opening of Kadem's ear.

'Regard this tiny insect.' In the jaws of the tweezers Batula held up an ant. 'The venom of his sting will make a lion roll on the ground roaring with agony. Tell me, you who call yourself Kadem, who are you and who sent you to commit this deed?'

Kadem looked at the wriggling insect. A clear drop of venom oozed out between the serrated jaws of its mandibles. It had a sharp, chemical odour that would drive any other ant that smelt it into an aggressive frenzy.

'I am a true follower of the Prophet,' Kadem replied, 'and I was sent by God to carry out His divine purpose.'

Mansur nodded to Batula. 'Let the ant whisper the question more clearly in the ear of this true follower of the Prophet.'

Kadem's eyes swivelled towards Mansur and he tried to spit again, but his mouth had dried. Batula placed the ant in the opening of the reed tube in his ear and closed the end with a plug of whittled soft wood.

'You will hear the ant as it comes down the tube,' Batula told Kadem. 'Its footsteps will sound like the hoofs of a horse. Then you will feel it walking in your eardrum. It will stroke the membrane of your inner ear with the sharp tips of its feelers. Then it will sting you.'

They watched Kadem's face. His lips twitched, then his eyes rolled back in their sockets until the whites showed and his whole face worked furiously.

'Allah!' he whispered. 'Arm me against the blasphemers!'

The sweat burst out from the pores of his skin like the first drops of monsoon rain, and he tried to shake his head as the footfalls of the ant in his eardrum were magnified a thousand times. But the thong held his head in a vice-like grip.

'Answer, Kadem,' Batula urged him. 'I can still wash out the ant before it stings. But you must answer swiftly.' Kadem closed his eyes to shut out Batula's face.

'Who are you? Who sent you?' Batula came closer and whispered in his open ear. 'Swiftly, Kadem, or the pain will be beyond even your crazed imagining.'

Then, deep in the recesses of the eardrum the ant humped its back and a fresh globule of venom oozed out between its curved mandibles. It sank the barbed points into the soft tissue at the spot where the auditory nerve was closest to the surface.

Kadem al-Jurf was consumed by waves of agony, and they were fiercer than Batula had warned him. He screamed once, a sound that was not human but something from a nightmare. Then the pain froze the muscles and vocal cords in his throat, his jaws clamped together in such a rock-hard spasm that one of the rotten teeth at the back of his mouth burst, filling his mouth with splinters and bitter pus. His eyes rolled back in his skull like those of a blind man. His back arched until Mansur feared that his spine would crack, and his body juddered so that his bonds cut deeply into his flesh.

'He will die,' Mansur asked anxiously.

'A *shaitan* is hard to kill,' Batula answered. The three squatted in a half-circle in front of Kadem and studied his suffering. Although it was dreadful to behold, none of them felt the slightest twinge of compassion.

'Regard, lord!' said Kumrah. 'The first spasm passes.' He was right. Kadem's spine slowly relaxed, and although a series of convulsions still shook him, each was less violent than the one before.

'It is finished,' Mansur said.

'No, lord. If God is just, soon the ant will sting again,' Batula said softly. 'It will not finish so swiftly.' As he said it, so it happened: the tiny insect struck again.

This time Kadem's tongue was caught between his teeth as they snapped closed. He bit through it, and the blood streamed down his chin. He shuddered and leaped against the chain. His bowels loosened with a spluttering rush, and even Mansur's lust for vengeance faltered. The dark veils of hatred and grief parted and his instinct for humanity shone through. 'Enough, Batula. End it now. Wash out the ant.'

Batula withdrew the wood plug from the end of the reed and filled his mouth with water. Through the hollow reed he spurted a jet into Kadem's eardrum, and in the overflow the drowned red body of the insect was washed down Kadem's straining neck.

Slowly Kadem's tortured body relaxed, and he hung inert in his bonds. His breathing was rapid and shallow, and every few minutes he let out a harsh, ragged exhalation, half sigh and half groan.

Once again, his captors squatted in a semi-circle in front of him and watched him carefully. Late in the afternoon, as the sun touched the tops of the forest trees Kadem groaned again. His eyes opened and focused slowly on Mansur.

'Batula, give him water,' Mansur ordered. Kadem's mouth was black and crusted with the blood. His torn tongue protruded between his lips like a lump of rotten liver. Batula held the waterskin to his mouth, and Kadem choked and gasped as he drank. Once he vomited up a gush of the jellied black blood he had swallowed, but then he drank again.

Mansur let him rest until sunset, then ordered Batula to let him drink again. Kadem was stronger now, and followed their movements with his eyes. Mansur ordered Batula and Kumrah to relax his bonds to allow the blood to flow back, and to chafe his hands and feet before gangrene killed off the living flesh. The pain of the returning blood must have been agonizing but Kadem bore it stoically. After a while they tightened the leather thongs again.

Mansur came to stand over him. 'You know well that I am the son of the Princess Yasmini whom you murdered,' he said. 'In the eyes of God and of men, vengeance is mine. Your life belongs to me.'

Kadem stared back at him.

'If you do not reply to me, I will order Batula to place another insect in your good ear.'

Kadem blinked, but his face remained impassive.

'Answer my question,' Mansur demanded. 'Who are you and who sent you to our home?'

Kadem's swollen tongue filled his mouth, so his reply was slurred and barely intelligible. 'I am a true follower of the Prophet,' he said, 'and I was sent by God to carry out His divine purpose.'

'That is the same answer, but it is not the one I wait for,' Mansur said. 'Batula, select another insect. Kumrah, place another reed in Kadem's ear.' When they had done as he ordered, Mansur asked Kadem, 'This time the pain may kill you. Are you ready for death?'

'Blessed is the martyr,' Kadem replied. 'I long with all my heart to be welcomed by Allah into Paradise.'

Mansur took Batula aside. 'He will not yield,' he said.

Batula looked dubious. His tone was uncertain as he replied, 'Lord, there is no other way.'

'I think there is.' Mansur turned to Kumrah. 'We do not need the reed.' Then, to both of them, 'Stay with him. I shall return.'

He rowed back down the stream. It was almost dark by the time he reached the encampment, but the full moon was already lighting the eastern sky with a marvellous golden glow as it pushed over the tops of the trees. 'Even the moon hastens to assist our enterprise,' Mansur murmured, as he went ashore on the beach below the camp. He saw the lamplight shine in chinks through the thatched wall of his father's hut and he hurried there.

His uncle Tom and aunt Sarah sat by the mattress on which Dorian lay. Mansur knelt beside his father and kissed his forehead. He stirred but did not open his eyes.

Mansur leaned close to Tom and whispered low, 'Uncle, the assassin will not yield. Now I need your help.'

Tom rose to his feet and jerked his head for Mansur to follow him outside. Swiftly Mansur told him what he wanted, and at the end said simply, 'This is something that I would do myself, but Islam forbids it.'

'I understand.' Tom nodded and looked up at the moon. ''Tis favourable. I saw a place in the forest close by here where

415

they feed each night on the tubers of the arum lily plant. Tell your aunt Sarah what I am about, and that she is not to fret. I shall not be too long gone.'

Tom went to the armoury and selected his big double-barrelled German four to the pound musket. He drew the charge and reloaded the weapon with a handful of Big Looper, the formidable lion shot. Then he checked the flint and the priming, made sure that his knife was on his belt and loosened the blade in its sheath.

He selected ten of his men and told them to wait for his call, but he left the camp alone: silence and stealth were vital to success. When he waded across the stream he stooped to take up a handful of black clay and smear it over his face, for pale skin shines in the moonlight and his quarry was stealthy and cunning. Although it was a huge creature he was hunting it was nocturnal in its habits, and for that reason few men ever laid eyes on it.

Tom followed the far bank of the stream for almost a mile. As he came closer to the swamp in which the arum lilies grew his steps slowed and he paused every fifty paces to listen intently. At the edge of the swamp he squatted and held the big gun across his lap. He waited patiently, never moving even to flick away the mosquitoes that whined around his head. The moon rose higher and its light grew stronger so that the shadows thrown by each tree and shrub had sharp edges.

Abruptly there came a grunt and a squeal from close at hand, and his pulse tripped. He waited, as still as one of the dead tree stumps, as the silence fell again. Then he heard the squelch of hoofs in the mud, more grunts, the sound of hog-like rooting and the champing of tusked jaws.

Tom eased forward towards the sounds. Without warning they ceased as abruptly as they had begun, and he froze. He knew that this was the customary behaviour of the bush pigs. The entire sounder would freeze together and listen for pred-ators. Although Tom was on one leg, he froze in that attitude, still as an ungainly statue as the silence drew out. Then the grunting and feeding started again.

With relief he lowered his foot, his thigh muscles burning,

and crept forward again. Then he saw the sounder just ahead of him: there were several dozen, dark hump-backed sows, with their piglets underfoot, rooting and wallowing. None was large enough to be a mature boar.

Tom moved with infinite care to a mound of harder earth at the edge of the swamp and crouched there, waiting for the big boars to come out of the forest. A cloud blew across the moon, and suddenly, in the utter darkness, he sensed a presence close by. He turned all his attention upon it and vaguely made out massive movement so close that he felt he could touch it with the muzzle of his musket. He inched the butt-stock to his shoulder, but dared not cock the hammers. The beast was too close. It would hear the click as the sear engaged. He stared into the darkness, not sure if it was real or his imagination. Then the clouds overhead blew open and the moonlight burst through.

In front of him loomed a gigantic hog. Along its mountain-ous back rose a mane of coarse bristles, shaggy and black in the moonlight. Its jaws were armed with curved tusks, sharp enough to rip the belly out of a man or to slice through the femoral artery in his groin and bleed him white within minutes.

Tom and the boar saw each other in the same moment. Tom swept back the hammers of the musket to full cock, and the boar squealed and charged straight at him. Tom fired the first barrel into its chest, and the heavy leaden loopers thudded into flesh and bone. The boar staggered and dropped on to its front knees but in an instant it bounded to its feet and came straight in. Tom fired the second barrel, then smashed the empty musket into the pig's face and dived to one side. One tusk hooked into his coat and split it like a razor, but the point missed his flesh. The beast's heavy shoulder struck him a glancing blow, which was powerful enough nevertheless to send him rolling into the mud.

Tom struggled to his feet with his knife clutched in his right hand, ready to meet the next attack. All around him there was the rush of dark bodies and squeals of alarm as the pigs scattered back into the forest.

Silence fell almost immediately after they were gone. Then

417

Tom heard a much softer sound: laboured gasping and snuffling and the convulsive thrashing of back legs in the reeds of the swamp. Cautiously he went towards the sounds, and found the boar down, kicking his last in the mud.

Tom hurried back to the camp and found his ten chosen men where he had left them, waiting his summons. None of them was a Muslim, so they had no religious qualms about touching a pig. Tom led them back to the swamp and they lashed the huge evil-smelling carcass to a carrying pole. It took all ten to stagger with this burden along the bank of the river to where Kadem was still tied to the tree and Mansur was waiting beside him with Batula and Kumrah.

By this time the dawn was breaking, and Kadem stared at the pig carcass as they dropped it in front of him. He said nothing but his expression clearly showed his horror and repugnance.

The bearers of the carcass had brought spades with them. Mansur put them to work at once digging a grave beside the carcass. None of them spoke to Kadem, and they barely glanced in his direction while they worked. However, Kadem's agitation increased as he watched them. He was again sweating and shivering, but this was not only the effects of the shock and agony of the ant stings. He had begun to understand the fate that Mansur was preparing for him.

When the grave was deep enough, the men laid aside their spades at Tom's order, and gathered around the carcass of the boar. Two stropped the blades of their skinning knives while the others rolled the boar on to its back and held all four legs widely separated to make the job of the skinners easier. They were expert, and the thick bristly hide was soon flayed away from pink and purple muscle and the white fat of the belly. At last it was free and the skinners stretched it open on the ground.

Mansur and the two sea captains kept well clear, careful not to let a drop of the vile creature's blood splatter them. Their revulsion was as evident as that of their captive. The stench of the old boar's fatty flesh was rank in the early-morning air, and Mansur spat the taste of it out of his mouth before he spoke to Kadem for the first time since they had brought in the carcass.

'O nameless one who calls himself a true follower of the Prophet, sent by God to carry out His divine purpose, we have no further need of you and your treachery. Your life on this earth has come to an end.' Kadem began to exhibit more distress than the agony that the insect's sting had inflicted upon him. He gibbered like an idiot, and his eyes rolled from side to side. Mansur ignored his protests and went on mercilessly, 'At my command, you will be stitched into this wet and reeking skin of the pig, and buried alive in the grave we have prepared for you. We will place the flayed carcass of this beast on top of you so that as you suffocate its blood and fat will drip into your face. As you and the pig rot your stinking bodily juices will mingle and you will become one. You will be fouled, *harom* for ever. The faces of God and all his prophets will be turned away from you for all eternity.'

Mansur gestured to the men who were waiting ready, and they came forward. Mansur unlocked Kadem's chains, but left him pinioned at wrists to ankles. The men carried him to the open pigskin and laid him upon it. The ship's sailmaker threaded his needle and donned his leather palm to sew Kadem into the winding sheet formed by the skin.

As Kadem felt the wet and greasy folds embrace him, he screeched like a condemned soul cast into eternal darkness. 'My name is Kadem ibn Abubaker, eldest son of Pasha Suleiman Abubaker. I came here to seek vengeance for the murder of my father and to carry out the will of my master Caliph Zayn al-Din ibn al-Malik.'

'What was the will of your master?' Mansur insisted.

'The execution of the Princess Yasmini and of her incestuous lover, al-Salil.'

Mansur turned to Tom who was squatting close by. 'That is all we need to know. May I kill him now, Uncle?'

Tom rose to his feet and shook his head. 'His life belongs not to me but to your father. Besides, we may have further need of this assassin yet, if we are to avenge your mother.'

With his damaged eardrum Kadem was unable to keep his

balance and he staggered and toppled over when they lifted him out of the folds of pigskin, cut loose his bonds and placed him on his feet. Tom ordered him to be strapped to the carrying pole on which they had brought in the pig's carcass. The bearers carried him like dead game back to the beach of the lagoon.

'It will be more difficult for him to escape from the ship. Take him out to the *Gift*,' Tom told Batula. 'Chain him in the orlop, and see to it that he is guarded day and night by your most reliable men.'

They stayed on in the encampment beside the lagoon during the forty days of mourning for Yasmini. For the first ten Dorian hung suspended over the black void of death, drifting from delirium into coma, then rallying again. Tom, Sarah and Mansur took turns to wait by his bedside.

On the tenth morning Dorian opened his eyes and looked at Mansur. He spoke weakly but clearly: 'Is your mother buried? Have you said the prayers?'

'She is buried and I have prayed over her grave, for you and for myself.'

'That is good, my son.' Dorian sank away, but within an hour he woke again and asked for food and drink.

'You will live,' Sarah told him as she brought a bowl of broth. 'You ran it very fine, Dorian Courtney, but now you will live.'

Relieved of the terrible anxiety over Dorian's condition, Tom let Sarah and the women servants take over his share of the vigil at the bedside, and he and Mansur devoted themselves to other business.

Every day Tom ordered Kadem to be brought up from the orlop deck, and exercised in the sunlight and open air. He made sure he was well fed, and that the gash in his scalp healed cleanly. He felt no compassion for the prisoner, but he wanted to ensure his survival in good condition: he was an important part of Tom's plans for the future.

Tom had ordered the bush-pigskin to be salted and hung in the *Gift*'s rigging. He questioned Kadem almost every day in fluent Arabic, forcing him to squat in the shadow of the pigskin that flapped over his head, a constant reminder of the fate that awaited him if he refused to answer.

'How did you learn that this ship belonged to me and my brother?' he demanded, and Kadem named the merchant in Zanzibar who had given him this information, before the life was choked out of him by the garotte.

Tom passed the information to Dorian, when he was strong enough to sit up unaided. 'So our identity is now known by the spies of Zayn al-Din at every anchorage along the coast from Good Hope to Hormuz and the Red Sea.'

'The Dutch know us also,' Dorian agreed. 'Keyser promised that every VOC port in the Orient would be closed to us. We must change the cut of our jibs.'

Tom set about altering the appearance of the two ships. One after the other they warped them to the beach. Tom used the rise and fall of the tide to careen them over. First they scraped away the heavy infestation of weed and treated the shipworm that had already taken firm hold in the hulls. Some of these loathsome creatures were as thick as a man's thumb and as long as his arm. They could riddle the timbers with holes until the ship was rotten as cheese and might easily break up in rough weather. They tarred the ship's bottom and renewed the copper sheathing where strips had been torn off, allowing the worm to enter. It was the only effective cure. Then Tom changed the masts and rigging. He stepped a mizzen on the *Gift*. This was something he and Dorian had discussed before: the additional mast altered the appearance and performance of the ship completely. When he took her out to sea for her trials, she sailed a full point closer to the wind and logged an additional two knots of speed through the water. Tom and Batula were delighted and reported the success gleefully to Dorian, who insisted on being allowed to hobble to the head of the beach to look at her.

'In God's name, she is as fresh as a virgin again.'

421

'She must have a new name, brother,' Tom agreed. 'What shall it be?'

Dorian barely hesitated. 'The *Revenge*.'

Tom saw by his expression what he was thinking, and gave him no argument. 'That is an illustrious name.' He nodded. 'Our great-great-grandfather sailed with Sir Richard Grenville on the old *Revenge*.'

They repainted the hull in sky blue, for that was the hue of the paint they had brought with them in abundance, and chequered the gunports in darker blue. It gave the *Revenge* a saucy air.

Then they began work on the *Maid of York*. She had always shown a flighty inclination to broach-to when driven hard before the wind. Tom took this opportunity to add an additional ten feet to the mainmast and give it five degrees more rake. He also lengthened the bowsprit and moved the jib stay and the staysail stay a touch forward. He repositioned the cradles of the water casks in the holds nearer to the stern to alter her trim. This not only changed her profile but made her more responsive to the helm and corrected her tendency to being down by the head.

Tom gave her the contrary colour scheme to the *Revenge*: a dark blue hull and sky blue gunports.

'She was named after you, the *Maid of York*,' Tom reminded Sarah. 'Fair is fair, you must rename her now.'

'*Water Sprite*,' she said immediately, and Tom blinked.

'How did you hit on that? 'Tis a quirky name.'

'And I am a quirky lady.' She laughed.

'That you are.' He laughed with her. 'But just plain *Sprite* might be better.'

'Are you naming her, or am I?' Sarah asked sweetly.

'Let's say rather, we are.' Sarah threw up both her hands in capitulation.

When the forty days of mourning for Yasmini had passed, Dorian was sufficiently recovered to walk unaided to the far end of the beach and swim back across the channel. Although he had recovered much of his strength, the loneliness and deep sadness had marked him. Whenever Mansur could find time from his duties he and Dorian spent it sitting together and talking quietly.

Each evening the entire family gathered around the campfire and discussed their plans. Soon it became obvious that none of them wished to make the lagoon their new home. As they were without horses Tom and Mansur's scouting expeditions on foot did not penetrate far inland, and they encountered none of the tribes that had once inhabited this country. The old villages were burned and deserted.

'There's no trade, unless you have someone to trade with,' Tom pointed out.

'It is a sickly place. Already we have lost one of our people to the fever.' Sarah supported him. 'I had hoped so much to meet our Jim Boy here, but in all this time there has been neither sign nor sight of him. He must have moved on further to the north.' There were a hundred other possible reasons why Jim had disappeared, but she put them out of her mind. 'We will find him there,' she said firmly.

'I, for another, cannot remain here,' Mansur said. In these last weeks he had taken his place quite naturally at the family councils. 'My father and I have a sacred obligation to find the man who ordered the death of my mother. I know who he is. My destiny lies to the north, in the kingdom of Oman.' He looked at his father enquiringly.

Slowly Dorian nodded agreement. 'Yasmini's murder has changed everything. I now share your sacred obligation of vengeance. We will go northwards together.'

'So, it's settled, then.' Tom spoke for all of them. 'When we reach Nativity Bay, we can decide again.'

'When can we sail?' Sarah asked eagerly. 'Name a day!'

'The ships are almost ready, and so are we. Ten days from now. The day after Good Friday,' Tom suggested. 'A propitious day.'

Sarah composed a letter to Jim. It ran to twelve pages of heavy parchment in her elegant close-written script. She stitched it into a canvas cover and painted the packet with sky blue ship's paint and sealed the seams with hot tar. She printed his name on it in white paint and block capitals: James

Archibald Courtney Esq. Then she carried it up the hill and, with her own hand, hid it in the recess below the post stone. She built a tall cairn on top to signal to Jim when he came that a letter was waiting for him.

Mansur hunted far up the valley and killed five more Cape buffalo. The women salted, pickled and dried the meat, then made spiced sausage for the voyage ahead. Mansur supervised the crews as they refilled all the water casks on both ships. When this was done, Tom and the Arab captains were rowed around the ships to check their trim. Though heavily laden, both vessels rode well. They looked wonderfully elegant in their new paint.

Chained and heavily guarded, Kadem al-Jurf was allowed on deck for a few hours each day. Tom and Dorian took turns to interrogate him. With the dried pigskin casting its shadow across the deck Kadem responded to their questions, if not willingly at least with some show of respect. However, that disconcerting stare never faded from his eyes. Though Tom and Dorian phrased the same questions in different guises, Kadem's replies were consistent and he avoided the traps they set for him. He must have known what his eventual fate would be. The law allowed Dorian and Mansur little discretion of mercy: when they stared at him Kadem saw death in their eyes, and all he could hope for was that when the time came they would grant him a swift, dignified execution, without the horror of dismemberment or the sacrilege of the pigskin.

Over the weeks, Kadem's incarceration in the orlop developed its own routine and rhythm. Three Arab seamen shared the duty of acting as his warders during the night, each taking a shift of four hours. They had been carefully chosen by Batula, and at first they were mindful of his orders. While themselves remaining mute, they reported Kadem's most casual remarks to Batula. However, the nights were long and the guard duty as dull as the need to remain awake was onerous. Kadem had been trained by the most famous mullahs of the Royal House of Oman in dialectic and religious debate. The things he whispered in the darkness to his warders while the rest of the crew were ashore or sleeping on the upper deck were compelling to those devout young men. The truths he spoke were too poignant and moving to report to Batula. They could not close their ears to him, and they listened at first with awe when he spoke of the truth and beauty of God's way. Then they began, against their own will, to respond to his whispers with their own. From the fire in his eyes they knew Kadem to be a holy man. By the fervour of his own devotion and the unassailable logic of his words they were convinced. Slowly they were held in thrall by Kadem ibn Abubaker.

Meanwhile, the excitement of impending departure built up in the rest of the company. The last sticks of furniture and goods were taken from the huts at the forest edge and ferried on board. On Good Friday Tom and Mansur applied torches to the empty huts. The thatch had dried out and they burned like bonfires. The day after Good Friday they sailed early in the morning watch, so that Tom had light enough to make out the channel. The wind stood fair offshore, and he led the little flotilla out through the heads into the open sea.

It was midday and the land was low and blue on the western horizon before one of the crew came up from below decks in a state of terrible agitation. Tom and Dorian were on the quarter-deck together, Dorian seated in the sling chair Tom had rigged for him. At first neither could understand the man's wild shouts.

'Kadem!' Tom caught the gist of it. He went bounding down the companionway to the orlop deck. Locked securely in the wooden cage that the carpenters had built for him, Kadem was curled in sleep upon the straw mattress. His chains were still secured to the ring bolts in the deck. Tom seized a corner of the single blanket that covered the prisoner from the top of his head to his feet, jerked it aside and then kicked the dummy that lay beneath it. It was cunningly made of two sacks filled with oakum and tied with short pieces of old rope to give it the outline of a human body beneath the blanket.

They searched the ship swiftly from stem to stern, Tom and Dorian with swords in hand raging through the holds and probing every corner and cranny.

'Three other men are missing,' Batula reported with a shamed face.

'Who are they?' Dorian demanded.

Batula hesitated before he could bring himself to answer. 'Rashood, Pinna and Habban,' he croaked, 'the same three men I set to guard him.'

Tom altered course and steered alongside the *Revenge*. Through the speaking tube, he hailed Mansur who had command of her. Both vessels went about and headed back towards the entrance of the lagoon, but the winds that had allowed them to clear the lagoon so handily now blocked them offshore. For days more they beat back and forth across the entrance. Twice they were almost piled up to the reef as Tom in frustration tried to force the passage.

It was six days after they had sailed that at last they dropped anchor off the beach of the lagoon once again. Since their departure it had rained heavily, and when they went ashore they found that any sign left by the fugitives had been washed away. 'Yet there is only one direction they would have taken.' Tom pointed up the valley. 'But they have almost nine days' start on us. If we are to catch up with them we must march at once.'

He ordered Batula and Kumrah to check the weapons lockers and the magazines. They came ashore with sorry expressions to report that four muskets were missing, with the same number of cutlasses, bullet bags and powder flasks. Tom stopped himself reviling the two captains further, for they had already suffered enough.

Dorian argued vehemently when Tom told him he must stay behind to take care of the ships and Sarah while they chased the fugitives. In the end, Sarah joined in to convince him that he was not yet strong enough for such an expedition, which would call for hard marches and perhaps even harder fighting. Tom selected ten of his best men to go with him, those who were proficient with sword, musket and pistol.

426

An hour after they had first stepped ashore all was ready. Tom kissed Sarah, and they left the beach heading inland. Tom and Mansur strode out at the head of the line of armed men.

'I would that little Bakkat were with us,' Tom muttered. 'He would follow them though they grew wings and flew ten feet above the ground.'

'You are a famous elephant hunter, Uncle Tom. I have heard you tell it since I was a child.'

'That was more than a year or two ago,' Tom smiled ruefully, 'and you must not remember all I tell you. Boasts and brags are like debts and childhood sweethearts – they often come back to plague the man who made them.'

At noon on the third day they stood on the crest of the range of mountains that ran in an unbroken rampart north and south. The slopes below them were covered with banks of purple heather. This was the dividing line between the littoral and the inland plateau of the continental shield. Behind, the forests lay like a green carpet down to the edge of the ocean. Ahead, the hills were harsh and rocky and the plains were endless, stretching for ever to the horizon, blue with distance. The tiny dustclouds kicked up by the moving herds of game drifted in the warm breezes.

'Any one of those might mark the path of the men we are hunting, but the hoofs of the herds will have wiped out their tracks,' Tom told Mansur. 'Still and all, I doubt they would have headed into that great emptiness. Kadem would have the sense at least to try to find human habitation.'

'The Cape colony?' Mansur looked southwards.

'More likely the Arab forts along the Fever Coast or the Portuguese territory of Mozambique.'

'The land is so big.' Mansur scowled. 'They could have gone anywhere.'

'We will wait for the scouts to come in before we decide what next to do.'

Tom had sent his best men to cast north and south, ordering them to try to cut Kadem's trail. He would not say so to Mansur, not yet at least, but he knew that their chances

427

were remote. Kadem had too long a start on them and, as Mansur had remarked, the land was big.

The rendezvous Tom had set at which to meet the scouts was a distinctive peak shaped like a cocked hat that could be seen from twenty leagues in any direction. They camped on the southern slope at the edge of the treeline, and the scouts came dribbling back during the night. None had been able to cut human sign.

'They have got clean away, lad,' Tom told his nephew. 'I think we can do naught else but let them go, and turn back for the ships. But I would like your agreement. 'Tis your duty to your mother that dictates what we do next.'

'Kadem was only the messenger,' Mansur said. 'My blood feud is with his master in Lamu, Zayn al-Din. I agree, Uncle Tom. This is fruitless. Our energies may best be expended elsewhere.'

'Think on this also, lad. Kadem will fly straight back to his master, the pigeon to its loft. When we find Zayn, Kadem will be at his side, if the lions have not eaten him first.'

Mansur's face brightened and his shoulders straightened. 'In God's Name, Uncle, I had not considered that. Of course you are right. As for Kadem perishing in the wilderness, it seems to me that he has the animal tenacity and fanatical faith to survive. I feel sure we will meet him again. He will not escape my vengeance. Let's hurry back to the ships.'

Before first light Sarah left her bunk in the little cabin of the *Sprite*. Then, as she had done every morning since Tom left, she went ashore and climbed to the hilltop above the lagoon. From there she watched for Tom's return. From afar she recognized his tall, straight figure and his swinging walk at the head of his men. The image blurred as her eyes filled with tears of joy and relief.

'Thank you, God, that you paid heed to my prayers,' she cried aloud, and ran down the hillside straight into his arms. 'I was so worried that you would get yourself into trouble again, without me to look after you, Tom Courtney.'

'I had no chance for trouble, Sarah Courtney,' he hugged her hard, 'more's the pity.' He looked to Mansur. 'You are

428

faster than me, lad. Run ahead to warn your father that we are returning, and to have the ships ready to sail again as soon as I set foot aboard.' Mansur set off at once.

As soon as he was out of earshot Sarah said, 'You're the crafty one, aren't you, Thomas? You did not want to be the one who gave the bitter news to Dorry that Yassie's murder is unrevenged.'

''Tis Mansur's duty more than mine,' Tom replied breezily. 'Dorry would have it no other way. The only profit in this bloody business is that it might bring father and son closer than they have ever been before – and that was mighty close.'

They sailed with the ebb of the tide. The wind stood fair and they had made good their offing before darkness fell. The ships were within two cables' length of each other, with the wind fresh on the quarter, their best point of sailing. The *Revenge* showed her new turn of speed and began to pull ahead of the *Sprite*. Thus it was with reluctance that Tom gave the order to shorten sail for the night. It seemed a pity not to take full advantage of the wind that was bearing them so swiftly towards Nativity Bay.

'But I am a trader and not a man-o'-war,' Tom consoled himself. As he gave the order to shorten sail he saw Mansur in the *Revenge* furl his staysail and reef his mizzen and main. Both ships hoisted lanterns to their maintops, to enable them the better to keep night stations on each other.

Tom was ready to give over the quarter-deck to Kumrah and go down to the small saloon for the supper that he could smell Sarah was cooking: he recognized the rich aroma of one of her famous spiced boobooties and saliva flooded into his mouth. He spent a few more minutes checking the set of the sails and the pointing of the helmsman. Satisfied at last, he turned towards the head of the companionway, then stopped abruptly.

He stared at the dark eastern horizon and muttered, mystified, 'There is a great fire out there. Is it a ship ablaze? No, it's something greater than that. The fires of a volcano?'

The crew on deck had seen it too and crowded to the rail, gawking and gabbling. Then, to Tom's utter astonishment, there burst over the dark horizon a monstrous ball of celestial fire. It lit the dark surface of the sea. Across the water the sails of the *Revenge* glowed palely in this ghostly emanation.

'A comet, by God!' Tom shouted in wonder, and stamped on the deck above the saloon. 'Sarah Courtney, come up here at once. You have never seen aught such as this, nor will you ever again.'

Sarah came flying up the ladder with Dorian close behind her. They stopped and stared in wonder, struck speechless by the splendour of the sight. Then Sarah came to Tom and placed herself within the protective circle of his arms. 'It is a sign,' she whispered. 'It's a benediction from on high for the old life we have left behind at Good Hope, and a promise of the new life that lies ahead of us.'

Dorian left them, moved slowly down the deck until he reached the bows and sank to his knees. He turned his face up to the sky. 'All the days of mourning have passed,' he said. 'Your time here on earth with me is over. Go, Yasmini, my little darling, I commit you to the arms of God, but you must know that my heart and all my love go with you.'

Across the dark water Mansur Courtney saw the comet, and he ran to the main shrouds and leaped into them. He clambered swiftly upwards until he reached the maintop. He threw an arm around the top-gallant mast, balancing lithely against the roll and pitch of the hull, which were magnified by the sixty feet that separated him from the surface of the sea. He lifted his face to the sky and his long, thick hair streamed back in the wind. 'The death of kings!' he cried. 'The destruction of tyrants! All these portentous events heralded by God's finger writing in the heavens.' Then he filled his lungs and shouted into the wind, 'Hear me, Zayn al-Din! I am Nemesis, and I am coming for you.'

Night after night as the two little ships sailed northwards the comet climbed overhead, seeming to light their way, until at last they picked out a tall bluff of land that rose out of the dark waters ahead of their bows like the back of a monstrous whale. At the northern end of the promontory, the whale's mouth opened. They sailed through this entrance into a huge landlocked bay, far greater in extent than the Lagoon of the Elephants. On one side the land was steep-to, on the other it stretched in dense mangrove swamps, but between them lay the lovely embouchure of a river of sweet, clear water flanked by gently sloping beaches that offered a natural landing place.

'This is not our first visit to this place. Dorian and I have been here many times before. The natives hereabouts call this river Umbilo,' Tom told Sarah, as he steered for the beach and dropped his anchor in three fathoms. Looking over the side they could watch the steel flukes burying themselves in the pale, sandy bottom and the brilliant shoals of fish swirling as they feasted on the small crabs and shrimps disturbed from their burrows by the anchor.

When all the canvas was furled, the yards sent down and both ships at rest, Tom and Sarah stood by the rail and watched Mansur row ashore from the *Revenge*, eager to explore these new surroundings.

'The restlessness of youth,' Tom said.

'If restlessness is the sign of tender age, then you are an infant in arms, Master Tom,' she replied.

'That is most unfair to me,' he chuckled, 'but I shall let it pass.'

She shaded her eyes and studied the shoreline. 'Where is the mail stone?'

'There, at the foot of the bluff, but do not set your hopes too high.'

'Of course not!' she snapped at him, but she thought, he need not try to protect me from disappointment. I know, with a mother's sure instinct, that Jim is close. Even if he has not yet reached this spot, he soon will. I need only be patient, and my son will come back to me.

Tom offered an olive branch by changing the subject in a placatory tone: 'What do you think of this spot upon the globe, Sarah Courtney?'

'I like it well enough. Perhaps I will grow to like it even more if you allow me to rest here more than a day and a night.' She accepted his peace-offering with a smile.

'Then Dorian and I will begin to mark out the site for our

new fort and trading post immediately.' Tom lifted his glass to his eye. He and Dorian had done most of this work on their last visit to Nativity Bay. He ran the glass over the site they had chosen then. It was on a promontory in a meander of the river. Because the Umbilo waters enclosed three sides, it was easy to defend. A constant supply of fresh water was also assured, and there was a good field of fire in all directions. In addition, it was under the guns of the anchored ships and would benefit from their support in the event of an attack by savage tribesmen or other enemies.

'Yes!' He nodded with satisfaction. 'It will suit our purpose well enough. We will start work tomorrow at the latest, and you shall design our private quarters for me just as you did at Fort Providence twenty years ago.'

'That was our honeymoon,' she said, with awakening enthusiasm.

'Aye, lass.' Tom smiled down at her. 'And this shall be our second of that ilk.'

The small band of horsemen moved slowly across the veld, dwarfed by the infinite landscape that surrounded them. They led the pack-horses and let the small herd of remounts follow at their own pace. Animals and men were lean and hardened by the journey. Their clothing was ragged and patched, their boots long ago worn out and discarded, to be replaced by new ones crudely sewn from the skins of the kudu antelope. The tack of the horses was abraded by their passage through the thorn thickets, the seats of the saddles polished by the riders' sweaty backsides.

The faces and arms of the three Dutchmen were burned as dark as those of the Hottentot troopers. They rode in silence, strung out behind the tiny trotting figure of Xhia, the Bushman. Onwards, ever onwards, following the tracks of the wagon wheels that ran ahead like an endless serpent across the plains and the hills.

The troopers had long ago given up any thought of desertion. It was not only the implacable determination of their leader that prevented them but also the thousands of leagues of wilderness that had already unfurled behind them. They knew that a lone horseman would have little chance of ever reaching the colony. They were herd animals, forced to stay together to survive. They were not only the prisoners of Captain Herminius Koots's obsession, but also of the great empty distances.

Koots's worn leather jacket and breeches were patched and stained with sweat, rain and red dust. His lank hair hung down to his shoulders. It was bleached white by the sun, and the ends were raggedly trimmed with a hunting knife. With his gaunt sun-darkened features and his pale, staring eyes he seemed indeed a man possessed.

For Koots the lure of the reward had long ago faded: he was driven onwards by the need to quench his hatred in the blood of his quarry. He would allow nothing, neither man nor beast nor the burning distances, to cheat him of that ultimate fulfilment.

His chin was sunk on his chest, but now he lifted it and stared ahead, eyes narrowed behind the colourless lashes. There was a dark cloud across the horizon. He watched it climb higher into the sky and roll towards them across the plain. He reined in and called to Xhia: 'What is this that fills the sky? It is not dust or smoke.'

Xhia cackled with laughter and broke into a gleeful dance, shuffling and stamping. The distances and hardships of the journey had not wearied him: he had been born to this life. Enclosing walls and the company of hordes of his fellow men would have jaded him and chafed his spirit. The wilderness was his hearth, the open sky his roof.

He broke into another of his paeans of self-praise and vilification of his mad, cruel master that he alone of all the company could understand. 'Slimy white worm, you creature with skin the colour of pus and curdled milk, do you know nothing at all of this land? Must Xhia, the mighty hunter and slayer of elephants, nurse you like a blind, mewling infant?' Xhia jumped high and deliberately broke flatus, with such force that the wind stirred the back flap of his loincloth. He knew that this would drive Koots into a rage. 'Must Xhia, who stands so tall that his long shadow terrifies his enemies, Xhia beneath whose mighty prong women squeal with joy, must Xhia always lead you by the hand? You understand nothing that is written plain upon the earth, you understand nothing that is blazoned in the very heavens.'

'Stop that monkey chatter at once,' Koots shouted. He could not understand the words but he recognized the mockery in the tone, and knew that Xhia had farted only to provoke him. 'Shut your filthy mouth, and answer me straight.'

'I must shut my mouth but answer your questions, great master?' Xhia switched into the patois of the colony, a mixture of all the languages. 'Am I then a magician?' Over the months of their enforced companionship they had learned to understand each other much better than they had at the beginning, both in words and in intent.

Koots touched the hilt of the long hippopotamus-hide *sjambok* that hung by its thong from the pommel of his saddle. This was another gesture well understood by them both. Xhia changed his tone and expression again, and danced just beyond the reach of the whip. 'Lord, this a gift from the Kulu Kulu. Tonight we will sleep with full bellies.'

'Birds?' Koots asked, and watched the shadow of this cloud sweep across the plain towards them. He had been amazed by the flocks of the tiny quelea bird, but this was far greater in height and extent.

'Not birds,' Xhia told him. 'These are locusts.'

Koots forgot his anger, and leaned back in the saddle to take in the size of the approaching swarm. It filled half of the bowl of the sky from horizon to horizon. The sound of wings was like that of a gentle breeze in the high branches of the forest, but it mounted swiftly, becoming next a murmur, a rising roar and then a thunder. The great swarm of insects formed a moving curtain whose trailing skirts swept the earth. Koots's fascination turned to alarm as the first insects, buzzing low to earth, slammed into his chest and face. He ducked and

434

cried out, for the locust's hind legs are barbed with sharp red spikes. One left a bloody welt across his cheek. His horse reared and plunged under him, and Koots threw himself from the saddle and seized the reins. He turned the horse's rump towards the approaching swarm, and shouted to his men to do the same. 'Hold the pack-horses and knee-halter the spares, lest they are driven away before this pestilence.'

They forced the animals to their knees, then shouted and jerked the reins until reluctantly they rolled flat on their sides and stretched out in the grass. Koots cowered behind the body of his own horse. He pulled his hat well down over his ears, and turned up the collar of his leather coat. Despite the partial protection afforded by the horse, the flying creatures slapped against any exposed parts of his body in a continuous hail-storm, each with the strength to sting painfully through the folds of his coat.

The rest of the band followed his example and lay behind their mounts, taking cover as though from enemy musket balls. Only Xhia seemed oblivious to the rain of hard bodies. He sat out in the open, snatching up the locusts that hit him and were stunned by the impact. He broke off their legs and goggle-eyed heads and stuffed the bodies into his mouth. The carapaces crunched as he chewed and the tobacco-coloured juices ran down his chin. 'Eat!' he called to them as he chewed. 'After the locust comes famine.'

From noon to sundown the locust swarm roared over them like the waters of a great river in flood. The sky was darkened by them so that the dusk came on them prematurely. Xhia's appetite seemed insatiable. He gobbled down the living bodies until his belly bulged, and Koots thought he must succumb to his own greed. However, Xhia was possessed of the same digestive tract as a wild animal. When his belly was stretched tight and shiny as a ball he staggered to his feet and tottered away a few paces. Then, still in full sight of Koots and with the breeze blowing directly to where Koots lay, Xhia lifted the tail flap of his loincloth and squatted again.

It seemed this abundance of food served only to lubricate

435

the action of his bowels. He defecated copiously and thunder-ously, and at the same time picked up more of the fluttering insects and stuffed them into his mouth.

'You disgusting animal,' Koots shouted at him, and drew his pistol, but Xhia knew that even if Koots thrashed him regularly, he could not kill him, not thousands of leagues from the colony and civilization.

'Good!' He grinned at Koots, and made the gesture of inviting him to join the feast.

Koots holstered his weapon and buried his nose in the crook of his arm. 'When he has served his purpose I will strangle the little ape with my own hands,' Koots promised himself, and gagged on the odours that wafted over him.

As darkness fell, the mighty locust swarm sank down out of the air and settled to roost wherever it came to earth. The deafening buzzing of their wings faded, and Koots rose to his feet at last and stared about.

For as far as he could see in every direction the earth was covered waist deep with a living carpet of bodies, reddish brown in the light of the sunset. The trees of the forest had changed shape as the swarms settled upon them. They were transformed into amorphous haystacks of living locusts, seeth-ing and growing larger as more insects settled upon those already at roost. With a crackle like volleys of musketry the main branches of the nearest trees gave way under the weight and came crashing down to earth, but still the locusts piled on to them and devoured the leaves.

From their burrows and lairs the carnivores emerged to feast upon this bounty. Koots watched in wonder as hyena, jackal and leopard became bold with greed and rushed upon the mounds of insects, gobbling them down.

Even a pride of eleven lions joined the banquet. They passed close to where Koots stood, but took not the slightest notice of the men or the horses, for they were preoccupied with the feast. Like grazing cattle they spread out across the plain, their noses to the earth, devouring the seething heaps of locusts, champing them between their great jaws. The lion cubs, their bellies stuffed full, stood up on their back legs and playfully batted the flying creatures out of the air as they were disturbed into flight again.

Koots's troopers swept a clear patch of earth, and built a fire on it. They used the blades of their spades as frying pans, and on these they roasted the locusts crisp and brown. Then they crunched them up with a relish almost as keen as Xhia's. Even Koots joined in and made a meal of these titbits. When night fell the men tried to compose themselves to rest, but the insects swarmed over them. They crawled into their faces, and their spiked feet rasped and scratched any exposed part of their skin and kept them from sleep.

The next morning when the sun rose it revealed a strange antediluvian landscape of dull featureless red-brown. Swiftly the sun warmed the motionless masses of locusts that had been chilled into a stupor during the night. They began to stir, to undulate and hum like a disturbed hive. Suddenly, as if at a signal, the entire horde rose into the air and roared away towards the east, borne on the morning breeze. For many hours the dark torrents streamed overhead, but as the sun reached its zenith the last had passed on. Once more the sky was brilliant blue and unsullied.

Yet the landscape they left behind was altered out of all recognition. It was bare earth and rock. The trees were denuded of their foliage, the bare branches snapped off to lie tangled below the stark boles and twisted trunks. It was as though a conflagration had consumed every leaf and green sprig. The golden grasses that had undulated in the breeze like the scend of the ocean were gone. In their place was this stony desolation.

The horses snuffled the bare earth and pebbles, then stood disconsolately, their empty bellies already rumbling with gases. Koots climbed to the top of the nearest bare hillock and played his telescope over the stony desert. The herds of antelope and quagga that had infested the land the previous day were gone. In the distance Koots made out a pale mist of drifting dust that might have been raised by the exodus of the last herds from this starvation veld. They were moving south-wards to search for other grasslands that had not been devastated by the locusts.

He went back down the hill and his men, who had been arguing animatedly, fell silent as he walked into the camp. Koots studied their faces as he filled his mug with coffee from the black kettle. The last grain of sugar had been used up weeks before. He sipped from the mug, then snapped, 'Ja, Oudeman? What is it that is worrying you? You have the same pained expression as an old woman with bleeding piles.'

'There is no grazing for the horses,' Oudeman blurted.

Koots made a show of amazement at this revelation. 'Sergeant Oudeman, I am grateful to you for pointing this out to me. Without your sharp sense of perception I might have overlooked it.'

Oudeman scowled at the laboured sarcasm. He was not sufficiently glib or well enough educated to match Koots in word-play. 'Xhia says that the herds of wild game will know which way to go to find grazing. If we follow them they will lead us to it.'

'Please go on, Sergeant. I never tire of gleaning these jewels of your wisdom.'

'Xhia says that since last night the game herds have started moving southwards.'

'Yes.' Koots nodded, and blew noisily into the mug of hot coffee. 'Xhia is right. I saw that from the hilltop up there.' He pointed with the mug.

'We must go southwards to find grazing for the horses,' Oudeman went on stubbornly.

'One question, Sergeant. Which way are the tracks of Jim Courtney's wagon heading?' Using the mug again, he pointed out the deep ruts, which were even more obvious now that the grass no longer screened them.

Oudeman lifted his hat and scratched his bald pate. 'North-east,' he grunted.

'So, if we go southwards will we catch up with Courtney?' Koots asked, in a kindly tone.

'No, but . . .' Oudeman's voice trailed off.

'But what?'

'Captain, sir, without the horses we will never get back to the colony.'

Koots stood up and flicked the coffee grounds out of his mug. 'The reason we are here, Oudeman, is to catch Jim Courtney, not to return to the colony. Mount!' He looked at Xhia. 'Good, so! You, yellow baboon, take the spoor again and eat the wind.'

There was water in the streams and the rivers they crossed, but no grass on the veld. They rode for fifty and then a hundred leagues without finding grazing. In the larger rivers they found aquatic weeds and lily stems beneath the surface of the water. They waded out to harvest them with their bayonets, and fed them to the horses. In one steep, narrow valley the sweet-thorn trees had not been entirely stripped of their foliage. They climbed into the trees and cut down the branches that the locusts had not torn down with their weight. The horses ate the green leaves hungrily, but this was not their normal diet and they derived only small benefit from it.

By now the animals were showing all the signs of slow starvation, but Koots never wavered in his determination. He led them on across the desolation. The horses were so weakened that the riders were forced to dismount and lead them up any sharp incline to husband their strength.

The men were hungry too. The game had disappeared along with the grass. The once teeming veld was deserted. They ate the last few handfuls in the leather grain sacks, and then were reduced to any windfall that the ruined veld might provide.

With his slingshot Xhia knocked down the prehistoric blue-headed lizards that lived among the rocks, and they dug up the burrows of moles and spring-rats that were surviving on subterranean roots. They roasted them without skinning or cleaning the carcasses. This would have wasted precious nourishment. They simply threw them whole upon the coals, let the fur frizzle off, the skin blacken and burst open. Then they picked the half-cooked flesh off the tiny bones with their fingers. Xhia chewed the discarded bones like a hyena.

He discovered a treasure in an abandoned ostrich nest. There were seven ivory-coloured eggs in the rude scrape in the ground. Each egg was almost the size of his own head. He capered around the nest, screeching with excitement. 'This is another gift that clever Xhia brings to you. The ostrich, which is my totem, has left this for me.' He changed his totem with as little compunction as he would take a new woman. 'Without Xhia you would have perished long ago.'

He selected one of the ostrich eggs, set it on end in the sand, then looped his bowstring around the shaft of an arrow. He placed the point of the arrow on the top of the shell. By sawing the bow rapidly back and forth he spun the arrow. The point drilled neatly through the thick shell. As it broke through there was a sharp hiss of escaping gas and a yellow fountain erupted high in the air, like champagne from a bottle that had been shaken violently. Xhia clapped his open mouth over the hole and sucked out the contents of the egg.

The men around him leaped backwards, exclaiming with alarm and disgust as a sulphurous stench engulfed them.

'Mother of a mad dog!' Koots swore. 'The thing is rotten.'

Xhia rolled his eyes with relish, but did not remove his mouth from the hole, lest the rest of the yellow liquid spray out on to the dry earth and be lost. He gulped it down greedily.

'Those eggs have lain there since the last breeding season – six months in the hot sun. They are so badly addled that they would poison a dog hyena.' Oudeman choked and turned away.

Xhia sat beside the nest and drank two of the eggs without pause, except to belch or chuckle with pleasure. Then he packed those that remained into his leather bag. He slung it over his shoulder and set off again along the wheel ruts of Jim Courtney's wagon train.

The men and horses grew daily weaker and more emaciated. Only Xhia was plump and his skin shone with health and vigour. The addled ostrich eggs, the castings of owls, the dung of lions and jackals, bitter roots and herbs, the maggots of blow-flies, the larvae of wasps and hornets – food that only he could stomach – sustained him.

Wearily the band climbed another denuded hillside and came upon yet another of Jim Courtney's camps. This one was different from the hundreds they had found before. The wagon train had paused here long enough to build grass huts and set up long smoking racks of raw timber over beds of what was by now cold black ash, most of it scattered on the wind.

'Here Somoya killed his first elephant,' Xhia announced, after only a cursory examination of the abandoned campsite.

'How do you know that?' Koots demanded, as he dismounted stiffly. He stood with clenched fists pressed into his aching back, and gazed around him.

'I know it because I am clever and you are stupid,' Xhia said, in the language of his people.

'None of that monkey talk,' Koots snarled at him. But he was too tired to cuff him. 'Answer me straight!'

'They have smoked a mountain of meat on these racks, and these are the knucklebones of the elephant from which they have made a stew.' He picked a bone out of the grass. A few shreds of sinew adhered to it and Xhia gnawed at them before he went on: 'I will find the rest of the carcass nearby.'

He disappeared like a tiny puff of yellow smoke, a way he had that never failed to take Koots by surprise. One moment he was standing in plain sight, the next he was gone. Koots sank down in the meagre shade of a bare tree. He did not have long to wait. Xhia appeared again, as suddenly as he had vanished, with the huge white thigh bone of a bull elephant.

'A great elephant!' he confirmed. 'Somoya has become a mighty hunter, as his father was before him. He has cut the tusks from the skull. By the holes in the jawbone I can tell that each tusk was as long as two men, one standing on the shoulders of the other. They were as thick around as my chest.' He puffed it out to illustrate.

Koots had little interest in the subject, and jerked his head to indicate the abandoned huts. 'How long did Somoya camp here?'

Xhia glanced at the depth of the ash in the pits, at the midden heaps and the worn footpaths between the huts, and showed the fingers of both hands twice. 'Twenty days.'

'Then we have gained that much upon them,' Koots said, with grim satisfaction. 'Find something for us to eat before we go on.'

Under Xhia's direction the troopers dug up a spring-hare and a dozen blind golden moles. A pair of white-collared crows was attracted by this activity, and Oudeman brought them down with a single musket shot. The moles tasted like chicken but the flesh of the crows was disgusting, tainted with the carrion of their diet. Only Xhia ate it with relish.

They were sick with weariness, and saddle sore, and after they had eaten the scraps of flesh they rolled into their blankets just as the sun was setting. Xhia woke them with squeals of excitement, and Koots staggered to his feet with his pistol in one hand, drawn sword in the other. 'To arms! On me!' he shouted, before he was fully awake. 'Fix your bayonets!'

Then he stopped short and gazed into the eastern sky. It was alight with a weird glow. The Hottentots whimpered with superstitious awe and cowered in their kaross blankets. 'It is a warning,' they told each other, but softly so that Koots could not hear them. 'It is a warning that we should turn back to the colony, and abandon this mad chase.'

'It is the burning eye of the Kulu Kulu,' Xhia sang, and danced for the great shining deity in the sky above him. 'He is watching over us. He promises rain and the return of the herds. There will be sweet green grass, and rich red meat. Soon, very soon.'

Instinctively the three Dutchmen moved closer together.

'This is the star that guided the three wise men to Bethlehem.' Koots was an atheist, but he knew the other two were devout, so he turned the phenomenon deftly to his advantage. 'It is beckoning us on.'

Oudeman grunted, but he did not want to provoke his captain with argument. Richter crossed himself furtively, for he was a clandestine Catholic in the company of Lutherans and heathens.

Some in fear, others in joyous anticipation, they all watched the comet's stately progress across the heavens. The stars paled and then disappeared, obliterated by its splendour.

Before dawn the trail of the comet stretched in an arc from one horizon to the other. Then, abruptly, it was in turn obscured by dense banks of cloud that rolled in from the east, off the warm Ocean of the Indies. As a murky day broke, thunder rolled against the hills and a blade of vivid lightning ripped open the belly of the clouds. The rain came down. The horses turned their tails into the wind and the men huddled under their tarpaulins as icy squalls swept over them. Only Xhia threw off his loincloth and pranced naked in the rain, throwing back his head and letting the waters fill his open mouth.

It rained for a day and a night without ceasing. The earth dissolved under them, and each gully and *donga* became a raging river, every depression and hollow in the earth became a lake. Incessantly the rain raked them and the thunder bemused them, like a cannonade of heavy guns. Huddled in their blankets, they shivered with the wet and the cold, their guts cramped and churned with the sour fluids of starvation. At intervals the rain froze before it hit the ground, and hailstones as big as knucklebones rattled against their tarpaulins and drove the horses frantic. Some snapped their ropes and galloped away in front of the sweeping grey squall.

Then on the second day, the clouds broke up and streamed away in dirty grey tatters and the sun burst through, hot and bright. They roused themselves, mounted and sallied out to retrieve the missing horses, which were scattered away for leagues across the veld. One had been killed by a pair of young lions. The two big cats were still on the body, so Koots and Oudeman rode them down and shot both of them in furious retribution. It was another three days wasted before Koots could resume the chase. Though the rain had eroded and, in places, obliterated the wagon trail, Xhia never faltered and led them on without check.

The veld responded joyously to the rain and the hot sun that followed it. Within the first day a soft green fuzz covered the gaunt outlines of the hills, and the trees lifted their drooping bare branches. Before they had gone another hundred leagues the horses' bellies were distended with sweet new grass, and they encountered the first influx of returning wild game.

From afar Xhia spotted a herd of over fifty hartebeest, each animal the size of a pony, their red coats shining in the sunlight, their thick horns sweeping up then twisting back, tall as a bishop's mitre. The three Dutchmen spurred out to meet the herd. The strength of the horses was restored by the fresh grazing, and they ran them down swiftly. Musket fire boomed out across the plains.

They butchered the hartebeest where they fell, and built fires beside the carcasses. They threw bleeding hunks of flesh on to the coals and then, half crazed with hunger, they gorged on the roasted meat. Although he was sleek, well fed and only half the size of the troopers, Xhia ate more than any two of them, and for once not even Koots grudged it to him.

Kadem knelt behind a fallen log beside a rain-swollen rill of sweet water. He had laid the musket over the top of the log, with his turban folded into a cushion beneath it. Without this padding the weapon might bounce off the hardwood log at the discharge and the shot fly wide. The musket was one of those they had taken from the powder magazine in the *Revenge*. Rashood had only managed to steal four small powder bags. The mighty rainstorm that had drenched them for a day and a night had also soaked and caked most of the powder that remained. Kadem had crumbled and sorted the damaged remnants with his fingers, but in the end he had only been able to retrieve a single bag of the precious stuff. To conserve what remained, he had used only half a measure to charge the musket.

Through the riverine bush he watched a small herd of impala antelope feeding. They were the first game he had seen since the locust swarms had passed. They were nibbling the sprigs of new green growth that the rains had brought forth. Kadem picked out one of the rams from the herd, a velvety brown creature with lyre-shaped horns. He was an expert musketeer, but his weapon was half charged and he had loaded only a few lead pellets of goose-shot on top of the powder. For these to be effective he had to let the animal come in close. His moment came and Kadem fired. Through the whirling cloud of gunsmoke he saw the ram stagger, and then, bleating pitifully, it tottered in a circle with its front leg dangling from the shattered shoulder. Kadem dropped the musket and darted forward with the cutlass in his hand. He stunned the ram with a blow of the heavy brass pommel, then rolled it over swiftly and slit its throat while it still lived.

'In God's Name!' He blessed it and the flesh was halal, no longer profane, fit to be eaten by believers. He whistled softly and his three followers came up the bank of the rill, from where they had hidden. Swiftly they butchered the carcass, then roasted strips of meat from either side of the spine over the small fire Kadem allowed them to build. As soon as the meat was cooked he ordered them to extinguish it. Even in this vast, uninhabited wilderness he was always careful to remain hidden. This was a part of his desert training, where almost every tribe was in a blood feud with all its neighbours.

They ate quickly and sparingly, then rolled the remaining cold cooked meat in their turbans, draped them over their shoulders and knotted them round their waists.

'In God's Name, we go on.' Kadem stood up and led his three followers along the bank of the stream. It cut through a steep, rugged barrier of hills. By now their robes were stained and the hems so tattered that they seemed to have been nibbled away by rats, barely covering their knees. They had made sandals for themselves from the hides of game they had killed before the locusts came. The ground was harsh and stony underfoot. There were areas carpeted with the three-pointed devil thorns, which always presented one of their spikes uppermost. The auger points could pierce even the most leathery sole to the bone.

By now the rains had repaired most of the damage wreaked by the locust swarms. However, they had no horses and they had travelled hard on foot, from before dawn until sunset each day. Kadem had decided that they must head northwards, and try to reach one of the coastal Omani trading centres beyond the Pongola river before their powder ran out. They were still a thousand leagues or more short of their goal.

They halted again at midday, for even these indefatigable travellers must stop to pray at the appointed times. They had no prayer mats with them, but Kadem estimated the direction of Mecca from the position of the noon sun and they prostrated themselves on the rugged earth. Kadem led the prayers. They affirmed that God was one and Muhammad his last true Prophet. They asked no boon or favour in return for their faith. When their worship was completed in the pure, strict form, they squatted in the shade and ate a little more of the cold roasted venison. Kadem led the quiet conversation, then instructed them in religious and philosophical matters. At last he glanced up at the sun again. 'In God's Name, let us continue the journey.'

They rose and girded themselves, then froze together as they heard, faint but unmistakable, the sound of musket fire.

'Men! Civilized men, with muskets and powder!' Kadem whispered. 'To have ventured this far inland they must have horses. All the things we need to save ourselves from perishing in this dreadful place.'

The gunfire came again. He cocked his head and slitted his wild eyes as he tried to pinpoint the source of the sound. He turned in that direction. 'Follow me. Move like the wind, swift and unseen,' he said. 'They must not know we are here.'

In the middle of that afternoon, Kadem found the spoor of many horses moving towards the north-east. The hoofs were shod with steel and had left clear prints in the rain-damp earth. They followed them at a trot across the plains, which danced and wavered with mirage. In the late afternoon they saw the dark smear of smoke from a campfire ahead. They went forward more cautiously. In the gathering dusk they could make out the twinkle of red flames below the smoke. Closer still, Kadem saw the shapes of men moving in front of the fire. Then the wind of the day faded away, and the night breeze puffed from another direction. Kadem sniffed the air and caught the unmistakable ammoniac tang.

'Horses!' he whispered, with excitement.

Koots leaned back against the bole of the camel-thorn tree and carefully pressed shreds of crumbling dry shag into his clay pipe. His tobacco bag was made from the scrotum of a bull buffalo with a drawn string of sinew to close the mouth. It was less than half full, and he was rationing himself to this half-pipe a day. He lit it with a coal from the fire and coughed softly with pleasure as the first powerful inhalation filled his lungs.

His troopers were spread out under the surrounding trees; each man had picked his own spot to lay out his fur kaross. Their bellies were stuffed with the meat of the hartebeest, the first time in over a month that they had eaten their fill. So that they could better savour this feast, Koots had allowed an early halt to the day's march. There was almost an hour left of daylight. In the normal run of events they would have camped only when the dusk obscured the wagon ruts they were following.

From the corner of his eye Koots picked up a flicker of movement and he glanced around quickly, then relaxed again. It was only Xhia. Even as Koots watched him he vanished into the darkening veld. A Bushman, with every hand turned against him all his life, would never lie down to sleep until he had swept his back trail. Koots knew he would make a wide circle out across the ground that they had already travelled. If an enemy was following them, Xhia would have cut his tracks.

Koots smoked his pipe down to the last crumb, savouring every breath. Then, regretfully, he knocked out the ash. With a sigh he settled down under his kaross and closed his eyes. He did not know how long he had slept, but he woke with a light touch on his cheek. As he started up Xhia made a soft, clucking sound to calm him.

'What is it?' Instinctively Koots kept his voice low.

'Strangers,' Xhia replied. 'They follow us.'

'Men?' Koots's wits were still fuddled with sleep. Xhia did not deign to answer such an inanity. 'Who? How many?' Koots insisted, as he sat up.

Quickly Xhia twisted a spill of dried grass. Before he lit it he held up a corner of Koots's kaross as a screen from watching eyes. Then he held the spill to the dying ash of the fire. He blew on the coals, and when the spill burst into flame he screened it with the kaross and his own body. He held something in his free hand. Koots peered at it. It was a scrap of soiled white cloth.

'Ripped from a man's clothing by thorns,' Xhia told him. Then he showed his next trophy, a single strand of black hair. Even Koots realized at once that it was a human hair, but it was too black and coarse to have come from the head of a northern European and it was too straight, free of kinks, to have come from the head of a Bushman or an African tribesman.

'This rag comes from a long robe such as Mussulmen wear. This hair from his head.'

'Mussulman?' Koots asked in surprise, and Xhia clicked in assent. Koots had learned better than to argue.

'How many?'

'Four.'

'Where are they now?'

'Lying close. They are watching us.' Xhia let the burning spill drop and rubbed out the last sparks in the dust with the palm of his childlike hand.

'Where have they left their horses?' Koots asked. 'If they had smelt ours they would have whinnied.'

'No horses. They come on foot.'

'Arabs on foot! Then, whoever they are, that is what they are after.' Koots pulled on his boots. 'They want our horses.'

448

Careful to keep a low profile, he crawled to where Oudeman was snoring softly and shook him. Once Oudeman was fully awake he grasped quickly what was happening, and understood Koots's orders.

'No gunfire!' Koots repeated. 'In the dark there is too much risk of hitting the horses. Take them with cold steel.'

Koots and Oudeman crept to each of the troopers, and whispered the orders. The men rolled out of their blankets, and slipped singly down to the horse pickets. With drawn sabres they lay up among shrub and low brush.

Koots placed himself on the southern perimeter furthest from the faint glow of the dying campfire. He lay flat against the earth, so that any man approaching the pickets would be silhouetted against the stars and the fading traces of the great comet, by now only an ethereal ghost in the western sky. Orion was no longer obliterated by its light: at this season of the year he was standing on his head below the dazzle of the Milky Way. Koots covered his eyes to enhance his night vision. He listened with all his attention, and opened his eyes only briefly, so that they would not be tricked by the light.

Time passed slowly. He measured it by the turning of the heavenly bodies. For any other man it might have been hard to keep his level of concentration screwed up to the main, but Koots was a warrior. He had to close his ears to the mundane sounds made by the horses as they shifted their weight or cropped a mouthful of grass.

The last glimmer of the great comet was low on the western horizon before Koots heard the click of two pebbles striking together. Every nerve in his body snapped taut. A minute later, and much closer, there came the slither of a leather sandal on the soft earth. He kept his head low, and saw a dark shape move against the stars.

He is closing in, he thought. Let him start to work on the ropes.

The intruder paused when he reached the head of the horselines. Koots saw his head turn slowly as he listened. He wore a turban and his beard bushed and curled. After a long minute he stooped over the running line to which the head halters of the horses were secured by steel rings. Two of the animals jerked their heads free as the line slipped through the rings.

As soon as Koots guessed that the intruder was absorbed in unravelling the next knot he rose to his feet and moved towards him. But he lost sight of him as he crouched below the skyline. He was no longer where Koots expected him to be, and abruptly Koots stumbled up against him in the darkness. Koots shouted to warn his men, then the two of them were struggling chest to chest, too close for Koots to use his blade.

Koots realized at once that the man he was wrestling was a formidable adversary. He twisted like an eel in his grip, and he felt all hard muscle and sinew. Koots tried to knee his groin, but his kneecap was almost torn loose as it struck the hard, rubbery muscle of the man's thigh instead of the soft bunch of his genitals. In an instantaneous riposte the man slammed the heel of his right hand up under Koots's jaw. His head snapped back and it felt as though his neck was broken as he went over backwards and sprawled on the ground. He saw the intruder rearing over him and the glint of his blade as it went up high for the forehand cut to his head. Koots threw up his own sabre in an instinctive parry, and steel thrilled on steel as the blades met.

The intruder broke off the attack and disappeared into the darkness. Koots crawled to his knees, still half stunned. There were shouts and the sound of blows from all around, and he heard both Oudeman and Richter bellowing orders and encouragement to the others. Then there was the bang and flash of a pistol shot. That galvanized Koots.

'Don't shoot, you fools! The horses! Have a care for the horses!' He pulled himself to his feet, and at that moment heard the clatter of shod hoofs behind him. He glanced around and saw the dark outline of a horseman bearing down upon him at full gallop. A sword glinted dully in the starlight and Koots ducked. The blade hissed past his cheek, and he glimpsed the turbaned head and beard of the rider as he raced by.

Wildly he looked about him. Nearby, the grey mare was a pale blob against the darker background. She was the fastest and strongest of the entire string. He sheathed his sword, and checked the pistol in the holster at his hip as he ran to her. As soon as he was astride her back he listened for the sound of hoofs, turned her with his knees and kicked her into a full gallop.

Every few minutes during the next hours he was forced to stop and listen for the fugitive's hoofbeats. Although the Arab often twisted and turned to throw off Koots's pursuit he always headed back towards the north. An hour before dawn Koots lost the sound of him altogether. Either he had turned again or he had slowed his mount to a walk.

North! He is set on north, he decided.

He placed the great Southern Cross squarely over his shoulder and rode into the north, keeping to a steady canter that would not burn up the mare. The dawn came up with startling rapidity. His horizon expanded as the darkness drew back, and his heart bounced as he made out the dark shape moving not a pistol shot ahead of him. He knew at once that it was not one of the larger species of antelope, for the shape of the rider upon its back was plain to see against the lightening veld. Koots pushed the mare harder and came up on him swiftly. The rider was not yet aware of him and was holding his horse to a walk. Koots recognized the bay gelding, a good strong mount, almost a match for his mare.

'Son of the great whore!' Koots laughed with triumph. 'The bay has gone lame. No wonder he had to slow down.' Even in this poor light it was plain to see that the gelding was favouring his off fore. He must have picked up a sharp stone or a thorn in the frog, and he was making heavy weather of it. Koots raced down upon them, and the fugitive swivelled round. Koots saw that he was a hawk-faced Arab, with a curling bush of beard. He took one quick look at Koots, then flogged the gelding into a laboured gallop.

Koots was close enough to risk a pistol shot and try to end it swiftly. He threw up his weapon and fired for the centre of the Arab's broad back. It must have been close for the Arab ducked and shouted, 'Swords, infidel! Man to man!'

As an ensign Koots had spent years with the VOC army in

the Orient. His Arabic was fluent and colloquial. 'Those are sweet words!' he shouted back. 'Stand and let me thrust them down your throat.'

Within two hundred yards the gelding was pulled up. The Arab slipped off his back, and turned to face Koots, flourishing the naval cutlass in his right hand. Koots realized he had no firearm: if he had carried a musket when he entered the camp, he had lost it somewhere along the way. He was dismounted, and had only the cutlass – and, of course, a dagger. An Arab always had a dagger. Koots had a great advantage, and no quixotic notions ever entered his calculations. He would exploit it to the full. He charged straight down on the Arab, leaning out to sabre him from horseback.

The Arab was quicker than he anticipated. As soon as he read Koots's intention, he feinted away from the charge and then, at the last moment, darted back under his sword arm, brushing down the flank of the running mare with the grace of a toreador leaning inside the horns of the charging bull. At the same time he reached up, grabbed a handful of the skirt of Koots's leather coat and threw all his weight on it. It was so sudden and unexpected that Koots was taken by surprise. He was leaning far out from his mount's bare back, without stirrups or reins to steady himself, and he was hauled bodily off the mare.

But Koots was a fighting man too, and, like a cat, he landed on his feet with his grip on the hilt of his sabre. The Arab went for the forehand cut to the head again. Then immediately he reversed and cut low for the Achilles tendon. Koots met the first stroke, deflecting it with a twist of the wrist, but the second was so fast that he had to jump over the swing of the cutlass. He was in balance when he landed and thrust straight at the Arab's dark glittering eyes. The Arab rolled his head and let the stroke fly over his shoulder, but so close that it razored a tuft of his beard from below his ear. They sprang apart and circled each other. Neither was even breathing hard: two warriors in peak condition.

'What is your name, son of the false prophet?' Koots asked easily. 'I like to know who I am killing.'

'My name is Kadem ibn Abubaker al-Jurf, infidel,' he said softly, but his eyes glittered at the insult. 'And, apart from Eater-of-Dung, what do men call you?'

'I am Captain Herminius Koots of the army of the VOC.'

'Ah!' said Kadem. 'Your fame goes ahead of you. You are married to the pretty little whore named Nella who has been fucked by every man who ever visited Good Hope. Even I had a few guilders' worth of her behind the hedge of the Company gardens when I was in the colony only a short while ago. I commend you. She knows her trade and enjoys her work.'

The insult was so barbed and unexpected that Koots gaped at him – the Arab even knew her name. His sword arm faltered with the shock. On the instant Kadem was at him again, and he had to scramble backwards to avoid the attack. They circled and came together, and this time Koots managed a touch high on his left shoulder. But it barely scratched the skin and no more than a few scarlet drops showed through the thin soiled cotton sleeve of Kadem's robe.

They essayed a dozen more passes without a hit, and then Kadem scored, slicing open Koots's hip, but only skin deep. The blood made it look worse than it was. Nevertheless Koots gave ground for the first time, and his sword arm ached. He regretted that wasted pistol shot. Kadem was smiling, a thin reptilian curl of the lips, and suddenly, as Koots had expected, a thin curved dagger appeared in his left hand.

Then Kadem came on again, very fast, leading with his right foot, his blade turning into a darting sunbeam, and Koots went back before it. His heel caught on a patch of thorns and he nearly fell, but recovered with a sideways twist that jarred his spine. Kadem broke off again and circled out left. He had read Koots accurately. Left was his weak side. Kadem was not to know that, years ago, during the fighting before Jaffna, he had taken a ball through that knee. It was aching now and he was panting for breath. Kadem came on again, steely and relentless.

By now Koots was flailing his blade a little, not thrusting straight and hard. His breath whistled in his own ears. He

453

knew that it would not be much longer. The sweat burned his eyes, and Kadem's face blurred.

Then, abruptly, Kadem pulled back and lowered his cutlass. He was staring over Koots's shoulder. It might have been a ruse, and Koots refused to respond. He watched the dagger in Kadem's left hand, trying to steady and compose himself for the next pass.

Then he heard the sound of hoofs behind him. He turned slowly, and there were Oudeman and Richter mounted and fully armed, Xhia leading them. Kadem let both the dagger and the cutlass drop from his hand, but still he stood with his chin lifted and his shoulders squared.

'Shall I kill the swine-pig, Captain?' Oudeman asked, as he rode up. His carbine was resting across the saddle in front of him. Koots almost gave the order. He was shaken and angry. He knew how close he had come, and Kadem had called Nella a whore. It was the truth, but death to any man who uttered it in Koots's hearing. Then he checked himself. The man had spoken of Good Hope. There was something to learn from that, and later Koots would kill him with his own hands. That would give him more pleasure than letting Oudeman do it for him.

'I want to hear more from him. Tie him behind your horse.'

It was almost two leagues back to camp. They bound Kadem's wrists together and tied the other end of the rope to the snap-ring on the wing of Oudeman's saddle. He dragged Kadem at a trot. When he fell Oudeman jerked him to his feet again, but each time Kadem lost a piece of skin from where his elbows or his knees struck the hard ground. He was coated with a paste of dust, sweat and blood when Oudeman dragged him into the camp.

Koots swung down from the back of the grey mare, and went to inspect the other three Arab prisoners that Oudeman had captured.

'Names?' he demanded of the two who seemed uninjured.

'Rashood, *effendi*.'

'Habban, *effendi*.' They touched their foreheads and breasts in respect and submission. He went to the third prisoner, who was wounded. He lay groaning, curled like a foetus in the womb.

'Name?' Koots said, and kicked him in the belly. The wounded man groaned louder, and fresh blood trickled from between his fingers where he was clutching his stomach. Koots glanced at Oudeman.

'Stupid Goffel,' Oudeman explained. 'He was carried away with excitement. Forgot your orders and shot him. It's in the belly. He won't live until tomorrow.'

'So! Better this than one of the horses,' Koots said, and drew the pistol from the holster on his sword belt. He cocked it and held the muzzle to the back of the wounded man's head. At the shot the prisoner stiffened, his eyes rolled back in their sockets. His legs kicked spasmodically, then lay still.

'Waste of good powder,' said Oudeman. 'Should have let me use the knife.'

'I haven't had my breakfast yet, and you know how squeamish I can be.' Koots smiled at his own sense of humour and returned the smoking pistol to its holster. He waved his hand towards the other prisoners, 'Give them each ten with the *sjambok* across the soles of both feet to put them in a friendlier mood, and as soon as I have finished my breakfast I will speak to them again.'

Koots ate a bowl of stew made from the shanks of the hartebeest, and watched Oudeman and Richter lay on the *sjambok* to the bare feet of the Arab captives.

'Hard men.' Koots gave grudging approval when the only sound they made was a small grunt to the fall of each stroke. He knew what agony they were enduring. Koots wiped out the bowl with a finger and sucked it as he went back to squat in front of Kadem. Despite his torn and dusty robe, the cuts and abrasions that covered his limbs, Kadem was so obviously the leader that Koots wasted no time on the others. He glanced up at Oudeman and indicated Rashood and Habban. 'Take these pig-swine away.'

Oudeman knew that he wanted them out of earshot while he questioned Kadem so that they would not hear his replies. Later he would question them separately and compare their responses. Koots waited until the Hottentot troopers had dragged them, limping on their swollen feet, to a tree and tied them to its trunk. Then he turned back to Kadem. 'So you visited the Cape of Good Hope, Beloved of Allah?'

Kadem stared back at him with fanatical, glittering eyes in his dusty face. However, the mention of the place stirred something in Oudeman's sluggish mind. He fetched one of the muskets they had captured from the Arabs and handed it to his captain. Koots's first glance at the weapon was perfunctory.

'The butt-stock.' Oudeman directed his attention. 'See the emblem in the wood?'

Koots's eyes narrowed and his lips formed a thin, hard line as he traced the design that had been burned into the wood with a branding iron. It depicted a cannon, a long-barrelled nine-pounder on a two-wheeled carriage, and in the ribbon below it the initials CBTC.

'Good, so!' Koots looked up and stared at Kadem. 'You are one of Tom and Dorian Courtney's men.'

Koots saw something flare in the depths of those dark eyes, but it was so swiftly hidden again that he could not be certain of it, but the emotion the names had engendered was passionate. It might have been loyalty, dedication or something different. Koots sat and stared at him. 'You know my wife,' Koots reminded him, 'and I might have to castrate you for the way you spoke of her. But do you know the Courtney brothers, Tom and Dorian? If you do, it might just save your balls.'

Kadem stared back at him, and Koots spoke to Oudeman: 'Sergeant, lift his skirts that we can judge how big is the knife we must use for the job.'

Oudeman grinned and knelt beside Kadem, but before he could touch him Kadem spoke.

'I know Dorian Courtney, but his Arabic name is al-Salil.'

'The Red-headed One,' Koots agreed. 'Yes, I have heard him called that. What of his brother, Tom? The one whom men also call Klebe, the hawk.'

'I know them both,' Kadem affirmed.

'You are their hireling, their creature, their lackey, their lickspittle?' Koots chose his words with care to provoke him.

'I am their implacable enemy.' Kadem rushed into the trap, his pride bristling. 'If Allah is kind, then one day I will be their executioner.'

He said it with such fierce sincerity that Koots believed him. He said nothing, for often silence is the best form of interrogation.

Kadem was by now so agitated that he burst out: 'I am the bearer of the sacred *fatwa* entrusted to me by my master the ruler of Oman, Caliph Zayn al-Din ibn al-Malik.'

'Why would such a noble and mighty monarch entrust such a mission to a miserable slice of rancid pork fat such as you?' Koots gave a mocking laugh. Although Oudeman had not understood a word of the Arabic exchanges he laughed like an echo.

'I am a prince of the royal blood,' Kadem avowed angrily. 'My father was the Caliph's brother. I am his nephew. The Caliph trusts me because I command his legions and I have proven myself to him a hundred times over in war and in peace.'

'Yet you have failed to accomplish this sacred *fatwa* of yours,' Koots taunted him. 'Your enemies still flourish, and you are in rags, tied to a tree and covered with filth. Is that the Omani ideal of a mighty warrior?'

'I have slain the incestuous sister of the Caliph, which was part of the task I was given, and I have stabbed al-Salil so deeply and grievously that he might still perish of the wound. If he does not, I will not rest until my duty is accomplished.'

'All this is the raving of a madman.' Koots smirked at him. 'If you are driven by this sacred duty, why do I find you wandering like a beggar in the wilderness, dressed in filthy rags, carrying a musket with al-Salil's emblem branded on it, trying to steal a horse on which to escape?'

Skilfully Koots milked the information out of his captive. Kadem boasted of how he had inveigled himself on board the *Gift of Allah*. How he had waited his opportunity, and how he had struck. He described his assassination of the Princess Yasmini, and how he had come so close to killing al-Salil also. Then he described how, with the help of his three followers,

457

he had escaped from the Courtney ship while it lay in the lagoon, how they had avoided the pursuit and at last had stumbled on Koots's troop.

There was much in this account that was entirely new to Koots, especially the flight of the Courtneys from the colony of Good Hope. This must have taken place long after he had left in pursuit of Jim Courtney. However, all of it was logical and he could detect no weak spots in the story, nor any attempt to deceive him in Kadem's rendition of it. Everything seemed to fit neatly into what he knew of Keyser and his intentions. It was also the kind of resourceful enterprise that Tom and Dorian Courtney between them might devise.

He believed it, with reservations. There were always reservations. Yes! he gloated inwardly, without letting it show in his expression. This is an extraordinary stroke of fortune, he thought. I have been sent an ally I can bind to me by chains of steel, a religious *fatwa* and a burning hatred beside which even my own determination pales.

Koots stared hard at Kadem while he made his decision. He had lived among the Mussulmen, fought for and against them long enough to understand the teachings of Islam and the immutable codes of honour that bound them.

'I also am the sworn enemy of the Courtneys,' he said at last. He saw the naked passion in Kadem's eyes veiled immediately.

Have I made a fatal mistake? he wondered. Have I rushed too swiftly to my purpose, and startled my quarry? He watched Kadem's suspicion growing stronger. However, I have taken the plunge now, and I cannot go back. Koots turned to Oudeman. 'Loosen his bonds,' he ordered, 'and bring water for him to wash and drink. Give him food to eat and let him pray. But watch him carefully. I don't think he will try to escape, but do not give him the chance.'

Oudeman looked mystified by these orders. 'What about his men?' he asked uncertainly.

'Keep them tied up and under close guard,' Koots told him. 'Don't let Kadem speak to them. Don't let him go near them.'

Koots waited until after Kadem had bathed, eaten and

carried out the solemn ritual of the midday prayers. Only then did he send for him to continue their conversation.

Koots observed the polite form of greeting and, in so doing, changed Kadem's status from that of captive to guest, with all the responsibilities that that relationship placed on both of them. Then he went on. 'The reason why you find me here, in the wilderness so far from the civilized abodes of men, is that I am following the same quest as you. Behold these wagon tracks.' He pointed them out, and Kadem glanced at them. Of course he had noticed them while he had stalked the horses and closed in on the camp.

'Do you see them?' Koots insisted.

Kadem's face set in a stony expression. He was already regretting his previous indiscretions. He should never have let his emotions run away with his tongue and revealed so much to the infidel. By now he had recognized that Koots was a clever, dangerous man.

'These tracks were made by four wagons that are being driven by the only son of Tom Courtney, whom you know as Klebe.' Kadem blinked but showed no other expression. Koots let him think about that for a while. Then he explained why Jim Courtney had been forced to leave the colony.

Although Kadem listened in silence and his eyes showed no more emotion than those of a cobra, he was thinking furiously. While he had been masquerading as a lowly seaman aboard the *Gift of Allah* he had heard all this discussed by his companions. He knew about Jim Courtney's flight from Good Hope.

'If we follow these wagon tracks, we can be certain that they will lead us to the place somewhere on the coast where father and son have agreed to meet,' Koots finished, and again they were silent.

Kadem thought about what Koots had told him. He turned it over and back and forth in his mind, the way a jeweller examines a precious stone for impurities. He could detect no false notes in Koots's version of events. 'What do you want of me?' he asked, at last.

'We share the same purpose,' Koots answered. 'I propose a

459

pact, an alliance. Let us take the oath together in the sight of God and his Prophet. Let us dedicate ourselves to the total destruction of our mutual enemies.'

'I agree to that,' said Kadem, and the mad glitter he had so carefully masked returned to his eyes. Koots found it unsettling, more menacing than the cutlass and dagger in the Arab's hands when they had fought that morning.

They took the oath beneath the towering branches of a camel-thorn tree, in which new growth had already burgeoned to replace that which had been devoured by the locust swarms. They swore on the blade and the haft of Kadem's Damascus-steel dagger. Each placed a pinch of coarse salt on the other's tongue. They shared a slice of venison, swallowing a morsel each. With the razor-sharp Damascus blade they opened a vein in their right wrists, then massaged the arm until the blood was flowing bright and warm down into their cupped palms. Then they clasped hands so that their blood mingled, and maintained the grip while Kadem recited the wondrous names of God. At last they embraced.

'You are my brother in blood,' said Kadem, and his voice trembled in awe at the binding power of the oath.

'You are my brother in blood,' Koots said. Though his voice was firm and clear and his gaze into Kadem's eyes was steady, the oath sat lightly upon his conscience. Koots recognized no God, especially not the foreign deity of a dark-skinned, inferior race. The profit in the bargain was all his for he could turn away from it when the time came, even kill his new blood-brother with impunity if it were called for. He knew that Kadem was bound by his hope of salvation and the wrath of his God.

Deep in his heart Kadem recognized the fragility of the bond between them. That evening as they shared the campfire and ate meat together, he showed how astute he was. He gave Koots an undertaking more poignant than any religious oath. 'I have told you that I am the favourite of my uncle, the Caliph. You know also the power and riches of the Omani empire. Its realm encompasses a great ocean and the Red and Persian Seas. My uncle has promised me great reward if I carry his *fatwa* to a successful conclusion. You and I have sworn, as brothers in blood, to dedicate ourselves to that end. Once it is done we will return together to the Caliph's palace on Lamu island, and to his gratitude. You will embrace Islam. I will request my uncle to place you in command of all his armies on the African mainland. I will ask him to make you governor of the provinces of Monamatapa, the land from which come the gold and slaves of Opet. You will become a man of power and wealth uncountable.'

The spring tides of Herminius Koots's life were beginning to flow strongly.

Now they moved along the wagon trail with renewed determination. Even Xhia was infected with this enhanced sense of purpose. Twice they cut the trail of herds of elephant coming down out of the north lands. Perhaps in some mysterious way the elephant were aware of the bounty the rains had brought upon the land. From afar Koots surveyed the massed herds of these grey giants through the lens of his telescope, but he showed only a passing interest in them. He would not let a hunt for a few ivory tusks deter him from his main quest.

He ordered Xhia to detour round the herds and they went onwards, leaving them unmolested. Both Koots and Kadem grudged every hour of delay and they drove horses and men hard along the tracks of their quarry.

They passed out of the wide swath that the locusts had cut through the land and left the great plains behind them. They entered a lovely land of rivers and lush forests, and the air tasted as sweet as the perfume of wild flowers. Scenes of great beauty and grandeur surrounded them, and the promise of riches and glory led them onwards.

'We are not far behind the wagons now,' Xhia promised them, 'and each day we draw closer.'

Then they came to a confluence of two rivers, a wide, deep flow and a smaller tributary. Xhia was amazed by what he

461

found there. He led Koots and Kadem through the field of rotting, sun-dried human remains, which had been chewed and scattered by the hyena and other scavengers. He did not have to point out to them the discarded spears and *assegais* and the rawhide shields, most of them shot through by musket fire. 'There was great battle here,' Xhia told them. 'These shields and weapons are those of the fierce Nguni tribes.'

Koots nodded. No man who had lived and travelled in Africa as he had could have been ignorant of the legend of the warrior tribes of the Nguni. 'Good, so!' he said. 'Tell us what else you see here.'

'The Nguni attacked the wagons Somoya had drawn up here, across the neck between the two rivers. That was a good place for him, his back and both his sides protected by the water. The Nguni had to come at him from the front. He killed them like chickens.' Xhia giggled and shook his head with admiration.

Koots walked across to the crater in the middle of the area of devastated ground in front of which the wagons had stood. 'What is this?' he asked. 'What happened here?'

Xhia picked a short length of charred slow-match out of the dirt, and brandished it. Even though he had seen fuse and explosives used before, he did not have the vocabulary to describe it. Instead he mimed the act of lighting the slow-match and made a sizzling sound as he ran along the path the flame must have taken. When he reached the crater he shouted, 'Ba-poof!' and leaped high into the air to illustrate the explosion. Then he fell on his back and kicked both legs, shrieking with laughter. It was so expressive that even Koots had to laugh.

'By the pox-ridden vagina of the great whore,' he guffawed, 'the Courtney puppy let off a mine under the *impis* as they stormed the wagons. We will have to take care when we catch up with him. He has grown as crafty as his father.'

It took Xhia the rest of the day to unravel all the secrets of the battlefield, spread out as it was over such a vast stretch of the veld. He showed Koots the path the routed *impis* had taken, and how Jim Courtney and his men had chased them on horseback and shot them down as they ran.

They came at last to the abandoned Nguni encampment, and Xhia became almost incoherent as he realized the extent of the cattle herds Jim had captured. 'Like the grass! Like the locusts!' he squeaked, as he pointed out the spoor the herds had trodden as they were driven away eastwards.

'A thousand?' Koots wondered. 'Five thousand, or maybe more?'

He tried to form a rough estimate of the value of these cattle if he could get them to Good Hope.

There are not enough guilders in the Bank of Batavia, he concluded. One thing is certain. When I catch up with them, Oudeman and these stinking Hottentots will not see a single centime. I will kill them first, before I hand over a guilder. By the time I am finished here I will make Governor van de Witten look like a pauper in comparison.

That was not the end of it. When they entered the camp Xhia led him to the far side of the encampment where a stockade stood, made of stout timber poles lashed together with strips of bark.

Koots had never seen such a sturdy construction, even in the permanent villages of the tribes. Is it a grain store? he wondered, as he dismounted and entered. He was further puzzled when he found that it contained what seemed to be drying or smoking racks. However, there was no sign of ash or scorched areas beneath them. As with the construction of the walls, the timber used seemed too massive for such a simple purpose. It was clear that the racks had been designed to support a much greater weight than strips of meat.

Xhia was trying to tell him something. He jumped up on the racks and repeated the word 'chicken'. Koots frowned irritably. This was no hen coop, nor even an ostrich coop. Koots shook his head. Xhia began another mime, holding one arm in front of his face like a long nose, and flapping his other hand from the side of his head like an ear. Koots puzzled over the meaning, then remembered that the San words for 'chicken' and 'elephant' were almost identical.

'Elephant?' he asked, and touched the elephant-hide belt at his waist.

'Yes! Yes! You stupid man.' Xhia nodded vigorously.

'Are you mad?' Koots asked in Dutch. 'An elephant would never fit through that doorway.'

Xhia leaped down from the rack and ferreted around under it. Then he crawled out again. He showed Koots what he had found. It was an immature tusk, taken from an elephant calf. It was only as long as Xhia's forearm and so slim that he could encircle it at the thickest point with thumb and finger. It must have been overlooked when the storeroom was emptied. Xhia waved it in Koots's face.

'Ivory?' Koots began to understand. Five years previously, when he was acting as aide-de-camp to the governor of Batavia, the governor had made an official visit to the Sultan of Zanzibar. The Sultan was proud of his collection of ivory tusks. He had invited the governor and his staff to tour his treasury and view the contents. The ivory had been laid out on racks much like these, to keep it off the damp floor.

'Ivory!' Koots breathed hard. 'These are ivory racks!' He imagined the tusks stacked high, and tried to estimate the value of such a treasure. 'In the name of the black angel, this is another great fortune to match the plundered herds of cattle.'

He turned and strode out of the shed. 'Sergeant!' he bellowed. 'Sergeant Oudeman, get the men mounted up. Kick the brown backsides of our Arab friends. We ride at once. We must catch Jim Courtney before he reaches the coast and comes under the protection of the guns on his father's ships.'

They rode eastwards along the spoor of the cattle herds, a beaten roadway almost a mile wide, along which the cattle had grazed and trodden down the grass.

'A blind man could follow this on a moonless night,' Koots told Kadem, who rode beside him.

'What a fine bait this piglet of the great hog will make for our trap,' Kadem agreed, with grim determination. They expected to come up with the wagons and the herds of plundered cattle at any moment. However, day succeeded day, and although they rode hard and Koots took every opportunity to spy out the land ahead through his telescope they caught no glimpse of either cattle or wagons.

Each day Xhia assured them that they were gaining rapidly. From the sign he was able to tell Koots that Jim Courtney was hunting for elephant while his caravan was on the march.

'This is slowing him down?' Koots asked.

'No, no, he hunts far ahead of the wagons.'

'Then we can surprise the caravan while he is not with them to defend them.'

'We have to catch up with them first,' said Kadem, and Xhia cautioned Koots that if they approached Jim Courtney's caravan too closely before they were ready to attack it, Bakkat would immediately discover their presence. 'In just the same way as I discovered that these brown baboons,' he indicated Kadem and his Arabs disdainfully, 'were creeping up on us. Although Bakkat is no match for Xhia, the mighty hunter, in stealth and wizard-craft, neither is he a fool. I have seen his footprints and his sign where he swept his back trail every evening before the wagons went into camp.'

'How do you know it is Bakkat's sign?' Koots demanded.

'Bakkat is my enemy, and I can pick out his footprints from those of any other man that walks this land.' Then Xhia pointed out other circumstances that Koots had not taken into consideration before. The signs showed clearly that Jim Courtney had made other additions to his retinue apart from the herds of captured cattle: men, many men – Xhia thought there were at least fifty and that there might be as many as a hundred additional men to face them when they attacked the wagons. Xhia had employed all his genius and wizardry to determine the character and condition of these new men.

'They are big, proud men. That I can tell by the manner in which they carry themselves, by the size of their feet and the length of their stride,' he told Koots. 'They bear arms and are freemen, not captives or slaves. They follow Somoya willingly and they guard and care for his herds. It comes to me that these are Nguni who will fight like warriors.' Koots was learning from experience that it was best to accept the little

Bushman's opinion. So far he had never been wrong in such matters.

With such quantity and quality of reinforcements added to the hard core of mounted musketeers, Jim Courtney had now mustered a formidable force which Koots dared not underestimate.

'We are outnumbered many times over. It will be a hard fight.' Koots weighed these new odds.

'Surprise,' said Kadem. 'We have the element of surprise. We can choose our time and place to attack.'

'Yes,' Koots agreed. By this time his opinion of the Arab as a warrior had been much enhanced. 'We must not waste that advantage.'

Eleven days later they came to the brink of a deep escarpment. There were tall snow-capped mountain peaks to the south, but ahead the land dropped away steeply in a confusion of hills, valleys and forest. Koots dismounted and steadied his spyglass on Xhia's shoulder. Then, suddenly, he shouted aloud as he picked out in the blue distance the even bluer tint of the ocean. 'Yes!' he cried. 'I was right all along. Jim Courtney is headed for Nativity Bay to join up with his father's ships. That is the coast less than a hundred leagues ahead.' Before he could fully articulate his satisfaction at having pursued the quest so far, something even more compelling caught Koots's eye.

In the wide expanse of land and forest below him he descried drifts of pale dust dispersed over a wide area, and when he turned the glass on these clouds he saw beneath them the movement of the massed herds of cattle, slow and dark as spilled oil spreading on the carpet of the veld.

'Mother of Satan!' he cried. 'There they are! I have them at last.' With a mighty effort he checked his warlike instinct to ride down on them immediately. Instead he cautioned himself to consider all the circumstances and eventualities that he and Kadem had discussed so earnestly over the past days.

'They are moving slowly, at the speed of the grazing herds. We can afford the time to rest our own men and horses and prepare ourselves for the attack. In the meantime I will send Xhia ahead to scout Jim Courtney's dispositions, to learn his line of march, the character of his new men, and the order of battle of his horsemen.'

Kadem nodded agreement as he surveyed the ground below them. 'We might circle out ahead and lie in ambush. Perhaps in a narrow pass through the hills or at a river crossing. Order Xhia to have an eye for a place such as that.'

'Whatever happens, we must not let them join up with the ships that might already be waiting for them in Nativity Bay,' said Koots. 'We must attack before that happens, or we will be facing cannon and grape-shot as well as muskets and spears.'

Koots lowered the telescope, and grabbed Xhia by the scruff of his neck to impress upon him the seriousness of his orders. Xhia listened earnestly, and understood at least every second word that Koots growled at him.

'I will find you here when I return,' Xhia agreed, when Koots ended his harangue. Then he trotted away down the escarpment wall without looking back. He did not have to make any further preparations for the task ahead of him, for Xhia carried upon his sturdy back every possession he owned.

It was a little before noon when he set out, and late afternoon before he was close enough to the cattle herds to hear their distant lowing. He was careful to cover his own sign, and not to approach any closer. Despite his braggadocio he held Bakkat's powers in high respect. He circled round the herds to find the exact position of Somoya's wagons. The cattle had trodden the tracks and confused the sign, so it was difficult even for him to read as much from them as he wanted.

He came up level with the wagons but a league out to the north of their line of march when suddenly he stopped. His heart began to pound like the hoofbeats of a galloping herd of zebra. He stared down at the dainty little footprint in the dust.

'Bakkat,' he whispered. 'My enemy. I would know your sign anywhere, for it is imprinted on my heart.'

All Koots's orders and exhortations were wiped from his mind and he concentrated all his powers on the spoor. 'He goes quickly and with purpose. In a straight line, not pausing

467

or hesitating. He shows no caution. If ever I can surprise him, this is the day.'

Without another thought he turned aside from his original purpose and followed the tracks of Bakkat, whom he hated above all else in his world.

In the early morning Bakkat heard the honey-guide. It was fluttering in the treetops, chittering and uttering that particular whirring sound that could mean only one thing. His mouth watered.

'I greet you, my sweet friend,' he called, and ran to stand beneath the tree in which the drab little bird was performing its seductive gyrations. Its movements became more frenzied when it saw that it had attracted Bakkat's attention. It left the branch on which it was displaying and flitted to the next tree.

Bakkat hesitated, and glanced round at the square of wagons laagered at the edge of the forest on the far side of the glade, a mile away. If he were to take the time to run back merely to tell Somoya where he was going, the bird might become discouraged and fly away before he returned. Somoya might forbid him to follow it. Bakkat smacked his lips: he could almost taste the sweet, viscous honey on his tongue. He lusted for it. 'I will not be away long,' he consoled himself. 'Somoya will not even know that I am gone. He and Welanga are probably playing with their little wooden dolls.' This was Bakkat's opinion of the carved chessmen that so often occupied the couple to the exclusion of everything around them. Bakkat ran after the bird.

The honey-guide saw him coming and sang to him as it flitted on to the next tree, then the next. Bakkat sang as he followed: 'You lead me to sweetness, and I love you for it. You are more beautiful than the sunbird, wiser than the owl, greater than the eagle. You are the lord of all birds.' Which was not true, but the honey-guide would be flattered to hear it.

Bakkat ran through the forest for the rest of that morning,

and in the noonday when the forest sweltered in the heat, and all the animals and birds were silent and somnolent, the bird stopped at last in the top branches of a tambootie tree, and changed its melody.

Bakkat understood what it was telling him: 'We have arrived. This is the place of the hive, and it overflows with golden honey. Now you and I will eat our fill.'

Bakkat stood beneath the tambootie and threw back his head as he peered upwards. He saw the bees, highlighted by the low sunlight like golden dust motes, as they darted into the cleft in the tree trunk. Bakkat took from his shoulder his bow and quiver, his axe and leather carrying bag. He laid them carefully at the base of the tree. The honey-guide would understand that this was his guarantee that he would return. However, to make certain there was no misunderstanding, Bakkat explained it to the bird: 'Wait for me here, my little friend. I will not be gone long. I must gather the vine to lull the bees.'

He found the plant he needed growing on the bank of a nearby stream. It climbed the trunk of a lead-wood tree, wrapping round it like a slender serpent. The leaves were shaped like teardrops, and the tiny flowers were scarlet. Bakkat was gentle as he harvested the leaves he needed, careful not to damage the plant more than he had to for it was a precious thing. To kill it would be a sin against nature and his own people, the San.

With the wad of leaves in his pouch he moved on until he reached a grove of fever trees. He picked out one whose trunk was the right girth for his needs and ring-barked it. Then he peeled off a section and rolled it into a tube, which he secured with twists of bark string. He ran back to the honey tree. When the bird saw him return, it burst into hysterical chitterings of relief.

Bakkat squatted at the foot of the tree and made a tiny fire inside the bark tube. He blew into one end to create a draught, and the coals glowed hotly. He scattered a few of the flowers and the leaves of the vine on to them. As they smouldered they emitted clouds of pungent smoke. Bakkat stood up, hooked the blade of the axe over his shoulder and began to climb the tree. He went up as swiftly as a vervet monkey. Just below the cleft in the trunk he found a convenient branch and took a seat on it. He sniffed the waxy odour of the hive and listened for a moment to the deep murmurous voice of the swarm in the depths of the hollow trunk. He studied the entrance to the hive and marked his first cut, then placed one end of the bark tube into the opening and gently blew puffs of the smoke into it. After a while the humming of the swarm fell into silence as the bees were sedated and lulled.

Bakkat laid aside the smoke tube and braced himself, balancing easily on the narrow branch. He swung the axe. As the blow reverberated through the trunk a few bees came out and buzzed around his head, but the smoke of the vine leaves had dulled their warlike instincts. One or two stung him, but Bakkat ignored them. With quick, powerful axe strokes he cut a square hatchway in the hollow trunk, and exposed the serried ranks of honeycombs.

Then he climbed down to the ground and laid aside the axe. He returned to his perch on the branch with the leather bag over his shoulder. He scattered more vine leaves on the coals in the fire tube, and blew clouds of the thick, pungent smoke into the enlarged entrance. When the swarm was silent again he reached deep into the hive. With bees flowing over his arms and shoulders, he lifted out the combs one at a time and laid them gently in the bag. When the hive was empty he thanked the bees for their bounty, and apologized to them for his cruel treatment.

'Very soon you will recover from the smoke I have given you, and you will be able to repair your hive and fill it once again with honey. Bakkat will always be your friend, and he feels only great respect and gratitude towards you,' he told the bees.

He climbed down to the ground and cut a curl of bark from the trunk of the tambootie tree to form a tray on which he could lay out the honey-guide's share of the booty. He selected the choicest comb for his little friend and accomplice, one that was full of the yellow grubs, for he knew the bird loved these almost as much as he did.

He gathered up all his possessions and slung the bulging leather bag over his shoulder. For the last time he thanked the bird and bade it farewell. As soon as he stepped back the bird dropped down from the top of the tree, fell upon the fat golden comb and pecked out the juicy grubs at once. Bakkat smiled and watched it indulgently for a while. He knew it would eat it all, even the wax, for it was the only creature that was able to digest this part of the bounty.

He reminded the little bird of the legend of the greedy San who had cleaned out the hive and left nothing for the bird. The next time the bird had led him to a hole in the trunk of a tree in which was coiled a huge black mamba. The snake stung the cheating San to death.

'The next time we meet, remember that I treated you well and fairly,' Bakkat told the bird. 'I will look for you again. May the Kulu Kulu watch over you.' And he set off back towards the wagons. As he went, he reached into the bag, broke off pieces of comb and stuffed them into his mouth, humming with deep pleasure.

Within half a mile he stopped abruptly at a crossing place on the stream and stared in astonishment at the prints of human feet in the clay of the bank. The people who had passed this way recently had made no effort to hide their tracks. They were San.

Bakkat's heart leaped like a gazelle. Only when he saw the fresh footprints did he realize how he had pined for his own people. He examined the sign avidly. There were five of them, two men and three women. One man was old, and the other much younger. He divined this from the reach and alacrity of their separate strides. One of the women was ancient, and hobbled along on gnarled, twisted feet. Another was in her prime, with a strong, determined step. She led the Indian file of her family.

Then Bakkat's eyes fell on the fifth and last set of prints, and he felt a great longing squeeze his heart. They were dainty

471

and as enchanting as any of the paintings of the artists of his tribe. Bakkat felt that he might weep with the beauty of them. He had to sit down for a while and stare at one until he could recover from the effect that they had had upon him. In his mind's eye he could see the girl who had left these signs for him to find. He divined with all his instincts that she was very young, but graceful, limber and nubile. Then he stood up again and followed her footprints into the forest.

On the far bank of the stream he came to the point where the two men had separated from the women and gone off among the trees to hunt. From that point the women had begun gathering the wild harvest of the veld. Bakkat saw where they had broken off the fruit from the branches, and dug out the edible tubers and roots with the sharp, pointed stakes that each carried.

He followed the tracks that the girl had left, and saw how swiftly and surely she worked. She made no false digs, wasting no effort, and it was clear to Bakkat that she knew every plant and tree she came upon. She passed by the poisonous and tasteless, and picked out the sweet and nourishing.

Bakkat giggled with admiration. 'This is a clever little one. She could feed her whole family with what she has gathered since she crossed the stream. What a wife she would make for a man.'

Then he heard voices in the forest ahead, feminine voices calling to each other as they worked. One was as musical and sweet as the call of the oriole, that golden songster of the high galleries of the forest.

It led him as irresistibly as the honey-guide had. Silent and unseen he crept towards the girl. She was working in a clump of thick scrub. He could hear her digging stick thudding into the earth. At last he was close enough to make out her movements, veiled by the latticework of branches and leaves. Then, suddenly, she moved into the open, directly in front of Bakkat. All the solitary years and loneliness were swept away like debris in the new, surging flow of his emotions.

She was exquisite, tiny and perfect. Her skin glowed in the noonday sunlight. Her face was a golden flower. Her lips were full and petal-shaped. She lifted one graceful hand and, with her thumb, wiped the clinging drops of perspiration from her arched eyebrow and flicked them away. They sparkled as they flew through the air. He was so close that one splashed on his dusty shin. She was oblivious of his presence, and began to walk away. Then one of the other women called to her from nearby, 'Are you thirsty, Letee? Shall we go back to the stream?' The girl stopped and looked back. She wore only a tiny leather apron in front, decorated with cowrie shells and beads made from chippings of ostrich-egg shell. The pattern of the shells and beads proclaimed that she was a virgin, and that no man had yet spoken for her.

'My mouth is as dry as a desert stone. Let us go.' Letee laughed as she replied to her mother. Her teeth were small and very white.

In that moment Bakkat's entire existence changed. As she walked away her little breasts joggled merrily and her plump, naked buttocks undulated. He made no attempt to stop or delay her. He knew that he could find her again anywhere and at any time.

When she had disappeared, he stood up slowly from his hiding-place. Suddenly he gave a leap of joy high into the air, and rushed away to make himself a love arrow. He selected a perfect reed from the edge of the stream, and lavished upon it all his talents as an artist. He painted it with mystic patterns and designs. The colours he chose from his paint horns were yellow, white, red and black. He fledged it with the purple feathers of the lourie, and padded the tip with a ball of tanned springbuck skin stuffed with sunbird feathers so that it would inflict no pain or injury on Letee.

'It is beautiful!' Bakkat admired his own handiwork when it was finished. 'But not as beautiful as Letee.'

That night he found the encampment of Letee's family. They were temporarily inhabiting a cave in the rocky cliff above the stream. He crept close in the darkness and listened to their banal inconsequential chatter. From it he learned that the old man and woman were her grandparents, and the other couple her mother and father. Her elder sister had recently

473

found herself a fine husband and left the clan. The others were teasing Letee. She had seen her first menstrual moonrise fully three months previously, yet she was still a virgin and unmarried. Letee hung her head in shame at her failure to find herself a man.

Bakkat left the mouth of the cave and found a place to sleep further down the stream. But he was back before dawn, and when the women left the cave to go out into the forest he followed them at a discreet distance. When they started to forage they kept in touch with each other by calling and whistling, but after a while Letee became separated from them. Bakkat closed in on her with all his stalking skills.

She was digging for the fat tuber of the tiski plant, a variety of wild manioc. She kept her legs straight as she bent over and rocked to the rhythm of her digging stick. The protruding lips of her sex peeped out from between the backs of her thighs, and her plump little rear end was pointed to the sky.

Bakkat crept close. His hands shook as he raised the tiny ceremonial bow and aimed his love arrow. Yet his aim was true as ever and Letee squeaked with surprise, and sprang high in the air as the arrow smacked into her bottom. She wheeled round clutching herself with both hands, her expression betraying her astonishment and outrage. Then she saw the arrow lying at her feet and gazed around her at the silent bush. Bakkat had disappeared like a puff of smoke. The stinging in her bottom abated as she rubbed it. Then, slowly, she was overcome with shyness.

Suddenly Bakkat appeared, so close that she gasped with shock. She stared at him. His chest was broad and deep. His legs and arms were sturdy. She saw at an instant, by the easy way in which he bore his weapons, that he was a mighty hunter, and that he would provide well for a family. He carried the colour pots of the artist on his belt, which meant that he would have high standing and much prestige within all the tribes of the San. She dropped her eyes demurely and whispered, 'You are so tall. I saw you from afar.'

'I also saw you from afar,' Bakkat replied, 'for your beauty lights the forest like the rising of the sun.'

474

'I knew you would come,' she answered him, 'for your face was painted on my heart on the day of my birth.' Letee came forward timidly, took his hand and led him to her mother. In her other hand she carried the love arrow. 'This is Bakkat,' she told her mother, and held up the arrow. Her mother shrieked, which brought the grandmother running, cackling like a hen guinea-fowl. The two older women went ahead of them to the cave, singing, dancing and clapping. Bakkat and Letee followed them, still holding hands.

Bakkat gave Letee's grandfather the bag of wild honey. He could not have brought them a more acceptable gift. Not only were they all addicted to the sweetness, but it proved Bakkat's ability to provide for a wife and children. The family feasted on it, but Bakkat ate none because he was the giver. With every mouthful Letee smacked her lips and smiled at him. They talked until late in the light of the campfire. Bakkat told them who he was, the totem of his tribe and the list of his ancestors. The grandfather knew many of them, and clapped his hands as he recognized their names. Letee sat with the other women and they did not join in the talk of the men. At last, Letee stood up and crossed to where Bakkat sat between the other two men. She took his hand and led him to where she had laid out her sleeping mat at the back of the cave.

The two left early in the morning. All Letee's possessions were packed into the roll of her sleeping mat, and she carried it balanced effortlessly on her head. Bakkat went ahead of her. They moved at a trot, a pace they could keep up from morning until evening. Bakkat sang the hunting songs of his tribe as he ran, and Letee joined in the chorus in her sweet, childlike voice.

Xhia was concealed in the thickets across the stream from the mouth of the cave. He watched the couple emerge into the early sunlight. He had been spying on Bakkat during all the preceding days of his courtship. Despite his hatred for Bakkat, Xhia was intrigued by the ancient marriage ritual. He felt a lascivious thrill from watching the man and woman play out their appointed roles. He wanted to witness the final act of mating before he interceded, and exacted his revenge from Bakkat.

'Bakkat has plucked himself another pretty flower.' The fact that she was the woman of his enemy made her all the more desirable to Xhia. 'But he will not enjoy her long.'

Xhia hugged himself with glee, and let the couple trot off into the forest. He would not follow too closely for he knew that although Bakkat was distracted by his new companion he was still a formidable adversary. Xhia was in no hurry. He was a hunter and the first attribute of the hunter is patience. He knew there would be a time when Bakkat and the girl were separated, if only for a short time. That would be his chance.

A little before noon Bakkat came upon a small herd of buffalo. Xhia watched as he left his bag and accoutrements in Letee's care, and crept forward. He picked out a half-grown heifer whose flesh would be sweet and tender, not gamey and tough as that of an older beast. She was also much smaller in size so that the poison would work more swiftly. Keeping downwind, Bakkat manoeuvred skilfully into a position directly behind the heifer so that he could send an arrow into the thin skin surrounding her anus and genitals. The thicker hide of her body would resist the frail arrow. The network of veins around the heifer's body openings would convey the poison swiftly to her heart. His shot was true, and the animal galloped away in alarm with the rest of the herd. The shaft of the arrow broke off, but the barbed, poisoned head was buried deeply. She ran for only a short distance before the poison started to take effect, and she slowed to a walk.

Bakkat and Letee followed patiently. The sun had moved only a few fingers across the sky before the heifer halted and lay down. Bakkat and his little woman squatted nearby. At last the beast groaned and rolled over on to her side. Bakkat and Letee broke into a song of praise and thanks to the heifer for giving them her flesh to sustain them, and ran forward to butcher the carcass.

That evening while it was still light they made their camp

beside it. No matter that the flesh would soon turn in the heat, they would remain here until the entire cow was consumed, guarding it from the vultures and other scavengers. Letee made the fire and roasted strips of liver and the backstraps of meat. When they had finished eating, Bakkat led her to the sleeping mat and they coupled. Xhia crept closer to spy upon this final act of the courtship. In the end, when Bakkat and Letee writhed together as one and cried out in a single voice, he doubled over and, in a shuddering spasm, ejaculated in concert with them. Then, before Bakkat could recover, he slipped back into the bushes.

'It has been done,' Xhia whispered to himself, 'and now the time has come for Bakkat to die. He is lulled and softened by love. There will never be a better time than this.'

In the dawn Xhia was watching when Letee rose from the mat beside her husband and knelt before the ashes of the fire to blow life back into them. When the flames burned up brightly, she left the camp and came into the bushes close to where Xhia waited. She looked about her carefully, then untied the string of her beaded apron, laid it aside and squatted. While she was busy, Xhia crept up on her. As she stood again he sprang upon her from behind. Xhia was swift and powerful. She had no chance to cry out before he had covered her mouth and nose with her own apron. He held her down easily while he gagged and trussed her with the bark rope he had plaited the previous evening. Then he lifted her on to his shoulder and carried her away. He made no effort to cover his tracks. The girl was the bait. Bakkat would follow her and Xhia would be ready for him.

Xhia had scouted the ground the previous evening, and he knew exactly where to take the girl. He had chosen an isolated *kopje* not far from the campsite. The sides were sheer and rocky, so that from the heights he could keep a watch over the approaches. He had discovered only one path to the top, and its entire length was exposed to an archer on the summit.

The girl was small and light. Xhia ran with her easily. At first she kicked and struggled, but he chuckled and told her, 'Every time you do that I will punish you.' She took no heed

477

of the warning and kicked wildly with both legs. She was moaning and mumbling into her gag.

'Xhia warned you to be still,' he told her, and pinched one of her nipples with his fingernails. They were sharp as flint knives, and blood oozed from the wounds they inflicted. She tried to scream, her face contorted with the effort. She writhed and fought, and tried to bump him in the face with her head. He took her other nipple and pinched it until his nails almost met in her tender flesh. She froze with agony and he started up the steep pathway to the top of the *kopje*. Just below the summit there was a cleft between two rocks. He laid her in it, then examined her bonds. He had tied them in haste. Now he retied the knots at ankles and wrists. Satisfied that they were tight, he removed the folds of her leather apron from between her jaws. Immediately she screamed with all the force of her lungs.

'Yes!' He laughed at her. 'Do that again. It will bring Bakkat to me even as the squeals of a wounded gazelle bring the leopard.'

She hissed and spat at him. 'My husband is a mighty hunter. He will kill you for this.'

'Your husband is a coward and a braggart. Before the sun sets today, I will make you a widow. Tonight you will share my sleeping mat. Tomorrow you will be married again.' He performed a few shuffling dance steps, and lifted his apron to show her that he was already tumescent.

Xhia had hidden his axe, bow and quiver among the rocks and he retrieved them. He tested his bowstring, flexing the bow to full draw. Then he removed the leather cover of his quiver and brought out his arrows. They were frail reeds, fletched with eagle feathers. Each of the arrowheads was carefully wrapped with a leather covering bound in place with twine. Xhia cut the twine and unwrapped the covers. He worked with great care. The arrowheads were carved from bone, barbed and needle sharp. They were blackened with poison made from the body juices of the larvae of a particular beetle boiled until they were thick and sticky as honey. A scratch from one of the poisoned arrows would inflict a death

478

so certain and agonizing that Xhia kept the tips covered in case he accidentally scratched himself.

Letee knew these deadly weapons. She had seen her father and grandfather bring down the heaviest game with them. From infancy she had been warned that she must not touch even the quiver that contained them. She stared at them now in dread. Xhia held up one in front of her face. 'This is the one I have chosen for Bakkat.' He stabbed the deadly point at her face, stopping it only a finger's length before her eyes. She recoiled in horror against the rocks, and screamed again with all her strength.

'Bakkat, my husband! Danger! An enemy waits for you!'

Xhia stood up with his bow across his muscular shoulder and the unbarred arrows in his quiver, ready to hand. 'My name is Xhia,' he said to Letee. 'Tell him my name, so he will know who it is that waits for him.'

'Xhia!' she screamed. 'It is Xhia!' and the echoes flung the name back at her. 'Xhia! Xhia!'

'Xhia!' Bakkat heard the name, which only confirmed what he had already read in the sign. It was the sound of Letee's voice that cut him to the heart, with both joy and dread: joy that she was alive, and dread that she had fallen into the hands of such a terrible enemy. He looked up at the kopje from which her cries had come. He made out the one sure and easy route to the summit, and the urge to rush up it was almost too strong to resist. He dug the nails of his right hand into the palm so that the pain would steady him, then studied the bare cliffs of the hill.

'Xhia has chosen his ground well,' he said aloud. Once again he considered that single route to the summit and saw it was a deathtrap. Xhia would be perched above him, shooting his arrows down at him all the way.

Bakkat circled the kopje, and on the far side he picked out an alternative route. It was difficult – parts of it were so steep and dangerous that they might be impassable: a slip would mean he would plunge down on to the rocks below. However, most of the path was concealed from above by an overhang, jutting out just below the summit. Only the last part of the climb would be exposed to a watcher at the top of the *kopje*.

Bakkat ran back to the camp. He laid aside his bow and quiver. He would be on the summit and the range was too close for bow work before he and Xhia came together. He selected only his knife and the axe, both better suited to close fighting. Then he laid out the wet buffalo skin, and from it swiftly shaped and cut out a cape that would cover his head and shoulders. The thick hide had already begun to stink in the heat, but it would provide an effective armour against a reed arrow. He rolled the heavy cape and strapped it on to his back. Then he ran back to the *kopje*, but circled round to come directly to the protected route he had chosen. Stealthily he crept through the bush at the foot of the hill and reached the cliff under cover of the overhang, almost certain that Xhia had not spotted him. But with Xhia you could never be certain.

He rested for only a few moments, gathering himself for the climb, but before he could begin Letee's screams rang out again, high above him. Then Xhia's voice called down to him: 'Watch me, Bakkat. See what I am doing to this woman of yours. Ah, yes! There! My fingers are deep inside her. She is tight and slippery.'

Bakkat tried to close his ears to Xhia's taunts, but he could not. 'Listen to your woman, Bakkat. These are only my fingers, but next she will feel something much bigger. How she will squeal when she feels that.'

Letee was sobbing and shrieking, and Xhia was giggling. The stone cliffs of the *kopje* magnified and echoed the dreadful sounds. Bakkat had to force himself to remain silent. He knew that Xhia wanted him to voice his rage, and in so doing betray his position. Xhia could not be sure which path Bakkat would use to try to reach the summit.

Bakkat went to the wall of red rock and began to climb it. He went swiftly at first, running up the wall like a gecko lizard. Then he reached the overhang, and was hanging out backwards reaching for every finger- and toe-hold, dragging himself round by the strength of his arms. The axe and the roll of wet skin hampered his movements, and gradually his progress slowed. The drop gaped beneath his dangling feet.

He reached for another handhold, but as he placed his weight on it, it broke off. A lump of rock twice his own size came loose from the roof above him. It grazed his head, and hurtled down the cliff to crash against the wall lower down. The echoes boomed out across the valley as it bounded on, kicking up a storm of dust and rock splinters every time it struck.

For terrible seconds Bakkat hung by the fingers of one hand. He scrabbled desperately with the other, and at last found a hold. He hung there for a while, trying to gather himself.

There were no more taunts from Xhia. He knew now exactly where Bakkat was, and would be waiting for him at the top of the cliff, a poison arrow nocked to his bow. Bakkat had no choice. The slab that had broken away had altered the shape of the wall, and cut off his retreat. There was only one route open to him, and that was upwards, to where Xhia was waiting.

Painfully slowly, Bakkat worked his way over the last stretch, and round the outer angle of the overhang. At any instant he would have a view to the summit ridge, but Xhia would be able to see him. Then, with a rush of relief, Bakkat found a narrow ledge below the lip. It was only just wide enough for him to squeeze himself on to it. He crouched there for what seemed a lifetime, and slowly the strength returned to his numbed, shaking arms. Carefully he unrolled the buffalo-skin cape and draped it over his head and shoulders. He made certain that his knife and axe were still in his belt. He came gingerly to his feet on the tiny ledge and flattened his body against the wall to maintain his balance. He was standing on his toes, his heels hanging out over the drop. He reached up and ran both hands along the lip of the cliff as high as he could reach. He found a niche just wide and deep enough for him to insert both hands and take a firm grip. He pulled himself upwards and his toes left the ledge. For a long, terrible interlude his feet dabbed against the face without finding purchase. Then he pulled himself just high enough to throw one arm over the top of the cliff.

As his head came up he looked towards the summit ledge just above. Xhia was watching him: he was smiling and his eyes were slitted as he sighted over the arrow. His bow was at full draw, the arrowhead aimed at Bakkat's face. It was so close that Bakkat could see each of the carved barbs, as sharp as the eyetooth of the striped tigerfish: the dung-brown poison dried into a thick paste between each barb.

Xhia loosed his arrow. It came with a flitting sound as fast as a darting swallow, and Bakkat was unable to duck or dodge. It seemed that the point would find the opening in his hide cape and strike him in the throat, but at the last instant it drifted off course and struck his shoulder. He felt the jerk as the point of the arrowhead snagged in a fold of the tough buffalo hide. The shaft snapped off and fell away, but the head stayed buried in the cape. Bakkat was galvanized by the threat of horrible death. He threw himself upwards the last few feet but as he teetered on the brink of the cliff Xhia nocked another arrow and aimed from a distance of only a few paces.

Bakkat hurled himself forward, and Xhia loosed the second arrow. Once again Bakkat caught it in the heavy folds of his cape. Though the arrowhead was stuck in the tough hide, the shaft broke off. Xhia reached for another arrow from his quiver, but Bakkat charged into him, and sent him reeling backwards. He dropped the bow and clung to Bakkat, pinning his arms before Bakkat could draw the knife from his belt. Chest to chest they struggled, turning in tight circles as they tried to swing each other off their feet.

Letee lay where Xhia had thrown her after he heard the fall of loose rock that had marked Bakkat's position for him. She was still trussed at hand and foot, and she was bleeding where Xhia had forced his fingers into her and his ragged fingernails had torn her most tender flesh. She watched the two men wrestling each other, powerless to help her husband. Then she saw Xhia's axe lying nearby, where he had left it.

With two quick rolls she reached it. She used her bare toes to tilt the axe-head until the sharp blade was uppermost. Then, holding it securely between her feet, she laid the bark ropes that held her wrists across it and sawed at them with all her strength.

Every few seconds she glanced up. She saw Xhia manage to hook one foot behind Bakkat's heels and trip him over backwards. They both fell heavily on to the rocks, but Bakkat was pinned under Xhia's lithe, muscular body. He could not throw him off and, powerless to intervene, Letee watched Xhia reach for the knife on his belt. Then, suddenly, unaccountably, Xhia screamed and released his grip. He recoiled from Bakkat and stared down at his own chest.

It took Bakkat a moment to realize what had happened. The arrowhead that had broken off in the folds of his cape had come between them as they wrestled, and Xhia's weight had driven the poisoned barbs deeply into his own flesh.

Xhia sprang to his feet and tried with both hands to claw the arrowhead free of his flesh, but the barbs held fast. Each time he tore at them a bright trickle of blood snaked down his bare chest.

'You are a dead man, Xhia,' Bakkat croaked, as he came to his knees.

Xhia let out another scream, but this was rage not terror. 'I will take you with me to the land of shadows!' He drew the knife from the sheath on his belt and rushed at Bakkat who was still on his knees. He lifted the knife, but when Bakkat tried to dodge the blow his legs caught in the folds of the heavy cape and he toppled backwards.

'You will die with me,' Xhia screamed, as he stabbed at his adversary's chest. Bakkat flung himself aside and the knife point grazed his upper arm. Xhia poised for the next blow, but Letee came to her feet behind him. Her ankles were still tied but her hands were free, and she held the axe. She took one hop forward and swung the axe from overhead. The blade glanced off Xhia's skull, shaving away a thick slice of his scalp and one of his ears, then went on to bite deeply into the joint between his shoulder and knife arm. The knife dropped from his paralysed fingers and the arm dangled uselessly at his side. He whirled round to face the tiny girl, clutching his wounded scalp with one hand, blood springing from between his fingers in a fountain.

'Run!' Bakkat shouted at her and started to his feet. 'Run, Letee!'

Letee ignored him. Although her ankles were tied, she jumped straight at Xhia. Fearless as a honey badger, she flew at his face and swung the axe again. Xhia reeled backwards and lifted his other arm to protect himself. The axe blade crunched into his forearm just below the elbow and the bone snapped.

Xhia staggered back, both arms maimed and useless. Letee bent swiftly and hacked away the ropes that held her ankles. Before Bakkat could intervene, she rushed at Xhia again. He saw her coming, a small fury, naked and outraged. Grievously wounded, he was tottering on the edge of the cliff. As he tried to dodge her next attack he lost his balance and went over backwards. He had no arms to save himself and he rolled down to the lip of the overhang, his blood staining the rock. He reached the edge and went over, disappearing from their view. They heard his scream receding in volume until there was a meaty thump and silence.

Bakkat ran to Letee. She dropped the axe and threw herself into his embrace. They clung together for a long time, until Letee had stopped shaking and shivering. Then Bakkat asked, 'Shall we go down, woman?' She nodded vehemently.

He led her to the head of the pathway, and they climbed down to the bottom of the hill. They paused beside Xhia's corpse. He lay on his back, and his eyes were wide and staring. His own arrow-head still protruded from his chest, and his half-severed arm was twisted under his back at an impossible angle.

'This man is of the San, as we are. Why did he try to kill us?' Letee asked.

'I will tell you the story one day,' Bakkat promised her, 'but for now let us leave him to his totem, the hyenas.' They turned away, and neither looked back as they broke into the quick trot that eats the wind.

Bakkat was taking his new woman to meet Somoya and Welanga.

Jim Courtney woke slowly in the semi-darkness before sunrise, and stretched voluptuously on the cardell bed. Then, instinctively he reached for Louisa. She was still asleep but she rolled over and threw an arm across his chest. She mumbled something that might have been either an endearment or a protest at being awakened.

Jim grinned and held her closer, then opened his eyes fully and started up. 'Where in God's name do you think you have been?' he roared. Louisa shot bolt upright beside him and they both stared at the two tiny figures perched on the foot of the bed, like sparrows on a fence pole.

Bakkat laughed merrily. It was so good to be back and have Somoya bellowing at him again. 'I saw you and Welanga from afar,' he greeted them.

Jim's expression softened. 'I thought the lions had got you. I rode after you but I lost your spoor in the hills.'

'I have been able to teach you nothing about following tracks.' Bakkat shook his head sadly.

Both Jim and Louisa turned their attention to his companion. 'Who is this?' Jim demanded.

'This is Letee, and she is my woman,' Bakkat told them.

Letee heard her name mentioned and broke into a sunny golden smile.

'She is very beautiful, and so tall,' said Louisa. Since leaving the colony she had learned to speak the patois fluently. She knew all the expressions of San courtesy.

'No, Welanga,' Bakkat contradicted her. 'She is truly very small. For my sake, it is best that Letee is not encouraged to believe that she is tall. Where might such a notion lead us?'

'Is she not at least beautiful?' Louisa insisted.

485

Bakkat looked at his woman and nodded solemnly. 'Yes, she is as beautiful as a sunbird. I dread the day she looks into a mirror for the first time, and discovers just how beautiful she is. That day might mark the beginning of my woes.'

At that Letee piped up in her sweet treble.

'What does she say?' Louisa demanded.

'She says she has never seen such hair or skin as yours. She wants to know if you are a ghost. But enough of woman's talk.' Bakkat turned to Jim. 'Somoya, a strange and terrible thing has happened.'

'What is it?' Jim became deadly serious.

'Our enemies are here. They have found us out.'

'Tell me,' Jim ordered. 'We have many enemies. Which ones are these?'

'Xhia,' Bakkat answered. 'Xhia stalked Letee and me. He tried to kill us.'

'Xhia!' Jim looked grave. 'Keyser and Koots's hunting dog? Is it possible? We have come three thousand leagues since we last laid eyes on him. Could he have followed us that far?'

'He has followed us, and we can be sure that he has led Keyser and Koots to us.'

'Have you seen them, those two Dutchmen?'

'No, Somoya, but they cannot be far off. Xhia would never come so far if he were alone.'

'Where is Xhia now?'

'He is dead, Somoya. I killed him.'

Jim blinked with surprise, then said in English, 'So he will not be answering any questions, then.' Then he reverted to the patois: 'Take your beautiful little woman with you and let Welanga and me dress without the benefit of your eyes upon us. I will talk to you again as soon as I have my breeches on.'

Bakkat was waiting by the campfire when Jim emerged from his wagon a few minutes later. Jim called him and they walked away into the forest were no one would overhear them.

'Tell me everything that happened,' Jim ordered. 'Where and when did Xhia attack you?' He listened intently to Bakkat's account. By the time the little man had finished, Jim's complacency had been shaken. 'Bakkat, if Keyser's men

486

are after us, you must find them. Can you backtrack Xhia and find where he came from?'

'That I know already. Yesterday, while Letee and I were on our way back to you, I came upon Xhia's old spoor. He had been following me for days. Ever since I left the wagons to follow a honey-guide I found.'

'Before that?' Jim demanded. 'Where did he come from before he began to follow you?'

'That way.' Bakkat pointed back at the escarpment, which was now only a faint, hazy line against the sky. 'He came along our wagon tracks, as though he had been shadowing us all the way from the Gariep river.'

'Go back!' Jim ordered. 'Find out if Keyser and Koots were with him. If they were, I want to know where they are now.'

'It is eight days since Xhia left,' said Captain Herminius Koots bitterly. 'I truly believe he has made a run for it.'

'Why would he do that?' Oudeman asked reasonably. 'Why now, when we are on the very brink of success, after all these hard and bitter months? The reward you promised him is almost in his hands.' A crafty look came into Oudeman's eyes. It was time to remind Koots about the reward once again. 'All of us have earned our share of the reward. Surely Xhia would not desert at this point, and forfeit his share?'

Koots frowned. He did not enjoy discussing the reward. These last months he had been pondering every possible expedient to avoid having to make good his promises in that regard. He turned to Kadem. 'We cannot wait here longer. The fugitives will get clean away from us. We must go on after them without Xhia. Do you not agree?' Since their first meeting the two had swiftly forged an alliance of convenience. Koots had in the front of his mind Kadem's promise to open the way for him into the favoured service of the Caliph of Oman, the power and riches that would spring from that position.

Kadem knew that Koots was his only chance of finding

Dorian Courtney again. 'I think you are right, Captain. We no longer need the little barbarian. We have found the enemy. Let us go forward and attack them.'

'Then we are in accord,' Koots said. 'We will ride hard and get well ahead of Jim Courtney. We will lay an ambush for them on ground where we have the advantage.'

It was a simple matter for Koots to keep track of Jim's caravan without closing in on him and disclosing his own presence. The dust kicked up by the cattle herds could be seen from leagues away. Having convinced himself that he no longer needed Xhia, Koots led his troop down the escarpment, then made a wide, cautious detour into the south to come out ten leagues ahead of the caravan. Now they started back to intercept it head-on. This way they would leave no tracks for Jim Courtney's Bushman tracker to pick up before they had a chance to spring their ambush.

The ground was favourable to them. It was evident that Jim Courtney was following a river valley down towards the ocean. There was grazing and good water for his herds along this way. However, at one point the river was pinched into a narrow gorge where it ran through a line of rugged hills. Koots and Kadem surveyed the bottleneck from the height of the hills above.

'They will have to come through here with the wagons,' Koots said, with satisfaction. 'The only other passage through these hills is four days' travel to the south.'

'It will take them days to traverse the gorge, which means that they must laager the wagons for at least one night in its confines,' Kadem agreed. 'We will be able to make a night attack. They will not be expecting that. The Nguni warriors they have with them will not fight in the dark. We will be the foxes in the hen coop, it will all be over before dawn breaks.'

They waited on the high ground, and at last watched the slow line of wagons enter the mouth of the gorge below them and follow the bank of the river deeper into the narrow way. Koots recognized Jim Courtney and his woman riding ahead of the lead wagon, and his smile was savage. He watched them make camp and outspan in the gut of the gorge. Koots was relieved to see that they made no attempt to laager the wagons, but merely parked them casually among the trees on the river bank, widely separated from each other. Behind the wagons the herds of cattle flowed into the mouth of the gorge. They watered at the river and the Nguni herders began to unload the ivory tusks each beast carried on its back.

This was the first time that Koots had been close enough to the caravan to see the quantity of the booty. He tried to count the cattle, but in the dust and confusion that was not possible. It was like trying to count the individual fish in a shoal of sardines. He turned his spyglass on the mounds of ivory piled up on the bank of the river. Here was a treasure greater than he had allowed himself to imagine.

He watched as the cattle settled down for the night, guarded by their Nguni herders. Then, as the sun sank and the light began to fade, Koots and Kadem left their hiding-place on the high ground and sneaked back from the skyline to where Sergeant Oudeman was holding the horses.

'Good, so, Oudeman,' Koots told him as he mounted. 'They are in a perfect position for the attack. We will go back now to join the others.'

They crossed the next ridgeline, then dropped down a steep game trail into the river gorge.

Bakkat watched them go. Even then he waited until the bottom limb of the sun touched the horizon before he stirred from his own place of concealment on the higher hilltop across the gorge. He was taking no chance on Koots doubling back. In the dusk he dropped swiftly and silently down the steep side of the gorge to report to Jim.

Jim listened until Bakkat had concluded. 'That does it,' he said, with satisfaction. 'Koots will attack tonight. Now that he has seen the cattle and the ivory, he will not be able to contain his greed. Follow them, Bakkat. Watch their every move. I will listen for your signals.'

As soon as it was dark enough to hide them from any

watcher on the hilltops, Jim inspanned the wagons again and moved them into a narrow re-entrant at the foot of the hills, with steep cliffs on three sides. They worked as silently as possible, without whipcracking or shouting. In this readily defensible position they laagered the wagons securely and lashed them wheel to wheel. They drove the herd of spare horses into the centre of the square. The horses they would ride tonight were hitched to the outside of the wagons, saddled and with muskets and cutlasses in the scabbards, ready for an instant sortie.

Then Jim went out to where Inkunzi, the head herdsman, and his Nguni waited. Under Jim's orders they bunched up the cattle and moved them quietly another three cables' length up the gorge from the bedding ground Koots had spied out at sundown. Jim spoke to the herders and explained exactly what he wanted of them. There was some muttered protest from these men, who looked upon the cattle as their children and were highly solicitous of their welfare, but Jim snarled at them and their protests subsided.

The cattle had sensed the mood of their herders, and they were restless and fretful. Inkunzi moved among them and played them a lullaby on his reed flute. They began to settle and some couched for the night. However, they kept bunched up together; in these nervous hours they needed the mutual assurance of the herd.

Jim went back to the wagons and made sure that all his men had eaten their dinner, and that they were booted and armed, ready to ride. Then he and Louisa climbed a short way up the cliff above the laager. From there they would be able to hear Bakkat's signals. They sat close together, sharing a woollen cape against the sudden night chill and talked quietly.

'They won't come before moonrise,' Jim predicted.

'When is that?' Louisa asked. Earlier in the evening they had consulted the almanac together, but she asked again mainly to hear his voice.

'A few minutes before ten of the clock. We are seven days from full moon. Just enough light for it.'

At last the moonrise lightened the eastern horizon. Jim stiffened and threw off the cape. On the hills on the far side of the gorge an eagle owl hooted twice. An eagle owl never hoots twice. 'That is Bakkat,' Jim said quietly. 'They are coming.'

'Which side of the river?' Louisa asked, as she stood up beside him.

'They will come to where they saw the wagons at sunset, on this side of the river.' The eagle owl hooted again, much closer.

'Koots is coming on fast.' Jim turned to the path down to the laager. 'Time to mount up.'

The men were waiting beside the horses, darkly muffled figures. Jim spoke a few words to each quietly. Some of the herd-boys had grown enough to be able to ride and handle a musket. The smallest, led by Izeze, the flea, would bring up the pack-horses with spare powder, shot and the waterbags, in case there was heavy fighting. Tegwane had twenty of the Nguni warriors under his command and he would stay to guard the wagons.

Intepe, Tegwane's granddaughter, was standing beside Zama, helping him secure his equipment on Crow's back. These days, the two spent much of their time together. Jim went to him now, and spoke low: 'Zama, you are my other arm. One of us must ride beside Welanga every minute. Do not become separated from her.'

'Welanga should stay in the laager with the other women,' Zama replied.

'You are right, old friend.' Jim grinned. 'She should do as I tell her, but I have never been able to find the words to convince her of that.'

The eagle owl hooted again, three times. 'They are close now.' Jim looked at the gibbous moon sailing above the hills.

'Mount!' he ordered. Every man knew what he had to do. Quietly they swung up on to the horses' backs. On Drumfire and Trueheart, Jim and Louisa led them to where Inkunzi waited with his warriors, guarding the bedded herds.

491

'Are you ready?' Jim asked, as he rode up. Inkunzi's shield was on his shoulder, and his *assegai* glinted in the moonlight. His men pressed up close behind him.

'I will lay a feast for your hungry blades tonight. Let them eat and drink their fill,' Jim told them. 'Now you know what you have to do. Let us begin.'

Quickly and silently, in an orderly, disciplined evolution, the warriors formed into an extended double rank across the breadth of the gorge, from river bank to cliff wall. The horsemen drew up behind them.

'We are ready, great lord!' Inkunzi sang out. Jim drew his pistol from the holster on the front of his saddle and fired a shot into the air. Immediately the still night was plunged into hubbub and uproar. The Nguni drummed on their shield with the blades of their *assegais* and shouted their war-cries. The horsemen fired their muskets and yelled like banshees. They surged forward down the gorge, and the cattle lumbered to their feet. The bulls bellowed in alarm for they were sensitive to the temper and mood of their herders. The breeding cows lowed plaintively, but when the ranks of yelling, drumming warriors bore down on them they panicked and whirled away before them.

These were all heavy beasts with great humps and swinging dewlaps. The span of their horns was twice the reach of a man's spread arms. Over the centuries the Nguni had bred them for this attribute, so that the cattle might better defend themselves against lions and other predators. They could run like wild antelope and when threatened they would defend themselves with those great racks of horn. In a dark and solid mass they stampeded down the valley. The running warriors and galloping horsemen pressed close behind them.

Koots was well satisfied that they had made a silent approach, and that they had not been detected by Jim Courtney's pickets. There was a good moon and, apart from

492

the usual night sounds of birds and small nocturnal animals, all was silent and still.

Koots and Kadem were riding stirrup to stirrup. They knew that they had still more than a mile to cover before they reached the spot on the river bank where they had seen the wagons outspanned. All of the Hottentots and the three Arabs knew exactly what to do. Before the alarm went up, they must get among the wagons and shoot down Jim Courtney's people as they emerged. Then they could deal with the Ngunis. Even though they were greater in number, they were armed only with spears. They were the lesser threat.

'No quarter,' Koots had ordered. 'Kill them all.'

'What about the women?' Oudeman asked. 'I haven't had a taste of the honey-pot since we left the colony. You promised us a go at the blonde girl.'

'If you can catch yourself a bit of *poesje*, well and good. But make sure all of the men are dead before you drop your pants. If not, you might get a cutlass up your arse end to help you along while you're pumping cream.' They had all laughed. At times Koots could show the common touch and speak to them in the language they understood best.

Now the troopers pressed forward eagerly. Earlier that day, from the heights above the gorge, some had glimpsed the cattle, the ivory and the women. They had told their companions and all were fired by the promise of pillage and rape.

Suddenly a single musket shot thudded out in the darkness ahead and, without waiting for the order, the column reined in. They peered ahead uneasily.

'Son of the great whore!' Koots swore. 'What was that?' He did not have long to wait for his answer. Abruptly the night was filled with uproar and clamour. None of them had ever heard before the sound of drumming on war-shields, and that made it more alarming. Moments later there was a fusillade of musket fire, wild shouts and screams, the bellowing and lowing of hundreds of cattle, then the rising thunder of hoofs bearing down on them out of the night.

In the fallible light of the moon it seemed that the earth

493

was moving, a flowing mass like black lava bearing down on them, stretching across the full breadth of the gorge from wall to cliff wall. The sound of hoofs was deafening, and they saw the humped backs of the monstrous herd looming closer and faster, the moonlight glinting on their horns.

'Stampede!' Oudeman yelled in terror, and the others took up the cry. 'Stampede!'

The tight-knit group of riders whirled round, broke up and scattered away before the solid wall of great horned heads and pounding hoofs. Within a dozen strides Goffel's horse hit an antbear burrow with his off fore. The leg snapped as the horse went down. Goffel was thrown forward to hit the earth with one shoulder. In terror he dragged himself to his feet with his arm dangling from the shattered bones, just as the front rank of cattle swept over him. One of the lead bulls hooked at him as it passed. The point of the horn slid in under his ribs and out of the small of his back at the level of his kidneys. The bull tossed its head and Goffel was thrown high, to drop back under the hoofs of the herd, then trampled and kicked to a boneless pulp. Three other troopers were trapped against an angle of the cliff. When they tried to turn back the herd engulfed them, and their mounts were gored by the enraged bulls. The frenzied horses reared, kicked and threw their riders, and men and horses were overwhelmed by the thrusting of horns and went down under the pounding hoofs.

Habban and Rashood raced side by side, but when Habban's horse stepped in a hole and fell with a broken leg Rashood turned back and, right under the horns of the stampede, dragged him up behind his saddle. They rode on, but the double-loaded horse could not keep ahead of the cattle, and was swallowed up by a wave of swinging horns and bellowing beasts. Habban was gored deeply in the thigh and dragged from his perch behind his companion's saddle.

'Ride on!' he screamed at Rashood, as he hit the ground. 'I am lost. Save yourself!' But Rashood tried to turn back, and his horse was horned again and again until it also fell in a tangle of legs and loose equipment. On hands and knees Rashood crawled through the dust and flying hoofs. Though he was kicked repeatedly, felt muscle and sinew tear in his back and chest and his ribs snap, he reached his fallen comrade and dragged him behind the bole of one of the larger trees. They huddled there, choking and coughing in the dustclouds while the stampede thundered by.

Even after the stampede had passed they could not leave their hiding-place because a wave of howling Nguni spearmen followed hard on the heels of the herds. Just when it seemed that they would find the two Arabs, an unhorsed Hottentot trooper broke from cover and tried to make a run for it. Like hounds on the fox the Nguni went after him, and were drawn away from Rashood and Habban. They stabbed the trooper repeatedly, washing their blades in his blood.

Koots and Kadem spurred their horses at full gallop along the bank of the river to keep ahead of the stampede. Oudeman stuck close behind them. He knew that Koots had the animal instinct for survival, and trusted him to find an escape for them from this disaster. Suddenly the horses ran into stands of hook-thorn and were slowed by the dense thickets. The herd leaders coming on close behind them crashed through the thorn without check, and swiftly overhauled them.

'Into the river!' Koots bellowed. 'They'll not follow us in there.'

As he shouted he swerved his mount towards the bank and lashed him over the top. They dropped twelve feet and hit the surface of the water with a high splash. Kadem and Oudeman followed him over. They surfaced together and saw Koots already half-way across the river. Swimming beside the horses, they reached the south bank after Koots had landed.

They climbed out and stood in a sodden, exhausted group and watched the herd still careering by on the far bank. Then in the moonlight they saw Jim Courtney's horsemen galloping close on the heels of the herd, and heard the thud and saw the muzzle flashes of their muskets as they caught up with the surviving riders of Koots's troop and shot them down.

'Our powder is wet,' Koots gasped. 'We cannot stand and fight.'

'I have lost my musket,' said Oudeman.

'It is over,' Kadem agreed, 'but there will be another day and another place when we shall finish this business.' They mounted and rode on swiftly into the east, away from the river, the stampeding herd and the enemy musketeers.

'Where are we going?' Oudeman asked at last, but neither of the other two answered him.

I t took the Nguni herdsmen many days to round up the scattered herds. They discovered that thirty-two of the great hump-backed beasts had died or been hopelessly maimed in the stampede. Some had fallen over precipices, run into holes, drowned in the rapids of the river or been killed by the lions when they had become separated from the herd. The Nguni mourned them. Lovingly they drove back those cattle that had survived the dreadful night. They moved among them, soothing and gentling them. They dressed their injuries, the horn wounds of their peers and the rips and contusions where they had run into trees or other objects.

Inkunzi, the head herdsman, was determined to express his outrage to Jim in the strongest terms he dared. 'I will demand that he suspend the march and rest in this place until all the cattle are recovered,' he assured his herders, and they all agreed staunchly with him. Despite his threats, the request when he made it to Jim was couched in much milder terms, and Jim agreed with him without quibble.

As soon as it was light, Jim and his men rode over the battlefield. They came upon four dead horses of Koots's troop with horn stabs, and two others so badly hurt that they had to be destroyed. However, they retrieved eleven more that were either unhurt or so little injured that they could be treated and added to Jim's own remount herd.

They also found the corpses of five of Koots's men. The features of three were so battered as to be unrecognizable, but from items of their clothing and equipment, and the pay books Jim found in the pockets of two, he could be certain that they were VOC cavalrymen, wearing mufti rather than military uniform. 'These are all Keyser's men. Although he did not come after us himself, Keyser sent them,' Jim assured Louisa.

Smallboy and Muntu recognized some of the corpses. The Cape colony was a small community where everyone knew his neighbours.

'Goffel! Now there was a truly bad *kerel*,' said Smallboy, as he prodded one of the battered corpses with his toe. His expression was stern and he shook his head. Smallboy himself was no angel of purity, and if he disapproved, thought Jim, Goffel must have been a veritable tower of vice.

'There are still five missing,' Bakkat told Jim. 'No sign yet of Koots and the bald sergeant, or of the three strange Arabs we saw with them yesterday. I must cast the far side of the river.' He waded across and Jim watched him scurry along the bank and peer at the ground as he read sign. Suddenly he stopped, like a pointer dog getting the scent of the bird.

'Bakkat! What have you found there?' Jim yelled across.

'Three horses, running hard,' Bakkat called back.

Jim, Louisa and Zama crossed the river to join him and they studied the tracks of galloping horses. 'Can you read who the riders were, Bakkat?' Jim asked. It seemed impossible but Bakkat responded to the question as though it were commonplace. He squatted by the tracks.

'These two are the horses that Koots and the bald one were riding yesterday. The other is one of the Arabs, the one with the green turban,' he declared, with finality.

'How can he tell?' Louisa asked, with wonder. 'They are all steel-shod horses. Surely the tracks are identical?'

'Not to Bakkat,' Jim assured her. 'He can tell from the uneven wear of the horseshoes, and dents and chips in the metal. To his eye each horse has a distinctive gait, and he can read it in the spoor.'

'So Koots and Oudeman have got away. What are you going to do now, Jim? Are you going to follow them?'

Jim did not reply at once. To delay the decision he ordered Bakkat to follow the spoor and make sure of the run of it.

After a mile the tracks turned determinedly towards the north. Jim ordered a halt and asked Bakkat and Zama for their opinion. It was a long debate.

'They are riding fast,' Bakkat pointed out. 'They have a start of almost half a night and a day. It will take many days to catch them, if you ever do. Let them go, Somoya.'

'I think they are beaten,' Zama said. 'Koots will not come back. But if you catch him, he will fight like a leopard in a trap. You will lose men.'

Louisa thought about that. Jim might be one of those wounded or killed. She thought of intervening, but she knew that might harden Jim's resolve. She had found a wide streak of contrariness in his nature. She bit back her pleas to make him stay, and instead said quietly, 'If you go after him, I shall go with you.'

Jim looked at her. The warlike gleam in his eye faded, and he smiled in defeat, but it was still a conditional surrender. 'I have a feeling that Bakkat is right, as usual. Koots has abandoned his hostile intentions towards us, for the present at least. Most of his men have been wiped out. But he still has a formidable force with him. There are five still unaccounted for: Koots, Oudeman and the three Arabs. They could make a bitter fight of it if we cornered them. Zama is also right. We can't hope to get away scot-free a second time. If we do catch up with them some of our people will be killed or hurt. On the other hand, what seems to be flight might be a trick to draw us away from the wagons. We know Koots is a crafty animal. If we follow, Koots might circle round and attack the wagons before we can get back to intervene.' He drew breath and conceded, 'We will keep on for the coast and see what we find at Nativity Bay.' They crossed the river and headed back down the narrow gut of the gorge along the path of the cattle stampede.

Now that she knew Jim would not ride off after Koots, Louisa was happy and chatted easily as they rode side by side. Zama was anxious to return to the wagons, and he drew steadily ahead, until he was almost obscured by the trees.

'In a hurry to get back to the lovely lily.' Louisa laughed.

'Who?' Jim was puzzled.

'Intepe.'

'Tegwane's granddaughter? Is Zama—'

'Yes, he is,' Louisa confirmed. 'Sometimes men are blind. How could you not have noticed?'

'You are the only thing in my eye, Hedgehog. I see nothing but you.'

'My love, that was neatly said.' Louisa leaned out of the saddle and offered her mouth. 'You shall have a kiss as a reward.'

But before he could claim it, there was a wild shout and the crash of a musket shot ahead. They saw Frost rear and shy under Zama as he reeled in the saddle.

'Zama's in trouble!' Jim shouted, and spurred forward. As he caught up he saw that Zama was wounded. He was hanging half out of the saddle, and blood was shining at the back of his coat. Before Jim could reach him he keeled over and fell to earth in a limp heap.

'Zama!' Jim shouted, and rode for him, but at that moment he saw a flash of movement to one side. There was danger there and Jim turned Drumfire to meet it. One of the Arabs, in a ragged robe stained with dirt and dried blood, was crouched behind the trunk of a fever tree. He was frantically reloading his long-barrelled musket, ramrodding a ball down the muzzle. He looked up as horse and rider charged down on him. Jim recognized him. 'Rashood!' he shouted. He was one of the crewmen from the family schooner, *Gift of Allah*, Jim had sailed with him more than once, and knew him well, yet here he was riding with a company of the enemy, treacherously attacking the Courtney wagons – and he had shot Zama.

At the same moment Rashood recognized Jim. He dropped the musket, sprang to his feet and ran. Jim unsheathed his cutlass, and steered Drumfire after him. When he realized he could not escape Rashood dropped to his knees and spread his arms in a gesture of surrender.

Jim rose over him in the stirrups.

'You treacherous, murderous bastard!' He was angry enough

499

to use the edge and split the man's skull, but at the last moment he controlled himself and swung the flat of the blade across Rashood's temple. The steel cracked against the bone with such force that Jim feared he might have killed him anyway. Rashood collapsed face forward on to the earth.

'Don't you dare die,' Jim threatened him, as he swung down from the saddle, 'not until you have answered my questions. Then I will give you a royal send-off.'

Louisa rode up, and Jim shouted, 'See to Zama. I think he is hard hit. I will come to you as soon as I have this swine secured.'

Louisa sent Bakkat to call for help from the men at the laager, and they carried Zama back on a litter. He had received a dangerous wound at an oblique angle through the chest and Louisa feared for his life, but she hid her anxiety. As soon as they reached the laager Intepe came running to help her nurse him.

'He is hurt, but he will live,' she told the weeping girl, as they laid Zama on the cardell bed in the spare wagon. With the help of the books and the medicine chest Sarah Courtney had given her, and by dint of much practice and experience, Louisa had become a proficient physician over the months since they had left the Gariep river. She made a more thorough examination of the wound, and exclaimed, with relief, 'The ball has gone clean through and out the other side. That's most propitious. We won't have to cut for it, and the danger of mortification and gangrene is much reduced.'

Jim left Zama to the women and took out his concern and anger on Rashood. With arms and legs spreadeagled like a starfish, they lashed him to the spokes of one of the big rear wagon wheels and jacked the rim clear of the ground. Jim waited for him to recover consciousness.

In the meantime Smallboy brought in the body of another Arab they had found lying close to where he had captured Rashood. This one had died from loss of blood: a horn wound in his groin had severed the big artery there. When they turned him face up, Jim recognized him as another of the sailors from the *Gift*. 'This one is Habban,' he said.

'It is indeed Habban,' agreed Smallboy.

'There is something going on here that stinks like rotten fish,' Jim said. 'I know not what it is, but this one can give us the answers.' He glared at Rashood, still hanging unconscious on the rear wheel of the wagon. 'Throw a bucket of water over him.' It needed not one but three buckets flung into his face to revive him.

'Salaam, Rashood,' Jim greeted him, as he opened his eyes. 'The beauty of your countenance lightens my heart. You are a servant of my family. Why did you attack our wagons and try to kill Zama, a man you know well as my friend?'

Rashood shook the water from his beard and long, lank hair. He stared back at Jim: he did not speak but the expression in his eyes was eloquent.

'We must loosen your tongue, Beloved of the Prophet.' Jim stepped back, and nodded to Smallboy. 'Give him a hundred turns of the wheel.'

Smallboy and Muntu spat on their hands and seized the rim. They began to spin it between them. Smallboy counted the turns. The speed built up swiftly until the image of Rashood's revolving body blurred before their eyes. Smallboy lost the count after fifty and had to start again. When at last he called the hundred and they braked the wheel, Rashood was writhing weakly against his bonds, his dirty robe drenched with sweat. His eyes were unfocused and he was heaving and gasping with vertigo.

'Rashood, why were you riding with Koots? When did you join his band? Who was the strange Arab with you, the man with the green turban?'

Despite his distress Rashood turned his eyes towards Jim and tried to focus on him. 'Infidel!' he blurted. '*Kaffir*! I act by virtue of the sacred *fatwa* of the Caliph Zayn al-Din of Muscat and at the command of his pasha, General Kadem ibn Abu-baker. The Pasha is a great and holy man, a mighty warrior and beloved of God and the Prophet.'

501

'So the one in the green turban is a pasha? What are the terms of this *fatwa?*' Jim demanded.

'They are too sacred to be spoken into the ear of the profane.'

'Rashood has discovered religion.' Jim shook his head sadly. 'I have never heard him prate such bigoted and venomous nonsense before.' He nodded to Smallboy. 'Give him another hundred turns on the wheel to cool his ardour.'

The wheel blurred again, but before they reached the count of a hundred, Rashood vomited in a long, sustained jet. Smallboy grunted at Muntu: 'Don't stop!' Then Rashood's bowels loosed and his bodily excretions erupted simultaneously from both ends of his body, like a deck hose.

At the hundred count they braked the wheel, but Rashood's befuddled senses could not tell the difference. The sensation of violent movement seemed to become stronger and he moaned and vomited until his stomach was empty. Then he heaved and dry-retched painfully.

'What were the terms of the *fatwa?*' Jim insisted.

'Death to the adulterers.' Rashood's voice was barely audible and yellow bile ran down his chin into his beard. 'Death to al-Salil and Princess Yasmini.'

Jim recoiled at the mention of those two beloved names. 'My uncle and aunt? Are they dead? Tell me they are still alive or I shall spin your black soul loose from your foul body.'

Rashood recovered his scattered senses and once more tried to oppose Jim's questions, but gradually the wheel broke down his resistance, and he answered freely. 'The Princess Yasmini was executed by the Pasha. She died with a thrust through her adulterous heart.' Even in his extreme condition Rashood mouthed the words with relish. 'And al-Salil was wounded to the brink of death.'

Jim's anger and sorrow were overwhelming, so much so that he lost all stomach for further punishment that day. Rashood was cut down from the wheel but chained and guarded for the rest of the night. 'I will question him again in the morning,' Jim said and went to tell Louisa the terrible news.

'My aunt Yasmini was the essence of kindness and goodness. I only wish you could have met her,' he said that night, as they lay in each other's arms. His tears soaked her nightdress. 'Thank God my uncle Dorian seems to have survived the assassination attempt by this fanatic, Kadem ibn Abubaker.'

In the morning Jim ordered the wagon to be towed well away from the laager so that Louisa could not hear Rashood on the wheel. They lashed him to the spokes, but Rashood broke down before Jim had ordered a single spin. 'Pity, *effendi*. Enough, Somoya! I will tell you all you wish to know, only take me down from this accursed wheel.'

'You will stay on the wheel until you have answered all my questions straight and true. If you hesitate or lie, the wheel will turn. When did this creature Kadem murder the princess? Where did this happen? What of my uncle? Has he recovered? Where is my family now?'

Rashood answered each question as though his life depended on it. Which indeed it does, Jim thought grimly.

When he heard the whole story of how his family had fled from Good Hope in the two schooners, and that they had sailed north after leaving the Lagoon of the Elephants, Jim's sorrow for Yasmini was tempered with relief and his anticipation of an imminent reunion.

'Now I know that we shall find my parents at Nativity Bay, and my uncle Dorian and Mansur with them. I count the days in my heart before I shall see them again. We must resume the journey again tomorrow at first light.'

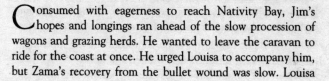

Consumed with eagerness to reach Nativity Bay, Jim's hopes and longings ran ahead of the slow procession of wagons and grazing herds. He wanted to leave the caravan to ride for the coast at once. He urged Louisa to accompany him, but Zama's recovery from the bullet wound was slow. Louisa insisted that he still needed her care and she could not leave him.

'You go on ahead,' she told him. Even though he was sure she did not truly mean him to leave her, and that she expected him to refuse, he was sorely tempted to take her at her word. But then he recalled that Koots, Oudeman and the Arab assassin, Kadem, were still at large and might be in the offing. He could not leave Louisa alone. Each morning he and Bakkat rode out far ahead of the caravan to scout the road path, and he made certain that he returned before sunset each evening to be with Louisa.

They emerged from the bottom end of the narrow gorge into a country lush with grasslands and fair hills interspersed with green forests. Each day Bakkat found sign of the elephant herds but none fresh enough to follow up until the morning of the fifth day after leaving the gorge. As usual he was riding just ahead of Jim, breaking trail and scanning ahead for sign, when suddenly he turned Crow aside and reined him to a standstill. Jim came up beside him. 'What is it?' Bakkat pointed wordlessly at the damp earth and the tracks deeply trodden into it. Jim felt his pulse jump with excitement. 'Elephant!'

'Three big bulls,' Bakkat agreed, 'and very fresh. They passed this way in the dawn of this very morning, not long since.' Jim felt his anxiety to reach Nativity Bay abate as he stared at the spoor. 'They are very big,' he said.

'One is a king of all elephants,' Bakkat said. 'It may be as large as the first great beast you slew.'

'They cannot be too far ahead of us,' Jim suggested hopefully. There had been many successful hunts since the battle with Manatasee's *impis* on the river bank. Each time they caught up with the great ivory-bearing bulls Jim added to his fund of experience and knowledge of their habits. By now he had honed his skills as a hunter, and in so doing had become addicted to the dangers and the fascination of the chase after this most noble quarry.

'How long will it take to catch up with them?' he asked Bakkat.

'They are feeding as they go, moving slowly,' Bakkat pointed out the torn branches of the trees from which the bulls had fed, 'and they are heading down towards the coast, along our own line of march. We need not detour to follow them.' Bakkat spat thoughtfully and looked up at the sky. He held up his right hand and measured his spread fingers against the angle of the sun. 'If the gods of the hunt are kind, we might catch them before noon, and still be back at the wagons before nightfall.' These days Bakkat showed a reluctance equal to Jim's to spend a night away from the wagons, and the golden charms of Letee.

Jim was torn. Despite his passion for the chase, his love and concern for Louisa were stronger. He knew that the vagaries of the hunt were unpredictable. To follow the bulls might add a day or more to the journey to the coast. They might not be able to return to the wagons before the onset of night. On the other hand there had been no sign of Koots and his Arab ally since that disastrous night attack. Bakkat had swept the back trail for many leagues and it was clear. There seemed no longer to be a threat from that direction. Even so, dare he leave Louisa for so long?

He wanted desperately to follow the tracks. In the months of hunting he had learned to read the spoor so vividly that he could picture them in his mind's eye, and he knew that these were magnificent bulls. He vacillated for a while longer while Bakkat squatted patiently beside the huge oval pad marks, and waited for him to make up his mind.

Then Jim thought of the small army of men who were with the wagons, to guard and protect Louisa. Koots's force had been routed and decimated. Surely he would not return so soon. At last he convinced himself that Koots was heading either for Portuguese or Omani territory, that he would not double back to attack them again.

'Every minute I dither here the bulls are walking away from me.' He made up his mind. 'Bakkat, take the spoor, and eat the wind.'

They rode hard and closed the gap swiftly. The spoor headed steadily through the low hills and forest towards the

505

coast. In places the raw trunks of the trees from which the elephant had stripped the bark shone like mirrors a cable's length ahead of them and they could push Drumfire and Crow into a canter. A little before noon they came upon a huge mound of spongy yellow dung, composed mostly of half-digested bark. It was lying in a puddle of urine that had not yet soaked away into the earth. The dung was covered by a swarm of butterflies with gorgeous white, yellow and orange wings.

Bakkat dismounted and thrust his bare toe into the moist pile to test the temperature. The butterflies rose around him in a cloud. 'The dung is still hot from his belly.' He grinned up at Jim. 'If you called his name the bull is so close he would hear your voice.'

The words were no sooner out of Bakkat's mouth than they both froze and their heads turned together. 'Ha!' Jim grunted. 'He heard you speak.'

In the forest not far ahead the elephant trumpeted again, high and clear as a bugle blast. Agile as a cricket Bakkat sprang into the saddle.

'What has alarmed them?' Jim asked, as he drew his big German four-to-the-pound gun from its sheath under his knee. 'Why did he trumpet? Did he catch our wind?'

'The wind is in our faces,' Bakkat replied. 'They have not smelt us, but something else has done it.'

'Sweet Mary!' Jim shouted with astonishment. 'That is musket fire!'

The heavy reports of the guns boomed out and the echoes were flung back by the surrounding hills.

'Is it Koots?' Jim demanded, then answered himself, 'It cannot be. Koots would never give himself away while he knows we're close. These are strangers, and they are attacking our herd.' Jim felt a flare of anger: these were his elephant – the interlopers had no right to intervene in his hunt. He felt a strong urge to rush forward, but he quelled that dangerous inclination. He did not know who these other hunters might be. Judging by the fusillade of gunfire he knew that there was more than one. Any stranger in the wilderness might be a deadly threat. Suddenly there was another sound, the crackle of breaking branches and the rush of an enormous body bearing down on them through the thick underbrush ahead.

'Be ready, Somoya!' Bakkat called urgently. 'They have driven one of the bulls back towards us. He may be wounded and dangerous.'

Jim had only time enough to swing Drumfire to face the sound, when the green forest wall ahead burst open and a bull elephant was upon him at full charge. In that moment of sudden danger, time seemed to slow as though he were caught in the coils of a nightmare. He saw curved tusks that seemed as massive as the main beams of a cathedral roof high above him, and the ears spread wide as the mainsail of a man-o'-war, tattered by shot after a close-fought battle. There was fresh blood smeared down the elephant's flank and fury in his tiny, gleaming eyes as they fastened on Jim.

Bakkat had guessed correctly: the gigantic animal was wounded and enraged. Jim realized that flight would be fatal for Drumfire would not be able to use his speed in the confines of the thorn underbrush while the bull would crash through it without check. Jim could not fire from the saddle. Drumfire was dancing in a circle under him and tossing his head. His antics would upset Jim's aim. Holding the heavy gun high above his head so that it would not hit him in the face as he landed, Jim threw one leg back over the cantle of the saddle and dropped to the ground, landing like a cat facing the charge.

He cocked the gun as his feet touched the earth. His fear was gone in that instant, replaced by a strange feeling of detachment, as though he stood outside himself and watched the gun come up.

Without conscious thought he knew that if he sent a ball through the beast's heart its stride would not even check. It would still rip him limb from limb as effortlessly as a butcher dismembers a chicken carcass, then walk another mile before it succumbed.

After his first near-fatal experience with the head shot, Jim had spent hours and days carefully dissecting and studying the

507

skulls of all the other elephant he had killed since then. Now he could visualize the exact location of the brain in the massive casket of the skull as though it was not solid bone but clear glass. As the butt-stock came into his shoulder he seemed not to see the iron sights of the weapon, but he looked through them to his tiny concealed target.

The shot thundered out. He was instantly blinded by the dense fog of gunsmoke, and driven back on his heels by the recoil. Then, out of the smoke bank, a grey avalanche toppled down on him. He was struck by an enormous slack weight.

The heavy gun was wrenched from his grip and he was hurled backwards. He rolled twice head over heels until he hit a low bush, which brought him up short. He struggled up just as the light breeze blew aside the curtains of silver gunsmoke, and saw the bull elephant kneeling before him on its front legs with the curve of the huge tusks resting on the earth and the tips pointing up to the sky. It seemed to be in an attitude of submission, like a trained elephant waiting to be mounted by a mahout. It was as still and motionless as a granite boulder. There was a round dark hole low between its eyes. It was so close that he reached up and thrust his forefinger full length into it. The pewter-hardened ball, a quarter of a pound in weight, had cleaved the massive frontal bones of the skull and driven through to the brain. When he withdrew his finger it was smeared with custard-yellow brain tissue.

Jim stood up and leaned heavily on one of the tusks. Now that the danger was past his breathing came hard and ragged, and his legs shook under him so that they could scarcely bear his weight. While he clung to the great curve of ivory and swayed on his feet Bakkat rode in and seized Drumfire before he could bolt. He brought him back to Jim and handed him the reins.

'My teaching begins to bear fruit.' He giggled. 'Now you must give thanks and respect to your quarry.'

It was some minutes before Jim could gather himself to complete the ancient ritual of the hunt. Under Bakkat's approving eye he broke off a leafy twig of the sweet thorn and placed it between the bull's lips. 'Eat your last meal to sustain you on the journey to the shadow land. Take with you my respect,' he said. Then he cut off the tail like his father before him. Jim had not forgotten the other musket shots he had heard. But as he stooped to retrieve his fallen musket, he noticed again the thick coating of blood down the bull's flank, and saw a bullet wound high in its right shoulder.

'Bakkat, this animal has been wounded before my shot,' he called sharply. Before Bakkat could reply another human voice close at hand shouted a challenge or a question. It was so unexpected, yet so familiar, that Jim stood with the empty gun in his hand and gaped at the tall athletic figure striding towards him through the undergrowth. A white man, dressed in European-style breeches and jacket, boots and a wide-brimmed straw hat.

'Hey there, fellow. What the devil do you think you're playing at? I drew first blood. The kill is mine.' The voice rang as joyously as church bells in Jim's ears. Under the brim of the hat the interloper's beard curled red and wild as a bush fire.

Jim recovered his wits at once and shouted back just as belligerently, 'By God, you saucy knave!' It required an effort to keep the laughter out of his tone. 'You will have to fight me for it, and I will crack your pate as I have done fifty times before.'

The saucy knave stopped dead in his tracks and stared at Jim, then let out a wild hurrah and rushed at him. Jim dropped his musket and charged headlong to meet him. They came together with a violence that rattled their teeth.

'Jim! Oh, what joy! I thought we would never find you.'

'Mansur! I hardly recognized you with that fluffy red bush sprouting all over your face. Where in the name of the devil have you been?'

They gabbled incoherently as they hugged and buffeted each other, and tried to pull handfuls of hair from each other's heads and faces. Bakkat watched them, shaking his head and slapping his sides with amusement.

'And you, you little hooligan!' Mansur seized him, lifted him off his feet and tucked him under his arm, then embraced Jim again. It took some time for them to begin to behave like sensible persons, but gradually they got themselves under a semblance of control. Mansur replaced Bakkat on his feet, and Jim released Mansur from the headlock in which he had pinned him.

They sat shoulder to shoulder, leaning against the dead elephant's side in the shadow cast by the massive carcass and talked, cutting in on each other, hardly waiting for the reply to one question before asking another. Every now and then Mansur would tug at Jim's beard and Jim would punch him affectionately in the chest or slap his hairy cheek. Though neither mentioned it, each of them was amazed at the changes that had taken place in the other during the time they had been apart. They had become men.

Then the retinue who had accompanied Mansur came looking for him. They were all servants from High Weald or sailors from the schooners. They were astonished to find Jim with their master. After Jim had greeted them affectionately, he set them to work under the supervision of Bakkat to cut out the tusks from the fallen bull. Then he and Mansur could continue their exchange of news, trying to cover in minutes all that had overtaken them and the family since their last meeting nearly two years ago.

'Where is Louisa, the girl you ran off with? Did she have the sense to send you packing?' Mansur demanded.

'By God, coz, I tell you that is a pearl of a lass. Presently I'll take you back to the wagons to be properly introduced to her. You will not credit your eyes when you see her, how lovely she has grown.' Then Jim broke off and his expression changed. 'I know not how best to tell you, coz, but only a few weeks past I fell in with a deserter from the *Gift of Allah*. You must remember the rogue. His name is Rashood. He had a strange and terrible tale to tell, once I could drag it out of him.'

The colour drained from Mansur's face and for a minute he could not speak. Then he blurted out, 'He must have been in the company of two other of our sailors, all three deserters, and there would have been a strange Arab with them.'

'One named Kadem ibn Abubaker al-Jurf.'

510

Mansur started up. 'Where is he? He murdered my mother, and almost killed my father.'

'I know it. I forced the whole story from Rashood.' Jim tried to calm him. 'My heart breaks for you. I loved Aunt Yassie almost as much as you did. But the assassin has escaped.'

'Tell me all of it,' Mansur demanded. 'Spare me not a single detail.'

There was so much to tell, and they sat so long telling it that the sun was low on the horizon before Jim stood up. 'We must get back to the wagons before nightfall. Louisa will be beside herself.'

Louisa had hung lighted lanterns in the trees to guide Jim home, and she rushed out of the wagon where she and Intepe were nursing Zama as soon as she heard the horses. At last she broke from Jim's embrace when she became aware that a stranger was with him, watching their uninhibited display of affection for each other.

'There is someone with you?' She tucked the loose strands of her silky hair under her bonnet, and straightened her clothing, which Jim had rumpled.

''Tis no one of consequence,' Jim assured her. ''Tis only my cousin Mansur, of whom I have spoken and whom you have seen before. Mansur, this is Louisa Leuven. She and I are affianced.'

'I thought you had over-extolled her virtues,' Mansur bowed to Louisa, then stared at her face in the lantern-light, 'but she is more lovely than you warned me.'

'Jim has told me much about you,' Louisa said shyly. 'He loves you better than a brother. When we saw each other before, on the deck of *Het Gelukkige Meeuw*, there was no opportunity for me to know you better. I hope that in the future we will be able to put that to rights.'

Louisa fed the two men, but as soon as they had eaten she left them to talk without interruption far into the night. It was after midnight when Jim came to join her in the wide cardell bed. 'Forgive me, Hedgehog, that I have neglected you this evening.'

'I would have it no other way, for I know what he means to you and how close you are to each other,' she whispered, as she held out her arms to him. 'But now is my time to be closer still.'

They were all astir before sunrise. While Louisa supervised the preparation of a celebratory breakfast to welcome Mansur to the laager, Mansur was at Zama's bedside. Jim joined them, and all three chatted and reminisced. Zama was so much encouraged by Mansur's arrival that he declared he was ready to leave his sickbed.

Smallboy and Muntu inspanned the wagons, and the caravan moved off. Louisa relinquished care of Zama to Intepe, and for the first time since Zama's wounding she saddled Trueheart and rode out with Jim and Mansur. They passed through the herds of cattle and Mansur was amazed by their numbers and by the weight of the ivory they carried on the pack-saddles strapped to their backs.

'Even though Uncle Tom and my father were able to escape from the colony with much of the family wealth, you have multiplied it many times over with what you have captured. Tell me how it happened. Tell me of the battle against this Nguni queen, Manatasee, and her legions.'

'I described it to you last night,' Jim protested.

'It is too good a tale to be told only once,' Mansur insisted. 'Tell it to me again.'

This time Jim embellished Louisa's role in the fighting, despite her protests that he was exaggerating. 'I warn you, coz, you must not anger this lady. She is a veritable Valkyrie once she is aroused. She is not feared far and wide as the Dreaded Hedgehog for no good reason.'

They rode to the crest of the next hill and looked down towards the ocean. It was so close that they could just make out the windswept white horses that danced on the horizon. 'How far are we from Nativity Bay?' Jim demanded.

'It took me less than three days on foot,' Mansur answered. 'Now that I have this good horse under me I could be there before nightfall.'

Jim looked at Louisa with a wistful air, and she smiled. 'I know what you are thinking, James Archibald,' she said.

'And what do you think about what I am thinking, Hedgehog?'

'I think we should leave Zama, the wagons and the cattle to come on at their best speed and that we should eat the wind.'

Jim let out a happy shout. 'Follow me, my love. This way for Nativity Bay.'

It took less time than Mansur had predicted and the sun was still above the horizon when they reined in on the hills above the wide, glittering bay. The two schooners were anchored off the mouth of the Umbilo river and Jim shaded his eyes with his hat against the sun's reflection off the water.

'Fort Auspice,' Mansur told them, and pointed out the newly erected buildings on the banks of the river. 'Your mother chose the name. She wanted to call it Fort Good Auspice, but Uncle Tom said, "That's a mouthful, and we all know that it an't a bad auspice, any which way you look at it." So that was it. Fort Auspice.'

As they rode closer they were able to make out the palisade of sharpened stakes that enclosed the high ground on which the fort was set. The earth was still raw around the gun emplacements that covered all the approaches to the fortifications.

'Our fathers have taken every precaution against attack by Keyser or other enemies. We have brought ashore most of the guns off the ships,' Mansur explained.

The roofs of the buildings it enclosed showed above the top of the palisade. 'There are barracks for the servants and each of our families have their own quarters.' Mansur pointed them out as they trotted down the hill. 'Those are the stables.

513

That is the warehouse, and there are the godown and the counting-house.'

All the roofs were still bright and unweathered with new-cut thatch.

'Father has the delusions of Nero.' Jim chuckled. 'He has built himself a city, not a trading post.'

'Aunt Sarah did little to dissuade him,' Mansur said. 'In fact you could say she was an active accomplice.' He snatched off his hat and waved it over his head. 'And there she is now!' A matronly figure had appeared in the gateway of the fort and was staring across at the little band of approaching riders. As soon as Jim waved she threw all dignity to the winds and came running down the path like a schoolgirl released from the classroom.

'Jim! Oh, Jim boy!' Her joyous cries echoed off the cliffs of the bluff. Jim sent Drumfire into a wild gallop to meet her. He jumped from the saddle while the stallion was still at full charge and gathered his mother into his arms.

When they heard Drumfire's hoofs Dorian and Tom Court-ney came running out through the gates of the fort. Mansur and Louisa hung back to let the first frenzy of greeting abate.

It took another five days for the wagons and cattle to reach Fort Auspice. The entire family stood together on the firing platform of the palisade. The herd of spare horses led the way, and Tom and Dorian cheered as they galloped past. 'It will be good to have a horse under me again,' Tom exulted. 'I have felt that half of me was missing for lack of a good mount. Now we will be able to range through this land and claim it as our own.'

Then they gazed in awed silence as the dark mass of the cattle herds poured down the hills towards them. When Inkunzi and his Nguni herders began to offload the ivory on the open parade in front of the gates, Tom climbed down the ladder from the platform and walked among the tall stacks of tusks, marvelling at the quantity and size of some of them. Then he came back and scowled at Jim. 'For the love of all that's holy, lad! Have you no sense of moderation? Did you not give a thought to where we were going to store all this?

We shall have to build another warehouse, and you are solely to blame.' Tom's scowl faded and he laughed at his own wit, then folded his son in a bear-hug. 'After this haul, I think we will have no choice but to declare you a full partner in the company.'

Over the following months, there was employment for all, and much besides to plan and arrange. The main work on the fort was completed, including the extension to the warehouse to accommodate the abundance of captured ivory. Sarah was able at last to bring her furniture ashore. She set up her harpsichord in the hall, which was to serve as the dining and common room to both families. That night she played all their favourite tunes, while they joined in the choruses. Tone-deaf Tom made up in volume for what he lacked in tuneful-ness, until Sarah tactfully distracted him by asking him to turn the pages of her music book.

For lack of grazing, such a great number of cattle could not be held in the immediate vicinity of the fort. Jim split them into seven smaller herds, and ordered Inkunzi to move them out into the surrounding country, as far as twenty leagues distant from Fort Auspice, wherever good grazing and water could be found. The Nguni herders built their villages close to these new grazing grounds.

'They will form a buffer round the fort,' Jim pointed out to Tom and Dorian, 'and they will give us good warning of the approach of an enemy before they come within twenty leagues.' Then he added, as if in afterthought, 'Of course, I will have to ride out to inspect them at regular intervals.'

'And that will provide you with a fine excuse to run off hunting elephants.' Tom nodded sagely. 'Your devotion to company duty is moving, lad.'

However, after only a few such expeditions the elephant responded to Jim's attentions by moving out of this country and vanishing into the fastness of the deep interior.

Within a month of their arrival at Fort Auspice, Jim and

Louisa waylaid Sarah in her kitchen. After a long and emotional discussion, which left both women in tears of joy, Sarah went off immediately to speak to Tom.

'My oath, Sarah Courtney, I know not what to say,' said Tom, which she knew was his most forceful expression of amazement. 'There can be no mistake?'

'Louisa is certain. Women are seldom mistaken in such matters,' Sarah replied.

'We shall need somebody to splice the knot, and make it all shipshape and legal.' Tom looked worried.

'Well, you are a ship's captain,' Sarah pointed out tartly, 'so you have that power vested in you.'

The longer Tom thought about it, the more the idea of having a grandson appealed to him. 'Well, it seems Louisa has passed her trials fair enough,' he conceded, with a convincing show of nonchalance.

Sarah placed her fists on her hips, a storm warning. 'If that was meant as a jest, Thomas Courtney, it fell far short of the mark. As far as you and I, or anyone else in the world, is concerned, Louisa Leuven will be a virgin bride,' she said.

He gave ground rapidly. 'I am convinced of that, and I will fight any man who says different. As you and I are well aware, premature birth runs strongly on both sides of our family. On top of that, Louisa is a comely and likely lass. I daresay our Jim would have to sail a long way to find another better.'

'Does that mean you will do it?' Sarah demanded.

'I suspect I will not have much peace until I do.'

'For once you suspect correctly,' she said, and he picked her up and bussed her on both cheeks.

Tom married them on the quarter-deck of the *Sprite*. There was not space aboard for all the company so the overflow watched from the rigging of the *Revenge* or from the palisade walls of the fort. Jim and Louisa spoke their vows, then signed the ship's log. When Jim brought his bride ashore, Mansur and his men fired a salute of twenty-one guns from the cannons of the fort, which scattered the Nguni warriors in confusion, and reduced little Letee to hysteria until Bakkat could reassure her that the sky was not falling in upon them.

'Well!' said Tom, with satisfaction. 'That should hold them, until they can find a priest to do the job properly.' And he doffed his captain's cocked hat and exchanged the job of clergyman for that of bartender, by knocking the bung out of a cask of Cape brandy.

Smallboy slaughtered an ox, and they roasted it whole on a spit on the beach below the fort. The festivities went on until it was consumed and the brandy cask was at last drunk dry.

Jim and Louisa began work on the construction of their own private quarters within the walls of the fort. With so many willing hands to join in the work, it was less than a week before they vacated the wagon that for so long had been their home, and moved under a thatched roof between solid walls of sun-baked brick.

Then there were darker matters to address. Rashood was brought out in his chains from the cell in the fort, which had originally been intended as a cellar. Dorian and Mansur who were, by the law of Islam, the judges and the executioners, took him into the forest far out of sight and earshot of the fort. They were gone for only a few hours, but when they returned they were grim of countenance, and Rashood was no longer with them.

The next day Tom convened a session of the family council. For the first time Louisa Courtney attended as the newest addition to the clan. As the eldest, Tom explained the decisions that faced them. 'Thanks to Jim and Louisa we are heavily overstocked with ivory. The best markets are still Zanzibar, the factories on the Coromandel Coast or at Bombay in the realm of the Great Mogul. Zanzibar is in the hands of Caliph Zayn al-Din, so that port is closed to us. I will stay on here at Fort Auspice to conduct company business, and I will need Jim to help me. Dorian will take the ships north, laden with as much of the ivory as they can carry, though I doubt that will be even a quarter of our total stock. When it has been sold he has even more pressing business in Muscat.' He looked at his younger brother. 'I will ask Dorian to explain it to you.'

Dorian removed the ivory mouthpiece of his hookah from

between his teeth, which were still white, even and without gaps. He looked around the circle of well-beloved faces. 'We know that Zayn al-Din was ousted by a revolutionary junta in Muscat. Both Batula and Kumrah were able to obtain certain confirmation of that on their last voyage to Oman. Kadem ibn Abubaker,' Dorian's handsome features darkened as he pronounced the name of Yasmini's murderer, 'purported to bring me an invitation from the junta, to take Zayn al-Din's place on the Elephant Throne, and to lead the battle against him. We don't know if the junta are truly trying to find me, or if it was merely another lie to try to entice me into Zayn's clutches. In any event, I refused for the sake of Yasmini, but in attempting to protect her I condemned her to death.'

Dorian's voice faltered, and Tom cut in gruffly, 'You are too harsh on yourself, brother. No man living could have foreseen the consequences.'

'Nevertheless Yasmini is dead by Zayn's orders and by the bloody hands of Kadem. There is no surer way for me to avenge her death than by sailing to Oman and throwing in my lot with the revolutionaries in Muscat.'

Mansur got up from his stool at the foot of the long table and went to stand at Dorian's shoulder. 'If you will allow it, I will sail with you, Father, and take my place at your right hand.'

'Not only will I allow it, I will welcome you with all my heart.'

'That is settled, then,' said Tom briskly. 'Jim and his bride will be here to help Sarah and me, so we will not be short-handed and we can spare Mansur. When do you plan on sailing, brother?'

'The trade winds will give way to the monsoon within six weeks. The winds should stand fair towards the end of next month,' Dorian replied. 'That will give us time to make the preparations.'

'We will strip all the remaining cannon out of the ships to give you more burthen for the ivory,' Tom said. 'Besides, we can use them here in the fort to bolster our defences. We can never be certain that Keyser has not smelt us out. Then there are these marauding Nguni *impis* sweeping through the land. Jim has routed one group under Manatasee, but we know from the fugitives who have come in to us that there are others just as savage running amok out there. Once you have sold the ivory you will be able to buy new guns in India. There are handy armourers in the Punjab. I have seen their work, and they make excellent nine-pounders. Just the right weight and length of barrel for our hulls.'

When the guns had been lifted out of the schooners, and all the powder and shot with them, they were ferried ashore in the longboats, dragged up the hill by teams of oxen and set in the earth emplacements around the fort.

'Well, that should do nicely.' Tom eyed the new defences with satisfaction. 'It would take an army with siege machines to subdue us. I think we are safe from marauding tribes, or even from any force that Keyser might care to send against us once he gets wind of where we are.'

Relieved of the cannon, the schooners rode lightly at anchor, showing much of the copper sheeting on their bottoms. 'We will soon find ballast to restore their trim,' Dorian promised, and he ordered the loading of the ivory and the refilling of the water casks.

Since Yasmini's murder Dorian had been cast into sudden moods of deep melancholy. He seemed prematurely aged by grief. There were new strands of pure silver in his red-gold hair and beard, and fresh lines deeply etched in his brow. But now, with a definite goal in mind and Mansur beside him, he seemed rejuvenated, once more abounding in vigour and determination.

They began to load the ivory aboard the schooners, and to lay in fresh stores and top up the water casks for the voyage ahead. The pickle barrels were refilled with sides of beef from the captured herds, and the hulls of the two ships settled deeper in the water. Dorian and his captains, Batula and Kumrah, agonized over the trim to wring the best speed and handiness from them.

'Until we have new guns to defend ourselves, we will have to rely on speed to run from any enemy that we encounter.

Despite our father's and brother Tom's best intentions and effort twenty years ago, there are still pirates at work in the Ocean of the Indies.'

'Keep well offshore from the African coast. That's where they have their nests,' Tom advised, 'and with the monsoon in your sails you will be well able to outrun any pirate dhow.'

They were all so busily employed, the women ordering their new homes, Tom and Jim occupied with the cattle and horses, Dorian and Mansur making the ships ready, that the days sped by.

'It does not seem like six weeks,' Jim told Mansur, as they stood on the beach together and looked out at the two little schooners. The yards were crossed and the crews had gone aboard. All was ready for them to catch the tide on the morrow.

'It seems, these days, that we no sooner set eyes upon each other than it is time to part again,' Mansur agreed.

'I have a feeling that this time it will be for more than just a short while, coz,' Jim said sadly. 'I believe that an adventure and a new life await you over the blue horizon.'

'You also, Jim. You have your woman, soon you will have a son, and you have made this land your own. I am alone, and I still seek the country of my heart.'

'No matter how many leagues of sea or land come between us, I shall always feel close to you in spirit,' said Jim.

Mansur knew how great an effort it had taken him to make such a sentimental declaration. He seized his cousin and hugged him hard. Jim hugged him back just as fiercely.

The two schooners sailed with the dawn and the tide, and all the family was on board the *Revenge* as they cleared the mouth of the bay. A mile offshore Dorian hove to, and Tom and Sarah, Jim and Louisa went down into the longboat and watched the two ships sail on and grow tiny with distance. At last they disappeared over the horizon and Jim turned the longboat back for the bay.

The fort seemed strangely empty without Dorian and Mansur, and they missed their marvellous voices at the family singsongs around Sarah's harpsichord in the evenings.

The voyage across the Ocean of the Indies was swift and almost without incident. With Mansur commanding the *Sprite* and Dorian the *Revenge*, the two schooners sailed in close company and the monsoon wind was kind to them. They gave the island of Ceylon a wide berth, mindful of Keyser's threats to warn the Dutch governor in Trincomalee of their trespasses in the colony of Good Hope, and they sailed on to the Coromandel Coast of south-eastern India, to reach it before the change of season. They called in at the competing trading factories of the English, French and Portuguese, without admitting their true identity. Both Dorian and Mansur adopted Arabic dress and in public spoke only that language. In each port Dorian judged the demand for ivory precisely, and was at pains not to flood the market with abundance. They did much better than he and Tom had calculated. With the ships' coffers charged with silver rupees and gold mohurs, and still a quarter of their ivory unsold, they turned back southwards and rounded the southern tip of India, sailing through the Palk between Ceylon and the mainland, then northwards again along the western coast until they reached the territories of the Great Mogul. Here they sold the remainder of the ivory in Bombay where the English East India Company had its headquarters, and in the other markets of the western ports of the crumbling Mogul empire.

The once mighty empire, the richest and most glorious that had ever flourished in the great continent, was now in decay and dissolution as lesser emperors than Babur and Akbar struggled for dominance. Despite the political upheavals, the new Persian influence at the court of Delhi made for a favourable trading climate. The Persians were traders to the marrow of their bones, and the prices for ivory exceeded those that they had received in the factories of the Carnatic.

Dorian was now in a position to rearm the two schooners, fill their empty holds with powder and shot, and transform them from trading vessels into fighting ships. They sailed on northwards and anchored in the roads of Hyderabad, through which the Indus river ran to the Arabian Sea. Dorian and Mansur went ashore with an armed party under Batula. They hired a carriage in the main souk, and an interpreter, to take them to one of the outlying areas of the sprawling, bustling city. The iron foundry of one of the most famous gun manufacturers in all the Punjab and the Indus basin – which meant in all India – was located on this flat and featureless alluvial plain. The proprietor was a Sikh of imperial mien, one Pandit Singh.

Over the following weeks Dorian and Mansur selected from his stores a battery of guns, twelve for each ship. These were all long-barrelled, with a four-inch bore and an eleven-foot-long barrel that fired an iron ball of nine pounds weight. With such a narrow bore relative to the length of barrel it was an accurate, long-ranged weapon.

Dorian measured and bore-gauged each of the barrels so that he could be certain that the same size of round-shot would fit them all, and that there were no discrepancies in the casting. Then, much to the indignation of Pandit Singh who took it as a slur on his workmanship, he insisted on firing the selected guns, to satisfy himself that there were no flaws in the metal. Two barrels burst on the first discharge. Pandit Singh explained that this had nothing to do with his manufacture, but was indubitably caused by the malignant influence of a *goppa*, the most pernicious variety of *shaitan*.

Dorian ordered gun carriages to be built by local carpenters to his own design. Then the guns on their own carriages were towed by bullock teams to the harbour, and at last carried out to the ships in lighters. Pandit Singh cast several hundred rounds of iron shot to fit the new guns, as well as great quantities of grape- and chain-shot. He was also able to supply any amount of gunpowder, which he personally guaranteed to be of the best quality. Dorian opened and sampled every barrel, rejecting over half before sending the remainder on board the schooners.

Next he turned his attention to the appearance of his flotilla, which in these seas was a consideration almost as important as its armament. He sent Mansur ashore to bargain for bolts of the finest quality green and burgundy canvas in the souks of Hyderabad. The sailmakers made up resplendent suits of sails, to replace the faded and weather-stained articles. The tailors of the souk were also put to work fitting the crews of the schooners with wide-legged cotton breeches and jackets to match the new sails. The results were impressive.

Being so close to Oman, Hyderabad was a hothouse of political and military rumour. While they bargained with the merchants, Dorian and Mansur drank their coffee and listened to the gossip. Dorian learned that the revolutionary junta still held power in Muscat, but that Caliph Zayn al-Din had consolidated his hold on Lamu and Zanzibar and all the other ports of the Omani empire. On every hand he heard that Zayn was planning an attack on Muscat to overthrow the junta and to recover his lost throne. In this endeavour he would have the assistance of the English East India Company and the Sublime Porte in Constantinople, seat of the Ottoman Turkish empire.

Dorian was also able to learn the identity of the new rulers in Muscat. They were a council of ten, of whom Dorian recognized most by name. They were men with whom he had eaten bread and salt, and ridden into battle in years gone by. His spirits soared when at last he was ready for sea.

Even after they sailed he did not immediately set a course for Muscat, which lay less than seven hundred miles away, west along the Tropic of Cancer in the Gulf of Oman. Instead, they sailed back and forth just out of sight of land while he drilled the crews of both ships in serving the new guns. Dorian had spared no expense on powder and shot, and kept them hard at it until they were almost as swift and expert as the gun-crews of a British Royal Navy frigate.

The flotilla made an impressive show when at last it sailed into the harbour of Muscat with the pristine sails set to the royals and the crew manning the yards in their new uniforms. The schooners flew the gold and royal-blue colours of Oman at their masthead. Dorian ordered the top sails struck and the new guns fired as a salute to the palace and the fortress. The gun-crew had grown fond of the sound of their own fire. Once begun, the honours continued enthusiastically until, in the end, they were persuaded to stop wasting further powder and shot only by the strenuous application of the rope's end.

All this created a great stir on the shore. Through his telescope Dorian watched the scurrying of messengers along the waterfront, and the gunners running to man the batteries on the parapets of the fortress. He knew that there would be a long delay while the junta decided how to react to the arrival of this strange flotilla of warships, so he settled down to wait.

Mansur launched the cutter and had himself rowed across to join his father. The two stood by the rail and turned their attention to the other shipping anchored in the inner harbour. In particular they studied a handsome, well-appointed three-masted ship that flew the Union flag, together with the pennant of his Britannic Majesty's consul general at her maintop. At first he presumed that such a fine ship must belong to the English East India Company, but her defaced blue ensign showed she was a privately owned vessel, like his own.

'A wealthy owner. That plaything must have cost five thousand pounds at the very least.' He read her name on her stern: '*Arcturus*. Of course, we would not find a ship belonging to John Company here in Muscat, because the Company has openly allied itself with Zayn al-Din in Zanzibar,' he pointed out to his son.

The blue-jacketed officers on the deck of the *Arcturus* turned their telescopes on them with equal interest. For the most part they seemed to be Indian or Arab for they were dark-skinned and most were bearded. Dorian picked out the captain by his cocked hat and the gold frogging on his sleeves. He was the exception, a ruddy-faced, clean-shaven European. Mansur swept his glass from the quarter-deck towards the bows and stopped with surprise. 'They have white women on board.'

Two ladies were strolling along the deck, accompanied by a fashionably dressed gentleman in a frock coat and high white stock. He wore a tall black hat and carried a cane with a gold head with which he illustrated some point he was making to his female companions.

'That's your rich owner for you,' Mansur observed, 'dressed like a dandy and very much satisfied with himself.'

'You can tell so much from so far?' Dorian asked, with a smile, but he studied the man carefully. Of course, it was highly unlikely that he had ever seen him before, but there seemed something hauntingly familiar about him.

Mansur laughed lightly. 'Cannot you see how he struts along like a penguin with a lighted candle stuck up its arse? I can tell that the plum pudding waddling along beside him in all the frippery and furbelows is his wife. They make a splendid couple—' Mansur broke off abruptly. Dorian lowered his glass and glanced at him. Mansur's eyes had narrowed and his suntanned cheek was suddenly stained a darker bronze. Dorian had seldom seen his son blush, but that was what was happening to him now. He lifted his telescope and studied the second woman, who was clearly the cause of his son's change of mood. More a girl than a woman, he thought, though tall enough. Waist like an hourglass but, then, she can probably afford an expensive French corset. Graceful deportment and lithe walk. Then he spoke aloud: 'What do you make of the other one?'

'Which one is that?' Mansur feigned indifference.

'The skinny one in the cabbage-coloured dress.'

'She is not skinny, and it's emerald,' said Mansur furiously, and was cast into confusion as he realized he had been caught out. 'Well, not that I am in the least concerned.'

The man in the tall hat seemed to take offence at their bold appraisal for he glared across the water at them, then took the arm of his plump companion and led her across to the starboard rail of the *Arcturus*. The girl in the green dress hesitated and looked back towards them.

Mansur watched her avidly. The wide-brimmed straw hat must have protected her complexion from the tropical sun. Even so, it was tanned to a soft peach colour. Though he was too far away to make out detail, he could see that her features were regular and finely proportioned. Her light brown hair was gathered up in a net on her shoulders. It was thick and lustrous. Her brow was wide and deep and her expression serene and intelligent. He felt strangely breathless, and wished he could tell the colour of her eyes. But then she tossed her head impatiently and gathered up her green skirts. She followed the older couple across the deck and out of Mansur's sight.

Mansur lowered the telescope, feeling oddly deprived.

'Well, the show is over for now,' Dorian said. 'I am going below. Call me if there is any change.'

An hour passed, then another, before Mansur hailed through the skylight of the stern cabin: 'Boat putting out from the palace jetty.'

It was a small lateen-rigged felucca with a crew of six, but there was a passenger in the stern sheets. He was dressed in snowy robes and turban, and at his waist was a scimitar in a gold scabbard. As they drew closer Dorian could make out the sparkle of a large ruby in his turban. This was a man of importance.

The felucca came in alongside and one of the crew hooked on to *Revenge*'s chains. After a short interval the visitor came up through the entry-port. He was probably a little older than Dorian. He had the sharp, hard features of one of the desert tribes, and the open, direct gaze of one who looked to far horizons. He crossed the deck towards Dorian with a long, supple stride.

'Peace unto you, bin-Shibam.' Dorian addressed him in the familiar form, as one comrade in arms might greet another. 'It is many years since you stood at my shoulder in the pass of the Bright Gazelle and let no enemy through.'

The tall warrior stopped in mid-stride and stared at Dorian in utter astonishment.

'I see that God has favoured you. You are as strong as you were when we were young. Do you still bear the lance against the tyrant and the patricide?' Dorian went on.

The warrior cried out and rushed forward to throw himself at Dorian's feet. 'Al-Salil! True prince of the royal house of

526

Caliph Abd Muhammad al-Malik. God has heard our fervent prayers. The prophecy of Mullah al-Allama is fulfilled. You have come back to your people in the time of their great sorrow, when most they need you.'

Dorian lifted bin-Shibam to his feet and embraced him. 'What are you, an old desert hawk, doing in the fleshpots of the city?' He held him at arm's length. 'You are dressed like a pasha. You who were once a fighting sheikh of the Saar, the fiercest of all the tribes of Oman.'

'My heart longs for the open desert, al-Salil, and to feel a racing camel under me,' bin-Shibam confessed, 'but instead I spend my time here in endless debate, when I should be riding free and wielding the long lance.'

'Come, old friend.' Dorian led him towards his cabin. 'Let us go where we can speak freely.'

In the cabin they reclined on the piled rugs and a servant brought them tiny brass cups of treacly coffee.

'To my sorrow and discomfort, I am now one of the war council of the junta. There are ten of us, one elected by each of the ten tribes of Oman. Ever since we toppled that murderous monster Zayn al-Din from the Elephant Throne, I have been sitting here in Muscat talking until my jaw aches and my gut grows slack.'

'Tell me the subject of these talks,' Dorian said, and over the next hours bin-Shibam confirmed almost everything that Dorian already knew.

He told of how Zayn al-Din had murdered all the heirs and descendants of Dorian's adoptive father Caliph al-Malik. He related many of his other unconscionable atrocities and the sufferings he had inflicted upon his people. 'In God's Name, the tribes rose up against his tyranny. We met his minions in battle and triumphed over them. Zayn al-Din fled the city and took refuge on the Fever Coast. We should have prosecuted our campaign against him to the end, but we were split by controversy over who should lead us. There were no heirs of the true Caliph left alive.' Here bin-Shibam bowed to Dorian. 'God forgive us, al-Salil, but we did not know your where-

527

abouts. It is only in the past few years that we heard whispers you were still alive. We have sent out messengers to every port in the Ocean of the Indies to seek you.'

'I have heard your pleas, though they were faint and far-off, and I have come to join your cause.'

'God's benevolence upon you, for we have been in grievous circumstances. Each of the ten tribes wants their own sheikh to take the caliphate. Zayn escaped with most of the fleet so we could not follow him to Zanzibar. While we talked end-lessly we grew weaker, and Zayn al-Din grew stronger. Seeing that we delayed, his minions, whom we had scattered, rallied and flocked back to him. He conquered the ports of the African mainland, and massacred those who supported us there.'

'It is the first principle of warfare that you should never give an enemy grace to gather his strength,' Dorian reminded him.

'Even as you say, al-Salil. Zayn has gathered powerful allies to his cause.' Bin-Shibam stood up and crossed to the porthole of the cabin. He drew aside the curtain. 'There is one of them who has come to us in all arrogance, purporting to act as a peace-maker, but in truth bringing an ultimatum and a deadly threat.' He pointed at the *Arcturus* anchored in the inner harbour.

'Tell me, who is aboard that ship? I see he flies the flag of a consul general.'

'He is the representative of the English monarch, his consul general to the Orient, one of the most powerful men in these seas. He comes purporting to mediate between us and Zayn al-Din, but we know this man well by reputation. As some merchants trade in rugs, he trades in nations, armies and all the weapons of war. He moves secretly from the conclaves of the English East India Company in Bombay to the court of the Great Mogul in Delhi, from the bosom of the Sublime Porte to the Emperor's cabinet in Peking. His wealth equals any of theirs. He has amassed it by dealing in power and war, and the lives of men.' Bin-Shibam spread his hands expressively. 'How can we children of the sands deal with such a one as this?'

'Have you heard his terms? Do you know what message he brings?'

'We have not yet met him. We have promised that we will do so on the first day of Ramadan. But we are afraid. We know that we will have the worst of any treaty we make with him.' He came back to kneel before Dorian. 'Perhaps in our hearts we were waiting for you to come to us, and to lead us into battle as you did so many times before. Give me your permission to go back to the council and tell them who you are, and why you have come.'

'Go, old friend. Tell them that al-Salil wishes to address the council.'

Bin-Shibam returned after nightfall. As soon as he entered the cabin he prostrated himself before Dorian. 'I would have come sooner but the council does not wish the English consul to see you come ashore. They bade me convey to you their deepest respect and, for your father's sake, they profess their loyalty to your family. They are waiting now in the throne room of the palace. I beg you, come with me and I will take you to them. From them you will learn more to your great profit and to ours.'

Dorian left Mansur in command of the flotilla. He threw a cloak of camel-hair over his head and shoulders and followed bin-Shibam down into the felucca. On the way to the palace jetty they passed close to the anchored *Arcturus*. The captain was on deck. Dorian saw his face in the light from the compass binnacle. He was giving orders to the officer of the watch. His was a fruity West Country accent, but it sounded strangely alien in Dorian's ears. I am already returning to the ties and loyalties of my childhood, he thought, and then his mind took another turning. If only Yasmini were with me now to share this homecoming.

Guards were waiting for them when they landed at the stone jetty, and they led Dorian through a heavy iron-grid door, and up a circular staircase into a maze of narrow passages.

The walls were of stone blocks and lit by torches guttering in wall brackets. It smelt of mould and rodents. At last they reached a heavily barred door. His escort beat upon it with the hilts of their lances, and when it swung open they went on down corridors that were wider and under high-domed ceilings. Now there were rushes on the floors and tapestries of silk and fine wool on the walls. They reached another doorway, with armoured sentries standing before it, who crossed their lance blades to deny them entrance.

'Who seeks admittance to the war council of Oman?'

'Prince al-Salil ibn al-Malik.'

The guards drew aside and made deep obeisance. 'Pass through, Your Highness. The council attends your arrival.'

The doors swung open slowly, creaking on their hinges, and Dorian stepped into the hall beyond. It was lit by hundreds of small ceramic lamps, the wicks floating in perfumed oil. But the light they shed was not sufficient to disperse the shadows that cloaked the far recesses, and left the high ceiling in darkness.

A circle of robed men was seated on cushions at a low table. The tabletop was cast from pure silver in the geometric patterns of Islamic religious art. The men rose as Dorian stood before them. One, who was clearly the elder and most senior of the council, came forward. His beard was shining white and he walked with the deliberate and venerable gait of age. He stared into Dorian's face.

'God's blessings on you, Mustapha Zindara,' Dorian greeted him, 'my father's trusted councillor.'

'It is him. In God's name, it is verily him,' cried the old man. He fell upon his face and kissed the hem of Dorian's robe. Dorian lifted him to his feet and embraced him.

One at a time the others came forward, and Dorian greeted most by name, asked after their families, and reminded them of desert crossings they had made together, battles they had fought as brothers in arms.

Then each took up a lamp. They all gathered around him and led him down the length of the long hall. As they approached the far end, something tall and massive glowed with a pearly lustre in the lamplight. Dorian knew what it was, for the last time he had seen it his father had been seated upon it.

They led Dorian up the steps and placed him on the piles of tigerskins and silken cushions embroidered with gold and silver thread that covered the summit platform of that tall structure. It had been carved three hundred years before from one hundred and fifty massive ivory tusks: the Elephant Throne of the Caliphate of Oman.

O ver the following days and weeks, from before dawn until after midnight, Dorian sat in council with his councillors and ministers. They reported to him on every facet of the affairs of the kingdom, from the mood of the populace and the desert tribes to the coffers of the treasury, the condition of the fleet and the strength of the army. They told him of the virtual breakdown in trade, and explained the diplomatic and political dilemmas that confronted them.

Swiftly Dorian grasped the desperate straits to which their cause had been reduced. What remained of the fleet that had made Oman a great seafaring nation had sailed with Zayn al-Din to the Fever Coast. Many tribes had become disheartened by the endless procrastination of the council, and most of their squadrons had disappeared like mist into desert fastness. The treasury was almost bare, for Zayn had ransacked it before he fled.

Dorian listened, then gave his orders. They were succinct and direct. It all seemed so natural and familiar, as though he had never ceased to command. His reputation for political and military genius was multiplied tenfold as it was repeated in the streets and souks of the city. His appearance was handsome and noble. He had the air of command. His sure manner and confidence were infectious. He froze what remained of the contents of the treasury, and issued bills backed by his own authority to meet long-overdue expenses. He took charge of the granaries, rationed the food supplies and prepared the city for siege.

He sent messages by swift camel to the sheikhs of the desert tribes, and rode out into the desert to meet them when they came to him to swear their allegiance. He sent them back into the interior to summon their battle array.

Inspired by his example, his military captains plunged with fresh vigour into planning the defence of the city. He replaced those who were clearly incompetent with men he knew from experience that he could trust.

When he toured the defences and ordered immediate repairs, the populace thronged about him joyously. They held up their children for a glimpse of the legendary al-Salil, and touched his robes as he passed.

Three times Dorian sent messages to the *Arcturus*, begging the consul general's indulgence, pleading the excuse that he was so recently elevated to the caliphate that he had not been able to acquaint himself with all the affairs of state. He fobbed off the inevitable meeting for as long as possible. Every day he could delay made his position that much stronger.

Finally, a boat came from the *Arcturus* to the palace jetty, bearing a letter from the English consul general. It was written in beautiful flowing Arabic script, and Mansur thought he recognized a feminine touch, and that he knew who had penned it. It was addressed not to the Caliph but to the President for the Time Being of the Revolutionary Council of Oman, and pointedly made no acknowledgement of Dorian's existence or of his title, Caliph al-Salil ibn al-Malik, although by now the English consul, through his spies, must certainly have been aware of all that was taking place.

The letter was brusque, and eschewed any attempt at flowery diplomacy. His Britannic Majesty's consul general to the Orient regretted that the council had been unable to grant him audience. Other more pressing matters made it necessary for the consul general to sail from Muscat to Zanzibar in the near future, and it was uncertain as to when he would return to Muscat.

Dorian was untroubled by the veiled threat the letter contained, but he was flabbergasted when he read the signature appended to it. Wordlessly he handed the letter back to Mansur and pointed out the name and signature that had been written in English.

'He has the same name as us.' Mansur was puzzled. 'Sir Guy Courtney.'

'The same name, yes,' Dorian's face was still pale and tight with the shock, 'and the same blood too. The moment I set eyes on him, I thought there was something familiar about him. He is your uncle Tom's twin brother, and my half-brother. That makes him another uncle of yours into the bargain.'

'I have never heard his name mentioned before this day,' Mansur protested, 'and I do not understand it at all.'

'There is every good reason that you have not heard Guy Courtney's name. Dark deeds and bad blood run deep.'

'Might I not know now?' Mansur asked.

Dorian was silent for a while before he sighed. 'It is a sad and sorry tale of treachery and deceit, jealousy and bitter hatred.'

'Tell me, Father,' Mansur insisted quietly.

Dorian nodded. 'Yes, I must, though it gives me no pleasure to relive these dire affairs. It is only fair that you should know.' He reached for the comfort of his hookah and did not speak again until the fire glowed in the bowl, and the blue smoke bubbled through the scented water of the glass reservoir.

'It's over thirty years ago now that Tom, Guy and I, all brothers together, sailed from Plymouth bound for Good Hope. We were with your grandfather Hal in the old *Seraph*. I was the baby, scarcely ten years of age, but Tom and Guy were almost grown men. There was another family on board. We were giving them passage to Bombay where Mr Beatty was to take up a high appointment with John Company. He had with him his daughters. The eldest girl was Caroline, sixteen and a beautiful vixen.'

'Surely you do not speak of the plum pudding we saw on the deck of the *Arcturus* in the harbour?' Mansur exclaimed.

'It seems so.' Dorian nodded. 'I assure you she was once lovely. Time changes all things.'

'Forgive me, Father, I should not have interrupted you. You were about to tell me of the other daughters.'

'The youngest was Sarah, and she was sweet and lovable.'

'Sarah?' Mansur looked askance.

'I know what you are thinking and you are correct in your assumption. Yes, she is now your aunt Sarah, but wait, I shall come to it – if you give me half a chance to get in a word edgewise.' Mansur looked repentant, and Dorian went on: 'Hardly had the *Seraph* cleared Plymouth harbour when Guy fell hopelessly in love with Caroline. She, on the other hand, had sheep's eyes for Tom. Your uncle Tom being Tom obliged her. He double-shotted her dainty cannon, stoked her fireplace, rattled her timbers and finally placed a large fruit cake to bake in her hot little oven.'

Mansur smiled, despite the seriousness of the subject. 'I am aghast that my own father should be familiar with such vulgar terms.'

'Forgive me for offending your sensitive feelings – but to continue. Guy was infuriated that his brother had so treated the object of his love and devotion and challenged Tom to a duel. Even in those early days Tom was a fine swordsman. Guy was not. Tom did not want to kill his brother, but on the other hand he wanted nothing further to do with the fruit cake Caroline was baking. For Tom it had been nothing more than a bit of fun. I was only a child at the time, and not certain as to what was happening, but I can still remember the storm that rocked and split the family. Our father forbade the duel, luckily for Guy.'

Mansur could see how Dorian was suffering at the memory, although he tried to cover his distress with a flippant air. He remained silent, respecting his father's feelings.

At last Dorian continued: 'In the end Guy broke away from us. When we reached Good Hope, he married Caroline and took on board Tom's bastard as his own. Then he left us and went on with the Beatty family to India. I never saw him again until now when we spied him and Caroline on the deck of the *Arcturus*.' He was silent again, brooding in the blue clouds of tobacco smoke.

'That was not the end of it. In Bombay, with his father-in-law's patronage, Guy rose swiftly to consular rank. When I was abducted at the age of twelve and fell into the hands of the slavers, Tom went to Guy and asked for his help to find me and rescue me. Guy refused, and tried to have Tom arrested for murder and other crimes he had not committed. Tom made a run for it, but not before he had swept up Sarah and eloped with her. This only fanned the flames of Guy's hatred. Sir Guy Courtney, his Britannic Majesty's consul general to the Orient, is a fine hater. My brother he may be, but in name alone. In fact, he is a bitter enemy and the ally of Zayn al-Din. But now I need your help in composing a letter to him.'

They took great pains with it. It was in Arabic style, filled with flowery compliments and protestations of goodwill. It went on to offer profuse apologies for any unintended offence that had been given. It expressed the greatest respect for the power and dignity of the consul general's office. Finally it went on to beg the consul general to attend an audience with the Caliph at a date and time of his own choice, but preferably at the first convenient opportunity.

'I would go out to the *Arcturus* myself but, of course, that would not be diplomatically correct. You must deliver the message. Whatever you do, do not let him suspect that we are blood relatives, nor that you speak English. I want you to assess his mood and intentions. Ask him if we can supply his ship with water, meat or fresh produce. Offer him and his crew the freedom and hospitality of the city. If they come ashore our spies will be able to milk news and intelligence from them. We must try to delay him here as long as possible, until we are ready to confront Zayn al-Din.'

Mansur dressed carefully for the visit, in the style befitting the eldest son of the Caliph of Oman. He wore the green turban of the believer with an emerald pin, one of the few notable gems that remained in the palace treasury after Zayn al-Din's depredations. Over his white robes, his waistcoat was of tanned camelskin embroidered with gold thread. His sandals, sword-belt and scabbard were all worked with filigree by the skilled goldsmiths of the city.

When Mansur mounted the ladder to the deck of the *Arcturus* with his red beard glowing in the sunlight, he cut such a magnificent figure that the captain and his officers gaped at him, and took a minute to recover.

'My compliments, sir, I am William Cornish, captain of this vessel.' The English captain's Arabic was poor and heavily accented. 'May I enquire who I have the honour of addressing?' His large red face, which had earned him the name 'Ruby' Cornish in the fleet of the English East India Company, glowed in the sunlight.

'I am Prince Mansur ibn al-Salil al-Malik,' Mansur replied, in flowing Arabic, touching his heart and lips in greeting. 'I come as an emissary of my father, Caliph al-Salil ibn al-Malik. I have the honour to bear a message for His Excellency the Consul General of His Britannic Majesty.'

Ruby Cornish looked uncomfortable. He followed what Mansur had said only with difficulty, and he had been severely enjoined not to acknowledge any titles of royalty to which these Omani rebels might lay claim.

'Please ask your retainers to remain in the barge,' he said. Mansur dismissed them with a gesture, and Cornish went on, 'If you will come this way, sir.' He led Mansur to where a sail had been rigged over the midships section of the upper-deck as a sun shade.

Sir Guy Courtney sat in a comfortable armchair covered with a leopardskin. His cocked hat was laid on the table beside him, and his sword was between his knees. He made no effort to rise from his chair as Mansur approached. He wore a burgundy-coloured jacket of fine broadcloth with solid gold buttons, and a high stock. His shoes were square-toed with silver buckles, and his white silk hose reached to his knees, and were held by garters that exactly matched the colour of his jacket. His tight-fitting trousers were also white, with a codpiece that flattered his masculinity. He wore the ribbons and stars of the Order of the Garter and some Oriental decorations.

536

Mansur made the polite gesture of greeting: 'I am honoured by your condescension, Your Excellency.'

Guy Courtney shook his head irritably. Mansur knew now that he was Tom's twin and must therefore be in his late forties, but he looked younger. Although his hair was thinning and receding, his figure was slim and his belly flat. But there were liver-coloured bags under his eyes, and one of his front teeth was discoloured. His expression was sour and unfriendly. 'My daughter will translate,' he said in English, and indicated the girl who stood behind his chair. Mansur pretended not to understand. He had been acutely aware of her presence since the moment he had stepped aboard the yacht, but now he looked directly at her for the first time.

He had the greatest difficulty in keeping his face expressionless. The first thing he noticed was that her eyes were large and green, lively and searching. The whites were clear, and the lashes long and densely curled.

Mansur tore away his gaze and addressed Sir Guy again. 'Forgive my ignorance but I speak no English,' he apologized. 'I do not understand what it was Your Excellency said.'

The girl spoke in beautiful classical Arabic, making music of the words: 'My father speaks no Arabic. With your forbearance I will translate for him.'

Mansur bowed again. 'I compliment you, my lady. Your command of our tongue is perfection. I am Prince Mansur ibn al-Salil al-Malik, and I come as the messenger of my father, the Caliph.'

'I am Verity Courtney, the consul general's daughter. My father bids you welcome aboard the *Arcturus*.'

'We are honoured by the emissary of such a powerful monarch, and such an illustrious nation.' For a while longer they exchanged compliments and expressions of esteem and respect, but Verity Courtney managed not to acknowledge any royal titles or honours. She was weighing him as carefully as he was her. She was much more handsome than when he had seen her through the lens of a telescope. Her complexion was lightly sun-gilded but otherwise of English perfection, and her features were strong and determined, without being heavy or

537

coarse. Her neck was long and graceful, her head perfectly balanced upon it. When she smiled politely her mouth was large and her lips full. Her two upper front teeth were slightly misaligned, but the imperfection was arresting and attractive.

Mansur asked if there was anything that they needed that he might be able to supply. Sir Guy told Verity, 'We are short of water, but don't let him know it.'

She relayed the request: 'A ship always needs water, *effendi*. It is not a pressing need, but my father would be grateful for your generosity.' Then she gave Mansur's answer to her father.

'The Prince says he will send out the water tender immediately.'

'Don't call him a prince. He is a dirty little rebel, and Zayn will feed him to the sharks. The water he sends out to us will probably be half camel piss.'

Verity did not even blink at her father's choice of words. Obviously she was accustomed to his phraseology. She turned back to Mansur. 'Of course, *effendi*, the water will be sweet and potable? You would not send us camel's piss?' she asked not in Arabic but in English. It was so artlessly done, her tone so level and her green eyes so candid that Mansur might have been taken in, had he not been ready for it. Yet he was so taken aback by those words on her ladylike lips that he only just managed to keep his own expression polite but neutral. He cocked his head slightly in blank enquiry. 'My father is grateful for your generosity.' She switched back to Arabic, having carried out this test of his linguistic skills.

'You are honoured guests,' Mansur replied.

'He speaks no English,' Verity said to her father.

'See what the blighter is after. They're a slippery bunch of eels, these wogs.' It was only recently that a secretary at Government House had penned this acronym for Worthy Oriental Gentleman, and as a mildly derogatory term it had been adopted throughout the Company.

'My father asks after the health of your father.' Verity avoided saying the forbidden word 'Caliph'.

'The Caliph is blessed with the strength and vigour of ten ordinary men.' Mansur emphasized his father's title. He was

538

enjoying the battle of wits. 'It is a virtue embodied in the royal blood of Oman.'

'What does he say?' Sir Guy demanded.

'He is trying to make me acknowledge that his father is the new ruler.' Verity smiled and nodded.

'Make the correct response.'

'My father hopes that your father will enjoy a hundred more summers in such robust health and in the sunshine of God's favour, and that his conscience will always lead him in the loyal and honourable path.'

'The Caliph, my father, wishes that your father shall have one hundred strong and noble sons, and that all his daughters grow to be as beautiful and clever as the one who stands before me now.' It was unsubtle and bordering on insolence, except of course that he was a prince and might take such liberties. He saw the quick shadow of annoyance in the depths of her green eyes.

Aha! he thought, without a smile of triumph. First blood to me.

But her riposte was quick and pointed. 'May all your father's sons be blessed with good manners and show respect and courtesy towards all women,' she replied, 'even if it is not in their true nature.'

'What's all that about?' Sir Guy demanded.

'He is being solicitous of your health.'

'Find out when his rascally father will see me. Warn him that I will brook no more nonsense from them.'

'My father enquires when he may present his compliments and duty in person to your illustrious father.'

'The Caliph would welcome such an occasion. It would also be an opportunity for him to enquire how it is that the consul general's daughter speaks the language of the Prophet with such a mellifluous tongue.'

Verity almost smiled. He was such a beautiful man. Even his insults were titillating, and his manner was so engaging that, despite herself, she could not take real offence. The simple answer to his implied question was that since her childhood on Zanzibar island, where her father had at one time been stationed, she had been fascinated by all things Oriental. She had learned to love the Arabic language with its poetic, expressive vocabulary. This was, however, the first time she had ever been even vaguely attracted to an Oriental man.

'If your honoured father would receive me and my father I would be pleased to respond to any question of his personally, rather than send my answers through one of his children.'

Mansur bowed to concede that she had taken the bout. He did not smile but his eyes sparkled as he took the letter from his sleeve and handed it to her.

'Read it to me,' Sir Guy ordered, and Verity translated it into English, listened to her father's reply, then turned back to Mansur. She made no further pretence at feminine modesty but looked him directly in the eye.

'The consul general wishes to have all the members of the council present at the meeting,' Verity told him.

'The Caliph would be delighted and honoured to accede to that request. He values the advice of his councillors.'

'How long will it take to arrange this meeting?' Verity demanded.

Mansur thought for a moment. 'Three days. The Caliph would be further honoured if you would join him in an expedition into the desert to fly his falcons against the bustard.'

Verity turned to Sir Guy. 'The rebel leader wants you to go out hawking in the wilderness. I am not certain that you would be safe.'

'This new fellow would be insane to offer me any violence.' Sir Guy shook his head. 'What he is after is a chance to speak in privacy to try to win my support. You can be certain that the palace is a hive of intrigue and a nest of spies. Out in the desert I might learn something from him to my great advantage. Tell him that we will go.'

Mansur listened to her polite rendition as though he had not understood a single word that Sir Guy had said. Then he touched his lips. 'I will personally arrange everything in a manner befitting the importance of the occasion. I will send a barge to collect your luggage tomorrow morning. It will be taken out to the hunting encampment to await your arrival.'

'That would be acceptable.' Verity gave Sir Guy's consent.

'We are honoured. I thirst for the day when I shall set eyes upon your face once again,' he murmured, 'as the hard-run stag thirsts after cool waters.' He backed away with a graceful gesture of farewell.

'You are flushed.' Sir Guy showed a touch of concern for his daughter. 'It is the heat. Your mother is also quite prostrated.'

'I am perfectly well. I thank you for your concern, Father,' Verity Courtney replied smoothly. She, who took great pride in her cool nerves even in the most difficult circumstances, found her emotions most confused.

As the prince went down into the royal barge, she did not want to stare after him. However, she could not leave her father standing alone by the ship's rail.

Mansur looked up at her so suddenly that she could not look away without appearing guilty. She held his gaze defiantly, but as the sail of the felucca caught the breeze and swelled out, it came between them like a screen and cut them off from each other.

Verity found herself breathlessly angry but strangely elated. I am not some brainless simpering Oriental *houri*, not some plaything for him to dally with. I am an Englishwoman and I will be treated as such, she determined silently, then turned to her father, and took a breath to steady herself before she spoke. 'Perhaps I should stay with Mother while you go to parley with the rebels. She really is feeling poorly. Captain Cornish can translate for you,' she said. She did not want to be mocked again by those dancing green eyes and that enigmatic smile.

'Don't be daft, child. Cornish doesn't know how to ask the time of day. I need you. You are coming with me, and no arguments.'

Verity was both annoyed and relieved by his insistence. At

541

least I will have an opportunity for another passage of arms with the pretty princeling. This time we will see who is quicker with the tongue, she thought.

Before dawn on the third morning the Caliph's barge conveyed the guests to the palace wharf, where Mansur was waiting with a large bodyguard of armed horsemen and grooms to greet them. After another lengthy exchange of compliments, he led Sir Guy to an Arab stallion with a glistening sable coat. Then the grooms led forward a chestnut mare for Verity. She seemed a tractable animal, although she had the legs and deep chest that bespoke both speed and stamina. Verity mounted astride with the ease and grace of an accomplished horsewoman. When they moved out through the city gates it was still dark, and outriders went ahead with torches to light the road. Mansur rode in close attendance on Sir Guy, elegant in his English hunting dress, Verity at her father's left hand.

She wore an intriguing mixture of English and Oriental hunting dress. Her high silk hat was held in place by a long blue scarf, the loose ends thrown back over one shoulder. Her blue coat reached below her knees but the tails were pleated to allow her freedom of movement while preserving her modesty. Beneath it she had on loose cotton trousers and soft knee-boots. Mansur had chosen for her a jewelled saddle with high pommel and cantle. At the jetty she had greeted him frostily and barely glanced at him while she chatted easily with her father. Excluded from her conversation, Mansur was able to study her quite openly. She was one of those unusual Englishwomen who flourish in the tropics. Rather than wilting and sweating and succumbing to the prickly heat, she was cool and poised. Even her costume, which might have been dowdy or outrageous on another, she wore with *élan*.

At first they rode through the date-palm groves and culti-vated fields outside the city walls where, in the first light of dawn, veiled women drew water from deep wells and carried it away in pots balanced on their heads. Herds of camels and beautiful horses drank together from the irrigation canals. On the fringe of the desert they came upon encampments of tribesmen who had come in from the wilderness in response to the Caliph's summons to arms. They came out of their tents and shouted loyal greetings to the prince and fired joy shots in the air as he passed.

But soon they were out in the true desert. When the day broke over the dunes, they were all awed by its majesty. The fine dustclouds suspended in the air reflected the sun's rays and set the eastern sky on fire. Although Verity rode with her head thrown back to gaze upon this celestial splendour, she was acutely aware that the prince was watching her. His importunity no longer annoyed her so intensely. Despite herself, she was beginning to find his attention amusing, although she was determined not to give him the slightest encouragement.

Ahead of them a large group of riders came over the dunes to meet them. The huntsmen led them. Their horses were gaily caparisoned in the gold and blue colours of the caliphate, and they carried hooded falcons on their wrists. Behind them came the musicians, with lutes, horns and the big bass drums suspended on each side of their saddles, then a rabble of grooms leading spare horses, water-carriers and other retainers. They welcomed the consul general with shouting and musket shots, fanfares and the booming beat of the drums, then fell in behind the prince's party.

After several hours' riding, Mansur led them across a wide, arid plain to where a steep valley fell away to a dry riverbed far below. On the top of these cliffs stood a weird cluster of massive rock monoliths. As they drew closer Verity realized that they were the remains of an ancient city that was perched above the valley, guarding a long-forgotten trade route.

'What ruins are these?' Verity asked Mansur, the first words she had spoken directly to him all that morning.

'We call it Isakanderbad, the City of Alexander. The Macedonian passed this way three thousand years ago. His army built this fortress.'

They rode in among the tumbled walls and monuments where once mighty armies had celebrated their triumphs. Now they were inhabited only by the lizard and the scorpion.

However, a flock of servants had arrived during the preceding days, and in the courtyard where, perhaps, the conqueror had once held sway, they had set up the hunting camp, a hundred coloured pavilions furnished with all the luxuries and amenities of a royal palace. There were servants to meet the guests too. Perfumed water was poured for them from golden ewers so that they might wash away the dust of the ride and refresh themselves.

Then Mansur led them to the largest of the grand tents. When they entered Verity saw it was hung with draperies of gold and blue silk, and that the floors were covered with precious rugs and cushions.

The Caliph and his councillors rose to greet them. Verity's skills as an interpreter were tested by the exchanges of compliments and good wishes. Nevertheless she took the opportunity to study the Caliph, al-Salil.

Like his son he was red-bearded and handsome, yet there were the marks of care and sorrow etched deeply into his features, and silver threads in his beard, which he had not covered with henna dye. There was something else she found impossible to fathom. She felt a sense of *déjà vu* when she looked into his eyes. Was it simply that Prince Mansur so closely resembled him? She thought not. It was more than that. Added to this disconcerting impression, something strange was taking place between her father and al-Salil also. They stared at each other as though they were not strangers meeting for the first time. There was a brittle tension between them. It was as though the summer thunderstorms were brewing and the air was heavy with humidity and the sense that the lightning would flash out at any moment.

Al-Salil led her father to the centre of the tent and seated him on a pile of cushions. He took the place beside him. Servants brought them aniseed-flavoured sherbet in golden goblets, and they nibbled at sugared dates and pomegranates.

The silk draperies kept out the worst of the desert heat,

and the conversation was polite. The royal cooks served the midday meal. Dorian helped Sir Guy to titbits from huge salvers, which overflowed with saffron rice, tender lamb and baked fish, then waved away what remained to be taken to his retinue seated in ranks outside the pavilion.

Now the talk became more earnest. Sir Guy nodded at Verity to come to sit between him and al-Salil. Then, while the sun rose to its zenith and outside all the world drowsed in the heat, they conversed in low tones. Sir Guy warned al-Salil of how fragile was the alliance of desert tribes that he was building. 'Zayn al-Din has enlisted the support of the Sublime Porte in Constantinople. Already there are twenty thousand Turkish troops in Zanzibar, and the ships to convey them to these shores as soon as the monsoon turns.'

'What of the English Company? Will they side with Zayn?' al-Salil asked.

'They have not yet committed themselves,' Sir Guy replied. 'As you are probably aware, the governor in Bombay awaits my recommendation before he decides.' He might just as well have used the word 'order' rather than 'recommendation'. Al-Salil and every one of his council could be in no doubt as to where the power lay.

Verity was so absorbed with her work of translating that again Mansur could study her intimately. For the first time he became aware of strange depths and undercurrents between her and her father. Could it be that she was afraid of him? he wondered. He could not be certain, but he sensed something dark and chilling to the spirit.

As they talked on through the heat of the afternoon, Dorian listened, nodded and gave the appearance of being moved by Sir Guy's logic. In reality he was listening for the hidden truths and meanings behind the flowery phrases that Verity translated to them. Gradually he was starting to understand how his half-brother had achieved such power and circumstance.

He is like a serpent, he twists and turns, and always you are aware of the venom in him, Dorian thought. In the end he nodded wisely and made reply: 'All of what you say is true. I can only pray to God that your wisdom and benign interest in these dire affairs of Oman will lead us to a just and lasting solution. Before we go further I would like to assure Your Excellency of the deep gratitude I feel towards you personally and on behalf of my people. I hope that I will be able to demonstrate these warm feelings in a more substantial manner than by mere words.' He saw the avaricious gleam in his brother's eye.

'I am not here for material rewards,' Sir Guy replied, 'but we have a saying in my country that the workman is worthy of his wage.'

'It is an expression that we in this country understand well,' Dorian said. 'But now the heat passes. There will be time for us to speak again on the morrow. We can ride out to fly my falcons.'

The hawking party, a hundred horsemen strong, left Isak-anderbad and rode along the edge of the cliff that looked down upon the dry river-course hundreds of feet below. The lowering sun cast mysterious blue shadows over the splendid chaos of tumbled walls and cliffs, and serpentine wadis.

'Why would Alexander choose such a wild and desolate place to build a city?' Verity wondered aloud.

'Three thousand years ago there was a mighty river and the valley floor would have been a garden of green,' Mansur replied.

'It is sad to think that so little is left of such a mighty enterprise. He built so much and it was destroyed in a single lifetime by the lesser men who inherited it from him.'

'Even Isakander's tomb is lost.' Gradually Mansur lured her into conversation, and slowly she lowered her guard and responded to him more readily. He was delighted to find in her a companion who shared his love of history, but as their discussion deepened he found that she was a scholar and her knowledge exceeded his own. He was content to listen to her rather than express his own opinions. He enjoyed the sound of her voice, and her use of the Arabic language.

The huntsmen had scouted the desert for days before and they were able to lead the Caliph to the most likely area in which they might find game. This was a wide, level plain, studded with clumps of low saltbush. It stretched away to the limit of the eye. Now, as it cooled, the air was sweet and clear as a mountain stream, and Verity felt alive and vital. Yet there was a restlessness in her, as though something extraordinary was about to happen, something that might change her life for ever.

Suddenly al-Salil called for a gallop and the horns rang out. They spurred forward together like a squadron of cavalry. Hoofs drummed on the hard-baked sand, and the wind sang past Verity's ears. The mare ran lightly under her, seeming to skim the ground like a swallow in flight, and she laughed. She looked over at Mansur, who rode beside her, and they laughed together for no other reason than that they were young and full of the joy of life.

Suddenly there was a shriller horn blast. A shout of excitement went up from the huntsmen. Ahead of the line a pair of bustards had been started from the cover of the saltbushes by the thunder of hoofs. They ran with their necks out-thrust, their heads held low to the ground. They were huge birds, larger than a wild goose. Although their plumage was cinnamon brown, blue and dark red it was so cunningly blended to match the desert terrain that they seemed ethereal and as insubstantial as wraiths.

At the sound of the horn the line of riders reined in. The horses milled, circled and chewed their bits, eager to run again, but they held their places in the line while al-Salil rode forward with a falcon on his wrist. It was a desert saker, the loveliest and fiercest of all falcons.

In the short time since they had been in Oman, Dorian had made this particular bird his favourite. It was a tercel, and therefore the more beautiful gender of the species. At three

547

years of age, it was at the peak of its strength and swiftness. He had named it Khamseen, after the furious desert wind.

With the line of horsemen halted, the bustards had not been driven into flight. They had gone back into cover in the saltbush. They must have been lying flat against the earth with their long necks thrust out. They remained still as the desert rocks that surrounded them, concealed from the eyes of the hunters by their colouring.

Al-Salil walked his mount slowly towards the patch of scrub where they had last been seen. Excitement built in the line of watchers. Although Verity did not share the passion of the true falconer, she found her breath coming short and the hand that held the reins was trembling slightly. She glanced sideways at Mansur and his features were rapt. For the first time she felt herself completely in tune with him.

Suddenly there was a harsh, croaking cry, and from under the front hoofs of al-Salil's stallion a huge body launched itself into flight. Verity was astonished at how swiftly and strongly the bustard rose into the air. The whistling beat of the wings carried clearly in the silence. Their span was as wide as the full stretch of a man's arms, blunt at the tips and deep as they hurled the bird aloft.

The watchers began a soft chant as the Caliph slipped the hood off the tercel's marvellously savage head. It blinked its yellow eyes and looked to the sky. The bass drummer began a slow beat that boomed out across the plain, exciting both watchers and falcon.

'Khamseen! Khamseen!' they chanted. The tercel saw the bustard outlined against the hard blue and bated against the jesses that restrained him. He hung for a moment upside down, beating his wings as he struggled to be free. The Caliph lifted him high, slipped the jesses and launched him into the air.

On swift blade-sharp wings the tercel rose, higher and higher, circling. His head moved from side to side as he watched the huge flapping bird that sped across the plain below him. The drummer increased the beat and the watchers raised their voices: 'Khamseen! Khamseen!'

548

The tercel reached the heights, a tiny black shape on sickle wings against the steely blue, towering over his massive prey. Then, abruptly, he cocked his wings back and dropped like a javelin, plummeting towards the earth. The drummer beat a frenetic crescendo, then abruptly cut it short.

In the silence they heard the wind fluting over the wings, and the tercel's stoop was so swift as to cheat the eye. He hit the bustard with a sound like the clash of fighting stags' antlers. The bustard seemed to burst into a cloud of feathers that streamed away on the breeze.

A triumphant cry went up from a hundred throats. Verity found that she was gasping as though she had surfaced from a deep dive below the sea.

Al-Salil recovered his falcon, fed him the bustard's liver and stroked him while he gulped it down. Then he called for another bird. With it on his wrist, he rode ahead with Sir Guy and most of his councillors. In the passion of the hunt that gripped them all, there was no discussion. Verity was no longer needed to translate for them, and she lingered with Mansur. Subtly he slowed his horse and she kept pace with him, so rapt in their talk that she seemed not to realize they were falling further and further behind the Caliph's party.

The antagonism between them evaporated as they talked, and both were animated by the other's proximity. When Verity laughed it was a fetching sound that delighted Mansur, and her handsome, rather austere features were enlivened almost to the point of beauty.

Slowly they forgot the large, colourful entourage in which they rode, and became isolated in the midst of the multitude. A distant shout and the beat of the war drum jerked them back to reality. Mansur rose in his stirrups and shouted with astonishment, 'Look! Do you not see them?' The men around them were shouting and the horns blared out; the drummers beat a frenzy.

'What is it? What has happened?' His change of mood was infectious and Verity pressed up close beside him. Then she saw what had caused the pandemonium. On the far slope of the valley the small party of huntsmen led by al-Salil was at full gallop. While casting for bustard they had put up much more dangerous game.

'Lions!' Mansur cried. 'Ten at least, maybe more! Come, follow me. We must not miss this sport.' Verity pushed her mare to keep pace with him as they raced down their side of the valley.

The pride that al-Salil and his hunters were driving before them, were swift, tawny shapes darting through the patches of saltbush, flitting in and out of the steep-sided wadis that rent the tortured desert ground.

The Caliph had passed his falcon to one of the hunters, and they had all snatched their long weapons from the lance-bearers. They were in full chase after the pride, their cries thin and faint with distance. Then there was a sudden terrible roar of pain and fury as al-Salil leaned from the saddle and speared one of the swift shapes. Verity saw the lion bowled over by the lance thrust, rolling and bellowing in a cloud of pale dust. Al-Salil cleared his weapon with an expert backward sweep and rode on after his next victim, leaving the downed lion grunting its last with the lung blood pumping from its jaws. The riders coming up behind him lanced the dying beast again and again.

Then another of the huntsmen scored with the lance, and another, and all became a wild confusion of racing horses and fleeing yellow cats. The hunters shouted each time they hit. The horses whinnied and shrilled under them, driven mad by the smell of lion blood mingled with the roaring of the wounded cats. The horns blew, the drums pounded and the dust shrouded it all.

Mansur snatched a lance from the bearer who rode behind him and galloped after his father. Verity kept pace with him but the hunt swept away over the crest of the hill before they could join in with the sport.

They passed two dead lions stretched out among the saltbush. Their carcasses were riddled with wounds, and the horses shied at the terrifying scent. By the time they reached the ridge and looked over, the hunt was scattered across the plain. Almost a mile away, they could make out al-Salil's distinctive figure in his flowing white robes leading the hunt, but there was no longer any sign of the lion pride. They had disappeared like brown smoke into the vastness of the desert.

'Too late,' Mansur lamented, and reined in his mount. 'They have run away from us. We will simply use up the horses to no profit if we try to chase after them.'

'Your Highness!' In her agitation Verity did not seem aware that she had used his title. 'I had a glimpse of one of the lions breaking away along the ridge.' She pointed off towards the left. 'It seemed to be heading back towards the river.'

'Come, then, my lady.' Mansur turned his stallion back. 'Show me where you saw it.'

She led him along the high ground, and then at an angle off the skyline. Within a quarter of a mile they were out of sight of the rest of the entourage, cantering alone through the wilderness. The excitement was still high in both of them, and they laughed together without reason. Verity's hat blew from her head and when Mansur would have turned back to retrieve it, she called, 'Leave it! We shall find it later.' She tossed her blue silk scarf into the air. 'This will mark the spot for us when we return.'

As she cantered on she shook out her hair. Until now she had covered it with a wide-meshed silk net. Mansur was astonished by its length as it floated over her shoulders in a dense honey-brown cloud, thick and lustrous in the soft evening sunlight. With her hair down her appearance was completely altered. She seemed to have become a wild thing, free and unfettered by the restraints of society and convention.

Mansur had fallen a little behind her, but he was content to follow and watch her. He felt a deep longing welling within him. This is my woman. This is the one I have waited and longed for. As he thought it, he caught a flicker of movement ahead of her running horse. It might have been the flit of the wings of one of the drab little thrushes, but he knew it was not.

He concentrated his attention and the complete picture leaped into his mind. It was a lion: the lash of its tail had alerted him. It was crouching in a shallow gully directly in

551

Verity's path. It was flattened against the ground, which was the same pale brown as its sleek hide. Its ears were laid flat against its skull, so that it looked like a monstrous serpent coiled to strike. Its eyes were an implacable gold. There was pink froth on its thin black lips, and a lance wound high in its shoulder, which had angled down to pierce the lung.

'Verity!' Mansur screamed. 'It's there, right in your path. Turn back! For God's sake, turn back!'

She looked back over her shoulder, her green eyes wide with surprise. He did not realize that he had shouted at her in English. Perhaps she was so taken aback by his change of language that she did not understand the import. She made no effort to check her mare, and galloped on towards the crouching lion.

Mansur spurred his stallion to the top of his speed, but he had dropped too far back to catch them. At the last moment the mare sensed the presence of the lion, and shied violently to one side. Verity was almost hurled from the saddle, but she snatched at the pommel and prevented herself going right over. She lost her seat, however, and one foot was out of its stirrup. As she was thrown forward over the mare's neck she hung on with both arms. The mare threw her head at the stench of the lion and the reins were jerked from Verity's hand. She was no longer in control.

The lion charged at the mare from the side. It was uttering deep chesty grunts and with each one bloody froth burst from its lips. The mare pivoted away and Verity was flung to one side, hanging down her flank with one foot trapped in the stirrup. The lion sprang upwards with both front paws reaching out, the claws fully extended, great yellow hooks that could slice through hide and muscle to the bone.

It struck the mare with a force that sent her staggering back on her haunches, but the lion's claws were sunk into her hindquarters. The mare shrilled with terror and agony and kicked out with both back legs. Verity was trapped between the two plunging bodies and her screams cut across Mansur's nerves. It sounded as though she was mortally wounded.

His stallion was already at full charge. Mansur couched his

lance and steered the horse under him with his heels, altering the angle of his attack, reaching forward with the bright lance-head dancing before him like a silver insect. The lion humped up over the mare's back, hanging on to her with the strength of those massive forelegs as she reared and bucked. It was roaring in a continuous bellow of sound. Its flanks were roped with muscle and the rack of its ribs was clearly outlined beneath the skin. He aimed the lance just behind the straining shoulder. It struck cleanly exactly at the spot he had intended. He ran the steel in with the impetus of the stallion's weight. It was almost effortless, just the jar as the steel touched bone, then glided on to transfix the lion from shoulder to shoulder. The beast arched its spine backwards in mortal agony, and the shaft of the lance snapped like a reed. The mare tore herself free of the hooked claws and raced away, the blood from her wounds slicked down her quarters. Still writhing and contorting the lion rolled in the low scrub.

Verity was half under the mare, clinging to the side of her neck, one foot still trapped in a stirrup. If she lost her grip she would be thrown to the ground and dragged along, with the back of her head bouncing along on the stones until her skull cracked open like an eggshell. She had no more breath to spare for screams. She hung on with all her strength, as the mare bolted.

Despite the bloody gashes in her hindquarters the horse ran hard. She was mad with terror, her eyeballs rolled back until the red lining of the sockets glared and silver ropes of saliva trailed from her open mouth. Verity tried to pull herself back into the saddle but her efforts merely goaded the mare to greater speed. In extreme terror she seemed endowed with fresh strength.

Mansur dropped the broken stub of the lance and shouted at the stallion, hammering his heels into the animal's heaving flanks, whipping him across the shoulders with the loose ends of his reins, but he could not catch the mare. They raced back down the slope, and at the bottom the mare turned towards the ancient riverbed. Mansur sent the stallion after her.

For half a mile they ran on, and the gap between the horses

never changed, until the mare's dreadful injuries began to tell. Her stride shortened almost imperceptibly and her back hoofs began to throw outside the line of her run.

'Hold hard, Verity!' Mansur shouted encouragement. 'I am gaining on you now. Don't let go!'

Then he saw the brink of the precipice open directly ahead of the mare, and he looked down the sheer wall of rock into the river valley two hundred feet below. Black despair clamped down on his heart as he imagined mare and girl hurled out over the cliff and dropping to the rocks far beneath.

He drove the stallion on with the strength of his arms and legs, and fierce resolve in his heart. The mare weakened visibly and the gap between them closed, but only slowly. At the last moment the mare saw the earth open ahead of her and tried to turn away, but as her front hoofs bit into the loose earth of the rim it broke away under her. She reared and teetered in wild panic, then toppled backwards.

As the mare went over Mansur threw himself from the back of the stallion and on the edge of the precipice he reached out and grabbed Verity's ankle. He was almost jerked out over the drop, but then her stirrup leather snapped and her leg was free. Still her weight dragged him face down on the sill, but he held on with all his strength. The mare fell away under them, dropping fifty feet before striking the cliff face and screaming in terror as she bounded out into the void.

Verity swung like a pendulum, dangling upside down from his right hand by one leg. The skirts of her coat fell over her head, but she dared not move, knowing that it might break his precarious grip on her ankle. She could hear his harsh panting above her, but she dared not look up. Then his voice reached her. 'Stay like that. I am going to pull you up.' His voice was strangled with the effort.

Even in her dreadful predicament she took note that he was still speaking English, unaccented and sweet in her ears, the voice of home. If I must die, let that be the last sound I hear, she thought, but could not trust her own voice to reply to him. She looked down through dizzying space to the valley floor so far below her. Her head swam with vertigo, but she hung quiescent and felt his hard fingers biting into her ankle through the soft leather of her boot. Above her Mansur grunted with the effort, and the rough rock of the cliff scraped against her hip as she was drawn upwards a few inches by his strength.

Blindly Mansur groped backwards with one leg and found a narrow cleft in the rock. He shoved his knee and thigh deeply into it. It anchored him, and now he could release his left hand with which he had been clinging to a precarious hold. He reached down over the sill of the cliff and locked both hands on to Verity's ankle.

'I have you now with both hands.' His voice was harsh with the effort. 'Courage, girl!' More decisively she was pulled upwards. He paused to gather himself.

'And a tiger!' Mansur gasped out the old nautical exhortation to encourage himself and her.

She wanted to scream at him to shut his mouth, to eschew the childish nonsense and use all his strength to lift her. She knew that the difficult part still lay ahead when he had to heave her backwards over the rock rim. He pulled again and she was dragged up another short space. There was a pause and she felt him adjusting and strengthening his position, using his hips to wriggle backwards, trying to wedge his other leg into the cleft in the rock. He pulled again more strongly from his enhanced position, and she was lifted higher.

'God love you for this,' she whispered, just loud enough for him to hear, and he heaved again so hard that she felt her leg might be pulled out of its socket in her hip.

'Nearly there, Verity,' he said, and pulled, but this time she did not move. A small shrub had taken root in a crack in the cliff face. Now its branches had hooked into her breeches. He pulled again but he could not budge her. She was firmly held by the wiry bush.

'Can't move you,' Mansur grunted. 'Something holding you.'

'It's a bush, catching my legs,' she whispered.

'Try to reach it,' he ordered.

'Hold me!' she replied, and bent her body at the waist,

555

reaching up with one hand. She felt the branches under her fingers, and made a quick grab at them.

'Got them?' he demanded.

'Yes!' But her grip was one-handed and tenuous. Then her heart turned to ice in her chest as she felt the boot he was holding begin to slide slowly off her foot.

'Boot's coming off!' she sobbed out.

'Give me your other hand,' he panted. Before she could refuse she felt him release one hand from her ankle and reach down along her leg. Her foot slid further out of the soft leather boot.

'Your hand!' he pleaded. His fingers were scrabbling urgently down her thigh towards where the bush had come up against her and blocked her way. She felt the back of her boot ride down under her heel.

'Boot's going! I shall fall!'

'Your hand! For the love of God, give me your hand.'

She lunged upwards and their fingers locked. She still had a grip on the bush with her other hand. Mansur was hanging on to the ankle of the boot, but now his right hand was linked to hers. Verity was doubled up, suspended by both arms and one leg. The skirts of her coat fell away from her face so she could see again. His face above her was flushed and swollen. His beard was dark, sodden with sweat. It dripped into her upturned face. Neither dared move.

'What must I do?' she said, but before he could answer it was decided for them. The boot slid off her foot. Her lower body dropped forcefully, then flicked round. Now she was stretched out arms upwards and feet down. Although the jerk had loosened her grip, she was still clinging to his right hand and to the bush.

Both were drenched with sweat, which greased their skin. His fingers began to slide through hers.

'I can't hold on to you,' she gasped.

'The bush,' he said. 'Don't let go of the bush.'

Though she felt as though he were crushing the bones of her fingers, their grip parted like a faulty chain link, and she dropped again until the bush broke her fall. It cracked and bent with her weight.

'It will not hold,' she screamed.

'I can't reach you.' He was groping for her with both hands and she was stretching up with her free hand, but she was just beyond his reach.

'Pull! You must pull yourself up so I can get you,' he grated. She felt the ice in her heart numbing her muscles. She knew it was over. He saw the despair in her eyes, saw her grip on the bush start to fail. She was going to let go.

He snarled at her savagely, trying to shock her into a last effort, 'Pull, you feeble creature! Pull, damn your lily liver!'

The insults stung her and anger gave her the strength for one more attempt. But she knew it was useless. Even if she could reach him their sweat-slimy hands could not hold together. She lunged for the branch and found a double hold, but the bush could no longer bear her weight. It crackled and snapped as it tore.

'I am going!' she sobbed.

'No, damn you, no!' he shouted, but the bush gave way. She started to fall, but suddenly both her wrists were seized and held. Her fall was arrested with a strength that made the joints of her upper arms pop in their sockets.

Mansur had made his last effort. He had freed his legs from the cleft in which he had wedged them, and threw himself forward over the lip of the cliff. At the full stretch of body and arms he had just reached her. He was hanging head down, only his toes hooked into the rock cleft held him. But he had to raise her before she slipped through his fingers again. He braced his elbows against the face of the cliff and slowly bent his arms, raising her until they were face to face. His features were swollen and contorted with the agony of his straining muscles, and with the rush of blood into his inverted head. 'I cannot lift you higher,' he breathed, with their lips almost touching. 'Climb up my body. Use me as a ladder.'

She locked one arm through his, the bend of her elbow through the bend in his. This left his other hand free. He

557

reached down and took hold of her leather belt and pulled her a little higher. She grabbed his belt buckle and they pulled together. He reached lower and took a handful of the seat of her breeches. She hooked her other arm between his legs and again they heaved. Now her face was level with his waist and she could see over the top of the cliff. He reached down, linked his fingers together and made a stirrup for her bare foot. With the purchase this gave her she could drag herself up and over the lip.

She sprawled on the rock for only an instant, then whipped round. 'Can you get back?' she gasped. He was fully extended, powerless to pull himself backwards and regain the crest.

He was almost too far gone to articulate coherently. 'Get the horse,' he gasped. 'Rope on saddle. Pull me back with the horse.'

She glanced around and saw the stallion a quarter of a mile away, trotting back up the valley. 'Your horse is gone.'

Mansur reached backwards and tried to find a fingerhold on the rock, but it was smooth. There was a tiny rasping sound as the toe of one boot moved in the rock crack. He slid forward an inch towards the edge of the cliff. Then his foot caught again. She was frozen with horror. His toehold was all that held him from the drop. She seized his ankle with both hands, but she knew it was hopeless. She could never hope to hold the weight of such a big man. She tried to brace herself as she watched his foot slip again and then his hold in the cleft broke. He slid forward irresistibly, and his ankle was plucked from her hands.

He shouted as he went over the edge, and she flung herself forward across the rock sill to peer down, expecting to see him falling away with his robes ballooning around him. Then she stared in disbelief. The hem of his white robe had snagged on a shard of granite on the lip of the cliff. It had broken his fall, and now he was swinging like a pendulum just below her, dangling over that dizzying void. She stretched down with one hand to try to reach him.

'Give me your hand!' she called. She was weak with her own efforts to escape, and her hand shook wildly.

'You will never hold me.' He looked up at her, and there was no fear in his eyes.

That touched her deeply. 'Let me try,' she pleaded.

'No,' he said. 'One of us will go, not both.'

'Please!' she whispered, and the hem of his robe tore with a sharp, ripping sound. 'I could not bear it if you died for me.'

'Worth it,' he said softly, and she felt her heart break. She sobbed and looked behind her. Then hope bloomed again. She slid back from the edge and wedged herself firmly into the rock cleft. She reached back over her shoulders and seized a double handful of her dense brown hair, pulled it forward and twisted it into a loose rope that hung below her waist. Then she threw herself flat on to the rock sill. She was just able to see over the edge. The rope of her hair tumbled forward.

'Take my hair,' she shouted. He swivelled his head and stared up at her as it brushed lightly against his face.

'Do you have purchase? Can you hold me?'

'Yes, I am wedged into the rock cleft.' She tried to sound confident, but she thought, Even if I can't we will go together. He twisted her hair round his wrist, and with a final crack of tearing cloth the hem of his robe gave way. She had just time to brace herself before the shock of his full weight dropping on to her hair half stunned her. Her head was jerked forward and her cheek slammed into the rock with a force that jarred her teeth. She was pinned down. She felt the vertebrae in her neck popping, as though she were hanged on the gallows.

Mansur hung on the rope of her hair only for the seconds it took him to orient. Then he climbed up, hand over hand, swiftly as a topyard sailor going up the main shrouds. She screamed involuntarily for it seemed that her scalp was being torn from her skull. But then he reached past her, found a handhold in the rock cleft and heaved himself over the rim of the cliff.

He turned instantly, seized her in his arms and dragged her back to safety. He held her to his chest and pressed his face against the top of her head, knowing how intense must be the agony of her scalp. She lay in his arms, weeping as though in bitter mourning. He rocked her gently as though she were an infant, mumbling incoherent words of comfort and gratitude. After a while she stirred against him and he thought she was trying to escape his embrace. He opened his arms to free her, but she reached up and slipped her arms around the back of his neck. She pressed herself to his chest, and their bodies seemed to melt together like hot wax through their sweat-soaked clothing. Her sobbing stilled and then, without pulling away from him, she lifted her face and looked into his eyes. 'You saved my life,' she whispered.

'And you saved mine,' he replied. The tears still cascaded down her face and her lips were trembling. He kissed her, and her lips opened without resistance. Her tears tasted of salt, and her mouth of fragrant herbs. Her hair fell in a tent over them. It was a lingering kiss, and ended only when they were forced to breathe.

'You are not an Arab,' she whispered. 'You are an Englishman.'

'You have found me out,' he said, and kissed her again.

When they drew apart, she said, 'I am so confused. Who are you?'

'I will tell you,' he promised, 'but later.' He sought her lips again, and she gave them willingly.

After a while she placed both her hands on his shoulders and pushed him back gently. 'Please, Mansur, we must stop this. If we don't something will happen that will spoil everything before it has begun.'

'It has begun already, Verity.'

'Yes, I know it has,' she said.

'It began when first I laid eyes on you on the deck of the *Arcturus*.'

'I know,' she said again, and stood up quickly. With both hands she flung the glorious profusion of her hair back from her face and over her shoulders.

'They are coming.' She pointed back up the valley at the band of horsemen who were galloping towards them.

560

As they rode back to Isakanderbad, al-Salil and Sir Guy listened to Verity's account of the near tragedy. When al-Salil asked Mansur for his version of events, Mansur replied quite naturally in Arabic, and Verity was obliged to go along with the deception that he spoke no English. She translated for her father his praises of her courage and resourcefulness, and could omit none of his hyperbole now that she knew Mansur understood every word.

At the end Sir Guy smiled tightly and nodded to Mansur. 'Please tell him that we are in his debt.' Then his expression turned bleak. 'You were at fault. You should not have been alone in his company, child. Your behaviour was scandalous. It will not happen again.' Once again Mansur saw fear in her eyes.

The sun had set and it was almost dark when they reached the encampment. Verity found her tent lit with lamps whose wicks floated in perfumed oil and her clothing from the ship had been unpacked. Three handmaidens were waiting to attend her. When she was ready for her bath they poured warm, perfumed pitchers of water over her, and giggled as they marvelled at the whiteness and beauty of her naked body.

The evening meal was laid out under a dazzle of stars, and the desert air had cooled. They sat cross-legged on cushions while the musicians played softly. After they had eaten, servants offered hookahs to the Caliph and Sir Guy. Only al-Salil indulged. Sir Guy lit a long black cheroot from the gold case that Verity carried for him. Politely she offered one to Mansur. 'Thank you, my lady, but I have never found tobacco to my taste.'

'I agree with you. I also find the odour of the smoke unpleasant in the extreme.' Instinctively she had lowered her voice, even though her father spoke no Arabic.

Now Mansur was certain she was terrified of him. There was more to her feelings than simply that Sir Guy was a daunting figure, hard and unyielding, and Mansur knew he

561

would have to be circumspect in what he now had in mind. He kept his voice on the same even level when he spoke again. 'At the end of this street there lies an ancient temple to Aphrodite. The moon rises a little before midnight. Although dedicated to a pagan deity, in the moonlight the temple is very lovely.'

Verity had not heard him, or so it seemed from her lack of reaction. She turned back to translate a remark that Sir Guy had made to al-Salil, and the two men continued their earnest conversation. They were discussing the extent of the Caliph's gratitude to Sir Guy for his intervention with the Company and the British government. In what manner could the Caliph best demonstrate it? al-Salil asked. Sir Guy suggested delicately that five lakhs of gold rupees might be appropriate, which should be followed by an annual payment of another lakh.

The Caliph began to understand how his brother had amassed such vast wealth. It would take two oxcarts to carry that amount of gold. The treasury in Muscat no longer held a tenth of that amount, but he did not inform Sir Guy of this. Instead he brought the subject to a close. 'These are matters we can discuss again, for I hope to enjoy many more days of your company. But now, if we are to rise again before the sun tomorrow, we should repair to our sleeping mats. May pleasant dreams attend your slumbers.'

Verity took her father's arm as he escorted her to her tent with torch-bearers leading them through the encampment. In turmoil, Mansur watched her go: he had no indication that she would honour their assignation.

Later, dressed in a dark cloak, he waited in the temple of Aphrodite. Through a hole in the dilapidated roof the moonlight played full on the statue of the goddess. The pearly marble glowed as though with internal life. Both her arms were missing, for the ages had taken their toll, but the figure was graceful and the battered head smiled in eternal ecstasy.

Mansur had stationed Istaph, his trusted coxswain from the *Sprite*, on the roof to keep guard. Now Istaph whistled softly. Mansur caught his breath and his pulse beat faster. He stood up from his seat on one of the tumbled stone blocks and moved to the centre of the temple so that she would see him at once and not be startled by his sudden appearance from out of the shadows. He saw the dim light of the lamp she carried as she came down the narrow alley, stepping over the rubble and debris of three thousand years.

At the entrance she paused and looked across at him, then set her lamp in a niche in the doorway and threw back her hood. She had braided her hair in a single rope that hung down over one shoulder, and in the moonlight her face was as pale as that of the goddess. He let his own cloak fall open to hang from his shoulders, and went to meet her. He saw that her expression was serious and remote.

When he was within arm's length she put out a hand to stop him coming closer. 'If you touch me I shall have to leave at once,' she said. 'You heard my father's rebuke. I was never again to be alone with you.'

'Yes, I heard. I understand your predicament,' he assured her. 'I am grateful you have come.'

'What happened today was wrong.'

'I am to blame,' he said.

'There is no blame on either of us. We had been close to death. Our expressions of relief and gratitude towards each other were only natural in the circumstances. However, I said foolish things. You must forget my words. This is the last time we shall meet like this.'

'I shall fall in with your wishes.'

'Thank you, Your Highness.'

Mansur switched to English. 'Will you not at least treat me as a friend and call me Mansur, and not by the title that sits so uncomfortably on your lips?'

She smiled, and answered in the same language. 'If that is indeed your true name. It seems to me that you are a great deal more than you seem, Mansur.'

'I have promised to explain it to you, Verity.'

'Yes, indeed you have. That is why I have come.' Then she added, as though she was trying to convince herself, 'And for no other reason.'

She turned away and took a seat on a fallen stone block

just large enough to accommodate her alone, and she gestured to another at a discreet distance. 'Will you not be seated and make yourself at ease? It seems to me that your tale will take some telling.' He sat, facing her. She leaned forward with one elbow on her knee and her chin in the palm of her hand. 'You have all of my attention.'

He laughed and shook his head. 'Where to begin? How will I ever make you believe me?' He paused to gather his thoughts. 'Let me start with the most preposterous. If I can convince you of those parts of it, then the rest of the medicine will not be so difficult for you to swallow.'

She inclined her head in invitation, and he drew breath. 'Like yours my English surname is Courtney. I am your cousin.'

She burst out laughing. 'In all fairness, you did warn me. None the less 'tis bitter medicine that you are trying to dole out to me.' She made as if to rise. 'I see that this is but a prank, and you take me for the fool.'

'Wait!' he entreated. 'Give me a fair hearing.' She sank back on the stone. 'Have you heard the names Thomas and Dorian Courtney?' The smile vanished from her lips and she nodded wordlessly. 'What have you heard?'

She thought for a moment, her expression troubled. 'Tom Courtney was a terrible rogue. He was my father's twin brother. He murdered his other brother, William, and had to fly from England. He died somewhere in the African wilderness. His grave is unmarked and his passing unmourned.'

'Is that all you know of him?

'No, there is more,' Verity admitted. 'He is guilty of something even more heinous.'

'What is worse than the murder of your own brother?'

Verity shook her head. 'I know none of the details, only that it was so foul a deed that his name and his memory are blackened for ever. I do not know the full extent of his wickedness, but since we were children we have been forbidden to mention his name.'

'When you say we, Verity, who is the other person?'

'My older brother, Christopher.'

'It pains me to be the one to tell you, but what you have

been told about Tom Courtney is but a sad travesty of the truth,' Mansur said, 'but before we discuss it further, please tell me what you know of Dorian Courtney.'

Verity shrugged. 'Very little, for there is little to know. He was my father's youngest brother. No, that is not correct, he was my father's half-brother. In a tragic turn of events he fell into the hands of Arab pirates when he was but a child of ten or twelve years. Tom Courtney, that craven rogue, was to blame for his abduction and did nothing to prevent it, or to save him. Dorian died of fever, neglect and a broken heart while he was a captive in the lair of the pirates.'

'How do you know all this?'

'My father told us about it, and with my own eyes I have seen Dorian's grave in the old cemetery on Lamu island. I placed flowers upon it and said a prayer for his poor little soul. I take comfort in the words of Christ, "Suffer little children to come to me". I know he rests in the bosom of Jesus.'

In the moonlight Mansur saw a tear tremble on her bottom eyelid. 'Please don't weep for little Dorian,' he said quietly. 'Today you rode out hawking in his company and you dined this very evening at his board.'

She recoiled so violently that the tear fell from her eyelid and slid down her cheek. She stared at him. 'I do not understand.'

'Dorian is the Caliph.'

'If this be true, which it cannot be, we are cousins.'

'Bravo, coz! You have arrived at where we started our conversation.'

She shook her head. 'It cannot be ... yet there is something about you—' She broke off, then began again: 'At our very first meeting I felt something, an affinity, a bond that I could not explain to myself.' She looked distraught. 'If all this is a jest, then it is a cruel one.'

'No jest, I swear it to you.'

'I need more than that to convince me.'

'There is more, a great deal more. You shall have as much of it as you can possibly desire. Shall I tell you first how Dorian was sold by the pirates to the Caliph al-Malik, and how the Caliph came to love him so that he adopted him as his own son? Shall I tell you how Dorian fell in love with his adoptive half-sister Princess Yasmini and they eloped together? How she bore him a son, whom they named Mansur? How Yasmini's half-brother Zayn al-Din became caliph after the death of al-Malik? How, not a year past, Zayn al-Din sent an assassin to murder my mother Yasmini?'

'Mansur!' Verity's face was as white as the marble Aphrodite's. 'Your mother? Zayn al-Din murdered her?'

'This is the main reason we have returned to Oman, my father and I. To avenge my mother's death, and to deliver our people from tyranny. But now I must tell you the truth about my uncle Tom. He is not the monster you paint him.'

'My father told us—'

'I last saw Uncle Tom scarcely a year ago, hale and flourishing in Africa. He is a kind person, brave and true. He is married to your aunt Sarah, your mother Caroline's younger sister.'

'Sarah is dead!' Verity exclaimed.

'She is very much alive. If you knew her you would love her as I do. She is so much like you, strong and proud. She even looks a great deal like you. She is tall and very beautiful.' He smiled and added softly, 'She has your nose.' Verity touched her own and smiled faintly.

'With such a nose as mine she cannot be so beautiful.' The little smile faded. 'They told me – my mother and father told me they were all dead, Dorian, Tom and Sarah . . .' Verity covered her eyes with one hand as she tried to assimilate what he had told her.

'Tom Courtney made two mistakes in his life. He killed his brother William in a fair fight, defending himself when Black Billy tried to murder him.'

'I heard that Tom stabbed William while he slept.' She dropped her hand and stared at him.

'Tom's other mistake was to father your brother Christopher. That is the reason your mother and father hated him so.'

'No.' She leaped to her feet. 'My brother is no bastard! My mother is no whore!'

'Your mother conceived in love. That is not harlotry,' Mansur said, and she sank down again. She reached across the gap between them and laid her hand on his arm. 'Oh, Mansur! This is too much for me to endure. Your words tear my world apart.'

'I do not tell you this to torment you, Verity, but for both our sakes.'

'I do not understand.'

'I have fallen in love with you,' Mansur said. 'You asked who I am, and because I love you I must tell you.'

'You delude yourself and me,' she whispered. 'Love is not something that falls like manna from the sky, full formed and complete. It grows between two persons—'

'Tell me you feel nothing, Verity.'

She would not reply. Instead she sprang to her feet and looked to the night sky as if seeking escape. 'The dawn is breaking. My father must not learn I have been with you. I must go back to my tent at once.'

'Answer my question before you go,' he insisted. 'Tell me you feel nothing and I will trouble you no further.'

'How can I tell you that when I know not what I feel? I owe you my life, but beyond that I cannot yet tell.'

'Verity! Give me one small grain of hope.'

'No, Mansur. I must go! Not another word.'

'Will you come to meet me here again, tomorrow evening?'

'You do not know my father—' She stopped herself. 'I can promise you nothing.'

'There is so much more that I must tell you.'

She laughed shortly, then stopped herself. 'Have you not told me sufficient to last me a lifetime?'

'Will you come?'

'I will try. But only to hear the rest of your story.' She snatched up the lamp and pulled the hood of her cloak over her head, covering her face, and ran from the temple.

In the dawn the Caliph rode out with his guests and all his entourage to fly the falcons. They killed three times before the heat came down and they were forced back into the shelter of the tents.

During the noonday heat Sir Guy spoke to the council, explaining to them how he could save Oman from the tyrant, and from the clutches of the Turk and the Mogul. 'You must place yourselves under the suzerainty of the English monarch and his Company.'

The desert sheikhs listened and argued among themselves. They were free men, and proud. At last Mustapha Zindara asked for all of them, 'We have driven out the jackal from our sheepfold. Shall we now allow the leopard to take his place? If this English monarch wants us as his subjects, will he come to us so that we can see him ride and wield the lance? Will he lead us into battle as al-Salil has done?'

'The English king will hold his shield over you, and protect you from your enemies.' Sir Guy avoided a direct answer.

'And what is the price in gold of his protection?' Mustapha Zindara asked.

Al-Salil had seen that Mustapha's temper was rising like the heat outside the tent. He looked across at Verity and said gently, 'I ask your father for his indulgence. We must discuss all he has told us, and I must explain to my people what it means, and set their fears at rest.' He turned to his councillors. 'The heat has passed and the huntsmen have found much game on the high ground across the river. We shall talk more on the morrow.'

Mansur found that Verity was avoiding him assiduously. She would not even glance in his direction. Whenever he came close to her she turned all her attention on her father or the Caliph. He saw how she looked on Dorian in a changed light now that she knew he was her uncle. She stared into his face and watched his eyes when he spoke to her. She followed his every gesture with attention, yet she would not even glance in Mansur's direction. During the afternoon's hunt she would not allow him to separate her from her father, but rode close at Sir Guy's side. In the end Mansur was forced to contain himself until the evening meal. He was not hungry and it seemed interminable. Only once did he catch Verity's eyes and, with a tilt of his head, asked a silent question of her. She arched an eyebrow enigmatically, and gave him no reply.

When at last the Caliph dismissed the company, Mansur escaped to his own tent with relief. He waited until all was quiet, for he knew that even if she intended to keep the assignation she would not move before then. That night there was a restless feeling in the camp with men passing back and forth, loud voices and singing. It was well after midnight before Mansur could leave his own tent, and start for the temple. Istaph was waiting for him beside the stone doorway. 'Is all well?' Mansur asked.

Istaph came closer and whispered, 'There are others abroad this night.'

'Who are they?'

'Two men came out of the desert while the Caliph and his guests were at dinner. They hid themselves in the horselines. When the English *effendi* and his daughter left the company, the girl did not go to her own tent as she did last night. Instead she went with her father to his. Then the two strangers came secretly to them.'

'They are set on mischief?' Mansur demanded, with horror. Was Verity to die as his own mother had, under the assassin's blade?

'No!' Kumrah assured him quickly. 'I heard the *effendi* greet them when they entered and they are together still.'

'You are certain you have never seen these men before tonight?'

'They are strangers. I do not know them.'

'How were they dressed?'

'They wore Arab robes, but only one was an Omani.'

'How did the other look?'

Kumrah shrugged. 'I saw him only for a moment. It is not possible to tell much from a man's face alone, but he was a *ferengi*.'

'A European?' Mansur exclaimed, with surprise. 'Are you sure?'

Istaph shrugged again. 'I am not sure, but so it seemed to me.'

'They are still in the tent of the consul? Is the woman with them?' Mansur demanded.

'They were all still there when I came to meet you here.'

'Come with me, but we must not be seen,' Mansur said decisively.

'There are watchmen only on the outer perimeter of the camp,' Istaph answered.

'We know where they are. We can avoid them.' Mansur turned back and went quietly down the narrow alley, the way he had come. He made as if he was returning to his own tent, then ducked behind a pile of ancient masonry and waited there until he was certain they had not been seen or followed. Then he and Istaph crept up silently behind Sir Guy's pavilion. There was light within, and Mansur could hear voices.

He recognized Verity's. She was speaking to her father, clearly translating, 'He says that the rest will arrive within the week.'

'A week!' Sir Guy's voice was louder. 'They should have been ready at the beginning of the month.'

'Father, lower your voice. You will be heard throughout the entire camp.'

For a while their voices sank to a soft mumble and they spoke with suppressed urgency. Then another voice spoke in Arabic. Even though it was so low and muted that he could not make out the words, Mansur knew he had heard it before, but where and when he could not be sure.

In a barely audible whisper Verity translated for Sir Guy, and his voice rose again sharply. 'He must not even think of it now. Tell him it could dash all our plans. His private concerns must wait until afterwards. He must restrain his pugnacious instincts until the main business has been taken care of.'

Mansur strained his ears but could catch only snatches of what followed. At one stage Sir Guy said, 'We must sweep up the whole shoal in our net. We must not allow a single fish to slip through.'

Then, abruptly, Mansur heard the strangers take leave of him. Once again the familiar Arab voice tugged at his memory. This time it whispered the formal words of farewell.

I know him, Mansur thought. He was certain of this, but still could not place him. The second stranger spoke for the first time. Istaph had been correct. This was a European speaking Arabic with a German or guttural Dutch accent. He could not remember having heard it before. He ignored it, and tried to concentrate instead on exchanges between Sir Guy and the Arab. There was silence, and he realized that the strangers had left Sir Guy's pavilion as quietly as they had come. He jumped up from where he was crouched and ran to the corner of the tent wall. Then he had to shrink back, for not ten paces away Sir Guy and Verity were standing at the entrance talking quietly and looking in the direction in which their visitors had gone. If Mansur and Istaph tried to follow, Sir Guy would spot them. Father and daughter remained in the doorway for some minutes longer before they went back inside. By this time the strange visitors had vanished among the closely huddled pavilions of the encampment.

Mansur turned to Istaph, who was close behind him. 'We must not let them get away. Search the far side of the camp, down towards the river, and see if they went that way. I shall take the northern perimeter.'

He broke into a run. Something about the stranger's voice had filled him with a sense of foreboding. I have to find out who that Arab is, he thought.

When he reached the last ruined buildings he saw two of the night watchmen standing together in the shadows cast by the wall. They were leaning on their jezails and talking quietly. He called to them, 'Did two men pass this way?'

They recognized his voice and ran to him. 'No, Highness,

no man passed us.' It seemed that they had been awake and alert, so Mansur had to believe them.

'Shall we raise the alarm?' one demanded.

'No,' Mansur said. 'It was nothing. Return to your post.'

The strangers must have gone down towards the river. He ran back through the dark camp and, in the moonlight, saw Istaph running back towards him along the causeway. He sprinted to meet him and called to him while still far off, 'Have you found them?'

'This way, Highness.' Istaph's voice was harsh with exertion. Together they raced down the hillside, then Istaph turned off the path and led Mansur towards a clump of thorn trees.

'They have camels,' he gasped.

As he said it two riders burst from the clump of trees. Mansur came up short and stood panting, gazing after them as they rode diagonally across the hillside below him. They passed not more than a pistol shot from where he stood. Their mounts were both beautiful racing camels and carried bulky saddlebags and waterbags for a desert crossing. They were ghostly in the silvery moonlight, moving away in uncanny silence towards the open desert.

In desperation Mansur bellowed after them, 'Stop! In the Caliph's name, I order you to halt!'

Both riders turned swiftly in their high saddles at the sound of his voice. They stared back at him. Mansur recognized them both. He had not seen the man with the European features, whom Istaph had called the *ferengi*, for some years. However, it was the Arab who commanded his attention. He had thrown the hood of his cloak upon his shoulders and, for a fleeting moment, the slanting rays of the moon struck full into his face. He and Mansur stared at each other for a heartbeat, then the Arab leaned forward over the neck of his camel and, with the long riding stick he carried, urged it into the long, elegant gait that covered the ground at an astonishing speed. His dark cloak billowed behind him as he whirled away down the valley with his *ferengi* companion riding hard behind him.

A shock of recognition and disbelief paralysed Mansur's

legs. He stood and stared after them Then, black thoughts swirled through his head and seemed to batter his senses like the flapping wings of vultures, until at last he rallied himself. I must get back to my father and warn him of what is afoot, he thought. But he waited while the camels dwindled into the distance, flitting like moths across the moonlit landscape, and then were gone.

Mansur ran all the way. He had to stop in the shadow of the walls to regain his breath. Then he went on swiftly but quietly among the tents so as not to raise the alarm. There were two sentries at the door to the Caliph's, but at a quiet word from Mansur they sheathed their swords and stood aside to let him pass. He went through into the inner chamber of the pavilion. A single oil lamp was burning on a metal tripod that shed a soft light.

'Father!' he called.

Dorian sat up from his sleeping mat. He wore only a light loincloth and his naked body was slim and muscled, like an athlete's, in the lamplight. 'Who is it?' he called.

'It is Mansur.'

'What ails you at this hour?' Dorian had recognized the urgency in his tone.

'There were two strangers in our camp this night. They were with Sir Guy.'

'Who were they?'

'I recognized them both. One was Captain Koots from the garrison at Good Hope, the man who pursued Jim across the wilderness.'

'Here in Oman?' Dorian came fully awake. 'It does not seem possible. Are you certain?'

'I am even more certain of the other man. His face is graven upon my mind until the day I die.'

'Tell me!' Dorian commanded.

'It was the assassin, Kadem ibn Abubaker, the swine who murdered my mother.'

'Where are they now?' Dorian's voice was harsh.

'They fled into the desert before I could confront them.'

'We must follow at once. We cannot let Kadem escape

573

again.' The glazed pink knife-scar on Dorian's chest caught the lamplight as he reached for his robes.

'They are mounted on racing camels,' Mansur answered. 'We have none, and they were headed into the dunes. We can never hope to catch them in the sands.'

'Nevertheless we must try.' Dorian raised his voice and shouted for the guards.

The dawn was a lemon and orange glow in the eastern sky before bin-Shibam had gathered together a punitive party of his desert warriors and they were all mounted and ready to ride. They swept down the causeway from the camp to where Mansur had seen the fugitives disappear. The ground was sun-baked and stony and held no tracks of the camels passing, but they could not afford further time for the skilled huntsmen to search every inch.

With Mansur leading, they followed the direction in which Kadem had headed into the wilderness. Within two hours' ride they saw the dunes rising ahead of them, in flowing and fantastic shapes. The slip faces down which the sand cascaded were blue and purple and amethyst in the early light. The crests were sharp and sinuous as the back of a gigantic iguana.

Here they found the tracks of two camels trodden into deep saucers in the liquid sand where they had climbed the first dune and disappeared over the crest. They tried to follow, but the horses sank over their hocks with each pace and, in the end, even Dorian had to admit that they were defeated.

'Enough, bin-Shibam!' he told the grizzled old warrior. 'We cannot go on. Wait for me here.'

Dorian would not allow even Mansur to accompany him as he rode up the face of the next dune. His tired horse had to lunge upwards with each pace and only reached the crest with great effort. There he dismounted. From the sand valley below Mansur watched his father. He was a tall, lonely figure staring out into the desert with the early-morning breeze blowing his robes out behind him. He stood like that for a long time, then sank to his knees in prayer. Mansur knew he was praying for Yasmini, and his own sorrow for the loss of his mother welled up almost to suffocate him.

At last Dorian remounted and came down the dune with his stallion sliding in the soft-running sands on braced haunches and stiff front legs. He said not a word as he passed them, and rode on with his chin sunk on his chest. They fell in behind him and he led them back to Isakanderbad.

Dorian dismounted in the horselines and the grooms took his stallion. He strode to Sir Guy's tent with Mansur close behind him. His intention was to confront his half-brother and disclose his true identity, to throw in his face the ancient memories of his vicious treatment of Tom, Sarah and himself as a child, and to demand from him a full explanation of the nocturnal and clandestine presence of Kadem ibn Abubaker in the camp.

Before he reached the tent he realized that things had changed during their absence. A party of strangers was gathered before the entrance. They all wore seafaring dress and were heavily armed. At their head was Captain William Cornish of the *Arcturus*. Dorian was so angry that he almost hailed him in English. With an effort he prevented his anger boiling over, but it simmered dangerously close to the surface.

Mansur followed close behind him as he stormed into the tent. Sir Guy and Verity stood in the centre of the room. They were in riding garb, and were deep in conversation. Both of them looked up, startled, at the precipitate entrance of the two grim-faced figures.

'Ask them what they want,' Guy said to his daughter. 'Make them understand that this behaviour is insulting.'

'My father welcomes you. He hopes nothing is seriously amiss.' Verity was pale and seemed distraught.

Dorian made a perfunctory gesture of greeting, then glanced around the tent. The handmaidens were packing the last of Sir Guy's possessions.

'You are leaving?'

'My father has received tidings of the gravest import. He must return to the *Arcturus* and sail at once. He asks me to present his most sincere apologies. He tried to inform you of this change in his plans, but he was informed that you and your son had left Isakanderbad.'

'We were in pursuit of bandits,' Dorian explained, 'but we are desolate that your honoured father must leave before we have reached an accord.'

'My father is also put out. He asks you to accept his thanks for the generosity and hospitality you have extended to him.'

'Before he leaves I would be most grateful for his assistance. We have learned that there were dangerous bandits in the camp last night. Two men, one an Arab, the other a European, perhaps a Dutchman. Did your father speak to these men? I have had a report that they were seen leaving this tent during the night.'

Sir Guy smiled at the question, but the smile was on his lips only and his eyes were cold. Verity said, 'My father wishes to assure you that the two men who came to the camp last night were not bandits. They were the messengers who brought him the news that has necessitated his change of plans. They were with him for a short time only.'

'Does your father know these men well?' Dorian insisted. Sir Guy's reply was without obvious guile.

'My father has never seen them before.'

'What were their names?'

'They did not give their names, nor did my father ask. Their names were of no interest or importance. They were merely messengers.'

Mansur was watching Verity's face intently as she answered these questions. Her expression was calm, but there was a latent tension in her voice, and shadows in her eyes as though dark thoughts lurked in her mind. She avoided looking at Mansur. He sensed that she was lying, perhaps for her father's sake and perhaps for her own.

'May I ask His Excellency the nature of the message they brought him?'

Sir Guy shook his head regretfully. Then he drew from his inner pocket a parchment packet that bore the heavily embossed royal coat-of-arms with the legend 'Honi soit qui mal y pense' and two red wax seals. 'His Excellency regrets that this is an official, privileged document. Any foreign power who attempted to seize it would be committing an act of war.'

'Please assure His Excellency that no one is contemplating an act of war.'

Dorian dared press the matter no further. 'I much regret His Excellency's sudden departure. I wish him a safe journey and a swift return to Oman. I hope I shall be allowed to ride in company with him upon the first mile of his journey?'

'My father would be greatly honoured.'

'I will leave you now to make your final preparations. I shall wait with a guard of honour on the perimeter of the camp.'

Both men bowed to each other as the Caliph withdrew. As he left the tent Verity shot a single, anguished glance at Mansur. He knew that, at last, she was desperate to talk to him.

Sir Guy and Verity, escorted by Captain Cornish and his armed seamen, rode up to where Dorian and Mansur waited beside the eastern road to escort them. Dorian had brought his anger firmly under control. They set out again in company. Although Mansur fell in beside her, Verity stayed close to her father, translating the polite but inconsequential conversation between him and Dorian. But as they topped the first rise, the wind off the sea blew into their faces, cool and refreshing. As though to adjust it, Verity loosened the scarf that held her high hat in place. She seemed to lose her grip on it, and the breeze snatched it from her head. It tumbled away down the hillside, rolling like a wheel on its stiff brim.

Mansur turned his horse and raced after it. He leaned far out of the saddle and grabbed the hat from the ground without checking the stallion's speed. He turned back and handed it to Verity as she rode to meet him. She nodded her thanks, and as she replaced it on her head she used the silk scarf to veil her face for a moment. She had contrived to separate them from the rest of the party by at least a hundred paces.

'We have but a moment before my father becomes suspicious. You did not come last night,' she said. 'I waited for you.'

'I could not,' he replied, and he would have explained further, but she cut him off brusquely.

'I have left a letter under the pedestal of the goddess.'

'Verity!' Sir Guy called sharply. 'Come here, child! I need you to interpret.'

With her hat again firmly on her head, the brim tilted to a saucy angle, Verity kicked her mare forward and trotted up beside her father's horse. She did not look directly at Mansur again, not even when, with an exchange of compliments, the two bands of horsemen parted. Sir Guy went on towards Muscat while the Caliph and his escort turned back to Isakanderbad.

By the merciless light of midday the goddess's expression was melancholy and her beauty marred by the ravages of millennia. With one last glance around the temple to make certain that he was unobserved, Mansur went down on one knee before her. Wind-blown sand was piled along one side of the pedestal base. Someone had arranged five small chips of white marble in the shape of an arrowhead. It pointed at a spot where the sand had been recently disturbed, then carefully smoothed over again.

He swept away the sand. There was a narrow crack between the marble base of the statue and the stone flags of the floor. When he lowered his face to floor level he saw that a folded sheet of parchment had been pushed deep into the crack. He had to use his dagger to prise it out. He unfolded the sheet and saw that both sides were written upon in an elegant, feminine script. He refolded the sheet, hid it in his sleeve, hurried back to his own tent and went into the inner room. He spread out the letter on his sleeping mat and pored over it. There was no salutation.

I hope you will be there tonight. If you are not I will leave this for you. I heard the alarm a short while ago and the horsemen riding out, and I must believe that you went with them. I suspect that you are chasing the two men

who came to my father this night. They are generals in
the army of Zayn al-Din. One is named Kadem ibn
Abubaker. The other is a renegade Dutchman whose name
I do not know. They command the Turkish infantry who
will lead the assault on Muscat. The news they brought
my father is that, at this very moment, the fleet and the
transports carrying Zayn's army are no longer lying in
Zanzibar roads. They sailed two weeks ago, and they are
already at anchor off Boomi island. My father and I will
return on board the *Arcturus* with all despatch so that we
are not trapped in the city when the Turks attack. It is my
father's purpose to join Zayn's fleet, so that he might be
present when Zayn enters the city.

Mansur felt his heart turn cold with dread. Boomi island
lay a mere ten sea miles from the entrance to Muscat harbour.
The enemy had come secretly upon them, and the city lay
under a terrible threat. He read on quickly:

Zayn himself is aboard the flagship. He has fifty great
dhows and seven thousand Turkish soldiers on board. They
plan to land on the peninsula and march on the city from
the landward side, to surprise the defences and avoid the
batteries of cannon on the seaward walls. By the time you
read this, they may have already launched their attack.
Zayn has another fifty dhows crammed with troops and the
munitions of war following. They will be in Muscat within
the next week.

Mansur was so stricken that he could barely bring himself
to read the rest of the letter before rushing out to warn his
father.

It is with deep sadness and guilt that I must tell you that
my father's offer of assistance to the junta was a ruse to lull
them and to keep the desert sheikhs in Muscat until Zayn
could fall upon them and capture all of them together.
They will receive no mercy from him. Nor shall you and

your father. I knew nothing of this until an hour ago. I truly believed that the offer of British protection my father made was genuine. I am ashamed by what he has done to his brothers, Tom and Dorian, down the years. I knew nothing of this either, not until you told me of it. I have always known he was an ambitious man, but I had no idea of the true extent of his ruthlessness. I wish there was some way in which I could make amends.

'There is, Verity, Oh, yes, there is,' Mansur whispered, as he read on.

There is more that it pains me to relate. I learned tonight that Kadem ibn Abubaker is the villain who assassinated your mother, Princess Yasmini. He boasted of the heinous murder. Tonight he wanted to kill your father and you also. My father prevented him doing so, not on grounds of compassion but lest the plot he has hatched with Zayn al-Din to recapture the city be jeopardized. If my father had not stopped him, I swear to you on my hope of salvation that I would have managed to warn you somehow. You cannot know how deep is my repugnance for the deeds my father has committed. In one short hour I have come to hate him. I fear him even more. Please forgive me, Mansur, for the hurt we have done you.

'You are not to blame,' he whispered, and turned over the sheet of parchment. He read the last few lines.

Last night you asked me if I did not feel anything between you and me. I would not answer you then, but I answer you now. Yes, I do.

If we never meet again, I hope you will always believe that I never intended to cause you hurt. Your affectionate cousin, Verity Courtney.

They drove the horses without mercy, riding in full force back to Muscat. They were still too late. As they came within sight of the city towers and minarets they heard the cannon fire and saw the dun smoke of battle sully the sky above the harbour.

With Dorian, al-Salil, at the head of the troop they drove the exhausted horses through the palm groves, and now they could hear musket fire, shouting and screaming below the city walls. Onwards they raced, and the roadway ahead was crammed with women, children and old men fleeing the city. They turned off and galloped on through the groves, while the din of battle grew louder. At last they saw the glint of spearheads, scimitars and bronze Turkish helmets surging forward towards the city gates.

They flogged the last ounce of speed from their horses, and in a tight column they raced for the gates. The Turks ran through the palm grove to head them off. The gates were swinging closed.

'The gates will shut before we can reach them!' Mansur called to his father.

Dorian ripped off his turban. 'Show them who we are!' he cried. Mansur pulled off his own turban and they rode on with their bright red hair streaming behind them like banners.

A cry went up from the parapets: 'Al-Salil! It is the Caliph!'

The gates began slowly to open again as the men on the winches bent to the handles.

The Turks saw that they could not cut them off on foot. Their cavalry had not yet arrived: it was following in the second fleet. They halted and unslung their short recurved bows. The first flight of arrows rose dark against the blue and hissed like a pitful of serpents as it fell among the racing horses. One was struck, and went down as though it had run full-tilt into a tripwire. Mansur turned back, hauled Istaph from the saddle of the floundering horse, swung him up on to

581

his stallion's withers and raced on. The gates started to close again the moment the Caliph had galloped through. Mansur shouted to the winchmen as he came through the storm of Turkish arrows. They seemed not to hear him and inexorably the gates continued to shut in his face.

Then, suddenly, Dorian turned back into the opening and stopped his horse full in the path of the great mahogany gates, which creaked to a standstill. Mansur galloped through with inches to spare. The gates slammed as the wave of Turkish attackers reached them, and the defenders on the parapets above fired muskets and arrows down into them. They fled back into the palm grove.

Dorian galloped at once through the narrow alleys to the mosque and climbed the spiral staircase to the top balcony of the tallest minaret. On one side he had a sweeping view over the harbour and peninsula, and on the other over cultivated fields and groves. Earlier he had devised a system of flag signals to communicate with the gunners on the parapets and his two ships in the bay so that he could co-ordinate their actions.

From this height he could make out through his telescope the forest of masts of Zayn al-Din's fleet showing above the high ground of the peninsula. He lowered the glass and turned to Mansur. 'Our ships are still safe,' he pointed to the *Sprite* and the *Revenge* at anchor, 'but as soon as Zayn brings his war dhows round the peninsula and enters the bay they will be exposed and vulnerable. We must bring them close in under the protection of the battery on the sea wall.'

'How long can we hold out, Father?' Mansur lowered his voice and spoke in English so that bin-Shibam and Mustapha Zindara, who had followed them, could not understand him.

'We have not had enough time to finish the work on the south wall,' Dorian replied. 'They will discover our weak places soon enough.'

'Zayn almost certainly knows of them already. The city is swarming with his spies. Look!' Mansur pointed at the corpses hanging on the outer wall like washing. 'Although Mustapha Zindara is taking care of as many as he can lay his hands on, no doubt he has overlooked one or two.'

Dorian surveyed the gaps in the defences, which had been hurriedly stopped up with timber balks and gabions filled with sand. The repairs were temporary, and would not withstand a determined attack by seasoned troops. Then he lifted his spyglass and ran the lens over the palm groves to the south of the city. Suddenly he stiffened and handed the glass to Mansur. 'The first attack is gathering already.' They could make out the sparkle of sunlight on the helmets and spearheads of the Turkish troops, who were massing under cover of the groves. 'Mansur, I want you to go aboard the *Sprite* and take overall command of both our ships. Bring them in as close to the shore as is safe. I want your guns to cover the approaches to the south wall.'

Later, Dorian watched him being rowed out to the *Sprite* in the longboat. Almost as soon as he stepped aboard, both ships swung round as their anchor cables were hauled in. Under topsails they sailed deeper into the bay, Mansur in the *Sprite* leading Batula in the *Revenge*.

In the light breeze they were barely under steerage way, and they loafed in over the sparkling water, their hulls dappled turquoise green by the reflection of sunlight off the white sand of the lagoon bottom. Then Dorian looked to the south, and saw the first wave of the Turkish assault swarming across the open fields towards the walls. He ordered a red flag hoisted to the pinnacle of the minaret: the prearranged signal to the squadron that an attack was imminent. He saw Mansur look up at the flag, waved down at him and pointed to the south. Mansur waved back in acknowledgement, and sailed on sedately.

Then the ships turned in succession just below the harbour wall. Dorian watched the gunports fall open and the guns run out, like the fangs of a snarling monster. Mansur's tall figure was pacing along the gundeck. He paused occasionally to speak to his crew as they gathered tensely around the gun carriages.

The south wall and its approaches were still hidden by the angle of the tall stone ramparts, but as the *Sprite* cleared the range and angled in towards the beach the view opened before Mansur's eyes.

The Turks were bunched up as they carried in the long scaling ladders. Some of them looked across the narrow strip of water as the two pretty little ships emerged from behind the citadel walls. The Turkish infantry had never seen the effect of shot from a naval nine-pounder. Some even waved, and Mansur ordered his crews to wave back to lull their fears.

It happened with dreamlike deliberation. Mansur had time to walk down his deck and lay each gun with his own hand, turning down the elevation screws. He found it difficult to convince some of his crew that the power of the guns was not enhanced when the screws were turned up to maximum. Closer and closer they crept in towards the beach and Mansur listened with one ear to the leadsman in the chains calling the soundings: 'By the mark, five.'

'Close enough,' Mansur murmured, and then to Kumrah, 'Bring her up a point.'

The *Sprite* settled on the new course parallel to the shore. 'We will now serve out a taste of Mr Pandit Singh's very best,' he murmured, without lowering the glass. The *Sprite*'s guns began to bear by the bows. Still he waited. Mansur knew that the first broadside would do the most damage. After that the enemy would scatter into cover.

They were so close that through the lens he could see the links in the chain-mail of the nearest Turks and the individual feathers in the plumed helmets of the officers.

He lowered the glass and walked back down the battery. Every gun was bearing and the gun-crews were watching him, waiting on his command. He lifted the scarf of scarlet silk in his right hand, and held it high.

'Fire!' he shouted, and snapped it down.

Kadem ibn Abubaker and Herminius Koots, that unlikely couple, stood on a rocky eminence and looked across the open ground towards the southern ramparts of the city. Their staff were gathered around them, among them the Turkish officers whose authority they had usurped when Zayn al-Din had promoted them.

They watched the assault troops moving forward in three columns of two hundred men each. They carried the scaling ladders, and on their shoulders were strapped the round bronze targes to defend them against the missiles that would rain down on them from the walls as soon as they were within range. Close behind them, in massed quarter columns, followed the battalions that would surge forward to exploit any foothold they won on the parapets. 'It is worth the risk of losing a few hundred men against the chance of a quick break-in,' Koots said.

'We can afford the loss,' Kadem agreed. 'The rest of the fleet will arrive within days, another ten thousand men. If we fail today, we can begin the formal siege works on the morrow.'

'You must prevail on your revered uncle, the Caliph, to bring his warships round to begin the blockade of the bay and the harbour.'

'He will give the order as soon as he has seen the outcome of this first assault,' Kadem assured the Dutchman. 'Have faith, General. My uncle is a seasoned commander. He has been waging war on his enemies since the day he ascended the Elephant Throne. The treacherous revolution of these pork-eating swine we see before us,' he pointed to the lines of defenders on the city wall, 'was the only defeat he has ever suffered — through treason and betrayal within his own court. It will not happen again.'

'The Caliph is a great man. I never said different,' Koots assured him hastily. 'We shall hang those traitors by their own entrails on the walls of the city.'

'With God's favour, thanks be to God,' Kadem intoned.

The first tenuous bond between them had been tempered to steel links over the two years they had been together. That terrible journey, forced upon them after they were routed by Jim Courtney in the disastrous night attack, was one that lesser men could not have survived. They had braved disease and starvation across thousands of leagues of wild country. Their horses died of sickness and exhaustion, or had been killed by hostile tribesmen. They had covered the last stages on foot through swamps and mangrove forest before they reached the coast again. There they had come across a fishing village. They attacked it in the night and slaughtered all the men and children at once, but they killed the five women and the three little girls only after Koots and Oudeman had expended their pent-up lust on them. Kadem ibn Abubaker had kept aloof from this orgy. He had prayed upon the beach while the women screamed and sobbed, then gave one last shriek as Koots and Oudeman slit their throats.

They had embarked in the captured fishing-boats that were nothing more than ancient, dilapidated outrigger canoes. After another arduous journey, they at last reached Lamu harbour. There they prostrated themselves before Zayn al-Din in the throne room of his palace.

Zayn al-Din had welcomed his nephew warmly. He had thought him dead, and was delighted by the tidings he brought of Yasmini's execution. As Kadem had promised, the Caliph looked with favour on Kadem's new companion and listened to accounts of his ruthless warlike talents with attention.

As a trial he had sent Koots with a small force to subdue the remaining strongholds of the rebels who still held out upon the African mainland. He expected him to fail, as all the others before him had done. However, true to his reputation, within two months Koots had brought all the ringleaders back to Lamu in chains. There, with his own hands and in Zayn's royal presence, he had disembowelled them alive. As his reward Zayn gave him half a lakh of gold rupees from the plunder, and his pick of the female slaves he had captured. Then he had promoted him to general and given him command of four battalions of the army that he was assembling to attack Muscat.

'The Caliph comes to us now. As soon as he arrives you can order the assault to begin.' Kadem turned and went to meet the palanquin that eight slaves were carrying up the hill. It was covered with a sun canopy of gold and blue, and when they set it down Zayn al-Din stepped out.

He was no longer the chubby child whom Dorian had thrashed in the harem on Lamu island and whose foot he had maimed in the struggle to protect Yasmini from the torments Zayn had heaped upon her. He still limped, but the puppy-fat had fallen away long ago from his frame. A lifetime of intrigue and constant strife had hardened his features as it had sharpened his wits. His eyes were quick and acquisitive, his manner imperious. If it were not for the cruel lines of his mouth and the fierce cunning in his dark eyes, he might have been handsome. Kadem and Koots prostrated themselves before him. In the beginning Koots had found this form of respect abhorrent. However, like the Oriental attire he had adopted, it had become part of his new existence.

Zayn gestured to his two generals to rise. They followed him to the brow of the hill, and looked down over the open ground on which the assault force was drawn up. Zayn studied the dispositions of the troops with a practised eye. Then he nodded. 'Proceed!' His voice was high-pitched, almost girlish. When he had first heard it, Koots had despised Zayn for it, but the voice was the only feminine thing about him. He had fathered a hundred and twenty-three children, and only sixteen were girls. He had slain his enemies in thousands, many with his own sword.

'One red rocket.' Koots nodded to his aide-de-camp. Swiftly the order was relayed down the back slope of the hill to the signallers. The rocket sparkled like a ruby as it rose into the cloudless sky on a long silver tail of smoke. From the foot of the hill they heard faint cheering, and the massed troops swarmed forward towards the walls. A slave stood in front of Zayn, who rested his long brass telescope on the man's shoulder, using him as a living bipod.

The leading ranks of Turks had reached the ditch below the walls when suddenly the *Sprite* came into view from behind the stone ramparts. She was followed almost immediately by the *Revenge*. Zayn and the officers switched their telescopes to the two ships.

'Those are the ships in which the traitor, al-Salil, arrived in Muscat,' snapped Kadem. 'Our spies warned us of their presence.'

Zayn said nothing, but his features altered at the mention of the name. He felt a stab of pain in his crippled foot, and the acid taste of hatred rose in the back of his throat.

'Their guns are run out.' Koots stared at them through the glass. 'They have our battalions in enfilade. Send a galloper to warn them,' he snarled at his aide-de-camp.

'We have no horses,' the man reminded him.

'Go yourself!' Koots seized his shoulder and shoved him away down the slope. 'Run, you useless dog, or I shall have you shot from a cannon's mouth.' His Arabic was becoming more fluent every day. The man raced away down the slope, shouting, waving his arms and pointing towards the small squadron of warships. However, the Turks were fully launched upon the attack, and none looked back.

'Signal the recall?' Kadem suggested, but they all knew it was too late for that. They watched in silence. Suddenly the leading ship erupted in a cloud of white powder smoke. She heeled slightly to the broadside of her long black cannons, then came back on even keel, but her hull was blotted out by the billowing smoke cloud. Only her masts showed high above it. The thunderous sound of the blast reached their ears only seconds after the discharge, then rolled away in diminishing echoes among the distant hills.

The watchers on the hilltop turned their telescopes back to the dense pack of humanity on the plain below. The havoc shocked even these old soldiers, who were hardened to the carnage of the battlefield. The grape-shot spread so that each blast cut a swathe twenty paces wide through the massed battalions. Like the scythe blade through a field of ripe wheat, it left not a single one standing in its path. Chain-mail and

588

bronze armour offered the same protection as a sheet of brittle parchment. Severed heads, bearded and still wearing their soup-bowl helmets, were tossed into the air. Torsos, with arms and legs torn off, were piled upon each other. The cries of the dying and wounded carried clearly to the men on the hilltop.

The *Sprite* put up her helm and tacked round into the open waters of the bay. The *Revenge* sailed serenely into her place. On shore the survivors stood in stunned dismay, unable to fathom the extent of the disaster that had swept through their ranks. As the *Revenge* levelled her cannon on them, the moans of the wounded were drowned out by the survivors' wails of despair. Few had the presence of mind to throw themselves flat against the earth. They dropped the scaling ladders, turned their backs on the menace of the guns and ran.

The *Revenge* loosed her broadside upon them. Her shot swept the field. She put up her helm and followed her sister ship round.

The *Sprite* completed her tack across the wind, then came back on the other leg, offering her port battery to the fleeing Turks. Meanwhile her starboard battery had reloaded with canvas bags of grape, and the gunners were standing ready to take their next turn.

Like dancers performing a stately minuet, the two ships went through a series of elaborate figures-of-eight. Each time their guns bore they loosed another thunderclap of smoke, flame and cast-iron grape-shot across the narrow strip of open water.

After the *Sprite* had completed her second pass, Mansur snapped his telescope shut and told Kumrah, 'There is nothing more to fire at. Run in the guns, take her out into the bay.' The two ships sailed back blithely to their anchorage under the protection of the guns on the parapets of the city walls.

Zayn and his two generals surveyed the field. Corpses littered the ground, thick as autumn leaves.

'How many?' asked Zayn, in his high girlish voice.

'Not more than three hundred,' Kadem hazarded.

'No, no! Fewer.' Koots shook his head. 'A hundred and fifty, two hundred at the most.'

'They are only Turks, and another hundred dhows full of them will arrive before the week is out.' Zayn nodded dispassionately. 'We must begin digging the approach trenches and throw up a wall of gabions filled with sand along the bayside to protect our men from the ships.'

'Will Your Majesty order the fleet to take up a blockading station across the entrance to the bay?' Kadem asked respectfully. 'We must bottle up those two ships of al-Salil and, at the same time, prevent supplies of food reaching the city by sea.'

'The orders have already been given,' Zayn told him loftily. 'The English consul will place his own ship at the head of the fleet. His is the only vessel to match those of the enemy for speed. Sir Guy will prevent them breaking out through our blockade and escaping to the open ocean.'

'Al-Salil and his bastard must not be allowed to escape.' Kadem's eyes lit with the dark mesmeric glare as he said the name.

'My own hatred for him exceeds yours. Abubaker was my brother and al-Salil murdered him. There are other old scores, too, almost as compelling, which I still have to settle with him,' Zayn reminded him. 'Despite this setback, we have the noose round his neck. Now we will draw it tight.'

Over the next weeks Dorian watched the development of the siege from his command post on the minaret. The enemy fleet sailed round the peninsula and deployed across the entrance to the bay, just out of range of the batteries on the walls or even of the long nine-pounders on the two schooners. Some of the larger, less manoeuvrable dhows were anchored on the twenty-fathom line where the sea bottom shelved in. The more nimble vessels patrolled back and forth in the deeper waters, ready to seize any supply ships trying to enter the bay, or to intercept the two schooners if they tried to break through.

The graceful hull and the elegant raked masts of the

Arcturus hovered in the distance, sometimes hidden by the cliffs, sometimes dropping below the horizon. At intervals Dorian heard the distant rumble of her cannons as she fell on some unfortunate small vessel attempting to bring supplies in to Muscat. Then she reappeared from a different quarter. Mansur and Dorian discussed her as they watched her through their telescopes.

'She points well up into the wind when she is close-hauled, unlike any of the dhows. She can carry a spread of canvas nearly half as large again as either of our ships. She has eighteen guns to our twelve,' Dorian murmured. 'She is a lovely ship.'

Mansur found himself wondering if Verity was aboard her. Then he thought, If Sir Guy is there, of course she must be with him. She is his voice. He could not do without her. He thought of having to turn his guns on the *Arcturus* if Verity were standing on the open deck. I will worry about that when the time comes, he decided, then answered his father. 'The *Sprite* and the *Revenge* are able to point higher. Between them they have twenty-four guns to Sir Guy's eighteen. Both Kumrah and Batula know these waters like lovers. Ruby Cornish is a babe in arms compared to them.' Mansur smiled with the reckless abandon of youth. 'Besides, we will make our stand here. We will send Zayn and his Turks running like curs with live coals tucked under their tails.'

'I wish I had the same confidence.' Dorian turned his spyglass inland, and they watched the besieging army inch inexorably towards the walls. 'Zayn has done this many times before. He will make few mistakes. See how he has begun to sap forward? Those trenches and the lines of gabions will protect his assault forces until they are right under the walls.' Each day he instructed Mansur on the ancient science of siege-making. 'See there, they are bringing up their great guns to position them in the emplacements they have prepared. Once they begin firing in earnest they will smash through the weak spots in our defences and shoot away any repairs faster than we can make them. When they have opened the breaches they will rush them from the head of the assault trenches.'

They watched the guns being dragged forward by the teams of oxen. Weeks earlier the remainder of Zayn's fleet had arrived from Lamu and had landed his horses, draught animals and the rest of his men on the other side of the peninsula. Now his cavalry patrolled the palm groves and the foothills of the interior. Their dust was always visible.

'What can we do?' Mansur sounded less certain of the outcome.

'Very little,' Dorian replied. 'We can sortie and raid the earthworks. But they are expecting us to do that. We will take heavy losses. We can shoot away a few of the gabions, but they will repair any damage we can inflict within hours.'

'You sound despondent,' Mansur said, accusingly. 'I am unaccustomed to that, Father.'

'Despondent?' Dorian said. 'No, not of the eventual outcome. However, I should never have allowed Zayn to trap us in the city. Our men do not fight well from behind walls. They love to be the attackers. They are the ones losing heart. Mustapha Zindara and bin-Shibam are having difficulty keeping them here. Even they want to be out in the open desert, fighting the way they know best.'

That night a hundred of bin-Shibam's men threw open the city gates and, in a tight group, galloped through the Turkish lines and escaped into the desert. The guards were only just able to close the gates before the attackers rushed to exploit this opportunity.

'Could you not have stopped them going?' Mansur demanded, next morning.

Bin-Shibam shrugged at his lack of understanding, and Dorian answered him. 'The Saar do not accept orders, Mansur. They follow a sheikh just as long as they agree with what he asks of them. If they don't, they go home.'

'Now that it has begun, more will leave. The Dahm and the Awamir are restless also,' Mustapha Zindara warned.

At dawn the following day the enemy batteries in their deep, heavily fortified emplacements began to bombard the southern wall. Counting the flashes and the spurts of gunsmoke with each discharge, Dorian and Mansur determined

592

that there were eleven guns of cavernous calibre. The stone balls they fired must have weighed well over a hundred pounds each. It was possible to watch the flight of the massive projectiles with the naked eye. Mansur timed the rate of fire: it took almost twenty minutes for each gun to be swabbed, loaded, primed, then run out, relaid and fired. Once the enemy guns had ranged in, the massive balls smashed into their target with disturbing accuracy, each one striking within a few feet of its predecessor. A single ball might crack a block in the wall, and the second, striking on the same spot, dislodged it entirely. If it struck the timber balks, which the defenders had used to repair the weak sections, it splintered them to toothpicks. By nightfall of the first day two breaches had been knocked through the walls. As soon as it was dark, teams of workmen under Mansur's command rushed forward to begin the repairs.

With the dawn the bombardment began again. By noon the repairs had been swept away, and the stone balls were chipping away to enlarge the breaches. Dorian's gunners dragged half of their guns round from the harbour side to reinforce the battery on the south wall, and steadily returned the fire. However, Zayn's guns were well set in their emplacements, with deep banks of sand-filled gabions protecting them. Only the gaping bronze muzzles were visible, and these were tiny targets to hit at such ranges. When the defenders' balls struck the gabions, the sand-filled baskets of woven cane absorbed the shot so completely that it made almost no impression at all.

However, half-way through the afternoon they scored their first direct hit. One of their twenty-pound iron balls struck the extreme left-hand gun full on the muzzle. The bronze rang like a church bell, and even that weight of metal was hurled backwards off its carriage, crushing the gun-crew behind it to mincemeat. The barrel stuck straight up in the air. On the city walls the gunners cheered themselves hoarse, and redoubled their efforts. But by dusk they had not achieved another hit, and the breaches in the walls gaped wide.

As soon as the moon set, bin-Shibam and Mansur led a

sortie into the enemy lines. They took twenty men each and crept up on the battery emplacement. Even though the Turks were expecting the raid, Mansur's party had almost reached the wall of the emplacement before they were spotted and one of the sentries fired his musket. The ball hummed past Mansur's head and he shouted at his men, 'Follow me!'

As he scrambled in through the embrasure, jumped up on the barrel of the gun, and ran along the top of it, he stabbed at the throat of the man who had fired the shot at him. He dropped the musket he was trying to reload and grabbed the naked blade with both hands. When Mansur pulled it back the steel ran through the man's fingers, severing flesh and tendons to the bone. Mansur jumped over his twitching body and down among the Turkish gunners, who were dulled with sleep, and struggling out of their blankets. He killed another, and wounded a third before they ran howling with terror into the night. His men followed him in to join the attack. While they were busy, Mansur plunged the point of one of the iron spikes he carried in his pouch into the touch-hole of the gun, and another of his men drove it home with a dozen lusty blows of the hammer.

Then they ran down the connecting trench to the adjoining emplacement. Here the gunners were fully awake, waiting to meet them with pikes and battleaxes. Within seconds they were a shouting, struggling mass, and Mansur knew they would never be able to reach the second gun. More of the enemy were rushing up the communication trench from the rear to repel them.

'Back!' Mansur yelled, and they clambered over the front wall, just as Istaph and the other grooms rode up with horses. They galloped back through the city gates with bin-Shibam coming in close behind them.

There they found they had lost five men killed and another dozen wounded. In the dawn light they saw that the Turks had stripped the corpses of the missing men and displayed them on the front wall of the emplacement. Between them, Mansur and bin-Shibam had managed to spike only two of the guns, and the remaining eight opened fire again. Within hours the stone balls had ripped away all the repairs that had been thrown up during the night. In the middle of the afternoon a single lucky shot brought twenty feet of wall tumbling down in a heap of masonry and rubble. Surveying the damage from the top of the minaret, Dorian estimated, 'Another week at the latest, and Zayn will be ready to launch his attack.'

That night two hundred of the Awamir and the Dahm saddled their horses and rode out of the city. The next day, as was customary, the muezzin gave his wailing call to the faithful from the minaret of the main mosque in the city. Both sides responded: the big guns stopped firing, the Turks took off their round helmets and knelt among the palm groves, while on the parapets the defenders did the same. Before he joined in the worship, Dorian smiled ironically at the notion that both sides prayed to the same God for the victory.

This time there was a new development to the ritual. After the prayers Zayn's heralds rode around the perimeter of the walls shouting a warning to the defenders on the parapets: 'Hear the words of the true Caliph. "Those of you who wish to leave this doomed city may do so without let. I grant you pardon for their treachery. You may take with you your horse and your weapons and return to your tents and your wives. Any man who brings me the head of the incestuous usurper al-Salil, I will reward with a lakh of gold rupees."'

The defenders jeered at them. However, that night another thousand warriors rode out through the gates. Before they went, two of the lesser sheikhs came to take their leave of Dorian. 'We are not traitors or cowards,' they told him, 'but this is not a fight for a man. Out in the desert we will ride with you unto death. We love you as we loved your father, but we will not die here like caged dogs.'

'Go with my blessing,' Dorian told them, 'and may you always find favour in the sight of God. Know you that I will come to you again.'

'We shall wait for you, al-Salil.'

The next day, at the time of prayers when the guns fell silent the heralds circled the walls again.

'The true Caliph Zayn al-Din has declared a sack of the

city. Any man or woman who is found within the walls when the Caliph enters will be put to death by torture.'

This time only a few voices jeered back. That night almost half of the remaining defenders left. The Turks lined the road as they passed and made no effort to prevent them.

'You are distracted, my darling.' Caroline Courtney watched her daughter's face quizzically. 'What is it that troubles you so?'

Apart from a vague greeting, Verity had not spoken to her mother since she had come up on the deck of the *Arcturus* from her father's great cabin. The meeting with the Caliph's military commander, Kadem ibn Abubaker, had lasted most of the morning. Now Verity stood at the ship's side and watched the fast felucca conveying the general back to the shore. She had translated Abubaker's report to her father, and relayed to him the Caliph's orders to tighten the blockade of the bay to prevent any enemy ships escaping when at last the city was captured from the usurper.

She sighed and turned to her mother. 'The siege is entering its final stages, Mother,' she answered dutifully. The two had never been close. Caroline was a nervous, hysterical woman. She was dominated by her husband and had little time or energy remaining for her role as mother. Like a child, she seemed unable to concentrate on a single matter for any extended period, and her mind flitted from one subject to the next like a butterfly in a spring garden.

'I will be so relieved when this awful business is over and your father has dealt properly with this al-Salil rascal. Then we can have done with the whole dreadful business and go back home.' For Caroline, home was the consulate in Delhi. Behind the stone walls, in the manicured gardens and cool courtyards with bubbling fountains, she was safe and shielded from the cruel, alien world of the Orient. She scratched at her throat, and moaned softly. There was a scarlet rash on the white skin. The humid tropical airs and confinement in the hot little cabin had aggravated her prickly heat again.

'Shall I help you with some of the cooling lotion?' Verity asked. She wondered how her mother could so easily make her feel guilty. She went to where Caroline lay on the wide hammock that Captain Cornish had had rigged for her in a corner of the quarter-deck. A canvas sun-screen shaded her, but allowed the cooling airs of the trade wind to flow over her plump, moist body.

Verity knelt beside her and dabbed the white liquid on to the inflamed and itching rash. Caroline waved a hand languidly. Her diamond rings were deeply embedded in pasty white skin. The slim brown Indian maid in her beautiful silk sari knelt on the opposite side of the hammock from Verity and offered her a dish of sweetmeats. Caroline picked out a pink cube of Turkish Delight. When the maid began to rise to her feet Caroline stopped her with a peremptory snap of her fingers and selected two more of the flower-flavoured jellies and popped them into her mouth. She chewed with unbridled pleasure, and the fine white icing sugar dusted her lips.

'What do you suppose will happen to al-Salil and his son Mansur if they are captured by Kadem ibn Abubaker?' Verity asked mildly.

'I have no doubt that it will be something utterly detestable,' Caroline said, without interest. 'The Caliph does beastly things to his enemies, trampling by elephants, shooting from cannon.' She shuddered and reached for the glass of honey sherbet that the maid offered her. 'I really do not want to discuss it.' She sipped, and brightened. 'If this business is over by the end of the month, then we might be back in Delhi for your birthday. I am planning a ball for you. Every eligible bachelor in the Company will attend. It is high time we found a husband for you, my dear. By the time I was your age, I had been married four years and had two children.'

Suddenly Verity was angry with this vapid, fatuous woman as she had never been before. She had always treated her mother with weary deference, making allowance for her gluttony and other weaknesses. Not until her meeting with Mansur had she understood the depths of her mother's subservience to her father, the guilt that had placed her in his power. But now she was outraged by her smug, mindless complacency. Her anger boiled over before she could check it.

'Yes, Mother,' she said bitterly. 'And the first of those two children was Tom Courtney's bastard.' No sooner were the words past her lips than she wished them back.

Caroline stared at her with huge, swimming eyes. 'Oh, you wicked, wicked child! You have never loved me!' she whimpered and a mixture of sherbet and half-chewed Turkish Delight dribbled down the front of her lace blouse.

All Verity's sense of deference vanished. 'You do remember Tom Courtney, Mother?' Verity asked. 'And what tricks the two of you played while you were on passage to India in Grandfather's ship the *Seraph*?'

'You never— Who told you? What have you heard? It isn't true!' Caroline blubbered hysterically.

'What about Dorian Courtney? Do you remember how you and my father left him to rot in slavery when he was a child? How you and Father lied to Uncle Tom? How you told him that Dorian had died of the fever? You told me the same lie. You even showed me the grave on Lamu island where you said he was buried.'

'Stop this!' Caroline clapped her hands over her ears. 'I will not listen to such filth.'

''Tis filth, is it, Mother?' Verity asked coldly. 'Then who do you think is this al-Salil, whom you wish trampled by elephants or shot from a cannon? Do you not know that he is Dorian Courtney?'

Caroline stared at her, her face white as buttermilk, the inflamed rash more evident in contrast. 'Lies!' she whispered. 'All terrible wicked lies.'

'And, Mother, al-Salil's son is my cousin, Mansur Courtney. You want a husband for me? Look no further. If ever Mansur does me the honour of asking me to marry him, I shall not hesitate. I shall fly to his side.'

Caroline let out a strangled shriek, and fell out of the

hammock on to the deck. The maid and two of the ship's officers ran forward to help her to her feet. As soon as she was up, she struggled out of their grip, the fat quivering beneath her lace and pearl-studded dress, and heaved herself to the companionway that led down to the great cabin.

Sir Guy heard her shrieks of anguish and rushed out of the doorway in his shirtsleeves. He seized his wife's arm and drew her into the cabin.

Verity waited alone by the ship's rail for the retribution that she knew must surely follow. She stared beyond the rest of the blockading fleet of war dhows, into the entrance of Muscat bay to the distant spires and minarets of the city.

In her mind she went over once again the dreadful news that Kadem ibn Abubaker had brought to her father, and which she had translated to him. Muscat would be in the hands of Zayn al-Din before the month was out. Mansur was in the most dire danger, and there was nothing she could do to help him. Her dread and frustration had led her to the gross indiscretion with her mother she had just perpetrated. 'Please, God!' she whispered. 'Do not let anything befall Mansur.'

Within the hour her father's steward came to summon her.

In the cabin her mother sat in the seat below the stern window. She held a moist, crumpled handkerchief, wiped her eyes and blew her nose loudly.

Her father stood in the centre of the cabin. He was still in his shirtsleeves. His expression was severe and hard. 'What poisonous lies have you been telling your mother?' he demanded.

'No lies, Father,' she answered him defiantly. She knew what the consequences of provoking him must be, but she felt a reckless abandon.

'Repeat them to me,' Sir Guy ordered. In quiet, measured tones she described to him all that Mansur had told her. At the end he was silent. He went to the stern window and stared out at the low swells of the azure sea. He did not look at his wife. The silence drew out. Verity knew that this silence was one of his ploys to intimidate her and force her to lower her defences and her resistance to him.

'You kept this from me,' he said at last. 'Why did you not tell me at once what you had learned? That was the duty you owe to me, child.'

'You do not deny any of it, Father?' she asked.

'I do not have to deny or affirm anything to you. I am not on trial. You are.'

Silence fell again. It was hot and airless in the cabin, and the ship rolled sickeningly on the slow, greasy undulations of the current. She felt breathless and nauseated, but was determined not to show it.

Sir Guy spoke again: 'You have given your mother a severe shock with these wild stories.' Caroline sobbed dramatically and blew her nose again. 'A fast packet boat arrived from Bombay this morning. I am sending her back to the consulate.'

'I will not go with her,' Verity said evenly.

'No,' Sir Guy agreed. 'I will keep you here. It might be a summary example for you to witness the execution of the rebels in whom you have expressed such an unhealthy interest.' He was silent again for a while as he considered how much Verity knew of his affairs. Her knowledge was so extensive that it might prove lethal if she chose to use it against him. He dared not let her escape his immediate control.

'Father, these rebels are your own brother,' Verity broke the silence, 'and his son.'

Sir Guy showed no reaction. Instead he went on quietly, 'It seems, from what your mother tells me, you have been playing the harlot with the younger Arab. Have you forgotten that you are an Englishwoman?'

'You demean yourself by making that accusation.'

'You demean me and your family by your unconscionable behaviour. For that alone you must be punished.'

He went to his desk and picked up the whalebone riding crop that lay upon it. He turned back to her. 'Disrobe!' he ordered. She stood motionless, her face expressionless.

'Do as your father orders,' said Caroline, 'you blatant hussy.' She had stopped weeping and her tone was vindictive and gloating.

600

'Disrobe at once,' Guy said again, 'or I shall summon two of the seamen to do it for you.'

Verity lifted her hands to her throat and untied the ribbon that held her blouse closed. When at last she stood naked before them she raised her chin defiantly, shook out her hair and let it hang forward over her shoulders to screen her proud young breasts, and cover her pudenda.

'Lie face down over the daybed,' her father ordered.

She went to it with a firm tread. She stretched out on the buttoned green leather. The lines of her body were sweet and smooth as those of a Michelangelo marble. I will not cry out, she told herself, but her muscles convulsed instinctively as the whip hissed and clapped across her buttocks. I will not grant him that pleasure, she promised herself, and closed her eyes as the next stroke fell across the back of her thighs. It stung like the bite of a scorpion. She bit her lip until blood seeped salty and metallic into her mouth.

At last Sir Guy stood back, his breath fast and ragged with the effort. 'You may dress yourself, you shameless harlot,' he gasped.

She sat up slowly, and tried to ignore the fire that raged down her back and her legs. The front of her father's breeches was on a level with her eyes and she smiled with cold contempt as she noticed the tumescent evidence of his arousal.

He turned away hurriedly and threw the whip on to the desk top. 'You have been deceitful and disloyal to me. I can no longer trust you. I shall keep you confined to your cabin until such time as I have decided what additional punishment is appropriate,' he warned her.

Dorian and Mansur stood with the sheikhs on the balcony of the minaret, and watched the plumes and tops of the bronze soup-bowl helmets of the Turkish assault troops showing above the parapets as they moved up the approach trenches. As they massed below the walls Zayn al-Din's heavy batteries redoubled their rate of fire. They had changed their ammunition. Instead of stone balls, they swept the parapets and breaches with cartloads of fist-sized pebbles and cast-iron potlegs. The guns fell silent and the Turkish trumpeters sounded the charge; the drums pounded out an urgent beat.

A mass of shrieking Turks erupted from the head of the trenches. As they raced forward across the last few yards before the breaches, the guns of the defenders on the parapets blazed down upon them, and the archers loosed flights of arrows.

The leading attackers were across the open ground before the gunners could reload. They left dead and wounded littered upon the shot-torn earth, but wave after wave ran forward to take the place of the fallen.

They clambered over the rubble and the shattered stone blocks, and swarmed through the breaches. As soon as they were through they found themselves in a maze of narrow alleys and dead-end lanes. Dorian had ordered barricades built across every one. The Turks had to take each by storm, running into a hail of close-range musket fire as they charged. As soon as they scaled an obstruction, the defenders ran back to the next line of defence and the Turks were forced to attack again. It was gruelling and bloody work, but gradually Mansur and bin-Shibam's depleted forces were driven back into the main souk, and the Turks were able to outflank them, and reach the main city gate. They slaughtered the men who tried to defend the winches and forced the gates wide. Kadem and Koots, at the head of two thousand Turks, were waiting outside and the moment the gates swung open they rushed in.

From the top of the minaret Dorian saw them pouring like floodwaters down the narrow streets. He was relieved that over the past months he had been able to spirit most of the women and children out of the city and into the desert, for they would have been lambs to these wolves. As soon as the gates were open, he ordered the hoisting of the previously prepared flag signal to the *Sprite* and the *Revenge*. Then he turned to his councillors and captains. 'It is over,' he told them. 'I thank you for your courage and loyalty. Take your men and escape if you can. We will fight again another day.' One at a time they came forward to embrace him.

Bin-Shibam was covered with dust and black with smoke; his robe was stained with the dried blood of half a dozen flesh wounds. It mingled with the blood of the Turks he had slain. 'We shall wait for your return,' he said.

'You know where you can find me. Send a messenger to me when all is in readiness. I shall return to you at once,' Dorian told him, 'if God is willing. Praise God.'

'God is great,' they replied.

The horses were waiting in the lanes before the small north gate. When it was thrown open Mustapha Zindara, bin-Shibam and the rest of the council rode out at the head of their men. They fought their way through the attackers who raced forward to cut them off, then galloped away through the palm groves and irrigated fields. Dorian watched them go from the minaret. He heard footsteps on the marble stairs and turned with his sword in his hand. For a moment he hardly recognized his own son under the coating of grime and soot.

'Come, Father,' Mansur said, 'we must hurry.'

Together they ran down the stairs to where Istaph and ten men were waiting for them in the mosque.

'This way.' An imam stepped from the shadows and gesticulated. They hurried after him, and he led them through a labyrinth of passages until they reached a small iron gate. He unlocked it and Mansur kicked it open.

'Stay with God's blessing,' Dorian told the imam.

'Go with God's blessing,' he replied, 'and may He bring you swiftly back to Oman.'

They ran through the door and found themselves in a gloomy alleyway so narrow that the latticed balconies of the top floors of the deserted buildings almost met overhead.

'This way, Majesty!' Istaph had been born in the city, and these alleys had been his childhood playground. They raced after him and burst out into the sunlight again. The open waters of the harbour lay before them, and the *Sprite*'s longboat was waiting out in the bay to take them off. Mansur shouted and waved to Kumrah who stood at the helm. The oarsmen pulled together and the longboat shot in towards them.

At that moment there was an angry din behind them. A

mob of Turkish and Omani attackers poured out from the mouth of one of the alleys on to the wharf. They charged towards them, their front rank bristling with long pikes and bright-edged weapons. Dorian glanced over his shoulder and saw that the longboat was still a pistol shot away across the green waters. 'Stand together!' he cried, and they formed a tight circle at the head of the landing steps, shoulder to shoulder, facing outwards.

'Al-Salil!' shouted the Arab who led the attack. He was tall and lean, and he moved like a leopard. His long, lank hair whipped out behind him and his beard curled on to his chest.

'Al-Salil!' he shouted again. 'I have come for you.' Dorian recognized that fierce, fanatical glare.

'Kadem.' Mansur recognized him at the same moment, and his voice rang with the force of his hatred.

'I have come for you also, you bastard puppy of a dog and an incestuous bitch in heat!' Kadem shouted again.

'You must take me first.' Dorian stepped forward a pace, and Kadem hurled himself upon him. Their blades clashed as Dorian blocked the cut for his head, and then sent a riposte at Kadem's throat. Steel rang and scraped on steel. It was the first time they had matched blades, but Dorian knew at once that Kadem was a dangerous opponent. His right arm was quick and powerful, and in his left hand he held a curved dagger, poised to strike through any opening.

'You murdered my wife!' Dorian snarled, as he thrust again.

'I give thanks that I was able to do that duty. I should have killed you also,' Kadem answered, 'for my father's sake.'

Mansur fought at Dorian's right hand and Istaph on the left, guarding his flanks but careful not to block or impede his sword arm. Step by step they gave ground, retreating to the head of the landing, and the attackers pressed them hard.

Dorian heard the bows of the longboat bump against the stone wall below them, and Kumrah shouted, 'Come, al-Salil!'

The steps were greasy with green algae and Kadem, seeing Dorian about to escape his vengeance a second time, leaped in furiously. Dorian was driven back another pace on to the top step, and his right foot slipped on the greasy surface. He went down on one knee and was forced to save his balance by dropping his point for an instant. Kadem saw his chance. He launched himself, all his weight on his right foot, lunging for Dorian's heart.

The moment his father had gone down, Mansur anticipated Kadem's response. He turned, poised and ready. Kadem swung his body forward and for an instant his left flank was open as he launched himself into the attack. Mansur hit him, going in under his raised arm. He put all his anger, hatred and grief for his mother behind the thrust. He expected to feel his point slide in deeply, that clinging reluctance of living flesh opening to the steel. Instead his sword arm jarred to the strike of steel on the bone of Kadem's ribs, and his wrist twisted slightly as the point was deflected. Nevertheless, the thrust ran along the outside of Kadem's ribcage, and up under his scapula. It touched no vital organ but the force of it spun Kadem sideways, throwing off-line the thrust he aimed at Dorian. Kadem reeled away, and Mansur pulled his blade free and struck again. But with a violent effort Kadem blocked the second blow, and Dorian leaped back to his feet.

Father and son went at Kadem together, eager for the kill. Blood was pouring from the wound under Kadem's arm and cascading down his flank. The shock of the blow and the realization that he was in mortal danger from two skilled swordsmen blanched his face a dirty treacle colour.

'*Effendi*!' Kumrah shouted, from the longboat. 'Come! We will be trapped. There are more Turks coming.' The enemy was thronging out of the mouth of the alleyway, and rushing towards them.

Realizing their predicament, Dorian hesitated and that was all Kadem needed to break off and leap out of play. Instantly two swarthy, armoured Turks jumped forward in his place and rushed at Dorian. When he struck at them his blade skidded off their chain-mail.

'Enough!' Dorian grunted. 'Get back to the boat!' Mansur feinted at the bearded face of one of the Turks, and when he ducked back Mansur stepped across to cover his father.

'Run!' he snapped, and Dorian bounded down the steps.

Istaph and the others were already on board, and Mansur was left alone at the head of the landing. A line of pikes and scimitars pressed him back. He had a glimpse of Kadem ibn Abubaker glaring at him from the back row of the attackers; the wound had not dimmed his hatred.

'Kill him!' he screamed. 'Let not the pig-swine escape.'

'Mansur!' He heard his father call from the bows of the longboat. Yet he knew that if he tried to run down the steps one of the pike men would send a thrust into his exposed back. He turned and jumped, launching himself out over the stone edge of the wharf. He dropped ten feet and landed feet first on one of the thwarts. The heavy planking cracked under his weight, and he toppled forward. The longboat rocked violently and Mansur almost went over the side, but Dorian grabbed and steadied him.

The oarsmen heaved together and the longboat shot away. Dorian looked back over the stern just as Kadem staggered to the edge of the wharf. He had dropped his sword and was clutching the wound under his arm. The blood flowed through his fingers. 'You shall not escape my vengeance!' he shrieked after them. 'You have my father's blood on your hands and your conscience. I have sworn your death in the sight of Allah. I will follow you to the gates of hell.'

'He does not understand the true meaning of hatred,' Dorian whispered. 'One day I hope to teach it to him.'

'I share your oath,' said Mansur, 'but now we have to get our ships out of the bay and into the open sea, with Zayn's entire fleet to oppose us.'

Dorian shook himself, throwing off the debilitating throes of grief and hatred. He turned to look at the mouth of the bay. Four of the big war-dhows were anchored in sight, and two more under sail.

'No sighting of the *Arcturus*?' he asked Mansur.

'Not these past three days,' Mansur replied, 'but we can be sure she is not far off, lurking just below the horizon.'

Dorian went up on to the deck of the *Revenge*, then called down to Mansur in the longboat. 'We must try at all times to keep one another in sight, but there is sure to be fighting. Should we become separated, you know the rendezvous.'

Mansur waved at him. 'Sawda island, north tip. I will wait for you there.' He broke off at the sullen boom of a cannon, and looked back at the city walls above the harbour. Powder smoke bloomed on the parapet but was swiftly blown aside by the wind. Moments later a fountain of spray leaped from the surface of the sea close alongside the *Sprite*.

'The enemy have seized the batteries,' Dorian shouted. 'We must get under way at once.'

Another cannon shot bellowed out before Mansur reached the *Sprite*. Although this ball fell well short, Mansur knew that the gunners would soon have the range.

'Pull!' he shouted to the rowers. 'Pull or you will be forced to swim!'

The crew of the *Sprite*, urged on by the fall of shot around them, had the anchor cable singled up and the falls dangling overside from the davits, ready to retrieve the longboat. As Mansur bounded up on to the deck, he ordered the jib set to bring her round to face the entrance to the bay. As the *Sprite* turned on to the wind Kumrah broke out all sails to the royals.

The evening offshore wind had set in and was blowing steadily from the west. It was on their best point of sailing and they flew down towards the mouth of the bay. As they came up with the *Revenge*, she backed her mainsail to allow the *Sprite* to take the lead. The entrance was treacherous with hidden shoals, but Kumrah knew these waters better even than Batula in the *Revenge*. He would lead them out.

Mansur had not realized until then how swiftly the day had sped away. The sun was already low on the peaks of the mountains behind them, and the light was rich and golden. The batteries on the parapets of Muscat were still blazing away at them, and one lucky shot punched a neat hole in the mizzen topmast staysail, but they drew steadily out of range and could look ahead to the blockading ships across the entrance. Two of the war-dhows had hoisted their anchors, set their huge lateen sails and were moving out into the channel to meet them. Their passage through the water was sluggish compared to the two much smaller schooners, and they fell away noticeably even though they were not pointing high up into the stiff evening breeze. In contrast, the two schooners had set all sail and were tearing down the length of the bay.

Mansur looked along his deck and saw that his gunners were all at their action stations, although they had not yet run out the guns, which were loaded with round-shot. The slow-match was smouldering in the sand tubs and the men were laughing and talking excitedly. The days of gunnery practice and their successful attack on the Turkish infantry had imbued them with confidence. They were chafed by the inactivity of the last few weeks while they had been forced to lie at anchor, but now that Mansur and al-Salil were back in command of the flotilla they were eager for a fight.

Kumrah made a small adjustment to their course. Although Mansur trusted his judgement, he felt a twinge of unease. On this heading Kumrah would take them into the boiling white surf below the cliffs that guarded the entrance to the bay.

The nearest war-dhow altered her course towards them as soon as Kumrah's turn became apparent. They began to converge swiftly. Mansur raised his glass and studied the dhow. It was crammed with men. They lined the windward rail and brandished their weapons. She had already run out her big guns.

'She is armed with short-barrelled Ostras,' Kumrah told Mansur.

'I do not know them.'

'That does not surprise me. They must be older than your grandfather.' Kumrah laughed. 'And with a great deal less power.'

'Then it seems we are in greater danger of striking the reef than receiving a ball from those ancient weapons,' Mansur said pointedly. They were still charging straight in towards the cliffs.

'Highness, you must have faith in Allah.'

'In Allah I have faith. I worry only about the captain of my ship.'

608

Kumrah smiled and held his course. The dhow fired her first ragged broadside from all fifteen of her starboard guns. The range was still too far by half. Mansur spotted the fall of only one shot, and that was short by half a musket. However, the faint cheering of the dhow's crew carried to them faintly.

Still the huge dhow and the two small ships converged. Gradually as they bore down on the breaking white water the cheering from the dhow subsided and the pugnacious display with it.

'You have terrified the enemy, as you have me,' said Mansur. 'Do you intend scuttling us on the reef, Kumrah?'

'I fished these waters as a boy, as did my father and his father before me,' Kumrah assured him. The reef was still dead ahead, and they were closing rapidly. The dhow fired another broadside, but it was clear that the gunners were distracted by the menace of the coral. Only a single large stone ball howled over the *Sprite* and severed a mizzen shroud. Quickly Kumrah sent two men to replace it.

Then, without reducing sail, Kumrah steered into a narrow channel in the reef that Mansur had not noticed. It was barely wide enough to accept the beam of the schooner. As they tore through, Mansur stared with dread fascination overside and saw huge mushroom heads of coral skimming by less than a fathom below the churning surface. Any one of them would have ripped the *Sprite*'s belly out of her.

This was too much for the nerves of the dhow captain. Mansur could see him in the stern of his ship, screaming and gesticulating wildly. His crew deserted their posts at the guns and scrambled to take in the billowing lateen sail and bring their ship on to the other tack. With the sail down they had to run the boom back to bring its butt round the mast, then home again on the port side. This was a laborious business and while they were about it the dhow wallowed helplessly.

'Stand by to go about!' Kumrah gave the order and his men ran to the stays. He was staring ahead, shading his eyes with one hand, judging his moment finely. 'Up helm!' he called to his helmsman, who spun the wheel until the spokes blurred. The *Sprite* pirouetted and shot through the dogleg turn in the channel. They raced out of the far end into the deeper water, and the helpless dhow wallowed directly ahead of them with her sail in disarray and her guns unmanned.

'Run out the starboard guns!' Mansur gave the order, and the lids of the gunports crashed open. They crossed the dhow's stern so closely that Mansur could have thrown his hat on to her deck.

'Fire as you bear!'

In quick succession the cannons roared out, and each ball smashed into the dhow's stern. Mansur could see the timbers shatter and burst open in clouds of flying wood splinters. One of them as long as his arm pegged like an arrow into the mast beside his ear. At that range not a single shot missed the mark, and the iron balls raked through the dhow from stem to stern. There were screams of terror and agony from the crew as the *Sprite* sailed on past her into the open sea.

Following her closely through the channel in the coral, the *Revenge* bore down on the stricken vessel in her turn. As she passed she raked her again, and the dhow's single mast toppled and fell overside.

Mansur looked ahead. The way was clear. Not one of the other dhows was in position to head them off. Kumrah's seemingly suicidal manoeuvre had taken them by surprise. 'Run in the guns!' he ordered. 'Close the ports and secure the gun tackles.'

He looked back and saw the *Revenge* only half a cable's length behind them. A long way back the dismasted dhow was drifting on to the reef, driven before the wind. She struck and heeled over violently. Through the glass Mansur saw her crew abandon her. They were leaping over the side, hitting the water with tiny white splashes, then striking out for the shore. Mansur wondered how many would survive the rip current at the foot of the cliffs, and the sharp fangs of the coral.

He backed his mainsail and let the *Revenge* come up alongside, close enough to enable his father to hail them through the speaking trumpet: 'Tell Kumrah never to play that trick on us again! He took us through the gates of hell.'

Kumrah made a deep and penitent obeisance, but Dorian

lowered the trumpet and saluted his cool head and nerves. Then he lifted the trumpet again. 'It will be dark in an hour. I shall burn a single lantern in my stern port for you to keep your station on me. If we should become separated during the night, the rendezvous will be the same as always, Sawda island.'

The *Revenge* forged ahead and the *Sprite* fell in behind her. Weeks before Dorian had decided on their final destination. There was only one port in all the Ocean of the Indies open to them now. Zayn had all the Fever Coast and the harbours of Oman under his thrall. The Dutch had Ceylon and Batavia. The English East India Company controlled all the coast of India. Sir Guy would close that to them. There remained only the safe haven of Fort Auspice in Nativity Bay. There they would be able to gather their reserves and make plans for the future. He had marked the chart and given Mustapha Zindara and bin-Shibam the sailing directions for Fort Auspice: they would send a ship to find him there as soon as they had united the desert tribes and made all the preparations for his return. They would need gold rupees and strong allies. Dorian was as yet uncertain as to where he would find men and money, but there would be time to ponder this later.

He turned to his immediate concerns, and the course that he set now was east by south-east to clear the Gulf of Oman. Once they were into the open ocean they could steer directly for Madagascar and pick up the Mozambique current to carry them southwards. Mansur took up close station on the *Revenge* and they sailed on beneath a sunset of awe-inspiring grandeur. Mountainous anvil-headed thunderclouds marched along the darkling western horizon to the sound of distant thunder, and the sinking sun costumed them with suits of rosy gold and glittering cobalt blue.

Yet all this beauty could not lift from Mansur's shoulder the sudden oppressive weight of the melancholia that bore down upon him. He was leaving the land and the people he had swiftly learned to love. The promise of a kingdom and of the Elephant Throne had been snatched from them. Yet all that was of little account when he thought of the woman he

611

had lost before he had won her. He took from the inner pocket of his robe the letter he carried close to his heart, and read yet again her words: 'Last night you asked me if I did not feel anything between you and me. I would not answer you then, but I answer you now. Yes, I do.'

It seemed to him that those were the most beautiful words ever written in the English language.

Darkness fell with the dramatic suddenness that is seen only in the tropics, and the stars showed through the gaps left in the high canopy of the stormclouds. Within a short time they were closed by the rolling thunderheads and the darkness was complete, except for the tiny firefly of light that was the lantern on the stern of the *Revenge*.

Mansur leaned on the compass pinnacle and let himself lapse into romantic fantasy, dreaming half the night away without seeking his bunk. Suddenly, he was roused by a stroke of forked lightning that flew from the cloud ceiling to the surface of the sea, and was followed immediately by a sky-shattering thunderclap. For an instant the *Revenge* appeared out of the darkness ahead, shimmering in vivid blue light, each detail of her rigging and sails stark and clear. Then the darkness fell over her again even more heavily than before.

Mansur jumped erect from his slouch over the binnacle and ran to the starboard rail. In that blinding lightning flash he thought he had seen something else. It had been an evanescent flash of reflected light, almost on the far horizon.

'Did you see it?' he shouted at Kumrah, who stood beside him at the rail.

'The *Revenge*?' Kumrah answered, from the darkness, and his tone was puzzled. 'Yes, Highness. She is not more than a single cable's length ahead. There – you can see the glimmer of her stern light still.'

'No, no!' Mansur cried. 'Not on our bow. Abaft our beam. Something else.'

'Nay, master. I saw nothing.'

Both men peered out into the night, and again the lightning cracked overhead like a gigantic whip, then thunder deafened them and seemed to shiver the surface of the dark sea with its monstrous discharge. In that fleeting moment of diamond-sharp clarity Mansur saw it again.

'There!' Mansur seized Kumrah's shoulder and shook him violently. 'There! Did you see it this time?'

'A ship! Another ship!' Kumrah cried. 'I saw it clear.'

'How far off?'

'Two sea miles, no more than that. A tall ship. Square-rigged. That is no dhow.'

''Tis the *Arcturus*! Lying here in ambuscade.' Desperately Mansur looked to his father's ship, and saw that the tell-tale lantern still burned on her stern. 'The *Revenge* has not seen the danger.'

'We must catch up with her and warn her,' Kumrah exclaimed.

'Even if we clap on all our canvas we will not overhaul the *Revenge* and be within hail of her in less than a hour. By then it may be too late.' Mansur hesitated a moment longer, then made his decision: 'Beat to action quarters. Fire a gun to alert the *Revenge*. Then bring her on to the starboard tack and run in to intercept the enemy. Do not light the battle lanterns until I give the order. God grant we can take the enemy by surprise.'

The war drums boomed out into the dark, and as the crew scrambled to their stations a single peremptory gunshot thudded. As the *Sprite* came about, Mansur peered across at the other ship, waiting for her to extinguish her lantern or show some sign that she had taken heed of the warning, but at that instant the thunderclouds burst open and the rain teemed down. All was lost in the warm, smothering cascade of water. It seemed to fill the air they breathed, cutting out any faint glimmer of light and muting all sound other than the roar of the heavy drops on the canvas overhead and the deck timbers underfoot.

Mansur ran back to the binnacle and took a hasty bearing, but he knew that it was not accurate, and that the enemy ship might also have spotted them and changed her course and heading. His chances of coming upon her in this deluge were remote. They might pass each other by half a pistol shot without either being aware of the other's presence.

'Turn the hourglass and mark the traverse-board,' he ordered the helmsman. Perhaps he could intercept her on dead reckoning. Then he snapped at Kumrah, 'Put two good men on the wheel.'

He hurried to the bows, and through the sheets of blinding rain tried for a glimpse of the stern lantern of the *Revenge*. He took little comfort from the fact that he could see and hear nothing.

'God grant that Father is aware of the danger, and that he has doused the lantern. Otherwise it might guide Sir Guy to him, and he could be taken unawares.' He considered firing another gun to emphasize the urgency of the danger, but discarded the idea almost at once. A second gun would confuse the warning. His father might be led to believe that the *Sprite* had already engaged an enemy. It might alert the *Arcturus* and bring her down upon them. Instead he sailed on into the darkness and the torrents of blood-warm rain.

'Send your sharpest lookouts aloft,' he ordered Kumrah grimly, 'and have the gunners ready to run out on the instant. We will not have much warning if we come upon the enemy.'

The hourglass was turned twice, and still they sailed on in darkness, every man aboard straining all his senses for some warning of the enemy ship. And the rain never let up.

The enemy might have sailed on without spotting us, Mansur thought. He pondered the chances and the choices that were open to him. Or she might have turned to intercept us, and have passed us close at hand. She might even now be creeping up on the unsuspecting *Revenge*.

He reached a decision, and called to Kumrah, 'Heave the ship to, and warn every man to keep his eyes peeled and his ears open.'

They lay dark and silent, and another hour passed, measured by the soft slide of the sand in the hourglass. The rain abated, and the freshening breeze veered into the north, bringing with it the spicy odour of the desert, which was still not far off. The rain ceased. Mansur was about to give the order to set sail again, when a flickering glow lit the darkness far over their stern. It played like candlelight on the underbelly of the lowering cloud masses. Mansur held his breath and counted slowly to five. Then came the sound, the unmistakable rumbling roar of the guns.

'The *Arcturus* has slipped by us and she has found the *Revenge*. They are engaged,' he shouted. 'Wear ship and bring her round on to the port tack.'

With the night breeze on their quarter the *Sprite* tore through the darkness, both Mansur and Kumrah straining to coax every knot of speed from her. Ahead of them the flickering light and rumble of gun salvos grew brighter and louder as they sailed towards them.

'God grant we are in time,' Mansur prayed, and as he stared ahead the wind of their passage in his face brought tears to his eyes, or it may have been some other emotion. The two persons he loved most were caught up in that maelstrom of shot and flame, and he was still powerless to intervene. Even though the *Sprite* lay well over and ran before the breeze like a stag hard pressed by the hounds, she was still too slow for Mansur's heart.

Yet the distance between them narrowed steadily and, standing in the bows, balancing to the ship's urgent motion, Mansur was at last able to make out the shapes of the two ships. They were locked in conflict, lit by the muzzle flashes of their cannon.

Mansur saw that they were on the opposite tack to the *Sprite*, crossing their bows at an acute angle, so he yelled to Kumrah to bring the *Sprite* round two points on to an interception course. Now the range began to close more rapidly, and he could make out the more intimate details of the battle.

In the *Revenge*, Dorian had somehow wrested the weather gauge from Captain Cornish, and was holding him off, frustrating his efforts to bring the *Arcturus* alongside and to board him. But Cornish was blocking any effort that Dorian might make to bring the *Revenge* before the wind on to her best point of sailing and to run away from his superior adversary. In this formation the two ships were almost perfectly matched for speed, and the *Revenge* could not evade the bigger ship for much longer. In a duel of attrition like this the heavier weight of cannon must tell in the end.

However, the *Sprite* was closing rapidly, and soon she would throw her own weight into the unequal contest. The balance then would swing in their favour – if Mansur could reach them before the *Arcturus* grappled and boarded the smaller ship.

Closer and closer Mansur edged the *Sprite* towards the two ships. Even though his impulse was to rush in recklessly and hurl himself at the *Arcturus*, he restrained his warlike instincts, and manoeuvred across the wind.

He knew that he was still shrouded in the night, invisible to the captains and crews of either ship. He must take the utmost advantage of the surprise element. There were many minutes still before he was in position to put up his helm and charge out of the darkness, to cross the *Arcturus*'s stern, then to grapple and board her from across her port quarter. Mansur watched the development of the conflict through the lens of his spyglass.

Although the guns were firing steadily, the range was still too long for them to inflict telling damage on each other. He saw that a number of the *Revenge*'s shots had smashed holes in her opponent's hull above the waterline. The shattered timbers were bright with fresh splinters. There were rips and holes in some of her sails, and a few spars had been knocked away in her rigging, but all her guns were firing steadily.

Opposite her the *Revenge* was in no worse a case. In the light of the cannons, Mansur could pick out his father's figure in the distinctive green robes as he directed his gunners. Batula stood beside the helm, endeavouring to milk the last turn of speed from his ship.

Then Mansur turned his glass back on the quarter-deck of the *Arcturus*. With dread he searched for a glimpse of Verity's tall slim figure. He felt a small lift of relief when he could not find her, although he guessed that Sir Guy had confined her below decks where she would have some protection from the screaming round-shot.

Then he picked out Captain Cornish's face, red and angry in the glare of gunfire. He was pacing his deck with ponderous dignity, occasionally shooting a glance at his adversary, then turning back to harangue his gunners through the speaking trumpet he held to his lips. Even as Mansur watched, a lucky shot from the *Revenge* took away a spar in the *Arcturus*'s rigging and her main course came billowing down across the quarter-deck, smothering officers and helmsman under its heavy canvas folds.

There were a few moments of pandemonium as the crew rushed to hack away the flapping canvas. The fire from her batteries dwindled, and the blinded helmsman allowed her head to pay off a point before the wind as he tried to struggle out from under the sail. Then, from the far side of the quarter-deck, Mansur saw Sir Guy Courtney run forward into Cornish's place, and take command. Mansur heard faintly his shouts and saw that order was being swiftly restored. He must act at once to take advantage of the moment. He called an order to Kumrah, who was already poised for it. The *Sprite* turned like a polo pony and charged out of the darkness. She passed close under the stern of the *Revenge* and Mansur jumped up in the shrouds and called across the narrow gap of water to Dorian, 'Father!' Dorian spun round with a startled expression as the *Sprite* appeared miraculously out of the darkness so close at hand. 'I will cross his bows and rake him. Then I will board him from his port side. You close from the other hand and split his force.' Dorian's features lit with the old battle madness and he grinned at Mansur as he waved acknowledgement.

Mansur ordered the guns run out as he steered boldly across the *Arcturus*'s bows. For almost five minutes, which seemed a lifetime, he came directly under her fire, but her gun-crews were still in disarray and only three balls crashed into the *Sprite*'s upper deck. Although they ripped open the heavy planking and the splinters buzzed like a swarm of hornets, not a single man of the *Sprite*'s crew was struck down. Then he was under the *Arcturus*'s bows and screened from her fire by her own hull.

Mansur ran forward as his guns began to bear, then walked back along his battery, making certain that each one was aimed true before he gave the order to fire. One after the other the huge bronze weapons bellowed flame and shot, then crashed back against their tackles. Every ball struck home.

Mansur had cut his attack a shade too fine, and he passed so closely under Arcturus's bows that the larger ship's bowsprit snagged in the *Sprite*'s mizzen mast shrouds and snapped off, but the hulls missed each other by only an arm's length before the *Sprite* was past.

Immediately he was clear Mansur spun the *Sprite* round and laid her neatly alongside the *Arcturus*. The lids of the gunports on her port side were still closed, for the *Arcturus* was unprepared for an attack from this quarter. As the grappling irons were hurled over the *Arcturus*'s bulwarks and the two hulls were lashed together, Mansur fired another point-blank salvo from his starboard battery, then led his men across in a howling berserker rush. The gun-crews of the *Arcturus* turned to face them, but no sooner were they locked in the desperate hand-to-hand fighting than the *Revenge* took advantage of her weather gauge and came gliding in to grapple on to her starboard side. The *Arcturus*'s batteries on that side had not been reloaded after the last discharge, and the crews had abandoned them to meet Mansur's attack. The *Arcturus* was caught in the jaws of the barracuda.

The fighting raged back and forth across the main deck, but the combined crews of the two schooners outnumbered that of the larger *Arcturus* and slowly they began to wrest the upper hand. Mansur sought out Cornish and the two locked blades. Mansur tried to drive him back across the deck, and pin him against the shrouds. But Ruby Cornish was a wily old dog sailor. He came back at Mansur hard and fast, and they circled each other.

Dorian killed a man with a quick thrust, then looked around for Guy. He was not certain what he would do if he found him. Perhaps, deep in his heart, he longed for a battlefield reconciliation. He could not see him in the ruck of fighting men, but he realized that the battle was swinging in their favour. The crew of the *Arcturus* were giving up the fight. He saw two throw aside their weapons and, quick as rabbits, scuttle down the nearest hatchway. When a crew ran below decks they were beaten.

'In God's Name the battle is ours,' he exhorted the men around him. 'Have at them!' His voice filled them with fresh strength and they threw themselves at the enemy. Dorian looked for Mansur, and saw him on the far side of the deck. He was heavily engaged with Cornish. There was blood on his robe but Dorian hoped that it was not his own. Then he saw Ruby Cornish break off, and run back to attempt to rally his fleeing men. Mansur was too exhausted to follow him and rested on his sword. In the light of the battle lanterns, sweat shone on his face and his chest heaved with the effort of breathing. Dorian shouted across the deck to him, 'What happened to Guy? Where is my brother? Have you seen him?'

'No, Father,' Mansur shouted back hoarsely. 'He must have run below with the rest of them.'

'We have them beaten,' Dorian cried. 'It will take one last charge, and the *Arcturus* is ours. Come on!'

The men around him gave a ragged cheer and started forward, but then they came up short again as Guy Courtney's high-pitched yell cut through the hubbub of the battle. He stood at the rail of the poop deck. In one hand he carried a burning length of slow-match and on the other shoulder he balanced a keg of black powder. The bung had been knocked from the keg and a thick trail of powder poured from it to the deck at his feet.

'This powder trail runs to the ship's main powder magazine,' he shouted. Though he spoke in English his meaning was clear

619

to every Arab seaman aboard. The fighting ceased and all stared at him, aghast. A deathly silence fell over the *Arcturus*'s deck.

'I will strike this ship, and blow up every one of you with it,' Guy screamed, and lifted the smoking, spluttering slow-match high. 'As God is my witness, I shall do it.'

'Guy!' Dorian shouted up at him, 'I am your brother, Dorian Courtney!'

'I know it well!' Guy yelled back, and there was a bitter, hard edge to his voice. 'Verity has confessed her deceit and complicity to me. That will not save you.'

'No, Guy!' Dorian cried. 'You must not do it.'

'There is naught you can say to dissuade me,' Guy shouted back, and hurled the powder keg down on to the deck at his feet. It burst open. Gunpowder spilled across the deck. Slowly he brought down the flaring slow-match and a wail of fear went up from the crowded main deck. One of the men from the *Revenge* turned and raced back to the ship's side. He sprang across the narrow gap, to the illusory safety of the deck of his own ship.

His example was infectious. They fled back to the smaller ships. As soon as they were aboard they hacked with their swords at the grappling lines that held them bound to the doomed *Arcturus*.

Only Kumrah, Batula and a few other staunch sailors stood their ground beside Dorian and Mansur.

'It's a ruse! He will not do it,' Dorian told them. 'Follow me!' But as he ran to the foot of the ladder that led up to the poop deck, Guy Courtney hurled the slow-match into the powder trail. In a dense, hissing tail of smoke the gunpowder ignited and ran back swiftly along the deck until it reached the open hatchway and shot down into the interior of the ship.

The pluck of even the stalwart captains and their officers deserted them, and they turned and ran. The last of the grappling lines were parting, popping like cotton threads. In a moment the two smaller ships would be free of the *Arcturus* and drift away into the night.

'Even if it is a ruse, we shall still be stranded here,' Mansur called to his father. There were hostile sailors all around them. Their predicament would prove fatal.

'Not a moment to lose,' Dorian shouted back. 'Run for it, Mansur.'

Both of them turned and leaped across to the decks of their own ships, just as the last grappling lines parted and the hulls drifted apart. On the poop deck Guy Courtney stood alone. The powder smoke swirled in clouds around him, giving him a satanical appearance. The sparks of burning powder and debris took hold in the rigging and ran up the shrouds.

The first cannon salvo had jarred the timbers of the hull and startled Verity awake. The *Arcturus* had come to battle stations so silently that in her barred cabin she had not realized what was happening on deck until this moment. She scrambled from her bunk and turned up the wick on the lantern that hung on gimbals from the deck above. She reached for her clothing and pulled on a cotton shirt and the breeches she preferred to skirts and petticoats when she needed freedom of movement.

She was busy with her boots when the hull heeled sharply to the next broadside of cannon. She ran to the door of her cabin and beat upon it with her fists. 'Let me out!' she screamed. 'Open this door!' But there was no one to hear her.

She picked up the heavy silver candelabrum from the table and tried to break open the door panels so that she could reach the locking bar on the outside, but the sturdy teak timbers resisted her efforts. She was forced to give up and retreat to the far side of her cabin. She opened the porthole and peered out. She knew that escape by this route was hopeless. She had considered it many times during the weeks of her captivity. The surface of the sea creamed by close below her face, and it was six feet to the rail of the deck above her. She gazed out into the night and tried to follow the battle by the flare and flicker of gunfire. She caught glimpses of the other ship that was engaging them, and recognized it at once as the *Revenge*. She could see no sign of Mansur's ship.

She winced every time the cannon salvos roared out from the deck above her cabin, or when an enemy ball crashed into their hull. The battle seemed to rage interminably, and her senses were dulled by the uproar. The stench of burnt powder permeated her cabin like some dreadful incense burned to the god Mars, and she coughed in its acrid fumes.

Then, suddenly, she saw another dark apparition appear silently out of the darkness, another ship.

'The *Sprite*!' she whispered, and her heart bounded. Mansur's ship! She had thought never to see it again. Then it began to fire upon them, and she was so excited that she felt no fear at all. One after another the iron round-shot smashed into the *Arcturus*, and each time she shuddered to the strike.

Then, abruptly, Verity was flung to the deck as a ball ripped through the bulkhead beside her doorway, and the cabin was filled with smoke and wood-dust. When it cleared she saw that the door had been shot away. She jumped to her feet, clambered through the wreckage and forced her way out into the open passageway. She heard the hand-to-hand fighting on the deck above her as the crew of the *Sprite* boarded the ship over her port rail. The shouts and cries mingled with the clash of steel blades and the report of pistols and muskets. She looked about her for a weapon but there was nothing. Then she saw that her father's door stood open. She knew he kept his pistols in the drawer of his desk, and hurried to it.

Now she stood directly below the skylight, and her father's voice carried clearly through the opening: 'This powder trail runs to the ship's main powder magazine,' he shouted. A deathly silence fell over the *Arcturus*'s deck, and Verity froze. 'I will strike this ship, and blow up every one of you with it,' her father screamed again. 'As God is my witness, I shall do it.'

'Guy!' Verity recognized the voice that answered him. 'I am your brother, Dorian Courtney!'

'I know it well!' Guy yelled back. 'Verity has confessed her deceit and complicity to me. That will not save you.'

'No, Guy!' Dorian cried. 'You must not do it.'

'There is naught you can say to dissuade me,' Guy shouted back.

Verity listened to no more. She dashed out into the passage and immediately saw the thick trail of black powder running down the treads of the companionway and along the passage to the lower deck and the magazine.

'He is telling the truth,' she cried aloud. 'He truly means to strike the ship.' She acted without hesitation. She seized one of the fire buckets that stood at the foot of the companionway. The ship's wooden hull was a mortal fire hazard, and the buckets filled with seawater were placed at every convenient point whenever the ship went into battle. Verity sloshed the water across the powder trail, washing a wide gap in it.

She was only just in time. With a sizzling rush the flames came shooting down the companionway, then checked in a cloud of blue smoke as they reached the gap she had made. She jumped upon them, stamping on the smouldering grains. Then she seized another bucket of seawater and emptied it over them. She made sure she had doused every spark before she ran up the ladder to the quarter-deck.

'Father! This is madness!' Verity cried, as she stepped out of the smoke behind him.

'I ordered you to remain in your cabin.' He rounded on her. 'You disobeyed me.'

'If I had not, you would have blown me and yourself to glory,' she shrieked at him, almost beside herself with terror at how close they had been to death.

He saw how her clothing was scorched and blackened and sodden with seawater. 'You treacherous, evil woman,' he screamed. 'You have gone over completely to my enemies.'

He struck her full in the face with a clenched fist, and sent her reeling across the deck until she crashed into the bulwark. She stared at him in horror and outrage. Since childhood she had been accustomed to the beatings with his riding crop across her legs and buttocks when she displeased him, but only twice before had he struck her with his fist. She knew in that moment that she could never let it happen again. That had been the third and last time. She wiped her mouth with the back of her hand and glanced at the thick smear of blood from her torn lips. Then she turned her head and looked down on to the deck of the *Sprite* below her.

The last grappling lines that held the two ships together parted and the *Sprite*'s sails filled with the night breeze. She began to bear away. Her deck was a shambles of shot damage, some of her crew were wounded, others scurrying to their gun stations, and still more were jumping back into her from the taller side of the *Arcturus* as the gap between them widened.

Then she saw Mansur below her on the deck of the *Sprite* and, despite her injuries and her father's rage, her heart hammered wildly against her ribs. During all the time since they had parted, she had tried to subdue her feelings for him. She had had no expectation of ever laying eyes upon him again, and thought she had succeeded in putting him out of her mind. But now, when she saw him again, handsome and tall in the light thrown by the burning rigging, she remembered the secrets he had imparted to her and the protestation of his feelings for her, and she could deny him no longer.

In the same moment he looked up and recognized her. She saw his astonishment give way immediately to grim determination. He leaped across the deck of the *Sprite* to the wheel and shoved aside the helmsman. He seized the spokes and spun it in a blur back the opposite way. The *Sprite*'s turn away to port checked and then she answered her rudder, turning back slowly. Once more her bows collided heavily against the *Arcturus*'s mid-section, but she did not rebound for Mansur held the wheel over. She began to drag down the side of the larger vessel.

Mansur shouted up at her, 'Jump, Verity! Come to me!' For a long moment she remained frozen, and then it was almost too late. 'Verity, in God's Name, you cannot deny me. I love you. Jump!'

She hesitated no longer. She came up on her feet as quick as a cat, and sprang to the top of the bulwark, balancing there for an instant with her arms outspread. Guy realized what she was about, and ran across the poop to her.

'I forbid it!' he screamed, and snatched at her leg, but she kicked away his hand. He grabbed a fistful of her shirt, and she tried to pull free, but he clung on stubbornly. As they struggled, Mansur left the wheel and ran to the *Sprite*'s side. He was directly below her, holding his arms wide in invitation.

'Jump!' he called. 'I will catch you.'

She flung herself out over the ship's side. Her father did not release his grip, and her shirt ripped, leaving him holding a handful of cloth. Verity dropped into Mansur's arms and her weight bore him to his knees, but he straightened and, for a moment, held her tightly to his chest. Then he set her on her feet and dragged her to safety. The crew's bundled hammocks had been piled along the bulwark as some protection from splinters and musket balls, and Mansur pushed her down behind this barricade. Then he ran back to the wheel and spun it the opposite way.

The two ships drew apart swiftly. The *Revenge* had also disentangled herself, and was under sail. The *Arcturus* was still ablaze, but Mansur saw Ruby Cornish striding down her deck, taking charge of the salvage. His men were swarming out of the hatchways again. Within minutes they had brought down the flaming canvas and doused it with seawater from the pumps.

With her guns reloaded and run out, the *Arcturus* turned in pursuit of the *Sprite* once more, but her rigging was heavily damaged and Cornish had not had time to bring up new canvas from the sail lockers and bend it on to the bare, scorched yards. The *Arcturus* made slow progress through the water and both the *Sprite* and the *Revenge* drew away from her.

Then, as swiftly as it had risen, the night wind died away. Almost as if they had anticipated the dawn, the clouds opened and allowed the paling stars to shine through. A hush descended on the ocean, the roiling surface seemed to freeze into a sheet of polished ice. All three of the battered ships slowed, then came to a gradual standstill. Even in the faint light of the stars they were within sight of each other, becalmed, swinging slowly and aimlessly on the silent currents beneath that glassy surface. However, the *Sprite* and the

Revenge were out of hail of each other, so Dorian and Mansur were unable to confer and decide their next course of action.

'Let the men eat their breakfast as they work, but we must repair our damage swiftly. This calm will not last long.' Mansur saw the work put in hand, then went to find Verity. She stood alone by the ship's side, staring across at the dim shape of the *Arcturus*, but she turned to him at once.

'You came,' he said.

'Because you called,' she replied softly, and held out her hand to him. He took it, and was surprised by how cool and smooth her skin was, how narrow and supple her hand.

'There is so much I want to tell you.'

'We will have a lifetime for that,' she said, 'but let me savour this first moment to the full.' They looked into each other's eyes.

'You are beautiful,' he said.

'I am not. But my heart sings to hear you say it.'

'I would kiss you.'

'But you cannot,' she answered. 'Not under the eyes of your crew. They would not approve.'

'Fortunately, we will have a lifetime for that also.'

'And I will rejoice in every minute of it.'

The dawn broke and the first shafts of sunlight beamed through the gaps in the thunderheads and turned the waters of the ocean to glowing amethyst. It played full upon the three ships. They lay motionless, like toys on a village pond. The sea was glassy smooth, its surface marred only by the skittering flight of the flying fish and the swirls of the great silver and gold tuna that pursued them.

The shot-torn sails hung slack and empty. From each ship the sounds of the carpenters' hammers and saws rang out as they hurriedly repaired the battle damage. The sailmakers laid out the damaged canvas on the decks and squatted over it, long needles flying as they cobbled up the tears and rents. They all knew that this respite would not last long, that the morning breeze would rise and the next phase of the conflict must begin.

Through the telescope Mansur watched the crew of the *Arcturus* extinguish the last flames, then send new spars aloft to replace the broken bowsprit and the yards that had been burned or shot away.

'Is your mother aboard the *Arcturus*?' Mansur asked Verity.

'Six weeks ago my father sent her back to the safety of the consulate in Bombay,' Verity answered. She did not want to think about Caroline now, or of the circumstances in which she had last seen her. To change the subject she asked, 'Will you fight again?'

'Are you afraid?' he asked.

She turned to him. Her eyes were green and her gaze was direct. 'That question is unkind.'

'Forgive me,' he said at once. 'I do not doubt your courage, for you proved it to me last night. I wanted only to know your feelings.'

'I am not afraid for myself. But my father is aboard the other ship, and you are on this one.'

'I saw him strike you.'

'He has struck me many times before, but he is still my father.' Then she lowered her eyes. 'More important than that, though, you are now my man. I am afraid for both of you. But I will not flinch.'

He reached out and touched her arm. 'I will do my utmost to avoid further battle,' he assured her. 'I would have done so last night but my own father was in danger. I had no choice but to come to his aid. However, I doubt that Sir Guy will let you and me escape without he does everything in his power to prevent it.' He nodded grimly towards the distant *Arcturus*.

'Here comes the morning wind,' she said. 'Now my father's intentions will be made plain.'

The wind scoured the polished azure surface with cats' paws. The *Arcturus*'s sails bulged and she began to glide forward. All her yards were standing, and bright new canvas had replaced much of that which had been scorched and blackened. The wind left her behind and she slowed gradually, then came once more to a standstill. Her mainsail flapped and drooped. The squall of wind came on and picked up the two smaller ships, carried them a short distance, then dropped them.

Again stillness and silence fell on the three vessels. All their sails were set, and the upper yardmen were poised to make the final adjustments when the wind came again.

This time it came out of the east, hard and steady. It caught up the *Arcturus* first and bore her on. The instant she had steerage way she put up her helm and charged straight towards the two smaller ships. Her guns were still run out and her intentions manifest.

'I am afraid your father is spoiling for a fight.'

'And so are you!' Verity accused him.

'You misjudge me.' He shook his head. 'I have already taken the prize. Sir Guy has nothing more that I want from him.'

'Then let us hope that the wind reaches us before he does.' As Verity spoke it puffed against her cheek and blew a long strand of hair across her eyes. She tucked it back into the silk hairnet. 'Here it comes.'

The wind struck the *Sprite* and she heeled to it. Her canvas slatted and her blocks rattled as her sails filled and bulged. They could feel the force of it in the eager trembling of the deck beneath their feet and, despite the exigencies of the moment, Verity laughed aloud with excitement. 'We are off!' she cried, and for a moment clung to his arm. Then she saw Kumrah's disapproving expression and stepped back. 'I need no chaperon aboard this ship for I have a hundred already.'

The *Sprite* raced down towards the *Revenge*, which still lay becalmed, but then the wind reached her also. The two ships bore away together, the *Revenge* leading by two cables' length. Mansur looked back over the stern at the pursuit.

'With the wind coming from this quarter your father can never catch us,' he told Verity exultantly. 'We will run him below the horizon before nightfall.' He took her arm and led her gently towards the companionway. 'I can safely leave the deck to Kumrah now, and we can go below to find suitable accommodation for you.'

'There are too many eyes here,' she agreed, and followed him willingly.

At the bottom of the ladder he turned her to face him. She was only a few inches shorter than he was, and the thick, lustrous coils of her hair made the difference even less obvious. 'There are no other eyes here,' he said.

'I fear I have been gullible,' her cheeks blushed pink as rose petals, 'but you would never take advantage of my innocence, would you, Your Highness?'

'I am afraid you may have overestimated my chivalry, Miss Courtney. It is my intention to do exactly that.'

'I suppose that it would be of no avail if I should scream, would it?'

'I am very much afraid that it would not,' he said.

She swayed towards him. 'Then I shall save my breath,' she whispered, 'for perhaps I will find better employment for it later.'

'Your lip is swollen.' He touched it gently. 'I will not hurt you?'

'We Courtneys are a hardy lot,' she said.

He kissed her, but softly.

It was Verity who pulled him closer, and parted her swollen lips to him. 'It hurts not at all,' she said, and he lifted her in his arms and carried her through into his cabin.

Kumrah stamped three times on the deck above Mansur's bunk. He sat up quickly. 'I am wanted on deck,' he said.

'Not as much as you are wanted here,' she murmured, with drowsy contentment, 'but I know that when duty calls I must let you go for the moment.'

He stood up and she watched him, her eyes growing bigger and her interest quickening. 'I have never seen a man in his natural state before,' she said. 'Only now do I realize I have been deprived, for 'tis a sight much to my liking.'

'I could think of far better,' he demurred, and stooped to kiss her belly. It was smooth as cream and her navel was a neat pit in the taut sleek muscle. He thrust the tip of his tongue into it.

She sighed and writhed voluptuously. 'You must stop that at once, or I shall never let you go.'

He straightened and then his eyes flew wide with alarm. 'There is blood on the sheet. Have I injured you?'

She raised herself on one elbow, looked down at the bright stain and smiled complacently. 'It is the flower of my maidenhood, which I bring to you as proof that I have always belonged to you and to none other.'

'Oh, my darling.' He sat on the edge of the bunk and smothered her face with kisses.

She pushed him away. 'Go to your duty. But come back to me the instant it is done.'

Mansur ran up the ladder and it seemed that his feet were winged, but he stopped at the head of the companionway in alarm. He had expected to see the *Revenge* still far ahead of him, for in speed she had the edge on the *Sprite*, but she was almost alongside. He snatched up his telescope from its bucket beside the binnacle and strode to the side. He saw at once that the *Revenge* sat low in the water, and that all her pumps were manned. Seawater was spurting white over the side from the outlet pipes. As he watched in consternation, Dorian appeared on deck, stepping out from the hatch over the main hold. Mansur snatched up the speaking trumpet and hailed him. His father looked across, then came to the near rail.

'What's amiss?' Mansur called again.

'We have taken a ball below the waterline, and we are taking in water faster than the pumps can discharge it.' His father's reply was faint on the wind.

So great was the disparity in speed between the two ships that in the short time that Mansur had been on deck the *Sprite* had gained a few yards on the *Revenge*. Already his father's voice carried more clearly across the gap. He looked back over the stern and judged that the *Arcturus* had lost little distance in the hours that he and Verity had been below. She was making much better speed through the water than the crippled *Revenge*.

'What can I do to assist you?' he asked his father. There was a long pause.

'I have shot an angle on the *Arcturus*'s mainmast every hour,' Dorian called back. 'At this rate she will be within cannon shot before nightfall. Even in the darkness we cannot hope to elude her.'

'Can we repair the damage?'

'The shot-hole is awkwardly placed.' Dorian shook his head. 'If we heave to, *Arcturus* will be upon us before we can plug it.'

'What, then, must we do?'

'Unless something unforeseen happens, we shall be forced to fight again.'

Mansur thought about Verity in the cabin below this deck, and had a picture of that perfect pale body torn to bloody tatters by round-shot. He forced the image from his mind. 'Wait!' he called to Dorian, then beckoned to Kumrah.

'What can we do, old friend?' They talked quickly and earnestly, but while they did so the *Revenge* dropped back a little further and Mansur was obliged to order a reef in his main sail to slow the *Sprite* enough to keep his station with the *Revenge*. Then he hailed his father. 'Kumrah has a plan. Conform to me as best you are able, but I will moderate my speed if you fall too far behind.'

Kumrah brought the *Sprite*'s bows around another three points into the west until they were on a direct heading for Ras al-Had, the point of land where the gulf opened out into the ocean proper.

For the rest of that morning Mansur kept his crew busy repairing the battle damage they had suffered, cleaning and servicing the guns, bringing up more round-shot from the orlop deck, filling the powder bags to replace that which had been fired away. Then, with block and tackle, they hoisted one of the guns up from the main deck to the poop where the carpenters had made a temporary gunport for it. Trained back over the stern the cannon could now be used as a stern chaser to bring the *Arcturus* under fire as soon as she drew within range.

Almost imperceptibly the *Revenge* was settling lower in the water and losing speed as the men at the pumps battled to hold at bay the inflow of water through her pierced hull. Mansur closed in on her and they passed a line across. Then he was able to send over twenty fresh seamen to relieve the *Revenge*'s crew, who were exhausted from the unremitting work at the pump handles. At the same time he sent over Baris, one of Kumrah's junior officers, a young Omani who was also a native of this coast and knew every rock and reef almost as intimately as Kumrah did. While the two ships sailed in such close company, Mansur explained to his father the plan he and Kumrah had devised.

Dorian understood at once that this was perhaps their best chance, and he endorsed it without hesitation. 'Go to it, lad,' he called back, through the speaking trumpet.

Within the next hour Mansur was obliged to take in another reef so as not to head-reach on the *Revenge* during the night. As darkness fell he gazed back at the *Arcturus* and calculated that she had closed the gap between them to only a little over two sea miles.

It was almost midnight before he went below to his cabin, but even then Mansur and Verity could not sleep. They made love as though it would never happen again, then lay naked in each other's arms, sweating in the tropical night, and they talked softly. Sometimes they laughed and more than once Verity wept. There was so much they had to tell, their whole lifetimes to relate to each other. At last, though, even their new love could no longer keep them awake, and they slept with their limbs entwined.

An hour before first light Mansur slipped from their bunk and left her to go back on deck. But within minutes Verity, too, came up the companionway and took a place in the angle of the quarter-deck and the poop, where she could be near him but unobtrusive.

Mansur ordered the cooks to give the men their breakfast

and while they ate he went down the deck and spoke to them, giving them encouragement, making them laugh and others smile, even though they knew that the *Arcturus* was close behind them in the darkness and they would soon be called upon to fight her again.

As soon as the dawn sky began to pale Mansur and Kumrah were at the stern rail on the poop deck beside the stern chaser. The lantern on the main truck of the *Revenge* showed close astern, but as the circle of their vision opened they all stared beyond her for the first glimpse of the *Arcturus*. They were not disappointed. As the light strengthened they caught the loom of her against the still dark horizon, and Mansur had to check himself from giving voice to his disappointment. She had gained almost a mile on them during the hours of darkness, and now she was within long cannon shot. Even as Mansur stared at her through the lens of his telescope there was a flash from her bows, and a puff of white smoke.

'Your father is firing at us with bow chasers. Though I fancy the range is a trifle too long for him to do us any real damage for a while yet,' Mansur told Verity.

At that moment there was a hail from the masthead: 'Land ho!' and they left the stern and went up into the bows to scan ahead with the spyglass.

'You excel yourself, Captain,' Mansur told Kumrah. 'Unless I am very much mistaken, that is Ras al-Had dead ahead.' They went back to the chart table beside the traverse-board and pored over the chart. This masterpiece of the cartographer's art had been drawn up by Kumrah himself, the work of a lifetime spent on the sea.

'Where is this Kos al-Heem?' Mansur asked. The name meant the Deceiver in the dialect of the Omani coast.

'I have not marked it on the chart.' Kumrah pricked the waxed leather with the point of his dividers. 'Some things are best kept from the eyes of the world. But it is here.'

'How much longer to run?' Mansur asked.

'If this wind holds, we will be there an hour after noon.'

'By then the *Arcturus* will have overhauled the *Revenge*.' Mansur glanced across his father's ship.

'If it is God's will,' said Kumrah, with resignation, 'for God is great.'

'We must try to shield the *Revenge* from the fire of the *Arcturus* until we reach the Deceiver.' Mansur gave Kumrah his orders, then went back to the stern where the gun-crew were gathered around the nine-pounder.

Kumrah shortened sail again and dropped back until he could interpose the *Sprite* between the other two ships. During that time the *Arcturus* fired twice with her bow chaser. Both shots fell short. However, the *Arcturus*'s next splashed heavily alongside the *Revenge*.

'Very well.' Mansur nodded. 'We can try a ranging shot at her now.'

He chose a round-shot from the locker, rolling it under his foot to check its symmetry. Then he measured the charge of powder with care, and had his crew swab the bore carefully to remove as much powder residue as possible.

Once the gun was loaded and run out he stood behind it and noted how the stern of the *Sprite* lifted and yawed as she rode over the swells. He calculated the adjustments necessary to counteract these movements. Then, slow-match in hand, he stood well clear of the breech and watched for the next swell. As the *Sprite* kicked up her heels and lifted her stern, like a flirtatious girl swishing her skirts, he pressed the burning end of the match to the quill of powder in the touch-hole. The elevation would give the iron ball the extra carry.

The long cannon bellowed and slammed back into its tackle. Verity and Kumrah were watching for the fall of shot.

Seconds later they picked out the tiny feather of white that jumped from the surface of the dark sea. 'Short by a hundred yards and about three degrees left,' Verity called sharply.

Mansur grunted and wound the elevation screw to its maximum height. They fired again. 'Under again, but on line.' They kept firing steadily.

The *Revenge* had joined in the bombardment. The *Arcturus* closed in slowly, firing her bow chasers as she came on. However, by the middle of the morning none of the ships had managed a hit, although some of the shot had fallen close.

Mansur and his gun-crew were stripped to the waist in the rising heat: their bodies were shining with sweat, and their faces were blackened with gunsmoke. The barrel of the cannon was too hot to touch. The wet swab sizzled and steamed as it was thrust down the bore. For the twenty-third time that morning they ran out the long nine-pounder and Mansur laid it with care. The *Arcturus* appeared much taller as he squinted at it over the sights. He stood back and waited for the pitch and roll of the hull under him before he fired.

The gun carriage bounded back violently and slammed against its tackle. This time, though they strained their eyes through the lens, there was no splash of falling shot. Instead Verity saw shattered timbers explode from the *Arcturus*'s bows and one of her chaser cannon knocked from its carriage and upended.

'"A hit! A very palpable hit!"'

'Say Miss Verity and the Bard!' Mansur laughed and gulped down a mouthful from the water dipper before laying the next shot.

Seemingly in retaliation, the *Arcturus* dropped a ball from the remaining bow chaser so close under the *Sprite*'s stern that a fountain of spray rose high into the air, then cascaded over them, drenching them to the skin.

All this time the rocky cape of Ras al-Had was rising higher out of the sea, and *Arcturus* was slowly overhauling them from astern.

'Where is Kos al-Heem?' Mansur asked impatiently.

'You will not see it until you are about to strike. That is how it was given the name, but these are the landmarks. The white streak in the cliff face, there. The tip of the egg-shaped rock that stands to the left of it, there!'

'I want you to take the helm now, Kumrah. Luff her a little and spill your wind. I want to let the *Arcturus* close up to us, without making it obvious that it is deliberate.'

The raging duel between the ships carried on. Mansur hoped to distract Cornish's attention from the hazard ahead, and to let the *Revenge* draw further ahead. The *Arcturus* came on eagerly, and within the hour she was so close that through the glass Mansur and Verity could recognize the burly figure and distinctive features of Captain Ruby Cornish.

'And there is Sir Guy!' Mansur had been about to say 'your father', but he changed the words at the last moment. He did not want to emphasize the relationship of his enemy to his love.

In comparison to Ruby Cornish, Guy Courtney cut a slim, elegant figure. He had changed his attire, and even in this heat he wore a cocked hat and a blue coat with scarlet lapels, tight-fitting white breeches and black boots. He stood staring across at them. His expression was set and hard, and there was a deadly purpose about him that chilled Verity to the marrow: she well knew this mood of his and dreaded it like the cholera.

'Kumrah!' Mansur called to him. 'Where is this Deceiver? Where is Kos al-Heem? Is it something you dreamed after a pipe of hashish?'

Kumrah glanced at the Revenge, which had forged slowly ahead. She was now leading them by a quarter of a sea mile.

'The Caliph, your revered father, is almost upon the Deceiver.'

'I can see no sign of it.' Minutely Mansur studied the waters ahead of the other ship, but the swells marched on inexorably, and there was no break or check in their ranks; no swirl nor flurry of white water that he was able to descry.

'That is why it is called the Deceiver,' Kumrah reminded him. 'It keeps its secrets well. It has murdered a hundred ships and more, including the galley of Ptolemy, the general and favourite of the mighty Isakander. It was only by God's favour that he survived the wreck.'

'God is great,' Mansur murmured automatically.

'Praise God,' Kumrah agreed and, as he spoke, the Revenge abruptly put up her helm and turned her bows into the wind. With all her sails backed and shuddering, she hove to.

'Ah!' cried Kumrah. 'Baris has found and marked the Deceiver for us.'

'Run out the port battery and prepare to come about on the starboard tack,' Mansur ordered. While the crew ran to their battle stations, he eyed the approaching Arcturus.

636

She was rushing in towards them jubilantly, with every stitch of canvas set. Even as he watched, Mansur saw the lids of her gunports crash open and the muzzles of her cannon poke out menacingly along her sides. He turned and strode forward until he had a full view of the *Revenge*, hove-to dead ahead; she also had run out her guns, offering battle.

Mansur went back to the helm. He was conscious that from the angle below the poop Verity was watching him intently. Her expression was calm and she showed no fear.

'I would like you to go below, my love,' he told her quietly. 'We will very soon be under fire.'

She shook her head. 'The ship's timbers offer no protection from nine-pound iron balls. This I know from experience,' she replied, with a naughty sparkle in her eyes, 'when you fired upon me.'

'I have never apologized for my bad manners in so doing.' He smiled back at her. 'It was unforgivable. But I swear I will make it up to you in spades and trumps.'

'All other things apart, from now on my place is at your side, not cowering under the bunk.'

'I shall always treasure your presence,' he said, and turned to look back at the *Arcturus*. She was within easy cannon shot at last. Now he must engage all her attention, and lure her on at the top of her speed. Kumrah was watching for his order.

'Up helm,' Mansur snapped, and the *Sprite* turned like a dancer. Suddenly she had turned her full broadside on the *Arcturus*.

'Steady, gunners!' Mansur shouted, through the trumpet. 'Make good your aim!' One after the other the captains raised their right arms to show that they had laid their pieces true.

'Fire!' Mansur cried, and the broadside bellowed out like a single clap of thunder. Gunsmoke poured back across the deck in a thick grey cloud, but was almost at once blown away by the wind and they could see a single spout of seawater rise from under the *Arcturus*'s bows, but the rest of the broadside smashed into her stem, tearing holes in her timbers. The ship seemed to tremble to these terrible blows but came on without a check in her speed.

'Bring her about on the old course,' Mansur ordered, and the *Sprite* obeyed her helm at once. They sped away towards where the *Revenge* lay waiting for them. Bows on to them, the *Arcturus* had not been able to fire her own broadside in return, but the manoeuvre had cost the *Sprite* almost all of her lead, and the enemy was scarcely more than a cable's length behind her. She fired her bow chaser, and the *Sprite* shuddered as the ball struck her stern and tore through her hull.

Kumrah was staring ahead with slitted eyes, but Mansur could see no sign of the Deceiver. Kumrah called a correction to the helm and the man on the wheel eased her over to port a trifle. This cleared the range for the *Revenge*, and now she could fire without fear of hitting the *Sprite*. She was still presenting her broadside to the enemy, and disappeared momentarily behind the curtain of her own gunsmoke as she let fly with all her cannon.

The range was long but she hit with at least some of her shot. The *Arcturus* was so close by now that Mansur could hear the iron round-shot strike against her timbers like heavy hammer strokes.

'That will invite all Cornish's attention,' Verity said, and her voice was clear in the sudden silence that followed the broadside. Mansur did not answer. He was gazing ahead with a worried frown.

'Where is this triple-damned Deceiver—' He broke off as he saw the sparkle of bright specks like drifting snowflakes deep in the blue waters directly under their bows. They were so unexpected that for a moment he was at a loss. Then it dawned upon him.

'Fusiliers!' he exclaimed. These shoals of tiny, jewelled fish always hung over submerged reefs, even out here in the mid-water at the edge of the continental shelf. The shoals scattered as the *Sprite*'s hull cut through them, and Mansur saw the dark, terrible shadows rising from the depths, like blackened fangs, directly in the ship's path. Kumrah stepped across and pushed away the helmsman. Then he took the wheel of his ship in lover's hands to steer her through.

Mansur saw the dark shapes harden as they rushed down

upon them. They were three horns of granite that reached up from dark waters to within a fathom of the sunlit surface. So sharp were the points that they offered little resistance to the flow and push of currents and waves. This accounted for the lack of surface turbulence.

Instinctively Mansur held his breath as Kumrah steered into the centre of this cruel crown of stone. He felt Verity's hand on his arm as she clung to him for comfort, her fingernails digging painfully into his flesh.

The *Sprite* touched the rock. To Mansur it felt as though he had ridden a horse at full gallop through the forest and a thornbush had tugged at his sleeve. The deck shuddered softly under his feet, and he heard the granite horn rasp against their bottom timbers. Then the *Sprite* pulled herself free and they were through. Mansur let the air out of his lungs with a sigh, and beside him Verity cried, 'That was as close as I ever want to be.'

Mansur seized her hand and they ran back to the stern rail. They watched the *Arcturus* run into the trap at full tilt. Despite her battle damage and her soot-blackened rigging she presented a beautiful picture, with every sail drawing and a tall white bow wave sparkling and curling back from her forefoot.

She hit the stone pinnacles and stopped dead in the water, transformed in a single instant from a thing of airy grace to a shambles. Her foremast snapped off level with the deck and half her yards came tumbling down. Her underwater timbers crackled and roared as they shattered and she hung in the water like part of the reef. The granite horns of the Deceiver were driven deep into her belly. The top yardsmen in her rigging were hurled from their perches, like pellets from a slingshot, to splash into the water half a pistol shot from the ship's side. The rest of her crew were skittled down the deck to slam into the masts and bulwarks. Their own cannons were turned against them as they were catapulted into the unyielding metal with the full impetus of the ship's way. Arms, legs and ribs broke like green twigs, and skulls cracked like eggs dropped on to a stone-flagged floor. The crews of the two smaller vessels lined the sides, and stared in awe at the devastation they had wrought, too overwhelmed to cheer the destruction of the enemy.

Mansur hove to alongside his father's ship. 'What now, Father?'

'We cannot leave Guy in such a state,' Dorian shouted back. 'We must render what help we can. I shall go across in the longboat.'

'No, Father!' Mansur called back. 'You can spend no more time here. Your ship is also in extremes. You must go on to find the safe harbour at Sawda island, where we can repair the underwater damage before she founders and sinks.'

'But what of Guy and his men?' Dorian hesitated. 'What is to become of them?'

'I shall take care of that business,' Mansur promised. 'You can be certain that I will not let your brother, Verity's father, perish here.'

Dorian and Batula conferred quickly, and then Dorian returned to the Revenge's side. 'Very well! Batula agrees that we must get into safe anchorage before another storm brews up. We cannot ride out rough seas in the shape we are now in.'

'I shall take off the survivors from the Arcturus, and follow you with all speed.'

Dorian put the Revenge once more before the wind, and headed in towards the mainland. Mansur handed over command to Kumrah, and went down into the longboat. He stood in the stern sheets as they rowed in towards the stranded and heavily listing Arcturus. As soon as they were within easy hail he ordered the boat crew to rest on their oars. 'Arcturus! I have a surgeon with me. What help do you need?'

Cornish's red face appeared over the top of the canted bulwark. 'We have many broken limbs. I need to get the wounded back to the infirmary on Bombay island, or they will die.'

'I am coming on board!' Mansur shouted back.

But another voice rang out angrily: 'Stand off, you filthy rebel scum!' Sir Guy Courtney was clinging to the main shrouds with one hand. His other arm was thrust into the front of his jacket, using it as a makeshift sling. He had lost his hat, and fresh blood caked his hair and the side of his face from the deep lacerations in his scalp. 'If you try to board this ship I shall fire into you.'

'Uncle Guy!' Mansur called. 'I am your brother Dorian's son. You must allow me to help you and your men.'

'In God's Holy Name, you are no kith or kin of mine. You are a heathen bastard, an abductor and violator of innocent English womanhood.'

'Your men need help. You yourself are wounded. Let me take you and your men to the port of Bombay island.'

Guy did not reply but staggered along the listing deck to the nearest cannon. He snatched a smoking slow-match from the sand tub. The heavy weapon still poked its gleaming bronze barrel through the open gunport, but Mansur was not alarmed. The weapon was harmless. The angle of the deck pointed the muzzle down into the water close alongside.

'Listen to reason, Uncle. My father and I wish you no harm. You are of our blood. See! I am unarmed.' He held up his open hands to prove it. But with a chill of horror he realized that Guy was not intending to fire the great cannon. Instead he seized the long handle of the murderer that sat squat and ugly in its gimbal fixed to the bulwark: it was a hand-cannon, designed to repel enemy boarders, loaded with a hatful of lead goose-shot. At short range its name described its gruesome capabilities accurately.

The longboat was close under the side of the *Arcturus*. Guy swivelled the murderer towards them and squinted over the crude notch-and-pin sights at Mansur. The flared muzzle of the gun seemed to leer at them obscenely.

'I gave you fair warning, you lecherous swine.' He thrust the burning match into the touch-hole.

'Down!' shouted Mansur, and flung himself on to the deck. His crew was slow to follow his example and the blast of goose-shot swept through them. In the screams of the wounded Mansur pulled himself upright again. His shirt was splashed by the brains of his coxswain, and three dead men lay piled

641

against the boat's side. Two others were clutching their wounds and struggling in puddles of their own blood. Seawater spurted in through the holes the goose-shot had torn in the planking.

Mansur rallied those of the crew who were unharmed. 'Pull back for the Sprite!' and they flung themselves on the oars with a will. From the stern sheets Mansur shouted back at the figure that still clung to the handle of the smoking hand-cannon: 'Rot your black soul, Guy Courtney. You bloody butcher! These were unarmed men on an errand of mercy.'

Mansur stormed back on to the deck of the Sprite. His face was white and set with rage. 'Kumrah,' he snarled, 'get our dead and wounded on board, then load all our guns with grape. I am going to give that murderous swine a taste of his own dung.'

Kumrah brought the Sprite round on to the port tack and at Mansur's direction steered in to pass the stranded wreck of the Arcturus at a distance of a hundred paces, the optimum range in which the grape would wreak the most slaughter.

'Stand by to fire as you bear!' Mansur called to his gunners. 'Sweep her deck clean. Kill them all. When you have done we will put fire into her and burn her down to the water-line.' He was still trembling with rage.

The crew of the Arcturus saw death coming down upon them, and scattered across the deck. Some ran below and others threw themselves over the side and thrashed around clumsily in the water. Only Captain Cornish and his master Sir Guy Courtney stood four-square and faced the Sprite's gaping broadside.

Mansur felt a light touch on his arm and glanced down. Verity stood beside him. Her face was pale but expressionless. 'This is murder,' she said.

'Your father is the murderer.'

'Yes. And he is my father. If you do this thing, you will never wash his blood from your conscience or from mine, not if we live a hundred years. This might be the one act that will destroy our love.'

Her words struck deep as a dagger. He looked up and saw

the number-one gunner about to touch off his weapon, the smoking slow-match only inches from the flash-hole. 'Hold your fire!' Mansur roared at him, and the man lifted his hand. All the gun captains turned to look back at Mansur. He took Verity by the hand and led her to the rail. He raised the speaking trumpet to his lips.

'Guy Courtney! You are saved only by the intervention of your daughter,' he called across.

'That treacherous bitch is no daughter of mine. She is naught but a common street whore.' Guy's face was livid, the clotted blood upon it dark crimson in contrast. 'Filth and filth have found their own level in the cesspool. Take her, and a black pox on both of you.'

With an effort that strained all his natural instincts, Mansur kept his temper from boiling over again. 'I thank you, sir, for your daughter's hand in marriage. A boon so graciously granted is one I will guard with my life.' Then he looked to Kumrah. 'We will leave them here to rot. Lay the ship on a course for Sawda island.'

As they drew away Ruby Cornish touched his forehead in a salute, silently acknowledging his defeat and Mansur's compassion in holding his fire.

They found the *Revenge* lying at anchor in the tiny bay, enclosed by the cliffs of Sawda island. This grim buttress of black rock reared three hundred feet sheer from the deep waters at the edge of the continental shelf, six miles off the coast of the Arabian peninsula. Kumrah had chosen it for good reasons. The island was uninhabited and isolated from the mainland, secure from casual discovery by an enemy. The bay was sheltered from the easterly gales. The enclosed waters were calm, and the narrow beach of black volcanic sand made a good platform on which to careen a ship's hull. There was even a secret seep of sweet water from a cleft at the foot of the cliff.

As soon as they dropped anchor, Mansur had himself and

Verity rowed across to the *Revenge*. Dorian was at the entry-port to welcome him aboard.

'Father, there is no call for me to present your niece Verity to you. You are well enough acquainted already.'

'My greetings and respect, Your Majesty.' Verity dropped him a curtsy.

'Now at last we are able to converse in English, and I can greet you as your uncle.' He embraced her. 'Welcome to your family, Verity. I know there will be much opportunity for us to come to know each other better.'

'I hope so, Uncle. But I realize that now you and Mansur have much else to do.'

Standing on the open deck they swiftly devised a plan of action, and at once set it in motion. Mansur brought the *Sprite* alongside his father's ship and they lashed the hulls together. Now all the pumps of both ships could be applied to pumping out the flooded hull. At the same time they dragged a sheet of the heaviest canvas under the *Revenge*'s hull. The pressure of the water held it firmly in place, plugging the underwater shot hole. With the inflow choked off they were able to dry out the hull within a few hours.

Then they hoisted all her heavy cargo out of her – cannon, powder and shot, spare canvas, masts and spars – and deck-loaded the *Sprite*. Relieved of her burden the *Revenge* floated high and light as a cork. With the boats they towed her on to the beach and, with the help of the tide, careened her over so that the shot damage was exposed. The carpenters and their mates fell to work.

It took two days and nights working by the light of the battle lanterns for them to complete the repairs. When they had finished, the replaced section of timber was stronger than the original. They took the opportunity to scrape the weed from her hull, recaulk her joints and renew the copper sheeting that kept the shipworm from attacking her underwater timber. When they floated her off she was tight and dry. They warped her out into the bay, reloaded her cargo and remounted her weapons. By evening they had topped up all the water-kegs of both ships from the spring, and were ready to sail. However,

Dorian decreed that the crews had earned a respite of two days to celebrate the Islamic festival of Id, a joyous occasion when an animal is sacrificed and the flesh shared among the celebrants.

That evening they assembled on the beach, and Dorian killed one of the milk goats that were kept in a cage on board the *Revenge*. Its meagre flesh provided only a mouthful for each of them, but they supplemented it with fresh fish roasted on the coals while the musicians among the crews sang, danced and praised God for their escape from Muscat, and their victory over the *Arcturus*. Verity sat between Dorian and Mansur on silk prayer mats spread on the black sand.

Like most people who came to know Dorian, Verity couldn't resist the warmth of his spirit, his quiet humour. She empathized with the tragic loss of his wife, and the sadness with which it had marked him.

He was equally taken by her lively intelligence, the courage she had demonstrated so amply, and her forthright, pleasing manner. Now, as he studied her in the firelight he thought, She has inherited all the virtues of both her parents – her mother's beauty before it was marred by gluttony, Guy's bright mind. She has been spared their failings – Caroline's shallow, fatuous personality, and Guy's avaricious and vicious instincts, his dearth of humanity. Then he put aside deep thoughts and picked up the light mood. They laughed and sang together, clapping and swaying in time to the music.

When at last the musicians faltered, Dorian dismissed them with thanks and a gold coin for their trouble. But the three were too elated for sleep. They were to sail on the morrow for Fort Auspice. Mansur began to describe to Verity the life they would live in Africa, and the relatives she would meet there for the first time. 'You will love Aunt Sarah and Uncle Tom.'

'Tom is the best of us three brothers,' Dorian agreed. 'He was always the leader, while Guy and myself—' He broke off as he realized that Guy's name would throw a pall over their mood. The awkward silence drew out and none of them knew how to break it.

Then Verity spoke: 'Yes, Uncle Dorian. My father is not a

645

good man, and I know that he is ruthless. I cannot hope to excuse his murderous behaviour when he fired on the long-boat. Perhaps I can explain why it happened.'

The two men were silent and embarrassed. They stared into the coals of the fire and did not look at her. After a while she resumed, 'He was desperate that no one should discover the cargo he carries in the main hold of the *Arcturus*.'

'What cargo is that, my dear?' Dorian looked up.

'Before I answer, I must explain to you how my father has amassed such a fortune as to exceed that of any potentate in the Orient, save perhaps the Great Mogul and the Sublime Porte in Constantinople. He is a power-broker. He uses his position as consul general to enthrone and dethrone kings. He wields the power of the English monarchy and the English East India Company to deal in armies and nations as some men deal in cattle and sheep.'

'Those powers you speak of, the monarchy and the Company, are not in his gift,' Dorian demurred.

'My father is a conjuror, a master of illusion. He can make others believe what he wants them to believe, although he cannot even speak the languages of his client kings and emperors.'

'For that he uses you,' Mansur interjected.

She inclined her head. 'Yes, I was his tongue, but his is the gift of political perception.' She turned to Dorian. 'You, Uncle, have listened to him and you must have understood how persuasive he can be and how uncanny his instincts are.'

Dorian nodded silently, and she went on, 'Had you not been forewarned you would have been eager to sample his wares, even though his fee was exorbitant. Well, Zayn al-Din has paid many times more than that to him. The sheer genius of my father is that not only was he able to milk Zayn but the Sublime Porte and the East India Company have paid him almost as much again to act as their emissary. For the work he has done in Arabia during these last three years my father has received fifteen lakhs in gold specie.'

Mansur whistled, and Dorian looked grave. ''Tis almost a

quarter of a million guineas,' he said softly, 'an emperor's ransom.'

'Yes.' Verity dropped her voice to a whisper. 'And all of it is stored in the main hold of the *Arcturus*. That is why my father would have died rather than allow you to board his ship, why he was prepared to strike his powder magazine when that cargo was threatened.'

'Sweet heavenly angels, my love,' Mansur whispered, 'why did you not tell us this before?'

She looked steadily into his eyes. 'One reason only. I have lived all my adult life with a man whose soul is consumed by greed. I know full well the effects of that corrosive affliction. I did not want to infect the man I love with the same disease.'

'That would never happen,' Mansur said hotly. 'You do me an injustice.'

'My darling,' she replied, 'if you could but see your own face at this very moment.' Shamefaced Mansur dropped his eyes. He knew that her arrow had struck close to the mark, for he could feel the emotions she had warned of churning in his guts.

'Verity, my dear,' Dorian intervened, 'would it not be a rich justice if we could use Zayn al-Din's blood-soaked gold to topple him from the Elephant Throne and set his people free?'

'This is what I have been brooding on endlessly since I threw in my lot so irrevocably with you and Mansur. The reason I have told you about the gold on board the *Arcturus* is because I reached the same conclusion as you. Please, God, that if we seize that blood money, we use it in a noble cause.'

From afar they saw that much of the *Arcturus*'s damaged rigging had been replaced or repaired, but as they sailed closer it became clear that she still lay impaled upon the granite horns of the Deceiver like a sacrifice on the altar of Mammon. Closer still they saw a small, forlorn group standing at the foot of the mainmast on the heavily canted deck.

Through the lens of the telescope Dorian picked out the burly figure and bright features of Ruby Cornish.

It was obvious that the *Arcturus* offered no threat. She was immobilized and the heavy list in her deck rendered her batteries useless. The cannons along her port side pointed into the water and the starboard side at the sky. However, Dorian took no chances: he ordered both the *Revenge* and the *Sprite* cleared for action and the guns run out. They closed in and hove to on each side of the *Arcturus*, covering her with their broadsides.

As soon as he was within hail Dorian called across to Cornish. 'Will you yield your ship, sir?'

Ruby Cornish was astonished to be addressed by the rebel Caliph in perfect English, toned with the sweet accents of Devon. He recovered swiftly, removed his hat and stepped to the rail, balancing there against the listing deck. 'You leave me no choice, Your Majesty. Do you wish to take my sword as well?'

'No, Captain. You fought bravely and acquitted yourself with honour. Please keep it.' Dorian was hoping for Cornish's co-operation.

'You are gracious, Your Majesty.' Cornish was mollified by these compliments. He clapped his hat back on his head and tightened his sword-belt. 'I await your instructions.'

'Where is Sir Guy Courteney? Is he below decks?'

'Nine days ago Sir Guy took the ship's boats and a party of my best men. He set off for Muscat where he purposes to find assistance. He will return as speedily as is possible to salvage the *Arcturus*. In the meantime, he left me to guard the vessel and protect her cargo.' This was a long message to shout, and Cornish's face was as bright as a jewel by the time he had finished.

'I am sending a boarding party to you. I intend to salvage your vessel and float her off the reef. Will you co-operate with my officers?' Cornish fidgeted for a moment, then seemed to make up his mind.

'Majesty, I have yielded to you. I will follow your orders.'

They laid the *Sprite* and the *Revenge* along each side of the

648

Arcturus and unloaded her, divesting her of her cannon, shot and water. Then they ran the heaviest anchor cables under her hull as slings. They tightened these with the windlasses on the *Revenge* and the *Sprite* until they were rigid as bars of iron. The *Arcturus* lifted slowly, and they heard the timbers popping and crackling as the granite horns eased their grip in her vitals. The tides were only two days from high springs, and in these waters the tidal variation was almost three fathoms. Before making the final effort, Dorian waited until slack water was at the bottom of the ebb. Then he sent every able-bodied man to his place at the pumps. At his signal they threw themselves on the long handles. The bilge water flew in sheets over the sides, faster than the inflow through rents in the *Arcturus*'s hull. As she lightened, she strained to tear herself free of the rock. The rising tide added its irresistible impulse to the buoyancy of the hull and, with a last, terrible rending sound from below, the *Arcturus* slowly righted and floated free.

Immediately all three vessels set their mainsails and, still lashed together, glided out of the Deceiver's clutches. With fifty fathoms of water under their hulls Dorian brought the linked vessels slowly around on a course for Sawda island. Then he placed an armed guard over the hatches of the *Arcturus*'s main hold with strict orders that no man be allowed to pass.

The steering was clumsy and erratic, and the three ships staggered along like drinking companions returning homeward from a night of revelry. As the dawn broke they had raised the black massif of Sawda over the horizon, and before noon they had dropped anchor in the bay.

The first task was to draw a heavy canvas sail under the *Arcturus*'s hull and cover the terrible tears through her bottom timbers; only then could the pumps of all three ships dry her out. Before they warped her into the beach to careen her and complete the repairs, Dorian, Mansur and Verity went aboard her.

Verity went directly to her own cabin. She was appalled by the damage that the battle had wrought. Her clothing was in disarray, torn by wood splinters, stained by seawater. Perfume

649

bottles had shattered, powder pots cracked, and the contents had spilled over her petticoats and stockings. However, all of this could be replaced. It was her books and manuscripts that were her prime concern. Chief of these was a set of rare, beautifully illustrated and centuries-old volumes of the *Ramayana*. This had been a personal gift from Muhammad Shah, the Great Mogul, in recognition of her services as interpreter during his negotiations with Sir Guy. She had already translated the first five volumes of this mighty Hindu epic into English.

Among her other treasures was a copy of the Qur'an. This had been given to her by Sultan Obied, when she and her father had last visited him in the Topkapi Saray Palace in Constantinople. The gift had been made on condition that she translate it into English. This was reputed to be one of the original copies of the authoritative text revisions commissioned by the Caliph Uthman in AD 644 to 656, twelve years after the death of Muhammad, and it was known as the Uthmanic Recension. True to her promise to the Sultan, Verity had almost completed the translation of this seminal work. Her manuscripts were an investment of two years' painstaking labour. With her heart in her mouth she dragged out the chest in which she kept them from under a pile of fallen timbers and other debris. She exclaimed with relief when she opened the lid and found them undamaged.

In the meantime Dorian and Mansur were searching Sir Guy's great cabin next door. Ruby Cornish had handed over the key to them. 'I have removed nothing,' he told them. They found him as good as his word. Dorian took custody of the *Arcturus*'s logbooks and all her other papers. In the locked drawers of Guy's desk they found his private papers and his journals.

'These will afford us much valuable evidence about my brother's activities,' Dorian said, with grim satisfaction, 'and of his dealings with Zayn al-Din and the East India Company.'

Then they went back on deck, and broke open the seals on the hatches of the main hold. They lifted off the covers and went down into it. They found it filled with great quantities of muskets, swords and lance heads, new and unused, still packed in the manufacturers' grease. There was also powder and shot by the ton, twenty light field-artillery pieces, and much other military stores.

'Enough to start a war or a revolution,' Dorian remarked drily.

'Which is Uncle Guy's purpose,' Mansur agreed.

Much of this had been damaged by seawater. It was a lengthy business to clear the hold of this cargo, but at last they were down to the deck timbers, and there was no trace of the gold Verity had promised them.

M ansur climbed out of the hot, fetid hold, and went to find her. She was in her cabin. He paused in the entrance. In this short time she had restored the shambles of her cabin to a remarkable state of order and cleanliness. She sat at the mahogany desk under the skylight. She was no longer clad like an orphan in his oversized cast-off clothing. Instead she was wearing a fresh blue organza dress with leg-o'-mutton sleeves and trimmed with fine lace. Around her throat was a lustrous string of pearls. She was reading a book in a jewelled, engraved silver cover, and making notes in another with a plain vellum cover. Mansur saw that the pages were closely written with her small, elegant script. She looked up at him and smiled sweetly. 'Ah, Your Highness, do I have your attention for the moment? I am greatly honoured.'

Despite his disappointment in finding the hold bare, Mansur gaped at her in admiration. 'There is not a shadow of doubt in my mind that you are the most beautiful woman I have ever laid eyes upon,' he said, with awe in his tone. In this setting she seemed to him a perfect jewel.

'While you, sir, are rather sweaty and grubby.' She laughed at him. 'But I am sure that is not what you came to hear.'

'There isn't a single coin down there,' he said lamely.

'Have you taken the trouble to look beneath the floor-boards, or should that be the deck? I am a little at sea with these nautical terms, if you will forgive the play on words.'

'I love you more each hour, my clever darling,' he cried, and ran back to the hold, shouting for the carpenters to come to him.

Verity waited until the banging and hammering in the hold ceased abruptly and she heard the squeal of timbers being prised loose. Then she laid aside the *Ramayana* and went up on deck. She strolled across to the open hatch. She was just in time to watch the first chest being brought reverentially out of its snug hiding-place beneath the deck. It was so weighty that it took the combined strength of Mansur and five hefty seamen to lift it. As one of the carpenters unscrewed the lid, seawater poured out through the joints, for the chest had been submerged since the ship had run on to the horns of the Deceiver.

There were exclamations of astonishment and wonder as Mansur lifted off the lid. From directly above, Verity caught the wanton shine of pure gold before the men crowded forward and cut off her view. She gazed instead at Mansur's bare back. His muscles were oiled with sweat, and when he reached down to pick out one of the bright yellow bars, she glimpsed the tuft of coppery hair in his armpit.

The sight of the gold had not moved her in the least, but his body did. She felt that strange but particular feeling melting her loins, and had to go back to her book in an attempt to alleviate it. This helped not at all. The warm and pleasant sensation grew stronger.

'You have become a shameless and lascivious woman, Verity Courtney,' she whispered primly, but her smug little smile gave the lie to her self-deprecatory tone.

652

Mansur and Dorian removed fifteen chests of gold from the bilges of the *Arcturus*. When they weighed them they found that, as Verity had said, each one contained a lakh of the precious metal.

'My father is a neat, fastidious man,' Verity explained. 'Originally the gold was delivered to him from the treasuries of Oman and Constantinople in a profusion of coins of various dates and empires and denominations, in bars, beads and coils of wire. My father had it melted down and recast into standard bars of ten pounds weight, with his crest and the assayed purity stamped into each.'

'This is a vast fortune,' Dorian murmured, as the fifteen chests were lowered into the hold of the *Revenge*, where they would be under his direct charge. 'My brother was a rich man.'

'Do not feel sorry on his behalf,' Verity said. 'He is a rich man still. This is but a small part of his wealth. There is much more than this in the strongroom of the consulate in Bombay. It is zealously guarded by my brother, Christopher, who sets greater store by it even than my father does.'

'You have my word on it, Verity, that what we do not use in the struggle to free Muscat from Zayn's baleful thrall will be returned to the treasury in Muscat whence most of it was stolen. It will be used for the benefit of my people.'

'I trust your word on that, Uncle, but the truth is that I am sickened by it, for I have been party to its acquisition by a man who prizes it above humanity.'

Once the gold was out of her they could warp the *Arcturus* on to the beach and careen her. Then the work went swiftly, for they had gathered much experience from the repairs they had carried out on the *Revenge*. This time they were also able to call upon the expertise of Captain Cornish. He cherished his ship like a beautiful mistress, and his advice and assistance were given unstintingly. Dorian came more and more to rely on him, although by rights he was an enemy prisoner-of-war.

In his own bluff, bucolic manner Ruby Cornish was Verity's

ardent admirer. He sought the first opportunity to be alone with her. This was while she was sitting on the black sands of the beach, sketching the scene as the workmen swarmed over the careened hull of the *Arcturus*. The patterns of lines and ropes stretched over the graceful hull reminded her of a spider's web, and the contrast of clean white planed timbers against the jagged black rock intrigued her.

'May I take a few minutes of your time, Mistress Courtney?' Cornish stood before her and doffed his hat, holding it across his chest. Verity looked up from her easel and smiled as she laid aside her pencils.

'Captain Cornish! What a pleasant surprise. I thought you had quite forgotten me.'

Cornish turned an impossible shade of scarlet. 'I have come to beg a favour of you.'

'You have only to ask, Captain, and I will do my best on your behalf.'

'Mistress, at the moment I am without employment, as my ship has been seized by Caliph al-Salil, who, I understand, is an Englishman and related to you.'

'It is all very confusing, I agree, but, yes, al-Salil is my uncle.'

'He has expressed the intention of sending me back to Bombay or to Muscat. I have lost your father's ship, which was in my charge,' Cornish went on doggedly, 'and, begging your pardon, your father is not a man who forgives readily. He will hold me directly responsible.'

'Yes, I rather suspect he may do so.'

'I would not like to explain the loss of the ship to him.'

'That might indeed be prejudicial to your continued good health.'

'Mistress Verity, you have known me since you were a young girl. Could you find it in your conscience to recommend me to your uncle, the Caliph, for continued employment as the captain of the *Arcturus*? I think you know that in the circumstances I will be loyal to my new employer. In addition, it would give me the greatest pleasure to think that our long acquaintance will not end here.'

They had, indeed, known each other for several years. Cornish was a fine seaman, and a loyal servant. She also had a special affection for him, in that he had on many occasions proved himself her staunch but discreet ally. Whenever possible he had shielded her from her father's perverted malice.

'I shall see what can be done, Captain Cornish.'

'You are very kind,' he muttered gruffly, clapped his hat back on his head and saluted her. Then he stamped away through the loose black sand.

Dorian did not have to ponder long on the request. As soon as the *Arcturus* was refitted and floated off the beach, Cornish resumed command of her. Only ten of his seamen refused to come with him. When the little flotilla sailed from Sawda island, it headed south-west to pick up the warm, benign waters of the Mozambique current which, with the monsoon winds, bore them rapidly southwards along the Fever Coast.

Some weeks later, they hailed a large trading dhow on an easterly heading. When Dorian exchanged news with him, her captain explained that he was on a trading expedition to the distant ports of Cathay. He was delighted to add the ten reluctant seamen from the *Arcturus* to his own crew. Dorian was content with the knowledge that it might take years for their report to filter back to Muscat, or to the English consulate in Bombay.

Then they set all sail that the monsoon winds would allow, and went on southwards, through the channel between the long island of Madagascar and the African mainland. Slowly the wild, unexplored coastline unfolded on their right hand, until at last they raised the high whale-backed bluff that guarded Nativity Bay, and sailed in through the narrow entrance.

It was the middle of the day, but there was no evidence of human presence at the fort: no smoke from chimneys, no washing flapping on the lines, no children playing on the beach. Dorian was concerned for the welfare of his family. It was almost three years since they had sailed away and much might have happened in that time. There were many enemies,

655

and in their absence the fort might have been overwhelmed by man, famine or pestilence. Dorian fired a gun as they glided in towards the beach, and was relieved to see the sudden stir of activity around the fort. A row of heads popped up along the parapet, the gates were flung open and a motley crowd of servants and children ran out. Dorian lifted his telescope and trained it on the gates. His heart leaped with joy as he saw the big, bear-like figure of his brother Tom striding through, and heading down the path towards the beach, waving his hat over his head. He had not reached the edge of the water before Sarah followed him, running out of the gates. When she caught up with him, she linked her arm through his. Her happy cries of welcome carried across the water to the ships as they anchored.

'You were right again,' Verity told Mansur. 'If that is my aunt Sarah, I already like her passing fair.'

'Can we trust this man?' Zayn al-Din asked, in his high, feminine voice.

'Your Majesty, he is one of my best captains. I vouch for him with my own life,' Muri Kadem ibn Abubaker replied. Zayn had bestowed upon him the title of Muri, High Admiral, after the capture of Muscat.

'You might have to do just that.' Zayn stroked his beard as he studied the man they were discussing. He was prostrated before the throne, his forehead pressed to the stone floor. Zayn made a gesture with his bony forefinger.

Kadem translated it at once. 'Lift your head. Let the Caliph see your face,' he told his captain, and the man sat back on his heels. However, his eyes were downcast for he dared not look directly into the eyes of Zayn al-Din.

Zayn studied his face carefully. The man was young enough still to have the vigour and dash of a warrior, but old enough to have tempered it with experience and judgement. 'What is your name?'

'I am Laleh, Your Majesty.'

'Very well, Laleh,' Zayn nodded, 'let us hear your report.'

'Speak,' Kadem ordered.

'Majesty, on the orders of Muri Kadem, six months ago I sailed south along the Africa mainland, until I reached the bay known by the Portuguese as the Nativity. I had been sent by the Muri to ascertain if, as our spies had told us, this was indeed the hiding place of al-Salil, the traitor and enemy of the Caliph and the people of Oman. At all times I was at great pains to make certain that my dhow should not be seen from the shore. During the day I cruised well below the horizon. Only after nightfall did I approach the entrance to the bay. If it so please Your Majesty.' Laleh prostrated himself again, his forehead pressed to the stone floor.

The men seated on cushions facing the throne were all listening intently. Sir Guy Courtney sat closest to the Caliph. Despite the loss of his ship, and the huge fortune in gold it contained, his power and influence were undiminished. He remained the chosen emissary of both the English East India Company and King George of England.

Sir Guy had found a new interpreter to replace Verity, a writer of long employment in the Bombay headquarters of the Company. He was a lanky, balding fellow, his skin pitted with smallpox scars, and his name was Peter Peters. Although his grasp of half a dozen languages was excellent, Sir Guy could not trust him as he had his daughter.

Below Sir Guy sat Pasha Herminius Koots. He also had been promoted after the capture of the city from al-Salil. Koots had accepted Islam, for he knew full well that without Allah and His Prophet he could never be fully inducted into the Caliph's favour. He was now the supreme commander of the Caliph's army. All three men, Kadem, Koots and Sir Guy, had pressing political and personal reasons to be present at this war council.

Zayn al-Din made an impatient gesture, and Muri Kadem stirred Captain Laleh with his toe. 'Continue, in the name of the Caliph.'

'May Allah always smile upon him, and shower him with good fortune,' Laleh intoned, and sat up again. 'During the

657

night I went ashore and hid myself in a secret place on the bluff above the bay. I sent my ship away so that it should not be seen by the followers of al-Salil. From this place I watched over the stronghold of the enemy, if it so please you, Your Majesty.'

'Continue!' This time Kadem did not wait for the Caliph to give the word, and kicked Laleh in the ribs.

He gasped, and went on hurriedly, 'I beheld three ships at anchor in the bay. One of these was the tall ship that was captured from the English *effendi*.' Laleh turned his head to indicate the consul, and Sir Guy frowned darkly to be reminded of his loss. 'The other vessels were those in which al-Salil fled after his defeat by the illustrious Caliph Zayn al-Din, beloved of the Prophet.' Laleh prostrated himself again, and this time Kadem caught him a full swing of his nailed sandals.

Laleh bounced upright and his voice was wheezy with the pain of his bruised ribcage. 'Towards evening I saw a small fishing-boat leave the bay and anchor on the reef outside the mouth. When darkness fell the three men of the boat-crew began fishing by lantern-light. When I went back on board my dhow I sent my men to capture them. They killed one man when he fought against capture, but they took the two others prisoner. I towed the fishing-boat many leagues offshore before filling it with ballast stones and scuttling it. I did this so that al-Salil would believe it had been overwhelmed by the sea during the night and the men drowned.'

'Where are these prisoners?' Zayn demanded. 'Bring them before me.'

Muri Kadem clapped his hands and the two men were led in by the guards. They were dressed only in filthy loincloths and their emaciated bodies bore the marks of heavy beatings. One had lost an eye. The raw, black-scabbed pit was uncovered, except for the metallic blue flies that swarmed into it. Both shuffled along under the weight of the leg irons that were riveted to their ankles.

The guards threw them full length on the flags at the foot of the throne. 'Abase yourselves before the favourite of the

Prophet, the ruler of Oman and all the islands of the Ocean of the Indies, Caliph Zayn al-Din.' The prisoners writhed before him and whined their protestations of fealty and duty.

'Majesty, these are the men I captured,' Laleh said. 'Unfortunately the one-eyed rogue lost his wits but the other, who is named Omar, is made of stouter stuff and he will be able to answer any questions you may deign to ask him.' Laleh unhooked from his belt a long hippopotamus-hide whip and uncoiled it. As soon as he shook out the lash, the idiot prisoner began gibbering and drooling with terror.

'I have learned that both these men were sailors aboard the ship commanded by al-Salil. They have been in his service for many years and know much of that traitor's affairs.'

'Where is al-Salil?' Zayn al-Din demanded. Laleh cracked the whiplash, and the one-eyed idiot defecated down his own legs with terror. Zayn turned away his face with disgust and ordered the guards, 'Take him out and kill him.' They dragged him, shrieking, from the throne room and Zayn turned all his attention on Omar, and repeated the question: 'Where is al-Salil?'

'Majesty, when last I saw him, al-Salil was at Nativity Bay, in the fort that they call Auspice. He had with him his son, his elder brother and their women.'

'What are his intentions? How long will he remain in this place?'

'Majesty, I am a humble seaman. Al-Salil did not discuss these matters with me.'

'Were you with al-Salil when the ship called *Arcturus* was captured? Did you see the gold chests that were part of her cargo?'

'Majesty, I was with al-Salil when he lured the *Arcturus* on to the rocks called the Deceiver. I was one of those who lifted the gold chests out of the hold and carried them on board the *Revenge*.'

'The *Revenge*?' Zayn demanded.

Omar explained hurriedly, 'That is the name of the flagship of al-Salil.'

'Where are those gold chests now?'

'Majesty, they were taken ashore as soon as the ships anchored in Nativity Bay. Once again I helped to carry them. We placed them in a strongroom under the foundations of the fort.'

'How many men are with al-Salil? How many of these are fighting men who are trained in the use of the sword and musket? How many cannon does al-Salil have? Are there only the three ships you have spoken of or does the traitor have others?' In his squeaky little voice, Zayn questioned Omar patiently, often repeating his questions. Whenever Omar faltered or hesitated Laleh sent the lash curling and snapping across his ribs. By the time Zayn sat back and nodded with satisfaction, blood was dripping from the freshly opened wounds that criss-crossed the seaman's back.

Zayn turned his attention from the prisoner to the three men who sat on silk cushions below his throne. He studied their faces, and a knowing smile twitched at his lips. They were like a circle of hungry hyena watching a great black-maned lion feed, waiting to rush in and gobble the scraps after he had eaten his fill.

'It may be that I have neglected to ask this wretch questions, the answers to which are important to our deliberations?' He turned the statement into a question, and looked at Sir Guy.

Peters translated, and Sir Guy made a small bow before he replied, 'Your Majesty's questions have shown his deep perception and understanding. There are a few small items of intelligence, personal matters, of which this loathsome creature might have knowledge. With your gracious permission?' He bowed again.

Zayn waved at him to continue. Peters turned to Omar and put the first question to him. It was a laborious business, but slowly Sir Guy drew from him every detail of the treasure and the strongroom where it was stored. At last he was satisfied that all his lost gold was in Fort Auspice and that none had been hidden in some other secret location. His only remaining concern was how to regain possession of it without having to relinquish inordinate amounts to his allies, who sat with him before the throne of Zayn al-Din. He would find the solution to this problem later. For the moment he put it aside, and instead questioned Omar minutely on the identity of every *ferengi* who was within the walls of Fort Auspice. Omar's pronunciation of the names was barely recognizable, but he understood enough to be certain that Tom and Sarah Courtney were with Dorian and Mansur.

The years had done little to dim the bitter hatred he harboured for his twin brother. He remembered vividly the adolescent adoration he had felt towards Caroline, and his devastation when he spied upon Tom and Caroline's midnight coupling in the powder magazine of the old *Seraph*. Of course he had married Caroline in the end, but she came to him as Tom's reject, carrying Tom's bastard in her belly. He had tried to expunge his hatred of Tom with the subtle torments he had inflicted upon Caroline over the years of their marriage. Although time had taken the heat out of it, the hatred persisted, hard and cold as obsidian from an extinct volcano.

Then his questions moved on to Mansur Courtney and Verity. Verity was the other great love of his life, but it was a dark, twisted love. He longed to possess her in every way, even those beyond law and nature. Her voice and beauty assuaged some deep hunger in his soul. However, he had never known such transports as when he sent the whip cracking over her sweet, pale flesh and watched the crimson welts rise on her perfect skin. Then his love for her had been fierce and all-consuming. Mansur Courtney had stolen the paragon of his desire away from him.

'What of the *ferengi* woman who was captured by al-Salil during the battle with my ship?' Sir Guy's voice trembled with the pain the question caused him.

'Does the *effendi* refer to his own daughter?' Omar asked, with childlike naïvety. Sir Guy could not bring himself to answer, but he nodded abruptly.

'She has become the woman of al-Salil's son, Mansur,' Omar replied. 'They share the same sleeping quarters and spend much time laughing and speaking privately together.' He hesitated before he could bring himself to recount a matter so indelicate, but then he went on, 'He treats her as an equal, even though she is a woman. He allows her to walk ahead of him and to interrupt him when he is speaking, and he embraces and caresses her in the sight of others. Although he is of Islam, he behaves towards her like an infidel.'

Sir Guy's stomach churned with the acid of outrage and anger. He thought of Verity's body, so pale and perfect. His imagination ran out of his control. He was unable to close his mind to the vivid images that assailed him, of the filthy and obscene acts Verity and Mansur performed together. He shuddered with disgust and with the perverse arousal that seized his loins in an agonizing vice. When I capture her I will flog her until the white skin hangs from her body in tatters, he promised himself. And as for the swine who has perverted her, I shall make him scream for the mercy of death.

His imaginings were so vivid that he was afraid the men around him must sense them as powerfully as he did. He could stomach no more.

'I have finished with this piece of excrement, Your Majesty.' He scrubbed his hands in the bowl of warm water scented with flower petals that stood beside him, as if cleansing himself from the repulsive contact.

Zayn al-Din looked at Pasha Koots. 'Is there aught you wish to know from the prisoner?'

'If Your Majesty graciously permits.' He bowed. At first the questions he had for Omar were those that would concern a soldier. He wanted to know how many sailors had been on board the three ships, and how many men were in the fort, how loyal they were, and how prepared to fight. He asked about the armaments, the placement of the cannon and the field guns that had been captured from the holds of the *Arcturus*. How much powder did al-Salil have in his magazine, how many muskets?

Then his questions changed. 'The one you call Klebe, the Hawk, and whose *ferengi* name is Tom, you say you know him?'

'Yes, I know him well,' Omar agreed.

'He has a son.'

'Him I know also. We call him Somoya, for he is like the storm wind,' Omar told him.

'Where is he?' Koots asked, with a stony face, although behind the mask his anger burned brightly.

'I have heard it said within the fort that he has gone on a journey into the interior of the country.'

'Has he gone to hunt ivory?' Koots asked.

'They say that Somoya is a mighty hunter. He has a great store of ivory in the fort.'

'Have you seen this store with your own eyes?'

'I have seen the five capacious storerooms of the fort packed to the rafters with its abundance.'

Koots nodded with satisfaction. 'That is all I wish to know at present, but there will be many more questions later.'

Kadem bowed to his uncle. 'Your Majesty, I request that this prisoner be given into my personal charge and custody.'

'Take him away. Make sure he does not die, not yet at least. Not until he has served his purpose.' The guards hauled Omar to his feet and dragged him out through the great bronze doors. Zayn al-Din looked at Laleh, who had crept away, trying to efface himself among the shadows at the rear of the throne room. 'You have done good work. Now go and prepare your ship for sea. I will need your services as a scout when you lead the fleet to this Nativity Bay.'

Laleh retreated backwards, bowing and making obeisance with each few steps towards the doors.

When the guards and all lesser men had gone, a silence fell on the council. All three waited for Zayn's next pronouncement. He seemed sunk in a deep reverie, like that of the bhang smoker. But at last he roused himself, and looked to Kadem ibn Abubaker.

'You are bound by a blood oath to avenge the death of your father at the hands of al-Salil.'

Kadem bowed deeply. 'That oath is more dear to me than my life.'

'Your soul has been desecrated by al-Salil's brother, Tom Courtney. He wrapped you in the skin of a pig, and threatened to bury you alive in the same grave as the obscene animal.'

Kadem ground his teeth at the memory. He could not bring himself to admit how he had been defiled and humiliated, but he sank to his knees. 'I beg you, my Caliph and brother of my father, to allow me to seek satisfaction for these terrible wrongs that have been perpetrated against me by these two diabolical brothers.'

Zayn nodded thoughtfully, and turned to Sir Guy. 'Consul General, your daughter has been abducted by the son of al-Salil. Your magnificent ship has been pirated and your great store of wealth stolen from you.'

'All this is true, Majesty.'

Zayn turned at last to Pasha Herminius Koots. 'You have suffered humiliation and your honour has been besmirched at the hands of this same family.'

'I have suffered all these afflictions.'

'As for me, the list of my own grievances against al-Salil goes back to my childhood,' Zayn al-Din said. 'It is too long and painful for me to recite here. We have a common purpose, and that is the eradication of this nest of venomous reptiles and pork-eaters. We know that they have accumulated a considerable store of gold and ivory. Let that be only the pepper sauce that piques our appetite for retribution.' He paused again, and looked from one to the other of his generals.

'How long will you need to draw up a battle plan?' he asked them.

'Mighty Caliph, before whom all your enemies are turned into dust and ashes, Pasha Koots and I will not sleep or eat until we are able to lay the battle order before you for your approval,' Kadem promised.

Zayn smiled. 'I would have accepted nothing less from you. We will meet here again after tomorrow's evening prayers to hear your plan.'

'We will be ready for you at that hour,' Kadem assured him.

The war council continued by the light of five hundred lamps, whose wicks floated in perfumed oils to drive away the clouds of mosquitoes that, as soon as the sun touched the horizon, swarmed from the swamps and cesspools outside the city walls.

Peter Peters fell into his accustomed place behind Sir Guy Courtney as they made their way through the labyrinth of passages towards the royal harem at the rear of the vast sprawling palace. The walls smelt of rot, fungus and two hundred years of neglect. Rats scurried away ahead of the torch-bearers as they escorted the Caliph to his bedchamber, and the tramp of the bodyguard echoed hollowly from the domes and cavernous recesses of the walls.

The Caliph kept up a high-pitched monologue, and Peters translated the words almost as they fell from his lips. When the Caliph paused, Peters translated Sir Guy's response just as swiftly. At last they reached the doors to the harem where a party of armed eunuchs waited to take over the escort duty, for no natural man other than the Caliph was permitted beyond this point.

The aroma of incense floated from behind the ivory screens and mingled with the scent of lusty young womanhood. Listening intently, Peters fancied he heard the whisper of small bare feet on the flags and the sound of girlish laughter tinkling like tiny golden bells. His fatigue fell away as the cat's claws of lust pricked at his manhood. The Caliph could go to his delights and Peters did not envy him: tonight the palace vizier had promised him something special. 'She is a daughter of the Saar, the fiercest of all the tribes of Oman. Although she has seen only fifteen summers she is peculiarly gifted. She is a creature of the desert, a gazelle with pubescent breasts and long slim legs. She has the face of a child and the instincts of a harlot. She delights in the wiles and wonders of love. She will open to you all three of her passageways to bliss.' The vizier sniggered. It was part of his duty to learn every personal detail of every inhabitant of the palace. He knew full well in which direction lay Peter Peters's tastes. 'Even through the forbidden nether passage she will welcome you. She will treat you like the great lord you truly are, *effendi*.' He knew how much this worthless little clerk enjoyed being given that title.

When at last Sir Guy dismissed him, Peters hurried to his own quarters. In Bombay he lived in three tiny cockroach-infested rooms at the back of the Company compound. The only female companions he could afford on his miserly salary were the women of the night in their cheap, gaudy saris and brass bangles, their lips and gums stained bloody crimson as sword wounds from betel nut, smelling of cardamom, garlic, curry and the musk of their unwashed genitals.

Here in the palace of Muscat he was treated with honour. Men called him *effendi*. He had two house slaves to wait upon his every whim. His quarters were sumptuous, and the girls the vizier sent to keep him company were young, sweet and compliant. There was always a new one available as soon as he tired of the old.

When he reached his bedchamber Peters felt the chill of disappointment slide down his spine, for the room was empty. Then he caught the smell of her, like the perfume of a citrus orchard in blossom. He stood in the centre of the room and searched it with his eyes, waiting for her to show herself. For a while nothing moved, and there was no sound except the rustle of the leaves of the tamarind tree that stood on the terrace below the balcony.

Softly Peters quoted a stanza of the Persian poet: '"Her bosom shines like the snowfields of Mount Tabora, her buttocks are bright and round as rising moons. The dark eye that nestles between them gazes implacably into the depth of my soul."'

The curtains that screened the balcony stirred and the girl giggled. It was a childlike sound, and he knew even before he set eyes on her that the vizier had not overstated her age. When she stepped out from behind the curtains, the moonlight struck through the flimsy stuff of her robe and the outline of her body was waiflike. She came to him and rubbed herself against him like a cat. When he stroked her small rounded backside through the thin cloth she purred.

'What is your name, my pretty child?'

'I am called Nazeen, *effendi*.' The vizier had instructed her carefully as to Peters's special tastes, and her skills far surpassed her tender years. Many times during the remainder of that long night she made him bawl and bleat like a weaning calf.

In the dawn Nazeen curled into his lap as he sat in the centre of the mattress of goose down. She selected one of the ripe loquats from the silver dish that stood beside the bed, and bit it in half with her small white teeth. She spat out the glossy brown pip and placed the rest of the sweet fruit between Peters's lips. 'You made me wait so long last night before you came to me. I thought my heart would break.' She pouted.

'I was with the Caliph and his generals until after midnight.' Peters could not resist the urge to impress her.

'The Caliph himself?' She stared at him with awe. Her eyes were huge and dark. 'Did he speak to you?'

'Of course.'

'You must be a great lord in your own country. What did the Caliph want of you?'

'He wanted my opinion and advice on matters of the utmost secrecy and importance.' She wriggled excitedly in his naked lap, and giggled as she felt him swell and stiffen under her. She rose on to her knees and reached down behind herself with both hands. She spread her tight brown buttocks, then sank back into his lap.

'I do so love secrets,' she whispered, and thrust her pink tongue deep into his ear.

Nazeen spent five more nights with Peters, and when they were not otherwise engaged they talked a great deal – or, more accurately, Peters talked and the girl listened.

On the fifth morning when he came to fetch her, while it was still dark, the vizier promised Peters, 'She will return to you again tonight,' and led her away by the hand to a side gate of the palace, where an old man of the Saar waited, kneeling patiently beside an equally ancient camel. The vizier swathed Nazeen in a dark camel-hair shawl and lifted her on to the dilapidated saddle.

The city gates opened with the sunrise, and there followed

the usual exodus and influx of desert folk who had come in to sell their wares, or who were returning into the vast wilderness: pilgrims and petty officials, traders and travellers. Among those leaving were the two riders on the old camel. There was nothing about them to excite interest or envy. Nazeen looked like the old man's grandchild. It was not easy to tell her gender under the shabby robe that covered her head and body. They rode away through the palm groves and none of the guards at the gate bothered to watch them go.

A little before noon the travellers spied a goatherd squatting on a crag of the barren hills. His herd of a dozen motley beasts was spread out among the rocks below him, nibbling at the desiccated twigs of the saltbush. The goatherd was playing a mournful little tune on his reed pipes. The old rider halted his camel and prodded its neck with his goad until it hissed, bellowed a protest and knelt in the sand. Nazeen slipped off its back and ran lightly up the rocky crag, throwing back the hood of her robe as she went towards the goatherd.

She prostrated herself before him and kissed the hem of his robe. 'Mighty Sheikh bin-Shibam, father of all my tribe, may Allah sweeten every day of your life with the perfume of jasmine blossom.'

'Nazeen! Sit up, child. Even here in the wilderness there may be eyes watching us.'

'My lord, I have much to relate,' Nazeen babbled. Her dark eyes sparkled with excitement. 'Zayn is sending no less than fifteen war-dhows!'

'Nazeen, draw a deep breath, then speak slowly but miss nothing, not a word of what the *ferengi* Peters has told you.'

As she prattled away bin-Shibam's face darkened with concern. Little Nazeen had an extraordinary memory, and she had been able to milk the most minute details from Peters. Now she effortlessly recited the numbers of men and the names of the dhow captains whose ships would carry them southwards. She gave him the exact date and state of the tide on which the fleet would sail, and the date on which they expected to arrive at Nativity Bay. When she finished, the sun was half-way down the sky. However bin-Shibam had one last question for her: 'Tell me, Nazeen, has Zayn al-Din announced who is to command the expedition? Is it to be Kadem ibn Abubaker or the *ferengi* Koots?'

'Great Sheikh, Kadem ibn Abubaker is to command the ships, and the *ferengi* Koots the warriors who go ashore. But Zayn al-Din in person will sail with the fleet and take the supreme command.'

'Are you sure, child?' he demanded. It seemed too great a stroke of good fortune.

'I am certain. He told his war council, and these are the exact words that Peters repeated to me, "My throne will never be secure as long as al-Salil still lives. I want to be there at the day of his death, and to wash my hands in his heart blood. Only then will I believe that he is dead."'

'As your mother has said to me, Nazeen, you are worth a dozen warriors in the battle against the tyrant.'

Nazeen hung her head shyly. 'How is my mother, great Sheikh?'

'She is well cared-for, as I promised. She asked me to tell you how much she loves you and how proud she is of what you are doing.'

Nazeen's dark eyes glowed with pleasure. 'Tell my mother that I pray for her every day.' Nazeen's mother was blind: the flies had laid their eggs under her eyelids, and the maggots had burrowed into her eyeballs. Without Nazeen she would long ago have been abandoned, for the desert life is pitiless. Now, however, she lived under the personal protection of Sheikh bin-Shibam.

Bin-Shibam watched the girl go back down the hill and mount behind the camel rider. They set off again in the direction of the city. He felt no guilt or remorse for what he had required Nazeen to do. When it was over, when al-Salil sat once more upon the Elephant Throne, he would find her a good husband. If that was what she wanted.

Bin-Shibam smiled and shook his head. He sensed that she was one of those born with a natural talent and appetite for her vocation. Deep down, he knew that she would never give up the excitement of the city for the austere, aesthetic life of the tribe. She was not a woman who would place herself willingly under the domination of a husband.

'That little one could take care of a hundred men. Perhaps I could do better for her simply by taking care of her blind mother, and leaving her to work out her own destiny. Go in peace, little Nazeen, and be happy,' he whispered after the distant shape of the camel, as it disappeared in the purple haze of fading day. Then he whistled and after a while the true goatherd came out of his hiding-place among the rocks. He knelt before bin-Shibam and kissed his sandalled feet. Bin-Shibam shrugged off the faded robe, and handed it back to him.

'You heard nothing. You saw nothing,' he said.

'I am deaf, blind and dumb,' the goatherd agreed. Bin-Shibam gave him a coin, and the man wept with gratitude.

Bin-Shibam crossed the ridge and went down to where he had left his own camel knee-haltered. He mounted, turned her head southwards, and rode through the night and the following day without pause. He ate a handful of dates and drank thick curds of camel's milk from the skin bladder that hung behind his saddle. He even prayed on the march.

In the evening he smelt the sea salt. Still without check he rode on through the night. In the dawn the ocean lay spread before him like an infinite shield of silver. From the hills he saw the fast felucca anchored just off the beach. The captain, Tasuz, was a man who had proven himself many times over. He sent a small boat to the beach to fetch bin-Shibam aboard.

Bin-Shibam had brought with him writing materials. He sat cross-legged on the deck with the scroll before him and wrote down all that Nazeen had been able to tell him. He ended with the words, 'Majesty, may God grant you victory and glory. I shall wait with all the tribes to welcome you when you return to us.' By the time he had finished, the day was far spent. He gave the scroll to Tasuz. 'Surrender this only into the hands of Caliph al-Salil. Give your own life rather than this scroll to another,' he ordered. Tasuz could neither read nor write, so the report was safe with him. He already had detailed sailing directions for Nativity Bay. Like many illiterate

670

people, he had an infallible memory. He would not forget a single detail.

'Go with God, and may He fill your sail with His sacred breath.' Bin-Shibam dismissed him.

'Stay with God, and may angels spread their wings over you, great sheikh,' Tasuz replied.

It was one hundred and three days later that Tasuz picked out the towering whale-backed bluff that his sailing orders had described, and as he steered into the lagoon he recognized the three tall ships that he had last seen anchored in Muscat harbour.

The entire Courtney family were gathered in the refectory, the central room in the main block of Fort Auspice where they spent much of their leisure time. It had taken Sarah four years to furnish it to its present state of homely comfort. The floor and all the furniture had been lovingly made by the carpenters from indigenous timber, stinkwood, tambootie and blackwood, magnificently grained and polished with beeswax to a warm lustre. The women had embroidered the cushions and stuffed them with wild kapok. The floors were covered with tanned animal skins. The walls were decorated with framed paintings, most of which had been executed by Sarah and Louisa, although Verity, during her short stay at the fort, had made a substantial contribution to the gallery. Sarah's harpsichord had pride of place against the main wall, and now that Dorian and Mansur were back the family choir was at full strength once again.

This evening there was no singing. They were concerned with far more dire affairs. They sat in intent silence and listened to Verity translate into English the long, detailed report that Tasuz had brought them from bin-Shibam in the north. Only one member of the family was less than enthralled by this recital.

George Courtney was now almost three, highly mobile and articulate, harbouring no doubts about his needs and desires and unafraid to make them known. He circled the table with his chubby buttocks showing under the vest that was his only garment. In front his uncircumcised penis waggled like a small white worm. George was accustomed to having the full attention of all, from the lowliest black servant to that godlike being, Grandpa Tom.

'Wepity!' He tugged imperiously at Verity's skirts. He was still having difficulty with the pronunciation of her name. 'Talk to me too!'

Verity faltered. George was not easily appeased. She broke off the recital of lists of men, ships and cannon, and looked down at him. He had his mother's golden hair, and his father's green eyes. He looked so angelic that he squeezed her heart and awakened in her instincts so deep-seated that she had only recently become aware of them. 'I will tell you a story after,' she offered.

'No! Now!' said George.

'Don't be a pest,' said Jim.

'Georgie baby, come to Mama,' said Louisa.

George ignored both his parents. 'Now, Wepity, now!' he said again, his voice rising. Sarah reached into the pocket of her apron and brought out a piece of shortbread. She showed it to him under the table. For the moment George lost all interest in Verity, dropped on to all fours, and shot among their feet to snatch the bribe out of his grandmother's hand.

'You have a wonderful way with children, Sarah Courtney.' Tom grinned at her. 'Just spoil 'em rotten, an't that so?'

'I learned the art from dealing with you,' she answered tartly. 'For you are the greatest baby of all.'

'Will you two stop squabbling for a moment? You're worse than Georgie by far,' Dorian told them. 'There's an empire at stake and all our lives at risk, while you are playing at being doting grandparents.'

Verity raised her voice and took up from where she had been interrupted, and they all became serious again. At last she read out bin-Shibam's final salutation to his Caliph. '"Majesty, may God grant you victory and glory. I shall wait with all the tribes to welcome you when you return to us."'

Tom broke the silence at last. 'Can we trust this fellow? How did he find out so much?'

'Yes, brother, we can trust him,' Dorian replied. 'I do not know how he has come by this news, I only know that if bin-Shibam says it is so, then it must be true.'

'In that case we cannot remain here to be attacked by an overwhelming fleet of war-dhows crammed with battle-hardened Omani troops. We will have to move on.'

'Do not even think it, Tom Courtney,' said Sarah. 'I have spent my whole married life on the move. This is my home, and this creature Zayn al-Din will not drive me out of it. I am staying here.'

'Woman, will you not listen to reason for once in your life?'

'I hate to take sides in such a domestic furore,' Dorian took his pipe out of his mouth and smiled at them fondly, 'but Sarah is right. We will never be able to run far enough to escape the wrath of Zayn and the men with him. Their enmity will encompass oceans and continents.'

Tom frowned darkly and tugged at one large ear. Then he sighed. 'Maybe you're right, Dorry. The hatred they bear this family goes back too far. Sooner or later we must stand and face them.'

'We will never have such an opportunity presented to us again,' Dorian went on. 'Bin-Shibam has given us Zayn al-Din's complete battle plan. Zayn will come to fight us on our own ground. When he disembarks his army it will be at the end of a voyage of two thousand leagues. He will have only those of his horses that have survived the rigours of the journey. We, on the other hand, will be prepared, our men rested, armed and well mounted.' Dorian laid his hand on his brother's shoulder. 'Believe me, Tom, this is our best chance and probably the only one we will get.'

'You think like a warrior,' Tom conceded, 'while I think like a merchant. I relinquish command to you. The rest of us, Jim and Louisa, Mansur and Verity, will follow your orders. I would like to say the same for my dear wife, but following orders has never been one of her strengths.'

'Very well, Tom, I accept the task. We have but a little

time to lay our plans,' Dorian said, 'and will need to take advantage of every minute of it. My first concern will be to survey the field, to pick out those areas where we are strongest and avoid those where we are weakest.'

Tom nodded approval. He liked the way Dorian had so swiftly taken the reins. 'Go on, brother. We are all listening.'

Dorian spoke through puffs of tobacco smoke. 'We know from bin-Shibam that when Zayn brings his ships into the lagoon and bombards the fort, it will be a diversion. The main force under Koots's command will land on the coast and march overland to surround us and prevent us breaking out to retreat inland. What we have to do first is find the most likely spot for Koots to land, then survey the route he will be forced to take to reach the fort.'

The next day Dorian and Tom went on board the *Revenge* and sailed in a northerly direction along the coast. They stood together at the chart table, studying the coastline as it passed, refreshing their memories as to all the salient features.

'Koots must try to land as close to the fort as possible. Every mile he is forced to march will compound his difficulties ten times over,' Dorian muttered.

This was a dangerous, treacherous coast: the steeply shelving beaches and rocky headlands were exposed to a high surf and open to sudden gales. Nativity Bay was almost the only secure harbour within a hundred miles. The one other possible landing was at the mouth of a large river, which ran into the sea only a few miles north of the entrance to Nativity Bay. The local tribes called this river Umgeni. Large war-dhows would not be able to negotiate the shallow bar at the entrance, but smaller boats could do so with ease.

'That is where Koots will land,' Dorian told Tom with finality. 'In his longboats, he could send five hundred men up the river in a few hours.'

Tom nodded. 'However, once he got them ashore, they would still face a march of many miles through rugged country to reach the fort.'

'We had best find out just how rugged it really is,' Dorian said, and he put the *Revenge* about and they sailed back

674

southwards, keeping as close inshore as the wind and tide would allow. They stood at the starboard rail and studied the shore through their telescopes.

There was a continuous sweep of beach all the way, sugary brown sands pounded by an unremitting surf. 'If they stuck to the beach, carrying their own armour, weapons and supplies, they would make heavy weather of marching through that deep sand,' Tom opined. 'What is more they would be vulnerable for the whole march to the cannonade of our ships.'

'Added to which is that, if he is trying to surprise us, Koots would never send them along the open beach. He knows we would spot such a large force at once. He must detour inland,' Dorian decided. 'Tell me, brother, the bush above the beach seems impenetrable. Is it really so?'

'It is very thick, but not impenetrable,' Tom told him. 'Also there are marshy and swampy areas. The bush is infested with buffalo and rhino, and the swamps are filled with crocodile. However, there are game paths along a ridge of slightly higher ground that runs parallel to the shore, about two cables' length inland from the beach. It remains dry and firm at all seasons and states of the tide.'

'Then we must go over the ground carefully and mark that path,' Dorian said, and they sailed back into the bay. The following morning, accompanied by Jim and Mansur, they rode along the beach until they reached the mouth of the Umgeni river.

'That was easy going.' Mansur checked his pocket watch. 'We covered the ground in less than three hours.'

'That may be so. But the enemy will be marching on foot, not mounted,' Jim pointed out, 'and we will have them in easy grape-shot range from the ships.'

'Yes,' Dorian acknowledged. 'Tom and I have already agreed that they must move inland. We want to scout that route now.'

They followed the south bank of the Umgeni river upstream for a mile or so until it entered the hills and the banks became steep and high, making the going difficult even for their small party.

'No, they will not come this far inland. They will be trying to invest the fort with all the speed they can. They must cut through the littoral swamps,' Dorian decided.

They returned downstream, and Jim pointed out the beginning of the low causeway through the swamps. The trees along it were taller than the surrounding forest. They left the river, and headed towards it. Almost immediately the horses plunged into the black mud of the mangrove swamps. They were forced to dismount and lead them through until they reached the ridge of firmer ground. Even here there were potholes of treacherous mud hidden under an innocuous-seeming scum of green slime. The bush grew so densely that the horses were unable to force their way through. The twisted stems of ancient milkwood trees formed serried ranks like armoured warriors and their branches hung down and entwined with the amatimgoola shrub, whose long, sturdy thorns could pierce the leather of their boots and inflict deep, painful wounds.

They were forced to move along the game paths that criss-crossed this jungle, which were nothing more than narrow tunnels of vegetation forged by buffalo and rhinoceros. The thorny roofs were so low that again they were forced to dismount and lead the horses. Even then they had to stoop and the thorns rasped on their empty saddles, scoring the leather. The mosquitoes and biting midges rose in black clouds from the mudholes and swarmed around their sweating faces, crawling into their ears and nostrils.

'When Kadem and Koots drew up their battle plan, neither of them had tried to march through this.' Tom lifted his hat and mopped his face and shiny pate.

'We can make him pay for every yard in heavy coin,' Jim said. Until now, he had been silent since they left the beach. 'In here it will all be close work, hand to hand. Bows and spears will have the advantage over muskets and cannon.'

'Bows and spears?' Dorian demanded, with sudden interest. 'Who will wield them?'

'My good friend and brother in blood and war, King Beshwayo and his bloodthirsty savages,' said Jim proudly.

'Tell me about him,' Dorian ordered.

676

'It's a long story, Uncle. It will have to wait until we get back to the fort. That is, if we can ever find our way home through this hellish tangle.'

That evening, after dinner, all the family remained in the refectory. Sarah stood behind Tom's chair with one arm draped over his shoulder. At intervals she rubbed the mosquito bites on his bald pate. When she did that, he closed his eyes in quiet enjoyment. At the other end of the table Dorian sat with Mansur on one side of him and his hookah on the other.

Verity had never looked upon herself as a domesticated creature, but since her arrival at Fort Auspice she had found a deep satisfaction in homemaking and caring for Mansur. She and Louisa, who were so different in nearly every way, had taken to each other from their first meeting. Now they moved quietly around the big room, clearing away the dinner dishes, serving endless cups of coffee to their menfolk, or coming to sit close to them and listen to their talk, from time to time adding their own opinions to the conversation. Louisa was well occupied with Master George. This was the time of the day that they all enjoyed most.

'Tell me about Beshwayo,' Dorian ordered Jim, and he laughed,

'Ah! You have not forgotten.' He picked up his son from the floor and placed him comfortably in his lap. 'You have raised enough hell for one day, my boy. Now I am going to tell a story,' he said.

'Story!' said George, and subsided at once. He laid his golden curls against Jim's shoulder, and thrust his thumb into his mouth.

'After you and Mansur sailed away in the *Revenge* and the *Sprite*, Louisa and I loaded up our wagons and set off into the wilderness to look for elephant and try to make contact with the tribes so that we could open trade with them.'

'Jim makes it sound as though I went willingly,' Louisa protested.

'Come now, Hedgehog, be honest. You have been bitten by the wander bug as deeply as I have.' Jim smiled. 'But let me go on. I knew that there were many large war parties of Nguni coming down with their herds from the north.'

'How did you discover that?' Dorian demanded.

'Inkunzi told me, and I sent Bakkat out far northwards to read the sign.'

'Bakkat I know well, of course. But Inkunzi? I only vaguely remember the name.'

'Then let me remind you, Uncle. Inkunzi was Queen Manatasee's chief herdsman. When I captured her cattle, he came with me rather than be parted from his beloved animals.'

'Of course! How could I ever forget it, Jim boy. Wonderful story.'

'Inkunzi and Bakkat guided us into the hinterland to find the other rampaging tribes of Nguni. Some were hostile and dangerous as nests of poisonous cobras or man-eating lions. We had a few scrapes with them, I can tell you. Then we came across Beshwayo.'

'Where did you find him?'

'About two hundred leagues north-west of here,' Jim explained. 'He was bringing his tribe and all their cattle down the escarpment. Our meeting was most propitious. I had just come upon three big elephant bulls. I did not know that Beshwayo was spying upon us from a nearby hilltop. He had never seen mounted men or a musket before. For me it was a most fortunate hunt. I was able to drive the elephant out of the thick forest into the open grassland. There, I rode them down one after the other, with Bakkat loading and passing me the guns. I managed to kill all three within a two-mile gallop on Drumfire. From his lookout Beshwayo watched it all. Afterwards he told me that it had been his intention to attack the wagons and massacre us all, but having seen the way I shot and rode he decided against it. He's a forthright rascal, is King Beshwayo.'

'He's a terrifying monster of a man,' Louisa corrected him. 'That is why he and Jim get along so well together.'

'Not true.' Jim chuckled. 'It was not I who won him over.

678

It was Louisa. He had never seen hair like hers, or anything to match this cub to whom she had just given birth. Beshwayo loves cattle and sons.' They both looked down fondly at the child in his arms. George had not been able to stay the course. The comforting warmth of his father's body and the sound of his voice was always a powerful soporific and he had fallen into a deep sleep.

'By this time I had learned enough of the Nguni language from Inkunzi, to be able to converse with Beshwayo. Once he had changed his warlike intentions, and prevented his warriors attacking the wagons, he set up his kraal close to us and we camped together for several weeks. I showed him the delights of cloth, glass beads, mirrors and the usual trifles of trade. These he enjoyed, but he was wary of our horses. Try as I might, I could not prevail on him to mount one. Beshwayo is fearless, except when invited to take part in equestrian activity. However, he was fascinated by the power of gunpowder, and I was required to demonstrate it to him at every opportunity, as if he needed further convincing after watching the elephant hunt.'

Louisa tried to lift George out of his father's arms and take him to his bed, but as she touched him he came fully awake and let out a bellow of protest. It took some minutes and the reassurances of the entire family to quieten him again to the point where Jim could resume his tale.

'As we came to know each other better, Beshwayo confided in me that he was having his differences with another Nguni tribe called the Amahin. These were a cunning, unscrupulous bunch of rogues who had committed the unforgivable sin of stealing several hundred of Beshwayo's cattle. This sin was compounded by the fact that in the process they had murdered a dozen or so of his herd-boys, of whom two were his sons. Beshwayo had not yet been able to avenge his sons and recover his cattle because the Amahin were ensconced in an impregnable natural fortress, which the erosion of the ages had carved from the sheer wall of the escarpment face. Beshwayo offered me two hundred head of prime cattle if I would assist him to assault the fortress of the Amahin. I told him that as I

679

now looked upon him as my friend, I would be pleased to fight alongside him without payment.'

'No payment, except the exclusive right of trade with his tribe,' Louisa smiled softly, 'and the right to hunt ivory through all the king's domain, and a treaty of alliance in perpetuity.'

'Perhaps I should have said little payment, rather than none at all,' Jim admitted, 'but let us not be pedantic. I took Smallboy and Muntu and the rest of my fellows and we rode with Beshwayo to the lair of the Amahin. I discovered that it was a massif of rock detached from the main escarpment and secured on all sides by sheer cliffs. The only avenue of approach was across a bridge of rock so narrow that it would allow the passage of only four men at a time. It was overlooked by the Amahin from the higher ground on the far side, and they were able to shower rocks, stones and poisoned arrows on any attackers who attempted to force the passage. Some hundred or so of Beshwayo's men had perished already, shot with poisoned arrows or their skulls crushed by rocks. I found a place on the face of the main escarpment from which my fellows were able to fire upon the defenders. The Amahin proved a doughty lot. Our musket balls served to dampen their ardour a little, but did not prevent them sweeping the attackers off the exposed bridgeway as soon as they ventured on to it.'

'I am certain that at this stage you conceived the solution to the insoluble, great military genius that you are.' Mansur laughed, and Jim grinned back at him.

'Not so, coz. I was at my wits' end, so naturally I did what we all do in these cases. I sent for my wife!' All three women applauded this gem of wisdom with such merry laughter that George was startled awake again and added his voice to the uproar. Louisa picked him up, helped him find his thumb and he collapsed back into oblivion.

'I had never heard of a Roman testudo until Louisa explained it. She had read of it in Livy. Although many of Beshwayo's men carried shields of rawhide, their use was frowned upon by the king as unmanly. Each warrior fights as an individual and not as part of a formation, and in the moment of greatest danger he is wont to throw aside his shield and hurl himself unprotected upon his enemy, relying on the fury of his charge and his fearsome aspect to drive his enemy from the field and carry him through unscathed. Beshwayo was at first appalled by such cowardly tactics as we suggested. In his view only women hid behind shields. However, he was desperate to avenge his sons and retrieve his stolen cattle. His men learned swiftly how to overlap their shields and hold them above their heads to form the tortoiseshell of protection. My men kept up a lively fire on the Amahin, and under their testudo Beshwayo's *impis* charged across the bridge. As soon as they had a foothold on the far side, we galloped across on the horses, firing from the saddle. The Amahin had never seen a horse before, nor had they faced cavalry, but by now they had learned of the power of our firearms. They broke at our first charge. Those Amahin warriors who did not leap from the cliffs voluntarily were helped to do so by Beshwayo's.'

'You will be pleased to know that the Amahin women did no jumping. They stayed with their children and most found husbands among Beshwayo's men soon after the end of the battle,' Louisa assured Sarah and Verity.

'Sensible creatures,' said Sarah, and stroked Tom's head. 'I would have done the same.'

Tom winked at Jim. 'Take no notice of your mother. She has a good heart. The only pity is that it does not match her tongue. Go on with the story, lad. I have heard it before, but it's a good one.'

'It was a rewarding day for all those who took part,' Jim resumed, 'except the Amahin warriors. Apart from a score of cattle that the Amahin had killed and feasted upon, we recovered the rest of the stolen herd and the king was delighted. He and I shared millet beer from the same pot, but only after we had diluted it with our commingled blood. We are now brothers of the warrior blood. My enemies are his enemies.'

'Having heard that account, there is no doubt in my mind that I should leave the defence of the swamps between here and the Umgeni river to you and your blood-brother Besh-wayo,' Dorian told him. 'And God help Herminius Koots when he tries to find his way through.'

'Just as soon as the wagons are made ready I shall leave to find Beshwayo and enlist his support and that of his spearmen,' Jim agreed.

'I hope, husband, that you do not intend to leave me here, while you wander off into the blue yet again?' Louisa asked sweetly.

'How can you think so poorly of me? Besides, I would meet with a cold welcome at the kraal of Beshwayo if I did not have you and Georgie with me.'

Bakkat went out into the hills to summon Inkunzi. The chief herder and his helpers wandered at large with the cattle herds, and no one else would have been able to find him as readily as the little Bushman. In the meantime Smallboy greased the wheel hubs of the wagons and brought in the draught oxen. Within five days Inkunzi had come into the fort with two dozen Nguni warriors and they were ready to leave.

The rest of the family stood on the palisade and watched the wagon train head for the hills. Louisa and Jim rode ahead on Trueheart and Drumfire. George was tucked into the leather carrying sling on his father's back. He waved one chubby little arm at them. 'Bye-bye, Grandpapa! Bye-bye, Grandmama! 'Bye, Uncle Dowy. 'Bye, Manie and Wepity!' he sang out, and his curls danced and sparkled to Drumfire's easy canter. 'Don't cry, Grandmama. Georgie will come back soon.'

'You heard your grandson,' said Tom gruffly. 'Stop blubbering, woman!'

'I am doing no such thing,' Sarah snapped. 'A midge flew into my eye, that is all.'

Bin-Shibam had warned Dorian in his report that it was Zayn's intention to set sail from Muscat as soon as the south-easterly *kusi* winds swung round the compass and became the *kaskazi*, blowing steadily out of the north-east to wing his fleet down the coast. That time of change was only weeks away. However, there were worrying signs. Already the black-headed gulls had arrived in their dense flocks to set up their nesting colonies on the heights of the bluff. They were the harbingers of an early change in season. For all Dorian knew Zayn's fleet might already be at sea.

Dorian and Mansur sent for their ships' captains. They studied the chart together. Although Tasuz was illiterate he could understand the shapes of islands and mainland and the arrow symbols of winds and currents, for these were the elements that guided his existence.

'At first, when the enemy leave Oman they will keep well offshore, to pick up the *kaskazi* wind and the main flow of the Mozambique current,' Dorian said, with certainty. 'It would take a large fleet to find them in that great expanse of water.' He spread his hand on the chart. 'The only place that you will be able to waylay them is here.' He moved his hand southwards on to the fish-shaped island of Madagascar. 'Zayn's fleet will be forced through the narrows of the channel between the mainland and the island, like sand through the hourglass. You will guard the narrows. Your three ships can cover the inshore passage, for such an assembly of war-dhows will be spread out over many miles. You will also be able to enlist the help of the local fishermen to help you keep watch.'

'When we discover the fleet should we attack them?' Batula asked, and Dorian laughed.

'I know you would enjoy that, you old *shaitan*, but you must keep your ships well below the horizon and out of sight of the enemy at all times. You must not let Zayn know that his advance has been discovered. As soon as you sight his fleet you will break off all contact and hurry back here as fast as wind and current can bring you.'

'What of the *Arcturus*?' asked Ruby Cornish, with a peeved expression. 'Am I also to act as a guard dog?'

'I have not forgotten you, Captain Cornish. Your ship is the most powerful, but not as fast as the *Sprite* and the *Revenge*, or even Tasuz's little felucca. I want you here in Nativity Bay and you can be sure that when the time comes I will have

683

much employment for you.' Cornish looked suitably mollified, and Dorian went on, 'Now, I want to go over the plans to engage the enemy as soon as they show themselves in the offing.' They spent the rest of that day and most of the night in conclave, going over every conceivable eventuality.

'Our fleet is so small, and the enemy so numerous, that our success will depend on each ship working in concert with the others. At night I will use signal lanterns and, during the day, smoke and Chinese rockets. I have drawn up a list of the signal codes we will employ, with copies for Batula and Kumrah written out fair in Arabic by Mistress Verity.'

In the dawn the three little ships, *Sprite*, *Revenge* and Tasuz's felucca, took advantage of the ebb of the tide and the offshore wind and sailed out of the bay, leaving only the *Arcturus* at anchor under the guns of the fort.

Beshwayo had moved his kraal fifty miles further downriver, but Bakkat had no difficulty in leading them directly to it, for every footpath and all the cattle tracks fanned out from it like the strands of a web, with King Beshwayo, the royal spider, at the centre. The lush and rolling grasslands through which they rode were heavily populated by his herds.

Regiments of the king's warriors were guarding the cattle. Many had fought with Jim against the Amahin. They all knew that Beshwayo had made him his blood-brother, and their greetings were enthusiastic. Each regimental *induna* detached fifty men to join the escort that led the wagons towards the royal kraal. The swiftest runners raced ahead to alert the king of their imminent arrival.

Thus Jim's entourage was several hundred strong by the time they crossed the last ridge and looked down into the basin of hills where Beshwayo's new kraal stood. It was laid out in an enormous circle, divided internally into rings within rings like an archery target. Jim guessed that it might take even Drumfire almost half an hour to gallop around the outer circumference.

The kraal was surrounded by a high stockade, and at its heart was a vast cattle pen in which all the royal herds could be contained. Beshwayo liked to live close to his beasts, and he had explained to Jim how the inner enclosure also served as a fly trap. The insects laid their eggs in the fresh cattle dung where they were trodden under the hoofs of the milling herd and could not hatch.

The outer circles of the kraal were filled with the closely spaced beehive huts that housed Beshwayo's court. The king's bodyguard lived in the smaller huts. The larger huts of the king's numerous wives stood within an enclosure of woven thorn branches. In a separate smaller enclosure were fifty elaborate structures that housed the *indunas*, Beshwayo's councillors and senior captains, and their families.

All these were dwarfed by the king's palace. It could not, by any stretch of semantics, be called a hut: it stood as tall as an English country church – it did not seem possible that sticks and reeds could have been built up so high without collapsing. Every single reed used in its construction had been selected by the master thatchers. It was a perfect hemisphere.

'It looks like the egg of the roc!' Louisa exclaimed. 'See how it catches the sunlight.'

'What's a roc, Mama?' demanded George, from the sling on his father's back. 'An't that the same as a stone?' He had picked up that form of negative from his grandfather, and clung to it stubbornly despite her protests.

'A roc is a huge and fabulous bird,' Louisa answered.

'Can I have one, please?'

'Ask your father.' She smiled sweetly at Jim.

He pulled a wry face. 'Thank you, Hedgehog. No peace for me for the next month.' To distract George he touched Drumfire with his heels and they trotted down the last hill. The escorting warriors burst into a full-throated anthem of praise to their king. Their voices were deep and melodious, stirring the blood with their magnificence. The long column of men, horses and wagons snaked down across the golden grassland, the warriors keeping perfect step. Their headdresses waved and nodded in unison; each regiment had its own totem: heron, vulture, eagle and owl, and they wore the feathers of their clan. Around their upper arms they wore the cow tails of honour, awarded by Beshwayo for killing an enemy in combat. Their shields were matched, some dappled, some black, others red, while a few of the élite regiments carried pure white ones. They beat upon them with their *assegais* as they approached the kraal across a parade-ground. At the far end of this wide expanse the imposing figure of Beshwayo waited for them, seated on a carved ebony stool. He was stark naked, displaying to all the world the proof that the dimensions of his manhood exceeded those of any of his subjects. His skin was anointed with beef fat and he shone in the sunlight like a beacon. The captains of his regiments were drawn up behind him, his *indunas* crowned with the rings of authority on their shaven heads, his witch doctors and his wives.

Jim reined in and fired a musket shot into the air. Beshwayo loved to be saluted thus, and he let forth a bull bellow of laughter. 'I see you, Somoya my brother!' he shouted, and his voice carried three hundred yards across the parade-ground.

'I see you, great black bull!' Jim shouted back, and urged Drumfire into a gallop. Louisa pushed Trueheart up alongside him. Beshwayo clapped his hands with delight to see the horses run. In the sling on his father's back George was kicking and struggling with excitement to be free.

'Beshie!' he yelled. 'My Beshie!'

'You had best let him down,' Louisa called across to Jim, 'before he does you or himself an injury.'

Jim hauled the stallion to a skidding halt on his haunches, lifted the child out of the sling with one hand and leaned out of the saddle to lower him to the ground. George took off at a run straight at the Great Bull of Earth and the Black Thunder of the Sky.

King Beshwayo came to meet him half-way, picked him up and hurled him high into the air. Louisa gasped and closed her eyes in trepidation, but George shrieked with delight as the king caught him before he hit the ground, and sat him firmly upon his gleaming muscular shoulder.

That night Beshwayo slaughtered fifty fat oxen and they feasted and drank huge clay pots of frothing beer. Jim and Beshwayo boasted and laughed and told each other amazing tales of their feats and adventures.

'Manatasee!' Beshwayo encouraged Jim. 'Tell me again how you killed her. Tell me how her head sailed up into the air like a bird.' He demonstrated with an extravagant sweep of his arms.

Louisa had heard the story repeated so often, for it was Beshwayo's favourite, that she pleaded the duties of motherhood as an excuse to leave the royal presence. She carried George, protesting sleepily, to his cot in the wagon.

Beshwayo listened to Jim's account of the battle with even more pleasure than the first time he had heard it. 'I wish I had met that mighty black cow,' he said, when the tale was told. 'I would have put a fine son in her belly. Can you imagine what a mighty warrior he would have been, with such a father and mother?'

'Then you would have been forced to live with Manatasee, the raging lioness.'

'No, Somoya. After she had given me my son, I would have made her head fly even higher into the sky than you did.' He roared with laughter and thrust the beer pot into Jim's hands.

When at last Jim came to join her in the cardell bed, Louisa had to help him climb over the afterclap. He collapsed on the mattress, and she removed his boots for him. The next morning it required two mugs of strong coffee before Jim announced dubiously that, if she nursed him well, he might just survive the day.

'I hope so, my darling husband, for I am sure you recall that this very day the king has invited you to attend the Festival of the First Flowers,' she told him, and Jim groaned.

'Beshwayo drank twice as much of that infernal brew as I did. Do you not think he may have the good sense to cancel the festival?'

'No,' said Louisa, with an angelic smile. 'I do not think he will for here come his *indunas* to escort us.'

They led Louisa and Jim back to the parade-ground. The

open expanse was lined with dense ranks of young warriors dressed in all the finery of feathers and animal-skin kilts. They sat upon their shields, silent and still as statues carved from anthracite. At the entrance to the great kraal, carved stools were set out for Jim and Louisa beside the empty stool of the king. Behind that the king's wives were squatting in double ranks. Many were beautiful young women, and nearly all were in some stage of gravidity, from a gentle swelling to full bloom, breasts bursting with abundance, belly buttons popping out. They exchanged knowing smiles with Louisa, and watched the antics of golden-headed George, their dark eyes swimming with the strength of their maternal feelings.

Louisa sighed and leaned across to Jim on his stool. 'Does not a woman have a peculiar type of beauty when she is to have a baby?' she asked ingenuously.

Jim groaned. 'You pick the oddest times to become subtly suggestive,' he whispered. 'Think you not that one George is about all this world can stomach?'

'She might be a girl,' Louisa pointed out.

'Would she look like you?' Despite the glare he opened his eyes a little wider.

'As like as not.'

'That bears some thought,' he conceded, but at that moment there sounded from within the walls of the kraal a shattering fanfare of kudu-horn trumpets and a crash of drums. Instantly the warriors sprang to their feet and their voices echoed against the hills with the royal salute, 'Bayete! Bayete!'

The king's musicians came out through the gates, rank upon rank, dipping and swaying, flirting their headdresses like the courtship dancing of crowned cranes, stamping until the dust powdered their legs to the knees. Then they froze in midstep and the only movement was the ruffle of the feathers in their headdresses.

King Beshwayo paced out through the gates. He wore a simple kilt of white cow tails, and war rattles on his ankles and wrists. His head was shaven and his skin had been polished with a mixture of fat and red-ochre clay. His tread was stately. He shimmered like a god as he walked.

He reached his place and looked upon his subjects with such a terrible mien that they shrank before his gaze. Then, suddenly, he hurled the spear he carried into the air. Driven by his massive shoulders it rose to an impossible height. It reached its zenith and then, in a graceful parabola, fell back to peg its glittering head into the sun-baked clay of the parade-ground.

Still there was no sound, no man or woman moved. Then a single voice broke the silence: sweetly and softly it rose from the riverbed at the far end of the parade-ground. A sigh went up from the throats of all the assembled warriors and their feathers danced as they turned their heads towards that sound.

A line of young maidens came shuffling up and over the river bank. Each one had her hands on the hips of the girl in front of her and followed her movements with mirror-like precision. They wore very short skirts of combed grass and crowns of wild flowers. Their breasts were bare and shining with oil. They kept snaking out of the riverbed, until it seemed they were not individuals but a single sinuous creature.

'These are the first flowers of the tribe,' Louisa said softly. 'Each one has seen her moon for the first time, and now they are ready for marriage.'

The girl who led the line of dancers reached the end of the first verse of the song, and all the others came in together with the chorus. Their voices soared high, then fell and languished, and rose again, achingly pure, cleaving the hearts of their listeners. The line of dancing virgins came to a halt before the ranks of young warriors. They turned to face them, and the song changed. The rhythm became as urgent as the act of love, the words suggestive and lewd.

'How sharp are your spears?' they asked the warriors. 'How long the shaft? How deep your thrust? Can you stab to the heart? Will blood flow when you pull out your blade from the wound?'

Then they began to dance again, at first swaying like long grass in the wind, then throwing back their heads and laughing with white teeth and flashing eyes. They held out their breasts, one cupped in each hand, and offered them to the young men.

Then they retreated and whirled away until their skirts flew waist high. They wore nothing beneath them, and they had plucked their pudenda so that their unmasked clefts were clearly defined. Then they faced away from the men, and bowed over until their foreheads touched their knees, writhing and rolling their hips.

The warriors danced in time to the girls, working themselves into a storm of lust. They stamped until the earth jumped under their feet. They shook their shoulders. Their eyes rolled back in their skulls and froth creamed on their contorted lips. They thrust their hips into the air like mating dogs, and their engorged sexes probed rigidly through the fur strips of their kilts.

Suddenly Beshwayo sprang high from his stool and landed on legs as straight and powerful as the trunks of two leadwood trees. 'Enough!' he bellowed.

Warriors and maidens, everyone on the parade, threw themselves to the ground and lay still as death, no sound or movement but the quivering of headdress feathers and grass skirts, the panting of their breath.

Beshwayo strode along the ranks of girls. 'These are my prime heifers,' he roared. 'These are the treasures of Beshwayo.' He gazed down on them with a fierce, possessive pride.

'They are beautiful and strong. They are full women. They are my daughters. From their hot wombs will come forth regiments of my warriors to conquer all the earth, and their sons shall shout my name to the skies. Through them my name will live for ever.' He threw back his head and let forth such a volume of sound from the barrel of his chest that it rang and echoed off the hills. 'Beshwayo!'

Not another person moved and the echoes faded away into silence. Then Beshwayo turned and strode back along the regiments of prostrated warriors. 'Who are these?' The question was filled with contempt. 'Are these men who grovel before me in the dust?' he bellowed, with mocking laughter. 'No!' he answered himself. 'Men stand tall and are full of pride. These are little children. Are these warriors?' he demanded of the sky, and laughed at the absurdity of the question. 'These are not warriors. Warriors have quenched their spears in the blood of the king's enemies. These are but snot-nosed children.' He walked down the line and spurned them with his foot.

'Stand up, you small boys!' he cried. They leaped to their feet with the agility of acrobats, their young bodies forged to perfection by a lifetime of rigorous training. Beshwayo shook his head with contempt. He walked away. Then, suddenly, he leaped high in the air and landed with the elegance of a panther. 'Stand up, my daughters,' he shouted, and the girls rose and swayed before him like a field of dark lilies.

'See how their beauty outshines the sun. Can the king allow those unweaned calves to mount his beautiful heifers?' he harangued them. 'No, for there is nothing between their legs of any account. These magnificent cows need bulls of power. Their wombs crave the seed of great warriors.'

He strode back down the alley between them. 'The sight of these young calves so displeases me that I am sending them away. They shall not look upon my heifers again until they have become bulls.'

'Go!' he bellowed at them. 'Go! And do not return until you have washed your spears in the blood of the king's enemies. Go! And return only when you have killed your man and wear the cow tail on your right arm.' He paused and looked down on them with disdainful hauteur. 'The sight of you displeases me. Be gone!'

'*Bayete!*' they shouted, with a single voice, and again, '*Bayete!* We have heard the voice of the Black Thunder of the Sky, and we will obey.'

In a close column they swung away, keeping perfect step, singing the praises of Beshwayo. Like a dark serpent, they wound up the slope of the hill and disappeared over the crest. Beshwayo strode back and took his seat on the carved stool. He was scowling hideously, but without changing his expression he said softly to Jim, 'Did you see them, Somoya? They are young lions and hot for blood. These are the finest fruits of any circumcision year in all my reign. No enemy can stand against them.' He turned on his stool towards Louisa. 'Did you see them, Welanga? Is there any maiden in all my realm who can resist them?'

'They are fine young men,' she agreed.

'Now I lack only an enemy to send them against.' Beshwayo's scowl became even more terrifying. 'I have scoured the land for twenty days' march in every direction, and found no more fodder for my spears.'

'I am your brother,' said Jim. 'I cannot allow you to suffer such lack. I have an enemy. Because you are my brother, I shall share this enemy with you.' Beshwayo stared at him for a long moment. Then he let fly such a bellow of laughter that all his *indunas* and his pregnant wives cachinnated in slavish imitation of him.

'Show me our enemy, Somoya. Like a pair of black-maned lions on a gazelle, you and I shall devour him.'

Three days later, when the wagons started back for the coast, Beshwayo went with them, singing his war anthems at the head of his new regiments and their battle-hardened *indunas*.

Faithful to Dorian's orders, once the *Sprite* and the *Revenge* entered the Mozambique channel, the two ships separated. Kumrah sailed up the west coast of the island of Madagascar, and Batula along the east coast of the African mainland. They called at each of the fishing villages along the way. From the headmen of these villages they hired, for payment of beads, rolls of copper wire and other stores such as fishing line, rope and bronze nails, a motley flotilla of feluccas and outrigger fishing-dhows. By the time they met again at the rendezvous off the north tip of the long island they were like ducks followed by a straggling line of ducklings. Most of these craft were ancient and decrepit and many could only be kept afloat by constant bailing.

Batula and Kumrah placed them in a thin screen from island to mainland, then took their own ships well to the south so that they were only just able to maintain visual contact with them. In this way they hoped to prevent the desertion of any of the frail vessels, and to receive their signals when Zayn's convoy of war-dhows appeared on the northern horizon, without being forced to reveal their own presence. They hoped that if Zayn's lookouts spotted one or two of these tiny vessels they would think them nothing more than innocent fishing-craft, the likes of which were common in these offshore waters.

The weeks passed slowly in such unrewarding activity. There was constant attrition among the scouting vessels. They were unsuited for such long periods at sea. The crews mutinied against the perils, discomfort and boredom, or their boats fell apart, or the rough weather of the *kaskazi* drove them into port. The screen became so perilously thin that in the heavy seas or in darkness even such a large fleet as Zayn's might slip through the holes in it unremarked.

Batula had placed Tasuz in the most likely position, within sight of the low blue outline of the African mainland. He guessed that Zayn would keep well within reach of the Omani trading settlements that for centuries had been sited at every convenient river mouth and sheltered bay and lagoon along this coast. From these bases Zayn would be able to revictual his ships with fresh water and supplies.

Batula fretted away these long, uneventful days. In the first light of each dawn he climbed to the main truck of the *Revenge* and stared into the dispersing darkness for the first sight of Tasuz's felucca. He was never disappointed. Even in the worst weather when all the other small craft had been driven to seek shelter, Tasuz was doggedly holding his position. Although his ship seemed at times to be buried under the grey, breaking swells of the Mozambique current, his dirty lateen sail always reappeared out of the gloom.

This morning the wind had dropped to a gentle zephyr. A bank of sea fret covered the horizon, and the current had settled into long swells that marched down from the north. Batula searched anxiously for his first sight of the felucca, but he was unprepared when the ghostly outline of the lateen sail

693

appeared out of the mist less than a sea mile dead ahead. 'She is flying the blue!' he exclaimed, with excitement. The long blue banner at her masthead writhed like a flying serpent in the gentle airs. It was the sky blue of al-Salil's colours. 'It is the signal. Tasuz has discovered the approach of the enemy fleet.'

He was aware at once of the danger. The sea mist would disperse as soon as the sun rose, and it would be a day of bright sunshine with visibility stretching to the horizon. He could not be certain how far behind the felucca was the enemy fleet.

He slid down the shrouds so rapidly that the rope scorched his palms, and as his feet hit the deck he shouted his orders to bring the ship about and head her southwards. Tasuz followed in his wake, but rapidly the speed of the felucca narrowed the gap. Within the hour the two ships were close together, and Tasuz shouted his report across to Batula: 'There are at least five large ships coming straight down the channel. There may be others following them. I cannot tell for certain, but I thought I glimpsed beyond them the peaks of other sails just showing over the horizon.'

'When did you last have sight of them?' Batula shouted back.

'At last light yesterday evening.'

'Did they hail you or try to intercept?'

'They paid me no heed. I think they took me for a coastal trader or a fisherman. I did not alter course until darkness hid me from them.'

Tasuz was a good man. Without arousing the suspicions of the enemy, he had been able to slip away from them and warn the two larger ships.

'The mist is beginning to lift, *effendi*,' the lookout called down to the deck, and Batula saw that it was thinning and breaking up. He seized his telescope and clambered back to the main truck. He had hardly settled himself there before the mist rolled aside like a translucent curtain and the morning sun burst through.

Swiftly he swept his lens across the northern horizon.

Beyond the felucca the channel seemed deserted, a wide blue expanse of water. Madagascar was out of sight to the east. Africa was an ethereal blue shadow in the west, and outlined against it he picked out the top sails of the *Sprite* holding her station. They were the only two ships in sight.

'We have run clear away from the enemy during the night.' His heart sang with relief. Then he turned his eye northwards again with more attention and studied the sharp line of the horizon.

'Ah!' he grunted, and then, 'Ah, yes!' He saw the tiny specks of white flash momentarily in the lens like the wings of a gull, then disappear. The leading ships of Zayn's fleet were there, hull down, showing only the very tops of their sails.

He hailed the felucca again. 'Tasuz, go across to the *Sprite* with all speed and recall her. Fire a gun to catch her attention—' He broke off and stared across at the distant schooner. 'No! You need not do it. Kumrah has already seen what we are about. He hastens to join us.'

Perhaps Kumrah had already seen the enemy sails to the north or he might have been alerted by the *Revenge*'s unusual behaviour. Whatever the reason, he had come about and was heading southwards with all sail set.

During the rest of that day the *kaskazi* wind increased in strength until, once more, it was blowing with its customary vigour and the ships were flying on course for Nativity Bay. By noon there was no longer any sight of Zayn's ships on the empty sea they left behind them. By late afternoon Kumrah had steered across on a converging course and the two schooners were in close company, but Tasuz in the felucca was almost out of sight ahead.

Batula watched his lateen sail grow tiny and disappear at last in the dusk. He stooped once more over his chart and made his calculations. 'With this wind Tasuz should reach Nativity Bay in seven more days. It will take us ten, and Zayn will be three or four behind us. We will be able to bring al-Salil fair warning.'

Zayn al-Din sat cross-legged on a bed of cushions and silk prayer mats, which were piled on the lee deck of his flagship under a canvas screen, spread to shelter him from the sun and from the wind and spray that blew back every time the *Sufi* thrust her shoulder into the green swells. The name of the flagship signified the mysticism central to fundamental Islamic thought. She was a ship of force, the most formidable in the entire Omani fleet. Rahmad, the captain who commanded her, had been selected by the Caliph himself for this venture.

Rahmad prostrated himself. 'Majesty, the whaleback that guards the bay in which lies the stronghold of the traitor is in sight.'

Zayn nodded with satisfaction and dismissed him, then turned to Sir Guy Courtney, who sat opposite. 'If Rahmad has brought us directly to our destination without sight of land for twenty days, he has done well. Let us see if it is truly so.' The two stood up and crossed to the weather rail. Rahmad and Laleh bowed respectfully as they approached.

'What do you make of the landfall?' Zayn demanded of Laleh. 'Is this the same bay in which you discovered the ships of al-Salil?'

'Great one, it is the same. This is indeed the lair of al-Salil. From the height of that very headland I looked down upon the bay where he has built his fort and where he anchors his ships.'

With a deep bow, Rahmad handed Zayn his brass telescope. Zayn al-Din balanced easily against the ship's motion. Over the past months his sea-legs had grown strong. He levelled the telescope and studied the distant shore. Then he closed the glass with a snap and smiled. 'We can be certain that our arrival has struck fear into the heart of your traitorous brother and mine. We have not been forced to grope around within sight of the shore to take our bearings. We have given him no warning of our presence and will appear suddenly before him, the deck of my lovely *Arcturus* before this day is done.' While Peters relayed this, Sir Guy had another thought that was almost as poignant. Not only would he recover his ship but his daughter too. Verity would come back to him. Even if she was no longer virgin, sullied and dirtied, no matter. His breath rasped in his throat as he imagined how she must be punished, and how sweet would be the reconciliation that followed. Their previous close and happy state would be restored. She would love him again, as he still loved her.

'Majesty, Muri Kadem's division is heaving to,' Rahmad reported.

Zayn roused himself, and walked back to the stern. This was how he had planned it. Kadem had the five smaller war-dhows under his command and the fifteen troop transports and supply ships. None of the transports was armed: they were merchant vessels Zayn had commandeered for this expedition, crammed with soldiers.

Kadem would lie offshore until the first division entered the bay and attacked the rebel fort. When he heard the guns open up, that would be the signal for him to take in the second division, and to land Koots and his troops in the Umgeni river mouth. When Koots had secured the landing, they could bring in the supply ships that were transporting the horses and land them through the surf. The cavalry would follow the infantry, and mop up any survivors who tried to fly from the doomed fort.

However, the long voyage in the heavy seas of the *kaskazi* had been terribly hard on the horses. They had already lost almost two in every five, and those that had survived were in poor condition. Weak and emaciated, they could still be used to pursue the fugitives. However, it would take many weeks for them to recover fully.

Many of the infantry were in scarcely better condition. The ships were overcrowded and the troops were ravaged by sea-sickness, the half-rotted rations they had to eat, and the water that was thick with green slime. However, Koots would stiffen them up once he had them ashore. Koots could get a corpse

in all our multitudes and power. By now he must know in his heart that at last retribution has found him out.'

'He has had no time to hide his stolen booty,' Sir Guy agreed happily. 'His ships will still be at anchor in the bay, and this wind will hold them landlocked until we attack.'

'What the English *effendi* says is right. The wind is steady out of the east, mighty Caliph.' Rahmad looked up to the huge sail. 'It will bear us in on this single tack. We will be able to enter the mouth of the lagoon before noon.'

'Where is this river Umgeni in which the main force of Pasha Koots will disembark and go ashore?'

'Majesty, it is not plain to see from this distance. There, slightly to the north of the entrance to the bay.' Abruptly Rahmad broke off, and his expression changed. 'There is a ship!' He pointed. It took Zayn a few moments to pick out the fleck of canvas against the background of the land.

'What ship is it?'

'I cannot be certain. A felucca, perhaps. It is small, but that type is fast on the wind. See! It is coming up and escaping out to sea.'

'Can you send one of our ships to capture it?' Zayn asked.

Rahmad looked dubious. 'Majesty, we have no vessel in the fleet fast enough to catch her in a stern chase. She has a lead of many miles. She will be over the horizon in an hour.'

Zayn thought for a moment, and then shook his head. 'It can do us no harm. The lookouts on the bluff must already have given the alarm to the enemy, and the felucca can pose no additional threat even to the smallest of our vessels. Let her go.'

Zayn turned away and looked back at his own ships. 'Make the signal to Muri Kadem ibn Abubaker,' he ordered.

Zayn had divided the fleet into two divisions. He had taken personal command of the first. This comprised the five largest war-dhows, all armed with heavy batteries of cannon.

At every opportunity since leaving Oman, Kadem ibn Abubaker and Koots had come on board the *Sufi* to attend his war councils. Zayn had been able to adjust his plans to take into account every new detail of intelligence they had gathered at all their ports of call along the way. Now, on the eve of battle, there was no need for Zayn to summon his commanders for another meeting. Every man knew in perfect detail what Zayn required of him. Like most good plans it was simple.

Zayn's first division would sail directly into Nativity Bay, and fall upon the enemy ships they found anchored there. With their superior numbers and firepower, and the advantage of surprise, they would engage them at close range and overpower them swiftly. Then all their guns would be turned upon the fort. In the meantime Kadem would land the infantry in the river mouth and Koots would march them swiftly round to attack the fort from the rear. As soon as Koots launched his attack, Sir Guy would lead a second landing party from the ships in the bay to support him. He had volunteered for this duty: he wanted to be there when the attackers broke into the treasury under the fort where his fifteen chests of gold bars were stored. He wanted to protect his property from looting.

There was one possible flaw in this plan. Would the rebel ships be in the bay? Zayn had not jumped to a hasty conclusion. He had gathered all the intelligence from his spies in every port and harbour in the Ocean of the Indies, including Ceylon and the Red Sea. Not one had been able to report a sighting of al-Salil's ships during the many months since his capture of the *Arcturus*. It seemed that they had vanished without trace.

'They could not have disappeared from the sight of so many eyes,' Zayn reasoned. 'They are hiding, and there is only one place for them to hide.' He wanted to believe this, but doubt itched like a flea in his undershirt. He wanted a final assurance. 'Send for the holy mullah. We shall ask him to pray for guidance. Then I will ask Kadem ibn Abubaker for a sign.' Mullah Khaliq was a saint of vast sanctity and power. His prayers had been a shield to Zayn over the years, and his faith had lit the way to victory in some of his darkest hours.

Kadem ibn Abubaker had the gift of prophecy, one of the reasons that Zayn al-Din valued him so highly. He relied on the revelations that sprang from him.

In the great cabin of the *Sufi*, the three, calip
admiral, prayed together through that long ni
expression was rapt, his single eye glittering, as he
most holy texts in his nasal, singsong voice.

While he listened and made the responses, K
Abubaker felt himself falling into that familiar dreaml
He knew that the angel of God was near. Just before
dawn he fell into a sudden, heavy sleep, and the ange
to him. Gabriel lifted him out of his body and bore him
white, rustling wings to a high place, a mountain shape
the back of a whale.

The angel pointed down and his voice echoed weirdly
Kadem's head: 'Behold, the ships are in the bay!'

They floated on a circle of bright waters, and on the dec
of the largest stood a tall, familiar figure. When Kade
recognized al-Salil, the hatred flowed through his veins li
poison. Al-Salil raised his bare head and looked up at him;
hair and his beard were red gold.

'I shall destroy you!' Kadem shouted down at him, an
he said the words al-Salil's head burst into flame, and bur
like a torch. The flame leaped up into the rigging, and sp
swiftly, consuming everything, man and ships. The wate
the bay boiled, the steam rose in a great cloud and blotte
the dream.

Kadem woke with a deep sense of religious joy, and
himself once more in the great cabin with Zayn al-Di
Khaliq watching him for the sign.

'My uncle, I have seen the ships,' he told his caliph
angel has shown them to me. They are in the bay an
shall be destroyed by fire.'

After that Zayn had no more doubts. The angel
deliver his enemy to him. Now he looked across the
flecked sea at the distant mountain.

'Al-Salil is here. I can smell him in the wind, an
him in my mouth,' he muttered. 'I have waited a lifet
this moment.'

Peter Peters translated his words and Sir Guy a
once. 'I have the same conviction. I shall stand once

to stand up and fight until it was killed again. Zayn smiled wolfishly.

They left the second division hove-to and Zayn's division forged ahead, straight for the entrance to the bay. As they closed in under the brooding height of the bluff, Zayn could pick out the calmer water of the channel. On either side of it the white surf broke, lashed into a fury by the onshore wind.

'They cannot escape us,' he gloated. 'Even if they spot us now, it will be too late for them.'

'I long for sight of my *Arcturus*.' Sir Guy stared ahead eagerly. Verity might still be aboard. He imagined her lying on her bunk in the beautifully decorated cabin, her long hair trailing over her shoulders and her soft white bosom.

'May I beat to quarters, my caliph?' Rahmad asked respectfully.

'Do so!' Zayn nodded. 'Run out the guns. By now the enemy must have seen us. They will be waiting for us in their ships and on the parapets of the fort.'

With all her great cannon loaded, and the gun crews crouching behind them, the *Sufi* led the line of warships up the centre of the channel. Laleh was the pilot, for he was the only one aboard who knew the channel well. He stood beside the helmsman at the wheel and listened to the chant of the man in the bows who was calling the soundings. The bulk of the bluff towered at their left hand, and on their right spread the jungle and mangroves of the littoral. Laleh judged the turn in the channel and gave the order to the helm.

The *Sufi* slatted her canvas, then filled it again with a subdued thunder, and they were round the rump of the bluff. But their speed through the water was scarcely diminished. Zayn stared ahead eagerly: he seemed to snuffle the air like a hunting dog hard on the heels of his quarry. Before them opened the wide sweep of the inner waters of the bay. Slowly Zayn's warlike glare faded and was replaced by an expression of disbelief. The vision that the angel had shown Kadem could not have been false.

'They are gone!' Sir Guy whispered.

701

The waters of the bay were empty. There was not even a fishing-boat at anchor in its whole wide expanse. The silence was ominous.

Still the line of five ships tore on, straight towards the walls of the fort on which the muzzles of the enemy guns stared at them blankly from a mile away. Zayn fought off the sense of foreboding that threatened to debilitate him. The angel had shown Kadem a vision, yet the ships were gone. He closed his eyes and prayed aloud: 'Hear me, Holiest of All. I pray you, great Gabriel, answer me.' Both Sir Guy and Rahmad looked at him strangely. 'Where are the ships?'

'In the bay!' He heard the voice reverberate in his head, but there was a sly, sardonic tone to it. 'The ships that shall burn are already in the bay.'

Zayn looked back, and saw that the fifth and last of his war-dhows was coming through the deep-water channel into the bay.

'You are not Gabriel,' Zayn blurted. 'You are the *shaitan* Iblis, the Fallen One. You have lied to us.' Rahmad stared at him in astonishment. 'You showed us our own fleet,' Zayn cried out. 'You have led us into a trap. You are not Gabriel. You are the Black Angel.'

'Nay, great caliph,' Rahmad protested. 'I am the most loyal of all your subjects. I would never think to lead you into a trap.'

Zayn stared at him. Rahmad's consternation was so comical that he was forced to laugh, but it was a bitter sound. 'Not you, you poor fool. Another more cunning than you.'

A single cannon shot boomed out across the waters of the bay, and forced Zayn's attention back to the present. Powder smoke rolled from the parapet of the fort and the ball struck the water and ricocheted across the surface of the bay. It crashed into the hull of the *Sufi* and there was a scream of agony from the lower decks.

'Anchor the fleet in line and open fire on the fort,' Zayn ordered. He felt a sense of relief that at last the battle had begun.

As each of the war-dhows dropped anchor and took in its

canvas, it rounded up to the wind, and turned its starboard battery on the fort. One after another they opened the bombardment and the heavy stone balls kicked showers of dust and loose earth from the glacis, or smashed into the log walls. It was immediately obvious that the fortifications could not withstand such furious fire for long. The timbers shattered and burst open to each massive impact.

'I had been made to believe that it was an impregnable fortress,' Sir Guy watched the effects of the bombardment with grim satisfaction, 'but those walls will be down before nightfall. Peters, tell the caliph that I must assemble the assault party at once to be ready to go ashore as soon as the fort is breached.'

'The traitor's defence is pathetically inadequate.' Zayn had to shout above the crash and thunder of the guns. 'I can see only two cannon returning our fire.'

'There!' Sir Guy shouted back. 'One of their guns has been hit.' Both men focused their glasses on the gaping hole that had been blown in the parapet of log poles. They could see that the gun carriage had been overturned, and the broken body of one of the enemy gunners was hanging like beef on a butcher's hook from the splintered stumps.

'Sweet Name of Allah!' Rahmad shouted. 'They are deserting the fort. They have given up. They are running for their very lives.'

The gates of the fort were dragged open and out rushed a panic-stricken mob. They scattered into the jungle, leaving the gates wide, the parapet deserted. The enemy guns fell silent as the last gunner fled his post.

'At once!' Zayn turned to Sir Guy. 'Take your battalion ashore and storm the fort.'

The enemy's capitulation had taken them all by surprise. Zayn had expected them to put up a more determined resistance. Valuable time was wasted while the boats were launched, and the assault party scrambled down into them.

Guy stood impatiently at the head of the gangway, shouting orders at the detachment of men he had chosen as his own. They were all hard men: he had seen them at work and they were like a pack of hunting dogs. Added to that, many of them understood and even spoke a little English. 'Come, waste no more time! Your enemy is getting clean away from you. Every minute and your booty is being taken.'

They understood that, and for those who did not Peters repeated it in Arabic. From somewhere Peters had found a sword and pistol and they were belted around his skinny waist, sagging so that the point of the scabbard dragged on the deck, and his jacket was pulled out of shape. He cut an absurd figure.

The bombardment raged on without pause, and the great stone balls crashed mercilessly into the ruined walls of the fort. The last few defenders fled back into the forest, and the building was deserted. But at last all the boats were loaded and Guy and Peters scrambled down into the largest.

'Pull!' Guy shouted. 'Straight for the beach.' He was desperate to reach the treasury, and his gold chests. As soon as they were half-way across, the ships ceased firing for fear of hitting them. A heavy silence fell over the bay, while the small boats streamed towards the beach. Guy's longboat was first to reach it. As the bows touched the sand he leaped out and waded ashore.

'Come on!' he yelled. 'Follow me!' With the information they had wrung out of Omar, the prisoner captured by Laleh, he had been able to draw up a detailed map of the interior of the fort. He knew exactly where he was going.

As soon as they were through the open gates, he sent men up to the parapets to secure the walls, and others to search the buildings to make sure none of the enemy remained. Then he hurried to the powder magazine. The defenders might have placed a time fuse to blow it up. Four of the men with him carried heavy crow-bars and prised the door off its hinges. The magazine was empty. This should have been a warning to Guy, but he could think of nothing but the gold. He ran to the main building. The staircase that led down to the strongrooms was concealed behind the fireplace in the kitchens. It was cunningly built and even though he knew it was there it took him some time to find it. Then he kicked open the door and went down the circular staircase. An iron grating set in the arched ceiling let in a little light, and he stopped in astonishment at the foot of the stairs. The long low room ahead of him was filled to the roof with neatly stacked ivory.

'The devil take me, but Koots was right! There's tons of the stuff here. If they abandoned such a wealth of ivory, then did they also leave my gold?'

Omar had explained how Tom Courtney had used the ivory to conceal the door to the inner strongroom. But Guy would not rush ahead blindly: before going further he waited for one of his captains to come down the stairwell and report to him. The man was panting with exertion and excitement, but there was no blood on his clothing or the blade of his weapon. 'Ask him if they have secured the fort,' Guy ordered, but the man knew enough English to understand the question.

'All gone, *effendi*. Nothing! No man or dog left inside the walls.'

'Good!' Guy nodded. 'Now get twenty of the men down here to clear the ivory from the right-hand wall of this chamber.'

The most massive tusks had been used to cover the entrance to the inner strongroom and it took almost two hours of hard work to reveal the small iron door, and another hour to batter it open.

As the door toppled out of its frame and crashed to the stone floor in a dense cloud of dust, Guy stepped forward and peered into the room. As the dust settled the interior was revealed. With a stab of angry disappointment he saw that the room was bare.

No, not quite bare. A sheet of parchment was nailed to the far wall. The writing on it was in a distinctive bold hand, which he recognized immediately, even after nearly two decades. Guy tore down the sheet and scanned it swiftly. His face darkened and twisted with fury.

RECEIPT FOR GOODS

I, the undersigned, gratefully acknowledge fair
receipt of the following goods from Sir Guy Courtney:
15 Chests of Fine Gold bars.
Signed on behalf of Courtney Brothers Trading
Company at Nativity Bay this 15th day of November in
the year 1738,
Thomas Courtney esq

Guy crumpled the sheet in his fist and hurled it at the wall. 'God rot your thieving soul, Tom Courtney,' he said, quivering with fury. 'You dare to mock me? You shall find the interest that I will collect from you to be far from any joke.'

He stormed back up the stairs and climbed to the parapet overlooking the bay.

The flotilla of dhows still rode at anchor. He saw that they were unloading the horses, lifting them out of the holds, swinging them overside then lowering them to the water and turning them loose to swim to the beach. A considerable herd was already ashore, and the grooms were tending them.

He saw Zayn al-Din standing by the rail of the *Sufi*. Guy knew he should go back aboard to report to him, but first he had to control his anger and frustration. 'No *Arcturus*, no Verity and, more important still, no gold. Where have you hidden with my gold, Tom Courtney, you bitch-born lecher? Was it not enough that you rutted on the belly of my wife, and saddled me with your bastard? Now you rob me of what is rightfully mine.'

He looked down from the parapet and his eyes followed the wagon track that ran out through the open gates of the fort and immediately forked. One track ran down to the beach, the other turned inland. It wound its way through patches of denser forest and swamp and, convoluted as a

706

scotched serpent, climbed the far hills to vanish over the crest.

'Wagons!' Guy whispered. 'You would need wagons to carry away fifteen lakhs of gold.' He rounded on Peters. 'Tell these men to follow me.' He led them at a run through the gates of the fort, and down to the head of the landing where the horses stood. The grooms were unloading the saddlery from the boats.

'Tell them I will need twenty horses,' he told Peters, 'and I will pick the men I want to go with me.' He hurried among them and slapped each of those he chose on the shoulder. They were all heavily armed and carried extra powder flasks. 'Tell them to fetch saddles from the boats.'

When the head groom realized that Sir Guy intended to take the best of his horses, he shouted a protest into his face. Guy tried to push him away, shouting back at him in English, but the man grabbed his arm and shook it violently, still protesting. 'I've no time to argue,' Guy said, drew the pistol from his belt and cocked the hammer. He thrust the muzzle into the groom's startled face and fired into his open mouth. The man collapsed. Guy stepped over his twitching corpse and ran to the horse that one of his men was holding ready for him.

'Mount!' he shouted, and Peters and twenty Arabs followed his example. He led them off the beach, along the wagon trail, heading into the hills and the hinterland. 'Hear me, Tom Courtney,' he said, 'and hear me well! I am coming to retrieve my stolen gold. Nothing that you or anyone else can do will stop me.'

From the quarter-deck of the *Sufi*, Zayn al-Din watched with anticipation as Sir Guy led his men into the deserted fort. There was no sound of fighting, and no further sight of the fugitives who had escaped from the fort. He waited impatiently for a report from Sir Guy as to what was taking place within the walls. After an hour he had to send a man ashore to enquire. He returned with a message. 'Mighty Caliph, the

English *effendi* has discovered that the fort has been stripped of all furniture and stores except much ivory. There is a hidden door in the cellars below the building. His men are forcing it open, but it is of iron and very strong.'

An hour passed during which Zayn ordered the horses to be sent ashore. Then, suddenly, Sir Guy appeared on the parapet of the fort. Zayn could tell at once from his demeanour that he had been unsuccessful. Then, abruptly, Sir Guy seemed to become galvanized. He rushed out of the fort followed by most of his detachment. Zayn expected him to come back to report to him and was puzzled when he did not, but then Sir Guy's men began to saddle most of the horses. There was a scuffle on the beach and a pistol shot rang out. Zayn saw a body lying on the sand. To his astonishment, Sir Guy and most of his men mounted and rode up from the water's edge then out along the wagon road.

'Stop them!' he snapped at Rahmad. 'Send a messenger ashore immediately to order those men to return.' Rahmad shouted to his boatswain, but before he could give the man his instructions Sir Guy's desertion became irrelevant.

A cannon shot startled them all. The echoes duplicated themselves along the cliffs of the bluff. Zayn jerked round and stared across the waters of the bay to where smoke still hung in the air. A hidden cannon had fired upon them from the tangle of dense vegetation that covered the slope of the bluff. He could not see the weapon, even though he searched through the lens of his spyglass. It was too cunningly concealed, probably in some deep emplacement dug into the hillside.

Then, suddenly, his view through the glass was momentarily obscured by a tall spout of water that leaped up directly in front of him. He dropped the glass to see that a cannon-ball had struck close alongside the anchored *Sufi*. As he stared, a strange phenomenon took place before his eyes. In the centre of the spreading ripples where the enemy cannon-ball had sunk, the shallow water began to seethe and boil, like a kettle, and steam rose in a dense cloud from the surface. For a long moment Zayn was at a loss to explain it. Then it came in all our multitudes and power. By now he must know in his heart that at last retribution has found him out.'

'He has had no time to hide his stolen booty,' Sir Guy agreed happily. 'His ships will still be at anchor in the bay, and this wind will hold them landlocked until we attack.'

'What the English *effendi* says is right. The wind is steady out of the east, mighty Caliph.' Rahmad looked up to the huge sail. 'It will bear us in on this single tack. We will be able to enter the mouth of the lagoon before noon.'

'Where is this river Umgeni in which the main force of Pasha Koots will disembark and go ashore?'

'Majesty, it is not plain to see from this distance. There, slightly to the north of the entrance to the bay.' Abruptly Rahmad broke off, and his expression changed. 'There is a ship!' He pointed. It took Zayn a few moments to pick out the fleck of canvas against the background of the land.

'What ship is it?'

'I cannot be certain. A felucca, perhaps. It is small, but that type is fast on the wind. See! It is coming up and escaping out to sea.'

'Can you send one of our ships to capture it?' Zayn asked.

Rahmad looked dubious. 'Majesty, we have no vessel in the fleet fast enough to catch her in a stern chase. She has a lead of many miles. She will be over the horizon in an hour.'

Zayn thought for a moment, and then shook his head. 'It can do us no harm. The lookouts on the bluff must already have given the alarm to the enemy, and the felucca can pose no additional threat even to the smallest of our vessels. Let her go.'

Zayn turned away and looked back at his own ships. 'Make the signal to Muri Kadem ibn Abubaker,' he ordered.

Zayn had divided the fleet into two divisions. He had taken personal command of the first. This comprised the five largest war-dhows, all armed with heavy batteries of cannon.

At every opportunity since leaving Oman, Kadem ibn Abubaker and Koots had come on board the *Sufi* to attend his war councils. Zayn had been able to adjust his plans to take into account every new detail of intelligence they had

In the great cabin of the *Sufi*, the three, caliph, mullah and admiral, prayed together through that long night. Khaliq's expression was rapt, his single eye glittering, as he recited the most holy texts in his nasal, singsong voice.

While he listened and made the responses, Kadem ibn Abubaker felt himself falling into that familiar dreamlike state. He knew that the angel of God was near. Just before break of dawn he fell into a sudden, heavy sleep, and the angel came to him. Gabriel lifted him out of his body and bore him up on white, rustling wings to a high place, a mountain shaped like the back of a whale.

The angel pointed down and his voice echoed weirdly in Kadem's head: 'Behold, the ships are in the bay!'

They floated on a circle of bright waters, and on the deck of the largest stood a tall, familiar figure. When Kadem recognized al-Salil, the hatred flowed through his veins like poison. Al-Salil raised his bare head and looked up at him; his hair and his beard were red gold.

'I shall destroy you!' Kadem shouted down at him, and as he said the words al-Salil's head burst into flame, and burned like a torch. The flame leaped up into the rigging, and spread swiftly, consuming everything, man and ships. The waters of the bay boiled, the steam rose in a great cloud and blotted out the dream.

Kadem woke with a deep sense of religious joy, and found himself once more in the great cabin with Zayn al-Din and Khaliq watching him for the sign.

'My uncle, I have seen the ships,' he told his caliph. 'The angel has shown them to me. They are in the bay and they shall be destroyed by fire.'

After that Zayn had no more doubts. The angel would deliver his enemy to him. Now he looked across the white flecked sea at the distant mountain.

'Al-Salil is here. I can smell him in the wind, and taste him in my mouth,' he muttered. 'I have waited a lifetime for this moment.'

Peter Peters translated his words and Sir Guy agreed at once. 'I have the same conviction. I shall stand once more on the deck of my lovely *Arcturus* before this day is done.' While Peters relayed this, Sir Guy had another thought that was almost as poignant. Not only would he recover his ship but his daughter too. Verity would come back to him. Even if she was no longer virgin, sullied and dirtied, no matter. His breath rasped in his throat as he imagined how she must be punished, and how sweet would be the reconciliation that followed. Their previous close and happy state would be restored. She would love him again, as he still loved her.

'Majesty, Muri Kadem's division is heaving to,' Rahmad reported.

Zayn roused himself, and walked back to the stern. This was how he had planned it. Kadem had the five smaller wardhows under his command and the fifteen troop transports and supply ships. None of the transports was armed: they were merchant vessels Zayn had commandeered for this expedition, crammed with soldiers.

Kadem would lie offshore until the first division entered the bay and attacked the rebel fort. When he heard the guns open up, that would be the signal for him to take in the second division, and to land Koots and his troops in the Umgeni river mouth. When Koots had secured the landing, they could bring in the supply ships that were transporting the horses and land them through the surf. The cavalry would follow the infantry, and mop up any survivors who tried to fly from the doomed fort.

However, the long voyage in the heavy seas of the *kaskazi* had been terribly hard on the horses. They had already lost almost two in every five, and those that had survived were in poor condition. Weak and emaciated, they could still be used to pursue the fugitives. However, it would take many weeks for them to recover fully.

Many of the infantry were in scarcely better condition. The ships were overcrowded and the troops were ravaged by seasickness, the half-rotted rations they had to eat, and the water that was thick with green slime. However, Koots would stiffen them up once he had them ashore. Koots could get a corpse to stand up and fight until it was killed again. Zayn smiled wolfishly.

They left the second division hove-to and Zayn's division forged ahead, straight for the entrance to the bay. As they closed in under the brooding height of the bluff, Zayn could pick out the calmer water of the channel. On either side of it the white surf broke, lashed into a fury by the onshore wind.

'They cannot escape us,' he gloated. 'Even if they spot us now, it will be too late for them.'

'I long for sight of my *Arcturus*.' Sir Guy stared ahead eagerly. Verity might still be aboard. He imagined her lying on her bunk in the beautifully decorated cabin, her long hair trailing over her shoulders and her soft white bosom.

'May I beat to quarters, my caliph?' Rahmad asked respectfully.

'Do so!' Zayn nodded. 'Run out the guns. By now the enemy must have seen us. They will be waiting for us in their ships and on the parapets of the fort.'

With all her great cannon loaded, and the gun crews crouching behind them, the *Sufi* led the line of warships up the centre of the channel. Laleh was the pilot, for he was the only one aboard who knew the channel well. He stood beside the helmsman at the wheel and listened to the chant of the man in the bows who was calling the soundings. The bulk of the bluff towered at their left hand, and on their right spread the jungle and mangroves of the littoral. Laleh judged the turn in the channel and gave the order to the helm.

The *Sufi* slatted her canvas, then filled it again with a subdued thunder, and they were round the rump of the bluff. But their speed through the water was scarcely diminished. Zayn stared ahead eagerly: he seemed to snuffle the air like a hunting dog hard on the heels of his quarry. Before them opened the wide sweep of the inner waters of the bay. Slowly Zayn's warlike glare faded and was replaced by an expression of disbelief. The vision that the angel had shown Kadem could not have been false.

'They are gone!' Sir Guy whispered.

701

The waters of the bay were empty. There was not even a fishing-boat at anchor in its whole wide expanse. The silence was ominous.

Still the line of five ships tore on, straight towards the walls of the fort on which the muzzles of the enemy guns stared at them blankly from a mile away. Zayn fought off the sense of foreboding that threatened to debilitate him. The angel had shown Kadem a vision, yet the ships were gone. He closed his eyes and prayed aloud: 'Hear me, Holiest of All. I pray you, great Gabriel, answer me.' Both Sir Guy and Rahmad looked at him strangely. 'Where are the ships?'

'In the bay!' He heard the voice reverberate in his head, but there was a sly, sardonic tone to it. 'The ships that shall burn are already in the bay.'

Zayn looked back, and saw that the fifth and last of his war-dhows was coming through the deep-water channel into the bay.

'You are not Gabriel,' Zayn blurted. 'You are the *shaitan* Iblis, the Fallen One. You have lied to us.' Rahmad stared at him in astonishment. 'You showed us our own fleet,' Zayn cried out. 'You have led us into a trap. You are not Gabriel. You are the Black Angel.'

'Nay, great caliph,' Rahmad protested. 'I am the most loyal of all your subjects. I would never think to lead you into a trap.'

Zayn stared at him. Rahmad's consternation was so comical that he was forced to laugh, but it was a bitter sound. 'Not you, you poor fool. Another more cunning than you.'

A single cannon shot boomed out across the waters of the bay, and forced Zayn's attention back to the present. Powder smoke rolled from the parapet of the fort and the ball struck the water and ricocheted across the surface of the bay. It crashed into the hull of the *Sufi* and there was a scream of agony from the lower decks.

'Anchor the fleet in line and open fire on the fort,' Zayn ordered. He felt a sense of relief that at last the battle had begun.

As each of the war-dhows dropped anchor and took in its

702

canvas, it rounded up to the wind, and turned its starboard battery on the fort. One after another they opened the bombardment and the heavy stone balls kicked showers of dust and loose earth from the glacis, or smashed into the log walls. It was immediately obvious that the fortifications could not withstand such furious fire for long. The timbers shattered and burst open to each massive impact.

'I had been made to believe that it was an impregnable fortress,' Sir Guy watched the effects of the bombardment with grim satisfaction, 'but those walls will be down before nightfall. Peters, tell the caliph that I must assemble the assault party at once to be ready to go ashore as soon as the fort is breached.'

'The traitor's defence is pathetically inadequate.' Zayn had to shout above the crash and thunder of the guns. 'I can see only two cannon returning our fire.'

'There!' Sir Guy shouted back. 'One of their guns has been hit.' Both men focused their glasses on the gaping hole that had been blown in the parapet of log poles. They could see that the gun carriage had been overturned, and the broken body of one of the enemy gunners was hanging like beef on a butcher's hook from the splintered stumps.

'Sweet Name of Allah!' Rahmad shouted. 'They are deserting the fort. They have given up. They are running for their very lives.'

The gates of the fort were dragged open and out rushed a panic-stricken mob. They scattered into the jungle, leaving the gates wide, the parapet deserted. The enemy guns fell silent as the last gunner fled his post.

'At once!' Zayn turned to Sir Guy. 'Take your battalion ashore and storm the fort.'

The enemy's capitulation had taken them all by surprise. Zayn had expected them to put up a more determined resistance. Valuable time was wasted while the boats were launched, and the assault party scrambled down into them.

703

Guy stood impatiently at the head of the gangway, shouting orders at the detachment of men he had chosen as his own. They were all hard men: he had seen them at work and they were like a pack of hunting dogs. Added to that, many of them understood and even spoke a little English. 'Come, waste no more time! Your enemy is getting clean away from you. Every minute and your booty is being taken.'

They understood that, and for those who did not Peters repeated it in Arabic. From somewhere Peters had found a sword and pistol and they were belted around his skinny waist, sagging so that the point of the scabbard dragged on the deck, and his jacket was pulled out of shape. He cut an absurd figure.

The bombardment raged on without pause, and the great stone balls crashed mercilessly into the ruined walls of the fort. The last few defenders fled back into the forest, and the building was deserted. But at last all the boats were loaded and Guy and Peters scrambled down into the largest.

'Pull!' Guy shouted. 'Straight for the beach.' He was desperate to reach the treasury, and his gold chests. As soon as they were half-way across, the ships ceased firing for fear of hitting them. A heavy silence fell over the bay, while the small boats streamed towards the beach. Guy's longboat was first to reach it. As the bows touched the sand he leaped out and waded ashore.

'Come on!' he yelled. 'Follow me!' With the information they had wrung out of Omar, the prisoner captured by Laleh, he had been able to draw up a detailed map of the interior of the fort. He knew exactly where he was going.

As soon as they were through the open gates, he sent men up to the parapets to secure the walls, and others to search the buildings to make sure none of the enemy remained. Then he hurried to the powder magazine. The defenders might have placed a time fuse to blow it up. Four of the men with him carried heavy crow-bars and prised the door off its hinges. The magazine was empty. This should have been a warning to Guy, but he could think of nothing but the gold. He ran to the main building. The staircase that led down to the strongrooms was concealed behind the fireplace in the kitchens. It was cunningly built and even though he knew it was there it took him some time to find it. Then he kicked open the door and went down the circular staircase. An iron grating set in the arched ceiling let in a little light, and he stopped in astonishment at the foot of the stairs. The long low room ahead of him was filled to the roof with neatly stacked ivory.

'The devil take me, but Koots was right! There's tons of the stuff here. If they abandoned such a wealth of ivory, then did they also leave my gold?'

Omar had explained how Tom Courtney had used the ivory to conceal the door to the inner strongroom. But Guy would not rush ahead blindly: before going further he waited for one of his captains to come down the stairwell and report to him. The man was panting with exertion and excitement, but there was no blood on his clothing or the blade of his weapon. 'Ask him if they have secured the fort,' Guy ordered, but the man knew enough English to understand the question.

'All gone, *effendi*. Nothing! No man or dog left inside the walls.'

'Good!' Guy nodded. 'Now get twenty of the men down here to clear the ivory from the right-hand wall of this chamber.'

The most massive tusks had been used to cover the entrance to the inner strongroom and it took almost two hours of hard work to reveal the small iron door, and another hour to batter it open.

As the door toppled out of its frame and crashed to the stone floor in a dense cloud of dust, Guy stepped forward and peered into the room. As the dust settled the interior was revealed. With a stab of angry disappointment he saw that the room was bare.

No, not quite bare. A sheet of parchment was nailed to the far wall. The writing on it was in a distinctive bold hand, which he recognized immediately, even after nearly two decades. Guy tore down the sheet and scanned it swiftly. His face darkened and twisted with fury.

RECEIPT FOR GOODS

I, the undersigned, gratefully acknowledge fair receipt of the following goods from Sir Guy Courtney:
15 Chests of Fine Gold bars.
Signed on behalf of Courtney Brothers Trading Company at Nativity Bay this 15th day of November in the year 1738,
Thomas Courtney esq

Guy crumpled the sheet in his fist and hurled it at the wall. 'God rot your thieving soul, Tom Courtney,' he said, quivering with fury. 'You dare to mock me? You shall find the interest that I will collect from you to be far from any joke.'

He stormed back up the stairs and climbed to the parapet overlooking the bay.

The flotilla of dhows still rode at anchor. He saw that they were unloading the horses, lifting them out of the holds, swinging them overside then lowering them to the water and turning them loose to swim to the beach. A considerable herd was already ashore, and the grooms were tending them.

He saw Zayn al-Din standing by the rail of the *Sufi*. Guy knew he should go back aboard to report to him, but first he had to control his anger and frustration. 'No *Arcturus*, no Verity and, more important still, no gold. Where have you hidden with my gold, Tom Courtney, you bitch-born lecher? Was it not enough that you rutted on the belly of my wife, and saddled me with your bastard? Now you rob me of what is rightfully mine.'

He looked down from the parapet and his eyes followed the wagon track that ran out through the open gates of the fort and immediately forked. One track ran down to the beach, the other turned inland. It wound its way through patches of denser forest and swamp and, convoluted as a scotched serpent, climbed the far hills to vanish over the crest.

'Wagons!' Guy whispered. 'You would need wagons to carry away fifteen lakhs of gold.' He rounded on Peters. 'Tell these men to follow me.' He led them at a run through the gates of the fort, and down to the head of the landing where the horses stood. The grooms were unloading the saddlery from the boats.

'Tell them I will need twenty horses,' he told Peters, 'and I will pick the men I want to go with me.' He hurried among them and slapped each of those he chose on the shoulder. They were all heavily armed and carried extra powder flasks. 'Tell them to fetch saddles from the boats.'

When the head groom realized that Sir Guy intended to take the best of his horses, he shouted a protest into his face. Guy tried to push him away, shouting back at him in English, but the man grabbed his arm and shook it violently, still protesting. 'I've no time to argue,' Guy said, drew the pistol from his belt and cocked the hammer. He thrust the muzzle into the groom's startled face and fired into his open mouth. The man collapsed. Guy stepped over his twitching corpse and ran to the horse that one of his men was holding ready for him.

'Mount!' he shouted, and Peters and twenty Arabs followed his example. He led them off the beach, along the wagon trail, heading into the hills and the hinterland. 'Hear me, Tom Courtney,' he said, 'and hear me well! I am coming to retrieve my stolen gold. Nothing that you or anyone else can do will stop me.'

From the quarter-deck of the *Sufi*, Zayn al-Din watched with anticipation as Sir Guy led his men into the deserted fort. There was no sound of fighting, and no further sight of the fugitives who had escaped from the fort. He waited impatiently for a report from Sir Guy as to what was taking place within the walls. After an hour he had to send a man ashore to enquire. He returned with a message. 'Mighty Caliph, the

English *effendi* has discovered that the fort has been stripped of all furniture and stores except much ivory. There is a hidden door in the cellars below the building. His men are forcing it open, but it is of iron and very strong.'

An hour passed during which Zayn ordered the horses to be sent ashore. Then, suddenly, Sir Guy appeared on the parapet of the fort. Zayn could tell at once from his demeanour that he had been unsuccessful. Then, abruptly, Sir Guy seemed to become galvanized. He rushed out of the fort followed by most of his detachment. Zayn expected him to come back to report to him and was puzzled when he did not, but then Sir Guy's men began to saddle most of the horses. There was a scuffle on the beach and a pistol shot rang out. Zayn saw a body lying on the sand. To his astonishment, Sir Guy and most of his men mounted and rode up from the water's edge then out along the wagon road.

'Stop them!' he snapped at Rahmad. 'Send a messenger ashore immediately to order those men to return.' Rahmad shouted to his boatswain, but before he could give the man his instructions Sir Guy's desertion became irrelevant.

A cannon shot startled them all. The echoes duplicated themselves along the cliffs of the bluff. Zayn jerked round and stared across the waters of the bay to where smoke still hung in the air. A hidden cannon had fired upon them from the tangle of dense vegetation that covered the slope of the bluff. He could not see the weapon, even though he searched through the lens of his spyglass. It was too cunningly concealed, probably in some deep emplacement dug into the hillside.

Then, suddenly, his view through the glass was momentarily obscured by a tall spout of water that leaped up directly in front of him. He dropped the glass to see that a cannonball had struck close alongside the anchored *Sufi*. As he stared, a strange phenomenon took place before his eyes. In the centre of the spreading ripples where the enemy cannon-ball had sunk, the shallow water began to seethe and boil, like a kettle, and steam rose in a dense cloud from the surface. For a long moment Zayn was at a loss to explain it. Then it came to him in a dread flash. 'Red-hot shot! The pork-eaters are firing heated shot!' He trained his glass on the hillside where the smoke still drifted. Now that he was searching for it, he saw a shimmering column of heated air rising into the sky, like a desert mirage. There was no visible smoke. He knew what that meant.

'Charcoal furnaces!' he exclaimed. 'Rahmad, we must get our ships out to sea at once. This is a terrible trap we are in. The entire flotilla will be in flames within the hour unless we can clear the bay at once.'

In a wooden ship, fire was the most terrifying hazard. Rahmad shouted his orders, but before they could get the anchor aboard, another red-hot iron ball hurtled down towards them from the heights of the bluff. It left a trail of sizzling sparks behind it and struck the last dhow in the line of anchored ships. It plunged through her maindeck deep into her hull, shedding splinters of red-hot iron in its path which buried themselves deep in the dry planking. Almost immediately they began to smoulder. Then the air reached them. With miraculous rapidity dozens of fires blossomed in the hull, and spread swiftly.

On board the *Sufi* all was pandemonium as men rushed to the pumps and the anchor capstan, and still others clambered aloft to set the sails. The anchor broke out of the sandy bottom, Rahmad set his lateen sail and the ship came round slowly towards the exit from the bay. Then a hail rang out from the lookout at the *Sufi*'s masthead. It was wild and incoherent. 'Deck below! In the Name of Allah! Beware, it is the curse of *shaitan*.'

Zayn looked up, and his voice was shrill with anger as he shouted, 'What have you seen? Make your report clear, you imbecile.' But the man was still jabbering, and pointing over the bows towards the exit channel from the bay.

Every man on deck followed the direction of his out-thrust arm. A groan of superstitious terror went up from them. 'A sea monster! The great snake from the depths that devours ships and men!' screamed a voice, and men dropped to their knees to pray, or simply stared in mute terror at the ophidian creature that uncoiled from one side of the channel. Its massive body seemed to undulate in endless humps as it swam through the water towards the far bank.

'It will attack us!' Rahmad shouted in terror. 'Kill it! Shoot it! Open fire!'

The gun-crews scrambled to their cannons, and the guns roared out from every ship in the squadron. Smoke and flame flew in sheets. Tall columns of seawater sprang up in a forest around the swimming monster. In such a storm of shot some of the balls struck home. Clearly they heard the crack of impact. However, the creature swam on without any sign that it was injured. The head reached the far shore but the long serpentine body stretched from one bank of the channel to the other and bobbed and rolled in the flow and push of the current. The cannon-balls fell about it like hail. Some glanced off the surface and ricocheted out to sea.

Zayn was the first man aboard to recover his wits. He ran to the near rail and stared at the thing through the lens of his telescope. Then he shrieked, in his high, penetrating voice, 'Cease fire! Stop this madness!' The bombardment petered out.

Rahmad ran to his caliph's side. 'What is it, Majesty?'

'The enemy have drawn a boom across the mouth of the bay. We are bottled in here like pickled fish in a tub.'

As he spoke another heated shot came flying from high on the slope of the bluff, glowing sparks snapping and popping in the air behind it. It plunged into the water only feet from their stern. Zayn looked about him. The first ship that had been hit was burning furiously. Even as he watched its great lateen sail caught fire and the flames engulfed it swiftly. The canvas collapsed over the deck trapping shrieking men under its weight, and incinerating them like insects in the flue of an oil lamp. Without the push of its sail, the vessel started a slow and aimless turn across the bay until it struck the beach and heeled over steeply. The surviving men of the crew sprang over the side and splashed and crawled ashore.

Yet another heated shot came swooping towards the *Sufi* in a smoking parabola. It passed only feet from their mainmast, then flew on to smash into the other war-dhow that sailed beside them. Almost at once her deck split open and tall flames burst out through her timbers. Her crew were already at the pumps, but the streams of water they aimed at the fire had no effect. The flames jumped higher.

'Steer closer to that ship. I will speak to her captain,' Zayn ordered Rahmad. The *Sufi* veered across to her, and as they drew alongside the burning ship Zayn called to the captain, 'Your ship is stricken and doomed. You must use it to clear an avenue of escape for the other ships of the squadron. Ram the enemy boom. Break it open.'

'As you command, Majesty!' The captain ran to the wheel and pushed aside the helmsman. While the other three ships backed their sails and let him forge ahead of them, he steered straight at the line of massive logs attached to a heavy ship's cable that sealed off the channel. Smoke and flame streamed back from the burning hull.

The officers on the deck of the *Sufi* cheered aloud as it struck, and the heavy log boom was plucked below the surface. The dhow heeled over. The top of her mast snapped off and her flaming sail ballooned down over the deck. She had stopped dead in the water, but even though her sail and rigging were in a shambles, she came slowly back on an even keel. Then the line of heavy logs that made up the boom surfaced again. They were intact. They had resisted the dhow's charge. The ship itself swung round aimlessly. She no longer had steerage way. She was not answering her rudder.

'She is mortally damaged below the waterline,' Rahmad said softly. 'See? She is already sinking by the bows. The boom has torn the guts clean out of her. The flames will devour the hull to the waterline.'

The crew of the doomed vessel had managed to launch two of their boats. They clambered down into them, and rowed for the shore. Zayn looked back at the rest of his squadron. Another of his ships was in flames. It headed towards the shore and piled on to the sand with its sails and rigging burning like a funeral pyre. Then another dhow was hit, and black smoke billowed into the sky above her. The blaze drove

most of her crew into the bows. A few were overpowered by
the smoke, collapsed on the deck and fire swept over them.
The rest leaped over the side. Those who were able to swim
struck out for the beach, but the others drowned almost at
once.

There was a shout of fear from the officers clustered around
Zayn and they all looked up towards the heights of the bluff.
Another red hot ball came sparkling in a meteoric arc towards
them. This one could not miss them.

The thunder of the cannon echoed from the cliffs of the
tall bluff, and rolled out across the waters to where Kadem
ibn Abubaker lay hove to a mile off the mouth of the Umgeni
river.

'The Caliph has begun his attack on the fort. Good! Now
you must land your battalions,' Kadem told Koots, then turned
to shout an order to the helm: 'Bring her back on the wind.'
Obediently the dhow came round to the thrust of the big
lateen, and they headed in towards the beach. The rest of the
convoy followed his lead.

The transports were towing their boats, which were already
packed with armed men. Others were waiting on the decks of
the ships for their turn to embark in the boats as they returned
empty from the beach. They sailed into the stain of yellow-
brown effluent that poured from the mouth of the river and
sullied the blue sea for miles along the coast. Both Kadem
and Koots studied the beach through their glasses as they
approached.

'Deserted!' Koots grunted.

'There is no reason for it to be otherwise,' Kadem told him.
'You will meet no opposition until you reach the fort. According to Laleh, the enemy guns are all aimed to fire out across
the bay to cover the entrance channel. They are not sited to
meet any attack from the landward side.'

'One quick rush while the enemy is busy with the attacking
dhows and we will be over the walls and into the fort.'

'*Inshallah!*' Kadem agreed. 'But you must move swiftly. My uncle, the Caliph, is already engaged. You must drive your men hard to encircle the fort before any of the defenders can escape with the booty.'

The crew took in the sail, and the anchor went overside. A cable's length beyond the first line of breakers the dhow settled quietly to ride the long swells running into the beach.

'And now, my old comrade in arms, it is time for us to part,' Kadem said, 'but always remember your promise to me, if you should be so fortunate as to capture al-Salil or his puppy.'

'Yes, I shall remember it well.' Koots smiled like a cobra. 'You want them for yourself. I swear, if it is within my power, I shall deliver them to you. For myself I want only Jim Courtney and his pretty wench.'

'Go with God!' Kadem said, and watched Koots go down into the crowded boat and head for the shore. A swarm of small craft followed him. As they approached the river mouth, the swells sent them swooping in over the sandbar that guarded it. As soon as they were into the protected water, the boats turned into the bank. From each one twenty men jumped overside into the waist-deep water and waded ashore, their weapons and packs held high.

They assembled in their platoons above the high-water mark and squatted in patient ranks. The empty boats returned to the anchored ships, the oarsmen driving them through the lines of waves at the river mouth. As soon as they were alongside the transports the next wave of men swarmed down into them from the high deck. As the boats ferried back and forth, and more and more men went ashore, the stretch of beach grew more crowded, but still none ventured into the thick jungle beyond.

Kadem watched through his telescope and began to fret. What is Koots doing? he wondered. Every minute now, the enemy will be rallying. He is throwing away his chances. Then he turned his head and listened. The distant sound of the bombardment had ceased and there was silence from the direction of the bay. What has happened to the Caliph's

713

attack? Surely he could not have overpowered the fort so swiftly. He looked back at the men on the beach. As for Koots, Kadem thought, he must move now. He cannot afford to waste more time.

Since he had landed, Koots had been able to form a better estimate of the kind of terrain that lay ahead of him, and had been most unpleasantly surprised. He had sent scouting parties into the bush to find the easiest way through, but they had still not returned. Now he was waiting anxiously at the edge of the jungle, thumping a clenched fist into the palm of the other hand with frustration. He understood as well as Kadem how dangerous it was to allow the momentum of his attack to dissipate, but on the other hand he dared not rush into the unknown.

Would it be better to take them along the beach? he wondered, and looked along the sweep of honey-brown sand. Then he glanced at his own feet. He was ankle-deep in it and the effort of walking even a few paces was demanding. Such a march under heavy packs would exhaust even the hardest of his men.

An hour past low tide, he estimated. Soon the tide will be in full flow. It will flood the sand and force us off it and into the bush.

While he still hesitated, one of the scouting parties pushed their way through the thick wall of vegetation and into the open. 'Where have you been?' Koots bellowed at the leader. 'Is there a way through?'

'It is very bad for three hundred yards. There is a deep swamp directly ahead. One of my men was taken by a crocodile. We tried to save him.'

'You idiot.' With his scabbard Koots struck the man across the side of the head, and he dropped to his knees in the sand. 'Is that what you have been doing all this time, trying to save another useless bastard like yourself? You should have let the crocodile have him. Did you find a path?'

714

The man came to his feet, swaying slightly and holding his injured face. 'Have no fear, Pasha *effendi*,' he mumbled. 'After the swamp there is a spur of dry ground that leads towards the south. There is an open path running along it, but it is narrow. It will take only three men abreast.'

'Any sign of the enemy?'

'None, great Pasha, but there are many wild beasts.'

'Lead us to the path at once, or I will find a crocodile for you also.'

'I f we attack them now, we will sweep them with a single charge back into the sea whence they came,' said Beshwayo, fiercely.

'No, great king, that is not our purpose. There are still many more of them coming ashore. We want all of them,' said Jim, in a reasonable tone. 'Why kill a few of them when, if we wait awhile, we will kill them all?'

Beshwayo chuckled and shook his head so that the earrings Louisa had given him jangled. 'You are right, Somoya. I have many young warriors seeking the right to wed and I do not want to deprive them of that honour.'

Jim and Beshwayo had waited on the hills above the coast from where they had an uninterrupted view out to sea. They watched Zayn's fleet sail in and separate into two divisions. The five largest ships sailed into the bay, and the gunsmoke billowed up as they began to bombard the fort. It seemed that this was the signal for which the second, larger division had been waiting out at sea, for they immediately came directly in towards the mouth of the Umgeni river. Jim waited until they anchored close inshore. He watched them launch their boats, filled with men, and send them in towards the beach.

'Here is the meat I promised you, mighty black lion,' Jim told Beshwayo.

'Then let us go down to the feast, Somoya, for my belly growls with hunger.'

The *impis* of young warriors poured down on to the flat

715

lands of the littoral strip. Silently as a pride of panthers they moved into their forward positions. Jim and Beshwayo ran ahead of the leading *impi* to the lookout position. They climbed high into the branches of the tall wild fig tree they had chosen days before. Its twisted serpentine air-roots and branches formed a natural ladder, and the bunches of yellow fruit and dense foliage sprouted directly from the trunk to screen them effectively. From their perch in one of the main forks they had a view through the foliage along the entire sweep of the beach south of the river mouth.

Jim had his eye to his spyglass. Suddenly he exclaimed in astonishment, 'Sweet Mother Mary, if it's not Koots himself, all dressed up like a Mussulman grandee. No matter what his disguise, I would know that evil jib anywhere.'

He spoke in English, and Beshwayo scowled. 'Somoya, I do not understand what you say,' he rebuked Jim. 'Now that I have taught you to speak the language of heaven, there is no reason for you still to jabber like a monkey in that strange tongue of yours.'

'Do you see that man on the beach down there in the headdress with the bright and shining band, the one closest to us? He is speaking to the other two. There! He has just struck one in the face.'

'I see him,' Beshwayo said. 'Not a good blow, for his victim is standing up again. Who is he, Somoya?'

'His name is Koots,' Jim answered grimly, 'my enemy to the death.'

'Then I will leave him for you,' Beshwayo promised.

'Ah, it seems as though at last they have all their troops ashore, and that Koots has made up his mind to move.'

Even above the sound of the surf breaking on the sandbar, they could hear the Arab captains shouting their orders. The squatting ranks rose to their feet, hefting their weapons and packs. Quickly they formed up into columns and began to move into the bush and swamp. Jim tried to count them, but could not do so accurately. 'Over two hundred,' he decided.

Beshwayo whistled and two of his *indunas* climbed up to him swiftly. They wore the head-rings of their rank, their short

716

beards were grizzled and their bare chests and arms carried the scars of many battles. Beshwayo gave them a rapid string of orders. To each they replied in unison, 'Yehbo, Nkosi Nkulu! Yes, great king!'

'You have heard me,' Beshwayo told them. 'Now obey!'

Beshwayo dismissed them, and they slid down the trunk of the wild fig and disappeared into the undergrowth. Minutes later, Jim saw the surreptitious movements in the bush below as the regiments of Beshwayo warriors began to creep forward. They were well spread out, and even from above there was only the brief flash of oiled dark skin, or the glint of bare steel as they closed in quietly on each flank of the marching Omani columns.

A detachment of Turks in their bronze bowl-shaped helmets passed almost directly under the fig tree in which they sat, but they were so intent on finding their way through the matted bush that none looked up. Suddenly there was a commotion of grunts, breaking branches and splashing mud. A small herd of buffalo, disturbed in their mud wallows, burst out of the swamp and thundered away in a solid mass of black, mud-caked bodies and curved, gleaming horns, smashing a road through the forest. There was a scream and Jim saw the body of one of the Arabs tossed high as he was gored by the old cow buffalo that led the herd. Then they were gone.

A few of his companions gathered about the man's crushed body, but the captains yelled at them angrily. They left him lying where he had fallen and went on. By this time the leading platoons had disappeared into the jungle, while the rear echelons were only just leaving the open beach and starting into the swamp.

Once they were into the bush, none of them was able to see further ahead than the man in front of him, and they followed each other blindly. Already they were falling into mudholes in the swamp, and losing any but the most general sense of direction as they were forced to skirt the densest patches of thorny scrub. The insects swarmed off the algae-green puddles that steamed in the heat. The Turks sweated under their steel mail. The bronze helmets reflected

717

arrows of light. The officers had to raise their voices to keep contact with their platoons, and any attempt at stealth was abandoned.

On the other hand, this was the kind of terrain in which the Beshwayo hunted and fought best. They were invisible to the columns of Koots's men. They shadowed them on each flank. The *indunas* never uttered a word of command. To guide their *impis* in for the kill, they used only birdcalls or the piping of tree frogs, which sounded so natural that it was difficult to believe they issued from a human throat.

Beshwayo listened to these sounds intently. Cocking his huge shaven head first on one side then the other, he understood what they were telling him as if they spoke in plain language. 'It is time, Somoya,' he said at last. He threw back his head and filled his lungs; his barrel chest swelled, then contracted at the force with which he uttered the high, chanting cry of a fish-eagle. Almost immediately, from far out and much closer at hand, his cry was repeated from a dozen places in the thick jungle below where they sat. His *indunas* were acknowledging the king's order to attack.

'Come, Somoya!' said Beshwayo softly. 'Unless we are quick we will miss the sport.' When Jim reached the ground he found Bakkat squatting beside the trunk of the fig tree.

He greeted Jim with a sparkling grin. 'I heard the fish eagle cry. So, now there is work to do, Somoya.' He handed Jim his sword belt. Jim buckled it about his waist, then thrust the pair of double-barrelled pistols through the leather loops. Like a dark shadow Beshwayo had already disappeared into a dense stand of reeds. Jim turned back to Bakkat. 'Koots is here. He leads the enemy brigade,' he told him. 'Find him for me, Bakkat.'

'He will be at the head of his troops,' Bakkat said. 'We must circle out around the main fighting so that we are not trapped in it, like a bull elephant in quicksand.'

Suddenly the jungle around them echoed and resonated with the clamour of fighting men: the thudding reports of musket and pistol, the thunder of *assegai* and *kerrie* drumming on rawhide shield, wild splashing in the swamps, and the crackle of breaking brush as men charged through it. Then the war chant of Beshwayo's men was answered by shouted challenges in Arabic and Turkish.

Bakkat darted away, avoiding the sounds of battle, circling out towards the river to get ahead of the Omani brigades. Jim ran hard to keep up with him. Once or twice he lost sight of him in the denser patches of jungle, but Bakkat whistled softly to lead him on.

They reached the spur of dry ground at the far side of the swamp. Bakkat found a narrow game path and ran back along it. After a few hundred paces he stopped again, and they both stood listening. Jim was panting like a dog, and his shirt was dark with sweat, plastered to his body like a second skin. The battle was so close that, underlying the uproar, they could clearly make out the more intimate sounds of death, the crunch of a skull splitting at the blow from a *kerrie*, the grunt as a spearman thrust home, the hiss of a scimitar blade through the air, the gush of blood spilling upon the earth, the thud of a falling body, the groans and laboured breath of the maimed and dying.

Bakkat looked at Jim, and made a gesture of closing in upon the battle, but Jim raised a hand to restrain him and cocked his head. His breath was returning swiftly. He loosed his pistols in their loops, and drew his sword.

Suddenly there was a bull-like bellow from the thickets close at hand. 'Come, my sons! Come, the children of heaven! Let us devour them!'

Jim grinned, it could be none other than Beshwayo. He was answered by another voice, crying out in heavily accented Arabic: 'Steady! Steady! Hold your fire! Let them come in close!'

'That's him!' Jim nodded at Bakkat. 'Koots!'

They left the game path and plunged into the undergrowth. Jim forced his way through a wall of thorns, and before him stretched an opening of bright green swamp grass. In its centre there was a tiny island not more than twenty paces across. On this last refuge Koots was making his stand with a dozen of his men, Arabs in mud-soaked robes and Turks in splattered half-armour. They had formed a ragged line, some kneeling, others standing with their muskets at high port. Koots was striding up and down behind the second rank, carrying his musket at the trail. A bloody cloth was wrapped round his forehead, but he was grinning like a skull, a fearsome rictus that exposed his clenched teeth.

Across the narrow neck of swamp they were confronted by a mass of Beshwayo's warriors, with the Great Bull at their head. Beshwayo threw back his head and gave one last bellow: 'Come, my children. This way lies the road to glory!' He bounded forward into the pools, scummed with thick clumps of stinking green algae. His warriors raced after him and the swamp exploded into spray under their charge.

'Steady!' Koots shouted. 'One shot and they will be on us.'

Beshwayo never faltered: he galloped forward, straight into the levelled muskets like a charging buffalo.

'The mad fool,' Jim lamented. 'He knows the power of the gun.'

'Wait!' Koots called, quite softly. 'Wait for it!' Jim saw that he had chosen the king, and was aiming at his chest. He snatched one of his pistols from the loop on his belt and fired instinctively, without seeing the iron sights. It was a forlorn effort. Koots did not even flinch as the ball flew past his head. Instead, his voice rang out harshly, 'Fire!' The volley crashed out, and in the smoke Jim saw at least four of the charging warriors go down, two killed outright, the others thrashing around in the mud. Their companions ran over the top of them. Jim searched desperately for a glimpse of Beshwayo. Then as the smoke cleared he saw him untouched and undaunted still in the front of the charge, bawling lustily as he came: 'I am the Black Death. Look upon me, and know fear!' He hurled himself into the front rank of Arabs, and knocked two flat on to the earth with a sweep of his shield. He stood over them and stabbed down so swiftly that his blade blurred. Each time he drew it out again a bright crimson tide followed the steel.

Koots threw aside his empty musket, and whirled round. He crossed the island with long, loping strides and plunged into the swamp, heading straight back towards where Jim stood. Jim stepped out from the thicket of thorns. He drew his sword, and waited for him at the edge of marshy ground. Koots recognized him and stopped ankle deep in the mud.

'The Courtney puppy!' He was still smiling. 'I have waited long for this moment. Keyser will still pay good gold guilders for your head.'

'You'll have to reap it first.'

'Where is your blonde whore? I have something for her also.' Koots took a handful of his crotch and shook it lewdly.

'I will hack it off and take it to her,' Jim promised him grimly.

Koots glanced over his shoulder. His men were all dead. With slashes of the *assegai*, the Beshwayo were disembowelling their corpses, allowing their spirits to escape: a last tribute to men who had fought well. But some had already started in pursuit of Koots, splashing towards him through the swamp.

Koots hesitated no longer. He came straight at Jim, stepping high through the mud, still smiling, those pale eyes staring into Jim's face to read his intentions. His first thrust came with no warning, straight at Jim's throat. Jim touched his blade, just enough to turn it off line so that the point flew over his shoulder. In the moment that Koots was at full extension, he shot his own blade forward, steel rasped on steel, and guided Jim's point home. He felt the hit, cloth and flesh splitting, then the shock of bone. Koots leaped back.

'*Liefde tot* God!' His smile had given way to a startled expression. Fresh blood spread on his muddy shirt-front. 'The puppy has become a dog.'

Surprise gave way to anger and he rushed at Jim again. Their blades clashed and scraped as he tried to drive Jim back, so that he could find firm footing. But Jim stood solid, and kept him pinned in the soft mud. It clung to Koots's boots and hampered each step he took.

'I am coming, Somoya,' shouted Beshwayo, as he bounded across the narrow neck of swamp.

'I do not take the food from your mouth,' Jim shouted back. 'Leave me this morsel.'

721

Beshwayo stopped and held up his hand, to restrain his men who swarmed eagerly after him.

'Somoya is hungry,' he said. 'Let him eat in peace.' And he laughed.

Koots dropped back a pace, trying to draw Jim forward into the mud. Jim smiled into his pale eyes and, with a scornful flick of his head, declined the invitation. Koots circled left and as soon as Jim turned to meet him he broke the other way, but he was slow in the mud. Jim hit him again, raking his flank. Beshwayo's men roared approval.

'You bleed as freely as the great pig you are,' Jim taunted him. The blood was sliding down Koots's leg and dripping into the mud. He glanced down at it and his expression was grim. Both wounds were shallow and light, but together they would drain him swiftly. Jim lunged at him.

When Koots jumped back he felt the weakness in his legs. He knew he must try for a quick decision. He looked at the man who confronted him, and for one of the few times in his life he felt a twinge of fear. This was no longer the stripling he had chased across half of Africa. This was a man, tall and broad-shouldered, forged like steel in the furnace of life.

Koots gathered his courage and the last of his strength and rushed at Jim, trying by sheer weight and strength to drive him back. Jim stood to meet him. It seemed that only an evanescent barrier of darting metal separated them. The clash and scrape of the blades rose to a dreadful crescendo. Beshwayo's warriors were enthralled by this novel form of combat. They recognized the skill and strength it demanded, and they chanted encouragement, drumming their *assegais* upon their shields, dancing and swaying with excitement.

It could not last much longer. Koots's pale eyes were covered by the sheen of despair. Sweat diluted the blood that streamed down his side. He felt the slackness in his wrist, and the give of his muscles when he tried to press Jim harder. Jim blocked his next desperate thrust high in the natural line of attack, and locked their blades in front of their eyes. They stared at each other through the cross of silver formed by the quivering steel. They formed a statue group that seemed carved from marble. The Beshwayo sensed the high drama of the moment and fell silent.

Koots and Jim both knew that whichever one tried to break away would expose himself to the killing stroke. Then Jim felt Koots break. Koots shifted his feet and, with a heave of both shoulders, tried to throw Jim back and disengage. Jim was ready for it, and as Koots released, Jim shot forward like the strike of an adder. Koots's eyes flew wide, but they were colourless and blind. His fingers opened, and he let his sword drop into the mud.

Jim stood with his wrist locked and the point of his own steel buried deep in Koots's chest. He felt the hilt thump softly in his hand, and thought for an instant that it was his own pulse. Then he realized that his blade had transfixed Koots's heart, and it was the pumping of his opponent's lifeblood that he could feel transmitted up the blade.

Koots's expression was puzzled. He opened his mouth to speak, then closed it again. Slowly his knees buckled and, as he sagged, Jim allowed him to slip off the blade. He fell face down in the mud, and Beshwayo's men roared like a pride of lions at the kill.

Weeks before, the three ships, *Revenge*, *Sprite* and *Arcturus*, had sailed out of Nativity Bay on the dawn tide. They left Tasuz in his little felucca within sight of the bluff to watch for the arrival of Zayn's fleet while they went on to lie in ambush out of sight of land below the eastern horizon. The endless days that followed were of unrelieved monotony and uncertainty, patrolling back and forth along the edge of the oceanic shelf, watching for Tasuz to summon them to battle.

Ruby Cornish in the *Arcturus* made his sun shot at noon each day, but the instincts of Kumrah in the *Sprite* and Batula in the *Revenge* were almost as accurate as his navigational instruments at keeping them on their station.

Mansur spent almost all the hours of daylight high in *Arcturus*'s main top, watching the horizon through the lens of his telescope until his right eye was bloodshot with the strain and the glare of the sun off the water. Each evening, after an early dinner with Cornish, he went to Verity's cabin. He sat late at her writing bureau. She had given him the key to the drawers when they parted on the beach of Nativity Bay. 'No one else has ever read my journals. I wrote them in Arabic, so that neither my father nor my mother could decipher them. You see, my darling, I never trusted either of them very far.' She laughed as she said it. 'I want you to be the first to read them. Through them you will be able to share my life and my innermost thoughts and secrets.'

'I feel humble that you should do me such great honour.' His voice choked as he said it.

'It is not about honour, it is about love,' she replied. 'From now onwards, I shall never keep a secret from you.'

Mansur found that the journals spanned the last ten years of her life, since she had turned nine. They were a monumental record of a young girl's emotions as she groped her way towards womanhood. He sat late each night, and by the light of the oil lamp he shared her yearnings and her bewilderment at life, her girlish disasters and petty triumphs. There were outpourings of joy, and others of such poignancy that his heart ached for her. There were dark, enigmatic passages when she pondered her relationship with her parents. He felt his flesh creep when she hinted fearfully at the unspeakable as she wrote of her father. She spared no detail when she described the punishments he had inflicted on her, and his hands shook with anger as he turned the perfumed pages. There were other passages that brought him up short with their brilliant revelations. Always her fresh, inspired use of words amazed him. At times she made him laugh aloud, and at others his vision blurred with tears.

The last pages of the penultimate volume covered the period from their first meeting on the deck of the *Arcturus* in Muscat harbour until their parting on the road back from Isakanderbad. At one point she had written of him, 'Though he does not yet know it, already he owns a part of me. From this time onwards our footsteps will be printed side by side in the sands of time.'

When at last she had burnt out his emotions with her words, he blew out the lamp and went dazed with emotional exhaustion to her bunk. The rich fragrance of her hair still lingered on her pillow and the sheets were perfumed by her skin. In the night he woke and reached for her, and when he realized that she was not there the agony made him groan. Then he hated his own father for not allowing her to stay with him, and sending her away in the wagons with Sarah, Louisa and little George into the wild hills of the hinterland.

No matter how little he had slept he was always on *Arcturus*'s deck when eight bells sounded in the middle watch, and before the first blush of dawn he was at the masthead, watching and waiting.

As the most powerful but slowest ship in the squadron, the *Arcturus* kept the windward station, and Mansur had the sharpest pair of eyes on board. It was he who spotted the tiny fleck of the felucca's sail as she came up over the horizon. The moment that they were certain of her identity Ruby Cornish brought the *Arcturus* about and they ran down to intercept her.

Tasuz answered his hail: 'Zayn al-Din is here, with twenty-five great dhows.' Then he turned and led the squadron back towards the African mainland, which now lay low on the horizon, dark blue and as menacing as some monster of the deep. Again it was Mansur who first picked out the shapes of the enemy flotilla anchored off the mouth of the Umgeni river. Their sails were furled and their dark hulls blended with the background of hills and forest.

'They are lying exactly where your father expected them.' Cornish studied them carefully as they raced down upon them. 'They are already sending their boats in to the beach. The attack has begun.'

Swiftly they closed the gap, and it seemed that the enemy were so intent on their landing that they were neglecting the watch they should have kept on the open sea behind them.

'Those are the five war-dhows of the escort.' Mansur pointed them out. 'The others are transports.'

'We have the weather gauge.' Cornish smiled comfortably and his face glowed with satisfaction. 'The same wind that blows to our advantage has them pinned against the lee shore. If they hoist their anchors they will go aground almost immediately. We have Kadem ibn Abubaker at our mercy. How should we proceed, Your Highness?' Cornish looked at Mansur. Dorian had given his son the overall command of the squadron: Mansur's royal rank dictated that. The Arab captains would not have understood or accepted any other in place of him.

'My instinct is to go straight at the war-dhows while we have them at our mercy. If we can destroy them, the transports will fall into our laps like overripe fruit. Would you agree, Captain Cornish?'

'With all my heart, Your Highness.' Cornish showed his appreciation of Mansur's tact by touching the brim of his hat.

'Then, if you please, let us close with the other ships so that I may pass the order to them. I shall allot an enemy ship to each. We in the *Arcturus* will engage the largest of them,' Mansur pointed to the dhow in the centre of the line of anchored ships, 'for that is almost certainly commanded by Kadem ibn Abubaker. I shall board immediately and capture it, while you sail on and do the same to the next in line.'

The *Sprite* and the *Revenge* were sailing a little ahead, backing their sails slightly so as not to head-reach too far on the *Arcturus*. Mansur hailed them, and pointed out which of the dhows were their separate targets. As soon as they understood what he wanted of them they barged ahead, charging at the line of anchored ships.

At last the enemy saw them coming, and confusion spread swiftly through their fleet. Three of the transports were occupied with landing the horses they were carrying. They were winching them out of the holds with slings passed under their bellies, then lowering them over the side into the water. When they reached it, they turned them loose to swim unaided. The sailors waiting for them in the small boats drove them into the breaking surf to fight their way to the beach as best they were able. Already more than a hundred of the sick, exhausted animals were in the water, struggling to keep afloat.

When they saw the tall ships bearing down on them with all their guns run out, the captains of the horse transports panicked. With a few axe strokes they severed their anchor cables, and tried to bear away. Two collided, and in the confusion they drifted into the line of heaving white surf. Still locked together, the waves broke over their decks. One capsized and took the other with it. The surface of the water was covered with wreckage, struggling men and horses. One or two of the other troop ships managed to cut their cables and hoist their sails. It was close work but they cleared the lee shore and made good their offing.

'They are unarmed and no danger to us,' Mansur told Cornish. 'Let them go. We can run them down later. First we must deal with the war-dhows.' He left Cornish, and went forward to take command of the boarding party. The five war-dhows had kept their positions at anchor. They were too large and ungainly to risk the dangerous manoeuvre of trying to clear the lee shore in the face of such a powerful enemy. They had no option but to stay and fight.

The *Arcturus* ran straight at the largest. Mansur stood in the bows and surveyed the deck of the other ship as the gap between them closed. 'There he is!' he shouted suddenly, and pointed with his sword. 'I knew he must be here!'

The ships were so close that Kadem heard his voice and glared back at him. The shaft of pure hatred that passed between them was almost tangible.

'One broadside, Captain Cornish,' Mansur looked back at the quarter-deck, 'and we will board her over her bows through the smoke.' Cornish waved acknowledgement and steered his ship in.

The direction of the wind held Kadem's dhow with her bows pointing out to sea, her stern towards the beach. Although the Omani crew ran out their guns defiantly, they could not bring them to bear. Cornish crossed the bows of Kadem's dhow to rake her at point-blank range. The *Arcturus*

727

stood higher out of the water than the dhow, and her guns were able to fire down on her. Cornish had loaded with grape-shot, and the broadside crashed out. A thick bank of grey gunsmoke shot through with lumps of burning wadding billowed out and obscured her open deck. The wind blew it aside and revealed a scene of utter devastation. The timbers of the dhow's deck had been ripped as though by the claws of a monstrous cat. The gunners were piled in bloody heaps upon their unfired weapons. The splintered scuppers ran crimson with their blood.

Mansur looked for Kadem in the carnage. With a small jolt of disbelief he saw that he was unharmed and still on his feet, trying to muster the stunned survivors of that terrible blast of iron balls. Skilfully Cornish let the hulls of the two ships kiss, then held them together with a delicate play on the helm. Mansur led his boarders across in a rush, and Cornish toyed with the wheel and disengaged. Leaving Mansur and his men to seize the dhow, he sailed on down the line of anchored ships to attack the next war-dhow before it could escape out to sea. He had a respite of a few minutes to look round and see how the other two ships were faring.

After battering them with unrelenting broadsides at close range, the crews of the *Revenge* and the *Sprite* had boarded their chosen adversaries. Three more of the troop transports had drifted into the surf and capsized; some of the others were still at anchor. Cornish counted six more who had avoided the attackers and were clawing desperately out to sea. Then he looked back over his stern and saw the bitter fighting that surged over the deck of Kadem's anchored dhow. He thought he saw Mansur in the front of the battle, but it was so fluid and confused that he could not be sure. The prince might have done better to let me give them a few more doses of grape, before he boarded, he thought, and then with admiration, but he is a hotblood. Kadem ibn Abubaker murdered his mother. Honour allows him no other course than to go after him, man to man.

The *Arcturus* was coming down fast on the next war-dhow in the line, and Cornish gave her all his attention. 'The same

medicine, lads,' he called to his gunners. 'A goodly draught of
the grape, and then we will board her.'

Although the grape-shot had killed or wounded half of the
men on the deck of Kadem ibn Abubaker's ship, the
moment Mansur's boarding party swung across from the *Arcturus*, Kadem shouted the order and the rest of his crew came
pouring out of the hatchways from the lower decks and
launched themselves into the fight.

In numbers boarders and defenders were almost evenly
matched. They were so closely packed that there was scarce
enough space in which to swing the sword or thrust with the
pike. They surged back and forth, slipping on the bloody
decks, shouting and hacking at each other.

Mansur looked for Kadem in the ruck, but almost immediately he was confronted by three men. They came at him in a
rush. Mansur hit one low in the chest, driving his point up
under the ribs. He heard the air hiss from the man's punctured
lungs before he toppled to the deck. Mansur only just had
time to recover his blood-smeared blade and come back on
guard before the other two were upon him.

One of these was a wiry fellow whose long arms were roped
with stringy muscle. His naked chest was tattooed with a *sura*
from the Qur'an. Mansur recognized him: he had fought beside
him on the ramparts of Muscat. He feinted, then cut overhand
at Mansur's head. Mansur blocked him and locked his blade.
He swung him round like a shield to hold off his comrade,
who was trying to intervene.

'So, Zaufar! You could not wait for the return of al-Salil,
your true caliph,' Mansur snarled into his face. 'Last time we
met I saved your life. This time I shall take it from you.'

Zaufar leaped back in consternation. 'Prince Mansur, is it
you?' In reply Mansur pulled off his turban and shook out his
copper golden hair.

'It is the prince,' Zaufar screamed. His comrades paused and
drew back. They stared at Mansur.

'It is the son of al-Salil,' one cried. 'Yield to him!'

'He is the spawn of the traitor! Kill him!' a pot-bellied rogue bellowed, and forced his way through their ranks. Zaufar turned and sent a thrust deeply into his bulging gut. In a moment the enemy was divided against each other. Mansur's men rushed forward to take advantage of the confusion.

'Al-Salil!' they shouted, and some of the dhow's crew took up the cry, while the others yelled back defiantly, 'Zayn al-Din!'

With so many of Kadem's men changing sides, those still loyal to him were outnumbered and they were swept back down the deck. Mansur led the charge, his face and robe splattered by the blood of his victims, his eyes ferocious. He searched for Kadem in the rabble. As he fought his way forward more of the enemy recognized him. They threw down their weapons and grovelled on the deck.

'Mercy in the name of al-Salil!' they screamed.

At last Kadem ibn Abubaker stood alone at the stern rail of the dhow. He stared across at Mansur.

'I have come for retribution,' Mansur called to him. 'I have come to purge your evil soul with steel.' He started forward again and the men between them shrank out of his way. 'Come, Kadem ibn Abubaker, meet me now.'

Kadem reared back, then swung forward and hurled his scimitar at Mansur's head. The curved blade, clotted with the blood of his victims, cartwheeled through the air with a vicious whirring sound. Mansur ducked under it and it went on to thud into the base of the mast.

'Not now, puppy. First I will kill your dog-sire, then only will I have time to deal with you.'

Before Mansur realized what he was about, Kadem pulled his robe over his head and threw it to the deck. He wore only a loincloth round his waist. His torso was lean and hard. Under his arm was the raised purple scar of the sword-thrust that Mansur had inflicted on him on the quay at Muscat harbour. Kadem turned to the rail and leaped far out. He hit the water, went under, then surfaced and struck out strongly for the beach.

730

Mansur ran down the deck to the stern, stripping off his own clothing as he went. He dropped his sword, but thrust the curved dagger still in its gold and silver sheath into the back of his loincloth where it would not hamper his swimming stroke. He knotted it there securely. Then, with hardly a check, he dived head first over the rail. Both Mansur and Jim had learned to swim in the turbulent waters of the Benguela current that sweeps the shores of Good Hope. As mere lads the two had kept the household of High Weald supplied with abalone and giant crayfish. They took these not by pot or net, but dived for them in the deep waters of the reef. At the end of many hours spent in the icy waters they would race each other back to the shore dragging the bulging sacks of their catch through the water with them.

Mansur came to the surface and, with a shake of his head, flicked his sodden mane out of his eyes. He saw Kadem fifty yards ahead of him. From experience, he knew that, even though they were accomplished seamen, few Arabs learned to swim, so he was surprised by how strongly Kadem forged through the water. Mansur struck out after him, swinging into a powerful overhead rhythm.

He heard the cries of encouragement from his men on the dhow, but he ignored them and put all his heart, sinew and muscle into the effort. Every dozen strokes he snatched a glance ahead and saw that he was slowly closing in on Kadem.

As they drew nearer to the beach the swells started to hump under them. Kadem reached the break-line first. The tumbling white surf caught and smothered him, then threw him up again, coughing and disoriented. Now, instead of going with the current, he fought against it.

Mansur looked behind him, and saw the next set of waves rearing their backs against the blue of the sky. He stopped swimming and hung in the water, treading gently and paddling with his hands. He watched the first wave come down to him, then let it pass under him. It lifted him so that he had a clear view of Kadem only thirty yards ahead. The wave went on and dropped Mansur into its trough. The next wave came at him, taller and more powerful.

'The first a piddle, the second a fountain, the third will wash you up the mountain.' He almost heard Jim call the doggerel to him as he had so often before while they played together in the surf. 'Wait for the third wave!'

Mansur let the second lift him even higher than the first. From the top he saw Kadem tumble end over end in the boil of the leading wave, his legs and then his flailing arms flashing out of the creaming surf. The wave sped on and left him struggling in its wake. Mansur looked back and saw the third wave bearing down on him. It arched up like the portals of the sky, its crest trembled, translucent green.

He turned with it and began to swim again, kicking hard and tearing at the water with both hands, building up his momentum. The wave picked him up and he found himself caught in its high frontal wall, racing onwards with his head and the top half of his body free.

Kadem was still floundering in the break and Mansur steered towards him with arms and legs, cutting across the face of the wave. At the last moment Kadem saw him and his eyes flew wide with astonishment. Mansur filled his own lungs with air and crashed into him. He locked his arms and legs around Kadem's body, as both of them were swallowed by the wave and carried deep beneath the surface.

Mansur felt his eardrums creak with the pressure and the pain was like a skewer being driven through his skull. He did not release his grip on Kadem, but he swallowed extravagantly and his eardrums made a popping sound as the pressure released. They were driven still deeper and he touched the bottom with one foot. All the time he was tightening his grip around Kadem's chest like the coils of a python.

They sank to the bottom and rolled together along the sandy floor. Mansur opened his eyes and looked upwards. His vision was blurred, and the surface seemed as remote as the stars. He gathered all his strength and squeezed again. He felt Kadem's ribs creaking and bending in the circle of his arms. Then suddenly Kadem opened his mouth wide with the agony of it, and there was an explosive rush of air out of his throat.

Drown, you swine! Mansur thought, as he watched the

732

silver bubbles of expelled wind racing up towards the surface. But he should have been ready for the last extremes of a dying animal. Somehow Kadem planted both feet on the sandy bottom, and thrust with all the strength of his legs. Still locked together they shot upwards, and the speed of their ascent increased as they approached the surface.

They broke out, and Kadem sucked in air. It gave him new strength, and he twisted in Mansur's arms and reached for his face with hooked fingers. His nails were sharp as augers and they raked Mansur's forehead and cheeks, groping for his eyes.

Mansur felt one hard fingertip force aside his tightly closed eyelid, and slip deeply into the socket. The pain was beyond belief as the nail scored his eyeball and Kadem began to prise it out of Mansur's skull. Mansur released his grip and jerked his head away just before the eyeball popped clean out. He was half blinded by the blood that welled up out of the wound. He emptied his lungs in a scream of agony. With renewed strength Kadem heaved himself on top of Mansur. He locked one arm around his throat in a strangler's grip and forced him under. He was kicking and driving his knees into Mansur's lower body, smothering him with blows and holding his head below the surface. Mansur's lungs were empty, and the urge to breathe was as powerful as the will for life. Kadem's arm was an iron band around his neck. He knew that he would waste the last of his strength if he continued to grapple with him.

He reached behind his back with one hand and drew his dagger from its scabbard. With his left hand he groped under the edge of Kadem's ribcage seeking the lethal point. With all his remaining strength he drove the dagger into the indentation below the sternum. The knife-maker had curved the steel to facilitate just this kind of disembowelling stroke, and the edge was so sharp that Kadem's tensed stomach muscles could offer little resistance to it. The steel ran into its full length, until Mansur felt the hilt strike against Kadem's lowest rib. Then he drew the razor edge down and like a purse opened Kadem's belly from his ribs to his pelvic bone.

With a massive convulsion of his whole body Kadem released his strangling grip, and broke away, rolling on to his back. He floundered on the surface and with both hands tried to stuff his bulging entrails back into the gaping wound. In blue and slippery ropes they kept pouring out and unwinding, until they tangled in his legs as he kicked to stay afloat. His face pointed to the sky and his mouth gaped in a silent cry of anger and despair.

Mansur looked around for him, but his injured eye was blurred and the image of Kadem's face was faceted, like the multiple reflections in a cracked mirror. Pain filled Mansur's skull so that it felt as though it was about to burst. With dread of what he might find, he touched his face. His relief was immense when he found that his eye was still in its socket, not hanging out on his cheek.

Another wave broke over Mansur's head and when he surfaced again he had lost sight of Kadem. He saw something more horrifying. The mouths of these African rivers that poured effluent and offal into the sea were the natural feeding grounds of the Zambezi shark. Mansur knew them well, and instantly recognized the distinctive blunt dorsal fin that sliced towards him, drawn by the taint of blood and split intestines. The next wave lifted the beast high, and for a moment Mansur saw its shape clearly outlined in the window of green water. It seemed to stare at him with an implacable dark eye. There was a kind of obscene beauty in the hard, sculpted lines of its body, and the sleek coppery hide. Its tail and fins were shaped like giant blades, and its mouth seemed set in a cruel, calculating sneer.

With a flick of its tail it shot past Mansur, brushing lightly against his legs. Then it was gone. Its disappearance was even more terrifying than its presence. He knew it was circling under him. This was the prelude to an attack. He had spoken to a few survivors of encounters with these ferocious animals, all missing limbs or bearing other hideous mutilations, and they had all told the same tale. 'They touch you first, and then they hit you.'

Mansur rolled on to his belly, ignoring the pain in his eye socket. Fortuitously another wave rolled down upon him and he swam with it until he felt it lift him, carry him in its arms like an infant, and bear him swiftly in towards the beach. He felt the sand under his feet and staggered up the slope with successive waves crashing into him.

He was cupping one hand over his eye, grunting with the pain, and as soon as he was above the high-water line he dropped to his knees. He ripped a strip from his loincloth and wrapped it round his head, knotting it tightly over the eye to try to ease the agony.

Then he peered back into the churning surf. Fifty yards out, he saw something pale break through the surface and realized it was an arm. There was a disturbance under it, a ponderous, weighty movement in the discoloured waters. The arm vanished again, seeming to be plucked under.

Mansur stood up unsteadily and saw that there were now two sharks feeding on Kadem's corpse. They fought over it like a pair of dogs with a bone. As they worried it, they drove themselves with thrashing tails into the shallow water. At last a larger wave threw the lump of tattered flesh that was all that remained of Kadem Abubaker high up the beach, and left it stranded. The sharks prowled along the edge of the surf for a while then dived and vanished again.

Mansur went down to gaze upon the remains of his enemy. Great half-moons of flesh had been bitten out of his body. The seawater had washed away the blood, so that his stomach cavity was a clean pink pit, his dangling entrails pale and shining. Even in death his eyes were fixed in a malevolent stare, and his mouth in a snarl of hatred.

'I have fulfilled my duty,' Mansur whispered. 'Perhaps now my mother's shade can find peace.' He prodded the mutilated corpse with his foot. 'As for you, Kadem ibn Abubaker, half your flesh is in the belly of the beast. You can never find peace. May your suffering last through all eternity.'

He turned away and looked out to sea. The battle was almost over. Three of the war-dhows had been captured, and the blue banners of al-Salil flew at their mastheads. The wreckage of one more was mingled with that of the transports, being battered to kindling in the surf. *Arcturus* was pursuing the remaining war-dhow out to sea, and her cannons boomed out as she overtook it. The *Revenge* was following the fleeing transports, but they were already scattered over a wide swathe of ocean.

Then he saw the *Sprite* hovering off the mouth of the river, and waved to it. He knew good, faithful Kumrah was searching for him, and that even from this distance he would recognize the colour of his hair. Almost at once he was proved right as he saw the *Sprite* lower a boat and send it in through the surf to pick him up. His vision was still blurred, but he thought he recognized Kumrah himself in the bows.

Mansur looked from the approaching boat back along the beach. Thrown upon the sands, scattered over a mile at the water's edge, were the carcasses of drowned men and horses from the destroyed dhows. Some of the enemy had survived. Men squatted singly or stood in small disconsolate groups along the shore, but it was clear that there was no fight left in them. Stray horses wandered about at the edge of the jungle.

He had lost his dagger in the surf. He felt utterly vulnerable, half blind, naked and unarmed. Trying to ignore the pain in his eye, Mansur ran to one of the nearest corpses. It still wore a short robe and a weapon was strapped around its waist. Mansur stripped off these pathetic relics and pulled the robe over his head. Then he drew the scimitar from its sheath and tested the blade. It was of fine Damascus steel. To test the edge he shaved a few hairs from his wrist before he ran the blade back into its scabbard. For the first time he became aware of a distant hubbub of voices. These came from the depths of the vegetation above the beach.

It's not over yet! he realized. Just then a rabble of running men burst out of the jungle. They were almost a furlong further up the beach, between him and the river mouth, but he saw that they were a mixed bunch of Arabs and Turks. They were being driven down towards the water's edge by a pack of Beshwayo's warriors. The stabbing spears flashed, then were buried in living flesh, and the triumphant shouts of the warriors mingled with the screams and desperate cries of the enemy.

'*Ngi dhla*! I have eaten!'

Mansur realized the fresh danger he was in. Beshwayo's forces were in a killing frenzy. None would recognize him as friendly: he was just another pale, bearded face and they would stab him with as much glee as they would any one of the Omani.

The wet sand along the edge of the water was hard and compacted. He ran along it towards the river mouth. The Arab survivors of the battle realized they were being driven into the sea and they turned at bay. In a last bitter stand they faced Beshwayo's men. There was only a narrow gap behind them but Mansur raced through it, although the pain in his eye made him grunt at each pace. He was almost clear, and the boat from the *Sprite* was through the surf and into the calm water. It would be on the beach before he reached it.

Then there was a shout behind him and he glanced back. Three of the black warriors had spotted him. They had left the surrounded Arabs to their comrades, and they were racing after him, yelping with excitement, hounds on the scent of the hare.

From ahead there were shouts of encouragement: 'We are here, Highness. Run, in the Name of God!' He recognized the voice and saw Kumrah in the bows of the boat.

Mansur ran, but his ordeal in the surf and the agony in his eye weakened him, and he could hear bare feet slapping on the wet sand close behind him. He could almost feel the glide of the steel through his flesh as an *assegai* stabbed between his shoulder-blades. Kumrah, in the boat, was thirty paces ahead, but that might just as well have been thirty leagues. He could hear the hoarse breathing of one man close behind his shoulder. He had to turn to face them and defend himself. He drew the scimitar from its scabbard and spun round.

The leading warrior was so close that he had already drawn back his *assegai*, low underhand, for the killing stroke. But with Mansur at bay he checked his rush, and called softly to his two companions, 'The horns of the bull!' This was their favourite tactic. They fanned out on each side of him, and in that instant Mansur was surrounded. Whichever way he turned his back would be exposed to a long blade. He knew he was a

737

dead man, but he rushed at the man before him. Before he could cross blades with him he heard Kumrah shout behind him: 'Down, Highness!' Mansur did not hesitate but threw himself flat on the sand.

His adversary stood over him and lifted the *assegai* high. '*Ngi dhla!*' he screamed.

Beshwayo's men had not yet realized the effects of close-range musketry. Before the warrior could make the stroke, a volley of musket fire swept over where Mansur lay. A ball hit the warrior in his elbow and his arm broke like a green twig. The *assegai* flew from his grip and he reeled back as another ball slapped into his chest. Mansur rolled over swiftly to face the other two warriors but one was on his knees clutching his belly and the other was on his back, kicking convulsively, half his head shot away.

'Come, Prince Mansur!' Kumrah called, through the veil of gunsmoke that had enveloped the boat. It blew aside, and Mansur saw that every man of the crew had fired the volley that had saved him. He dragged himself to his feet and staggered to the boat. Now that mortal danger was past he lacked the strength to pull himself over the gunwale, but many strong hands reached out for him.

Tom and Dorian had knelt side by side in the gun emplacement and rested their telescopes on the parapet. They studied Zayn's squadron of ships, which were anchored in a group below the walls of the fort on the far side of the bay and bombarding the walls.

Dorian had sited the long nine-pounder cannons with great care. From this height they could bring every part of the bay under fire. Once it came through the entrance no ship was safe from them. It had been a Herculean task to get the guns up to this eyrie. The sides of the bluff were too high and steep, and the guns too heavy, to lift them straight up from the shore.

Tom had cut a track through the thick forest along the

738

rising spine of the ridge and, using this as a ramp, he had dragged the guns up with teams of oxen until they were directly above the chosen site. Then, on heavy anchor cable, he lowered them down into the concealed emplacements. Once the guns were sited they ranged them on targets set up around the shore of the bay. Their first shots had flown far over and crashed into the forest beyond.

Once they were satisfied with the position of the guns, they built the charcoal furnace fifty paces from the powder magazine to reduce the danger of sparks flying from one to the other. They plastered the furnace with river clay. They made the bellows with fifty tanned ox hides, sealing the seams with tar. A gang of cooks, labourers and riff-raff worked the handles to force air into the furnace. Once it reached full blast, it was not possible to look with the naked eye into the white-hot glare of the interior so Dorian had smoked a sheet of glass with the flame of an oil lamp: peering through this, they could judge when the shot was hot enough. Then they manhandled each cannon ball out of the furnace with long-handled tongs. The men doing the job wore thick leather mittens and aprons to protect them from the heat. They dropped each glowing ball into a specially prepared cradle, with long handles. These were carried by two men across to the gun, which was waiting with its barrel raised to the maximum possible elevation.

Once the ball was dropped down the muzzle, it was not long before it burned away the wet wads and spontaneously ignited the powder charge behind them. A premature discharge while the barrel was pointed skywards would tear it off its carriage, wreck the gun emplacement and kill or maim the gun-crews. This allowed only the briefest respite to lay the gun on its target and fire it. Then the whole dangerous, lengthy process had to be repeated. After a few shots the barrel overheated until it was on the point of bursting and the recoil was monstrous; it had to be sponged out and buckets of sea-water poured down the sizzling muzzle before they dared ram a fresh charge of powder into it.

Over the previous weeks, while they awaited the arrival of Zayn al-Din's fleet, Dorian had instructed and exercised the gunners in handling hot shot. They had encountered all these complications for themselves and learned by hard experience, which culminated with the explosion of one of the guns. Two men had been killed by flying fragments of the bronze barrel. All of the crews now had a deep respect for the glowing cannon-balls, and none was looking forward to firing the remaining three weapons in earnest.

The foreman had come from the furnace to report to Dorian with an expression of awe and dread: 'We have twelve balls ready, mighty Caliph.'

'You have done well, Farmat, but I am not yet ready to open fire. Keep the furnaces hot.' He and Tom turned back to continue their surveillance of the action taking place below them. The bombardment from Zayn's ships covered the whole bay and the edges of the forest with smoke, but through it they saw the defenders abandon the fort and run out through the gates.

'Good!' said Dorian, with satisfaction. 'They have remembered their orders.' He had ordered a token defence of the fort merely to lure Zayn's fleet deep into the bay.

'I hope they remembered to spike the guns on the parapets before they left,' Tom growled. 'I do not fancy them being turned on us.'

The bombardment died away, and they watched the boats filled with the assault party leave the war-dhows and head in for the beach, to occupy the deserted fort. Both Tom and Dorian recognized Guy Courtney in the bows of the leading boat.

'His Britannic Majesty's honourable consul general in the flesh!' Dorian exclaimed. 'The scent of the gold was too strong for him to ignore. He has come in person to retrieve it.'

'My beloved twin brother!' Tom agreed. 'It does my heart good to see him again after all these years. When we last parted he was trying to kill me. It seems that things have changed not at all since then.'

'It will not take him long to find that the cupboard is bare,' Dorian said, 'so now it is time to slam the door shut behind them.' He called to the runner who waited eagerly at the back of the redoubt for just this summons. He was one of Sarah's orphans, and he rushed forward grinning widely and trembling with eagerness to please. 'Go down to Smallboy, and tell him it is time to close the gate.' Dorian had barely finished speaking before the boy had jumped over the wall and was racing down the steep pathway. Dorian had to shout after him, 'Don't let them see you!'

Smallboy and Muntu waited with the teams of oxen already hitched to the heavy anchor cable. This was strung out across the entrance of the bay to the heavy piles of logs on the far bank. The slack cable was weighted to lie on the bottom of the channel until pulled taut. The war-dhows had sailed in over it without being aware of its presence under their keels.

The boom was made up of seventy huge logs. Many had been felled the previous year and stacked in the sawmill yard at the back of the fort, ready to be sawn into planks. Even with this stockpile, they were still short of twenty logs to span the channel.

Jim and Mansur had taken every available man into the forest to cut down more of the giant trees, and Smallboy's ox teams had dragged them to the beach. There, they had bolted them lengthwise to the spare anchor cable that they had lifted out of *Arcturus*'s orlop. The cable was almost twenty inches in diameter and had a test strain of over thirty tons. The logs, some of them three feet in diameter and forty feet in length, were strung along this massive hemp rope like pearls on a necklace. They would form a barricade that Tom and Dorian calculated would resist the onslaught of even the largest of Zayn's dhows. The heavy line of logs would tear out a ship's bottom before it could break through.

As soon as Zayn's fleet was sighted from the top of the bluff Smallboy and Muntu inspanned the ox teams and led them round to the south bank of the entrance channel. They kept the teams hidden in the dense bush, and watched the five big dhows sail past within easy pistol shot of where they lay. When the messenger lad had come racing down from the gun emplacements with the order from Dorian, he was so out of breath and wild with excitement that he was incoherent. Smallboy had to grab him by the shoulders and shake him. 'Master Klebe says to close the gate!' the child had squeaked.

Smallboy fired his long whiplash and the ox teams took the strain, then plodded away with the end of the boom cable. As it came up taut, the cable rose to the surface of the channel and the oxen had to lean into the traces. The line of logs answered the pull. They slithered down the far bank from where they had been stacked, and snaked across the channel. The head of the boom reached the north side of the channel, and Smallboy chained it fast to the trunk of a huge tambootie hardwood. The mouth of the bay was corked up tightly.

Tom and Dorian had watched as Guy led his shore party at a rush through the gates of the captured fort and disappeared from their view. Then they turned their telescopes on the entrance to the bay and saw the massive cable rise to the surface of the channel as the oxen drew it tight.

'We can load the first gun,' Dorian told his gunners, who responded without marked enthusiasm. The gun captain relayed the order to the foreman in charge of the furnace. It was a lengthy business to fish the first shot from the furnace, and while they waited Tom kept a watch on the enemy.

Suddenly he called to Dorian. 'Guy is back on the parapet of the fort. He must have discovered the epistle I left for him in the treasury.' He chuckled aloud. 'Even from this distance I can see he's fit to burst with rage.' Then his expression changed. 'Now what's the crafty swine up to? He is heading back to the beach. He is saddling up the horses that have come ashore. There is some kind of fracas. By God! You will not believe this, Dorry. Guy has shot one of his own men.' The distant pop of the pistol shot carried to them on the heights, and Dorian left the cannon to join Tom.

'He has mounted.'

'He is taking at least twenty men with him.'

'Where in the name of the devil is he going?'

They watched the troop of horsemen, with Guy at the head, set out along the wagon road. It dawned on both Tom and Dorian at the same moment.

'He has seen the wagon tracks.'

'He is going after the wagons and the gold.'

'The women and little George! They are with the wagons. If Guy catches them—' Tom broke off. The thought was too painful to express. Then he went on bitterly, 'I blame myself. I should have considered this possibility. Guy does not give up readily.'

'The wagons have had a start of many days. They will be leagues away by now.'

'Only twenty miles,' Tom said bitterly. 'I told them to go as far as the river gorge, and make laager there.'

'It's my fault more than yours,' said Dorian. 'The safety of the women should have been my first concern. What a fool I am.'

'I must go after them.' Tom jumped to his feet. 'I must stop them falling into Guy's clutches.'

'I will ride with you.' Dorian stood up beside him.

'No, no!' Tom shoved him back. 'The battle is in your hands. Without you all is lost. You cannot desert your command. That goes for Jim and Mansur too. They must not come rushing after me. I can take care of brother Guy without their help. You must keep the lads here with you until the job is done. Give me your word on it, Dorry.'

'Very well. But you must take Smallboy and his musketeers with you. By the time you reach them, their job with the boom will be done.' He slapped Tom on the shoulder. 'Ride for all you are worth, and God go with you every step of the way.' Tom sprang over the bank of the gun emplacement and ran to where the horses were tethered.

743

As Tom galloped away down the track, two men came staggering from the furnace. They carried between them by its long handles the cradle on which lay the cannon-ball red as a ripe apple. Dorian could spare only one more quick glance after his elder brother, then hurried to supervise the gunners as they began the dangerous task of coaxing the ball into the muzzle of the gun. As it rolled down the smooth bore, two gunners rodded it up hard against the wet wadding and it sizzled and hissed. Clouds of steam poured out of the muzzle as they lowered the barrel.

Dorian wound down the elevation screw himself, trusting no other with this precise adjustment. Two other men with crowbars levered the barrel, traversing it as Dorian called to them, 'Left, and a hair more left!' Then, satisfied that the largest enemy dhow lay exactly in his sights, Dorian yelled, 'Stand clear!' and seized the lanyard. The gun-crew responded to his command with alacrity. Dorian yanked the lanyard, and the huge gun leaped like a wild animal charging the bars of its cage.

They could all follow the flight of the sparkling ball as it arced out across the waters of the bay, then fell towards the anchored dhow. A ragged cheer went up as they thought it must strike, then turned into a groan of disappointment as a tall white fountain jumped up close alongside the dhow's hull.

'Wet her down well!' Dorian had ordered. 'You have seen what will happen if you do not.'

He scrambled out of the emplacement and ran to the second gun. Already the next ball was being carried from the furnace and the crew was waiting for him. Before they could load and lay the gun, the five vessels had fled their moorings and were headed back across the bay towards the channel. Dorian peered over the sights. He had marked the angles of elevation in white paint on the gauge, and the men on the crow-bars nudged the long barrel round. He fired.

This time there was a roar of triumph from every man on

the hill as, even from this range, they saw the shower of bright sparks as the ball struck the hull of one of the dhows and the shot ripped through her timbers. Dorian ran to the third gun, leaving the crews of the other two sponging out. By the time they had loaded again, the stricken dhow was blazing like a bonfire on Guy Fawkes night.

'They are trying to break through the boom!' one of the men shouted, as they saw the burning ship steer into the entrance channel and, without checking its speed, bear down on the line of floating logs. They cheered again as it struck the boom, the mast tumbled down and the fire spread through her. Her crew leaped over the sides.

Dorian was bathed in sweat as he worked over the guns, loading and laying. Even though the crews doused them with buckets of water, the metal still crackled like a frying pan, and at each successive shot the guns leaped more violently on their carriages. However, within the next hour they fired another twenty hot balls, and four of the dhows were ablaze. The vessel that had struck the boom had burned down to the waterline, another drifted aimlessly across the bay, abandoned by her crew, who had rowed ashore in the boats. Two more had been beached and the crews had abandoned them to burn while they escaped into the forest, all too aware that the ships' magazines were crammed with kegs of black powder. Only the largest dhow had so far escaped the fire Dorian aimed at it. But it was locked into the bay, and could only tack back and forth across the open water.

'You can't dodge me for ever,' Dorian muttered. As the next ball was carried from the furnace, he spat on it for luck. The globule of saliva hit the heated metal and disappeared in a puff of steam, and at the same moment a huge shockwave of hot air blew across the hillside. It thumped painfully into their eardrums, and every man stared down into the bay in awe.

The drifting dhow had blown up as the powder in her magazine ignited. A tall mushroom-shaped cloud of smoke boiled up into the sky until it reached higher than the hilltop. Then, as if in sympathy, one of the beached dhows blew up with even greater force. The blast tore across the bay and lifted creaming waves from the surface. It raced through the forest above the beach, flattening the smaller trees, tearing off branches from the larger trees, raising a storm of dust, leaves and twigs. The men who watched it were struck dumb by the extent of the damage they had created. They did not cheer again but stood and gaped.

'One more left.' Dorian broke the spell. 'There she is, pretty as a bride on her wedding day.' He pointed down at the big dhow as she came about and started back towards the beach below the fort.

The cradle men lifted the ball, smoking and crackling, to roll it into the muzzle of the gun. Before they could do so another shout went up from every man: 'She is scuttling herself. Praise God and his angels, the enemy has had enough.'

The captain of the remaining dhow had seen the fate of the rest of the squadron. He made no effort to tack again but bore straight down on the sloping beach. At the last moment the dhow dropped her sail and went aground with such force that they heard her belly timbers snapping. She canted over heavily and lay quiescent, transformed in the instant from a thing of grace to a broken hulk. Her crew swarmed out of her, and left her lying abandoned at the water's edge.

'Enough!' Dorian called to his men. 'We have no more need of that.' With obvious relief they tipped the hot ball out on to the earth. Dorian scooped a ladleful from one of the buckets of drinking water and poured it over his head, then wiped his streaming face in the crook of his arm.

'Behold!' screamed the foreman of the furnace and pointed down. Immediately there was an excited clamour from the gun-crews, as they recognized the tall figure in cloud-white robes who clambered down from the stranded dhow and, with his distinctive limp, led his men along the beach towards the fort.

'Zayn al-Din!' they shouted.

'Death and damnation to the tyrant!'

'Power and glory to al-Salil.'

'God has given us the victory. God is great.'

'No.' Dorian jumped to the top of the emplacement wall

where they could all see him. 'The victory is not ours yet. Like a wounded jackal into his hole, Zayn al-Din has taken refuge in the fort.'

They saw the enemy seamen who had escaped from the other ships creep out of the forest, then hurry more boldly after Zayn al-Din. They streamed into the deserted fort after him.

'We must smoke him out,' Dorian told them, and jumped down from the wall. He called his gun captains to him and gave them swift orders. 'No more need for heated shot. Use only cold balls, but keep up a lively fire on the walls of the fort. Give them no rest. I am going down to round up all our men and lay siege to the fort. They have no food or water. We left no powder in the magazine, and the guns on the parapets have been spiked. Zayn cannot hold out for more than a day or two.'

A groom had already saddled his horse and Dorian rode down with every man who could be spared from the guns trooping after him. The men who had put up the token defence of the fort were waiting at the bottom of the hill to swell his ranks. He sent them to surround the building and make certain that none of the enemy could escape.

He saw Muntu coming through the forest from the direction of the entrance channel, and rode to meet him. 'Where is Smallboy?'

'He has taken ten men and gone with Klebe to follow the wagons.'

'Have you opened the boom, so that our ships can re-enter the bay?'

'Yes, master. The channel is clear.' Dorian lifted his telescope and checked the entrance. He saw that Muntu had severed the cable and the current had pushed the boom aside.

'Well done, Muntu. Now take your oxen.' He pointed down the shore to where Zayn's dhow lay stranded. 'Get the cannon out of that ship, and drag them round to cover the fort. We will pound the enemy from all sides. Knock a breach through the walls, so that when Jim arrives with Beshwayo's *impis* they can storm in and finish the business.'

By late afternoon the captured cannons from the stranded dhow had been towed by the oxen into position and the first shots knocked clods of earth and shattered timbers from the walls of the fort. They kept up the bombardment all night, giving the besieged enemy no rest.

In the dawn the *Sprite* sailed into the bay through the channel. She was followed by the *Arcturus* and the *Revenge*, shepherding all the captured Omani dhows and transports ahead of them. The warships anchored, and immediately turned all their guns on the fort. The three long nine-pounders on the heights of the bluff and the captured carronades from Zayn's own ships were already hammering away. Between them they directed a withering fire on the fort.

No sooner had the *Revenge* dropped her anchor than Mansur came ashore. Dorian was waiting to greet him on the beach, and ran forward when he saw his son's head swathed in the bandage. He embraced him and asked anxiously, 'You are hurt. How badly?'

'A scratch on my eyeball.' Mansur shrugged it off. 'It is almost healed. But Kadem, who inflicted the injury, is dead.'

'How did he die?' Dorian demanded, holding him at arm's length and staring into his face.

'By the knife. The same way that he murdered my mother.'

'You killed him?'

'Yes, Father. I killed him, and he did not die an easy death. My mother is avenged.'

'No, my son. There is still another. Zayn al-Din is holding out within the fort.'

'Can we be certain he is in there? Have you seen him with your own eyes?' They both stared along the shore at the battered palisades of the building. They could make out the heads of a few doughty defenders behind the parapets. However, Zayn had no artillery and most of his men were crouching behind the walls. The thudding of their muskets was a feeble response to the thunder of the cannon.

'Yes, Mansur. I have seen him. I will not leave this place until he also has paid the price in full, and gone to join his minion Kadem ibn Abubaker in hell.'

They both became aware of a new sound, faint at first but growing louder with every minute. Half a mile down the shores of the bay a dense column of men trotted out of the forest. They ran in a precise military formation. Like the foam on the crest of a dark wave, their feather headdresses danced in rhythm to their step. The early sunlight sparkled on their *assegais*, and on their oiled torsos. They were singing, a deep warlike chant that thrilled the blood and rumbled across the top of the forest. A lone horseman rode at the head of the leading column. He was mounted on a dark stallion whose long mane and tail streamed back in the wind of his canter.

'Jim on Drumfire.' Mansur laughed. 'Thank God he's safe.' A diminutive figure ran beside one of Jim's stirrups, and beside the other a giant of a man.

'Bakkat and Beshwayo,' said Dorian. Mansur ran to meet Jim, who swung down from the saddle and took him in a bear-hug.

'What is this rag you wear, coz? Is it some new fashion you have struck upon? It suits you not at all, you should take my word on it.' Then he turned to Dorian with his arm still around Mansur's shoulder.

'Uncle Dorry, where is my father?' His expression changed to dread. 'He is not hurt or killed? Tell me, I beg of you.'

'Nay, Jim lad. Breathe easy. Our Tom is impervious to shot and steel. As soon as his work here was done, he went to take care of the women and little Georgie.'

Dorian knew that if he told them the full truth about Guy's intervention, he would not be able to fulfil his promise to Tom and keep the boys with him. They would rush off immediately to defend their womenfolk. Quickly he glossed over his deception. 'But what of your side of the battle?'

'It is over, Uncle Dorry. Herminius Koots, who commanded the enemy, is dead. I saw to that myself. Beshwayo's men have cleared the forests of the rest of them. The pursuit took all of yesterday and most of the night. They chased some of the Turks a league up the beach and over the hills before they caught up with them.'

'Where are the prisoners?' Dorian demanded.

749

'Beshwayo does not understand the meaning of that word, and I was unable to educate him.' Jim laughed. But Dorian did not laugh with him: he could imagine the slaughter that had taken place in the forest, and his conscience troubled him. Those Omani who had perished under the *assegais* were his own subjects. He could not rejoice in their deaths. His anger towards Zayn al-Din flared even higher. Here was more blood for which he must pay.

Jim did not notice his uncle's expression. He was still buoyed up by the wild excitement of battle and intoxicated with the taste of victory. 'Look at him now.' He pointed to where Beshwayo was already parading his *impis* before the walls of the fort.

The guns had knocked a wide breach through them and Beshwayo strode down the ranks, stabbing his *assegai* towards the breach and haranguing his warriors: 'My children, some of you have not yet earned the right of marriage. Did I not give you opportunity enough? Were you slow? Were you unlucky?' He paused and glared at them. 'Or were you afraid? Did you piss down your own legs when you saw the feast I laid for you?'

His *impis* shouted an angry denial. 'We are thirsty still. We hunger still.'

'Give us to eat and drink again, Great Black Bull.'

'We are your faithful hunting dogs. Let us slip, great king. Let us run!' they pleaded.

'Before Beshwayo can send in an *impi* through the breach,' Jim said to Dorian, 'you must order the batteries to cease firing so as not to endanger his men.'

Dorian sent his runners out to the gun captains with the order. One after the other the batteries ceased firing. It took the message longer to reach the three guns on the heights of the bluff, but at last a tense, heavy silence fell over the bay.

The only movement was the waving of the feather head-dresses of the Beshwayo. The Arab defenders on the parapets looked down on this array, poised so menacingly before their walls, and their desultory musket-fire dried up. They stared bleakly upon implacable death.

Then, abruptly, a ram's-horn trumpet blared out from the walls of the fort. The ranks of black warriors stirred restlessly. Dorian turned his telescope to see a flag waved from the parapets.

'Surrender?' Jim smiled. 'Beshwayo does not understand that word either. A white flag will not save one of the men inside those walls.'

'Not a surrender.' Dorian shut his telescope. 'I know the man waving that flag. His name is Rahmad. He is one of the Omani admirals, a good sailor and a brave man. He was not able to choose the master he serves. He will not cravenly surrender. He wants to parley.'

Jim shook his head impatiently. 'I cannot keep Beshwayo in check much longer. What is there to speak about?'

'I intend to find out,' Dorian said.

'By God, Uncle! You cannot trust Zayn al-Din. This might be a trap.'

'Jim is right, Father,' cried Mansur. 'Don't give yourself into Zayn's power.'

'I must speak to Rahmad, if there is some small chance that I can end the bloodshed now and save the lives of those wretches trapped within the walls.'

'Then I must go with you,' said Jim.

'I also.' Mansur stepped up beside him.

Dorian's expression softened and he placed a hand on each of their shoulders. 'Stay here, both of you. I will need someone to avenge me, if things go awry.' He dropped his hands and loosened his sword-belt. He handed the weapon to Mansur. 'Keep this for me.' Then he looked at Jim: 'Can you hold your friend Beshwayo and his hunting hounds on a leash for just a little longer?'

'Be quick, Uncle. Beshwayo is not famous for his forbearance. I know not how long I can hold him.' Jim went with Dorian to where Beshwayo stood at the front of his impis, and

751

spoke to him earnestly. At last Beshwayo grunted reluctantly, and Jim told Dorian, 'Beshwayo agrees to wait until you return.'

Dorian strode through the ranks of the Beshwayo *impis*. They opened before him, for those warriors recognized the quality of nobility in him. Dorian's step was measured and stately as he strode towards the walls and stopped within easy pistol shot. He looked up at the figure on the parapet.

'Speak, Rahmad!' he ordered.

'You remember me?' Rahmad sounded amazed.

'I know you well. I would not have trusted you otherwise. You are a man of honour.'

'Majesty!' Rahmad bowed deeply. 'Mighty Caliph.'

'If you address me thus, why do you fight against me?'

Rahmad seemed for a moment overcome with shame. Then he raised his head. 'I speak not only for myself but for every man within these walls.'

Dorian raised his hand to stop him. 'This is strange, Rahmad. You speak for the men? You do not speak for Zayn al-Din? Explain this to me.'

'Mighty al-Salil, Zayn al-Din is . . .' Rahmad seemed to search for the right words. 'We have requested Zayn al-Din to demonstrate to us and all the world that he, not you, is indeed the Caliph of Oman.'

'In what way can he prove this?'

'In the traditional manner, when two men have an equal claim to the throne. In the sight of God, and before all this array, man to man in single combat, we have requested Zayn al-Din to fight to the death to prove that claim.'

'You propose a duel between us?'

'We have taken an oath of allegiance to Zayn al-Din. We cannot surrender his person to you. We are bound to defend him with our own lives. However, if he were defeated in a traditional duel, we would be released from our vow. Gladly then we would become your liege men.'

Dorian understood their dilemma. They were holding Zayn al-Din prisoner, but they were unable to execute him or hand him over. He must kill Zayn himself in single combat. The alternative would be for him to allow the Beshwayo to slaughter Rahmad and all the Omani.

'Why should I place myself in such peril? You and Zayn al-Din are in my power.' Dorian pointed at the black ranks of Beshwayo. 'Why should I not send them in to massacre you all here and now?'

'A lesser man might do that. I know you will not, for you are the son of Sultan Abd Muhammad al-Malik. You will not desecrate our honour, or your own.'

'What you say is true, Rahmad. It is my destiny to unite the kingdom of Oman, not split it asunder. I must take up that destiny with honour. I will fight Zayn al-Din for the caliphate.'

W ith white ash the Omani elders and headmen marked out the duelling ring on the hard-baked ground below the walls of the fort. This was a circle twenty paces in diameter.

All the Arabs who had fought with Zayn al-Din and been trapped within the fort now lined the parapets. Dorian's forces, including the crews from the captured dhows who had declared their loyalty to him, were drawn up on the bayside of the ring, facing the opposing forces on the walls of the fort.

Jim had explained the rules and the object of the duel to Beshwayo, and he was enthralled. He no longer resented being deprived of the right to storm the fort and wipe out the defenders. For him this gladiatorial contest was even greater sport.

'This is a fine way to solve a dispute, Somoya. It is truly a warrior's thing. I shall make it my own custom in the future.'

The entire Beshwayo army squatted in ranks behind Dorian's legions. The high parapet and the slope of the ground afforded every man present an unobstructed view of the ring.

Dorian, flanked by Jim and Mansur, stood at the forefront

of this array, facing the closed gates of the fort. He wore only a simple white robe and his feet were bare. In accordance with the rules of the contest he was unarmed.

There was another blast on the ram's horn and the gates of the fort swung open. Four men marched out and came down the hill. They were in half-armour, bronze helmets and chain-mail overshirts, with greaves protecting their lower legs. They were big men with cold eyes and brutal faces, the executioners of the Omani court. Torture and death were their vocation. They took up their positions at the four points of the circle, and leaned on the hilts of their drawn swords.

There was a pause and then another trumpet blast. A second procession came down the slope. It was led by Mullah Khaliq. Behind him came Rahmad and four other tribal headmen. Then, with an escort of five armed men, the tall figure of Zayn al-Din limped after them. They stopped on the far side of the ring, facing Dorian.

Rahmad advanced into the centre of the ring. 'In the Name of the One God and his True Prophet we are met here this day to decide the fate of our nation. Al-Salil!' He bowed towards Dorian. 'And Zayn al-Din.' He turned and bowed again. 'This day one of you will die and the other will ascend the Elephant Throne of Oman.'

He held out his hands and the two headmen who flanked him passed Rahmad a pair of scimitars. Rahmad stabbed the point of one of these weapons into the earth just inside the ash line of the ring, and left it standing upright. Then he crossed the circle and placed the other weapon exactly opposite it.

'Only one of you will be permitted to leave this ring alive. The four referees,' he pointed to the waiting executioners, 'have been strictly charged with the duty of killing immediately whichever of you is driven or thrown outside this line of ashes.' He touched the line with the toe of his sandal. 'Now Mullah Khaliq will lead the prayers begging for the guidance of God in these affairs.'

The holy man's voice droned in the silence as he commended the combatants to God and their fate. Dorian and

Zayn stared across the ring at each other. Their faces were expressionless but their eyes burned with hatred and anger. The mullah ended his prayer: 'In God's Name let it begin!'

'In God's Name, make ready!' Rahmad called.

Jim and Mansur lifted the loose robe over Dorian's head. He wore only a white loincloth under it. Where the sun had not touched him his skin was smooth and white as cream in a jug. At the same time his escort helped Zayn remove his robe. Now he wore only a loincloth, and his skin was the colour of old ivory. Dorian knew that Zayn was his senior by only two years. They were both in their middle forties, and the effects of age were becoming apparent on their bodies. There were streaks of grey in their hair and beards, and a fleshiness round their waistlines. However, their limbs were clean and hard and their movements were lithe as they stepped into the ring. Even the impediment in Zayn's step seemed more sinister than inhibiting. They were matched in height but Zayn was the heavier man, bigger boned and wider in the shoulder. Since childhood both had been trained in the warrior's way, but they had matched against each other once only before this day. However, they had been children then, and they and the world about them were altered.

They stood just out of arm's reach of each other. Neither spoke, but they assessed each other carefully. Rahmad stepped between them. He carried a length of silken cord, light as gossamer and strong as steel. He had measured its length and cut it precisely five paces shorter than the diameter of the ring.

Rahmad went to Zayn first. Though he knew full well that he was left-handed, Rahmad asked formally, 'Which hand?'

Disdaining a reply Zayn proffered his right hand. Rahmad tied the end of the cord round his wrist. He was a sailor and the knot would neither tighten nor slip, yet it would hold like a steel cuff. Rahmad came to Dorian with the other end of the cord. Dorian gave him his left hand and he tied it with the same type of knot. The two combatants were linked together: only the death of one could part them now.

'Mark your swords!' Rahmad ordered them, and they

glanced back at the scimitar that stood behind each man on the perimeter of the ring. The silk cord was too short to allow them simultaneously to reach a weapon.

'A blast on the ram's horn will begin this contest, but only death will end it,' intoned Rahmad. He and the four headmen left the ring. A terrible silence descended on the field. Even the breeze seemed to still, and the gulls ceased their mewing cries. Rahmad looked to the trumpeter on the parapet and raised his hand. The trumpeter lifted the curled horn to his lips. Rahmad dropped his hand and the blast sobbed and echoed off the cliffs of the bluff. A huge wave of sound swept over the ring as every man in the convocation shouted together.

Neither contestant moved. They faced each other still, leaning back on the cord, keeping it taut, taking the strain, assessing each other's weight and strength, the way a fisherman feels a heavy fish after the strike. Neither could reach his scimitar unless he could force the other to give ground. They strained silently. Suddenly Dorian darted forward, and Zayn reeled back as the cord went slack. Then he whirled and ran for his sword. Grimly Dorian noted the slight clumsiness as he turned into his crippled side. Dorian ran after him and gathered in a double arm's length of the slack in the cord. He gained the centre of the ring, and shortened the length of cord between them by almost half. From this position he dominated the ring, but he had sacrificed precious ground for that. Zayn was reaching out for the hilt of his scimitar. Dorian took a turn of the cord round his wrist and planted his feet. He anchored the cord and Zayn came up hard against the end of it with such force that it snapped him round on to his bad side. For a moment he was off-balance and Dorian heaved him backwards and gained another arm's length of the cord.

Abruptly Dorian changed the angle of his pull. He made himself the fulcrum around which Zayn pivoted. Like the stone on the end of a slingshot, Dorian used the impetus to launch Zayn towards the white ash line, straight at one of the executioners who waited with drawn sword to meet him. As it seemed he must be hurled backwards out of the ring, Zayn found purchase with his stronger leg and checked the slingshot effect. He teetered on the line and raised a puff of white ash, but he managed to stop himself going out. The executioner stood behind him with the blade raised to make the stroke. Now there was slack in the cord and Dorian had lost the leverage. He raced forward to crash into Zayn with his shoulder and drive him that last yard across the line. Zayn saw him coming, braced his legs and dropped his shoulder to meet him.

They came together with a force that jarred every bone in their bodies, and stood like a carving in marble, straining and grunting. Dorian had the heel of his right hand under Zayn's chin and forced his head back. Slowly Zayn's spine arched over the line, and the executioner moved forward a pace to meet him as he stepped over it. Zayn drew a hissing breath and summoned the last vestige of his strength. His face seemed to darken and swell with the effort, but slowly his back straightened. He pushed Dorian back a step.

The noise was deafening. A thousand voices joined in, and the Beshwayo warriors were dancing and drumming on their shields. A hurricane of sound swept over the ring. Zayn exerted his greater weight and gradually worked his shoulder down under Dorian's armpit, then suddenly heaved upwards. He took the weight off Dorian's legs and forced him to lose traction and grip. The bare soles of his feet skidded in the dust, and he was driven back a yard, then another. Dorian was pitting all his strength against Zayn's thrust. Abruptly Zayn jumped back. Dorian staggered forward off-balance. Swift as a lizard on his crippled foot Zayn darted away, straight back to where his sword was pegged into the earth.

Dorian tried to snatch up the slack in the cord to restrain him again, but before he could bring it tight Zayn had reached the weapon and had a firm grip on the hilt. Dorian jerked him backwards, but Zayn came willingly, rushing at him with the point of the blade levelled at Dorian's throat. Dorian ducked under it and they circled each other. They were still linked by the umbilical cord of silk.

Zayn was laughing silently, but it was a sound without joy.

He mock-charged at Dorian, forcing him to dodge back, and as soon as he had made slack in the cord for the move Zayn darted to where Dorian's scimitar was still standing at the far end of the circle. Before Dorian could bring the rope tight, Zayn had grabbed the second weapon out of the ground. Now he turned to face Dorian with a blade in each hand.

A silence fell over the multitude and they watched in awful fascination as Zayn stalked Dorian round the ring, while the executioners shadowed him from behind, waiting for him to step out of the ash circle. Watching him carefully, Dorian realized that though he favoured his left hand Zayn was almost as dexterous with his right. As if to demonstrate this he rushed forward and cut right-handed at Dorian's head. When Dorian ducked out of the stroke he thrust with his left and Dorian could not avoid it. Although he twisted aside, the point scored his ribs and the crowd howled to see blood spurt.

Mansur clutched at Jim's arm with such strength that his fingernails cut through the skin. 'He is hurt. We must stop it.'

'No, coz,' Jim said softly. 'We cannot intervene.'

The pair in the ring kept turning, as though the cord that linked them was a spoke of a wheel. Dorian still held the slack of the line between his hands.

Zayn was quivering with eagerness for the kill, his mouth working, his eyes burning darkly. 'Bleed, pig, and when you have shed your last drop, I will hack your carcass into fifty pieces and send each bit to the furthest corners of my empire so that all men will know the penalty for treachery.'

Dorian did not reply. He held his end of the cord lightly in the fingers of his right hand. With total concentration he watched Zayn's eyes for the signal that he would charge again. Zayn feigned a move with his bad leg, then sprang forward off his strong side. It was exactly what Dorian had anticipated. He flicked out the bight in the cord, and then, with a snap of his wrist, shot the loop forward like a whiplash. The silk cord slashed across Zayn's right eye with such force that the blood vessels burst, the pupil and the cornea shattered, and in an instant the eyeball was transformed into a fragile pink sack of jelly.

Zayn screamed, high-pitched and shrill as a girl. He dropped both swords and cupped his hands over his injured eye. He stood blind and shrieking in the centre of the ring. Dorian stooped and picked up one of the scimitars. As he came upright again, as gracefully as a dancer, he drove the point into Zayn's belly.

The shriek was cut off from Zayn's lips. One hand was still clasped over his eye but with the other hand he groped down and found the gaping wound in his guts from which blood, intestinal gas and detritus bubbled. He sank forward on to his knees and bowed his head. His neck was stretched forward. Dorian raised the scimitar on high, then swung it down. The air fluted, softly as the call of a mourning dove, over the steel, which found the joint of the vertebrae and sheared through. Zayn's head jumped from his shoulders and thumped on to the hard-baked earth. His trunk remained kneeling for a moment, with the severed arteries pumping, then toppled forward.

Dorian stooped, took a handful of the silver-streaked hair, then lifted high the severed head. The eyes were wide open and darted from side to side with a louche expression.

'Thus I avenge the Princess Yasmini. Thus I claim the Elephant Throne of Oman,' Dorian shouted in triumph.

A thousand voices joined in the cry: 'Hail to al-Salil! Hail to the Caliph!'

Beshwayo's *impis* leaped to their feet and, led by the king himself, thundered out the royal salute: '*Bayete, Inkhosi! Bayete!*'

Dorian dropped the head, and reeled from the effects of his wound. The blood was still streaming down his flank and he might have fallen, had not Mansur and Jim rushed into the ring and supported him at each side. They half carried him into the fort. The rooms had been stripped of every stick of furniture, but they took Dorian to his own bedroom and laid him on the bare floor. Mansur ordered Rahmad to call Zayn al-Din's personal surgeon, who had been waiting at the door for this summons. He hurried in at once.

While he bathed the wound and stitched it closed with cat-gut, Dorian spoke softly to Mansur and Jim. 'Tom made

759

me give my word that I would not tell you this until the fighting here was over. Now I am released from that promise. As soon as our defenders abandoned the fort, our brother Guy came ashore with a squad of armed men. They stormed into the fort. When Guy found that we had emptied the treasury, he came out on to the parapet and saw the wagon tracks. He must have realized we had sent the gold away. Zayn had already landed his horses on the beach by this time. Guy commandeered mounts for himself and twenty of his men, and rode out along the wagon road. There can be no doubt that he intends to capture the wagons.' The two young men stared at him aghast.

Jim found his voice first. 'The women! Little Georgie!'

'As soon as we realized what was happening, Tom took Smallboy and his musketeers. They chased after Guy.'

'Oh, God!' Mansur groaned. 'That was yesterday. There is no way of telling what has happened since then. Why did you not tell us before?'

'You know why I could not, but now I am freed of my promise to Tom.'

As he turned to Mansur, Jim's voice cracked with anxiety for his family – Sarah, Louisa and Georgie: 'Are you with me, coz?'

'Will you let me go, Father?'

'Of course, my son, and all my blessings with you,' Dorian replied.

Mansur sprang to his feet. 'I am with you, coz!' They ran to the door.

Jim was already shouting for Bakkat: 'Saddle up Drumfire. We ride at once.'

In addition to being at a safe distance from the coast, the gorge was a lovely place. Sarah had chosen it as the campsite for that reason. The river came down out of the mountains in a series of cascades and waterfalls. The pools below each of these were clear and placid, filled with yellow fish. Tall trees shaded the site of their laager. Flowering fruits in the leafy canopy attracted birds and vervet monkeys.

Although Tom had prevailed on Sarah to cache most of the furniture and her other possessions within a few miles of the fort, in the same hiding-place as some of the ivory, Sarah had insisted on loading all her real treasures on to the wagons. She did not look upon the chests of gold bars that Tom had foisted on her as being of especial importance. When they reached the campsite she had not even bothered to have them unloaded. When Louisa and Verity politely queried the wisdom of this, Sarah laughed. 'Wasted effort. We will just have to load them all up again when it's time to go home.'

On the other hand, she spared no effort in providing the camp with all the comforts of home. Chief of these was a fine mud-walled kitchen and refectory. The roof was a masterpiece of the thatcher's art. The floor was plastered with clay and cow dung. Sarah's harpsichord had pride of place in the centre of the room and every evening they gathered around it to sing while Sarah played.

During the days they picnicked beside the pool, and watched George swim like a naked little fish, and applauded as he jumped in from the high bank with the loudest splash he could make. They painted and sewed. Louisa gave George riding lessons, perched up on Trueheart's back like a flea. Verity worked on her translations of the Qur'an and the *Ramayana*. Sarah took George with her to collect wild flowers. Back in the laager she sketched the plants and wrote descriptive notes of them to add to her collection. Verity had brought a box of her favourite books from her cabin in the *Arcturus*, and she read aloud to the other women. They marvelled over James Thomson's *Seasons* and giggled together like schoolgirls over *Rage on Rage*.

Some mornings Louisa left George in the care of Sarah and Intepe, the lily, while she and Verity went out riding. This was an arrangement that suited George very well. Grandmama Sarah was an unending source of biscuits, toffee and other delights. She was also a captivating raconteur. Gentle Intepe was in George's thrall and obeyed his lordly instructions

761

without quibble. She was now Zama's wife and had already borne him one lusty son. The baby was still at her breast, but her older boy was George's liege man. Zama had made for each of them a miniature bow, and a sharpened stick to use as a spear. They spent a great amount of time hunting around the perimeter of the camp. To date they had only achieved one kill: a fieldmouse had made the mistake of running under George's feet and, in an effort to avoid it, he had stood on its head. They cooked the tiny carcass in the flames of a large fire they built expressly for the purpose, and devoured the scorched, blackened flesh with relish.

These seemed idyllic days, but they were not. A dark shadow hung over the camp. Even in the midst of laughter the women would fall suddenly silent and look back along the wagon track that led down to the coast. When they mentioned the names of the men they loved, which they did often, their eyes were sad. In the night they started up at the whicker of one of the horses, or the sound of hoofs in the darkness. They called from one wagon to the other: 'Did you hear aught, Mother?'

'It was only one of our own horses, Louisa. Sleep now. Jim will come soon.'

'Are you well, Verity?'

'As well as you, but I miss Mansur as much as you miss Jim.'

'Do not fret, girls,' Sarah calmed them. 'They are Courtneys and they are tough. They'll be back soon.'

Every four or five days a rider came up from Fort Auspice with a leather satchel over his shoulder that contained letters for them. His arrival was the highlight of their lives. Each of the women seized the letter addressed to her and rushed to her own wagon to read it alone. They emerged much later, flushed and smiling, filled with ephemeral high spirits to discuss the news they had received. Then they began the long, lonely wait until the rider came again.

Intepe's grandfather, Tegwane, was the night-watchman. At his age he slept little and took his duties seriously. He prowled endlessly around the wagons on his stork thin legs with his spear over his shoulder. Zama was the camp overseer. He had eight men under him, including the wagon drivers and the armed *askari*. Izeze, the flea, was growing into a robust youth, and a fine musket shot. He was the sergeant of the guard.

On Jim's orders Inkunzi had moved all the cattle herds up from the coast into the hills where they would be safe from any incursion by Zayn al-Din's expeditionary force. He and all his Nguni herders were close at hand if any emergency arose.

After twenty-eight days in the river camp the women should have felt secure, but they did not. They should have been able to sleep soundly, but they were not. The premonition of evil hung over them all.

That particular night Louisa had not been able to sleep. She had hung a blanket over George's cot to shield him from the light, while she lay on the cardell bed propped up on her pillows and read Henry Fielding by the light of the oil lamp. Suddenly she cast aside the book and rushed to the afterclap of the wagon. She pulled open the curtains and listened until she was certain, then she called, 'Rider coming. It must be the mail.'

The lamps in the other wagons flared as the wicks were turned up, and all three women jumped down and stood in a huddle in front of the kitchen. They were talking excitedly as Zama and Tegwane piled logs on the fire and a shower of sparks flew upwards.

Sarah was the first to grow uneasy. 'There is more than one horse.' She cocked her head to listen.

'Do you think it may be the men?' Louisa asked eagerly.

'I don't know.'

'Perhaps we should take precautions,' Verity suggested. 'We should not presume that because they are mounted and come without stealth they are friendly.'

'Verity is right. Louisa, fetch Georgie! Everyone else into the kitchen! We will lock ourselves in there until we know who they are.'

Louisa gathered up the skirts of her nightgown and raced back to her wagon, her long pale hair flying out behind her.

Intepe came running from her hut with her children, and Sarah and Verity shepherded them into the kitchen. Sarah snatched a musket from the rack and stood at the doorway.

'Hurry, Louisa!' she shouted urgently. The sound of hoofs swelled louder, and out of the night galloped a large band of horsemen. They charged into the camp and reined in, their horses milling about, knocking over buckets and chairs, kicking up a haze of dust in the firelight.

'Who are you?' Sarah called sharply, still standing four-square in the doorway. 'What do you want with us?'

The leader of the band rode towards her and pushed his hat on to the back of his head so that she could see he was a white man. 'Put down that gun, woman. Get all your people out here in the open. I am taking charge here.'

Verity stepped up beside Sarah. 'It's my father,' she told Sarah softly. 'Guy Courtney.'

'Verity, you treacherous child. Come out of there. You have much to answer for.'

'You leave her be, Guy Courtney. Verity is under my protection.'

Guy laughed bitterly as he recognized her. 'Sarah Beatty, my beloved sister-in-law. It's been many a long year since we parted.'

'Not long enough for my taste,' Sarah told him grimly. 'I'll have you know that I am no longer Beatty, but Mrs Tom Courtney. Now be gone and leave us alone.'

'You should not boast of marriage to such a black rogue and lecher, Sarah. However, I cannot leave so soon. You have in your possession things that have been stolen from me. My gold and my daughter. I have come to reclaim them.'

'You will have to kill me before you get your hands on either of them.'

'That would cause me no hardship, I assure you.' He laughed again and looked back at Peters. 'Tell the men to search the wagons.'

'Stop!' Sarah raised the musket.

'Shoot!' Guy invited her. 'But I swear it will be the last thing you ever do.'

While Sarah hesitated, Guy's men jumped off their horses and rushed to the wagons. There was a shout and Peters told Guy, 'They have found the gold chests.'

Then there was a scream and two of the Arabs dragged Louisa from her wagon. She had George in her arms and she was struggling wildly with her captors. 'Leave me! Leave my baby.'

'Who is this brat?' Guy reached down, grabbed the child by one arm and tore him from Louisa's grip. He looked at Sarah across the fire. 'Do you know anything about this little bastard?'

Verity tugged surreptitiously at the back of Sarah's night-dress, and whispered urgently, 'Don't let him know what George means to you. He will use him ruthlessly.'

'So, my darling daughter is conniving with her father's enemies. Shame on you, child.' His eyes swivelled back to Sarah's face. He saw that it had turned frosty pale, and he smiled coldly. 'No relation of yours, Sarah? You make no claim to him? Then let's get rid of him.'

He leaned from the saddle and dangled George over the flames of the campfire. The child felt the heat on his bare legs and shrieked at the pain. Louisa screamed as loudly, and Verity shouted, 'No, Daddy, please let him go.'

'No, Guy, no.' Sarah's reaction was the strongest of all. She rushed forward. 'He is my grandson. Please, do not hurt him. We will do as you say, only let Georgie go.'

'That is so much more reasonable.' Guy lifted the child away from the flames.

'Give him to me, Guy.' Sarah held up both arms to him. 'Please, Guy.'

'Please, Guy!' He mimicked her. 'That is much more civil. But I fear I must keep young George with me to make certain that you do not have a change of heart. Now, I want all your servants to throw down their weapons and come out from wherever they are hiding with their hands over their heads. Give them the order!'

'Zama! Tegwane! Izeze! All of you. Do as he says,' Sarah ordered. They came shuffling out reluctantly from among the

765

wagons and the surrounding trees. Guy's men grabbed their muskets, tied their hands behind their backs and led them away.

'Now, Sarah, you, Verity and this other wench,' he pointed at Louisa, 'get back inside the hut. Remember, I have this fine fellow with me.' He pinched George's cheek between his nails until the tender skin tore and the child shrieked in pain. The women struggled in the arms of the men who held them, but they were dragged back into the kitchen. The door slammed shut, and two of Guy's men stood guard over it.

Guy swung down from the saddle and threw his reins to one of the men. He dragged George along with him and when the child balked he stooped over him and shook him until his teeth rattled together and he lost his breath so that he could no longer yell. 'Shut your mouth, you little swine, or I will shut it for you.' He straightened up and called to Peters, 'Tell them to unload the gold chests. I want to check the contents for myself.'

It took longer than Guy expected for his men to manhandle the heavy crates out of the wagons and unscrew the lids, but when he stood over them at last and gazed down on the shining yellow bars his face took on a deeply religious expression. 'It's all here,' he whispered dreamily, 'every last ounce.' Then he roused himself. 'Now, it remains only to get it safely back to the ships. We will need at least two of these wagons.' He tucked George under one arm, and strode across to where the servants huddled under armed guard. 'Which of you are the wagon drivers?' He picked them out. 'Go with my men and bring in your oxen. Inspan them to these two wagons. Work quickly. If you try to escape you will be shot.'

As soon as the kitchen door slammed shut behind them Sarah turned to the girls. Verity was pale but calm. Louisa was shaking and weeping softly.

'Verity, you stay by the door and warn us if anyone tries to

766

open it.' She put one arm round Louisa. 'Come, darling, be brave. This won't help George.'

Louisa straightened her shoulders and sniffed back her tears. 'What do you want me to do?'

'Help me.' Sarah went across to the military chest that stood against the side wall. She rummaged in the bottom drawer and brought out a blue leather case. When she opened it a pair of silver duelling pistols lay in their velvet-lined nests. 'Tom taught me to shoot with these.' She handed one to Louisa. 'Help me load.'

Now that she had a task, Louisa pulled herself together quickly and loaded the weapon with swift, sure hands. Sarah had watched her at practice and knew that Jim had made her an expert shot.

'Hide it in your bodice,' Sarah ordered, and tucked the other pistol down the front of her night clothes. She went back to the door and listened. 'Have you heard anything?'

'The two Arab guards are talking,' Verity whispered back.

'What are they saying?'

'There has been fighting at the bay. They are very worried. While they were on the road here they heard the sound of a battle raging behind them, heavy cannon fire and a number of explosions that they think were Zayn's ships blowing up. They are discussing deserting my father and trying to make a run for it to the coast. They don't want to be abandoned here if Zayn is defeated.'

'So all is not lost, then. Tom and Dorian are still fighting.'

'It sounds as if that is what is happening,' Verity agreed.

'Keep listening, Verity. I want to try the window.'

Sarah left her at the door and placed a chair under the single high window. While Louisa held it steady she climbed on to it. She lifted aside the edge of the kudu-skin curtain that covered it and peered out.

'Can you see George?' Louisa's voice shook.

'Yes, Guy has him. He looks frightened but not badly hurt.'

'My poor baby,' Louisa sobbed.

'Now, don't start that again,' Sarah snapped. To keep the

minds of the two girls occupied, she began a commentary of all that she could see taking place outside. 'They are unloading the gold chests from the wagons and opening the lids. Guy is checking them.'

She described how, once the chests had been sealed and reloaded into the two wagons, the drivers brought in the ox teams and, under the scrutiny of Guy's henchmen, inspanned them.

'They are ready to leave,' Sarah said with relief. 'Guy has all that he came for. Surely he must give George back to us now and leave us in peace.'

'I don't think he will do that, Aunt,' Verity disagreed reluctantly. 'I think we are his passport back to the coast. From what I overheard the guards saying, our men are still fighting. My father will know that as long as he has us women and Georgie as his hostages they will be powerless to attack him.'

Within minutes she was proved right. There was a tramp of feet outside and the door was thrown open. Five Arabs crowded through it and one spoke harshly to Verity. She translated for the others: 'He says we must dress quickly in warmer clothes and be ready to leave at once.'

They were led to their wagons and the guards stood over them as they pulled on heavy coats over their nightdresses and hastily threw a few necessities into a valise. Then the three were led out to where horses had been saddled for them. The two wagons carrying the gold were drawn up one behind another, pointed back along the track. Guy was at the head of his men.

'Let me take George from you,' Sarah pleaded.

'Once, long ago, you played me for the fool, Sarah Beatty. It will not happen again. I shall keep your grandson firmly under my hand.' He drew the dagger from the sheath on his belt and held the blade to George's throat. The child was too terrified to cry out. 'You must not doubt for a minute that I shall slit his throat without compunction if you give me cause. If we meet Tom or Dorian or any of their vile brood on the road you will tell them that. Now hold your tongue.'

They mounted the horses that Zama, Izeze and Tegwane were holding for them. As Louisa settled on Trueheart's back she leaned forward and whispered to Zama, 'Where are Intepe and her children?'

'I have sent them into the forest,' he answered quietly. 'No one tried to stop them.'

'Thank God for that at least.'

Guy called out the order to advance, and Peters repeated it in a loud voice. The trek whips popped and the wagons rolled forward. Guy led the convoy, with George carried awkwardly on his hip. The escort of Arabs forced the women to follow close behind him. They crowded them together so that their knees touched. The rumble of the wheels and the creak and rattle of equipment covered Sarah's voice as she whispered to the girls, 'Have you the pistol ready, Louisa?'

'Yes, Mother. I have my hand upon it.'

'Good. Then this is what we must do.' She went on speaking softly, and the two girls murmured acknowledgement. 'Wait for my word,' Sarah warned them. 'Our only chance is to take them by surprise. We must act in concert to have any chance of success.'

The cavalcade wound down the hills towards the littoral. The horses were constrained to the speed of the plodding oxen. After a while nobody spoke. Captors and prisoners rode in a lethargic silence, which slowly became torpor. George had long ago sunk into an exhausted sleep. His head lolled on Guy's shoulder. Every time Sarah looked at him her heart squeezed with dread.

Every once in a while she would reach across and touch one of the girls to keep them awake and alert. She had been studying the horses that the Arab captors rode. They were thin and in poor condition, and she guessed they had endured a long, debilitating voyage in small ships. They would be no match for the mounts that she and the girls rode. Of their three horses Trueheart was the swiftest. Louisa was a light weight to carry and she and Trueheart would run away from any of them, even if she was carrying George with her.

The Arab riding next to Sarah let his head drop forward

on his chest. He started to slide sideways out of the saddle. Sarah knew that he had fallen asleep. Before he toppled from his horse's back, the man's head flew up as he woke with a start.

They are all exhausted, Sarah told herself. They have had no rest since they left the coast. Their horses are in no better case. It is nearly time for us to break away, and make a run for it.

In the moonlight she recognized this section of the road. They were approaching a ford over one of the tributaries of the main river. On the outward journey up from Fort Auspice, Zama and his men had spent days digging out the banks. It was a narrow and steep crossing that the wagons could only negotiate with difficulty. She knew that they would not find a better place at which to make the break. She estimated that there was still an hour of darkness to cover their escape, and by that time she hoped they would be clear of the weakened, exhausted horses of their pursuers.

She reached stealthily across to each of the girls in turn. She squeezed their hands and shook them lightly to alert them. The three pressed their mounts gently and moved up together until they were riding within touching distance of the rump of Guy's horse.

Sarah reached under her coat and slipped the duelling pistol out of her bodice. She used the folds of her sheepskin coat to muffle the click as she drew back the hammer to half-cock. The trigger of the weapon was set very lightly and she dared not cock it fully until the moment of firing. Fifty yards ahead she saw the gap in the river bank appear out of the darkness, with the road running down into it. She waited until Guy reined in his horse as he studied the cutting that led down to the ford.

Before Guy could call out, Sarah deliberately rode into his horse. The girls on each side of her pressed forward, and for a moment there was confusion as the horses bumped each other and milled about.

'Keep your damned horses under control,' Guy exclaimed with annoyance.

Then another voice roared from the darkness of the cutting just ahead. 'Stand where you are! I have fifty muskets loaded with goose-shot trained on you.'

'Tom!' Sarah exulted. 'It's Tom!' Of course he had heard the wagons from a mile off, and he would choose the river crossing to ambush them.

'Tom Courtney!' Guy shouted back. 'I have your grandson, and my dagger to his throat. My men have your wife Sarah, and the other women of your family. Stand aside and let us pass if you want any of them alive.'

To reinforce the threat he lifted George off his shoulder and held him up with both hands. 'It's your grandfather, child. Speak to him. Tell him you are safe.' He pricked George's arm with the dagger. From behind Guy's shoulder Sarah saw the blood start on the white skin, black and shiny in the moonlight.

'Grandpapa!' George shrieked at the top of his lungs. 'There is a horrid man hurting me.'

'By God, Guy! You touch a hair of that child's head and I'll kill you with my bare hands,' Tom's voice rang out with angry frustration.

'Hear the piglet squeal,' Guy shouted back, and pricked George again. 'Throw down your weapons and show yourselves, or I will send you your grandson's guts on a silver tray.'

Sarah drew the pistol from under her coat and cocked the hammer. She reached forward and pressed the muzzle into the small of Guy's back at the level of the kidneys. She fired and the shot was muffled by Guy's clothing and flesh. Guy's back arched in his agony as the ball shattered his vertebrae. He loosened his grip and George fell out of his raised hands.

'Now, Louisa!' Sarah screamed.

But Louisa did not need the order. She leaned out of the saddle and caught George as he fell. She clasped him to her bosom and kicked her heels into Trueheart's ribs. 'Ha! Ha!' she shouted to the mare. 'Run, Trueheart! Run!'

Trueheart jumped forward. One of the Arabs reached out to seize her, but Louisa fired the second pistol into his bearded face, and he fell backwards out of the saddle. Verity turned her horse in behind Trueheart to screen George and his mother from any musket bullets fired by the escort. She was only just quick enough. One of the Arabs, more alert than his companions, threw up his jezail and the long flame of the discharge ripped through the darkness. Sarah heard the ball strike flesh. Verity's horse collapsed under her, and she was thrown forward over its head.

Sarah spurred forward just as Guy toppled backwards and fell limply from the saddle into her path. Her horse tried to jump over him, but one of the metal-shod hoofs struck Guy's temple and she heard the brittle bone break like ice. Her horse recovered its balance and Sarah steered it towards where Verity was struggling to her feet.

'I am coming, Verity!' Sarah called to her, and made an arm for her. Verity hooked hers through Sarah's as the horse swept past her. Neither of them had the strength to swing Verity up astride, but she managed to throw her free arm over the horse's withers and cling on desperately as they followed Trueheart down into the river ford.

'Tom!' Sarah yelled. 'It's us. Don't shoot!'

The rest of the Arab escort had recovered their wits and were galloping after Sarah in a tight band. Suddenly a volley of musket fire erupted from the edge of the bank where Smallboy and the rest of Tom's men were lying. Three horses went down in a tangle, and the rest of the Arabs reined in and turned back. They raced for the shelter of the wagons and huddled behind them.

Tom jumped down from the bank and, as Sarah reined in, he seized her and Verity and dragged them down. He pulled them into safety behind the bank.

'Louisa!' Sarah gasped. 'Catch Louisa and George.'

'No one can catch Trueheart when she has the bit between her teeth. But they are safe out there as long as we keep the Arabs pinned down here.' Tom embraced Sarah. 'By God, I'm pleased to see you, woman.'

Sarah pushed him away. 'There'll be plenty of time for that nonsense later, Tom Courtney. You still have work to do here.'

'Right you are!'

Tom ran back to the top of the bank, and called to the dark wagons behind which the Arabs were sheltering: 'Guy! Do you hear me?'

'He's dead, Tom,' Sarah interrupted him. 'I shot him.'

'Then you beat me to it,' Tom said grimly. 'I was looking forward to it myself.' He realized that Verity was standing beside him, 'I'm sorry, my dear. He was your father.'

'If I had had a pistol in my hand, I would have done it myself,' Verity said calmly. 'What he has done to me over the years is of no account, but when he started torturing Georgie . . . No, Uncle Tom, he deserved that and more.'

'You are a brave girl, Verity.' He hugged her spontaneously.

'We Courtneys are made of rawhide,' she said, and hugged him back. Tom chuckled and released her.

'Now, if you call those blackguards out from behind the wagons, I would be much obliged. You can tell them that we will not harm them and they will have free passage back to the coast as long as they abandon the wagons. Tell them I have a hundred men with me, which is a lie. If they don't surrender we will attack and wipe them out to the man.'

Verity called the message across to them in Arabic. There was a delay while they discussed what she had said. She could hear their heated voices and she caught some of the words. Some were arguing that the *effendi* was dead, and there was no reason to remain here. Others were talking about the amount of gold, and what Zayn al-Din would do when he learned that they had lost it. One loud voice reminded them of the sounds of battle they had heard coming from the bay. 'Perhaps Zayn al-Din is dead also,' the speaker said.

Guy Courtney's body was still lying where it had fallen and the dawn light was strengthening so that Verity could see her father's dead face. Despite her brave words she had to turn away her eyes.

At last one of the Arabs called back their reply: 'Let us go in peace and we will hand over our weapons and surrender the wagons.'

J im and Mansur pushed their horses hard, riding through the night. They were leading spare horses and when their mounts tired they changed saddles quickly and went on. They rode mostly in silence, locked in their own thoughts, which were darker than the night. When they spoke it was mostly in monosyllables or in curt sentences, and their eyes were fixed ahead.

'Less than six miles to the laager at the gorge,' Jim said, as they climbed a steep rise. In the first light of morning he recognized the tree that stood on the skyline. 'We will be there in an hour.'

'Please God!' said Mansur, and they rode up on to the crest and looked ahead. They saw the river winding below them, but then the first rays of the sun touched the belly of the cloud and lit the valley with dramatic suddenness. They both saw the dust at the same moment.

'Rider coming at the gallop!' Jim exclaimed.

'Only a messenger rides like that,' Mansur said softly. 'Let us hope he has favourable tidings.'

They both reached for their telescopes, and for a moment were struck speechless as they picked up the rider in the lens.

'Trueheart!' Jim shouted.

'In the Name of God! It's Louisa on her back. Look at her hair shine in the sunlight,' Mansur agreed. 'She carries something in her arms. It's Georgie.'

Jim waited for no more. He turned loose the spare horse he was leading and shouted to Drumfire, 'Run, my lovely! Run with all your heart.'

Mansur could not keep pace with them as they raced down the track.

George saw them coming and wriggled and twisted in Louisa's arms like a fish. 'Papa!' he screamed. 'Papa!'

Jim jumped down from Drumfire's back the moment the horse slid to a halt, lifted them down from Trueheart's saddle and hugged them both, crushing Louisa and George to his chest.

Mansur rode up. 'Where is Verity? Is she safe?'

'At the ford of the river with the wagons. Tom and Sarah have her.'

'God love you, Louisa.' Mansur spurred on, and left Louisa and Jim weeping with happiness in each other's arms, and George tugging with both hands at Jim's beard.

They dug a grave for Guy Courtney beside the wagon road, and wrapped his body in a blanket before they lowered him into it.

'He was a vile bastard,' Tom murmured, in Sarah's ear. 'He deserved to be left for the hyena, but he was my brother.'

'And my brother-in-law on both sides – and I was the one who killed him. That will be on my conscience for the rest of my life.'

'Let it sit lightly, for you are without guilt,' Tom said, and they looked across to where Verity and Mansur stood hand in hand on the far side of the open grave.

'We are doing the right thing, Thomas,' Sarah said.

'It does not feel like it,' he grunted. 'Let's get it over with and head out for Fort Auspice. Dorian is wounded, and even if he is now a king, he needs us with him.'

They left Zama and Muntu to fill in the grave and cover it with rocks to stop the hyena digging it open, and Mansur and Verity followed them down the hill to where Smallboy had the two gold wagons inspanned. Mansur and Verity walked hand in hand, but though her face was pale Verity's eyes were dry.

Jim and Louisa were waiting at the wagons. Both had refused to attend the burial. 'Not after what he did to Louisa and Georgie.' Jim scowled when Tom had suggested it. Now Jim looked enquiringly at his father, and Tom nodded. 'It is done.'

They mounted and turned the horses' heads down towards the coast and Fort Auspice.

It took several weeks to repair the stranded war-dhow, the *Sufi*, and float her off the beach. Rahmad and his crew took her out and anchored her in the middle of the bay. Already the captured transport dhows were ready for the long voyage back to Muscat, their holds crammed with ivory.

Dorian leaned heavily on Tom's shoulder as he hobbled down to the beach. The wound he had received from Zayn al-Din was not yet entirely healed and Sarah was in close attendance on her royal patient. When they were settled in the longboat, Jim and Mansur rowed them out to the *Arcturus*. Verity and Louisa, with George chirping on her hip, were waiting to welcome them aboard. Verity had the farewell banquet laid out on trestle tables on the quarter-deck. They laughed and ate and drank together for the last time, but Ruby Cornish was watching for the turning of the tide. At last he stood up regretfully and said, 'Forgive me, Your Majesty, but the tide and the wind stand fair.'

'Give us one last toast, brother Tom,' Dorian said.

Tom stood up just a trifle unsteadily. 'A swift and safe voyage. May we all meet again, and that right soon.'

They drank the toast and embraced, then those who were remaining at Fort Auspice went down into the longboat. From the beach they watched the *Arcturus* weigh anchor. Dorian was at the rail supported by Mansur and Verity. Suddenly he began to sing, his voice as strong and beautiful as ever:

'Farewell and adieu to you, fair Spanish ladies,
Farewell and adieu to you, ladies of Spain,
For we've received orders to sail for old England,
But we hope in a short time to see you again.

The *Arcturus* led the fleet of dhows out through the channel. When the mainland was a low blue outline on the horizon Ruby Cornish came to where Dorian sat against the windward rail. 'Your Majesty, we have made good our offing.'

'Thank you, Captain Cornish. Will you be good enough to lay the ship on course for Muscat? We have some unsettled business there.'

The wagons were loaded and Smallboy and Muntu led the oxen in from the pasture and inspanned them. 'Where are you going?' Sarah asked.

Louisa shook her head. 'Mother, you must ask that of Jim, for I know not the answer.'

They both looked at him and he laughed. 'Beyond the next blue horizon,' he replied, picking up George and placing him on his shoulder. 'But fear not, we will be back soon enough with the wagons groaning under the weight of the ivory and diamonds they carry.'

Tom and Sarah stood on the parapet of Fort Auspice and watched the wagon convoy wind away up the hills, heading into the hinterland. Jim and Louisa were in the van, with Bakkat and Zama riding a short distance behind them. Intepe and Letee were walking beside the lead wagon, the children clustered about their legs.

At the crest of the hill Jim turned in the saddle and waved back at them. Sarah whipped off her bonnet and waved it furiously until they dropped out of sight over the far side.

'Well, Thomas Courtney, it's just you and I again,' she said softly.

'I like it well enough that way,' he said, and placed his arm round her waist.

Jim looked ahead and his eyes shone with wanderlust. Perched on his shoulders George yelled, 'Horsy! Giddy-up, horsy.'

'Hedgehog, you have given birth to a monster,' Jim said.

Louisa leaned across and squeezed his arm, smiling secretively. 'I shall hope to do better on my next attempt.'

Jim stopped dead in his tracks, and stared back at her. 'No, you aren't! Are you?'

'Oh yes, I am!' she replied.

'Why did you not tell me before this?'

'Because you might have left me behind.'

'Never!' he said, with great force.

HUNGRY AS
THE SEA

This book is for my wife and the jewel
of my life, Mokhiniso, with all
my love and gratitude for the enchanted
years that I have been married to her

Nicholas Berg stepped out of the taxi on to the floodlit dock and paused to look up at the *Warlock*. At this state of the tide she rode high against the stone quay, so that even though the cranes towered above her, they did not dwarf her.

Despite the exhaustion that fogged his mind and cramped his muscles until they ached, Nicholas felt a stir of the old pride, the old sense of value achieved, as he looked at her. She looked like a warship, sleek and deadly, with the high flared bows and good lines that combined to make her safe in any seaway.

The superstructure was moulded steel and glittering armoured glass, behind which her lights burned in carnival array. The wings of her navigation bridge swept back elegantly and were covered to protect the men who must work her in the cruellest weather and most murderous seas.

Overlooking the wide stern deck was the second navigation bridge, from which a skilled seaman could operate the great winches and drums of cable, could catch and control the hawser on the hydraulically operated rising fairleads, could baby a wallowing oil rig or a mortally wounded liner in a gale or a silky calm.

Against the night sky high above it all, the twin towers replaced the squat single funnel of the old-fashioned salvage tugs – and the illusion of a man-of-war was heightened by the fire cannons on the upper platforms from which the *Warlock* could throw fifteen hundred tons of sea water an hour on to a burning vessel. From the towers themselves could be swung the boarding ladders over which men could be sent aboard a hulk, and between them was painted the small circular target that marked the miniature heliport. The whole of it, hull and upper decks, was fireproofed so she could survive in the inferno of burning petroleum from a holed tanker or the flaming chemical from a bulk carrier.

Nicholas Berg felt a little of the despondency and spiritual exhaustion slough away, although his body still ached and his legs carried him stiffly, like those of an old man, as he started towards the gangplank.

'The hell with them all,' he thought. 'I built her and she is strong and good.'

Although it was an hour before midnight, the crew of the *Warlock* watched him from every vantage point they could find; even the oilers had come up from the engine room when the word reached them, and now loafed unobtrusively on the stern working deck.

David Allen, the First Officer, had placed a hand at the main harbour gates with a photograph of Nicholas Berg and a five-cent piece for the telephone call box beside the gate, and the whole ship was alerted now.

David Allen stood with the Chief Engineer in the glassed wing of the main navigation bridge and they watched the solitary figure pick his way across the shadowy dock, carrying his own case.

'So that's him.' David's voice was husky with awe and respect. He looked like a schoolboy under his shaggy bush of sun-bleached hair.

'He's a bloody film star.' Vinny Baker, the Chief Engineer, hitched up his sagging trousers with both elbows, and his spectacles slid down the long thin nose, as he snorted. 'A bloody film star,' he repeated the term with utmost scorn.

'He was first to Jules Levoisin,' David pointed out, and again the note of awe as he intoned that name, 'and he is a tug man from way back.'

'That was fifteen years ago.' Vinny Baker released his

elbow grip on his trousers and pushed his spectacles up on to the bridge of his nose. Immediately his trousers began their slow but inexorable slide deckwards. 'Since then he's become a bloody glamour boy – and an owner.'

'Yes,' David Allen agreed, and his baby face crumpled a little at the thought of those two legendary animals, master and owner, combined in one monster. A monster which was on the point of mounting his gangway to the deck of *Warlock*.

'You'd better go down and kiss him on the soft spot,' Vinny grunted comfortably, and drifted away. Two decks down was the sanctuary of his control room where neither masters nor owners could touch him. He was going there now.

David Allen was breathless and flushed when he reached the entry port. The new Master was halfway up the gangway, and he lifted his head and looked steadily at the mate as he stepped aboard.

Though he was only a little above average, Nicholas Berg gave the impression of towering height, and the shoulders beneath the blue cashmere of his jacket were wide and powerful. He wore no hat and his hair was very dark, very thick and brushed back from a wide unlined forehead. The head was big-nosed and gaunt-boned, with a heavy jaw, blue now with new beard, and the eyes were set deep in the cages of their bony sockets, underlined with dark plum-coloured smears, as though they were bruised.

But what shocked David Allen was the man's pallor. His face was drained, as though he had been bled from the jugular. It was the pallor of mortal illness or of exhaustion close to death itself, and it was emphasized by the dark eye-sockets. This was not what David had expected of the legendary Golden Prince of Christy Marine. It was not the face he had seen so often pictured in newspapers and magazines around the world. Surprise made him mute and the man stopped and looked down at him.

3

'Allen?' asked Nicholas Berg quietly. His voice was low and level, without accent, but with a surprising timbre and resonance.

'Yes, sir. Welcome aboard, sir.'

When Nicholas Berg smiled, the edges of sickness and exhaustion smoothed away at his brow and at the corners of his mouth. His hand was smooth and cool, but his grip was firm enough to make David blink.

'I'll show you your quarters, sir.' David took the Louis Vuitton suitcase from his grip.

'I know the way,' said Nick Berg. 'I designed her.'

He stood in the centre of the Master's day cabin, and felt the deck tilt under his feet, although the *Warlock* was fast to the stone dock, and the muscles in his thighs trembled.

'The funeral went off all right?' Nick asked.

'He was cremated, sir,' David said. 'That's the way he wanted it. I have made the arrangements for the ashes to be sent home to Mary. Mary is his wife, sir,' he explained quickly.

'Yes,' said Nick Berg. 'I know. I saw her before I left London. Mac and I were shipmates once.'

'He told me. He used to boast about that.'

'Have you cleared all his gear?' Nick asked, and glanced around the Master's suite.

'Yes sir, we've packed it all up. There is nothing of his left in here.'

'He was a good man.' Nick swayed again on his feet and looked longingly at the day couch, but instead he crossed to the port and looked out on to the dock. 'How did it happen?'

'My report—'

'Tell me!' said Nicholas Berg, and his voice cracked like a whip.

'The main tow-cable parted, sir. He was on the after-deck. It took his head off like a bullwhip.'

Nick stood quietly for a moment, thinking about that terse description of tragedy. He had seen a tow part under stress once before. That time it had killed three men.

'All right.' Nick hesitated a moment, the exhaustion had slowed and softened him so that for a moment he was on the point of explaining why he had come to take command of *Warlock* himself, rather than sending another hired man to replace Mac.

It might help to have somebody to talk to now, when he was right down on his knees, beaten and broken and tired to the very depths of his soul. He swayed again, then caught himself and forced aside the temptation. He had never whined for sympathy in his life before.

'All right,' he repeated. 'Please give my apologies to your officers. I have not had much sleep in the last two weeks, and the flight out from Heathrow was murder, as always. I'll meet them in the morning. Ask the cook to send a tray with my dinner.'

The cook was a huge man who moved like a dancer in a snowy apron and a theatrical chef's cap. Nick Berg stared at him as he placed the tray on the table at his elbow. The cook wore his hair in a shiny carefully coiffured bob that fell to his right shoulder, but was drawn back from the left cheek to display a small diamond earring in the pierced lobe of that ear.

He lifted the cloth off the tray with a hand as hairy as that of a bull gorilla, but his voice was as lyrical as a girl's, and his eyelashes curled soft and dark on to his cheek.

'There's a lovely bowl of soup, and a *pot-au-feu*. It's one of my little special things. You will adore it,' he said, and stepped back. He surveyed Nick Berg with those huge hands on his hips. 'But I took one look at you as you came aboard and I just knew what you really needed.' With a magician's flourish, he produced a half-bottle of Pinch Haig from the deep pocket of his apron. 'Take a nip of that with

5

your dinner, and then straight into bed with you, you poor dear.'

No man had ever called Nicholas Berg 'dear' before, but his tongue was too thick and slow for the retort. He stared after the cook as he disappeared with a sweep of his white apron and the twinkle of the diamond, and then he grinned weakly and shook his head, weighing the bottle in his hand.

'Damned if I don't need it,' he muttered, and went to find a glass. He poured it half full, and sipped as he came back to the couch and lifted the lid of the soup pot. The steaming aroma made the little saliva glands under his tongue spurt.

The hot food and whisky in his belly taxed his last reserves, and Nicholas Berg kicked off his shoes as he staggered into his night cabin.

He awoke with the anger on him. He had not been angry in two weeks which was a measure of his despondency.

But when he shaved, the mirrored face was that of a stranger still, too pale and gaunt and set. The lines that framed his mouth were too deeply chiselled, and the early sunlight through the port caught the dark hair at his temple and he saw the frosty glitter there and leaned closer to the mirror. It was the first time he had noticed the flash of silver hair – perhaps he had never looked hard enough, or perhaps it was something new.

'Forty,' he thought. 'I'll be forty years old next June.'

He had always believed that if a man never caught the big one before he was forty, he was doomed never to do so. So what were the rules for the man who caught the big wave before he was thirty, and rode it fast and hard and high, then lost it again before he was forty and was washed

6

out into the trough of boiling white water. Was he doomed also? Nick stared at himself in the mirror and felt the anger in him change its form, becoming directed and functional.

He stepped into the shower, and let the needles of hot water sting his chest. Through the tiredness and disillusion, he was aware, for the first time in weeks, of the underlying strength which he had begun to doubt was still there. He felt it rising to the surface in him, and he thought again of what an extraordinary sea creature he was, how it needed only a deck under him and the smell of the sea in his throat.

He stepped from the shower and dried quickly. This was the right place to be now. This was the place to recuperate – and he realized that his decision not to replace Mac with a hired skipper had been a gut decision. He needed to be here himself.

Always he had known that if you wanted to ride the big wave, you must first be at the place where it begins to peak. It's an instinctive thing, a man just knows where that place is. Nick Berg knew deep in his being that this was the place now, and, with his rising strength, he felt the old excitement, the old 'I'll show the bastards who is beaten' excitement, and he dressed swiftly and went up the Master's private companionway to the upper deck.

Immediately, the wind flew at him and flicked his dark wet hair into his face. It was force five from the south-east, and it came boiling over the great flat-topped mountain which crouched above the city and harbour. Nick looked up at it and saw the thick white cloud they called the 'table-cloth' spilling off the heights, and swirling along the grey rock cliffs.

'The Cape of Storms,' he murmured. Even the water in the protected dock leaped and peaked into white crests which blew away like wisps of smoke.

The tip of Africa thrust southwards into one of the most treacherous seas on all the globe. Here two oceans swept

7

turbulently together off the rocky cliffs of Cape Point, and then roiled over the shallows of the Agulhas bank.

Here wind opposed current in eternal conflict. This was the breeding ground of the freak wave, the one that mariners called the 'hundred-year wave', because statistically that was how often it should occur.

But off the Agulhas bank, it was always lurking, waiting only for the right combination of wind and current, waiting for the inphase wave sequence to send its crest rearing a hundred feet high and steep as those grey rock cliffs of Table Mountain itself.

Nick had read the accounts of seamen who had survived that wave, and, at a loss for words, they had written only of a great hole in the sea into which a ship fell helplessly. When the hole closed, the force of breaking water would bury her completely. Perhaps the *Waratah Castle* was one which had fallen into that trough. Nobody would ever know – a great ship of 9,000 tons burden, she and her crew of 211 had disappeared without trace in these seas.

Yet here was one of the busiest sea lanes on the globe, as a procession of giant tankers ploughed ponderously around that rocky Cape on their endless shuttle between the Western world and the oil Gulf of Persia. Despite their bulk, those supertankers were perhaps some of the most vulnerable vehicles yet designed by man.

Now Nick turned and looked across the wind-ripped waters of Duncan Dock at one of them. He could read her name on the stern that rose like a five-storied apartment block. She was owned by Shell Oil, 250,000 dead weight tons, and, out of ballast, she showed much of her rust-red bottom. She was in for repairs, while out in the roadstead of Table Bay, two other monsters waited patiently for their turn in the hospital dock.

So big and ponderous and vulnerable – and valuable. Nick licked his lips involuntarily – hull and cargo together, she was thirty million dollars, piled up like a mountain.

That was why he had stationed the *Warlock* here at Cape Town on the southernmost tip of Africa. He felt the strength and excitement surging upwards in him.

All right, so he had lost his wave. He was no longer cresting and racing. He was down and smothered in white water. But he could feel his head breaking the surface, and he was still on the breakline. He knew there was another big wave racing down on him. It was just beginning to peak and he knew he still had the strength to catch her, to get up high and race again.

'I did it once – I'll damned well do it again,' he said aloud, and went down for breakfast.

He stepped into the saloon, and for a long moment nobody realized he was there. There was an excited buzz of comment and speculation that absorbed them all.

The Chief Engineer had an old copy of *Lloyd's List* folded at the front page and held above a plate of eggs as he read aloud. Nicholas wondered where he had found the ancient copy.

His spectacles had slid right to the end of his nose, so he had to tilt his head far backwards to see through them, and his Australian accent twanged like a guitar.

'In a joint statement issued by the new Chairman and incoming members of the Board, a tribute was paid to the fifteen years of loyal service that Mr Nicholas Berg had given to Christy Marine.'

The five officers listened avidly, ignoring their breakfasts, until David Allen glanced up at the figure in the doorway.

'Captain, sir,' he shouted, and leapt to his feet, while with the other hand, he snatched the newspaper out of Vinny Baker's hands and bundled it under the table.

'Sir, may I present the officers of *Warlock*.'

Shuffling, embarrassed, the younger officers shook hands hurriedly and then applied themselves silently to their congealing breakfasts with a total dedication that precluded any conversation, while Nick Berg took the Master's seat at the head of the long table in the heavy silence and David Allen sat down again on the crumpled sheets of newsprint.

The steward offered the menu to the new Captain, and returned almost immediately with a dish of stewed fruit.

'I ordered a boiled egg,' said Nick mildly, and an apparition in snowy white appeared from the galley, with the chef's cap at a jaunty angle.

'The sailor's curse is constipation, Skipper. I look after my officers – that fruit is delicious and good for you. I'm doing you your eggs now, dear, but eat your fruit first.' And the diamond twinkled again as he vanished.

Nick stared after him in the appalled silence.

'Fantastic cook,' blurted David Allen, his fair skin flushed pinkly and the *Lloyd's List* rustled under his backside. 'Could get a job on any passenger liner, could Angel.'

'If he ever left the *Warlock*, half the crew would go with him,' growled the Chief Engineer darkly, and hauled at his pants with elbows below the level of the table. 'And I'd be one of them.'

Nick Berg turned his head politely to follow the conversation.

'He's almost a doctor,' David Allen went on, addressing the Chief Engineer.

'Five years at Edinburgh Medical School,' agreed the Chief solemnly.

'Do you remember how he set the Second's leg? Terribly useful to have a doctor aboard.'

Nick picked up his spoon, and tentatively lifted a little of the fruit to his mouth. Every officer watched him intently as he chewed. Nick took another spoonful.

'You should taste his jams, sir,' David Allen addressed Nick directly at last. 'Absolutely Cordon Bleu stuff.'

'Thank you, gentlemen, for the advice,' said Nick. The

smile did not touch his mouth, but crinkled his eyes slightly. 'But would somebody convey a private message to Angel that if he ever calls me "dear" again I'll beat that ridiculous cap down about his ears.'

In the relieved laughter that followed, Nick turned to David Allen and sent colour flying to his cheeks again by asking, 'You seem to have finished with that old copy of the *List*, Number One. Do you mind if I glance at it again?'

Reluctantly, David lifted himself and produced the newspaper, and there was another tense silence as Nick Berg rearranged the rumpled sheets and studied the old headlines without any apparent emotion.

THE GOLDEN PRINCE OF CHRISTY MARINE DEPOSED

Nicholas hated that name. It had been old Arthur Christy's quirk to name all of his vessels with the prefix 'Golden' and twelve years ago, when Nick had rocketed to head of operations at Christy Marine, some wag had stuck that label on him.

ALEXANDER TO HEAD THE CHRISTY
BOARD OF DIRECTORS

Nicholas was surprised by the force of his hatred for the man. They had fought like a pair of bulls for dominance of the herd and the tactics that Duncan Alexander had used had won. Arthur Christy had said once, 'Nobody gives a damn these days whether it is moral or fair, all that counts is, will it work and can you get away with it?' For Duncan it had worked, and he had got away with it in the grandest possible style.

As Managing Director in charge of operations, Mr Nicholas Berg helped to build Christy Marine from a

11

small coasting and salvage company into one of the five largest owners of cargo shipping operating anywhere in the world.

After the death of Arthur Christy in 1968, Mr Nicholas Berg succeeded him as Chairman, and continued the company's spectacular expansion.

At present, Christy Marine has in commission eleven bulk carriers and tankers in excess of 250,000 dead weight tons, and is building the 1,000,000 ton giant ultra-tanker *Golden Dawn*. It will be the largest vessel ever launched.

There it was, stated in the baldest possible terms, the labour of a man's lifetime. Over a billion dollars of shipping, designed, financed and built almost entirely with the energy and enthusiasm and faith of Nicholas Berg.

Mr Nicholas Berg married Miss Chantelle Christy, the only child of Mr Arthur Christy. However, the marriage ended in divorce in September of last year and the former Mrs Berg has subsequently married Mr Duncan Alexander, the new Chairman of Christy Marine.

He felt the hollow nauseous feeling in his stomach again, and in his head the vivid image of the woman. He did not want to think of her now, but could not thrust the image aside. She was bright and beautiful as a flame – and, like a flame, you could not hold her. When she went, she took everything with her, everything. He should hate her also, he really should. Everything, he thought again, the company, his life's work, and the child. When he thought of the child, he nearly succeeded in hating her, and the newsprint shook in his hand.

He became aware again that five men were watching him, and without surprise he realized that not a flicker of his emotions had shown on his face. To be a player for fifteen years in one of the world's highest games of chance, inscrutability was a minimum requirement.

In a joint statement issued by the new Chairman and incoming members of the Board, a tribute was paid.

Duncan Alexander paid the tribute for one reason, Nick thought grimly. He wanted the 100,000 Christy Marine shares that Nick owned. Those shares were very far from a controlling interest. Chantelle had a million shares in her own name, and there were another million in the Christy Trust, but insignificant as it was, Nick's holding gave him a voice in and an entry to the company's affairs. Nick had bought and paid for every one of those shares. Nobody had given him a thing, not once in his life. He had taken advantage of every stock option in his contract, had bartered bonus and salary for those options, and now those 100,000 shares were worth three million dollars, meagre reward for the labour which had built up a fortune of sixty million dollars for the Christy father and daughter.

It had taken Duncan Alexander almost a year to get those shares. He and Nicholas had bargained with cold loathing. They had hated each other from the first day that Duncan had walked into the Christy Building on Leadenhall Street. He had come as old Arthur Christy's latest *Wunderkind*, the financial genius fresh from his triumphs as financial controller of International Electronics, and the hatred had been instant and deep and mutual, a fierce smouldering chemical reaction between them.

In the end Duncan Alexander had won, he had won it all, except the shares, and he had bargained for those from overwhelming strength. He had bargained with patience and skill, wearing his man down over the months. Using all Christy Marine's reserves to block and frustrate Nicholas, forcing him back step by step, taxing even his strength to its limits, driving such a bargain that at the end Nicholas was forced to bow and accept a dangerous price for his shares. He had taken as full payment the subsidiary of Christy Marine, Christy Towage and Salvage, all its assets and all its debts. Nick had felt like a fighter who had been battered for fifteen rounds, and was now hanging desperately to the ropes with his legs gone, blinded by his own sweat and blood and swollen flesh; so he could not see from whence the next punch would come. But he had held on just long enough. He had got Christy Towage and Salvage – he had walked away with something that was completely and entirely his.

Nicholas Berg lowered the newspaper, and immediately his officers attacked their breakfasts ravenously and there was the clatter of cutlery.

'There is an officer missing,' he said.

'It's only the Trog, sir,' Dave Allen explained.

'The Trog?'

'The Radio Officer, sir. Speirs, sir. We call him the Troglodyte.'

'I'd like all the officers present.'

'He never comes out of his cave,' Vinny Baker explained helpfully.

'All right,' Nick nodded. 'I will speak to him later.'

They waited now, five eager young men, even Vin Baker could not completely hide his interest behind the smeared lenses of his spectacles and the tough Aussie veneer.

'I wanted to explain to you the new set-up. The Chief has kindly read to you this article, presumably for the benefit of those who were unable to do so for themselves a year ago.'

Nobody said anything, but Vin Baker fiddled with his porridge spoon.

'So you are aware that I am no longer connected in any way with Christy Marine. I have now acquired Christy Towage and Salvage. It becomes a completely independent

14

company. The name is being changed.' Nicholas had resisted the vanity of calling it Berg Towage and Salvage. 'It will be known as Ocean Towage and Salvage.'

He had paid dearly for it, perhaps too dearly. He had given up his three million dollars' worth of Christy shares for God alone knew what. But he had been tired unto death.

'We own two vessels. The *Golden Warlock* and her sister ship which is almost ready for her sea trials, the *Golden Witch*.'

He knew exactly how much the company owed on those two ships, he had agonized over the figures through long and sleepless nights. On paper the net worth of the company was around four million dollars; he had made a paper profit of a million dollars on his bargain with Duncan Alexander. But it was paper profit only, the company had debts of nearly four million more. If he missed just one month's interest payments on those debts – he dismissed the thought quickly, for on a forced sale his residue in the company would be worth nothing. He would be completely wiped out.

'The names of both ships have been changed also. They will become simply *Warlock* and *Sea Witch*. From now onwards "Golden" is a dirty word around Ocean Salvage.'

They laughed then, a release of tension, and Nick smiled with them, and lit a thin black cheroot from the crocodile-skin case while they settled down.

'I will be running this ship until *Sea Witch* is commissioned. It won't be long, and there will be promotions then.'

Nick superstitiously tapped the mahogany mess table as he said it. The dockyard strike had been simmering for a long time. *Sea Witch* was still on the ways, but costing interest, and further delay would prove him mortal.

'I have got a long oil-rig tow. Bight of Australia to

South America. It will give us all time to shake the ship down. You are all tug men, I don't have to tell you when the big one comes up, there will be no warning.'

They stirred, and the eagerness was on them again. Even the oblique reference to prize money had roused them.

'Chief?' Nick looked across at him, and the Engineer snorted, as though the question was an insult.

'In all respects ready for sea,' he said, and tried simultaneously to adjust his trousers and his spectacles.

'Number One?' Nick looked at David Allen. He had not yet become accustomed to the Mate's boyishness. He knew that he had held a master mariner's ticket for ten years, that he was over thirty years of age and that MacDonald had hand-picked him – he had to be good. Yet that fair unlined face and quick high colour under the unruly mop of blond hair made him look like an undergraduate.

'I'm waiting on some stores yet, sir,' David answered quickly. 'The chandlers have promised for today, but none of it is vital. I could sail in an hour, if it is necessary.'

'All right.' Nick stood up. 'I will inspect the ship at 0900 hours. You'd best get the ladies off the ship.' During the meal there had been the faint tinkle of female voices and laughter from the crew's quarters.

Nick stepped out of the saloon and Vin Baker's voice was pitched to reach him. It was a truly dreadful imitation of what the Chief believed to be a Royal Naval accent.

'0900, chaps. Jolly good show, what?'

Nick did not miss a step, and he grinned tightly to himself. It's an old Aussie custom; you needle and needle until something happens. There is no malice in it, it's just a way of getting to know your man. And once the boots and fists have stopped flying, you can be friends or enemies on a permanent basis. It was so long since he had been in elemental contact with tough physical men, straight hard men who shunned all subterfuge and sham, and he found the novelty stimulating. Perhaps that was what he really

16

needed now, the sea and the company of real men. He felt his step quicken and the anticipation of physical confrontation lift his spirits off the bottom.

He went up the companionway to the navigation deck, taking the steps three at a time, and the doorway opposite his suite opened. From it emerged the solid grey stench of cheap Dutch cigars and a head that could have belonged to some prehistoric reptile. It too was pale grey and lined and wrinkled, the head of a sea-turtle or an iguana lizard, with the same small dark glittery eyes.

The door was that of the radio room. It had direct access to the main navigation bridge and was merely two paces from the Master's day cabin.

Despite appearances, the head was human, and Nick recalled clearly how Mac had once described his radio officer. 'He is the most anti-social bastard I've ever sailed with, but he can scan eight different frequencies simultaneously, in clear and Morse, even while he is asleep. He is a mean, joyless, constipated son of a bitch – and probably the best radio man afloat.'

'Captain,' said the Trog, in a reedy petulant voice. Nick did not ponder the fact that the Trog recognized him instantly as the new Master. The air of command on some men is unmistakable. 'Captain, I have an "all ships signify".'

Nick felt the heat at the base of his spine, and the electric prickle on the back of his neck. It is not sufficient merely to be on the break line when the big wave peaks, it is also necessary to recognize your wave from the hundred others that sweep by.

'Coordinates?' he snapped, as he strode down the passageway to the radio room.

'72° 16' south 32° 12' west.'

Nick felt the jump in his chest and the heat mount up along his spine. The high latitudes down there in the vast and lonely wastes. There was something sinister and

17

menacing in the mere figures. What ship could be down there?

The longitudinal coordinates fitted neatly in the chart that Nick carried in his mind, like a war chart in a military operations room. She was south and west of the Cape of Good Hope – down deep, beyond Gough and Bouvet Island, in the Weddell Sea.

He followed the Trog into the radio room. On this bright, sunny and windy morning, the room was dark and gloomy as a cave, the thick green blinds drawn across the ports; the only source of light was the glowing dials of the banked communication equipment, the most sophisticated equipment that all the wealth of Christy Marine could pack into her, a hundred thousand dollars' worth of electronic magic, but the stink of cheap cigars was overpowering.

Beyond the radio room was the operator's cabin, the bunk unmade, a tray of soiled dishes on the deck beside it.

The Trog hopped up into the swivel seat, and elbowed aside a brass shell-casing that acted as an ashtray and spilled grey flakes of ash and a couple of cold wet chewed cigar butts on to the desk.

Like a wizened gnome, the Trog tended his dials; there was a cacophony of static and electronic trash blurred with the sharp howl of Morse.

'The copy?' Nick asked, and the Trog pushed a pad at him. Nick read off quickly.

CTMZ. 0603 GMT. 72° 16′ S. 32° 12′ W. All ships in a position to render assistance, please signify. CTMZ.

He did not need to consult the RT Handbook to recognize that call sign 'CTMZ'.

With an effort of will he controlled the pressure that caught him in the chest like a giant fist. It was as though he had lived this moment before. It was too neat. He forced himself to distrust his instinct, forced himself to think with his head and not his guts.

Beyond him he heard his officers' voices on the navigation bridge, quiet voices – but charged with tension. They were up from the saloon already.

'Christ!' he thought savagely. 'How do they know? So quickly?' It was as though the ship itself had come awake beneath his feet and trembled with anticipation.

The door from the bridge slid aside and David Allen stood in the opening with a copy of *Lloyd's Register* in his hands.

'CTMZ, sir, is the call sign of the *Golden Adventurer*. Twenty-two thousand tons, registered Bermuda 1975. Owners Christy Marine.'

'Thank you, Number One,' Nick nodded. Nicholas knew her well; he personally had ordered her construction before the collapse of the great liner traffic. Nick had planned to use her on the Europe-to-Australia run.

Her finished cost had come in at sixty-two million dollars, and she was a beautiful and graceful ship under her tall light alloy superstructure. Her accommodation was luxurious, in the same class as the *France* or the *United States*, but she had been one of Nick's few miscalculations.

When the feasibility of operation on the planned run had shown up prohibitive in the face of rising costs and diminishing trade, Nick had switched her usage. It was this type of flexible and intuitive planning and improvisation that had built Christy Marine into the Goliath she was now.

Nick had innovated the idea of adventure cruises – and changed the ship's name to *Golden Adventurer*. Now she carried rich passengers to the wild and exotic corners of the globe, from the Galapagos Islands to the Amazon, from the remote Pacific islands to the Antarctic, in search of the unusual.

She carried guest lecturers with her, experts on the environments and ecology of the areas she was to visit, and she was equipped to take her passengers ashore to study the monoliths of Easter Island or to watch the mating displays of the wandering albatross on the Falkland Islands.

She was probably one of the very few cruise liners that was still profitable, and now she stood in need of assistance.

Nicholas turned back from the Trog. 'Has she been transmitting prior to this signify request?'

'She's been sending in company code since midnight. Her traffic was so heavy that I was watching her.'

The green glow of the sets gave the little man a bilious cast, and made his teeth black, so that he looked like an actor from a horror movie.

'You recorded?' Nick demanded, and the Trog switched on the automatic playback of his tape monitors, recapitulating every message the distressed ship had sent or received since the previous midnight. The jumbled blocks of code poured into the room, and the paper strip printed out with the clatter of its keys.

Had Duncan Alexander changed the Christy Marine code? Nick wondered. It would be the natural procedure, completely logical to any operations man. You lose a man who has the code, you change immediately. It was that simple. Duncan had lost Nick Berg; he should change. But Duncan was not an operations man. He was a figures and paper man, he thought in numbers, not in steel and salt water.

If Duncan had changed, they would never break it. Not even with the Decca. Nick had devised the basis of the code. It was a projection that expressed the alphabet as a mathematical function based on a random six-figure master, changing the value of each letter on a progression that was impossible to monitor.

Nick hurried out of the stinking gloom of the radio room with the printout in his hands.

The navigation bridge of *Warlock* was gleaming chrome and glass, as bright and functional as a modern surgical theatre, or a futuristic kitchen layout.

The primary control console stretched the full width of the bridge, beneath the huge armoured windows. The old-fashioned wheel was replaced by a single steel lever, and the remote control could be carried out on to the wings of the bridge on its long extension cable, like the remote on a television set, so that the helmsman could con the ship from any position he chose.

Illuminated digital displays informed the master instantly of every condition of his ship: speed across the bottom at bows and stern, speed through the water at bows and stern, wind direction and strength, together with all the other technical information of function and malfunction. Nick had built the ship with Christy money, and stinted not at all.

The rear of the bridge was the navigational area, and the chart-table divided it neatly with its overhead racks containing the 106 big blue volumes of the *Global Pilot* and as many other volumes of maritime publications. Below the table were the multiple drawers, wide and flat to contain the spread Admiralty charts that covered every corner of navigable water on the globe.

Against the rear bulkhead stood the battery of electronic navigational aids, like a row of fruit machines in a Vegas gambling hall.

Nick switched the big Decca Satellite Navaid into its computer mode and the display lights flashed and faded and relit in scarlet.

He fed it the six-figure control, numbers governed by the moon phase and date of dispatch. The computer digested this instantaneously, and Nick gave it the last arithmetical proportion known to him. The Decca was ready to decode and Nick gave it the block of garbled transmission – and waited for it to throw back gibberish at him. Duncan *must* have altered the code. He stared at the printout.

Christy Marine from Master of *Adventurer*. 2216 GMT. 72° 16′ S. 32° 05′ W. Underwater ice damage sustained midships starboard. Precautionary shutdown mains. Auxiliary generators activated during damage survey. Stand by.

So Duncan had let the code stand then. Nick groped for the croc-skin case of cheroots, and his hand was steady and firm as he held the flame to the top of the thin black tube. He felt the intense desire to shout aloud, but instead, he drew the fragrant smoke into his lungs.

'Plotted,' said David Allen from behind him. Already on the spread chart of the Antarctic he had marked in the reported position. The transformation was complete, the First Officer had become a grimly competent professional. There remained no trace of the high-coloured undergraduate.

Nick glanced at the plot, saw the dotted ice line far above the *Adventurer*'s position, saw the outline of the forbidding continent of Antarctica groping for the ship with merciless fingers of ice and rock.

The Decca printed out the reply:

Master of *Adventurer* from Christy Marine. 2222 GMT. Standing by.

The next message from the recording tape was flagged nearly two hours later, but was printed out almost continuously from the Trog's recording.

Christy Marine from Master of *Adventurer*. 0005 GMT. 72° 18′ S. 32° 05′ W. Water contained. Restarted

mains. New course CAPE TOWN direct. Speed 8 knots.
Stand by.

Dave Allen worked swiftly with parallel rulers and protractor.

'While she was without power she drifted thirty-four nautical miles, south-south-east – there is a hell of a wind or big current setting down there,' he said, and the other deck officers were silent and strained. Although none of them would dare crowd the Master at the Decca, yet in order of seniority they had taken up vantage points around the bridge best suited to follow the drama of a great ship in distress.

The next message ran straight out from the computer, despite the fact that it had been dispatched many hours later.

Christy Marine from Master of *Adventurer*. 0546 GMT.
72° 16′ S. 32° 12′ W. Explosion in flooded area.
Emergency shutdown all. Water gaining. Request your
clearance to issue 'all ships signify'. Standing by.

Master of *Adventurer* from Christy Marine. 0547 GMT.
You are cleared to issue signify. Break. Break. Break.
You are expressly forbidden to contract tow or salvage
without reference Christy Marine. Acknowledge.

Duncan was not even putting in the old chestnut, 'except in the event of danger to human life'.

The reason was too apparent. Christy Marine underwrote most of its own bottoms through another of its subsidiaries, the London and European Insurance and Finance Company. The self-insurance scheme had been the brainchild of Alexander Duncan himself when first he arrived at Christy Marine. Nick Berg had opposed the

23

scheme bitterly, and now he might live to see his reasoning being justified.

'Are we going to signify?' David Allen asked quietly.

'Radio silence,' snapped Nick irritably, and began to pace the bridge, the crack of his heels muted by the cork coating on the deck.

'Is this my wave?' Nick demanded of himself, applying the old rule he had set for himself long ago, the rule of deliberate thought first, action after.

The *Golden Adventurer* was drifting in the ice-fields two thousand and more miles south of Cape Town, five days and nights of hard running for the *Warlock*. If he made the go decision, by the time he reached her, she might have effected repairs and restarted, she might be under her own command again. Again, even if she was still helpless, *Warlock* might reach her to find another salvage tug had beaten her to the scene. So now it was time to call the roll.

He stopped his pacing at the door to the radio room and spoke quietly to the Trog.

'Open the telex line and send to Bach Wackie in Bermuda quote call the roll unquote.'

As he turned away, Nick was satisfied with his own forethought in installing the satellite telex system which enabled him to communicate with his agent in Bermuda, or with any other selected telex station, without his message being broadcast over the open frequencies and monitored by a competitor or any other interested party. His signals were bounced through the high stratosphere where they could not be intercepted.

While he waited, Nicholas worried. The decision to go would mean abandoning the Esso oil-rig tow. The tow fee had been a vital consideration in his cash-flow situation. Two hundred and twenty thousand sterling, without which he could not meet the quarterly interest payment due in sixty days' time – unless, unless . . . He juggled figures in his head, but the magnitude of the risk involved was growing momentarily more apparent – and the figures did not add up. He needed the Esso tow. God, how badly he needed it!

'Bach Wackie are replying,' called the Trog above the chatter of the telex receiver, and Nick spun on his heel.

He had appointed Bach Wackie as the agents for Ocean Salvage because of their proven record of quick and aggressive efficiency. He glanced at his Rolex Oyster and calculated that it was about two o'clock in the morning local time in Bermuda, and yet his request for information on the disposition of all his major competitors was now being answered within minutes of receipt.

For Master *Warlock* from Bach Wackie latest reported positions. *John Ross* dry dock Durban. *Woltema Wolteraad* Esso tow Torres Straits to Alaska Shelf –

That took care of the two giant Safmarine tugs; half of the top opposition was out of the race.

Wittezee Shell exploration tow Galveston to North Sea. *Grootezee* lying Brest –

That was the two Dutchmen out of it. The names and positions of the other big salvage tugs, each of them a direct and dire threat to *Warlock*, ran swiftly from the telex and Nicholas chewed his cheroot ragged as he watched, his eyes slitted against the spiralling blue smoke, feeling the relief rise in him as each report put another of his competitors in some distant waters, far beyond range of the stricken ship.

'*La Mouette*,' Nick's hands balled into fists as the name sprang on to the white paper sheet, '*La Mouette* discharged Brazgas tow Golfo San Jorge on 14th reported en route Buenos Aires.'

Nick grunted like a boxer taking a low blow, and turned

25

away from the machine. He walked out on to the open wing of the bridge and the wind tore at his hair and clothing.

La Mouette, the seagull, a fanciful name for that black squat hull, the old-fashioned high box of superstructure, the traditional single stack; Nick could see it clearly when he closed his eyes.

There was no doubt in his mind at all. Jules Levoisin was already running hard for the south, running like a hunting dog with the scent hot in its nostrils.

Jules had discharged in the southern Atlantic three days ago. He would certainly have bunkered at Comodoro. Nick knew how Jules' mind worked, he was never happy unless his bunkers were bulging.

Nick flicked the stub of his cigar away, and it was whisked far out into the harbour by the wind.

He knew that *La Mouette* had refitted and installed new engines eighteen months before. With a nostalgic twinge, he had read a snippet in *Lloyd's List*. But even nine thousand horsepower couldn't push that tubby hull at better than eighteen knots, Nick was certain of that. Yet even with *Warlock's* superior speed, *La Mouette* was better placed by a thousand miles. There was no room for complacency. And what if *La Mouette* had set out to double Cape Horn instead of driving north up the Atlantic? If that had happened, and with Jules Levoisin's luck it might just have happened, then *La Mouette* was a long way inside him already.

Anybody else but Jules Levoisin, he thought, why did it have to be him? And oh God, why now? Why now when I am so vulnerable – emotionally, physically and financially vulnerable. Oh God, why did it come now?

He felt the false sense of cheer and well-being, with which he had buoyed himself that morning, fall away from him like a cloak, leaving him naked and sick and tired again.

I am not ready yet, he thought; and then realized that it was probably the first time in his adult life he had ever said that to himself. He had always been ready, good and ready, for anything. But not now, not this time.

Suddenly Nicholas Berg was afraid, as he had never been before. He was empty, he realized, there was nothing in him, no strength, no confidence, no resolve. The depth of his defeat by Duncan Alexander, the despair of his rejection by the woman he loved, had broken him. He felt his fear turn to terror, knowing that his wave had come, and would sweep by him now, for he did not have the strength to ride it.

Some deep instinct warned him that it would be the last wave, there would be nothing after it. The choice was go now, or never go again. And he knew he could not go, he could not go against Jules Levoisin, he could not challenge the old master. He could not go – he could not reject the certainty of the Esso tow, he did not have the nerve now to risk all that he had left on a single throw. He had just lost a big one, he couldn't go at risk again.

The risk was too great, he was not ready for it, he did not have the strength for it.

He wanted to go to his cabin and throw himself on his bunk and sleep – and sleep. He felt his knees buckling with the great weight of his despair, and he hungered for the oblivion of sleep.

He turned back into the bridge, out of the wind. He was broken, defeated, he had given up. As he went towards the sanctuary of his day cabin, he passed the long command console and stopped involuntarily.

His officers watched him in a tense, electric silence.

His right hand went out and touched the engine telegraph, sliding the pointer from 'off' to 'stand by'.

'Engine Room,' he heard a voice speak in calm and level tones, so it could not be his own. 'Start main engines,' said the voice.

Seemingly from a great distance he watched the faces of his deck officers bloom with unholy joy, like old-time pirates savouring the prospect of a prize.

The strange voice went on, echoing oddly in his ears, 'Number One, ask the Harbour Master for permission to clear harbour immediately – and, Pilot, course to steer for the last reported position of *Golden Adventurer*, please.'

From the corner of his eye, he saw David Allen punch the Third Officer lightly but gleefully on the shoulder before he hurried to the radio telephone.

Nicholas Berg felt suddenly the urge to vomit. So he stood very still and erect at the navigation console and fought back the waves of nausea that swept over him, while his officers bustled to their seagoing stations.

'Bridge. This is the Chief Engineer,' said a disembodied voice from the speaker above Nick's head. 'Main engines running.' A pause and then that word of special Aussie approbation. 'Beauty!' – but the Chief pronounced it in three distinct syllables, 'Be-yew-dy!'

*W*arlock's wide-flared bows were designed to cleave and push the waters open ahead of her and in those waters below latitude 40° she ran like an old bull otter, slick and wet and fast for the south.

Uninterrupted by any landmass, the cycle of great atmospheric depressions swept endlessly across those cold open seas, and the wave patterns built up into a succession of marching mountain ranges.

Warlock was taking them on her starboard shoulder, bursting through each crest in a white explosion that leapt from her bows like a torpedo strike, the water coming aboard green and clear over her high foredeck, and sweeping her from stern to stern as she twisted and broke out, dropping sheer into the valley that opened ahead of her.

Her twin ferro-bronze propellers broke clear of the surface, the slamming vibration instantly controlled by the sophisticated variable-pitch gear, until she swooped forward and the propellers bit deeply again, the thrust of the twin Mirrlees diesels hurtling her towards the slope of the next swell.

Each time it seemed that she could not rise in time to meet the cliff of water that bore down on her. The water was black under the grey sunless sky. Nick had lived through typhoon and Caribbean hurricane, but had never seen water as menacing and cruel as this. It glittered like the molten slag that pours down the dump of an iron foundry and cools to the same iridescent blackness.

In the deep valleys between the crests, the wind was blanketed so they fell into an unnatural stillness, an eerie silence that only enhanced the menace of that towering slope of water.

In the trough, *Warlock* heeled and threw her head up, climbing the slope in a gut-swooping lift, that buckled the knees of the watch. As she went up, so the angle of her bridge tilted back, and that sombre cheerless sky filled the forward bridge windows with a vista of low scudding cloud.

The wind tore at the crest of the wave ahead of her, ripping it away like white cotton from the burst seams of a black mattress, splattering custard-thick spume against the armoured glass. Then *Warlock* put her sharp steel nose deeply into it. Gouging a fat wedge of racing green over her head, twisting violently at the jarring impact, dropping sideways over the crest, and breaking out to fall free and repeat the cycle again.

Nick was wedged into the canvas Master's seat in the corner of the bridge. He swayed like a camel-driver to the thrust of the sea and smoked his black cheroots quietly, his head turning every few minutes to the west, as though he expected at any moment to see the black ugly hull of *La*

Mouette come up on top of the next swell. But he knew she was a thousand miles away still, racing down the far leg of the triangle which had at its apex the stricken liner.

'If she *is* running,' Nick thought, and knew that there was no doubt. *La Mouette* was running as frantically as was *Warlock* – and as silently. Jules Levoisin had taught Nick the trick of silence. He would not use his radio until he had the liner on his radar scan. Then he would come through in clear, 'I will be in a position to put a line aboard you in two hours. Do you accept "Lloyd's Open Form"?'

The Master of the distressed vessel, having believed himself abandoned without succour, would overreact to the promise of salvation, and when *La Mouette* came bustling up over the horizon, flying all her bunting and with every light blazing in as theatrical a display as Jules could put up, the relieved Master would probably leap at the offer of 'Lloyd's Open Form' – a decision that would surely be regretted by the ship's owners in the cold and unemotional precincts of an arbitration court.

When Nick had supervised the design of *Warlock*, he had insisted that she look good as well as being able to perform. The master of a disabled ship was usually a man in a highly emotional state. Mere physical appearance might sway him in the choice between two salvage tugs coming up on him. *Warlock* looked magnificent; even in this cold and cheerless ocean, she looked like a warship. The trick would be to show her to the master of *Golden Adventurer* before he struck a bargain with *La Mouette*.

Nick could no longer sit inactive in his canvas seat. He judged the next towering swell and, with half a dozen quick strides, crossed the bridge deck in those fleeting moments as *Warlock* steadied in the trough. He grabbed the chrome handrail above the Decca computer.

On the keyboard he typed the function code that would set the machine in navigational mode, coordinating the transmissions she was receiving from the circling satellite stations high above the earth. From these were calculated *Warlock*'s exact position over the earth's surface, accurate to within twenty-five yards.

Nick entered the ship's position and the computer compared this with the plot that Nick had requested four hours previously. It printed out quickly the distance run and the ship's speed made good. Nick frowned angrily and swung round to watch the helmsman.

In this fiercely running cross sea, a good man could hold *Warlock* on course more efficiently than any automatic steering device. He could anticipate each trough and crest and prevent the ship paying off across the direction of the swells, and then kicking back violently as she went over, wasting critical time and distance.

Nick watched the helmsman work, judging each sea as it came aboard, checking the ship's heading on the big repeating compass above the man's head. After ten minutes, Nick realized that there was no wastage; *Warlock* was making as good a course as was possible in these conditions.

The engine telegraph was pulled back to her maximum safe power-setting, the course was good and yet *Warlock* was not delivering those few extra knots of speed that Nick Berg had relied on when he had made the critical decision to race *La Mouette* for the prize.

Nick had relied on twenty-eight knots against the Frenchman's eighteen, and he was not getting it. Involuntarily, he glanced out to the west as *Warlock* came up on the top of the next crest. Through the streaming windows, from which the spinning wipers cleared circular areas of clean glass, Nick looked out across a wilderness of black water, forbidding and cold and devoid of other human presence.

Abruptly Nick crossed to the R/T microphone.

'Engine Room confirm we are top of the green.'

'Top of the green, it is, Skipper.'

The Chief's casual tones floated in above the crash of the next sea coming aboard.

'Top of the green' was the maximum safe power-setting recommended by the manufacturers for those gigantic Mirrlees diesels. It was a far higher setting than top economical power, and they were burning fuel at a prodigious rate. Nick was pushing her as high as he could without going into the 'red' danger area above eighty per cent of full power, which at prolonged running might permanently damage her engines.

Nick turned away to his seat, and wedged himself into it. He groped for his cheroot case, and then checked himself, the lighter in his hand. His tongue and mouth felt furred over and dry. He had smoked without a break every waking minute since leaving Cape Town, and God knows he had slept little enough since then. He ran his tongue around his mouth with distaste before he returned the cheroot to his case, and crouched in his seat staring ahead, trying to work out why *Warlock* was running slow.

Suddenly he straightened and considered a possibility that brought a metallic green gleam of anger into Nick's eyes.

He slid out of his seat, nodded to the Third Officer who had the deck and ducked through the doorway in the back of the bridge into his day cabin. It was a ploy. He didn't want his visit below decks announced, and from his own suite he darted into the companionway.

The engine control room was as modern and gleaming as *Warlock*'s navigation bridge. It was completely enclosed with double glass to cut down the thunder of her engines. The control console was banked below the windows, and all the ship's functions were displayed in green and red digital figures.

The view beyond the windows into the main engine

room was impressive, even for Nick who had designed and supervised each foot of the layout.

The two Mirrlees diesel engines filled the white-painted cavern with only walking space between, each as long as four Cadillac Eldorados parked bumper to bumper and as deep as if another four Cadillacs had been piled on top of them.

The thirty-six cylinders of each block were crowned with a moving forest of valve stems and con-rod ends, each enormous powerhouse capable of pouring out eleven thousand usable horsepower.

It was only custom that made it necessary for any visitor, including the Master, to announce his arrival in the engine room to the Chief Engineer. Ignoring custom, Nick slipped quietly through the glass sliding doors, out of the hot burned-oil stench of the engine room into the cooler and sweeter conditioned air of the control room.

Vin Baker was deep in conversation with one of his electricians, both of them kneeling before the open doors of one of the tall grey steel cabinets which housed a teeming mass of coloured cables and transistor switches. Nick had reached the control console before the Chief Engineer uncoiled his lanky body from the floor and spun round to face him.

When Nick was very angry, his lips compressed in a single thin white line, the thick dark eyebrows seemed to meet above the snapping green eyes and large slightly beaked nose.

'You pulled the override on me,' he accused in a flat, passionless voice that did not betray his fury. 'You're governing her out at seventy per cent of power.'

'That's top of the green in my book,' Vin Baker told him. 'I'm not running my engines at eighty per cent in this sea. She'll shake the guts out of herself.' He paused and the stern was flung up violently as *Warlock* crashed over the top of another sea. The control room shuddered with the vibration of the screws breaking out of the surface, spinning wildly in the air before they could bite again.

'Listen to her, man. You want me to pour on more of it?'

'She's built to take it.'

'Nothing's built to run that hard, and live in this sea.'

'I want the override out,' said Nick flatly, indicating the chrome handle and pointer with which the engineer could cancel the power settings asked for by the bridge. 'I don't care when you do it – just as long as it's any time within the next five seconds.'

'You get out of my engine room – and go play with your toys.'

'All right,' Nick nodded, 'I'll do it myself.' And he reached for the override gear.

'You take your hands off my engines,' howled Vin Baker, and picked up the iron locking handle off the deck. 'You touch my engines and I'll break your teeth out of your head, you ice-cold Pommy bastard.'

Even in his own anger, Nick blinked at the epithet. When he thought about the blazing passions and emotions that seethed within him, he nearly laughed aloud. *Ice-cold*, he thought, so that's how he sees me.

'You stupid Bundaberg-swilling galah,' he said quietly, as he reached for the override. 'I don't really care if I have to kill you first, but we are going to eighty per cent.'

It was Vin Baker's turn to blink behind his smeared glasses, he had not expected to be insulted in the colloquial. He dropped the heavy steel handle to the deck. It fell with a clang.

'I don't need it,' he announced, and tucked his spectacles into his back pocket and hoisted his trousers with both elbows. 'It will be more fun to take you to pieces by hand.'

It was only then that Nick realized how tall the engineer was. His arms were ridged with the lean wiry taut muscle of hard physical labour. His fists, as he balled them, were lumpy with scar tissue across the knuckles and the size of a pair of nine-pound hammers. He went down into a fighter's crouch, and rode the plunging deck with an easy flexing of the long powerful legs.

As Nicholas touched the chrome override handle, the first punch came from the level of Baker's knees, but it came so fast that Nick only just had time to sway away from it. It whistled up past his jaw and scraped the skin from the outside corner of his eye, but he counter-punched instinctively, swaying back and slamming it in under the armpit, feeling the blow land so solidly that his teeth jarred his own head. The Chief's breath hissed, but he swung left-handed and a bony fist crushed the pad of muscle on the point of Nick's shoulder, bounced off and caught him high on the temple.

Even though it was a glancing blow, it felt as though a door had slammed in Nick's head, and resounding darkness closed behind his eyes. He fell forward into a clinch to ride the darkness, grabbing the lean hard body and smothering it in a bear hug as he tried to clear the singing darkness in his head.

He felt the Chief shift his weight, and was shocked at the power in that wiry frame, it took all his own strength to hold him. Suddenly and clearly he knew what was going to happen next. There were little white ridges of scar tissue half hidden by the widow's peak of flopping sandy hair on the Chief's forehead. Those scars from previous conflicts warned Nick.

Vin Baker reared back, like a cobra flaring for the strike, and then flung his head forward; it was the classic butt aimed for Nick's face and, had it landed squarely, it would have crushed in his nose and broken his teeth off level to the gums – but Nick anticipated, and dropped his own chin, tucking it down hard so that their foreheads met with a crack like a breaking oak branch.

The impact broke Nick's grip, and both of them reeled apart across the heaving deck, Vin Baker howling like a moon-sick dog and clutching his own head.

'Fight fair, you Pommy bastard!' he howled in outrage, and he came up short against the steel cabinets that lined the far side of the control room. The astonished electrician dived for cover under the control console, scattering tools across the deck.

Vin Baker lay for a moment gathering his lanky frame, and then, as *Warlock* swung hard over, rolling viciously in the cross sea, he used her momentum to hurl himself down the steeply tilting deck, dropping his head again like a battering ram to crush in Nick's ribs as he charged.

Nick turned like a cattle man working an unruly steer. He whipped one arm round Vin Baker's neck and ran with him, holding his head down and building up speed across the full length of the control room. They reached the armoured glass wall at the far end, and the top of Vin Baker's head was the point of impact with the weight of both their bodies behind it.

The Chief Engineer came round at the prick of the needle that Angel forced through the thick flap of open flesh on top of his head. He came round fighting drunkenly, but the cook held him down with one huge hairy arm.

'Easy, love.' Angel pulled the needle through the torn red weeping scalp and tied the stitch.

'Where is he, where is the bastard?' slurred the Chief.

'It's all over, Chiefie,' Angel told him gently. 'And you

are lucky he bashed you on the head – otherwise he might have hurt you.' He took another stitch.

The Chief winced as Angel pulled the thread up tight and knotted it. 'He tried to mess with my engines. I taught the bastard a lesson.'

'You've terrified him,' Angel agreed sweetly. 'Now you take a swig of this and lie still. I want you in this bunk for twelve hours – and I might come and tuck you in.'

'I'm going back to my engines,' announced the Chief, and drained the medicine glass of brown spirit, then whistled at the bite of the fumes.

Angel left him and crossed to the telephone. He spoke quickly into it, and as the Chief lumbered off the bunk, Nick Berg stepped into the cabin, and nodded to the cook.

'Thank you, Angel.'

Angel ducked out of the cabin and left them facing each other. The Chief opened his mouth to snarl at Nick.

'Jules Levoisin in *La Mouette* has probably made five hundred miles on us while you have been playing prima donna,' said Nick quietly, and Vin Baker's mouth stayed open, although no sound came out of it.

'I built this ship to run fast and hard in just this kind of contest, and now you are trying to do all of us out of prize money.'

Nick turned on his heel and went back up the companionway to his navigation deck. He settled into his canvas chair and fingered the big purple swelling on his forehead tenderly. His head felt as though a rope had been knotted around it and twisted up tight. He wanted to go to his cabin and take something for the pain, but he did not want to miss the call when it came.

He lit another cheroot, and it tasted like burned tarred rope. He dropped it into the sandbox and the telephone at his shoulder rang once.

'Bridge, this is the Engine Room.'

'Go ahead, Chief.'

'We are going to eighty per cent now.'

Nick did not reply, but he felt the change in the engine vibration and the more powerful rush of the hull beneath him.

'Nobody told me *La Mouette* was running against us. No way that frog-eating bastard's going to get a line on her first,' announced Vin Baker grimly, and there was a silence between them. Something more had to be said.

'I bet you a pound to a pinch of kangaroo dung,' challenged the Chief, 'that you don't know what a galah is, and that you've never tasted a Bundaberg rum in your life.'

Nick found himself smiling, even through the blinding pain in his head.

'Be-yew-dy!' Nick said, making three syllables of it and keeping the laughter out of his voice, as he hung up the receiver.

D ave Allen's voice was apologetic. 'Sorry to wake you, sir, but the *Golden Adventurer* is reporting.'

'I'm coming,' mumbled Nick, and swung his legs off the bunk. He had been in that black death-sleep of exhaustion, but it took him only seconds to pull back the dark curtains from his mind. It was his old training as a watch-keeping officer.

He rubbed away the last traces of sleep, feeling the rasping black stubble of his beard under his fingers as he crossed quickly to his bathroom. He spent forty seconds in bathing his face and combing his tousled hair, and regretfully decided there was no time to shave. Another rule of his was to look good in a world which so often judged a man by his appearance.

When he went out on to the navigation bridge, he knew at once that the wind had increased its velocity. He guessed it was rising force six now, and *Warlock*'s motion was more violent and abandoned. Beyond the warm, dimly lit capsule of the bridge, all those elements of cold water and vicious racing winds turned the black night to a howling tumult.

The Trog was crouched over his machines, grey and wizened and sleepless. He hardly turned his head to hand Nick the message flimsy.

'Master of *Golden Adventurer* to Christy Marine,' the Decca decoded swiftly, and Nick grunted as he saw the new position report. Something had altered drastically in the liner's circumstances. 'Main engines still unserviceable. Current setting easterly and increasing to eight knots. Wind rising force six from north-west. Critical ice danger to the ship. What assistance can I expect?'

There was a panicky note to that last line, and Nick saw why when he compared the liner's new position on the spread chart.

'She's going down sharply on the lee shore,' David muttered as he worked quickly over the chart. 'The current and wind are working together – they are driving her down on to the land.'

He touched the ugly broken points of Coatsland's shoreline with the tip of one finger.

'She is eighty miles offshore now. At the rate she is drifting, it will take her only another ten hours before she goes aground.'

'If she doesn't hit an iceberg first,' said Nick. 'From the Master's last message, it sounds as though they are into big ice.'

'That's a cheerful thought,' agreed David, and straightened up from the chart.

'What's our time to reach her?'

'Another forty hours, sir,' David hesitated and pushed

the thick white-gold lock of hair off his forehead, 'if we can make good this speed – but we may have to reduce when we reach the ice.'

Nick turned away to his canvas chair. He felt the need to pace back and forward, to release the pent-up forces within him. However, any movement in this heavy pounding sea was not only difficult but downright dangerous, so he groped his way to the chair and wedged himself in, staring ahead into the clamorous black night.

He thought about the terrible predicament of the liner's Captain. His ship was at deadly risk, and the lives of his crew and passengers with it.

How many lives? Nick cast his mind back and came up with the figures. The *Golden Adventurer's* full complement of officers and crew was 235, and there was accommodation for 375 passengers, a possible total of over six hundred souls. If the ship was lost, *Warlock* would be hard put to take aboard that huge press of human life.

'Well, sir, they signed on for adventure,' David Allen spoke into his thoughts as though he had heard them, 'and they are getting their money's worth.'

Nick glanced at him, and nodded. 'Most of them will be elderly. A berth on that cruise costs a fortune, and it's usually only the oldsters who have that sort of gold. If she goes aground, we are going to lose life.'

'With respect, Captain,' David hesitated, and blushed again for the first time since leaving port, 'if her Captain knows that assistance is on the way, it may prevent him doing something crazy.'

Nick was silent. The Mate was right, of course. It was cruel to leave them in the despair of believing they were alone down there in those terrible icefields. The *Adventurer's* Captain could make a panic decision, one that could be averted if he knew how close succour was.

'The air temperature out there is minus five degrees, and if the wind is at thirty miles an hour, that will make it a lethal chill factor. If they take to the boats in that—' David was interrupted by the Trog calling from the radio room.

'The owners are replying.'

It was a long message that Christy Marine were sending to their Captain. It was filled with those same hollow assurances that a surgeon gives to a cancer patient, but one paragraph had relevance for Nick:

'All efforts being made to contact salvage tugs reported operating South Atlantic.'

David Allen looked at him expectantly. It was the right humane thing to do. To tell them he was only eight hundred miles away, and closing swiftly.

Nervous energy fizzed in Nick's blood, making him restless and angry. On an impulse he left his chair and carefully crossed the heaving deck to the starboard wing of the bridge.

He slid open the door and stepped out into the gale. The shock of that icy air took his breath away and he gasped like a drowning man. He felt tears streaming from his eyes across his cheeks and the frozen spray struck into his face like steel darts.

Carefully he filled his lungs, and his nostrils flared as he smelt the ice. It was that unmistakeable dank smell, he remembered so well from the northern Arctic seas. It was like the body smell of some gigantic reptilian sea monster – and it struck the mariner's chill into his soul.

He could endure only a few seconds more of the gale, but when he stepped back into the cosy green-lit warmth of the bridge, his mind was clear, and he was thinking crisply.

'Mr Allen, there is ice ahead.'

'I have a watch on the radar, sir.'

'Very good,' Nick nodded, 'but we'll reduce to fifty per cent of power.' He hesitated, and then went on, 'and maintain radio silence.'

The decision was hard made, and Nick saw the

accusation in David Allen's eyes before he turned away to give the orders for the reduction in power. Nick felt a sudden and uncharacteristic urge to explain the decision to him. He did not know why – perhaps he needed the Mate's understanding and sympathy. Instantly Nick saw that as a symptom of his weakness and vulnerability. He had never needed sympathy before, and he steeled himself against it now.

His decision to maintain radio silence was correct. He was dealing with two hard men. He knew he could not afford to give an inch of sea room to Jules Levoisin. He would force him to open radio contact first. He needed that advantage.

The other man with whom he had to deal was Duncan Alexander, and he was a hating man, dangerous and vindictive. He had tried once to destroy Nick – and perhaps he had already succeeded. Nick had to guard himself now, he must pick with care his moment to open negotiations with Christy Marine and the man who had displaced him at its head. Nick must be in a position of utmost strength when he did so.

Jules Levoisin must be forced to declare himself first, Nick decided. The Captain of the *Golden Adventurer* would have to be left in the agonies of doubt a little longer, and Nick consoled himself with the thought that any further drastic change in the liner's circumstances or a decision by the Master to abandon his ship and commit his company to the lifeboats would be announced on the open radio channels and would give him a chance to intervene.

Nick was about to caution the Trog to keep a particular watch on Channel 16 for *La Mouette*'s first transmission, then he checked himself. That was another thing he never did – issue unnecessary orders. The Trog's grey wrinkled head was wreathed in clouds of reeking cigar smoke but was bowed to his mass of electronic equipment, and he adjusted a dial with careful lover's fingers; his little eyes were bright and sleepless as those of an ancient sea turtle.

Nick went to his chair and settled down to wait out the few remaining hours of the short Antarctic summer night.

The radar screen had shown strange and alien capes and headlands above the sea clutter of the storm, strange islands, anomalies which did not relate to the Admiralty charts. Between these alien masses shone myriad other smaller contacts, bright as fireflies, any one of which could have been the echo of a stricken ocean liner – but which was not.

As *Warlock* nosed cautiously down into this enchanted sea, the dawn that had never been far from the horizon flushed out, timorous as a bride, decked in colours of gold and pink that struck splendorous splinters of light off the icebergs.

The horizon ahead of them was cluttered with ice, some of the fragments were but the size of a billiard table and they bumped and scraped down the *Warlock*'s side, then swung and bobbed in her wake as she passed. There were others the size of a city block, weird and fanciful structures of honeycombed white ice, that stood as tall as *Warlock*'s upperworks as she passed.

'White ice is soft ice,' Nick murmured to David Allen beside him, and then caught himself. It was an unnecessary speech, inviting familiarity, and before the Mate could answer, Nick turned quickly away to the radar-repeater and lowered his face to the eyepiece in the coned hood. For a minute he studied the images of the surrounding ice in the darkened body of the instrument, then went back to his seat and stared ahead impatiently.

Warlock was running too fast, Nick knew it; he was

relying on the vigilance of his deck officers to carry her through the ice. Yet still this speed was too slow for his seething impatience.

Above their horizon rose another shoreline, a great unbroken sweep of towering cliff which caught the low sun, and glowed in emerald and amethyst, a drifting tableland of solid hard ice, forty miles across and two hundred feet high.

As they closed with that massive translucent island, so the colours that glowed through it became more hauntingly beautiful. The cliffs were rent by deep bays, and split by crevasses whose shadowy depths were dark sapphire, blue and mysterious, paling out to a thousand shades of green.

'My God, it's beautiful!' said David Allen with the reverence of a man kneeling in a cathedral.

The crests of the ice cliffs blazed in clearest ruby; to windward, the big sea piled in and crashed against those cliffs, surging up them in explosive bursts of white spray. Yet the iceberg did not dip nor swing or work, even in that murderous sea.

'Look at the lee she is making.' Dave Allen pointed. 'You could ride out a force twelve behind her.'

On the leeward side, the waters were protected from the wind by that mountain of sheer ice. Green and docile, they lapped those mysterious blue cliffs, and *Warlock* went into the lee, passing in a ship's length from the plunging rearing action of a wild horse into the tranquillity of a mountain lake, calm, windless and unnatural.

In the calm, Angel brought trays piled with crisp brown-baked Cornish pasties and steaming mugs of thick creamy cocoa, and they ate breakfast at three in the morning, marvelling at the fine pale sunlight and the towers of incredible beauty, the younger officers shouting and laughing when a school of five black killer whales passed so close that they could see their white cheek patterns and wide grinning mouths through the icy clear waters.

The great mammals circled the ship, then ducked beneath her hull, surging up on the far side with their huge black triangular fins shearing the surface as they blew through the vents in the top of their heads. The fishy stink of their breath pervaded the bridge, and then they were gone, and *Warlock* motored calmly along in the lee of the ice, like a holiday launch of day-trippers.

Nicholas Berg did not join the spontaneous gaiety. He munched one of Angel's delicious pies full of meat and thick gravy, but he could not finish it. His stomach was too tense. He found himself resenting the high spirits of his officers. The laughter offended him, now when his whole life hung in precarious balance. He felt the temptation to quell them with a few harsh words, conscious of the power he had to plunge them into instant consternation.

Nick listened to their carefree banter and felt old enough to be their father, despite the few years' difference in their ages. He was impatient with them, irritated that they should be able to laugh like this when so much was at stake – six hundred human lives, a great ship, tens of millions of dollars, his whole future. They would probably never themselves know what it felt like to put a lifetime's work at risk on a single flip of the coin – and then suddenly, unaccountably, he envied them.

He could not understand the sensation, could not fathom why suddenly he longed to laugh with them, to share the companionship of the moment, to be free of pressure for just a little while. For fifteen years, he had not known that sort of hiatus, had never wanted it.

He stood up abruptly, and immediately the bridge was silent. Every officer concentrating on his appointed task, not one of them glancing at him as he paced once, slowly, across the wide bridge. It did not need a word to change the mood, and suddenly Nick felt guilty. It was too easy, too cheap.

Carefully Nick steeled himself, shutting out the weakness,

building up his resolve and determination, bringing all his concentration to bear on the Herculean task ahead of him, and he paused at the door of the radio room. The Trog looked up from his machines, and they exchanged a single glance of understanding. Two completely dedicated men, with no time for frivolity.

Nick nodded and paced on, the strong handsome face stern and uncompromising, his step firm and measured – but when he stopped again by the side windows of the bridge and looked up at the magnificent cliff of ice, he felt the doubts surging up again within him.

How much had he sacrificed for what he had gained, how much joy and laughter had he spurned to follow the high road of challenge, how much beauty had he passed along the way without seeing it in his haste, how much love and warmth and companionship? He thought with a fierce pang of the woman who had been his wife, and who had gone now with the child who was his son. Why had they gone, and what had they left him with – after all his strivings?

Behind him, the radio crackled and hummed as the carrier beam opened Channel 16, then it pitched higher as a human voice came through clearly.

'Mayday. Mayday. Mayday. This is the *Golden Adventurer*.'

Nick spun and ran to the radio room as the calm masculine voice read out the coordinates of the ship's position.

'We are in imminent danger of striking. We are preparing to abandon ship. Can any vessel render assistance? Repeat, can any vessel render assistance?'

'Good God,' David Allen's voice was harsh with anxiety, 'the current's got them, they're going down on Cape Alarm at nine knots – she's only fifty miles offshore and we are still two hundred and twenty miles from that position.'

'Where is *La Mouette?*' growled Nick Berg. 'Where the hell is she?'

'We'll have to open contact now, sir,' David Allen looked up from the chart. 'You cannot let them go down into the boats – not in this weather, sir. It would be murder.'

'Thank you, Number One,' said Nick quietly. 'Your advice is always welcome.' David flushed, but there was anger and not embarrassment beneath the colour. Even in the stress of the moment, Nick noted that, and adjusted his opinion of his First Officer. He had guts as well as brains.

The Mate was right, of course. There was only one thing to consider now, the conservation of human life.

Nick looked up at the top of the ice cliff and saw the low cloud tearing off it, roiling and swirling in the wind, pouring down over the edge like boiling milk frothing from the lip of a great pot.

He had to send now. *La Mouette* had won the contest of silence. Nick stared up at the cloud and composed the message he would send. He must reassure the Master, urge him to delay his decision to abandon ship and give *Warlock* the time to close the gap, perhaps even reach her before she struck on Cape Alarm.

The silence on the bridge was deepened by the absence of wind. They were all watching him now, waiting for the decision, and in that silence the carrier beam of Channel 16 hummed and throbbed.

Then suddenly a rich Gallic accent poured into the silent bridge, a full fruity voice that Nick remembered so clearly, even after all the years.

'Master of *Golden Adventurer*, this is the Master of salvage tug *La Mouette*. I am proceeding at best speed your assistance. Do you accept Lloyd's Open Form "No cure no pay"?'

Nick kept his face from showing any emotion, but his heart barged wildly against his ribs. Jules Levoisin had broken silence.

'Plot his position report,' he said quietly.

'God! She's inside us.' David Allen's face was stricken as he marked *La Mouette*'s reported position on the chart. 'She's a hundred miles ahead of us.'

'No.' Nick shook his head. 'He's lying.'

'Sir?'

'He's lying. He always lies.' Nick lit a cheroot and when it was drawing evenly, he spoke again to his radio officer.

'Did you get a bearing?' and the Trog looked up from his radio direction-finding compass on which he was tracing *La Mouette*'s transmissions.

'I have only one coordinate, you won't get a fix—'

But Nick interrupted him, 'We'll use his best course from Golfo San Jorge for a fix.' He turned back to David Allen. 'Plot that.'

'There's a difference of over three hundred nautical miles.'

'Yes.' Nick nodded. 'That old pirate wouldn't broadcast an accurate position to all the world. We are inside him and running five knots better, we'll put a line over *Golden Adventurer* before he's in radar contact.'

'Are you going to open contact with Christy Marine now, sir?'

'No, Mr Allen.'

'But they will do a deal with *La Mouette* – unless we bid now.'

'I don't think so,' Nick murmured, and almost went on to say, 'Duncan Alexander won't settle for Lloyd's Open Form while he is the underwriter, and his ship is free and floating. He'll fight for daily hire and bonus, and Jules

Levoisin won't buy that package. He'll hold out for the big plum. They won't do a deal until the two ships are in visual contact – and by that time I'll have her in tow and I'll fight the bastard in the awards court for twenty-five per cent of her value—' But he did not say it. 'Steady as she goes, Mr Allen,' was all he said, as he left the bridge.

He closed the door of his day cabin and leaned back against it, shutting his eyes tightly as he gathered himself. It had been so very close, a matter of seconds and he would have declared himself and given the advantage to *La Mouette*.

Through the door behind him, he heard David Allen's voice. 'Did you see him? He didn't feel a thing – not a bloody thing. He was going to let those poor bastards go into the boats. He must piss ice-water.' The voice was muffled, but the outrage in it was tempered by awe.

Nick kept his eyes shut a moment longer, then he straightened up and pushed himself away from the door. He wanted it to begin now. It was the waiting and the uncertainty which was eroding what was left of his strength.

'Please God, let me reach them in time.' And he was not certain whether it was for the lives or for the salvage award that he was praying.

Captain Basil Reilly, the Master of the *Golden Adventurer*, was a tall man, with a lean and wiry frame that promised reserves of strength and endurance. His face was very darkly tanned and splotched with the dark patches of benign sun cancer. His heavy moustache was silvered like the pelt of a snow fox, and though his eyes were set in webs of finely wrinkled and pouchy skin, they were bright and calm and intelligent.

He stood on the windward wing of his navigation bridge and watched the huge black seas tumbling in to batter his helpless ship. He was taking them broadside now, and each time they struck, the hull shuddered and heeled with a sick dead motion, giving reluctantly to the swells that rose up and broke over her rails, sweeping her decks from side to side, and then cascading off her again in a tumble of white that smoked in the wind.

He adjusted the life jacket he wore, settling the rough canvas more comfortably around his shoulders as he reviewed his position once more.

Golden Adventurer had taken the ice in that eight-to-midnight watch traditionally allotted to the most junior of the navigating officers. The impact had hardly been notice-able, yet it had awoken the Master from deep sleep – just a slight check and jar that had touched some deep chord in the mariner's instinct.

The ice had been a growler, one of the most deadly of all hazards. The big bergs standing high and solid to catch the radar beams, or the eye of even the most inattentive deck watch, were easily avoided. However, the low ice lying awash, with its great bulk and weight almost com-pletely hidden by the dark and turbulent waters, was as deadly as a predator in ambush.

The growler showed itself only in the depths of each wave trough, or in the swirl of the current around it, as though a massive sea-monster lurked there. At night, these indications would pass unnoticed by even the sharpest eyes, and below the surface, the wave action eroded the body of the growler, turning it into a horizontal blade that lay ten feet or more below the water level and reached out two or three hundred feet from the visible surface indications.

With the Third Officer on watch, and steaming at cautionary speed of a mere twelve knots, the *Golden Adventurer* had brushed against one of these monsters, and although the actual impact had gone almost unnoticed on board, the ice had opened her like the knife stroke which splits a herring for the smoking rack.

50

It was classic *Titanic* damage, a fourteen-foot rent through her side, twelve feet below the Plimsoll line, shearing two of her watertight compartments, one of which was her main engine-room section.

They had held the water easily until the electrical explosion, and since then, the Master had battled to keep her afloat. Slowly, step by step, fighting all the way, he had yielded to the sea. All the bilge pumps were running still, but the water was steadily gaining.

Three days ago he had brought all his passengers up from below the main deck, and he had battened down all the watertight bulkheads. The crew and passengers were accommodated now in the lounges and smoking rooms. The ship's luxury and opulence had been transformed into the crowded, unhygienic and deteriorating conditions of a city under siege.

It reminded him of the catacombs of the London underground converted to air-raid shelters during the blitz. He had been a lieutenant on shore-leave and he had passed one night there that he would remember for the rest of his life.

There was the same atmosphere on board now. The sanitary arrangements were inadequate. Fourteen toilet bowls for six hundred, many of them seasick and suffering from diarrhoea. There were no baths nor showers, and insufficient power for the heating of water in the hand-basins. The emergency generators delivered barely sufficient power to work the ship, to run the pumps, to supply minimal lighting, and to keep the communicational and navigational equipment running. There was no heating in the ship and the outside air temperature had fallen to minus twenty degrees now.

The cold in the spacious public lounges was brutal. The passengers huddled in their fur coats and bulky life jackets under mounds of blankets. There were limited cooking facilities on the gas stoves usually reserved for adventure tours ashore. There was no baking or grilling, and most of the food was eaten cold and congealed from cans; only the soup and beverages steamed in the cold clammy air, like the breaths of the waiting and helpless multitude.

The desalination plants had not been in use since the ice collision and now the supply of fresh water was critical; even hot drinks were rationed.

Of the 368 paying passengers, only forty-eight were below the age of fifty, and yet the morale was extraordinary. Men and women who before the emergency could and did complain bitterly at a dress shirt not ironed to crisp perfection or a wine served a few degrees too cold, now accepted a mug of beef tea as though it were a vintage Château Margaux, and laughed and chatted animatedly in the cold, shaming with their fortitude the few that might have complained. These were an unusual sample of humanity, men and women of achievement and resilience, who had come here to this outlandish corner of the globe in search of new experience. They were mentally prepared for adventure and even danger, and seemed almost to welcome this as part of the entertainment provided by the tour.

Yet, standing on his bridge, the Master was under no illusion as to the gravity of their situation. Peering through the streaming glass, he watched a work party, led by his First Officer, toiling heroically in the bows. Four men in glistening yellow plastic suits and hoods, drenched by the icy seas, working with the slow cold-numbed movements of automatons as they struggled to stream a sea anchor and bring the ship's head up into the sea, so that she might ride more easily, and perhaps slow her precipitous rush down onto the rocky coast. Twice in the preceding days, the anchors they had rigged had been torn away by sea and wind and the ship's dead weight.

Three hours before, he had called his engineering

officers up from below, where the risk to their lives had become too great to chance against the remote possibility of restoring power to his main engines. He had conceded the battle to the sea and now he was planning the final moves when he must abandon his command and attempt to remove six hundred human beings from this helpless hulk to the even greater dangers and hardships of Cape Alarm's barren and storm-rent shores.

Cape Alarm was one of those few pinnacles of barren black rock which thrust out from beneath the thick white mantle of the Antarctic cap, pounded free of ice like an anvil beneath the eternal hammering assault of storm and sea and wind.

The long straight ridge protruded almost fifty miles into the eastern extremity of the Weddell Sea, was fifty miles across at its widest point, and terminated in a pair of bull's horns which formed a small protected bay named after the polar explorer Sir Ernest Shackleton.

Shackleton Bay, with its steep purple-black beaches of round polished pebbles, was the nesting ground of a huge colony of chin-strap penguin, and for this reason was one of *Golden Adventurer*'s regular ports of call.

On each tour, the ship would anchor in the deep and calm waters of the bay, while her passengers went ashore to study and photograph the breeding birds and the extraordinary geological formations, sculptured by ice and wind into weird and grotesque shapes.

Only ten days earlier, *Golden Adventurer* had weighed anchor in Shackleton Bay and stood out into the Weddell Sea. The weather had been mild and still, with a slow oily swell and a bright clear sun. Now, before a force seven gale, in temperatures forty-five degrees colder, and borne on the wild dark sweep of the current, she was being carried back to that same black and rocky shore.

There was no doubt in Captain Reilly's mind – they

were going to go aground on Cape Alarm, there was no avoiding that fate with this set of sea and wind, unless the French salvage tug reached them first.

La Mouette should have been in radar contact already, if the tug's reported position was correct, and Basil Reilly let a little frown of worry crease the brown parchment skin of his forehead and shadows were in his eyes.

'Another message from head office, sir.' His Second Officer was beside him now, a young man with the shape of a teddy bear swathed in thick woollen jerseys and marine blue top coat. Basil Reilly's strict dress regulations had long ago been abandoned and their breaths steamed in the frigid air of the navigation bridge.

'Very well.' Reilly glanced at the flimsy. 'Send that to the tug master.' The contempt was clear in his voice, his disdain for this haggling between owners and salvors, when a great ship and six hundred lives were at risk in the cold sea.

He knew what he would do if the salvage tug made contact before *Golden Adventurer* struck the waiting fangs of rock, he would override his owner's express orders and exercise his rights as Master by immediately accepting the offer of assistance under Lloyd's Open Form.

'But let him come,' he murmured to himself. 'Please God, let him come,' and he raised his binoculars and slowly swept a long jagged horizon where the peaks of the swells seemed black and substantial as rock. He paused with a leap of his pulse when something white blinked in the field of the glasses and then, with a little sick slide, realized that it was only a random ray of sunlight catching a pinnacle of ice from one of the floating bergs.

He lowered the glasses and crossed from the windward wing of the bridge to the lee. He did not need the glasses now, Cape Alarm was black and menacing against the sow's-belly grey of the sky. Its ridges and valleys picked out with gleaming ice and banked snow, and against her steep shore, the sea creamed and leapt high in explosions of purest white.

'Sixteen miles, sir,' said the First Officer, coming to stand beside him. 'And the current seems to be setting a little more northerly now.' They were both silent, as they balanced automatically against the violent pitch and roll of the deck.

Then the Mate spoke again with a bitter edge to his voice, 'Where is that bloody frog?' And they watched the night of Antarctica begin to shroud the cruel lee shore in funereal cloaks of purple and sable, picked out with the ermine collars and cuffs of ice.

She was very young, probably not yet twenty-five years of age, and even the layers of heavy clothing topped by a man's anorak three sizes too big could not disguise the slimness of her body, that almost coltish elegance of long fine limbs and muscle toned by youth and hard exercise.

Her head was set jauntily on the long graceful stem of her neck, like a golden sunflower, and the profuse mane of long hair was sun-bleached, streaked with silver and platinum and copper gold, twisted up carelessly into a rope almost as thick as a man's wrist and piled on top of her head. Yet loose strands floated down on to her forehead and tickled her nose so that she pursed her lips and puffed them away.

Her hands were both occupied with the heavy tray she carried, and she balanced like a skilled horsewoman against the ship's extravagant plunging as she offered it.

'Come on, Mrs Goldberg,' she wheedled. 'It will warm the cockles of your tum.'

'I don't think so, my dear,' the white-haired woman faltered.

'Just for me, then,' the girl wheedled.

'Well,' the woman took one of the mugs and sipped it tentatively. 'It's good,' she said, and then quickly and furtively, 'Samantha, has the tug come yet?'

'It will be here any minute now, and the Captain is a dashing Frenchman, just the right age for you, with a lovely tickly moustache. I'm going to introduce you first thing.'

The woman was a widow in her late fifties, a little overweight and more than a little afraid, but she smiled and sat up a little straighter.

'You naughty thing,' she smiled.

'Just as soon as I've finished with this,' Samantha indicated the tray, 'I'll come and sit with you. We'll play some klabrias, okay?' When Samantha Silver smiled, her teeth were very straight and white against the peach of her tanned cheeks and the freckles that powdered her nose like gold dust. She moved on.

They welcomed her, each of them, men and women, competing for her attention, for she was one of those rare creatures that radiate such warmth, a sort of shining innocence, like a kitten or a beautiful child, and she laughed and chided and teased them in return and left them grinning and heartened, but jealous of her going, so they followed her with their eyes. Most of them felt she belonged to them personally, and they wanted all of her time and presence, making up questions or little stories to detain her for a few extra moments.

'There was an albatross following us a little while ago, Sam.'

'Yes, I saw it through the galley window—'

'It was a wandering albatross, wasn't it, Sam?'

'Oh, come on, Mr Stewart! You know better than that. It was *Diomedea melanophris*, the black-browed albatross, but still it's good luck. All albatrosses are good luck – that's a scientifically proven fact.'

Samantha had a doctorate in biology and was one of the

ship's specialist guides. She was on sabbatical leave from the University of Miami where she held a research fellowship in marine ecology.

Passengers thirty years her senior treated her like a favourite daughter most of the time. However, in even the mildest crisis they became childlike in their appeal to her and in their reliance on her natural strength which they recognized and sought instinctively. She was to them a combination of beloved pet and den-mother.

While a ship's steward refilled her tray with mugs, Samantha paused at the entrance to the temporary galley they had set up in the cocktail room and looked back into the densely packed lounge.

The stink of unwashed humanity and tobacco smoke was almost a solid blue thing, but she felt a rush of affection for them. They were behaving so very well, she thought, and she was proud of them.

'Well done, team,' she thought, and grinned. It was not often that she could find affection in herself for a mass of human beings. Often she had pondered how a creature so fine and noble and worthwhile as the human individual could, in its massed state, become so unattractive.

She thought briefly of the human multitudes of the crowded cities. She hated zoos and animals in cages, remembering as a little girl crying for a bear that danced endlessly against its bars, driven mad by its confinement. The concrete cages of the cities drove their captives into similar strange and bizarre behaviour. All creatures should be free to move and live and breathe, she believed, and yet man, the super-predator, who had denied that right to so many other creatures, was now destroying himself with the same single-mindedness, poisoning and imprisoning himself in an orgy that made the madness of the lemmings seem logical in comparison. It was only when she saw human beings like these in circumstances like these that she could be truly proud of them – and afraid for them.

She felt her own fear deep down, at the very periphery of her awareness, for she was a sea-creature who loved and understood the sea – and knew its monumental might. She knew what awaited them out there in the storm, and she was afraid. With a deliberate effort she lifted the slump of her shoulders, and set the smile brightly on her lips and picked up the heavy tray.

At that moment the speakers of the public-address system gave a preliminary squawk, and then filtered the Captain's cultured and measured tones into the suddenly silent ship.

'Ladies and gentlemen, this is your Captain speaking. I regret to inform you that we have not yet established radar contact with the salvage tug *La Mouette*, and that I now deem it necessary to transfer the ship's company to the lifeboats.'

There was a sigh and stir in the crowded lounges, heard even above the storm. Samantha saw one of her favourite passengers reach for his wife and press her silvery-grey head to his shoulder.

'You have all practised the lifeboat drill many times and you know your teams and stations. I am sure I do not have to impress upon you the necessity to go to your stations in orderly fashion, and to obey explicitly the orders of the ship's officers.'

Samantha set down her tray and crossed quickly to Mrs Goldberg. The woman was weeping, softly and quietly, lost and bewildered, and Samantha slipped her arm around her shoulder.

'Come now,' she whispered. 'Don't let the others see you cry.'

'Will you stay with me, Samantha?'

'Of course I will.' She lifted the woman to her feet. 'It will be all right – you'll see. Just think of the story you'll be able to tell your grandchildren when you get home.'

Captain Reilly reviewed his preparations for leaving the ship, going over them item by item in his mind. He now knew by heart the considerable list he had compiled days previously from his own vast experience of Antarctic conditions and the sea.

The single most important consideration was that no person should be immersed, or even drenched by sea water during the transfer. Life expectation in these waters was four minutes. Even if the victim were immediately pulled from the water, it was still four minutes, unless the sodden clothing could be removed and heating provided. With this wind blowing, rising eight of the Beaufort scale at forty miles an hour and an air temperature of minus twenty degrees, the chill factor was at the extreme of stage seven, which, translated into physical terms, meant that a few minutes' exposure would numb and exhaust a man, and that mere survival was a matter of planning and precaution.

The second most important consideration was the physiological crisis of his passengers, when they left the comparative warmth and comfort and security of the ship for the shrieking cold and the violent discomfort of a life-raft afloat in an Antarctic storm.

They had been briefed, and mentally prepared as much as was possible. An officer had checked each passenger's clothing and survival equipment, they had been fed high-sugar tablets to ward off the cold, and the life-raft allocations had been carefully worked out to provide balanced complements, each with a competent crew member in command. It was as much as he could do for them, and he turned his attention to the logistics of the transfer.

The lifeboats would go first – six of them, slung three on each side of the ship, each crewed by a navigation officer and five seamen. While the great drogue of the sea-anchor held the ship's head into the wind and the sea, they would be swung outboard on their hydraulic derricks and the winches would lower them swiftly to the surface of a sea temporarily smoothed by the oil sprayed from the pumps in the bows.

Although they were decked-in, powered, and equipped with radio, the lifeboats were not the ideal vehicles for survival in these conditions. Within hours, the men aboard them would be exhausted by the cold. For this reason, none of the passengers would be aboard them. Instead, they would go into the big inflatable life-rafts, self-righting even in the worst seas and enclosed with a double skin of insulation. Equipped with emergency rations and battery-powered locator beacons, they would ride the big black seas more easily and each provide shelter for twenty human beings, whose body warmth would keep the interior habitable, at least for the time it took to tow the rafts to land.

The motor lifeboats were merely the shepherds for the rafts. They would herd them together and then tow them in tandem to the sheltering arms of Shackleton Bay.

Even in these blustering conditions, the tow should not take more than twelve hours. Each boat would tow five rafts, and though the crews of the motor boats would have to change, brought into the canopy of the rafts and rested, there should be no insurmountable difficulties; Captain Reilly was hoping for a tow-speed of between three and four knots.

The lifeboats were packed with equipment and fuel and food sufficient to keep the shipwrecked party for a month, perhaps two on reduced rations, and once the calmer shores of the bay had been reached, the rafts would be carried ashore, the canopies reinforced with slabs of packed snow and transformed into igloo-type huts to shelter the survivors. They might be in Shackleton Bay a long time, for even when the French tug reached them, it could not take aboard six hundred persons; some would have to remain and await another rescue ship.

Captain Reilly took one more look at the land. It was very close now, and even in the gloom of the onrushing night, the peaks of ice and snow glittered like the fangs of some terrible and avaricious monster.

'All right,' he nodded to his First Officer, 'we will begin.'

The Mate lifted the small two-way radio to his lips. 'Foredeck. Bridge. You may commence laying the oil now.'

From each side of the bows, the hoses threw up silver dragonfly wings of sprayed diesel oil, pumped directly from the ship's bunkers; its viscous weight resisted the wind's efforts to tear it away, and it fell in a thick coating across the surface of the sea, broken by the floodlights into the colour spectrum of the rainbow.

Immediately, the sea was soothed, the wind-riven surface flattened by the weight of oil, so the swells passed in smooth and weighty majesty beneath the ship's hull.

The two officers on the wing of the bridge could feel the sick, waterlogged response of the hull. She was heavy with the water in her, no longer light and quick and alive.

'Send the boats away,' said the Captain, and the mate passed the order over the radio in quiet conversational tones.

The hydraulic arms of the derricks lifted the six boats off their chocks and swung them out over the ship's side, suspended one moment high above the surface; then, as the ship fell through the trough, the oil-streaked crest raced by only feet below their keels. The officer of each lifeboat must judge the sea, and operate the winch so as to drop neatly onto the back slope of a passing swell – then instantly detach the automatic clamps and stand away from the threatening steel cliff of the ship's side.

In the floodlights, the little boats shone wetly with spray, brilliant electric yellow in colour, and decorated with garlands of ice like Christmas toys. In the small armoured-glass windows the officers' faces also glistened whitely with the strain and concentration of these terrifying moments, as each tried to judge the rushing black seas.

Suddenly the heavy nylon rope that held the cone-shaped drogue of the sea-anchor snapped with a report like a cannon shot, and the rope snaked and hissed in the air, a vicious whiplash which could have sliced a man in half.

It was like slipping the head halter from a wild stallion. *Golden Adventurer* threw up her bows, joyous to be freed of restraint. She slewed back across the scend of the sea, and was immediately pinned helplessly broadside, her starboard side into the wind, and the three yellow lifeboats still dangling.

A huge wave reared up out of the darkness. As it rushed down on the ship, one of the lifeboats sheared her cables and fell heavily to the surface, the tiny propeller churning frantically, trying to bring her round to meet the wave – but the wave caught her and dashed her back against the steel side of the ship.

She burst like a ripe melon and the guts spilled out of her; from the bridge they saw the crew swirled helplessly away into the darkness. The little locator lamps on their lifejackets burned feebly as fireflies in the darkness and then blinked out in the storm.

The forward lifeboard was swung like a door-knocker against the ship, her forward cable jammed so she dangled stern upmost, and as each wave punched into her, she was smashed against the hull. They could hear the men in her screaming, a thin pitiful sound on the wind, that went on for many minutes as the sea slowly beat the boat into a tangle of wreckage.

The third boat was also swung viciously against the hull. The releases on her clamps opened, and she dropped twenty feet into the boil and surge of water, submerging completely and then bobbing free like a yellow fishing float after the strike. Leaking and settling swiftly, she limped away into the clamorous night.

'Oh, my God,' whispered Captain Reilly, and in the harsh lights of the bridge, his face was suddenly old and haggard. In a single stroke he had lost half his boats. As yet he did not mourn the men taken by the sea, that would come later – now it was the loss of the boats that appalled him, for it threatened the lives of nearly six hundred others.

'The other boats' – the First Officer's voice was ragged with shock – 'the others got away safely, sir.'

In the lee of the towering hull, protected from both wind and sea, the other three boats had dropped smoothly to the surface and detached swiftly. Now they circled out in the dark night, with their spotlights probing like long white fingers. One of them staggered over the wildly plunging crests to take off the crew of the stricken life-boat, and they left the cracked hull to drift away and sink.

'Three boats,' whispered the Captain, 'for thirty rafts.' He knew that there were insufficient shepherds for his flock – and yet he had to send them out, for even above the wind, he thought he could hear the booming artillery barrage of high surf breaking on a rocky shore. Cape Alarm was waiting hungrily for his ship. 'Send the rafts away,' he said quietly, and then again under his breath, 'And God have mercy on us all.'

'Come on, Number 16,' called Samantha. 'Here we are, Number 16.' She gathered them to her, the eighteen passengers who made up the complement of her allotted life-raft. 'Here we are – all together now. No stragglers.'

They were gathered at the heavy mahogany doors that opened on to the open forward deck.

'Be ready,' she told them. 'When we get the word, we have to move fast.'

With the broadsiding seas sweeping the deck and cascading down over the lee, it would be impossible to embark from landing-nets into a raft bobbing alongside.

The rafts were being inflated on the open deck, the passengers hustled across to them and into the canopied interior between waves and then the laden rafts were lifted over the side by the clattering winches and dropped into the quieter waters afforded by the tall bulk of the ship. Immediately, one of the lifeboats picked up the tow and took each raft out to form the pitiful little convoy.

'Right!' the Third Officer burst in through the mahogany doors and held them wide. 'Quickly!' he shouted. 'All together.'

'Let's go, gang!' sang out Samantha, and there was an awkward rush out on to the wet and slippery deck. It was only thirty paces to where the raft crouched like a monstrous yellow bullfrog, gaping its ugly dark mouth, but the wind struck like an axe and Samantha heard them cry out in dismay. Some of them faltered in the sudden merciless cold.

'Come on,' Samantha shouted, pushing those ahead of her, half-supporting Mrs Goldberg's plump body that suddenly felt as heavy and unco-operative as a full sack of wheat. 'Keep going.'

'Let me have her,' shouted the Third Officer, and he grabbed Mrs Goldberg's other arm. Between them they tumbled her through the entrance of the raft.

'Good on you, love,' the officer grinned at Samantha briefly. His smile was attractive and warm, very masculine and likeable. His name was Ken and he was five years her senior. They would probably have become lovers fairly soon, Samantha knew, for he had pursued her furiously since she stepped aboard in New York. Although she knew she did not love him, yet he had succeeded in arousing her and she was slowly succumbing to his obvious charms and her own passionate nature. She had made the decision to have him, and had been merely savouring it up until then. Now, with a pang, she realized that the moment might never come.

'I'll help you with the others.' She raised her voice above the hysterical shriek of the wind.

'Get in,' he shouted back, and swung her brusquely towards the raft. She crept into the crowded interior and looked back at the brightly lit deck that glistened in the arc lamps.

Ken had started back to where one of the women had slipped and fallen. She sprawled helplessly on the wet deck, while her husband stooped over her, trying to lift her back to her feet.

Ken reached them and lifted the woman easily; the three of them were the only ones out on the open deck now, and the two men supported the woman between them, staggering against the heavy sullen roll of the waterlogged hull.

Samantha saw the wave come aboard and she shrieked a warning.

'Go back, Ken! For God's sake go back!' But he seemed not to hear her. The wave came aboard; over the windward rail like some huge black slippery sea-monster, it came with a deep silent rush.

'Ken!' she screamed, and he looked over his shoulder an instant before it reached them. Its crest was higher than his head. They could reach neither the raft, nor the shelter of the mahogany doors. She heard the clatter of the donkey-winch and the raft lifted swiftly off the deck, with a swooping tug in her guts. The operator could not let the rushing power of the wave crash into the helpless raft, throwing it against the superstructure or tearing its belly out on the ship's railing, for the frail plastic skin would rupture and it would collapse immediately.

Samantha hurled herself to the entrance and peered down. She saw the sea take the three figures in a black glittering rush. It cut them down, and swept them away. For a moment, she saw Ken clinging to the railing while the waters poured over him, burying his head in a tumbling fall of white and furious water. He disappeared and when the ship rolled sullenly back, shaking herself clear of the water, her decks were empty of any human shape.

With the next roll of the ship, the winch-operator high up in his glassed cabin swung the dangling raft outboard and lowered it swiftly and dexterously to the surface of the sea where one of the lifeboats circled anxiously, ready to take them in tow.

Samantha closed and secured the plastic door-cover, then she groped her way through the press of packed and terrified bodies until she found Mrs Goldberg.

'Are you crying, dear?' the elderly woman quavered, clinging to her desperately.

'No,' said Samantha, and placed one arm around her shoulders. 'No, I'm not crying.' And with her free hand, she wiped away the icy tears that streamed down her cheeks.

The Trog lifted his headset and looked at Nick through the reeking clouds of cigar smoke.

'Their radio operator has screwed down the key of his set. He's sending a single unbroken homing beam.'

Nick knew what that meant – they had abandoned *Golden Adventurer*. He nodded once but remained silent. He had wedged himself into the doorway from the bridge. The restless impatience that consumed him would not allow him to sit or be still for more than a few moments at a time. He was slowly facing up to the reality of disaster. The dice had fallen against him and his gamble had been with very survival. It was absolutely certain that *Golden Adventurer* would go aground and be beaten into a total wreck by this storm. He could expect a charter from Christy Marine to assist *La Mouette* in ferrying the survivors back to Cape Town, but the fee would be a small fraction of the Esso tow fee that he had forsaken for this wild and desperate dash south.

The gamble had failed and he was a broken man. Of course, it would take months still for the effects of his folly to become apparent, but the repayments of his loans and the construction bills for the other tug still building would slowly throttle and bring him down.

'We might still reach her before she goes aground,' said David Allen sturdily, and nobody else on the bridge spoke. 'I mean there could be a backlash of the current close inshore which could hold her off long enough to give us a chance—' His voice trailed off as Nick looked across at him and frowned.

'We are still ten hours away from her, and for Reilly to make the decision to abandon ship, she must have been very close indeed. Reilly is a good man.' Nick had personally selected him to command the *Golden Adventurer*. 'He was a destroyer captain on the North Atlantic run, the youngest in the navy, and then he was ten years with P & O. They pick only the best—' He stopped talking abruptly. He was becoming garrulous. He crossed to the radarscope and adjusted it for maximum range and illumination before looking down into the eyepiece. There was much fuzz and sea clutter, but on the extreme southern edge of the circular screen there showed the solid luminous glow of the cliffs and peaks of Cape Alarm. In good weather they were a mere five hours' steaming away, but now they had left the shelter of that giant iceberg and were staggering and plunging wildly through the angry night. She could have taken more speed, for *Warlock* was built for big seas, but always there was the deadly menace of ice, and Nick had to hold her at this cautionary speed, which meant ten hours more before they were in sight of *Golden Adventurer* – if she was still afloat.

Behind him, the Trog's voice crackled rustily with excitement. 'I'm getting voice – it's only strength one, weak and intermittent. One of the lifeboats is sending on a battery-powered transmitter.' He held his earphones pressed to his head with both hands as he listened.

'They are towing a batch of life-rafts with all survivors aboard to Shackleton Bay. But they've lost a life-raft,' he said. 'It's broken away from their towline, and they haven't got enough boats to search for it. They are asking *La Mouette* to keep a watch for it.'

'Is *La Mouette* acknowledging?'

The Trog shook his head. 'She's probably still out of range of this transmission.'

'Very well.' Nick turned back into the bridge. He had still not broken radio silence, and could feel his officers' disapproval, silent but strong. Again he felt the need for human contact, for the warmth and comfort of human conversation and friendly encouragement. He didn't yet have the strength to bear his failure alone.

He stopped beside David Allen and said, 'I have been studying the Admiralty sailing directions for Cape Alarm, David,' and pretended not to notice that the use of his Christian name had brought a startled look and quick colour to the mate's features. He went on evenly, 'the shore is very steep-to and she is exposed to this westerly weather, but there are beaches of pebble and the glass is going up sharply again.'

'Yes, sir,' David nodded enthusiastically. 'I have been watching it.'

'Instead of hoping for a cross-current to hold her off, I suggest you offer a prayer that she goes up on one of those beaches and that the weather moderates before she is beaten to pieces. There is still a chance we can put ground tackle on her before she starts breaking up.'

'I'll say ten Hail Marys, sir,' grinned David. Clearly he was overwhelmed by this sudden friendliness from his silent and forbidding Captain.

'And say another ten that we hold our lead on *La Mouette*,' said Nick, and smiled. It was one of the few times that David Allen had seen him smile, and he was amazed at the change it made to the stern features. They lightened with a charm and warmth and he had not before noticed the clear green of Nick Berg's eyes and how white and even were his teeth.

'Steady as she goes,' said Nick. 'Call me if anything changes,' and he turned away to his cabin.

'Steady as she goes, it is, sir,' said David Allen with a new friendliness in his voice.

The strange and marvellous lights of the aurora australis quivered and flickered in running streams of red and green fire along the horizon, and formed an incredible backdrop for the death agonies of a great ship.

Captain Reilly looked back through the small portholes of the leading lifeboat and watched her going to her fate. It seemed to him she had never been so tall and beautiful as in these terrible last moments. He had loved many ships, as if each had been a wonderful living creature, but he had loved no other ship more than *Golden Adventurer*, and he felt something of himself dying with her.

He saw her change her action. The sea was feeling the land now, the steep bank of Cape Alarm, and the ship seemed to panic at the new onslaught of wave and wind, as though she knew what fate awaited her there.

She was rolling through thirty degrees, showing the dull red streak of her belly paint as she came up short at the limit of each huge penduluming arc. There was a headland, tall black cliffs dropping sheer into the turbulent waters and it seemed that *Golden Adventurer* must go full on to them, but in the last impossible moments she slipped by, borne on the backlash of the current, avoiding the cliffs and swinging her bows on into the shallow bay beyond where she was hidden from Captain Reilly's view.

He stood for many minutes more, staring back across the leaping wave-tops and in the strange unnatural light of the heavens his face was greenish grey and heavily furrowed with the marks of grief.

Then he sighed once, very deeply, and turned away, devoting all his attention to guiding his pathetic limping little convoy to the safety of Shackleton Bay.

Almost immediately it was apparent that the fates had relented, and given them a favourable inshore current to carry them up on to the coast. The lifeboats were strung out over a distance of three miles, each of them with its string of bloated and clumsy rafts lumbering along in its wake. Captain Reilly had two-way VHF radio contact with each of them, and despite the brutal cold, they were all in good shape and making steady and unexpectedly rapid progress. Three or four hours would be sufficient, he began to hope. They had lost so much life already, and he could not be certain that there would be no further losses until he had the whole party ashore and encamped.

Perhaps the tragic run of bad luck had changed at last, he thought, and he picked up the small VHF radio. Perhaps the French tug was in range at last and he began to call her.

'*La Mouette*, do you read me? Come in, *La Mouette* . . .'

The lifeboat was low down on the water and the output of the little set was feeble in the vastness of sea and ice, yet he kept on calling.

They had accustomed themselves to the extravagant action of the disabled liner, her majestic roll and pitch, as regular as a gigantic metronome. They had adjusted to the cold of the unheated interior of the great ship, and the discomfort of her crowded and unsanitary conditions.

They had steeled themselves and tried to prepare themselves mentally for further danger and greater hardship, but not one of the survivors in life-raft Number 16 had imagined anything like this. Even Samantha, the youngest, probably physically the toughest and certainly the one most prepared by her training and her knowledge and love of the sea, had not imagined what it would be like in the raft.

It was utterly dark, not the faintest glimmer of light penetrated the insulated domed canopy, once its entrance was secured against the sea and the wind.

Samantha realized almost immediately how the darkness would crush their morale and, more dangerously, would induce disorientation and vertigo, so she ordered two of them at a time to switch on the tiny locator bulbs on their life jackets. It gave just a glimmering of light, enough to let them see each others' faces and take a little comfort in the proximity of other humans.

Then she arranged their seating, making them form a circle around the sides with all their legs pointing inwards, to give the raft better balance and to ensure that each of them had space to stretch out.

Now that Ken had gone, she had naturally taken command, and, as naturally, the others had turned to her for guidance and comfort. It was Samantha who had gone out through the opening into the brutal exposure of the night to take aboard and secure the tow rope from the lifeboat. She had come in again half-frozen, shaking in a palsy of cold, with her hands and face numbed. It had taken nearly half an hour of hard massage before feeling

71

returned and she was certain that she had avoided frost-bite.

Then the tow began, and if the movement of the light raft had been wild before, it now became a nightmare of uncoordinated movement. Each whim of sea and wind was transmitted directly to the huddling circle of survivors, and each time the raft pulled away or sheered off, the tow rope brought it up with a violent lurch and jerk. The wave crests whipped up by the wind and feeling the press of the land were up to twenty feet high, and the raft swooped over them and dropped heavily into the troughs. She did not have the lateral stability of a keel, so she spun on her axis until the tow rope jerked her up and she spun the other way. The first of them to start vomiting was Mrs Goldberg and it spurted in a warm jet down the side of Samantha's anorak.

The canopy was almost airtight, except for the small ventilation holes near the apex of the roof, and immediately the sweetish acrid stench of vomit permeated the raft. Within minutes, half a dozen of the other survivors were vomiting also.

It was the cold, however, that frightened Samantha. The cold was the killer. It came up even through the flexible insulated double skin of the deck, and was trans-ferred into their buttocks and legs. It came in through the plastic canopy and froze the condensation of their breaths, it even froze the vomit on their clothing and on the deck.

'Sing!' Samantha told them. 'Come on, sing! Let's do "Yankee Doodle Dandy", first. You start, Mr Stewart, come on. Clap your hands, clap hands with your neighbour.' She hectored them relentlessly, not allowing any of them to fall into that paralytic state which is not true sleep but the trance caused by rapidly dropping body temperature. She crawled among them, prodding them awake, popping barley sugar from the emergency rations into their mouths.

'Suck and sing!' she commanded them, the sugar would

72

combat the cold and the seasickness. 'Clap your hands. Keep moving, we'll be there soon.'

When they could sing no more, she told them stories – and whenever she mentioned the word 'dog' they must all bark and clap their hands, or crow like the rooster, or bray like the donkey.

Samantha's throat was scratchy with singing and talking, and she was dizzy with fatigue and sick with cold, recognizing in herself the first symptoms of disinterest and lethargy, the prelude to giving up. She roused herself, struggling up into the sitting position from where she had slumped.

'I'm going to try and light the stove and get us a hot drink.' she sang out brightly. Around her there was only a mild stir and somebody retched painfully.

'Who's for a mug of beef tea—' she stopped abruptly. Something had changed. It took her a long moment to realize what it was. The sound of the wind had muted and the raft was riding more easily now, it was moving into a more regular rhythm of sweep and fall, without the dreadful jerk of the tow rope snapping it back.

Frantically she crawled to the entrance of the raft, and with cold crippled fingers she tore at the fastenings.

Outside the dawn had broken into a clear cold sky of palest ethereal pinks and mauves. Although the wind had dropped to a faint whisper, the seas were still big and unruly, and the waters had changed from black to the deep bottle green of molten glass.

The tow rope had torn away at the connecting shackle, leaving only a dangling flap of plastic. Number 16 had been the last raft in the line being towed by number three, but of the convoy, Samantha could now see no sign – though she crawled out through the entrance and clung precariously to the side of the raft, scanning the wave-caps about her desperately.

There was no sign of a lifeboat, no sight even of the

rocky, ice-capped shores of Cape Alarm. They had drifted away, during the night, into the vast and lonely reaches of the Weddell Sea.

Despair cramped her belly muscles, and she wanted to cry out in protest against this further cruelty of fate, but she prevented herself doing so, and stayed out in the clear and frosty air, drawing it in carefully for she knew that it could freeze her lung tissue. She searched and searched until her eyes streamed with the cold and the wind and concentration. Then at last the cold drove her back into the dark and stinking interior of the raft. She fell wearily among the supine and quiescent bodies, and pulled the hood of her anorak more tightly around her head. She knew it would not take long for them to start dying now, and somehow she did not care. Her despair was too intense, she let herself begin sinking into the morass of despondency which gripped all the others, and the cold crept up her legs and arms. She closed her eyes, and then opened them again with a huge effort.

'I'm not going to die,' she told herself firmly. 'I refuse to just lie down and die,' and she struggled up onto her knees. It felt as though she wore a rucksack filled with lead, such was the physical weight of her despair.

She crawled to the central locker that held all their emergency rations and equipment.

The emergency locator transmitter was packed in polyurethane and her fingers were clumsy with cold and the thick mittens, but at last she brought it out. It was the size of a cigar-box, and the instructions were printed on the side of it. She did not need to read them, but switched on the set and replaced it in its slot. Now for forty-eight hours, or until the battery ran out, it would transmit a DF homing-signal on 121,5 megahertz.

It was possible, just possible, that the French tug might pick up that feeble little beam, and track it down to its source. She set it out of her mind, and devoted herself to the Herculean task of trying to heat half a mug of water on the small solid-fuel stove without scalding herself as she held the stove in her lap and balanced it against the raft's motion. While she worked, she searched for the courage and the words to tell the others of their predicament.

The *Golden Adventurer*, deserted of all human beings, her engines dead, but with her deck lights still burning, her wheel locked hard over, and the Morse key in the radio room screwed down to transmit a single unbroken pulse, drifted swiftly down on the black rock of Cape Alarm.

The rock was of so hard a type of formation that the cliffs were almost vertical, and even exposed as they were to the eternal onslaught of this mad sea, they had weathered very little. They still retained the sharp vertical edges and the glossy polished planes of cleanly fractured faults.

The sea ran in and hit the cliff without any check. The impact seemed to jar the very air, like the concussion of bursting high explosive, and the sea shot high in a white fury against the unyielding rock of the cliff, before rolling back and forming a reverse swell.

It was these returning echoes from the cliff that held *Golden Adventurer* off the cliff. The shore was so steep-to that it dropped to forty fathoms directly below the cliffs. There was no bottom on which the ship could gut herself.

The wind was blanketed by the cliff and in the eerie stillness of air, she drifted in closer and closer, rolling almost to her limits as the swells took her broadside. Once she actually touched the rock with her superstructure on one of those rolls, but then the echo-wave nudged her away. The next wave pushed her closer, and its smaller weaker offspring pushed back at her. A man could have jumped from a ledge on the cliff on to her deck as she drifted slowly, parallel to the rock.

The cliff ended in an abrupt and vertical headland, where it had calved into three tall pillars of serpentine, as graceful as the sculptured columns of a temple of Olympian Zeus.

Again, *Golden Adventurer* touched one of those pillars, she bumped it lightly with her stern. It scraped paint from her side and crushed in her rail, but then she was past.

The light bump was just sufficient to push her stern round, and she pointed her bows directly into the wide shallow bay beyond the cliffs.

Here a softer, more malleable rock-formation had been eroded by the weather, forming a wide beach of purple-black pebbles, each the size of a man's head and water-worn as round as cannon balls.

Each time the waves rushed up this stony beach, the pebbles struck against each other with a rattling roar, and the brash of rotten and mushy sea ice that filled the bay susurrated and clinked, as it rose and fell with the sea.

Now *Golden Adventurer* was clear of the cliff, she was more fully in the grip of the wind. Although the wind was dying, it still had force enough to move her steadily deeper into the bay, her bows pointed directly at the beach.

Unlike the cliff shore, the bay sloped up gently to the beach and this allowed the big waves to build up into rounded sliding humps. They did not curl and break into white water because the thick layer of brash ice weighted and flattened them, so that these swells joined with the wind to throw the ship at the beach with smoothly gathering impetus.

She took the ground with a great metallic groan of her straining plates and canted over slowly, but the moving pebble beach moulded itself quickly to her hull, giving gradually, as the waves and wind thrust her higher and higher until she was firmly aground; then, as the short night ended so the wind fell further, and in sympathy the swells moderated also and the tide drew back, letting the ship settle more heavily.

By noon of that day, *Golden Adventurer* was held firmly by the bows on the curved purple beach, canted over at an angle of 10°. Only her after end was still floating, rising and falling like a see-saw on the swell patterns which still pushed in steadily, but the plummeting air temperature was rapidly freezing the brash ice around her stern into a solid sheet.

The ship stood very tall above the glistening wet beach. Her upperworks were festooned with rime and long rapier-like stalactites of shining translucent ice hung from her scuppers and from the anchor fair-leads.

Her emergency generator was still running, and although there was no human being aboard her, her lights burned gaily and piped music played softly through her deserted public rooms.

Apart from the rent in her side, through which the sea still washed and swirled, there was no external evidence of damage, and beyond her the peaks and valleys of Cape Alarm, so wild and fierce, seemed merely to emphasize her graceful lines and to underline how rich a prize she was, a luscious ripe plum ready for the picking.

Down in her radio room, the transmitting key continued to send out an unbroken beam that could be picked up for 500 miles around.

Two hours of deathlike sleep – and then Nick Berg woke with a wild start, knowing that something of direct consequence was about to happen. But it took fully ten seconds for him to realize where he was.

He stumbled from his bunk, and he knew he had not slept long enough. His skull was stuffed with the cotton-wool of fatigue, and he swayed on his feet as he shaved in the shower, trying to steam himself awake with the scalding water.

When he went out on to the bridge, the Trog was still at his equipment. He looked up at Nick for a moment with his little rheumy pink eyes, and it was clear that he had not slept at all. Nick felt a prick of shame at his own indulgence.

'We are still inside *La Mouette*,' said the Trog, and turned back to his set. 'I reckon we have an edge of almost a hundred miles.'

Angel appeared on the bridge, bearing a huge tray, and the saliva jetted from under Nick's tongue as he smelled it.

'I did a little special for your brekker, Skipper,' said Angel. 'I call it "Eggs on Angel's Wings".'

'I'm buying,' said Nick, and turned back to the Trog with his mouth full and chewing. 'What of the *Adventurer*?'

'She's still sending a DF, but her position has not altered in almost three hours.'

'What do you mean?' Nick demanded, and swallowed heavily.

'No change in position.'

'Then she's aground,' Nick muttered, the food in his hand forgotten, and at that moment David Allen hurried on to the bridge still shrugging on his pea-jacket. His eyes were puffy and his hair was hastily wetted and combed, but spiky at the back from contact with his pillow. It had not taken him long to hear that the Captain was on the bridge.

'And in one piece, if her transmitter is still sending.'

'It looks like those Hail Marys worked, David.' Nick

flashed his rare smile and David slapped the polished teak top of the chart table.

'Touch wood, and don't dare the devil.'

Nick felt his early despair slipping away with his fatigue, and he took another big mouthful and savoured it as he strode to the front windows and stared ahead.

The sea had flattened dramatically, but a weak and butter-yellow sun low on the horizon gave no warmth, and Nick glanced up at the thermometer and read the outside air temperature at minus thirty degrees.

Down here below 60° south, the weather was so unstable, caught up on the wheel of endlessly circling atmospheric depressions, that a gale could rise in minutes and drop to a flat calm almost as swiftly. Yet foul weather was the rule. For a hundred days and more each year, the wind was at galeforce or above. The photographs of Antarctica always gave a completely false impression of fine days with the sun sparkling on pristine snow fields and lovely towering icebergs. The truth was that you cannot take photographs in a blizzard or a white-out.

Nick distrusted this calm, and yet found himself praying that it would hold. He wanted to increase speed again, and was on the point of taking that chance, when the officer of the watch called a sharp alteration of course.

Ahead of them, Nick made out the sullen swirl of hidden ice below the surface, like a lurking monster, and as *Warlock* altered course to avoid it, the ice broke the surface. Black ice, striated with bands of glacial mud, ugly and deadly. Nick did not pass the order for the increase in speed.

'We should be raising Cape Alarm within the hour,' David Allen gloated beside him. 'If this visibility holds.'

'It won't,' said Nick. 'We'll have fog pretty soon,' and he indicated the surface of the sea, which was beginning to steam, emitting ghostly tendrils and eddies of seafret, as the difference between sea and air temperature widened.

'We'll be at the *Golden Adventurer* in four hours more.' David was bubbling with renewed excitement, and he slapped the teak table again. 'With your permission, sir, I'll go down and double-check the rocket-lines and tow equipment.'

While the air around them thickened into a ghostly white soup, and blotted out all visibility to a few hundred yards, Nick paced the bridge like a caged lion, his hands clasped behind his back and a black unlit cheroot clamped between his teeth. He broke his pacing every time that the Trog intercepted another transmission from either Christy Marine, Jules Levoisin or Captain Reilly on his VHF radio.

At mid-morning, Reilly reported that he and his slow convoy had reached Shackleton Bay without further losses, that they were taking full advantage of the moderating weather to set up an encampment, and he ended by urging *La Mouette* to keep a watch on 121,5 megahertz to try and locate the missing life-raft that had broken away during the night. *La Mouette* did not acknowledge.

'They aren't reading on the VHF,' grunted the Trog.

Nick thought briefly of the hapless souls adrift in this cold, and decided that they would probably not last out the day unless the temperature rose abruptly. Then he dismissed the thought and concentrated on the exchanges between Christy Marine and *La Mouette*.

The two parties had diametrically changed their bargaining standpoints.

While *Golden Adventurer* was adrift on the open sea, and any salvage efforts would mean that the tug should merely put a rocket-line across her, pass a messenger wire to carry the big steel hawser and then take her in tow, Jules Levoisin had pressed for Lloyd's Open Form 'No cure no pay' contract.

Since the 'cure' was almost certain, 'pay' would follow as a matter of course. The amount of payment would be fixed by the arbitration of the committee of Lloyd's in

London under the principles of international maritime law, and would be a percentage of the salved value of the vessel. The percentage decided upon by the arbitrator would depend upon the difficulties and dangers that the salvor had overcome. A clever salvor in an arbitration court could paint a picture of such daring and ingenuity that the award would be in millions of dollars.

Christy Marine had been desperately trying to avoid a 'No cure no pay' contract. They had been trying to wheedle Levoisin into a daily hire and bonus contract, since this would limit the total cost of the operation, but they had been met by a Gallic acquisitiveness – right up to the moment when it became clear that *Golden Adventurer* had gone aground.

When that happened, the roles were completely reversed. Jules Levoisin, with a note of panic in his transmission, had immediately withdrawn his offer to go Lloyd's Open Form. For now the 'cure' was far from certain, and the *Adventurer* might already be a total wreck, beaten to death on the rocks of Cape Alarm, in which case there would be 'no pay'.

Now Levoisin was desperately eager to strike a daily hire contract, including the run from South America and the ferrying of survivors back to civilization. He was offering his services at $10,000 a day, plus a bonus of 2½ per cent of any salved value of the vessel. They were fair terms, for Jules Levoisin had given up the shining dream of millions and he had returned to reality.

However, Christy Marine, who had previously been offering a princely sum for daily hire, had just as rapidly withdrawn that offer.

'We will accept Lloyd's Open Form, including ferrying of survivors,' they declared on Channel 16.

'Conditions on site have changed,' Jules Levoisin sent back, and the Trog got another good fix on him.

'We are head-reaching on him handsomely,' he

announced with satisfaction, blinking his pink eyes rapidly while Nick marked the new relative positions on the chart.

The bridge of *Warlock* was once again crowded with every officer who had an excuse to be there. They were all in working rig, thick blue boiler suits and heavy sea boots, bulked up with jerseys and balaclava helmets, and they watched the plot with total fascination, arguing quietly among themselves.

David Allen came in carrying a bundle of clothing. 'I've got working rig for you, sir. I borrowed it from the Chief Engineer. You are about the same size.'

'Does the Chief know?' Nick asked.

'Not exactly, I just borrowed it from his cabin—'

'Well done, David,' Nick chuckled. 'Please put it in my day cabin.' He felt himself warming more and more to the younger man.

'Captain, sir,' the Trog sang out suddenly. 'I'm getting another transmission. It's only strength one, and it's on 121,5 megahertz.'

'Oh, shit!' David Allen paused in the entrance to the Captain's day cabin. 'Oh, shit!' he repeated, and his expression was stricken. 'It's that bloody missing life-raft.'

'Relative bearing!' snapped Nick angrily.

'She bears 280° relative and 045° magnetic,' the Trog answered instantly, and Nick felt his anger flare again.

The life-raft was somewhere out on their port beam, eighty degrees off their direct course to the *Golden Adventurer*.

The consternation on the bridge was carried in a babble of voices, that Nick silenced with a single black glance – and they stared at the plot in dismayed hush.

The position of each of the tugs was flagged with a coloured pin – and there was another, a red flag, for the position of the *Golden Adventurer*. It was so close ahead of them now, and their lead over *La Mouette* so slender, that one of the younger officers could not remain silent.

'If we go to the raft, we'll be handing it to the bloody frog on a plate.'

The words ended the restraint and they began to argue again, but in soft controlled tones. Nick Berg did not look up at them, but remained bowed over the chart, with his fist on the tabletop bunched so fiercely that the knuckles were ivory white.

'Christ, they have probably all had it by now. We'd be throwing it all away for a bunch of frozen stiffs.'

'There is no telling how far off course they are, those sets have a range of a hundred miles.'

'*La Mouette* will waltz away with it.'

'We could pick them up later – after we put a line on *Golden Adventurer*.'

Nick straightened slowly and took the cheroot out of his mouth. He looked across at David Allen and spoke levelly, without change of expression.

'Number One, will you please instruct your junior officers in the rule of the sea.'

David Allen was silent for a moment, then he answered softly 'The preservation of human life at sea takes precedent over all other considerations.'

'Very well, Mr Allen,' Nick nodded. 'Alter 80° to port and maintain a homing course on the emergency transmission.'

He turned away to his cabin. He could control his anger until he was alone, and then he turned and crashed his fist into the panel above his desk.

Out on the navigation bridge behind him nobody spoke nor moved for fully thirty seconds, then the Third Officer protested weakly.

'But we are so close!'

David Allen roused himself, and spoke angrily to the helmsman.

'New course 045° magnetic.'

And as *Warlock* heeled to the change, he flung the

armful of clothing bitterly on to the chart-table and went to stand beside the Trog.

'Corrections for course to intercept?' he asked.

'Bring her on to 050°,' the Trog instructed, and then cackled without mirth. 'First you call him an ice-water pisser – now you squeal like a baby because he answers a mayday.'

And David Allen was silent as the *Warlock* turned away into the fog, every revolution of her big variable-pitch propellers carrying her directly away from her prize, and *La Mouette*'s triumphant transmissions taunted them as the Frenchman raced across the last of the open water that separated her from Cape Alarm, bargaining furiously with the owners in London.

The fog seemed so thick that it could be chopped into chunks like cheese. From the bridge it was not possible to see *Warlock*'s tall bows. Nick groped his way into it like a blind man in an unfamiliar room, and all around him the ice pressed closely.

They were in the area of huge tabular icebergs again. The echoes of the great ice islands flared green and malevolently on the radar screen and the awful smell and taste of the ice was on every breath they drew.

'Radio Officer?' Nick asked tensely, without taking his eyes from the swirling fog curtains ahead.

'Still no contact,' the Trog answered, and Nick shuffled on his feet. The fog had mesmerized him, and he felt the shift of vertigo in his head. For a moment he had the illusion that his ship was listing heavily to one side, almost as though it were a space vehicle. He forcibly rejected the hallucination and stared fixedly ahead, tensing himself for the first green loom of ice through the fog.

'No contact for nearly an hour now,' David muttered beside him.

'Either the battery on the DF has run down, or they have snagged ice and sunk—' volunteered the Third Officer, raising his voice just enough for Nick to hear.

' – or else their transmitter is blanketed by an iceberg,' Nick finished for him, and there was silence on the bridge for another ten minutes, except for the quietly requested changes of course that kept *Warlock* zigzagging between the unseen but omnipresent icebergs.

'All right,' Nick made the decision at last. 'We'll have to accept that the raft has floundered and break off the search.' And there was a stir of reawakening interest and enthusiasm. 'Pilot, new course to *Golden Adventurer*, please, and we'll increase to fifty per cent power.'

'We could still beat the frog.' Again speculation and rising hope buoyed the young officers. 'She could run into ice and have to reduce—' They wished misfortune on *La Mouette* and her Captain, and even the ship beneath Nick's feet seemed to regain its lightness and vibrancy as she turned back for a last desperate run for the prize.

'All right, David,' Nick spoke quietly. 'One thing is certain now, we aren't going to reach the prize ahead of Levoisin. So we are going to play our ace now—' he was about to elaborate, when the Trog's voice squeaked with excitement.

'New contact, on 121,5,' he cried, and the dismay on the bridge was a tangible thing.

'Christ!' said the Third Officer. 'Why won't they just lie down and die!'

'The transmission was blanked by that big berg north of us,' the Trog guessed. 'They are close now. It won't take long.'

'Just long enough to make certain we miss the prize.'

The berg was so big that it formed its own weather

system about it, causing eddies and currents of both air and water, enough to stir the fog.

The fog opened like a theatre curtain, and directly ahead there was a heart-stopping vista of green and blue ice, with darker strata of glacial mud banding cliffs which disappeared into the higher layers of fog above as though reaching to the very heavens. The sea had carved majestic arches of ice and deep caverns from the foot of the cliff.

'There they are!'

Nick snatched the binoculars from the canvas bin and focused on the dark specks that stood out so clearly against the backdrop of glowing ice.

'No,' he grunted. Fifty emperor penguins formed a tight bunch on one of the flat floes, big black birds standing nearly as tall as a man's shoulder; even in the lens, they were deceptively humanoid.

Warlock passed them closely, and with sudden fright they dropped on to their bellies and used their stubby wings to skid themselves across the floe, and drop into the still and steaming waters below the cliff. The floe eddied and swung on the disturbance of *Warlock*'s passing.

Warlock nosed on through solid standing banks of fog and into abrupt holes of clear air where the mirages and optical illusions of Antarctica's flawed air maddened them with their inconsistencies, transforming flocks of penguins into herds of elephants or bands of waving men, and placing in their path phantom rocks and bergs which disappeared again swiftly as they approached.

The emergency transmissions from the raft faded and silenced, then beeped again loudly into the silence of the bridge, and seconds later were silent again.

'God damn them,' David swore quietly and bitterly, his cheeks pink with frustration. 'Where the hell are they? Why don't they put up a flare or a rocket?' And nobody answered as another white fog monster enveloped the ship, muting all sound aboard her.

'I'd like to try shaking them up with the horn, sir,' he said, as *Warlock* burst once more into sparkling and blinding sunlight. Nick grunted acquiescence without lowering his binoculars.

David reached up for the red-painted foghorn handle above his head, and the deep booming blast of sound, the characteristic voice of an ocean-going salvage tug, reverberated through the fog, seeming to make it quiver with the volume of the sound. The echoes came crashing back off the ice cliffs of the bergs like the thunder of the skies.

S amantha held the solid-fuel stove in her lap using the detachable fibreglass lid of the locker as a tray. She was heating half a pint of water in the aluminium pannikin, balancing carefully against the wallowing motion of the raft.

The blue flame of the stove lit the dim cavern of plastic and radiated a feeble glow of warmth insufficient to sustain life. They were dying already.

Gavin Stewart held his wife's head against his chest, and bowed his own silver head over it. She had been dead for nearly two hours now, and her body had already cooled, the face peaceful and waxen.

Samantha could not bear to look across at them, she crouched over the stove and dropped a cube of beef into the water, stirring it slowly and blinking against the tears of penetrating cold. She felt thin watery mucus run down her nostrils and it required an effort to lift her arm and wipe it away on her sleeve. The beef tea was only a little above blood warmth, but she could not waste time and fuel on heating it further.

The metal pannikin passed slowly from mittened hand to numbed and clumsy hand. They slurped the warm liquid and passed it on reluctantly, though there were some who had neither the strength nor the interest to take it.

'Come on, Mrs Goldberg,' Samantha whispered painfully. The cold seemed to have closed her throat, and the foul air under the canopy made her head ache with grinding, throbbing pain. 'You must drink—' Samantha touched the woman's face, and cut herself off. The flesh had a putty-like texture and was cooling swiftly. It took long lingering minutes for the shock to pass, then carefully Samantha pulled the hood of the old woman's parka down over her face. Nobody else seemed to have noticed. They were all too far sunk into lethargy.

'Here,' whispered Samantha to the man beside her – and she pressed the pannikin into his hands, folding his stiff fingers around the metal to make certain he had hold of it. 'Drink it before it cools.'

The air around her seemed to tremble suddenly with a great burst of sound, like the bellow of a dying bull, or the rumble of cannon balls across the roof of the sky. For long moments, Samantha thought her mind was playing tricks with her, and only when it came again did she raise her head.

'Oh God,' she whispered. 'They've come. It's going to be all right. They've come to save us.'

She crawled to the locker, slowly and stiffly as an old woman.

'They've come. It's all right, gang, it's going to be all right,' she mumbled, and she lit the globe on her life jacket. In its pale glow, she found the packet of phosphorus flares.

'Come on now, gang. Let's hear it for Number 16.' She tried to rouse them as she struggled with the fastenings of the canopy. 'One more cheer,' she whispered, but they were still and unresponsive, and as she fumbled her way out into the freezing fog, the tears that ran down her cheeks were not from the cold.

She looked up uncomprehendingly, it seemed that from the sky around her tumbled gigantic cascades of ice, sheer sheets of translucent menacing green ice. It took her moments to realize that the life-raft had drifted in close beneath the precipitous lee of a tabular berg. She felt tiny and inconsequential beneath that ponderous mountain of brittle glassy ice.

For what seemed an eternity, she stood, with her face lifted, staring upwards – then again the air resonated with the deep gut-shaking bellow of the siren. It filled the swirling fog-banks with solid sound that struck the cliff of ice above her and shattered into booming echoes, that bounded from wall to wall and rang through the icy caverns and crevices that split the surface of the great berg.

Samantha held aloft one of the phosphorus flares, and it required all the strength of her frozen arm to rip the igniter tab. The flare spluttered and streamed acrid white smoke, then burst into the dazzling crimson fire that denotes distress at sea. She stood like a tiny statue of liberty, holding the flare aloft in one hand and peering with streaming eyes into the sullen fog-banks.

Again the animal bellow of the siren boomed through the milky, frosted air; it was so close that it shook Samantha's body the way the wind moves the wheat on the hillside, then it went on to collide solidly with the cliff of ice that hung above her.

The working of sea and wind, and the natural erosion of changing temperatures had set tremendous forces at work within the glittering body of the berg. Those forces had found a weak point, a vertical fault line, that ran like an axe-stroke from the flattened tableland of the summit, five hundred feet down to the moulded bottom of the berg far below the surface.

The booming sound waves of *Warlock*'s horn found a sympathetic resonance with the body of the mountain that set the ice on each side of the fault vibrating in different frequencies.

Then the fault sheared, with a brittle cracking explosion of glass bursting under pressure, and the fault opened. One hundred million tons of ice began to move as it broke away from the mother berg. The block of ice that the berg calved was in itself a mountain, a slab of solid ice twice the size of Saint Paul's Cathedral – and as it swung out and twisted free, new pressures and forces came into play within it, finding smaller faults and flaws so that ice burst within ice and tore itself apart, as though dynamited with tons of high explosive.

The air itself was filled with hurtling ice, some pieces the size of a locomotive and others as small and as sharp and as deadly as steel swords; and below this plunging toppling mass, the tiny yellow plastic raft bobbed helplessly.

'There,' called Nick. 'On the starboard beam.' The phosphorus distress flare lit the fog-banks internally with a fiery cherry red and threw grotesque patterns of light against the belly of lurking cloud. David Allen blew one last triumphant blast on the siren.

'New heading 150°,' Nick told the helmsman and *Warlock* came around handily, and almost instantly burst from the enveloping bank of fog into another arena of open air.

Half a mile away, the life-raft bobbed like a fat yellow toad beneath a glassy green wall of ice. The top of the iceberg was lost in the fog high above, and the tiny human figure that stood erect on the raft and held aloft the brilliant crimson flare was an insignificant speck in this vast wilderness of fog and sea and ice.

'Prepare to pick up survivors, David,' said Nick, and the mate hurried away while Nick moved to the wing of the bridge from where he could watch the rescue.

Suddenly Nick stopped and lifted his head in bewilderment. For a moment he thought it was gunfire, then the explosive crackling of sound changed to a rending shriek as of the tearing of living fibre when a giant redwood tree is falling to the axes. The volume of sound mounted into a rumbling roar, the unmistakeable roar of a mountain in avalanche.

'Good Christ!' whispered Nick, as he saw the cliff of ice begin to change shape. Slowly sagging outwards, it seemed to fold down upon itself. Faster and still faster it fell, and the hissing splinters of bursting ice formed a dense swirling cloud, while the cliff leaned further and further beyond its point of equilibrium and at last collapsed and lifted pressure waves from the green waters that raced out one behind the other, flinging *Warlock*'s bows high as she rode them and then nosed down into the troughs between.

Since Nick's oath, nobody had spoken on the bridge. They clutched for balance at the nearest support and stared in awe at that incredible display of careless might, while the water still churned and creamed with the disturbance and pieces of broken jagged ice, some the size of a country house, bobbed to the surface and revolved slowly, finding their balance as they swirled and bumped against each other.

'Closer,' snapped Nick. 'Get as close as you can.'

Of the yellow life-raft there was no longer any sign. Jagged shards of ice had ripped open its fragile skin and the grinding, tumbling lumps had trodden it and its pitiful human cargo deep beneath the surface.

'Closer,' urged Nick. If by a miracle anybody had survived that avalanche, then they had four minutes left of life, and Nick pushed *Warlock* into the still rolling and roiling mass of broken ice – pushing it open with ice-strengthened bows.

Nick flung open the bridge doors beside him and stepped out into the freezing air of the open wing. He ignored the cold, buoyed up by new anger and frustration. He had paid the highest price to make this rescue, he had given up his chance at *Golden Adventurer* for the lives of a handful of strangers, and now, at this last moment, they had been snatched away from him. His sacrifice had been in vain, and the terrible waste of it all appalled him. Because there was no other outlet for his feelings, he let waves of anger sweep over him and he shouted at David Allen's little group on the foredeck.

'Keep your eyes open. I want those people—'

Red caught his eye, a flash of vivid red, seen through the green water, becoming brighter and more hectic as it rose to the surface.

'Both engines half astern!' he screamed. And *Warlock* stopped dead as the twin propellers changed pitch and bit into the water, pulling her up in less than her own length.

In a small open area of green water the red object broke out. Nick saw a human head in a red anorak hood, supported by the thick inflated life jacket. The head was thrown back, exposing a face as white and glistening with wetness as the deadly ice that surrounded it. The face was that of a young boy, smooth and beardless, and quite incredibly beautiful.

'Get him,' Nick yelled, and at the sound of his voice the eyes in that beautiful face opened. Nick saw they were a misty green and unnaturally large in the glistening pale oval framed by the crimson hood.

David Allen was racing back, carrying life-ring and line.

'Hurry. God damn you.' The boy was still alive, and Nick wanted him. He wanted him as fiercely as he had wanted anything in his life, he wanted at least this one young life in return for all he had sacrificed. He saw that the boy was watching him. 'Come on, David,' he shouted again.

'Here!' called David, bracing himself at the ship's rail and he threw the life-ring. He threw it with an expert round arm motion that sent it skimming forty feet to where the hooded head bobbed on the agitated water. He threw it so accurately that it hit the bobbing figure a glancing blow on the shoulder and then plopped into the water alongside, almost nudging the boy.

'Grab it,' yelled Nick. 'Grab hold!'

The face turned slowly, and the boy lifted a gloved hand clear of the surface, but the movement was blunderingly uncoordinated.

'There. It's right next to you,' David encouraged. 'Grab it, man!'

The boy had been in the water for almost two minutes already, he had lost control of his body and limbs; he made two inconclusive movements with the raised hand, one actually bumped the ring but he could not hold it and slowly the life-ring bobbed away from him.

'You bloody idiot,' stormed Nick. 'Grab it!' And those huge green eyes turned back to him, looking up at him with the total resignation of defeat, one stiff arm still raised – almost a farewell salute.

Nick did not realize what he was going to do until he had shrugged off his coat and kicked away his shoes; then he realized that if he stopped to think about it, he would not go.

He jumped feet first, throwing himself far out to miss the rail below him, and as the water closed over his head he experienced a terrified sense of disbelief at the cold.

It seized his chest in a vice that choked the air from his lungs, it drove needles of agony deep into his forehead, and blinded him with the pain as he rose to the surface again. The cold rushed through his light clothing, it crushed his testicles and his stomach was filled with nausea. The marrow in the bones of his legs and arms ached so that he found it difficult to force his limbs to respond, but he struck out for the floating figure.

It was only forty feet, but halfway there he was seized by a panic that he was not going to make it. He clenched his teeth and fought the icy water as though it was a mortal enemy, but it sapped away his strength with the heat of his body.

He struck the floating figure with one outflung arm before he realized he had reached him, and he clung desperately to him, peering up at *Warlock*'s deck.

David Allen had retrieved the ring by its line and he threw it again. The cold had slowed Nick down so that he could not avoid the ring and it struck him on the forehead, but he felt no pain, there was no feeling in his face or feet or hands.

The fleeting seconds counted out the life left to them as he struggled with the inert figure, slowly losing command of his own limbs as he tried to fit the ring over the boy's body. He did not accomplish it. He got the boy's head and one arm through, and he knew he could do no more.

'Pull,' he screamed in rising panic, and his voice was remote and echoed strangely in his own ears.

He took a twist of line around his arm, for his fingers could no longer hold, and he clung with the remains of his strength as they dragged them in.

Jagged ice brushed and snatched at them, but he held the boy with his free arm.

'Pull,' he whispered. 'Oh, for God's sake, pull!' And then they were bumping against *Warlock*'s steel side, were being lifted free of the water, the twist of line smearing the wet skin from his forearm, staining his sleeve with blood that was instantly dissolved to pink by sea water. He felt no pain.

With the other arm, he hung on to the boy, holding him from slipping out of the life-ring. He did not feel the hands that grabbed at him. There was no feeling in his legs and he collapsed face forward, but David caught him before he struck the deck and they hustled him into the steaming warmth of Angel's galley, his legs dragging behind him.

'Are you okay, Skipper?' David kept demanding, and when Nick tried to reply, his jaw was locked in a frozen rictus and great shuddering spasms shook his whole body.

'Get their clothes off,' grated Angel, and, with an easy swing of his heavily muscled shoulders, lifted the boy's body on to the galley table and laid it out face upwards. With a single sweep of a Solingen steel butcher's knife he split the crimson anorak from neck to crutch and stripped it away.

Nick found his voice, it was ragged and broken by the convulsions of frozen muscles.

'What the hell are you doing, David? Get your arse on deck and get this ship on course for *Golden Adventurer*,' he grated, and would have added something a little more forceful, but the next convulsion caught him, and anyway David Allen had already left.

'You'll be all right.' Angel did not even glance up at Nick as he worked with the knife, ripping away layer after layer of the boy's clothing. 'A tough old dog like you – but I think we've got a ripe case of hypothermia here.'

Two of the seamen were helping Nick out of his sodden clothing, the cloth crackled with the thin film of ice that had already formed. Nick winced with the pain of returning circulation to half-frozen hands and feet.

'Okay,' he said, standing naked in the middle of the galley and scrubbing at himself with a rough towel. 'I'll be all right now, return to your stations.' He crossed to the kitchen range, tottering like a drunk, and welcomed the blast of heat from it, rubbing warmth into himself, still shaking and shuddering, his body mottled puce and purple with cold and his genitals shrunken and drawn up into the dense black bush at his crotch.

'Coffee's boiling. Get yourself a hot drink, Skip,' Angel

told him, glancing up at Nick from his work. He ran a quick appreciative glance over Nick's body, taking in the wide rangy shoulders, the dark curls of damp hair that covered his chest, and the trim lines of hard muscle that moulded his belly and waist.

'Put lots of sugar in it – it will warm you the best possible way,' Angel instructed him, and returned his attention to the slim young body on the table.

Angel had put aside his camp airs, and worked with the brusque efficiency of a man who had been trained at his task.

Then suddenly he stopped and stood back for a moment. 'Would you believe! No fun gun!' Angel sighed.

Nick turned just as Angel spread a thick woollen blanket over the pale naked body on the table and began to massage it vigorously.

'You better leave us girls alone together, Skipper,' said Angel with a sweet smile and a twinkle of his diamond earrings, and Nick was left with the memory of a single fleeting glimpse of the stunningly lovely body of a young woman below the pale face and the thick sodden head of copper and gold hair.

Nick Berg was swaddled in a grey woollen blanket, over the boiler suit and bulk jerseys. His feet were in thick Norwegian trawlerman's socks and heavy rubber working boots. He held a china mug of almost boiling coffee in both hands, bending over it to savour the aroma of the steam. It was the third cup he had drunk in the last hour – and yet the shivering spasms still shook him every few minutes.

David Allen had moved his canvas chair across the bridge so he could watch the Trog and work the ship at the same time. Nick could see the loom of the black rock cliffs of Cape Alarm close on their port beam.

The Morse beam squealed suddenly, a long sequence of code to which every man on the bridge listened with complete attention, but it needed the Trog to say it for them.

'*La Mouette* has reached the prize.' He seemed to take a perverse relish in seeing their expressions. 'She's beaten us to it, lads. 12½ per cent salvage to her crew—'

'I want it word for word,' snapped Nick irritably, and the Trog grinned spitefully at him before bowing over his pad.

'*La Mouette* to Christy Marine. *Golden Adventurer* is hard aground, held by ice and receding tides. Stop. Ice damage to plating appears to be below surface. Stop. Hull is flooded and open to sea. Stop. Under no circumstances will Lloyd's Open Form be acceptable. Emphasize importance of beginning salvage work immediately. Stop. Worsening weather and sea conditions. My final hire offer of $8,000 *per diem* plus 2½ per cent of salvaged value open until 1435 GMT. Standing by.'

Nick lit one of his cheroots and irrelevantly decided he must conserve them in future. He had opened his last box that morning. He frowned through the blue smoke and pulled the blanket closer around his shoulders.

Jules Levoisin was playing it touch and hard now. He was dictating terms and setting ultimatums. Nick's own policy of silence was paying off. Probably by now, Jules felt completely safe that he was the only salvage tug within two thousand miles, and he was holding a big-calibre gun to Christy Marine's head.

Jules had seen the situation of the *Golden Adventurer*'s hull. If he had been certain of effecting salvage – no, even if there had been a fifty-fifty chance of a good salvage, Jules would have gone Open Form.

So Jules was not happy with his chances, and he had the shrewdest and most appraising eye in the salvage business. It was a tough one then. *Golden Adventurer* was probably held fast by the quicksand effect of beach and ice, and *La Mouette* could build up a mere nine thousand horse-power.

It would mean throwing out ground-tackle, putting power on *Adventurer*'s pumps – the problems and solutions passed in review through Nick's mind. It was going to be a tough one, but *Warlock* had twenty-two thousand rated horsepower and a dozen other high cards.

He glanced at his gold Rolex Oyster, and he saw that Jules had set a two-hour ultimatum.

'Radio Officer,' he said quietly, and every man on the bridge stiffened and swayed closer, so as not to miss a word.

'Open the telex line direct to Christy Marine, London, and send quote "Personal for Duncan Alexander from Nicholas Berg Master of *Warlock*. Stop. I will be alongside *Golden Adventurer* in one hour forty minutes. Stop. I make firm offer Lloyd's Open Form Contract Salvage. Stop. Offer closes 1300 GMT".'

The Trog looked up at him startled, and blinked his pink eyes swiftly.

'Read it back,' snapped Nick, and the Trog did it in a high penetrating voice and when he finished, waited quizzically, as if expecting Nick to cancel.

'Send it,' said Nick, and rose to his feet. 'Mr Allen,' he turned to David, 'I want you and the Chief Engineer in my day cabin right away.'

The buzz of excitement and speculation began before Nick had closed the door behind him.

David knocked and followed him three minutes later, and Nick looked up from the notes he was making.

'What are they saying?' Nick asked. 'That I am crazy?'

'They're just kids,' shrugged David. 'What do they know?'

'They know plenty, and they're right. I am crazy to go Open Form on a site unseen! But it's the craziness of a man with no other option. Sit down, David.

'When I made the decision to leave Cape Town on the chance of this job – that was when I did the crazy thing.' Nick could no longer keep the steely silence. He had to say it, to talk it out. 'I was throwing dice for my whole bundle. When I turned down the Esso tow, that was when I went on the line for the whole company, *Warlock* and her sister, the whole thing depended on the cash from the Esso tow—'

'I see,' muttered David, and his colour was pink and high, embarrassed by this confidence from Nick Berg.

'What I am doing now is risking nothing. If I lose now, if I fail to pull *Golden Adventurer* out of there, I have lost nothing that is not already forfeit.'

'We could have offered daily hire at a better rate than *La Mouette*,' David suggested.

'No. Duncan Alexander is my enemy. The only way I can get the contract is to make it so attractive that he has no alternative. If he refuses my offer of Open Form, I will take him up before Lloyd's Committee and his own shareholders. I will make a rope of his own guts and hoist it around his neck. He has to go with me – whereas, if I had offered daily hire at a few thousand dollars less than *La Mouette*—' Nick broke off, reached for the box of cheroots on the corner of his desk, then arrested the gesture and swivelled in his chair at the heavy knock on the cabin door.

'Come!'

Vin Baker's overalls were pristine blue, but the bandage around his head was smeared with engine grease, and he had recovered all the bounce and swagger that Nick had banged out of him against the engine-room windows.

'Jesus!' he said. 'I hear you just flipped. I hear you blew your mind and jumped overboard – and when they fished

99

you out, you up and went Open Form on a bomber that's beating herself to death on Cape Alarm.'

'I'd explain it to you,' offered Nick solemnly, 'only I don't know enough words of one syllable.' The Chief Engineer grinned wickedly at that and Nick went on quickly, 'Just believe me when I tell you that I'm playing with someone else's chips. I'm not risking anything I haven't lost already.'

'That's good business,' the Australian agreed handsomely, and helped himself to one of Nick's precious cheroots.

'Your share of 12½ per cent of daily hire is peanuts and apple jelly,' Nick went on.

'Too right,' Vin Baker agreed, and hoisted at his waistline with his elbows.

'But if we snatch *Golden Adventurer* and if we can plug her and pump her out, and if we can keep her afloat for three thousand miles, there will be a couple of big "M's" – and that's beef and potatoes.'

'You know something,' Vin Baker grunted. 'For a Pommy, I'm beginning to like the sound of your voice.' He said it reluctantly and shook his head, as if he didn't really believe it.

'All I want from you now,' Nick told him, 'are your plans for getting power on to *Golden Adventurer*'s pumps and anchor-winch. If she's up on the beach, we will have to kedge her off and we won't have much time.'

Kedging off was the technique of using a ship's own anchor and power winch to assist the pull of the tug in dragging her off a stranding.

Vin Baker waved the cheroot airily. 'Don't worry about that, I'm here.' And at that moment the Trog put his head through the doorway again, this time without knocking.

'I have an urgent and personal for you, Skipper.' He brandished the telex flimsy like a royal flush in spades.

Nick glanced through it once, then read it aloud:

'Master of *Warlock* from Christy Marine. Your offer Lloyd's Open Form "No cure no pay" accepted. Stop. You are hereby appointed main salvage contractor for wreck of *Golden Adventurer*. ENDS.'

Nick grinned with that rare wide irresistible flash of very white teeth. 'And so, gentlemen, it looks as though we are still in business – but the devil knows for just how much longer.'

*W*arlock rounded the headland, where the three black pillars of serpentine rock stood into a lazy green sea, across which low oily swells marched in orderly ranks to push in gently against the black cliffs.

They came round to the sudden vista of the wide, ice-choked bay. The abandoned hulk of *Golden Adventurer* was so majestic, so tall and beautiful that not even the savage mountains could belittle her. She looked like an illustration from a child's book of fairy tales, a lovely ice ship, glistening and glittering in the yellow sunlight.

'She's a beauty,' whispered the Chief Engineer, and his voice captured the sorrow they all felt for a great ship in mortal distress. To every single man on the bridge of *Warlock*, a ship was a living thing for which at best they could feel love and admiration; even the dirtiest old tramp roused a grudging affection. But *Golden Adventurer* was like a lovely woman. She was something rare and special, and all of them felt it.

For Nick Berg, the bond was much more deeply felt. She was child of his inspiration, he had watched her lines take shape on the naval architect's drawingboard, he had seen her keel laid and her bare skeleton fleshed out with lovingly worked steel, and he had watched the woman who had once been his wife speak the blessing and then smash

101

the bottle against her bows, laughing in the sunlight while the wine spurted and frothed.

She was his ship, and now, as he would never have believed possible, his destiny depended upon her.

He looked away from her at last to where *La Mouette* waited in the mouth of the bay at the edge of the ice. In contrast to the liner, she was small and squat and ugly, like a wrestler with all the weight in his shoulders. Greasy black smoke rose straight into the pale sky from her single stack, and her hull seemed to be painted the same greasy black.

Through his glasses, Nick saw the sudden bustle of activity on her bridge as *Warlock* burst into view. The headland would have blanketed *La Mouette*'s radar and, with Nick's strict radio silence, this would be the first that Jules Levoisin knew of *Warlock*'s presence. Nick could imagine the consternation on her navigation bridge, and he noted wryly that Jules Levoisin had not even gone through the motions of putting a line on to *Golden Adventurer*. He must have been completely sure of himself, of his unopposed presence. In maritime law, a line on to a prize's hull bestowed certain rights, and Jules should have made the gesture.

'Get *La Mouette* in clear,' he instructed, and picked up the hand microphone as the Trog nodded to him.

'*Salut Jules, ca va?* You pot-bellied little pirate, haven't they caught and hung you yet?' Nick asked kindly in French, and there was a long disbelieving silence on Channel 16 before the fruity Gallic tones boomed from the overhead speaker.

'Admiral James Bond, I think?' and Jules chuckled, but unconvincingly. 'Is that a battleship or a floating whorehouse? You always were a fancy boy, Nicholas, but what kept you so long? I expected to get a better run for my money.'

'Three things you taught me, *mon brave*: the first was to

take nothing for granted; the second was to keep your big yap shut tight when running for a prize; and the third was to put a line on it when you got there – you've broken your own rules, Jules.'

'The line is nothing. I am arrived.'

'And I, old friend, am arrived also. But the difference is that I am Christy Marine's contractor.'

'*Tu rigoles!* You are joking!' Jules was shocked. 'I heard nothing of this!'

'I am not joking,' Nick told him. 'My James Bond equipment lets me talk in private. But go ahead, call Christy Marine and ask them – and while you are doing it, move that dirty old greaser of yours out of the way. I've got work to do.' Nick tossed the microphone back to the Trog. 'Tape everything he sends,' he instructed, and then to David Allen, 'We are going to smash up that ice before it grabs too tight a hold on *Golden Adventurer*. Put your best man on the wheel.'

Nick was a man transformed, no longer the brooding, moody recluse, agonizing over each decision, uncertain of himself and reacting to each check with frustrated and undirected anger.

'When he starts moving – he really burns it up,' thought David Allen, as he listened to Nick on the engine-room intercom.

'I want flank power on both, Chief. We are going to break ice. Then I want you in full immersion with helmet, we are going on board her to take a peek at her engine room.' He swung back to David Allen. 'Number One, you can stand by to take command.' The man of action glorying in the end to inactivity, he almost seemed to dance upon his feet, like a fighter at the first bell. 'Tell Angel I want a hot meal for us before we go into the cold, plenty of sugar in it.'

'I'll ask the steward,' said David, 'Angel is no good at

the moment. He's playing dolls with the lass you pulled out the water. God, he'll be dressing her up and wheeling her around in a pram—'

'You tell Angel, I want food – and good food,' growled Nick, and turned away to the window to study the ice that blocked the bay, 'or I'll go down personally and kick his backside.'

'He'd probably enjoy that,' muttered David, and Nick rounded on him.

'How many times have you checked out the salvage gear since we left Cape Town?'

'Four times.'

'Make it five. Do it again. I want all the diesel auxiliaries started and run up, then shut down for freezing and rigged to be swung out. I want to have power on *Adventurer* by noon tomorrow.'

'Sir.'

But before he could go, Nick asked, 'What is the barometric reading?'

'I don't know—'

'From now until the end of this salvage, you will know, at any given moment, the exact pressure and you will inform me immediately of any variation over one millibar.'

'Reading is 1018,' David checked hastily.

'It's too high,' said Nick. 'And it's too bloody calm. Watch it. We are going to have a pressure bounce. Watch it like an eagle scout.'

'Sir.'

'I thought I asked you to check the gear.'

The Trog called out, 'Christy Marine has just called *La Mouette* and confirmed that we are the main contractor – but Levoisin has accepted daily hire to pick up a full load of survivors from Shackleton Bay and ferry them to Cape Town. Now he wants to speak to you again.'

'Tell him I'm busy.' Nick did not take his attention from

the ice-packed bay, then he changed his mind. 'No, I'll talk to him.' He took the hand microphone. 'Jules?'

'You don't play fair, Nicholas. You go behind the back of an old friend, a man who loves you like a brother.'

'I'm a busy man. Did you truly call to tell me that?'

'I think you made a mistake, Nicholas. I think your'e crazy to go Lloyd's Open on this one. That ship is stuck fast – and the weather! Did you read the met from Gough Island? You got yourself a screaming bastard there, Nicholas. You listen to an old man.'

'Jules I've got twenty-two thousand horses running for me—'

'I still think you made a mistake, Nicholas. I think you're going to burn more than just your fingers.'

'*Au revoir*, Jules. Come and watch me in the awards court.'

'I still think that's a whorehouse, not a tug, you are sailing. You can send over a couple of blondes and a bottle of wine—'

'Goodbye, Jules.'

'Good luck, *mon vieux*.'

'Hey, Jules – you say "good luck" and it's the worst possible luck. You taught me that.'

'*Oui*, I know.'

'Then good luck to you also, Jules.' For a minute Nick looked after the departing tug. It waddled away over the oily swells, small and fat-bottomed and cheeky, for all the world like its Master – and yet there was something dejected and crestfallen about her going.

He felt a prick of affection for the little Frenchman, he had been a true and good friend as well as a teacher, and Nick felt his triumph softening to regret.

He crushed it down ruthlessly. It had been a straight, hard but fair run, and Jules had been careless. Long ago, Nick had taught himself that anybody in opposition was an enemy, to be hated and beaten, and when you had done so, you despised them. You did not feel compassion, it weakened your own resolve.

He could not quite bring himself to despise Jules Levoisin. The Frenchman would bounce back, probably snatching the next job out from under Nick's nose, and anyway he had the lucrative contract to ferry the survivors from Shackleton Bay. It would pay the costs of his long run southwards and leave some useful change over.

Nick's own dilemma was not as easily resolved. He put Jules Levoisin out of his mind, turning away before the French tug had rounded the headland and he studied the ice-choked bay before him with narrow eyes and a growing feeling of concern. Jules had been right – this was going to be a screaming bastard of a job.

The high seas that had thrown *Golden Adventurer* ashore had been made even higher by the equinoctial spring tides. Both had now abated and she was fast.

The liner's hull had swung also, so she was not aligned neatly at right angles to the beach. *Warlock* would not be able to throw a straight pull on to her. She would have to drag her sideways. Nick could see that now as he closed.

Still closer, he could see how the heavy steel hull, half filled with water, had burrowed itself into the yielding shingle. She would stick like toffee to a baby's blanket.

Then he looked at the ice, it was not only brash and pancake ice, but there were big chunks, bergie bits, from rotten and weathered icebergs, which the wind had driven into the bay, like a sheepdog with its flock.

The plunging temperatures had welded this mass of ice into a whole; like a monstrous octopus, it was wrapping thick glistening tentacles around *Adventurer*'s stern. The ice had not yet had sufficient time to become impenetrable, and *Warlock*'s bows were ice-strengthened for just such an emergency – yet Nick knew enough not to underestimate the hardness of ice. 'White ice is soft ice' was the old adage, and yet here there were big lumps and hummocks of green and striated glacial ice in the mass, like fat plums in a pudding, any one of which could punch a hole through *Warlock*'s hull.

Nick grimaced at the thought of having to send Jules Levoisin a mayday.

He spoke to the helmsman quietly. 'Starboard five – midships,' lining *Warlock* up for a fracture-line in the ice-pack. It was vital to come in at a right angle, to take the ice fully on the stem; a glancing blow could throw the bows off line and bring the vulnerable hull in contact with razor ice.

'Stand by, engine room,' he alerted them, and *Warlock* bore down on the ice at a full ten knots and Nick judged the moment of impact finely. Half a ship's length clear, he gave a crisp order.

'Both half back.'

Warlock checked, going up on to the ice as she decelerated, but still with a horrid rasping roar that echoed through the ship. Her bows rose, riding up over the ice. It gave with a rending crackle, huge slabs of ice upending and tumbling together.

'Both full back.'

The huge twin propellers changed their pitch smoothly into reverse thrust, and the wash boiled into the broken ice, sweeping it clear, as *Warlock* drew back into open water and Nick steadied her and lined her up again.

'Both ahead full.'

Warlock charged forward, checking at the last moment, and again thick slabs of white ice broke away, and grated along the ship's side. Nick swung her stern first starboard then port, deftly using the twin screws to wash the broken ice free, then he pulled *Warlock* out and lined up again.

Butting and smashing and pivoting, *Warlock* worked her way deeper into the bay, opening a spreading web of cracks across the white sheet of ice.

David Allen was breathless, as he burst on to the bridge.

'All gear checked and ready, sir.'

'Take her,' said Nick. 'She's broken it up now – just keep it stirred up.' He wanted to add a warning that the big variable-pitch propellers were *Warlock's* most vulnerable parts, but he had a high enough opinion now of his Mate's ability, so he went on instead, 'I'm going down now to kit up.'

Vin Baker was in the aft salvage hold ahead of him, he had already half finished the tray of rich food and Angel hovered over him, but, as Nick came down the steel ladder, he lifted the cover off another steaming tray.

'It's good,' said Nick, although he could hardly force himself to swallow. The nerves in his stomach were bunched up too tightly. Yet food was one of the best defences against the cold.

'Samantha wants to talk to you, Skip.'

'Who the hell is Samantha?'

'The girl – she wants to thank you.'

'Use your head, Angel, can't you see I have other things on my mind?'

Nick was already pulling on the rubber immersion suit over a full-length woollen undersuit. He needed the assistance of a seaman to enter the opening in the chest of the suit.

He had already forgotten about the girl as they closed the chest opening of the suit with a double ring seal, and then over the watertight bootees and mittens went another full suit of polyurethane. Nick and Vin Baker looked like a pair of fat Michelin men, as their dressers helped them into the full helmets, with wraparound visors, built-in radio microphones and breathing valves.

'Okay, Chief?' Nick asked, and Vin Baker's voice squawked too loudly into his headphones.

'Clear to roll.'

Nick adjusted the volume, and then shrugged into the oxygen rebreathing set. They were not going deeper than thirty feet, so Nick had decided to use oxygen rather than the bulky steel compressed-air cylinders.

'Let's go,' he said, and waddled to the ladder.

The Zodiac sixteen-foot inflatable dinghy swung overboard with the four of them in it, two divers and two picked seamen to handle the boat. Vin pushed one of them aside and primed the outboard himself.

'Come on, beauty,' he told it sternly, and the big Johnson Seahorse fired at the first kick. Gingerly, they began to feel their way through an open lead in the ice, with the two seamen poling away small sharp pieces that would have ripped the fabric of the Zodiac.

In Nick's radio headset, David Allen's voice spoke suddenly.

'Captain, this is the First Officer. Barometric pressure is 1021 – it looks like it's going through the roof.'

The pressure was bouncing, as Nick had predicted. What goes up, must come down – and the higher she goes, the lower she falls.

Jules Levoisin had warned him it was going to be a screamer.

'Did you read the last met from Gough Island?'

'They have 1005 falling, and the wind at 320° and thirty-five knots.'

'Lovely,' said Nick. 'We've got a big blow coming.' And through the visor of his helmet he looked up at the pale and beautiful sun. It was not bright enough to pain the eye, and now it wore a fine golden halo like the head of a saint in a medieval painting.

'Skipper, this is as close as we can get,' Vin Baker told

him, and slipped the motor into neutral. The Zodiac coasted gently into a small open pool in the ice pack, fifty yards from *Golden Adventurer*'s stern.

A solid sheet of compacted ice separated them, and Nick studied it carefully. He had not taken the chance of working *Warlock* in closer until he could get a look at the bottom here. He wanted to know what depth of water he had to manoeuvre in, and if there were hidden snags, jagged rock to rip through the *Warlock*'s hull, or flat shingle on which he could risk a bump.

He wanted to know the slope of the bottom, and if there was good holding for his ground-tackle, but most of all, he wanted to inspect the underwater damage to *Golden Adventurer*'s hull.

'Okay, Chief?' he asked, and Vin Baker grinned at him through the visor.

'Hey, I just remembered – my mommy told me not to get my feet wet. I'm going home.'

Nick knew just how he felt. There was thick sheet ice between them and *Adventurer*, they had to go down and swim below it. God alone knew what currents were running under the ice, and what visibility was like down there. A man in trouble could not surface immediately, but must find his way back to open water. Nick felt a claustrophobic tightening of his belly muscles, and he worked swiftly, checking out his gear, cracking the valve on his oxygen tank to inflate the breathing bag, checking the compass and Rolex Oyster on his wrist and clipping his buddy line on to the Zodiac, a line to return along, like Theseus in the labyrinth of the Minotaur.

'Let's go,' he said, and flipped backwards into the water. The cold struck through the multiple layers of rubber and cloth and polyurethane almost instantly, and Nick waited only for the Chief Engineer to break through the surface beside him in a cloud of swirling silver bubbles.

'God,' Vin Baker's voice was distorted by the earphones,

'it's cold enough to crack the gooseberries off a plaster saint.'

Paying out the line behind him, Nick sank down into the hazy green depths, looking for bottom. It came up dimly, heavy shingle and pebble, and he checked his depth gauge – almost six fathoms – and he moved in towards the beach.

The light from the surface was filtered through thick ice, green and ghostly in the icy depths, and Nick felt unreasonable panic stirring deep in him. He tried to thrust it aside and concentrate on the job, but it flickered there, ready to burst into flame.

There was a current working under the ice, churning the sediment so that the visibility was further reduced, and they had to fin hard to make headway across the bottom, always with the hostile ceiling of sombre green ice above them, cutting them off from the real world.

Suddenly the *Golden Adventurer*'s hull loomed ahead of them, the twin propellers glinting like gigantic bronze wings in the gloom.

They moved in within arm's length of the steel hull and swam slowly along it. It was like flying along the outer wall of a tall apartment block, a sheer cliff of riveted steel plate – but the hull was moving.

The *Golden Adventurer* was hogging on the bottom, the stern dipping and swaying to the pulse of the sea, the heaving groundswell that came in under the ice; her stern bumped heavily on the pebbly bottom, like a great hammer beating time to the ocean.

Nick knew that she was settling herself in. Every hour now was making his task more difficult and he drove harder with his swim fins, pulling slightly ahead of Vin Baker. He knew exactly where to look for the damage. Reilly had reported it in minute detail to Christy Marine, but he came across it without warning.

It looked as though a monstrous axe had been swung

horizontally at the hull, a clean slash, the shape of an elongated teardrop. The metal around it had been depressed, and the paint smeared away so that the steel gleamed as though it had been scoured and polished.

At its widest, the lips of the fifteen-foot rent gaped open by three feet or a little more, and it breathed like a living mouth – for the force of the groundswell pushing into the gap built up pressure within the hull, then as the swell subsided the trapped water was forcibly expelled, sucking in and out with tremendous pressure.

'It's a clean hole,' Vin Baker's voice squawked harshly. 'But it's too long to pump with cement.'

He was right, of course, Nick had seen that at once. Liquid cement would not plug that wicked gash, and anyway, there wasn't time to use cement, not with weather coming. An idea began forming in his mind.

'I'm going to penetrate.' Nick made the decision aloud, and beside him the Chief was silent for long incredulous seconds, then he covered the edge of fear in his voice with,

'Listen, cobber, every time I've ever been into an orifice shaped like that, it's always meant big trouble. Reminds me of my first wife—'

'Cover for me,' Nick interrupted him. 'If I'm not out in five minutes—'

'I'm coming with you,' said the Chief. 'I've got to take a look at her engine room. This is as good a time as any.'

Nick did not argue with him.

'I'll go first,' he said and tapped the Chief's shoulder. 'Do what I do.'

Nick hung four feet from the gash, finning to hold himself there against the current.

He watched the swirl of water rushing into the opening, and then gushing out again in a rash of silver bubbles. Then, as she began to breathe again, he darted forward.

The current caught him and he was hurled at the gap,

with only time to duck his helmeted head and cover the fragile oxygen bag on his chest with both arms.

Raw steel snagged at his leg; there was no pain, but almost instantly he felt the leak of sea water into his suit. The cold stung like a razor cut, but he was through into the total darkness of the cavernous hull. He was flung into a tangle of steel piping, and he anchored himself with one arm and groped for the underwater lantern on his belt.

'You okay?' The Chief's voice boomed in his headphones.

'Fine.'

Vin Baker's lantern glowed eerily in the dark waters ahead of him.

'Work fast,' instructed Nick. 'I've got a tear in my suit.'

Each of them knew exactly what to do and where to go. Vin Baker swam first to the watertight bulkheads and checked all the seals. He was working in darkness in a totally unfamiliar engine room, but he went unerringly to the pump system, and checked the valve settings; then he rose to the surface, feeling his way up the massive blocks of the main engines.

Nick was there ahead of him. The engine room was flooded almost to the deck above and the surface was a thick stinking scum of oil and diesel, in which floated a mass of loose articles, most of them undefinable, but in the beam of his lantern Nick recognized a gumboot and a grease pot floating beside his head. The whole thick stinking soup rose and fell and agitated with the push of the current through the rent.

The lenses of their lanterns were smeared with the oily filth and threw grotesque shadows into the cavernous depths, but Nick could just make out the deck above him, and the dark opening of the vertical ventilation shaft. He wiped the filth from his visor and saw what he wanted to see and the cold was spreading up his leg. He asked brusquely, 'Okay, Chief?'

113

'Let's get the hell out of here.'

There were sickening moments of panic when Nick thought they had lost the line to the opening. It had sagged and wrapped around a steam pipe. Nick freed it and then sank down to the glimmer of light through the gash.

He judged his moment carefully, the return was more dangerous than the entry, for the raw bright metal had been driven in by the ice, like the petals of a sunflower – or the fangs in a shark's maw. He used the suck of water and shot through without a touch, turning and finning to wait for Vin Baker.

The Australian came through in the next rush of water, but Nick saw him flicked sideways by the current, and he struck the jagged opening a touching blow. There was instantly a roaring rush of escaping oxygen from his breathing bag, as the steel split it wide, and for a moment the Chief was obscured in the silver cloud of gas that was his life's breath.

'Oh God, I'm snagged,' he shouted, clutching helplessly at his empty bag, plummeting sharply into the green depths at the drastic change in his buoyance. The heavily leaded belt around his waist had been weighted to counter the flotation of the oxygen bag, and he went down like a gannet diving on a shoal of sardine.

Nick saw instantly what was about to happen. The current had him – it was dragging him down under the hull, sucking him under that hammering steel bottom, where he would be crushed against the stony beach by twenty-two thousand tons of pounding steel.

Nick went head down, finning desperately to catch the swirling body which tumbled like a leaf in high wind. He had a fleeting glimpse of Baker's face, contorted with terror and lack of breath, the glass visor of his helmet already swamping with icy water as the pressure spurted through the non-return valve. The Chief's headset microphone squealed once and then went dead as the water shorted it out.

'Drop your belt,' yelled Nick, but Baker did not respond; he had not heard, his headset had gone and instead he fought ineffectually in the swirling current, drawn inexorably down to brutal death.

Nick got a hand to him and threw back with all his strength on his fins to check their downward plunge, but still they went down and Nick's right hand was clumsy with cold and the double thickness of his mittens as he groped for the quick-release on the Chief's belt.

He hit the rounded bottom of the great hull with his shoulder, and felt them dragged under to where clouds of sediment blew like smoke from the working of the keel. Locked together like a couple of waltzing dancers, they swung around and he saw the keel, like the blade of a guillotine, rise up high above them. He could not reach the Chief's release toggle.

There were only microseconds in which to go for his one other chance. He hit his own release and the thick belt with thirty-five pounds of lead fell away from Nick's waist; with it went the buddy line that would guide them back to the waiting Zodiac, for it had been clipped into the back of the belt.

The abrupt loss of weight checked their downward plunge, and fighting with all the strength of his legs, Nick was just able to hold them clear of the great keel as it came swinging downwards.

Within ten feet of them, steel struck stone with a force that rang in Nick's eardrum like a bronze gong but he had an armlock on the Chief's struggling body, and now at last his right hand found the release toggle on the other man's belt.

He hit it, and another thirty-five pounds of lead dropped away. They began to rise, up along the hogging steel hull, faster and faster as the oxygen in Nick's bag expanded with the release of pressure. Now their plight was every bit as desperate, for they were racing upwards to a roof of solid ice with enough speed to break bone or crack a skull.

Nick emptied his lungs, exhaling on a single continuous breath, and at the same time opened the valve to vent his bag, blowing away the precious life-giving gas in an attempt to check their rise – yet still they went into the ice with a force that would have stunned them both, had Nick not twisted over and caught it on his shoulder and outflung arm. They were pinned there under the ice by the cork-like buoyancy of their rubber suits and the remaining gas in Nick's bag.

With mild and detached surprise Nick saw that the lower side of the ice pack was not a smooth sheet, but was worked into ridges and pinnacles, into weird flowing shapes like some abstract sculpture in pale green glass. It was only a fleeting moment that he looked at it, for beside him Baker was drowning.

His helmet was flooded with icy water and his face was empurpled and his mouth contorted into a horrible rictus; already his movements were becoming spasmodic and uncoordinated, as he struggled for breath.

Nick realized that haste would kill them both now. He had to work fast but deliberately – and he held Baker to him as he cracked the valve on his steel oxygen bottle, reinflating his chest bag.

With his right hand, he began to unscrew the breathing pipe connection into the side of Baker's helmet. It was slow, too slow. He needed touch for this delicate work.

He thought, 'This could cost me my right hand,' and he stripped off the thick mitten in a single angry gesture. Now he could feel – for the few seconds until the cold paralysed his fingers. The connection came free and while he worked, Nick was pumping his lungs like a bellows, hyper-ventilating, washing his blood with pure oxygen until he felt light-headed and dizzy.

One last sweet breath, and then he unscrewed his own hose connection; icy water flooded through the valve but he held his head at an angle to trap oxygen in the top of his helmet, keeping his nose and eyes clear, and he rescrewed his own hose into Baker's helmet with fingers that no longer had feeling.

He held the Chief's body close to his chest, embracing like lovers, and he cracked the last of the oxygen from his bottle. There was just sufficient pressure of gas left to expunge the water from Baker's helmet. It blew out with an explosive hiss through the valve, and Nick watched carefully with his face only inches from Baker's.

The Chief was choking and coughing, gulping and gasping at the rush of cold oxygen, his eyes watery and unseeing, his spectacles blown awry and the lenses obscured by sea water, but then Nick felt his chest begin to swell and subside. Baker was breathing again, 'which is more than I am doing,' Nick thought grimly – and then suddenly he realized for the first time that he had lost the guide line with his weight belt.

He did not know in which direction was the shore, nor which way to swim to reach the Zodiac. He was utterly disorientated, and desperately he peered through his half-flooded visor for sight of the *Golden Adventurer*'s hull to align himself. She was not there, gone in the misty green gloom – and he felt the first heave of his lungs as they demanded air. And as he denied his body the driving need to breathe, he felt the fear that had flickered deep within him flare up into true terror, swiftly becoming cold driving panic.

A suicidal urge to tear at the green ice roof of this watery tomb almost overwhelmed him. He wanted to try and rip his way through it with bare freezing hands to reach the precious air.

Then, just before panic completely obliterated his reason, he remembered the compass on his wrist. Even then his brain was sluggish, beginning to starve for oxygen, and it took precious seconds working out the reciprocal of his original bearing.

As he leaned forward to read the compass, more sea water spurted into his helmet, spiking needles of icy cold agony into the sinuses of his cheeks and forehead, making the teeth ache in his jaws, so he gasped involuntarily and immediately choked.

Still holding Baker to him, linked by the thick black umbilical cord of his oxygen hose, Nick began to swim out on the reciprocal compass heading. Immediately his lungs began to pump, convulsing in involuntary spasms, like those of childbirth, craving air, and he swam on.

With his head thrown back slightly he saw that the sheet of ice moved slowly above him; at times, when the current held them, it moved not at all, and it required all his self-control to keep finning doggedly, then the current relaxed its grip and they moved forward again, but achingly slowly.

He had time then to realize how exquisitely beautiful was the ice roof; translucent, wondrously carved and sculptured – and suddenly he remembered standing hand in hand with Chantelle beneath the arched roof of Chartres Cathedral, staring up in awe. The pain in his chest subsided, the need to breathe passed, but he did not recognize that as the sign of mortal danger, nor the images that formed before his eyes as the fantasy of a brain deprived of oxygen and slowly dying.

Chantelle's face was before him then, glowing hair soft and thick and glossy as a butterfly's wing, huge dark eyes and that wide mouth so full of the promise of delight and warmth and love.

'I loved you,' he thought. 'I really loved you.'

And again the image changed. He saw again the

118

incredible slippery explosive liquid burst with which his son was born, heard the first querulous cry as he dangled pink and wet and hairless from the rubber-gloved hand, and felt again the soul-consuming wonder and joy.

'A drowning man—' Nick recognized at last what was happening to him. He knew then he was dying, but the panic had passed, as the cold had passed also, and the terror. He swam on, dreamlike, into the green mists. Then he realized that his own legs were no longer moving; he lay relaxed not breathing, not feeling, and it was Baker's body that was thrusting and working against him.

Nick peered into the glass visor still only inches from his eyes, and he saw that Baker's face was set and determined. He was gulping the pure sweet oxygen and gaining strength with each breath, driving on strongly.

'You beauty,' whispered Nick dreamily, and felt the water shoot into his throat, but there was no pain.

Another image formed before him, an Arrowhead-class yacht with spinnaker set, running free across a bright Mediterranean sea, and his son at the tiller, the dense tumble of curls that covered his small neat head fluttering in the wind, and the same velvety dark eyes as his mother's in the suntanned oval of his face as he laughed.

'Don't let her run by the lee, Peter,' Nicholas wanted to shout to his son, but the image faded into blackness. He thought for a moment that he had passed into unconsciousness, but then he realized suddenly that it was the black rubber bottom of the Zodiac only inches from his eyes, and that the rough hands that dragged him upwards, lifting him and tearing loose the fastening of his helmet, were not part of the fantasy.

Propped against the pillowed gunwale of the Zodiac, held by the two boatmen from falling backwards, the first breaths of sub-zero air were too rich for his starved lungs, and Nick coughed and vomited weakly down the front of his suit.

Nick came out of the shower cabinet. The cabin was thick with steam, and his body glowed dull angry red from the almost boiling water. He wrapped the towel around his waist as he stepped through into his night cabin.

Baker slouched in the armchair at the foot of his bunk. He wore fresh overalls, his hair stood up in little damp spikes around the shaven spot where Angel's catgut stitches still held the scabbed wound closed. One of the side frames of his spectacles had snapped during those desperate minutes below *Golden Adventurer*'s stern, and Baker had repaired it with black insulating tape.

He held two glasses in his left hand, and a big flat brown bottle of liquor in the other. He poured two heavy slugs into the glasses as Nick paused in the bathroom door, and the sweet, rich aroma smelled like the sugar-cane fields of northern Queensland.

Baker passed a glass to Nick, and then showed him the bottle's yellow label.

'Bundaberg rum,' he announced, 'the dinky die stuff, sport.'

Nick recognized both the offer of liquor and the salutation as probably the highest accolade the Chief would ever give another human being.

Nick sniffed the dark honey-brown liquor and then took it in a single toss, swirled it once around his mouth, swallowed, shuddered like a spaniel shaking off water droplets, exhaled harshly and said: 'It's still the finest rum in the world.' Dutifully he said what was expected of him, and held out his glass.

'The Mate asked me to give you a message,' said Baker as he poured another shot for each of them. 'Glass hit 1035 and now it's diving like a dingo into its hole – back to 1020 already. It's going to blow – is it ever going to blow!'

They regarded each other over the rims of the glasses.

'We've wasted almost two hours, Beauty,' Nick told

him, and Baker blinked at the unlikely name, then grinned crookedly as he accepted it.

'How are you going to plug that hull?'

'I've got ten men at work already. We are going to fother a sail into a collision mat.'

Baker blinked again, then shook his head in disbelief. 'That's Hornblower stuff—'

'The *Witch of Endor*,' Nick agreed. 'So you can read?'

'You haven't got pressure to drive it home,' Baker objected. 'The trapped air from the engine room will blow it out.'

'I'm going to run a wire down the ventilation shaft of the engine room and out through the gash. We'll fix the collision mat outside the hull and winch it home with the wire.'

Baker stared at him for five seconds while he examined the proposition. A sail was fothered by threading the thick canvas with thousands of strands of unravelled oakum until it resembled a huge shaggy doormat. When this was placed over an aperture below a ship's waterline, the pressure of water forced it into the hole, and the water swelled the mass of fibre until it formed an almost watertight plug.

However, in *Golden Adventurer*'s case the damage was extensive and as the hull was already flooded, there was no pressure differential to drive home the plug. Nick proposed to beat that by using an internal wire to haul the plug into the gash.

'It might work.' Beauty Baker was noncommittal.

Nick took the second rum at a gulp, dropped the towel and reached for his working gear laid out on the bunk.

'Let's get power on her before the blow hits us,' he suggested mildly, and Baker lumbered to his feet and stuffed the Bundaberg bottle into his back pocket.

'Listen, sport,' he said. 'All that guff about you being a Pommy, don't take it too seriously.'

'I won't,' said Nick. 'Actually, I was born and educated

in Blighty, but my father's an American. So that makes me one also.'

'Christ.' Beauty hitched disgustedly at his waist with both elbows. 'If there's anything worse than a bloody Pom, it's a goddamned Yank.'

Now that Nick was certain that the bottom of the bay was clean and free of underwater snags, he handled *Warlock* boldly but with a delicately skilful touch which David Allen watched with awe.

Like a fighting cock, the *Warlock* attacked the thicker ice line along the shore, smashing free huge lumps and slabs, then washing them clear with the propellers, giving herself space to work about *Golden Adventurer*'s stern.

The ominous calm of both sea and air made the work easier, although the vicious little current working below *Adventurer*'s stern complicated the transfer of the big alternator.

Nick had two Yokohama fenders slung from *Warlock*'s side, and the bloated plastic balloons cushioned the contact of steel against steel as Nick laid *Warlock* alongside the stranded liner, holding her there with delicate adjustments of power and rudder and screw pitch.

Beauty Baker and his working party, swaddled in heavy Antarctic gear, were already up on the catwalk of *Warlock*'s forward gantry, seventy feet above the bridge and overlooking *Adventurer*'s sharply canted deck.

As Nick nudged *Warlock* in, they dropped the steel boarding-ladder across the gap between the two ships and Beauty led them across in single file, like a troop of monkeys across the limb of a forest tree.

'All across,' the Third Officer confirmed for Nick, and then added, 'Glass has dropped again, sir. Down to 1005.'

'Very well,' Nick drew *Warlock* gently away from the liner's stern, and held her fifty feet off. Only then did he flick his eyes up at the sky. The midnight sun had turned into a malevolent jaundiced yellow, while the sun itself was a ball of dark satanic red above the peaks of Cape Alarm, and it seemed that the snowfields and glaciers were washed with blood.

'It's beautiful.' Suddenly the girl was beside him. The top of her head was on a level with his shoulder, and in the ruddy light, her thick roped hair glowed like newly minted sovereigns in red gold. Her voice was low and a little husky with shyness, and touched a chord of response in Nick, but when she lifted her face to him he saw how young she was.

'I came to thank you,' she said softly. 'It's the first chance I've had.'

She wore baggy, borrowed men's clothing that made her look like a little girl dressing up, and her face, free of cosmetics, had that waxy plastic glow of youth, like the polished skin of a ripe apple.

Her expression was solemn and there were traces of her recent ordeal beneath her eyes and at the corners of her mouth. Nick sensed the tension and nervousness in her.

'Angel wouldn't let me come before,' she said, and suddenly she smiled. The nervousness vanished and it was the direct warm unselfconscious smile of a beautiful child that has never known rejection. Nick was shocked by the strength of his sudden physical desire for her, his body moved, clenching like a fist in his groin, and he felt his heart pound furiously in the cage of his ribs.

His shock turned to anger, for she looked but fourteen or fifteen years of age; almost she seemed as young as his own son, and he was shamed by the perversity of his attraction. Since the good bright times with Chantelle, he had not experienced such direct and instant involvement

123

with a woman. At the thought of Chantelle, his emotions collapsed in a disordered tangle, from which only his lust and his anger emerged clearly.

He cupped the anger to him, like a match in a high wind, it gave him strength again. Strength to thrust this aside, for he knew how vulnerable he still was and how dangerous a course had opened before him, to be led by this child-woman. Suddenly he was aware that he had swayed bodily towards the girl and had been staring into her face for many long seconds, that she was meeting his gaze steadily and that something was beginning to move in her eyes like cloud shadow across the sunlit surface of a green mountain lake. Something was happening which he could not afford, could not chance – and then he realized also that the two young deck officers were watching them with undisguised curiosity, and he turned his anger on her.

'Young lady,' he said. 'You have an absolute genius for being in the wrong place at the wrong time.' And his tone was colder and more remote than even he had intended it.

Before he turned away from her, he saw the moment of her disbelief turn to chagrin, and the green eyes misted slightly. He stood stiffly staring down the foredeck where David Allen's team was opening the forward salvage hold.

Nick's anger evaporated almost at once, to be replaced by dismay. He realized clearly that he had completely alienated the girl and he wanted to turn back to her and say something gracious that might retrieve the situation, but he could think of nothing and instead lifted the hand microphone to his lips and spoke to Baker over the VHF radio.

'How's it going, Chief?'

There were ten seconds of delay, and Nick was very conscious of the girl's presence near him.

'Their emergency generator has burned out, it will need two days' work to get it running again. We'll have to take on the alternator,' Beauty told him.

'We are ready to give it to you,' Nick told him, and then called David Allen on the foredeck.

'Ready, David?'

'All set.'

Nick began edging *Warlock* back towards the liner's towering stern, and now at last he turned back to the girl. Unaccountably, he now wanted her approbation, so his smile was ready – but she had already gone, taking with her that special aura of brightness.

Nick's voice had a jagged edge to it as he told David Allen, 'Let's do this fast and right, Number One.'

Warlock nuzzled *Adventurer*'s stern, the big black Yokohama fenders gentling her touch, and on her foredeck the winch whined shrilly, the lines squealing in their blocks and from the open salvage hatch the four-ton alternator swung out. It was mounted on a sledge for easy handling. The diesel tanks were charged and the big motor primed and ready to start.

It rose swiftly, dangling from the tall gantry, and a dozen men synchronized their efforts, in those critical moments when it hung out over *Warlock*'s bows. A nasty freaky little swell lifted the tug and pushed her across, for the dangling burden was already putting a slight list on her, and it would have crashed into the steel side of the liner had not Nick thrown the screws into reverse thrust and given her a burst of power to hold her off.

The instant the swell subsided, he closed down and slid the pitch to fine forward, pressing the cushioned bows lightly back against *Adventurer*'s side.

'He's good!' David Allen watched Nicholas work. 'He's better than old Mac ever was.' Mackintosh, *Warlock*'s previous skipper, had been careful and experienced, but Nicholas Berg handled the ship with the flair and intuitive touch that even Mac's vast experience could never have matched.

David Allen pushed the thought aside and signalled the

winchman. The huge dangling machine dropped with the control of a roosting seagull on to the liner's deck. Baker's crew leapt on it immediately, releasing the winch cable and throwing out the tackle, to drag it away on its sledge.

Warlock drew off, and when Baker's crew was ready, she went in to drop another burden, this time one of the high-speed centrifugal pumps which would augment *Golden Adventurer*'s own machinery – if Baker could get that functioning. It went up out of *Warlock*'s forward hold, followed ten minutes later by its twin.

'Both pumps secured.' Baker's voice had a spark of jubilation in it, but at that moment a shadow passed over the ship, as though a vulture wheeled above on widespread pinions, and as Nick glanced up he saw the men on the foredeck lift their heads also.

It was a single cloud seeming no bigger than a man's fist, a thousand or fifteen hundred feet above them, but it had momentarily obscured the lowering sun, before scuttling on furtively down the peaks of Cape Alarm.

'There is still much to do,' Nick thought, and he opened the bridge door and stepped out on to the exposed wing. There was no movement of air, and the cold seemed less intense although a glance at the glass confirmed that there were thirty degrees still of frost. No wind here, but high up it was beginning.

'Number One,' Nick snapped into the microphone. 'What's going on down there – do you think this is your daddy's yacht?'

And David Allen's team leapt to the task of closing down the forward hatch, and then tramped back to the double salvage holds on the long stern quarter.

'I am transferring command to the stern bridge.' Nick told his deck officers and hurried back through the accommodation area to the second enclosed bridge, where every control and navigational aid was duplicated, a unique feature of salvage-tug construction where so much of the work took place on the afterdeck.

This time from the aft gantries, they lifted the loaded pallets of salvage gear on to the liner's deck, another eight tons of equipment went aboard *Golden Adventurer*. Then they pulled away and David Allen battened down again. When he came on to the bridge stamping and slapping his own shoulders, red-cheeked and gasping from the cold, Nick told him immediately.

'Take command, David, I'm going on board.' Nick could not bring himself to wait out the uncertain period while Beauty Baker put power and pumps into action.

Anything mechanical was Baker's responsibility, as seamanship was strictly Nick's, but it could take many hours yet, and Nick could not remain idle that long.

From high on the forward gantry, Nick looked out across that satiny ominous sea. It was a little after midnight now and the sun was halfway down behind the mountains, a two-dimensional disc of metal heated to furious crimson. The sea was sombre purple and the icebergs were sparks of brighter cherry red. From this height he could see that the surface of the sea was crenellated, a small regular swell spreading across it like ripples across a pond, from some disturbance far out beyond the horizon.

Nick could feel the fresh movement of *Warlock*'s hull as she rode this swell, and suddenly a puff of wind hit Nick in the face like the flit of a bat's wing, and the metallic sheen of the sea was scoured by a cat's-paw of wind that scratched at the surface as it passed.

He pulled the drawstring of the hood of his anorak up more tightly under his chin and stepped out on to the open boarding-ladder, like a steeplejack, walking upright and balancing lightly seventy feet above *Warlock*'s slowly rolling foredeck.

He jumped down on to *Golden Adventurer*'s steeply

canted, ice-glazed deck and saluted *Warlock*'s bridge far below in a gesture of dismissal.

'I tried to warn you, dearie,' said Angel gently, as she entered the steamy galley, for with a single glance he was aware of Samantha's crestfallen air. 'He tore you up, didn't he?'

'What are you talking about?' She lifted her chin, and the smile was too bright and too quick. 'What do you want me to do?'

'You can separate that bowl of eggs,' Angel told her, and stooped again over twenty pounds of red beef, with his sleeves rolled to the elbows about his thick and hairy arms, clutching a butcher's knife in a fist like that of Rocky Marciano.

They worked in silence for five minutes, before Samantha spoke again.

'I only tried to thank him—' And again there was a grey mist in her eyes.

'He's a lower-deck pig,' Angel agreed.

'He is not,' Samantha came in hotly. 'He's not a pig.'

'Well, then, he's a selfish, heartless bastard – with jumped-up ideas.'

'How *can* you say that!' Samantha's eyes flashed now. 'He is not selfish – he went into the water to get me—'

Then she saw the smile on Angel's lips and the mocking quizzical expression in his eyes, and she stopped in confusion and concentrated on cracking the eggshells and slopping the contents into the mixing basin.

'He's old enough to be your father,' Angel needled her, and now she was really angry; a ruddy flush under the smooth gloss of her skin made the freckles shine like gold dust.

'You talk the most awful crap, Angel.'

'God, dearie, where did you learn that language?'

'Well, you're making me mad.' She broke an egg with such force that it exploded down the front of her pants. 'Oh, shit!' she said, and stared at him defiantly. Angel tossed her a dishcloth, she wiped herself violently and they went on working again.

'How old is he?' she demanded at last. 'A hundred and fifty?'

'He's thirty-eight,' Angel thought for a moment, 'or thirty-nine.'

'Well, smart arse,' she said tartly, 'the ideal age is half the man's age, plus seven.'

'You aren't twenty-six, dearie,' Angel said gently.

'I will be in two years' time,' she told him.

'You really want him badly, hey? A fever of lust and desire?'

'That's nonsense, Angel, and you know it. I just happen to owe him a rather large debt – he saved my life – but as for wanting him, ha!' She dismissed the idea with a snort of disdain and a toss of her head.

'I'm glad,' Angel nodded. 'He's not a very nice person, you can see by those ferrety eyes of his—'

'He has beautiful eyes—' she flared at him, and then stopped abruptly, saw the cunning in his grin, faltered and then collapsed weakly on the bench beside him, with a cracked egg in one hand.

'Oh, Angel, you are a horrible man and I hate you. How can you make fun of me now?'

He saw how close she was to tears, and became brisk and businesslike.

'First of all, you better know something about him—' and he began to tell her, giving her a waspish biography of Nicholas Berg, embellished by a vivid imagination and a wicked sense of humour, together with a quasi-feminine love of gossip, to which Samantha listened avidly, making an occasional exclamation of surprise.

'His wife ran away with another man, she could be out of her mind, don't you think?'

'Dearie, a change is like two weeks at the seaside.'

Or asking a question. 'He owns this ship, actually owns it? Not just Master?'

'He owns this ship, and its sister, and the company. They used to call him the Golden Prince. He's a high flyer, dearie, didn't you recognize it?'

'I didn't—'

'Of course you did. You're too much woman not to. There is no more powerful aphrodisiac than success and power, nothing like the clink of gold to get a girl's hormones revving up, is there?'

'That's unfair, Angel. I didn't know a thing about him. I didn't know he was rich and famous. I don't give a damn for money—'

'Ho! Ho!' Angel shook his curls and the diamond studs flashed in his ears. But he saw her anger flare again. 'All right, dearie, I'm teasing. But what really attracts you is his strength and air of purpose. The way other men obey, and follow and fear him. The air of command, of power and with it, success.'

'I didn't—'

'Oh, be honest with yourself, love. It was not the fact he saved your life, it wasn't his beautiful eyes nor the lump in his jeans—'

'You're crude, Angel.'

'You're bright and beautiful, and you just can't help yourself. You're like a nubile little gazelle, all skittish and ready, and you have just spotted the herd bull. You can't help yourself, dearie, you're just a woman.'

'What am I going to do, Angel?'

'We'll make a plan, love, but one thing is certain, you're not going to trail around behind him, dressed like an escapee from a junk shop, breathing adoration and hero-worship. He's doing a job. He doesn't need to trip over you every time he turns. Play hard to get.'

Samantha thought about it for a moment. 'Angel, I don't want to play it that hard that I never get around to being got – if you follow me.'

Beauty Baker had the work in hand, well organized and going ahead as fast as even Nick, in his over-whelming impatience, could expect.

The alternator had been manhandled through the double doors into the superstructure on B deck, and it had been secured against a steel bulkhead and lashed down.

'As soon as I have power, we'll drill the deck and bolt her down,' he explained to Nick.

'Have you got the lines in?'

'I'll bypass the main junction box on C deck, and I will select from the temporary box—'

'But you've identified the foredeck winch circuit, and the pumps?'

'Jesus, sport, why don't you go sail your little boat and leave me to do my work?'

On the upper deck one of Baker's gangs was already at work with the gas welding equipment. They were opening access to the ventilation shaft of the main engine room. The gas cutter hissed viciously and red sparks showered from the steel plate of the tall dummy smokestack. The stack was merely to give the *Golden Adventurer* the tra-ditional rakish lines, and now the welder cut the last few inches of steel plating. It fell away into the deep, dark cavern, leaving a roughly square opening six feet by six feet which gave direct access into the half-flooded engine room fifty feet below.

Despite Baker's advice, Nick took command here,

131

directing the rigging of the winch blocks and steel wire cable that would enable a cable to be taken down into the flooded engine room and out again through that long, viciously fanged gash in the ship's side. When he looked at his Rolex Oyster again, almost an hour had passed. The sun had gone and a luminous green sky filled with the marvellous pyrotechnics of the *Aurora Australis* turned the night eerie and mysterious.

'All right, bosun, that's all we can do now. Bring your team up to the bows.'

As they hurried forward along the open foredeck, the wind caught them, a single shrieking gust that had them reeling and staggering and grabbing for support; then it was past and the wind settled down to nag and whine and pry at their clothing as Nick directed the work at the two huge anchor winches; but he heard the rising sea starting to push and stir the pack-ice, making it growl and whisper menacingly.

They catted the twin sea-anchors and with two men working over *Adventurer*'s side they secured collars of heavy chain to the crown of each anchor. *Warlock* would now be able to drag those anchors out, letting them bump along the bottom, but in the opposite direction to that in which they had been designed to drag, so that the pointed flukes would not be able to dig in and hold.

Then, when the anchors were out to the full reach of their own chains, *Warlock* would drop them, the flukes would dig in and hold. This was the ground-tackle which might resist the efforts of even a force twelve wind to throw *Golden Adventurer* further ashore.

When Baker had power on the ship, the anchor winches would be used to kedge *Golden Adventurer* off the bank. Nick placed much reliance on these enormously powerful winches to assist *Warlock*'s own engines, for even as they worked, he could feel through the soles of his feet how heavily grounded the liner was.

It was a tense and heavy labour, for they were working with enormous weights of dead-weight steel chain and shackles. The securing shackle, which held the chain collar on the anchor crown, alone weighed three hundred pounds and had to be manhandled by six men using complicated tackle.

By the time they had the work finished, the wind was rising force six, and wailing in the superstructure. The men were chilled and tired, and tempers were flashing.

Nick led them back to the shelter of the main super-structure. His boots seemed to be made of lead, and his lungs pumped for the solace of cheroot smoke, and he realized irrelevantly that he had not slept now for over fifty hours – since he had fished that disturbing little girl from the water. Quickly he pushed the thought of her aside, for it distracted him from his purpose, and, as he stepped over the door-sill into the liner's cold but wind-protected main accommodation, he reached for his cheroot-case.

Then he arrested the movement and blinked with surprise as suddenly garish light blazed throughout the shipdeck lights and internal lights, so that instantly a festival air enveloped her and from the loudspeakers on the deck above Nicholas' head wafted soft music as the broad-casting equipment switched itself in. It was the voice of Donna Summer, as limpid and ringing clear as fine-leaded crystal. The sound was utterly incongruous in this place and in these circumstances.

'Power is on!'

Nick let out a whoop and ran through to B deck. Beauty Baker was standing beside his roaring alternator and hug-ging himself with glee.

'Howzat, sport?' he demanded. Nick punched his shoulder.

'Right on, Beauty.' He wasted a few moments and a cheroot by placing one of the precious black tubes between Baker's lips and flashing his lighter. The two of them smoked for twenty seconds in close and companionable silence.

'Okay,' Nick ended it. 'Pumps and winches.'

'The two emergency portables are ready to start, and I'm on my way to check the ship's main pumps.'

'The only thing left is to get the collision mat into place.'

'That is your trick,' Baker told him flatly. 'You're not getting me into the water again, ever. I've even given up bathing.'

'Yeah, did you notice I'm standing upwind?' Nick told him. 'But somebody has got to go down again to pass the wire.'

'Why don't you send Angel?' Baker grinned evilly. 'Excuse me, cobber – I've got work to do.' He inspected the cheroot. 'After we've pulled this dog off the ground, I hope you will be able to afford decent gaspers.' And he was gone into the depths of the liner, leaving Nick with the one task he had been avoiding even thinking about. Somebody had to go down into that engine room. He could call for volunteers, of course, but then it was another of his own rules never to ask another man to do what you are afraid to do yourself.

'I can leave David to lay out the ground-tackle, but I can't let anybody else put the collision mat in.' He faced it now. He would have to go down again, into the cold and darkness and mortal danger of the flooded engine room.

The ground-tackle that David Allen had laid was holding *Golden Adventurer* handsomely, even in the aggravated swell which was by now pouring into the open mouth of the bay, driven on by the rising wind that was inciting it to wilder abandon.

David had justified Nick's confidence in the seamanlike

manner in which he had taken the Golden Adventurer's twin anchors out and dropped them a cable's length offshore, at a finely judged angle to give the best purchase and hold.

Beauty Baker had installed and test-run the two big centrifugals and he had even resuscitated two of the liner's own forward pump assemblies which had been protected by the watertight bulkhead from the sea break-in. He was ready now to throw the switch on this considerable arsenal of pumps, and he had calculated that if Nick could close that gaping rent in the hull, he would be able to pump the liner's hull dry and clean in just under four hours.

Nick was in full immersion kit again, but this time he had opted for a single-bottle Drager diving-set; he was off oxygen sets for life, he decided wryly.

Before going down, he paused on the open deck with the diving helmet under his arm. The wind must be rising seven now, he decided, for it was kicking off the tops of the waves in bursts of spray and a low scudding sky of dirty grey cloud had blotted out the rising sun and the peaks of Cape Alarm. It was a cold dark dawn, with the promise of a wilder day to follow.

Nick took one glance across at Warlock. David Allen was holding her nicely in position, and his own team was ready, grouped around that ugly black, freshly burned opening in Adventurer's stack. He lifted the helmet on to his head, and while his helpers closed the fastenings and screwed down the hose connections, he checked the radio.

'Warlock, do you read me?'

Allen's voice came back immediately, acknowledging and confirming his readiness, then he went on, 'The glass just went through the floor, Skipper, she's 996 and going down. Wind's force six rising seven and backing. It looks like we are fair in the dangerous quadrant of whatever is coming.'

'Thank you, David,' Nick replied. 'You warm my heart.'

He stepped forward, and they helped him into the canvas bosun's chair. Nick checked the tackle and rigging, that 'once-more-for-luck' check, and then he nodded.

The interior of the engine room was no longer dark, for Baker had rigged floodlights high above in the ventilation shaft, but the water was black with engine oil, and as Nick was lowered slowly down, with legs dangling from the bosun's chair, it surged furiously back and across like some panic-stricken monster trying to break out of its steel cage. That wind-driven swell was crashing into *Golden Adventurer*'s side and boiling in through the opening, setting up its own wave action, forming its own currents and eddies which broke and leaped angrily against the steel bulkheads.

'Slower,' Nick spoke into the microphone. 'Stop!'

His downward progress was halted ten feet above the starboard main engine block, but the confined surge of water broke over the engine as though it were a coral reef, covering it entirely at one instant, and then sucking back and exposing it again at the next.

The rush of water could throw a man against that machinery with force enough to break every bone in his body, and Nick hung above it and studied the purchases for his blocks.

'Send down the main block,' he ordered, and the huge steel block came down out of the shadows and dangled in the floodlights.

'Stop.' Nick began directing the block into position. 'Down two feet. Stop!'

Now waist-deep in the oily, churning water, he struggled to drive the shackle pin and secure the block to one of the main frames of the hull. Every few minutes a stronger surge would hurl the water over his head, forcing him to cling helplessly, until it relinquished its grip, and his visor cleared sufficiently to allow him to continue his task.

He had to pull out and rest after forty minutes of it. He

sat as close as he could to the heat-exchangers of the running diesel engine of the alternator, taking warmth from them and drinking Angel's strong sweet Thermos coffee. He felt like a fighter between rounds, his body aching, every muscle strained and chilled by the efforts of fighting that filthy churned emulsion of sea water and oil, his flanks and ribs bruised from harsh contact with the submerged machinery. But after twenty minutes, he stood up again.

'Let's go,' he said and resettled the helmet. The hiatus had given him a chance to replan the operation, thinking his way around the problems he had found down there; now the work seemed to fall more readily into place, though he had lost all sense of time alone in the infernal resounding cavern of steel and he was not sure of the hour, or the phase of the day, when at last he was ready to carry the messenger out through the gap.

'Send it down,' he ordered into his headset, and the reel of light line came down, swinging and circling under the glaring floodlights to the ship's motion and throwing grotesque shadows into the far corners of the engine room.

The line was of finely plaited Dacron, with enormous strength and elasticity in relation to its thinness and lightness. One end was secured on the deck high above, and Nick threaded it into the sheave blocks carefully, so that it was free to run.

Then he clamped the reel of line on to his belt, riding it on his hip where it could be protected from snagging when he made the passage of the gap.

He realized then how close to final exhaustion he was, and he considered breaking off the work to rest again, but the heightened action of the sea into the hull warned him against further delay. An hour from now the task might be impossible, he had to go, and he reached for the reserve of strength and purpose deep inside himself, surprised to find that it was still there – for the icy chill of the water seemed to have penetrated his suit and entered his soul, dulling every sense and turning his very bones brittle and heavy.

It must be day outside, he realized, for light came through the gash of steel, pale light further obscured by the filthy muck of mixed oil and water contained in the hull.

He clung to one of the engine-room stringers, his head seven feet from the opening, breathing in the slow, even rhythm of the experienced scuba diver, feeling the ebb and flow through the hull, and trying to find some pattern in the action of the water. But it seemed entirely random, a hissing, bubbling ingestion followed by three or four irregular and weak inflows, then three vicious exhalations of such power that they would have windmilled a swimming man end over into those daggers of splayed steel. He had to choose and ride a middling-sized swell, strong enough to take him through smoothly, without the dangerous power and turbulence of those viciously large swells.

'I'm ready to go now, David,' he said into his helmet. 'Confirm that the work boat is standing by for the pick-up outside the hull.'

'We are all ready.' David Allen's voice was tense and sharp.

'Here we go,' said Nick, this was his wave now. There was no point in waiting longer.

He checked the reel on his belt, ensuring that the line was free to run, and watched the gash suck in clean green water, filled with tiny bright bubbles, little diamond chips that flew past his head to warn him of the lethal speed and power of that flood.

The inflow slowed and stopped as the hull filled to capacity, building up great pressures of air and water, and then the flow reversed abruptly as the swell on the far side subsided, and trapped water began to rush out again.

Nick released his grip on the stringer and instantly the water caught him. There was no question of being able to swim in that mill-race, all he could hope for was to keep his arms at his sides and his legs straight together to give himself a smoother profile, and to steer with his fins.

The accelerating speed appalled him as he was flung head first at that murderous steel mouth, he could feel the nylon line streaming out against his leg, the reel on his belt racing as though a giant marlin had struck and hooked upon the other end.

The rush of his progress seemed to leave his guts behind him as though he rode a fairground rollercoaster, and then a flick of the current turned him, he felt himself beginning to roll – and he fought wildly for control just as he hit.

He hit with a numbing shock, so his vision starred in flashing colour and light. The shock was in his shoulders and left arm, and he thought it might have been severed by that razor steel.

Then he was swirling, end over end, completely disorientated so he did not know which direction was up. He did not know if he was still inside *Golden Adventurer*'s hull, and the nylon line was wrapping itself around his throat and chest, around the precious air tubes and cutting off his air supply like a stillborn infant strangled by its own umbilical cord.

Again he hit something, this time with the back of his head, and only the cushioning of his helmet saved his skull from cracking. He flung out his arms and found the rough irregular shape of ice above him.

Terror wrapped him again, and he screamed soundlessly into his mask, but suddenly he broke out into light and air, into the loose scum of slush and rotten ice mixed with bigger, harder chunks, one of which had hit him.

Above him towered the endless steel cliff of the liner's side and beyond that, the low bruised wind-sky, and as he struggled to disentangle himself from the coils of nylon, he realized two things. The first was that both his arms were still attached to his body, and still functioning, and the second was that *Warlock*'s work boat was only twenty feet away and butting itself busily through the brash of rotten broken ice towards him.

The collision mat looked like a five-ton Airedale terrier curled up to sleep in the bows of the work boat, just as shaggy and shapeless, and of the same wiry, furry brown colour.

Nick had shed his helmet and pulled an Arctic cloak and hood over his bare head and suited torso. He was balanced in the stern of the work boat as she plunged and rolled and porpoised in the big swells; chunks of ice crashed against her hull, knocking loose chips off her paintwork, but she was steel-hulled, wide and sea-kindly. The helmsman knew his job, working her with calm efficiency to Nick's handsignals, bringing her in close through the brash ice, under the tall sheer of *Golden Adventurer*'s stern.

The thin white nylon line was the only physical contact with the men on the liner's towering stack of decks, the messenger which would carry heavier tackle. However it was vulnerable to any jagged piece of pancake ice, or the fangs of that voracious underwater steel jaw.

Nick paid out the line through his own numbed hands, feeling for the slightest check or jerk which could mean a snag and a break-off.

With handsignals, he kept the work boat positioned so that the line ran cleanly into the pierced hull, around the sheave blocks he had placed with such heart-breaking labour in the engine room, from there up the tall ventilation shaft, out of the burned square opening in the stack and around the winch, beside which Beauty Baker was supervising the recovery of the messenger.

The gusts tore at Nick's head so that he had to crouch

to shield the small two-way radio on his chest, and Baker's voice was tinny and thin in the buffeting boom of wind.

'Line running free.'

'Right, we are running the wire now,' Nick told him. The second line was as thick as a man's index finger, and it was of the finest Scandinavian steel cable. Nick checked the connection between nylon and steel cable himself, the nylon messenger was strong enough to carry the weight of steel, but the connection was the weakest point.

He nodded to the crew, and they let it go over the side; the white nylon disappeared into the cold green water and now the black steel cable ran out slowly from the revolving drum.

Nick felt the check as the connection hit the sheave block in the engine room. He felt his heart jump. If it caught now, they would lose it all; no man could penetrate that hull again, the sea was now too vicious. They would lose the tackle, and they would lose *Golden Adventurer*; she would break up in the seas that were coming.

'Please God, let it run,' Nick whispered in the boom and burst of sea wind. The drum halted, made a half turn and jammed. Somewhere down there, the cable had snagged and Nick signalled to the helmsman to take the work boat in closer, to change the angle of the line into the hull.

He could almost feel the strain along his nerves as the winch took up the pull, and he could imagine the fibres of the nylon messenger stretching and creaking.

'Let it run! Let it run!' prayed Nick, and then suddenly he saw the drum begin to revolve again, the cable feeding out smoothly, and streaming down into the sea.

Nick felt light-headed, almost dizzy with relief, as he heard Baker's voice over the VHF, strident with triumph.

'Wire secured.'

'Stand by,' Nick told him. 'We are connecting the two-inch wire now.'

Again, the whole laborious, touchy, nerve-scouring process as the massive two-inch steel cable was drawn out by its thinner, weaker forerunner – and it was a further forty vital minutes, with the wind and sea rising every moment, before Baker shouted, 'Main cable secured, we are ready to haul!'

'Negative,' Nick told him urgently. 'Take the strain and hold.' If the collision mat in the bows hooked and held on the work boat's gunwale, Baker would pull the bows under and swamp her.

Nick signalled to his crew and the five of them shambled up into the bows, bulky and clumsy in their electric-yellow oilskins and work boots. With handsignals, Nick positioned them around the shaggy head-high pile of the collision mat before he signalled to the helmsman to throw the gear in reverse and pull back from *Golden Adventurer*'s side.

The mass of unravelled oakum quivered and shook as the two-inch cable came up taut and they struggled to heave the whole untidy mass overboard.

There was nearly five tons of it and the weight would have been impossible to handle were it not for the reverse pull of the work boat against the cable. Slowly, they heaved the mat forward and outward, and the work boat took on a dangerous list under the transfer of weight. She was down at the bows and canting at an angle of twenty degrees, the diesel motor screaming angrily and her single propeller threshing frantically, trying to pull her out from under her cumbersome burden.

The mat slid forward another foot, and snagged on the gunwale, sea water slopped inboard, ankle-deep around their rubber boots as they strained and heaved at the reluctant mass of coarse fibre.

Some instinct of danger made Nick look up and out to sea. *Warlock* was lying a quarter of a mile farther out in the bay, at the edge of the ice, and beyond her, Nick saw the rearing shape of a big wave alter the line of the horizon. It was merely a forerunner of the truly big waves that the storm was running before her, like hounds before the hunter, but it was big enough to make *Warlock* throw up her stern sharply, and even then the sea creamed over the tug's bows and streamed from her scuppers.

It would hit the exposed and hampered work boat in twenty-five seconds, it would hit her broadside while her bows were held down and anchored by mat and cable. When she swamped, the five men who made up her crew would die within minutes, pulled down by their bulky clothing, frozen by the icy green water.

'Beauty,' Nick's voice was a scream in the microphone, 'heave all – pull, damn you, pull.'

Almost instantly the cable began to run, drawn in by the powerful winch on *Golden Adventurer*'s deck; the strain pulled the work boat down sharply and water cascaded over her gunwale.

Nick seized one of the oaken oars and thrust it under the mat at the point where it was snagged, and using it as a lever he threw all his weight upon it.

'Lend a hand,' he yelled at the man beside him, and he strained until he felt his vision darkening and the fibres of his back muscles creaking and popping.

The work boat was swamping, they were almost knee-deep now and the wave raced down on them. It came with a great silent rush of irresistible power, lifting the mass of broken ice and tossing it carelessly aside without a check.

Suddenly, the snag cleared and the whole lumpy massive weight of oakum slid overboard. The work boat bounded away, relieved of her intolerable burden, and Nick windmilled frantically with both arms to get the helmsman to bring her bows round to the wave.

They went up the wave with a gut-swooping rush that threw them down on to the floorboards of the half-flooded work boat, and then crashed over the crest.

Behind them the wave slogged into *Golden Adventurer*'s stern, and shot up it with an explosion of white and furious water that turned to white driven spray in the wind.

The helmsman already had the work boat pushing heavily through the pack-ice, back towards the waiting *Warlock*.

'Stop,' Nick signalled him. 'Back up.'

Already he was struggling out of his hood and oilskins, as he staggered back to the stern.

He shouted in the helmsman's face, 'I'm going down to check,' and he saw the disbelieving, almost pleading, expression on the man's face. He wanted to get out of there now, back to the safety of *Warlock*, but relentlessly Nick resettled the diving helmet and connected his air hose.

The collision mat was floating hard against *Golden Adventurer*'s side, buoyant with trapped air among the mass of wiry fibre.

Nick positioned himself beneath it, twenty feet from the maelstrom created by the gashed steel.

It took him only a few seconds to ensure that the cable was free, and he blessed Beauty Baker silently for stopping the winch immediately it had pulled the mat free of the work boat. Now he could direct the final task.

'She's looking good,' he told Baker. 'But take her up slowly, fifty feet a minute on the winch.'

'Fifty feet, it is,' Baker confirmed.

And slowly the bobbing mat was drawn down below the surface.

'Good, keep it at that.'

It was like pressing a field-dressing into an open bleeding wound. The outside pressure of water drove it deep into the gash, while from the inside the two-inch cable plugged it deeper into place. The wound was staunched almost instantly and Nick finned down, and swam carefully over it.

The deadly suck and blow of high pressure through the gap was killed now, and he detected only the lightest movement of water around the edges of the mat; but the oakum fibres would swell now they were submerged and, within hours, the plug would be watertight.

'It's done,' said Nick into his microphone. 'Hold a twenty-ton pull on the cable – and you can start your pumps and suck the bitch clean.'

It was a measure of his stress and relief and fatigue that Nick called that beautiful ship a bitch, and he regretted the word as soon as it was spoken.

Nick craved sleep, every nerve, every muscle shrieked for surcease, and in his bathroom mirror his eyes were inflamed, angry with salt and wind and cold; the smears of exhaustion that underlined them were as lurid as the fresh bruises and abrasions that covered his shoulders and thighs and ribs.

His hands shook in a mild palsy with the need for rest and his legs could hardly carry him as he forced himself back to *Warlock*'s navigation bridge.

'Congratulations, sir,' said David Allen, and his admiration was transparent.

'How's the glass, David?' Nick asked, trying to keep the weariness from showing.

'994 and dropping, sir.'

Nick looked across at *Golden Adventurer*. Below that dingy low sky, she stood like a pier, unmoved by the big swells that marched on her in endless ranks, and she shrugged aside each burst of spray, hard aground and heavy with the water in her womb. However, that water was being flung from her, in solid white sheets.

Baker's big centrifugals were running at full power, and from both her port and starboard quarters the water poured. It looked as though the floodgates had been opened on a concrete dam, so powerful was the rush of expelled water.

The oil and diesel mixed with that discharge formed a sullen, iridescent slick around her, sullying the ice and the pebble beach on which she lay. The wind caught the jets from the pump outlets and tore them away in glistening plumes, like great ostrich feathers of spray.

'Chief,' Nick called the ship. 'What's your discharge rate?'

'We are moving nigh on five hundred thousand gallons an hour.'

'Call me as soon as she alters her trim,' he said, and then glanced up at the pointer of the anemometer above the control panel. The wind force was riding eight now, but he had to blink his stinging swollen eyes to read the scale.

'David,' he said, and he could hear the hoarseness in his voice, the flat dead tone. 'It will be four hours before she will be light enough to make an attempt to haul her off, but I want you to put the main towing cable on board her and make fast, so we will be ready when she is.'

'Sir.'

'Use a rocket-line,' said Nick, and then stood dumbly, trying to think of the other orders he must give, but his brain was blank.

'Are you all right, sir?' David asked with quick concern, and immediately Nick felt the prick of annoyance. He had never wanted sympathy in his life, and he found his voice again. But he stopped the sharp words that came so quickly to his lips.

'You know what to do, David. I won't give you any other advice.' He turned like a drunkard towards his quarters. 'Call me when you've done it, or if Baker reports alteration of trim – or if anything else changes, anything, anything at all, you understand.'

He made it to the cabin before his knees buckled and he dropped his terry robe as he toppled backwards on to his bunk.

At 60° south latitude, there runs the only sea lane that circumnavigates the entire globe, unbroken by any land mass. This wide girdle of open water runs south of Cape Horn and Australasia and the Cape of Good Hope, and it has the fearsome reputation of breeding the wildest weather on earth. It is the meeting-ground of two vast air masses, the cold slumping Antarctic air, and the warmer, more buoyant airs of the subtropics. These are flung together by the centrifugal forces generated by the earth as it revolves on its own axis, and their movement is further complicated by the enormous torque of the Coriolis force. As they strike each other, the opposing air masses split into smaller fragments that retain their individual characteristics. They begin to revolve upon themselves, gigantic whirlpools of tortured air, and as they advance, so they gain in strength and power and velocity.

The high-pressure system which had brought that ominously calm and silken weather to Cape Alarm, had bounced the pressure right up to 1035 millibars, while the great depression which pursued it so closely and swiftly had a centre pressure as low as 985 millibars. Such a sharp contrast meant that the winds along the pressure gradient were ferocious.

The depression itself was almost fifteen hundred miles across its circumference, and it reached up to the high troposphere, thirty thousand feet above the level of the sea. The mighty winds it contained reached right off the maximum of the Beaufort scale of force twelve, gusting 120 miles an hour and more. They roared unfettered upon a terrible sea, unchecked by the bulwark of any land mass, nothing in their path, but the sudden jagged barrier of Cape Alarm.

While Nicholas Berg slept the deathlike sleep of utter exhaustion, and Beauty Baker tended his machines, driving them to their limits in an effort to pump *Golden Adventurer* free of her burden of salt water, the storm rushed down upon them.

When her knock was unanswered, Samantha stood uncertainly, balancing the heavy tray against the *Warlock*'s extravagant action as she rode the rising swells at the entrance to the bay.

Her uncertainty lasted not more than three seconds, for she was a lady given to swift decisions. She tried the door-latch and when it turned, she pushed it open slowly enough to warn anybody on the far side, and stepped into the Captain's day cabin.

'He ordered food,' she justified her intrusion, and closed the door behind her, glancing swiftly around the empty cabin. It had been furnished in the high style of the old White Star liners. Real rosewood panelling and the couch and chairs were in rich brown calf hide, polished and buttoned, while the deck was carpeted in thick shaggy wool, the colour of tropical forest leaves.

Samantha placed the tray on the table that ran below the starboard portholes, and she called softly. There was no reply, and she stepped to the open doorway into the night cabin.

A white terry robe lay in a heap in the centre of the deck, and she thought for one disturbing moment that the body on the bed was naked, but then she saw he wore a thin pair of white silk boxer shorts.

'Captain Berg,' she called again, but softly enough not to disturb him, and with a completely feminine gesture picked up the robe from the floor, folded it and dropped it over a chair, moving forward at the same time until she stood beside his bunk.

She felt a quick flare of concern when she saw the bruises which stood out so vividly on the smooth pale skin, and concern turned to dismay when she realized how he lay like a dead man, his legs trailing over the edge of the bunk and his body twisted awkwardly, one arm thrown back over his shoulder and his head lolling from side to side as *Warlock* rolled.

She reached out quickly and touched his cheek, experiencing a lift of real relief as she felt the warmth of his flesh and saw his eyelids quiver at her touch.

Gently she lifted his legs and he rolled easily on to his side, exposing the sickening abrasion that wrapped itself angrily across back and shoulder. She touched it with a light exploring fingertip and knew that it needed attention, but she sensed that rest was what he needed more.

She stood back and for long seconds gave herself over to the pleasure of looking at him. His body was fined down, he carried no fat on his belly or flanks; clearly she could see the rack of his ribs below the skin, and the muscles of his arms and legs were smooth but well defined, a body that had been cared for and honed by hard exercise. Yet there was a certain denseness to it, that thickening of shoulder and neck, and the distinctive hair patterns of the mature man.

It might not have the grace and delicacy of the boys she had known, yet it was more powerful than that of even the strongest of the young men who had until then filled her world. She thought of one of them whom she had believed she loved. They had spent two months in Tahiti together on the same field expedition. She had surfed with him, danced and drunk wine, worked and slept sixty consecutive days and nights with him; in the same period they had become engaged to marry, and had argued, and parted, with surprisingly little regret on her part – but he had had the most beautifully tanned and sculptured body she had ever known. Now, looking at the sleeping figure on the bunk, she knew that even he would not have been able to match this man in physical determination and strength.

Angel had been right. It was the power that attracted her so strongly. The powerful, rangy body with the dark coarse hair covering his chest and exploding in flak bursts in his armpits – this, together with the power of his presence.

She had never known a man like this, he filled her with a sense of awe. It was not only the legend that surrounded him, nor the formidable list of his accomplishments that Angel had recounted for her, nor yet was it only the physical strength which he had just demonstrated while the entire crew of *Warlock*, she among them, had watched and listened avidly over the VHF relay. She leaned over him again, and she saw that even in repose, his jawline was hard and uncompromising, and the little creases and lines and marks that life had chiselled into his face, around the eyes at the corners of the mouth, heightened the effect of power and determination, the face of a man who dictated his own terms to life.

She wanted him. Angel was right, oh God, how she wanted him! They said there was no love at first sight – they had to be mad.

She turned away and unfolded the eiderdown from the foot of the bunk, spreading it over him, and then once again she stooped and gently lifted the fall of thick dark hair from his forehead, smoothing it back with a maternally protective gesture.

Although he had slept on while she lifted and covered him, strangely this lightest of touches brought him to the edge of consciousness and he sighed and twisted, then whispered hoarsely, 'Chantelle, is that you?'

Samantha recoiled at the bitter sharp pang of jealousy with which another woman's name stabbed her. She turned away and left him, but in the day cabin she paused again beside his desk.

There were a few small personal items thrown carelessly on the leather-bound blotter – a gold money clip holding a mixed sheath of currency notes, five pounds sterling, fifty US dollars, Deutschmarks and francs, a gold Rolex Oyster perpetual watch, a gold Dunhill lighter with a single white diamond set in it, and a billfold of the smoothest finest calf leather. They described clearly the man who owned them and, feeling like a thief, she picked up the billfold and opened it.

There were a dozen cards in their little plastic envelopes, American Express, Diners, Bank American, Carte Blanche, Hertz No. 1, Pan Am VIP and the rest. But opposite them was a colour photograph. Three people: a man, Nicholas in a cable-stitch jersey, his face bronzed, his hair windruffled; a small boy in a yachting jacket with a mop of curly hair and solemn eyes above a smiling mouth – and a woman. She was probably one of the most beautiful women Samantha had ever seen, and she closed the billfold, replaced it carefully, and quietly left the cabin.

David Allen called the Captain's suite for three minutes without an answer, slapping his open palm on the mahogany chart table with impatience and staring through the navigation windows at the spectacle of a world gone mad.

For almost two hours, the wind had blown steadily from

the north-west at a little over thirty knots, and although the big lumpy seas still tumbled into the mouth of the bay, *Warlock* had ridden them easily, even connected, as she was, to *Golden Adventurer* by the main tow-cable.

David had put a messenger over the liner's stern, firing the nylon line from a rocket gun, and Baker's men had retrieved the line and winched across first the carrier wire and then the main cable itself.

Warlock had let the main cable be drawn out of her by *Adventurer*'s winches, slowly revolving off the great winch drums in the compartment under the tug's stern deck, out through the cable ports below the after navigation bridge where David stood controlling each inch of run and play with light touches on the controls.

A good man could work that massive cable like a fly-fisherman playing a big salmon in the turbulent water of a mountain torrent, letting it slip against the clutchplates, or run free, or recover slack, bringing it up hard and fast under a pull of five hundred tons – or, in dire emergency, he could hit the shear button, and snip through the flexible steel fibre, instantaneously relinquishing the tow, possibly saving the tug itself from being pulled under or being rushed by the vessel it was towing.

It had taken an hour of delicate work, but now the tow was in place, a double yoke made fast to *Golden Adventurer*'s main deck bollards, one on her starboard and one on her port stern quarters.

The yoke was Y-shaped, drooping over the high stern to join at the white nylon spring, three times the thickness of a man's thigh and with the elasticity to absorb sudden shock which might have snapped rigid steel cable. From the yoke connection, the single main cable looped back to the tug.

David Allen was lying back a thousand yards from the shore, holding enough strain on the tow-cable to prevent it from sagging to touch and possibly snag on the unknown bottom. He was holding his station with gentle play on the pitch and power of the twin screws, and checking his exact position against the electronic dials which gave him his speed across the ground in both directions, accurate to within a foot a minute.

It was all nicely under control, and every time he glanced up at the liner, the discharge of water still boiled from her pump outlets.

Half an hour previously, he had been unable to contain his impatience, for he knew with a seaman's deep instinct what was coming down upon them out of the dangerous quadrant of the wind. He had called Baker to ask how the work on the liner was progressing. It had been a mistake.

'You've got nothing better to do than call me out of the engine room to ask about my piles, and the FA Cup final? I'll tell you when I'm ready, believe me, sonny, I'll call you. If you are bored, go down and give Angel a kiss, but for God's sake, leave me alone.'

Beauty Baker was working with two of his men in that filthy, freezing steel box deep down in the liner's stern that housed the emergency steering-gear. The rudder was right across at full port lock. Unless he could get power on the steering machinery, she would be almost unmanageable, once she was under tow, especially if she was pulled off stern first. It was vital that the big ship was responding to her helm when *Warlock* tried to haul her off.

Baker cursed and cajoled the greasy machinery, knocking loose a flap of thick white skin from his knuckles when a spanner slipped, but working on grimly without even bothering to lift the injury to his mouth to suck away the welling blood. He let it drop on to the spanner and thicken into a sticky jelly, swearing softly but viciously as he concentrated all his skills on the obdurate steel mass of the steering gear. He knew every bit as well as the First Officer what was coming down upon them.

The wind had dropped to a gentle force four, a moderate

153

steady breeze that blew for twenty minutes, just long enough for the crests of the waves to stop breaking over on themselves. Then slowly, it veered north – and without any further warning, it was upon them.

It came roaring like a ravening beast, lifting the surface of the sea away in white sheets of spray that looked as though red-hot steel had been quenched in it. It laid *Warlock* right over, so that her port rail went under and she was flung up so harshly on her main cable that her stern was pulled down sharply, water pouring in through her stern scuppers.

It took David by surprise, so that she paid off dangerously before he could slam open the port throttle and throw the starboard screw into full reverse thrust. As she came up, he hit the call to the Captain's suite, watching with rising disbelief as the mad world dissolved around him.

Nick heard the call from far away, it only just penetrated to his fatigue-drugged brain, and he tried to respond, but it felt as though his body was crushed under an enormous weight and that his brain was slow and sluggish as a hibernating reptile.

The buzzer insisted, a tinny, nagging whine and he tried to force his eyes open, but they would not respond. Then dimly, but deeply, he felt the wild anguished action of his ship and the tumult that he believed at first was in his own ears, but was the violent uproar of the storm about the tug's superstructure.

He forced himself up on one elbow, and his body ached in every joint. He still could not open his eyes but he groped for the handset.

'Captain to the after bridge!' He could hear something in David Allen's voice that forced him to his feet.

When Nick staggered on to the after navigation bridge, the First Officer turned gratefully to him.

'Thank God you've come, sir.'

The wind had taken the surface off the sea, had stripped it away, tearing each wave to a shrieking fog of white spray and mingling it with the sleet and snow that drove horizontally across the bay.

Nick glanced once at the dial of the wind anemometer, and then discounted the reading. The needle was stuck at the top of the scale. It made no sense, a wind speed of 120 miles an hour was too much to accept, the instrument had been damaged by the initial gusts of this wind, and he refused to believe it; to do so now would be to admit disaster, for nobody could salvage an ocean-going liner in wind velocities right off the Beaufort scale.

Warlock stood on her tail, like a performing dolphin begging for a meal, as the cable brought her up short and the bridge deck became a vertical cliff down which Nick was hurled. He crashed into the control panel and clung for purchase to the foul-weather rail.

'We'll have to shear the cable and stand out to sea.' David Allen's voice was pitched too high and too loud, even for the tumult of the wind and the storm.

There were men on board *Golden Adventurer*; Baker and sixteen others, Nick thought swiftly, and even her twin anchors could not be trusted to hold in this.

Nick clung to the rail and peered out into the storm. Frozen spray and sleet and impacted snow drove on the wind, coming in with the force of buckshot fired at point-blank range, cracking into the armoured glass of the bridge and building up in thick clots and lumps that defeated the efforts of the spinning 'clear vision' panels.

He looked across a thousand yards and the hull of the liner was just visible, a denser area in the howling, swirling, white wilderness.

'Baker?' he asked into the hand microphone. 'What is your position?'

'The wind's got her, she's slewing. The starboard anchor is dragging.' And then, while Nick thought swiftly, 'You'll

155

not be able to take us off in this.' It was a flat statement, an acceptance of the fact that the destinies of Baker and his sixteen men were inexorably linked to that of the doomed ship.

'No,' Nick agreed. 'We won't be able to get you off.' To approach the stricken ship was certain disaster for all of them.

'Shear the cable and stand off,' Baker advised. 'We'll try to get ashore as she breaks up.' Then, with a hangman's chuckle, he went on, 'Just don't forget to come and fetch us when the weather moderates – that is if there is anybody to fetch.'

Abruptly Nick's anger came to the surface through the layers of fatigue, anger at the knowledge that all he had risked and suffered was now to be in vain, that he was to lose *Golden Adventurer*, and probably with her sixteen men, one of whom had become a friend.

'Are you ready to heave on the anchor winches?' he asked. 'We are going to pull the bitch off.'

'Jesus!' said Baker. 'She's still half flooded—'

'We will have a lash at it, cobber,' said Nick quietly.

'The steering-gear is locked, you won't be able to control her. You'll lose *Warlock* as well as—' but Nicholas cut Baker short.

'Listen, you stupid Queensland sheep-shagger, get on to those winches.' As he said it, *Golden Adventurer* disappeared, her bulk blotted out completely by the solid, white curtains of the blizzard.

'Engine room,' Nick spoke crisply to the Second Engineer. 'Disengage the override, and give me direct control of both power and pitch.'

'Control transferred to bridge, sir,' the Engineer confirmed, and Nick touched the shining stainless-steel levers with fingers as sensitive as those of a concert pianist. *Warlock*'s response was instantaneous. She pivoted, shrugging aside a green slithering burst of water which came in

156

over her shoulder and thundered down the side of her superstructure.

'Anchor winches manned.' Beauty Baker's tone was almost casual.

'Stand by,' said Nick, and felt his way through that white inferno. It was impossible to maintain visual reference, the entire world was white and swirling, even the surface of the sea was gone in torn streamers of white; the very pull of gravity, that should have defined even a simple up or down, was confused by the violent pitch and roll of the deck.

Nick felt his exhausted brain begin to lurch dizzily in the first attacks of vertigo. Swiftly he switched his attention to the big compass and the heading indicator.

'David,' he said, 'take the wheel.' He wanted somebody swift and bright at the helm now.

Warlock plunged suddenly, so viciously that Nick's bruised ribs were brought in brutal contact with the edge of the control console. He grunted involuntarily with the pain. *Warlock* was feeling her cable, she had come up hard.

'Starboard ten,' said Nick to David, bringing her bows up into that hideous wind.

'Chief,' he spoke into the microphone, his voice still ragged with the pain in his chest. 'Haul starboard winch, full power.'

'Full power starboard.'

Nick slid pitch control to fully fine, and then slowly nudged open the throttles, bringing in twenty-two thousand horse-power.

Held by her tail, driven by the great wind, and tortured by the sea, lashed by her own enormous propellers, *Warlock* went berserk. She corkscrewed and porpoised to her very limits, every frame in her hull shook with the vibration of her screws as her propellers burst out of the surface and spun wildly in the air.

Nick had to clench his jaws as the vibration threatened to crack his teeth, and when he glanced across at the forward and lateral speed-indicators, he saw that David Allen's face was icy white and set like that of a corpse.

Warlock was slewing down on the wind, describing a slow left-hand circle at the limit of the cable as the engine torque and the wind took her around.

'Starboard twenty,' Nick snapped, correcting the turn, and despite the rigour of his features, David Allen's response was instantaneous.

'Twenty degrees of starboard wheel on, sir.'

Nick saw the lateral drift stop on the ground speed-indicator, and then with a wild lurch of elation he saw the forward speed-indicator flicked into green. Its electronic digital read out, changing swiftly – they were moving forward at 150 feet a minute.

'We are moving her,' Nick cried aloud, and he snatched up the microphone.

'Full power both winches.'

'Both full and holding,' answered Baker immediately.

And Nick glanced back at the forward speed across the ground, 150, 110, 75 feet a minute, *Warlock*'s forward impetus slowed, and Nick realized with a slide of dismay that it was merely the elasticity of the nylon spring that had given them that reading. The spring was stretching out to its limit.

For two or three seconds, the dial recorded a zero rate of speed. *Warlock* was standing still, the cable drawn out to the full limit of her strength, then abruptly the dial flicked into vivid red; they were going backwards, as the nylon spring exerted pressures beyond that of the twin diesels and the big bronze screws – *Warlock* was being dragged back towards that dreadful shore.

For another five minutes, Nick kept both clenched fists on the control levers, pressing them with all his strength to the limit of their travel, sending the great engines shrieking, driving the needles up around the dials, deep into the red 'never exceed' sectors.

He felt tears of anger and frustration scalding his swollen eyelids, and the ship shuddered and shook and screamed under him, her torment transmitted through the soles of his feet and the palms of his hands.

Warlock was held down by cable and power, so she could not rise to meet the seas that came out of the roaring whiteness. They tumbled aboard her, piling up on each other, so she burrowed deeper and more dangerously.

'For God's sake, sir,' David Allen was no longer able to contain himself. His eyes looked huge in his bone-white face. 'You'll drive her clean under.'

'Baker,' Nick ignored his Mate, 'Are you gaining?'

'No recovery either winch,' Beauty told him. 'She is not moving.'

Nick pulled back the stainless steel levers, the needles sank swiftly back around their dials, and *Warlock* reacted gratefully, shaking herself free of the piled waters.

'You'll have to shear the tow.' Baker's disembodied voice was muted by the clamour of the storm. 'We'll take our chances, sport.'

Beside him, David Allen reached for the red-painted steel box that housed the shear button. It was protected by the box from accidental usage; David Allen opened the box and looked expectantly, almost pleadingly, at Nick.

'Belay that!' Nick snarled at him, and then to Baker, 'I'm shortening tow. Be ready to haul again, when I am in position.'

David Allen stared at him, his right hand still on the open lid of the red box.

'Close that bloody thing,' Nick said, and turned to the main cable controls. He moved the green lever to reverse, and felt the vibration in the deck as below him in the main cable room the big drums began to revolve, drawing the thick ice-encrusted cable up over *Warlock*'s stern.

Fighting every inch of the way like a wild horse on a head halter, *Warlock* was drawn in cautiously by her own winches, and the officers watched in mounting horror as out of the white terror of the blizzard emerged the mountainous ice-covered bulk of *Golden Adventurer*.

She was so close that the main cable no longer dipped below the surface of the sea, but ran directly from the liner's stern to the tug's massive fairleads on her stern quarter.

'Now we can see what we are doing,' Nick told them grimly. He could see now that much of *Warlock*'s power had been wasted by not exerting a pull on exactly the same plane as *Golden Adventurer*'s keel. He had been disoriented in the white-out of the blizzard, and had allowed *Warlock* to pull at an angle. It would not happen now.

'Chief,' he said. 'Pull, pull all, pull until she bursts her guts!' And again he slid the throttle handles fully home.

Warlock flung up against the elastic yoke, and Nick saw the water spurt from the woven fibres and turn instantly to ice crystals as it was whipped away on the shrieking wind.

'She's not moving, sir,' David cried beside him.

'No recovery either winch,' Baker confirmed almost immediately. 'She's solid!'

'Too much water still in her,' said David, and Nick turned on him as though to strike him to the deck.

'Give me the wheel,' he said, his voice cracking with his anger and frustration.

With both engines boiling the sea to white foam, and roaring like dying bulls, Nick swung the wheel to full port lock.

Wildly *Warlock* dug her shoulder in, water pouring on board her as she rolled, instantly Nick spun the wheel to full starboard lock and she lurched against the tow, throwing an extra ton of pressure on to it.

Even above the storm, they heard *Golden Adventurer* groan, the steel of her hull protesting at the weight of water in her and the intolerable pressure of the anchor winches and *Warlock*'s tow cable.

The groan became a crackling hiss as the pebble bottom gave and moved under her.

'Christ, she's coming!' shrieked Baker, and Nick swung her to full port lock again, swinging *Warlock* into a deep trough between waves, then a solid ridge of steaming water buried her, and Nick was not certain she could survive that press of furious sea. It came green and slick over the superstructure and she shuddered wearily, gone slow and unwieldy. Then she lifted her bows and, like a spaniel, shook herself free, becoming again quick and light.

'Pull, my darling, pull,' Nick pleaded with her.

With a slow reluctant rumble, *Golden Adventurer*'s hull began to slide over the holding, clinging bottom.

'Both winches recovering,' Baker howled gleefully, and *Warlock*'s ground speed-indicator flicked into the green, its little angular figures changing in twinkling electronic progression as *Warlock* gathered way.

They all saw *Golden Adventurer*'s stern swinging to meet the next great ridge of water as it burst around her. She was floating, and for moments Nick was paralysed by the wonder of seeing that great and beautiful ship come to life again, become a living, vital sea creature as she took the seas and rose to meet them.

'We've done it, Christ, we've done it!' howled Baker, but it was too soon for self-congratulation. As *Golden Adventurer* came free of the ground and gathered sternway under *Warlock*'s tow, so her rudder bit and swung her tall stern across the wind.

She swung, exposing the enormous windage of her starboard side to the full force of the storm. It was like setting a mainsail, and the wind took her down swiftly on the rocky headland with its sentinel columns that guarded the entrance to the bay.

Nick's first instinct was to try and hold her off, to oppose

161

the force of the wind directly, and he flung *Warlock* into the task, relying on her great diesels and the two anchors to keep the liner from going ashore again – but the wind toyed with them, it ripped the anchors out of the pebble bottom and *Warlock* was drawn stern first through the water, straight down on the jagged rock of the headland.

'Chief, get those anchors up,' Nick snapped into the microphone. 'They'll never hold in this.'

Twenty years earlier, bathing off a lonely beach in the Seychelles, Nick had been caught out of his depth by one of those killer currents that flow around the headlands of oceanic islands, and it had sped him out into the open sea so that within minutes the silhouette of the land was low and indistinct on his watery horizon. He had fought that current, swimming directly against it, and it had nearly killed him. Only in the last stages of exhaustion had he begun to think, and instead of battling it, he had ridden the current, angling slowly across it, using its impetus rather than opposing it.

The lesson he had learned that day was well remembered, and as he watched Baker bring *Golden Adventurer*'s dripping anchors out of the wild water he was driving *Warlock* hard, bringing her around on her cable so the wind was no longer in her teeth, but over her stern quarter.

Now the wind and *Warlock*'s screws were no longer opposed, but *Warlock* was pulling two points off the wind, as fine a course as Nick could judge barely to clear the most seaward of the rocky sentinels; now the liner's locked rudder was holding her steady into the wind – but opposing *Warlock*'s attempt to angle her away from the land.

It was a problem of simple vectors of force, that Nick tried to work out in his head and prove in physical terms, as he delicately judged the angle of his tow and the direction of the wind, balancing them against the tremendous leverage of the liner's locked rudder, the rudder which was dragging her suicidally down upon the land.

Grimly, he stared ahead to where the black rock cliffs were still hidden in the white nothingness. They were invisible, but their presence was recorded on the cluttered screen of the radar repeater. With both wind and engines driving them, their speed was too high, and if *Golden Adventurer* went on to the cliffs like this, her hull would shatter like a watermelon hurled against a brick wall.

It was another five minutes before Nick was absolutely certain they would not make it. They were only two miles off the cliffs now, he glanced again at the radar screen, and they would have to drag *Golden Adventurer* at least half a mile across the wind to clear the land. They were just not going to make it.

Helplessly, Nick stood and peered into the storm, waiting for the first glimpse of black rock through the swirling eddies of snow and frozen spray, and he had never felt more tired and unmanned in his entire life as he moved to the shear button, ready to cut *Golden Adventurer* loose and let her go to her doom.

His officers were silent and tense around him, while under his feet *Warlock* shuddered and buffeted wildly, driven to her mortal limits by the sea and her own engines, but still the land sucked at them.

'Look!' David Allen shouted suddenly, and Nick spun to the urgency in his voice.

For a moment he did not understand what was happening. He knew only that the shape of *Golden Adventurer*'s stern was altered subtly.

'The rudder,' shouted David Allen again. And Nick saw it revolving slowly on its stock as the ship lifted on another big sea.

Almost immediately, he felt *Warlock* making offing from under that lee shore, and he swung her up another point into the wind, *Golden Adventurer* answering her tow with a more docile air, and still the rudder revolved slowly.

'I've got power on the emergency steering gear now,' said Baker.

'Rudder amidships,' Nick ordered.

'Amidships it is,' Baker repeated, and now he was pulling her out stern first, almost at right angles across the wind.

Through the white inferno appeared the dim snow-blurred outline of the rock sentinels, and the sea broke upon them like the thunder of the heavens.

'God, they are close,' whispered David Allen. So close that they could feel the backlash of the gale as it rebounded from the tall rock walls, moderating the tremendous force that was bearing them down – moderating just enough to allow them to slide past the three hungry rocks, and before them lay three thousand miles of wild and tumultuous water, all of it open sea room.

'We made it. This time we really made it,' said Baker, as though he did not believe it was true, and Nick pulled back the throttle controls taking the intolerable strain off her engines before they tore themselves to pieces.

'Anchors and all,' Nick replied. It was a point of honour to retrieve even the anchors. They had taken her off clean and intact – anchors and all.

'Chief,' he said, 'instead of sitting there hugging yourself, how about pumping her full of Tannerax?' The anti-corrosive chemical would save her engines and much of her vital equipment from further sea-water damage, adding enormously to her salvaged value.

'You just never let up, do you?' Baker answered accusingly.

'Don't you believe it,' said Nick. He felt stupid and frivolous with exhaustion and triumph. Even the storm that still roared about them seemed to have lost its murderous intensity. 'Right now I'm going down to my bunk to sleep for twelve hours – and I'll kill anybody who tries to wake me.'

164

He hung the handmike on its bracket and put his hand on David Allen's shoulder. He squeezed once, and said:

'You did well – you all did very well. Now take her, Number One, and look after her.'

Then he stumbled from the bridge.

It was eight days before they saw the land again. They rode out the storm in the open sea, eight days of unrelenting tension and heart-breaking labour.

The first task was to move the two-cable to *Golden Adventurer*'s bows. In that sea, the transfer took almost 24 hours, and three abortive attempts before they had her head-on to the wind. Now she rode more easily, and *Warlock* had merely to hang on like a drogue, using full power only when one of the big icebergs came within dangerous range, and it was necessary to draw her off.

However, the tension was always there and Nick spent most of those days on the bridge, watchful and worried, nagged by the fear that the plug in the gashed hull would not hold. Baker used timbers from the ship's store to shore up the temporary patch, but he could not put steel in place while *Golden Adventurer* plunged and rolled in the heavy seas, and Nick could not go aboard to check and supervise the work.

Slowly, the great wheel of low pressure revolved over them, the winds changed direction, backing steadily into the west, as the epicentre marched on down the sea lane towards Australasia – and at last it had passed.

Now *Warlock* could work up towing speed. Even in those towering glassy swells of black water that the storm had left them as a legacy, she was able to make four knots.

Then one clear and windy morning under a cold yellow sun, she brought *Golden Adventurer* into the sheltered waters of Shackleton Bay. It was like a diminutive guide-dog leading a blinded colossus.

As the two ships came up into the still waters under the sheltering arm of the bay, the survivors came down from their encampment to the water's edge, lining the steep black pebble beach, and their cheers and shouts of welcome and relief carried thinly on the wind to the officers on Warlock's bridge.

Even before the liner's twin anchors splashed into the clear green water, Captain Reilly's boat was puttering out to Warlock, and when he came aboard, his eyes were haunted by the hardship and difficulties of these last days, by the disaster of a lot command and the lives that had been ended with it. But when he shook hands with Nick, his grasp was firm.

'My thanks and congratulations, sir!'

He had known Nicholas Berg as Chairman of Christy Marine, and, as no other, he was aware of the magnitude of this most recent accomplishment. His respect was apparent.

'It's good to see you again,' Nick told him. 'Naturally you have access to my ship's communications to report to your owners.'

Immediately he turned back to the task of manoeuvring Warlock alongside, so that steel plate could be swung up from her salvage holds to the liner's deck; it was another hour before Captain Reilly emerged from the radio room.

'Can I offer you a drink, Captain?' Nick led him to his day cabin, and began with tact to deal with the hundred details which had to be settled between them. It was a delicate situation, for Reilly was no longer Master of his own ship. Command had passed to Nicholas as salvage master.

'The accommodation aboard Golden Adventurer is still quite serviceable, and, I imagine, a great deal warmer and more comfortable than that occupied by your passengers at

166

present—' Nick made it easier for him while never for a moment letting him lose sight of his command position, and Reilly responded gratefully.

Within half an hour, they had made all the necessary arrangements to transfer the survivors aboard the liner. Levoisin on La Mouette had been able to take only one hundred and twenty supernumeraries on board his little tug. The oldest and weakest of them had gone and Christy Marine was negotiating for a charter from Cape Town to Shackleton Bay to take off the rest of them. Now that charter was unnecessary, but the cost of it would form part of Nick's claim for salvage award.

'I won't take up more of your time.' Reilly drained his glass and stood. 'You have much to do.'

There were another four days and nights of hard work. Nick went aboard Golden Adventurer and saw the cavernous engine room lit by the eye-scorching blue glare of the electric welding flames, as Baker placed his steel over the wound and welded it into place. Even then, neither he nor Nick was satisfied until the new patches had been shored and stiffened with baulks of heavy timber. There was a hard passage through the roaring forties ahead of them, and until they had Golden Adventurer safely moored in Cape Town docks, the salvage was incomplete.

They sat side by side among the greasy machinery and the stink of the anti-corrosives, and drank steaming Thermos coffee laced with Bundaberg rum.

'We get this beauty into Duncan Docks – and you are going to be a rich man,' Nick said.

'I've been rich before. With me it never lasts long – and it's always a relief when I've spent the stuff.' Beauty gargled the rum and coffee appreciatively, before he went on, shrewdly. 'So you don't have to worry about losing the best goddamned engineer afloat.'

Nick laughed with delight. Baker had read him accurately. He did not want to lose this man.

Nick left him and went to see to the trim of the liner, studying her carefully and using the experience of the last days to determine her best points of tow, before giving his orders to David Allen to raise her slightly by the head.

Then there was the transfer from the liner's bunkers of sufficient bunker oil to top up *Warlock*'s own tanks against the long tow ahead, and Bach Wackie in Bermuda kept the telex clattering with relays from underwriters and Lloyd's, with the first tentative advances from Christy Marine; already Duncan Alexander was trying out the angles, manoeuvring for a liberal settlement of Nick's claims, without, as he put it, the expense of the arbitration court.

'Tell him I'm going to roast him,' Nick answered with grim relish. 'Remind him that as Chairman of Christy Marine I advised against underwriting our own bottoms – and now I'm going to rub his nose in it.'

The days and nights blurred together, the illusion made complete by the imbalance of time down here in the high latitudes, so that Nick could often believe neither his senses nor his watch when he had been working eighteen hours straight and yet the sun still burned, and his watch told him it was three o'clock in the morning.

Then again, it did not seem part of reality when his senior officers, gathered around the mahogany table in his day cabin, reported that the work was completed – the repairs and preparation, the loading of fuel, the embarkation of passengers and the hundred other details had all been attended to, and *Warlock* was ready to drag her massive charge out into the unpredictable sea, thousands of miles to the southernmost tip of Africa.

Nick passed the cheroot-box around the circle and while the blue smoke clouded the cabin, he allowed them all a few minutes to luxuriate in the feeling of work done, and done well.

'We'll rest the ship's company for twenty-four hours,' he

announced in a rush of generosity. 'And take in tow at 0800 hours Monday. I'm hoping for a two speed of six knots – twenty-one days to Cape Town, gentlemen.'

When they rose to leave, David Allen lingered self-consciously. 'The wardroom is arranging a little Christmas celebration tonight, sir, and we would like you to be our guest.'

The wardroom was the junior officers' club from which, traditionally, the Master was excluded. He could enter the small panelled cabin only as an invited guest, but there was no doubt at all about the genuine warmth of the welcome they gave him. Even the Trog was there. They stood and applauded him when he entered, and it was clear that most of them had made an early start on the gin. David Allen made a speech which he read haltingly from a scrap of paper which he tried to conceal in the palm of one hand. It was a speech full of hyperbole, clichés and superlatives, and he was clearly mightily relieved once it was over.

Then Angel brought in a cake he had baked for the occasion. It was iced in the shape of *Golden Adventurer*, a minor work of art, with the figures '$12\frac{1}{2}$%' picked out in gold on its hull, and they applauded him. That $12\frac{1}{2}$ per cent had significance to set them all grinning and exclaiming.

Then they called on Nick to speak, and his style was relaxed and easy. He had them hooting with glee within minutes – a mere mention of the prize money that would be due to them once they brought *Golden Adventurer* into Cape Town had them in ecstasy.

The girl was wedged into a corner, almost swallowed in the knot of young officers who found it necessary to press as closely around her as was possible without actually smothering her.

She laughed with a clear unaffected exuberance, her voice ringing high above the growl of masculine mirth, so that Nick found it difficult not to keep looking across at her.

She wore a dress of green clinging material, and Nick wondered where it had come from, until he remembered that *Golden Adventurer*'s passenger accommodation was intact and that earlier that morning, he had noticed the girl standing beside David Allen in the stern of the work boat as it returned from the liner, with a large suitcase at her feet. She had been to fetch her gear and she probably should have stayed aboard the liner. Nick was pleased she had not.

Nick finished his little speech, having mentioned every one of his officers by name and given to each the praise they deserved, and David Allen pressed another large whisky into his one hand and an inelegant wedge of cake into the other, and then left hurriedly to join the tight circle around the girl. It opened reluctantly, yielding to his seniority and Nick found himself almost deserted.

He watched with indulgence the open competition for her attention. She was shorter than any of them, so Nick saw only the top of that magnificent mane of sun-streaked hair, hair the colour of precious metal that shone as she nodded and tilted her head, catching the overhead lights.

Beauty Baker was on one side of her, dressed in a ready-made suit of shiny imitation sharkskin that made a startling contrast to his plaid shirt and acid-yellow tie; the trousers of the suit needed hoisting every few minutes and his spectacles glittered lustfully as he hung over the girl.

David Allen was close on her other side, blushing pinkly every time she turned to speak to him, plying her with cake and liquor – and Nick found his indulgence turning to irritation.

He was irritated by the presence of a tongue-tied fourth

officer who had clearly been delegated to entertain him, and was completely awed by the responsibility. He was irritated by the antics of his senior officers. They were behaving like a troupe of performing seals in their competition for the girl's attention.

For a few moments, the tight circle around her opened, and Nick was left with a few vivid impressions. The green of her dress matched exactly the brilliant sparkling green of her eyes. Her teeth were very white, and her tongue as pink as a cat's when she laughed. She was not the child he had imagined from their earlier encounters; with colour touched to her lips and pearls at her throat, he realized she was in her twenties, early twenties perhaps, but a full woman, nevertheless.

She looked across the wardroom and their eyes met. The laughter stilled on her lips, and she returned his gaze. It was a solemn enigmatic gaze, and he found himself once again regretting his previous rudeness to her. He dropped his gaze from hers and saw now that under the clinging green material, her body was slim and beautifully formed, with a lithe athletic grace. He remembered vividly that one nude glimpse he had been given.

Although the green dress was high-necked, he saw that her breasts were large and pointed, and that they were not trussed by any undergarments; the young shapely flesh was as strikingly arresting as if it had been naked.

It made him angry to see her body displayed in this manner. It did not matter that every young girl in the streets of New York or London went so uncorseted, here it made him angry to see her do the same, and he looked back into her eyes. Something charged there, a challenge perhaps, his own anger reflected? He was not sure. She tilted her head slightly, now it was an invitation – or was it? He had known and handled easily so many, many women. Yet this one left him with a feeling of uncertainty,

171

perhaps it was merely her youth, or was it some special quality she possessed? Nicholas Berg was uncertain and he did not relish the feeling.

David Allen hurried to her with another offering, and cut off the gaze that passed between them, and Nick found himself staring at the Chief Officer's slim, boyish back, and listening to the girl's laughter again, sweet and high. But somehow it seemed to be directed tauntingly at Nick, and he said to the young officer beside him,

'Please ask Mr Allen for a moment of his time.' Patently relieved the officer went to fetch him.

'Thank you for your hospitality, David,' said Nick, when he came.

'You aren't going yet, sir?' Nick took a small sadistic pleasure in the Mate's obvious dismay.

He sat at the desk in his day cabin and tried to concentrate. It was the first opportunity he had had to consider the paperwork that awaited him. The muted sounds of revelry from the deck below distracted him, and he found himself listening for the sounds of her laughter while he should have been composing his submissions to his London attorneys, which would be taken to the arbitrators of Lloyd's, a document and record of vital importance, the whole basis of his claim against *Golden Adventurer*'s underwriters. And yet he could not concentrate.

He swung his chair away from the desk and began to pace the thick, sound-deadening carpet, stopping once to listen again as he heard the girl's voice calling gaily, the words unintelligible, but the tone unmistakable. They were dancing, or playing some raucous game which consisted of a great deal of bumping and thumping and shrieks of laughter.

He began to pace again, and suddenly Nick realized he was lonely. The thought stopped him dead again. He was lonely, and completely alone. It was a disturbing realization, especially for a man who had travelled much of life's journey as a loner. Before it had never troubled him, but now he felt desperately the need for somebody to share his triumph. Triumph it was, of course. Against the most improbable odds, he had snatched spectacular victory, and he crossed slowly to the cabin portholes and looked across the darkened bay to where *Golden Adventurer* lay at anchor, all her lights burning, a gay and festive air about her.

He had been knocked off his perch at the top of the tree, deprived of a life's work, a wife and a son – yet it had taken him only a few short months to clamber back to the top.

With this simple operation, he had transformed Ocean Salvage from a dangerously insecure venture, a tottering cash-starved, problem-hounded long chance, into something of real value. He was off and running again now, with a place to go and the means of getting there. Then why did it suddenly seem of so little worth? He toyed with the idea of returning to the revelry in the wardroom, and grimaced as he imagined the dismay of his officers at the Master's inhibiting intrusion.

He turned away from the porthole and poured whisky into a glass, lit a cheroot and dropped into the chair. The whisky tasted like toothpaste and the cheroot was bitter. He left the glass on his desk and stubbed the cheroot before he went through on to the navigation bridge.

The night lights were so dim after his brightly lit cabin that he did not notice Graham, the Third Officer, until his eyes adjusted to the ruby glow.

'Good evening, Mr Graham.' He moved to the chart-table and checked the log. Graham was hovering anxiously, and Nick searched for something to say.

'Missing the party?' he asked at last.

'Sir.'

It was not a promising conversational opening, and despite his loneliness of a few minutes previously, Nick suddenly wanted to be alone again.

'I will stand the rest of your watch. Go off and enjoy yourself.'

The Third Officer gawped at him.

'You've got three seconds before I change my mind.'

'That's jolly decent of you, sir,' called Graham over his shoulder as he fled.

The party in the wardroom had by now degenerated into open competition for Samantha's attention and approbation.

David Allen, wearing a lampshade on his head and, for some unaccountable reason, with his right hand thrust into his jacket in a Napoleonic gesture, was standing on the wardroom bar counter and declaiming Henry's speech before Agincourt, glossing over the passages which he had forgotten with a 'dum-de-dum'. However, when Tim Graham entered, he became immediately the First Officer. He removed the lampshade and inquired frostily.

'Mr Graham, am I correct in believing that you are officer of the watch? Your station at this moment is on the bridge—'

'The old man came and offered to stand my watch,' said Tim Graham.

'Good Lord!' David replaced his lampshade, and poured a large gin for his Third Officer. 'The old bastard must have come over all soft suddenly.'

Beauty Baker, who was hanging off the wall like a gibbon ape, dropped to his feet and drew himself up with rather unsteady dignity, hitched his trousers and announced ominously,

'If anybody calls the old bastard a bastard, I will personally kick his teeth down his throat.' He swept the wardroom with an eye that was belligerent and truculent, until it alighted on Samantha. Immediately it softened. 'That one doesn't count, Sammy!' he said.

'Of course not,' Samantha agreed. 'You can start again.'

Beauty returned to the starting point of the obstacle course, fortified himself with a draught of rum, pushed up his spectacles with a thumb and spat on his palms.

'One to get ready, two to get steady – and three to be off,' sang out Samantha, and clicked the stopwatch. Beauty Baker swung dizzily from the roof, clawing his way around the wardroom without touching the deck, cheered on by the entire company.

'Eight point six seconds!' Samantha clicked the watch, as he ended up on the bar counter, the finishing post. 'A new world record.'

'A drink for the new world champion.'

'I'm next, time me, Sammy!'

They were like schoolboys. 'Hey, watch me, Sammy!' But after another ten minutes, she handed the stopwatch to Tim Graham, who as a late arrival was still sober.

'I'll be back,' she lied, picked up a plate with a large untouched hunk of Angel's cake upon it and was gone before any of them realized it was happening.

N ick Berg was working over the chart-table, so intently that he was not aware of her for many seconds. In the dramatic lighting of the single overhead lamp, the strength of his features was emphasized. She saw the hard line of his jawbone, the heavy brow and the alert, widely spaced set of his eyes. His nose was large and slightly hooked, like that of a plains Indian or a desert Bedouin, and there were lines at the corners of his mouth and around his eyes that were picked out in dark shadow. In his complete absorption with the charts and *Admiralty Pilot*, he had relaxed his mouth from its usual severe line.

She saw now that the lips were full without being fleshy, and there was a certain sensitivity and voluptuousness there that she had not noticed before.

She stood quietly, enchanted with him, until he looked up suddenly, catching the rapt expression upon her face.

She tried not to appear flustered, but even in her own ears her voice was breathless.

'I'm sorry to disturb you. I brought some cake for Timmy Graham.'

'I sent him below to join the party.'

'Oh, I didn't notice him. I thought he was here.'

She made no move to leave, holding the plate in one hand, and they were silent a moment longer.

'I don't suppose I could interest you in a slice? It's going begging.'

'Share it,' he suggested, and she came to the chart-table.

'I owe you an apology,' he said, and was immediately aware of the harshness in his own voice. He hated to apologize, and she sensed it.

'I picked a bad moment,' she said, and broke off a piece of the cake. 'But this seems a better time. Thank you again, and I'm sorry for all the trouble I caused. I understand now that it nearly cost you the *Golden Adventurer*.'

They both turned to look out of the big armoured glass windows to where she lay.

'She is beautiful, isn't she?' said Nick, and his voice had lost its edge.

'Yes, she's beautiful,' Samantha agreed, and suddenly they were very close in the intimate ruddy glow of the night lights.

He began to talk, stiffly and self-consciously at first, but she drew him on, and with secret joy, she sensed him warming and relaxing. Only then did she begin to put her own ideas forward.

Nick was surprised and a little disconcerted at the depth

176

of her view, and at her easy coherent expression of ideas, for he was still very much aware of her youth. He had expected the giddiness and the giggle, the shallowness and uninformed self-interest of immaturity, but it was not there, and suddenly the difference in their ages was of no importance. They were very close in the night, touching only with their minds, but becoming each minute so much more closely involved in their ideas that time had no significance.

They spoke about the sea, for they were both creatures of that element and as they discovered this, so their mutual delight in each other grew.

From below came the faint unmelodious strains of Beauty Baker leading the ship's officers in a chorus of:

> '—*The working class can kiss my arse*
> *I've got my 12½ per cent at last!*'

And at another stage in the evening, a very worried Tim Graham appeared on the bridge and blurted out,

'Captain, sir, Doctor Silver is missing. She's not in her cabin and we have searched—' He saw her then, sitting in the Captain's chair and his worry turned to consternation. 'Oh, I see. We didn't know – I mean we didn't expect – I'm sorry, sir. Excuse me, sir. Goodnight, sir.' And again he fled the bridge.

'Doctor?' Nick asked.

'I'm afraid so,' she smiled, and then went on to talk about the university, explaining her research project, and the other work she had in mind. Nicholas listened silently, for like all highly competitive and successful men, he respected achievement and ambition.

The chasm that he imagined existed between them shrank rapidly, so that it was an intrusion when the eight-to-twelve watch ended, and the relief brought other human presence to the bridge, shattering the fragile mood they had created around themselves, and denying them further excuse for remaining together.

'Goodnight, Captain Berg,' she said.

'Goodnight, Doctor Silver,' he answered reluctantly. Until that night, he had not even known her name, and there was so much more he wanted to know now, but she was gone from the bridge. As he entered his own suite, Nick's earlier loneliness returned, but with even more poignancy.

During the long day of getting Golden Adventurer under tow, the hours of trim and accommodation to the sea, until she was following meekly settling down to the long journey ahead, Nick thought of the girl at unlikely moments; but when he changed his usual routine and dined in the saloon rather than his own cabin, she was surrounded by a solidly attentive phalanx of young men and, with a small shock of self-honesty, Nick realized that he was actually jealous of them. Twice during the meal, he had to suppress the sharp jibes that came to his lips, and would have plunged the unfortunate recipient into uncomprehending confusion.

Nick ate no desert and took coffee alone in his day cabin. He might have relished Beauty Baker's company, but the Australian was aboard Golden Adventurer, working on her main engines. Then, despite the tensions and endeavours of the day, his bunk had no attractions for him. He glanced at the clock on the panelled bulkhead above his desk and saw that it was a few minutes after eight o'clock.

On impulse he went through to the navigation bridge, and Tim Graham leapt guiltily to his feet. He had been sitting in the Master's chair, a liberty which deserved at the least a sharp reprimand, but Nick pretended not to notice and made a slow round of the bridge, checking every detail from the cable tensions of the tow and power settings of *Warlock*'s engines, to the riding lights on both ships and the last log entry.

'Mr Graham,' he said, and the young officer stiffened to attention like the victim before a firing squad, 'I will stand this watch – you may go and get some dinner.'

The Third Officer was so thunderstruck that he needed a large gin before he could bring himself to tell the wardroom of his good fortune.

Samantha did not look up from the board but moved a bishop flauntingly across the front of David Allen's queen, and when David pounced on it with a gurgle of glee, she unleashed her rook from the rear file and said, 'Mate in three, David.'

'One more, Sam, give me my revenge,' pleaded David, but she shook her head and slipped out of the wardroom.

Nicholas became aware of the waft of her perfume. It was an inexpensive but exuberant fragrance – 'Babe', that was it, the one advertised by Hemingway's granddaughter. It suited Samantha perfectly. He turned to her, and it was only then that he was honest enough to admit to himself that he had relieved his Third Officer with the express intention of luring the girl up to the bridge.

'There are whales ahead,' he told her, and smiled one of those rare, irresistible smiles that she had come to treasure. 'I hoped you might come up.'

'Where? Where are they?' she asked with unfeigned excitement, and then they both saw the spout, a golden feather of spray in the low night sunlight two miles ahead.

'*Balaenoptera musculus!*' she exclaimed.

'I'll take your word for it, Doctor Silver, but to me it's still a blue whale.' Nick was still smiling, and she looked abashed for a moment.

'Sorry, I wasn't trying to dazzle you with science.' Then she looked back at the humpy, uninviting cold sea as the whale blew again, a far and ethereal column of lonely spray.

179

'One,' she said, 'only one.' And the excitement in her voice cooled. 'There are so few of them left now – that might be the last one we will ever see.'

'So few that they cannot find each other in the vastness of the ocean to breed.' Nick's smile was gone also, and again they talked of the sea, of their own involvement with it, their mutual concern at what man had done to it, and what he was still doing to it.

'When the Marxist government of Mozambique took over from the Portuguese colonists, it allowed the Soviets to send in dredgers – not trawlers, but dredgers – and they dredged the weed beds of Delagoa Bay. They actually *dredged* the breeding grounds of the Mozambique prawn. They took out a thousand tons of prawn, and destroyed the grounds for ever – and they drove an entire species into extinction in six short months.' Her outrage was in her voice as she told it.

'Two months ago the Australians arrested a Japanese trawler in their territorial waters. She had in her freezers the meat of 120,000 giant clams that her crew had torn from the barrier reef with crowbars. The calm population of a single coral reef would not exceed 20,000. That means they had denuded six oceanic reefs in one expedition – and they fined the Captain a thousand pounds.'

'It was the Japanese who perfected the "long line",' Nick agreed, 'the endless floating line, armed with specially designed hooks, and laid across the lanes of migration of the big pelagic surface-feeding fish, the tuna and the marlin. They wipe out the shoals as they advance – wipe them out to the last fish.'

'You cannot reduce any animal population beyond a certain point.' Samantha seemed much older as she turned her face up to Nick. 'Look what they did to the whales.'

Together they turned back to the windows, gazing out in hope of another glimpse of that gentle monster, doomed now to extinction, one last look at another creature that would disappear from the seas.

'The Japanese and the Russians again,' said Nick. 'They would not sign the whaling treaty until there were not enough blues left in the seas to make their killing an economic proposition. Then they signed it. When there were two or three thousand blue whales left in all the oceans, that is when they signed.'

'Now they will hunt the fin and the sei and the minke to extinction.'

As they stood side by side staring into the bizarre sun-lit night, searching vainly for that spark of life in the watery wilderness, without thinking Nick lifted his arm; he would have placed it around her shoulders, the age-old protective attitude of man to his woman, but he caught himself at the last moment before he actually touched her. She had felt his movement and tensed for it, swaying slightly towards him in anticipation, but he stepped away, letting his arm fall and stooped over the radarscope. She only realized then how much she had wanted him to touch her, but for the rest of that evening he stayed within the physical limits which he seemed to have set for himself.

The next evening she declined the wardroom's importunate invitations, and after dinner waited in her own cabin, the door an inch ajar so she heard Tim Graham leave the bridge, clattering down the companionway with exuberance, relieved once more of his watch. The moment he entered the wardroom, Samantha slipped from her cabin and ran lightly up to the bridge.

She was with him only minutes after he had assumed the watch and Nick was amused by the strength of his pleasure. They grinned at each other like schoolchildren in a successful piece of mischief.

Before the light went, they passed close by one of the big tabular bergs, and she pointed out the line of filth that marked the white ice like the ring around a bathtub that had been used by a chimney sweep.

'Paraffin wax,' she said,' and undissolved hydrocarbons.'

'No,' he said, 'that's only glacial striation.'

'It's crude oil,' she answered him. 'I've sampled it. It was one of the reasons I took the guide job on *Golden Adventurer*, I wanted first-hand knowledge of these seas.'

'But we are two thousand miles south of the tanker lanes.'

'The beach at Shackleton Bay is thick with wax balls and crude droplets. We found oil-soaked penguins on Cape Alarm, dead and dying. They hit an oil slick within fifty miles of that isolated shore.'

'I can hardly believe—' Nick started, but she cut across him.

'That's just it!' she said. 'Nobody wants to believe it. Just walk on by, as though it's another mugging victim lying on the sidewalk.'

'You're right,' Nick admitted grudgingly. 'Very few people really care.'

'A few dead penguins, a few little black tar balls sticking to your feet on the beach. It doesn't seem much to shout about, but it's what we cannot see that should terrify us. Those millions of tons of poisonous hydrocarbons that dissolve into the sea, that kill slowly and insidiously, but surely. That's what should really terrify us, Nicholas!'

She had used his given name for the first time, and they were both acutely aware of it. They were silent again, staring intently at the big iceberg as it passed slowly. The sun had touched it with ethereal pinks and dreaming amethyst, but that dark line of poisonous filth was still there.

'The world has to use fossil fuels, and we sailors have to transport them,' he said at last.

'But not at such appalling risks, not with an eye only to the profits. Not in the same greedy thoughtless grabbing petty way as man wiped out the whale, not at the cost of turning the sea into a stinking festering cesspool.'

'There are unscrupulous owners—' he agreed, and she cut across him angrily.

'Sailing under flags of convenience, without control, ships built to dangerous standards, equipped with a single boiler—' she reeled out the charges and he was silent.

'Then they waived the winter load-line for tankers rounding the Cape of Good Hope in the southern winter, to enable them to carry that extra fifty thousand tons of crude. The Agulhas Bank, the most dangerous winter sea in the world, and they send overloaded tankers into it.'

'That was criminal,' he agreed.

'Yet you were Chairman of Christy Marine, you had a representative on the Board of Control.'

She saw that she had made a mistake. His expression was suddenly ferocious. His anger seemed to crackle like electricity in the ruby gloom of the bridge. She felt an unaccountable flutter of real fear. She had forgotten what kind of man he was.

But he turned away and made a slow circuit of the bridge, elaborately checking each of the gauges and instruments, and then he paused at the far wing and lit a cheroot. She ached to offer some token of reconciliation, but instinctively she knew not to do so. He was not the kind of man who respected compromise or retreat.

He came back to her at last, and the glow of the cheroot lit his features so that she could see the anger had passed.

'Christy Marine seems like another existence to me now,' he said softly, and she could sense the deep pain of unhealed wounds. 'Forgive me, your reference to it took me off balance. I did not realize that you know of my past history.'

'Everybody on board knows.'

'Of course,' he nodded, and drew deeply on the cheroot before he spoke again. 'When I ran Christy Marine, I insisted on the highest standards of safety and seamanship for every one of our vessels. We opposed the Cape winter-line decision, and none of my tankers loaded to their summer-line on the Good Hope passage. None of my tankers made do with only one boiler, the design and engineering of every Christy Marine vessel was of the same standard as that ship there,' he pointed back at *Golden Adventurer*, 'or this one here,' and he stamped once on the deck.

'Even the *Golden Dawn?*' she asked softly, braving his anger again – but he merely nodded.

'*Golden Dawn*,' he repeated softly. 'It sounds such an absurdly presumptuous name, doesn't it? But I really thought of her as that, when I conceived her. The first million-ton tanker, with every refinement and safety feature that man has so far tested and proved. From inert gas scrubbers to independently articulated main tanks, not one boiler but four, just like one of the old White Star liners – she was really to be the golden dawn of crude oil transportation.

'However, I am no longer Chairman of Christy Marine, and I am no longer in control of *Golden Dawn*, neither her design nor her construction.' His voice was hollow, and in the dim light his eyes seemed shrunken into their cavities like those of a skull. 'Nor yet am I in control of her operation.'

It was all turning out so badly; she did not want to argue with him, nor make him unhappy. However, she had stirred memories and regrets within him, and she wished vainly that she had not disturbed him so. Her instinct warned her she should leave him now.

'Goodnight, Doctor Silver,' he nodded non-committally at her sudden plea of tiredness.

'My name is Sam,' she told him, wishing that she could comfort him in some way, any way, 'or Samantha, if you prefer it.'

'I do prefer it,' he said, without smiling. 'Goodnight, Samantha.'

She was angry with both herself and him, angry that the good feeling between them had been destroyed, so she flashed at him:

'You really are old-fashioned, aren't you?' and hurried from the bridge.

The following evening she almost did not go up to him, for she was ashamed of those parting words, for having pointed up their age difference so offensively. She knew he was sufficiently aware of their differences, without being reminded. She had done herself harm, and she did not want to face him again.

While she was in the shower of the guest cabin, she heard Tim Graham come clattering down the stairs on the other side of the thin bulkhead. She knew that Nicholas had relieved him.

'I'm not going up,' she told herself firmly, and took her time drying and talcuming and brushing out her hair before she clambered naked and still pink from the hot water into her bunk.

She read for half an hour, a western that Beauty Baker had lent her, and it required all her concentration to follow the print, for her mind kept trying to wander. At last she gave an exclamation of self-disgust, threw back the blankets and began dressing.

His relief and pleasure, when she appeared beside him, were transparent, and his smile was a princely welcome for her. She was suddenly very glad she had come, and this night she effortlessly steered past all the pitfalls.

She asked him to explain how the Lloyd's Open Form contract worked, and she followed his explanations swiftly.

'If they take into consideration the danger and difficulties involved in the salvage,' she mused, 'you should be able to claim an enormous award.'

'I'm going to ask for twenty per cent of the hull value—'

'What is the hull value of *Golden Adventurer?*'

And he told her. She was silent a moment as she checked his mental arithmetic.

'That's six million dollars,' she whispered in awe.

'Give or take a few cents,' he agreed.

'But there isn't that much money in the world!' She turned and stared back at the liner.

'Duncan Alexander is going to agree with you.' Nick smiled a little grimly.

'But,' she shook her head, 'what would anybody do with that much money?'

'I'm asking for six – but I won't get it. I'll walk away with three or four million.'

'Still, that's too much. Nobody could spend that much, not if they tried for a lifetime.'

'It's spent already. It will just about enable me to pay off my loans, launch my other tug, and to keep Ocean Salvage going for another few months.'

'You owe three or four million dollars?' She stared at him now in open wonder. 'I'd never sleep, not one minute would I be able to sleep—'

'Money isn't for spending,' he explained. 'There is a limit to the amount of food you can eat, or clothes you can wear. Money is a game, the biggest most exciting game in town.'

She listened attentively to it all, happy because tonight he was gay and excited with grand designs and further plans, and because he shared them with her.

'What we will do is this, we'll come down here with both tugs and catch an iceberg.'

She laughed. 'Oh, come on!'

'I'm not joking,' he assured her, but laughing also. 'We'll put tow-lines on a big berg. It may take a week to build up tow speed, but once we get it moving nothing will stop it.

We will guide it up into the middle forties, catch the roaring forties and, just like the old wool clippers on the Australian passage, we will run our eastings down.' He moved to the chart-table, selected a large-scale chart of the Indian Ocean and beckoned her to join him.

'You're serious.' She stopped laughing, and stared at him again. 'You really are serious, aren't you?'

He nodded, still smiling, and traced it out with his finger. 'Then we'll swing northwards, up into the Western Australian current, letting the flow carry us north in a great circle, until we hit the easterly monsoon and the north equatorial current.' He described the circle, but she watched his face. They stood very close, but still not touching and she felt herself stirred by the timbre of his voice, as though to the touch of fingers. 'We will cross the Indian Ocean to the east coast of Africa with the current pushing all the way, just in time to catch the south-westerly monsoon drift – right into the Persian Gulf.' He straightened up and smiled again.

'A hundred billion tons of fresh water delivered right into the driest and richest corner of the globe.'

'But – but—' she shook her head, 'it would melt!'

'From a helicopter we spray it with a reflective polyurethane skin to lessen the effect of the sun, and we moor it in a shallow specially prepared dock where it will cool its own surrounds. Sure, it will melt, but not for a year or two and then we'll just go out and catch another one and bring it in, like roping wild horses.'

'How would you handle it?' she objected. 'It's too big.'

'My two tugs hustle forty-four thousand horses – we could pull in Everest, if we wanted.'

'Yes, but once you get it to the Persian Gulf?'

'We cut it into manageable hunks with a laser lance, and lift the hunks into a melting dam with an overhead crane.'

She thought about it. 'It could work,' she admitted.

'It will work,' he told her. 'I've sold the idea to the Saudis already. They are already building the dock and the dams. We'll give them water at one hundredth the cost of using nuclear condensers on sea water, and without the risk of radioactive contamination.'

She was absorbed with his vision, and he with hers. As they talked deep into the long watches of the night, they drew closer in spirit only.

Although each of them treasured those shared hours, somehow neither could bridge the narrow chasm between friendliness and real intimacy. She was instinctively aware of his reserves, that he was a man who had considered life and established his code by which to live it. She guessed that he did nothing unless it was deeply felt, and that a casual physical relationship would offer no attraction to him; she knew of the turmoil to which his life had so recently been reduced, and that he was pulling himself out of that by main strength, but that he was now wary of further hurt. There was time, she told herself, plenty of time – but *Warlock* bore steadily north by north-east, dragging her crippled ward up through the roaring forties; those notorious winds treated her kindly and she made good the six knots that Nick had hoped for.

On board *Warlock*, the attitude of the officers towards Samantha Silver changed from fawning adulation to wistful respect. Every one of them knew of the nightly ritual of the eight-to-midnight watch.

'Bloody cradle-snatcher,' groused Tim Graham.

'Mr Graham, it is fortunate I did not hear that remark,' David Allen warned him with glacial coldness – but they all resented Nicholas Berg, it was unfair competition, yet they kept a new respectful distance from the girl, not one of them daring to challenge the herd bull.

The time that Samantha had looked upon as endless was running out now, and she closed her mind to it. Even when David Allen showed her the fuzzy luminescence of the African continent on the extreme range of the radar screen, she pretended to herself that it would go on like this — if not for ever, at least until something special happened.

During the long voyage up from Shackleton Bay, Samantha had streamed a very fine-meshed net from *Warlock*'s stern, collecting an incredible variety of krill and plankton and other microscopic marine life. Angel had grudgingly given her a small corner of his scullery in return for her services as honorary assistant under-chef and unpaid waitress, and she spent many absorbed hours there each day, identifying and preserving her specimens.

She was working there when the helicopter came out to *Warlock*. She looked up at the buffeting of the machine's rotors as they changed into fine pitch for the landing on *Warlock*'s heli-deck, and she was tempted to go up like every idle and curious hand on board, but she was in the middle of staining a slide, and somehow she resented the encroachment on this little island of her happiness. She worked on, but now her pleasure was spoiled, and she cocked her head when she heard the roar of the rotors as the helicopter rose from the deck again and she was left with a sense of foreboding.

Angel came in from the deck, wiping his hands on his apron and he paused in the doorway.

'You didn't tell me he was going, dearie.'

'What do you mean?' Samantha looked up at him, startled.

'Your boyfriend, darling. Socks and toothbrush and all.' Angel watched her shrewdly. 'Don't tell me he didn't even kiss you goodbye.'

She dropped the glass slide into the stainless steel sink and it snapped in half. She was panting as she gripped the rail of the upper deck and stared after the cumbersome yellow machine.

It flew low across the green wind-chopped sea, hump-backed and nose low, still close enough to read the operating company's name 'COURT' emblazoned on its fuselage, but it dwindled swiftly towards the far blue line of mountains.

N ick Berg sat in the jump seat between the two pilots of the big S. 58T Sikorsky and looked ahead towards the flat silhouette of Table Mountain. It was overlaid by a thick mattress of snowy cloud, at the south-easterly wind swirled across its summit.

From their altitude of a mere thousand feet, there were still five big tankers in sight, ploughing stolidly through the green sea on their endless odyssey, seeming to be alien to their element, not designed to live in harmony with it, but to oppose every movement of the waters. Even in this low sea, they wore thick garlands of white at their stubby rounded bows, and Nick watched one of them dip suddenly and take spray as high as her foremast. In any sort of blow, she would be like a pier with pylons set on solid ground. The seas would break right over her. It was not the way a ship should be, and now he twisted in his seat and looked back.

Far behind them, *Warlock* was still visible. Even at this distance, and despite the fact that she was dwarfed by her charge, her lines pleased the seaman in him. She looked good, but that backward glance invoked a pang of regret that he had been so stubbornly trying to ignore – and he had a vivid image of green eyes and hair of platinum and gold.

His regret was spiced by the persistent notion that he

had been cowardly. He had left *Warlock* without being able to bring himself to say goodbye to the girl, and he knew why he had done so. He would not take the chance of making a fool of himself. He grimaced with distaste as he remembered her exact words, 'You really are old-fashioned, aren't you?'

There was something vaguely repulsive in a middle-aged man lusting after young flesh – and he supposed he must now look upon himself as middle-aged. In six months he would be forty years of age, and he did not really expect to live to eighty. So he was in the middle of the road.

He had always scorned those grey, lined, balding, unattractive little men with big cigars, sitting in expensive restaurants with pretty young girls beside them, the young thing pretending to hang on every pearl-like word, while her eyes focused beyond his shoulder – on some younger man.

But still, it had been cowardice. She had become a friend during those weeks, and she could hardly have been aware of the emotions that she had aroused in him during those long dark hours on *Warlock's* bridge. She was not to blame for his unruly passions, in no way had she encouraged him to believe that he was more than just an older man, not even a father figure, but just someone with whom to pass an otherwise empty hour. She had been as friendly and cheerful to everyone else on board *Warlock*, from the Mate to the cook.

He really had owed her the common courtesy of a handshake and an assurance of the pleasure he had taken from her company, but he had not been certain he could restrict it to that.

He winced again as he imagined her horror as he blurted out some sort of declaration, some proposal to prolong their relationship or alter its structure into something more intimate, her disenchantment when she realized that behind the façade of the mature and cultured man, he was just as grimy an old lecher as the furtive drooling browsers in the porno-shops of Times Square.

'Let it go,' he had decided. No matter that he was probably in better physical shape now than he had been at twenty-five, to Dr Samantha Silver he was an old man – and he had a frightening vision of an episode from his own youth.

A woman, a friend of his mother's, had trapped the nineteen-year-old Nicholas alone one rainy day in the old beach house at Martha's Vineyard. He remembered his own revulsion at the sagging white flesh, the wrinkles, the lines of stria across her belly and breasts, and the *oldness* of her. She would then have been a woman of forty, the same age as he was now, and he had done her the service she required out of some obligation of pity, but afterwards he had scrubbed his teeth until the gums bled and he had stood under the shower for almost an hour.

It was one of the cruel deceits of life that a person aged from the outside inwards. He had thought of himself in the fullness of his physical and mental powers, especially now after bringing in *Golden Adventurer*. He was ready for them to lead on the dragons and he would tear out their jugulars with his bare hands – then she had called him an old-fashioned thing, and he had realized that the sexual fantasy which was slowly becoming an obsession must be associated with the male menopause, a sorry symptom of the ageing process of which he had not been conscious until then. He grinned wryly at the thought.

The girl would probably hardly notice that he had left the ship, at the worst might be a little piqued by his lack of manners, but in a week would have forgotten his name. As for himself, there was enough, and more than enough to fill the days ahead, so that the image of a slim young body and that precious mane of silver and gold would fade until it became the fairy tale it really was.

Resolutely he turned in the jump seat and looked ahead. Always look ahead, there are never regrets in that direction.

They clattered in over False Bay, crossing the narrow isthmus of the Cape Peninsula under the bulk of the cloud-capped mountain, from the Indian Ocean to the Atlantic in under ten minutes.

He saw the gathering, like vultures at the lion kill, as the Sikorsky lowered to her roost on the helipad within the main harbour area of Table Bay.

As Nick jumped down, ducking instinctively under the still-turning rotors, they surged forward, ignoring the efforts of the Courtline dispatcher to keep the pad clear; they were led by a big red-faced man with a scorched-looking bald head and the furry arms of a tame bear.

'Larry Fry, Mr Berg,' he growled. 'You remember me?'

'Hello, Larry.' He was the local manager for Bach Wackie & Co, Nick's agents.

'I thought you might say a few words to the Press.' But the journalists swarmed around Nick now, demanding, importuning, jostling each other, their minions firing flash bulbs.

Nick felt his irritation flare, and he needed a deep breath and a conscious effort to control his anger.

'All right, lads and ladies.' He held up both hands, and grinned that special boyish grin. They were doing a tough job, he reminded himself. It couldn't be easy to be forced daily into the company of rich and successful men, grabbing for tidbits, and being grossly underpaid for your efforts with the long-term expectation of ulcers and cirrhosis of the liver.

'Play the game with me and I'll play it with you,' he promised, and thought for a moment how it would be if they *didn't* want to speak with him, how it would be if they didn't know who he was, and didn't care.

'Where have you booked me?' he asked Larry Fry now,

and turned back to them. 'In two hours' time I'll be in my suite at the Mount Nelson Hotel. You're invited, and there'll be whisky.'

They laughed and tried a few more half-hearted questions, but they had accepted the compromise – at least they had got the pictures.

As they went up the palm-lined drive to the gracious old hotel, built in the days when space included five acres of carefully groomed gardens, Nick felt the stir of memory, but he suppressed that and listened intently to the list of appointments and matters of urgency from which Larry Fry read. The change in the big man's attitude was dramatic. When Nick had first arrived to take command of *Warlock*, Larry Fry had given him ten minutes of his time and sent a deputy to complete the business.

Then Nick had been touched by the mark of the beast, a man on his way down, with as much appeal as a leper. Larry Fry had accorded him the minimum courtesy due the master of a small vessel, but now he was treating him like visiting royalty, limousine and fawning attention.

'We have chartered a 707 from South African Airways to fly *Golden Adventurer*'s passengers to London, and they will take scheduled commercial flights to their separate destinations from there.'

'What about berthing for *Golden Adventurer*?'

'The Harbour Master is sending out an inspector to check the hull before he lets her enter harbour.'

'You have made the arrangements?' Nick asked sharply. He had not completed the salvage until the liner was officially handed over to the company commissioned to undertake the repairs.

'Court are flying him out now,' Larry Fry assured him. 'We'll have a decision before nightfall.'

'Have the underwriters appointed a contractor for the repairs?'

'They've called for tenders.'

The hotel manager himself met Nicholas under the entrance portico.

'Good to see you again, Mr Berg.' He waived the registration procedures. 'We can do that when Mr Berg has settled in.' And then he assured Nick, 'We have given you the same suite.'

Nick would have protested, but already they were ushering him into the sitting room. If it had been a room lacking completely in character or taste, the memories might not have been so poignant. However, unlike one of those soulless plastic and vinyl coops built by the big chains and so often offered to travellers under the misnomer of 'inns', this room was furnished with antique furniture, oil-paintings and flowers. The memories were as fresh as those flowers, but not as pleasing.

The telephone was ringing as they entered, and Larry Fry seized it immediately, while Nick stood in the centre of the room. It had been two years since last he stood here, but it seemed as many days, so clear was the memory.

'The Harbour Master has given permission for *Golden Adventurer* to enter harbour.' Larry Fry grinned triumphantly at Nick, and gave him the thumbs-up signal.

Nick nodded, the news was an anti-climax after the draining endeavours of the last weeks. Nick walked through to the bedroom. The wallpaper was a quietly tasteful floral design with matching curtains.

From the four-poster bed, Nick remembered, you could look out over the lawns. He remembered Chantelle sitting under that canopy, with a gossamer-sheer bed-robe over her creamy shoulders, eating thin strips of marmaladed toast and then delicately and carefully licking each slim tapered finger with a pink pointed tongue.

Nicholas had come out to negotiate the transportation of South African coal from Richards Bay, and iron ore from

Saldanha Bay to Japan. He had insisted that Chantelle accompany him. Perhaps he had the premonition of imminent loss, but he had overridden her objections.

'But Africa is such a primitive place, Nicky, they have things that bite.'

And she had in the end gone with him. He had been rewarded with four days of rare happiness. The last four days ever, for though he did not then even suspect it, he was already sharing her bed and body with Duncan Alexander. He had never tired in thirteen years of that lovely smooth creamy body; rather, he had delighted in its slow luscious ripening into full womanhood, believing without question that it belonged to him.

Chantelle was one of those unusual women who grew more beautiful with time; it had always been one of his pleasures to watch her enter a room filled with other internationally acclaimed beauties, and see them pale beside his wife. And suddenly, for no good reason, he imagined Samantha Silver beside Chantelle – the girl's coltish grace would be transmuted to gawkiness beside Chantelle's poise, her manner as gauche as a schoolgirl's beside Chantelle's mature control, a warm lovable little bunny beside the sleekly beautiful mink—

'Mr Berg, London.' Larry Fry called from the sitting room interrupting him, and with relief Nick picked up the telephone. 'Just keep going forward,' he reminded himself, and before he spoke, he thought again of the two women, and wondered suddenly how much that thick rich golden mane of Samantha's hair would pale beside Chantelle's lustrous sable, and just how much of the mother-of-pearl glow would fade from that young, clear skin—

'Berg,' he said abruptly into the telephone.

'Mr Berg, good morning. Will you speak to Mr Duncan Alexander of Christy Marine?'

Nick was silent for five full seconds. He needed that long to adjust to the name, but Duncan Alexander was the natural extension of his previous thoughts. In the silence he heard the banging of doors and rising clamour of voices, as the journalists converged on the liquor cabinet next door.

'Mr Berg, are you there?'

'Yes,' he said, and his voice was steady and cool. 'Put him on.'

'Nicholas, my dear fellow.' The voice was glossy as satin, slow as honey, Eton and King's College, a hundred thousand pound accent, impossible to imitate, not quite foppish nor indolent, razor steel in a scabbard of velvet encrusted with golden filigree and precious stones – and Nicholas had seen the steel bared. 'It seems that it is impossible to hold a good man down.'

'But you tried, young Duncan,' Nick answered lightly. 'Don't feel bad about it, indeed you tried.'

'Come, Nicholas. Life is too short for recriminations. This is a new deck of cards, we start equal again.' Duncan chuckled softly. 'At least be gracious enough to accept my congratulations.'

'Accepted,' Nicholas agreed. 'Now what do we talk about?'

'Is *Golden Adventurer* in dock yet?'

'She has been cleared to enter. She'll be tied up within twenty-four hours – and you'd better have your cheque book ready.'

'I hoped that we might avoid going up before the Committee. There has been too much bitterness already. Let's try and keep it in the family, Nicholas.'

'The family?'

'Christy Marine is the family – you, Chantelle, old Arthur Christy – and Peter.'

It was the very dirtiest form of fighting, and Nick found suddenly that he was shaking like a man in fever and that his fist around the receiver was white with the force of his grip. It was the mention of his son that had affected him so.

'I'm not in that family any more.'

'In a way you will always be part of it. It is as much your achievement as any man's, and your son—'

Nick cut across him brusquely, his voice gravelly.

'You and Chantelle made me a stranger. Now treat me like one.'

'Nicholas—'

'Ocean Salvage as main contractor for the recovery of *Golden Adventurer* is open to an offer.'

'Nicholas—'

'Make an offer.'

'As bluntly as that?'

'I'm waiting.'

'Well now. My Board has considered the whole operation in depth, and I am empowered to make you an outright settlement of three-quarters of a million dollars.'

Nick's tone did not alter. 'We have been set down for a hearing at Lloyd's on the 27th of next month.'

'Nicholas, the offer is negotiable within reasonable limits—'

'You are speaking a foreign language,' Nick cut him off. 'We are so far apart that we are wasting each other's time.'

'Nicholas, I know how you feel about Christy Marine, you know the company is underwriting its own—'

'Now you are really wasting my time.'

'Nicholas, it's not a third party, it's not some big insurance consortium, it's Christy Marine—'

He used his name again, though it scalded his tongue.

'Duncan, you're breaking my heart. I'll see you on the 27th of next month, at the arbitration court.' He dropped the receiver on to its bracket, and moved across to the mirror, swiftly combing his hair and composing his features, startled to see how hard and bleak his expression was, and how fierce his eyes.

However, when he went through to the lounge of the suite, he was relaxed and urbane and smiling.

'All right, ladies and gentlemen. I'm all yours,' and one of the ladies of the press, blonde, pretty and not yet thirty but with eyes as old as life itself, took another sip of her whisky as she studied him, then murmured huskily, 'I wouldn't mind at all, duckie.'

Golden Adventurer stood tall and very beautiful against the wharf of Cape Town harbour, waiting her turn to go into the dry dock.

Globe Engineering, the contractors who had been appointed to repair her, had signed for her and legally taken over responsibility from Warlock's First Officer. But David Allen still felt an immense proprietary pride in her.

From Warlock's navigation bridge, he could look across the main harbour basin and see the tall, snowy superstructure glistening in the bright hot summer sunshine, towering as high as the giraffe-necked steel wharf cranes; and in gloating self-indulgence, David dwelt on a picture of the liner, wreathed in snow, half obscured by driving sleet and sea fume, staggering in the mountainous black seas off Antarctica. It gave him a solid feeling of achievement, and he thrust his hands deeply into his pockets and whistled softly to himself, smiling and watching the liner.

The Trog thrust his wrinkled head from the radio room.

'There's a call for you on the landline,' he said, and David picked up the handset.

'David?'

'Yessir.' He drew himself to his full height as he recognized Nicholas Berg's voice.

'Are you ready for sea?'

David gulped, then glanced at the bulkhead clock. 'We discharged tow an hour and ten minutes ago.'

'Yes, I know. How soon?'

David was tempted to lie, estimate short, and then fake it for the extra time he needed. Instinct warned him against lying deliberately to Nicholas Berg.

'Twelve hours,' he said.

'It's an oil-rig tow, Rio to the North Sea, a semi-submersible rig.'

'Yessir,' David adjusted quickly, thank God he had not yet let any of his crew ashore. He had arranged for bunkering at 1300 hours. He could make it. 'When are you coming aboard, sir?'

'I'm not,' said Nick. 'You're the new Master. I'm leaving for London on the five o'clock flight. I won't even get down to shout at you. She's all yours, David.'

'Thank you, sir,' David stuttered, feeling himself flush hot scarlet.

'Bach Wackie will telex you full details of the tow at sea, and you and I will work out your own contract later. But I want you running at top economic power for Rio by dawn tomorrow.'

'Yessir.'

'I've watched you carefully, David.' Nick's voice changed, becoming personal, warmer. 'You're a damn good tug-man. Just keep telling yourself that.'

'Thank you, Mr Berg.'

S amantha had spent half the afternoon helping with the arrangements for taking off the remaining passengers from *Golden Adventurer* and embarking them in the waiting fleet of tourist buses which would distribute them to hotels throughout the city while they waited for the London charter flight.

It had been a sad occasion, farewell to many who had become friends, and remembering those who had not come back from Cape Alarm with them – Ken, who might have been her lover, and the crew of raft Number 16 who had been her special charges.

Once the final bus had left, with the occupants waving for the last time to Samantha, 'Take care, honey!' 'You come and visit with us now, you hear?' she was as lonely and forlorn as the silent ship. She stood for a long time staring up the liner's high side, examining the damage where sea and ice had battered her – then she turned and picked her way dejectedly along the edge of the basin, ignoring the occasional whistle or ribald invitation from the fishermen and crew members of the freighters on their moorings.

Warlock seemed as welcoming as home, rakish and gallant, wearing her new scars with high panache, already thrusting and impatient at the restraint of her mooring lines. And then Samantha remembered that Nicholas Berg was no longer aboard her, and her spirits sagged again.

'God,' Tim Graham met her at the gangplank. 'I'm glad you got back. I didn't know what to do with your gear.'

'What do you mean?' Samantha demanded. 'Are you throwing me off the ship?'

'Unless you want to come with us to Rio.' He thought about that for a moment, and then he grinned, 'Hey, that's not a bad idea, how about it, old girl? Rio in Carnival time, you and me—'

'Don't get carried away, Timothy,' she warned him. 'Why Rio?'

'The Captain—'

'Captain Berg?'

'No, David Allen, he's the new skipper,' and she lost interest.

'When are you sailing?'

'Midnight.'

'I'd best go pack up.' She left him on the quarterdeck, and Angel pounced on her as she passed the galley.

'Where have you been?' He was in a flutter, all wrists and tossing hair, 'I've been beside myself, darling.'

'What is it, Angel?'

'It's probably too late already.'

'What is it?' She caught his urgency. 'Tell me.'

'He's still in town.'

'Who?' But she knew, they spoke of only one person in these emotional terms.

'Don't be dense, luv. Your crumpet.' She hated it when he referred to Nick like that, but now she let him go on. 'But he won't be very much longer. His plane leaves at five o'clock, he is making the local flight to Johannesburg, and connecting there for London.'

She stared at him.

'Well what are you waiting for?' Angel keened. 'It's almost four o'clock now, and it will take you at least half an hour to reach the airport.'

She did not move. 'But, Angel,' she almost wrung her hands in anguish, 'but what do I do when I get there?'

Angel shook his head and twinkled his diamonds in exasperation. 'Sweet merciful heavens, duckie.' Then he sighed. 'When I was a boy I had two guinea pigs, and they also refused to get it on. I think they were retarded, or something. I tried everything, even hormones, but neither of them survived the shots. Alas, their love was never consummated—'

'Be serious, Angel.'

'You could hold him down while I give him a hormone shot—'

'I hate you, Angel.' She had to laugh, even in her anxiety.

'Dearie, every night for the past month you have tried to set him on fire with your dulcet silvery voice – and we haven't even passed "GO" and collected our first $200—'

'I know, Angel. I know.'

'It seems to me, sweetie, that it's time now to cut out the jawing and to ignite him with that magic little tinderbox of yours.'

'You mean right there in the departure lounge of the airport?' She clapped her hands with delight, then struck a lascivious pose. 'I'm Sam – fly me!'

'Hop, poppet there is a taxi on the wharf – he's been waiting an hour, with his meter running.'

There is no first-class lounge in Cape Town's DF Malan Airport, so Nicholas sat in the snake-pit, amongst the distraught mothers and their whining, sticky offspring, the harassed tourists loaded like camels with souvenirs and the florid-faced commercial travellers, but he was alone in a multitude; with unconscious deference they allowed him a little circle of privacy and he used the Louis Vuitton briefcase on his knee as a desk.

It occurred to him suddenly how dramatically the balance had swung in the last mere forty days, since he had recognized his wave peaking, but had almost not been able to find the strength for it.

A shadow passed across his eyes, and the little creased crow's foot appeared between them as he remembered the physical and emotional effort that it had taken to make the 'Go' decision on *Golden Adventurer*, and he shivered slightly in fear of what might have happened if he had not gone. He would have missed his wave, and there would never have been another.

With a small firm movement of his head, he pushed that memory of fear behind him. He had caught his wave, and he was riding high and fast. Now it seemed that the fates were intent on smothering him with largesse: the oil-rig for *Warlock*, Rio to the Bravo Sierra field off Norway – then a back-to-back tow from the North Sea through Suez to the new South Australian field, would keep *Warlock* fully employed for the next six months. That was not all, the threatening dockyard strike at Construction Navale

Atlantique had been smoothed over and the delivery date for the new tug had come forward by two months. At midnight the night before, a telephone call from Bach Wackie had awakened him to let him know Kuwait and Qatar were now also studying the iceberg-to-water project with a view to commissioning similar schemes; he would have to build himself another two vessels if they decided to go.

'All I need now is to hear that I have won the football pools,' he thought, and turned his head, started and caught his breath with a hiss, as though he had been punched in the ribs.

She stood by the automatic doors, and the wind had caught her hair and torn it loose from its thick twisted knot so that fine gold tendrils floated down on to her cheeks – cheeks that were flushed as though she had run fast, and her chest heaved so that she held one hand upon it, fingers spread like a star between those fine pointed breasts. She was poised like a forest animal that has scented the leopard, fearful, tremulous, but not yet certain in which direction to run. Her agitation was so apparent that he thrust aside his briefcase and stood up.

She saw him instantly, and her face lit with an expression of such unutterable joy, that he was halted in his intention of going towards her, while she in contrast wheeled and started to run towards him.

She collided with a portly, sweating tourist, nearly flooring him and shaking loose a rain of carved native curios and anonymous packets which clattered to the floor around him like ripe fruit.

He snarled angrily, then his expression changed as he looked at her. 'Sorry!' She stooped swiftly, picked up a packet, thrust it into his arms, hit him with her smile, and left him beaming bemusedly after her.

However, now she was more restrained, her precipitous rush calmed to that long-legged, thrusting, hip-swinging walk of hers, and the smile was a little uncertain as she pushed vainly at the loose streamers of golden hair, trying to tuck them up into the twisted rope on top of her head.

'I thought I'd missed you.' She stopped a little in front of him.

'Is something wrong?' he asked quickly, still alarmed by her behaviour.

'Oh no,' she assured him hurriedly. 'Not any more,' and suddenly she was awkward and coltish again. 'I thought,' her voice hushed, 'it was just that I thought I'd missed you.' And her eyes slid away from him. 'You didn't say goodbye—'

'I thought it was better that way.' And now her eyes flew back to his face, sparkling with green fire.

'Why?' she demanded, and he had no answer to give her.

'I didn't want to—' How could he say it to her, without making the kind of statement that would embarrass them both?

Above them, the public address system squawked into life.

'South African Airways announces the departure of their Airbus flight 235 to Johannesburg. Will passengers please board at Gate Number Two.'

She had run out of time. 'I'm Sam – Fly Me! Please!' she thought, and felt the urge to giggle, but instead she said:

'Nicholas, tomorrow you'll be in London – in mid-winter.'

'It's a sobering thought,' he agreed, and for the first time smiled; his smile closed like a fist around her heart and her legs felt suddenly weak.

'Tomorrow or at least the day after, I'll be riding the long sea at Cape St Francis,' she said. They had spoken of that, on those enchanted nights. He had told her how he had first ridden the surf at Waikiki Beach long ago before the sport had become a craze, and it had been part of their shared experience, part of their love of the sea, drawing them closer together.

'I hope the surf's up for you,' he said. Cape St Francis was three hundred and fifty miles north of Cape Town, simply another beach and headland in a shoreline that stretched in unbroken splendour for six thousand miles, and yet it was unique in all the world. The young and the young-at-heart came in almost religious pilgrimage to ride the long sea at Cape St Francis. They came from Hawaii and California, from Tahiti and Queensland, for there was no other wave quite like it.

At the departure gate, the shuffling queue was shortening, and Nick stooped to pick up his briefcase, but she reached out and laid her hand on his biceps, and he froze.

It was the first time she had deliberately touched him, and the shock of it spread through his body like ripples on a quiet lake. All the emotions and passions which he had so strenuously denied came tumbling back upon him, and it seemed that their strength had grown a hundredfold while under restraint. He ached for her, with a deep, yearning, wanting ache.

'Come with me, Nicholas,' she whispered, and his own throat closed so he could not answer. He stared at her, and already the ground hostesses at the gate were peering around irritably for their missing passenger.

She had to convince him and she shook his arm urgently, startled at the hardness of the muscle under her fingers.

'Nicholas, I really want,' she began, intending to finish, 'you to,' but her tongue played a Freudian trick on her, and she said, 'I really want you.'

'Oh God,' she thought, as she heard herself say it, 'I sound like a whore,' and in panic she corrected herself.

'I really want you to,' and she flushed, the blood came

up from her neck, dark under the peach of her tan so the freckles glowed on her skin like flakes of gold-dust.

'Which one is it?' he asked, and then smiled again.

'There isn't time to argue.' She stamped her foot, feigning impatience, hiding her confusion, then added, 'Damn you!' for no good reason.

'Who is arguing?' he asked quietly, and suddenly, like magic, she was in his arms, trying to burrow herself deeper and deeper into his embrace, trying to draw all the man smell of him into her lungs, amazed at the softness and warmth of his mouth and the hard rasp of new beard on his chin and cheek, making little soft mewing sounds of comfort deep in her throat as she clung to him.

'Passenger Berg. Will passenger Berg please report to the departure gate,' chanted the public address.

'They're calling me,' Nicholas murmured.

'They can go right to the back of the queue,' she mumbled into his lips.

Sunlight was made for Samantha. She wore it like a cloak that had been woven especially for her. She wore it in her hair, sparkling like jewellery, she used it to paint her face and body in lustrous shades of burnt honey and polished amber, she wore it glowing in golden freckles on her cheeks and nose.

She moved in sunlight with wondrous grace, barefooted in the white sand, so that her hips and buttocks roistered brazenly under the thin green stuff of her bikini.

She sprawled in the sunlight like a sleeping cat, offering her face and her naked belly to it, so he felt that if he laid his hands against her throat he would feel her purr deep inside her chest.

She ran in the sunlight, light as a gull in flight, along the hard wet sand at the water's edge, and he ran beside her, tirelessly, mile after mile, the two of them alone in a world of green sea and sun and tall pale hot skies. The beach curved away in both directions to the limit of the eye, smooth and white as the snows of Antarctica, devoid of human life or the scars of man's petty endeavours, and she laughed beside him in the sunlight, holding his hand as they ran together.

They found a deep, clear rock pool in a far and secret place. The sunlight off the water dappled her body, exploding silently upon it like the reflections of light from a gigantic diamond, as she cast aside the two green wisps of her bikini, let down the thick rope of her hair and stepped into the pool, turning, knee-deep, to look back at him. Her hair hung almost to her waist, springing and thick and trying to curl in the salt and wind, it cloaked her shoulders and her breasts peeped through the thick curtains of it. Her breasts, untouched by the sun, were rich as cream and tipped in rose, so big and full and exuberant that he wondered that he had ever thought her a child; they bounced and swung as she moved, and she pulled back her shoulders and laughed at him shamelessly when she saw the direction of his eyes.

She turned back to the pool and her buttocks were white with the pinkish sheen of a deep-sea pearl, round and tight and deeply divided, and, as she bent forward to dive, a tiny twist of copper gold curls peeped briefly and coyly from the wedge where the deep cleft split into her tanned smooth thighs.

Through the cool water, her body was warm as bread fresh from the oven, cold and heat together, and when he told her this, she entwined her arms around his neck.

'I'm Sam the baked Alaska, eat me!' she laughed, and the droplets clung to her eyelashes like diamond chips in the sunlight.

Even in the presence of others, they walked alone; for

them, nobody else really existed. Among those who had come from all over the world to ride the long sea at Cape St Francis were many who knew Samantha, from Florida and California, from Australia and Hawaii, where her field trips and her preoccupation with the sea and the life of the sea had taken her.

'Hey, Sam!' they shouted, dropping their boards in the sand and running to her, tall muscular men, burned dark as chestnuts in the sun. She smiled at them vaguely, holding Nicholas' hand a little tighter, and replied to their chatter absentmindedly, drifting away at the first opportunity.

'Who was that?'

'It's terrible, but I can't remember – I'm not even sure where I met him or when.' And it was true, she could concentrate on nothing but Nicholas, and the others sensed it swiftly and left them alone.

Nicholas had not been in the sun for over a year, his body was the colour of old ivory, in sharp contrast to the thick dark body hair which covered his chest and belly. At the end of that first day in the sun, the ivory colour had turned to a dull angry red.

'You'll suffer,' she told him, but the next morning his body and limbs had gone the colour of mahogany and she drew back the sheets and marvelled at it, touching him exploringly with the tip of her fingers.

'I'm lucky, I've got a hide like a buffalo,' he told her.

Each day he turned darker, until he was the weathered bronze of an American Indian, and his high cheekbones heightened the resemblance.

'You must have Indian blood,' she told him, tracing his nose with her fingertip.

'I only know two generations back,' he smiled at her. 'I've always been terrified to look further than that.'

She sat over him, cross-legged in the big bed and touched him, exploring him with her hands, touching his lips and the lobes of his ears, smoothing the thick dark curve of his eyebrows, the little black mole on his cheek, and exclaiming at each new discovery.

She touched him when they walked, reaching for his hand, pressing her hip against him when they stood, on the beach sitting between his spread knees and leaning back against his chest, her head tucked into his shoulder – it was as if she needed constant physical assurance of his presence.

When they sat astride their boards, waiting far out beyond the three-mile reef for the set of the wave, she reached across to touch his shoulder, balancing the board under her like a skilled horsewoman, the two of them close and spiritually isolated from the loose assembly of thirty or forty surf-riders strung out along the line of the long set.

This far out, the shore was a low dark green rind, above the shaded green and limpid blues of the water. In the blue distance, the mountains were blue on the blue of the sky and above them, the thunderheads piled dazzling silver, tall and arrogant enough to dwarf the very earth.

'This must be the most beautiful land in the world,' she said, moving her board so that her knee lay against his thigh.

'Because you are here,' he told her.

Under them, the green water breathed like a living thing, rising and falling, the swells long and glassy, sliding away towards the land.

Growing impatient, one of the inexperienced riders would move to catch a bad swell, kneeling on the board and paddling with both hands, coming up unsteadily on to his feet and then toppling and falling as the water left him, and the taunts and friendly catcalls of his peers greeted him as he surfaced, grinning sheepishly, and crawled back on to his board.

Then the ripple of excitement, and a voice calling, 'A three set!' the boards quickly rearranging themselves, sculled by cupped bare hands, spacing out for running room, the riders peering back eagerly over their dark burned shoulders, laughing and kidding each other as the wave set bumped up on the horizon, still four miles out at sea, but big enough so that they could count the individual swells that made up the set.

Running at fifty miles an hour, the swells took nearly five minutes, from the moment when they were sighted, to reach the line, and during that time Samantha had a little ritual of preparation. First, she hoisted the bottom of her bikini which had usually slipped down to expose a pair of dimples and a little of the deep cleft of her buttocks, then she tightened her top hamper, pulling open the brassière of her costume and cupping each breast in turn, settling it firmly in its sheath of thin green cloth, grinning at Nick as she did it.

'You're not supposed to watch.'

'I know, it's bad for my heart.'

Then she plucked out a pair of hairpins and held them in her mouth as she twisted the wrist-thick plait of hair tighter until it hung down between her shoulder blades and pinned back the wisps over her ears.

'All set?' he called, and she nodded and answered,

'Ride three?'

The third wave in the set was traditionally the big one, and they let the first one swing them high and drop them again into its trough. Half the other riders were up and away, only their heads still visible above the peak of the wave, the land obscured by the moving wall of water.

The second wave came through, bigger, more powerful, but swooping up and over the crest and most of the other riders went on it, two or three tumbling on the steep front of water, losing their boards, dragged under as the ankle lines came up taut.

'Here we go!' exulted Samantha, and three came rustling, green and peaking, and in the transparent wall of water four big bottle-nosed porpoises were framed, in perfect motion, racing in the wave, pumping their flat delta-shaped tails and grinning that fixed porpoise grin of delight.

'Oh look!' sang Samantha. 'Just look at them, Nicholas!'

Then the wave was upon them and they sculled frantically, weight high on the board, the heart-stopping moment when it seemed the water would sweep away and leave them, then suddenly the boards coming alive under them and starting to run, tipping steeply forward, with the hiss of the waxed fibreglass through the water.

Then they were both up and laughing in the sunlight, dancing the intricate steps that balanced and controlled the boards, lifted high on the crest, so they could see the sweep of the beach three miles ahead, and the ranks of other riders on the twin waves that had gone before them.

One of the porpoises frolicked with them on the racing crest, ducking under the flying boards, turning on its side to grin up at Samantha, so she stooped and stretched out a hand to touch him, lost her balance, and almost fell while the porpoise grinned at her mischievously and flipped away to rise fin up on her far side.

Now, out on their right hand, the wave was feeling the reef and starting to curl over on itself, the crest arching forwards, holding that lovely shape for long moments, then slowly collapsing.

'Go left,' Nick called urgently to her, and they kicked the boards around and danced up on to the stubby prows, bending at the knees to ride the hurtling craft, their speed rocketing as they cut across the green face of the wave, but behind them the arching wave spread rapidly towards them, faster than they could run before it.

Now at their left shoulders, the water formed a steep vertical wall, and, glancing at it, Samantha found the porpoise swimming head-high beside her, his great tail pumping powerfully, and she was afraid, for the majesty and strength of that wave belittled her.

'Nicholas!' she screamed, and the wave fanned out over her head, arcing across the sky, cutting out the sunlight, and now they flew down a long, perfectly rounded tunnel of roaring water. The sides were smooth as blown glass, and the light was green and luminous and weird as though they sped through a deep submarine cavern, only ahead of them was the perfect round opening at the mouth of the tunnel – while behind her, close behind her, the tunnel was collapsing in a furious thunder of murderous white water, and she was as terrified and as exulted as she had ever been in her life.

He yelled at her, 'We must beat the curl,' and his voice was far away and almost lost in the roar of water, but obediently she went forward on her board until all her bare toes were curled over the leading edge.

For long moments they held their own, then slowly they began to gain, and at last they shot out through the open mouth of the tunnel into the sunlight again, and she laughed wildly, still high on the exultation of fresh terror.

Then they were past the reef and the wave firmed up, leaving the white water like lace on the surface far behind.

'Let's go right!' Samantha sang out to stay within the good structure of the wave, and they turned and went back, swinging across the steep face. The splatter of flung water sparkled on her belly and thighs, and the plait of her hair stood out behind her head like the tail of an angry lioness, her arms were extended and her hands held open, unconsciously making the delicate finger gestures of a Balinese temple dancer as she balanced; and miraculously the porpoise swam, fin up, beside her, following like a trained dog.

Then at last, the wave felt the beach and ran berserk, tumbling wildly upon itself, booming angrily, and churning

213

the sand like gruel, and they kicked out of the wave, falling back over the crest and dropping into the sea beside the bobbing boards, laughing and panting at each other with the excitement and terror and the joy of it.

Samantha was a sea-creature with a huge appetite for the fruits of the sea, cracking open the crayfish legs in her fingers and sucking the white sticks of flesh into her mouth with a noisy sensuality, while her lips were polished with butter sauce, not taking her eyes from his face as she ate.

Samantha in the candlelight gulping those huge Knysna oysters, and then slurping the juice out of the shells.

'You're talking with your mouth full.'

'It's just that I've still got so much to tell you,' she explained.

Samantha was laughter, laughter in fifty different tones and intensities, from the sleepy morning chortle when she awoke and found him beside her, to the wild laughter yelled from the crest of a racing wave.

Samantha was loving. With a face of thundering innocence and the virginal, guileless green eyes of a child, she combined hands and a mouth whose wiles and wicked cunning left Nick stunned and disbelieving.

'The reason I ran away without a word was that I did not want to have your ravishment and violation on my conscience,' he shook his head at her disbelievingly.

'I wrote my PhD thesis in those subjects,' she told him blithely, using her forefinger to twist spit-curls in his sweat-dampened chest hairs. 'And what's more, buster, that was just the introductory offer – now we sign you up for a full course of treatment.'

Her delight in his body was endless, she must touch and examine every inch of it, exclaiming and revelling in it without a trace of self-consciousness, holding his hand in her lap and bending her head studiously over it, tracing the lines of his palm with her fingernail.

'You are going to meet a beautiful wanton blonde, give her fifteen babies and live to be a hundred and fifty.'

She touched the little chiselled lines around his eyes and at the corners of his mouth with the tip of her tongue, leaving cool damp smears of saliva on his skin.

'I always wanted a real craggy man all for myself.'

Then, when her examination became more intimate and clinical and he demurred, she told him severely, 'Hold still, this is a private thing between me and himself.'

Then a little later.

'Oh wow! He's real poison!'

'Poison?' he demanded, his manhood denigrated.

'Poison,' she sighed. 'Because he just slays me!'

In fairness, she offered herself for his touch and scrutiny, guiding his hands, displaying herself eagerly.

'Look, touch, it's yours – all yours,' wanting his approval, not able to give him sufficient to satisfy her own need to give. 'Do you like it, Nicholas? Is this good for you? Is there anything else you want, Nicholas, anything at all that I can give you?'

And when he told her how beautiful she was, when he told her how much he wanted her, when he touched and marvelled over the gifts she brought to him, she glowed and stretched and purred like a great golden cat so that when he learned that the zodiacal sign of her birthday was Leo, he was not at all surprised.

Samantha was loving in the early slippery grey-pearl light of dawn, soft sleepy loving, with small gasps and murmurs and chuckles of deep contentment.

Samantha was loving in the sunlight, spread like a beautiful starfish in the fierce reflected sunlight of the sculptured dunes. The sand coated her body like crystals of sugar, and their cries rose together, high and ecstatic as those of the curious seagulls that floated above them on motionless white wings.

Samantha was loving in the green cool water, their two heads bobbing beyond the first line of breakers, his toes only just touching the sandy bottom and she twined about him like sea kelp about a submerged rock, clutching both their swimsuits in one hand and gurgling merrily.

'What's good enough for a lady blue whale is good enough for Samantha Silver! Thar blows Moby Dick!'

And Samantha was loving in the night, with her hair brushed out carefully and spread over him, lustrous and fragrant, a canopy of gold in the lamplight, and she kneeling astride him in almost religious awe, like a temple maid making the sacrifice.

But more than anything else, Samantha was vibrant, bursting life – and youth eternal.

Through her, Nicholas recaptured those emotions which he had believed long atrophied by cynicism and the pragmatism of living. He shared her childlike delight in the small wonders of nature, the flight of a gull, the presence of the porpoise, the discovery of the perfect translucent fan of papery nautilus shell washed up on the white sand with the rare tentacled creature still alive within the convoluted interior.

He shared her outrage when even those remote and lonely beaches were invaded by an oil slick, tank washings from a VLCC out on the Agulhas current, and the filthy clinging globules of spilled crude oil stuck to the soles of their feet, smeared the rocks and smothered the carcasses of the jackass penguins they found at the water's edge.

Samantha was life itself, just to touch the warmth of her and to drink the sound of her laughter was to be rejuvenated. To walk beside her was to feel vital and strong.

Strong enough for the long days in the sea and sun, strong enough to dance to the loud wild music half the night, and then strong enough to lift her when she faltered and carry her down to their bungalow above the beach, she in his arms like a sleepy child, her skin tingling with the memory of the sun, her muscles aching deliciously with fatigue, and her belly crammed with rich food.

'Oh Nicholas, Nicholas – I'm so happy I want to cry.'

Then Larry Fry arrived; he arrived on a cloud of indignation, red-faced and accusing as a cuckolded husband.

'Two weeks,' he blared. 'London and Bermuda and St Nazaire have been driving me mad for two weeks!' And he brandished a sheath of telex flimsies that looked like the galley proofs for the *Encyclopaedia Britannica*.

'Nobody knew what had happened to you. You just disappeared.' He ordered a large gin and tonic from the white-jacketed bartender and sank wearily on to the stool beside Nick. 'You nearly cost me my job, Mr Berg, and that's the truth. You'd have thought I'd bumped you off personally and dumped your body in the bay. I had to hire a private detective to check every hotel register in the country.' He took a long, soothing draught of the gin.

At that moment, Samantha drifted into the cocktail lounge. She wore a loose, floating dress the same green as her eyes, and a respectful hush fell on the pre-luncheon drinkers as they watched her cross the room. Larry Fry forgot his indignation and gaped at her, his bald scorched head growing shining under a thin film of perspiration.

'Godstrewth,' he muttered. 'I'd rather feel that, than feel sick.' And then his admiration turned to consternation when she came directly to Nicholas, laid her hand on his shoulder and in full view of the entire room kissed him lingeringly on the mouth.

There was a soft collective sigh from the watchers and Larry Fry knocked over his gin.

'We must go now, today,' Samantha decided. 'We mustn't stay even another hour, Nicholas, or we will spoil it. It was perfect, but now we must go.'

Nicholas understood. Like him she had the compulsion to keep moving forward. Within the hour, he had chartered a twin-engined Beechcraft Baron. It picked them up at the little earth strip near the hotel and put them down at Johannesburg's Jan Smuts Airport an hour before the departure of the UTA flight for Paris.

'I always rode in the back of the bus before,' said Samantha, as she looked around the first-class cabin appraisingly. 'Is it true that up this end you can eat and drink as much as you like, for free?'

'Yes.' Then Nick added hastily, 'But you don't have to take that as a personal challenge.' Nicholas had come to stand in awe of Samantha's appetites.

They stayed overnight at the Georges V in Paris and caught the mid-morning TAT flight down to Nantes, the nearest airfield to the shipyards at St Nazaire, and Jules Levoisin was there to meet them at the Château Bougon field.

'Nicholas!' he shouted joyfully, and stood on tiptoe to buss both his cheeks, enveloping him in a fragrant cloud of eau de Cologne and pomade. 'You are a pirate, Nicholas, you stole that ship from under my nose. I hate you.' He held Nicholas at arm's length. 'I warned you not to take the job, didn't I?'

'You did, Jules, you did.'

'So why do you make a fool of me?' he demanded, and twirled his moustaches. He was wearing expensive cashmere and an Yves St Laurent necktie; ashore, Jules was always the dandy.

'Jules, I am going to buy lunch for you at La Rôtisserie,' Nicholas promised.

'I forgive you,' said Jules, it was one of his favourite

eating-places – but at that moment Jules became aware that Nicholas was not travelling alone.

He stood back, took one long look at Samantha and it seemed that tricolours unfurled around him and brass bands burst into the opening bars of 'La Marseillaise'. For if dalliance was the national sport, Jules Levoisin considered himself veteran champion of all France.

He bowed over her hand, and tickled the back of it with his still black moustache. Then he told Nicholas, 'She is too good for you, *mon petit*, I am going to take her away from you.'

'The same way you did *Golden Adventurer?*' Nick asked innocently.

Jules had his ancient Citroën in the car park. It was lovingly waxed and fitted with shiny gewgaws and dangling mascots. He handed Samantha into the front seat as though it was a Rolls Camargue.

'He's beautiful,' she whispered, as he scampered around to the driver's door.

Jules could not devote attention to both the road ahead and to Samantha, so he concentrated solely upon her, without deviating from the Citroën's top speed, only occasionally turning to shout, '*Cochon!*' at another driver or jerk his fist at them with the second finger pointed stiffly upwards in ribald salutation.

'Jules' great-grandfather charged with the Emperor's cavalry at Quatre Bras,' Nick explained. 'He is a man without fear.'

'You will enjoy La Rôtisserie,' Jules told Samantha. 'I can only afford to eat there when I find somebody rich who wishes a favour of me.'

'How do you know I want a favour?' Nick asked from the back seat, clinging to the door-handle.

'Three telegrams, a telephone call from Bermuda – another from Johannesburg,' Jules chuckled fruitily and winked at Samantha. 'You think I believe Nicholas Berg wants to discuss old times? You think I believe he feels so deeply for his old friend, who taught him everything he knows? A man who treated him like a son, and whom he blatantly robbed—' Jules sped across the Loire bridge and plunged into that tangled web of narrow one-way streets and teeming traffic which is Nantes; a way opened for him miraculously.

In the Place Briand, he handed Samantha gallantly from the Citroën, and in the restaurant he puffed out his cheeks and made little anxious clucking and tut-tutting noises, as Nicholas discussed the wine list with the *sommelier* – but he nodded reluctant approval when they settled on a Chablis Moutonne and a Chambertin-Clos-de-Bèze, then he applied himself with equal gusto to the food, the wine and Samantha.

'You can tell a woman who is made for life and love, by the way she eats,' and when Samantha made wide lascivious eyes at him over her trout, Nicholas expected him to crow like a cockerel.

Only when the cognac was in front of them, and both he and Nick had lit cheroots, did he demand abruptly:

'So, now, Nicholas, I am in a good mood. Ask me.'

'I need a Master for my new tug,' said Nick, and Jules veiled his face behind a thick blue curtain of cigar smoke.

They fenced like masters of épée all the way from Nantes to St Nazaire.

'Those ships you build, Nicholas, are not tugs. They are fancy toys, floating bordellos – all those gimmicks and gadgets—'

'Those gimmicks and gadgets enabled me to deal with Christy Marine while you still hadn't realized that I was within a thousand miles.' Jules blew out his cheeks and muttered to himself.

'Twenty-two thousand horsepower, *c'est ridicule!* They are over-powered—'

'I needed every single one of those horses when I pulled *Golden Adventurer* off Cape Alarm.'

'Nicholas, do not keep reminding me of that shameful episode.' He turned to Samantha. 'I am hungry, *ma petite*, and in the next village there is a *pâtisserie*,' he sighed and kissed his bunched fingers, 'you will adore the pastry.'

'Try me,' she invited, and Jules had found a soulmate.

'Those fancy propellers – variable pitch – ouf!' Jules spoke through a mouthful of pastry, and there was whipped cream on his moustache.

'I can make twenty-five knots and then slam *Warlock* into reverse thrust and stop her within her own length.'

Jules changed pace, and attacked from a new direction.

'You'll never find full employment for two big expensive ships like that.'

'I'm going to need four, not two,' Nick contradicted him. 'We are going to catch icebergs,' and Jules forgot to chew, as he listened intently for the next ten minutes. 'One of the beauties of the iceberg scheme is that all my ships will be operating right on the tanker lanes, the busiest shipping lanes in all the oceans—'

'Nicholas,' Jules shook his head in admiration, 'you move too fast for me. I am an old man, old-fashioned—'

'You're not old,' Samantha told him firmly. 'You're only just in your prime.' And Jules threw up both hands theatrically.

'Now you have a pretty girl heaping flattery on my bowed grey head,' he looked at Nicholas; 'is no trick too deceitful for you?'

It was snowing the next morning, a slow sparse sprinkling from a grey woollen sky, when they drove into St Nazaire from the little seaside resort of La Baule twenty-five kilometres up the Atlantic coast.

Jules had a small flat in one of the apartment blocks. It was a convenient arrangement, for *La Mouette*, his command, was owned by a Breton company and St Nazaire was her home port. It was a mere twenty-minute drive before they made out the elegant arch of the suspension bridge which crosses the estuarine mouth of the Loire river at St Nazaire.

Jules drove through the narrow streets of that area of the docks just below the bridge which comprises the sprawling shipbuilding yard of Construction Navale Atlantique, one of the three largest shipbuilding companies in Europe.

The slipways for the larger vessels, the bulk carriers and naval craft, faced directly on to the wide smooth reach of the river; but the ways for the small vessels backed on to the inner harbour.

So Jules parked the Citroën at the security gates nearest the inner harbour, and they walked through to where Charles Gras was waiting for them in his offices overlooking the inner basin.

'Nicholas, it is good to see you again.' Gras was one of Atlantique's top engineers, a tall stooped man with a pale face and lank black hair that fell to his eyebrows, but he had the sharp foxy Parisian features and quick bright eyes that belied the morose unsmiling manner.

He and Nicholas had known each other many years, and they used the familiar 'tu' form of address.

Charles Gras changed to heavily accented English when he was introduced to Samantha, and back to French when he asked Nicholas,

'If I know you, you will want to go directly to see your ship now, *n'est-ce pas?*'

Sea Witch stood high on her ways, and although she

was an identical twin to *Warlock*, she seemed almost twice her size with her underwater hull exposed. Despite the fact that the superstructure was incomplete and she was painted in the drab oxide red of marine primer, yet it was impossible to disguise the symmetrically functional beauty of her lines.

Jules puffed, and muttered '*Bordello*' and made remarks about 'Admiral Berg and his battleship', but he could not hide the gleam in his eye as he strutted about the incomplete navigation bridge, or listened intently as Charles Gras explained the electronic equipment and the other refinements that made the ship so fast, efficient and manoeuvrable.

Nick realized that the two experts should be left alone now to convince each other; it was clear that although this was their first meeting the two of them had established an immediate rapport.

'Come.' Nick quietly took Samantha's arm and they stepped carefully around the scaffolding and loose equipment, picking their way through groups of workmen to the upper deck.

The snow had stopped, but a razor of a wind snickered in from the Atlantic. They found a sheltered corner, and Samantha pressed close to Nick, snuggling into the circle of his arm.

High on her ways, *Sea Witch* gave them a sweeping view, through the forest of construction cranes, over the roofs of the warehouses and offices to the river slipways where the keels of the truly big hulls were laid down.

'You spoke about *Golden Dawn*,' Nick said. 'There she is.'

It took some moments for Samantha to realize she was looking at a ship.

'My God,' she breathed. 'It's so big.'

'They don't come bigger,' he agreed.

The structure of steel was almost a mile and a half long,

three city blocks, and the hull was as tall as a five-storey building, while the navigation tower was another 100 feet higher than that.

Samantha shook her head. 'It's beyond belief. It looks like – like a city! It's terrifying to think of that thing afloat.'

'That is only the main hull, the tank pods have been constructed in Japan. The last I heard is that they are under tow direct to the Persian Gulf.'

Nick stared solemnly across the ship, blinking his eyes against the stinging wind.

'I must have been out of my mind,' he whispered, 'to dream up a monster like that.' But there was a touch of defiant pride in his tone.

'It's so big – beyond imagination,' she encouraged him to talk about it. 'How big *is* it?'

'It's not a single vessel,' he explained. 'No harbour in the world could take a ship that size, it could not even approach the continental United States, for that matter, there is just not enough water to float it.'

'Yes?' She loved to listen to him expound his vision, she loved to hear the force and power of his convictions.

'What you're seeing is the carrying platform, the accommodation and the main power source.' He held her closer. 'On to that, we attach the four tank pods, each one of them capable of carrying a quarter of a million tons of crude oil, each tank almost as large as the biggest ship afloat.'

He was still explaining the concept while they sat at lunch, and Charles Gras and Jules Levoisin listened as avidly as she did.

'A single rigid hull of those dimensions would crack and break up in heavy seas,' he took the cruet set and used it to demonstrate, 'but the four individual pods have been designed so that they can move independently of each other. This gives them the ability to ride and absorb the movement of heavy seas. It is the most important principle of ship construction, a hull must ride the water – not try to oppose it.'

Across the table, Charles Gras nodded lugubrious agreement.

'The tank pods hive on to the main hull, and are carried upon it like remora on the body of a shark, not using their own propulsion systems, but relying on the multiple boilers and quadruple screws of the main hull to carry them across the oceans.' He pushed the cruet set around the table and they all watched it with fascination. 'Then, when it reaches the continental shelf opposite the shore discharge site, the main hull anchors, forty or fifty, even a hundred miles offshore, detaches one or two or all of its pod tanks, and they make those last few miles under their own propulsion. In protected water and in chosen weather conditions, their propulsion systems will handle them safely. Then the empty pod ballasts itself and returns to hook on to the main hull.'

As he spoke, Nicholas detached the salt cellar from the cruet and docked it against Samantha's plate. The two Frenchmen were silent, staring at the silver salt cellar, but Samantha watched Nick's face. It was burned dark by the sun now, lean and handsome, and he seemed charged and vital, like a thoroughbred horse in the peak of training, and she was proud of him, proud of the force of his personality that made other men listen when he spoke, proud of the imagination and the courage it took to conceive and then put into operation a project of this magnitude. Even though it were no longer his – yet his had been the vision.

Now Nicholas was talking again. 'Civilization is addicted to liquid fossil fuels. Without them, it would be forced into a withdrawal trauma too horrible to contemplate. If then we have to use crude, let's pipe it out of the earth, transport and ship it with all possible precautions to protect ourselves from its side effects—'

'Nicholas,' Charles Gras interrupted him abruptly. 'When last did you inspect the drawings of *Golden Dawn*?'

Nick paused, taken in full stride and a little off balance. He frowned as he cast back, 'I walked out of Christy Marine just over a year ago.' And the darkness of those days settled upon him, making his eyes bleak.

'A year ago we had not even been awarded the contract for the construction of *Golden Dawn*.' Charles Gras twisted the stem of his wineglass between his fingers, and thrust out his bottom lip. 'The ship you have just described to us is very different from the ship we are building out there.'

'In what way, Charles?' Nick's concern was immediate, a father hearing of radical surgery upon his first-born.

'The concept is the same. The mother vessel and the four tank pods, but—' Charles shrugged, that eloquent Gallic gesture, 'it would be easier to show it to you. Immediately after lunch.'

'*D'accord*,' Jules Levoisin nodded. 'But on the condition that it does not interfere with the further enjoyment of this fine meal.' He nudged Nicholas. 'If you eat with a scowl on your face, *mon vieux*, you will grow yourself ulcers like a bunch of Loire grapes.'

Standing beneath the bulk of *Golden Dawn*, she seemed to reach up into that low grey snow-sky, like a mighty alp of steel. The men working on the giddy heights of her scaffolding were small as insects, and quite unbelievably, as Samantha stared up at them, a little torn streamer of wet grey cloud, coming up the Loire basin from the sea, blew over the ship, obscuring the top of her navigation bridge for a few moments.

'She reaches up to the clouds,' said Nick beside her, and the pride was in his voice as he turned back to Charles Gras. 'She looks good?' It was a question, not a statement. 'She looks like the ship I planned—'

'Come, Nicholas.'

The little party picked its way through the chaos of the yard. The squeal of power cranes and the rumble of heavy steel transporters, the electric hissing crackle of the huge automatic running welders combined with the roaring gunfire barrage of the riveters into a cacophony that numbed the senses. The scaffolding and hoist systems formed an almost impenetrable forest about the mountainous hull, and steel and concrete were glistening wet and rimmed with thin clear ice.

It was a long walk through the crowded yard, almost twenty minutes merely to round the tanker's stern – and suddenly Nicholas stopped so abruptly that Samantha collided with him and might have fallen on the icy concrete, but he caught her arm and held her as he stared up at the bulbous stern.

It formed a great overhanging roof like that of a medieval cathedral, so that Nick's head was flung back, and the grip on her arm tightened so fiercely that she protested. He seemed not to hear, but went on staring upwards.

'Yes,' Charles Gras nodded, and the lank black hair flopped against his forehead. 'That is one difference from the ship you designed.'

The propeller was in lustrous ferro-bronze, six-bladed, each shaped with the beauty and symmetry of a butterfly's wing, but so enormous as to make the comparison laughable. It was so big that not even the bulk of *Golden Dawn*'s own hull could dwarf it, each separate blade was longer and broader than the full wingspan of a jumbo-jet airliner, a gargantuan sculpture in gleaming metal.

'One!' whispered Nick. 'One only.'

'Yes,' Charles Gras agreed. 'Not four – but one propeller only. Also, Nicholas, it is fixed pitch.'

They were all silent as they rode up in the cage of the hoist. The hoist ran up the outside of the hull to the level of the main deck, and though the wind searched for them remorselessly through the open mesh of the cage, it was not the cold that kept them silent.

The engine compartment was an echoing cavern,

harshly lit by the overhead floodlights, and they stood high on one of the overhead steel catwalks looking down fifty feet on to the boiler and condensers of the main engine.

Nick stared down for almost five minutes. He asked no questions, made no judgements, but at last he turned to Charles Gras and nodded once curtly.

'All right. I've seen enough,' he said, and the engineer led them to the elevator station. Again they rode upwards. It was like being in a modern office block – the polished chrome and wood panelling of the elevator, the carpeted passageways high in the navigation tower along which Charles Gras led them to the Master's suite and unlocked the carved mahogany doorway with a key from his watch chain.

Jules Levoisin looked slowly about the suite and shook his head wonderingly. 'Ah, this is the way to live,' he breathed. 'Nicholas, I absolutely insist that the Master's quarters of *Sea Witch* be decorated like this.'

Nick did not smile, but crossed to the view windows that looked forward along the tanker's main deck to her round, blunt, unlovely prow a mile and a quarter away. He stood with his hands clasped behind his back, legs apart, chin thrust out angrily and nobody else spoke while Charles Gras opened the elaborate bar and poured cognac into the crystal brandy balloons. He carried a glass to Nick who turned away from the window.

'Thank you, Charles. I need something to warm the chill in my guts.' Nick sipped the cognac and rolled it on his tongue as he looked slowly around the opulent cabin.

It occupied almost half the width of the navigation bridge, and was large enough to house a diplomatic reception. Duncan Alexander had picked a good decorator to do the job, and without the view from the window it might have been an elegant Fifth Avenue New York apartment, or one of those penthouses high on the cliffs above Monte Carlo, overlooking the harbour.

Slowly Nick crossed the thick green carpet, woven with the house device, the entwined letters C and M for Christy Marine, and he stopped before the Degas in its place of honour above the marble fireplace.

He remembered Chantelle's bubbling joy at the purchase of that painting. It was one of Degas' ballet pieces, soft, almost luminous light on the limbs of the dancers, and, remembering the unfailing delight that Chantelle had taken in it during the years, he was amazed that she had allowed it to be used on board one of the company ships, and that it was left here virtually unguarded and vulnerable. That painting was worth a quarter of a million pounds.

He leaned closer to it, and only then did he realize how clever a copy of the original it was. He shook his head in dismissal.

'The owners were advised that the sea air may damage the original,' Charles Gras shrugged, and spread his hands deprecatingly, 'and not many people would know the difference.'

That was typical of Duncan Alexander, Nicholas thought savagely. It could only be his idea, the sharp accountant's brain. The conviction that it was possible to fool all of the people all of the time.

Everybody knew that Chantelle owned that work, therefore nobody would doubt its authenticity. That's the way Duncan Alexander would reason it. It could not be Chantelle's idea. She had never been one to accept anything that was sham or dross; it was a measure of the power that he exerted over her, for her to go along with this cheap little fraud.

Nicholas indicated the forgery with his glass and spoke directly to Charles Gras.

'This is a cheat,' he spoke quietly, his anger contained and controlled, 'but it is harmless.' Now he turned away from it and, with a wider gesture that embraced the whole ship, went on, 'But this other cheat, this enormous fraud,' he paused to control the metallic edge that had entered his tone, going on quietly again, 'this is a vicious, murderous gamble he is taking. He has bastardized the entire concept of the scheme. One propeller instead of four – it cannot manoeuvre a hull of these dimensions with safety in any hazardous situation, it cannot deliver sufficient thrust to avoid collision, to fight her off a lee shore, to handle heavy seas.' Nick stopped, and his voice dropped even lower, yet somehow it was more compelling. 'This ship cannot, by all moral and natural laws, be operated on a single boiler. My design called for eight separate boilers and condensers, the standard set for the old White Star and Cunard Lines. But Duncan Alexander has installed a single boiler system. There is no back-up, no fail-safe – a few gallons of sea water in the system could disable this monster.'

Nicholas stopped suddenly as a new thought struck him. 'Charles,' his voice sharper still, 'the pod tanks, the design of the pod tanks. He hasn't altered that, has he? He hasn't cut the corners there? Tell me, old friend, they are still self-propelled, are they not?'

Charles Gras brought the Courvoisier bottle to where Nicholas stood, and when Nick would have refused the addition to his glass, Charles told him sorrowfully, 'Come, Nicholas, you will need it for what I have to tell you now.'

As he poured, he said, 'The pod tankers, their design has been altered also.' He drew a breath to tell it with a rush. 'They no longer have their own propulsion units. They are now only dumb barges that must be docked and undocked from the main hull and manoeuvred only by attendant tugs.'

Nicholas stared at him, his lips blanched to thin white lines. 'No. I do not believe it. Not even Duncan—'

'Duncan Alexander has saved forty-two million dollars by redesigning *Golden Dawn* and equipping her with only

230

a single boiler and propeller.' Charles Gras shrugged again. 'And forty-two million dollars is a lot of money.'

There was a pale gleam of wintry sunlight that flickered through the low grey cloud and lit the fields not far from the River Thames with that incredibly vivid shade of English green.

Samantha and Nicholas stood in a thin line of miserably cold parents and watched the pile of struggling boys across the field in their coloured jerseys; the light blue and black of Eton, the black and white of St Paul's, were so muddied as to be barely distinguishable.

'What are they doing?' Samantha demanded, holding the collar of her coat around her ears.

'It's called a scrum,' Nick told her. 'That's how they decide which team gets the ball.'

'Wow. There must be an easier way.'

There was a flurry of sudden movement and the slippery egg-shaped ball flew back in a lazy curve that was snapped up by a boy in the Etonian colours. He started to run.

'It's Peter, isn't it?' cried Samantha.

'Go it, Peter boy!' Nick roared, and the child ran with the ball clutched to his chest and his head thrown back. He ran strongly with the reaching coordinated stride of an older boy, swerving round a knot of his opponents, leaving them floundering in the churned mud, and angling across the lush thick grass towards the white-painted goal line, trying to reach the corner before a taller, more powerfully built lad who was pounding across the field to intercept him.

Samantha began to leap up and down on the same spot, shrieking wildly, completely uncertain of what was happening, but wild with excitement that infected Nicholas.

231

The two runners converged at an angle which would bring them to the white line at the same moment, at a point directly in front of where Nick and Samantha stood.

Nick saw the contortion of his son's face, and realized that this was a total effort. He felt a physical constriction of his own chest as he watched the boy drive himself to his utmost limits, the sinews standing out in his throat, his lips drawn back in a frozen rictus of endeavour that exposed the teeth clenched in his jaw.

From infancy, Peter Berg had brought to any task that faced him the same complete focus of all his capabilities. Like his grandfather, old Arthur Christy, and his own father, he would be one of life's winners. Nick knew this instinctively, as he watched him run. He had inherited the intelligence, the comeliness and the charisma, but he bolstered all that with this unquenchable desire to succeed in all he did. The single-minded determination to focus all his talents on the immediate project. Nick felt the pressure in his chest swell. The boy was all right, more than all right, and pride threatened to choke him.

Sheer force of will had driven Peter Berg a pace ahead of his bigger, longer-legged adversary, and now he leaned forward with the ball held in both hands, arms fully extended, reaching for the line to make the touchdown.

He was ten feet from where Nick stood, a mere instant from success, but he was unbalanced, and the St Paul's boy dived at him, crashing into the side of his chest, the impact jarring and brutal, hurling Peter out of the field of play with the ball spinning from his hands and bouncing away loosely, while Peter smashed into the earth on both knees, then rolled forward head over heels, and sprawled face down on the soggy turf.

'It's a touchdown!' Samantha was still leaping up and down.

'No,' said Nick. 'No, it isn't.'

Peter Berg dragged himself upright. His cheek was

streaked with chocolate mud and both his knees were running blood, the skin smeared open by the coarse grass.

He did not glance down at his injuries, and he shrugged away the St Paul boy's patronizing hand, holding himself erect against the pain as he limped back on to the field. He did not look at his father, and the moisture that filled his eyes and threatened to flood over the thick dark lashes were not tears of pain, but of humiliation and failure. With an overwhelming feeling of kinship, Nick knew that for his son those feelings were harder to bear than any physical agony.

When the game ended he came to Nicholas, all bloodied and mud-smeared, and shook hands solemnly.

'I am so glad you came, sir,' he said. 'I wish you could have watched us win.'

Nick wanted to say: 'It doesn't matter, Peter, it's only a game.' But he did not. To Peter Berg, it mattered very deeply, so Nicholas nodded agreement and then he introduced Samantha.

Again Peter shook hands solemnly and startled her by calling her, 'M'am.' But when she told him, 'Hi, Pete. A great game, you deserved to slam them,' he smiled, that sudden dazzling irresistible flash that reminded her so of Nicholas that she felt her heart squeezed. Then when the boy hurried away to shower and change, she took Nick's arm.

'He's a beautiful boy, but does he always call you "sir"?'

'I haven't seen him in three months. It takes us both a little while to relax.'

'Three months is a long time—'

'It's all tied up by the lawyers. Access and visiting rights – what's good for the child, not what's good for the parents. Today was a special concession from Chantelle, but I still have to deliver him to her at five o'clock. Not five past five, five o'clock.'

They went to the Cockpit teashop and Peter startled

Samantha again by pulling out her chair and seating her formally. While they waited for the best muffins in Britain to be brought to the table, Nicholas and Peter engaged each other in conversation that was stiff with self-consciousness.

'Your mother sent me a copy of your report, Peter. I cannot tell you how delighted I was.'

'I had hoped to do better, sir. There are still three others ahead of me.'

And Samantha ached for them. Peter Berg was twelve years of age. She wished he could just throw his arms around Nicholas' neck and say, 'Daddy, I love you,' for the love was transparent, even through the veneer of public-school manners. It shone behind the thick dark lashes that fringed the boy's golden brown eyes, and glowed on the cheeks still as creamy and smooth as a girl's.

She wanted desperately to help them both, and on inspiration she launched into an account of *Warlock*'s salvage of *Golden Adventurer*, a tale with emphasis on the derring-do of *Warlock*'s Master, not forgetting his rescue of Samantha Silver from the icy seas of Antarctica.

Peter's eyes grew enormous as he listened, never leaving her face except to demand of Nicholas, 'Is that true, Dad?' And when the story was told, he was silent for a long moment before announcing, 'I'm going to be a tug captain when I'm big.'

Then he showed Samantha how to spread strawberry jam on her muffins in the correct way, and chewing together heartily with cream on their lips the two of them became fast friends, and Nicholas joined their chatter more easily, smiling his thanks to Samantha and reaching under the table to squeeze her hand.

He had to end it at last. 'Listen, Peter, if we are to make Lynwood by five—' and the boy sobered instantly.

'Dad, couldn't you telephone Mother? She might just let me spend the weekend in London with you.'

'I already tried that.' Nick shook his head. 'It didn't work,' and Peter stood up, his feeling choked by an expression of stoic resignation.

From the back of Nick's Mercedes 450 Coupé the boy leaned forward into the space between the two bucket seats, and the three of them were very close in the snug interior of the speeding car, their laughter that of old friends.

It was almost dark when Nicholas turned in through Lynwood's stone gateway, and he glanced at the luminous dial of his Rolex. 'We'll just make it.'

The drive climbed the hill in a series of broad, even curves through the carefully tended woods, and the three-storied Georgian country house on the crest was ablaze with light in every window.

Nick never came here without that strange hollow feeling in the bottom of his stomach. Once this had been his home, every room, every acre of the grounds had its memories, and now, as he parked under the white columned portico, they came crowding back.

'I have finished the model Spitfire you sent me for Christmas, Dad.' Peter was playing desperately for time now. 'Won't you come up and see it?'

'I don't think so—' Nicholas began, and Peter blurted out before he could finish.

'It's all right, Uncle Duncan won't be here. He always comes down late from London on Friday nights, and his Rolls isn't in the garage yet.' Then, in a tone that tore at Nick like thorns, 'Please . . . I won't see you again until Easter.'

'Go,' said Samantha. 'I'll wait here.' And Peter turned on her, 'You come too, Sam, please.'

Samantha felt herself infected by that fatal curiosity, the desire to see, to know more of Nick's past life; she knew he was going to demur further, but she forestalled him, slipping quickly out of the Mercedes.

'Okay, Pete, let's go.'

Nick must follow them up the broad steps to the double oaken doors, and he felt himself carried along on a tide of events over which he had no control. It was a sensation that he never relished.

In the entrance hall Samantha looked around her quickly, feeling herself overcome by awe. It was so grand, there was no other word to describe the house. The stairwell reached up the full height of the three storeys, and the broad staircase was in white marble with a marble balustrade, while on each side of the hall, glass doors opened on to long reception rooms. But she did not have a chance to look further, for Peter seized her hand and raced her up the staircase, while Nick followed them up to Peter's room at a more sedate pace.

The Spitfire had place of honour on the shelf above Peter's bed. He brought it down proudly, and they examined it with suitable expressions of admiration. Peter responded to their praise like a flower to the sun.

When at last they descended the staircase, the sadness and restraint of parting was on them all, but they were stopped in the centre of the hall by the voice from the drawing-room door on the left.

'Peter, darling.' A woman stood in the open doorway, and she was even more beautiful than the photograph that Samantha had seen of her.

Dutifully Peter crossed to her. 'Good evening, Mother.'

She stooped over him, cupping his face in her hands, and she kissed him tenderly, then she straightened, holding his hand so he was ranged at her side, a subtle drawing of boundaries.

'Nicholas,' she tilted her head, 'you look marvellous – so brown and fit.'

Chantelle Alexander was only a few inches taller than her son, but she seemed to fill and light the huge house with a shimmering presence, the way a single beautiful bird can light a dim forest.

Her hair was dark and soft and glowing, and her skin and the huge dark sloe eyes were a legacy from the beautiful Persian noblewoman that old Arthur Christy had married for her fortune, and come to love with an obsessive passion.

She was dainty. Her tiny, narrow feet peeped from below the long, dark green silk skirt, and the exquisite little hand that held Peter's was emphasized by a single deep throbbing green emerald the size of a ripe acorn.

Now she turned her head on the long graceful neck, and her eyes took the slightly oriental slant of a modern-day Nefertiti as she looked at Samantha.

For seconds only, the two women studied each other, and Samantha's chin came up firmly as she looked into those deep dark gazelle eyes, touched with all the mystery and intrigue of the East. They understood each other instantly. It was an intuitive flash, like a discharge of static electricity, then Chantelle smiled, and when she smiled the impossible happened – she became more beautiful than before.

'May I present Dr Silver?' Nick began, but Peter tugged at his mother's hand.

'I asked Sam to see my model. She's a marine biologist, and she's a professor at Miami University—'

'Not yet, Pete,' Samantha corrected him, 'but give me time.'

'Good evening, Dr Silver. It seems you have made a conquest.' Chantelle let the statement hang ambiguously as she turned back to Nick. 'I was waiting for you, Nicholas, and I'm so glad to have a chance to speak to you.' She glanced again at Samantha. 'I do hope you will excuse us for a few minutes, Dr Silver. It is a matter of some urgency. Peter will be delighted to entertain you. As a biologist, you will find his guinea pigs of interest, I'm sure.'

The commands were given so graciously, by a lady in such control of her situation, that Peter went to take Samantha's hand and lead her away.

It was one of the customs of Lynwood that all serious discussion took place in the study. Chantelle led the way, and went immediately to the false-fronted bookcase that concealed the liquor cabinet, and commenced the ritual of preparing a drink for Nicholas. He wanted to stop her. It was something from long ago, recalling too much that was painful, but instead, he watched the delicate but precise movements of her hands pouring exactly the correct measure of Chivas Royal Salute into the crystal glass, adding the soda and the single cube of ice.

'What a pretty young girl, Nicholas.'

He said nothing. On the ornate Louis Quatorze desk was a silver-framed photograph of Duncan Alexander and Chantelle together, and he looked away and moved to the fireplace, standing with his back to the blaze as he had done on a thousand other evenings.

Chantelle brought the glass to him, and stood close, looking up at him – and her fragrance touched a deep nostalgic chord. He had first bought *Calèche* for her on a spring morning in Paris; with an effort he forced the memory aside.

'What did you want to speak to me about, is it Peter?'

'No. Peter is doing as well as we can hope for, in the circumstances. He still resents Duncan – but—' she shrugged, and moved away. He had almost forgotten how narrow was her waist, he would still be able to span it with both hands.

'It's hard to explain, but it's Christy Marine, Nicholas. I desperately need the advice of someone I can trust.'

'You can trust me?' he asked.

'Isn't it strange? I would still trust you with my life.' She came back to him, standing disconcertingly close, envel-

238

oping him with her scent and heady beauty. He sipped at the whisky to distract himself.

'Even though I have no right to ask you, Nicholas, still I know you won't refuse me, will you?'

She wove spells, he could feel the mesh falling like gossamer around him.

'I always was a sucker, wasn't I?'

Now she touched his arm. 'No, Nicholas, please don't be bitter.' She held his gaze directly.

'How can I help you?' Her touch on his arm disturbed him, and, sensing this, she increased the pressure of her fingers for a moment, then lifted her hand and glanced at the slim white gold Piaget on her wrist.

'Duncan will be home soon – and what I have to tell you is long and complicated. Can we meet in London early next week?'

'Chantelle,' he began.

'Nicky, please.' *Nicky*, she was the only one who ever called him that. It was too familiar, too intimate.

'When?'

'You are meeting Duncan on Tuesday morning to discuss the arbitration of *Golden Adventurer*.'

'Yes.'

'Will you call me at Eaton Square when you finish? I'll wait by the telephone.'

'Chantelle—'

'Nicky, I have nobody else to turn to.'

He had never been able to refuse her – which was part of the reason he had lost her, he thought wryly.

There was no engine noise, just the low rush of air past the body of the Mercedes.

'Damn these seats, they weren't made for lovers,' Samantha said.

'We'll be home in an hour.'

'I don't know if I can wait that long,' Samantha whispered huskily. 'I want to be closer to you.'

And they were silent again, until they slowed for the weekend traffic through Hammersmith.

'Peter is a knockout. If only I were ten years old, I'd cash in my dolls.'

'My guess is he would swop his Spitfire.'

'How much longer?'

'Another half-hour.'

'Nicholas, I feel threatened,' her voice had a sudden panicky edge to it. 'I have this terrible foreboding—'

'That's nonsense.'

'It's been too good – for too long.'

James Teacher was the head of Salmon, Peters and Teacher, the lawyers that Nick had retained for Ocean Salvage. He was a man with a formidable reputation in the City, a leading expert on maritime law – and a tough bargainer. He was florid and bald, and so short that his feet did not touch the floorboards of the Bentley when he sat on the back seat.

He and Nick had discussed in detail where this preliminary meeting with Christy Marine should be held, and at last they had agreed to go to the mountain, but James Teacher had insisted on arriving in his chocolate-coloured Bentley, rather than a cab.

'Smoked salmon, Mr Berg, not fish and chips – that's what we are after.'

Christy House was one of those conservative smoke-stained stone buildings fronted on to Leadenhall Street, the centre of Britain's shipping industry. Almost directly opposite was Trafalgar House, and a hundred yards further was Lloyd's of London. The doorman crossed the pavement to open Nicholas' door.

'Good to see you again, Mr Berg sir.'

'Hello, Alfred. You taking good care of the shop?'

'Indeed, sir.'

The following cab, containing James Teacher's two juniors and their bulky briefcases, pulled up behind the Bentley and they assembled on the pavement like a party of raiding Vikings before the gates of a medieval city. The three lawyers settled their bowler hats firmly and then moved forward determinedly in spearhead formation.

In the lobby, the doorman passed them on to a senior clerk who was waiting by the desk.

'Good morning, Mr Berg. You are looking very well, sir.'

They rode up at a sedate pace in the elevator with its antique steel concertina doors. Nicholas had never brought himself to exchange them for those swift modern boxes. And the clerk ushered them out on to the top-floor landing.

'Will you follow me, please, gentlemen?'

There was an antechamber that opened on to the board room, a large room, panelled and hung with a single portrait of old Arthur Christy on the entrance wall – fighting jaw and sharp black eyes under beetling white eyebrows. A log fire burned in the open grate, and there was sherry and Madeira in crystal decanters on the central table – another one of the old man's little traditions – that both James Teacher and Nick refused curtly.

They waited quietly, standing facing the door into the Chairman's suite. They waited for exactly four minutes before the door was thrown open and Duncan Alexander stepped through it.

His eyes flicked across the room and settled instantly on Nick, locking with his, like the horns of two great bull buffalo, and the room was very still.

The lawyers around Nick seemed to shrink back and the men behind Duncan Alexander waited, not yet following him into the antechamber, but all of them watched and waited avidly; this meeting would be the gossip of the City for weeks to come. It was a classic confrontation, and they wanted to miss not a moment of it.

Duncan Alexander was a strikingly good-looking man, very tall, two inches taller than Nick, but slim as a dancer, and he carried his body with a dancer's control. His face also was narrow, with the long lantern jaw of a young Lincoln, already chiselled by life around the eyes and at the corners of the mouth.

His hair was very dense and a metallic blond; though he wore it fashionably long over the ears, yet it was so carefully groomed that each gleaming wave seemed to have been sculptured.

His skin was smooth and tanned darker than his hair, sunlamp or skiing at Chantelle's lodge at Gstaad perhaps, and now when he smiled his teeth were dazzlingly white, perfect large teeth in the wide friendly mouth – but the eyes did not smile though they crinkled at the corners. Duncan Alexander watched from behind the handsome face like a sniper in ambush.

'Nicholas,' he said, without moving forward or offering a hand.

'Duncan,' said Nick quietly, not answering the smile, and Duncan Alexander adjusted the hang of his lapel. His clothes were beautifully cut, and the cloth was the finest, softest wool, but there were foppish little touches: the hacking slits in the tails of the jacket, the double-flapped pockets, and the waistcoat in plum-coloured velvet. Now he touched the buttons with his fingertips, another little distracting gesture, the only evidence of any discomfort.

Nicholas stared at him steadily, trying to measure him dispassionately, and now for the first time he began to see how it might have happened. There was a sense of excitement about the man, a wicked air of danger, the fascination of the leopard – or some other powerful predator. Nick could understand the almost irresistible attraction he had for women, especially for a spoiled and bored lady, a matron of thirteen years who believed there was still excitement and adventure in life that she was missing. Duncan had done his cobra dance, and Chantelle had watched like a mesmerized bird of paradise – until she had toppled from the branch – or that's how Nicholas liked to think it had happened. He was wiser now, much wiser and more cynical.

'Before we begin,' Nick knew that anger was seething to his still surface, must soon bubble through unless he could give it release, 'I should like five minutes in private.'

'Of course.' Duncan inclined his head, and there was a hurried scampering as his minions cleared the doorway into the Chairman's suite. 'Come through.'

Duncan stood aside, and Nick walked through. The offices had been completely redecorated, and Nick blinked with surprise, white carpets and furniture in chrome and perspex, stark abstract geometrical art in solid primary colours on the walls; the ceiling had been lowered by an eggcrate design in chrome steel and free-swivelling studio spotlights gave selected light patterns on wall and ceiling. It was no improvement, Nick decided.

'I was in St Nazaire last week.' Nicholas turned in the centre of the wide snowy floor and faced Duncan Alexander as he closed the door.

'Yes, I know.'

'I went over *Golden Dawn*.'

Duncan Alexander snapped open a gold cigarette case and offered it to Nick, then when he shook his head in refusal, selected one himself. They were a special blend, custom-made for him by Benson and Hedges.

'Charles Gras exceeded his authority,' Duncan nodded. 'Visitors are not allowed on *Golden Dawn*.'

'I am not surprised you are ashamed of that death-trap you are building.'

'But you do surprise me, Nicholas.' Duncan showed his teeth again. 'It was your design.'

'You know it was not. You took the idea, and bastardized it. Duncan, you cannot send that,' Nick sought the word, 'monster on to the open sea. Not with one propulsion unit, and a single screw. The risk is too appalling.'

'I tell you this for no good reason, except perhaps that this was once your office,' Duncan made a gesture that embraced the room, 'and because it amuses me to point out to you the faults in your original planning. The concept was sound, but you soured the cream by adding those preposterous, shall we call them Bergean, touches. Five separate propulsion units, and a forest of boilers. It wasn't viable, Nicholas.'

'It was good, the figures were right.'

'The whole tanker market has changed since you left Christy Marine. I had to rework it.'

'You should have dropped the whole concept if the cost-structure changed.'

'Oh no, Nicholas, I restructured. My way, even in these hard times, I will recover capital in a year, and with a five-year life on the hull there is two hundred million dollars' profit in it.'

'I was going to build a ship that would last for thirty years,' Nick told him. 'Something of which we could be proud—'

'Pride is an expensive commodity. We aren't building dynasties any more, we are in the game of selling tanker space.' Duncan's tone was patronizing, that impeccable accent drawn out, emphasizing the difference in their backgrounds. 'I'm aiming at a five-year life, two hundred million profit, and then we sell the hull to the Greeks or Japs. It's a one-time thing.'

'You always were a smash-and-grab artist,' Nick agreed. 'But it isn't like dealing in commodities. Ships aren't wheat and bacon, and the oceans aren't the orderly market floors.'

'I disagree, I'm afraid. The principles are the same – one buys, one sells.'

'Ships are living things, the ocean is a battleground of all the elements.'

'Come, Nicholas, you don't really believe that romantic nonsense.' Duncan drew a gold Hunter from his waist pocket, and snapped open the lid to read the dial, another of his affectations which irritated Nicholas. 'Those are very expensive gentlemen waiting next door.'

'You will be risking human life, the men who sail her.'

'Seamen are well paid—'

'You will be taking a monstrous risk with the life of the oceans. Wherever she goes *Golden Dawn* will be a potential—'

'For God's sake, Nicholas, two hundred million dollars is worth some kind of risk.'

'All right,' Nick nodded. 'Let's forget the environment, and the human life, and consider the important aspects – the money.'

Duncan sighed, and wagged that fine head, smiling as at a recalcitrant child.

'I have considered the money – in detail.'

'You will not get an A1 rating at Lloyd's. You will not get insurance on that hull – unless you underwrite yourself, the same way you did with *Golden Adventurer*, and if you think that's wise, just wait until I've finished with my salvage claim.'

Duncan Alexander's smile twisted slowly, and blood darkened his cheeks under the snow-tan. 'I do not need a Lloyd's rating, though I am sure I could get one if I wanted it. I have arranged continental and oriental underwriters. She will be fully insured.'

'Against pollution claims, also? If you burst that bag of crude on the continental shelf of America, or Europe, they'll hit you for half a billion dollars. Nobody would underwrite that.'

'*Golden Dawn* is registered in Venezuela, and she has no sister ships for the authorities to seize, like they did with the *Torrey Canyon*. To whom will they address the pollution bill? A defunct South American Company? No, Nicholas, Christy Marine will not be paying any pollution bills.'

'I cannot believe it, even of you.' Nick stared at him. 'You are cold-bloodedly talking about the possibility – no, the probability – of dumping a million tons of crude oil into the sea.'

'Your moral indignation is touching. It really is. However, Nicholas, may I remind you that this is family and house business – and you are no longer either family or house.'

'I fought you every time you cut a corner,' Nick reminded him. 'I tried to teach you that cheap is always expensive in the long run.'

'You taught me?' For the first time Duncan taunted him openly. 'What could you ever teach me about ships or money,' and he rolled his tongue gloating around the next words, 'or women?'

Nick made the first movement of lunging at him, but he caught himself, and forced himself to unclench his fists at his sides. The blood sang in his ears.

'I'm going to fight you,' he said quietly. 'I'm going to fight you from here to the maritime conference, and beyond.' He made the decision in that moment, he hadn't realized he was going to do it until then.

'A maritime conference has never taken less than five years to reach a decision restricting one of its members. By

246

that time *Golden Dawn* will belong to some Japanese, Hong-Kong-based company – and Christy Marine will have banked two hundred million.'

'I'll have the oil ports closed to you—'

'By whom? Oil-thirsty governments, with lobbies of the big oil companies?' Duncan laughed lightly, he had replaced the urbane mask. 'You really are out of your depth again. We have bumped heads a dozen times before, Nicholas – and I'm still on my feet. I'm not about to fold up to your fine threats now.'

After that, there was no hope that the meeting in the panelled boardroom would lead to conciliation. The atmosphere crackled and smouldered with the antagonism of the two leading characters, so that they seemed to be the only persons on the stage.

They sat opposite each other, separated by the glossy surface of the rosewood table top, and their gazes seldom disengaged. They leaned forward in their chairs, and when they smiled at each other, it was like the silent snarl of two old dog wolves circling with hackles erect.

It took an enormous effort of self-control for Nicholas to force back his anger far enough to be able to think clearly, and to allow his intuition to pick up the gut-impressions, the subtle hints of the thinking and planning that were taking place across the table behind Duncan Alexander's handsome mask of a face.

It was half an hour before he was convinced that something other than personal rivalry and antagonism was motivating the man before him. His counter-offer was too low to have any hope of being accepted, so low that it became clear that he did not want to settle. Duncan Alexander wanted to go to arbitration – and yet there was nothing he could gain by that. It must be obvious to everyone at the table, beyond any doubt whatsoever, that Nicholas' claim was worth four million dollars. Nicholas would have settled for four, even in his anger he would have gone for four – risking that an arbitration board might have awarded six, and knowing the delay and costs of going to litigation might amount to another million. He would have settled.

Duncan Alexander was offering two and a half. It was a frivolous offer. Duncan was going through the motions only. There was no serious attempt at finding a settlement. He didn't want to come to terms, and it seemed to Nicholas that by refusing to settle he was gaining nothing, and risking a great deal. He was a big enough boy to know that you never, but never, go to litigation if there is another way out. It was a rule that Nicholas had graven on his heart in letters of fire. Litigation makes only lawyers fat.

Why was Duncan baulking, what was he to gain by this obstruction? Nicholas crushed down the temptation to stand up and walk out of the room with an exclamation of disgust. Instead, he lit another cheroot and leaned forward again, staring into Duncan Alexander's steely grey eyes, trying to fathom him, needling, probing for the soft rotten spot – and thinking hard.

What had Duncan Alexander to gain from not settling now? Why did he not try with a low, but realistic offer – what was he to gain?

Then quite suddenly he knew what it was. Chantelle's enigmatic appeal for help and advice flashed back to him, and he knew what it was. Duncan Alexander wanted time. It was as simple as that. Duncan Alexander needed time.

'All right.' Satisfied at last, Nicholas leaned back in the deep leather-padded chair, and veiled his eyes. 'We are still a hundred miles apart. There will be only one meeting-ground. That's in the upper room at Lloyd's. It's set down for the 27th. Are we at least agreed on that date?'

'Of course.' Duncan leaned back also and Nicholas saw

the shift of his eyes, the little jump of nerves in the point of his clenched jaws, the tightening of the long pianist's fingers that lay before him on the leather-bound blotter. 'Of course,' Duncan repeated, and began to stand up, a gesture of dismissal. He lied beautifully; had Nicholas not known he would lie, he might have missed the little tell-tale signs.

In the ancient lift, James Teacher was jubilant, rubbing his little fat hands together. 'We'll give him a go!' Nicholas glanced at him sourly. Win, lose or draw, James Teacher would still draw his fee, and Duncan Alexander's refusal to settle had quadrupled that fee. There was something almost obscene about the little lawyer's exultation.

'They are going to duck,' Nick said grimly, and James Teacher sobered slightly.

'Before noon tomorrow, Christy Marine will have lodged for postponement of hearing,' Nick prophesied. 'You'll have to use *Warlock* with full power on both to pull them before the arbitration board.'

'Yes, you're right,' James Teacher nodded. 'They had me puzzled, I sensed something—'

'I'm not paying you to be puzzled,' Nick's voice was low and hard. 'I'm paying you to out-guess and out-jump them. I want them at the hearing on the 27th, get them there, Mr Teacher.' He did not have to voice the threat, and in a moment, the exultation on James Teacher's rotund features had changed to apprehension and deep concern.

The drawing-room in Eaton Square was decorated in cream and pale gold, cleverly designed as a frame for the single exquisite work of art which it contained, the original of the group of Degas ballet-dancers whose copy hung in *Golden Dawn*'s stateroom. It was the room's centrepiece; cunningly lit by a hidden spotlight, it glowed like a precious jewel. Even the flowers on the ivory grand piano were cream and white roses and carnations, whose pale ethereal blossoms put the painting into stronger contrast.

The only other flash of brightness was worn by Chantelle. She had the oriental knack of carrying vivid colour without it seeming gaudy. She wore a flaming Pucci that could not pale her beauty, and as she rose from the huge shaggy white sofa and came to Nicholas, he felt the soft warm melting sensation in his stomach spreading slowly through his body like a draught of some powerful aphrodisiac. He knew he would never be immune to her.

'Dear Nicky, I knew I could rely upon you.' She took his hand and looked up at him, and still holding his hand she led him to the sofa, and then she settled beside him, like a bright, lovely bird alighting. She drew her legs up under her, her calves and ankles flashed like carved and polished ivory before she tucked the brilliant skirt around them, and lifted the Wedgwood porcelain teapot.

'Orange pekoe,' she smiled at him. 'No lemon and no sugar.'

He had to smile back at her. 'You never forget,' and he took the cup.

'I told you that you looked well,' she said, slowly and unself-consciously studying him. 'And you really do, Nicholas. When you came down to Lynwood for Peter's birthday in June I was so worried about you. You looked terribly ill and tired – but now,' she tilted her head critically, 'you look absolutely marvellous.'

Now he should tell her that she was beautiful as ever, he thought grimly, and then they would start talking about Peter and their old mutual friends.

'What did you want to talk to me about?' he asked quietly, and there was a passing shadow of hurt in her dark eyes.

'Nicholas, you can be so remote, so—' she hesitated, seeking the correct word, 'so detached.'

'Recently someone called me an ice-cold Pommy bastard,' he agreed, but she shook her head.

'No. I know you are not, but if only—'

'The three most dangerous and inflammatory phrases in the English language,' he stopped her. 'They are "you always" and "you never" and "if only". Chantelle, I came here to help you with a problem. Let's discuss that – only.'

She stood up quickly, and he knew her well enough to recognize the fury in the snapping dark eyes and the quick dancing steps that carried her to the mantelpiece, and she stood looking up at the Degas with her small fists clenched at her sides.

'Are you sleeping with that child?' she asked, and now the fury was raw in her voice.

Nicholas stood up from the sofa.

'Goodbye, Chantelle.'

She turned and flew to him, taking his arm.

'Oh, Nicholas, that was unforgivable, I don't know what possessed me. Please don't go.' And when he tried to dislodge her hand. 'I beg you, for the first time ever, I beg you, Nicholas. Please don't go.'

He was still stiff with anger when he sank back on the sofa, and they were silent for nearly a minute while she regained her composure.

'This is all going so terribly badly. I didn't want this to happen.'

'All right, let's get on to safer ground.'

'Nicholas,' she started, 'you and Daddy created Christy Marine. If anything, it was more yours than his. The great days were the last ten years when you were Chairman, all the tremendous achievements of those years—'

He made a gesture of denial and impatience, but she went on softly.

251

'Too much of your life is locked up in Christy Marine, you are still deeply involved, Nicholas.'

'There are only two things I am involved with now,' he told her harshly. 'Ocean Salvage and Nicholas Berg.'

'We both know that is not true,' she whispered. 'You are a special type of man.' She sighed. 'It took me so long to recognize that. I thought all men were like you. I believed strength and nobility of mind were common goods on the market—' she shrugged. 'Some people learn the hard way,' and she smiled, but it was an uncertain, twisted little smile.

He said nothing for a moment, thinking of all that was revealed by those words, then he replied.

'If you believe that, then tell me what is worrying you.'

'Nicholas, something is terribly wrong with Christy Marine. There is something happening there that I don't understand.'

'Tell me.'

She turned her head away for a moment, and then looked back at him. Her eyes seemed to change shape and colour, growing darker and sadder. 'It is so difficult not to be disloyal, so difficult to find expression for vague doubts and fears,' she stopped and bit her lower lip softly. 'Nicholas, I have transferred my shares in Christy Marine to Duncan as my nominee, with voting rights.'

Nicholas felt the shock of it jump down his nerves and string them tight. He shifted restlessly on the sofa and stared at her, and she nodded.

'I know it was madness. The madness of those crazy days a year ago. I would have given him anything he asked for.'

He felt the premonition that she had not yet told him all and he waited while she rose and went to the window, looked out guiltily and then turned back to him.

'May I get you a drink?'

He glanced at his Rolex. 'The sun is over the yardarm, what about Duncan?'

'These days he is never home before eight or nine.' She went to the decanter on the silver tray and poured the whisky with her back to him, and now her voice was so low that he barely caught the words.

'A year ago I resigned as executrix of the Trust.'

He did not answer, it was what he had been waiting for, he had known there was something else. The Trust that old Arthur Christy had set up was the backbone and sinews of Christy Marine. One million voting shares administered by three executors: a banker, a lawyer and a member of the Christy family.

Chantelle turned and brought the drink to him.

'Did you hear what I said?' she asked, and he nodded and sipped the drink before he asked,

'The other executors? Pickstone of Lloyd's and Rollo still?'

She shook her head and again bit her lip.

'No, it's not Lloyd's any more, it's Cyril Forbes.'

'Who is he?' Nick demanded.

'He is the head of London and European.'

'But that's Duncan's own bank,' Nick protested.

'It's still a registered bank.'

'And Rollo?'

'Rollo had a heart attack six months ago. He resigned, and Duncan put in another younger man. You don't know him.'

'My God, three men and each of them is Duncan Alexander – he has had a free hand with Christy Marine for over a year, Chantelle, there is no check on him.'

'I know,' she whispered. 'It was a madness. I just cannot explain it.'

'It's the oldest madness in the world.' Nick pitied her then; for the first time, he realized and accepted that she had been under a compulsion, driven by forces over which she had no control, and he pitied her.

'I am so afraid, Nicholas. I'm afraid to find out what I have done. Deep down I know there is something terribly wrong, but I'm afraid of the truth.'

'All right, tell me everything.'

'There isn't anything else.'

'If you lie to me, I cannot help you,' he pointed out gently.

'I have tried to follow the new structuring of the company, it's all so complicated, Nicholas. London and European is the new holding company, and – and—' her voice trailed off. 'It just goes round and round in circles, and I cannot pry too deep or ask too many questions.'

'Why not?' he demanded.

'You don't know Duncan.'

'I am beginning to,' he answered her grimly. 'But, Chantelle, you have every right to ask and get answers.'

'Let me get you another drink.' She jumped up lightly.

'I haven't finished this one.'

'The ice has melted, I know you don't like that.' She took the glass and emptied the diluted spirit, refilled it and brought it back to him.

'All right,' he said. 'What else?'

Suddenly she was weeping. Smiling at him wistfully and weeping. There was no sobbing or sniffing, the tears merely welled up slowly as oil or blood from the huge dark eyes, broke from the thick, arched lashes and rolled softly down her cheeks. Yet she still smiled.

'The madness is over, Nicholas. It didn't last very long – but it was a holocaust while it did.'

'He comes home at nine o'clock now,' Nicholas said.

'Yes, he comes home at nine o'clock.'

He took the linen handkerchief from his inner pocket and handed it to her.

'Thank you.'

She dabbed away the tears, still smiling softly.

'What must I do, Nicholas?'

'Call in a team of auditors,' he began, but she shook her head and cut him short.

'You don't know Duncan,' she repeated.

'There is nothing he could do.'

'He could do anything,' she contradicted him. 'He is capable of anything. I am afraid, Nicholas, terribly afraid, not only for myself, but for Peter also.'

Nicholas sat erect then.

'Peter. Do you mean you are afraid of something physical?'

'I don't know, Nicholas. I'm so confused and alone. You are the only person in the world I can trust.'

He could no longer remain seated. He stood up and began to pace about the room, frowning heavily, looking down at the glass in his hand and swirling the ice so that it tinkled softly.

'All right,' he said at last. 'I will do what I can. The first thing is to find out just how much substance there is to your fears.'

'How will you do that?'

'It's best you don't know, yet.'

He drained his glass and she stood up, quick with alarm.

'You aren't going, are you?'

'There is nothing else to discuss now. I will contact you when or if I learn anything.'

'I'll see you down.'

In the hall she dismissed the uniformed West Indian maid with a shake of her head, and fetched Nicholas' top-coat from the closet herself.

'Shall I send for the car? You'll not get a cab at five o'clock.'

'I'll walk,' he said.

'Nicholas, I cannot tell you how grateful I am. I had forgotten how safe and secure it is to be with you.' Now she was standing very close to him, her head lifted, and her lips were soft and glossy and ripe, her eyes still flooded and bright. He knew he should leave immediately. 'I know it's going to be all right now.'

She placed one of those dainty ivory hands on his lapel, adjusting it unnecessarily with that proprietary feminine gesture, and she moistened her lips.

'We are all fools, Nicholas, every one of us. We all complicate our lives – when it's so easy to be happy.'

'The trick is to recognize happiness when you stumble on it, I suppose.'

'I'm sorry, Nicholas. That's the first time I've ever apologized to you. It's a day of many first times, isn't it? But I am truly sorry for everything I have ever done to hurt you. I wish with all my heart that it were possible to wipe it all out and begin again.'

'Unfortunately, it doesn't work that way.' With a major effort of will he broke the spell, and stepped back. In another moment he would have stooped to those soft red lips.

'I'll call you if I learn anything,' he said, as he buttoned the top of his coat and opened the front door.

Nicholas stepped out furiously with the cold striking colour into his cheeks, but her presence kept pace with him and his blood raced not from physical exertion alone.

He knew then, beyond all doubt, that he was not a man who could switch love on and off at will.

'You old-fashioned thing.' Samantha's words came back to him clearly – and she was right, of course. He was cursed by a constancy of loyalty and emotion that restricted his freedom of action. He was breaking one of his own rules now, he was no longer moving ahead. He was circling back.

He had loved Chantelle Christy to the limits of his soul, and had devoted almost half of his life to Christy Marine. He realized then that those things could never change, not for him, not for Nicholas Berg, prisoner of his own conscience.

Suddenly he found himself opposite the Kensington Natural History Museum in the Cromwell Road, and swiftly he crossed to the main gates – but it was a quarter to six and they were closed already. Samantha would not have been in the public rooms anyway, but in those labyrinthine vaults below the great stone building. In a few short days, she had made half a dozen cronies among the museum staff. He felt a stab of jealousy, that she was with other human beings, revelling in their companionship, delighting in the pleasures of the mind – had probably forgotten he existed.

Then suddenly the unfairness of it occurred to him, how his emotions of a minute previously had been stirring and boiling with the memories of another woman. Only then did he realize that it was possible to be in love with two different people, in two entirely different ways, at exactly the same time.

Troubled, torn by conflicting loves, conflicting loyalties, he turned away from the barred iron gates of the museum.

N icholas' apartment was on the fifth floor of one of those renovated and redecorated buildings in Queen's Gate.

It looked as though a party of gypsies were passing through. He had not hung the paintings, nor had he arranged his books on the shelves. The paintings were stacked against the wall in the hallway, and his books were pyramided at unlikely spots around the lounge floor, the carpet still rolled and pushed aside, two chairs facing the television set, and another two drawn up to the dining-room table.

It was an eating and sleeping place, sustaining the bare minima of existence; in two years he had probably slept here on sixty nights, few of them consecutive. It was impersonal, it contained no memories, no warmth.

He poured a whisky and carried it through into the bedroom, slipping the knot of his tie and shrugging out of his jacket. Here it was different, for evidence of Samantha's presence was everywhere. Though she had remade the bed that morning before leaving, still she had left a pair of shoes abandoned at the foot of it, a booby trap to break the ankles of the unwary; her simple jewellery was strewn on the bedside table, together with a book, Noel Mostert's *Supership*, opened face down and in dire danger of a broken spine; the cupboard door was open and his suits had been bunched up in one corner to give hanging space to her slacks and dresses; two very erotic and transparent pairs of panties hung over the bath to dry; her talcum powder still dusted the tiled floor and her special fragrance pervaded the entire apartment.

He missed her with a physical ache in the chest, so that when the front door banged and she arrived like a high wind, shouting for him, 'Nicholas, it's me!' as though it could possibly have been anyone else, her hair tangled and wild with the wind and high colour under the golden tan of her cheeks, he almost ran to her and seized her with a suppressed violence.

'Wow,' she whispered huskily. 'Who is a hungry baby, then.' And they tumbled on to the bed clinging to each other with a need that was almost desperation.

Afterwards they did not turn the light on in the room that had gone dark except for the dim light of the street lamps filtered by the curtains and reflected off the ceiling.

'What was that all about?' she asked, then snuggled against his chest, 'not that I'm complaining, mind you.'

'I've had a hell of a day. I needed you, badly.'

'You saw Duncan Alexander?'

'I saw Duncan.'

'Did you settle?'

'No. There was never really any chance.'

258

'I'm hungry,' she said. 'Your loving always makes me hungry.'

So he put on his pants and went down to the Italian restaurant at the corner for pizzas. They ate them in bed with a white Chianti from whisky tumblers, and when she was finished, she sighed and said:

'Nicholas, I have to go home.'

'You can't go,' he protested instantly.

'I have work to do – also.'

'But,' he felt a physical nausea at the thought of losing her, 'but you can't go before the hearing.'

'Why not?'

'It would be the worst possible luck, you are my fortune.'

'A sort of good-luck charm?' She pulled a face. 'Is that all I'm good for?'

'You are good for many things. May I demonstrate one of them?'

'Oh, yes please.'

An hour later Nick went for more pizzas.

'You have to stay until the 27th,' he said with his mouth full.

'Darling Nicholas, I just don't know—'

'You can ring them, tell them your aunt died, that you are getting married.'

'Even if I were getting married, it wouldn't lessen the importance of my work. I think you know that is something I will never give up.'

'Yes, I do know, but it's only a couple of days more.'

'All right, I'll call Tom Parker tomorrow.' Then she grinned at him. 'Don't look like that. I'll be just across the Atlantic, we'll be virtually next-door neighbours.'

'Call him now. It's lunchtime in Florida.'

She spoke for twenty minutes, wheedling and charming, while the blood-curdling transatlantic rumblings on the receiver slowly muted to reluctant and resigned mutterings.

'You're going to get me into trouble one of these days, Nicholas Berg,' she told him primly as she hung up.

'Now *there* is a happy thought,' Nick agreed, and she hit him with her pillow.

The telephone rang at two minutes past nine the next morning. They were in the bath together and Nicholas swore and went through naked and steaming and dripping suds.

'Mr Berg?' James Teacher's voice was sharp and business-like. 'You were right, Christy Marine petitioned for post-ponement of hearing late yesterday afternoon.'

'How long?' Nicholas snapped.

'Ninety days.'

'The bastard,' grunted Nick. 'What grounds?'

'They want time to prepare their submission.'

'Block them,' Nick instructed.

'I have a meeting with the Secretary at eleven. I'm going to ask for an immediate preliminary hearing to set down and confirm the return date.'

'Get him before the arbitrators,' said Nick.

'We'll get him.'

Samantha welcomed him back to the tub by drawing her knees up under her chin. Her hair was piled on top of her head, but damp wisps hung down her neck and on to her cheeks. She looked pink and dewy as a little girl.

'Careful where you put your toes, sir,' she cautioned him, and he felt the tension along his nerves easing. She had that effect on him.

'I'll buy you lunch at Les A if you can tear yourself away from your microscope and fishy-smelling specimens for an hour or two.'

'Les Ambassadeurs? I've heard about it! For lunch there I'd walk across London on freshly amputated stumps.'

'That won't be necessary, but you will have to charm a tribe of wild desert Sheikhs. I understand they are very sympathetic towards blondes.'

'Are you going to sell me into a harem – sounds fun, I've always fancied myself in baggy, transparent bloomers.'

'You, I'm not selling – icebergs, I am. I'll pick you up at the front gate of the museum at one o'clock sharp.'

She went with laughter and a great clatter and banging of doors and Nicholas settled at the telephone.

'I'd like to speak to Sir Richard personally, it's Nicholas Berg.' Sir Richard was at Lloyd's, an old and good friend.

Then he called and spoke to Charles Gras.

There were no new delays or threats to *Sea Witch*'s completion date.

'I am sorry for any trouble you had with Alexander.'

'*Ça ne fait rien*, Nicholas. Good luck at the hearing. I will be watching the *Lloyd's List*.' Nicholas felt a sense of relief. Charles Gras had risked his career to show him *Golden Dawn*. It could have been serious.

Then Nick spoke for nearly half an hour to Bernard Wackie of Bach Wackie in Bermuda. *Warlock* had reported on the telex two hours previously; she was making good passage with her oil-rig tow, would drop off at Bravo II on schedule and pick up her next tow as soon as she had anchored.

'David Allen is a good youngster,' Bernard told Nick. 'But have you got Levoisin for *Sea Witch*?'

'Jules is playing the prima donna, he has not said yes, but he'll come.'

'You'll have a good team, then. What's the latest date for *Sea Witch*?'

'End March.'

'The sooner the better, I've got contacts to keep both tugs running hard until the iceberg project matures.'

'I'm having lunch with the Sheikhs today.'

'I know. There's a lot of interest. I've got a good feeling.

There is something big brewing, but they are a cagey bunch. The inscrutable smile on the face of the sphinx – when do we see you?'

'I'll come across just as soon as I've got Duncan Alexander into the arbitration court – end of the month, hopefully.'

'We've got a lot to talk about, Nicholas.'

Nick hesitated for the time it took to smoke the first cheroot of the day before he called Monte Carlo – for the call would cost him at least fifty thousand dollars, probably closer to seventy-five. The best is always the cheapest, he reminded himself, picked up the receiver and spoke to a secretary in Monte Carlo, giving his name.

While he waited for the connection he thought how his life was complicating itself once more. Very soon Bach Wackie would not be enough, there would have to be a London branch of Ocean Salvage, offices, secretaries, files, accounts, and then a New York branch, a branch in Saudi, the whole cycle again. He thought suddenly of Samantha, uncluttered and simple happiness, life without its wearisome trappings – then the connection was made and he heard the thin, high, almost feminine voice.

'Mr Berg – Claud Lazarus.' No other greeting, no expressions of pleasure at the renewal of contact. Nick imagined him sitting at his desk in the suite high above the harbour, like a human foetus – preserved in spirits, bottled on the museum shelf. The huge bald, domed head, the soft, putty-coloured rudimentary features, the nose hardly large enough to support the thick spectacles. The eyes distorted and startled by the lens, changing shape like those of a fish in an aquarium as the light moved. The body underdeveloped, as that of a foetus, narrow shoulders, seemingly tapering away to the bowed question mark of a body.

'Mr Lazarus. Are you in a position to undertake an indepth study for me?' It was the euphemism for financial and industrial espionage; Claud Lazarus' network was not limited by frontiers or continents; it spanned the globe with delicately probing tentacles.

'Of course,' he piped softly.

'I want the financial structuring, the lines of control and management, the names of the nominees and their principals, the location and inter-relationship of all the elements of the Christy Marine Group and London European Insurance and Banking Co. Group, with particular reference to any changes in structure during the previous fourteen months. Do you have that?'

'This is being recorded, Mr Berg.'

'Of course. Further, I want the country of registration, the insurers and underwriters of all bottoms traceable to their holdings.'

'Please continue.'

'I want an accurate estimate of the reserves of London and European Insurance in relations to their potential liability.'

'Continue.'

'I am particularly interested in the vessel *Golden Dawn* presently building at the yards of Construction Navale Atlantique at St Nazaire. I want to know if she has been chartered or has contracted with any oil company for carriage of crude and, if so, on what routes and at what rates.'

'Yes?' Lazarus squeaked softly.

'Time is of the essence – and, as always, so is discretion.'

'You need not have mentioned that, Mr Berg.'

'My contact, when you are ready to pass information, is Back Wackie in Bermuda.'

'I will keep you informed of progress.'

'Thank you, Mr Lazarus.'

'Good day, Mr Berg.'

It was refreshing not to have to pretend to be the bosom comrade of somebody who supplied essentials but nonetheless revolted him, Nick thought, and comforting to know he had the best man in the world for the job.

He looked at his watch. It was lunchtime, and he felt the quick lift of his spirits at the thought of being with Samantha.

Lime Street is a narrow alleyway, with tall buildings down each side of it, which opens off Leadenhall Street. A few yards from the junction, on the left-hand side as you leave the street of shipping, is the covered entrance to Lloyd's of London.

Nicholas stepped out of James Teacher's Bentley and took Samantha on his arm. He paused a moment, with a feeling of certain reverence.

As a seaman, the history of this remarkable institution touched him intimately. Not that the building itself was particularly old or venerable. Nothing now remained of the original coffee house, except some of the traditions: the caller who intoned the brokers' names like the offertory in the temple of some exotic religion, the stalls in which the underwriters conducted their business and the name and uniform of the institution's servants, the 'waiters' with brass buttons and red collar tabs.

Rather it was the tradition of concern that was enshrined here, the concern for ships and for all men who went down to the sea in those ships and did their business in great waters.

Perhaps later, Nicholas would find time to take Samantha through the Nelson rooms and show her the displays of memorabilia associated with the greatest of Britain's sailors, the plate and letters and awards. Certainly he would have her as lunch guest in the big dining room, at the table set aside specifically for visiting sea captains.

But now there were more important considerations to

demand all his attention. He had come to hear the verdict given on his future – within a few hours he would know just how high and how fast the wave of his fortune had carried him.

'Come,' he said to Samantha, and led her up the short flight of steps into the lobby, where there was a waiter alerted to receive them.

'We will be using the Committee Room today, sir.'

The earlier submissions by both parties had been heard in one of the smaller offices, leading off the high gallery above the vast floor of the exchange with its rows of underwriters' stalls. However, due to the extraordinary nature of this action, the Committee of Lloyd's had made a unique decision – to have their arbitrators give their findings and make their award in surroundings more in keeping with the importance of the occasion.

They rode up in silence, all of them too tense to make the effort of smalltalk. and the waiter led them down the wide corridor, past the Chairman's suite of offices and through the double doors into the grandeur of the room designed by Adam for Bowood House, the country home of the Marquess of Lansdowne. It had been taken to pieces, panel by panel, floor, ceiling, fireplace and plaster mouldings, transported to London and re-erected in its entirety with such care and attention that when Lord Lansdowne inspected it, he found that the floorboards squeaked in exactly the same places as they had before.

At the long table, under the massive glittering pyramids of the three chandeliers, the two arbitrators were already seated. Both of them were master mariners, selected for their deep knowledge and experience of the sea, and their faces were toughened and leathery from the effects of sea and salt water. They talked quietly together, without acknowledging in any way the rows of quietly attentive faces in the rows of chairs facing them – until the minute hand of the antique clock on the Adam fireplace touched its zenith. Then the President of the Court looked across at the waiter who obediently closed the double doors and stood to attention before them.

'This Arbitration Court has been set up under the Committee of Lloyd's and empowered to receive evidence in the matter between the Christy Marine Steamship Co. Ltd. and the Ocean Salvage and Towage Co. Ltd. This Court finds common ground in the following areas:

'Firstly, a contract of salvage under Lloyd's Open Form "No cure no pay" for the recovery of the passenger liner *Golden Adventurer*, a ship of 22,000 tons gross burden and registered at Southampton, exists between the parties.

'Secondly, that the Master of the *Golden Adventurer* while steaming on a south-westerly heading during the night of December 16th at or near 72° 16' south and 32° 12' west—'

The President let no dramatics intrude on his assembly of the facts. He recounted it all in the driest possible terms, succeeding in making *Golden Adventurer*'s plight and the desperate endeavours of her rescuers sound boring. Indeed, his colleague seemed to descend into a condition of coma at the telling of it. His eyes slowly closed, and his head sagged gently sideways, his lips vibrating slightly at each breath – a volume not quite sufficient to make it a snore.

It took nearly an hour, with the occasional consultation of the ship's logbooks and a loose volume of handwritten and typed notes, before the President was satisfied that he had recounted all the facts, and now he rocked back in his chair and hooked his thumbs into his waistcoat. His expression became decisive, and while he surveyed the crowded room, his colleague stirred, opened his eyes, took out a white linen handkerchief and blew two sharp blasts, one for each nostril, like the herald angel sounding the crack of doom.

There was a stir of reawakened interest, they all recognized the moment of decision, and for the first time Duncan Alexander and Nicholas Berg looked directly at each other over the heads of the lawyers and company men. Neither of them changed expression, no smile nor scowl, but something implacable and clearly understood passed between them. They did not unlock their gaze, until the President began to speak again.

'Taking into consideration the foregoing, this Court is of the firm opinion that a fair and good salvage of the vessel was effected by the salvors, and that therefore, they are entitled to salvage awards commensurate with the services rendered to the owners and underwriters.'

Nicholas felt Samantha's fingers groping for his. He took her hand, and it was slim and cold and dry; he interlocked their fingers and laid their hands upon his upper thigh.

'This Court, in arriving at the value of the salvor's services, has taken into consideration, firstly, the situation and conditions existing on the site of operations. We have heard evidence that much of the work was carried out in extreme weather conditions. Temperatures of thirty degrees below freezing, wind forces exceeding twelve on the Beaufort scale, and extreme icing.

'We have also considered that the vessel *Golden Adventurer* was no longer under command. That she had been abandoned by her passengers, her crew and her Master. She was aground on a remote and hostile coast.

'We have further noted that the salvors undertook a voyage of many thousands of miles, without any guarantee of recompense, but merely in order to be in a position to offer assistance, should that have become necessary.'

Nicholas glanced across the aisle at Duncan Alexander. He sat at ease, as though he were in his box at Ascot. His suit was of sombre gunmetal grey, but on him it seemed flamboyant and the I Zingari tie as rakish as any of Cardin's fantasies.

Duncan turned that fine leonine head and looked directly at Nicholas again. This time Nicholas saw the deep angry glow in his eyes as when a vagrant breeze fans the coals of an open fire. Then Duncan turned his face back towards the President, and he balanced his thrusting square chin on the clenched, carefully manicured fingers of his right fist.

'Furthermore, we have taken into consideration the transportation of the survivors from the site of the striking, to the nearest port of succour, Cape Town in the Republic of South Africa.'

The President was summing up strongly in favour of Ocean Salvage. It was a dangerous sign; so often a judge about to deliver an unfavourable decision prefaced it by building a strong case for the loser and then tearing it down again.

Nicholas steeled himself; anything below three million dollars would not be sufficient to keep Ocean Salvage alive. That was the barest minimum he needed to keep *Warlock* afloat, and to put *Sea Witch* on the water for the first time. He felt the spasm of his stomach muscles as he contemplated his commitments – even with three million he would be at the mercy of the Sheikhs, unable to manoeuvre, a slave to any conditions they wished to set. He would not be off his knees even.

Nicholas squeezed Samantha's hand for luck, and she pressed her shoulder against his.

Four million dollars would give him a fighting chance, a slim margin of choice – but he would still be fighting hard, pressed on all sides. Yet he would have settled for four million, if Duncan Alexander had made the offer. Perhaps Duncan had been wise after all, perhaps he might yet see Nicholas broken at a single stroke.

'Three.' Nicholas held the figure in his head. 'Let it be three, at least let it be three.'

'This Court has considered the written reports of the Globe Engineering Co., the contractors charged with the repairing and refurbishing of Golden Adventurer, together with those of two independent marine engineering experts commissioned separately by the owners and the salvors to report on the condition of the vessel. We have also had the benefit of a survey carried out by a senior inspector of Lloyd's of London. From all of this, it seems apparent that the vessel sustained remarkably light damage. There was no loss of equipment, the salvors recovering even the main anchors and chains—'

Strange how that impressed a salvage court. 'We took her off, anchors and all,' Nick thought, with a stir of pride.

'Prompt anti-corrosion precautions by the salvors resulted in minimal damage to the main engines and ancillary equipment—'

It went on and on. Why cannot he come to it now? I cannot wait much longer, Nicholas thought.

'This Court has heard expert opinion and readily accepts that the residual value of the Golden Adventurer's hull, as delivered to the contractors in Cape Town can be fairly set at twenty-six million US dollars or fifteen million, three hundred thousand pounds sterling, and in consideration of the foregoing, we are further of the firm opinion that the salvors are entitled to an award of twenty per cent of the residual hull value—'

For long cold seconds Nicholas doubted his hearing, and then he felt the flush of exultation burning on his cheeks.

'In addition, it was necessary to compute the value of the passage provided to the survivors of the vessel—'

It was six – six million dollars! He was clear and running free as a wild albatross sweeping across the oceans on wide pinions.

Nicholas turned his head and looked at Duncan Alexander, and he smiled. He had never felt so strong and vital and alive in his life before. He felt like a giant, immortal, and at his side was the vibrant young body pressing to him, endowing him with eternal youth.

Across the aisle, Duncan Alexander tossed his head, a gesture of dismissal and turned to speak briefly with his counsel who sat beside him. He did not look at Nicholas, however, and there was a waxen cast to his skin now as though it had a fine sheen of perspiration laid upon it, and the blood had drained away beneath the tan.

'Anyway, another few days and you'd probably have started to find me a boring dolly-bird, or one of us would have had a heart attack.' Samantha smiled at him, a pathetic, lopsided little grin, nothing like her usual brilliant golden flashing smile. 'I like to quit while I'm still ahead.'

They sat close on the couch in the Pan Am Clipper Lounge at Heathrow.

Nicholas was shocked by the extent of his own desolation. It felt as though he were about to be deprived of the vital force of life itself, he felt the youth and strength draining away as he looked at her and knew that in a few minutes she would be gone.

'Samantha,' he said. 'Stay here with me.'

'Nicholas,' she whispered huskily, 'I have to go, my darling. It's not for very long but I have to go.'

'Why?' he demanded.

'Because it's my life.'

'Make me your life.'

She touched his cheek, as she countered his offer.

'I have a better idea, give up *Warlock* and *Sea Witch* — forget your icebergs and come with me.'

270

'You know I cannot do that.'

'No,' she agreed, 'you could not, and I would not want you to. But, Nicholas, my love, no more can I give up my life.'

'All right, then, marry me,' he said.

'Why, Nicholas?'

'So I don't lose my lucky charm, so that you'd damn well have to do what I tell you.'

And she laughed delightedly and snuggled against his chest. 'It doesn't work like that any more, my fine Victorian gentleman. There is only one good reason for marrying, Nicholas, and that's to have babies. Do you want to give me a baby?'

'What a splendid idea.'

'So that I can warm the bottles and wash the nappies while you go off to the ends of the oceans – and we'll have lunch together once a month?' She shook her head. 'We might have a baby together one day – but not now, there is still too much to do, there is still too much life to live.'

'Damn it.' He shook his head. 'I don't like to let you run around loose. Next thing you'll take off with some twenty-five-year-old oaf, bulging with muscles and—'

'You have given me a taste for vintage wine,' she laughed in denial. 'Come as soon as you can, Nicholas. As soon as you have done your work here, come to Florida and I'll show you my life.'

The hostess crossed the lounge towards them, a pretty smiling girl in the neat blue Pan Am uniform.

'Dr Silver? They are calling Flight 432 now.'

They stood and looked at each other, awkward as strangers.

'Come soon,' she said, and then she stood on tiptoe and placed her arms around his shoulders. 'Come as soon as you can.'

271

Nicholas had protested vigorously as soon as James Teacher advanced the proposition. 'I don't want to speak to him, Mr Teacher. The only thing I want from Duncan Alexander is his cheque for six million dollars, preferably guaranteed by a reputable bank – and I want it before the 10th of next month.'

The lawyer had wheedled and jollied Nicholas along. 'Think of the pleasure of watching his face – indulge yourself, Mr Berg, gloat on him a little.'

'I will obtain no pleasure by watching his face, offhand I can think of a thousand faces I'd rather watch.' But in the end Nicholas had agreed, stipulating only that this time the meeting should be at a place of Nicholas' choice, an unsubtle reminder of whose hand now held the whip.

James Teacher's rooms were in one of those picturesque, stone buildings in the Inns of Court covered with ivy, surrounded by small velvety lawns, bisected with paved walkways that connected the numerous blocks, the entire complex reeking of history and tradition and totally devoid of modern comforts. Its austerity was calculated to instil confidence in the clients.

Teacher's rooms were on the third floor. There was no elevator and the stairs were narrow, steep and dangerous. Duncan Alexander arrived slightly out of breath and flushed under his tan. Teacher's clerk surveyed him discouragingly from his cubicle.

'Mr who?' he asked, cupping his hand to one ear. The clerk was a man as old, grey and picturesque as the building. He even affected a black alpaca suit, shiny and greenish with age, together with a butterfly collar and a black string tie like that last worn by Neville Chamberlain as he promised peace in our time.

'Mr who?' and Duncan Alexander flushed deeper. He was not accustomed to having to repeat his name.

'Do you have an appointment, Mr Arbuthnot?' the clerk

enquired frostily, and laboriously consulted his diary before at last waving Duncan Alexander through into the spartan waiting room.

Nicholas kept him there exactly eight minutes, twice as long as he himself had waited in the board room of Christy Marine, and he stood by the small electric fire in the fireplace, not answering Duncan's brilliant smile as he entered.

James Teacher sat at his desk under the windows, out of the direct line of confrontation, like the umpire at Wimbledon, and Duncan Alexander barely glanced at him.

'Congratulations, Nicholas,' Duncan shook that magnificent head and the smile faded to a rueful grin. 'You turned one up for the books, you truly did.'

'Thank you, Duncan. However, I must warn you that today I have an impossible schedule to meet, I can give you only ten minutes.' Nicholas glanced at his watch. 'Fortunately I can imagine only one thing that you and I have to discuss. The tenth of next month, either a transfer to the Bermuda account of Ocean Salvage, or a guaranteed draft by registered airmail to Bach Wackie.'

Duncan held up his hand in mock protest. 'Come now, Nicholas – the salvage money will be there, on the due date set by the Court.'

'That's fine,' Nicholas told him, still smiling. 'I have no taste for another brawl in the debtors' court.'

'I wanted to remind you of something that old Arthur Christy once said—'

'Ah, of course, our mutual father-in-law.' Nicholas said softly, and Duncan pretended not to hear; instead he went on unruffled.

'He said, with Berg and Alexander I have put together one of the finest teams in the world of shipping.'

'The old man was getting senile towards the end.' Nicholas had still not smiled.

'He was right, of course. We just never got into step.

273

'My God, Nicholas, can you imagine if we had been working together, instead of against each other. You the best salt and steel man in the business, and I—'

'I'm touched, Duncan, deeply touched by this new and gratifying esteem in which I find myself held.'

'You rubbed my nose in it, Nicholas. Just as you said you would. And I'm the kind of man who learns by his mistakes, turning disaster to triumph is a trick of mine.'

'Play your trick now,' Nicholas invited. 'Let's see you turn six million dollars into a flock of butterflies.'

'Six million dollars and Ocean Salvage would buy you back into Christy Marine. We'd be on equal terms.'

The surprise did not show on Nicholas' face, not a flicker of an eyelid, not even a tightening of the lips, but his mind raced to get ahead of the man.

'Together we would be unstoppable. We would build Christy Marine into a giant that controlled the oceans, we'd diversify out into ocean oil exploration, chemical containers.' The man had immense presence and charm, he was almost – but not quite – irresistible, his enthusiasm brimming and overflowing, his fire flaring and spreading to light the dingy room, and Nicholas studied him carefully, learning more about him every second.

'Good God, Nicholas, you are the type of man who can conceive of a venture like the *Golden Dawn* or salvage a giant liner in a sub-zero gale, and I am the man who can put together a billion dollars on a wink and whistle. Nothing could stand before us, there would be no frontiers we could not cross.' He paused now and returned Nicholas' scrutiny as boldly, studying the effect of his words. Nicholas lit the cheroot he was holding, but his eyes watched shrewdly through the fine blue veil of smoke.

'I understand what you are thinking,' Duncan went on, his voice dropping confidentially. 'I know that you are stretched out, I know that you need those six big Ms to keep Ocean Salvage floating. Christy Marine will guarantee

Ocean Salvage outstandings, that's a minor detail. The important thing is us together, like old Arthur Christy saw it, Berg and Alexander.'

Nicholas took the cheroot from his mouth and inspected the tip briefly before he looked back at him.

'Tell me, Duncan,' he asked mildly, 'in this great sharing you envisage, do we put our women into the kitty also?'

Duncan's mouth tightened, and the flesh wrinkled at the corners of his eyes.

'Nicholas,' he began, but Nicholas silenced him with a gesture.

'You said that I need that six million badly, and you were right. I need three million of it for Ocean Salvage and the other three to stop you running that monster you have built. Even if I don't get it, I will still use it to stop you. I'll slap a garnishee order on you by ten minutes past nine on the morning of the eleventh. I told you I would fight you and *Golden Dawn*. The warning still stands.'

'You are being petty,' Duncan said. 'I never expected to see you join the lunatic fringe.'

'There are many things you do not know about me, Duncan. But, by God, you are going to learn – the hard way.'

C hantelle had chosen San Lorenzo in Beauchamp Place when Nicholas had refused to go again to Eaton Square. He had learned that it was dangerous to be alone with her, but San Lorenzo was also a bad choice of meeting-ground.

It carried too many memories from the golden days. It had been a family ritual, Sunday lunch whenever they were in town. Chantelle, Peter and Nicholas laughing together at the corner table. Mara had given them the corner table again.

275

'Will you have the *osso bucco*?' Chantelle asked, peeping at him over the top of her menu.

Nicholas always had the *osso bucco*, and Peter always had the *lasagne*, it was part of the ritual.

'I'm going to have a sole.' Nicholas turned to the waiter who was hovering solicitously. 'And we'll drink the house white.' Always the wine had been a Sancerre; Nicholas was deliberately downgrading the occasion by ordering the carafe.

'It's good.' Chantelle sipped it and then set the glass aside. 'I spoke to Peter last night, he is in the san with flu, but he will be up today, and he sent you his love.'

'Thank you,' he spoke stiffly, stilted by the curious glances from some of the other tables where they had been recognized. The scandal would fly around London like the plague.

'I want to take Peter to Bermuda with me for part of the Easter holidays,' Nicholas told her.

'I shall miss him – he's such a delight.'

Nicholas waited for the main course to be served before he asked bluntly, 'What did you want to speak to me about?'

Chantelle leaned towards him, and her perfume was light and subtle and evocative.

'Did you find out anything, Nicholas?'

'No,' he thought to himself. 'That's not what she wants.' It was the Persian in her blood, the love of secrecy, the intrigue. There was something else here.

'I have learned nothing,' he said. 'If I had, I would have called you.' His eyes bored into hers, green and hard and searching. 'That is not what you wanted,' he told her flatly.

She smiled and dropped her eyes from his. 'No,' she admitted, 'it wasn't.'

She had surprising breasts, they seemed small, but really they were too big for her dainty body. It was only their perfect proportions and the springy elasticity of the creamy flesh that created the illusion. She wore a flimsy silk blouse with a low lacy front, which exposed the deep cleft between them. Nicholas knew them so well, and he found himself staring at them now.

She looked up suddenly and caught his eyes, and the huge eyes slanted with a sly heart-stopping sexuality. Her lips pouted softly and she moistened them with the tip of her tongue.

Nick felt himself sway in his seat, it was a tell-tale mannerism of hers. That set of lips and movement of tongue were the heralds of her arousal, and instantly he felt the response of his own body, too powerful to deny, although he tried desperately.

'What was it?' He did not hear the husk in his voice, but she did and recognized it as readily as he had the flicker of her tongue. She reached across the table and took his wrist, and she felt the leap of his pulse under her fingers.

'Duncan wants you to come back into Christy Marine,' she said. 'And so do I.'

'Duncan sent you to me.' And when she nodded, he asked, 'Why does he want me back? God knows what pains the two of you took to get rid of me.' And he gently pulled his wrist from her fingers and dropped both hands into his lap.

'I don't know why Duncan wants it. He says that he needs your expertise.' She shrugged, and her breasts moved under the silk. He felt the tense ache of his groin, it confused his thinking. 'It isn't the true reason, I'm sure of that. But he wants you.'

'Did he ask you to tell me that?'

'Of course not.' She fiddled with the stem of her glass; her fingers were long and perfectly tapered, the painted nails set upon them with the brilliance of butterflies' wings. 'It was to come from me alone.'

'Why do you think he wants me?'

'There are two possibilities that I can imagine.' She

surprised him sometimes with her almost masculine appraisal. That was what made her lapse so amazing; as he listened to her now, Nicholas wondered again how she could ever have let control of Christy Marine pass to Duncan Alexander – then he remembered what a wild and passionate creature she could be. 'The first possibility is that Christy Marine owes you six million dollars, and he has thought up some scheme to avoid having to pay you out.'

'Yes,' Nicholas nodded. 'And the other possibility?'

'There are strange and exciting rumours in the City about you and Ocean Salvage – they say that you are on the brink of something big. Something in Saudi Arabia. Perhaps Duncan wants a share of that.'

Nicholas blinked. The iceberg project was something between the Sheikhs and himself, then he remembered that others knew. Bernard Wackie in Bermuda, Samantha Silver, James Teacher – there had been a leak somewhere then.

'And you? What are your reasons?'

'I have two reasons, Nicholas,' she answered. 'I want control back from Duncan. I want the voting rights in my shares, and I want my rightful place on the Trust. I didn't know what I was doing, it was madness when I made Duncan my nominee. I want it back now, and I want you to get it for me.'

Nicholas smiled, a bitter wintry smile. 'You're hiring yourself a gunman, just the way they do in the Western serials. Duncan and I alone on the deserted street, spurs clinking.' The smile turned to a chuckle, but he was thinking hard, watching her – was she lying? It was almost impossible to tell, she was so mysterious and unfathomable. Then he saw tears well in the depths of those huge eyes, and he stopped laughing. Were the tears genuine, or all part of the intrigue?

'You said you had two reasons.' And now his voice was

gentler. She did not answer immediately, but he could see her agitation, the rapid rise and fall of those lovely breasts under the silk, then she caught her breath with a little hiss of decision and she spoke so softly that he barely caught the words.

'I want you back. That's the other reason, Nicholas.' And he stared at her while she went on. 'It was all part of the madness. I didn't realize what I was doing. But the madness is over now. Sweet merciful God, you'll never know how much I've missed you. You'll never know how I've suffered.' She stopped and fluttered one small hand. 'I'll make it up to you, Nicholas, I swear it to you. But Peter and I need you, we both need you desperately.'

He could not answer for a moment, she had taken him by surprise and he felt his whole life shaken again and the separate parts of it tumbled like dice from the cup of chance.

'There is no road back, Chantelle. We can only go forward.'

'I always get what I want, Nicholas, you know that,' she warned him.

'Not this time, Chantelle.' He shook his head, but he knew her words would wear away at him.

Duncan Alexander slumped on the luxurious calf-hide seat of the Rolls, and he spoke into the telephone extension that connected him directly with his office in Leadenhall Street.

'Were you able to reach Kurt Streicher?' he asked.

'I'm sorry, Mr Alexander. His office was unable to contact him. He is in Africa on a hunting safari. They did not know when to expect him back in Geneva.'

'Thank you, Myrtle.' Duncan's smile was completely lacking in humour. Streicher was suddenly one of the world's most industrious sportsmen – last week he had been skiing and was out of contact, this week he was in Africa slaughtering elephant, perhaps next week he would be chasing polar bears in the Arctic. And by then, it would be too late, of course.

Streicher was not alone. Since the salvage award on *Golden Adventurer*, so many of his financial contacts had become elusive, veritable will-o'-the-wisps skipping ahead of him with their chequebooks firmly buttoned into their pockets.

'I shall not be back at the office again today,' he told his secretary. 'Please have my pending tray sent round to Eaton Square. I will work on it tonight, and do you think you could get in an hour earlier tomorrow morning?'

'Of course, Mr Alexander.'

He replaced the handset and glanced out of the window. The Rolls was passing Regent's Park, heading in the direction of St John's Wood; three times in the last six months he had taken this route, and suddenly Duncan felt that hot scalding lump deep under his ribs. He straightened up in his seat but the pain persisted, and he sighed and opened the rosewood liquor cabinet, spilled a spoonful of the powder into a glass and topped it with soda water.

He considered the turbid draught with distaste, then drank it at a gulp. It left an aftertaste of peppermint on his tongue, but the relief was almost immediate. He felt the acid burn subside, and he belched softly.

He did not need a doctor to tell him that it was a duodenal ulcer, probably a whole bunch of them – or was that the correct collective noun, a tribe of ulcers, a convocation? He smiled again, and carefully combed his brazen waves of hair, watching himself in the mirror.

The strain did not show on his face, he was sure of that. The façade was intact, devoid of cracks. He had always had the strength, the courage to ride with his decisions. This had been a hard ride, however, the hardest of his life.

He closed his eyes briefly, and saw *Golden Dawn* standing on her ways. Like a mountain. The vision gave him strength, he felt it rising deep within him, welling up to fill his soul.

They thought of him only as a money man, a paper man. There was no salt in his blood nor steel in his guts – that was what they said of him in the City. When he had ousted Berg from Christy Marine, they had shied off, watching him shrewdly, standing aside and waiting for him to show his guts, forcing him to live upon the fat of Christy Marine, devouring himself like a camel in the desert, running him thin.

'The bastards,' he thought, but it was without rancour. They had done merely what he would have done, they had played by the hard rules which Duncan knew and respected, and by those same rules, once he had shown his guts to be of steel, they would ply him with largesse. This was the testing time. It was so close now, two months still to live through – yet those sixty days seemed as daunting as the hard year through which he had lived already.

The stranding of *Golden Adventurer* had been a disaster. Her hull value had formed part of the collateral on which he had borrowed; the cash she generated with her luxury cruises was budgeted carefully to carry him through the dangerous times before *Golden Dawn* was launched. Now all that had altered drastically. The flow of cash had been switched off, and he had to find six million in real hard money – and find it before the 10th of the month. Today was the 6th, and time was running through his fingers like quicksilver.

If only he had been able to stall Berg. He felt a corrosive welling up of hatred again; if only he had been able to stall him. The bogus offer of partnership might have held him just long enough, but Berg had brushed it aside contemptuously. Duncan had been forced to scurry about in undignified haste, trying to pull together the money. Kurt

Streicher was not the only one suddenly unavailable, it was strange how they could smell it on a man, he had the same gift of detecting vulnerability or weakness in others so he understood how it worked. It was almost as though the silver blotches showed on his hands and face and he walked the city pavements chanting the old leper's cry, 'Unclean. Beware. Unclean.'

With so much at stake, it was a piddling amount, six million for two months, the insignificance of it was an insult, and he felt the tension in his belly muscles again and the rising hot acid sting of his digestive juices. He forced himself to relax, glancing again from the window to find that the Rolls was turning into the cul-de-sac of yellow-face brick apartments piled upon each other like hen-coops, angular and unimaginatively lower middle class.

He squared his shoulders and watched himself in the mirror, practising the smile. It was only six million, and for only two months, he reminded himself, as the Rolls slid to a halt before one of the anonymous buildings.

Duncan nodded to his chauffeur as he held the door open and handed Duncan the pigskin briefcase.

'Thank you, Edward. I should not be very long.'

Duncan took the case and he crossed the pavement with the long, confident stride of an athlete, his shoulders thrown back, wearing his topcoat like an opera cloak, the sleeves empty and the tails swirling about his legs, and even in the grey overcast of a March afternoon, his head shone like a beacon fire.

The man who opened the door to him seemed only half Duncan's height, despite the tall black Homburg hat that he wore squarely over his ears.

'Mr Alexander, shalom, shalom.' His beard was so dense and bushy black that it covered the starched white collar and white tie, regulation dress of the strict Hasidic Jew. 'Even though you come to me last, you still bring honour on my house,' and his eyes twinkled, a mischievous spark-ling black under thick brows.

'That is because you have a heart of stone and blood like iced water,' said Duncan, and the man laughed delightedly, as though he had been paid the highest compliment.

'Come,' he said, taking Duncan's arm. 'Come in, let us drink a little tea together and let us talk.' He led Duncan down the narrow corridor, and halfway they collided with two boys wearing yamulka on their curly heads coming at speed in the opposite direction.

'Ruffians,' cried the man, stooping to embrace them briefly and then send them on their way with a fond slap on their backsides. Still beaming and shaking the ringlets that dangled out from under the black Homburg, he ushered Duncan into a small crowded bedroom that had been converted to an office. A tall old-fashioned pigeon-holed desk filled one wall and against the other stood an overstuffed horsehair sofa on which were piled ledgers and box files.

The man swept the books aside, making room for Duncan. 'Be seated,' he ordered, and stood aside while a jolly little woman his size brought in the teatray.

'I saw the award court's arbitration on *Golden Adventurer* in *Lloyd's List*,' the Jew said when they were alone. 'Nicholas Berg is an amazing man, a hard act to follow – I think that is the expression.' He pondered, watching the sudden bloom of anger on Duncan's cheeks and the murderous expression in the pale eyes.

Duncan controlled his anger with an effort, but each time that somebody spoke that way of Nicholas Berg, he found it more difficult. There was always the comparison, the snide remarks, and Duncan wanted to stand up and leave this cluttered little room and the veiled taunts, but he knew he could not afford to, nor could he speak just yet for his anger was very close to the surface. They sat in silence for what seemed a long time.

'How much?' The man broke the silence at last, and Duncan could not bring himself to name the figure for it was too closely related to the subject that had just infuriated him.

'It is not a large amount, and for a short period – sixty days only.'

'How much?'

'Six million,' Duncan said. 'Dollars.'

'Six million is not an impossibly large amount of money, when you have it – but it is a great fortune when you do not.' The man tugged at the thick black bush of his beard. 'And sixty days can be an eternity.'

'I have a charter for *Golden Dawn*,' Duncan said softly. 'A ten-year charter.' He slipped the nine-carat gold catches on the slim, finely grained pigskin briefcase and brought out a batch of xeroxed sheets. 'As you see, it is signed by both parties already.'

'Ten years?' asked the man, watching the papers in Duncan's hand.

'Ten years, at ten cents a hundred ton miles and a guaranteed minimum annual of 75,000 miles.'

The hand on the man's thick black beard stilled. '*Golden Dawn* has a burden of a million tons – that will gross a minimum of seventy-five million dollars a year.' With an effort he managed to disguise his awe, and the hand resumed its gentle tugging at the beard. 'Who is the charterer?' The thick eyebrows formed two thick black question marks.

'Orient Amex,' said Duncan, and handed him the xeroxed papers.

'The El Barras field.' The man's eyebrows stayed up as he read swiftly. 'You are a brave man, Mr Alexander. But I never once doubted that.' He read on in silence for another minute, shaking his head slowly so that the ringlets danced on his cheeks. 'The El Barras field.' He folded the papers and looked up at Duncan. 'I think Christy Marine may have found a worthy successor to Nicholas Berg – perhaps the shoes are even a little small, maybe they will begin to pinch your toes soon, Mr Alexander.' He squirmed down in his chair thinking furiously, and Duncan watched him, hiding his trepidation behind a remotely amused half-smile.

'What about the environmentalists, Mr Alexander? The new American administration, this man Carter is very conscious of environmental dangers.'

'The lunatic fringe,' said Duncan. 'There is too much invested already. Orient Amex have nearly a billion in the new cadmium cracking plants at Galveston, and three of the other oil giants are in it. Let them fuss, we'll still carry in the new cad-rich crudes.'

Duncan spoke with the force of complete conviction. 'There is too much at stake, the potential profits are too large and the opposition is too weak. The whole world is sick of the doom-merchants, the woolly-headed sentimentalists,' he dismissed them with a short abrupt gesture. 'Man has already adjusted to a little oil on the beaches, a little smoke in the air, a few less fish in the sea or birds in the sky, and he will go on adjusting.'

The man nodded, listening avidly. 'Yes,' he nodded. 'You are a brave man. The world needs men like you.'

'The important thing is a cadmium catalyst cracking system which breaks down the high carbon atoms of crude and gives back a 90 per cent yield in low carbon instead of the 40 per cent we hope for now. 90 per cent yield, double-double profits, double efficiency—'

' – and double danger.' The man smiled behind his beard.

'There is danger in taking a bath. You might slip and crack your skull, and we haven't invested a billion dollars in bathing.'

'Cadmium in concentrations of 100 parts to the million is more poisonous than cyanide or arsenic; the cad-rich crudes of the El Barras field are concentrated 2,000 parts to the million.'

'That's what makes them so valuable,' Duncan nodded. 'To enrich crude artificially with cadmium would make the whole cracking process hopelessly uneconomic. We've turned what appeared to be a hopelessly contaminated oilfield into one of the most brilliant advances in oil refining.'

'I hope you have not underestimated the resistance to the transportation of—'

Duncan cut him short. 'There will be no publicity. The loading and unloading of the crude will be conducted with the utmost discretion, and the world will not know the difference. Just another ultra-tanker moving across the oceans with nothing to suggest that she is carrying cad-rich.'

'But, just suppose the news did leak?'

Duncan shrugged. 'The world is conditioned to accept anything, from DDT to Concorde, nobody really cares any more. Come hell and high water, we'll carry the El Barras oil. Nobody is strong enough to stop us.'

Duncan gathered his papers and went on softly, 'I need six million dollars for sixty days – and I need it by noon tomorrow.'

'You are a brave man,' the man repeated softly. 'But you are finely stretched out. Already my brothers and I have made a considerable investment in your courage. To be blunt, Mr Alexander, Christy Marine has exhausted its collateral. Even *Golden Dawn* is pawned down to her last rivet – and the charter for Orient Amex does not change that.'

Duncan took another sheaf of papers, bound in a brown folder, and the man lifted an eyebrow in question.

'My personal assets,' Duncan explained, and the man skimmed swiftly through the typed lists.

'Paper values, Mr Alexander. Actual values are 50 per cent of those you list, and that is not six million dollars of collateral.' He handed the folder back to Duncan. 'They will do for a start, but we'll need more than that.'

'What more is there?'

'Share options, stock options in Christy Marine. If we are to share risk, then we must have a share of the winnings.'

'Do you want my soul also?' Duncan demanded harshly, and the man laughed.

'We'll take a slice of that as well,' he agreed amiably.

It was two hours later that Duncan sank wearily into the leather-work of the Rolls. The muscles in his thighs trembled as though he had run a long way and there was a nerve in the corner of his eye that jumped as though a cricket was trapped beneath the skin. He had made the gamble, everything – Christy Marine, his personal fortune, his very soul. It was all at risk now.

'Eaton Square, sir?' the chauffeur asked.

'No,' Duncan told him. He knew what he needed now to smooth away the grinding, destroying tension that wracked his body, but he needed it quickly without fuss and, like the peppermint-tasting powder, like a medicine.

'The Senator Club in Frith Street,' he told the chauffeur.

Duncan lay face down on the massage table in the small green-curtained cubicle. He was naked, except for the towel, and his body was smooth and lean. The girl worked up his spine with strong skilled fingers, finding the little knots of tension in the sleek muscle and unravelling them.

'Do you want the soft massage, sir?' she asked.

'Yes,' he said and rolled on to his back. She lifted away the towel from around his waist. She was a pretty blonde girl in a short green tunic with the golden laurel leaf club insignia on the pocket, and her manner was brisk and business-like.

'Do you want any extras, sir?' Her tone was neutral, and she began to unbutton the green tunic automatically.

'No,' Duncan said. 'No extras,' and closed his eyes, surrendering himself completely to the touch of her expert fingers.

He thought of Chantelle, feeling the sneaking guilt of the moment, but it was so seldom these days that he had the energy for her smouldering, demanding Persian passions. He did not have the strength for her, he was drained and weary, and all he wanted was the release, swift and simple. In two months' time it would be different, he would have the strength and energy to pick the world up in his bare hands and shake it like a toy.

His mind was separated from his body, and odd disconnected images flitted across the red darkness of his closed eyelids. He thought again how long it had been since last he and Chantelle had made love together, and he wondered what the world would say if they knew of it.

'Nicholas Berg left a big empty place in his bed also,' they would say.

'The hell with them,' Duncan thought, but without the energy for real anger.

'The hell with all of them.' And he gave himself up to the explosion of light that burst against his eyelids and the dark, but too fleeting, peace that followed it.

Nicholas lay back in the rather tatty old brown leather armchair which was one of James Teacher's concessions to creature comfort and he stared at the cheap hunting prints on the faded wallpaper through a thin fug of cheroot smoke. Teacher could have afforded a decent Gauguin or a Turner, but such vulgar display was frowned on in the Inns of Court. It might lead prospective clients to ponder the amount of the fees that they were to be charged.

James Teacher replaced the telephone and stood up behind his desk. It did not make much difference to his height.

'Well, I think we have covered all the entrances to the warren,' he announced cheerfully, and he began to tick off the items on his fingers. 'The sheriff of the South African supreme court will serve notice of attachment on the hull of *Golden Adventurer* at noon local time tomorrow. Our French correspondent will do the same on *Golden Dawn*—' He spoke for three minutes more, and, listening to him, Nicholas reluctantly admitted to himself that he earned the greater proportion of his enormous fees.

'Well, there it is, Mr Berg. If your hunch is correct—'

'It's not a hunch, Mr Teacher. It's a certainty. Duncan Alexander has his backside pinched in the doorway. He's been rushing round the City like a demented man looking for money. My God, he even tried to stall me with that incredible offer of a partnership. No, Mr Teacher, it's not a hunch. Christy Marine is going to default.'

'I cannot understand that. Six millions is peanuts,' said James Teacher. 'At least it's peanuts to a company like Christy Marine, one of the healthiest shipping owners.'

'It was, a year ago,' Nicholas agreed grimly. 'But since then, Alexander has had a clear run, no checks, it's not a public company, he administers the shares in the Trust.' He drew on his cheroot. 'I'm going to use this to force a full investigation of the company's affairs. I'm going to have Alexander under the microscope and we'll have a close look at all his pimples and warts.'

Teacher chuckled and picked up the telephone at the first ring. 'Teacher,' he chuckled, and then laughed out loud, nodding, 'Yes,' and 'Yes!' again. He hung up and turned to Nicholas, his face bright red with mirth, fat and round as the setting sun.

'I have a disappointment for you, Mr Berg.' He guffawed. 'An hour ago a transfer was made to the credit of Ocean Salvage in Bermuda by Christy Marine.'

'How much?'

'Every penny, Mr Berg. In full and final payment. Six million and some odd dollars in the legal currency of the United States of America.'

Nicholas stared at him, uncertain as to which of his emotions prevailed – relief at having the money, or disappointment at being prevented from tearing Duncan Alexander to shreds.

'He's a high roller and very fast on his feet,' said Teacher. 'It wouldn't pay to underestimate a man like Duncan Alexander.'

'No, it would not,' Nicholas agreed quietly, knowing that he had done so more than once and each time it had cost him dearly.

'I wonder if your clerk could find out from British Airways when the next flight leaves for Bermuda?'

'You are leaving so soon? Will it be in order to mark my brief and send it direct to Bach Wackie in Bermuda?' Teacher asked delicately.

B ernard Wackie was waiting in person for Nicholas beyond the customs barrier. He was tall and lean and alert, burned dark as a stick of chew tobacco by the sun, and dressed in open-neck shirt and cotton trousers.

'Nicholas, it's good to see you.' His handshake was hard and dry and cool. He was under sixty and over forty; it was impossible to get nearer to his age. 'I'm taking you directly to the office, there is too much to discuss. I don't want to waste time.' And he took Nicholas' arm and hurried him through burning sunlight into the shivery cold of the Rolls's air-conditioning.

The car was too big for the island's narrow winding roads. Here ownership of automobiles was restricted to one per family unit, but Bernard made the most of his rights.

He was one of those men whose combination of energy and brilliance made it impossible for him to live in England and to subject himself to the punitive taxes of envy.

'It's hard to be a winner, in a society dedicated to the glorification of the losers,' he had told Nicholas, and had moved his whole operation to this taxless haven.

To a lesser man it would have been suicide, but Bernard had taken over the top floor of the Bank of Bermuda building, with a magnificent view across Hamilton Harbour, and had fitted it out with a marine operations room and a communications system the equal of NATO Command.

From it, he offered a service so efficient, so personally involved, so orientated to every single facet of ship ownership and operation, that not only had his old clients followed him, but others had come flocking.

'No taxes, Nicholas,' he smiled. 'And look at the view.' The picturesque buildings of Hamilton town were painted in candy colours, strawberries and limes, plum and lemon – and across the bay the cedar trees stood tall in the sunlight, and the yachts from the pink-painted clubhouse spread multicoloured sails across green waters. 'It's better than London in winter, isn't it?'

'The same temperature,' said Nicholas, and glanced up at the air-conditioning.

'I'm a hot-blooded man,' Bernard explained, and when his tall nubile secretary entered to his ring, bearing the Ocean Salvage files like a high priestess carrying the sacrament, Bernard fell into an awed silence, concentrating all his attention on her pneumatic bosoms; they bounced and strained against the laws of gravity as though filled with helium.

She flashed a dazzling, painted smile at Nicholas as she placed the files on Bernard's desk, and then she left with her perfectly rounded buttocks under the tightly tailored skirt, swinging and dancing to a distant music. 'She can type too,' Bernard assured Nick with a sigh, and shook his head as if to clear it. He opened the top file.

'Right,' he began. 'The deposit from Christy Marine—'

The money had come in, and only just in time. The next instalment on *Sea Witch* was already forty-eight hours overdue and Atlantique were becoming highly agitated.

'Son of a gun,' said Bernard. 'You would not think six million was an easy sum of money to get rid of, would you?'

'You don't even have to try,' Nick agreed. 'It just spends itself.' Then with a scowl, 'What's this?'

'They've invoked the escalation clause again, another 3 + 106 per cent.' *Sea Witch's* builders had included a clause that related the contract price to the index cost of steel and the Union labour rates. They had avoided the threatened dockyard strike by capitulating to Union demands, and now the figures came back to Nicholas. They were big fat ugly figures. The clause was a festering canker to Nicholas, draining his strength and money.

They worked on through the afternoon, paying, paying and paying. Bunkers and the other running costs of *Warlock*, interest and capital repayments on the debts of Ocean

Salvage, lawyers' fees, agents' fees, the six million whittled away. One of the few payments that gave Nicholas any pleasure was the 12½ per cent salvage money to the crew of *Warlock*. David Allen's share was almost thirty thousand dollars; Beauty Baker another twenty-five thousand – Nick included a note with that cheque, 'Have a Bundaberg on me!'

'Is that all the payments?' Nicholas asked at last.

'Isn't it enough?'

'It's enough.' Nick felt groggy with jetlag and from juggling with figures. 'What's next?'

'Good news, next.' Bernard picked up the second file. 'I think I've squared Esso. They hate you, they have threatened never to use your tugs again, but they are not going to sue.' Nicholas had breached contract when he deserted the Esso tow and ran south for *Golden Adventurer*; the breach of contract suit had been hanging since then. It was a relief to have it aside. Bernard Wackie was worth every penny of his hire.

'Okay. Next?'

It went on for another six unbroken hours, piled on top of the jetlag that Nicholas had accumulated across the Atlantic.

'You okay?' Bernard asked at last. Nicholas nodded, though his eyes felt like hard-boiled eggs, and his chin was dark and raspy with beard.

'You want something to eat?' Bernard asked, and then Nick shook his head and realized that it was dark outside. 'Drink? You'll need one for what comes next.'

'Scotch,' Nicholas agreed, and the secretary brought the tray through, and poured the drinks in another respectful hush.

'That will be all, Mr Wackie?'

'For now, honey.' Bernard watched her go, and then saluted Nicholas with his glass.

'I give you the Golden Prince!' And when Nicholas

scowled, he went on swiftly, 'No, Nicholas, I'm not shafting you. It's for real. You've done it again. The sheikhs are fixing to make you an offer. They want to buy you out, clean, take over the whole show, liabilities, everything. Of course, they'll want you to run it for them – two years, while you train one of their own men. A hell of a salary,' he went on crisply, and Nicholas stared at him.

'How much?'

'Two hundred grand, plus 2½ per cent profits.'

'Not the salary,' Nicholas told him. 'How much are they offering for the company?'

'They are Arabs. The first offer is just to stir the pot a little.'

'How much?' Nicholas asked impatiently.

'The sum of five was delicately mentioned.'

'What do you think they'll go to?'

'Seven, seven and half – eight, perhaps.'

Through the fuzz of fatigue, far off like a lantern in the window on a winter's night, Nicholas saw the vision of a new life, a life such as Samantha had shown him. A life uncluttered, uncomplicated, shorn of all but joy and purpose.

'Eight million dollars clear?' Nicholas' voice was husky, and he tried to wipe away the fatigue from his stinging eyelids with thumb and forefinger.

'Maybe only seven,' Bernard demurred, 'but I'd try for eight.'

'I'll have another drink,' Nicholas said.

'That's a splendid idea,' Bernard agreed, and rang for his secretary with an anticipatory sparkle in his eyes.

Samantha wore her hair in twin braids down her back, and hacked-off denim pants which left her long brown legs bare and exposed a pale sliver of tight round buttock at each step as she walked away. She had sandals on her feet and sunglasses pushed up on top of her head.

'I thought you were never coming,' she challenged Nick as he stepped through the barrier at Miami International. He dropped his bag and fielded her rush against his chest. She clung to him and he had forgotten the clean, sun-drenched smell of her hair.

She was trembling with a suppressed eagerness like a puppy, and it was only when a small quivering sob shook her shoulders that he realized she was weeping.

'Hey now!' He lifted her chin, and her eyes were flooded. She snuffled once loudly.

'What's the trouble, little one?'

'I'm just so happy,' Samantha told him, and Nicholas deeply envied the ability to live so near the surface. To be able to cry with joy seemed to him at that moment to be the supreme human accomplishment. He kissed her and she tasted salty with tears. With surprise he felt a choke deep in his own throat.

The jaded airport crowds had to open and trickle around the two of them like water around a rock, and they were oblivious to it all.

Even when they came out of the building into the Florida sunlight, she had both arms around his waist, hampering his stride, as she led him to her vehicle.

'Good God!' exclaimed Nicholas, and he shied when he saw it. It was a Chevy van, but its paintwork had been restyled. 'What's that?'

'It's a masterpiece,' she laughed. 'Isn't it?' It was rain-bowed, in layers of vibrant colour and panels of fantastic landscapes and seascapes.

'You did that?' Nick asked, and he took his dark glasses

from his breast pocket, and inspected the seagulls and palm trees and flowers through them.

'It's not that bad,' she protested. 'I was bored and depressed without you. I needed something to brighten my life.'

One of the panels depicted the translucent green of a curling wave, and on the face of the wave a pair of human figures on Hawaii boards and a graceful dolphin shape flew in formation together. Nick leaned closer and barely recognized the male figure as himself; each detail of the features had been rendered with loving attention, and he came out of it looking like something between Clark Gable and Superman – only a little more glamorous.

'From memory,' she said proudly.

'It's tremendous,' he told her. 'But I've got bigger biceps, and I'm more beautiful.'

Despite the wild choice of colour and the romantic style, he realized she had real talent.

'You don't expect me to ride in that – what if one of my creditors saw me!'

'Get your mind out of its stiff collar and blue suit, mister. You have just signed on for the voyage to Never-Never land by way of the moon.'

Before she started the engine she looked at him seriously out of those great shining green eyes.

'How long, Nicholas?' she asked. 'How long have we got together this time?'

'Ten days,' he told her. 'Sorry, but I must be back in London by the 25th. There is a big one coming up, *the* big one. I'll tell you about it.'

'No.' She covered her ears with both hands. 'I don't want to hear about it, not yet.'

She drove the Chevy with careless unforced skill, very fast and efficiently, acknowledging the homage of other male drivers with a grin and a shake of her braids.

When she slipped off Highway 95 and parked in the lot of a supermarket, Nicholas raised an eyebrow.

'Food,' she explained, and then with a lascivious roll of her eyes, 'I reckon to get mighty hungry later.'

She chose steaks, a bag full of groceries and a jug of California Riesling, and would not let him pay. 'In this town, you are my guest.'

Then she paid the toll and took the Rickenbacker causeway across the water to Virginia Key.

'That's the marine division of the University of Miami and that's my lab at the top of the jetty, just beyond that white fishing boat – see it?'

The low buildings were crowded into a corner of the island, between the seaquarium and the wharves and jetties of the University's own little harbour.

'We aren't stopping,' Nicholas observed.

'Are you kidding?' she laughed at him. 'I don't need a controlled scientific environment for the experiment I am about to conduct.'

And with no diminution of speed, the Chevy flew across the long bridge between Virginia Key and Key Biscayne, and three miles on she turned off sharply left on a narrow dirt track that twisted through a lush tropical maritime forest of banyan and palmetta and palm, and ended at a clapboard shack just above the water.

'I live close to the shop,' Samantha explained, as she clattered up on to the screened porch, her arms full of groceries.

'This is yours?' Nicholas asked. He could just make out the tops of big blocks of condominiums on each side; they were incompletely screened by the palms.

'Pa left it to me. He bought it the year I was born,' Samantha explained proudly. 'My ground stretches from there to there.'

A few hundred yards, but Nicholas realized the value of

it. Everybody in the world wants to live on the water, and those condominiums were pressing in closely.

'It must be worth a million.'

'There is no price on it,' she said firmly. 'That's what I tell those awful sweaty little men with their big cigars. Pa left it to me and it's not for sale.'

She had the door open now, bumping it with her denim-clad backside.

'Don't just stand there, Nicholas,' she implored him. 'We've only got ten days.'

He followed her into the kitchen as she dumped her load into the sink, and whirled back to him.

'Welcome to my house, Nicholas,' and then as she slid her arms around his waist, jerked his shirt tails out of his belt and slid her hands up his bare back, 'You'll never know just how welcome. Come, let me show you around – this is the living room.'

It had spartan furniture, with Indian rugs and pottery, and Samantha's chopped-off denims were discarded in the centre of the floor along with Nicholas' shirt.

'And this – surprise! surprise! – is the bedroom.' She dragged him by one hand, and under the short tee-shirt her bottom reminded him of a chipmunk with its cheeks stuffed with nuts, chewing vigorously.

The tiny bedroom overlooked the beach. The sea breeze fluffed out the curtains and the sound of the low surf breathed like a sleeping giant, a deep regular hiss and sigh that filled the air around them.

The bed was too big for the room, all ornate antique brass, with a cloudy soft mattress and an old-fashioned patchwork quilt in a hundred coloured and patterned squares.

'I don't think I could have lived another day without you,' she said, and unwound the thick plaits of her hair. 'You came like the cavalry, in the very nick of time.'

He reached up and took the golden tresses of hair,

winding them thickly around his wrist, twining them in his fingers, and he pulled her gently down beside him.

Suddenly Nick's life was uncluttered and simple again. Suddenly he was young and utterly carefree again. The petty strivings, the subterfuge, the lies and the cheating did not exist in this little universe that encompassed a tiny wooden shack on the edge of the ocean, and a huge brass bed that clanged and rattled and banged and squeaked with the wholesale, the completely abandoned happiness that was the special miracle called Samantha Silver.

S amantha's laboratory was a square room, built on piles over the water, and the soft hum of the electric pumps blended with the slap of the wavelets below and the burble and blurp of the tanks.

'This is my kingdom,' she told him. 'And these are my subjects.'

There were almost a hundred tanks, like the small glass-sided aquaria for goldfish, and suspended over each of them was a complicated arrangement of coils and bottles and electric wiring.

Nick sauntered across to the nearest of the tanks and peered into it. It contained a single large salt-water clam; the animal was feeding with the double shells agape, the pink soft flesh and frilly gills rippling and undulating in the gentle flow of pumped and filtered sea water. To each half of the shell, thin copper wires were attached with blobs of polyurethane cement.

Samantha came to stand beside him, touching, and he asked her, 'What's happening?'

She touched a switch and immediately the cylindrical scroll above the tank began to revolve slowly and a stylus, after a few preliminary jerks and quivers, began to trace out a regular pattern on the paper scroll, a trough and double peak, the second a fraction lower than the first, and then the trough again.

She said, 'He's wired and bugged.'

'You're a member of the CIA,' he accused.

And she laughed. 'His heartbeat. I'm passing an electric impulse through the heart – the heart is only a millimetre across – but each spasm changes the resistance and moves the stylus.' She studied the curve for a moment. 'This fellow is one very healthy cheerful *Spisula solidissima*.'

'Is that his name?' Nick asked. 'I thought he was a clam.'

'One of fifteen thousand bivalves who use that common generic,' she corrected.

'I had to pick an egghead,' said Nicholas ruefully. 'But what's so interesting about his heart?'

'It's the closest and cheapest thing to a pollution metre that we have discovered so far – or rather,' she corrected herself without false modesty, 'that I have discovered.'

She took his hand and led him down the long rows of tanks. 'They are sensitive, incredibly sensitive to any contamination of their environment, and the heartbeat will register almost immediately any foreign element or chemical, organic or otherwise, in such low concentrate that it would take a highly trained specialist with a spectroscope to detect otherwise.'

Nicholas felt his mild attention changing and growing into real interest as Samantha began to prepare samples of common pollutants on the single bench against the forewall of the cluttered little laboratory.

'Here,' she held up one test tube, 'aromatic carbons, the more poisonous elements of crude petroleum – and here,' she indicated the next tube, 'mercury in a concentration of 100 parts to the million. Did you see the photographs of the human vegetables and the Japanese children with the flesh falling off their bones at Kiojo? That was mercury. Lovely stuff.'

She picked up another tube. 'PCB, a by-product of the electrical industry, the Hudson River is thick with it. And these, tetrahydrofurane, cyclohexane, methylbenzene – all industrial by-products but don't let the fancy names throw you. One day they will come back to haunt us, in newspaper headlines, as THF or CMB – one day there will be other human cabbages and babies born without arms or legs.' She touched the other tubes. 'Arsenic, old-fashioned Agatha Christie vintage poison. And then here is the real living and breathing bastard daddy of them all – this is cadmium; as a sulphide so it's easily absorbed. In 100 parts to the million it's as lethal as a neutron bomb.'

While he watched, she carried the tray of tubes across to the tanks and set the ECG monitors running. Each began to record the normal double-peaked heartbeat of a healthy clam.

'Now,' she said, 'watch this.'

Under controlled conditions, she began to drip the weak poisoned solutions into the reticulated water systems, a different solution to each of the tanks.

'These concentrations are so low that the animals will not even be aware of trauma, they will continue to feed and breed without any but long-term indications of systemic poisoning.'

Samantha was a different person, a cool quick-thinking professional. Even the white dust-coat that she had slipped over her tee-shirt altered her image and she had aged twenty years in poise and authority as she passed back and forth along the row of tanks.

'There,' she said, with grim satisfaction as the stylus on one recording drum made a slightly double beat at its peak and then just detectably flattened the second peak. 'Typical aromatic carbon reaction.'

The distorted heartbeat was repeated endlessly on the slowly turning drum, and she passed on to the next tank.

'See the pulse in the trough, see the fractional speeding

up of the heart spasm? That's cadmium in ten parts to the million, at 100 parts it will kill all sea life, at five hundred it will kill man slowly, at seven hundred parts in air or solution it will kill him very quickly indeed.'

Nicholas' interest became total fascination, as he helped Samantha record the experiments and control the flow and concentration in the tanks. Slowly they increased the dosage of each substance and the moving stylus dispassionately recorded the increasing distress and the final convulsions and spasmodic throes that preceded death.

Nicholas voiced the tickle of horror and revulsion he felt at watching the process of degeneration.

'It's macabre.'

'Yes.' She stood back from the tanks. 'Death always is. But these organisms have such rudimentary nervous systems that they don't experience pain as we know it.' She shuddered slightly herself and went on. 'But imagine an entire ocean poisoned like one of these tanks, imagine the incredible agonies of tens of millions of seabirds, of the mammals, seals and porpoises and whales. Then think of what would happen to man himself—' Samantha shrugged off her white dust-coat.

'Now I'm hungry,' she announced, and then looking up at the fibreglass panels in the roof, 'No wonder! It's dark already!'

While they cleaned and tidied the laboratory, and made a last check of the pumps and running equipment, Samantha told him, 'In five hours we have tested over a hundred and fifty samples of contaminated water and got accurate indications of nearly fifty dangerous substances – at a probable cost of fifty cents a sample.' She switched out the lights. 'To do the same with a gas spectroscope would have cost almost ten thousand dollars and taken a highly specialized team two weeks of hard work.'

'It's a hell of a trick,' Nicholas told her. 'You're a clever lady – I'm impressed, I really am.'

At the psychedelic Chevy van she stopped him, and in the light of the street lamp, she looked up at him guiltily.

'Do you mind if I show you off, Nicholas?'

'What does that mean?' he asked suspiciously.

'The gang are eating shrimps tonight. Then they'll sleep over on the boat and have the first shot at fish tagging tomorrow – but we don't have to go. We could just get some more steaks and another jug of wine.' But he could see she really wanted to go.

She was fifty-five foot, an old purse-seiner with the ungainly wheelhouse forward looking like a sentry box or an old-fashioned pit latrine. Even with her coat of new paint, she had an old-fashioned look.

She was tied up at the end of the University jetty, and as they walked out to her, so they could hear the voices and the laughter coming up from below decks.

'Tricky Dicky,' Nicholas read her name on the high ugly rounded stern.

'But we love her,' Samantha said, and led him across the narrow, rickety gangplank. 'She belongs to the University. She's only one of our four research vessels. The others are all fancy modern ships, two-hundred-footers, but the *Dicky* is our boat for short field trips to the Gulf or down the Keys, and she's also the faculty clubhouse.'

The main cabin was monastically furnished, bare planking and hard benches, a single long table, but it was as crowded as a fashionable discotheque, packed solid with sunburned young people, girls and boys all in faded jeans and tee-shirts, impossible to judge sexes by clothing or by the length of their sun-tortured and wind-tangled hair.

The air was thick with the rich smell of broiling Gulf shrimps and molten butter, and there were gallon jugs of California wine on the table.

'Hey!' Samantha shouted above the uproar of voices raised in heated dispute and jovial repartee. 'This is Nicholas.'

A comparative silence descended on the gathering, and they looked him over with the curious veiled group hostility of any tribe for an interloper, an intruder in a closed and carefully guarded group. Nick returned the scrutiny calmly, met each pair of eyes, while realizing that despite the affected informality of their dress and some of the wildly unkempt hairstyles and the impressive profusion of beards, they were an élite group. There was not a face that was not intelligent, not a pair of eyes that was not alert and quick, and there was that special feeling of pride and self-confidence in all of them.

At the head of the table sat a big impressive figure, the oldest man in the cabin, perhaps Nick's age or a little older, for there were silver strands in his beard and his face was lined and beaten by sun and wind and time.

'Hi, Nick,' he boomed. 'I won't pretend we've never heard of you. Sam has given us all cauliflower ears—'

'You cut that out, Tom Parker,' Samantha stopped him sharply, and there was a ripple of laughter, a relaxation of tension and a casual round of greetings.

'Hi, Nick, I'm Sally-Anne.' A pretty girl with china-blue eyes behind wire-framed spectacles put a heavy tumbler of wine into his hand.

'We are short of glasses, guess you and Sam will have to share.'

She slid up along the bench and gave them a few inches of space and Samantha perched on Nicholas' lap. The wine was a rough fighting red, and it galloped, booted and spurred across his palate but Samantha sipped her share with the same relish as if it had been a '53 Château Lafitte, and she nuzzled Nicholas' ear and whispered:

'Tom is prof of the Biology Department. He's a honey. After you – he's my most favourite man in the world.'

A woman came through from the galley, carrying a huge platter piled high with bright pink shrimps and a bowl of molten butter. There was a roar of applause for her as she placed the dishes in the centre of the table, and they fell upon the food with unashamed gusto.

The woman was tall with dark hair in braids and a strong capable face, lean and supple in tight breeches, but she was older than the other women and she paused beside Tom Parker and draped one arm across his shoulders in a comfortable gesture of long-established affection.

'That's Antoinette, his wife.' The woman heard her name and smiled across at them, and with dark gentle eyes she studied Nicholas and then nodded and made the continental 'O' of thumb and forefinger at Samantha, before slipping back into the galley.

The food did not inhibit the talk, the lively contentious flow of discussion that swung swiftly from banter to deadly seriousness and back again, bright, trained, informed minds clicking and cannoning off each other with the crispness of ivory billiard balls, while at the same time buttery fingers ripped the whiskered heads off the shrimps, delving for the crescent of sweet white flesh, then leaving greasy finger-prints on the wine tumblers.

As each of them spoke, Samantha whispered their names and credentials. 'Hank Petersen, he's doing a PhD on the bluefin tuna – spawning and a trace of its migratory routes. He's the one running the tagging tomorrow.

'That's Michelle Rand, she's on loan from UCLA, and she's porpoises and whales.'

Then suddenly they were all discussing indignantly a rogue tanker captain who the week before had scrubbed his tanks in the middle of the Florida straits and left a thirty-mile slick down the Gulf Stream. He had done it under cover of night, and changed course as soon as he was into the Atlantic proper.

'We fingerprinted him,' Tom Parker spoke like an angry

bear, 'we had him made, dead in the cross-hairs.' Nick knew he was talking of the finger-printing of oil residues, the breakdown of samples of the slick under gas spectroscopy which could match them exactly to the samples taken by the Coast Guard from the offender's tanks. The identification was good enough to bear up in an international court of law. 'But the trick is getting the son-of-a-bitch into court.' Tom Parker went on. 'He was fifty miles outside our territorial waters by the time the Coast Guard got to him, and he's registered in Liberia.'

'We tried to cover cases like that in the set of proposals I put up to the last maritime conference.'

Nick joined the conversation for the first time. He told them of the difficulties of legislating on an international scale, of policing and bringing to justice the blatant transgressors; then he listed for them what had been done so far, what was in process and finally what he believed should still be done to protect the seas.

He spoke quietly, succinctly, and Samantha noticed again, with a swell of pride, how all the men listened when Nicholas Berg talked. The moment he paused, they came at him from every direction, using their bright young minds like scalpels, tearing into him with sharp lancing questions. He answered them in the same fashion, sharp and hard, armed with total knowledge of his subject, and he saw the shift in the group attitude, the blooming of respect, the subtle opening of ranks to admit him, for he had spoken the correct passwords and they recognized him as one of their own number, as one of the élite.

At the head of the table, Tom Parker sat and listened, nodding and frowning, sitting in judgement with his arm around Antoinette's slim waist and she stood beside him and played idly with a curl of thick wiry hair on the top of his head.

Tom Parker found fish forty miles offshore where the Gulf Stream was setting blue and warm and fast into the north. The birds were working, falling on folded wings down the backdrop of cumulonimbus storm clouds that bruised the horizon. The birds were bright, white pinpoints of light as they fell, and they struck the dark blue water with tiny explosions of white spray, and went deep. Seconds later they popped to the surface, stretching their necks to force down another morsel into their distended crops, before launching into flight again, climbing in steep circles against the sky to join the hunt again. There were hundreds of them and they swirled and fell like snowflakes.

'Anchovy,' grunted Tom Parker, and they could see the agitated surface of the water under the bird flock where the frenzied bait-fish churned. 'Could be bonito working under them.'

'No,' said Nick. 'They are blues.'

'You sure?' Tom grinned a challenge.

'The way they are bunching and holding the bait-fish, it's tuna,' Nick repeated.

'Five bucks?' Tom asked, as he swung the wheel over, and *Tricky Dicky*'s big diesel engine boomed as she went on to the top of her speed.

'You're on,' Nick grinned back at him, and at that moment, they both saw a fish jump clear. It was a brilliant shimmering torpedo, as long as a man's arm. It went six feet into the air, turned in flight and hit the water again with a smack they heard clearly above the diesel.

'Blues,' said Nick flatly. 'Shoal blues – they'll go twenty pounds each.'

'Five bucks,' Tom grunted with disgust. 'Son of a gun, I don't think I can afford you, man,' and he delivered a playful punch to the shoulder which rattled Nick's teeth, then he turned to the open window of the wheelhouse and bellowed out on to the deck, 'Okay, kids, they are blues'.

There was a scramble and chatter of excitement as they rushed for lines and tagging poles. It was Hank's show: he was the bluefin tunny expert; he knew as much about their sex habits, their migratory routes and food chains as any man living, but when it came to catching them, Nick observed drily, he could probably do a better job as a blacksmith.

Tom Parker was no fisherman either. He ran down the shoal, charging *Tricky Dicky* through the centre of it, scattering birds and fish in panic – but by sheer chance one of the gang in the stern hooked in, and after a great deal of heaving and huffing and shouted encouragement from his peers, dragged a single luckless baby bluefin tuna over the rail. It skittered and jumped around the deck, its tail hammering against the planking, pursued by a shrieking band of scientists who slid and slipped in the fish slime, knocked each other down and finally cornered the fish against the rail. The first three attempts to affix the plastic tag were unsuccessful, Hank's lunges with the dart pole becoming wilder as his frustration mounted. He almost succeeded in tagging Samantha's raised backside as she knelt on the deck trying to cradle the fish in both arms.

'You do this often?' Nicholas asked mildly.

'First time with this gang,' Tom Parker admitted sheepishly. 'Thought you'd never guess.'

By now the triumphant band was solicitously returning the fish to the sea, the barbed dart of the plastic tag embedded dangerously near its vitals; and if that didn't eventually kill it, the rough handling probably would. It had pounded its head on the deck so heavily that blood oozed from the gill covers. It floated away, belly up on the stream, oblivious of Samantha's anguished cries of:

'Swim, fish, get in there and swim!'

'Mind if we try it my way?' Nick asked, and Tom relinquished command without a struggle.

Nicholas picked the four strongest and best co-ordinated

of the young men, and gave them a quick demonstration and lecture on how to handle the heavy handlines with the Japanese feather lures, showing them how to throw the bait, and the recovery with an underhand flick that recoiled the line between the feet. Then he gave each a station along the starboard rail, with the second member of each team ready with a tagging pole and Hank Petersen on the roof of the wheelhouse to record the fish taken and the numbers of the tags.

They found another shoal within the hour and Nicholas circled up on it, closing steadily at good trolling speed, helping the feeding tuna bunch the shoal of frenzied anchovy on the surface, until he could lock *Tricky Dicky*'s wheel hard down starboard and leave her to describe her own sedate circles around the shoal. Then he hurried out on to the deck.

The trapped and surrounded fish thrashed the surface until it boiled like a porridge of molten, flashing silver; through it drove the fast dark torpedoes of the hungry tuna.

Within minutes Nick had his four fishermen working to the steady rhythm of throwing the lures into the frothing water, almost instantly striking back on the line as a tuna snatched the feathers, and then swinging hand over head, recovering and coiling line fast with minimum effort, swinging the fish out and up with both hands and then catching its streamlined body under the left armpit like a quarterback picking up a long pass, clamping it there firmly, although the cold, firm, silver bullet shape juddered and quivered and the tail beat in a blur of movement. Then he taught them to slip the hook from the jaw, careful not to damage the vulnerable gills, holding the fish firmly but gently while the assistant pressed the barbed dart into the thick muscle at the back of the dorsal fin. When the fish was dropped back over the side, there were so few after-effects that it almost immediately began feeding again on the packed masses of tiny anchovies.

Each plastic tag was numbered and imprinted with a request in five languages to mail it back to the University of Miami with details of the date and place of capture, providing a valuable trace of the movements of the shoals in their annual circumnavigation of the globe. From their spawning grounds somewhere in the Caribbean they worked the Gulf Stream north and east across the Atlantic, then south down and around the Cape of Good Hope with an occasional foray down the length of the Mediterranean Sea – although now the dangerous pollution of that landlocked water was changing their habits. From Good Hope east again south of Australia to take a gigantic swing up and around the Pacific, running the gauntlet of the Japanese long-liners and the California tunny men before ducking down under the terrible icy seas of the Horn and back to their spawning grounds in the Caribbean.

They sat up on the wheelhouse as the *Dicky* ran home in the sunset, drinking beer and talking. Nicholas studied them casually and saw that they possessed so many of the qualities he valued in his fellow humans; they were intelligent and motivated, they were dedicated and free of that particular avarice that mars so many others.

Tom Parker crumpled the empty beer can in a huge fist as easily as if it had been a paper packet, fished two more from the pack beside him and tossed one across to Nick. The gesture seemed to have some special significance and Nicholas saluted him with the can before he drank.

Samantha was snuggled down in luxurious weariness against his shoulder, and the sunset was a magnificence of purple and hot molten crimson. Nicholas thought idly how pleasant it would be to spend the rest of his life doing things like this with people like these.

Tom Parker's office had shelves to the ceiling, and they were sagging with hundreds of bottled specimens and rows of scientific papers and publications.

He sat well back in his swivel chair with ankles crossed neatly in the centre of the cluttered desk.

'I ran a check on you, Nicholas. Damned nerve, wasn't it? You have my apology.'

'Was it an interesting exercise?' Nicholas asked mildly.

'It wasn't difficult. You have left a trail behind you like a—' Tom sought for a comparison, 'like a grizzly bear through a honey farm. Son of a gun, Nicholas, that's a hell of a track record you've got yourself.'

'I've kept busy,' Nicholas admitted.

'Beer?' Tom crossed to the refrigerator in the corner that was labelled 'Zoological Specimens. DO NOT OPEN.'

'It's too early for me.'

'Never too early,' said Tom and pulled the tag on a dewy can of Millers and then picked up Nicholas' statement. 'Yes, you have kept busy. Strange, isn't it, that around some men things just happen.'

Nicholas did not reply, and Tom went on. 'We need a man around here who can *do*. It's all right thinking it out, then you need the catalyst to transform thought and intention into action.' Tom sucked at the can and then licked the froth off his moustache. 'I know what you have done. I've heard you speak, I've seen you move, and those things count. But most important of all, I know you care. I've been watching you carefully, Nick, and you really care, down deep in your guts, the way we do.'

'It sounds as though you're offering me a job, Tom.'

'I'm not going to horse around, Nick, I *am* offering you a job.' He waved a huge paw, like a bunch of broiled pork sausages. 'Hell, I know you're a busy man, but I'd like to romance you into an associate professorship. We'd want a little of your time when it came to hassling and negotiating up in Washington, we'd call for you when we needed real muscle to put our case, when we need the right contacts, somebody with a big reputation to open doors, when we need a man who knows the practical side of the oceans and the men that use them and abuse them.

'We need a man who is a hard-headed businessman, who knows the economics of sea trade, who has built and run tankers, who knows that human need is of paramount importance, but who can balance the human need for protein and fossil fuels against the greater danger of turning the oceans into watery deserts.' Tom lubricated his throat with beer, watching shrewdly for some reaction from Nicholas, and when he received no encouragement, he went on more persuasively. 'We are specialists, perhaps we have the specialist's narrow view; God knows, they think of us as sentimentalists, the lunatic fringe of doomsayers, long-haired intellectual hippies. What we need is a man with real clout in the establishment – shit, Nicholas, if you walked into a Congressional committee they'd really jerk out of their geriatric trance and switch on their hearing-aids.' Nicholas was silent still and Tom was becoming desperate. 'What can we offer in return? I know you aren't short of cash, and it would be a lousy 12,000 a year, but an associate professorship is a nice title. We start out holding hands with that. Then we might start going steady, a full professorship – chair of applied oceanology, or some juicy title like that which we'd think up. I don't know what else we can offer you, Nick, except perhaps the warm good feeling in your guts when you're doing a tough job that has to be done.' He stopped again, running out of words, and he wagged his big shaggy head sadly.

'You aren't interested, are you?' he asked.

Nick stirred himself. 'When do I start?' he asked, and as Tom's face split into a great beaming grin, Nick held out his hand. 'I think I'll take that beer now.'

The water was cool enough to be invigorating. Nick and Samantha swam so far out that the land was almost lost in the lowering gloom of dusk, and then they turned and swam back side by side. The beach was deserted; in their mood, the lights of the nearest condominiums were no more intrusive than the stars, the faint sound of music and laughter no more intrusive than the cry of gulls.

It was the right time to tell her, and he did it in detail beginning with the offer by the Sheikhs to buy out Ocean Salvage and Towage.

'Will you sell?' she asked quietly. 'You won't, will you?'

'For seven million dollars clear?' he asked. 'Do you know how much money that is?'

'I can't count that far,' she admitted. 'But what would you do if you sold? I cannot imagine you playing bowls or golf for the rest of your life.'

'Part of the deal is that I run Ocean Salvage for them for two years, and then I've been offered a part-time assignment which will fill any spare time I've got left over.'

'What is it?'

'Associate Professor at Miami University.'

She stopped dead and dragged him around to face her.

'You're having me on!' she accused.

'That's a start only,' he admitted. 'In two years or so, when I've finished with Ocean Salvage, there may be a full chair of applied oceanology.'

'It's not true!' she said, and took him by the arms, shaking him with surprising strength.

'Tom wants me to ramrod the applied aspects of the environmental research. I'll troubleshoot with legislators and the maritime conference, a sort of hired gun for the Greenpeacers—'

'Oh Nicholas, Nicholas!'

'Sweet Christ!' he accused. 'You're crying again.'

'I just can't help it.' She was in his arms still wet and

cold and gritty with beach sand. She clung to him, quivering with joy. 'Do you know what this means, Nicholas? You don't, do you? You just don't realize what this means.'

'Tell me,' he invited. 'What does it mean?'

'What it means is that, in future, we can do everything together, not just munch food and go boom in bed – but everything, work and play and, and *live* together like a man and woman should!' She sounded stunned and frightened by the magnitude of the vision.

'The prospect daunts me not at all,' he murmured gently, and lifted her chin.

They washed off the salt and the sand, crowding together into the thick, perfumed steam of the shower cubicle and afterwards they lay together on the patchwork quilt in the darkness with the sound of the sea as background music to the plans and dreams they wove together.

Every time they both descended to the very frontiers of sleep, one of them would think of something vitally important and prod the other awake to say it.

'I've got to be in London on Tuesday.'

'Don't spoil it all, now,' she murmured sleepily.

'And then we're launching *Sea Witch* on the 7th April.'

'I'm not listening,' she whispered. 'I've got my fingers in my ears.'

'Will you launch her – I mean break the bottle of bubbly and bless her?'

'I've just taken my fingers out again.'

'Jules would love it.'

'Nicholas, I cannot spend my life commuting across the Atlantic, not even for you. I've got work to do.'

'Peter will be there, I'll work that as a bribe.'

'That's unfair pressure,' she protested.

'Will you come?'

'You know I will, you sexy bastard. I wouldn't miss it for

all the world.' She moved across the quilt and found his ear with her lips. 'I am honoured.'

'Both of you are sea witches,' Nick told her.

'And you are my warlock.'

'Sea witch and warlock,' he chuckled. 'Together we will work miracles.'

'Look, I know it's terribly forward of me, but seeing that we are both wide awake, and it's only two o'clock in the morning, I would be super ultra-grateful if you could work one of your little miracles for me right now.'

'It will be a great pleasure,' Nick told her.

Nicholas was early, he saw as he came out of the American Consulate and glanced at his Rolex, so he moderated his pace across the Place de la Concorde, despite the gentle misty rain that settled in minute droplets on the shoulders of his trench coat.

Lazarus was at the rendezvous ahead of him, standing under one of the statues in the corner of the square closest to the French naval headquarters.

He was heavily muffled against the cold, dressed all in sombre blue with a long cashmere scarf wound around his throat and a dark blue hat pulled down so low as to conceal the pale smooth bulge of his forehead.

'Let's find a warm place,' Nick suggested, without greeting the little man.

'No,' said Lazarus, looking up at him through the thick distorting lenses of his spectacles. 'Let us walk.' And he led the way through the underpass on to the promenade above the embankment of the Seine, and set off in the direction of the Petit Palais.

In the middle of such an inclement afternoon they were the only strollers, and they walked in silence three or four hundred yards while Lazarus satisfied himself absolutely of this, and while he adjusted his mincing little steps to Nick's stride. It was like taking Toulouse-Lautrec for a stroll, Nick smiled to himself. Even when Lazarus began speaking, he kept glancing back over his shoulder, and once when two bearded Algerian students in combat jackets overtook them, he let them get well ahead before he went on.

'You know there will be nothing in writing?' he piped.

'I have a recorder in my pocket,' Nick assured him.

'Very well, you are entitled to that.'

'Thank you,' murmured Nick dryly.

Lazarus paused, it was almost as though a new reel was being fitted into the computer, and when he began talking again, his voice had a different timbre, a monotonous, almost electronic tone, as though he was indeed an automaton.

First, there was a recital of share movements in the thirty-three companies which make up the Christy Marine complex, every movement in the previous eighteen months.

The little man reeled them off steadily, as though he were actually reading from the share registers of the companies. He must have had access, Nicholas realized, to achieve such accuracy. He had the date, the number of the shares, the transferor and transferee, even the transfer of shares in Ocean Salvage and Towage to Nicholas himself, and the reciprocal transfer of Christy Marine stock was faithfully detailed, confirming the accuracy of Lazarus' other information. It was all an impressive exhibition of total knowledge and total recall, but much too complicated for Nicholas to make any sense of it. He would have to study it carefully. All that he would hazard was that somebody was putting up a smokescreen.

Lazarus stopped on the corner of the Champs Elysées and the rue de la Boétie. Nicholas glanced down at him and saw his shapeless blob of a nose was an unhealthy purplish pink in the cold, and that his breathing had coarsened and laboured with the exertion of walking. Nick realized suddenly that the little man was probably asthmatic, and as if to confirm this, he took a little silver and turquoise pill-box from his pocket and slipped a single pink capsule into his mouth before leading Nicholas into the foyer of a movie house and buying two tickets.

It was a porno movie, a French version of *Deep Throat* entitled *Gorge Profonde*. The print was scratched and the French dubbing was out of synchronization. The cinema was almost empty, so they found two seats in isolation at the rear of the stalls.

Lazarus stared unblinkingly at the screen, as he began the second part of his report. This was a detailed breakdown of cash movements within the Christy Marine Group, and Nick was again amazed at the man's penetration.

He drew a verbal picture of the assemblage of enormous sums of money, marshalled and channelled into orderly flows by a master tactician. The genius of Duncan Alexander was as clearly identifiable as that flourishing signature with the flamboyant 'A' and 'X' which Nicholas had seen him dash off with studied panache. Then suddenly the cashflow was not so steady and untroubled, there were eddies and breaks, little gaps and inconsistencies that nagged at Nicholas like the false chimes of a broken clock. Lazarus finished this section of his report with a brief summation of the Group's cash and credit position as at a date four days previously and Nicholas realized that the doubts were justified. Duncan had run the Group out along a knife-edge.

Nicholas sat hunched down in the threadbare velvet seat, both hands thrust into the pockets of his trenchcoat, watching the incredible feats of Miss Lovelace on the screen, without really seeing them, while beside him

Lazarus took an aerosol can from his pocket, screwed a nozzle on to it and noisily sprayed a fine mist down his own throat. It seemed to relieve him almost immediately.

'Insurance and marine underwriting of vessels owned by the Christy Marine Group of companies.' He began again with names and figures and dates, and Nicholas picked up the trend. Duncan was using his own captive company, London and European Insurance and Banking, to lead the risk on all his vessels, and then he was reinsuring in the marketplace, spreading part of the risk, but carrying a whacking deductible himself, the principle of self-insurance that Nicholas had opposed so vigorously, and which had rebounded so seriously upon Duncan's head with the salvage of *Golden Adventurer*.

The last of the vessels in Lazarus' recital was *Golden Dawn*, and Nicholas shifted restlessly in his seat at the mention of the name, and almost immediately he realized that something strange was taking place.

'Christy Marine did not apply for a Lloyd's survey of this vessel.' Nicholas knew that already. 'But she has been rated first class by the continental surveyors.' It was a much easier rating to obtain, and consequently less acceptable than the prestigious A1 at Lloyd's.

Lazarus went on, lowering his voice slightly as another patron entered the almost deserted cinema and took a seat two rows in front of them.

'And insurance has been effected outside Lloyd's.' The risk was led by London and European Insurance. Again, Duncan was self-insuring, Nicholas noted grimly, but not all of it. 'And further lines were written by—' Lazarus listed the other companies which carried a part of the risk, with whom Duncan had reinsured. But it was all too thin, too nebulous. Again, only careful study of the figures would enable Nicholas to analyse what Duncan was doing, how much was real insurance and how much was bluff to convince his financiers that the risk was truly covered, and their investment protected.

Some of the names of the reinsurers were familiar; they had been on the list of transferees who had taken stock positions in Christy Marine.

'Is Duncan buying insurance with capital?' Nicholas pondered. Was he buying at desperate prices? He must have cover, of course. Without insurance the finance houses, the banks and institutions which had loaned the money to Christy Marine to build the monstrous tanker, would dig in against Duncan. His own shareholders would raise such hell – No, Duncan Alexander had to have cover, even if it was paper only, without substance, a mere incestuous circle, a snake eating itself tail first.

Oh, but the trail was so cleverly confused, so carefully swept and tied up, only Nicholas' intimate knowledge of Christy Marine made him suspicious, and it might take a team of investigators years to unravel the tortured tapestry of deceit. In the first instant, it had occurred to Nicholas that the easiest way to stop Duncan Alexander was to leak his freshly gleaned suspicions to Duncan's major creditors, to those who had financed the building of *Golden Dawn*. But immediately he realized that this was not enough. There were no hard facts, it was all inference and innuendo. By the time the facts could be exhumed and laid out in all their putrefaction for autopsy, *Golden Dawn* would be on the high seas, carrying a million tons of crude. Duncan might have won sufficient time to make his profit and sell out to some completely uncontrollable Greek or Chinaman, as he had boasted he would do. It would not be so simple to stop Duncan Alexander; it was folly to have believed that for one moment. Even if his creditors were made aware of the flimsy insurance cover over *Golden Dawn*, were they too deeply in already? Would they not then accept the risks, spreading them where they could,

319

and simply twist the financial rope a little tighter around Duncan's throat? No, it was not the way to stop him. Duncan had to be forced to remodify the giant tanker's hull, forced to make her an acceptable moral risk, forced to accept the standard Nicholas had originally stipulated for the vessel.

Lazarus had finished the insurance portion of his report and he stood up abruptly, just as Miss Lovelace was about to attempt the impossible. With relief, Nick followed him down the aisle and into the chill of a Parisian evening, and they breathed the fumes that the teeming city exhaled as Lazarus led him back eastwards through the VIIIᵉ Arrondissement with those little dancing steps, while he recited the details of the charters of all Christy Marine's vessels, the charterer, the rates, the dates of expiry of contract; and Nicholas recognized most of them, contracts that he himself had negotiated, or those that had been renewed on expiry with minor alterations to the terms. He was relying on the recorder in his pocket, listening only with the surface layer of his mind, pondering all he had heard so far from this extraordinary little man – so that when it came he almost did not realize what he was hearing.

'On 10th January Christy Marine entered a contract of carriage with Orient Amex. The tenure is ten years. The vessel to be employed is the *Golden Dawn*. The rate is 10 cents US per hundred ton miles with a minimum annual guaranteed usage of 75,000 nautical miles.'

Nicholas registered the trigger word *Golden Dawn* and then he assimilated it all. The price, ten cents per hundred ton miles, that was wrong, high, much too high, ridiculously high in this depressed market. Then the name, Orient Amex – what was there about it that jarred his memory?

He stopped dead, and a following pedestrian bumped him. Nicholas shouldered him aside thoughtlessly and stood thinking, ransacking his mind for buried items of information. Lazarus had stopped also and was waiting patiently, and now Nicholas laid a hand on the little man's shoulder.

'I need a drink.'

He drew him into a brasserie which was thick with steam from the coffee machine and the smoke of Caporal and Disque Bleu, and sat him at a tiny table by the window overlooking the sidewalk.

Primly, Lazarus asked for a Vittel water and sipped it with an air of virtue, while Nicholas poured soda into his whisky.

'Orient Amex,' Nicholas asked, as soon as the waiter had left. 'Tell me about it.'

'That is outside my original terms of reference,' Lazarus demurred delicately.

'Charge me for it,' Nicholas invited, and Lazarus paused as the computer reels clicked in his mind, then he began to speak.

'Orient Amex is an American-registered company, with an issued capital of twenty-five million shares at a par value of ten dollars—' Lazarus recited the dry statistics. 'The company is presently undertaking substantial dry-land exploration in Western Australia and Ethiopia, and off-shore exploration within the territorial waters of Norway and Chile. It has erected a refinery at Galveston in Texas to operate under the new atomic catalyst-cracking process, first employed at its pilot plant on the same site. The plant is projected for initial operation in June this year, and full production in five years.'

It was all vaguely familiar to Nicholas, the names, the process of cracking the low-value high-carbon molecules, breaking up the carbon atoms and reassembling them in volatile low-carbon molecules of high value.

'The company operates producing wells in Texas, and in the Santa Barbara offshore field, in Southern Nigeria, and has proven crude reserves in the El Barras field of

321

Kuwait, which will be utilized by the new cracking plant in Galveston.'

'Good God,' Nicholas stared at him. 'The El Barras field – but it's cadmium-contaminated, it's been condemned by—'

'The El Barras field is a high cadmium field, naturally enriched with the catalyst necessary for the new process.'

'What are the cadmium elements?' Nicholas demanded.

'The western area of the El Barras field has sampled at 2,000 parts per million, and the north and eastern anticline have sampled as high as 42,000 parts per million.' Lazarus recited the figures pedantically. 'The American and Nigerian crudes will be blended with the El Barras crudes during the revolutionary cracking process. It is projected that the yield of low-carbon volatiles will be increased from 40 per cent to 85 per cent by this process, making it five to eight times more profitable, and extending the life of the world's known reserves of crude petroleum by between ten and fifteen years.'

As he listened, Nicholas had a vivid mental image of the stylus in Samantha's laboratory recording the death throes of a cadmium-poisoned clam. Lazarus was talking on dispassionately. 'During the cracking process, the cadmium sulphide will be reduced to its pure metallic, non-toxic form, and will be a valuable by-product, reducing the costs of refining.'

Nicholas shook his head in disbelief, and he spoke aloud. 'Duncan is going to do it. Across two oceans, a million tons at a time, in that vulnerable jerry-built monster of his, Duncan is going to do what no other shipowner has ever dared to do – he's going to carry the cad-rich crudes of El Barras!'

From the balcony windows of his suite in the Ritz, Nicholas could look out across the Place Vendôme at the column in the centre of the square with its spiral bas-relief made from the Russian and Austrian guns and commemorating the little Corsican's feats of arms against those two nations. While he studied the column and waited for his connection, he did a quick calculation and realized that it would be three o'clock in the morning on the eastern seaboard of North America. At least he would find her at home. Then he smiled to himself. If she wasn't at home, he'd want to know the reason why.

The telephone rang and he picked it up without turning away from the window.

There was a confused mumbling and Nicholas asked, 'Who is this?'

'It's Sam Silver – what's the time? Who is it? Good God, it's three o'clock. What do you want?'

'Tell that other guy to put his pants on and go home.'

'Nicholas!' There was a joyous squeal, followed immediately by a crash and clatter that made Nicholas wince and lift the receiver well away from his ear.

'Oh damn it to hell, I've knocked the table over. Nicholas, are you there? Speak to me, for God's sake!'

'I love you.'

'Say that again, please. Where are you?'

'Paris. I love you.'

'Oh,' her tone drooped miserably. 'You sound so close. I thought—' Then she rallied gamely. 'I love you too – how's himself?'

'On the dole.'

'Who is she?'

'Dole is unemployment insurance – welfare—' He sought the American equivalent. 'I mean he is temporarily unemployed.'

'Great. Keep him that way. Did I tell you I love you, I forget?'

'Wake up. Shake yourself. I've got something to tell you.'

'I'm awake – well, almost anyway.'

'Samantha, what would happen if somebody dumped a million tons of 40,000 parts concentration of cadmium sulphide in an emulsion of aromatic Arabian crude into the Gulf Stream, say thirty nautical miles off Key West?'

'That's a freaky question, Nicholas. For three in the morning, that's a bomber.'

'What would happen?' he insisted.

'The crude would act as a transporting medium,' she was struggling to project a scenario through her sleepiness, 'it would spread out on the surface to a thickness of a quarter of an inch or so, so you'd end up with a slick of a few thousand miles long and four or five hundred wide, and it would keep going.'

'What would be the results?'

'It would wipe out most of the marine life on the Bahamas and on the eastern seaboard of the States, no, correct that – it would wipe out all marine life, that includes the spawning grounds of the tuna, the freshwater eels and the sperm whale, and it would contaminate—' she was coming fully awake now, and a stirring horror altered her tone. 'You're macabre, Nicholas, what a sick thing to think about, especially at three in the morning.'

'Human life?' he asked.

'Yes, there would be heavy loss,' she said. 'As sulphide, it would be readily absorbed and in that concentration it would be poisonous on contact, fishermen, vacationers, anybody who walked on a contaminated beach.' She was truly beginning to realize the enormity of it. 'A large part of the population of the cities on the east coast – Nicholas, it could amount to hundreds of thousands of human beings, and if it was carried beyond America on the Gulf Stream, the Newfoundland Banks, Iceland, the North Sea, it would poison the cod fisheries, it would kill everything, man, fish, bird and animal. Then the tail of the Gulf Stream twists around the British Isles and the north continent of Europe – but why are you asking me this, what kind of crazy guessing game is this, Nicholas?'

'Christy Marine has signed a ten-year contract to carry one million ton loads of crude from the El Barras field on the South Arabian Gulf to the Orient Amex refinery in Galveston. The El Barras crude has a cadmium sulphide constituent of between 2,000 and 40,000 parts per million.'

Now there was trembling outrage in her voice as she whispered, 'A million tons! That's some sort of genocide, Nicholas, there has probably never been a more deadly cargo in the history of seafaring.'

'In a few weeks' time *Golden Dawn* will run down her ways at St Nazaire – and when she does, the seeds of catastrophe will be sewn upon the oceans.'

'Her route from the Arabian Gulf takes her around Good Hope.'

'One of the most dangerous seas in the world, the home of the hundred-year wave,' Nicholas agreed.

'Then across the southern Atlantic—'

' – and into the bottleneck of the Gulf Stream between Key West and Cuba, into the Devil's Triangle, the breeding ground of the hurricanes—'

'You can't let them do it, Nicholas,' she said quietly. 'You just have to stop them.'

'It won't be easy, but I'll be working hard on it this side, there are a dozen tricks I am going to try, but you have to take over on your side,' he told her. 'Samantha, you go get Tom Parker. Get him out of bed, if necessary. He has to hit Washington with the news, hit all the media – television, radio and the press. A confrontation with Orient Amex, challenge them to make a statement.'

Samantha picked up the line he was taking. 'We'll get the Greenpeacers to picket the Orient Amex refinery in Galveston, the one which will process the cadmium crudes.

We'll have every environmental agency in the country at work – we'll raise a stink like that of a million corpses,' she promised.

'Fine,' he said. 'You do all that, but don't forget to get your chubby little backside across here for the launching of *Sea Witch*.'

'Chubby obese, or chubby nice?' she demanded.

'Chubby beautiful,' he grinned. 'And I'll have room service ready to send up the food, in a front-end loader.'

Nicholas sat over the telephone for the rest of the day, having his meals brought up to the suite, while he worked systematically down the long list of names he had drawn up with the help of the tape recording of Lazarus' report.

The list began with all those who it seemed had loaned capital to Christy Marine for the construction of *Golden Dawn*, and then went on to those who had written lines of insurance on the hull, and on the pollution cover for the tanker.

Nicholas dared not be too specific in the summation he gave to each of them, he did not want to give Duncan Alexander an opportunity to throw out a smokescreen of libel actions against him. But in each case, Nicholas spoke to the top men, mostly men he knew well enough to use their Christian names, and he said just enough to show that he knew the exact amount of their involvement with Christy Marine, to suggest they re-examine the whole project, especially with regard to *Golden Dawn*'s underwriting and to her contract of carriage with Orient Amex.

In the quiet intervals between each telephone call, or while a name was tracked down by a secretary, Nicholas sat over the Place Vendôme and carefully re-examined himself and his reasons for what he was doing.

It is so very easy for a man to attribute to himself the most noble motives. The sea had given Nicholas a wonderful life, and had rewarded him in wealth, reputation and achievement. Now it was time to repay part of that debt, to use some of that wealth to protect and guard the oceans, the way a prudent farmer cherishes his soil. It was a fine thought, but when he looked below its shining surface, he saw the shape and movement of less savoury creatures, like the shadows of shark and barracuda in the depths.

There was pride. *Golden Dawn* had been his creation, the culmination of a lifetime's work, it was going to be the laurel crown on his career. But it had been taken from him, and bastardized – and when it failed, when the whole marvellous concept collapsed in disaster and misery, Nicholas Berg's name would still be on it. The world would remember then that the whole grandiose design had originated with him.

There was pride, and then there was hatred. Duncan Alexander had taken his woman and child. Duncan Alexander had wrested his very life from him. Duncan Alexander was the enemy, and by Nicholas' rules, he must be fought with the same single-mindedness, with the same ruthlessness, as he did everything in his life.

Nicholas poured himself another cup of coffee and lit a cheroot; brooding alone in the magnificence of his suite, he asked himself the question:

'If it had been another man in another ship who was going to transport the El Barras crudes – would I have opposed him so bitterly?'

The question needed no formal reply. Duncan Alexander was the enemy.

Nicholas picked up the telephone, and placed the call he had been delaying. He did not need to look in the red calf-bound notebook for the number of the house in Eaton Square.

'Mrs Chantelle Alexander, please.'

'I am sorry, sir. Mrs Alexander is at Cap Ferrat.'

'Of course,' he muttered. 'Thank you.'

'Do you want the number?'

'That's all right, I have it.' He had lost track of time. He dialled again, this time down to the Mediterranean coast.

'This is the residence of Mrs Alexander. Her son Peter Berg speaking.'

Nicholas felt the rush of emotion through his blood, so that it burned his cheeks and stung his eyes.

'Hello, my boy.' Even in his own ears his voice sounded stilted, perhaps pompous.

'Father,' undisguised delight. 'Dad, how are you – sir? Did you get my letters?'

'No, I didn't, where did you send them?'

'The flat – in Queen's Gate.'

'I haven't been back there for,' Nicholas thought, 'for nearly a month.'

'I got your cards, Dad, the one from Bermuda and the one from Florida. I just wrote to tell you—' and there was a recital of schoolboy triumphs and disasters.

'That's tremendous, Peter. I'm really proud.'

Nicholas imagined the face of his son as he listened, and his heart was squeezed – by guilt, that he could do so little, could give him so little of his time, squeezed by longing for what he had lost. For it was only at times such as these that he could admit how much he missed his son.

'That's great, Peter—' The boy was trying to tell it all at the same time, gabbling out the news he had stored so carefully, flitting from subject to subject, as one thing reminded him of another. Then, of course, the inevitable question:

'When can I come to you, Dad?'

'I'll have to arrange that with your mother, Peter. But it will be soon. I promise you that.' Let's get away from that, Nick thought, desperately. 'How is *Apache*? Have you raced her yet these holidays?'

'Oh yes, Mother let me have a new set of Terylene sails, in red and yellow. I raced her yesterday.' *Apache* had not actually been placed first in the event, but Nicholas gained the impression that the blame lay not with her skipper but rather on the vagaries of the wind, the unsporting behaviour of the other competitors who bumped when they had the weather gauge, and finally the starter who had wanted to disqualify *Apache* for beating the gun. 'But,' Peter went on, 'I'm racing again on Saturday morning—'

'Peter, where is your mother?'

'She's down at the boathouse.'

'Can you put this call through there? I must speak to her, Peter.'

'Of course.' The disappointment in the child's voice was almost completely disguised. 'Hey, Dad. You promised, didn't you? It will be soon?'

'I promised.'

'Cheerio, sir.'

There was a clicking and humming on the line and then suddenly her voice, with its marvellous timbre and serenity.

'*C'est Chantelle Alexander qui parle.*'

'*C'est Nicholas ici.*'

'Oh, my dear. How good to hear your voice. How are you?'

'Are you alone?'

'No, I have friends lunching with me. The Contessa is here with his new boyfriend, a matador no less!'

The 'Contessa' was an outrageously camp and wealthy homosexual who danced at Chantelle's court. Nicholas could imagine the scene on the wide paved terrace, screened from the cliffs above by the sighing pines and the rococo pink boathouse with its turrets and rusty-coloured tiles. There would be gay and brilliant company under the colourful umbrellas.

'Pierre and Mimi sailed across from Cannes for the day.'

Pierre was the son of the largest manufacturer of civil and military jet aircraft in Europe. 'And Robert—'

Below the terrace was the private jetty and small beautifully equipped yacht basin. Her visitors would have moored their craft there, the bare masts nodding lazily against the sky and the small Mediterranean-blue wavelets lapping the stone jetty. Nicholas could hear the laughter and the tinkle of glasses in the background, and he cut short the recital of the guest list.

'Is Duncan there?'

'No, he's still in London – he won't be out until next week.'

'I have news. Can you get up to Paris?'

'It's impossible, Nicky.' Strange how the pet name did not jar from her. 'I must be at Monte Carlo tomorrow, I'm helping Grace with the Spring Charity—'

'It's important, Chantelle.'

'Then there's Peter. I don't like to leave him. Can't you come here? There is a direct flight at nine tomorrow. I'll get rid of the house guests so we can talk in private.'

He thought quickly, then, 'All right, will you book me a suite at the Negresco?'

'Don't be silly, Nicky. We've thirteen perfectly good bedrooms here – we are both civilized people and Peter would love to see you, you know that.'

The Côte d'Azur was revelling in a freakish burst of early spring weather when Nicholas came down the boarding ladder at Nice Airport, and Peter was waiting for him at the boundary fence, hopping up and down and waving both hands above his head like a semaphore signaller. But when Nicholas came through the gate he regained his composure and shook hands formally.

'It's jolly good to see you, Dad.'

'I swear you've grown six inches,' said Nicholas, and on impulse stooped and hugged the child. For a moment they clung to each other, and it was Peter who pulled away first. Both of them were embarrassed by that display of affection for a moment, then quite deliberately Nicholas placed his hand on Peter's shoulder and squeezed.

'Where is the car?'

He kept his hand on the child's shoulder as they crossed the airport foyer, and as Peter became more accustomed to this unusual gesture of affection, so he pressed closer to his father, and seemed to swell with pride.

Characteristically, Nicholas wondered what had changed about him that made it easier for him to act naturally towards those he loved. The answer was obvious, it was Samantha Silver who had taught him to let go.

'Let go, Nicholas.' He could almost hear her voice now.

The chauffeur was new, a silent unobtrusive man, and there were only the two of them in the back seat of the Rolls on the drive back through Nice, and along the coast road.

'Mother has gone across to the Palace. She won't be back until dinner time.'

'Yes, she told me. We've got the day to ourselves,' Nicholas grinned, as the chauffeur turned in through the electric gates and white columns that guarded the entrance to the estate. 'What are we going to do?'

They swam and they played tennis and took Peter's Arrowhead-class yacht *Apache* on a long reach up the coast as far as Menton and then raced back, gull-winged and spinnaker set on the wind with the spray kicking up over the bows and flicking into their faces. They laughed a lot and they talked even more, and while Nicholas changed for dinner, he found himself caught up in the almost postcoital melancholy of too much happiness – happiness that was transitory and soon must end. He tried to push the sadness aside, but it persisted as he dressed in a white silk rollneck and double-breasted blazer and went down to the terrace room.

Peter was there before him, early as a child on Christmas morning, his hair still wet and slicked down from the shower and his face glowing pinkly from the sun and happiness.

'Can I pour you a drink, Dad?' he asked eagerly, already hovering over the silver drinks tray.

'Leave a little in the bottle,' Nicholas cautioned him, not wanting to deny him the pleasure of performing this grown-up service, but with a healthy respect for the elephantine tots that Peter dispensed in a sense of misplaced generosity.

He tasted the drink cautiously, gasped, and added more soda. 'That's fine,' he said, Peter looked proud, and at that moment Chantelle came down the wide staircase into the room.

Nicholas found it impossible not to stare. Was it possible she had grown more lovely since their last meeting, or had she merely taken special pains this evening?

She was dressed in ivory silk, woven gossamer fine, so it floated about her body as she moved, and as she crossed the last ruddy glow of the dying day that came in from the French windows of the terrace, the light struck through the sheer material and put the dainty line of her legs into momentary silhouette. Closer to him, he saw the silk was embroidered with the same thread, ivory on ivory, a marvellous understatement of elegance, and under it the shadowy outline of her breasts, those fine shapely breasts that he remembered so well, and the faint dusky rose suggestion of her nipples. He looked away quickly and she smiled.

'Nicky,' she said, 'I'm so sorry to have left you alone.'

'Peter and I have had a high old time,' he said.

She had emphasized the shape and size of her eyes, and the planes of the bone structure of her cheeks and jawline, with a subtlety that made it appear she wore no make-up, and her hair had a springing electrical fire to it, a rich glowing sable cloud about the small head. The honeyed ivory of her skin had tanned to the velvety texture of a cream-coloured rose petal across her bare shoulders and arms.

He had forgotten how relaxed and gracious she could be, and this magnificent building filled with its treasures standing in its pine forest high above the darkening ocean and the fairy lights of the coast was her natural setting. She filled the huge room with a special glow and gaiety, and she and Peter shared an impish sense of fun that had them all laughing at the old well-remembered jokes.

Nicholas could not sustain his resentment, could not bring himself to dwell on her betrayal in this environment, so the laughter was easy and the warmth uncontrived. When they went through to the small informal dining room, they sat at the table as they had done so often before; they seemed to be transported back in time to those happy almost forgotten years.

There were moments which might have jarred, but Chantelle's instinct was so certain that she could skirt delicately around these. She treated Nicholas as an honoured guest, not as the master of the house; instead she made Peter the host. 'Peter darling, will you carve for us?' and the boy's pride and importance was almost overwhelming, although the bird looked as though it had been caught in a combine harvester by the time he had finished with it. Chantelle served food and wine, a chicken stuffed in Creole style and a petit Chablis, that had no special associations from the past; and the choice of music was Peter's. 'Music to develop ulcers by,' as Nicholas remarked aside, to Chantelle.

Peter fought a valiant rearguard action to delay the passage of time, but finally resigned himself when Nicholas told him, 'I'll come and see you up to bed.'

He waited while Peter cleaned his teeth with an impressive vigour that might have continued beyond midnight if Nicholas had not protested mildly. When at last he was installed between the sheets, Nicholas stooped over him and the boy wrapped both arms around his neck with a quiet desperation.

'I'm so happy,' he whispered against Nicholas' neck and when they kissed he crushed Nicholas' lips painfully with his mouth – then, 'Wouldn't it be fabulous if we could be like this always?' he asked. 'If you didn't have to go away again, Dad?'

Chantelle had changed the wild music to the muted haunting melodies of Liszt, and as he came back into the room she was pouring cognac into a thin crystal balloon.

'Did he settle down?' she asked, and then answered herself immediately. 'He's exhausted, although he doesn't know it.'

She brought him the cognac and then turned away and went out through the doors on to the terrace. He followed her out, and they stood at the stone balustrade side by side. The air was clear but chill.

'It's beautiful,' she said. The moon paved a wide silver path across the surface of the sea. 'I always thought that the highway to my dreams.'

'Duncan,' he said. 'Let's talk about Duncan Alexander,' and she shivered slightly, folding her arms across her breasts and grasping her own naked shoulders.

'What do you want to know?'

'In what terms did you give him control of your shares?'

'As an agent, my personal agent.'

'With full discretion?'

She nodded, and he asked next, 'Did you have an escape clause? In what circumstances can you reclaim control?'

'The dissolution of marriage,' she said, and then shook her head. 'But I think I knew that no court would uphold the agreement if I wanted to change it. It's too Victorian. Anytime I want to I could simply apply to have the appointment of Duncan as my agent set aside.'

'Yes, I think you're right,' Nicholas agreed. 'But it might take a year or more, unless you could prove malafides, unless you could prove he deliberately betrayed the trust of agency.'

'Can I prove that, Nicky?' She turned to him now, lifting her face to him. 'Has he betrayed that trust?'

'I don't know yet,' Nicholas told her cautiously, and she cut in.

'I've made a terrible fool of myself, haven't I?' He kept silent, and she went on tremulously, 'I know there is no way I can apologize to you for – for what I did. There is no way that I can make it up to you, but believe me, Nicholas – please believe me when I tell you, I have never regretted anything so much in all my life.'

'It's past, Chantelle. It's over. There is no profit in looking back.'

'I don't think there is another man in the world who would do what you are doing now, who would repay deceit and betrayal with help and comfort. I just wanted to say that.'

She was standing very close to him now, and in the cool night he could feel the warmth of her flesh across the inches that separated them, and her perfume had a subtly altered fragrance on that creamy skin. She always wore perfume so well, the same way she wore her clothes.

'It's getting cold,' he said brusquely, took her elbow and steered her back into the light, out of that dangerous intimacy. 'We still have a great deal to discuss.'

He paced the thick forest-green carpet, quickly establishing a beat as regular as that of a sentry, ten paces from the glass doors, passing in front of where she sat in the centre of the wide velvet couch, turning just before he reached the headless marble statue of a Greek athlete from antiquity that guarded the double oaken doors into the lobby, and then back in front of her again. As he paced, he told her in carefully prepared sequence all that he had learned from Lazarus.

She sat like a bird on the point of flight, turning her head to watch him, those huge dark eyes seeming to swell larger as she listened.

It was not necessary to explain it to her in layman's language, she was Arthur Christy's daughter, she understood when he told her how he suspected that Duncan Alexander had been forced to self-insure the hull of *Golden Dawn* and how he had used Christy stock to buy re-insurance, stock that he had probably already pledged to finance construction of the vessel.

Nicholas reconstructed the whole inverted pyramid of Duncan Alexander's machinations for her to examine, and almost immediately she saw how vulnerable, how unstable it was.

'Are you certain of all this?' she whispered, and her face was drained of all its lustrous rose tints.

He shook his head. 'I've reconstructed the Tyrannosaurus from a jawbone,' he admitted frankly. 'The shape of it might be a little different, but one thing I am certain of is that it's a big and dangerous beast.'

'Duncan could destroy Christy Marine,' she whispered again. 'Completely!' She looked around slowly, at the house – at the room and its treasures, the symbols of her life. 'He has risked everything that is mine, and Peter's.'

Nicholas did not reply, but he stopped in front of her and watched her carefully as she absorbed the enormity of it all.

He saw outrage turn slowly to confusion, to fear and finally to terror. He had never seen her even afraid before – but now, faced with the prospect of being stripped naked of the armour which had always protected her, she was like a lost animal, he could even see that flutter of her heart under the pale swelling flesh of her bosom, and she shivered again.

'Could he lose everything, Nicholas? He couldn't, could he?' She wanted assurance, but he could not give it to her, all he could give her was pity. Pity was the one emotion, probably the only one she had never aroused in him, not once in all the years he had known her.

'What can I do, Nicholas?' she pleaded. 'Please help me. Oh God, what must I do?'

'You can stop Duncan launching *Golden Dawn* – until the hull and propulsion has been modified, until it has been properly surveyed and underwritten – and until you have taken full control of Christy Marine out of his hands again.' And his voice was gentle, filled with his compassion as he told her.

'That's enough for one day, Chantelle. If we go on now, we will begin chasing our tails. Tonight you know what could happen, tomorrow we will discuss how we can prevent it. Have you a Valium?'

She shook her head. 'I've never used drugs to hide from things.' It was true, he knew, that she had never lacked courage. 'How much longer can you stay?'

'I have a seat on the eleven o'clock plane. I have to be back in London by tomorrow night – we'll have time tomorrow morning.'

The guest suite opened on to the second-floor balcony which ran along the entire front of the building overlooking the sea and the private harbour. The five main bedrooms all opened on to this balcony, an arrangement from fifty years previously when internal security against kidnapping and forcible entry had been of no importance.

Nicholas determined to speak to Chantelle about that in the morning. Peter was an obvious target for extortion, and he felt the goose bumps of horror rise on his arms as he imagined his son in the hands of those degenerate monsters who were everywhere allowed to strike and destroy with impunity. There was a price to pay these days for being rich and successful. The smell of it attracted the hyenas and vultures. Peter must be better protected, he decided.

In the sitting-room, there was a well-stocked liquor cabinet concealed behind mirrors, nothing so obvious and resoundingly middle-class as a private bar. The daily papers, in English, French and German were set out on the television table, *France-Soir*, *The Times*, *Allgemeine Zeitung*, with even an airmail version of the *New York Times*.

Nicholas flipped open *The Times* and glanced quickly at the closing prices. Christy Marine common stock was at £5.32p, up 15p on yesterday's prices. The market had not sniffed corruption – yet.

He pulled off his silk rollneck, and even though he had bathed three hours previously, the tension had left his skin feeling itchy and unclean. The bathroom had been lavishly redecorated in green onyx panels and the fittings were eighteen-carat gold, in the shape of dolphins. Steaming water gushed from their gaping mouths at a touch. It could have been vulgar, but Chantelle's unerring touch steered it into Persian opulence instead.

He showered, turning the setting high so that the stinging needles of water scalded away his fatigue and the feeling of being unclean. There were half a dozen thick white terry towelling robes in the glass-fronted warming cupboard, and he selected one and went through into the bedroom, belting it around his naked waist. In his briefcase there was a draft of the agreement of sale of Ocean Salvage and Towage to the Sheikhs. James Teacher and his gang of bright young lawyers had read it, and made a thick sheaf of notes. Nicholas must study these before tomorrow evening when he met them in London.

He took the papers from his case and carried them through into the sitting room, glancing at the top page before dropping them carelessly on to the low coffee table while he went to pour himself a small whisky, heavily diluted. He brought the drink back with him and sprawled into the deep leather armchair, picked up the papers and began to work.

He became aware of her perfume first, and felt his blood quicken uncontrollably at the fragrance, and the papers rustled in his hand.

Slowly he lifted his head. She had come in utter silence on small bare feet. She had removed all her jewellery and had let down her hair brushing it out on to her shoulders.

It made her seem younger, more vulnerable, and the gown she wore was cuffed and collared in fine soft lace. She moved slowly towards his chair, timorous and for once uncertain, the eyes huge and dark and haunted, and when he rose from the armchair, she stopped and one hand went to her throat.

'Nicholas,' she whispered, 'I'm so afraid, and so alone.' She moved a step closer, and saw his eyes shift, his lips harden, and she stopped instantly.

'Please,' she pleaded softly, 'don't send me away, Nicky. Not tonight, not yet. I'm afraid to be alone – please.'

He knew then that this had been going to happen, he had hidden the certainty of it from himself all that evening, but now it was upon him, and he could do nothing to avoid it. It was as though he had lost the will to resist, as though he stood mesmerized, his resolve softening and melting like wax in the candle flame of her beauty, of the passions which she commanded so skilfully, and his thoughts lost coherence, began to tumble and swirl like storm surf breaking on rock.

She recognized the exact instant when it happened to him, and she came forward silently, with small gliding footsteps, not making the mistake of speaking again and pressed her face to his bare chest framed in the collar of his robe. The thick curling hair was springing over hard flat muscle, and she flared her nostrils at the clean virile animal smell of his skin.

He was still resisting, standing stiffly with his hands hanging at his sides. Oh, she knew him so well. The terrible conflict he must suffer before he could be made to act against that iron code of his own. Oh, she knew him, knew that he was as sexual and physical an animal as she was herself, that he was the only man who had ever been able to match her appetites. She knew the defences he had erected about himself, the fortressing of his passions, the controls and repressions, but she knew so well how to subvert these elaborate defences, she knew exactly what to do and what to say, how to move and touch. As she began now, she found the deliberate act of breaking down his resistance excited her so swiftly that it was pain almost, agony almost, and it required all her own control not to advance too swiftly for him, to control the shaking of her legs and the pumping of her lungs, to play still the hurt and bewildered and frightened child, using his kindness, the sense of chivalry which would not allow him to send her away, in such obvious distress.

Oh God, how her body churned, her stomach cramped with the strength of her wanting, her breasts felt swollen and so sensitive that the contact of silk and lace was almost too painfully abrasive to bear.

'Oh, Nicky, please – just for a moment. Just once, hold me. Please, I cannot go on alone. Just for a moment, please.'

She felt him lift his hands, felt the fingers on her shoulders, and the terrible pain of wanting was too much to bear, she could not control it – she cried out, it was a soft little whimper, but the force of it shook her body, and immediately she felt his reaction. Her timing had been immaculate, her natural womanly cunning had guided her. His fingers on her shoulders had been gentle and kindly, but now they hooked cruelly into her flesh.

His back arched involuntarily, his breath drummed from his chest under her ear, a single agonized exhalation like that of a boxer taking a heavy body punch. She felt his every muscle become taut, and she knew again the frightening power, the delirious giddy power she could still wield. Then, at last, joyously, almost fearfully, she experienced the great lordly lift and thrust of his loins – as though the whole world had moved and shifted about her.

She cried out again, fiercely, for now she could slip the hounds she had held so short upon the leash, she could let them run and hunt again. They had been too long denied, but now there was no longer need for care and restraint.

She knew exactly how to hunt him beyond the frontiers of reason, to course him like a flying stag, and his fingers tangled frantically in the foaming lace at her throat as he tried to free her tight swollen breasts. She cried out a third time, and with a single movement jerked open the fastening at his waist, exposing the full hard lean length of his body, and her hands were as frantic as his.

'Oh, sweet God, you're so hard and strong – oh sweet God, I've missed you so.'

There was time later for all the refinements and nuances of love, but now her need was too cruel and demanding to be denied another moment. It had to happen this instant before she died of the lack.

Nicholas rose slowly towards the surface of sleep, aware of a brooding sense of regret. Just before he reached consciousness, a dream image formed in his sleep-starved brain, he relived a moment from the distant past. A fragment of time, recaptured so vividly as to seem whole and perfect. Long ago he had picked a deep-sea trumpet shell at five fathoms from the oceanic wall of the coral reef beyond the Anse Baudoin lagoon of Praslin Island. It was the size of a ripe coconut and once again he found himself holding the shell in both cupped hands, gazing into the narrow oval opening, around which the weed-furred and barnacle-encrusted exterior changed dramatically, flaring into the pouting lips and exposing the inner mother-of-pearl surfaces that were slippery to the touch, a glossy satin sheen, pale translucent pink, folded and convoluted upon themselves, shading darker into fleshy crimsons and wine purples as the passage narrowed and sank away into the mysterious lustrous depths of the shell.

Then abruptly, the dream image changed in his mind. The projected opening in the trumpet shell expanded, articulating on jaw-hinges and he was gaping into the deep and terrible maw of some great predatory sea-creature, lined with multiple rows of serrated triangular teeth – shark-like, terrifying, so he cried out in half-sleep, startling himself awake, and he rolled quickly on to his side and raised himself on one elbow. Her perfume still lingered on his skin, mingled with the smell of his own sweat, but the bed beside him was empty, though warm and redolent with the memory of her body.

Across the room, the early sun struck a long sliver of light through a narrow chink in the curtains. It looked like a blade, a golden blade. It reminded him instantly of Samantha Silver. He saw her again wearing sunlight like a cloak, barefoot in the sand – and it seemed that the blade of sunlight was being driven up slowly under his ribs.

He swung his feet off the wide bed and padded softly

across to the gold and onyx bathroom. There was a dull ache of sleeplessness and remorse behind his eyes and as he ran hot water from the dolphin's mouth into the basin, he looked at himself in the mirror although the steam slowly clouded the image of his own face. There were dark smears below his eyes and his features were gaunt, harsh angles of bone beneath drawn skin.

'You bastard,' he whispered at the shadowy face in the mirror. 'You bloody bastard.'

They were waiting breakfast for him, in the sunlight on the terrace under the gaily coloured umbrellas. Peter had preserved the mood of the previous evening, and he ran laughing to meet Nicholas.

'Dad, hey Dad.' He seized Nicholas' hand and led him to the table.

Chantelle wore a long loose housegown, and her hair was down on her shoulders, so soft that it stirred like spun silk in even that whisper of breeze. It was calculated, Chantelle did nothing by chance; the intimately elegant attire and the loose fall of her hair set the mood of domesticity – and Nicholas found himself resisting it fiercely.

Peter sensed his father's change of mood with an intuitive understanding beyond his years, and his dismay was a palpable thing, the hurt and reproach in his eyes as he looked at Nicholas; and then the chatter died on his lips and he bent his head studiously over his plate and ate in silence.

Nicholas deliberately refused the festival array of food, took only a cup of coffee, and lit a cheroot, without asking Chantelle's permission, knowing how she would resent that. He waited in silence and as soon as Peter had eaten he said:

'I'd like to speak to your mother, Peter.'

The boy stood up obediently.

'Will I see you before you leave, sir?'

343

'Yes.' Nicholas felt his heart wrung again. 'Of course.'

'We could sail again?'

'I'm sorry, my boy. We won't have time. Not today.'

'Very well, sir.' Peter walked to the end of the terrace, very erect and dignified, then suddenly he began to run, taking the steps down two at a time, and he fled into the pine forest beyond the boathouse as though pursued, feet flying and arms pumping wildly.

'He needs you, Nicky,' said Chantelle softly.

'You should have thought about that two years ago.'

She poured fresh coffee into his cup. 'Both of us have been stupid – all right, worse than that. We've been wicked. I have had my Duncan, and you have had that American child.'

'Don't make me angry now,' he warned her softly. 'You've done enough for one day.'

'It's as simple as this, Nicholas. I love you, I have always loved you – God, since I was a gawky schoolgirl.' She had never been that, but Nicholas let it pass. 'Since I saw you that first day on the bridge of old *Golden Eagle*, the dashing ship's captain—'

'Chantelle. All we have to discuss is *Golden Dawn* and Christy Marine.'

'No, Nicholas. We were born for each other. Daddy saw that immediately, we both knew it at the same time – it was only a madness, a crazy whim that made me doubt it for a moment.'

'Stop it, Chantelle.'

'Duncan was a stupid mistake. But it's unimportant—'

'No, it's not unimportant. It changed everything. It can never be the same again, besides—'

'Besides, what? Nicky, what were you going to say?'

'Besides, I am building myself another life now. With another very different person.'

'Oh God, Nicky, you aren't serious?' She laughed then, genuine amusement, clapping her hands delightedly. 'My dear, she's young enough to be your daughter. It's the forty syndrome, the Lolita complex.' Then she saw his real anger, and she was quick, retrieving the situation neatly, aware that she had carried it too far.

'I'm sorry, Nicky. I should never have said that.' She paused, and then went on. 'I will say she's a pretty little thing, and I'm sure she's sweet – Peter liked her.' She damned Samantha with light condescension, and then dismissed her as though she were merely a childlike prank of Nicholas', a light and passing folly of no real significance.

'I understand, Nicholas, truly I do. However, when you are ready, as you will be soon, then Peter and I and Christy Marine are waiting for you still. This is your world, Nicholas.' She made a gesture which embraced it all. 'This is your world; you will never really leave it.'

'You are wrong, Chantelle.'

'No.' She shook her head. 'I am very seldom wrong, and on this I cannot be wrong. Last night proved that, it is still there – every bit of it. But let's discuss the other thing now, *Golden Dawn* and Christy Marine.'

Chantelle Alexander lifted her face to the sky and watched the big silver bird fly. It climbed nose high, glinting in the sunlight, twin trails of dark unconsumed fuel spinning out behind it as the engines howled under the full thrust. With the wind in this quarter, the extended centreline of the main Nice runway brought it out over Cap Ferrat.

Beside Chantelle, only an inch or two shorter than she was, Peter stood and watched it also and she took his arm, tucking her small dainty hand into the crook of his elbow.

'He stayed such a short time,' Peter said, and overhead the big airbus turned steeply on to its crosswind leg.

'We will have him with us again soon,' Chantelle

promised, and then she went on. 'Where were you, Peter? We hunted all over when it was time for Daddy to go.'

'I was in the forest,' he said evasively. He had heard them calling, but Peter was hidden in the secret place, the smuggler's cleft in the yellow rock of the cliff; he would have killed himself rather than let Nicholas Berg see him weeping.

'Wouldn't it be lovely if it was like the old times again?' Chantelle asked softly, and the boy stirred beside her, but unable to take his gaze from the aircraft. 'Just the three of us again?'

'Without Uncle Duncan?' he asked incredulously, and high above them the aircraft, with a last twinkle of sunlight, drove deeply into the banks of cumulus cloud that buttressed the northern sky. Peter turned at last to face her.

'Without Uncle Duncan?' he demanded again. 'But that's impossible.'

'Not if you help me, darling.' She took his face in her cupped hands. 'You will help me, won't you?' she asked, and he nodded once, a sharply incisive gesture of assent; she leaned forward and kissed him tenderly on the forehead.

'That's my man,' she whispered.

'Mr Alexander is not available. May I take a message?'

'This is Mrs Alexander. Tell my husband that it's urgent.'

'Oh, I'm terribly sorry, Mrs Alexander.' The secretary's voice changed instantly, cool caution becoming effusive servility. 'I didn't recognize your voice. The line is dreadful. Mr Alexander will speak to you directly.'

Chantelle waited, staring impatiently from the study

346

windows. The weather had changed in the middle of the morning with the cold front sweeping down off the mountains, and now icy wind and rain battered at the windows.

'Chantelle, my dear,' said the rich glossy voice that had once so dazzled her. 'Is this my call to you?'

'It's mine, Duncan. I must speak to you urgently.'

'Good,' he agreed with her. 'I wanted to speak to you also. Things are happening swiftly here. It's necessary for you to come up to St Nazaire next Tuesday, instead of my joining you at Cap Ferrat.'

'Duncan—'

But he went on over her protest, his voice as full of self-confidence, as ebullient as she had not heard it in over a year.

'I have been able to save almost four weeks on *Golden Dawn*.'

'Duncan, listen to me.'

'We will be able to launch on Tuesday. It will be a makeshift ceremony, I'm afraid, at such short notice.' He was inordinately proud of his own achievement. It annoyed her to hear him. 'What I have arranged is that the pod tanks will be delivered direct to the Gulf from the Japanese yards. They are towing them in their ballast with four American tugs. I will launch the hull here, with workmen still aboard her, and they will finish her off at sea during the passage around Good Hope, in time for her to take on her tanks and cargo at El Barras. We'll save nearly seven and a half million—'

'Duncan!' Chantelle cried again, and this time something in her tone stopped him.

'What is it?'

'This can't wait until Tuesday, I want to see you right away.'

'That's impossible,' he laughed, lightly, confidently. 'It's only five days.'

'Five days is too long.'

'Tell me now,' he invited. 'What is it?'

'All right,' she said deliberately, and the vicious streak of Persian cruelty was in her voice. 'I'll tell you. I want a divorce, Duncan, and I want control of my shares in Christy Marine again.'

There was a long, hissing crackling silence on the line, and she waited, the way the cat waits for the first movement of the crippled mouse.

'This is very sudden.' His voice had changed completely, it was bleak and flat, lacking any timbre or resonance.

'We both know it is not,' she contradicted him.

'You have no grounds.' There was a thin edge of fear now. 'Divorce isn't quite as easy as that, Chantelle.'

'How is this for grounds, Duncan?' she asked, and there was a spiteful sting in her voice now. 'If you aren't here by noon tomorrow, then my auditors will be in Leadenhall Street and there will be an urgent order before the courts—'

She did not have to go on, he spoke across her and there was a note of panic in his voice. She had never heard it before. He said, 'You are right. We do have to talk right away.' Then he was silent again, collecting himself, and his voice was once more calm and careful when he went on, 'I can charter a Falcon and be at Nice before midday. Will that do?'

'I'll have the car meet you,' she said, and broke the connection with one finger. She held the bar down for a second, then lifted her finger.

'I want to place an international call,' she said in her fluent rippling French when the operator answered. 'I do not know the number, but it is person to person. Doctor Samantha Silver at the University of Miami.'

'There is a delay of more than two hours, madame.'

'*J'attendrai*,' she said, and replaced the receiver.

348

The Bank of the East is in Curzon Street, almost opposite the White Elephant Club. It has a narrow frontage of bronze and marble and glass, and Nicholas had been there, with his lawyers, since ten o'clock that morning. He was learning at first hand the leisurely age-old ritual of oriental bargaining.

He was selling Ocean Salvage, plus two years of his future labour – and even for seven million dollars he was beginning to wonder if it was worth it – and it was not a certain seven million either. The words tripped lightly, the figures seemed to have no substance in this setting. The only constant was the figure of the Prince himself, seated on the low couch, in a Savile Row suit but with the fine white cotton and gold-corded headdress framing his dark handsome features with theatrical dash.

Beyond him moved a shadowy, ever-changing background of unctuous whispering figures. Every time that Nicholas believed that a point had been definitely agreed, another rose-pink or acid-yellow Rolls-Royce with Arabic script numberplates would deposit three or four more dark-featured Arabs at the front doors and they would hurry through to kiss the Prince on his forehead, on the bridge of his nose and on the back of his hand, and the hushed discussion would begin all over again with the newcomers picking up at the point they had been an hour previously.

James Teacher showed no impatience, and he smiled and nodded and went through the ritual like an Arab born, sipping the little thimbles of treacly coffee and watching patiently for the interminable whisperings to be translated into English before making a measured counter proposal.

'We are doing fine, Mr Berg,' he assured Nicholas quietly. 'A few more days.'

Nicholas had a headache from the strong coffee and the Turkish tobacco smoke, and he found it difficult to concentrate. He kept worrying about Samantha. For four days he had tried to contact her. He had to get out for a while and he excused himself to the Prince, and went down to the Enquiries Desk in the Bank's entrance hall and the girl told him,

'I'm sorry, sir, there is no reply to either of those numbers.'

'There must be,' Nicholas told her. One number was Samantha's shack at Key Biscayne and the other was her private number in her laboratory.

She shook her head. 'I've tried every hour.'

'Can you send a cable for me?'

'Of course, sir.'

She gave him a pad of forms and he wrote out the message.

'Please phone me urgently, reverse charges to—' he gave the number of the Queen's Gate flat and James Teacher's rooms, then he thought with the pen poised, trying to find the words to express his concern, but there were none.

'I love you,' he wrote. 'I really do.'

Since Nicholas's midnight call to tell her of the carriage of cad-rich crude petroleum, Samantha Silver had been caught up in a kaleidoscope whirl of time and events.

After a series of meetings with the leaders of Greenpeace, and other conservation bodies in an effort to publicize and oppose this new threat to the oceans, she and Tom Parker had flown to Washington and met with a deputy director of the Environmental Protection Agency and with two young senators who spearheaded the conservation lobby – but their efforts to go further had been frustrated by the granite walls of big oil interest. Even usually cooperative sources had been wary of condemning or speaking out against Orient Amex's new carbon-cracking technology. As one thirty-year-old Democrat senator had pointed out, 'It's tough to try and take a shot at something that's going to increase the fossil fuel yield by fifty per cent.'

'That's not what we are shooting at,' Samantha had flared, bitter with fatigue and frustration. 'It's this irresponsible method of carrying the cad-rich through sensitive and highly vulnerable seaways we are trying to prevent.' But when she presented the scenario she had worked out, picturing the effects on the North Atlantic deluged with a million tons of toxic crude, she saw the disbelief in the man's eyes and the condescending smile of the sane for the slightly demented.

'Oh God, why is common sense the hardest thing in the world to sell?' she had lamented.

She and Tom had gone on to meet the leaders of Greenpeace in the north, and in the west, and they had given advice and promises of support. The Californian Chapter counselled physical intervention as a last resort, as some of their members had successfully interposed small craft between the Russian whalers and the breeding minkes they were hunting in the Californian Gulf.

In Galveston, they met the young Texans who would picket the Orient Amex refinery as soon as they were certain the ultra-tanker had entered the Gulf of Mexico.

However, none of their efforts were successful in provoking confrontation with Orient Amex. The big oil company simply ignored invitations to debate the charges on radio or television, and stonewalled questions from the media. It's hard to stir up interest in a one-sided argument, Samantha found.

They managed one local Texas television show, but without controversy to give it zip, the producer cut Samantha's time down to forty-five seconds, and then tried to date her for dinner.

The energy crisis, oil tankers and oil pollution were joyless subjects. Nobody had ever heard of cadmium pollution, the Cape of Good Hope was half a world away, a million tons was a meaningless figure, impossible to visualize, and it was all rather a bore.

The media let it drop flat on its face.

'We're just going to have to smoke those fat cats at Orient Amex out into the open,' Tom Parker growled angrily, 'and kick their arses blue for them. The only way we are going to do that is through Greenpeace.'

They had landed back at Miami International, exhausted and disappointed, but not yet despondent. 'Like the man said,' Samantha muttered grimly, as she threaded her gaudy van back into the city traffic flow, 'we have only just begun to fight.'

She had only a few hours to clean herself up and stretch out on the patchwork quilt before she had to dress again and race back to the airport. The Australian had already passed through customs and was looking lost and dejected in the terminal lobby.

'Hi, I'm Sam Silver.' She pushed away fatigue, and hoisted that brilliant golden smile like a flag.

His name was Mr Dennis O'Connor and he was the top man in his field, doing fascinating and important work on the reef populations of Eastern Australian waters, and he had come a long way to talk to her and see her experiments.

'I didn't expect you to be so young.' She had signed her correspondence 'Doctor Silver' and he gave the standard reaction to her. Samantha was just tired and angry enough not to take it.

'And I'm a woman. You didn't expect that either,' she agreed. 'It's a crying bastard, isn't it? But then, I bet some of your best friends are young females.'

He was a dinky-die Aussie, and he loved it. He burst into an appreciative grin, and as they shook hands, he said, 'You are not going to believe this, but I like you just the way you are.'

He was tall and lean, sunburned and just a little grizzled

at the temples, and within minutes they were friends, and the respect with which he viewed her work confirmed that.

The Australian had brought with him, in an oxygenated container, five thousand live specimens of *E. digitalis*, the common Australian water snail, for inclusion in Samantha's experimentation. He had selected these animals for their abundance and their importance in the ecology of the Australian inshore waters, and the two of them were soon so absorbed in the application of Samantha's techniques to this new creature that when her assistant stuck her head through and yelled, 'Hey, Sam, there's a call for you.' She shouted back, 'Take a message. If they're lucky I'll call them back.'

'It's international, person to person!' and Samantha's pulse raced; instantly forgotten was the host of spiral-coned sea snails.

'Nicholas!' she shouted happily, spilled half a pint of sea water down the Australian's trouser leg and ran wildly to the small cubicle at the end of the laboratory.

She was breathless with excitement as she snatched up the receiver and she pressed one hand against her heart to stop it thumping.

'Is that Doctor Silver?'

'Yes! It's me.' Then correcting her grammar, 'It is she!'

'Go ahead, please,' said the operator, and there was a click and pulse on the line as it came alive.

'Nicholas!' she exulted. 'Darling Nicholas, is that you?'

'No.' The voice was very clear and serene, as though the speaker stood beside her, and it was familiar, disconcertingly so, and for no good reason Samantha felt her heart shrink with dread.

'This is Chantelle Alexander, Peter's mother. We have met briefly.'

'Yes.' Samantha's voice was now small, and still breathless.

'I thought it would be kind to tell you in person, before

353

you hear from other sources – that Nicholas and I have decided to remarry.'

Samantha sat down jerkily on the office stool.

'Are you there?' Chantelle asked after a moment.

'I don't believe you,' whispered Samantha.

'I'm sorry,' Chantelle told her gently. 'But there is Peter, you see, and we have rediscovered each other – discovered that we had never stopped loving each other.'

'Nicholas wouldn't—' her voice broke, and she could not go on.

'You must understand and forgive him, my dear,' Chantelle explained. 'After our divorce he was hurt and lonely. I'm sure he did not mean to take advantage of you.'

'But, but – we were supposed to, we were going to—'

'I know. Please believe me, this has not been easy for any of us. For all our sakes—'

'We had planned a whole life together.' Samantha shook her head wildly, and a thick skein of golden hair came loose and flopped into her face, she pushed it back with a combing gesture. 'I don't believe it, why didn't Nicholas tell me himself? I won't believe it until he tells me.'

Chantelle's voice was compassionate, gentle. 'I so wanted not to make it ugly for you, my child, but now what can I do but tell you that Nicholas spent last night in my house, in my bed, in my arms, where he truly belongs.'

It was almost miraculous, a physical thing, but sitting hunched on the hard round stool Samantha Silver felt her youth fall away from her, sloughed off like a glittering reptilian skin. She was left with the sensation of timelessness, possessed of all the suffering and sorrow of every woman who had lived before. She felt very old and wise and sad, and she lifted her fingers and touched her own cheek, mildly surprised to feel that the skin was not dried and withered like that of some ancient crone.

'I have already made the arrangements for a divorce

354

from my present husband, and Nicholas will resume his position at the head of Christy Marine.'

It was true, Samantha knew then that it was true. There was no question, no doubt, and slowly she replaced the receiver of the telephone, and sat staring blankly at the bare wall of the cubicle. She did not cry, she felt as though she would never cry, nor laugh, again in her life.

Chantelle Alexander studied her husband carefully, trying to stand outside herself, and to see him dispassionately. She found it easier now that the giddy insanity had burned away.

He was a handsome man, tall and lean, with those carefully groomed metallic waves of coppery hair. Even the wrist that he shot from the crisp white cuff of his sleeve was covered with those fine gleaming hairs. She knew so well that even his lean chest was covered with thick golden curls, crisp and curly as fresh lettuce leaves. She had never been attracted by smooth hairless men.

'May I smoke?' he asked, and she inclined her head. His voice had also attracted her from the first, deep and resonant, but with those high-bred accents, the gentle softening of the vowel sounds, the lazy drawling of consonants. The voice and the patrician manner were things that she had been trained to appreciate – and yet, under the mannered cultivated exterior was the flash of exciting wickedness, that showed in the wolfish white gleam of smile, and the sharp glittering grey steel of his gaze.

He lit the custom-made cigarette with the gold lighter she had given him – her very first gift, the night they had become lovers. Even now, the memory of it was piquant, and for a moment she felt the soft melting warmth in her lower belly and she stirred restlessly in her chair. There had been reason, and good reason for that madness, and even now it was over, she would never regret it.

It had been a period in her life which she had not been able to deny herself. The grand sweeping illicit passion, the last flush of her youth, the final careless autumn that preceded middle age. Another ordinary woman might have had to content herself with sweaty sordid gropings and grapplings in anonymous hotel bedrooms, but not Chantelle Christy. Her world was shaped by her own whims and desires, and, as she had told Nicholas, whatever she desired was hers to take. Long ago, her father had taught her that there were special rules for Chantelle Christy, and the rules were those she made herself.

It had been marvellous, she shivered slightly at the lingering sensuality of those early days, but now it was over. During the past months she had been carefully comparing the two men. Her decision had not been lightly made.

She had watched Nicholas retrieve his life from the gulf of disaster. On his own, stripped naked of all but that invisible indefinable mantle of strength and determination, he had fought his way back out of the gulf. Strength and power had always moved her, but she had over the years grown accustomed to Nicholas. Familiarity had staled their relationship for her. But now her interlude with Duncan had freshened her view of him, and he had for her all the novel appeal of a new lover – yet with the proven values and qualities of long intimate acquaintance. Duncan Alexander was finished; Nicholas Berg was the future.

But, no, she would never regret this interlude in her life. It had been a time of rejuvenation. She would not even regret Nicholas' involvement with the pretty American child. Later, it would add a certain perverse spice to their own sexuality, she thought, and felt the shiver run down her thighs and the soft secret stirring of her flesh, like the opening of a petalled rosebud. Duncan had taught her many things, bizarre little tricks of arousal, made more poignant by being forbidden and wicked. Unfortunately Duncan relied almost entirely on the tricks, and not all of them had worked for her – the corners of her mouth turned down with distaste as she remembered; perhaps it was just that which had begun the curdling process.

No, Duncan Alexander had not been able to match her raw, elemental sexuality and soaring abandon. Only one man had ever been able to do that. Duncan had served a purpose, but now it was over. It might have dragged on a little longer, but Duncan Alexander had endangered Christy Marine. Never had she thought of that possibility; Christy Marine was a fact of her life, as vast and immutable as the heavens, but now the foundations of heaven were being shaken. His sexual attraction had staled. She might have forgiven him that, but not the other.

She became aware of Duncan's discomfort. He twisted sideways in his chair, crossing and uncrossing his long legs, and he rolled the cigarette between his fingers, studying the rising spiral of blue smoke to avoid the level, expressionless gaze of her dark fathomless eyes. She had been staring at him, but seeing the other man. Now, with an effort, she focused her attention on him.

'Thank you for coming so promptly,' she said.

'It did seem rather urgent.' He smiled for the first time, glossy and urbane – but with fear down there in the cool grey eyes, and his tension was betrayed by the clenched sinew in the point of his jaw.

Looking closely, as she had not done for many months, she saw how he was fined down. The long tapered fingers were bony, and never still. There were new harder lines to his mouth, and a frown to the set of his eyes. The skin at the corners cracked like oil paint into hundreds of fine wrinkles that the deep brown snow-tan hid from a casual glance. Now he returned her scrutiny directly.

'From what you told me yesterday—'

She lifted her hand to stop him. 'That can wait. I merely wanted to impress you with the seriousness of what is happening. What is really of prime importance now is what you have done with control of my shares and those of the Trust.'

His hands went very still. 'What does that mean?'

'I want auditors, my appointed auditors, sent in—'

He shrugged. 'All this will take time, Chantelle, and I'm not certain that I'm ready to relinquish control.' He was very cool, very casual now and the fear was gone.

She felt a stir of relief, perhaps the horror story that Nicholas had told her was untrue, perhaps the danger was imaginary only. Christy Marine was so big, so invulnerable.

'Not just at the moment, anyway. You'd have to prove to me that doing so was in the best interest of the company and of the Trust.'

'I don't have to prove anything, to anyone,' she said flatly.

'This time you do. You have appointed me—'

'No court of law would uphold that agreement.'

'Perhaps not, Chantelle, but do you want to drag all this through the courts – at a time like this?'

'I'm not afraid, Duncan.' She stood up quickly, light on her feet as a dancer, the lovely legs in loose black silk trousers, soft flat shoes making her seem still smaller, a slim gold chain emphasizing the narrowness of the tiny waist. 'You know I'm afraid of nothing.' She stood over him, and pointed the accuser's finger. The nails tipped in scarlet, the colour of fresh arterial blood. 'You should be the one to fear.'

'And precisely what is it you are accusing me of?'

And she told him, reeling off swiftly the lists of guarantees made by the Trust, the transfer of shares and the issues of new shares and guarantees within the Christy Marine group of subsidiaries, she listed the known layering of underwriting cover on *Golden Dawn* that Nicholas had unearthed.

'When my auditors have finished, Duncan darling, not only will the courts return control of Christy Marine to me, but they will probably sentence you to five years of hard labour. They take this sort of thing rather seriously, you know.'

He smiled. He actually smiled! She felt her fury seething to the surface and the set of her eyes altered, colour tinted the smooth pale olive of her cheeks.

'You dare to grin at me,' she hissed. 'I will break you for that.'

'No,' he shook his head. 'No, you won't.'

'Are you denying—' she snapped, but he cut her off with a raised hand, and a shake of that handsome arrogant head.

'I am denying nothing, my love. On the contrary, I am going to admit it – and more, much more.' He flicked the cigarette away, and it hissed sharply in the lapping blue wavelets of the yacht basin. While she stared at him, struck speechless, he let the silence play out like a skilled actor as he selected and lit another cigarette from the gold case.

'For some weeks now I have been fully aware that somebody was prying very deeply into my affairs and those of the company.' He blew a long blue feather of cigarette smoke, and cocked one eyebrow at her, a cynical mocking gesture which increased her fury, but left her feeling suddenly afraid and uncertain. 'It didn't take long to establish that the trace was coming from a little man in Monte Carlo who makes a living at financial and industrial espionage. Lazarus is good, excellent, the very best. I have used him myself, in fact it was I who introduced him to Nicholas Berg.' He chuckled then, shaking his head indulgently. 'The silly things we do sometimes. The connection was immediate. Berg and Lazarus. I have run my own check on what they have come up with and I estimate that even Lazarus could not have uncovered more than twenty-five per cent of the answers.' He leaned forward and suddenly his voice snapped with a new authority. 'You see, Chantelle dear, I am probably one of the best in the world myself. They could never have traced it all.'

'You are not denying then—' She heard the faltering tone in her own voice, and hated herself for it. He brushed her aside contemptuously.

'Be quiet, you silly little woman, and listen to me. I am going to tell you just how deeply you are in – I am going to explain to you, in terms that even you can understand, why you will not send in your auditors, why you will not fire me, and why you will do exactly what I tell you to do.'

He paused and stared into her eyes, a direct trial of strength which she could not meet. She was confused and uncertain, for once not in control of her own destiny. She dropped her eyes, and he nodded with satisfaction.

'Very well. Now listen. I have put it all – everything that is Christy Marine – it is all riding on *Golden Dawn*.'

Chantelle felt the earth turn giddily under her feet and the sudden roaring rush of blood in her ears. She stepped back and the stone parapet caught the back of her knees. She sat down heavily.

'What are you talking about?' she whispered. And he told her, in substantial detail, from the beginning, how it had worked out. From the laying of *Golden Dawn*'s keel in the times of vast tanker tonnage demand. 'My calculations were based on demand for tanker space two years ago, and on construction costs of that time.'

The energy crisis and collapse in demand for tankers had come with the vicious rise in inflation, bloating the costs of construction of *Golden Dawn* by more than double. Duncan had countered by altering the design of the gigantic tanker. He had reduced the four propulsion units to one, he had cut down the steel structuring of the hull

360

reinforcement by twenty per cent, he had done away with elaborate safety functions and fail-safe systems designed by Nicholas Berg, and he had cut it too fine. He had forfeited the Al Lloyd's rating, the mark of approval from the inspectors of that venerable body; without the insurance backing of that huge underwriting market, he had been forced to look elsewhere to find the cover to satisfy his financiers. The premiums had been crippling. He had to pledge Christy Marine stock, the Trust stock. Then the spiralling cost of production had overtaken him again and he needed money and more money. He had taken it where he could find it, at rates of interest that were demanded, and used more Christy stock as collateral.

Then the insurance cover had been insufficient to cover the huge increase in the cost of the ultra-tanker's hull.

'When luck runs out—' Duncan shrugged eloquently, and went on. 'I had to pledge more Christy stock, all of it. It's all at risk, Chantelle, every single piece of paper, even the shares we retrieved from your Nicholas – and even that wasn't enough. I have had to write cover through front companies, cover that is worthless. Then,' Duncan smiled again, relaxed and unruffled, almost as though he was enjoying himself, 'then, there was that awful fiasco when *Golden Adventurer* went up on the ice, and I had to find six million dollars to pay the salvage award. That was the last of it, I went out for everything then, all of it. The Trust, the whole of Christy Marine.'

'I'll break you,' she whispered. 'I'll smash you. I swear before God—'

'You don't understand, do you?' He shook his head sorrowfully, as though at an obtuse child. 'You cannot break me, without breaking Christy Marine and yourself. You are in it, Chantelle, much much deeper than I am. You have everything, every penny, this house, that emerald on your finger, the future of your brat – all of it is riding on *Golden Dawn*'.

'No.' She closed her eyes very tightly, and there was no colour in her cheeks now.

'Yes. I'm afraid it's yes,' he contradicted. 'I didn't plan it that way. I saw a profit of 200 millions in it, but we have been caught up in circumstances, I'm afraid.'

They were both silent, and Chantelle swayed slightly as the full enormity of it overwhelmed her.

'If you whistle up your hounds now, if you call in your axemen, there will be plenty for them to work on,' he laughed again, 'buckets of dung for us all to wallow in. And my backers will line up to cancel out. *Golden Dawn* will never run down her ways – she is not fully covered, as I explained to you. It all hangs on a single thread, Chantelle. If the launching of *Golden Dawn* is delayed now, delayed by a month – no, by a week even, it will all come tumbling down.'

'I'm going to be sick,' she whispered thickly.

'No, you are not.' He stood up and crossed quickly to her. Coldly he slapped her face, two hard open-handed back and forth blows, that snapped her head from side to side, leaving the livid marks of his fingers on her pale cheeks. It was the first time ever that a man had struck her, but she could not find the indignation to protest. She merely stared at him.

'Pull yourself together,' he snarled at her, and gripped her shoulders fiercely, shaking her as he went on. 'Listen to me. I have told you the worst that can happen. Now, I will tell you the best. If we stand together now, if you obey me implicitly, without question, I will pull off one of the greatest financial coups of the century for you. All it needs is one successful voyage by *Golden Dawn* and we are home free – a single voyage, a few short weeks, and I will have doubled your fortune.' She was staring at him, sickened and shaken to the core of her existence. 'I have signed an agreement of charter with Orient Amex, that will pull us out from under a single voyage, and the day *Golden Dawn* anchors in Galveston roads and sends in her tank pods to discharge, I will have a dozen buyers for her.' He stepped back, and straightened the lapels of his jacket. 'Men are going to remember my name. In future when they talk of tankers, they are going to talk of Duncan Alexander.'

'I hate you,' she said softly. 'I truly hate you.'

'That is not important.' He waved it away. 'When it is over, I can afford to walk away – and you can afford to let me go. But not a moment before.'

'How much will you make from this, if it succeeds?' she asked, and she was recovering, her voice firmer.

'A great deal. A very great deal of money – but my real reward will be in reputation and achievement. After this, I will be a man who can write his own ticket.'

'For once, you will be able to stand comparison with Nicholas Berg. Is that it?' She saw she had scored immediately, and she pressed harder, trying to wound and destroy. 'But you and I both know it is not true. *Golden Dawn* was Nicholas' inspiration and he would not have had to descend to the cheat and sham—'

'My dear Chantelle—'

'You will never be, could never be the man Nicholas is.'

'Damn you.' Suddenly he was shaking with anger, and she was screaming at him.

'You're a cheat and a liar. For all your airs, you're still a cheap little barrow-boy at heart. You're small and shoddy—'

'I've beaten Nicholas Berg every time I've met him.'

'No, you haven't, Duncan. It was I who beat him for you—'

'I took you.'

'For a while,' she sneered. 'Just for a short fling, Duncan dear. But when he wanted me he took me right back again.'

'What do you mean by that?' he demanded.

363

'The night before last, Nicholas was here, and he loved me in a way you never could. I'm going back to him, and I'll tell the world why.'

'You bitch.'

'He is so strong, Duncan. Strong where you are weak.'

'And you are a whore.' He half turned away, and then paused. 'Just be at St Nazaire on Tuesday.' But she could see he was hurt, at last she had cut through the carapace and touched raw quick nerves.

'He loved me four times in one night, Duncan. Magnificent, soaring love. Did you ever do that?'

'I want you at St Nazaire, smiling at the creditors on Tuesday.'

'Even if you succeed with *Golden Dawn*, within six months Nicholas will have your job.'

'But until then you'll do exactly what I say.' Duncan braced himself, a visible effort, and began to walk away.

'You are going to be the loser, Duncan Alexander,' she screamed after him, her voice cracking shrilly with frustration and outrage. 'I will see to that – I swear it to you.'

He subdued the urge to run, and crossed the terrace, holding himself carefully erect, and the storm of her hatred and frustration burst around him.

'Go into the streets where you belong, into the gutter where I found you,' she screamed, and he went up the stone staircase and out of her sight. Now he could hurry, but he found his legs were trembling underneath him, his breath was ragged and broken, and there was a tight knot of anger and jealousy turning his guts into a ball.

'The bastard,' he spoke aloud. 'That bastard Berg.'

'Tom? Tom Parker?'

'That's right, who is this, please?' His voice was so clear and strong, although the Atlantic Ocean separated them.

'It's Nicholas, Nicholas Berg.'

'Nick, how are you?' the big voice boomed with genuine pleasure. 'God, I'm glad you called. I've been trying to reach you. I've got good news. The best.'

Nicholas felt a quick lift of relief.

'Samantha?'

'No, damn it,' Tom laughed. 'It's the job. Your job. It went up before the Board of Governors of the University yesterday. I had to sell it to them hard – I'll tell you that for free – but they okayed it. You're on, Nick, isn't that great?'

'It's terrific, Tom.'

'You're on the Biology faculty as an associate. It's the thin end of the wedge, Nicholas. We'll have you a chair by the end of next year, you wait and see.'

'I'm delighted.'

'Christ, you don't sound it,' Tom roared. 'What's bugging you, boy?'

'Tom, what the hell has happened to Samantha?'

And Nicholas sensed the mood change, the silence lasted a beat too long, and then Tom's tone was guileless.

'She went off on a field trip – down the Keys, didn't she tell you?'

'Down the Keys?' Nicholas' voice rose with his anger and frustration. 'Damn it, Tom. She was supposed to be here in France. She promised to come over for the launching of my new vessel. I've been trying to get in touch with her for a week now.'

'She left Sunday,' said Tom.

'What is she playing at?'

'That's a question she might want to ask you sometime.'

'What does that mean, Tom?'

'Well, before she took off, she came up here and had a good weep with Antoinette – you know, my wife. She plays den mother for every hysterical female within fifty miles, she does.'

Now it was Nicholas' turn to be silent, while the coldness settled on his chest, the coldness of formless dread.

'What was the trouble?'

'Good God, Nick, you don't expect me to follow the intimate details of the love life—'

'Can I speak to Antoinette?'

'She isn't here, Nick. She went up to Orlando for a meeting. She won't be back until the weekend.'

The silence again.

'All that heavy breathing is costing you a fortune, Nicholas. You're paying for this call.'

'I don't know what got into Sam.' But he did. Nicholas knew – and the guilt was strong upon him.

'Listen, Nick. A word to the wise. Get your ass across here, boy. Just as soon as you can. That girl needs talking to, badly. That is, if you care about it.'

'I care about it,' Nicholas said quickly. 'But hell, I am launching a tug in two days' time. I've got sea trials, and a meeting in London.'

Tom's voice had an air of finality. 'A man's got to do what he's got to do.'

'Tom, I'll be across there as soon as I possibly can.'

'I believe it.'

'If you see her, tell her that for me, will you?'

'I'll tell her.'

'Thanks, Tom.'

'The governors will want to meet you, Nicholas. Come as soon as you can.'

'It's a promise.'

Nicholas cradled the receiver, and stood staring out of the windows of the site office. The view across the inner

366

harbour was completely blocked by the towering hull of his tug. She stood tall on her ways. Her hull already wore its final coat of glistening white and the wide flaring bows bore the name *Sea Witch* and below that the port of registration, 'Bermuda'.

She was beautiful, magnificent, but now Nicholas did not even see her. He was overwhelmed by a sense of imminent loss, the cold premonition of onrushing disaster. Until that moment when he faced the prospect of losing her, he had not truly known how large a part that lovely golden girl had come to play in his existence, and in his plans for the future.

There was no way that Samantha could have learned of that single night of weakness, the betrayal that still left Nicholas sickened with guilt – there must be something else that had come between them. He bunched his right fist and slammed it against the sill of the window. The skin on his knuckles smeared, but he did not feel the pain, only the bitter frustration of being tied down here in St Nazaire, weighed down by his responsibilities, when he should have been free to follow the jack-o'-lantern of happiness.

The loudspeaker above his head gave a preliminary squawk, and then crackled out the message, 'Monsieur Berg. Will Monsieur attend upon the bridge?'

It was a welcome distraction, and Nicholas hurried out into the spring sunshine. Looking upwards, he could see Jules Levoisin on the wing of the bridge. His portly figure foreshortened against the open sky, like a small pugnacious rooster. He stood facing the electronics engineer who was responsible for the installation of *Sea Witch*'s communications system, and Jules' cries of 'Sacré bleu' and 'Merde' and 'Imbécile' carried clearly above the cacophony of shipyard noises.

Nicholas started to run as he saw the engineer's arms begin to wave and his strident Gallic cries blended with those of *Sea Witch*'s new Master. It was only the third time that Jules Levoisin had become hysterical that day, however it was not yet noon. As the hour of launching came steadily closer, so the little Frenchman's nerves played him tricks. He was behaving like a prima ballerina awaiting the opening curtain. Unless Nicholas reached the bridge within the next few minutes, he would need either a new Master or a new electronics engineer.

Ten minutes later, Nicholas had a cheroot in each of their mouths. The atmosphere was still tense but no longer explosive, and gently Nick took the engineer by the elbow, placed his other arm around Jules Levoisin's shoulders and led them both back into the wheelhouse.

The bridge installation was complete, and Jules Levoisin was accepting delivery of the special equipment from the contractors, a negotiation every bit as traumatic as the Treaty of Versailles.

'I myself authorized the modification of the MK IV transponder,' Nicholas explained patiently. 'We had trouble with the same unit on *Warlock*. I should have told you, Jules.'

'You should have,' agreed the little Master huffily.

'But you were perceptive to notice the change from the specification,' Nicholas soothed him, and Jules puffed out his chest a little and rolled the cheroot in his mouth.

'I may be an old dog, but I know all the new tricks.' He removed the cheroot and smugly blew a perfect smoke ring.

When Nicholas at last left them chatting amiably over the massed array of sophisticated equipment that lined the navigation area at the back of the bridge, they were paging him from the site office.

'What is it?' he asked, as he came in through the door.

'It's a lady,' the foreman indicated the telephone lying on the littered desk below the window.

'Samantha,' Nick thought, and snatched up the receiver.

'Nicky.' He felt the shock of quick guilt at the voice.

'Chantelle, where are you?'

'In La Baule.' The fashionable resort town just up the Atlantic coast was a better setting for Chantelle Alexander than the grubby port with its sprawling dockyards. 'Staying at the Castille. God, it's too awful. I'd forgotten how awful it was.'

They had stayed there together, once long ago, in a different life it seemed now.

'But the restaurant is still quite cute, Nicholas. Have lunch with me. I must speak to you.'

'I can't leave here.' He would not walk into the trap again.

'It's important. I must see you.' He could hear that husky tone in her voice, imagine clearly the sensuous droop of the eyelids over those bold Persian eyes. 'For an hour, only an hour. You can spare that.' Despite himself, he felt the pull of temptation, the dull ache of it at the base of his belly – and he was angry at her for the power she could still exert over him.

'If it's important, then come here,' he said brusquely, and she sighed at his intransigence.

'All right, Nicholas. How will I find you?'

The Rolls was parked opposite the dockyard gates and Nicholas crossed the road and stepped through the door that the chauffeur held open for him.

Chantelle lifted her face to him. Her hair was cloudy dark and shot with light like a bolt of silk, her lips the colour of ripe fruit, moist and slightly parted. He ignored the invitation and touched her cheek with his lips before settling into the corner opposite her.

She made a little moue, and slanted her eyes at him in amusement. 'How chaste we are, Nicky.'

Nicholas touched the button on the control console and the glass soundproof partition slid up noiselessly between them and the chauffeur.

'Did you send in the auditors?' he asked.

'You look tired, darling, and harassed.'

'Have you blown the whistle on Duncan?' he avoided the distraction. 'The work on *Golden Dawn* is still going ahead. The arc lights were burning over her all night and the talk in the yards is that she is being launched at noon tomorrow, almost a month ahead of schedule. What happened, Chantelle?'

'There is a little bistro at Mindin, it's just across the bridge—'

'Damn it, Chantelle. I haven't time to fool around.'

But the Rolls was already gliding swiftly through the narrow streets of the port, between the high warehouse buildings.

'It will take five minutes, and the Lobster Armoricaine is the local speciality – not to be confused with Lobster Américaine. They do it in a cream sauce, it's superb,' she chatted archly, and the Rolls turned out on to the quay. Across the narrow waters of the inner harbour humped the ugly camouflaged mounds of the Nazi submarine pens, armoured concrete so thick as to resist the bombs of the RAF and the efforts of all demolition experts over the years since then.

'Peter asked me to give you his love. He has got his junior team colours. I'm so proud.'

Nicholas thrust his hands deep into his jacket pockets and slumped down resignedly against the soft leather seat.

'I am delighted to hear it,' he said.

And they were silent then until the chauffeur checked the Rolls at the toll barrier to pay before accelerating out on to the ramp of the St Nazaire bridge. The great span of the bridge rose in a regal curve, three hundred feet above the waters of the Loire river. The river was almost three miles wide here, and from the highest point of the bridge there was an aerial view over the dockyards of the town.

There were half a dozen vessels building along the banks of the broad muddy river, a mighty forest of steel scaffolding, tall gantries and half-assembled hulls, but all of it insignificant under the mountainous bulk of *Golden Dawn*. Without her pod tanks, she had an incomplete gutted appearance, as though the Eiffel Tower had toppled over and somebody had built a modernistic apartment block at one end. It seemed impossible that such a structure was capable of floating. God, she was ugly, Nick thought.

'They are still working on her,' he said. One of the gantries was moving ponderously along the length of the ship like an arthritic dinosaur, and at fifty paces the brilliant blue electric fires of the welding torches flickered; while upon the grotesquely riven hull crawled human figures reduced to ant-like insignificance by the sheer size of the vessel.

'They are still working,' he repeated it as an accusation.

'Nicholas, nothing in this life is simple—'

'Did you spell it out for Duncan?'

' – except for people like you.'

'You didn't confront Duncan, did you?' he accused her bitterly.

'It's easy for you to be strong. It's one of the things that first attracted me.'

And Nicholas almost laughed aloud. It was ludicrous to talk of strength, after his many displays of weakness with this very woman.

'Did you call Duncan's cards?' he insisted, but she put him off with a smile.

'Let's wait until we have a glass of wine—'

'Now,' he snapped. 'Tell me right now. Chantelle, I haven't time for games.'

'Yes, I spoke to him,' she nodded. 'I called him down to Cap Ferrat, and I accused him – of what you suspected.'

'He denied it? If he denies it, I now have further proof—'

'No, Nicholas. He didn't deny a thing. He told me that I knew only the half of it.' Her voice rose sharply, and suddenly it all spilled out in a torrent of tortured words.

Her composure was eroded swiftly away as she relived the enormity of her predicament. 'He's gambled with my fortune, Nicholas. He's risked the family share of Christy Marine, the Trust shares, my shares, it's all at risk. And he gloated as he told me, he truly gloried in his betrayal.'

'We've got him now.' Nicholas had straightened slowly in his seat as he listened. His voice was grimly satisfied and he nodded. 'That's it. We will stop the *Golden Dawn*, like that—' he hammered his bunched fist into the palm of the other hand with a sharp crack. 'We will get an urgent order before the courts.'

Nicholas stopped suddenly and stared at her. Chantelle was shaking her head slowly from side to side. Her eyes slowly filled, making them huge and glistening, a single tear spilled over the lid and clung in the thick dark lashes like a drop of morning dew.

The Rolls had stopped now outside the tiny bistro. It was on the river front, with a view across the water to the dockyards. To the west the river debouched into the open sea and in the east the beautiful arch of the bridge across the pale blue spring sky.

The chauffeur held open the door and Chantelle was gone with her swift birdlike grace, leaving Nicholas no choice but to follow her.

The proprietor came through from his kitchen and fussed over Chantelle, seating her at the window and lingering to discuss the menu.

'Oh, let's drink the Muscadet, Nicholas.' She had always had the most amazing powers of recovery, and now the tears were gone and she was brittle and gay and beautiful, smiling at him over the rim of her glass. The sunlight through the leaded window panes danced in the cool golden wine and rippled on the smoky dark fall of her hair.

'Here's to us, Nicholas darling. We are the last of the great.' It was a toast from long ago, from the other life, and it irritated him now but he drank it silently and then set down the glass.

'Chantelle, when and how are you going to stop Duncan?'

'Don't spoil the meal, darling.'

'In about thirty seconds I'm going to start becoming very angry.'

She studied him for a moment, and saw that it was true. 'All right then,' she agreed reluctantly.

'When are you going to stop him?'

'I'm not, darling.'

He stared at her. 'What did you say?' he asked quietly.

'I'm going to do everything in my power to help him launch and sail the *Golden Dawn*.'

'You don't understand, Chantelle. You're talking about risking a million tons of the most deadly poison—'

'Don't be silly, Nicky. Keep that heroic talk for the newspapers. I don't care if Duncan dumps a million tons of cadmium in the water supply of Greater London, just as long as he pulls the Trust and me out of the fire.'

'There is still time to make the modifications to *Golden Dawn*.'

'No, there isn't. You don't understand, darling. Duncan has put us so deeply into it that a delay of a few days even would bring us down. He has stripped the cupboard bare, Nicky. There is no money for modifications, no time for anything, except to get *Golden Dawn* under way.'

'There is always a way and a means.'

'Yes, and the way is to fill *Golden Dawn*'s pod tanks with crude.'

'He's frightened you by—'

'Yes,' she agreed. 'I am frightened. I have never been so frightened in my life, Nicky. I could lose everything – I am terrified. I could lose it all.' She shivered with the horror of it. 'I would kill myself if that happened.'

'I am still going to stop Duncan.'

'No, Nicky. Please leave it, for my sake – for Peter's sake. It's Peter's inheritance that we are talking about. Let *Golden Dawn* make one voyage, just one voyage – and I will be safe.'

'It's the risk to an ocean, to God alone knows how many human lives, we are talking about.'

'Don't shout, Nicky. People are looking.'

'Let them look. I'm going to stop that monster.'

'No, Nicholas. Without me, you cannot do a thing.'

'You best believe it.'

'Darling, I promise you, after her first voyage we will sell *Golden Dawn*. We'll be safe then, and I can rid myself of Duncan. It will be you and I again, Nicky. A few short weeks, that's all.'

It took all his self-control to prevent his anger showing. He clenched his fists on the starched white tablecloth, but his voice was cool and even.

'Just one more question, Chantelle. When did you telephone Samantha Silver?'

She looked puzzled for a moment as though she was trying to put a face to a name. 'Samantha, oh, your little friend. Why should I want to telephone her?' And then her expression changed. 'Oh, Nicky, you don't really believe I'd do that? You don't really believe I would tell anybody about it, about that wonderful—' Now she was stricken, again those huge eyes brimmed and she reached across and stroked the fine black hairs on the back of Nicholas' big square hand. 'You don't think that of me! I'm not that much of a bitch. I don't have to cheat to get the things I want. I don't have to inflict unnecessary hurt on people.'

'No,' Nicholas agreed quietly. 'You'd not murder more than a million or poison more than a single ocean at a time, would you?' He pushed back his chair.

'Sit down, Nicky. Eat your lobster.'

'Suddenly I'm not hungry.' He stripped two one-hundred-franc notes from his money clip and dropped them beside his plate.

'I forbid you to leave,' she hissed angrily. 'You are humiliating me, Nicholas.'

'I'll send your car back,' he said, and walked out into the sunlight. He found with surprise that he was trembling, and that his jaws were clenched so tightly that his teeth ached.

The wind turned during the night, and the morning was cold with drifts of low, grey, fast-flying cloud that threatened rain. Nicholas pulled up his collar against the wind and the tails of his coat flogged about his legs, for he was exposed on the highest point of the arched bridge of St Nazaire.

Thousands of others had braved the wind, and the guardrail was lined two and three deep, all the way across the curve of the northern span. The traffic had backed up and half a dozen gendarmes were trying to get it moving again; their whistles shrilled plaintively. Faintly the sound of a band floated up to them, rising and falling in volume as the wind caught it, and even with the naked eye Nicholas could make out the wreaths of gaily coloured bunting which fluttered on the high cumbersome stern tower of *Golden Dawn*.

He glanced at his wristwatch, and saw it was a few minutes before noon. A helicopter clattered noisily under the grey belly of cloud, and hovered about the yards of Construction Navale Atlantique on the gleaming silver coin of its rotor.

Nicholas lifted the binoculars and the eyepieces were

painfully cold against his skin. Through the lens, he could almost make out individual features among the small gathering on the rostrum under the tanker's stern.

The platform was decorated with a tricolour and a Union Jack, and as he watched the band fell silent and lowered their instruments.

'Speech time,' Nicholas murmured, and now he could make out Duncan Alexander, his bared head catching one of the fleeting rays of sun, a glimmer of coppery gold as he looked up at the towering stern of *Golden Dawn*.

His bulk almost obscured the tiny feminine figure beside him. Chantelle wore that particular shade of malachite green which she so dearly loved. There was confused activity around Chantelle, half a dozen gentlemen assisting in the ceremony she had performed so very often. Chantelle had broken the champagne on almost all of Christy Marine's fleet; the first time had been when she was Arthur Christy's fourteen-year-old darling – it was another of the company's many traditions.

Nicholas blinked, believing for an instant that his eyes had tricked him, for it seemed that the very earth had changed its shape and was moving.

Then he saw that the great hull of *Golden Dawn* had begun to slide forward. The band burst into the 'Marseillaise', the heroic strains watered down by wind and distance, while *Golden Dawn* gathered momentum.

It was an incredible, even a stirring sight, and despite himself, Nicholas felt the goosebumps rise upon his forearms and the hair lift on the back of his neck. He was a sailor, and he was watching the birthing of the mightiest vessel ever built.

She was grotesque, monstrous, but she was part of him. No matter that others had bastardized and perverted his grand design – still the original design was his and he found himself gripping the binoculars with hands that shook.

He watched the massive wooden-wedged arresters kick

out from under that great sliding mass of steel as they served to control her stern-first rush down the ways. Steel cable whipped and snaked upon itself like the Medusa's hair, and *Golden Dawn*'s stern struck the water.

The brown muddy water of the estuary opened before her, cleaved by the irresistible rush and weight, and the hull drove deep, opening white-capped rollers that spread out across the channel and broke upon the shores with a dull roar that carried clearly to where Nicholas stood.

The crowd that lined the bridge was cheering wildly. Beside him, a mother held her infant up to watch, both of them screaming with glee.

While *Golden Dawn*'s bows were still on the dockyard's ways her stern was thrusting irresistibly a mile out into the river; forced down by the raised bows it must now be almost touching the muddy bottom for the wave was breaking around her stern quarters.

God, she was huge! Nicholas shook his head in wonder. If only he had been able to build her the right way, what a ship she would have been. What a magnificent concept!

Now her bows left the end of the slips, and the waters burst about her, seething and leaping into swirling vortices.

Her stern started to rise, gathering speed as her own buoyancy caught her, and she burst out like a great whale rising to blow. The waters spilled from her, creaming and cascading through the steelwork of her open decks, boiling madly in the cavernous openings that would hold the pod tanks when she was fully loaded.

Now she came up short on the hundreds of retaining cables that prevented her from driving clear across the river and throwing herself ashore on the far bank.

She fought against this restraint, as though having felt the water she was now eager to run. She rolled and dipped and swung with a ponderous majesty that kept the crowds along the bridge cheering wildly. Then slowly she settled and floated quietly, seeming to fill the Loire river from bank to bank and to reach as high as the soaring spans of the bridge itself.

The four attendant harbour tugs moved in quickly to assist the ship to turn its prodigious length and to line up for the roads and the open sea.

They butted and backed, working as a highly skilled team, and slowly they coaxed *Golden Dawn* around. Her sideways motion left a mile-wide sweep of disturbed water across the estuary. Then suddenly there was a tremendous boil under her counter, and Nicholas saw the bronze flash of her single screw sweeping slowly through the brown water. Faster and still faster it turned, and despite himself Nicholas thrilled to see her come alive. A ripple formed under her bows, and almost imperceptibly she began to creep forward, overcoming the vast inertia of her weight, gathering steerage way, under command at last.

The harbour tugs fell back respectfully, and as the mighty bows lined up with the open sea she drove forward determinedly.

Silver spouts of steam from the sirens of the tugs shot high, and moments later, the booming bellow of their salute crashed against the skies.

The crowds had dispersed and Nicholas stood alone in the wind on the high bridge and watched the structured steel towers of *Golden Dawn*'s hull blending with the grey and misted horizon. He watched her turn, coming around on to her great circle course that would carry her six thousand miles southward to Good Hope, and even at this distance he sensed her change in mood as she steadied and her single screw began to push her up to top economic speed.

Nicholas checked his watch and murmured the age-old Master's command that commenced every voyage.

'Full away at 1700 hours,' he said, and turned to trudge back along the bridge to where he had left the hired Renault.

It was after six o'clock and the site office was empty by the time Nicholas got back to *Sea Witch*. He threw himself into a chair and lit a cheroot while he thumbed quickly through his address book. He found what he wanted, dialled the direct London code, and then the number.

'Good afternoon. This is the *Sunday Times*. May I help you?'

'Is Mr Herbstein available?' Nicholas asked.

'Hold on, please.'

While he waited, Nicholas checked his address book for his next most likely contact, should the journalist be climbing the Himalayas or visiting a guerrilla training camp in Central Africa, either of which were highly likely – but within seconds he heard his voice.

'Denis,' he said. 'This is Nicholas Berg. How are you? I've got a hell of a story for you.'

Nicholas tried to bear the indignity of it with stoicism, but the thick coating of pancake make-up seemed to clog the pores of his skin and he moved restlessly in the make-up chair.

'Please keep still, sir,' the make-up girl snapped irritably; there was a line of unfortunates awaiting her ministrations along the bench at the back of the narrow room. One of them was Duncan Alexander and he caught Nicholas' eye in the mirror and raised an eyebrow in a mocking salute.

In the chair beside him, the anchorman of *The Today and Tomorrow Show* lolled graciously; he was tall and elegant with dyed and permanently waved hair, a carnation in his buttonhole, a high camp manner and an ostentatiously liberal image.

'I've given you the first slot. If it gets interesting, I'll run you four minutes forty seconds, otherwise I'll cut it off at two.'

Denis Herbstein's Sunday article had been done with high professionalism, especially bearing in mind the very short time he had to put it together. It had included interviews with representatives of Lloyd's of London, the oil companies, environmental experts both in America and England, and even with the United States Coast Guard.

'Try to make it tight and hard,' advised the anchorman. 'Let's not pussyfoot around.' He wanted sensation, not too many facts or figures, good gory horror stuff – or a satisfying punch-up. The *Sunday Times* article had flushed them out at Orient Amex and Christy Marine; they had not been able to ignore the challenge for there was a question tabled for Thursday by a Labour member in the Commons, and ominous stirrings in the ranks of the American Coast Guard service.

There had been enough fuss to excite the interest of *The Today and Tomorrow Show*. They had invited the parties to meet their accuser, and both Christy Marine and Orient Amex had fielded their first teams. Duncan Alexander with all his charisma had come to speak for Christy Marine, and Orient Amex had selected one of their directors who looked like Gary Cooper. With his craggy honest face and the silver hairs at his temples he looked like the kind of man you wanted flying your airliner or looking after your money.

The make-up girl dusted Nicholas' face with powder.

'I'm going to invite you to speak first. Tell us about this stuff – what is it, cadmium?' the interviewer checked his script.

Nicholas nodded, he could not speak for he was suffering the ultimate indignity. The girl was painting his lips.

The television studio was the size of an aircraft hangar, the concrete floor strewn with thick black cables and the roof lost in the gloomy heights, but they had created the illusion of intimacy in the small shell of the stage around which the big mobile cameras cluttered like mechanical crabs around the carcass of a dead fish.

The egg-shaped chairs made it impossible either to loll or to sit upright, and the merciless white glare of the arc lamps fried the thick layer of greasy make-up on Nicholas' skin. It was small consolation that across the table Duncan looked like a Japanese Kabuki dancer in make-up too white for his coppery hair.

An assistant director in a sweatshirt and jeans clipped the small microphone into Nicholas' lapel and whispered,

'Give them hell, ducky.'

Somebody else in the darkness beyond the lights was intoning solemnly, 'Four, three, two, one – you're on!' and the red light lit on the middle camera.

'Welcome to *The Today and Tomorrow Show*,' the anchorman's voice was suddenly warm and intimate and mellifluous. 'Last week in the French shipbuilding port of St Nazaire, the largest ship in the world was launched—' In a dozen sentences he sketched out the facts, while on the repeating screens beyond the cameras Nicholas saw that they were running newsreel footage of *Golden Dawn*'s launching. He remembered the helicopter hovering over the dockyard, and he was so fascinated by the aerial views of the enormous vessel taking to the water that when the cameras switched suddenly to him, he was taken by surprise and saw himself start on the little screen as the interviewer began introducing him, swiftly running a thumbnail portrait and then going on:

'Mr Berg has some very definite views on this ship.'

'In her present design and construction, she is not safe to carry even regular crude petroleum oil,' Nicholas said. 'However, she will be employed in the carriage of crude oil that has been contaminated by cadmium sulphide in such concentrations as to make it one of the more toxic substances in nature.'

'Your first statement, Mr Berg, does anyone else share your doubts as to the safety of her design?'

'She does not carry the A1 rating by the marine inspectors of Lloyd's of London,' said Nicholas.

'Now can you tell us about the cargo she will carry – the so-called cad-rich crudes?'

Nicholas knew he had perhaps fifteen seconds to draw a verbal picture of the Atlantic Ocean turned into a sterile poisoned desert; it was too short a time, and twice Duncan Alexander interjected, skilfully breaking up the logic of Nicholas' presentation and before he had finished, the anchor-man glanced at his watch and cut him short.

'Thank you, Mr Berg. Now Mr Kemp is a director of the oil company.'

'My company, Orient Amex, last year allocated the sum of two million U.S. dollars as grants to assist in the scientific study of world environmental problems. I can tell you folks, right now, that we at Orient Amex are very conscious of the problems of modern technology—' He was projecting the oil-company image, the benefactors of all humanity.

'Your company's profit last year, after taxation, was four hundred and twenty-five million dollars,' Nicholas cut in clearly. 'That makes point four seven per cent on environmental research – all of it tax deductible. Congratulations, Mr Kemp.'

The oil man looked pained and went on: 'Now we at Orient Amex,' plugging the company name again neatly, 'are working towards a better quality of life for all peoples. But we do realize that it is impossible to put back the clock a hundred years. We cannot allow ourselves to be blinded by the romantic wishful thinking of *amateur* environmentalists, the weekend scientists and the doomcriers who—'

'Cry *Torrey Canyon*,' Nicholas suggested helpfully, and the oil man suppressed a shudder and went on quickly.

' – who would have us discontinue such research as the

revolutionary cadmium cracking process, which could extend the world's utilization of fossil fuels by a staggering forty per cent and give the world's oil reserves an extended life of twenty years or more.'

Again the anchorman glanced at his watch, cut the oil man off in mid-flow and switched his attention to Duncan Alexander.

'Mr Alexander, your so-called ultra-tanker will carry the cad-rich crudes. How would you reply to Mr Berg?'

Duncan smiled, a deep secret smile. 'When Mr Berg had my job as head of Christy Marine, the Golden Dawn was the best idea in the world. Since he was fired, it's suddenly the worst.'

They laughed, even one of the cameramen out beyond the lights guffawed uncontrollably, and Nicholas felt the hot red rush of his anger.

'Is the Golden Dawn rated A1 at Lloyd's?' asked the anchorman.

'Christy Marine has not applied for a Lloyd's listing – we arranged our insurance in other markets.'

Even through his anger Nicholas had to concede how good he was. He had a mind like quicksilver.

'How safe is your ship, Mr Alexander?'

Now Duncan turned his head and looked directly across the table at Nicholas.

'I believe she is as safe as the world's leading marine architects and naval engineers can make her.' He paused, and there was a malevolent gleam in his eyes now, 'So safe, that I have decided to end this ridiculous controversy by a display of my personal confidence.'

'What form will this show of faith take, Mr Alexander?' The anchorman sensed the sensational line for which he had been groping and he leaned forward eagerly.

'On Golden Dawn's maiden voyage, when she returns from the Persian Gulf fully laden with the El Barras crudes, I and my family, my wife and my stepson, will travel aboard her for the final six thousand miles of her voyage – from Cape Town on the Cape of Good Hope to Galveston in the Gulf of Mexico.' As Nicholas gaped at him wordlessly, he went on evenly, 'That's how convinced I am that *Golden Dawn* is capable of performing her task in perfect safety.'

'Thank you.' The anchorman recognized a good exit line, when he heard one. 'Thank you, Mr Alexander. You've convinced me – and I am sure you have convinced many of our viewers. We are now crossing to Washington via satellite where—'

The moment the red 'in use' light flickered out on the television camera, Nicholas was on his feet and facing Duncan Alexander. His anger was fanned by the realization that Duncan had easily grandstanded him with that adroit display of showmanship, and by the stabbing anxiety at the threat to take Peter aboard *Golden Dawn* on her hazardous maiden voyage.

'You're not taking Peter on that death trap of yours,' he snapped.

'That's his mother's decision,' said Duncan evenly. 'As the daughter of Arthur Christy, she's decided to give the company her full support,' he emphasized the word 'full'.

'I won't let either of you endanger my son's life for a wild public-relations stunt.'

'I'm sure you will try to prevent it,' Duncan nodded and smiled, 'and I'm sure your efforts will be as ineffectual as your attempts to stop *Golden Dawn*.' He deliberately turned his back on Nicholas and spoke to the oil man. 'I do think that went off rather well,' he said, 'don't you?'

J ames Teacher gave a graphic demonstration of why
he could charge the highest fees in London and still
have his desk piled high with important briefs. He
had Nicholas' urgent application before a Judge-in-
Chambers within seventy-two hours, petitioning for a writ
to restrain Chantelle Alexander from allowing the son of
their former marriage, one Peter Nicholas Berg, aged twelve
years, to accompany her on an intended voyage from Cape
Town in the Republic of South Africa to Galveston in the
state of Texas aboard the bulk crude-carrier *Golden Dawn*,
and/or to prevent the said Chantelle Alexander from
allowing the child to undertake any other voyage aboard
the said vessel.

The Judge heard the petition during a recess in the
criminal trial of a young post-office worker standing accused
of multiple rape. The judge's oak-panelled book-lined
chambers were overcrowded by the two parties, their
lawyers, the judge's registrar and the considerable bulk of
the judge himself.

Still in his wig and robes from the public court, the
judge read swiftly through the written submission of both
sides, listened attentively to James Teacher's short address
and the rebuttal by his opposite number, before turning
sternly to Chantelle.

'Mrs Alexander.' The stern expression wavered slightly
as he looked upon the devastating beauty which sat
demurely before him. 'Do you love your son?'

'More than anything else in this life.' Chantelle looked
at him steadily out of those vast dark eyes.

'And you are happy to take him on this journey with
you?'

'I am the daughter of a sailor. If there was danger I
would understand it. I am happy to go myself and take my
son with me.'

The judge nodded, looked down at the papers on his
desk for a moment.

'As I understand the circumstances, Mr Teacher, it is common ground that the mother has custody?'

'That is so, my lord. But the father is the child's guardian.'

'I'm fully aware of that, thank you,' he snapped acidly. He paused again before resuming in the measured tones of judgement, 'We are concerned here exclusively with the welfare and safety of the child. It has been shown that the proposed journey will be made during the holidays and that no loss of schooling will result. On the other hand, I do not believe that the petitioner has shown that reasonable doubts exist about the safety of the vessel on which the voyage will be made. It seems to be a modern and sophisticated ship. To grant the petition would, in my view, be placing unreasonable restraint on the child's mother.' He swivelled in his chair to face Nicholas and James Teacher. 'I regret, therefore, that I see insufficient grounds to accede to your petition.'

I n the back seat of James Teacher's Bentley, the little lawyer murmured apologetically. 'He was right, of course, Nicholas. I would have done the same in his place. These domestic squabbles are always—'

Nicholas was not listening. 'What would happen if I picked up Peter and took him to Bermuda or the States?'

'Abduct him!' James Teacher's voice shot up an octave, and he caught Nicholas' arm with genuine alarm. 'I beg of you, dismiss the thought. They would have the police waiting for you – God!' Now he wriggled miserably in his seat. 'I can't bear to think of what might happen. Apart from getting you sent to gaol, your former wife might even get an order restraining you from seeing your boy again. She could get guardianship away from you. If you did that, you could lose the child, Nicholas. Don't do it. Please don't do it!'

Now he patted Nicholas' arm ingratiatingly. 'You'd be playing right into their hands.' And then with relief he switched his attention to the briefcase on his lap.

'Can we read through the latest draft of the agreement of sale again?' he asked. 'We haven't got much time, you know.' Then, without waiting for a reply, he began on the preamble to the agreement which would transfer all the assets and liabilities of Ocean Salvage and Towage to the Directors of the Bank of the East, as nominees for parties unnamed.

Nicholas slumped in the far corner of the seat, and stared thoughtfully out of the window as the Bentley crawled in the traffic stream out of the Strand, around Trafalgar Square with its wheeling clouds of pigeons and milling throngs of tourists, swung into the Mall and accelerated down the long straight towards the Palace.

'I want you to stall them,' Nicholas said suddenly, and Teacher broke off in the middle of a sentence and stared at him distractedly.

'I beg your pardon?'

'I want you to find a way to stall the Sheikhs.'

'Good God, man.' James Teacher was utterly astounded. 'It's taken me nearly a month – four hard weeks to get them ripe to sign,' his voice choked a little at the memory of the long hours of negotiation. 'I've written every line of the agreement in my own blood.'

'I need to have control of my tugs. I need to be free to act—'

'Nicholas, we are talking about seven million dollars.'

'We are talking about my son,' said Nicholas quietly. 'Can you stall them?'

'Yes, of course I can, if that's what you truly want.' Wearily James Teacher closed the file on his lap. 'How long?'

'Six weeks – long enough for *Golden Dawn* to finish her maiden voyage, one way or the other.'

'You realize that this may blow the whole deal, don't you?'

'Yes, I realize that.'

'And you realize also that there isn't another buyer?'

'Yes.'

They were silent then, until the Bentley pulled up before the Bank building in Curzon Street, and they stepped out on to the pavement.

'Are you absolutely certain?' Teacher asked softly.

'Just do it,' Nicholas replied, and the doorman held the bronze and glass doors open for them.

B ermuda asserted its calming influence over Nicholas the moment he stepped out of the aircraft into its comfortable warmth and clean, glittering sunlight. Bernard Wackie's gorgeous burnt-honey-coloured secretary was there to welcome him. She wore a thin cotton dress the colour of freshly cut pineapple and a flashing white smile.

'Mr Wackie's waiting for you at the Bank, sir.'

'Are you out of your mind, Nicholas?' Bernard greeted him. 'Jimmy Teacher tells me you blew the Arabs out of the window. Tell me it's not true, please tell me it's not true.'

'Oh, come on, Bernard,' Nicholas shook his head and patted him consolingly on the shoulder, 'your commission would only have been a lousy point seven million, anyway.'

'Then you did it!' Bernard wailed, and tried to pull his hand out of Nicholas' grip. 'You screwed it all up.'

'The Sheikhs have been screwing us up for over a month, Bernie baby. I just gave them a belt of the same medicine, and do you know what? They loved it. The

Prince sat up and showed real interest for the first time. For the first time we were speaking the same language. They'll still be around six weeks from now.'

'But why? I don't understand. Just explain to me why you did it.'

'Let's go into the plot, and I'll explain it to you.'

In the plot Nicholas stood over the perspex map of the oceans of the globe, and studied it carefully for fully five minutes without speaking.

'That's *Sea Witch*'s latest position. She's making good passage?'

The green plastic disc that bore the tug's number was set in mid-Atlantic.

'She reported two hours ago.' Bernie nodded, and then said with professional interest, 'How did her sea trials go off?'

'There were the usual wrinkles to iron out, that's what kept me in St Nazaire so long. But we got them straight – and Jules has fallen in love with her.'

'He's still the best skipper in the game.'

But already Nicholas' attention had switched halfway across the world.

'*Warlock*'s still in Mauritius,' his voice snapped like a whip.

'I had to fly out a new armature for the main generator. It was just bad luck that she broke down in that God-forsaken part of the world.'

'When will she be ready for sea?'

'Allen promises noon tomorrow. Do you want to telex him for an update on that?'

'Later.' Nicholas wet the tip of a cheroot carefully, without taking his eyes off the plot, calculating distances and currents and speeds.

'*Golden Dawn*?' he asked, and lit the cheroot while he listened to Bernard's reply.

'Her pod tanks arrived under tow at the new Orient Amex depot on El Barras three weeks ago.' Bernie picked up the pointer and touched the upper bight of the deep Persian Gulf. 'They took on their full cargoes of crude and lay inshore to await *Golden Dawn's* arrival.'

For a moment, Nicholas contemplated the task of towing those four gigantic pod tanks from Japan to the Gulf, and then he discarded the thought and listened to Bernard.

'*Golden Dawn* arrived last Thursday and, according to my agent at El Barras, she coupled up with her pod tanks and made her turn around within three hours.' Bernard slid the tip of the pointer southwards down the eastern coast of the African continent. 'I have had no report of her since then, but if she makes good her twenty-two knots, then she'll be somewhere off the coast of Mozambique, or Maputo as they call it now, and she should double the Cape within the next few days. I will have a report on her then. She'll be taking on mail as she passes Cape Town.'

'And passengers,' said Nicholas grimly; he knew that Peter and Chantelle were in Cape Town already. He had telephoned the boy the night before and Peter had been wildly elated at the prospect of the voyage on the ultra-tanker.

'It's going to be tremendous fun, Dad,' his voice cracking with the onset of both excitement and puberty. 'We'll be flying out to the ship in a helicopter.'

Bernard Wackie changed the subject, now picking up a sheaf of telex flimsies and thumbing swiftly through them.

'Right, I've confirmed the standby contract for *Sea Witch*.' Nicholas nodded, the contract was for Jules Levoi-sin and the new tug to stand by three offshore working rigs, standard exploration rigs, that were drilling in the Florida Bay, that elbow of shallow water formed by the sweep of the Florida Keys and the low swampy morass of the Everglades. 'It's ridiculous to use a twenty-two-thousand-horsepower ocean-going tug as an oil-rig standby,' Bernard lowered the file, and could no longer contain his irritation.

'Jules is going to go bananas sitting around playing nurse-maid. You are going to have a mutiny on your hands – and you'll be losing money. The daily hire won't cover your direct costs.'

'She will be sitting exactly where I want her,' said Nicholas, and switched his attention back to the tiny dot of an island in the middle of the Indian Ocean. 'Now *Warlock*.'

'Right. *Warlock*.' Bernie picked up another file. 'I have tendered for a deep-sea tow.'

'Cancel it,' said Nicholas. 'Just as soon as Allen has repaired his generator, I want him running top of the green for Cape Town.'

'For Cape Town – top of the green?' Bernard stared at him. 'Christ, Nicholas. What for?'

'He won't be able to catch *Golden Dawn* before she rounds the Cape, but I want him to follow her.'

'Nicholas, you're out of your mind – do you know what that would cost?'

'If *Golden Dawn* gets into trouble he'll be only a day or two behind her. Tell Allen he is to shadow her all the way into Galveston roads.'

'Nicholas, you're letting this whole thing get out of all proportion. It's become an obsession with you, for God's sake!'

'With her superior speed, *Warlock* should be up with her before she enters the—'

'Listen to me, Nicholas. Let's think this all out carefully. What are the chances of *Golden Dawn* suffering structural failure or crippling breakdown on her maiden voyage – a hundred to one against it? It's that high?'

'That's about right.' Nicholas agreed. 'A hundred to one.'

'What is it going to cost to hold one ocean-going salvage tug on standby, at a lousy 1,500 dollars a day – and then to send another halfway around the world at top of the green?'

Bernard clasped his brow theatrically. 'It's going to cost you a quarter of a million dollars, if you take into consideration the loss of earnings on both vessels – that's the very least it's going to cost you. Don't you have respect for money any longer?'

'Now you understand why I had to stall the Sheikhs,' Nicholas smiled calmly. 'I couldn't shoot their money on a hundred-to-one chance – but it's not their money yet. It's mine. *Sea Witch* and *Warlock* aren't their tugs, they are mine. Peter isn't their son, he's mine.'

'You're serious,' said Bernard incredulously. 'I do believe you are serious.'

'Right,' Nicholas agreed. 'Damned right, I am. Now get a telex off to David Allen and ask him for his estimated time of arrival in Cape Town.'

Samantha Silver had one towel wrapped around her head like a turban. Her hair was still wet from the luxurious shampooing it had just received. She wore the other towel tucked under her armpits, making a short sarong of it. She still glowed all over from the steaming tub and she smelled of soap and talcum powder.

After a long field trip, it took two or three of these soakings and scrubbings to get the salt and the smell of the mangroves out of her pores, and the Everglades mud from under her nails.

She poured the batter into the pan, the oil spitting and crackling with the heat and she sang out, 'How many waffles can you eat?'

He came through from the bathroom, a wet towel wrapped around his waist, and he stood in the doorway and grinned at her. 'How many have you got?' he asked. She had still not accustomed her ear to the Australian twang.

He was burned and brown as she was, and his hair was bleached at the ends, hanging now, wet from the shower, into his face.

They had worked well together, and she had learned much from him. The drift into intimacy had been gradual, but inevitable. In her hurt, she had turned to him for comfort, and also in deliberate spite of Nicholas. But now, if she turned her head away, she would not really be able to remember his features clearly. It took an effort to remember his name – Dennis, of course, Doctor Dennis O'Connor.

She was detached from it all, as though a sheet of armoured glass separated her from the real world. She went through the motions of working and playing, of eating and sleeping, of laughing and loving, but it was all a sham.

Dennis was watching her from the doorway now, with that slightly puzzled expression, the helpless look of a person who watches another one drowning and is powerless to give aid.

Samantha turned away quickly. 'Ready in two minutes,' she said, and he turned back into the bedroom to finish dressing.

She flipped the waffles on to a plate and poured a fresh batch of batter.

Beside her, the telephone rang and she sucked her fingers clean and picked it up with her free hand.

'Sam Silver,' she said.

'Thank God. I've been going out of my mind. What happened to you, darling?'

Her knees went rubbery under her, and she had to sit down quickly on one of the stools.

'Samantha, can you hear me?'

She opened her mouth, but no sound came out.

'Tell me what's happening—' She could see his face before her, clearly, each detail of it so vividly remembered, the clear green eyes below the heavy brow, the line of cheekbone and jaw, and the sound of his voice made her shiver.

'Samantha.'

'How is your wife, Nicholas?' she asked softly – and he broke off. She held the receiver to her ear with both hands, and the silence lasted only a few beats of her heart, but it was long enough. Once or twice, in moments of weakness during the last two weeks, she had tried to convince herself that it was not true. That it had all been the viciousness of a lying woman. Now she knew beyond any question that her instinct had been correct. His silence was the admission, and she waited for the lie that she knew would come next.

'Would it help to tell you I love you?' he asked softly, and she could not answer. Even in her distress, the felt the rush of relief. He had not lied. At that moment it was the most important thing in her life. He had not lied. She felt it begin to tear painfully, deep in her chest. Her shoulders shook spasmodically.

'I'm coming to get you,' he said into the silence.

'I won't be here,' she whispered, but she felt it welling up into her throat, uncontrollably. She had not wept before, she had kept it all safely bottled away – but now, the first sob burst from her, and with both hands she slammed the telephone back on to its cradle.

She stood there still, shaking wildly, and the tears poured down her cheeks and dripped from her chin.

Dennis came into the kitchen behind her, tucking his shirt into the top of his trousers, his hair shiny and wet with the straight lines of the comb through it.

'Who was that?' he asked cheerfully, and then stopped aghast.

'What is it, love?' He started forward again, 'Come on now.'

'Don't touch me, please,' she whispered huskily, and he

stopped again uncertainly. 'We are fresh out of milk,' she said without turning. 'Will you take the van down to the shopping centre?'

By the time Dennis returned, she was dressed and she had rinsed her face and tied a scarf around her head like a gypsy. They chewed cold, unappetizing waffles in silence, until she spoke.

'Dennis, we've got to talk—'

'No,' he smiled at her. 'It's all right, Sam. You don't have to say it. I should have moved on days ago, anyway.'

'Thanks,' she said.

'It was Nicholas, wasn't it?'

She regretted having told him now, but at the time it had been vitally necessary to speak to somebody.

She nodded, and his voice had a sting to it as he went on.

'I'd like to bust that bastard in the mouth.'

'We levelled the score, didn't we?' She smiled, but it was an unconvincing smile, and she didn't try to hold it.

'Sam, I want you to know that for me it was not just another quick shack job.'

'I know that.' Impulsively she reached out and squeezed his hand. 'And thanks for understanding – but is it okay if we don't talk about it any more?'

P eter Berg had twisted round in his safety straps, so that he could press his face to the round perspex window in the fuselage of the big Sikorsky helicopter.

The night was completely, utterly black.

Across the cabin, the Flight Engineer stood in the open doorway, the wind ripping at his bright orange overalls, fluttering them around his body, and he turned and grinned across at the boy, then he made a windmilling gesture with his hand and stabbed downwards with his thumb. It was impossible to speak in the clattering, rushing roar of wind and engine and rotor.

The helicopter banked gently and Peter gasped with excitement as the ship came into view.

She was burning all her lights; tier upon tier, the brilliantly lit floors of her stern quarters rose above the altitude at which the Sikorsky was hovering, and, seeming to reach ahead to the black horizon, the tank deck was outlined with rows of hooded lamps, like the street lamps of a deserted city.

She was so huge that she looked like a city. There seemed to be no end to her, stretched to the horizon and towering into the sky.

The helicopter sank in a controlled sweep towards the white circular target on the heliport, guided down by the engineer in the open doorway. Skilfully the pilot matched his descent to the forward motion of the ultra-tanker, twenty-two knots at top economical – Peter had swotted the figures avidly – and the deck moved with grudging majesty to the scend of the tall Cape rollers pushing in unchecked from across the length of the Atlantic Ocean.

The pilot hovered, judging his approach against the brisk north-westerly crosswind, and from fifty feet Peter could see that the decks were almost level with the surface of the sea, pressed down deeply by the weight of her cargo. Every few seconds, one of the rollers that raced down her length would flip aboard and spread like spilled milk, white and frothy in the deck lights, before cascading back over the side.

Made arrogant and unyielding by her vast bulk, the *Golden Dawn* did not woo the ocean, as other ships do. Instead, her great blunt bows crushed the swells, churning them under or shouldering them contemptuously aside.

Peter had been around boats since before he could walk.

He too was a sea-creature. But though his eye was keen, it was as yet unschooled, so he did not notice the working of the long wide deck.

Sitting beside Peter on the bench seat, Duncan Alexander knew to look for the movement in the hull. He watched the hull twisting and hogging, but so slightly, so barely perceptibly, that Duncan blinked it away, and looked again. From bows to stern she was a mile and a half long, and in essence she was merely four steel pods held together by an elaborate flexible steel scaffolding and driven forward by the mighty propulsion unit in the stern. There was small independent movement of each of the tank pods, so the deck twisted as she rolled, and flexed like a longbow as she took the swells under her. The crest of these swells were a quarter of a mile apart. At any one time, there were four separate wave patterns beneath *Golden Dawn*'s hull, with the peaks thrusting up and the troughs allowing the tremendous dead weight of her cargo to push downwards; the elastic steel groaned and gave to meet these shearing forces.

No hull is ever completely rigid, and elasticity had been part of the ultra-tanker's original design, but those designs had been altered. Duncan Alexander had saved almost two thousand tons of steel, by reducing the stiffening of the central pillar that docked the four pods together, and he had dispensed with the double skins of the pods themselves. He had honed *Golden Dawn* down to the limits at which his own architects had baulked; then he had hired Japanese architects to rework the designs. They had expressed themselves satisfied that the hull was safe, but had also respectfully pointed out that nobody had ever carried a million tons of crude petroleum in a single cargo before.

The helicopter sank the last few feet and bumped gently on to the insulated green deck, with its thick coat of plasticized paint which prevented the striking of spark.

Even a grain of sand trodden between leather sole and bare steel could ignite an explosive air and petroleum gas mixture.

The ship's party swarmed forward, doubled under the swirling rotor. The luggage in its net beneath the fuselage was dragged away and strong hands swung Peter down on to the deck. He stood blinking in the glare of deck lamps and wrinkling his nose to the characteristic tanker stench. It is a smell that pervades everything aboard one of these ships: the food, the furniture, the crew's clothing – even their hair and skin.

It is the thin, acrid chemical stench of under-rich fumes vented off from the tanks. Oxygen and petroleum gas are only explosive in a mixture within narrow limits: too much oxygen makes the blend under-rich and too much petroleum gas makes it over-rich, either of which mixtures are non-explosive, non-combustible.

Chantelle Alexander was handed down next from the cabin of the helicopter, bringing an instant flash of elegance to the starkly lit scene of bleak steel and ugly functional machinery. She wore a catsuit of dark green with a bright Jean Patou scarf on her head. Two ship's officers closed in solicitously on each side of her and led her quickly away towards the towering stern quarters, out of the rude and blustering wind and the helicopter engine roar.

Duncan Alexander followed her down to the deck and shook hands quickly with the First Officer.

'Captain Randle's compliments, sir. He is unable to leave the bridge while the ship is in the inshore channel.'

'I understand.' Duncan flashed that marvellous smile. The great ship drew almost twenty fathoms fully laden and she had come in very close, as close as was prudent to the mountainous coastline of Good Hope with its notorious currents and wild winds. However, Chantelle Christy must not be exposed to the ear-numbing discomfort of the helicopter flight for a moment longer than was necessary, and so *Golden Dawn* had come in through the inner channel, perilously close to the guardian rocks of Robben Island that stood in the open mouth of Table Bay.

Even before the helicopter rose and circled away towards the distant glow of Cape Town city under its dark square mountain, the tanker's great blunt bows were swinging away towards the west, and Duncan imagined the relief of Captain Randle as he gave the order to make the offing into the open Atlantic with the oceanic depths under his cumbersome ship.

Duncan smiled again and reached for Peter Berg's hand.

'Come on, my boy.'

'I'm all right, sir.'

Skilfully Peter avoided the hand and the smile, containing his wild excitement so that he walked ahead like a man, without the skipping energy of a little boy. Duncan Alexander felt the customary flare of annoyance. No, more than that – bare anger at this further rejection by Berg's puppy. They went in single file along the steel catwalk with the child leading. He had never been able to get close to the boy and he had tried hard in the beginning. Now Duncan stopped his anger with the satisfying memory of how neatly he had used the child to slap Berg in the face, and draw the fangs of his opposition.

Berg would be worrying too much about his brat to have time for anything else. He followed Chantelle and the child into the gleaming chrome and plastic corridors of the stern quarters. It was difficult to think of decks and bulkheads rather than floors and walls in here. It was too much like a modern apartment block, even the elevator which bore them swiftly and silently five storeys up to the navigation bridge helped to dispel the feelings of being shipborne.

On the bridge itself, they were so high above the sea as to be divorced from it. The deck lights had been extinguished once the helicopter had gone, and the darkness of the night, silenced by the thick double-glazed windows, heightened the peace and isolation. The riding lights in the bows seemed remote as the very stars, and the gentle lulling movement of the immense hull was only just noticeable.

The Master was a man of Duncan Alexander's own choosing. The command of the flagship of Christy Marine should have gone to Basil Reilly, the senior captain of the fleet. However, Reilly was Berg's man, and Duncan had used the foundering of *Golden Adventurer* to force premature retirement on the old sailor.

Randle was young for the responsibility – just a little over thirty years of age – but his training and his credentials were impeccable, and he was an honours graduate of the tanker school in France. Here top men received realistic training in the specialized handling of these freakish giants in cunningly constructed lakes and scale-model harbours, working thirty-foot models of the bulk carriers that had all the handling characteristics of the real ships.

Since Duncan had given him the command, he had been a staunch ally, and he had stoutly defended the design and construction of his ship when the reporters, whipped up by Nicholas Berg, had questioned him. He was loyal, which weighed heavily, tipping the balance for Duncan against his youth and inexperience.

He hurried to meet his important visitors as they stepped out of the elevator into his spacious, gleaming modern bridge, a short stocky figure with a bull neck and the thrusting heavy jaw of great determination or great stubbornness. His greeting had just the right mixture of warmth and servility, and Duncan noted approvingly that he treated even the boy with careful respect. Randle was bright enough to realize that one day the child would be head of Christy Marine. Duncan liked a man who could think so clearly and so far ahead, but Randle was not quite prepared for Peter Berg.

'Can I see your engine room, Captain?'

'You mean right now?'

'Yes.' For Peter the question was superfluous. 'If you don't mind, sir,' he added quickly. Today was for doing things and tomorrow was lost in the mists of the future. Right now, would be just fine.

'Well now,' the Captain realized the request was deadly serious, and that this lad could not be put off very easily, 'we go on automatic during the night. There's nobody down there now – and it wouldn't be fair to wake the engineer, would it? It's been a hard day.'

'I suppose not.' Bitterly disappointed, but amenable to convincing argument, Peter nodded.

'But I am certain the Chief would be delighted to have you as his guest directly after breakfast.'

The Chief Engineer was a Scot with three sons of his own in Glasgow, the youngest of them almost exactly Peter's age. He was more than delighted. Within twenty-four hours, Peter was the ship's favourite, with his own blue company-issue overalls altered to fit him and his name embroidered across the back by the lascar steward, 'PETER BERG'. He wore his bright yellow plastic hard hat at the same jaunty angle as the Chief did, and carried a wad of cotton waste in his back pocket to wipe his greasy hands after helping one of the stokers clean the fuel filters – the messiest job on board, and the greatest fun.

Although the engine control room with its rough camaraderie, endless supplies of sandwiches and cocoa and satisfying grease and oil that made a man look like a professional, was Peter's favourite station, yet he stood other watches.

Every morning he joined the First Officer on his inspection. Starting in the bows, they worked their way back, checking each of the pod tanks, every valve, and every one of the heavy hydraulic docking clamps that held the pod tanks attached to the main frames of the hull. Most important of all they checked the gauges on each compartment which gave the precise indication of the gas mixtures contained in the air spaces under the main deck of the crude tanks.

Golden Dawn operated on the 'inert' system to keep the trapped fumes in an over-rich and safe condition. The exhaust fumes of the ship's engine were caught, passed through filters and scrubbers to remove the corrosive sulphur elements and then, as almost pure carbon dioxide and carbon monoxide, they were forced into the air spaces of the petroleum tanks. The evaporating fumes of the volatile elements of the crude mingled with the exhaust fumes to form an over-rich, oxygen-poor, and unexplosive gas.

However, a leak through one of the hundreds of valves and connections would allow air into the tanks, and the checks to detect this were elaborate, ranging from an unceasing electronic monitoring of each tank to the daily physical inspection, in which Peter now assisted.

Peter usually left the First Officer's party when it returned to the stern quarters, he might then pass the time of day with the two-man crew in the central pump room.

From here the tanks were monitored and controlled, loaded and offloaded, the flow of inert gas balanced, and the crude petroleum could be pushed through the giant centrifugal pumps and transferred from tank to tank to make alterations to the ship's trim, during partial discharge, or when one or more tanks were detached and taken inshore for discharge.

In the pump room was kept a display that always fascinated Peter. It was the sample cupboard with its rows of screw-topped bottles, each containing samples of the cargo taken during loading. As all four of *Golden Dawn*'s tanks had been filled at the same offshore loading point and all with crude from the same field, each of the bottles bore the identical label.

EL BARRAS CRUDE

BUNKERS 'C'

HIGH CADMIUM

Peter liked to take one of the bottles and hold it to the light. Somehow he had always expected the crude oil to be treacly and tar-like, but it was thin as human blood and when he shook the bottle, it coated the glass and the light through it was dark red, again like congealing blood.

'Some of the crudes are black, some yellow and the Nigerians are green,' the pump foreman told him. 'This is the first red that I've seen.'

'I suppose it's the cadmium in it,' Peter told him.

'Guess it is,' the foreman agreed seriously; all on board had very soon learned not to talk down to Peter Berg. He expected to be treated on equal terms.

By this time it was mid-morning and Peter had worked up enough appetite to visit the gallery, where he was greeted like visiting royalty. Within days, Peter knew his way unerringly through the labyrinthine and usually deserted passageways. It was characteristic of these great crude-carriers that you might wander through them for hours without meeting another human being. With their huge bulk and their tiny crews, the only place where there was always human presence was the navigation bridge on the top floor of the stern quarters.

The bridge was always one of Peter's obligatory stops.

'Good morning, Tug,' the officer of the watch would greet him. Peter had been christened with his nickname when he had announced at the breakfast table on his first morning:

'Tankers are great, but I'm going to be a tug captain, like my dad.'

On the bridge the ship might be taken out of automatic to allow Peter to spell the helmsman for a while, or he would assist the junior deck officers while they made a sun shot as an exercise to check against the satellite navigational Decca; then, after socializing with Captain Randle for a while, it was time to report to his true station in the engine.

'We were waiting on you, Tug,' growled the Chief. 'Get your overalls on, man, we're going down the propeller shaft tunnel.'

The only unpleasant period of the day was when Peter's mother insisted that he scrub off the top layers of grease and fuel oil, dress in his number ones, and act as an unpaid steward during the cocktail hour in the elaborate lounge of the owner's suite.

It was the only time that Chantelle Alexander fraternized with the ship's officers and it was a painfully stilted hour, with Peter one of the major sufferers – but the rest of the time he was successful in avoiding the clinging restrictive rulings of his mother and the fiercely hated but silently resented presence of Duncan Alexander, his stepfather.

Still, he was instinctively aware of the new and disturbing tensions between his mother and Duncan Alexander. In the night he heard the raised voices from the master cabin, and he strained to catch the words. Once, when he had heard the cries of his mother's distress, he had left his bunk and gone barefooted to knock on the cabin door. Duncan Alexander had opened it to him. He was in a silk dressing gown and his handsome features were swollen and flushed with anger.

'Go back to bed.'

'I want to see my mother,' Peter had told him quietly.

'You need a damned good hiding,' Duncan had flared. 'Now do as you are told.'

'I want to see my mother.' Peter had stood his ground, standing very straight in his pyjamas with both his tone and expression neutral, and Chantelle had come to him in her nightdress and knelt to embrace him.

'It's all right, darling. It's perfectly all right.' But she had been weeping. After that there had been no more loud voices in the night.

However, except for an hour in the afternoon, when the swimming pool was placed out of bounds to officers and crew, while Chantelle swam and sunbathed, she spent the rest of the time in the owner's suite, eating all her meals there, withdrawn and silent, sitting at the panoramic windows of her cabin, coming to life only for an hour in the evenings while she played the owner's wife to the ship's officers.

Duncan Alexander, on the other hand, was like a caged animal. He paced the open decks, composing long messages which were sent off regularly over the telex in company code to Christy Marine in Leadenhall Street.

Then he would stand out on the open wing of *Golden Dawn*'s bridge, staring fixedly ahead at the northern horizon, awaiting the reply to his last telex, chafing openly at having to conduct the company's business at such long remove, and goaded by the devils of doubt and impatience and fear.

Often it seemed as though he were trying to forge the mighty hull onwards, faster and faster into the north, by the sheer power of his will.

In the north-western corner of the Caribbean basin, there is an area of shallow warm water, hemmed in on one side by the island chain of the Great Antilles, the bulwark of Cuba and Hispaniola, while in the west the sweep of the Yucatan peninsula runs south through Panama into the great land-mass of South America – shallow, warm, trapped water and saturated tropical air, enclosed by land masses which can heat very rapidly in the high hot sun of the tropics. However, all of it is gently cooled and moderated by the benign influence of the north-easterly trade winds – winds so unvarying in strength and direction that over the centuries, seafaring men have placed their lives and their fortunes at risk upon their balmy wings, gambling on the constancy of that vast moving body of mild air.

But the wind does fail; for no apparent reason and without previous warning, it dies away, often merely for an hour or two, but occasionally – very occasionally – for days or weeks at a time.

Far to the south and east of this devil's spawning ground, the *Golden Dawn* ploughed massively on through the sweltering air and silken calm of the doldrums, northwards across the equator, changing course every few hours to maintain the great circle track that would carry her well clear of that glittering shield of islands that the Caribbean carries, like an armoured knight, on its shoulder.

The treacherous channels and passages through the islands were not for a vessel of *Golden Dawn*'s immense bulk, deep draught and limited manoeuvrability. She was to go high above the Tropic of Cancer, and just south of the island of Bermuda she would make her westings and enter the wider and safer waters of the Florida Straits above Grand Bahamas. On this course, she would be constricted by narrow and shallow seaways for only a few hundred miles before she was out into the open waters of the Gulf of Mexico again.

But while she ran on northwards, out of the area of

equatorial calm, she should have come out at last into the sweet cool airs of the trades, but she did not. Day after day, the calm persisted, and stifling still air pressed down on the ship. It did not in any way slow or affect her passage, but her Master remarked to Duncan Alexander:

'Another corker today, by the looks of it.'

When he received no reply from his brooding, silent Chairman, he retired discreetly, leaving Duncan alone on the open wing of the bridge, with only the breeze of the ship's passage ruffling his thick coppery hair.

However, the calm was not merely local. It extended westwards in a wide, hot belt across the thousand islands and the basin of shallow sea they enclosed.

The calm lay heavily on the oily waters, and the sun beat down on the enclosing land masses. Every hour the air heated and sucked up the evaporating waters; a fat bubble like a swelling blister began to rise, the first movement of air in many days. It was not a big bubble, only a hundred miles across, but as it rose, the rotation of the earth's surface began to twist the rising air, spinning it like a top, so that the satellite cameras, hundreds of miles above, recorded a creamy little spiral wisp like the decorative-icing flower on a wedding cake.

The cameras relayed the picture through many channels, until at last it reached the desk of the senior forecaster of the hurricane watch at the meteorological headquarters at Miami in southern Florida.

'Looks like a ripe one,' he grunted to his assistant, recognizing that all the favourable conditions for the formation of a revolving tropical storm were present. 'We'll ask air force for a fly-through.'

At forty-five thousand feet the pilot of the US Air Force B52 saw the rising dome of the storm from two hundred miles away. It had grown enormously in only six hours.

As the warm saturated air was forced upwards, so the icy cold of the upper troposphere condensed the water vapour into thick, puffed-up silver clouds. They boiled upwards, roiling and swirling upon themselves. Already the dome of cloud and ferociously turbulent air was higher than the aircraft.

Under it, a partial vacuum was formed, and the surrounding surface air tried to move in to fill it. But it was compelled into an anticlockwise track around the centre by the mysterious forces of the earth's rotation. Compelled to travel the long route, the velocity of the air mass accelerated ferociously, and the entire system became more unstable, more dangerous by the hour, turning faster, perpetuating itself by creating greater wind velocities and steeper pressure gradients.

The cloud at the top of the enormous rising dome reached an altitude where the temperature was thirty degrees below freezing and the droplets of rain turned to crystals of ice and were smeared away by upper-level jetstreams. Long, beautiful patterns of cirrus against the high blue sky were blown hundreds of miles ahead of the storm to serve as its heralds.

The US Air Force B52 hit the first clear-air turbulence one hundred and fifty miles from the storm's centre. It was as though an invisible predator had seized the fuselage and shaken it until the wings were almost torn from their roots, and in one surge, the aircraft was flung five thousand feet straight upwards.

'Very severe turbulence,' the pilot reported. 'We have vertical wind speeds of three hundred miles an hour plus.'

The senior forecaster in Miami picked up the telephone and called the computer programmer on the floor above him. 'Ask Charlie for a hurricane code name.'

And a minute later the programmer called him back. 'Charlie says to call the bitch "Lorna".'

Six hundred miles south-west of Miami the storm began to move forward, slowly at first but every hour gathering power, spiralling upon itself at unbelievable velocities, its high dome swelling upwards now through fifty thousand feet and still climbing. The centre of the storm opened like a flower, the calm eye extended upwards in a vertical tunnel with smooth walls of solid cloud rising to the very summit of the dome, now sixty thousand feet above the surface of the wind-tortured sea.

The entire mass began to move faster, back towards the east, in a directly contrary direction to the usual track of the gentle trade winds. Spinning and roaring upon itself, devouring everything in its path, the she-devil called Lorna launched itself across the Caribbean Sea.

Nicholas Berg turned his head to look down upon the impressive skyline of Miami Beach. The rampart of tall, elegant hotel buildings followed the curve of the beach into the north, and behind it lay the ugly sprawled tangle of urban development and snarled highways.

The Eastern Airlines direct flight from Bermuda turned on to its base leg and then on to the final approach, losing height over the beach and Biscayne Bay.

Nicholas felt uncomfortable, the nagging of guilt and uncertainty. His guilt was of two kinds. He felt guilty that he had deserted his post at the moment when he was likely to be desperately needed.

Ocean Salvage's two vessels were out there somewhere in the Atlantic, *Warlock* running hard up the length of the Atlantic in a desperate attempt to catch up with *Golden Dawn*, while Jules Levoisin in *Sea Witch* was now approaching the eastern seaboard of America where he would refuel before going on to his assignment as standby tug on the exploration field in the Gulf of Mexico. At any moment, the Master of either vessel might urgently need to have his instructions.

Then there was *Golden Dawn*. She had rounded the Cape of Good Hope almost three weeks ago. Since then, even Bernard Wackie had been unable to fix her position. She had not been reported by other craft, and any communications she had made with Christy Main must have been by satellite telex, for she had maintained strict silence on the radio channels. However, she must rapidly be nearing the most critical part of her voyage when she turned west and began her approach to the continental shelf of North America and the passage of the islands into the Gulf. Peter Berg was on board that monster, and Nicholas felt the chill of guilt. His place was at the centre, in the control room of Bach Wackie on the top floor of the Bank of Bermuda building in Hamilton town. His post was there where he could assess changing conditions and issue instant commands to coordinate his salvage tugs.

Now he had deserted his post, and even though he had made arrangements to maintain contact with Bernard Wackie, still it would take him hours, perhaps even days, to get back to where he was needed, if there was an emergency.

But then there was Samantha. His instincts warned him that every day, every hour he delayed in going to her would reduce his chances of having her again.

There was more guilt there, the guilt of betrayal. It was no help to tell himself that he had made no marriage vows to Samantha Silver, that his night of weakness with Chantelle had been forced upon him in circumstances almost impossible to resist, that any other man in his position would have done the same, and that in the end the episode had been a catharsis and a release that had left him free for ever of Chantelle.

To Samantha, it had been betrayal, and he knew that much was destroyed by it. He felt terrible aching guilt, not for the act – sexual intercourse without love is fleeting and insignificant – but for the betrayal and for the damage he had wrought.

Now he was uncertain, uncertain as to just how much he had destroyed, how much was left for him to build upon. All that he was certain of was that he needed her, more than he had needed anything in his life. She was still the promise of eternal youth and of the new life towards which he was groping so uncertainly. If love was needing, then he loved Samantha Silver with something close to desperation.

She had told him she would not be there when he came. He had to hope now that she had lied. He felt physically sick at the thought that she meant it.

He had only a single Louis Vuitton overnight valise as cabin luggage so he passed swiftly through customs, and as he went into the telephone booths, he checked his watch. It was after six o'clock; she'd be home by now.

He had dialled the first four digits of her number before he checked himself.

'What the hell am I phoning for?' he asked himself grimly. 'To tell her I'm here, so she can have a flying start when she runs for the bushes?'

There is nothing so doomed as a timid lover. He dropped the receiver back on its cradle, and went for the Hertz desk at the terminal doors.

'What's the smallest you've got?' he asked.

'A Cougar,' the pretty blonde in the yellow uniform told him. In America, 'small' is a relative term. He was just lucky she hadn't offered him a Sherman tank.

The brightly painted Chevy van was in the lean-to shelter under the spread branches of the ficus tree, and he parked the Cougar's nose almost touching its tailgate. There was no way she could escape now, unless she went out through the far wall of the shed. Knowing her, that was always a possibility, he grinned mirthlessly.

He knocked once on the screen door of the kitchen and went straight in. There was a coffee pot beside the range, and he touched it as he passed. It was still warm.

He went through into the living room, and called:

'Samantha!'

The bedroom door was ajar. He pushed it open. There was a suit of denims, and some pale transparent wisps of underwear thrown carelessly over the patchwork quilt.

The shack was deserted. He went down the steps of the front stoop and straight on to the beach. The tide had swept the sand smooth, and her prints were the only ones. She had dropped her towel above the high-water mark but he had to shade his eyes against the ruddy glare of the lowering sun before he could make out her bobbing head – five hundred yards out.

He sat down beside her towel in the fluffy dry sand and lit a cheroot.

He waited, while the sun settled in a wild, fiery flood of light, and he lost the shape of her head against the darkening sea. She was half a mile out now, but he felt no urgency, and the darkness was almost complete when she rose suddenly, waist-deep from the edge of the gentle surf, waded ashore and came up the beach, twisting the rope of her hair over one shoulder to wring the water from it.

Nicholas felt his heart flop over and he flicked the cheroot away and stood up. She halted abruptly, like a startled forest animal, and stood completely still, staring uncertainly at the tall, dark figure before her. She was so young and slim and smooth and beautiful.

'What do you want?' she faltered.

'You,' he said.

'Why? Are you starting a harem?' Her voice hardened and she straightened; he could not see the expression of her eyes, but her shoulders took on a stubborn set.

He stepped forward and she was rigid in his arms and her lips hard and tightly unresponsive under his.

'Sam, there are things I'll never be able to explain. I don't even understand them myself, but what I do know very clearly is that I love you, that without you my life is going to be flat and plain goddamned miserable—'

There was no relaxation of the rigid muscles. Her hands were still held stiffly at her sides and her body felt cold and wet and unyielding.

'Samantha, I wish I were perfect – I'm not. But all I am sure of is that I can't make it without you.'

'I couldn't take it again. I couldn't live through this again,' she said tightly.

'I need you. I am certain of that,' he insisted.

'You'd better be, you son of a bitch. You cheat on me one time more and you won't have anything left to cheat with – I'll take it off clean, at the roots.' Then she was clinging to him. 'Oh God, Nicholas, how I hated you, and how I missed you – and how long you took to come back,' and her lips were soft and tasted of the sea.

He picked her up and carried her up through the soft sand. He didn't trust himself to speak. It would be so easy to say the wrong thing now.

'Nicholas, I've been sitting here waiting for your call.' Bernard Wackie's voice was sharp and alert, the tension barely contained. 'How soon can you get yourself back here?'

'What is it?'

'It is starting to pop. I've got to hand it to you, baby, you've got a nose for it. You smelled this coming.'

'Come on, Bernie!' Nicholas snapped.

'This call is going through three open exchanges,' Bernie told him. 'You want chapter and verse, or did nobody ever tell you that it's a tough game you are in? There is a lot of competition cluttering up the scene. The cheese-heads have one lying handy.' Probably *Wittezee* or one of the other big Dutch tugs, Nicholas thought swiftly. 'They could be streaming a towing wire within a couple of days. And the Yanks are pretty hot numbers. McCormick has one stationed in the Hudson River.'

'All right,' Nick cut through the relish with which Bernie was detailing the threat of hovering competition.

'There is a direct flight at seven tomorrow morning – if I can't make that, I'll connect with the British Airways flight from Nassau at noon tomorrow. Meet me,' Nick ordered.

'You shouldn't have gone running off,' said Bernard Wackie, showing amazing hindsight. Before he could deliver any more pearls of wisdom, Nicholas hung up on him.

Samantha was sitting up in the centre of the bed. She was stark naked, but she hugged her knees to her chest with both arms, and under the gorgeous tangle of her hair her face was desolate as that of a lost child and her green eyes haunted.

'You're going again,' she said softly. 'You only just came, and now you're going again. Oh God, Nicholas, loving you is the toughest job I've ever had in my life. I don't think I have got the muscle for it.'

He reached for her quickly and she clung to him, pressing her face into the thick pad of coarse dark hair that covered his chest.

'I have to go – I think it's *Golden Dawn*,' he said, and she listened quietly while he told it to her. Only when he finished speaking did she begin to ask the questions which kept them talking quietly, locked in each other's arms in the old brass bed, until long after midnight.

She insisted on cooking his breakfast for him, even though it was still dark outside and she was more than half asleep, hanging on to the range for support and turning up the early morning radio show so that the music might shake her awake.

'Good morning, early birds, this is WWOK with another lovely day ahead of you. A predicted 85° at Fort Lauderdale and the coast, and 80° inland with a 10 per cent chance of rain. We've got a report on Hurricane Lorna for you also. She's dipping away south, towards the lesser Antilles – so we can all relax, folks – relax and listen to Elton John.'

'I love Elton John,' Samantha said sleepily. 'Don't you?'

'Who is he?' Nicholas asked.

'There! I knew right away we had a lot in common.' She blinked at him owlishly. 'Did you kiss me good morning? I forget.'

'Come here,' he instructed. 'You're not going to forget this one.'

Then, a few minutes later, 'Nicholas, you'll miss your plane.'

'Not if I cut breakfast.'

'It would have been a grotty breakfast anyway.' She was coming awake fast now.

She gave him the last kiss through the open window of the Cougar. 'You've got an hour – you'll just about make it.'

He started the engine and still she held on to the sill.

'Nicholas, one day we will be together – I mean all the time, like we planned? You and me doing our own thing, our own way? We will, won't we?'

'It's a promise.'

'Hurry back,' she said, and he gunned the Cougar up the sandy driveway without looking back.

There were eight of them crowded into Tom Parker's office. Although there was only seating for three, the others found perches against the tiered shelves with their rows of biological specimens in bottles of formaldehyde or on the piles of reference books and white papers that were stacked against the walls.

Samantha sat on the corner of Tom's desk, swinging her long denim-clad legs, and answered the questions that were fired at her.

'How do you know she will take the passage of the Florida Straits?'

'It's an educated guess. She's just too big and clumsy to thread the needle of the islands.' Samantha's replies were quick. 'Nicholas is betting on it.'

'I'll go along with that then,' Tom grunted.

'The Straits are a hundred miles wide—'

'I know what you're going to say,' Samantha smiled, and turned to one of the other girls. 'Sally-Anne will answer that one.'

'You all know my brother is in the Coast Guard – all traffic through the Straits reports to Fort Lauderdale,' she explained. 'And the coastguard aircraft patrol out as far as Grand Bahama.'

'We'll have a fix on her immediately she enters the Straits – we've got the whole US Coast Guard rooting for us.'

They argued and discussed for ten minutes more, before Tom Parker slapped an open palm on the desk in front of him and they subsided reluctantly into silence.

'Okay,' he said. 'Do I understand the proposal to be that this Chapter of Greenpeace intercepts the tanker carrying cad-rich crudes before it enters American territorial waters and attempts to delay or divert the ship?'

'That's exactly it,' Samantha nodded, and looked about her for support. They were all nodding and murmuring in agreement.

'What are we trying to achieve? Do we truly believe that we will be able to hold up the delivery of toxic crudes to the refinery at Galveston? Let's define our objectives,' Tom insisted.

'In order for evil men to triumph it is necessary only that good men do nothing. We are doing something.'

'Bullshit, Sam,' Tom growled. 'Let's cut down on the rhetoric – it's one of the things that does us more harm than good. You talk like a nut and you discredit yourself before you have begun.'

'All right,' Samantha grinned. 'We are publicizing the dangers, and our opposition to them.'

'Okay,' Tom nodded. 'That's better. What are our other objectives?'

They discussed that for twenty minutes more, and then Tom Parker took over again.

'Fine, now how do we get out there in the Straits to confront this vessel – do we put on our waterwings and swim?'

Even Samantha looked sheepish now. She glanced around for support, but the others were studying their fingernails or gazing with sudden fascination out of the windows.

'Well,' Samantha began, and then hesitated. 'We thought—'

'Go on,' Tom encouraged her. 'Of course, you weren't thinking of using University property, were you? There is actually a law in this country against taking other people's ships – it's called piracy.'

'As a matter of fact—' Samantha gave a helpless shrug.

'And as a senior and highly respected member of the faculty, you would not expect me to be party to a criminal act.'

They were all silent, watching Samantha, for she was their leader, but for once she was at a loss.

'On the other hand, if a party of graduate researchers

put in a requisition, through the proper channels, I would be quite happy to authorize an extended field expedition across the Straits to Grand Bahama on board the *Dicky*.'

'Tom, you're a darling,' said Samantha.

'That's a hell of a way to speak to your Professor,' said Tom, and scowled happily at her.

'They came in on the British Airways flight from Heathrow yesterday afternoon. Three of them; here is a list of the names,' Bernard Wackie slid a notepad across the desk, and Nicholas glanced at it quickly.

'Charles Gras – I know him, he's Chief Engineer at Construction Navale Atlantique,' Nicholas explained.

'Right,' Bernard nodded. 'He gave his occupation and employer to Immigration.'

'Isn't that privileged information?'

Bernard grinned. 'I keep my ear to the ground,' and then he was deadly serious again. 'All right, so these three engineers have a small suitcase each and a crate in the hold that weighs three hundred and fifty kilos, and it's marked "Industrial Machinery".'

'Don't stop now,' Nicholas encouraged him.

'And there is an S61N Sikorsky helicopter sitting waiting for them on the tarmac. The helicopter has been chartered direct from London by Christy Marine of Leadenhall Street. The three engineers and the case of machinery are shuttled aboard the Sikorsky so fast that it looks like a conjuring trick, and she takes off and egg-beats for the south.'

'Did the Sikorsky pilot file a flight-plan?'

'Sure did. Servicing shipping, course 196° magnetic. ETA to be reported.'

'What's the range of the 61N – 500 nautical miles?'

418

'Not bad,' Bernard conceded. '533 for the standard, but this model has long-range tanks. She's good for 750. But that's one way, not the return journey. The helicopter hasn't returned to Bermuda yet.'

'She could refuel aboard – or, if they aren't carrying avgas, she could stay on until final destination,' Nicholas said. 'What else have you got?'

'You want more?' Bernard looked aghast. 'Doesn't anything ever satisfy you?'

'Did you monitor the communications between Bermuda Control, the chopper, and the ship she was servicing?'

'Nix,' Bernard shook his head. 'There was a box-up.' He looked shamefaced. 'It happens to the best of us.'

'Spare me the details. Can you get information from Bermuda Control of the time the chopper closed her flight-plan?'

'Jesus, Nicholas, you know better than that. It's an offence to listen in on the aviation frequencies, let alone ask them.'

Nicholas jumped up, and crossed swiftly to the perspex plot. He brooded over it, leaning on clenched fists, his expression smouldering as he studied the large-scale map.

'What does all this mean to you, Nicholas?' Bernard came to stand beside him.

'It means that a vessel at sea, belonging to the Christy Marine fleet, has requested its head office to send machinery spares and specialist personnel by the fastest possible means, without regard to expense. Have you figured the air freight on a package of 350 kilos?'

Nicholas straightened up and groped for the crocodile-skin cheroot case.

'It means that the vessel is broken down or in imminent danger of breakdown somewhere in an area south-west of Bermuda, within an arc of four hundred and fifty miles –

probably much closer, otherwise she would have requested service from the Bahamas, and it's highly unlikely they would have operated the chopper at extreme range.'

'Right,' Bernard agreed. Nicholas lit his cheroot and they were both silent a moment.

'A hell of a small needle in a bloody big haystack,' said Bernard.

'You let me worry about that,' Nicholas murmured, still without taking his eyes from the plot.

'That's what you are paid for,' Bernard agreed amiably. 'it's Golden Dawn, isn't it?'

'Has Christy Marine got any other vessels in the area?'

'Not as far as I know.'

'Then that was a bloody stupid question.'

'Take it easy, Nicholas.'

'I'm sorry.' Nicholas touched his arm. 'My boy's on that pig.' He took a deep draw on the cheroot, held it a moment, and then slowly exhaled. His voice was calm and businesslike, as he went on:

'What's our weather?'

'Wind at 060° and 15 knots. Cloud three eighths stratocumulus at four thousand feet. Long-range projection, no change.'

'Steady trade winds again,' Nicholas nodded. 'Thank God for all small mercies.'

'There is a hurricane warning out, as you know, but on its present position and track, it will blow itself out to sea a thousand miles south of Grand Bahama.'

'Good,' Nicholas nodded again. 'Please ask both Warlock and Sea Witch to report their positions, course, speed and fuel conditions.'

Bernard had the two telex flimsies for him within twenty minutes.

'Warlock has made a good run of it,' Nicholas murmured, as the position of the tug was marked on the plot.

'She crossed the equator three days ago,' said Bernard.

420

'And *Sea Witch* will reach Charleston late tomorrow,' Nicholas observed. 'Are any of the opposition inside us?'

Bernard shook his head. 'McCormick has one in New York and *Wittezee* is halfway back to Rotterdam.'

'We are in good shape,' Nicholas decided, as he balanced the triangles of relative speeds and distances between the vessels.

'Is there another chopper available on the island to get me out to *Warlock?*'

'No,' Bernard shook his head. 'The 61N is the only one based on Bermuda.'

'Can you arrange bunkering for *Warlock*, I mean immediate bunkering – here in Hamilton?'

'We can have her tanks filled an hour after she comes in.'

Nicholas paused and then made the decision. 'Please telex David Allen on *Warlock*, TO MASTER WARLOCK FROM BERG IMMEDIATE AND URGENT NEW SPEED TOP OF THE GREEN NEW COURSE HAMILTON HARBOUR BERMUDA ISLAND DIRECT REPORT EXPECTED TIME OF ARRIVAL ENDS.'

'You're going to run, then?' Bernard asked. 'You are going to run with both your ships?'

'Yes,' Nicholas nodded. 'I'm running with everything I've got.'

Golden Dawn wallowed with the dead heavy weight of one million tons of crude oil. Her motion was that of a waterlogged hulk. Broadside to the set of the swells, her tank decks were almost awash. The low seas broke against her starboard rail and the occasional crest flopped over and spread like pretty patches of white lace-work over the green plastic-coated decks.

She had been drifting powerlessly for four days now.

The main bearing of the single propeller shaft had begun to run hot forty-eight hours after crossing the equator, and the Chief Engineer had asked for shutdown to inspect the bearing and effect any repairs. Duncan Alexander had forbidden any shutdown, overriding the good judgement of both his Master and Chief Engineer, and had only grudgingly agreed to a reduction in the ship's speed.

He ordered the Chief Engineer to trace any fault and to effect what repairs he could, while under reduced power.

Within four hours, the Chief had traced the damaged and leaking gland in the pump that force-lubricated the bearing, but even the running under reduced power setting had done significant damage to the main bearing, and now there was noticeable vibration, jarring even *Golden Dawn*'s massive hull.

'I have to get the pump stripped down or we'll burn her clear out,' the Chief faced up to Duncan Alexander at last. 'Then you'll *have* to shut down and not just a couple of hours either. It will take two days to fit new bearing shells at sea.' The Chief was pale and his lips trembled, for he knew of this man's reputation. The engineer knew that he discarded those who crossed him, and he had the reputation of a special vindictiveness to hound a man until he was broken. The Chief was afraid, but his concern for the ship was just strong enough.

Duncan Alexander changed direction. 'What was the cause of the pump failure in the first place? Why wasn't it noticed earlier? It looks like a case of negligence to me.'

Stung at last, the Chief blurted out, 'If there had been a back-up pump on this ship, we could have switched to secondary system and done proper maintenance.'

Duncan Alexander flushed and turned away. The modifications he had personally ordered to *Golden Dawn*'s design had excluded most of the duplicated back-up systems; anything that kept down the cost of construction had been ordered.

422

'How long do you need?' He stopped in the centre of the owner's stateroom and glared at his engineer.

'Four hours,' the Scot replied promptly.

'You've got exactly four hours,' he said grimly. 'If you haven't finished by then you will live to regret it. I swear that to you.'

While the engineer stopped his engines, stripped, repaired and reassembled the lubrication pump, Duncan was on the bridge with the Master.

'We've lost time, too much time,' he said. 'I want that made up.'

'It will mean pushing over best economic speed,' Captain Randle warned carefully.

'Captain Randle, the value of our cargo is 85 dollars a ton. We have on board one million tons. I want the time made up.' Duncan brushed his objection aside. 'We have a deadline to meet in Galveston roads. This ship, this whole concept of carrying crude is on trial, Captain. I don't have to keep reminding you of that. The hell with the costs, I want to meet the deadline.'

'Yes, Mr Alexander,' Randle nodded. 'We'll make up the time.'

Three and a half hours later, the Chief Engineer came up to the bridge.

'Well?' Duncan turned on him fiercely as he stepped out of the elevator.

'The pump is repaired, but—'

'What is it, man?'

'I've got a feeling. We ran her too long. I've got a nasty feeling about that bearing. It wouldn't be clever to run her over 50 per cent of power, not until it's been taken down and inspected—'

'I'm ordering revolutions for 25 knots,' Randle told him uneasily.

'I wouldn't do that, man,' the Chief shook his head rather mournfully.

'Your station is in the engine room,' Duncan dismissed him brusquely, nodded to Randle to order resumption of sailing, and went out to his customary place on the open wing of the bridge. He looked back over the high round stern as the white turbulence of the great propeller boiled out from under the counter and then settled in a long slick wake that soon reached back to the horizon. Duncan stood out in the wind until after dark, and when he went below, Chantelle was waiting for him. She stood up from the long couch under the forward windows of the stateroom.

'We are under way again.'

'Yes,' he said. 'It's going to be all right.'

The engine control was switched to automatic at nine o'clock local time that night. The engine room personnel went up to dinner, and to bed, all except the Chief Engineer. He lingered for another two hours shaking his head and mumbling bitterly over the massive bearing assembly in the long, narrow shaft tunnel. Every few minutes, he laid his hand on the massive casting, feeling for the heat and vibration that would warn of structural damage.

At eleven o'clock, he spat on the steadily revolving propeller shaft. It was thick as an oak trunk and polished brilliant silver in the stark white lights of the tunnel. He pushed himself up stiffly from his crouch beside the bearing.

In the control room, he checked again that all the ship's systems were on automatic, and that all circuits were functioning and repeating on the big control board, then he stepped into the elevator and went up.

Thirty-five minutes later, one of the tiny transistors in the board blew with a pop like a champagne cork and a puff of grey smoke. There was nobody in the control room to hear or see it. The system was not duplicated, there was no back-up to switch itself in automatically, so that when the temperature of the bearing began to rise again, there was no impulse carried to the alarm system, no automatic shutdown of power.

The massive shaft spun on while the overheated bearing closed its grip upon the area of rough metal, damaged by the previous prolonged running. A fine sliver of metal lifted from the polished surface of the spinning shaft, and curled like a silver hairspring, was caught up and smeared into the bearing. The whole assembly began to glow a sullen cherry red and then the oxide paint that was daubed on the outer surfaces of the bearing began to blister and blacken. Still the tremendous power of the engine forced the shaft around.

What oil was still being fed between the glowing surfaces of the spinning shaft and the shells of the bearing turned instantly thin as water in the heat, then reached its flash-point and burst into flame and ran in little fiery rivulets down the heavy casting of the main bearing, flashing the blistered paintwork alight. The shaft tunnel filled with thick billows of stinking chemical-tainted smoke, and only then did the fire sensors come to life and their alarms repeated on the navigation bridge and in the quarters of Master, First Officer and Chief Engineer.

But the great engine was still pounding along at 70 per cent of power, and the shaft still turned in the disintegrating bearing, smearing heat-softened metal, buckling and distorting under unbearable strains.

The Chief Engineer was the first to reach the central console in the engine control room, and without orders from the bridge he began emergency shutdown of all systems.

It was another hour before the team under the direction of the First Officer had the fire in the shaft tunnel under control. They used carbon dioxide gas to smother the burning paint and oil, for cold water on the heated metal would have aggravated the damage done by heat distortion and buckling.

The metal of the main bearing casting was still so hot when the Chief Engineer began opening it up, that it scorched the thick leather and asbestos gloves worn by his team.

The bearing shells had disintegrated, and the shaft itself was brutally scored and pitted. If there was distortion, the Chief knew it would not be detected by eye. However, even a buckling of one ten thousandth of an inch would be critical.

He cursed softly as he worked, making the obscenities sound like a lullaby; he cursed the manufacturers of the lubricating pump, the men who had installed and tested it, the damaged gland and the lack of a back-up system, but mostly he cursed the stubbornness and intractability of the Chairman of Christy Marine whose ill-advised judgement had turned this functionally beautiful machinery into blackened, smoking twisted metal.

It was mid-morning by the time the Chief had the spare bearing shells brought up from stores and unpacked from their wood shavings in the wooden cases; but it was only when they came to fit them that they realized that the cases had been incorrectly stencilled. The half-shells that they contained were obsolete non-metric types, and they were five millimetres undersized for *Golden Dawn*'s shaft; that tiny variation in size made them utterly useless.

It was only then that Duncan Alexander's steely urbane control began to crack; he raged about the bridge for twenty minutes, making no effort to think his way out of the predicament, but abusing Randle and his engineer in wild and extravagant terms. His rage had a paralysing effect on all *Golden Dawn*'s officers and they stood white-faced and silently guilty.

Peter Berg had sensed the excitement and slipped up

unobtrusively to watch. He was fascinated by his stepfather's rage. He had never seen a display like it before, and at one stage he hoped that Duncan Alexander's eyeballs might actually burst like overripe grapes; he held his breath in anticipation, and felt cheated when it did not happen.

At last, Duncan stopped and ran both hands through his thick waving hair; two spikes of hair stood up like devil's horns. He was still panting, but he had recovered partial control.

'Now sir, what do you propose?' he demanded of Randle, and in the silence Peter Berg piped up.

'You could have new shells sent from Bermuda – it's only three hundred miles away. We checked it this morning.'

'How did you get in here?' Duncan swung round. 'Get back to your mother.'

Peter scampered, appalled at his own indiscretion, and only when he left the bridge did the Chief speak.

'We could have spares flown out from London to Bermuda—'

'There must be a boat—' Randle cut in swiftly.

'Or an aircraft to drop it to us—'

'Or a helicopter—'

'Get Christy Main on the telex,' snapped Duncan Alexander fiercely.

I t was good to have a deck under his feet again, Nicholas exulted. He felt himself coming fully alive again.

'I'm a sea-creature,' he grinned to himself. 'And I keep forgetting it.'

He looked back to the low silhouette of the Bermuda islands, the receding arms of Hamilton Harbour and the flecking of the multicoloured buildings amongst the cedar trees, and then returned his attention to the spread charts on the navigation table before him.

Warlock was still at cautionary speed. Even though the channel was wide and clearly buoyed, yet the coral reef on each hand was sharp and hungry, and David Allen's full attention was on the business of conning *Warlock* out into the open sea. But as they passed the 100 fathom line, he gave the order to his deck officer,

'Full away at 0900 hours, pilot,' and hurried across to join Nicholas.

'I didn't have much of a chance to welcome you on board, sir.'

'Thank you, David. It's good to be back.' Nicholas looked up and smiled at him. 'Will you bring her round on to 240° magnetic and increase to 80 per cent power?'

Quickly David repeated his order to the helm and then shifted from one foot to the other, beginning to flush under the salt-water tan.

'Mr Berg, my officers are driving me mad. They've been plaguing me since we left Cape Town – are we running on a job – or is this a pleasure cruise?'

Nicholas laughed aloud then. He felt the excitement of the hunt, a good hot scent in the nostrils, and the prospect of a fat prize. Now he had *Warlock* under him, his concern for Peter's safety had abated. Whatever happened now, he could get there very fast. No, he felt good, very good.

'We're hunting, David,' he told him. 'Nothing certain yet—' he paused, and then relented, 'Get Beauty Baker up to my cabin, tell Angel to send up a big pot of coffee and a mess of sandwiches – I missed breakfast – and while we are eating, I'll fill both of you in.'

Beauty Baker accepted one of Nicholas' cheroots.

'Still smoking cheap,' he observed, and sniffed at the four-dollar cheroot sourly, but there was a twinkle of pleasure behind the smeared lenses of his spectacles. Then, unable to contain himself, he actually grinned.

'Skipper tells me we are hunting, is that right?'

'This is the picture—' Nicholas began to spell it out to them in detail, and while he talked, he thought with comfortable self-indulgence, 'I must be getting old and soft – I didn't always talk so much.'

Both men listened in silence, and only when he finished did the two of them begin bombarding him with the perceptive penetrating questions he had expected.

'Sounds like a generator armature,' Beauty Baker guessed, as he puzzled the contents of the wooden case that had been flown out to *Golden Dawn*. I cannot believe that *Golden Dawn* doesn't carry a full set of mechanical spares.'

While Baker was fully preoccupied with the mechanics of the situation, David Allen concentrated on the problems of seamanship. 'What was the range of the helicopter? Has it returned to base yet? With her draught, she must be heading for the Florida Straits. Our best bet would be to shape a course for Matanilla Reef at the mouth of the Straits.'

There was a peremptory knock on the door of the guest cabin, and the Trog stuck his grey wrinkled tortoise head through. He glanced at Nicholas, but did not greet him. 'Captain, Miami is broadcasting a new hurricane alert. "Lorna" has kicked northwards, they're predicting a track of north north-west and a speed over the ground of twenty knots.'

He closed the door and they stared at each other in silence for a moment.

Nicholas spoke at last.

'It is never one single mistake that causes disaster,' he said. 'It is always a series of contributory errors, most of them of small consequence in themselves – but when taken with a little bad luck—' he was silent for a moment and then, softly, 'Hurricane Lorna could just be that bit of bad luck.'

He stood up and took one turn around the small guest cabin, feeling caged and wishing for the space of the Master's suite which was now David Allen's. He turned back to Beauty Baker and David Allen, and suddenly he realized that they were hoping for disaster. They were like two old sea wolves with the scent of the prey in their nostrils. He felt his anger rising coldly against them, they were wishing disaster on his son.

'Just one thing I didn't tell you,' he said. 'My son is on *Golden Dawn*.'

The immense revolving storm that was code-named Lorna was nearing full development. Her crest was reared high above the freezing levels so she wore a splendid mane of frosted white ice particles that streamed out three hundred miles ahead of her on the jet stream of the upper troposphere.

From one side to the other, she now measured one hundred and fifty miles across, and the power unleashed within her was of unmeasurable savagery.

The winds that blew around her centre tore the surface off the sea and bore it aloft at speeds in excess of one hundred and fifty miles an hour, generating precipitation that was as far beyond rain as death is beyond life. Water filled the dense cloud-banks so that there was no clear line between sea and air.

It seemed now that madness fed upon madness, and like a blinded and berserk monster, she blundered across the confined waters of the Caribbean, ripping the trees and buildings, even the very earth from the tiny islands which stood in her path.

But there were still forces controlling what seemed uncontrollable, dictating what seemed to be random, for, as she spun upon a spinning globe, the storm showed the primary trait of gyroscopic inertia, a rigidity in space that was constant as long as no outside force was applied.

Obeying this natural law, the entire system moved steadily eastwards at constant speed and altitude above the surface of the earth, until her northern edge touched the landmass of the long ridge of land that forms the greater Antilles.

Immediately another gyroscopic law came into force, the law of precession. When a deflecting force is applied to the rim of a spinning gyro, the gyro moves not away from, but *directly towards* that force.

Hurricane Lorna felt the land and, like a maddened bull at the flirt of the matador's cape, she turned and charged towards it, crossing the narrow high strips of Haiti in an orgy of destruction and terror until she burst out of the narrow channel of the Windward Passage into the open beyond.

Yet still she kept on spinning and moving. Now, barely three hundred miles ahead of her, across those shallow reefs and banks prophetically named 'Hurricane Flats' after the thousands of other such storms that had followed the same route during the memory of man, lay the deeper waters of the Florida Straits and the mainland of the continental United States of America.

At twenty miles an hour, the whole incredible heaven-high mass of crazed wind and churning clouds trundled north-westwards.

D uncan Alexander stood under the bogus Degas ballet dancers in the owner's stateroom. He balanced easily on the balls of his feet and his hands were clasped lightly behind his back, but his brow was heavily furrowed with worry and his eyes darkly under-scored with plum-coloured swollen bags of sleeplessness.

Seated on the long couch and on the imitation Louis Quatorze chairs flanking the fireplace, were the senior officers of *Golden Dawn* – her Captain, Mate and Chief Engineer, and in the leather-studded wing-backed chair across the wide cabin sat Charles Gras, the engineer from Atlantique. It seemed as though he had chosen his seat to keep himself aloof from the owner and officers of the crippled ultra-tanker.

He spoke now in heavily accented English, falling back on the occasional French word which Duncan translated quickly. The four men listened to him with complete attention, never taking their eyes from the sharp, pale Parisian features and the foxy bright eyes.

'My men will have completed the reassembly of the main bearing by noon today. To the best of my ability, I have examined and tested the main shaft. I can find no evidence of structural damage, but I must emphasize that this does not mean that no damage exists. At the very best, the repairs must be considered to be temporary.' He paused and they waited, while he turned deliberately to Captain Randle. 'I must urge you to seek proper repair in the nearest port open to you, and to proceed there at the lowest speed which will enable you efficiently to work the ship.'

Randle twisted uncomfortably in his seat, and glanced across at Duncan. The Frenchman saw the exchange and a little steel came into his voice.

'If there is structural distortion in the main shaft, operation at speeds higher than this may result in permanent and irreversible damage and complete breakdown. I must make this point most forcibly.'

Duncan intervened smoothly. 'We are fully burdened and drawing twenty fathoms of water. There are no safe harbours on the eastern seaboard of America, that is even supposing that we could get permission to enter territorial waters with engine trouble. The Americans aren't likely to welcome us. Our nearest safe anchorage is Galveston roads, on the Texas coast of the Gulf of Mexico – and then only after the tugs have taken off our pod tanks outside the 100-fathom line.'

The tanker's First Officer was a young man, probably not over thirty years of age, but he had so far conducted himself impeccably in the emergencies the ship had encountered. He had a firm jaw and a clear level eye, and he had been the first into the smoke-filled shaft tunnel.

'With respect, sir,' and they all turned their heads towards him, 'Miami has broadcast a revised hurricane alert that includes the Straits and southern Florida. We would be on a reciprocal course to the hurricane track, a directly converging course.'

'Even at fifteen knots, we would be through the Straits and into the Gulf with twenty-four hours to spare,' Duncan stated, and looked to Randle for confirmation.

'At the present speed of the storm's advance – yes,' Randle qualified carefully. 'But conditions may change—'

The Mate persisted. 'Again, with respect, sir. Our nearest safe anchorage is the lee of Bermuda Island—'

'Do you have any idea of the value of this cargo?' Duncan's voice rasped. 'No, you do not. Well, I will inform you. It is $85,000,000. The interest on that amount is in the region of $25,000 a day.' His voice rose a note, again that wild note to it. 'Bermuda does not have the facilities to effect major repairs—'

The door from the private accommodation opened silently and Chantelle Alexander stepped into the state-room. She wore no jewellery, a plain pearl silk blouse and a simple dark woollen skirt, but her skin had been gilded by the sun and she had lightly touched her dark eyes with a make-up that emphasized their size and shape. Her beauty silenced them all and she was fully aware of it as she crossed to stand beside Duncan.

'It is necessary that this ship and her cargo proceed directly to Galveston,' she said softly.

'Chantelle—' Duncan began, and she silenced him with a brusque gesture of one hand.

'There is no question about the destination and the route that is to be taken.'

Charles Gras looked to Captain Randle, waiting for him to assert the authority vested in him by law. But when the young Captain remained silent, the Frenchman smiled sardonically and shrugged a world-weary dismissal of further interest. 'Then I must ask that arrangements be made for my two assistants and myself to leave this ship immediately we have completed the temporary repairs.' Again Gras emphasized the word 'temporary'.

Duncan nodded. 'If we resume our sailing when you anticipate, and even taking into consideration the low fuel condition of the helicopter, we will be within easy range of the east coast of Florida by dawn tomorrow.'

Chantelle had not taken her eyes from the *Golden Dawn*'s officers during this exchange, and now she went on in the same quiet voice.

'I am quite prepared to accept the resignation of any of the officers of this ship who wish to join that flight.'

Duncan opened his mouth to make some protest at her assumption of his authority, but she turned to him with a small lift of the chin, and something in her expression and the set of her head upon her shoulders reminded him forcibly of old Arthur Christy. There was the same toughness and resilience there, the same granite determination; strange that he had not noticed it before.

'Perhaps I have never looked before,' he thought. Chantelle recognized the moment of his capitulation, and calmly she turned back to face *Golden Dawn*'s officers.

One by one, they dropped their eyes from hers; Randle was the first to stand up.

'If you will excuse me, Mrs Alexander, I must make preparations to get under way again.'

Charles Gras paused and looked back at her, and he

434

smiled again, as only a Frenchman smiles at a pretty woman.

'*Magnifique!*' he murmured, and lifted one hand in a graceful salute of admiration before he stepped out of the stateroom.

When Chantelle and Duncan were alone together, she turned to him slowly, and she let the contempt show in her expression.

'Any time you feel you have not got the guts for it, let me know, will you?'

'Chantelle—'

'You have got us into this, me and Christy Marine. Now you'll get us out of it, even if it kills you.' Her lips compressed into a thinner line and her eyes slitted vindictively. 'And it would be nice if it did,' she said softly.

The pilot of the Beechcraft Baron pulled back the throttles to 22" of boost on both engines, and slid the propellers into fully fine pitch, simultaneously beginning a gentle descending turn towards the extraordinary-looking vessel that came up swiftly out of the low early morning haze that spilled over from the islands.

The same haze had blotted the low silhouette of the Florida coast from the western horizon, and even the pale green water and shaded reefs of little Bahamas Bank were washed pale by the haze, and partially obscured by the intermittent layer of stratocumulus cloud at four thousand feet.

The Baron pilot selected 20° of flap to give the aircraft a nosedown attitude which would afford a better forward vision, and continued his descent down through the cloud. It burst in a brief grey puff across the windshield before they were out into sunlight again.

'What do you make of her?' he asked his co-pilot.

'She's a big baby,' the co-pilot tried to steady his binoculars. 'Can't read her name.'

The enormously wide low bows were pushing up a fat sparkling pillow of churning water, and the green decks seemed to reach back almost to the limits of visibility before rising sheer into the stern quarters.

'Son of a gun,' the pilot shook his head. 'She looks like the vehicle-assembly building on Cape Kennedy.'

'She does too,' agreed his co-pilot. The same square unlovely bulk of that enormous structure was repeated in smaller scale by the navigation bridge of the big ship. 'I'll give her a call on 16.' The co-pilot lowered his binoculars and thumbed the microphone as he lifted it to his lips.

'Southbound bulk carrier, this is Coast Guard November Charlie One Fife Niner overhead. Do you read me?'

There was the expected delay; even in confined and heavily trafficked waters, these big bastards kept a sloppy watch and the spotter fumed silently.

'Coast Guard One Fife Niner, this is *Golden Dawn*. Reading you fife by fife. Going up to 22.'

Two hundred miles away the Trog knocked over the shell-casing, spilling damp and stinking cigar butts over the deck, in his haste to change frequency to channel 22 as the operator on board *Golden Dawn* had stipulated, at the same time switching on both the tape recorder and the radio direction-finder equipment.

High up in *Warlock*'s fire-control tower, the big metal ring of the direction-finding aerial turned slowly, lining up on the transmissions that boomed so clearly across the ether, repeating the relative bearing on the dial of the instrument on the Trog's cluttered bench.

'Good morning to you, *Golden Dawn*,' the lilting Southern twang of the coastguard navigator came back. 'I would be mightily obliged for your port of registry and your cargo manifest.'

'This ship is registered Venezuela.' The Trog dexterously made the fine tuning, scribbled the bearing on his pad, ripped off the page and darted into *Warlock*'s navigation bridge.

'*Golden Dawn* is sending in clear,' he squeaked with an expression of malicious glee.

'Call the Captain,' snapped the deck officer, and then as an afterthought, 'and ask Mr Berg to come to the bridge.'

The conversation between coastguard and ultra-tanker was still going on when Nicholas burst into the radio room, belting his dressing gown.

'Thank you for your courtesy, sir,' the coastguard navigator was using extravagant Southern gallantry, fully aware that *Golden Dawn* was outside United States territorial waters, and officially beyond his government's jurisdiction. 'I would appreciate your port of final destination.'

'We are en route to Galveston for full discharge of cargo.'

'Thank you again, sir. And are you appraised of the hurricane alert in force at this time?'

'Affirmative.'

From *Warlock*'s bridge, David Allen appeared in the doorway, his face set and flushed.

'She must be under way again,' he said, his disappointment so plain that it angered Nicholas yet again. 'She is into the channel already.'

'I'd be obliged if you would immediately put this ship on a course to enter the Straits and close with her as soon as is possible,' Nicholas snapped, and David Allen blinked at him once then disappeared on to his bridge, calling for the change in course and increase in speed as he went.

Over the loudspeaker, the coastguard was being politely persistent.

'Are you further appraised, sir, of the update on that hurricane alert predicting storm passage of the main navigable channel at 1200 hours local time tomorrow?'

'Affirmative.' *Golden Dawn*'s replies had become curt.

'May I further trouble you, sir, in view of your sensitive cargo and the special weather conditions, for your expected time of arrival abeam of the Dry Tortugas Bank marine beacon and when you anticipate clearing the channel and shaping a northerly course away from the predicted hurricane track?'

'Standby.' There was a brief hum of static while the operator consulted the deck officer and then the *Golden Dawn* came back, 'Our ETA Dry Tortugas Bank beacon is 0130 tomorrow.'

There was a long pause now as the coastguard consulted his headquarters ashore on one of the closed frequencies, and then:

'I am requested respectfully, but officially, to bring to your attention that very heavy weather is expected ahead of the storm centre and that your present ETA Dry Tortugas Bank leaves you very fine margins of safety, sir.'

'Thank you, coastguard One Fife Niner. Your transmission will be entered in the ship's log. This is *Golden Dawn* over and out.'

The coastguard's frustration was evident. Clearly he would have loved to order the tanker to reverse her course. 'We will be following your progress with interest, *Golden Dawn*. Bon voyage, this is coastguard One Fife Niner over and out.'

Charles Gras held his blue beret on with one hand, while with the other he lugged his suitcase. He ran doubled up, instinctively avoiding the ear-numbing clatter of the helicopter's rotor.

He threw his suitcase through the open fuselage door and then hesitated, turned and scampered back to where the ship's Chief Engineer stood at the edge of the white-painted helipad target on *Golden Dawn*'s tank deck.

Charles grabbed the Engineer's upper arm and leaned close to shout in his ear.

'Remember, my friend, treat her like a baby, like a tender virgin – if you have to increase speed, do so gently – very gently.' The Engineer nodded, his sparse sandy hair fluttering in the down draught.

'Good luck,' shouted the Frenchman. '*Bonne chance!*' He slapped the man's shoulder. 'I hope you don't need it!'

He darted back and scrambled up into the fuselage of the Sikorsky, and his face appeared in one of the portholes. He waved once, and then the big ungainly machine rose slowly into the air, hovered for a moment and then banked away low over the water, setting off in its characteristic nose-down attitude for the mainland, still hidden by haze and distance.

D r Samantha Silver, dressed in thigh-high rubber waders and with her sleeves rolled up above the elbows, staggered under the weight of two ten-gallon plastic buckets of clams as she climbed the back steps of the laboratory building.

'Sam!' down the length of the long passageway, Sally-Anne screamed at her. 'We were going to leave without you!'

'What is it?' Sam dumped the buckets with relief, slopping salt water down the steps.

'Johnny called – the anti-pollution patrol bespoke *Golden Dawn* an hour ago. She's in the Straits. She was abeam Matanilla reef when they spotted her and she will be abeam of Biscayne Key before we can get out there, if we don't leave now.'

'I'm coming.' Sam hefted her heavy buckets, and broke into a rubber-kneed trot. 'I'll meet you down on the wharf – did you call the TV studio?'

'There's a camera team on the way,' Sally-Anne yelled back as she ran for the front doors. 'Hurry, Sam – fast as you like!'

Samantha dumped the clams into one of her tanks, switched on the oxygen and as soon as it began to bubble to the surface, she turned and raced from the laboratory and out of the front doors.

Golden Dawn's deck officer stopped beside the radarscope, glanced down at it idly, then stooped with more attention and took a bearing on the little glowing pinpoint of green light that showed up clearly inside the ten-mile circle of the sweep.

He grunted, straightened, and walked quickly to the front of the bridge. Slowly, he scanned the green windchopped sea ahead of the tanker's ponderous bows.

'Fishing boat,' he said to the helmsman. 'But they are under way.' He had seen the tiny flash of a bow wave. 'And they are right in the main navigational channel – they must have seen us by now, they are making a turn to pass us to starboard.' He dropped the binoculars and let them dangle against his chest. 'Oh thank you.' He took the cup of cocoa from the steward, and sipped it with relish as he turned away to the chart-table.

One of the tanker's junior officers came out of the radio room at the back of the bridge.

'Still no score,' he said, 'and only injury time left now,' and they fell into a concerned discussion of the World Cup soccer match being played under floodlights at Wembley Stadium on the other side of the Atlantic.

'If it's a draw then it means that France is in the—'

There was an excited shout from the radio room, and the junior officer ran to the door and then turned back with an excited grin. 'England has scored!'

The deck officer chuckled happily. 'That will wrap it up.' Then with a start of guilt he turned back to his duties, and had another start, this time of surprise, when he glanced into the radarscope.

'What the hell are they playing at!' he exclaimed irritably, and hurried forward to scan the sea ahead.

The fishing boat had continued its turn and was now bows on.

'Damn them. We'll give them a buzz.' He reached up for the handle of the foghorn and blew three long blasts that echoed out mournfully across the shallow greenish water of the Straits. There was a general movement among the officers to get a better view ahead through the forward bridge windows.

'They must be half asleep out there.' The deck officer thought quickly about calling the Captain to the bridge. If it came to manoeuvring the ship in these confined waters, he flinched from the responsibility. Even at this reduced speed, it would take *Golden Dawn* half an hour and seven nautical miles to come to a stop; a turn in either direction would swing through a wide arc of many miles before the ship was able to make a 90° change of course – God, then there was the effect of the wind against the enormously exposed area of the towering stern quarters, and the full bore of the Gulf Stream driving out of the narrows of the Straits. The problems of manoeuvring the vessel struck a chill of panic into the officer – and the fishing boat was on collision course, the range closing swiftly under the combined speeds of both vessels. He reached for the call button of the intercom that connected the bridge directly to the Captain's quarters on the deck below, but at that moment Captain Randle came bounding up the private staircase from his day cabin.

'What is it?' he demanded. 'What was that blast on the horn?'

'Small vessel holding on to collision course, sir.' The

officer's relief was evident, and Randle seized the handle of the foghorn and hung on to it.

'God, what's wrong with them?'

'The deck is crowded,' exclaimed one of the officers without lowering his binoculars. 'Looks as though they have a movie-camera team on the top deck.'

Randle judged the closing range anxiously; already the small fishing vessel was too close for the Golden Dawn to stop in time.

'Thank God,' somebody exclaimed. 'They are turning away.'

'They are streaming some sort of banner. Can anybody read that?'

'They are heaving-to,' the deck officer yelled suddenly. 'They are heaving-to right under our bows.'

Samantha Silver had not expected the tanker to be so big. From directly ahead, her bows seemed to fill the horizon from one side to the other, and the bow wave she threw up ahead of her creamed and curved like the set of the long wave at Cape St Francis when the surf was up.

Beyond the bows, the massive tower of her navigation bridge stood so tall that it looked like the skyline of The Miami Beach, one of those massive hotel buildings seen from close inshore.

It made her feel distinctly uneasy to be directly under that on-rushing steel avalanche.

'Do you think they have seen us?' Sally-Anne asked beside her, and when Samantha heard her own unease echoed by the pretty girl beside her, it steeled her.

'Of course they have,' she announced stoutly so that everyone in the small wheelhouse could hear her. 'That's why they blew their siren. We'll turn aside at the last minute.'

'They aren't slowing down,' Hank Petersen, the helmsman, pointed out huskily, and Samantha wished that Tom Parker had been on board with them. However, Tom was up in Washington again, and they had taken the *Dicky* to sea with a scratch crew, and without Tom Parker's written authorization. 'What do you want to do, Sam?' And they all looked at her.

'I know a thing that size can't stop, but at least we're going to make them slow down.

'Are the TV boys getting some stuff?' Samantha asked, to delay the moment of decision. 'Go up, Sally-Anne, and check them.' Then to the others, 'You-all get the banner ready. We'll let them get a good look at that.'

'Listen, Sam.' Hank Petersen's tanned intelligent face was strained. He was a tunny expert, and was not accustomed to handling the vessel except in calm and uncluttered waters. 'I don't like this, we're getting much too close. That thing could churn us right under, and not even notice the bump. I want to turn away now.' His voice was almost drowned by the sudden sky-crashing blast of the tanker's foghorns.

'Son of a gun, Sam, I don't like playing chicken-chicken with somebody that size.'

'Don't worry, we'll get out of their way at the last moment. All right!' Samantha decided. 'Turn 90° to port, Hank. Let's show them the signs. I'm going to help them on deck.'

The wind tore at the thin white canvas banner as they tried to run it out along the side of the deckhouse, and the little vessel was rolling uncomfortably while the TV producer was shouting confused stage directions at them from the top of the wheelhouse.

Bitterly Samantha wished there was somebody to take

command, somebody like Nicholas Berg – and the banner tried to wrap itself around her head.

The *Dicky* was coming around fast now, and Samantha shot a glance at the oncoming tanker and felt the shock of it strike in the pit of her stomach like the blow of a fist. It was huge, and very close – much too close, even she realized that.

At last she managed to get a turn of the thin line that secured the banner around the stern rail – but the light canvas had twisted so that only one word of the slogan was readable. 'POISONER', it accused in scarlet, crudely painted letters followed by a grinning skull and crossed bones.

Samantha dived across the deck and struggled with the flapping canvas; above her head the producer was shouting excitedly; two of the others were trying to help her; Sally-Anne was screaming 'Go back! Go back!' and waving both arms at the great tanker. 'You poison our oceans!'

Everything was becoming confused and out of control. The *Dicky* swung ahead into the wind and pitched steeply, the person next to her lost his footing and knocked painfully into Samantha, and at that moment she felt the change of the engine beat.

Tricky Dicky's diesel had been bellowing furiously as Hank opened the throttle to its stop, using full power to bring the little vessel around from under the menace of those steel bows.

The smoking splutter of the exhaust pipe that rose vertically up the side of the deckhouse had made all speech difficult – but now it died away, and suddenly there was only the sound of the wind.

Even their own raised voices were silenced, and they froze, staring out at *Golden Dawn* as she bore down on them without the slightest check in her majestic approach.

Samantha was the first one to recover, then she ran across the plunging deck to the wheelhouse.

Hank Petersen was down on his knees beside the bulkhead, struggling ineffectually with the conduit that housed the controls to the engine room on the deck below.

'Why have you stopped?' Samantha yelled at him, and he looked up at her as though he were mortally wounded.

'It's the throttle linkage,' he said. 'It's snapped again.'

'Can't you fix it?' and the question was a mockery. A mile away, Golden Dawn came down on them – silent, menacing, unstoppable.

For ten seconds Randle stood rigid, both hands gripping the foul weather rail below the sill of the bridge windows.

His face was set, pale and finely drawn, as he watched the stern of the wallowing fishing boat for the renewed churning of its prop.

He knew that he could not turn nor stop his ship in time to avoid collision, unless the small vessel got under way immediately, and took evasive action by going out to starboard under full power.

'Damn them to hell,' he thought bitterly, they were in gross default. He had all the law and the custom of the sea behind him; a collision would cause very little damage to Golden Dawn, perhaps she would lose a little paint, at most a slightly buckled plate in the reinforced bows – and they had asked for it.

He had no doubts about the object of this crazy, irresponsible seamanship. There had been controversy before the Golden Dawn sailed. He had read the objections and seen the nutcase environmentalists on television. The scarlet-painted banner with the ridiculously melodramatic Jolly Roger made it clear that this was a boatload of nutters who were attempting to prevent Golden Dawn from entering American waters.

He felt his anger boiling up fiercely. These people always made him furious. If they had their way, there would be no tanker trade, and now they were deliberately threatening him, placing him in a position which might prejudice his own career. He already had the task of taking his ship through the Straits ahead of the hurricane. Every moment was vital – and now there was this.

He would be happy to maintain course and speed, and to run them down. They were flaunting themselves, challenging him to do it – and, by God, they deserved it.

However, he was a seaman, with a seaman's deep concern for human life at sea. It would go against all his instincts not to make an effort to avoid collision, no matter how futile that effort would be. Then beside him one of his officers triggered him.

'There are women on board her – look at that! Those are women!'

That was enough. Without waiting for confirmation, Randle snapped at the helmsman beside him.

'Full port rudder!'

And with two swift paces he had reached the engine room telegraph. It rang shrilly as he pulled back the chromed handle to 'Full Astern'.

Almost immediately, the changed beat came up through the soles of his feet, as the great engine seven decks below the bridge thundered suddenly under all emergency power, and the direction of the spinning main propellor shaft was abruptly reversed.

Randle spun back to face ahead. For almost five minutes, the bows held steady on the horizon without making any answer to the full application of the rudder. The inertia of a million tons of crude oil, the immense drag of the hull through water and the press of wind and current held her on course, and although the single ferro-bronze propeller bit deeply into the green waters, there was not the slightest diminution of the tanker's speed.

Randle kept his hand on the engine telegraph, pulling back on the silver handle with all his strength, as though this might arrest the great ship's forward way through the water.

'Turn!' he whispered to the ship, and he stared at the fishing boat that still lay, rolling wildly, directly in *Golden Dawn*'s path. He noticed irrelevently that the tiny human figures along the rear rail were waving frantically, and that the banner with its scarlet denunciation had torn loose at one end and was now whipping and twisting like a Tibetan prayer flag over the heads of the crew.

'Turn,' Randle whispered, and he saw the first response of the hull; the angle between the bows and the fishing boat altered, it was a noticeable change, but slowly accelerating and a quick glance at the control console showed a small check in the ship's forward speed.

'Turn, damn it, turn.' Randle held the engine telegraph locked at full astern, and felt the sudden influence of the Gulf Stream current on the ship as she began to come across the direction of flow.

Ahead, the fishing boat was almost about to disappear from sight behind *Golden Dawn*'s high blunt bows.

He had been holding the ship at full astern for almost seven minutes now, and suddenly Randle felt a change in *Golden Dawn*, something he had never experienced before.

There was a harsh, tearing, pounding vibration coming up through the deck. He realized just how severe that vibration must be, when *Golden Dawn*'s monumental hull began to shake violently – but he could not release his grip on the engine telegraph, not with that helpless vessel lying in his track.

Then suddenly, miraculously, all vibration in the deck under his feet ceased altogether. There was only the calm press of the hull through the water, no longer the feel of the engine's thrust, a sensation much more alarming to a mariner than the vibration which had preceded it, and simultaneously, a fiery rash of red warning lights bloomed on the ship's main control console, and the strident screech of the full emergency audio-alarm deafened them all.

Only then did Captain Randle push the engine tele-graph to 'stop'. He stood staring ahead as the tiny fishing boat disappeared from view, hidden by the angle from the navigation bridge which was a mile behind the bows.

One of the officers reached across and hit the cut-out on the audio-alarm. In the sudden silence every officer stood frozen, waiting for the impact of collision.

Golden Dawn's Chief Engineer paced slowly along the engine-room control console, never taking his eyes from the electronic displays which monitored all the ship's mechanical and electrical functions.

When he reached the alarm aboard, he stopped and frowned at it angrily. The failure of the single transistor, a few dollars' worth of equipment, had been the cause of such brutal damage to his beloved machinery. He leaned across and pressed the 'test' button, checking out each alarm circuit, yet, while he was doing it, recognizing the fact that it was too late. He was nursing the ship along, with God alone knew what undiscovered damage to engine and main shaft only kept in check by this reduced power setting – but there was a hurricane down there below the southern horizon, and the Chief could only guess at what emergency his machinery might have to meet in the next few days.

It made him nervous and edgy to think about it. He searched in his back pocket, found a sticky mint humbug, carefully picked off the little pieces of lint and fluff before tucking it into his cheek like a squirrel with a nut, sucking noisily upon it as he resumed his restless prowling up and down the control console.

His on-duty stokers and the oilers watched him surreptitiously. When the old man was in a mood, it was best not to attract attention.

'Dickson!' the Chief said suddenly. 'Get your lid on. We are going down the shaft tunnel again.'

The oiler sighed, exchanged a resigned glance with one of his mates and clapped his hard-hat on his head. He and the Chief had been down the tunnel an hour previously. It was an uncomfortable, noisy and dirty journey.

The oiler closed the watertight doors into the shaft tunnel behind them, screwing down the clamps firmly under the Chief's frosty scrutiny, and then both men stopped in the confined headroom and started off along the brightly-lit, pale grey painted tunnel.

The spinning shaft in its deep bed generated a high-pitched whine that seemed to resonate in the steel box of the tunnel, as though it was the body of a violin. Surprisingly, the noise was more pronounced at this low speed setting. It seemed to bore into the teeth at the back of the oiler's jaw like a dentist's drill.

The Chief did not seem to be affected. He paused beside the main bearing for almost ten minutes, testing it with the palm of his hand, feeling for heat or vibration. His expression was morose, and he worried the mint humbug in his cheek and shook his head with foreboding before going on up the tunnel.

When he reached the main gland, he squatted down suddenly and peered at it closely. With a deliberate flexing of his jaw he crushed the remains of the humbug between his teeth, and his eyes narrowed thoughtfully.

There was a thin trickle of seawater oozing through the gland and running down into the bilges. The Chief touched it with his finger. Something had shifted, some balance was disturbed, the seal of the gland was no longer watertight – such a small sign, a few gallons of seawater, could be the first warning of major structural damage.

The Chief shuffled around, still hunched down beside the shaft bed, and he lowered his face until it was only inches from the spinning steel main shaft. He closed one eye, and cocked his head, trying once again to decide if the faint blurring of the shaft's outline was real or merely his over-active imagination, whether what he was seeing was distortion or his own fears.

Suddenly, startlingly, the shaft slammed into stillness. The deceleration was so abrupt that the Chief could actually see the torque transferred into the shaft bed, and the metal walls creaked and popped with the strain.

He rocked back on to his heels, and almost instantly the shaft began to spin again, but this time in reverse thrust. The whine built up swiftly into a rising shriek. They were pulling emergency power from the bridge, and it was madness, suicidal madness.

The Chief seized the oiler by the shoulder and shouted into his ear, 'Get back to control – find out what the hell they are doing on the bridge.'

The oiler scrambled away down the tunnel; it would take him ten minutes to negotiate the long narrow passage, open the watertight doors and reach the control room and as long again to return.

The Chief considered going after him, but somehow he could not leave the shaft now. He lowered his head again, and now he could clearly see the flickering outline of the shaft. It wasn't imagination at all, there was a little ghost of movement. He clamped his hands over his ears to cut out the painful shriek of the spinning metal, but there was a new note to it, the squeal of bare metal on metal and before his eyes he saw the ghost outline along the edge of the shaft growing, the flutter of machinery out of balance, and the metal deck under his feet began to quiver.

'God! They are going to blow the whole thing!' he shouted, and jumped up from his crouch. Now the deck was juddering and shaking under his feet. He started back along the shaft, but the entire tunnel was agitating so violently that he had to grab the metal bulkhead to steady himself, and he reeled drunkenly, thrown about like a captive insect in a cruel child's box.

Ahead of him, he saw the huge metal casting of the main bearing twisting and shaking, and the vibration chattered his teeth in his clenched jaw and drove up his spine like a jackhammer.

Disbelievingly he saw the huge silver shaft beginning to rise and buckle in its bed, the bearing tearing loose from its mountings.

'Shut down!' he screamed. 'For God's sake, shut down!' but his voice was lost in the shriek and scream of tortured metal and machinery that was tearing itself to pieces in a suicidal frenzy.

The main bearing exploded, and the shaft slammed it into the bulkhead, tearing steel plate like paper.

The shaft itself began to snake and whip. The Chief cowered back, pressing his back to the bulkhead and covering his ears to protect them from the unbearable volume of noise.

A sliver of heated steel flew from the bearing and struck him in the face, laying open his upper lip to the bone, crushing his nose and snapping off his front teeth at the level of his gums.

He toppled forward, and the whipping, kicking shaft seized him like a mindless predator and tore his body to pieces, pounding him and crushing him in the shaft bed and splattering him against the pale metal walls.

The main shaft snapped like a rotten twig at the point where it had been heated and weakened. The unbalanced weight of the revolving propeller ripped the stump out through the after seal, as though it were a tooth plucked from a rotting jaw.

The sea rushed in through the opening, flooding the tunnel instantly until it slammed into the watertight doors

– and the huge glistening bronze propeller, with the stump of the main shaft still attached, the whole unit weighing one hundred and fifty tons, plummeted downwards through four hundred fathoms to embed itself deeply in the soft mud of the sea bottom.

Freed of the intolerable goad of her damaged shaft, *Golden Dawn* was suddenly silent and her decks still and steady as she trundled on, slowly losing way as the water dragged at her hull.

Samantha had one awful moment of sickening guilt. She saw clearly that she was responsible for the deadly danger into which she had led these people, and she stared out over the boat's side at the *Golden Dawn*.

The tanker was coming on without any check in her speed; perhaps she had turned a few degrees, for her bows were no longer pointed directly at them, but her speed was constant.

She was achingly aware of her inexperience, of her helplessness in this alien situation. She tried to think, to force herself out of this frozen despondency.

'Life jackets!' she thought, and yelled to Sally-Anne out on the deck, 'The life jackets are in the lockers behind the wheelhouse.'

Their faces turned to her, suddenly stricken. Up to this moment it had all been a glorious romp, the old fun-game of challenging the money-grabbers, prodding the establishment, but now suddenly it was mortal danger.

'Move!' Samantha shrieked at them, and there was a rush back along the deck.

'Think!' Samantha shook her head, as though to clear it. 'Think!' she urged herself fiercely. She could hear the tanker now, the silken rustling sound of the water under its hull, the sough of the bow wave curling upon itself.

The *Dicky*'s throttle linkage had broken before, when they had been off Key West a year ago. It had broken between the bridge and the engine, and Samantha had watched Tom Parker fiddling with the engine, holding the lantern for him to see in the gloomy confines of the smelly little engine room. She had not been certain how he did it, but she remembered that he had controlled the revolutions of the engine by hand – something on the side of the engine block, below the big bowl of the air filter.

Samantha turned and dived down the vertical ladder into the engine room. The diesel was running, burbling away quietly at idling speed, not generating sufficient power to move the little vessel through the water.

She tripped and sprawled on the greasy deck, and pulled herself up, crying out with pain as her hand touched the red-hot manifold of the engine exhaust.

On the far side of the engine block, she groped desperately under the air filter, pushing and tugging at anything her fingers touched. She found a coil spring, and dropped to her knees to examine it.

She tried not to think of the huge steel hull bearing down on them, of being down in this tiny box that stank of diesel and exhaust fumes and old bilges. She tried not to think of not having a life jacket, or that the tanker could tramp the little vessel deep down under the surface and crush her like a matchbox.

Instead, she traced the little coil spring to where it was pinned into a flat upright lever. Desperately she pushed the lever against the tension of the spring – and instantly the diesel engine bellowed deafeningly in her ears, startling her so that she flinched and lost the lever. The diesel's beat died away into the bumbling idle and she wasted seconds while she found the lever again and pushed it hard against its stops once more. The engine roared, and she felt the ship picking up speed under her. She began to pray incoherently.

She could not hear the words in the engine noise, and she was not sure she was making sense, but she held the throttle open, and kept on praying.

She did not hear the screams from the deck above her. She did not know how close the *Golden Dawn* was; she did not know if Hank Petersen was still in the wheelhouse conning the little vessel out of the path of the onrushing tanker – but she held the throttle open and prayed.

The impact, when it came, was shattering, the crash and crackle of timbers breaking, the rending lurch and the roll of the deck giving to the tearing force of it.

Samantha was hurled against the hot steel of the engine, her forehead striking with such a force that her vision starred into blinding white light; she dropped backwards, her body loose and relaxed, darkness ringing in her ears, and lay huddled on the deck.

She did not know how long she was unconscious, but it could not have been for more than a few seconds; the spray of icy cold water on her face roused her and she pulled herself up on to her knees.

In the glare of the single bare electric globe in the deck above her, Samantha saw the spurts of water jets through the starting planking of the bulkhead beside her.

Her shirt and denim pants were soaked, salt water half blinded her, and her head felt as though the skull were cracked and someone was forcing the sharp end of a bradawl between her eyes.

Dimly she was aware that the diesel engine was idling noisily, and that the deck was sloshing with water as the boat rolled wildly in some powerful turbulence. She wondered if the whole vessel had been trodden under the tanker.

Then she realized it must be the wake of the giant hull which was throwing them about so mercilessly, but they were still afloat.

She began to crawl down the plunging deck. She knew

where the bilge pump was, that was one thing Tom had taught all of them – and she crawled on grimly towards it.

Hank Petersen ducked out of the wheelhouse, flapping his arms wildly as he struggled into the life jacket. He was not certain of the best action to take, whether to jump over the side and begin swimming away from the tanker's slightly angled course, or to stay on board and take his chances with the collision which was now only seconds away.

Around him, the others were in the grip of the same indecision; they were huddled silently at the rail staring up at the mountain of smooth rounded steel that seemed to blot out half the sky. Only the TV cameraman on the wheelhouse roof, a true fanatic oblivious of all danger, kept his camera running. His exclamations of delight and the burr of the camera motor blended with the rushing sibilance of *Golden Dawn*'s bow wave. It was fifteen feet high, that wave, and it sounded like wild fire in dry grass.

Suddenly the exhaust of the diesel engine above Hank's head bellowed harshly, and then subsided into a soft burbling idle again. He looked up at it uncomprehendingly, now it roared again, fiercely, and the deck lurched beneath him. From the stern he heard the boil of water driven by the propeller, and the *Dicky* shrugged off her lethargy and lifted her bows to the short steep swell of the Gulf Stream.

A moment longer Hank stood frozen, and then he dived back into the wheelhouse and spun the spokes of the wheel through his fingers, sheering off sharply, but still staring out through the side glass.

The *Golden Dawn*'s bows filled his whole vision now, but the smaller vessel was scooting frantically out to one side, and the tanker's bows were swinging majestically in the opposite direction.

A few seconds more and they would be clear, but the bow wave caught them and Hank was flung across the wheelhouse. He felt something break in his chest, and heard the snap of bone as he hit, then immediately afterwards there was the crackling rending tearing impact as the two hulls came together and he was thrown back the other way, sprawling wildly across the deck.

He tried to claw himself upright, but the little fishing boat was pitching and cavorting with such abandon that he was thrown flat again. There was another tearing impact as the vessel was dragged down the tanker's side, and then flung free to roll her rails under and bob like a cork in the mill race of the huge ship's wake.

Now, at last, he was able to pull himself to his feet, and doubled over, clutching his injured ribs. He peered dazedly through the wheelhouse glass.

Half a mile away, the tanker was lazily turning up into the wind, and there was no propeller wash from under her counter. Hank staggered to the doorway, and looked out. The deck was still awash, but the water they had taken on was pouring out through the scuppers. The railing was smashed, most of it dangling overboard and the planking was splintered and torn, the ripped timber as white as bone in the sunlight.

Behind him, Samantha came crawling up the ladder from the engine room. There was a purple swelling in the centre of her forehead, she was soaking wet and her hands were filthy with black grease. He saw a livid red burn across the back of one hand as she lifted it to brush tumbled blonde hair out of her face.

'Are you all right, Sam?'

'Water's pouring in,' she said. 'I don't know how long the pump can hold it.'

'Did you fix the motor?' he asked.

Samantha nodded. 'I held the throttle open,' she said, and then with feeling, 'but I'll be damned to hell if I'll do

456

it again. Somebody else can go down there, I've had my turn.'

'Show me how,' Hank said, 'and you can take the wheel. The sooner we get back to Key Biscayne, the happier I'll be.'

Samantha peered across at the receding bulk of *Golden Dawn*.

'My God!' she shook her head with wonder. 'My God! We were lucky!'

> *'Mackerel skies and mares' tails,*
> *Make tall ships carry short sails.'*

N icholas Berg recited the old sailor's doggerel to himself, shading his eyes with one hand as he looked upwards.

The cloud was beautiful as fine lacework; very high against the tall blue of the heavens it spread swiftly in those long filmy scrolls. Nicholas could see the patterns developing and expanding as he watched, and that was a measure of the speed with which the high winds were blowing. That cloud was at least thirty thousand feet high, and below it the air was clear and crisp – only out on the western horizon the billowing silver and the blue thunderheads were rising, generated by the land-mass of Florida whose low silhouette was still below their horizon.

They had been in the main current of the Gulf Stream for six hours now. It was easy to recognize this characteristic scend of the sea, the short steep swells marching close together, the particular brilliance of these waters that had been first warmed in the shallow tropical basin of the Caribbean, the increased bulk flooding through into the Gulf of Mexico and there heated further, swelling in volume until they formed a hillock of water which at last rushed out through this narrow drainhole of the Florida Straits, swinging north and east in a wide benevolent wash, tempering the climate of all countries whose shores it touched and warming the fishing grounds of the North Atlantic.

In the middle of this stream, somewhere directly ahead of *Warlock*'s thrusting bows, the *Golden Dawn* was struggling southwards, directly opposed to the current which would clip eighty miles a day off her speed, and driving directly into the face of one of the most evil and dangerous storms that nature could summon.

Nicholas found himself brooding again on the mentality of anybody who would do that; again he glanced upwards at the harbingers of the storm, those delicate wisps of lacy cloud.

Nicholas had sailed through a hurricane once, twenty years ago, as a junior officer on one of Christy Marine's small grain carriers, and he shuddered now at the memory of it.

Duncan Alexander was a desperate man even to contemplate that risk, a man gambling everything on one fall of the dice. Nicholas could understand the forces that drove him, for he had been driven himself – but he hated him now for the chances he was taking. Duncan Alexander was risking Nicholas' son, and he was risking the life of an ocean and of the millions of people whose existence was tied to that ocean. Duncan Alexander was gambling with stakes that were not his to place at hazard.

Nicholas wanted one thing only now, and that was to get alongside *Golden Dawn* and take off his son. He would do that, even if it meant boarding her like a buccaneer. In the Master's suite, there was a locked and sealed arms cupboard with two riot guns, automatic 12-gauge shotguns and six Walther PK.38 pistols. *Warlock* had been equipped for every possible emergency in any ocean of the world, and those emergencies could include piracy or mutiny aboard a vessel under salvage. Now Nicholas was fully prepared to take an armed party on board *Golden Dawn*, and to take his chances in any court of law afterwards.

Warlock was racing into the chop of the Gulf Stream and scattering the spray like startled white doves, but she was running too slowly for Nicholas and he turned away impatiently and strode into the navigation bridge.

David Allen looked up at him, a small frown of preoccupation marring the smooth boyish features.

'Wind is moderating and veering westerly,' he said, and Nicholas remembered another line of doggerel:

> *'When the wind moves against the sun*
> *Trust her not for back she'll run.'*

He did not recite it, however, he merely nodded and said:

'We are running into the extreme influence of Lorna. The wind will back again as we move closer to the centre.'

Nicholas went on to the radio room and the Trog looked up at him. It was not necessary for Nicholas to ask, the Trog shook his head. Since that long exchange with the coastguard patrol early that morning, *Golden Dawn* had kept her silence.

Nicholas crossed to the radarscope and studied the circular field for a few minutes; this usually busy seaway was peculiarly empty. There were some small craft crossing the main channel, probably fishing boats or pleasure craft scuttling for protection from the coming storm. All across the islands and on the mainland of Florida the elaborate precautions against the hurricane assault would be coming into force. Since the highway had been laid down on the spur of little islands that formed the Florida Keys, more than three hundred thousand people had crowded in there, in the process transforming those wild lovely islands into the Taj Mahal of ticky-tacky. If the hurricane struck there, the loss of life and property would be enormous. It was

459

probably the most vulnerable spot on a long exposed coastline. For a few minutes, Nicholas tried to imagine the chaos that would result if a million tons of toxic crude oil was driven ashore on a littoral already ravaged by hurricane winds. It baulked his imagination, and he left the radar and moved to the front of the bridge. He stood staring down the narrow throat of water at a horizon that concealed all the terrors and desperate alarms that his imagination could conjure up.

The door to the radio shack was open and the bridge was quiet, so that they all heard it clearly; they could even catch the hiss of breath as the speaker paused between each sentence, and the urgency of his tone was not covered by the slight distortion of the VHF carrier beam.

'Mayday! Mayday! Mayday! This is the bulk oil carrier *Golden Dawn*. Our position is 79° 50' West 25° 43' North.'

Before Nicholas reached the chart-table, he knew she was still a hundred miles ahead of them, and, as he pored over the table, he saw his estimate confirmed.

'We have lost our propeller with main shaft failure and we are drifting out of control.'

Nicholas' head flinched as though he had been hit in the face. He could imagine no more dangerous condition and position for a ship of that size – and Peter was on board.

'This is *Golden Dawn* calling the United States Coast Guard service or any ship in a position to afford assistance—'

Nicholas reached the radio shack with three long strides, and the Trog handed him the microphone and nodded.

'*Golden Dawn*, this is the salvage tug *Warlock*. I will be in a position to render assistance within four hours—'

Damn the rule of silence, Peter was on board her.

' – Tell Alexander I am offering Lloyd's Open Form and I want immediate acceptance.'

He dropped the microphone and stormed back on to

the bridge, his voice clipped and harsh as he caught David Allen's arm.

'Interception course and push her through the gate,' he ordered grimly. 'Tell Beauty Baker to open all the taps.' He dropped David's arm and spun back to the radio room.

'Telex Levoisin on *Sea Witch*. I want him to give me a time to reach *Golden Dawn* at his best possible speed,' and he wondered briefly if even the two tugs would be able to control the crippled and powerless *Golden Dawn* in the winds of a hurricane.

Jules replied almost immediately. He had bunkered at Charleston, and cleared harbour six hours previously. He was running hard now and he gave a time to *Golden Dawn*'s position for noon the next day, which was also the forecast time of passage of the Straits for Hurricane Lorna, according to the meteorological up-date they had got from Miami two hours before, Nicholas thought as he read the telex and turned to David Allen.

'David, there is no precedent for this that I know of – but with my son on board *Golden Dawn* I just have to assume command of this ship, on a temporary basis, of course.'

'I'd be honoured to act as your First Officer again, sir,' David told him quietly, and Nicholas could see he meant it.

'If there is a good salvage, the Master's share will still be yours,' Nicholas promised him, and thanked him with a touch on the arm. 'Would you check out the preparations to put a line aboard the tanker?'

David turned to leave the bridge, but Nicholas stopped him. 'By the time we get there, we will have the kind of wind you have only dreamed about in your worst nightmares – just keep that in mind.'

461

'Telex,' screeched the Trog. '*Golden Dawn* is replying to our offer.'

Nicholas strode across to the radio room, and read the first few lines of message as it printed out.

OFFER CONTRACT OF DAILY HIRE FOR TOWAGE THIS VESSEL FROM PRESENT POSITION TO GALVESTON ROADS

'The bastard,' Nicholas snarled. 'He's playing his fancy games with me, in the teeth of a hurricane and with my boy aboard.' Furiously he punched his fist into the palm of his other hand. 'Right!' he snapped. 'We'll play just as rough! Get me the Director of the US Coast Guard at the Fort Lauderdale Headquarters – get him on the emergency coastguard frequency and I will talk to him in clear.'

The Trog's face lit with malicious glee and he made the contact.

'Colonel Ramsden,' Nicholas said. 'This is the Master of *Warlock*. I'm the only salvage vessel that can reach *Golden Dawn* before passage of Lorna, and I'm probably the only tug on the eastern seaboard of America with 22,000 horsepower. Unless the *Golden Dawn*'s Master accepts Lloyd's Open Form within the next sixty minutes, I shall be obliged to see to the safety of my vessel and crew by running for the nearest anchorage – and you're going to have a million tons of highly toxic crude oil drifting out of control into your territorial waters, in hurricane conditions.'

The Coast Guard Director had a deep measured voice, and the calm tones of a man upon whom the mantle of authority was a familiar garment.

'Stand by, *Warlock*, I am going to contact *Golden Dawn* direct on Channel 16.'

Nicholas signalled the Trog to turn up the volume on

Channel 16 and they listened to Ramsden speaking directly to Duncan Alexander.

'In the event your vessel enters United States territorial waters without control or without an attendant tug capable of exerting that control, I shall be obliged under the powers vested in me to seize your vessel and take such steps to prevent pollution of our waters as I see fit. I have to warn you that those steps may include destruction of your cargo.'

Ten minutes later the Trog copied a telex from Duncan Alexander personal to Nicholas Berg accepting Lloyd's Open Form and requesting him to exercise all dispatch in taking *Golden Dawn* in tow.

'I estimate we will be drifting over the 100-fathom line and entering US territorial waters within two hours,' the message ended.

While Nicholas read it, standing out on the protected wing of *Warlock*'s bridge, the wind suddenly fluttered the paper in his hand and flattened his cotton shirt against his chest. He looked up quickly and saw the wind was backing violently into the east, and beginning to claw the tops of the Gulf Stream swells. The setting sun was bleeding copiously across the high veils of cirrus cloud which now covered the sky from horizon to horizon.

There was nothing more that Nicholas could do now. *Warlock* was running as hard as she could, and all her crew were quietly going about their preparations to pass a wire and take on tow. All he could do was wait, but that was always the hardest part.

Darkness came swiftly but with the last of the light, Nicholas could just make out a dark and mountainous shape beginning to hump up above the southern horizon like an impatient monster. He stared at it with awful fascination, until mercifully the night hid Lorna's dreadful face.

The wind chopped the Gulf Stream up into quick confused seas, and it did not blow steadily, but flogged them with squally gusts and rain that crackled against the bridge windows with startling suddenness.

The night was utterly black, there were no stars, no source of light whatsoever, and *Warlock* lurched and heeled to the patternless seas.

'Barometer's rising sharply,' David Allen called suddenly. 'It's jumped three millibars – back to 1005.'

'The trough,' said Nicholas grimly. It was a classic hurricane formation, that narrow girdle of higher pressure that demarcated the outer fringe of the great revolving spiral of tormented air. 'We are going into it now.'

And as he spoke the darkness lifted, the heavens began to burn like a bed of hot coals, and the sea shone with a sullen ruddy luminosity as though the doors of a furnace had been thrown wide.

Nobody spoke on *Warlock*'s bridge, they lifted their faces with the same awed expressions as worshippers in a lofty cathedral and they looked up at the skies.

Low cloud raced above them, cloud that glowed and shone with that terrible ominous flare. Slowly the light faded and changed, turning a paler sickly greenish hue, like the shine on putrid meat. Nicholas spoke first.

'The Devil's Beacon,' he said, and he wanted to rationalize it to break the superstitious mood that gripped them all. It was merely the rays of the sun below the western horizon catching the cloud peaks of the storm and reflected downwards through the weak cloud cover of the trough – but somehow he could not find the right words to denigrate that phenomenon that was part of the mariner's lore, the malignant beacon that leads a doomed ship on to its fate.

The weird light faded slowly away leaving the night even darker and more foreboding than it had been before.

'David,' Nicholas thought quickly of something to

distract his officers, 'have we got a radar contact yet?' and the new Mate roused himself with a visible effort and crossed to the radarscope.

'The range is very confused,' he said, his voice still subdued, and Nicholas joined him at the screen.

The sweeping arm lit a swirling mass of sea clutter, and the strange ghost echoes thrown up by electrical discharges within the approaching storm. The outline of the Florida mainland and of the nearest islands of the Grand Bahamas bank were firm and immediately recognizable. They reminded Nicholas yet again of how little sea-room there was in which to manoeuvre his tugs and their monstrous prize.

Then, in the trash of false echo and sea clutter, his trained eye picked out a harder echo on the extreme limits of the set's range. He watched it carefully for half a dozen revolutions of the radar's sweep, and each time it was constant and clearer.

'Radar contact,' he said. 'Tell *Golden Dawn* we are in contact, range sixty-five nautical miles. Tell them we will take on tow before midnight.' And then, under his breath, the old sailor's qualifications, 'God willing and weather permitting.'

T he lights on *Warlock*'s bridge had been rheostatted down to a dull rose glow to protect the night vision of her officers, and the four of them stared out to where they knew the tanker lay.

Her image on the radar was bright and firm, lying within the two mile ring of the screen, but from the bridge she was invisible.

In the two hours since first contact, the barometer had gone through its brief peak as the trough passed, and then fallen steeply.

From 1005 it had crashed to 900 and was still plummeting, and the weather coming in from the east was blustering and squalling. The wind mourned about them on a forever rising note, and torrential rain obscured all vision outside an arc of a few hundred yards. Even *Warlock*'s twin searchlights, set seventy feet above the main deck on the summit of the fire-control gantry, could not pierce those solid white curtains of rain.

Nicholas groped like a blind man through the rain fog, using pitch and power to close carefully with *Golden Dawn*, giving his orders to the helm in a cool impersonal tone which belied the pale set of his features and the alert brightness of his eyes as he reached the swirling bank of rain.

Abruptly another squall struck *Warlock*. With a demented shriek, it heeled the big tug sharply and shredded the curtains of rain, ripping them open so that for a moment Nicholas saw *Golden Dawn*.

She was exactly where he had expected her to be, but the wind had caught the tanker's high navigation bridge like the mainsail of a tall ship, and she was going swiftly astern.

All her deck and port lights were burning, and she carried the twin red riding lights at her stubby masthead that identified a vessel drifting out of control. The following sea driven on by the rising wind piled on to her tank decks, smothering them with white foam and spray, so that the ship looked like a submerged coral reef.

'Half ahead both,' Nicholas told the helmsman. 'Steer for her starboard side.'

He closed quickly with the tanker, staying in visual contact now; even when the rain mists closed down again, they could make out the ghostly shape of her and the glow of her riding lights.

David Allen was looking at him expectantly and

Nicholas asked, 'What bottom?' without taking his eyes from the stricken ship.

'One hundred sixteen fathoms and shelving fast.' They were being blown quickly out of the main channel, on to the shallow ledge of the Florida littoral.

'I'm going to tow her out stern first,' said Nicholas, and immediately David saw the wisdom of it. Nobody would be able to get up into her bows to secure a towline, the seas were breaking over them and sweeping them with ten and fifteen feet of green water.

'I'll go aft—' David began, but Nicholas stopped him.

'No, David. I want you here – because I'm going on board *Golden Dawn*.'

'Sir,' David wanted to tell him that it was dangerous to delay passing the towing cable – with that lee shore waiting.

'This will be our last chance to get passengers off her before the full hurricane hits us,' said Nicholas, and David saw that it was futile to protest. Nicholas Berg was going to fetch his son.

From the height of *Golden Dawn*'s towering navigation bridge, they could look directly down on to the main deck of the tug as she came alongside.

Peter Berg stood beside his mother, almost as tall as she was. He wore a full life-jacket and a corduroy cap pulled down over his ears.

'It will be all right,' he comforted Chantelle. 'Dad is here. It will be just fine now.' And he took her hand protectively.

Warlock staggered and reeled in the grip of wind as she came up into the tanker's lee, rain blew over her like dense white smoke and every few minutes she put her nose down and threw a thick green slice of sea water back along her decks.

In comparison to the tug's wild action, *Golden Dawn* wallowed heavily, held down by the oppressive weight of a million tons of crude oil, and the seas beat upon her with increasing fury, as if affronted by her indifference. *Warlock* edged in closer and still closer.

Duncan Alexander came through from the communications room at the rear of the bridge. He balanced easily against *Golden Dawn*'s ponderous motion but his face was swollen and flushed with anger.

'Berg is coming on board,' he burst out. 'He's wasting valuable time. I warned him that we must get out into deeper water.'

Peter Berg interrupted suddenly and pointed down at *Warlock*.

'Look!' he cried.

Until that moment, the night and the storm had hidden the small huddle of human shapes in the tug's high forward tower. They wore wet, glistening oilskins and their life jackets gave them a swollen pregnant look. They were lowering the boarding gantry into the horizontal position.

'There is Dad!' Peter shouted. 'That's him in front.'

At the extremity of her roll, *Warlock*'s boarding gantry touched the railing of the tanker's quarterdeck, ten feet above the swamped tank deck – and the leading figure on the tug's upperworks ran out lightly along the gantry, balanced for a moment high above the roaring, racing green water and then leapt across five feet of open space, caught a hand hold and then pulled himself over *Golden Dawn*'s rail.

Immediately the tug sheered off and fell in fifty yards off the tanker's starboard side, half hidden in the rain mists, but holding her station steadily, despite all the wind's and the sea's spiteful efforts to separate the two vessels.

The whole manoeuvre had been performed with an expertise which made it seem almost casual.

'Dad's carried a line across,' Peter said proudly, and Chantelle, looking down, saw that a delicate white nylon thread was being hove in by two seamen on the tanker's quarter deck, while from the tug's fire-control tower a canvas bosun's chair was being winched across.

The elevator doors slid open with a whine and Nicholas Berg strode on to the tanker's bridge. His oilskins still ran with rainwater that splattered on to the deck at his feet.

'Dad!' Peter ran to meet him and Nicholas stooped and embraced him fiercely before straightening; with one arm still about his son's shoulders, he confronted Chantelle and Duncan Alexander.

'I hope both of you are satisfied now,' he said quietly, 'but I for one don't rate our chances of saving this ship very highly, so I'm taking off everybody who is not needed on board to handle her.'

'Your tug,' burst out Duncan, 'you've got 22,000 horse-power, and can—'

'There is a hurricane on its way,' said Nicholas coldly, and he shot a glance at the roaring night. 'This is just the overture.' He turned back to Randle. 'How many men do you want to keep on board?'

Randle thought for a moment. 'Myself, a helmsman, and five seamen to handle the towlines and work the ship.' He paused and then went on, 'And the pump-room personnel to control the cargo.'

'You will act as helmsman, I will control the pump room, and I'll need only three seamen. Get me volunteers,' Nicholas decided. 'Send everybody else off.'

'Sir,' Randle began to protest.

'May I remind you Captain, that I am salvage master, my authority now supersedes yours.' Nicholas did not wait for his reply. 'Chantelle,' he picked her out, 'take Peter down to the quarterdeck. You'll go across first.'

'Listen here, Berg,' Duncan could no longer contain himself, 'I insist you pass the towing cable, this ship is in danger.'

'Get down there with them,' Nicholas snapped. 'I'll decide the procedures.'

'Do as he says, darling,' Chantelle smiled up at her husband vindictively. 'You've lost. Nicholas is the only winner now.'

'Shut up, damn you,' Duncan hissed at her.

'Get down to the afterdeck,' Nicholas' voice cracked like breaking ice.

'I'm staying on board this ship,' said Duncan abruptly. 'It's my responsibility. I said I'd see it out and by God I will. I am going to be here to make sure you do your job, Berg.'

Nicholas checked himself, studied him for a long moment, and then smiled mirthlessly.

'Nobody ever called you a coward,' he nodded reluctantly. 'Other things – but not a coward. Stay if you will, we might need an extra hand,' Then to Peter, 'Come, my boy.' And he led him towards the elevator.

At the quarterdeck rail, Nicholas hugged the boy, holding him in his arms, their cheeks pressed tightly together, and drawing out the moment while the wind cannoned and thrummed about their heads.

'I love you, Dad.'

'And I love you, Peter, more than I can ever tell you – but you must go now.'

He broke the embrace and lifted the child into the deep canvas bucket of the bosun's chair, stepped back and windmilled his right arm. Immediately, the winch party in *Warlock*'s upperworks swung him swiftly out into the gap between the two ships and the nylon cable seemed as fragile and insubstantial as a spider's thread.

As the two ships rolled and dipped, so the line tightened and sagged, one moment dropping the white canvas bucket almost to the water level where the hungry waves snatched at it with cold green fangs, and the next, pulling the line up so tightly that it hummed with tension, threatening to snap and drop the child back into the sea, but at last it reached the tug and four pairs of strong hands lifted the boy clear. For one moment, he waved back at Nicholas and then he was hustled away, and the empty bosun's chair was coming back.

Only then did Nicholas become aware that Chantelle was clinging to his arm and he looked down into her face. Her eyelashes were dewed and stuck together with the flying raindrops. Her face ran with wetness and she seemed very small and childlike under the bulky oilskins and life jacket. She was as beautiful as she had ever been but her eyes were huge and darkly troubled.

'Nicholas, I've always needed you,' she husked. 'But never as I need you now.'

Her existence was being blown away on the wind, and she was afraid.

'You and this ship are all I have left.'

'No, only the ship,' he said brusquely, and he was amazed that the spell was broken. That soft area of his soul which she had been able to touch so unerringly was now armoured against her. With a sudden surge of relief, he realized he was free of her, for ever. It was over; here in the storm, he was free at last.

She sensed it – for the fear in her eyes changed to real terror.

'Nicholas, you cannot desert me now. Oh Nicholas, what will become of me without you and Christy Marine?'

'I don't know,' he told her quietly, and caught the

bosun's chair as it came in over *Golden Dawn's* rail. He lifted her as easily as he had lifted his son and placed her in the canvas bucket.

'And to tell you the truth, Chantelle, I don't really care,' he said, and stepping back, he windmilled his right arm. The chair swooped out across the narrow water, swinging like a pendulum in the wind. Chantelle shouted something at him but Nicholas had turned away, and was already going aft in a lurching run to where the three volunteers were waiting.

He saw at a glance that they were big, powerful, competent-looking men.

Quickly Nicholas checked their equipment, from the thick leather gauntlets to the bolt cutters and jemmy bars for handling heavy cable.

'You'll do,' he said. 'We will use the bosun's tackle to bring across a messenger from the tug – just as soon as the last man leaves this ship.'

Working with men to whom the task was unfamiliar, and in rapidly deteriorating conditions of sea and weather, it took almost another hour before they had the main cable across from *Warlock* secured by its thick nylon spring to the tanker's stern bollards – yet the time had passed so swiftly for Nicholas that when he stood back and glanced at his watch, he was shocked. Before this wind they must have been going down very fast on the land. He staggered into the tanker's stern quarters, and left a trail of sea water down the passageway to the elevators.

On the bridge, Captain Randle was standing grim-faced at the helm, and Duncan Alexander snapped accusingly at him.

'You've cut it damned fine.' A single glance at the

472

digital printout of the depth gauge on the tanker's control console bore him out. They had thirty-eight fathoms of water under them now, and the Golden Dawn's swollen belly sagged down twenty fathoms below the surface. They were going down very swiftly before the easterly gale winds. It was damned fine, Nicholas had to agree, but he showed no alarm or agitation as he crossed to Randle's side and unhooked the hand microphone.

'David,' he asked quietly, 'are you ready to haul us off?'

'Ready, sir,' David Allen's voice came from the speaker above his head.

'I'm going to give you full port rudder to help your turn across the wind,' said Nicholas, and then nodded to Randle. 'Full port rudder.'

'Forty degrees of port rudder on,' Randle reported.

They felt the tiny shock as the tow-cable came up taut, and carefully Warlock began the delicate task of turning the huge ship across the rising gusting wind and then dragging her out tail first into the deeper water of the channel where she would have her best chance of riding out the hurricane.

It was clear now that Golden Dawn lay directly in the track of Lorna, and the storm unleashed its true nature upon them. Out there upon the sane and rational world, the sun was rising, but here there was no dawn, for there was no horizon and no sky. There was only madness and wind and water, and all three elements were so intermingled as to form one substance.

An hour – which seemed like a lifetime – ago, the wind had ripped away the anemometer and the weather-recording equipment on top of the navigation bridge, so Nicholas had no way of judging the wind's strength and direction.

Out beyond the bridge windows, the wind took the top off the sea; it took it off in thick sheets of salt water and lifted them over the navigation bridge in a shrieking white curtain that cut off visibility at the glass of the windows. The tank deck had disappeared in the racing white emulsion of wind and water, even the railing of the bridge wings six feet from the windows was invisible.

The entire superstructure groaned and popped and whimpered under the assault of the wind, the pressed aluminium bulkheads bulging and distorting, the very deck flexing and juddering at the solid weight of the storm.

Through the saturated, racing, swirling air, a leaden and ominous grey light filtered, and every few minutes the electrical impulses generated within the sixty-thousand-foot-high mountain of racing, spinning air released themselves in shattering cannonades of thunder and sudden brilliance of eye-searing white lightning.

There was no visual contact with *Warlock*. The massive electrical disturbance of the storm and the clutter of high seas and almost solid cloud and turbulence had reduced the radar range to a few miles, and even then it was unreliable. Radio contact with the tug was drowned with buzzing squealing static. It was possible to understand only odd disconnected words from David Allen.

Nicholas was powerless, caged in the groaning, vibrating box of the navigation bridge, blinded and deafened by the unleashed powers of the heavens. There was nothing any of them could do.

Randle had locked the ultra-tanker's helm amidships, and now he stood with Duncan and the three seamen by the chart-table, all of them clinging to it for support, all their faces pale and set as though carved from chalk.

Only Nicholas moved restlessly about the bridge; from the stern windows where he peered down vainly, trying to get a glimpse of either the tow-cable and its spring, or of the tug's looming shape through the racing white storm, then he came forward carefully, using the foul-weather rail to steady himself against the huge ship's wild and unpredictable motion, and he stood before the control console, studying the display of lights that monitored the pod tanks and the ship's navigational and mechanical functions.

None of the petroleum tanks had lost any crude oil and in all of them the nature of the inert gas was constant. There had been no ingress of air to them; they were all still intact then. One of the reasons that Nicholas had taken the tanker in tow stern first was so that the navigation tower might break the worst of wind and sea, and the fragile bloated tanks would receive some protection from it.

Yet desperately he wished for a momentary sight of the tank deck, merely to reassure himself. There could be malfunction in the pump control instruments, the storm could have clawed one of the pod tanks open, and even now *Golden Dawn* could be bleeding her poison into the sea. But there was no view of the tank decks through the storm, and Nick stooped to the radarscope. The screen glowed and danced and flickered with ghost images and trash – he wasn't too certain if even *Warlock*'s image was constant, the range seemed to be opening, as though the towline had parted. He straightened up and stood balanced on the balls of his feet, reassuring himself by the feel of the deck that *Golden Dawn* was still under tow. He could feel by the way she resisted the wind and the sea that the tow was still good.

Yet there was no means of telling their position. The satellite navigational system was completely blanketed, the radio waves were distorted and diverted by tens of thousands of feet of electrical storm, and the same forces were blanketing the marine radio beacons on the American mainland.

The only indication was the ship's electronic log which gave Nicholas the speed of the ship's hull through the water and the speed across the sea bottom, and the depth finder which recorded the water under her keel.

For the first two hours of the tow, *Warlock* had been able to pull the ship back towards the main channel at three and a half knots, and slowly the water had become deeper until they had 150 fathoms under them.

Then as the wind velocity increased, the windage of *Golden Dawn*'s superstructure had acted as a vast mainsail and the storm had taken control. Now, despite all the power in *Warlock*'s big twin propellers, both tug and tanker were being pushed once more back towards the 100-fathom line and the American mainland.

'Where is *Sea Witch*?' Nicholas wondered, as he stared helplessly at the gauges. They were going towards the shore at a little over two knots, and the bottom was shelving steeply. *Sea Witch* might be the ace that took the trick, if she could reach them through these murderous seas and savage winds, and if she could find them in this wilderness of mad air and water.

Again, Nicholas groped his way to the communications room, and still clinging to the bulkhead with one hand he thumbed the microphone.

'*Sea Witch. Sea Witch.* This is *Warlock*. Calling *Sea Witch*.'

He listened then, trying to tune out the snarl and crackle of static, crouching over the set. Faintly he thought he heard a human voice, a scratchy whisper through the interference and he called again and listened, and called again. There was the voice again, but so indistinct he could not make out a single word.

Above his head, there was a tearing screech of rending metal. Nicholas dropped the microphone and staggered through on to the bridge. There was another deafening banging and hammering and all of them stood staring up at the metal roof of the bridge. It sagged and shook, there

476

was one more crash and then with a scraping, dragging rush, a confused tangle of metal and wire and cable tumbled over the forward edge of the bridge and flapped and swung wildly in the wind.

It took a moment for Nicholas to realize what it was.

'The radar antennae!' he shouted. He recognized the elongated dish of the aerial, dangling on a thick coil of cable, then the wind tore that loose also, and the entire mass of equipment flapped away like a giant bat and was instantly lost in the teeming white curtains of the storm.

With two quick paces, he reached the radarscope, and one glance was enough. The screen was black and dead. They had lost their eyes now, and, unbelievably, the sound of the storm was rising again.

It boomed against the square box of the bridge, and the men within it cowered from its fury.

Then abruptly, Duncan was screaming something at Nicholas, and pointing up at the master display of the control console. Nicholas, still hanging on to the radarscope, roused himself with an effort and looked up at the display. The speed across the ground had changed drastically. It was now almost eight knots, and the depth was ninety-two fathoms.

Nicholas felt icy despair clutch and squeeze his guts. The ship was moving differently under him, he could feel her now in mortal distress; that same gust which had torn away the radar mast had done other damage.

He knew what that damage was, and the thought of it made him want to vomit, but he had to be sure. He had to be absolutely certain, and he began to hand himself along the foul-weather rail towards the elevator doors.

Across the bridge the others were watching him intently, but even from twenty feet it was impossible to make himself heard above the clamorous assault of the storm.

One of the seamen seemed suddenly to guess his intention. He left the chart-table and groped his way along the bulkhead towards Nicholas.

'Good man!' Nicholas grabbed his arm to steady him, and they fell forward into the elevator as *Golden Dawn* began another of those ponderous wallowing rolls and the deck fell out from under their feet.

The ride down in the elevator car slammed them back and forth across the little coffin-like box, and even here in the depths of the ship they had to shout to hear each other.

'The tow cable,' Nicholas yelled in the man's ear. 'Check the tow cable.'

From the elevator they went carefully aft along the central passageway, and when they reached the double storm doors, Nicholas tried to push the inner door open, but the pressure of the wind held it closed.

'Help me,' he shouted at the seaman, and they threw their combined weight against it. The instant that they forced the jamb open a crack, the vacuum of pressure was released and the wind took the three-inch mahogany doors and ripped them effortlessly from their hinges, and whisked them away, as though they were a pair of playing cards – and Nicholas and the seaman were exposed in the open doorway.

The wind flung itself upon them, and hurled them to the deck, smothering them in the icy deluge of water that ripped at their faces as abrasively as ground glass.

Nicholas rolled down the deck and crashed into the stern rail with such jarring force that he thought his lungs had been crushed, and the wind pinned him there, and blinded and smothered him with salt water.

He lay there helpless as a newborn infant, and near him he heard the seaman screaming thinly. The sound steeled him, and Nicholas slowly dragged himself to his knees, desperately clutching at the rail to resist the wind.

Still the man screamed and Nicholas began to creep

forward on his hands and knees. It was impossible to stand in that wind and he could move only with support from the rail.

Six feet ahead of him, the extreme limit of his vision, the railing had been torn away, a long section of it dangling over the ship's side, and to this was clinging the seaman. His weight driven by the wind must have hit the rail with sufficient force to tear it loose, and now he was hanging on with one arm hooked through the railing and the other arm twisted from a shattered shoulder and waving a crazy salute as the wind whipped it about. When he looked up at Nicholas his mouth had been smashed in. It looked as though he had half chewed a mouthful of blackcurrants, and the jagged stumps of his broken front teeth were bright red with the juice.

On his belly, Nicholas reached for him, and as he did so, the wind came again, unbelievably it was stronger still, and it took the damaged railing with the man still upon it and tore it bodily away. They disappeared instantly in the blinding white-out of the storm, and Nicholas felt himself hurled forward towards the edge. He clung with all his strength to the remaining section of the rail, and felt it buckle and begin to give.

On his knees still he clawed himself away from that fatal beckoning gap, towards the stern, and the wind struck him full in the face, blinding and choking him. Sightlessly, he dragged himself on until one outstretched arm struck the cold cast iron of the port stern bollard, and he flung both arms about it like a lover, choking and retching from the salt water that the wind had forced through his nose and mouth and down his throat.

Still blind, he felt for the woven steel of *Warlock*'s main tow-wire. He found it and he could not span it with his fist – but he felt the quick lift of his hopes.

The cable was still secured. He had catted and prevented it with a dozen nylon strops, and it was still holding. He crawled forward, dragging himself along the tow-cable, and immediately he realized that his relief had been premature. There was no tension in the cable and when he reached the edge of the deck it dangled straight down. It was not stretched out into the whiteness, to where he had hoped *Warlock* was still holding them like a great sea anchor.

He knew then that what he had dreaded had happened. The storm had been too powerful; it had snapped the steel cable like a thread of cotton, and *Golden Dawn* was loose, without control, and this wild and savage wind was blowing her down swiftly on to the land.

Nicholas felt suddenly exhausted to his bones. He lay flat on the deck, closed his eyes and clung weakly to the severed cable. The wind wanted to hurl him over the side; it ballooned his oilskins and ripped at his face. It would be so easy to open his fingers and to let go – and it took all his resolve to resist the impulse.

Slowly, as painfully as a crippled insect, he dragged himself back through the open, shattered doorway into the central passageway of the stern quarters – but still the wind followed him. It roared down the passageway, driving in torrents of rain and salt water that flooded the deck and forced Nicholas to cling for support like a drunkard.

After the open storm, the car of the elevator seemed silent and tranquil as the inner sanctum of a cathedral. He looked at himself in the wall mirror, and saw that his eyes were scoured red and painful-looking by salt and wind, and his cheeks and lips looked raw and bruised, as though the skin had been rasped away. He touched his face and there was no feeling in his nose nor in his lips.

The elevator doors slid open and he reeled out on to the navigation bridge. The group of men at the chart-table seemed not to have moved, but their heads turned to him.

Nicholas reached the table and clung to it. They were silent, watching his face.

'I lost a man,' he said, and his voice was hoarse and

roughened by salt and weariness. 'He went overboard. The wind got him.'

Still none of them moved nor spoke, and Nicholas coughed, his lungs ached from the water he had breathed. When the spasm passed, he went on.

'The tow-cable has parted. We are loose – and *Warlock* will never be able to re-establish tow. Not in this.'

All their heads turned now to the forward bridge windows, to that impenetrable racing whiteness beyond the glass, that was lit internally with its glowing bursts of lightning.

Nicholas broke the spell that held them all. He reached up to the signal locker above the chart-table and brought down a cardboard packet of distress flares. He broke open the seals and spilled the flares on to the table. They looked like sticks of dynamite, cylinders of heavily varnished waterproof paper. The flares could be lit, and would spurt out crimson flames, even if immersed in water, once the self-igniter tab at one end was pulled.

Nicholas stuffed half a dozen of the flares into the inner pockets of his oilskins.

'Listen,' he had to shout, even though they were only feet away. 'We are going to be aground within two hours. This ship is going to start breaking up immediately we strike.'

He paused and studied their faces; Duncan was the only one who did not seem to understand. He had picked up a handful of the signal flares from the table and he was looking inquiringly at Nicholas.

'I will give you the word; as soon as we reach the twenty-fathom line and she touches bottom, you will go over the side. We will try and get a raft away. There is a chance you could be carried ashore.'

He paused again, and he could see that Randle and his two seamen realized clearly just how remote that chance was.

'I will give you twenty minutes to get clear. By then, the pod tanks will have begun breaking up—' He didn't want this to sound melodramatic and he searched for some way to make it sound less theatrical, but could think of none. 'Once the first tank ruptures, I will ignite the escaping crude with a signal flare.'

'Christ!' Randle mouthed the blasphemy, and the storm censored it on his lips. Then he raised his voice. 'A million tons of crude. It will fireball, man.'

'Better than a million-ton slick down the Gulf Stream,' Nicholas told him wearily.

'None of us will have a chance. A million tons. It will go up like an atom bomb.' Randle was white-faced and shaking now. 'You can't do it!'

'Think of a better way,' said Nicholas and left the table to stagger across to the radio room. They watched him go, and then Duncan looked down at the signal flares in his hand for a moment before thrusting them into the pocket of his jacket.

In the radio room, Nicholas called quietly into the microphone. 'Come in, *Sea Witch* – *Sea Witch*, this is *Golden Dawn*.' And only the static howled in reply.

'*Warlock*. Come in, *Warlock*. This is *Golden Dawn*.'

Something else went in the wind, they heard it tear loose, and the whole superstructure shook and trembled. The ship was beginning to break up; it had not been designed to withstand winds like this.

Through the open radio room door, Nicholas could see the control console display. There were seventy-one fathoms of water under the ship, and the wind was punching her, flogging her on towards the shore.

'Come in, *Sea Witch*,' Nicholas called with quiet desperation. 'This is *Golden Dawn*. Do you read me?'

The wind charged the ship, crashing into it like a monster, and she groaned and reeled from the blow.

'Come in, *Warlock*.'

Randle lurched across to the forward windows, and clinging to the rail he bowed over the gauges that monitored the condition of the ship's cargo, checking for tank damage.

'At least he is still thinking.' Nicholas watched him, and above the Captain's head, the sounding showed sixty-eight fathoms.

Randle straightened slowly, began to turn, and the wind struck again.

Nicholas felt the blow in his stomach. It was a solid thing, like a mountain in avalanche, a defeaning boom of sound and the forward bridge window above the control console broke inwards.

It burst in a glittering explosion of glass shards that engulfed the figure of Captain Randle standing directly before it. In a fleeting moment of horror, Nicholas saw his head half severed from his shoulders by a guillotine of flying glass, then he crumpled to the deck and instantly the bright pulsing hose of his blood was diluted to spreading pale pink in the torrent of wind and blown water that poured in through the opening, and smothered the navigation bridge.

Charts and books were ripped from their shelves and fluttered like trapped birds as the wind blustered and swirled in the confines of glass and steel.

Nicholas reached the Captain's body, protecting his own face with an arm crooked across it, but there was nothing he could do for him. He left Randle lying on the deck and shouted to the others.

'Keep clear of the windows.'

He gathered them in the rear of the bridge, against the bulkhead where stood the Decca and navigational systems. The four of them kept close together, as though they gained comfort from the close proximity of other humans, but the wind did not relent.

It poured in through the shattered window and raged

about the bridge, tearing at their clothing and filling the air with a fine mist of water, flooding the deck ankle deep so that it sloshed and ran as the tanker rolled almost to her beam ends.

Randle's limp and sodden body slid back and forth in the wash and roll, until Nicholas left the dubious security of the after bulkhead, half-lifted the corpse under the arms, and dragged it into the radio room and wedged it into the radio operator's bunk. Swift blood stained the crisply ironed sheets, and Nicholas threw a fold of the blanket over Randle and staggered back into the bridge.

Still the wind rose, and now Nicholas felt himself numbed by the force and persistence of it.

Some loose material, perhaps a sheet of aluminium from the superstructure, or a length of piping ripped from the tank deck below, smashed into the tip of the bridge like a cannon ball and then flipped away into the storm, leaving a jagged rent which the wind exploited, tearing and worrying at it, enlarging the opening, so that the plating flapped and hammered and a solid deluge of rain poured in through it.

Nicholas realized that the ship's superstructure was beginning to go; like a gigantic vulture, soon the wind would begin stripping the carcass down to its bones.

He knew he should get the survivors down nearer the water line, so that when they were forced to commit themselves to the sea, they could do so quickly. But his brain was numbered by the tumult, and he stood stolidly. It needed all his remaining strength merely to brace himself against the tearing wind and the ship's anguished motion.

In the days of sail, the crew would tie themselves to the main mast, when they reached this stage of despair.

Dully, he registered that the depth of water under the ship was now only fifty-seven fathoms, and the barometer was reading 955 millibars. Nicholas had never heard of a reading that low; surely it could not go lower, they must be almost at the centre of the revolving hurricane.

With an effort, he lifted his arm and read the time. It was still only ten o'clock in the morning, they had been in the hurricane for only two and a half hours.

A great burning light struck through the torn roof, a light that blinded them with its intensity, and Nicholas threw up his hands to protect his eyes. He could not understand what was happening. He thought his hearing had gone, for suddenly the terrible tumult of the wind was muted, fading away.

Then he understood. 'The eye,' he croaked, 'we are into the eye,' and his voice resounded strangely in his own ears. He stumbled to the front of the bridge.

Although the *Golden Dawn* still rolled ponderously, describing an arc of almost forty degrees from side to side, she was free of the unbearable weight of the wind and brilliant sunshine poured down upon her. It beamed down like the dazzling arc lamps of a stage set, out of the throat of a dark funnel of dense racing swirling cloud.

The cloud lay to the very surface of the sea, and encompassed the full sweep of the horizon in an unbroken wall. Only directly overhead was it open, and the sky was an angry unnatural purple, set with the glaring, merciless eye of the sun.

The sea was still wild and confused, leaping into peaks and troughs and covered with a thick frothy mattress of spindrift, whipped into a custard by the wild winds. But already the sea was subsiding in the total calm of the eye and *Golden Dawn* was rolling less viciously.

Nicholas turned his head stiffly to watch the receding wall of racing cloud. How long would it take for the eye to pass over them, he wondered.

Not very long, he was sure of that, half an hour perhaps – an hour at the most – and then the storm would be on them again, with its renewed fury every bit as sudden as its passing. But this time, the wind would come from exactly the opposite direction as they crossed the hub and went into the far side of the revolving wall of cloud.

Nicholas jerked his eyes away from that racing, heaven-high bank of cloud, and looked down on to the tank deck. He saw at a single glance that *Golden Dawn* had already sustained mortal damage. The forward port pod tank was half torn from its hydraulic coupling, holding only by the bows and lying at almost twenty degrees from the line of the other three tanks. The entire tank deck was twisted like the limb of an arthritic giant. It rolled and pitched out of sequence with the rest of the hull.

Golden Dawn's back was broken. It had broken where Duncan had weakened the hull to save steel. Only the buoyancy of the crude petroleum in her four tanks was holding her together now. Nicholas expected to see the dark, glistening ooze of slick leaking from her; he could not believe that not one of the four tanks had ruptured, and he glanced at the electronic cargo monitor. Loads and gas contents of all tanks were still normal. They had been freakishly lucky so far, but when they went into the far side of the hurricane he knew that *Golden Dawn*'s weakened spine would give completely, and when that happened it must pinch and tear the thin skins of the pod tanks.

He made a decision then, forcing his mind to work, not certain how good a decision it was but determined to act on it.

'Duncan,' he called to him across the swamped and battered bridge. 'I'm sending you and the others off on one of the life-rafts. This will be your only chance to launch one. I'll stay on board to fire the cargo when the storm hits again.'

'The storm has passed,' suddenly Duncan was screaming at him like a madman. 'The ship is safe now. You're going to destroy my ship – you're deliberately trying to break me.'

He was lunging across the heaving bridge. 'It's deliberate. You know I've won now. You are going to destroy this ship. It's the only way you can stop me now.' He swung a clumsy round arm blow. Nicholas ducked under it and caught Duncan around the chest.

'Listen to me,' he shouted, trying to calm him. 'This is only the eye—'

'You'd do anything to stop me. You swore you would stop me—'

'Help me,' Nicholas called to the two seamen, and they grabbed Duncan's arms. He bucked and fought like a madman, screaming wildly at Nicholas, his face contorted and swollen with rage, sodden hair flopping into his eyes. 'You'd do anything to destroy me, to destroy my ship—'

'Take him down to the raft deck,' Nicholas ordered the two seamen. He knew he could not reason with Duncan now, and he turned away and stiffened suddenly.

'Wait!' he stopped them leaving the bridge.

Nicholas felt the terrible burden of weariness and despair slip from his shoulders, felt new strength rippling through his body, recharging his courage and his resolution – for a mile away, from behind that receding wall of dreadful grey cloud, *Sea Witch* burst abruptly into the sunlight, tearing bravely along with the water bursting over her bows and flying back as high as her bridgework, running without regard to the hazard of sea and storm.

'Jules,' Nicholas whispered.

Jules was driving her like only a tugman can drive a ship, racing to beat the far wall of the storm.

Nicholas felt his throat constricting and suddenly the scalding tears of relief and thankfulness half-blinded him – for a mile out on *Sea Witch*'s port side, and barely a cable-length astern of her, *Warlock* came crashing out of the storm bank, running every bit as hard as her sister ship.

'David,' Nicholas spoke aloud. 'You too, David.'

He realized only then that they must have been in radar

contact with him through those wild tempestuous hours of storm passage, hovering there, holding station on *Golden Dawn*'s crippled bulk and waiting for their first opportunity.

Above the wail and crackle of static from the overhead loudspeaker boomed Jules Levoisin's voice. He was close enough and in the clear eye the interference allowed a readable radio contact.

'*Golden Dawn*, this is *Sea Witch*. Come in, *Golden Dawn*.'

Nicholas reached the radio bench and snatched up the microphone.

'Jules.' He did not waste a moment in greeting or congratulations. 'We are going to take the tanks off her, and let the hull go. Do you understand?'

'I understand to take off the tanks,' Jules responded immediately.

Nicholas' brain was crisp and clear again. He could see just how it must be done. '*Warlock* takes off the port tanks first – in tandem.'

In tandem, the two tanks would be strung like beads on a string, they had been designed to tow that way.

'Then you will take off the starboard side—'

'You must save the hull.' Duncan still fought the two seamen who held him. 'Goddamn you, Berg. I'll not let you destroy me.'

Nicholas ignored his ravings until he had finished giving his orders to the two tug masters. Then he dropped the microphone and grabbed Duncan by the shoulders. Nicholas seemed to be possessed suddenly by supernatural strength, and he shook him as though he were a child. He shook him so his head snapped back and forth and his teeth rattled in his head.

'You bloody idiot,' he shouted in Duncan's face. 'Don't you understand the storm will resume again in minutes?'

He jerked Duncan's body out of the grip of the two

seamen and dragged him bodily to the windows overlooking the tank deck.

'Can't you see this monster you have built is finished, finished! There is no propeller, her back is broken, the superstructure will go minutes after the wind hits again.'

He dragged Duncan round to face him, their eyes were inches apart.

'It's over, Duncan. We will be lucky to get away with our lives. We'll be luckier still to save the cargo.'

'But don't you understand – we've got to save the hull – without it—' Duncan started to struggle, he was a powerful man, and quickly he was rousing himself, within minutes he would be dangerous – and there was no time, already *Warlock* was swinging up into her position on *Golden Dawn's* port beam for tank transfer.

'I'll not let you take off—' Duncan wrenched himself out of Nicholas' grip, there was a mad fanatic light in his eyes.

Nicholas swivelled; coming up on to his toes and swinging from the shoulders he aimed for the point of Duncan's jaw, just below the ear and the thick sodden wedge of Duncan's red-gold sideburns. But Duncan rolled his head with the punch, and the blow glanced off his temple, and *Golden Dawn* rolled back the other way as Nicholas was unbalanced.

He fell back against the control console, and Duncan drove at him, two running paces like a quarterback taking a field goal, and he kicked right-legged for Nicholas' lower body.

'I'll kill you, Berg,' he screamed, and Nicholas had only time to roll sideways and lift his leg, scissoring it to protect his crotch. Duncan's kick caught him in the upper thigh. An explosion of white pain shot up into his belly and numbed his leg to the thigh, but he used the control console and his good leg to launch himself into a counter-punch, hooking with his right again, under the ribs – and the wind went out of Duncan's lungs with a whoosh as he doubled. Nicholas transferred his weight smoothly and swung his left fist up into Duncan's face. It sounded like a watermelon dropped on a concrete floor, and Duncan was hurled backwards against the bulkhead, pinned there for a moment by the ship's roll. Nicholas followed him, hobbling painfully on the injured leg, and he hit him twice more. Left and right, short, hard, hissing blows that cracked his skull backwards against the bulkhead, and brought quick bright rosettes of blood from his lips and nostrils.

As his legs buckled, Nicholas caught him by the throat with his left hand and held him upright, searching his eyes for further resistance, ready to hit again, but there was no fight left in him.

Nicholas let him go, and went to the signal locker. He snatched three of the small walkie-talkie radios from the radio shelves and handed one to each of the two seamen.

'You know the pod tank undocking procedures for a tandem tow?' he asked.

'We've practised it,' one of them replied.

'Let's go,' said Nicholas.

It was a job that was scheduled for a dozen men, and there were three of them. Duncan was of no use to them, and Nicholas left him in the pump control room on the lowest deck of *Golden Dawn*'s stern quarter, after he had closed down the inert gas pumps, sealed the gas vents, and armed the hydraulic releases of the pod tanks for undocking.

They worked sometimes neck-deep in the bursts of green, frothing water that poured over the ultra-tanker's foredeck. They took on board and secured *Warlock*'s main cable, unlocked the hydraulic clamps that held the forward pod tank attached to the hull and, as David Allen eased it clear of the crippled hull, they turned and lumbered back along the twisted and wind-torn catwalk, handicapped by the heavy seaboots and oilskins and the confused seas that still swamped the tank-deck every few minutes.

On the after tank, the whole laborious energy-sapping procedure had to be repeated, but here it was complicated by the chain coupling which connected the two half-mile-long pod tanks. Over the walkie-talkie Nicholas had to co-ordinate the efforts of his seamen to those of David Allen at the helm of *Warlock*.

When at last *Warlock* threw on power to both of her big propellers and sheered away from the wallowing hull, she had both port pod tanks in tow. They floated just level with the surface of the sea, offering no windage for the hurricane winds that would soon be upon them again.

Hanging on to the rail of the raised catwalk Nicholas watched for two precious minutes with an appraising professional eye. It was an incredible sight, two great shiny black whales, their backs showing only in the troughs, and the gallant little ship leading them away. They followed meekly, and Nicholas' anxiety was lessened. He was not confident, not even satisfied, for there was still a hurricane to navigate – but there was hope now.

'*Sea Witch*,' he spoke into the small portable radio. 'Are you ready to take on tow?'

Jules Levoisin fired the rocket-line across personally. Nicholas recognized his portly but nimble figure high in the fire-control tower, and the rocket left a thin trail of snaking white smoke high against the backdrop of racing, grey hurricane clouds. Arching high over the tanker's tank-deck, the thin nylon rocket-line fell over the catwalk ten feet from where Nicholas stood.

They worked with a kind of restrained frenzy, and Jules Levoisin brought the big graceful tug in so close beside them that glancing up Nicholas could see the flash of a gold filling in Jules' white smile of encouragement. It was only a glance that Nicholas allowed himself, and then he raised his face and looked at the storm.

The wall of cloud was slippery and smooth and grey, like the body of a gigantic slug, and at its foot trailed a glistening white slimy line where the winds frothed the surface of the sea. It was very close now, ten miles, no more, and above them the sun had gone, cut out by the spiralling vortex of leaden cloud. Yet still that open narrow funnel of clear calm air reached right up to a dark and ominous sky.

There was no hydraulic pressure on the clamps of the starboard forward pod tank. Somewhere in the twisted damaged hull the hydraulic line must have sheared. Nicholas and one of the seamen had to work the emergency release, pumping it open slowly and laboriously by hand.

Still it would not release, the hull was distorted, the clamp jaws out of alignment.

'Pull,' Nicholas commanded Jules in desperation. 'Pull all together.' The storm front was five miles away, and already he could hear the deadly whisper of the wind, and a cold puff touched Nicholas' uplifted face.

The sea boiled under *Sea Witch*'s counter, spewing out in a swift white wake as Jules brought in both engines. The tow-cable came up hard and straight; for half a minute nothing gave, nothing moved – except the wall of racing grey cloud bearing down upon them.

Then, with a resounding metallic clang, the clamps slipped and the tank slid ponderously out of its dock in *Golden Dawn*'s hull – and as it came free, so the hull, held together until that moment by the tanks' bulk and buoyancy, began to collapse.

The catwalk on which Nicholas stood began to twist and tilt so that he had to grab for a handhold, and he stood frozen in horrified fascination as he watched *Golden Dawn* begin the final break-up.

The whole tank deck, now only a gutted skeleton, began to bend at its weakened centre, began to hinge like an enormous pair of nutcrackers – and caught between the jaws of the nutcracker was the starboard after pod tank. It was a nut the size of Chartres Cathedral, with a soft liquid centre, and a shell as thin as the span of a man's hand.

Nicholas broke into a lurching, blundering run down the twisting, tilting catwalk, calling urgently into the radio as he went.

'Shear!' he shouted to the seamen almost half a mile away across that undulating plane of tortured steel. 'Shear the tandem tow!'

For the two starboard pod tanks were linked by the heavy chain of the tandem, and the forward tank was linked to *Sea Witch* by the main tow-cable. So *Sea Witch* and the doomed *Golden Dawn* were coupled inexorably, unless they could cut the two tanks apart and let *Sea Witch* escape with the forward tank which she had just undocked.

The shear control was in the control box halfway back along the tank deck, and at that moment the nearest seaman was two hundred yards from it.

Nicholas could see him staggering wildly back along the twisting, juddering catwalk. Clearly he realized the danger, but his haste was fatal, for as he jumped from the catwalk, the deck opened under him, gaping open like the jaws of a steel monster and the seaman fall through, waist deep, into the opening between two moving plates, then as he squirmed feebly, the next lurch of the ship's hull closed the plates, sliding them across each other like the blades of a pair of scissors.

The man shrieked once and a wave burst over the deck, smothering his mutilated body in cold, green water. When it poured back over the ship's side there was no sign of the man. The deck was washed glisteningly clean.

Nicholas reached the same point in the deck, judged the gaping and closing movement of the steel plate and the next rush of sea coming on board, before he leapt across the deadly gap.

He reached the control box, and slid back the hatch, pressing himself into the tiny steel cubicle as he unlocked the red lid that housed the shear button. He hit the button with the heel of his hand.

The four heavy chains of the tandem tow lay between the electrodes of the shear mechanism. With a gross surge of power from the ship's generators and a flash of blue electric flame, the thick steel links sheared as cleanly as cheese under the cutting wire – and, half a mile away, *Sea Witch* felt the release and pounded ahead under the full thrust of her propellers, taking with her the forward starboard tank still held on main tow.

Nicholas paused in the opening of the control cubicle, hanging on to the sill for support and he stared down at the single remaining tank, still caught inextricably in the tangled moving forest of *Golden Dawn*'s twisting, contorting hull. It was as though an invisible giant had taken the Eiffel Tower at each end and was bending it across his knee.

Suddenly there was a sharp chemical stink in the air, and Nicholas gagged on it. The stink of crude petroleum oil gushing from the ruptured tank.

'Nicholas! Nicholas!' The radio set slung over his shoulder squawked, and he lifted it to his lips without taking his eyes from the *Golden Dawn*'s terrible death throes.

'Go ahead, Jules.'

'Nicholas, I am turning to pick you up.'

'You can't turn, not with that tow.'

'I will put my bows against the starboard quarterdeck rail, directly under the forward wing of the bridge. Be ready to jump aboard.'

'Jules, you are out of your head!'

'I have been that way for fifty years,' Jules agreed amiably. 'Be ready.'

'Jules, drop your tow first,' Nicholas pleaded. It would be almost impossible to manoeuvre the *Sea Witch* with that monstrous dead weight hanging on her tail. 'Drop tow. We can pick up again later.'

'You teach your grandfather to break eggs,' Jules blithely mangled the old saying, giving it a sinister twist.

'Listen Jules, the No. 4 tank has ruptured. I want you to shut down for fire. Do you understand? Full fire shut down. Once I am aboard, we will put a rocket into her and burn off cargo.'

'I hear you, Nicholas, but I wish I had not.'

Nicholas left the control cubicle, jumped the gaping, chewing gap in the decking and scrambled up the steel ladder on to the central catwalk.

Glancing over his shoulder, he could see the endlessly slippery grey wall of racing cloud and wind; its menace was overpowering, so that for a moment he faltered before forcing himself into running back along the catwalk towards the tanker's stern tower half a mile ahead.

The single remaining seaman was on the catwalk a hundred yards ahead of him, pounding determinedly back towards the pick-up point. He also had heard Jules Levoisin's last transmission.

A quarter of a mile across the roiling, leaping waters, Jules Levoisin was bringing *Sea Witch* around. At another time Nicholas would have been impressed by the consummate skill with which the little Frenchman was handling his ship and its burdensome tow, but now there was time and energy for one thing only.

The air stank. The heavy fumes of crude oil burned Nicholas' pumping lungs, and constricted his throat. He coughed and gasped as he ran, the taste and reek of it coated his tongue and seared his nostrils.

Below the catwalk, the bloated pod-tank was punctured in a hundred places by the steel lances of the disintegrating hull, pinched and torn by moving steel girders, and the dark red oil spurted and dribbled and oozed from it like the poisonous blood from the carcass of a mortally wounded dragon.

Nicholas reached the stern tower, barged in through the storm doors to the lowest deck and reached the pump control room.

Duncan Alexander turned to him, as he entered, his face swollen and bruised where Nicholas had beaten him.

'We are abandoning now,' said Nicholas. '*Sea Witch* is taking us off.'

'I hated you from that very first day,' Duncan was very calm, very controlled, his voice even, deep and cultured. 'Did you know that?'

'There's no time for that now.' Nicholas grabbed his arm, and Duncan followed him readily into the passageway.

'That's what the game is all about, isn't it, Nicholas, power and wealth and women – that's the game we played.'

Nicholas was barely listening. They were out on to the quarterdeck, standing at its starboard rail, below the bridge, the pick-up point that Jules had stipulated. *Sea Witch* was turning in, only five hundred yards out, and Nicholas had time now to watch Jules handle his ship.

He was running out the heavy tow cable on free spool, deliberately letting a long bight of it form between the tug and its enormous whalelike burden, and he was using the slack in the cable to cut in towards *Golden Dawn*'s battered, sagging hulk. He would be alongside for the pick-up in less than a minute.

'That was the game we played, you and I,' Duncan was still talking calmly. 'Power and wealth and women—'

Below them *Golden Dawn* poured her substance into the sea in a slick, stinking flood. The waves, battering against her side, churned the oil to a thick filthy emulsion, and it was spreading away across the surface, bleeding its deadly poison into the Gulf Stream to broadcast it to the entire ocean.

'I won,' Duncan went on reasonably. 'I won it all, every time—' He was groping in his pockets, but Nicholas hardly heard him, was not watching him. ' – until now.'

Duncan took one of the self-igniting signal flares from his pocket and held it against his chest with both hands, slipping his index finger through the metal ring of the igniter tab.

'And yet I win this one also, Nicholas,' he said. 'Game, set and match.' And he pulled the tab on the flare with a sharp jerk, and stepped back, holding it aloft.

It spluttered once and then burst into brilliant sparkling red flame, white phosphorescent smoke billowing from it.

Now at last Nicholas turned to face him, and for a moment he was too appalled to move. Then he lunged for Duncan's raised hand that held the burning flare, but Duncan was too fast for him to reach it.

He whirled and threw the flame in a high spluttering arc, out over the leaking, stinking tank-deck.

It struck the steel tank and bounced once, and then rolled down the canted oil-coated plating.

Nicholas stood paralysed at the rail staring down at it. He expected a violent explosion, but nothing happened; the flare rolled innocently across the deck, burning with its pretty red twinkling light.

'It's not burning,' Duncan cried. 'Why doesn't it burn?'

Of course, the gas was only explosive in a confined space, and it needed spark. Out here in the open air the oil had a very high flashpoint; it must be heated to release its volatiles.

The flare caught in the scuppers and fizzled in a black pool of crude, and only then the crude caught. It caught with a red, slow, sulky flame that spread quickly but not explosively over the entire deck, and instantly, thick billows of dark smoke rose in a dense choking cloud.

Below where Nicholas stood, the *Sea Witch* thrust her bows in and touched them against the tanker's side. The seaman beside Nicholas jumped and landed neatly on the tug's bows, then raced back along *Sea Witch*'s deck.

'Nicholas,' Jules' voice thundered over the loud hailer. 'Jump, Nicholas.'

Nicholas spun back to the rail, and poised himself to jump.

Duncan caught him from behind, whipping one arm around his throat, and pulling him backwards away from the rail.

'No,' Duncan shouted. 'You're staying, my friend. You are not going anywhere. You are staying here with me.'

A greasy wave of black choking smoke engulfed them, and Jules' magnified voice roared in Nicholas' ears.

'Nicholas, I cannot hold her here. Jump, quickly, jump!'

Duncan had him off-balance, dragging him backwards, away from the ship's side, and suddenly Nicholas knew what he must do.

Instead of resisting Duncan's arm, he hurled himself backwards and they crashed together into the superstructure – but Duncan bore the combined weight of both their bodies.

His armlock around the throat relaxed slightly and Nicholas drove his elbow into Duncan's side below the ribs, then wrenched his body forward from the waist, reached between his own braced legs and caught Duncan's ankles. He straightened up again, dragging Duncan off his feet and the same instant dropped backwards with his full weight on to the deck.

Duncan gasped and his arm fell away, as Nicholas bounced to his feet again, choking in the greasy billows of smoke, and he reached the ship's side.

Below him, the gap between *Sea Witch*'s bows and the tanker's side was rapidly widening and the thrust of the sea and the drag of the tug pulled them apart.

Nicholas vaulted on to the rail, poised for an instant and then jumped. He struck the deck and his teeth cracked together with the impact; his injured leg gave under him and he rolled once, then he was up on his hands and knees.

He looked up at *Golden Dawn*. She was completely enveloped now in the boiling column of black smoke. As the flames heated the leaking crude, so it burned more readily. The bank of smoke was shot through now with the satanic crimson of high, hot flame.

As *Sea Witch* sheered desperately away, the first rush of the storm hit them, and for a moment it smeared the smoke away, exposing the tanker's high quarterdeck.

Duncan Alexander stood at the rail above the roaring holocaust of the tank-deck. He stood with his arms extended, and he was burning; his clothing burned fiercely and his hair was a bright torch of flame. He stood like a ritual cross, outlined in fire, and then slowly he seemed to shrivel and he toppled forward over the rail into the bubbling, spurting, burning cargo of the monstrous ship that he had built – and the black smoke closed over him like a funeral cloak.

As the crude oil escaping from the pierced pod tank fed the flames, so the heat built up swiftly, still sufficient to consume only the volatile aromatic spirits which constituted less than half the bulk of the cargo.

The heavy carbon elements, not yet hot enough to burn, boiled off in that solid black column of smoke, and as the returning winds of the hurricane raced over the *Golden Dawn* once more, so that filthy pall was mixed with air and lifted into the cloud bank of the storm, rising first a thousand, then ten, then twenty thousand feet above the surface of the ocean.

And still *Golden Dawn* burned, and the temperatures of

the gas and oil mixture trapped in her hull rocketed steeply. Steel glowed red, then brilliant white, ran like molten wax, and then like water – and suddenly the flashpoint of heavy carbon smoke in a mixture of air and water vapour was reached in the womb of this mighty furnace.

Golden Dawn and her entire cargo turned into a fireball.

The steel and glass and metal of her hull disappeared in an instantaneous explosive combustion that released temperatures like those upon the surface of the sun. Her cargo, a quarter of a million tons of it, burned in an instant, releasing a white blooming rose of pure heat so fierce that it shot up into the upper stratosphere and consumed the billowing pall of its own hydrocarbon gas and smoke.

The very air burst into flame, the surface of the sea flamed in that white fireball of heat and even the clouds of smoke burned as the oxygen and hydrocarbon they contained exploded.

Once an entire city had been subjected to this phenomena of fireball, when stone and earth and air had exploded, and five thousand German citizens of the city of Cologne had been vaporized, and that vapour burned in the heat of its own release.

But this fireball was spawned by a quarter of a million tons of volatile liquids.

'Can't you get us further away?' Nicholas shouted above the thunder of the hurricane. His mouth was only inches from Jules Levoisin's ear.

They were standing side by side, hanging from the overhead railing that gave purchase on this wildly pitching deck.

'If I open the taps I will part the tow wire,' Jules shouted back.

Sea Witch was alternately standing on her nose and then

her tail. There was no forward view from the bridge, only green washes of sea water and banks of spray.

The full force of the hurricane was on them once more, and a glance at the radarscope showed the glowing image of *Golden Dawn*'s crippled and bleeding hull only half a mile astern.

Suddenly the glass of the windows was obscured by an impenetrable blackness, and the light in *Sea Witch*'s navigation bridge was reduced to only the glow of her fire-lights and the electronic instruments of her control console.

Jules Levoisin turned his face to Nicholas, his plump features haunted by green shadows in the gloom.

'Smoke bank,' Nicholas shouted an explanation. There was no reek of the filthy hydrocarbon in the bridge, for *Sea Witch* was shut down for fire drill, all her ports and ventilators sealed, her internal air-conditioning on a closed circuit, the air being scrubbed and recharged with oxygen by the big Carrier until above the main engine room. 'We are directly downwind of the *Golden Dawn*.'

A fiercer rush of the hurricane winds laid *Sea Witch* over on her side, the lee rail deep under the racing green sea, and held her there, unable to rise against the careless might of the storm for many minutes. Her crew hung desperately from any hand hold, the irksome burden of her tow helping to drag her down further; the propellers found no grip in the air, and her engines screamed in anguish.

But *Sea Witch* had been built to live in any sea, and the moment the wind hesitated, she fought off the water that had come aboard and began to swing back.

'Where is *Warlock*?' Jules bellowed anxiously. The danger of collision preyed upon him constantly, two ships and their elephantine tows manoeuvring closely in confined hurricane waters was nightmare on top of nightmare.

'Ten miles east of us.' Nicholas picked the other tug's image out of the trash on the radarscope. 'They had a start, ahead of the wind—'

He would have gone on, but the boiling bank of hydrocarbon smoke that surrounded *Sea Witch* turned to fierce white light, a light that blinded every man on the bridge as though a photograph flashlight had been fired in his face.

'Fireball!' Nicholas shouted, and, completely blinded, reached for the remote controls of the water cannons seventy feet above the bridge on *Sea Witch*'s fire-control tower.

Minutes before, he had aligned the four water cannons, training them down at their maximum angle of depression, so now as he locked down the multiple triggers, *Sea Witch* deluged herself in a pounding cascade of sea water.

Sea Witch was caught in a furnace of burning air, and despite the torrents of water she spewed over herself, her paintwork was burned away in instantaneous combustion so fierce that it consumed its own smoke, and almost instantly the bare scorched metal of her exposed upperworks began to glow with heat.

The heat was so savage that it struck through the insulated hull, through the double glazing of the two-inch armoured glass of her bridge windows, scorching and frizzling away Nicholas' eyelashes and blistering his lips as he lifted his face to it.

The glass of the bridge windows wavered and swam as they began to melt – and then abruptly there was no more oxygen. The fireball had extinguished itself, consumed everything in its twenty seconds of life, everything from sea level to thirty thousand feet above it, a brief and devastating orgasm of destruction.

It left a vacuum, a weak spot in the earth's thin skin of air; it formed another low pressure system smaller, but much more intense, and more hungry to be filled than the eye of Hurricane Lorna itself.

It literally tore the guts out of that great revolving storm, setting up counter winds and a vortex within the established system that ripped it apart.

New gales blew from every point about the fireball's vacuum, swiftly beginning their own dervish spirals and twenty miles short of the mainland of Florida, hurricane Lorna checked her mindless, blundering charge, fell in upon herself and disintegrated into fifty different willy-nilly squalls and whirlpools of air that collided and split again, slowly degenerating into nothingness.

O n a morning in April in Galveston roads, the salvage tug *Sea Witch* dropped off tow to four smaller harbour tugs who would take the *Golden Dawn* No. 3 pod tank up the narrows to the Orient Amex discharge installation below Houston.

Her sister ship *Warlock*, Captain David Allen commanding, had dropped off his tandem tow of No. 1 and No. 2 pod tanks to the same tugs forty-eight hours previously.

Between the two ships, they had made good salvage under Lloyd's Open Form of three-quarters of a million tons of crude petroleum valued at $85.50 US a ton. To the prize would be added the value of the three tanks themselves – not less than sixty-five million dollars all told, Nicholas calculated, and he owned both ships and the full share of the salvage award. He had not sold to the Sheikhs yet, though for every day of the tow from the Florida Straits to Texas, there had been frantic telex messages from James Teacher in London. The Sheikhs were desperate to sign now, but Nicholas would let them wait a little longer.

Nicholas stood on the open wing of *Sea Witch*'s bridge and watched the four smaller harbour tugs bustling importantly about their ungainly charge.

He lifted the cheroot to his lips carefully, for they were still blistered from the heat of the fireball – and he pondered the question of how much he had achieved, apart from spectacular riches.

He had reduced the spill from a million to a quarter of a million tons of cad-rich crude, and he had burned it in a fireball. Nevertheless, there had been losses, toxins had been lifted high above the fireball. They had spread and settled across Florida as far as Tampa and Tallahassee, poisoning the pastures and killing thousands of head of domestic stock. But the American authorities had been quick to extend the hurricane emergency procedures. There had been no loss of human life. He had achieved that much.

Now he had delivered the salvaged pod tanks to Orient Amex. The new cracking process would benefit all mankind, and nothing that Nicholas could do would prevent men from carrying the cad-rich crudes of El Barras across the oceans. But would they do so in the same blindly irresponsible manner that Duncan Alexander had attempted?

He knew then with utter certainty that it was his appointed life's work from now on, to try and ensure that they did not. He knew how he was to embark upon that work. He had the wealth that was necessary, and Tom Parker had given him the other instruments to do the job.

He knew, with equal certainty, who would be his companion in that life's work – and standing on the fire-scorched deck of the gallant little vessel he had a vivid image of a golden girl who walked forever beside him in sunlight and in laughter.

'Samantha.'

He said her name aloud just once, and suddenly he was very eager to begin.